Coming Home

Rosamunde PILCHER

Coming Home

A THOMAS DUNNE BOOK

ST. MARTIN'S PRESS
NEW YORK

Design by Jaye Zimet

Library of Congress Cataloging-in-Publication Data

Pilcher, Rosamunde.
    Coming home / Rosamunde Pilcher.
      p. cm.
    "A Thomas Dunne book."
    ISBN 0-312-13451-7 (hardcover)
    I. Title.
  PS6066.I38C66   1995
  823'.914—dc20   95-21656
                        CIP

First Edition: September 1995

10 9 8 7 6 5 4 3 2 1

Published simultaneously in Canada by McClelland & Stewart Inc. (ISBN 0-7710-7011-X)

This book is for my husband, Graham,
who served with the Highland Division.

And for Gordon, and for Judith, and for all of us
who were young together at the same time.

Part One

Coming Home

1935

*T*he Porthkerris Council School stood half-way up the steep hill which climbed from the heart of the little town to the empty moors which lay beyond. It was a solid Victorian edifice, built of granite blocks, and had three entrances, marked Boys, Girls, and Infants, a legacy from the days when segregation of the sexes was mandatory. It was surrounded by a Tarmac playground and a tall wrought-iron fence, and presented a fairly forbidding face to the world. But on this late afternoon in December, it stood fairly ablaze with light, and from its open doors streamed a flood of excited children, laden with boot-bags, book-bags, balloons on strings, and small paper bags filled with sweets. They emerged in small groups, jostling and giggling and uttering shrieks of cheerful abuse at each other, before finally dispersing and setting off for home.

The reason for the excitement was twofold. It was the end of the winter term, and there had been a school Christmas party. Singing games had been played, and relay races won, up and down the assembly hall, with bean bags to be snatched and delivered to the next person in the team. The children had danced Sir Roger de Coverley, to music thumped out on the tinny old school piano, and eaten a tea of splits and jam, saffron buns, and fizzy lemonade. Finally they had lined up and, one by one, had shaken Mr. Thomas, the headmaster, by the hand, wished him a Merry Christmas, and been given a bag of sweets.

It was a routine that was followed every year, but always happily anticipated and much enjoyed.

Gradually the noisy outflux of children was reduced to a trickle, the late-leavers, those delayed by a search for missing gloves or an abandoned shoe. Last of all, as the school clock chimed a quarter to five, there came, through the open door, two girls, Judith

3

Dunbar and Heather Warren, both fourteen years old, both dressed in navy-blue coats and rubber boots, and with woollen hats pulled down over their ears. But that was as far as the resemblance went, for Judith was fair, with two stubby pigtails, freckles, and pale-blue eyes; while Heather had inherited her colouring from her father, and through him, back over the generations of ancestors, from some Spanish sailor, washed ashore on the Cornish coast after the destruction of the Armada. And so her skin was olive, her hair raven-black, and her eyes dark and bright as a pair of juicy raisins.

They were the last of the revellers to depart because Judith, who was leaving Porthkerris School forever, had had to say goodbye not only to Mr. Thomas but all the other teachers as well, and to Mrs. Trewartha, the school cook, and old Jimmy Richards, whose lowly tasks included stoking the school boiler and cleaning the outside lavatories.

But finally, there was nobody else to say goodbye to, and they were on their way, across the playground and through the gates. The overcast day had slipped early into darkness and a thin drizzle fell, shimmering against glowing street lamps. The street sloped down the hill, black and wet, pooled with reflected light. They began to walk, descending into the town. For a bit neither of them spoke. Then Judith sighed.

"Well," she said in final tones, "that's it."

"Must feel a bit funny, knowing you're not coming back again."

"Yes, it does. But the funniest bit is feeling sad. I never thought I'd feel sad to leave any school, but I do now."

"It's not going to be the same without you."

"It's not going to be the same without you, either. But you're lucky, because at least you've still got Elaine and Christine for friends. I've got to start all over, brand new, trying to find someone I like at Saint Ursula's. And I have to wear that uniform."

Heather's silence was sympathetic. The uniform was almost the worst of all. At Porthkerris, everybody wore their own clothes, and very cheerful they looked too, in different-coloured sweaters, and the girls with bright ribbons in their hair. But Saint Ursula's was a private school and archaically old-fashioned. The girls wore dark-green tweed overcoats and thick brown stockings, and dark-green hats that were guaranteed to make even the prettiest totally plain, so unbecoming were they. Saint Ursula's took day-girls as well as boarders, and these unfortunate creatures were much despised by Judith and Heather and their contemporaries at Porthkerris, and considered fair bait for teasing and torment should they be unlucky enough to travel on the same bus. It was depressing to contemplate Judith having to join the ranks of those wet, goody-goody creatures who thought themselves so grand.

But worst of all was the prospect of boarding. The Warrens were an intensely close family, and Heather could not imagine a worse fate than to be torn from her parents and her two older brothers, both as handsome and raven-haired as their father. At Porthkerris School, they had been notorious for their devilment and wickedness, but since moving on to the County

School in Penzance, had been somewhat tamed by a terrifying headmaster, and been forced to settle down to their books and mend their ways. But still, they were the best fun in the world, and it was they who had taught Heather to swim and ride a bicycle and trawl for mackerel from their stubby wooden boat. And what fun could you possibly have with nothing but *girls?* It didn't matter that Saint Ursula's was in Penzance and so only ten miles away. Ten miles was forever if you had to live away from Mum and Dad and Paddy and Joe.

However, it seemed that poor Judith had no choice. Her father worked in Colombo, in Ceylon, and for four years Judith, her mother, and her little sister had lived apart from him. Now Mrs. Dunbar and Jess were returning to Ceylon, and Judith was being left behind, with little idea of when she would see her mother again.

But it was, as Mrs. Warren was wont to remark, no good crying over spilt milk. Heather cast about for something cheerful to say.

"There'll be holidays."

"With Aunt *Louise.*"

"Oh, come on, don't be so down in the dumps. At least you'll still be *here*. Living in Penmarron. Just think, your aunt might live somewhere awful, up-country, or in some town. And you wouldn't know anybody. As it is, we can go on seeing each other. You can come over, and we'll go down to the beach. Or go to the pictures."

"Are you sure?"

Heather was perplexed. "Sure about what?"

"Well, I mean . . . sure you're going to want to go on seeing me and being my friend. Going to Saint Ursula's and everything. You won't think I'm snobby and horrible?"

"Oh, you." Heather gave her a loving thump over the bottom with her boot-bag. "What do you think I am?"

"It would be a sort of escape."

"You make it sound like going to prison."

"You know what I mean."

"What's your aunt's house like?"

"It's quite big, and it's right up at the top of the golf course. And it's full of brass trays and tiger skins and elephants' feet."

"Elephants' feet? My dear life, what does she use them for?"

"An umbrella stand."

"I wouldn't like that. But I suppose you won't have to look at it much. Got your own room, have you?"

"Yes, I've got a room. It was her best spare room, and it's got its own wash-basin and there's room for my desk."

"Sounds all right to me. Don't know what you're making such a fuss about."

"I'm not making a fuss. It's just not *home*. And it's so cold up there, all bleak and windy. The house is called Windyridge, and no wonder. Even when it's dead calm everywhere else, there always seems to be a gale blowing at Aunt Louise's windows."

"Some spooky."

"And the other thing is, that it's so far from everywhere. I won't be able just to hop on the train any longer, and the nearest bus stop's two miles away. And Aunt Louise won't have time to drive me around, because she's always playing golf."

"Perhaps she'll teach you how."

"Oh, ha ha."

"Sounds to me as though what you need is a bike. Then you could go wherever you wanted, whenever. It's only three miles to Porthkerris over the top road."

"You are brilliant. I never thought of a bike."

"I don't know why you never had one before. My dad gave me mine when I was ten. Not that it's much good in this dratted place, with all the hills, but out where you are, it'd be just the thing."

"Are they very expensive?"

"About five pounds for a new one. But you could maybe pick one up second-hand."

"My mother's not very good at that sort of thing."

"Don't suppose any mother is, really. But it's not very difficult to go to a bicycle shop. Get her to give it to you for Christmas."

"I've already asked for a jersey for Christmas. One with a polo-neck."

"Well, ask for a bike as well."

"I couldn't."

"Course you could. She can scarcely say no. Going away, and not knowing when she's going to see you again, she'll give you anything you want. You just strike while the iron's hot"—another of Mrs. Warren's favourite sayings.

But Judith only said, "I'll see."

They walked on in silence for a bit, their footsteps ringing on the damp pavement. They passed the fish-and-chips shop, bright with cheerful light, and the warm smell of hot fat and vinegar which emanated from the open door was mouth-watering.

"This aunt of yours, Mrs. Forrester. Your mother's sister, is she?"

"No, my father's. She's much older. About fifty. She lived in India. That's where she got the elephant's foot."

"What about your uncle?"

"He's dead. She's a widow."

"Got any children?"

"No. I don't think they ever had children."

"Funny that, isn't it? Do you suppose it's because they don't want them, or because . . . something . . . doesn't happen? My Auntie May, she's got no children, and I heard Dad say it was because Uncle Fred hadn't got it in him. What do you suppose he meant by that?"

"I don't know."

6

"Think it's got something to do with what Norah Elliot told us? You know, that day behind the bicycle shed."

"She's just making it all up."

"How do you know?"

"Because it was too disgusting to be true. Only Norah Elliot could have thought up something so disgusting."

"Suppose so . . ."

It was a fascinating topic, around which the two girls had skirted from time to time without ever coming to any useful conclusion, except the fact that Norah Elliot smelt and her school blouses were always dirty. This was not, however, the time to unravel the conundrum, because their conversation had brought them down the hill, to the centre of the town, the public library and the parting of their ways. Heather would carry on in the direction of the harbour, down narrowing streets and baffling cobbled lanes, to the square granite house where the Warren family lived over Mr. Warren's grocery shop, and Judith would climb yet another hill, and head for the railway station.

They stood in the soaking drizzle beneath the street lamp and faced each other.

"I suppose it's goodbye, then," said Heather.

"Yes. I suppose so."

"You can write to me. You've got my address. And ring the shop if you want to leave a message. I mean . . . like coming over when it's holidays."

"I'll do that."

"I don't suppose that school'll be too bad."

"No. I don't suppose so."

"Bye then."

" 'Bye."

But neither moved, nor turned away. They had been friends for four years. It was a poignant moment.

Heather said, "Have a good Christmas."

Another pause. Abruptly, Heather leaned forward and planted a kiss on Judith's rain-damp cheek. Then, without saying anything more, she turned and went running away down the street, and the sound of her footsteps became fainter and fainter, until Judith could hear them no longer. Only then, feeling a bit bereft, did she continue on her solitary way, climbing the narrow pavement between small shops brightly illuminated, their windows decorated for Christmas with tinsel wound around boxes of tangerines and jars of bath salts tied with scarlet ribbons. Even the ironmonger had done his bit. USEFUL AND ACCEPTABLE GIFT said a handwritten card leaning against a ferocious claw-hammer which sported a sprig of artificial holly. She passed the last shop, at the very top of the hill, which was the local branch of W. H. Smith, where Judith's mother bought her monthly *Vogue* and came each Saturday to change her library book. After that the road levelled off and the houses fell away, and without their shelter the wind asserted itself. It came in soft gusts, laden with moisture, blowing the drenching mist into her face. In the darkness this wind had a special feel to it and brought with it the sound of break-ers booming up on the beach far below.

After a bit, she paused to lean her elbows on a low granite wall; to rest after the stiff climb and get her breath. She saw the blurred jumble of houses slipping away down to the dark goblet of the harbour, and the harbour road outlined by a curved necklace of street lamps. The red and green riding lights of fishing boats dipped in the swell and sent shimmering reflections down into the inky water. The far horizon was lost in the darkness, but the heaving, restless ocean went on forever. Far out, the lighthouse flashed its warning. A short beam, and then two long beams. Judith imagined the eternal breakers pouring in over the cruel rocks at its base.

She shivered. Too cold to stand in the dark, wet wind. The train would be leaving in five minutes. She began to run, her boot-bag thumping against her side; came to the long flight of granite steps which dropped to the railway station, and hurtled down them with the careless confidence of years of famil-iarity.

The little branch-line train waited at the platform. The engine, two third-class carriages, one first-class carriage, and the guard's van. She did not have to buy a ticket, because she had a School Season, and anyway Mr. William, the guard, knew her as well as his own daughter. Charlie, the engine driver, knew Judith too, and was good about holding the train at Penmarron Halt if she was late for school, tooting his whistle while she pelted down the garden of Riverview House.

Travelling to school and back in the little train was going to be one of the things that she was really going to miss, because the line ran, for three miles, along the edge of a spectacular stretch of coast, incorporating everything that one could possibly want to look at. Because it was dark, she couldn't look at it now as they rattled along, but knew it was there just the same. Cliffs and deep cuttings, bays and beaches, delectable cottages, little paths and tiny fields which in spring would be yellow with daffodils. Then the sand dunes and the huge lonely beach which she had come to think of as her own.

Sometimes, when people learned that Judith had no father, because he was on the other side of the world working for a prestigious shipping company called Wilson-McKinnon, they were sorry for her. How awful to be without a father. Didn't she miss him? How could it feel, not to have a man about the house, not even at weekends? When would she see him again? When would he come home?

She always answered the questions in a vague fashion, partly because she didn't want to discuss the matter, and partly because she didn't know exactly how she *did* feel. Only that she had known, always, that life would be like this, because this was how it was for every British India family, and the chil-dren absorbed and accepted the fact that, from an early age, long separations and partings would, eventually, be inevitable.

Judith had been born in Colombo and lived there until she was ten, which was two years longer than most British children were allowed to stay in the tropics. During that time, the Dunbars had travelled home once for a Long Leave, but Judith had been only four at the time, and memories of that sojourn in England were blurred by the passage of years. She was never to feel that England was Home. Colombo was, the spacious bungalow on the Galle Road, with a verdant garden, separated from the Indian Ocean by the single-track railway line that ran south to Galle. Because of the proximity of the sea, it never seemed to matter how hot it got, because there was always a fresh breeze blowing in with the breakers, and indoors were wooden ceiling fans to stir the air.

But, inevitably, the day came when they had to leave it all behind. To say goodbye to the house and the garden, and Amah and Joseph the butler, and the old Tamil who tended the garden. To say goodbye to Dad. *Why do we have to go?* Judith was asking even as he drove them to the harbour where the P & O boat, already getting up steam, lay at anchor. *Because it is time to go,* he had said; *there is a time for everything.* Neither parent told her that her mother was pregnant, and it was not until after the three-week voyage had been made and they were back in grey England, with the rain and the cold, that Judith was let into the secret that there was a new baby on the way.

Because they had no establishment of their own to return to, Aunt Louise, primed by her brother Bruce, had taken matters into her own hands, located Riverview House, and leased it as a furnished let. Soon after they took up residence, Jess was born in the Porthkerris Cottage Hospital. And now the time had come for Molly Dunbar to return to Colombo. Jess was going with her, and Judith was remaining behind. She envied them dreadfully.

Four years they had lived in Cornwall. Nearly a third of her life. And, by and large, they had been good years. The house was comfortable, with space for all of them, and it had a garden, large and rambling, which spilt down the hill in a series of terraces, lawns, stone steps, and an apple orchard.

Best of all, however, was the freedom which Judith had been allowed. The reason for this was twofold. Molly, with her new baby to care for, had little time to watch over Judith, and was content for her to entertain herself. As well, although she was by nature over-anxious and protective of her children, she soon came to realize that the sleepy little village, and its peaceful environs, held no threat for any child.

Exploring, Judith had tentatively ventured beyond the bounds of the garden, so that the railway line, the neighbouring violet-farm, and the shores of the estuary became her playground. Growing bolder, she found the lane which led to the eleventh-century church, with its square Norman tower and wind-torn graveyard filled with ancient lichened headstones. One fine day, as she crouched trying to decipher the hand-hewn inscription on one of these, she had been surprised by the vicar who, charmed by her interest, had taken her into the church, told her some of its history, and pointed out its salient features and simple treasures. Then they had climbed the tower and stood at the top in the buffeting wind, and he had pointed out interesting landmarks to her. It was like having all the world revealed, a huge and marvellously coloured map: farmland, patchworked like a quilt into small fields, green velvet for pasture and brown corduroy velvet for plough; distant hills, crowned with cairns of rock which dated back to a time, so long ago, that it was beyond comprehension; the estuary, its flood-waters blue with reflected sky, like a huge land-enclosed lake, but it wasn't a lake at all, for it filled and emptied with the tides, flowing out to sea down the deep-water passage known as the Channel. That day, the tide-race of the Channel was indigo-blue, but the ocean was turquoise, with rollers pouring in onto the empty beach. She saw the long coastline of dunes curving north to the rock where the lighthouse stood, and there were fishing boats out at sea, and the sky was full of screaming gulls.

The vicar explained that the church had been built upon this hillock above the beach so that its tower would be a beacon, a marker, for ships seeking a landfall and safe water, and it was not difficult to imagine those bygone galleons, their sails filled with wind, moving in from the open sea, and upstream with the running tide.

As well as discovering places, she got to know the local people. The Cornish love children, and wherever she turned up she was welcomed with such pleasure that her inherent shyness swiftly evaporated. The village fairly buzzed with interesting characters. Mrs. Berry, who ran the village shop and made her own ice-creams out of custard powder; old Herbie, who drove the coal-cart; and Mrs. Southey in the post office, who set a fire-guard on the counter to keep bandits at bay and could scarcely sell a stamp without giving the wrong change.

And there were others, even more fascinating, residing farther afield. Mr. Willis was one of them. Mr. Willis had spent a good chunk of his life tin-mining in Chile, but had finally returned to his native Cornwall after a life-time of adventure, and put down his roots in a wooden shack perched on the sandy dunes above the shore of the Channel. The narrow beach in front of his hut was littered with all sorts of interesting bits of flotsam: scraps of rope and broken fish boxes, bottles, and sodden rubber boots. One day, Mr. Willis had come upon Judith searching for shells, got talking, and invited her into his hut for a cup of tea. After that, she always made a point of looking out for him and having a chat.

But Mr. Willis was by no means an idle beachcomber, because he had two jobs. One of them was to watch the tides and raise a signal when the water rose high enough for the coal-boats to sail in over the sandbar, and the other was ferryman. Outside his house, he had rigged up an old ship's bell, and any person wishing to cross the Channel rang this, whereupon Mr. Willis would emerge from his shack, drag his balky row-boat down off the sand, and oar them over the water. For this service, fraught with discomfort, and even danger if there happened to be a roaring ebb-tide, he charged twopence.

Mr. Willis lived with Mrs. Willis, but she milked cows for the village farmer, and quite often wasn't there. Rumour had it that she wasn't Mrs. Willis at all, but Miss Somebody-or-other, and nobody talked to her much.

The mystery of Mrs. Willis was all bound up with the mystery of Heather's Uncle Fred who hadn't got it in him, but whenever Judith broached the matter with her mother, she was met with pursed lips and a change of subject.

Judith never talked to her mother about her friendship with Mr. Willis. Instinct told her that she might be discouraged from keeping company with him, and would certainly be forbidden to go into his hut and drink tea. Which was ridiculous. What harm could Mr. Willis do to anybody? Mummy, sometimes, was dreadfully stupid.

But then, she could be terribly stupid about a lot of things, and one of them was how she treated Judith exactly the way that she treated Jess, and Jess was four years old. At fourteen, Judith reckoned that she was mature enough to have really important decisions, that were going to affect *her*, shared and discussed.

But no. Mummy never discussed. She simply told.

I have had a letter from your father, and Jess and I are going to have to go back to Colombo.

Which had been a bit of a bombshell, to say the least of it.

But worse. *We have decided that you should go to Saint Ursula's as a boarder. The headmistress is called Miss Catto, and I have been to see her, and it's all arranged. The Easter term starts on the fifteenth of January.*

As though she were a sort of parcel, or a dog being put into a kennel.

"But what about the holidays?"

You'll stay with Aunt Louise. She's very kindly said that she'll take care of you, and be your guardian while we're all abroad. She's going to let you have her best spare room for your own, and you can take your own bits and pieces with you, and have them there.

Which was, perhaps, most daunting of all. It wasn't that she didn't *like* Aunt Louise. During their sojourn in Penmarron, they had seen quite a lot of her, and she had never been anything but kind. It was just that she was all *wrong*. Old—at least fifty—and faintly intimidating, and not cosy in the least. And Windyridge was an old person's house, orderly and quiet. Two sisters, Edna and Hilda by name, who worked for her as cook and house parlourmaid, were equally elderly and unforthcoming, not a bit like darling Phyllis, who did everything for them all at Riverview House, but still found time to play racing demon at the kitchen table and read fortunes with tea-leaves.

They would probably spend Christmas Day with Aunt Louise. They would go to church, and then there would be roast goose for lunch, and afterwards, before it grew dark, they would take a brisk walk over the golf course, to the white gate which stood high above the sea.

Not very exciting, but at fourteen Judith had lost some of her illusions about Christmas. It ought to be as it was in books and on Christmas cards, but it never was, because Mummy wasn't much good at Christmas, and invariably showed a sad disinclination to decorate with holly, or dress a tree. For two years now she had been telling Judith that she was really too old to have a stocking.

In fact, when Judith thought about it, Mummy wasn't really much good at anything like that. She didn't like picnics on the beach, and she would rather do anything than throw a birthday party. She was even timid about driving the car. They had a car, of course, a very small and shabby Austin, but Mummy would come up with any excuse rather than get it out of the garage, convinced as she was that she was about to drive it into some other vehicle, lose control of the brakes, or be unable to double de-clutch when they came to a hill.

Back to Christmas. However they spent it, Judith knew that nothing could be worse than that Christmas, two years ago, when Mummy insisted that they spend some time with *her* parents, the Reverend and Mrs. Evans.

Grandfather was incumbent of a tiny parish in Devon, and Grandmother a defeated old lady who had struggled all her life with genteel poverty and vicarages built for huge families of Victorian children. They had spent an inordinate amount of time treading to and from church, and Grandmother had given Judith a prayer-book for a Christmas present. *Oh, thank you, Grandmother*, Judith had said politely, *I've always wanted a prayer-book*. She had not added, *but not very much*. And Jess, who always ruined everything, had gone down with croup, and taken up all Mother's time and attention, and every other day there were stewed figs and blancmange for pudding.

No, nothing could be worse than that.

But even so (like a dog worrying a bone, Judith's thoughts turned back to her original grievance), the business of Saint Ursula's still rankled. Judith hadn't even been to see the school, nor to meet the probably terrifying Miss Catto. Perhaps Mother had feared an outburst of rebellion and taken the easiest course, but even that didn't make sense, because Judith had never, in all her life, rebelled against anything. It occurred to her that perhaps, at fourteen, she should give it a try. Heather Warren had known for years how to get her own way, and had her besotted father nicely twisted around her little finger. But then fathers were different. And, for the time being, Judith didn't have one.

The train was slowing down. It passed under the bridge (you could always tell by the different sound the wheels made) and ground to a hissing halt. She collected her bags and stepped out onto the platform in front of the station, which was tiny and looked like a wooden cricket pavilion with much fancy fretwork. Mr. Jackson, the station-master, stood silhouetted against the light which shone out from the open door.

"Hello there, Judith. You're late tonight."

"We had the school party."

"Lovely!"

The last bit of the journey was the shortest possible walk, because the station stood exactly opposite the bottom gate of the Riverview House garden. She went through the waiting-room, which always smelt distressingly of lavatories, and emerged into the unlit lane that lay beyond. Pausing for an instant to let her eyes get used to the darkness, she realized that the rain had stopped, and heard the wind soughing through the topmost branches of the pine coppice that sheltered the station from the worst of the weather. It was an eerie sound, but not a frightening one. She crossed the road, felt for the latch of the gate, opened it, and went into the garden and up the steeply sloping path, which rose in steps and terraces. At the top, the house loomed darkly before her, with curtained windows glowing in friendly fashion. The ornamental lantern which hung over the front door had been turned on, and in its light she saw an alien car parked on the gravel. Aunt Louise, come, no doubt, for tea.

A big black Rover. Standing there, it looked innocent enough, harmless, solid and dependable. But any person who ventured onto the narrow roads and lanes of West Penwith had reason to be wary of its appearance, because it had a powerful engine, and Aunt Louise, good citizen that she was, regular churchgoer and pillar of the golf club, underwent a sort of personality change the moment she got behind the wheel, roaring around blind corners at fifty miles an hour, and confidently certain that, provided she kept the heel of her hand on the horn, the letter of the law was on her side. Because of this, if her bumper grazed another person's mudguard, or she ran over a hen, she never for a moment considered the possibility that the fault might be hers, and so forceful were her accusations and admonitions that the injured parties usually lacked the guts to stand up to her, and slunk away from the encounter without daring to claim damages or demand reparation for the dead chicken.

Judith did not want, instantly, to be faced by Aunt Louise. Because of this, she did not go in through the front door, but made her way around to the back, through the yard and the scullery and so into the kitchen. Here she found Jess sitting at the scrubbed table with her crayons and her colouring book, and Phyllis, in her afternoon uniform of green dress and muslin apron, dealing with a pile of ironing.

After the cold outside, and the damp, the kitchen felt blissfully warm. It was, in fact, the warmest room in the house, because the fire in the black-leaded, brass-knobbed Cornish range never went out. Now it simmered, causing the kettle on the hob to sing. Opposite the range a dresser stood, arranged with a motley of meat platters, vegetable dishes, and a soup tureen, and by the side of the range was Phyllis's basket chair, in which she collapsed whenever she had a moment to get the weight off her legs, which was not often. The room smelt pleasantly of warm linen, and overhead hung a pulley, laden with airing laundry.

Phyllis looked up. "Hello there. What are you doing, sneaking in the back way?"

She smiled, showing her not very good teeth. She was a flat-chested and bony girl with pale skin and straight mousy hair, but had the sweetest disposition of any person Judith had ever known.

"I saw Aunt Louise's car."

"That's no reason. Have a good party, did you?"

"Yes." She delved in her coat pocket. "Here, Jess," and she gave Jess a bag of sweets.

Jess looked at them. "What are they?"

She was a beautiful child, chubby and silver-blonde, but dreadfully baby-ish, and Judith was constantly being exasperated by her.

"Sweets, of course, silly."

"I like fruit gums."

"Well, look and see if you can find one, then."

She pulled off her coat and her woollen hat and dumped them on a chair. Phyllis didn't say, "Hang them up." Sometime, she would probably hang them up for Judith herself.

"I didn't know Aunt Louise was coming for tea."

"Telephoned, she did, about two o'clock."

"What are they talking about?"

"Nosy Parker."

"Me, I suppose."

"You, and that school, and lawyers and fees, and half-terms and telephone calls. And talking of telephone calls, your Aunt Biddy called this morning. Spoke to your mother ten minutes or more."

Judith perked up. "Aunt Biddy?" Aunt Biddy was Mummy's own sister, and a favourite of Judith's. "What did she want?"

"I wasn't eavesdropping, was I? You'll have to ask your mum." She dumped down the iron and began to do up the buttons of Mummy's best blouse. "You'd better go through. I've laid a cup for you, and there's scones and lemon cake if you're hungry."

"Starving."

"As usual. Didn't they feed you at the party?"

"Yes. Saffron buns. But I'm still hungry."

"Off you go then, or your mother will be wondering."

"Wondering what?"

But Phyllis only said, "Go and get your shoes changed, and wash your hands first."

So she did this, washing her hands in the scullery, using Phyllis's California Poppy soap, and then, with some reluctance, left the snug companionship of the kitchen and crossed the hall. From beyond the sitting-room door came the low murmur of female voices. She opened the door, but silently, so that for a moment the two women remained unaware of her presence.

They sat, Molly Dunbar and her sister-in-law Louise Forrester, on either side of the hearth, with a folding tea-table set up between them. This had been laid with an embroidered linen cloth and the best china, as well as plates containing sandwiches, an iced lemon cake, hot scones spread with cream and strawberry jam, and two kinds of biscuit—shortbread and choco-late.

They had made themselves very comfortable, with velvet curtains closely drawn and the coal-fire flickering in the grate. The sitting-room was neither large nor grand, and, because Riverview House was a furnished let, nor was it specially well-appointed. Faded chintz graced the armchairs, a Turkey rug covered the floor, and occasional tables and bookcases were functional rather than decorative. But nevertheless, in the gentle lamplight, it looked quite feminine and pretty, for Molly had brought with her from Ceylon a selection of her favourite bits and pieces, and these, set about the place, did much to alleviate the impersonality of the room. Ornaments in jade and ivory; a red lacquer cigarette box; a blue-and-white bowl planted with hyacinths; and family photographs in silver frames.

". . . you'll have such a lot to do," Aunt Louise was saying. "If I can help . . ." She leaned forward to place her empty cup and saucer upon the table, and doing so, glanced up and saw Judith standing at the open door. "Well, look who's here . . ."

Molly turned. "Judith. I thought perhaps you'd missed the train."

"No. I've been talking to Phyllis." She closed the door and crossed the room. "Hello, Aunt Louise." She stooped to kiss Aunt Louise's proffered cheek. Aunt Louise accepted this but made no move to kiss Judith in return.

She was not one to show emotion. She sat there, a well-built woman in her early fifties, with legs of surprising thinness and elegance, and long narrow feet shod in brogues polished to a chestnut shine. She wore a tweed coat and skirt, and her short grey hair was marcel-waved and kept firmly in control with an invisible hairnet. Her voice was deep and husky from smoking, and even when she changed for the evening into more feminine attire, velvet dresses and embroidered bridge coats, there was something disconcertingly masculine about her, like a man who, for a joke or a fancy-dress party, puts on his wife's clothes and reduces the assembled company into shrieks of glee.

A handsome woman, but not beautiful. And, if old sepia photographs were to be believed, never beautiful, even in youth. Indeed, when she was twenty-three, still unengaged and unspoken for, her parents had been reduced to packing her off to India to stay with Army relations stationed in Delhi. When the hot weather came, the entire household decamped north to the cool hills and Poona, and it was there that Louise met Jack Forrester. Jack was a major in the Bengal Rifles and had just spent twelve months holed up in some remote mountain fort, skirmishing from time to time with warlike Afghans. He was in Poona on leave, desperate, after months of celibacy, for female companionship; and Louise—young, pink-cheeked, unattached, and athletic—glimpsed bounding about on a tennis court, seemed to his hungry and bedazzled eyes a most desirable creature. With enormous determination but little finesse—there was no time for finesse—he pursued her, and before he knew what was happening discovered himself engaged to be married.

Oddly enough, it was a sound marriage, although . . . or perhaps because . . . they were never blessed with children. Instead, they shared a love of the open-air life, and all the glorious opportunities for sport and game that India offered. There were hunting parties and expeditions up into the hills; horses for riding and playing polo, and every opportunity for tennis and the golf at which Louise excelled. When Jack was finally retired from the Army and they returned to England, they settled in Penmarron, simply because of the

15

proximity of the golf course, and the club became their home away from home. In inclement weather they played bridge, but most fine days saw them out on the fairways. As well, a certain amount of time was spent at the bar, where Jack earned the doubtful reputation of being able to drink any man under the table. He boasted of having a stomach like a bucket and all his friends agreed, until one bright Saturday morning, when he dropped dead on the fourteenth green. After that they weren't so sure.

Molly was in Ceylon when this sad event occurred, and wrote a letter of the deepest sympathy, being unable to imagine how Louise would manage without Jack. Such friends they had been, such pals. But when finally they did meet up again, she could find no change in Louise at all. She looked the same, lived in the same house, enjoyed the same life-style. Every day saw her out on the golf course, and because she had an excellent handicap and could thwack the ball as hard as any man, was never short of male partners.

Now, she reached for her cigarette case, opened it, and fitted a Turkish cigarette into an ivory holder. She lit it with a gold lighter which had once belonged to her late husband.

"How," she asked Judith through a cloud of smoke, "did the Christmas party go?"

"It was all right. We did Sir Roger de Coverley. And there were saffron buns." Judith eyed the tea-table. "But I'm still hungry."

"Well, we've left plenty for you to finish up," said Molly. Judith pulled up a low stool and settled herself between the two women, her nose on a level with all Phyllis's goodies. "Do you want milk or tea?"

"I'll have milk, thank you." She reached for a plate and a scone and began to eat, cautiously, because the thick cream and strawberry jam were spread so generously that they were liable to squidge out and drop all over the place.

"Did you say goodbye to all your friends?"

"Yes. And Mr. Thomas and everybody. And we all got a bag of sweets, but I've given mine to Jess. And then I walked down the hill with Heather—"

"Who is Heather?" asked Aunt Louise.

"Heather Warren. She's my special friend."

"You know," said Molly, "Mr. Warren, the grocer in the Market Place."

"Oh!" Aunt Louise raised her eyebrows and became arch. "The dashing Spaniard. Such a good-looking man. Even if he didn't sell my favourite Tip-trees marmalade, I think I should have to give him my custom."

She was obviously in a good mood. Judith decided that this was the right moment to broach the subject of the bicycle. Strike while the iron's hot, as Mrs. Warren liked to say. Take the bull by the horns.

"Actually, Heather had the most frightfully good idea. That I ought to have a bicycle."

"A *bicycle*?"

"Mummy, you sound as though I'm asking for a racing car, or a pony. And I think it's a really good idea. Windyridge isn't like this house, next door to the railway station, and it's miles to the bus stop. If I have a bicycle, then I can get myself about, and Aunt Louise won't have to drive me in her car. And," she added cunningly, "*then* she can get on with her golf."

Aunt Louise gave a snort of laughter. "You've certainly thought of everything."

"*You* wouldn't mind, would you, Aunt Louise?"

"Why should I mind? Glad to be rid of you," which was Aunt Louise's way of being funny.

Molly found her voice. "But Judith . . . isn't a bicycle dreadfully expensive?"

"Heather says about five pounds."

"I thought so. Dreadfully expensive. And we have so many other things to buy. We haven't even started on your uniform yet, and the clothes list for Saint Ursula's is yards long."

"I thought you could give it to me for Christmas."

"But I've already got your Christmas present. What you asked me to get for you—"

"Well, a bicycle could be my birthday present. You won't be here for my birthday, you'll be in Colombo, so that will save you having to post me a parcel."

"But you'll have to go on the main roads. You might have an accident . . ."

Here Aunt Louise intervened. "Can you ride a bicycle?"

"Yes, of course. But I've never asked for one before, because I haven't really needed it. But do admit, Aunt Louise, it would be terribly handy."

"But Judith . . ."

"Oh, Molly, don't be such a fuss-pot. What harm can the child come to? And if she drives herself under a bus, then it's her own fault. I'll stand you a bicycle, Judith, but because it's so expensive, it'll have to do for your birthday as well. Which will save *me* having to post you a parcel."

"Really?" Judith could scarcely believe that her argument had worked, that she had gone on pressing her point, and actually got her own way. "Aunt Louise, you are a brick."

"Anything to get you out from under my feet."

"When can we buy it?"

"What about Christmas Eve?"

Molly said faintly, "Oh, no." She sounded flustered, and Louise frowned. "What's the matter *now*?" she demanded. Judith thought there was no reason to speak so unkindly, but then Aunt Louise was often impatient with Molly, treating her more like an idiot girl than a sister-in-law. "Thought of more objections?"

"No . . . it's not that." A faint blush turned Molly's cheeks pink. "It's just that we won't be here. I haven't told you yet, Louise, but I wanted to tell Judith first." She turned to Judith. "Aunt Biddy rang."

"I know. Phyllis told me."

"She's asked us to go and spend Christmas and New Year with them in Plymouth. You and me and Jess."

Judith's mouth was full of scone. For a moment she thought she was going to choke, but managed to swallow it down before anything so awful should happen.

Christmas with Aunt Biddy.

"What did you *say?*"

"I said we would."

Which was so unbelievably exciting that all other thoughts, even the new bicycle, fled from Judith's head.

"When are we going?"

"I thought the day before Christmas Eve. The trains won't be so crowded then. Biddy would meet us at Plymouth. She said she was sorry that she'd left it so late, the invitation, I mean, but it was just an impetuous idea. And she thought that, as it will be our last Christmas for a bit, it would be a good idea to spend it all together."

If Aunt Louise hadn't been there, Judith would have jumped up and down and waved her arms and danced around the room. But it seemed a bit rude to be so elated when Aunt Louise hadn't been asked as well. Containing her excitement, she turned to her aunt.

"In that case, Aunt Louise, perhaps we could buy the bicycle *after* Christmas?"

"Looks as though we're going to have to, doesn't it? As a matter of fact, I was going to ask you all to spend Christmas with me, but now it looks as though Biddy's saved me the trouble."

"Oh, Louise, I'm sorry. Now I feel I've let you down."

"Rubbish. Better for us all to have a bit of a change. Will Biddy's boy be there?"

"Ned? Unfortunately, no. He's going to Zermatt to ski, with some of his term at Dartmouth."

Aunt Louise raised her eyebrows, not approving of expensive and extravagant gallivanting. But then, Biddy had always spoiled her only child quite appallingly, and could deny him no pleasure.

"Pity," was all she said. "He would have been a companion for Judith."

"Aunt Louise, Ned's sixteen! He wouldn't take any notice of me at all. I expect I shall enjoy myself much more without him there . . ."

"You're probably right. And knowing Biddy, you'll have a high old time. Haven't seen her for ages. When was she last here, Molly, staying with you?"

"At the beginning of last summer. You remember. We had that lovely heat wave . . ."

"Was that when she came to dinner with me in those extraordinary beach pyjamas?"

"Yes, that's right."

"And I found her in your garden sunbathing in a two-piece bathing suit. Flesh-pink. She might just as well have been naked."

"She's always very up-to-date." Molly felt moved to stand up for her flighty sister, however feebly. "I suppose before very long we'll all be wearing beach pyjamas."

"Heaven forbid."

"What will you do for Christmas, Louise? I do hope you won't feel abandoned."

"Heavens, no. I shall rather enjoy being on my own. I'll maybe ask Billy Fawcett over for a drink, and then we'll go down to the club for lunch. They usually put on quite a good do." Judith had a mental picture of all the golfers, in their knickerbockers and stout shoes, pulling crackers and donning paper hats. "And then, perhaps, have a rubber or two of bridge."

Molly frowned. "Billy Fawcett? I don't think I know him."

"No. You wouldn't. Old friend from the Quetta days. Retired now, and thought he'd give Cornwall a try. So he's rented one of those new bungalows they've built down my road. I'm going to introduce him around. You must meet him before you go. Keen golfer as well, so I've put him up for the club."

"That's nice for you, Louise."

"What's nice?"

"Well . . . having an old friend come to live nearby. And a golfer too. Not that you're ever short of a partner."

But Louise was not about to commit herself. She only played golf with the very best. "It depends," she said, forcefully stubbing out her cigarette, "on what sort of handicap he gets." She looked at her watch. "Heavens, is that the time? I must be on my way." She gathered up her handbag and pulled herself out of her chair, and Molly and Judith, as well, rose to their feet. "Tell Phyllis, a delicious tea. You'll miss that girl. Has she found another position yet?"

"I don't think she's tried very hard."

"A treasure for some lucky person. No, don't ring for her. Judith can see me out. And if I don't see you before Christmas, Molly, have a ripping time. Give me a tinkle when you get back. Let me know when you want to move Judith's belongings up to Windyridge. And, Judith, we'll buy the bicycle at the beginning of the Easter holidays. You won't need it before then, anyway . . ."

1936

*T*he black morning was so cold that, slowly waking, Judith was aware of her nose as a separate entity, frozen to her face. Last night, going to bed, the room had felt too icy even to open the window, but she had drawn back the curtains a bit, and now, beyond the frost-starred glass of the window, gleamed yellow light from the lamp in the street below. There was no sound. Perhaps it was still the middle of the night. And then she heard the clop of horses' hooves, the milk-delivery cart, and knew that it was not the middle of the night at all, but morning.

It was now necessary to make a huge effort of physical courage. One, two, three. She pulled her hand out of the warm bedclothes and reached out to turn on the bedside light. Her new clock—from Uncle Bob, and one of her best presents—told her seven forty-five.

She put her hand quickly back under the blankets and warmed it between her knees. A new day. The last day. She felt a bit depressed. Their Christmas holiday was over, and they were going home.

The room in which she lay was in the attics of Aunt Biddy's house, and Aunt Biddy's second-best spare room. Mother and Jess had been given the best room, on the first floor, but Judith preferred this one, with its sloping ceilings and dormer window, and flowery cretonne curtains. The cold had been the worst thing about it, because the meagre heating of the rooms below her did not permeate up the last flight of stairs, but Aunt Biddy had let her have a small electric fire, and with the aid of this and a couple of hot-water bottles, she had managed to keep snug.

For, just before Christmas, the temperature had dropped alarmingly. A cold snap was on its way, warned the weatherman on the wireless, but he had prepared nobody for the Arctic conditions which had prevailed ever since. As the Dunbars travelled up-country in the *Cornish Riviera*, Bodmin Moor had lain white with snow, and alighting at Plymouth had been a bit like arriving in Siberia, with bitter winds driving showers of sleet down the station platform.

Which was unfortunate, because Aunt Biddy and Uncle Bob lived in what had to be the coldest house in Christendom. This was not their fault, because it went with Uncle Bob's job, which was Captain (E) in charge of the Royal Naval Engineering College at Keyham. The house stood in a north-facing terrace, and was tall and thin and whistled with draughts. The warmest spot was the basement kitchen, but that was the territory of Mrs. Cleese, the cook, and Hobbs, the retired Royal Marine bandsman who came in each day to black the boots and heave coals. Hobbs was something of a character, with white hair smarmed down over his bald patch, and an eye as bright and knowing as a blackbird's. He had tobacco-stained fingers, and a face seamed and battered and brown, like an old bit of luggage. If there was a party in the evening, he spruced himself up, put on a pair of white gloves and handed round the drinks.

There had been a lot of parties because, despite the freezing cold, this had been a truly magical Christmas, just the way Judith had always imagined Christmas ought to be, and had begun to think that she would never experience. But Biddy, who never did things by halves, had dressed the house over-all—like a battleship, Uncle Bob remarked—and her Christmas tree, standing in the hall and filling the stairwell with lights and glitter and drifting tinsel and the smell of spruce, was the most magnificent that Judith had ever seen. Other rooms were just as festive, with hundreds of Christmas cards strung from scarlet ribbons, and swags of holly and ivy framing the fireplaces, and, in dining-room and drawing-room, great coal-fires burned non-stop, like ship's boilers, stoked by Hobbs and banked up each night with slack, so that they never went out.

And there had been so much to do, so much going on, all the time. Luncheon parties and dinner parties, with, afterwards, dancing to the gramophone. Friends kept dropping in, for tea, or for drinks, and if a lull should occur on an empty afternoon, Aunt Biddy never succumbed to a spot of peace, but instantly suggested a visit to the cinema, or an expedition to the indoor skating rink.

Her mother, Judith knew, had become quite exhausted, and from time to time would creep upstairs for a rest on her bed, having delivered Jess into the care of Hobbs. Jess liked Hobbs and Mrs. Cleese better than anybody, and spent most of her time in the basement kitchen, being fed unsuitable snacks. Which was something of a relief to Judith, who enjoyed herself a great deal more without her baby sister tagging along.

Every now and then, of course, Jess was included. Uncle Bob had bought tickets for the pantomime, and they had all gone, with another family, taking up a whole row of stalls, and Uncle Bob had bought programmes for everybody, and a vast box of chocolates. But then the Dame had appeared, in her red wig and her corsets and her great scarlet bloomers, and Jess had behaved most embarrassingly and burst into piercing howls of fear, and had had to be hurried out by Mummy and not returned again. Luckily that happened fairly near the beginning, so everybody else was able to settle down and enjoy the rest of the show.

Uncle Bob was the best. Being with him, getting to know him, was the undoubted high spot of the holiday. Judith had never known that fathers could be such good value, so patient, so interesting, so funny. Because it was a holiday, he didn't have to go to the College every day, and so had time to spare, and they had spent much of it in that holy-of-holies, his study, where he had shown her his photograph albums, let her play records on his wind-up gramophone, and taught her how to use his battered portable typewriter. And when they went skating, it was he who had helped her around the rink until she found what he called her sea-legs; and at parties he always made sure that she wasn't left out, but introduced her to his guests, just as though she were a grown-up.

Dad, although dear, and missed, had never been such fun. Admitting this to herself, Judith had felt a bit guilty, because, over the last couple of weeks, she had been having such a good time that she had scarcely thought of him. To make up for this, she thought of him now, very hard, but she had to think about Colombo first, because that was where he was, and that was the only place where she could bring his image to life. But it was difficult. Colombo had been a long time ago. You thought you could remember every detail, but time had blurred the sharpness of recall, just as light fades old photographs. She searched for some occasion on which she could latch her memory.

Christmas. Obvious. Christmas in Colombo was unforgettable, if only because it was so incongruous, with the brilliant tropic skies, the nailing heat, shifting waters of the Indian Ocean, and the breeze stirring the palm trees. In the house on the Galle Road, at Christmas, she had opened her presents on the airy veranda, within sound of the breaking waves, and Christmas dinner had not been turkey but a traditional curry lunch at the Galle Face Hotel. A lot of other people celebrated this way as well, so it was a bit like a huge children's party, with everybody wearing paper hats and blowing tooters. She thought of the dining-room filled with families, all eating and drinking far too much, and the cool sea breeze blowing in from the ocean, and the ceiling fans slowly turning.

It worked. Now she had a clear picture of him. Dad, sitting at the head of the table in a blue paper crown starred with gold. She wondered how he had spent this solitary Christmas. When they had left him, four years ago, a bachelor friend had moved in to keep him company. But somehow it was impossible to imagine the two of them indulging in seasonal cheer. They had probably ended up at the club, with all the other bachelors and grass-widowers. She sighed. She supposed she missed him, but it was not easy to go on missing a person when life had been lived without him for so long, with the only contact his monthly letters, which were three weeks old when they arrived, and not very inspiring even then.

The new clock now pointed to eight o'clock. Time to get up. Now. One, two, three. She flung back the covers, hopped out of bed, and fled to turn on the electric fire. And then, very quickly, bundled herself into her Jaeger dressing-gown and pushed her bare feet into sheepskin slippers.

Her Christmas presents were neatly lined up on the floor. She fetched her small suitcase, a Chinese one made of wicker, with a handle and little toggles to keep the lid shut, and set it down, all ready to contain her loot. She put the clock into it, and the two books which Aunt Biddy had given her. The new Arthur Ransome, called *Winter Holiday*, and, as well, a beautiful leather-bound copy of *Jane Eyre*. It seemed a very long book, with close print, but there were a number of illustrations, colour-plates protected by leaves of tissue paper, and so beguiling were they that Judith could scarcely bear to wait to start reading. Then the woollen gloves from her grandparents, and the glass bubble which, if you shook it, erupted into a snowstorm. That was from Jess. Mummy had given her a pullover, but this was a bit of a disappointment, because it had a round neck and she had wanted a polo. However, Aunt Louise had come up trumps, and despite the promised bicycle, there had been a holly-wrapped parcel under the tree for Judith, and inside a five-year diary, fat and leathery as a Bible. Her present from Dad had not come yet. He wasn't always very good about getting things on time, and the post took ages. Still, that was something to look forward to. Almost the best present was from Phyllis, and was exactly what Judith needed—a pot of sticky paste with its own little brush and a pair of scissors. She would keep them in the locked drawer of her desk, away from Jess's fiddling fingers, and then, whenever she felt creative and wanted to make something, or cut something out, or stick a postcard into her private scrapbook, she wouldn't have to go and ask her mother for scissors (which could never be located) or be reduced to making glue out of flour and water. It never worked properly and smelt disgusting. Owning for herself these two humble objects gave Judith a good feeling of self-sufficiency.

She placed everything neatly into the basket, and there was just room for it all, without the lid refusing to close. She fastened the little toggles and put the basket on her bed, and then, as swiftly as she could, got dressed. Breakfast would be waiting and she was hungry. She hoped it would be sausages and not poached eggs.

Biddy Somerville sat at the end of her dining-room table, drank black coffee, and tried to ignore the fact that she had a slight hangover. Yesterday evening, after dinner, two young engineer-lieutenants had dropped in to pay their respects, and Bob had produced a bottle of brandy, and in the consequent celebration Biddy had tossed back a snifter too many. Now, a faint throb in her temple reminded her that she should have stopped at two. She had not mentioned to Bob that she felt a little queasy, otherwise he would briskly tell her the same thing. He bracketed hangovers with sunburn: a punishable offence.

Which was all very well for him, because he had never suffered from a hangover in his life. He sat now at the other end of the table, hidden from her by the opened pages of *The Times*. He was fully dressed, in uniform, because his seasonal leave was over, and today he returned to work. In a moment, he would close the paper, fold it, lay it on the table, and announce that it was time he was off. The rest of their little house party had not yet appeared, and for this Biddy was grateful, because by the time they appeared, she would, with luck, have had her second cup of coffee and be feeling stronger.

They were leaving today, and Biddy found herself feeling quite sorry that the time had come to say goodbye. She had invited them to stay for a number of reasons. It was Molly's last Christmas before returning to the Far East, and she was Biddy's only sister. There was no knowing, the world being in the state that it was, when they would see each other again. As well, Biddy was a bit guilty, because she felt that she hadn't done enough for the Dunbars during the last four years; hadn't seen enough of them; hadn't made as much effort as she might. Finally, she had asked them because Ned was away skiing, and the thought of Christmas without youngsters around was a bleak one, and not to be countenanced.

The fact that she had little in common with her sister, and scarcely knew the two girls, had rendered her not too hopeful as to the outcome of the arrangement. But it had all been a surprising success. Molly, it was true, had wilted from time to time, defeated by the pace of Biddy's social whirl, and had retired to her bed to put her feet up; and Jess, it had to be admitted, was a spoilt and babied brat, dreadfully indulged and petted every time she cried.

But Judith had proved a real eye-opener, the sort of girl Biddy would have liked as a daughter of her own, if ever she had had one. Entertaining herself if necessary, never chipping into adult conversations, and enthusiastic about, and grateful for, any ploy suggested for her diversion. She was also, Biddy thought, extraordinarily pretty . . . or, at least, she would be in a few years. The fact that there was no one of her own age around the place had not fazed her in the very least, and at Biddy's parties she had made herself useful, handing round nuts and biscuits, and responding to anybody who paused to talk to her. The rapport she had struck up with Bob was an extra bonus, because it was obvious that she had given him as much pleasure as he had bestowed upon her. He liked her for old-fashioned reasons, for her good manners, and the way she spoke up and looked you in the eye; but as well, for both of them, there was a natural attraction and stimulation of being with a member of the opposite sex, a father-daughter relationship that both of them, one way or another, had missed out on.

Perhaps they should have had daughters. Perhaps they should have had a string of children. But there was only Ned, packed off to prep school when he was eight, and then to Dartmouth. The years flew by so fast, and it felt almost no time had passed since he was small, and precious, with baby cheeks and flaxen hair, and dirty knees and rough, warm little hands. Now he was sixteen and nearly as tall as his father. Before you could say Jack Robinson, he'd be done with his studies and sent to sea. Be grown up. Get married. Produce a family of his own. Biddy's imagination flew ahead. She sighed. Being a grandmother did not appeal to her. She was young. She *felt* young. Middle age must be kept, at all costs, at bay.

The door opened, and Hobbs trod creakily into the room, bearing the morning mail and a fresh pot of black coffee. He put this on the hotplate on the sideboard, and then came to lay the letters down on the table by her side. She wished that he would do something about his squeaking boots.

"Bitter cold this morning," he observed with relish. "All the gutters thick with ice. I've salted the front-door step."

But Biddy only said, "Thank you, Hobbs," because if she responded to his observation he might stand and chat forever. Frustrated by her lengthening silence, Hobbs sucked his teeth in a morose sort of way, straightened a fork on the table in order to justify his presence, but finally, defeated, took himself off. Bob continued to read his paper. Biddy leafed through her mail. Not so much as a postcard from Ned, but a letter from her mother, probably thanking her for the knitted knee-rug that Biddy had sent her for Christmas. She took up a knife to slit the envelope open. As she did this, Bob lowered his paper, folded it, and slapped it down on the table with some force.

Biddy looked up. "What's wrong?"

"Disarmament. The League of Nations. And I don't like the smell of what's happening in Germany."

"Oh dear." She hated him to be depressed or concerned. Herself, she only read cheerful news, and hastily turned the page if the headlines looked black.

He looked at his watch. "Time I was off." He pushed back his heavy chair and stood up, a tall and squarely built man, his bulk made yet more impressive by the dark, double-breasted, gold-buttoned jacket. His face, clean-shaven and craggy, was shadowed by a pair of bushy eyebrows, and his thick hair, iron-grey, lay smooth on his head, relentlessly barbered and firmly controlled by Royal Yacht hair oil and a pair of bristly brushes.

"Have a good day," Biddy told him.

He looked at the empty table. "Where is everybody?"

"Not down yet."

"What time is their train?"

"This afternoon. The *Riviera*."

"I don't think I can make it. Will you be able to take them?"

"Of course."

"You'll say goodbye for me. Say goodbye to Judith."

"You'll miss her."

"I . . ." An unemotional man—or, more accurately, a man who did not show his emotions—he searched for words. "I don't like to think of her being abandoned. Left on her own."

"She won't be on her own. Louise is there."

"She needs more than Louise is able to offer."

"I know. I've always thought the Dunbars were just about the dullest crew in the world. But there it is. Molly married into the family, and seems to have become absorbed by them. Not very much you and I can do about it."

He thought about this, standing gazing out of the window at the bleak, dark morning, and rattling the change in his trouser pocket.

"You could always ask her for a few days. Judith, I mean. During the holidays. Or would that be an awful bore for you?"

"No, not at all. But I doubt if Molly would agree. She'd make some excuse about not wanting to offend Louise. She's dreadfully under Louise's thumb, you know. Louise treats her like a nitwit, but she never says boo."

"Well, let's be honest, she is a bit of a nitwit. But have a try, anyway."

"I'll suggest it."

He came to drop a kiss on the top of her unruly head. "See you this evening, then." He never came home in the middle of the day, preferring to lunch in the Wardroom.

" 'Bye, darling."

He went. She was alone. She finished her coffee and went to pour another cup, then returned to the table to read her mother's letter. The writing was spidery and uncertain and looked like the hand of a very old lady.

My *dear Biddy*,

> Just a line to thank you for the rug. Just the thing for cold evenings, and with this spell of weather my rheumatism has been playing up again. We had a quiet Christmas. Small congregations, and the organist had 'flu, so Mrs. Fell had to fill in, and as you know, she's not very good. Father had a horrid skid in his car coming up the Woolscombe Road. The car is dented and he knocked his forehead on the windscreen. A nasty bruise. I had a card from poor Edith, her mother is failing . . .

Too early in the day for such gloom. She laid the letter down and returned to her coffee, sitting with her elbows on the table and her long fingers wrapped around the welcome warmth of the cup. She thought of that sad old pair who were her parents and found time to marvel anew at the fact that they had actually performed unimaginable acts of sexual passion, so producing their two daughters, Biddy and Molly. But even more miraculous was the fact that these daughters somehow or other had managed to escape the Vicarage, to find men to marry, and to be shed forever of the stifling dullness and genteel poverty in which they had been brought up.

For neither had been prepared for life. Neither had trained as a nurse, nor gone to University, nor learned how to type. Molly had longed for the stage, to be a dancer, a ballerina. At school, she had always been the star of the dancing class, and yearned to follow in the footsteps of Irina Baronova and Alicia Markova. But from the very beginning her feeble ambitions were thwarted by parental disapproval, by lack of money, and by the Reverend Evans's unspoken conviction that going on the stage was tantamount to becoming a harlot. If Molly hadn't been invited to that tennis party with the Luscombes, and there met Bruce Dunbar, home on his first long leave from Colombo and searching desperately for a wife, heaven alone knew what might have happened to the poor girl. A lifetime of spinsterhood, probably, helping Mother with the church flowers.

Biddy was different. She always knew what she wanted, and went out and got it. From an early age Biddy saw clearly that if she was going to have any sort of life, she was going to have to take care of herself. With this resolved, she became astute, and made friends only with the girls at school who she reckoned would, in the fullness of time, help her to achieve her ambitions. The friend who became her *best* friend was the daughter of a Naval Commander, living in a large house near Dartmouth. As well, she had brothers. Biddy decided that this was fertile ground, and after a few casual hints, managed to wangle an invitation to stay for the weekend. She was, as she had every intention of being, a social success. She was attractive, with long legs and bright, dark eyes, and a mop of curly brown hair, and young enough for it not to matter that she didn't have many of the right sort of clothes. As well, she had a sure instinct as to what was expected of her; when to be polite, and when to be charming, and how to flirt with the older men, who thought her a baggage and slapped her bottom. But the brothers were the best; the brothers had friends and these friends had friends. Biddy's circle of acquaintances expanded with marvellous ease, and before long she had become an accepted member of this surrogate family, spending more time with them than she did at home, and taking less and less notice of her anxious parents' admonitions and dire warnings.

Her careless life-style earned her something of a reputation, but she did not care. At nineteen she enjoyed the dubious fame of being engaged to two young sub-lieutenants at the same time, swapping their rings over as their different ships came into port, but at the end of the day, when she was twenty-one, she had married serious Bob Somerville, and had never lived to regret the decision. For Bob was not only her husband, the father of Ned, but her friend, turning a blind eye to a string of flighty associates, but always on hand when she needed him beside her.

They had had good times, for she loved to travel, and she was never unwilling to up sticks and pack and join Bob wherever he was sent. Two years in Malta had been the best, but none of it had been bad. No, there was no doubt. She had been very fortunate.

The clock on the dining-room mantelpiece struck the half-hour. Half past eight, and still Molly had not appeared. Biddy by now was feeling slightly less hung over and decided that she was ready for her first cigarette. She went to get one from the silver box on the sideboard, and on her way back to the table scooped up Bob's newspaper to open it and scan the headlines. It did not make cheerful reading, and she understood why Bob had appeared so uncharacteristically blue. Spain seemed headed for a blood-stained civil war, Herr Hitler was making noisy speeches about the remilitarization of the Rhineland, and in Italy Mussolini boasted of his growing naval strength in the Mediterranean. No wonder Bob was grinding his teeth. He could not stand Mussolini, whom he referred to as the Fat Fascist, and had no doubt that all that was needed to silence his bombast was a couple of salvoes from the foredeck of some British battleship.

It was all a bit frightening. She dropped the newspaper onto the floor and tried not to think about Ned, sixteen years old, committed to the Royal Navy, and ripe as a sweet fruit for combat. The door opened and Molly came into the dining-room.

Biddy did not dress for breakfast. She had a useful garment called a house-coat which, every morning, she pulled on over her night-gown. And so Molly's appearance, neatly turned out and shod, and with her hair carefully fluffed out, and a little discreet make-up on her face, engendered a sisterly dart of irritation.

"I'm sorry I'm late."

"Not late at all. No matter, anyway. Did you sleep in?"

"Not really. But I was up and down all night. Poor Jess had dreadful nightmares and kept waking. She dreamt that the Dame in the pantomime was in the room and trying to kiss her."

"What, corsets and all? I can't think of anything worse."

"She's still asleep, poor pet. Judith's not appeared either?"

"She's probably packing. Don't worry about her. She'll turn up in a moment."

"And Bob?"

"Been and gone. Work calls. Leave's over. He said to say goodbye to you. I'm going to drive you all to the station. Get something to eat—Mrs. Cleese has cooked sausages."

Molly went to the sideboard, lifted the lid of the sausage dish, hesitated, and then replaced it. She poured coffee and came to join her sister.

Biddy raised her eyebrows. "Not hungry?"

"Not really. I'll have a bit of toast."

Molly Dunbar's claim to beauty lay in her extraordinarily girlish appearance, the fluffy fair hair, the rounded cheeks, the eyes, which reflected only a sort of bewildered innocence. She was not a clever woman, always slow to see the point of a joke, and accepting any observation at face value, however loaded it might be with *double entendre*. Men were apt to find this rather charming, because it made them feel protective, but her patent transparency was a cause of irritation to Biddy. Now, however, she experienced a certain concern. She saw that, beneath the delicate dusting of face powder, there were dark shadows beneath Molly's eyes, and her cheeks were unusually pale.

"Are you feeling all right?"

"Yes. Just not hungry. And suffering from lack of sleep." She drank coffee. "I *hate* not sleeping in the middle of the night. It's like being in a different world, and everything becomes so much more awful."

"What's so awful in the first place?"

"Oh, I don't know. Just all the things that have to be done when I get home. Buying school clothes for Judith, and organizing everything. Closing the house. Trying to help Phyllis find a new job. Then getting myself to London, catching the boat, going back to Colombo. Everything. I'd put it all out of my mind while I was here with you; not thought about it. Now I've got to start being sensible again. And I think sometime I'm going to *have* to try to spend just a few days with the parents. Which makes another complication."

"Must you go?"

"Yes, I really think I must."

"You're a glutton for punishment. I've got a letter here from Mother."

"Everything all right?"

"No. All wrong as usual."

"I even feel guilty about them being on their own for Christmas."

"I don't," said Biddy shortly. "I asked them, of course. I always do, praying that they'll refuse. But, thank God, they came up with all the usual excuses. Father's busy time; snow on the roads; the car making a funny noise; Mother's little twinges of rheumatism. They're impossible. Dug deep into their rut. No point in trying to brighten their lives, because then they wouldn't have anything to moan about."

"They're old."

"No, they're not. They've simply embraced decrepitude. I shouldn't worry about them, when you've got so much else on your plate."

"I can't help it." Molly hesitated, and then said, quite violently, "The awful thing is that right now, at this moment, I think I'd give anything not to be going. I hate leaving Judith. I hate us all being torn apart. It makes me feel as though I don't belong anywhere. You know, sometimes I get this most extraordinary feeling . . . as though I were in a sort of limbo, without any identity. It happens just when I'm least expecting it. Riding on top of a London bus, or leaning over the rail of some P and O liner, watching the wake of the ship creaming away into the past. And I think, what am I doing here? And where am I meant to be? And who am I?"

Her voice cracked. For a dreadful moment Biddy feared that she was about to burst into tears.

"Oh, Molly . . ."

". . . and I know it's just this thing of living between two worlds, and the worst bits are when the two worlds come so close that they're nearly touching. Like now. I don't feel that I belong to either of them. Just . . . distracted . . ."

Biddy thought that she understood. "If it's any comfort, there are thousands of women like yourself, British India wives, facing just the same dilemma . . ."

"I know. And it isn't any comfort at all. I just go on feeling utterly isolated."

"It's just that you're tired. Not sleeping. It makes one depressed."

"Yes." Molly sighed, but at least she wasn't weeping. She drank more coffee, and laid down her cup. "But still I can't help wishing that Bruce worked in London, or Birmingham, or *anywhere,* so that we could live in England, and just be together."

"It's a bit late to start wishing that."

"Or even that we'd never married. That we'd never met. That he found some other girl. That he'd left me alone."

"It's unlikely *you'd* have met another man," Biddy told her brutally. "And imagine the alternative. Life at the Vicarage with Mother. And no beautiful daughters."

"It's just the thought of having to start . . . again. Picking up the pieces. Not belonging to myself any more . . ."

Her voice trailed into silence. The unsaid words hung between them. Molly lowered her eyes and a faint blush crept up into her cheeks.

Despite herself, Biddy was filled with sympathy. She knew exactly what was at the back of this distressing flood of uncharacteristic confidence. It had nothing to do with all the imminent practicalities of packing up and departure. It had nothing to do with saying goodbye to Judith. It had everything to do with Bruce. She felt sorry for Bruce, dull as he was. Four years separation did no marriage any good, and Biddy did not suppose that Molly, so feminine and fastidious and diffident, had ever been much good in bed. How on earth all those abandoned husbands dealt with their natural sexual desires was beyond her. But, on second thoughts, not beyond her at all. The obvious solution was simply some discreet arrangement, but even the wayward Biddy was ingrained with the inbred prejudices of her generation, so she reined in her imagination and firmly put the whole sorry business out of her mind.

Molly's blush had faded. Biddy decided to be positive. She said robustly, "You know, I am sure it will all work itself out." Which, even to her own ears, sounded fairly inconclusive. "I mean . . . I think it's all rather exciting. Once you get onto the boat, you'll feel a different woman. Just think of the bliss, three weeks with nothing whatever to do but lie in a deck-chair. And once you've stopped being sick in the Bay of Biscay, you'll probably have the time of your life. Going back to the sun, and the tropics, and lots of servants. Seeing all your old friends again. Why, I'm almost envious of you!"

"Yes." Molly managed an apologetic smile. "Yes, of course. I'm just being silly. I'm sorry . . . I know you think I'm being silly."

"No, I don't, you silly girl. I do understand. And I remember when we went to Malta, how I simply hated leaving Ned. But there it is. We can't be everywhere at once. The only thing to be certain about is that you're leaving Judith at a school that is sympathetic and caring. What's the name of this place you've found for her?"

"Saint Ursula's."

"Did you like the headmistress?"

"She has a very good reputation."

"Yes, but did you like her?"

"Yes, I think I did, once I'd stopped being frightened of her. Clever women always scare me to bits."

"Has she got a sense of humour?"

"I didn't tell her a joke."

"But you're happy with the school?"

"Oh, yes. Even if I hadn't been going back to Ceylon, I think I should have sent Judith to Saint Ursula's. The Porthkerris School has been excellent, academically, but the children there are a pretty mixed bunch. Her best friend was the grocer's daughter."

"Nothing wrong with that."

"No, but it doesn't *lead* anywhere, does it? Socially, I mean."

Biddy had to laugh. "Honestly, Molly, you always were the most appalling snob."

"I'm not a snob. But people matter."

"Yes, they certainly do."

"What are you getting at now?"

"Louise."

"Don't you like her?"

"About as much as she likes me. I certainly wouldn't want to spend my holidays with her."

This threw Molly into a state of instant agitation. "Oh, Biddy, *please* don't start interfering and raising objections. It's all been arranged, and cut and dried, and there's nothing to be said."

"Who said I was going to raise objections?" Biddy asked, and immediately started raising them. "She's such a tough old bird. So boring with her endless golf and her bridge and the Holy Temple of the Golf Club. She's so unfeminine, so set in her ways, so . . ." Biddy frowned, searching for the right word, but could only come up with "unwarm."

"Actually, you've got it wrong. She's very kind. She's been a tower of strength to me. And she offered to have Judith. I didn't have to ask. That's generous. And she's going to give Judith a bicycle. That's generous too, because they're dreadfully expensive. But most important, she's reliable. She'll give Judith security . . . I won't need to worry . . ."

"Perhaps Judith needs more than security."

"Such as?"

"Emotional space; freedom to grow in her own direction. She'll soon be fifteen. She'll need to spread wings, find herself. Make her own friends. Have some contact with the opposite sex . . ."

"Biddy, trust *you* to bring sex into the conversation. She's far too young to start thinking about that sort of thing . . ."

"Oh, come on, Molly, be your age. You've seen her, these last couple of weeks. She's literally flowered with all the fun we've had. You mustn't begrudge her the perfectly natural pleasures of life. You don't want her to be like we were, shut away by the circumstances of our upbringing, and bored stiff."

"It doesn't matter what I think. I said it's too late. She's going to Louise."

"Come hell or high water—I knew that would be your attitude."

"Then why bring the subject up in the first place?"

Biddy wanted to hit her, but thought of Judith, and managed to control her rising impatience. Instead she tried another, softer approach. Gentle persuasion. "But wouldn't it be fun for her to come to us from time to time? No, don't look so horrified, it's a perfectly viable suggestion. In fact, it was Bob's idea. He's taken a shine to Judith. It would be a nice little break for her, and it would be a nice little break for Louise."

"I . . . I'd have to discuss it with Louise . . ."

"Oh, for God's sake, Molly, have some gumption of your own . . ."

"I don't want to *upset* Louise . . ."

"Because Louise doesn't approve of *me*."

"No, because I don't want to rock the boat, have Judith unsettled. Not just now. Oh, please understand, Biddy. Perhaps later on . . ."

"There may not be a later on."

"What do you mean?" Molly demanded, in evident alarm.

"Read the papers. The Germans have embraced National Socialism, but Bob doesn't trust Herr Hitler further than he could throw him. And the same goes for fat old Mussolini."

"You mean . . ." Molly swallowed. ". . . a war?"

"Oh, I don't know. But I don't think we should fritter around with our private lives, because, perhaps very soon, we won't have any. And I think the reason you're frittering now is because you don't want Judith to come to me. You think I'm a bad influence, I suppose. All those wicked parties, and young lieutenants coming to call. That's it, isn't it? You might as well admit it."

"It isn't that!" It had turned into a proper row, with both of them raising their voices. "You know it isn't. And I am grateful. You and Bob have been so good . . ."

"For heaven's sake, you make it sound like a penance. We've had you for Christmas, and we've all had a great time. That's all. And I think you're being very feeble and very selfish. You're just like Mother . . . hating people to enjoy themselves."

"That's not true."

"Let's just forget it." And with this, Biddy, exasperated, reached for *The Times*, snapped its pages open, and retreated behind it.

Silence. Molly, quite shattered by the awfulness of everything, the possibility of another war, the confusions of her imminent future, and the fact that Biddy was now furious with her, sat in a state of trembling agitation. It wasn't fair. She was doing her best. It wasn't her fault. The loaded silence lengthened, and she discovered that she could not stand it for another second. She pushed back the cuff of her cardigan and looked at her watch.

"Where is *Judith*?" A relief to have thought of something, someone, on whom to unleash her misery. She stood abruptly, pushing back her chair, and went to the door to fling it open and call for her tardy daughter. But there was no need to call, for Judith was already there, just across the hall, sitting at the foot of the staircase.

"What *are* you doing?"

"Tying my shoelace."

She did not meet her mother's eyes, and Molly felt a coldness and, not always the most perceptive of women, realized that her daughter had been there for some time, halted by the raised voices from behind the closed dining-room door, and had heard every word of the acrimonious and regrettable exchange.

It was Jess who came to her rescue.

"Mummy."

She looked up and saw her younger child peering at her through the banister rail. Jess, awake at last, but still in her long cream night-dress and with her curls awry.

"Mummy!"

"I'm coming, darling."

"I want to get my *close* on."

"I'm coming." She crossed the hall, paused for an instant. "You'd better go and have breakfast," she told Judith. She went upstairs.

Judith waited until she was gone, then pulled herself to her feet and went into the dining-room. Aunt Biddy was sitting there, in her usual place, and, down the length of the room, they looked, bleakly, at each other.

Aunt Biddy said, "Oh, dear." She had been reading the newspaper. She folded it and dropped it on the floor. She said, "Sorry about that."

Judith was not used to having grown-ups apologize to her. "It's all right."

"Get yourself a sausage. I should think you need it."

Judith did as she was told, but hot sizzling sausages weren't much of a comfort. She carried her plate back to the table and sat down in her customary place, with her back to the window. She looked at the food, but didn't think that, just yet, she could eat it.

After a bit, "Did you hear it all?" Aunt Biddy asked.

"Most of it."

"It was my fault. My timing was rotten. I chose the wrong moment. Your mother's in no state to make any sort of a plan at the moment. I should have realized that."

"I shall be all right with Aunt Louise, you know."

"I know that. It isn't that I'm worried about your well-being, just the fact that, quite possibly, it won't be much fun."

Judith said, "I've never had proper grown-up fun before. Not before this Christmas."

"What you're trying to say is what you don't have, you don't miss."

"Yes, I suppose that's it. But I would love to come back."

"I'll try again. A little later."

Judith picked up her knife and fork and cut a sausage in two. She said, "Is there really going to be another war?"

"Oh, my dear, I don't expect so. You're far too young to be worrying about that."

"But Uncle Bob's worried?"

"Not so much worried, I think, as frustrated. Grinding his teeth at the very thought of the might of the British Empire being challenged. Roused, he can become a real old bulldog."

"If I came to stay, would I come here?"

"I don't know. Keyham's a two-year appointment, and we're due to move at the end of the summer."

"Where will you go?"

"No idea. Bob wants to go back to sea. If he does, I think I shall try to buy a little house of our own. We've never owned bricks and mortar, always lived in quarters. But I think it would be nice to have a permanent base. I thought, Devon. We have friends around here. Somewhere like Newton Abbot or Chagford, not too far from your grandparents."

"A little house of your own!" It was a charming prospect. "Oh, do get one in the country. And then I could come and stay with you there."

"If you want."

"I'll always want."

"No. That's the funny thing. You mightn't. At your age, everything changes so quickly, and yet a year can seem like a lifetime. I remember. And you'll make new friends; want different things. And in your case, it's even more important, because you're going to have to make your own decisions and make up your mind about what you want to do. You won't have your mother around, and although you're bound to feel a bit bereft and lonely, in a way, it's a good thing. I'd have given the world to be shed of my parents when I was fourteen, fifteen. As it was," she added with some satisfaction, "I didn't do too badly, but that was because I took matters into my own hands."

"It's not very easy to take matters into your own hands when you're at boarding-school," Judith pointed out. She thought Aunt Biddy was making it all sound far too easy.

"I think you must learn to precipitate situations, not be passive and simply let them happen to you. You must learn to be selective, about the friends you make and the books you read. An independence of spirit, I suppose that's what I'm talking about." She smiled. "George Bernard Shaw said that youth is wasted on the young. It's only when you get to be old that you begin to understand what he was talking about."

"You're not old."

"Maybe. But I'm certainly no longer a spring chicken."

Judith popped a bit of sausage into her mouth and chewed thoughtfully, ruminating over Aunt Biddy's advice. "What I really hate," she admitted at last, "is being treated as though I were the same age as Jess. I'm never *asked* about things, or *told* about things. If I hadn't heard you shouting at each other, I should never have known that you'd asked me to stay with you. She would never have told me."

"I know. It must be maddening. And I think you've got a genuine griev-ance. But you mustn't be too hard on your mother just now. At the moment, she's in a state of upheaval, and who can blame her if she does start twittering around like a wet hen?" She laughed, and was rewarded by the beginnings of a smile. "Between you and me, I think she's rather in awe of Louise."

"I know she is."

"And you?"

"I'm not frightened of her."

"Good girl."

"You know, Aunt Biddy, I've really loved staying with you. I won't ever forget it."

Biddy was touched. "We've liked having you. Bob in particular. He said to say goodbye. He was sorry not to see you. Now . . ." She pushed back her chair and got to her feet. "I can hear your mother and Jess on their way downstairs. Eat your breakfast and pretend we haven't been having a heart-to-heart. And remember, keep your spirits up. Now, I must go and put some clothes on . . ."

But before she reached the door, Molly and Jess had come into the room, Jess now dressed in a little smock and white socks, and with her silky curls smoothed by a hairbrush. Biddy paused to drop an airy kiss onto Molly's cheek. "Don't bother about a thing," she told her sister, which was the near-est she could get to an apology, and then she was gone, running up the stairs to the sanctuary of her bedroom.

And so the quarrel was swept away, under the carpet, and the day progressed. Judith was so relieved that the air was clear between her mother and her aunt, and that no bad feeling hung about in the atmosphere, that it was only when they were actually at the station, standing on the windswept platform and waiting for the *Riviera* to arrive to take them back to Cornwall, that she had time to regret the absence of Uncle Bob.

It was horrid going without saying goodbye to him. It was her own fault, for being so late coming down to breakfast, but it would have been nice if he could have waited, just five minutes, and said goodbye properly. And she wanted to thank him for so much, and thanks were never the same written in a letter.

The best had been his gramophone. Despite her mother's girlhood yearn-ings to go on the stage and become a ballerina, neither she nor Dad were musically inclined, but those afternoons spent with Uncle Bob in his study had awakened an awareness, an appreciation the existence of which Judith had never even suspected. He owned a huge variety of records, and although she had much enjoyed the Gilbert and Sullivan songs with their witty lyrics and catchy tunes, there were others which had lifted her heart, or made her feel so poignantly sad that she could scarcely keep the tears from brimming into her eyes. Puccini arias from *La Bohème,* the Rachmaninoff Piano Concerto, Tchaikovsky's *Romeo and Juliet* music. And, sheerest magic, Rimski-Korsakov's *Scheherazade*, the solo violin sending shivers down her spine. There was another record, by the same composer, which Uncle Bob referred to as the "Bum of the Flightle Bee," by Rip His Corsetsoff, a joke which reduced Judith to paroxysms of giggles. She had no idea that a grown-up could be so funny. But one thing was certain, which was that she simply had to have a gramophone of her own, and then she could collect records, just the way Uncle Bob had, and whenever she wanted, play them and be transported, as though led by the hand, into that other and previously unimagined land. She would start saving up right away.

Her feet were frozen. She tried to stamp some life into them, marking time on the greasy platform. Aunt Biddy and Mother were chatting inconsequently, as people do, while waiting for a train. They seemed to have run out of important things to say. Jess sat on the edge of a trolley and swung her white-gaitered fat legs. She hugged her golliwog, that revolting toy she took to bed every night. Judith was sure it must be filthy, but because it had a black face it didn't show the dirt. Not only filthy, but full of germs.

And then something really good happened. Aunt Biddy stopped chattering, looked up over Mother's head, and said, in quite a different voice, "Oh, look. There's Bob."

Judith's heart lifted. She swung around. Frozen feet were forgotten. And there he was, a huge, unmistakable figure in his British warm, coming down the platform towards them, with his brass hat cocked, Beatty fashion, over one bristling eyebrow, and a great grin on his craggy features. Judith's feet stopped feeling cold, and she had to stand very still to keep herself from running to meet him.

"Bob! What are you doing here?"

"Had a moment or two to spare, decided to come and see our little party on board." He looked down at Judith. "I couldn't let you go without saying goodbye properly."

She beamed up at him. She said, "I'm glad you came. I wanted to say thank you for everything. Especially for the clock."

"You'll have to remember to wind it."

"Oh, I will . . ." She couldn't stop smiling.

Uncle Bob cocked his head, listening. "I think that's the train now."

And indeed there was a sound—the railway lines were humming, and Judith looked and saw, around the distant curve beyond the end of the platform, the huge green-and-black steam engine surge into view, with its polished brass fixtures, its billowing plume of black smoke. Its approach was majestic and awe-inspiring as it crept alongside the platform. The engine driver, sooty-faced, leaned down from the footplate and Judith had a glimpse of the flickering flames of the boiler furnace. The massive pistons, like a giant's arms, revolved more and more slowly, until finally, with a hiss of steam, the monster stopped. It was, as always, dead on time.

A small pandemonium broke out. Doors were flung open, passengers alighted, lugging their baggage. A certain urgency prevailed, a flurry of departure. Then the porter heaved their suitcases on board and went in search of seats. Uncle Bob, with seamanlike thoroughness, followed him, just to make sure the job was done in a proper fashion. Molly, panicking slightly, lifted Jess into her arms and hopped up into the train, and had to lean down to kiss her sister goodbye.

"You've been so kind. We've had a wonderful Christmas. Wave goodbye to Aunt Biddy, Jess."

Jess, still clutching Golly, flapped a little white-furred paw.

Aunt Biddy turned to Judith. "Goodbye, dear child. You've been a little brick." She stooped and kissed Judith. "Don't forget. I'm always here. Your mother's got my telephone number in her book."

"Goodbye. And thank you so much."

"Quick. Up you get, or the train will go without you." She raised her voice. "Make sure Uncle Bob gets off, otherwise you'll have to take him with you." For a moment she had looked a bit serious, but now she was laughing again. Judith smiled back, gave a final wave, and then plunged down the corridor after the others.

A compartment had been found containing only one young man, who sat, with an open book on his knee, while the porter piled luggage in the racks over his head. Then, when all was stowed, Uncle Bob tipped the porter and sent him on his way.

"You must also go, quickly," Judith told him, "or the train will move, and you'll be caught."

He smiled down at her. "It's never happened yet. Goodbye, Judith." They shook hands. When she drew her hand away, she found, in the palm of her woollen glove, a ten-shilling note. A whole ten shillings.

"Oh, Uncle Bob, *thank you*."

"Spend it wisely."

"I will. Goodbye."

He was gone. A moment later, he and Aunt Biddy reappeared again, standing on the platform below their window. "Have a good journey." The train began to move. "Safe arrival!" It gathered speed. "Goodbye!" The platform and the station slid away behind them. Uncle Bob and Aunt Biddy were gone. It was all over. They were on their way.

The next few moments were taken up in getting themselves settled. The other occupant of the carriage, the young man, sat by the door, and so they had the window-seats. The heating was on full blast, and it was very warm, so gloves, coats, and hats were removed by the children; Molly kept her hat on. Jess was put by the window, where she knelt on the prickly plush and pressed her nose against the smutty glass. Judith sat opposite her. Her mother, once she had folded coats and stowed them in the rack, and then delved into her travelling bag for Jess's drawing-book and coloured pencils, finally sank down beside Jess and let out a sigh of relief, as though the whole operation had been almost too much for her. She closed her eyes, but after a little they fluttered open again, and she began to fan her face with her hand.

"Goodness, it's hot," she said to nobody in particular.

Judith said, "I think it's rather nice." Her feet hadn't even started to thaw.

But her mother was adamant. "I wonder . . ." Now she was addressing the young man, whose privacy and peace they had so rudely disturbed. He looked up from his book, and she smiled disarmingly. "I wonder, would you mind if we turned the heating down a little? Or even opened the window a chink?"

"Of course." He was very polite. He laid aside his book and stood up. "Which would you rather? Or, perhaps, both?"

"No, I think a little fresh air would do the trick . . ."

"Right." He moved to the window. Judith tucked her legs out of the way and watched as he unloosed the heavy leather strap, let the window down an inch, and then fixed the strap again.

"How's that?"

"Perfect."

"Be careful that your little girl doesn't get a smut in her eye."

"I hope she won't."

He went back to his seat and picked up his book again. Listening in to other people's conversations, watching strangers and trying to guess their lives, were two of Judith's favourite occupations. Mummy called it "staring." "Don't stare, Judith."

But Mummy was reading her magazine, so that was all right.

Covertly, she studied him. His book looked both large and dull, and she wondered why it so absorbed his interest, because he did not strike her as a studious type, being broad-shouldered and solidly built. Quite tough and fit, she decided. He was dressed in corduroys and a tweed jacket and a thick grey polo-necked sweater, and draped around his neck was an extremely long and startlingly striped woollen scarf. He had hair that was no particular colour, neither fair nor brown, and it was rather untidy and looked as though it needed a good cut. She could not see the colour of his eyes because he was reading, but he wore heavy horn-rimmed spectacles and there was a deep cleft, too masculine to be called a dimple, bang in the middle of his chin. She wondered how old he was and decided about twenty-five. But perhaps she was wrong. She hadn't much experience of young men, and it was hard to be sure.

She turned back to the window. In a moment they would be going over the Saltash Bridge, and she didn't want to miss the sight of all the naval men-of-war at anchor in the harbour.

But Jess had other thoughts. She was already bored with looking out of the window, and now searched for some different diversion. She began to jump up and down, and then scrambled down off the seat in order to be able to scramble up again. In doing so her shoe kicked Judith's shin, quite painfully.

"Oh, sit *still*, Jess."

Jess responded by flinging Golly at her sister. For two pins, Judith would have posted him out of the open crack at the top of the window and horrible Golly would have gone forever, but instead she picked him up and threw him back. Golly hit Jess in the face. Jess howled.

"Oh, *Judith*." Mother took Jess on her knee. When the howls had subsided, she apologized to the young man.

"I'm sorry. We've disturbed your peace."

He looked up from his book and smiled. It was a particularly charming smile, revealing even white teeth as good as a toothpaste advertisement, and it lit up his homely features and completely changed his face, so that quite suddenly he was almost good-looking.

"Not at all," he reassured her.

"Have you come from London?"

She was obviously in a conversational mood. The young man, as well, seemed to realize this, for he closed his book and set it aside.

"Yes."

"Have you been away for Christmas?"

"No, I was working over Christmas and the New Year. I'm taking my holiday now."

"Goodness, what a shame. Fancy having to work over Christmas. What do you do?"

Judith thought she was being rather nosy, but the young man didn't appear to think so. In fact, he looked quite happy to talk, as though he had had enough of his boring book.

"I'm a houseman at Saint Thomas's."

"Oh, a *doctor!*"

"That's right."

Judith was terrified she was going to say, "You look much too young to be a doctor," which would have embarrassed everybody, but she didn't. And it explained the reason for his solid, heavy book. He was probably studying the symptoms of some obscure disease.

"Not a very amusing Christmas for you."

"On the contrary. Christmas in hospital is great fun. Decorations in the wards and nurses singing carols."

"And now you're going home?"

"Yes. To Truro. My parents live there."

"We're going farther than that. Just about to the end of the line. We've been staying with my sister and her husband. He's a captain at the Engineering College."

It sounded a little as though she were bragging. To divert attention Judith said, "Here's the bridge coming now."

Rather to her surprise, the young man seemed as excited about this as she was. "I must have a look," he said, and he got to his feet and came to stand beside her, steadying himself with a hand on the window's edge. He smiled down at her, and she saw that his eyes were neither brown nor green, but speckled, like a trout. "It's too good to miss, isn't it?"

The wheels were slowing. The iron girders clanked past, and far below gleamed cold winter water, crammed with sleek grey cruisers and destroyers, and pinnaces, and small, busy launches, and ships' boats, all flying the White Ensign.

She said, "I think it's a special bridge."

"Why? Because it takes you over the river into a foreign land?"

"Not just that."

"Brunel's masterpiece."

"Sorry?"

"Brunel. He designed and built it for the Great Western Railway. The wonder of the day. Still is pretty wonderful, for that matter."

They fell silent. He stayed there until the train had crossed the bridge and steamed into Saltash on the Cornish side of the Tamar, and then he went back to his seat and picked up his book again.

After a bit, the man from the restaurant car came along to tell them that afternoon tea was being served. Molly asked the young doctor if he would like to join them, but he declined politely, so they left him on his own and made their way down the rackety, lurching corridors of the train until they came to the restaurant car. Here, they were ushered to a table covered in a white linen cloth and set with white china. There were little rose-shaded lights, and these had been turned on, which made it all very luxurious and cosy, because outside the winter afternoon was darkening to twilight. Then the waiter came, with tea in a china teapot, a little jug of milk, and a jug of hot water and a bowl of sugar lumps. Jess had eaten three lumps even before her mother noticed. And then another waiter appeared and served them sandwiches and hot buttered teacakes, and slabs of Dundee cake, and Jacob's chocolate biscuits wrapped up in silver paper.

Molly poured from the teapot and Judith drank the strong hot tea and ate the buttered teacakes. She gazed out into the deepening darkness and decided that, after all, it had not been such a bad day. It had started a bit gloomily, waking up and knowing that the holiday was over, and had become very nearly disastrous over breakfast-time, with her mother and Aunt Biddy having that terrible row. But they had patched it up, and gone on being nice to each other, and out of it had come the good knowledge that Aunt Biddy and Uncle Bob actually liked Judith enough to want to have her to stay again, even though it didn't seem that she was going to be allowed to. Aunt Biddy had been particularly kind and understanding, talking to Judith just as though she were a grown-up, and giving advice that she would always remember. Another good thing had been Uncle Bob appearing at the station, come to say goodbye and see them off, and leaving Judith with a ten-shilling note in her hand. The start of saving to buy a gramophone. And finally, talking to the young doctor in their compartment. It would have been nice if he had joined them for tea, but perhaps they would all have run out of things to say to each other. Still, he was pleasant, with his easy manner. As they crossed the Saltash Bridge, he had stood very close to Judith and she had smelt the Harris tweedy smell of his jacket, and the end of his long muffler had lain across her knee. Brunel, he had told her. Brunel built this bridge. It occurred to her that he was the sort of person one would like to have as a brother.

She finished the teacake and took a salmon-paste sandwich, and pretended to herself that Mummy and Jess did not belong to her, and that she was on her own, rattling across Europe in the *Orient Express*, with state secrets in her Chinese wicker basket, and all manner of exciting adventures in the offing.

Soon after they returned to their compartment, the train steamed into Truro, and their fellow passenger stowed his book into his zippered bag, wound his muffler around his neck, and said goodbye. Through the window, Judith watched him make his way down the busy lamp-lit platform. Then he was gone.

After that, it was a bit dull, but there wasn't far to go, and Jess had fallen asleep. At the junction, Judith found a porter, who carried their big suitcases, while Judith carried the smaller bags, and Molly carried Jess. Crossing the bridge which led to the other platform and the Porthkerris train, she felt the wind blowing in from the sea, and although it was cold, it was a different sort of cold from Plymouth, as though their short journey had brought them to another land. No longer intense and frosty, but soft and damp, and the night smelt of salt and earthy furrows and pine trees.

They piled into the small train, and presently, in an unhurried sort of way, they were off. *Clackety-clack.* Quite a different sound from the great London express. Five minutes later they were all piling out again at Penmarron Halt, and Mr. Jackson, with his lantern, was on the platform to meet them.

"Want me to give you a hand with your bags, Mrs. Dunbar?"

"No, I think we'll leave the big stuff here and just take our small bags. Just for the night, we can manage. Perhaps the carrier can bring them up on his cart in the morning."

"They'll be safe enough."

They walked through the waiting-room, across the dark dirt road, through the gate and up the shadowed garden. Jess was heavy, and every now and then Molly had to pause to catch her breath. But finally they reached the top terrace, and the light was on over the porch. As they came to the top of the path, the inner glass door was opened, and Phyllis was there to welcome them.

"Look who's here, turned up like a lot of bad pennies." She hurried down the steps. "Here, give me the child, madam, you must be exhausted. What are you thinking of, carrying her all the way up those steps, and her weighing more than she should, by the feel of her." Phyllis's shrill voice in her ear had finally woken Jess. She blinked sleepily with no idea where she was. "How much Christmas pudding have you eaten, Jess? Now come along, let's get you all in out of the cold. I've got the bath-water scalding, and there's a nice fire in the sitting-room, and a boiled fowl for your supper."

Phyllis, decided Molly, really was a treasure, and life without her was never going to be quite the same again. Once she had heard a brief run-down of their Christmas, and had imparted a few gobbets of village gossip of her own, she bore Jess upstairs to bathe her, feed her warm bread and milk, and put her to bed. Judith, carrying her Chinese wicker basket, followed, still chattering. "I got a clock from Uncle Bob, Phyllis, it's in a sort of leather case. I'll show you . . ."

Molly watched them go. Relieved at last of the responsibility of Jess, and with the journey behind her, she all at once felt totally exhausted. She took off her fur coat and slung it over the end of the banister. Then she gathered up the pile of mail which awaited her on the hall table, and went into the sitting-room. The coal-fire burnt brightly, and she stood in front of it for a moment, warming her hands, and trying to ease the stiffness out of her neck and shoulders. After a bit, she sat in her chair and leafed through her letters. There was one from Bruce, but she would not open it immediately. Just now, all she wanted to do was just sit, quite quietly, be warmed by the fire, and gather her wits.

For it had been something of a shattering day, and the dreadful row with Biddy, following on the heels of a sleepless night, had just about finished her. "Don't bother about a thing," Biddy had said, and kissed her, as though that were the end of ill feeling, but before lunch, she had started in on Molly again, while they were on their own, sipping a glass of sherry and waiting for Hobbs to ring the gong for luncheon.

She had done it quite kindly, almost teasing, but her message was loud and clear.

"Do take some notice of what I said. It's for your own good, and for Judith's as well. You can't leave her for four years, totally unprepared for what is always a fairly difficult time. I hated being fourteen—I always felt I was neither fish, fowl, nor good red herring."

"Biddy, she's not *totally* unprepared . . ."

Biddy lit one of her perpetual cigarettes. She blew smoke. She said, "Has she started the curse yet?"

Her bluntness was embarrassing, even from a sister, but Molly refused to be outfaced. "Yes, of course, six months ago."

"Well, that's a blessing anyway. And what about her clothes? She's going to need some attractive clothes, and I don't imagine Louise will be much use in that direction. Is she going to have a dress allowance . . . ?"

"Yes, I've made provision for that."

"That dress she wore the other evening. It was quite pretty, but a bit infantile. And then you told me that she wanted an Arthur Ransome book for Christmas, so I went and bought it."

"She loves Arthur Ransome . . ."

"Yes, but she should be into adult novels by now . . . or at least starting to read them. That's why I shot out on Christmas Eve and bought *Jane Eyre*. Once she's into that she won't come out of it until she's turned the last page. She'll probably fall madly in love with Mr. Rochester, just as every teenager does." Biddy's eyes teased, sparkling with amusement. "Or perhaps you didn't fall in love with him? Perhaps you were saving yourself for Bruce?"

Molly knew that she was being laughed at, but refused to be goaded. "That is my business."

"And then you saw him for the first time and your knees turned to water . . ."

She was sometimes quite outrageous, but funny too, and despite herself, Molly had to laugh. Even so, she had taken it all to heart, but what made it so upsetting was that Biddy's strictures, which Molly realized were perfectly justifiable, had come too late for Molly to do very much about improving the situation, because, as usual, she had left things to the very last moment, and, looming before her, there was so much to *do*.

She yawned enormously. The clock on the mantelpiece struck six o'clock. Time for the evening ritual of going upstairs, bathing, changing for dinner. She changed for dinner every night, as she had done all her married life, even though, for the last four years, there had been no person but Judith to eat it with. It was one of the small conventions that had propped up her lonely life, providing a sort of structure and order that she needed to give day-to-day existence, humdrum as it was, some sort of shape. This was something else that Biddy teased her about, because Biddy, left on her own, would, once she had bathed, fling on that housecoat, or even her ratty old dressing-gown, stuff her feet into a pair of slippers, and instruct Phyllis to serve the boiled fowl on a tray by the sitting-room fire.

She would also treat herself to a large whisky and soda. At Riverview House, Molly's evening tipple was a single glass of sherry, slowly savoured, but staying with Biddy had been a real eye-opener, and she had downed a whisky with the best of them, after a cold afternoon out of doors, or the distressingly unsuccessful visit to the pantomime. The very idea of whisky, now, when she felt so tired and washed out, was enormously tempting. She debated for a moment as to whether or not she *ought* to. And whether it was worth the effort needed to go through to the dining-room and assemble the whisky bottle, the soda siphon, and a tumbler. In the end, she decided that, for medicinal purposes, it was absolutely essential, so she stopped debating, pulled herself out of her chair, and went to pour the drink. She was only going to have one, so she made it fairly strong. Back by the fire and settled once more in her chair, she took a delicious, warming, and comforting mouthful, then set down the heavy glass and reached for her husband's letter.

While Phyllis dealt with Jess, Judith took reoccupation of her own bedroom, unpacked her night-things and her sponge-bag, and then her Chinese wicker basket with all her Christmas loot. She laid everything out on the top of her desk, so that when Phyllis was finished with Jess she could show it all off, and explain to Phyllis who had given her what. Uncle Bob's ten-shilling note she stowed away in a private drawer that had a little key, and his clock she set on the table by her bed. When Phyllis put her head around the door, she was sitting at her desk, writing her name on the flyleaf of her new diary.

"There's Jess," announced Phyllis. "Looking at her picture book. She'll be asleep again before she knows where she is."

She came into the room and plumped herself down on Judith's bed, which she had already turned down for the night, as she had drawn the curtains.

"Come and show me what you got."

"Yours was the best, Phyllis, it was kind of you."

"At least you won't have to come asking me for scissors all the time. You'll need to hide them from Jess. And I have to thank you for those bath salts. I like Evening in Paris better than California Poppy. Used one yesterday afternoon when I had my bath. Felt like a film star. Now let's have a look . . ."

It all took a bit of time because Phyllis, so generous of nature, had to inspect everything minutely, and marvel at its splendour. "Look at that book. It'll take you months to read. Some grown-up, that is. And feel that jumper. So soft! And that's your diary. It's got a leather jacket, you'll have secrets to put in that."

"Wasn't it kind of Aunt Louise, because she's already promised me a bicycle? I never expected two presents."

"And the little clock! No excuse for being late for breakfast now. What did you get from your dad?"

"I asked for a cedarwood box, with a Chinese lock, but it hasn't arrived yet."

"Oh, well, it'll come." Phyllis settled herself more comfortably on the bed. "Now . . ." She was agog with curiosity. "Tell me what you did."

So Judith told her, all about Aunt Biddy's house ("It was absolutely freezing cold, Phyllis, I've never been in such a cold house, but there were fires in the sitting-room, and somehow it didn't seem to matter because we were having such a good time"), and about the pantomime, and skating, and about Uncle Bob and his gramophone, typewriter, and interesting photographs, and about the parties and the Christmas tree, and the Christmas lunch table with a centre-piece of holly and Christmas roses, and red and gold crackers and little silver dishes of chocolates.

"Aw." Phyllis let out a sigh of envy. "It sounds *lovely*."

Which made Judith feel a bit guilty, because she was pretty sure that Phyllis's Christmas had been a fairly thin one. Phyllis's father was a tin miner out Saint Just way, and her mother a large-busted, large-hearted, pinafored woman, usually with a child tucked up onto her hip. Phyllis was the eldest of five children, and how they all squeezed into that tiny stone-built terrace house was something of a conundrum. Once Judith had accompanied Phyllis to Saint Just Feast, to watch the Hunt ride out for the first meet of the season, and afterwards they had gone for tea in her house. They had eaten saffron buns and drunk strong tea, seven of them all crammed around the kitchen table, while Phyllis's father sat in his chair by the range, drank his tea out of a pudding bowl, and rested his boots on the polished brass fender.

"What did *you* do, Phyllis?"

"Not much, really. My mum was poorly, she had 'flu, I think, so I had to do most of the work."

"Oh, I am sorry. Is she better?"

"Up and about but, aw, she's got a teasy cough."

"Did you get a Christmas present?"

"Yes, I got a blouse from my mum, and a box of hankies from Cyril."

Cyril Eddy was Phyllis's young man, another tin miner. She had known him since they went to school together, and they had been walking out ever since. They weren't exactly engaged, but Phyllis was busy crocheting a set of doilies for her bottom drawer. She and Cyril didn't see much of each other, because Saint Just was so far away, and he worked shifts, but when they did manage to get together, they went on bicycle rides, or sat, locked in each other's arms, in the back row of the Porthkerris cinema. Phyllis had a photograph of Cyril on the chest of drawers in her bedroom. He wasn't very good-looking, but Phyllis assured Judith that he had lovely eyebrows.

"What did you give him?"

"A collar for his whippet. He was some pleased." A coy expression came into her face. "You meet any nice young men, did you?"

"Oh, Phyllis, of course not."

"No need to talk in that tone. Nothing unnatural."

"Most of Aunt Biddy's friends are grown up. Except on the last night, two young lieutenants came in after dinner for a drink. But it was so late that I went to bed pretty soon, so I didn't talk to them much. Anyway," she added, determined to be truthful, "they were far too busy being amused by Aunt Biddy to look at me . . ."

"That's just your age. Not one thing nor another. Couple of years, you'll be grown up, have the boys round you like flies round a honey-pot. You'll catch their eye." Phyllis smiled. "You never fancy a boy?"

"I said I don't know any. Except . . ." She hesitated.

"Go on. Tell Phyllis."

"There was this man in our compartment coming down from Plymouth. He was a doctor but he looked terribly young. Mummy talked to him, and then he told me that the Saltash Bridge was built by somebody called Brunel. He was really nice. I wouldn't mind meeting somebody like that."

"Perhaps you will."

"Not at Saint Ursula's."

"You don't go to a place like that to meet boys, you go to get educated. And don't turn up your nose at that. I had to leave school when I was younger than you, go into service, and I can't do much more than read and write and add up a sum. By the time you're done, you'll be passing exams and winning prizes. Only prize I ever won was for growing cress on a damp flannel."

"I suppose with your mother being ill and everything, you didn't have time to look for another job?"

"Didn't have the heart, somehow. I suppose, the truth is, I don't really want to leave you all. Never mind, Madam said she'd help, give me a good reference. Thing is, I don't want to be any further away from home. As it is, takes most of my day off just to bike back to Saint Just. I couldn't manage more."

"Perhaps someone in Porthkerris needs a maid."

"That'd be better."

"You might get a much nicer job. With other people in the kitchen to chat to, and not nearly so much to do."

"I dunno. I don't want to end up skivvying for some bad-tempered old bitch of a cook. Rather do it all myself, even if I've a heavy hand with the pastry, and never could get the hang of that old egg-whisk. Madam always said . . ." She stopped short.

Judith waited. "What's wrong?"

"That's funny. She hasn't come up for her bath. Look, it's twenty past six. I hadn't realized I'd been sitting here for so long. Do you suppose she thinks I'm not done with Jess yet?"

"I don't know."

"Well, go down like a good girl, and tell her the bathroom's empty. Doesn't matter about the fowl, I can hold that back till she's ready to eat. Poor soul, she's probably catching her breath after that train journey, but it's not like her to miss her bath . . ." She pulled herself to her feet. "I'd better get down and see to those potatoes."

But when she was gone, Judith lingered for a little, putting everything away, straightening the crumpled eiderdown, laying the new diary in the middle of her desk. Since the first of January, she had written in it every day, in her neatest handwriting. Now, she stared at the flyleaf. Judith Dunbar. She thought about putting down her address, and then decided against it, because very soon she wouldn't have a proper address. She worked out that when she finished writing the diary, it would be December 1940. And she would be nineteen. Which was, somehow, rather frightening, so she put the diary away in a drawer, combed her hair, and ran downstairs to tell her mother that if she hurried, she would have time for a bath.

She burst into the sitting-room.

"Mummy, Phyllis says that if you want to—"

She got no further. Because something, obviously, was terribly wrong. Her mother sat there, in her armchair by the fire, but the face she turned to Judith was stricken with despair and made swollen and ugly by weeping. A half-emptied tumbler stood on the table by her side, and on the floor at her feet were shed, like leaves, the scattered flimsy pages of a close-written letter.

"Mummy!" Instinctively, she closed the door behind her. "Whatever is it?"

"Oh, *Judith*."

She was across the carpet and kneeling by her mother's side. "But what is it?" The horror of seeing her parent in tears was worse than anything she could possibly have to tell her.

"It's a letter from Dad. I just opened it. I can't bear it . . ."

"What's happened to him?"

"Nothing." Molly dabbed at her face with an already sodden scrap of handkerchief. "It's just that . . . we're not staying in Colombo. He's got a new job . . . we have to go to Singapore!"

"But why does that make you cry?"

"Because it's *another* move . . . as soon as I get there, we've got to pack up, and go on again. To somewhere else that's strange. And I shan't know anybody. It was bad enough going back to Colombo, but at least I'd have had my own house . . . and it's even further away . . . and I've never been there . . . and I shall have to . . . Oh, I know I'm being silly . . ." Her tears flowed anew. "But somehow it's the last straw. I'm feeling so tired, and there's so . . ."

But by now she was crying too hard to be able to say anything. Judith kissed her. She smelt of whisky. She never drank whisky. She put out her arm, and gave Judith a clumsy hug. "I really need a clean handkerchief."

"I'll get one."

She left her mother and went out of the room, ran upstairs to her bedroom, and took one of her own large, sensible school handkerchiefs out of her top drawer. Slamming the drawer shut, glancing up, she faced her own reflection in the mirror, and saw that she looked almost as distraught and anxious as her weeping mother downstairs. Which wouldn't do at all. One of them had to be strong and sensible, otherwise everything was going to fall to pieces. She took a deep breath or two and composed herself. What was it Aunt Biddy had said? You must learn to precipitate situations, not let them simply happen to you. Well, this was a situation, if ever there was one. She straightened her shoulders and went back downstairs.

She found Molly, as well, had made a similar effort, had gathered the letter up off the floor, and even managed a trembling smile as Judith came back into the room.

"Oh, dear, thank you . . ." She accepted the clean handkerchief gratefully and blew her nose. "I am sorry. I don't know what came into me. It's really been the most exhausting of days. I suppose I'm tired . . ."

Judith sat down on the fireside stool. "May I read the letter?"

"Of course." She handed it over.

Dearest Molly,

His writing was neat and even, and very black. He always used black ink.

> By the time you get this, Christmas will be over. I hope that you and the girls had an enjoyable time. I have fairly momentous news for you. The Chairman called me into his office yesterday morning, and told me that they want me to move to Singapore, as Company Manager for Wilson-McKinnon. It is a promotion, which means a better salary, and other bonuses like a larger house, a company car and a driver. I hope you will be as pleased and gratified as I am. The new job does not commence until the month after you and Jess arrive here, so you will be able to help pack up this house, and ready it for the man who is to be my replacement, and the three of us will sail to Singapore together. I know you will miss Colombo, as I will, and all the beauty of this lovely island, but I find it exciting to

think that we shall travel together, and be together when we set up in our new home. The job will be a great deal more responsible and probably demanding, but I feel I can do it and am capable of making a success of it. I am very much looking forward to seeing you and meeting Jess. I hope she won't be too strange with me, and will get used to the idea that I am her father.

Tell Judith that her Christmas present should be arriving any day now. I hope all the arrangements for Saint Ursula's are going according to plan, and that it isn't going to be too much of a wrench for you, saying goodbye.

I saw Charlie Peyton the other day at the club. He tells me that Mary is expecting a new baby in April. They want us to go and dine with them . . .

And so on. She did not need to read any more. She folded the pages and gave them back to her mother.

She said, "It sounds quite good. Good for Dad. I don't think you should be too sad about it."

"I'm not sad. I'm just . . . defeated. I know it's selfish, but I don't feel that I want to go to Singapore. It's so hot there and so damp, and a new house, and new servants . . . making new friends . . . everything. It's too much . . ."

"But you won't have to do it all yourself. Dad will be there . . ."

"I *know* . . ."

"It'll be exciting."

"I don't want to be excited. I want everything to be calm, and still, and not to change. I want a *home*, not moving all the time, and being torn apart. And everybody demanding things of me, and telling me I do things all wrong when I do them, and knowing that I'm incompetent and incapable . . ."

"But you're *not!*"

"Biddy thinks I'm an idiot. So does Louise."

"Oh, don't take any notice of Biddy and Louise . . ."

Molly blew her nose again, and took another mouthful out of her whisky tumbler.

"I didn't know you drank whisky."

"I don't usually. I just needed one. That's probably why I cried. I'm probably drunk."

"I don't think you are."

Her mother smiled, a bit sheepishly, trying to laugh at herself. And then she said, "I'm sorry about this morning. That silly row we had, Biddy and I. I didn't know you were listening, but even so, we should never have behaved so childishly."

"I wasn't eavesdropping."

"I know that. I do hope you don't think I'm being mean and selfish to you. I mean, about Biddy asking you to stay, and me being so uncooperative. It's just that Louise, well, it's true she doesn't approve of Biddy, and it just seemed another complication that I had to deal with . . . perhaps I didn't handle it very well."

Judith said truthfully, "I don't mind about any of that." And then she added, because it seemed as good a time as any to say it, "I don't mind about not going to Aunt Biddy, or staying with Aunt Louise, or any of it. What I do mind is that you never talk to me about what's going to happen. You never bother to ask me what *I* want."

"That's what Biddy said. Just before lunch, she started in again. And I feel so guilty, because perhaps I have left you on your own too much, and make plans for you without discussing them. School and everything, and Aunt Louise. And now I feel I've left it all too late."

"Aunt Biddy should never have scolded you. And it's not too late . . ."

"But there's so much to *do*." She was off again. "I've left everything to the last moment, I haven't even bought your uniform, and there's Phyllis, and packing up, and everything . . ."

She was so fraught, so hopeless, that Judith felt, all at once, enormously protective, organized, and strong. She said, "We'll help. I'll help. We'll all do it together. As for that awful school uniform, why don't we go and get it tomorrow? Where do we have to go?"

"Medways, in Penzance."

"All right, then, we'll go to Medways, and we'll get everything in one fell swoop."

"But we have to buy hockey sticks, and Bibles, and attaché cases . . ."

"Well, we'll get them too. We won't come back here until we've got every single thing. We'll take the car. You'll have to be very brave and drive us, we couldn't possibly bring it all home in the train."

Molly looked, instantly, a little less woebegone. It seemed that just making one decision *for* her rendered her more cheerful. She said, "All right." She thought about it. "We'll leave Jess with Phyllis, she'd never last the day. And have a bit of an outing, just the two of us. And we'll have lunch at the Mitre, for a treat. We'll deserve it by then."

"And as well," said Judith, with much firmness, "we'll drive to Saint Ursula's, and I can have a look at the place. I can't go to a school I've never even seen . . ."

"But it's holiday time. There won't be anybody there."

"All the better. We'll prowl and peer through windows. Now, that's all fixed, so cheer up. Are you feeling better now? Do you want a bath? Do you want to go to bed, and have Phyllis bring your supper up on a tray?"

But Molly shook her head. "No. No, none of those lovely things. I'm all right now. I'll have my bath later."

"In that case, I'll go and tell Phyllis that we'll eat her boiled fowl when she's ready for us."

"In a moment. Give me another moment or two. I don't want Phyllis to know I've been crying. Do I look as though I have been?"

"No. Just a bit red in the face from the fire."

Her mother leaned forward and kissed her. "Thank you. You've made me feel quite different. So sweet of you."

"That's all right." She tried to think of something reassuring to say. "You were just in a state."

Molly opened her eyes and faced the new day. It was scarcely light, and not yet time to rise, so she lay warm, and lapped in linen sheets, and was filled with gratitude because she had slept, without dreams, all through the night, sleeping as soon as her head touched the pillow, without interruption, and undisturbed by Jess. This in itself was a small miracle, for Jess was a demanding child. If she did not wake during the small hours and scream for her mother, then she was on the go hideously early, and clambering into Molly's bed.

But she, it seemed, had been as tired as her mother, and at half past seven, there was neither sight nor sound of her. Perhaps, thought Molly, it was the whisky. Perhaps I should drink whisky every night, and then I should always sleep. Or perhaps it was the fact that the overwhelming anxieties and apprehensions of the previous evening had been sublimated by her own physical exhaustion. Whatever. It had worked. She had slept. She felt refreshed, renewed, ready for whatever the day had to bring.

Which was shopping for the school uniform. She got out of bed and pulled on her dressing-gown and went to close the window, and draw back the curtains. She saw a pale and misty morning, not yet fully light, and very still. Below her window the sloping terraced garden lay quiet and damp, and from the shore beyond the railway line the curlews called. But the sky was clear, and it occurred to Molly that perhaps the morning would turn into one of those days that spring steals from a Cornish winter, so that all is imbued with the sense of things growing, pushing up through the soft dark earth; buds beginning to swell, and returning birds to sing. She would keep it whole, separate, an entity on its own, a single day spent with her elder daughter, set aside. Remembered, it would be sharp-edged and vivid, like a photograph neatly framed, with no intrusion to blur the image.

She turned from the window, sat at her dressing-table, and took from one of the drawers the bulky manila envelope which contained the Saint Ursula's clothes list, and a positive plethora of instructions for parents:

> The Easter term commences on the fifteenth of January. Boarders are asked to arrive no later than 2:30 P.M. on the afternoon of that day. Please make certain that your daughter's Health Certificate has been signed. Miss Catto's secretary will meet you in the Front Hall, and show you and your daughter to her dormitory. If you wish, Miss Catto will be pleased to offer any parent tea in her study from 3:30 P.M. onwards. Boarders are forbidden to bring any sweets or food into their dormitories. The ration of sweets is two pounds a term, and these should be handed over to Matron. PLEASE be certain that all boots and shoes are clearly marked with your daughter's name . . . [And so on and so on.]

The rules and regulations, it seemed, were as strict for parents as they were for the poor children. She picked up the clothes list and glanced through that. Three pages of it. "Items starred can be purchased at the authorized shop, Medways, Drapers and Outfitters, Penzance." Almost everything seemed to be starred. Regulation this, regulation that. Oh, well, if they could buy everything in one shop, then the whole performance wouldn't take so long. And it had to be done.

She put it all back into the envelope and went in search of Jess.

Over breakfast, she spooned boiled egg into Jess's mouth (one for Daddy, and one for Golly) and broke the news that she was to be abandoned for the day.

Jess said, "I don't want to."

"Of course you do; you'll have a lovely time with Phyllis."

"Don't want to . . ." Her bottom lip stuck out like a shelf.

"And you and Phyllis can take Golly for a walk, and buy fruit gums from Mrs. Berry . . ."

"You're bribing," Judith told her from the other side of the table.

"Anything's better than a scene . . ."

"Don't want to."

"It doesn't seem to be working."

"But, Jess, you love fruit gums . . ."

"Don't WANT to . . ." Tears poured down Jess's face, and her mouth went square. She howled. Judith said, "Oh, Lord, now she's off . . ." But just then Phyllis came in with some hot toast in a rack, and when she had put it on the table, she simply said, "What's all this, then," and scooped the howling Jess up into her arms, bore her firmly out of the room, and closed the door behind her. By the time she reached the kitchen, the wails had already started to subside.

"Thank goodness for that," said Judith. "Now we can finish our breakfast in peace. And you're not to go and say goodbye to her, Mummy, otherwise she'll start up all over again."

Which, Molly had to admit to herself, was perfectly true. Drinking coffee, she looked at Judith, who, this morning, had come downstairs with her hair done in a new way, tied back from her face with a navy-blue ribbon. Molly was not sure if the style suited her. It made her look quite different, not a little girl any longer, and her ears, now revealed, had never been her most attractive feature. But she said nothing, and knew that Biddy would approve of her tactful silence.

Instead, she said, "I think we'd better start out as soon as we've finished breakfast. Otherwise we're going to run out of time. You should just see the length of the clothes list! And then it's all got to be marked with name-tapes. Just think of all that tedious stitching. Perhaps Phyllis will help me."

"Why don't we use the sewing-machine?"

"That's a brilliant idea. Much quicker and neater. I never thought of that."

Half an hour later, they were ready to go. Molly armed herself with lists, instructions, handbag and cheque-book, and dressed prudently—because one never knew—for rain, in sensible shoes, and her Burberry and her dark-red Henry Heath hat. Judith wore her old navy-blue raincoat and a tartan scarf. The raincoat was too short and her long, thin legs seemed endless.

"Now have you *got* everything?" she asked.

"I think so."

They paused to listen, but from the kitchen came only contented sounds, Jess's piping voice in conversation with Phyllis, who was probably stirring a custard, or sweeping the floor. "We mustn't make a cheep, or she'll want to come with us." So they let themselves creepingly out of the front door and tiptoed over the gravel towards the wooden shed which was the garage. Judith opened the doors and Molly climbed gingerly in, behind the wheel of the little Austin Seven, and after one or two false starts managed to get the engine running, jam the gear-stick into reverse and back jerkily out. Judith got in beside her, and they set off. It took a moment or two for Molly to get her nerve up, and they had passed through the village and were well on their way before she finally achieved top gear and a speed of thirty miles an hour.

"I can't think why you're so frightened of driving. You do it very well."

"It's because I haven't had much practice. In Colombo we always had a driver."

They trundled on, and then ran into a bit of mist, so it was necessary to turn on the windscreen wipers, but there were very few cars on the road (just as well, Judith told herself), and Molly began to relax a little. At one moment a horse pulling a cartful of turnips loomed out of the drizzle ahead of them, but she managed to deal with this emergency, tooting her horn, putting on a little speed, and overtaking the creaking vehicle.

"Brilliant," said Judith.

Before long, the mist disappeared as swiftly as it had fallen, and the other sea came into view, a pearly blue in the thin morning sunshine, and they saw the great sweep of Mount's Bay, and Saint Michael's Mount like a fairy-tale castle on top of its rock. The tide was in, and so it was isolated by water. Then the road ran on between the railway line and the gentle slopes of farm-land, small fields green with broccoli, and the town lay ahead, and the harbour busy with fishing boats. They passed by hotels closed for the winter, and the railway station, and then Market Jew Street sloped up ahead of them, to the statue of Humphrey Davy with his miner's safety lamp, and the tall dome of the Lloyds Bank Building.

They parked the car in the Greenmarket by the fruit-and-vegetable shop. Outside its door stood tin buckets crammed with the first fragile bunches of the early daffodils, and from within wafted smells of earth and leeks and parsnips. The pavements were busy with shoppers, country women laden with heavy baskets, standing in little groups exchanging gossip.

"Lovely now, isn't it?"

"How's Stanley's leg?"

"Blown up like a balloon."

It would have been nice to linger, to listen in, but Molly was already on her way, not wanting to waste a moment, crossing the street and heading for Medways. Judith followed her, running to catch up.

It was an old-fashioned, sombre shop, with plate-glass windows displaying outdoor wear, tweeds, woollens, hats and raincoats for both ladies and gentlemen. Inside all was fitted in dark wood, and smelt of paraffin heaters, rubber waterproofs, and fusty assistants. One of these, who looked as though his head had been attached to his body by his high, throttling collar, came respectfully forward.

"May I be of assistance, madam?"

"Oh, thank you. We have to buy uniform, for Saint Ursula's."

"First floor, madam. If you'd like to take the stairs."

"Where does he want us to take the stairs *to?*" Judith hissed as they ascended.

"Be quiet, he'll hear you."

The staircase was wide and stately and had a portentous banister with a polished mahogany rail that would be perfect, under different circumstances, for sliding down. The children's department took up the whole of the first floor and was spacious, with a long, polished counter on either side and tall windows facing out over the street. This time it was a lady assistant who approached them. She wore a sad black dress and was quite elderly, and she walked as though her feet hurt, which they probably did, after years of standing.

"Good morning, madam. Want some help, do you?"

"Yes, we do." Molly fished in her bag for the clothes list. "The Saint Ursula's uniform. For my daughter."

"That's lovely, isn't it? Going to Saint Ursula's, are you? What are you needing?"

"Everything."

"That'll take some time." So two bentwood chairs were produced and arranged in place, and Molly, drawing off her gloves, found her fountain pen and settled down to the enormous shop.

"Where would you like to begin, madam?"

"At the top of the list, I think. One green tweed overcoat."

"Lovely material, the overcoats are. And I'll bring the coat and skirt as well. For Sundays, they are. For going to church . . ."

Judith, sitting with her back to the counter, heard their voices, but had stopped listening, because her attention had been caught by something infinitely more fascinating. On the other side of the department, and at the other counter, a second mother and her daughter were also shopping together, not as though the undertaking were a serious business, but something of a joke, because a lot of chat and laughter seemed to be taking place. As well, their shop lady was young and quite jolly-looking, and the three of them all appeared to be having the time of their lives. Which was extraordinary, because they too were buying the Saint Ursula's uniform in its entirety. Or, more accurately, had bought it, and come to the end of their marathon, for the piles of pristine garments, most of them in that deadly bottle-green, were being packed, rustling with fresh white tissue paper, into large cardboard dress boxes, and firmly tied up with yards of stout white string.

"I could have them delivered, if you want, Mrs. Carey-Lewis. The van goes out your way next Tuesday."

"No, we'll take them. Mary wants to sew on the name-tapes. And I've got the car. I'll just need some kindly body to help me down the street and load the boot."

"I'll fetch young Will from the stock-room. He'll give you a hand."

They sat with their backs to Judith, but this didn't matter too much because there was a large mirror on the far wall and, in a way, gazing at reflected faces was better because, with a bit of luck, she could stare without being observed.

Saint Ursula's. The girl was going to Saint Ursula's. Which raised possibilities and rendered Judith's scrutiny sharper and far more personal. Reckoning, she decided that she was probably about twelve, or perhaps thirteen; very thin, and long-legged and flat-chested as a boy. She wore scuffed Clark's Sandals and knee-stockings, a pleated tartan skirt, and a very old navy-blue sweater that looked as though it had once belonged to some male, and much larger, relation. A dreadfully shabby garment, with a ravelled hem and darned elbows. But it didn't matter, because she was so sensationally pretty and attractive, with a long and slender neck and curly dark hair cut quite short, that Judith was reminded of a flower-head on a stem, a shaggy chrysanthemum perhaps. Her eyes, beneath strong dark brows, were violet-blue, her skin the colour of honey (or perhaps just exactly the shade and texture of a perfect brown egg), and when she smiled, it was a wicked urchin's grin.

She sat leaning her elbows on the counter, with her bony shoulders hunched, and her spindly legs wound aroung the legs of the chair. Ungraceful, and yet not graceless, because there was such a lack of unselfconsciousness about her, such overweening confidence, that one knew instinctively that nobody, in all her life, had ever told her that she was clumsy, or stupid, or dull.

The last knot was tied, the string cut with a pair of huge scissors.

"How will you be paying this morning, Mrs. Carey-Lewis?"

"Oh, put it on my account, that's the simplest."

"*Mummy*. You know Pops said you had to pay for everything right away, because you always throw bills into the waste-paper basket."

Much laughter all round. "Darling, you mustn't give my secrets away."

Mrs. Carey-Lewis's voice was deep and ripe with amusement, and it was difficult to come to terms with the fact that she was anybody's mother. She looked like an actress, or a film star, or a glamorous older sister, even a dashing aunt. Anything but a mother. Fine-boned and very slender, her face was made up to porcelain paleness, with fine, arched eyebrows and a scarlet mouth. Her hair was corn-gold and silky straight, cut in a simple bob that had nothing to do with fashion, and everything to do with style. She wore . . . and this was particularly *outré* . . . trousers. Slacks, they were called. Grey flannel, snug around her narrow hips and then flaring to fullness at the ankle, like an undergraduate's Oxford bags. Over her shoulders was tossed a short fur jacket, dark brown and the softest and supplest of garments that could possibly be imagined. A red-tipped hand dangled by her side, loosely holding the loop of a scarlet leather leash, the other end of which was attached to a motionless, furry, cream-coloured cushion.

"Well, that's it, I suppose." She slid her arms into the sleeves of her fur jacket, and doing so, dropped the leash. "Come along, darling, we must be off. It hasn't taken nearly so long as I'd feared. We'll go and have coffee, and I'll buy you an ice-cream, or a Kunzle cake, or something equally disgusting."

The furry cushion on the floor, no longer tethered, decided to come to life, pulled itself onto four velvety feet, yawned enormously, and turned towards Judith a pair of dark, bulbous eyes, embedded like jewels in a flattened face. A plumy tail curled over its back. Having yawned, it shook itself, snuffled a bit, chumping on its little underhung jaw, and then, to Judith's delight, proceeded with much dignity across the carpet towards her, trailing the red leash like a royal train.

A dog. Judith adored dogs, but had never, for a number of perfectly viable reasons, been allowed one. A Pekingese. Irresistible. For the moment all else was forgotten. As he approached, she slid from the chair and crouched to greet him. "Hello." She laid her hand on the soft domed head, and it was like stroking cashmere. He raised his face to hers, and snuffled again, and she slid her fingers under his chin and gently rubbed his furry neck.

"Pekoe! What are you up to?" His mistress came after him, and Judith straightened up and tried not to look embarrassed. "He hates shopping," Mrs. Carey-Lewis told her, "but we didn't like to leave him on his own in the car." She stooped and picked up the leash, and Judith caught a drift of her perfume, which was sweet and heavy as the scent of remembered flowers in the gardens of Colombo, the temple flowers, which only loosed their fragrance into the darkness, after the sun had gone down. "Thank you for being kind to him. Do you like Pekes?"

"I like all dogs."

"He's very special. A lion dog. Aren't you, my darling?"

Her eyes were mesmerizing, brilliantly blue and unblinking, and fringed by bristly black lashes. Judith, stunned by their impact, could only stare, unable to think of anything to say. But Mrs. Carey-Lewis smiled, as though understanding, and turned to go, moving away like a queen, with her dog and her daughter and the shop assistant, who staggered slightly beneath the pile of boxes, forming a procession behind her. As she passed Molly, she paused for a moment.

"Are you kitting your child up for Saint Ursula's as well?"

Molly, caught unawares, seemed a little taken aback.

"Yes. Yes, I am actually."

"Have you *ever*, in *all* your life, seen so many hideous garments?" She was laughing. She did not wait for a reply. She raised her arm in a vague gesture of farewell and led her little party away, down the stairs, and so out of sight.

They watched her go. For a moment nobody said anything. Their departure left behind a sort of emptiness, an extraordinary vacuum. It was as though a light had been turned off, or the sun lost behind a cloud. It occurred to Judith that this probably always happened when Mrs. Carey-Lewis walked out of a room. She took her glamour with her, and left only the humdrum behind.

It was Molly who broke the silence. She cleared her throat. "Who was that?"

"That? That's Mrs. Carey-Lewis, of Nancherrow."

"Where's Nancherrow?"

"Out beyond Rosemullion, on the Land's End Road. It's a lovely place, right on the sea. I went there once, at hydrangea time. Chapel Sunday-school outing. We had a charabanc, and balloons, and a knife-and-fork tea, and screeches of fun. Never seen such gardens, though."

"And is that her daughter?"

"Yes, that's Loveday. That's her baby. She's got two other children, but they're nearly grown up. A girl and a boy."

"She's got grown-up children?" Disbelief rang in Molly's voice.

"You wouldn't believe it, would you, to look at her? Slim as a girl, she is, and not a line on her face."

Loveday. She was called Loveday Carey-Lewis. Judith Dunbar sounded like somebody plodding along, one flat foot in front of the other, but Loveday Carey-Lewis was a marvellous name, light as air, as butterflies on a summer breeze. You couldn't miss, with a name like that.

"Is she going to Saint Ursula's as a boarder?" Judith asked the lady in the sad black dress.

"No, I don't think so. Weekly boarder, I believe, going home on weekends. Apparently Colonel and Mrs. Carey-Lewis sent her to a big school up near Winchester, but she only stayed half a term, and then she ran away. Got herself home on the train, and said she wasn't going back, because she missed Cornwall. So they're sending her to Saint Ursula's instead."

"She sounds," said Molly, "a little spoilt."

"Being the baby, she's had her own way all her life."

"Yes," said Molly, and looked a bit uncomfortable. "I see." It was time to bring matters back to business. "Now. Where have we got to? Blouses. Four cotton and four silk. And, Judith, go into the fitting room and try on this gym tunic."

By eleven o'clock, all had been accomplished and they were done with Medways. Molly wrote and signed the enormous cheque, while the piles of uniform were folded and boxed, but for them there was no offer of a van, nor the suggestion that some minion should carry their purchases to their car, and help load them in. Perhaps, Judith thought, having an account at Medways made you more important, inviting respect, and even a sort of servility. But then Mrs. Carey-Lewis threw all her bills into the waste-paper basket, so she couldn't be a particularly welcome customer. No, it was simply because she was who she was, Mrs. Carey-Lewis of Nancherrow, and frightfully grand and beautiful. Molly could have had an account in a dozen shops and however promptly she paid her bills, she would never be treated, by any person, like royalty.

And so, laden like a couple of pack-horses, they carried the boxes themselves back to the Greenmarket, thankfully to unload their burdens onto the back seat of the Austin.

"A good thing we didn't bring Jess," Judith pointed out, slamming the door shut. "There'd have been nowhere for her to sit."

They were done with Medways, but yet by no means finished. Still the shoe-shop to visit, and the sports-shop (A hockey stick and shin-pads are essential for the Easter Term); the stationer (A pad of paper for writing letters, pencils, an eraser, a geometry set, a Bible); and the saddler (A writing-case). They looked at a lot of writing-cases, but of course the one which Judith really wanted was about four times as expensive as the others.

"Wouldn't this one do, with the zip-fastener?" Molly asked without much hope.

"I don't think it's big enough. And *this* is like a sort of attaché case. And it's got pockets to put things in the lid, and a darling little address book. Look. *And* it's got a lock and a key. I can keep things secret that way. I can keep my five-year diary in it . . ."

So, in the end, the attaché case it was. Leaving the saddler, "That was really sweet of you," Judith told her mother. "I know it's expensive, but if I take care of it it will last me all my life. And I've never had an address book of my own. It will be terribly useful."

Another trip to the Greenmarket, and another unloading of parcels. By now it was half past twelve, so they walked down Chapel Street to the Mitre, and there lunched splendidly on roast beef and Yorkshire pudding and fresh sprouts and roast potatoes and gravy, and for pudding there was apple charlotte and Cornish cream, and they each had a glass of cider.

As she paid the bill, "What do you want to do now?" Molly asked.

"Let's go to Saint Ursula's and have a look round."

"Is that what you really want?"

"Yes."

So they walked back to the car and got in, and drove on, through the town, and out the other side, to where the last of the houses thinned to a trickle and the countryside began again. They turned up into a side road which wound up a hill, and at the top of this came to a pair of gates on the left-hand side. A notice board said SAINT URSULA'S SCHOOL, STRICTLY PRIVATE, but they paid no heed to this, turned in through the gates and onto a driveway bordered by wide grass verges and stands of rhododendron as high as good-sized trees. It was not a long drive, and the house stood at the end of it, with a gravel sweep in front of the imposing front door. Two small cars were parked at the foot of the steps that led up to this, but otherwise there didn't seem to be anybody about.

"Do you think we should ring and let them know we're here?" Molly asked. She was always timid of trespassing, fearful of some angry figure appearing to give her a row.

"No, don't lets. If anybody asks us what we're doing, we'll simply tell them . . ."

She was looking at the house and saw that the main part was quite old, with stone sills to the windows, and an aged Virginia creeper clambering up the granite stone walls. But beyond this original building lay a new and much more modern wing, with rows of windows, and, at the far end, a stone arch-way leading into a small quadrangle.

They walked, their footsteps crunching alarmingly on the gravel, from time to time pausing to peer through windows. A form-room, desks with lids and ink-wells and a chalky blackboard; farther on, a science laboratory, with wooden counters and Bunsen burners.

"It looks a bit gloomy," Judith observed.

"Empty classrooms always do. Something to do with learning theorems and French verbs. Do you want to go inside?"

"Not particularly. Let's explore the garden."

Which they did, following a wandering path which led through shrubber-ies to a couple of grass tennis courts. These, in January unmarked and un-mown, looked forlorn, and did not induce images of spirited play. Otherwise, everything was very tidy, the gravel raked and verges trimmed.

"They must employ a lot of gardeners," said Molly.

"That'll be why the school fees are so enormous. Thirty pounds a term!"

After a bit, they came upon a cobbled sun-trap with a curved bench, and it seemed a good place to sit for a moment and enjoy the thin warmth of the winter sunshine. They faced a view of the bay, a glimpse of the sea and the pale sky, framed by a pair of eucalyptus trees. The bark of these was silvery and their aromatic leaves shivered in some mysterious unfelt breeze.

"The eucalyptus," Judith remembered. "They used to grow in Ceylon. They smelt of having your chest rubbed."

"You're right. Up-country. In Nuwara Eliya. Lemon-scented gum trees."

"I've never seen them anywhere else."

"I suppose it's mild here, so temperate." Molly leaned back in the seat, turned her face up to the sun, closed her eyes. After a bit, she said, "What do you think?"

"Think about what?"

"This place. Saint Ursula's."

"It's a beautiful garden."

Molly opened her eyes and smiled. "Is that a comfort?"

"Of course. If you have to be shut up somewhere, it helps if it's beautiful."

"Oh, don't say that. It makes me feel as though I were abandoning you in some sort of prison. And I don't want to leave you anywhere. I want to take you with me."

"I'll be all right."

"If . . . if you want to go to Biddy at any time . . . you can, you know. I'll speak to Louise. Have a word. It was a storm in a teacup and all I really want is for you to be happy."

"I do too, but it doesn't always happen."

"You must make it happen."

"So must you."

"What does that mean?"

"You mustn't be in such a state about going to Singapore. You'll probably simply love it, even more than you liked being in Colombo. It's like going to some party. The ones you dread very often turn out to be the best fun of all."

"Yes," Molly sighed, "you're right. I was silly. I don't know why I got into such a panic. I suddenly felt so dreadfully *afraid*. Perhaps I was just tired. I know I have to think of it as an adventure. Promotion for Dad, a better life. I know that. But I still can't help dreading it all, having to move everything, and meet new people and make new friends."

"You mustn't think so far ahead. Just think about tomorrow, and then take one thing at a time."

A vapour, too fine to be called a cloud, drifted over the face of the sun. Judith shivered. "I'm getting cold. Let's move."

They left the little sun-trap and strolled on, following a rooted lane which led back up the slope. At the top, they found a walled garden, but the flowers and vegetables had all disappeared and their place been taken by an asphalt netball court. A gardener was sweeping leaves from the path, and he had made a series of little bonfires, burning the leaves as he worked. The clean, sweet smoke smelt delicious. As they approached he glanced up, touched his cap and said, "Arternoon."

Molly paused. "A lovely day."

"Yes. Dry enough."

"We were just having a look around."

"Doing no harm as far as I can see."

They left him and went through a door in the high stone wall. It led out onto playing fields, with goal-posts for hockey, and a wooden games pavilion. Out of the shelter of the garden, it became, suddenly, much colder, quite chill and breezy. They walked faster, hunched against the sneaking wind, and crossed the fields, and came to farm buildings and cart-sheds, and a farm road that led, past a row of cottages, back to the main gate and so to the drive, and the forecourt of Saint Ursula's and their little Austin, waiting for them.

They got into the car and slammed the door shut. Molly reached for the ignition key, but did not turn it. Judith waited, but her mother only repeated what she had already said, as though repetition could somehow make it happen: "I really *do* want you to be happy."

"Do you mean happy at school, or happy ever after?"

"Both, I suppose."

"Happy ever after's a fairy-tale."

"I wish it wasn't." She sighed, and switched on the engine. "A silly thing to say."

"Not silly. Rather nice."

They set off for home.

It had been a good day, Molly decided. A constructive day, which left her feeling marginally better about everything. Ever since that heated exchange with Biddy, she had suffered from a nagging guilt, not simply because she was returning to Ceylon and leaving Judith behind, but because of past misunderstandings and her own lack of perception. Guilt was bad enough, but the knowledge that she had so little time left to make things right between them caused her more distress than she would admit, even to herself.

But somehow, it had worked out. Not just because they had achieved so much, but because it had been done under such pleasant and companionable circumstances. Both of them, she realized, had tried their hardest, and this alone was enough to fill her heart with grateful appreciation. Without Jess tagging along, demanding attention, being with Judith had been like spending time with a girl-friend, a contemporary, and all the small treats and extravagances—lunching at the Mitre, and buying the extremely expensive attaché case which was the one that Judith really wanted—were a small price to pay for the knowledge that, somehow, she had crossed a difficult bridge in the relationship with her elder daughter. Perhaps she had left it rather late, but at least it was done.

She felt much calmed and strengthened. Take one thing at a time, Judith had told her, and, encouraged and heartened by this co-operation, Molly took her advice and refused to be overwhelmed by all that was still left to do. She made lists, giving each task a priority number, and ticking things off as they were dealt with.

And so, over the following days, in strict sequence, plans were laid and carried out for the closing of Riverview House and the dispersal of its occupants. Personal possessions which Molly had brought home from Colombo, or gathered around her during her tenure, were collected from various rooms and cupboards, listed, and packed away to be put into store. Judith's new, brass-bound school trunk, marked with her initials, stood open on the upstairs landing, and as various garments were name-taped and folded, they were neatly stacked into this capacious piece of luggage.

"Judith, can you come and help?"

"I am helping," came Judith's voice from beyond her bedroom door.

"What are you doing?"

"Packing my books to take to Aunt Louise."

"All of them? All your baby books?"

"No, I'm putting them in another box. They can go into store with all your stuff."

"But you won't need your baby books again."

"Yes, I will. I want to keep them for my children."

Molly, torn between laughter and tears, hadn't the heart to argue. And what difference would a few extra boxes make anyway? She said, "Oh, all right," and put a tick alongside "hockey boots" on the endless clothes list.

"I've found another position for Phyllis. At least I think I have. She's going for an interview the day after tomorrow."

"Where?"

"In Porthkerris. Better, really. She'll be nearer home."

"Who with?"

"Mrs. Bessington."

"Who's Mrs. Bessington?"

"Oh, Judith, you know. We meet her sometimes shopping and she always chats. She carries a basket and has a white Highland terrier. She lives up at the top of the hill."

"She's old."

"Well . . . middle-aged. Perfectly lively. But the maid she's had for twenty years wants to retire because of her varicose veins. She's going to go and keep house for her brother. So I suggested Phyllis."

"Has Mrs. Bessington got a cook?"

"No. Phyllis will be cook-general."

"Well, that's something. She told me she'd rather be on her own. She didn't want to skivvy for some bad-tempered old bitch of a cook."

"Judith, you shouldn't use words like that."

"I'm simply telling you what Phyllis said to me."

"Well, she shouldn't."

"I think 'bitch' is rather a good word. And it only means a lady dog. There's nothing rude about that."

The last days slipped by with frightening speed. By now, rooms, stripped of photographs, pictures, and ornaments, became impersonal, as though already deserted. The sitting-room, empty of flowers and small personal touches, presented a bleak, cheerless face, and there seemed to be crates and packing-boxes everywhere. While Judith and Phyllis laboured valiantly, Molly spent much time on the telephone, speaking to the shipping company, the passport office, the storage firm, the railway station, the bank manager, the lawyer, Louise, her sister Biddy, and finally, her mother.

This last was the most exhausting call, because Mrs. Evans was becoming deaf, and she distrusted the telephone, suspecting that the female on the switchboard listened in to private conversations, and then repeated them to

Others. So it took some plain speaking and a good deal of frustration before the penny dropped and Mrs. Evans was made to comprehend.

"What was all that about?" Judith asked, coming in on the tail end of the conversation.

"Oh, she's impossible. But I think I've fixed it. After I've taken you to Saint Ursula's, then I'll close this house, and Jess and I will spend the last night with Louise. She's promised, very kindly, to drive us to the station in her car. And then we'll spend a week with your grandparents."

"Oh, Mummy, do you *have* to?"

"I feel it's the least I can do. They're getting so old, and heaven only knows when I shall see them again."

"You mean, they might die?"

"Well, not exactly." Molly thought this over. "Well, yes, they might," she admitted. "But I can't think about that."

"No, I suppose not. But I still think you're being very saintly. You haven't seen my rubber boots anywhere, have you . . . ?"

The station carrier arrived at the front door with his horse and his float, and onto this were loaded Judith's desk and other possessions that had to be transported to Aunt Louise's house. It took some time to rope it all securely, and Judith watched its departure, bumping up the road behind the ambling horse, to travel the three miles to Windyridge. Then the man who ran the village filling station appeared to make an offer for the Austin Seven. It was not much of an offer, but then it was not much of a car. The next day, he came to take delivery, handed over the puny cheque, and drove it away. Seeing it go for the last time felt a bit like watching an old dog being taken off by the vet to be put down.

"If we haven't got a car, how are you going to take me to Saint Ursula's?"

"We'll order a taxi. We'd never have got your trunk into the Austin, anyway. And then, once you're safely installed, it can bring Jess and me home again."

"I don't, actually, want Jess to come."

"Oh, Judith. Poor little Jess. Why ever not?"

"She'll just be a nuisance. Cry or something. And if she cries, then you will, and me too."

"You never cry."

"No, but I might. I can say goodbye to her here, when I say goodbye to Phyllis."

"It seems a little unfair."

"I think it's kind. Anyway, I don't suppose she'll even notice."

But Jess did notice. She was not a stupid child, and she witnessed the dismemberment of her home with considerable alarm. Everything was changing. Familiar objects disappeared, packing-cases stood in hall and dining-room, and her mother was too busy to pay much attention to her. Her doll's house, her red-painted hobby-horse, and her push-along dog on wheels, there one day, were gone the next. Only Golly was left to her, and she carried him everywhere, dangling by one leg, and with her thumb plugged into her mouth.

She had no idea what was happening to her small world, only knew that she liked none of it.

On the last day, because the dining-room had been stripped of silver and cutlery, and they were down to the barest basics, they had lunch in the kitchen, the four of them sitting around Phyllis's scrubbed table, and eating stew and blackberry crumble off the chipped and mismatched plates which went with the furnished let. Clinging to Golly, Jess let her mother feed her with a spoon, because she wanted to be a baby again, and when she had eaten her pudding, she was given a tiny packet of fruit gums, all to herself. The disposal of this, the opening of the packet and the choosing of the colours, occupied her attention while Phyllis cleared the table, and she scarcely noticed that her mother and Judith had disappeared upstairs.

And then the next upsetting thing occurred. Phyllis was in the scullery, rattling dishes and scouring saucepans, so it was Jess who, looking up, through the window saw the strange black car turn in at the gate, drive slowly across the gravel, and come to a halt outside the front door. With her cheeks bulging with sweets, she went to tell Phyllis.

"It's a *car*."

Phyllis shook water from her reddened hands and reached for a tea-towel on which to dry them.

"That'll be the taxi . . ."

Jess went with her, out into the hall, and they let the man into the house. He wore a peaked cap like a postman.

"Got luggage, have you?"

"Yes. All this."

It was piled at the foot of the stairs. The brass-bound trunk, suitcases and bags, the hockey stick, and Judith's new attaché case. He went to and fro, manhandling everything out to his taxi, stacking it into the opened boot, roping it all securely, so that it would not fall off.

Where was he taking it? Jess stood and stared. As he went in and out, the taxi-man smiled at her, and asked her what her name was, but she didn't smile back, and she wasn't going to tell him.

And then Mummy and Judith came downstairs, and that was the worst of all, because Mummy had her coat and hat on, and Judith was wearing a green suit that Jess had never seen before, and a collar and tie, like a man, and brown lace-up shoes, and it all looked so stiff and uncomfortable, and too big, and her appearance was so frighteningly strange, that all at once Jess was filled with terror, she could contain herself no longer, and burst into hysterical weeping.

They were both going to go away, and leave her forever. This was what she had obscurely suspected, and was now about to happen. She screamed for her mother to pick her up, and take her too, clinging to her coat, trying to climb up into her arms as though she were about to climb a tree.

But it was Judith who stepped forward and picked her up, and hugged her very tight, and Jess, with the desperation of the drowning man and his straw, put her arms around Judith's neck, pressed her teary cheeks into Judith's face, and sobbed bitterly.

"Where you *going?*"

Judith had never imagined anything so dreadful would happen, and realized that she had underestimated Jess. They had behaved towards her as though she were a baby, imagined that a few fruit gums would get them over any possible crisis. They had all been wrong, and this painful scene was the result of their mistake.

She held Jess close and rocked her to and fro.

"Oh, Jess, don't cry. It'll be all right. Phyllis is here, and Mummy will be back very quickly."

"I want to *come.*"

Her weight was sweet, the fat little arms and legs unbearably soft and dear. She smelt of Pears soap, and her hair silky as floss. It was no use recalling all the times that Judith had been impatient and cross with her little sister, those times were already over, and all that was important now was that they were saying goodbye, and that Judith really loved her. She pressed kisses onto Jess's cheeks.

"You mustn't cry," she implored. "I'll write you letters, and you must send me lovely drawings and pictures. And just think, when I see you again, you'll be eight years old, and nearly as tall as I am." The sobs abated slightly. Judith kissed her again, and then moved to hand her to Phyllis, untangling Jess's arms from around her neck. Jess sobbed on, but her screams had abated, and her thumb was back in her mouth.

"You take care of Golly now. Don't let him fall overboard. Goodbye, Phyllis darling."

They embraced, but Phyllis couldn't give Judith much of a cuddle because of having her arms full of Jess. And she didn't seem to be able to say anything much either, except "Good luck."

"Good luck too. I'll write."

"Mind you do."

They all trooped out of the house, to where the taxi waited. Her mother dropped a kiss on Jess's damp cheek. "I'll be back," she promised, "in a little while. You be a good girl to Phyllis."

"Don't come rushing back, madam. You take your time. You don't want to hurry nothing."

Then they were getting into the taxi, and the man slammed the doors shut behind them and climbed in behind the driving-wheel. The engine started. The exhaust pipe belched a cloud of smelly smoke.

"Wave goodbye, Jess," Phyllis told her. "Wave goodbye like a brave girl." So Jess flapped Golly, as though she were waving a flag, and the taxi went

64

crunching away over the gravel, and they saw Judith's face pressed against the back window, and Judith was waving too, and she went on waving until the taxi turned the corner and trundled away up the lane, out of sight and sound.

Windyridge,
Saturday, 18th January 1936.

Dearest Bruce,

I am writing this in my bedroom at Louise's. Jess is asleep, and in a moment I shall go downstairs and join Louise for a drink before supper. Riverview House is now behind us, closed and empty. Dear Phyllis has left us, to go home for a few days, and then start her new job in Porthkerris. On Monday morning Louise will drive Jess and me to the station and we'll spend a few days with my parents before heading for London and catching the boat. We sail on the thirty-first. On Wednesday I took Judith to Saint Ursula's and left her there. We did not take Jess with us, and there was a terrible scene at Riverview House before we got into the taxi. I had not expected such distress, and did not realize how much Jess was taking in about leaving. It was very upsetting, but Judith particularly did not want her coming to the school with us, and of course she was right. Better that it all happened in the privacy of our own home.

I was afraid that this scene would prove too much for Judith, but she handled it in a most adult way and was very loving and sweet to little Jess. In the taxi we talked of practicalities, because somehow I couldn't bring myself to talk of anything else. She looked quite smart in her new uniform, but so different that I felt in a strange way that I was taking some other person's daughter to school and not my own. Over the last few weeks she has suddenly grown up, and she has been the greatest help with all the packing and the arrangements that have had to be made. It is ironic that one spends so many years bringing up a child and then, just when she begins to be a friend and an equal, she has to be abandoned and life contin- ued without her. Four years, at this moment, seem endless. They stretch before me like eternity. Once I am on the boat and on my way to Colombo, I think I shall feel less depressed about it all; just now is not a good time.

At Saint Ursula's, I was meant to go into the school with her, settle her into her dormitory, and then have a cup of tea with Miss Catto. But in the taxi, already half-way to Penzance, Judith suddenly announced that she did not want me to do any of these things. She wanted our goodbyes to be quick and abrupt, and over as soon as possible. She could manage, she assured me. She did not want me to go into the school with her, because she said if I did, I would be part of the school, and she didn't want that. She didn't want her two worlds to touch, to impinge on each other in any way. It was a little embarrassing, because I felt I was *expected* to present myself and show some sort of interest, but I gave in because I thought that that was the least I could do.

And so it only took moments. We unloaded her luggage and a porter came with a trolley and dealt with her trunk and her suitcase. There were some other cars there, other parents and other children, all starting the new term. The girls all look alike in their green uniforms, and all at once Judith was one of them, as though she had lost all individuality and become homogenized. I don't know whether this made it easier or more difficult to say goodbye. I looked into her sweet face, and saw there the promise of a beauty which will be evident when I finally see her again. Her eyes had no tears in them. We kissed and hugged, promised to write, kissed again, and then she was gone, turning from me, walking away, up the steps and through the open door. She never looked back. She was carrying her book-bag and her hockey stick, and the little attaché case I bought her to keep her writing-paper in and her diary and her stamps.

I know you will think it silly of me, but I cried all the way home in the taxi, and didn't stop until Phyllis had given me a hot cup of tea. Then I rang Miss Catto to apologize for my rudeness. She said she understood and would keep us in touch as to Judith's well-being and progress. But we shall be so far away! And the mail-boats take so long.

Now she paused, to lay down her pen and read over what she had already written. It seemed, she decided, dreadfully emotional. She and Bruce had never found it easy to open their hearts to each other, nor to speak of intimacies, or shared secrets. She wondered if he would be upset by her clear distress, and debated as to whether she should tear up the pages and start all over again. But the writing of them had eased her, and she had neither the heart nor the energy to pretend coldly that all was well.

She picked up her pen and continued.

So it is all over, and I am putting on a cheerful face, for Jess's sake and for Louise. But I feel as though I were grieving for a child lost. For opportunities missed, and for the coming years which we are not going to be able to share. I know that I am going through what thousands of other women like myself have to endure, but for some reason or other, that doesn't make it any better.

Within a month, Jess and I will be with you. I await further news of our passage on to Singapore. You have done well, and I am delighted for you.

With my love,

Molly

PS   Judith's Christmas present from you has still not arrived. I have instructed Mrs. Southey at the Penmarron Post Office to forward it to Saint Ursula's when it does finally turn up.

Once more she read the letter through, then folded it, put it in an envelope, sealed and addressed it. It was done. She sat and listened to the rising wind outside, which thumped and whined at the window beyond the drawn curtain. It sounded as though a storm was blowing up. The small desk lay in a pool of light from the lamp which stood upon it, but behind her the bed-room was dim and quiet. In one of the twin beds Jess slept, Golly pressed to her cheek. Molly stood up and went to kiss her, and adjust the covers. Then she moved to the mirror over the dressing-table to touch her hair, and alter a little the drape of the silk scarf which she had knotted around her shoulders. Her pale reflection floated, like a wraith, in the dark glass. She went from the room, closing the door gently behind her. She crossed the landing, started down the stairs.

Windyridge, she had long decided, was a house which fell uncomfortably between two styles. Built just after the First World War, it was neither modern enough for convenience, nor old enough for charm, and its position, on the top of the hill above the golf course, ensured that it stood in the path of every wind that blew. But its most unhappy feature was the sitting-room, which the architect, suffering, Molly could only imagine, from an unfortunate rush of blood to the head, had designed as a lounge/hall, so that the staircase descended, and the front door opened, into it. This arrangement ensured both howling draughts and a sensation of impermanence, rather like sitting in a railway waiting-room.

However, Louise was there, ensconced in her easy chair by a roaring coal-fire, with her cigarettes and her whisky and soda conveniently to hand, and her knitting on the go. She was making shooting stockings. She was always making shooting stockings. When a pair was finished, she laid it in a drawer, ready for the next Church Sale, or Bring and Buy, and started again, casting on the next pair. She called it organized fidgeting, and clocked up her indus-try to Good Works.

Hearing Molly's step on the stair, she glanced up.

"Ah, there you are! Thought you'd lost yourself."

"I'm sorry. I was writing to Bruce."

"Jess asleep?"

"Yes. Fast."

"Have a drink. Help yourself."

A loaded tray stood at the side of the room, stacked with bottles, clean glasses, and a siphon of soda. It was a masculine touch, smacking of the memory of Jack Forrester, but then nothing had been changed since his death. His golf trophies still decorated the mantelpiece, his regimental photo-graphs, going back to India, hung on the walls, and everywhere were evi-dences of the hunt and the chase—the elephant's foot, the tiger-skin rugs, the horns of defunct deer.

Molly poured herself a small sherry and went to sit in the chair on the other side of the hearth. Louise stopped knitting and reached out her hand for her whisky. "Cheers," she said, and took a mouthful. She laid down the glass and looked at Molly over her spectacles. "You don't look too cheerful."

"I'm all right."

"Bit of a wrench for you, leaving Judith, I can see that. Never mind. Time heals. You'll get over it."

"I suppose so," Molly said faintly.

"At least it's behind you now. All over. It's done."

"Yes. It's done." She thought about it. "I suppose . . ."

But she got no further. A sound caught her attention, from out of doors, over the whine of the wind. A footstep, crunching on the gravel.

"There's somebody outside."

"That'll be Billy Fawcett. Asked him over for a snifter. Thought it'd cheer us up."

The front door opened, and a gust of cold air poured in upon them, causing rugs to flap and a cloud of sooty smoke to belch forth from the fireplace.

Louise raised her voice. "Billy, you old fool, close the *door*." It was slammed shut. The rugs stilled, the fire composed itself. "What a night to be out. Come along in."

Molly was both taken aback and irritated by this untimely and unexpected intrusion. The last thing she wanted, at this moment, was company. She did not feel like making conversation with strangers, and felt it unperceptive of Louise to invite her friend over on this of all evenings. However, there was nothing to be done about it, and so, with a sinking heart, she laid down her sherry glass, arranged her features into a pleasant expression, and turned in her chair to greet the visitor.

Louise raised her voice. "Good of you to come, Billy!"

He did not immediately appear, because he was, presumably, taking off his overcoat and hat. But when he finally made his entrance, rubbing his hands against the cold, it was with the air of a man bestowing kindly favours.

"Here I am, my dear, battered by the tempest."

He was not tall, but wirily built, and wore a plus-four suit of large and loud checks. The plus-fours were particularly voluminous, and emerging from their ample folds his skinny calves, in bright-yellow knitted stockings, resembled the legs of a bird. Molly wondered if Louise had knitted the stockings, and if so, which of them had chosen the colour. His hair was white, thinning over a leathery scalp, and his cheeks were netted with red veins. He sported a Regimental tie, a brisk moustache, and a merry twinkle in his light-blue eyes. She guessed his age to be around fifty.

"Molly, this is my neighbor, Billy Fawcett. Or Colonel Fawcett, if you wish to be formal. Billy, this is my sister-in-law, Molly Dunbar."

She put a smile on her face, held out her hand, and said, "How do you do," expecting him to shake it. But he grasped her fingers and bowed low. For a mad moment she thought he was going to kiss it, and very nearly snatched her hand away. But he was just being excessively courtly.

"Delighted to meet you . . . heard so much about you," he added, that rider which is guaranteed to freeze spontaneous conversation.

But Louise, abandoning her knitting and rising from her chair, took over. "Take a pew, Billy. After your efforts, you'll need a whisky and splash."

"Won't say no." He did not, however, sit down, but went to stand in front of the fire, slapping his thighs, and causing his baggy tweeds to steam slightly, and emanate a faint smell of old bonfires.

Molly resettled herself in her chair and reached for her sherry. Billy Fawcett smiled engagingly down at her. His teeth were even and yellow, rather
like those of a healthy horse.

"You've been having a bit of a time, I hear, getting your house in order
before you go back East."

"Yes. We're birds of passage now. Louise has very kindly let us come here
for a couple of nights before we set off on our journeys."

"I must say I envy you. Wouldn't mind a spot of the old sun again. Oh,
thank you, Louise my dear, just the ticket."

"You'd better sit down, Billy. Your trousers are going to catch fire. There,
on the sofa, between us."

"Just warming myself up a bit. Well, cheers, ladies." He took a mouthful of
the large and very dark drink, let out an appreciative sigh as though he had
been looking forward to it for a week, and only then did as he was told, and
moved from the fire's scorching blaze to settle himself against the cushions of
the sofa. He looked, thought Molly, extremely at home. She wondered how
often he popped over to see Louise, and whether he was contemplating moving into Windyridge on a more permanent basis.

"Louise tells me that you've only just come to live in Penmarron," she said.

"Been here three months now. Only a rented house, mind you."

"And you play golf?"

"Yes. Enjoy a round." He twinkled at Louise. "Not up to your sister-in-
law's standard, though. Eh, Louise? We used to play in India together. When
Jack was alive."

"How long have you been retired?" Not wanting to know in the very least,
but feeling that, for Louise's sake, she must show some polite interest.

"Couple of years. Chucked in my commission and came Home."

"Were you in India long?"

"All my service life." It was not hard to imagine him playing polo, and
hurling curses at his bearer. "As a nineteen-year-old subaltern, I was up on
the North-West Frontier. That was a hairy business, I can tell you, keeping
those Afghans toeing the line. A chap didn't want to get captured by one of
those blighters. Eh, Louise?" Louise, rather obviously, made no reply. It was
clear that she did not wish to follow this line of conversation. But Billy
Fawcett was in no way put down. "After India," he told Molly, "I decided I
couldn't stick the cold. Thought I'd give the Cornish Riviera a try. As well,
knowing Louise . . . made a bit of an entrée. Friends are short on the ground,
you know, when you've been abroad for so long."

"And is your wife of like mind?"

This threw him a bit, as it was meant to. "Sorry?"

"Your wife. Does she feel the cold?"

"I'm a bachelor, my dear. Never found the right little memsahib. Where I
was fighting, there were few enough pretty girls around."

"Yes," said Molly. "I suppose so."

"But then, you know all about the rigours of our Far-Flung Empire. Where
is it you're based? Rangoon, did Louise say?"

"No. Colombo. But my husband has a new job, and we're moving on to Singapore."

"Aha. The Long Bar in Raffles Hotel. That's the life."

"I think we're getting a home in Orchard Road."

"And you've got a young daughter? Coming to stay with Louise for the holidays? Look forward to meeting her. We could do with a bit of young blood about the place. Show her around."

"She's lived in Penmarron for the last four years," Molly told him coldly, "so she'll scarcely need showing around."

"No. No, of course not." Thick-skinned, he did not appear in any way discomfited by her small snub. "But it helps to have the old friend to turn to."

The very notion of Judith turning to Billy Fawcett for any sort of reason caused Molly to be overwhelmed by a sensation of deep repugnance. She did not like him. There was no reason that she could instantly put her finger on, just an instinctive antipathy. He was probably perfectly harmless, and as well, he was an old friend of Louise's. Louise was no fool, to be taken in. And yet how could she stand his company? Why did she not take him by the scruff of the neck and turn him out of the house, like a dog that has peed on a good carpet?

> I do not love thee, Dr. Fell
> The reason why I cannot tell.

The room, the fire became, all at once, unbearably hot. She could feel the flush creep up her body, reach her cheeks, turn them flaming red. She was sweating slightly. Quite suddenly, she could not bear it any longer. She had finished her sherry. Making a play of pushing back her cuff and glancing at her watch, she said, "I wonder if you would both excuse me for a moment." She must get out of doors, into the fresh air, or she would, quite likely, faint clean away. "Jess is such a restless sleeper . . . just go and check her." She stood up, backed away from them. ". . . I shan't be a moment."

Louise, blessedly, had not noticed her high colour, her discomfiture. "When you get back," she said, "you can have the other half."

She left them and went upstairs. In their bedroom, Jess still slept. She had not moved. Molly took a warm coat from the wardrobe and draped it around her shoulders. She went out of the room and made her way down the back stairs, and so through to the dining-room, where the table stood, already laid for two, for dinner with Louise. On the far side of the dining-room, French windows led out onto a small paved garden surrounded by a high hedge of escallonia, and so partially sheltered from the winds. Here Louise grew rock plants and scented thyme, and used the little terrace in the summertime for alfresco drinks or informal meals. Molly drew back the heavy velvet curtains and unlatched the French windows and let herself out, and the wind instantly pounced upon her, jerking at the glass door, so that she had to struggle to get it closed again before it slammed shut, and aroused attention. Then she turned to the darkness and let her fiery body be drenched in cold, and it was like stepping under an icy shower, and she filled her lungs with the clean sharp air, and smelt the distant sea, and was careless of the wind which blew her hair into disorder, away from her damp brow.

That was better. She closed her eyes and no longer felt as though she were about to suffocate. She was cooled, calmed, chilled. She opened her eyes and looked up at the sky. There was a half moon, blinking in and out as the black clouds raced across its face. Beyond were stars, the universe, space. She was reduced to nothing, a pin-point of humanity, and all at once was seized by a terrible fright, the old panic of disorientation, and nonentity. Who am I? Where am I? Where am I going and what will happen when I get there? She knew that this terror had nothing to do with the fury of the wild night. The wind and the darkness were elements known and recognized, but the fear and the apprehensions were rooted nowhere, except within herself.

She shivered. A frisson of pure terror. *A ghost going over your grave*, she told herself. She groped for her thick coat and drew it around her, hugging it across her chest. And she tried to think of Judith, but that was worst of all, because it was like remembering a child already dead, a child that she would never see again.

She began to weep, a mother grieving. The tears rose to her eyes and overflowed and poured down her face, and the gusty wind dried them as they fell, salty on her cheeks. To cry was a release of pain, and she let them fall and did not try to stop them. After a bit, it was all over and the panic was stilled, and she was herself again. She had no idea how long she had been standing here, and was by now too cold to remain any longer. She turned and let herself back into the house, closing the French windows and drawing the curtains. She went upstairs as she had descended, by the back stairs, treading softly, so as to make no sound. She hung up her coat and looked at her bed, and longed to crawl into it, to be alone, to sleep. But instead she washed her face with a scalding flannel, dabbed on powder, combed her hair. Thus, outwardly restored, she returned to the others.

As she came downstairs, Louise looked up.

"Molly. What kept you so long?"

"I sat with Jess."

"Everything all right?"

"Oh, yes," Molly told her. "Everything. Quite all right."

Saint Ursula's
February 2nd, 1936.

Dear Mummy and Dad,

Sunday is letter-writing day, so here I am writing a letter. Everything is fine, and I am settling down. Weekends are funny. We do prep on Saturday mornings, and play games out-of-doors on Saturday afternoons. Yesterday we played either netball or kick-the-can. Sunday mornings we have to walk to church in a crocodile, which is boring, and church is pretty boring too, with lots of kneeling. It is very High Church and they have incense and one girl fainted. Then back for Sunday lunch, then another walk (as though we needed it) and now letter-writing, and then tea. After tea is nice because we all go to the library and Miss Catto reads aloud to us. She is reading *The Island of Sheep*, by John Buchan, and it is very exciting. Can't wait to know what happens.

Lessons are all right, and I'm not too behind except in French, but I am having extra coaching. We do gym on Tuesdays but it is difficult climbing the rope. We have prayers every morning in the gym and sing a hymn. There is a lot of music and once a week we listen to classical gramophone records. On Fridays we have an hour of Community Singing, which is lovely, and we sing songs like "Sweet Lass of Richmond Hill" and "Early One Morning."

My form-mistress is called Miss Horner, and she teaches English and History. She is terribly strict and I am Blackboard Monitor and have to keep the blackboard clean and make sure there is plenty of chalk.

I am in a dorm with five other girls. Matron is not a bit kind, so I hope I am never sick. Do you remember the girl who was buying uniform when we did? She is called Loveday Carey-Lewis and she is in my dorm too, only she sleeps by the window and I am by the door. She is the only weekly boarder in the school. She is in a form lower than me, and I haven't talked to her much because she has a friend who is a day girl called Vicky Payton and they have known each other before.

I have had letters from Aunt Louise and Aunt Biddy. And a postcard from Phyllis. Half-term is the 6th March, we get four days, and Aunt Louise is going to buy me my bicycle then.

It is very cold and wet. Bits of the school are warmish but most of it is cold. Hockey is the worst because bare knees and no gloves. Some girls have chilblains.

My present from Dad has still not come. I hope it is not lost, or that Mrs. Southey has forgotten to send it on.

I hope you are all well and that the journey out in the boat was nice. I looked on the map and found Singapore. It is *miles* away.

Lots of love to everybody and Jess,

Judith

The head-girl of Saint Ursula's was a strapping and glorious creature who rejoiced in the name of Deirdre Ledingham. She had long brown pigtails and a splendid bust, and her dark-green gym tunic was well decorated with games colours and various badges of office. Rumour had it that when she left school, she was going to the Bedford School of Physical Training to learn how to be a games mistress, and to witness her leaping over the vaulting-horse was a sight not to be missed. As well, she sang solo in the choir, and it was not surprising that she was the object of violent crushes amongst the smaller and more impressionable girls, who wrote her anonymous love letters on paper torn from exercise books, and blushed furiously if in passing she threw them so much as a word.

Her duties were many and various and she took her responsibilities with great seriousness: ringing bells, escorting Miss Catto to Morning Prayers, and organizing the long, straggly crocodile that trod, weekly, to church. In addition, she was in charge of the daily distribution of letters and parcels which arrived, in the post-van, for the boarders. This event took place each day during the empty half-hour before lunch, when she stood behind a large oak table in the Main Hall, rather like a competent shopkeeper, and handed out the envelopes and packages.

"Emily Backhouse. Daphne Taylor. Daphne, you'd better go and do your hair before lunch, it's dreadfully untidy. Joan Betworthy. Judith Dunbar."

A large and heavy parcel, wrapped in thick hessian, strongly tied, labelled and plastered in foreign stamps. "Judith Dunbar?"

"She's not here," somebody said.

"Where is she?"

"I don't know."

"Well, why isn't she here? Someone go and fetch her. No, don't bother. Who's in her dorm?"

"I am."

Deirdre looked for the girl who had spoken, and saw, at the back of the shoving throng, Loveday Carey-Lewis. She frowned. She had taken against this wayward new-comer, who she had decided was altogether too big for her boots, having already caught her twice running in the corridors, a cardinal sin, as well as surprising her eating a peppermint in the cloakroom.

"Judith should be here."

"It's not my fault," said Loveday.

"Don't be cheeky." A small extra penance seemed to be the order of the day. "You'd better take it to her. And tell her that she should attend Letters every day. And it's jolly heavy, so mind you don't drop it."

"Where shall I find her?"

"No idea, you'll have to look. Rosemary Castle. A letter for you . . ."

Loveday moved forward and gathered the enormous parcel to her bony chest. It was extremely heavy. Clutching it tightly, she edged away from the table and set off across the polished floor, through the long dining-room, and so into the corridor which led to classrooms. She went to Judith's classroom first, but it was empty, so she turned back and started up the wide uncarpeted staircase, headed for the dormitories.

A prefect was descending.

"Heavens, what have you got there?"

"It's for Judith Dunbar."

"Who told you to take it?"

"Deirdre," Loveday told her smugly, safe in the knowledge that she had authority on her side. The prefect was discomfited. "Oh, well, all right. But don't either of you be late for lunch."

Loveday stuck out her tongue at the prefect's retreating back view and continued on her way. Her burden became heavier with each step. What on earth could be in it? She reached the landing, set off down another long passage, finally came to the door of the dormitory, pushed it open with her shoulder and staggered in.

Judith was there, washing her hands in the single basin which they all shared.

"I've found you," said Loveday, and she tipped the parcel onto Judith's bed, and, as though exhausted, collapsed beside it.

Her sudden and unexpected appearance, bouncing in like a jack-in-the-box, the reason for it, and the fact that, for the first time, they were alone together, with no other person to intrude, caused Judith to be overcome by a painful and maddening shyness. From that moment in Medways, when she had first set eyes on the Carey-Lewis mother and daughter, she had thought Loveday quite fascinating, and longed to get to know her. So the most disappointing aspect of her first couple of weeks at Saint Ursula's had been the fact that Loveday had totally ignored her presence, leaving Judith with the sad conviction that she was such a nonentity that Loveday did not even recognize her.

She has a friend who is a day girl called Vicky Payton, she had written to her mother, but the cool little sentence had been carefully framed to allay suspicion, because her natural pride would not allow her mother to think that she was hurt or upset by Loveday's indifference. At break, and after games, she had covertly watched Loveday and Vicky together, drinking their mid-morning milk, or walking back to school after hockey, chattering and laughing and enviably intimate.

It wasn't that Judith hadn't made friends of her own. She knew all the girls in her class by now, and the names of everybody in the Junior Common Room, but there was nobody special, not a real friend like Heather Warren, and she had no intention of making do with second-best. She remembered her father saying, "Beware of the first man who speaks to you on the P and O boat, for he will surely be the ship's bore," and his wise words had stayed with her. After all, boarding-school was not all that different, for one was thrown into the company of a lot of people with whom one had little in common, and it took time to sift out the grain from the sand.

But Loveday Carey-Lewis, obscurely, was different. *She* was special. And now she was here.

"I've been told to give you a row because you weren't at Letters."

"I was filling my pen and I got ink on my hands. And it simply won't come off."

"Try a pumice stone."

"I can't bear the feel."

"No, I know, it's horrible, isn't it? Anyway, Deirdre told me to find you and bring you this. It weighs a ton. Do come and open it, I want to know what's inside."

Judith shook the water from her hands, reached for a towel, and started to dry them.

"I think it's probably my father's Christmas present to me."

"Christmas present! But it's February."

"I know. It's taken ages." She joined Loveday on her bed, the impressive package parked between them. She saw the stamps, and the postmarks and the customs labels. She smiled. "That's what it is. I thought it was never coming."

"Why's it taken so long?"

"It's come from Colombo. In Ceylon."

"Does he live in Ceylon?"

"Yes. He works there."

"What about your mother?"

"She's just gone back to be with him. She's taken my little sister with her."

"You mean you're all *alone*? Where do you live?"

"Nowhere, just now. I mean, we haven't got a house in this country. So I stay with Aunt Louise."

"Who's she, when she's at home?"

"I told you. My aunt. She lives at Penmarron."

"Haven't you got brothers and sisters?"

"Just Jess."

"Is she the one who's gone with your mother?"

"That's right."

"Goodness, that's awful. I am sorry for you. I didn't know. When I saw you in the shop . . ."

"So you *did* see me?"

"Yes, of course I did. Do you think I'm blind?"

"No. It's just that you didn't talk to me. I thought perhaps you hadn't recognized me."

"Well, you haven't talked to *me*."

Which was true enough. Judith tried to explain. "You're always with Vicky Payton. I thought you were her friend."

"Of course I am. We were at baby school together. I've known her forever."

"I thought you were her *best* friend."

"Oh, best friends!" Loveday mocked, her vivid face alight with amusement. "You sound like someone out of an Angela Brazil book. Anyway," she pointed out, "we're talking now, so that's all right." She laid her hand on the parcel. "Do open it. I'm bursting to see what's inside, and as I've humped it all the way up the stairs, the least you can do is to get it unwrapped and show me."

"I know what's inside. It's what I asked for. A cedarwood box with a Chinese lock."

"Then hurry. Quickly. Or it'll be the lunch bell and we'll have to go."

But Judith knew that she couldn't open the present in a hurry. She had waited so long, and now it was here, and she wanted to keep the excitement going, and, once it was open, have time to examine every single detail of her new and longed-for possession.

"There's not time now. I'll do it later. Before supper."

Loveday became exasperated. "But I want to *see*."

"We'll open it together. I promise I won't look without you here. We'll change terribly quickly for supper, and then we'll have heaps of time. It's going to take ages to get all the wrappings off. I can tell, just by looking at it. Let's wait. And it'll be something lovely to look forward to all afternoon."

"Oh, all right." Loveday was persuaded, but obviously against her will. "How you can be so strong-minded I can't imagine."

"It just makes it last longer."

"Have you got a photo of your dad?" Loveday's eyes moved to Judith's white-painted chest of drawers, identical to the other five placed around the dormitory.

"Yes, but it's not very good." She reached for it and handed it to Loveday to inspect.

"Is that him, in the shorts? He looks quite nice. And is this your mother? Yes, of course it is. I recognize her, too. Why isn't Jess here?"

"Because she wasn't born. She's only four. Dad's never seen her."

"Never *seen* her? I can't believe it. What's he going to say when he does see her? She'll think he's just another man, or an uncle or something. Would you like to see my photographs?"

"Oh, yes, please."

They got up from the bed and went to Loveday's end of the dormitory, which was much nicer and lighter, being so close to the big windows. The school rule was that you were allowed two photographs, but Loveday had about six.

"This is Mummy, looking perfectly beautiful, all dressed up in her white fox furs. And this is Pops . . . isn't he heaven? It was taken one day when he was shooting pheasants, that's why he's got a gun. And he's got Tiger with him, Tiger's his Labrador. And this is my sister Athena, and this is my brother Edward, and this is Pekoe the Peke, and you met him in the shop too."

Judith found herself overwhelmed. She had never imagined anyone could have such a handsome, beautiful, and glamorous lot of relations, all looking as though they had stepped from the pages of some glossy society magazine, like *The Tatler*.

"How old is Athena?"

"She's eighteen. She had her London Season last year, and then she went off to Switzerland to learn French. She's still there."

"Is she going to be a French mistress or something?"

"Golly, no. She's never done a stroke of work in her life."

"What will she do when she comes back from Switzerland?"

"Stay in London, probably. Mummy's got a little house in Cadogan Mews. Athena's got strings of boy-friends, and she's always going away for the week-end and things."

It sounded an enviable existence. "She looks like a film star," Judith said a little wistfully.

"She does, a bit."

"And your brother?"

"Edward? He's sixteen. He's at Harrow."

"I've got a cousin of sixteen. He's at Dartmouth. He's called Ned. Your . . ." She hesitated. "Your mother doesn't look old enough to have almost grown-up children."

"Everybody says that. It's so boring." Loveday set the last photograph down, and then settled herself with a thump on her own narrow, white-covered bed. "Do you like this place?" she asked abruptly.

"What? School, you mean? It's all right."

"Did you want to come here?"

"Not particularly. But I had to. I had to start boarding-school."

"Because of your mother going away?"

Judith nodded.

"I wanted to come here," Loveday told her. "Because I wanted to be near home. Last September I was sent to the most dreadful place in Hampshire, and I was so homesick that I cried for weeks and then I ran away."

Judith, who already knew this, having been told by the shop assistant in Medways, was filled anew with admiration. "I can't imagine anyone being so brave."

"It wasn't particularly. I just made up my mind that I couldn't bear the horrible place for another instant. I had to get home. Running away always sounds so difficult, but it was actually quite easy. I just caught a bus to Winchester Station, and then got on a train."

"Did you have to change platforms?"

"Oh, yes, twice, but I just asked people. And then when I got to Penzance I rang up Mummy from the public call-box and told her to come and fetch me. And when we got home I told her she was never, ever to send me far away again and she promised she wouldn't. So I came here, and when Miss Catto heard about running away, she said I could be a weekly boarder, because she didn't want it happening again."

"So . . ." But there was no time for more of this fascinating conversation, as the whole building was suddenly rent by the clangour of the school bell, summoning them to lunch. "Oh, bother, I can't bear it. I hate that bell, and it's Tuesday, so there'll be prunes and custard for pudding. Come on, we'd better go or we'll get a row."

They sped downstairs, to assemble in their classrooms. But, before they parted, there was time for one last exchange.

"Before supper, in the dormitory. And we'll open the parcel together."

"I can't wait."

After that it felt as if the whole colour and the shape of the day had been miraculously changed. Judith had experienced, previously, the elations and swings of mood which affect every child; the sudden, reasonless gusts of happiness, even ecstasy. But this was different. An event. A series of events. Her Christmas present had come at last, and because of this, the first overtures of friendship with Loveday Carey-Lewis had been made, and there was still the ceremonial unwrapping of the cedarwood box to look forward to. As the afternoon progressed, her high spirits were compounded by other unexpected bonuses, and it began to seem as though her day had been charmed and nothing could go wrong. At lunch it wasn't prunes and custard—which she hated—for pudding, but vanilla sponge with syrup, which was a treat. Then she got eight out of ten for her French verb test, and when it was time to don games gear and head for the windy hockey pitches, she saw that the grey rain of the morning had blown away. The sky was clear, a pristine blue; the breeze was perfectly bearable; and early daffodils, lining the paths which led to the games fields, were beginning to open into full yellow flower. Brimming with physical energy, she even enjoyed the hockey, racing up and down the wing as the game moved to and fro, and whacking the leather ball with effortless precision whenever it came her way. So well did she perform that at the end of game she got a pat on the back from Miss Fanshaw, the games mistress, a sturdy lady with an Eton crop and pea-whistle, who was known for being grudging with her praise.

"Well done, Judith. Go on playing like that, and we'll have you on the team."

And then it was tea, and then prep, and at last time to change for supper. She fled upstairs, two at a time, to the dormitory, drew the white cotton curtains of her cubicle, and tore off her clothes. She even managed to grab a bathroom before anyone else got there first, but even so, by the time she returned to the dormitory, Loveday was waiting for her, sitting on Judith's bed, and already dressed in the drab green gabardine frock with the white linen collar and cuffs, which was their regulation garb for the evenings.

"Gosh, you've been quick," Judith exclaimed.

"It was only netball, so I wasn't too sweaty. Hurry up and get dressed, and then we can start. I've got my nail scissors here, to cut the string."

Judith flung on her clothes any old how, buttoning the front of her dress as she stuffed her feet into her shoes, then slapped a brush over her hair, tied it back with a ribbon, and was ready. She took the scissors and cut the string, but then had to pick away at the coarse stitches with which the hessian had been sewn into place. After the hessian was a layer of brown paper, and then a thick wadding of newspaper, which was exciting enough in itself, being covered with strange Eastern newsprint and characters. Everything smelt spicy and foreign. The last wrapping was shiny white paper. This was torn away, and, at last, the Christmas gift revealed. They sat in silence and gazed at it.

Finally, Loveday broke the silence. "It's divine," she breathed, and the words came out like a satisfied sigh.

And it was indeed very beautiful, more splendid than Judith had dared to hope. The wood was the colour of honey, smooth as satin and intricately carved all over. Its ornamental latch was silver, embossed in a flowerlike design, and the Chinese lock slipped into this like a little padlock. The key to the lock was fastened, by means of a strip of glued paper, to the lid of the box. Loveday instantly removed this and handed the key to Judith, and she slid it into the side of the lock and a hidden spring was touched and released, and the padlock opened. She lifted the latch and raised the lid and a mirror slid forward to prop the lid open. The front of the box could be parted, opening out like wings, to reveal two miniature chests of drawers. The scent of cedar filled the air. Loveday said, "Did you *know* it was going to be like this?"

"Something like this. My mother had one in Colombo. That's why I asked for it. But it wasn't anything *nearly* as lovely as this."

She opened one of the little drawers. It slid sweetly and smoothly, revealing dovetailed joints and a gleaming red lacquer finish within.

"What a place to keep your treasures! And you can lock it up. That's the best. And hang the key around your neck. Goodness, you're lucky . . . let's close it up again, and lock it, and then I can have a go with the key . . ."

They might have played with it forever had not Matron come bouncing into the dormitory. She heard their voices and flung back the cubicle curtains with an angry swish, and, much startled, they looked up to see her glaring down at them, her appearance not improved by the nurse's veil which she wore low on her eyebrows, as though she were a nun.

"What are you two doing, whispering away? You know perfectly well, you're not allowed in cubicles together."

Judith opened her mouth to apologize, because she was rather frightened of Matron, but Loveday wasn't frightened of anybody.

"Do look, Matron, isn't it gorgeous? Judith got it from her father in Ceylon, for Christmas, only it's taken ages to get here."

"And why are *you* in Judith's cubicle?"

"I was only helping her to open it. Oh, do look. It's got a lock, and darling little drawers . . ." Displaying its charms, she opened one to show Matron, and did this in such a beguiling manner that Matron's fury abated slightly, and she even took a step forward to peer through her spectacles at the object upon the bed.

"I must say," she admitted, "that's very neat. What a pretty thing." And then she reverted to her normal hectoring manner. "Where on earth are you going to keep it, Judith? There's no space in your locker."

This problem had not occurred to Judith. "I suppose . . . I could take it to Aunt Louise's at half-term."

"Haven't *you* got somewhere safe, Matron?" Loveday cajoled. "In the sickroom, or somewhere? One of those cupboards. Just for the time being?"

"Well. I'll see. Maybe. Meanwhile clear up all that mess and get it tidied away before the supper bell goes. And back you go to your own cubicle, Loveday, and don't let me catch you together again."

"No, Matron. I'm sorry, Matron. And thank you, Matron."

Loveday's tones were so sweet and repentant that Matron frowned. For a moment she stared suspiciously into Loveday's face. But Loveday only smiled, and after a little, unable to find anything more to complain about, Matron turned and stalked off. They kept straight faces until she was out of earshot, and then dissolved into uncontrollable giggles.

Saint Ursula's
Sunday, February 9th.

Dear Mummy and Dad,

My Christmas present from Dad came this week and thank you, thank you, it is exactly what I wanted and even better. I was so afraid it had got lost. There is nowhere to keep it in my cubicle or my locker, so Matron has taken it and put it in the bottom of the Red Cross cupboard, which I suppose is kind of her but means I can't go and gloat. When I go to Aunt Louise's for half-term (29th February), I shall take it and put it in my room there. Thank you again, I really love it.

And thank you, Mummy, for the letter you posted in London just before you sailed. I hope you are having a good trip, and that Jess is enjoying the boat.

Loveday Carey-Lewis helped me open my box, and she is really nice. She's naughty, but somehow manages to get away with it, and doesn't mind what anybody says to her or tells her to do. She's been sent here because she wants to be at a school near her home. It is called Nancherrow, and she's got a pony. In the Junior Common Room we have to do projects for Charity, and Loveday and me are making a patchwork cushion cover out of bits. I don't think she was a special friend of Vicky Payton, she just knew her before, and we are nice to Vicky when she talks to us, and she's got another friend who's a day girl, so I don't think she minds about Loveday and me.

Loveday has got a sister called Athena who is in Switzerland, and a brother called Edward who is at Harrow. Her father has got a dog called Tiger.

I am getting better at French verbs, and tomorrow am going to have a test to be in the choir.

Lots of love, and to Jess,

Judith

On the Wednesday of the following week, when Judith dutifully presented herself to collect any possible mail, she was told by Deirdre Ledingham that there were no letters for her but that Miss Catto wanted to see her now, right away, before the bell rang for luncheon.

Judith's heart instantly dropped, and her stomach churned with dread. She was aware of eyes turned towards her, filled with awe and a sort of reluctant respect, as though she had been incredibly brave and done something dreadfully wicked.

She did a quick dig-around in her conscience, and came up with nothing. No running in the corridor, no talking after lights. With a certain mouselike courage, "Why does she want to see me?" she managed.

"No idea, but you'll know soon enough. Off you go, quick sharp. She's in her study."

Judith, terrified but obedient, went.

Miss Catto, in her role as headmistress, was an ever-present influence in the school, and yet, perhaps deliberately, kept herself remote from the day-to-day activities of her establishment. While the rest of the staff made do with austere bedrooms, and a staff-room that was overcrowded with teachers, teacups, and exercise books, Miss Catto had her own set of rooms on the first floor of the old part of the building, but her study, on the ground floor, was the holy-of-holies, and the nerve-centre of everything that went on. She was held, by all, in much respect, and when she made an entrance, her black gown flowing behind her, at Morning Prayers, or meals in the dining-room, where she presided over the High Table, the entire school automatically fell silent and rose to their collective feet.

Because she taught only the senior girls, grappling with either School Certificate or matriculation, there was little or no personal contact with the younger children, and Judith had only spoken to her once, on her first day, when Miss Catto had said her name, greeted her, and wished her well. But, like every other girl in the school, she was perpetually aware of the headmistress, as a presence that loomed, was observed from a distance, was constantly there.

So being sent for was something of an ordeal.

Miss Catto's study stood at the end of the long corridor which led to the various classrooms. The door, brown-painted, stood closed. Dry-mouthed, Judith rapped on the panel with her knuckles.

"Come in."

She opened the door. Miss Catto sat behind her desk. She looked up, and laid down her pen.

"Oh, Judith. Come along."

Judith closed the door behind her and went into the room. It was a bright morning, the study faced south over the gardens and was flooded with sunlight. There was a jug of wild primroses on Miss Catto's desk, and behind her, on the wall, an oil painting of a cove and an indigo sea, and a boat pulled up onto a beach.

"Get a chair and sit down. And stop looking so agonized, because I'm not cross with you. Just wanted to have a word." She leaned back in the chair. "How are you getting on?"

For all her elevated position and heavy responsibilities, Miss Catto was comparatively young, not yet forty, and with the fresh complexion and springy gait of a woman who only feels truly relaxed when she is out of doors and taking exercise. Her hair was pepper-and-salt, and drawn back from her smooth brow into a neat and uncompromising bun. Her eyes were blue and clear, and her piercing gaze was capable of both charming and intimidating, depending on the circumstances of the interview. She wore, beneath her gown, a dark-blue coat and skirt and a silk blouse, with a bow at the throat. Her capable hands were ringless, but there were pearl studs in her ears, and a pearl brooch, like a man's tie-pin, was pinned to her businesslike lapel.

Judith, having found a chair, sat on it and faced her.

"All right, thank you, Miss Catto."

"You're getting quite satisfactory marks, and I'm pleased with your work."

"Thank you, Miss Catto."

Miss Catto smiled, and her severe expression was transformed to one of genuine warmth. "Have you heard from your mother?"

"Yes, I got a letter that was posted in London."

"Everything well?"

"I think so."

"I'm glad. Now, down to business. You seem to have made friends with Loveday Carey-Lewis?"

(Did she miss nothing?) "Yes."

"I had a feeling you two might get on, which is why I told Matron to put you in the same dormitory. Now, what's happened is that Mrs. Carey-Lewis has been on the telephone to me, because apparently Loveday wants to take you home for a weekend. Has she said anything to you about this plan?"

"No. Not a word."

"Good girl. Her mother made her promise not to mention it until she had spoken to me. Would you like to go?"

"Like to . . . ?" Judith could scarcely believe her ears. "Oh, Miss Catto, I'd *love* to."

"Now, you must understand that if I say you can go, it's a great privilege, because officially half-term is the only weekend that boarders are allowed away. But in the circumstances, with your family abroad, I think it might be good for you."

"Oh, thank you."

"You'll go with Loveday on Saturday morning, and come back with her on Sunday evening. And I'll telephone your Aunt Louise because she is your legal guardian, and she must know everything that you do."

"I'm sure she won't say No."

"I don't think she will, but it's important, and polite, to observe formalities. So . . ." Her smile was a dismissal. She rose to her feet, and Judith hastily scrambled to hers. "That's settled then. I'll let Mrs. Carey-Lewis know. Off you go now, and find Loveday and tell her the good news."

"Yes, Miss Catto, and thank you so much . . ."

"Remember"—Miss Catto raised her voice—"not to run in the corridor."

She finally ran Loveday to earth in her classroom, waiting, with the rest of her form, for the luncheon bell to sound.

"You beast, Loveday! You brute!"

But Loveday saw her rosy, ecstatic face, and shrieked with glee. "Pussy-Catto said *yes!*" They clung to each other, leapt up and down in a wild war dance of satisfaction and delight. "She said yes. I never thought she would."

"But you never *told* me that you'd asked your mother."

"I promised I wouldn't because we were afraid Miss Catto would refuse permission and being disappointed is the most horrible feeling in the world. And I've nearly *burst* keeping it secret. It was Mummy's idea. I told her about you, and she said 'Bring Judith home,' and I said you wouldn't be allowed, and she said, 'Leave it to me.' So I did. And it worked. It always works with Mummy. Pops always says she's the most persuasive woman in the world. Oh, it'll be fun. I can't wait to show you everything. I can't wait . . . What are you suddenly looking so gloomy about?"

"I've just remembered. I haven't any home clothes. All my things are at Aunt Louise's."

"Oh, heavens, that doesn't matter. You can borrow mine."

"You're thinner and shorter than me."

"Then you can borrow Athena's. Or Edward's. Doesn't matter what you look like. And I can show you—"

But there was no time for more, as the bell for luncheon began to clang.

"The best thing about going home," said Loveday in her loud and carrying voice, "is that there are no bloody bells," which earned her an order mark from her shocked form prefect, and reduced Loveday to her usual state of disrespectful giggles.

They were due to depart at ten o'clock in the morning; both dressed, packed, and ready to leave, when Loveday came up with one of her brilliant ideas.

"Your cedarwood box."

"What about it?"

"Let's take it with us. Then we can show Mummy."

Judith was doubtful. "But will she want to see it?"

"Oh, don't be silly, of course she will. I told her all about it."

"Matron will be furious."

"Nothing to be furious about. She'll be glad to get rid of it, cluttering up her cupboards. Anyway, it doesn't matter if she is furious. I'll go if you like . . ."

But in the end they both went. They found Matron in the sick-room, dosing some skinny child with a sticky spoonful of Malt Extract. As expected, she was not in the least pleased to see them.

"You two still here?" Matron did not approve of Miss Catto's bending of the rules and allowing Judith away for the weekend, and had made this perfectly clear since the moment she was told of the plan. "I should have thought you'd be off by now."

"We're just going, Matron," Loveday explained, in placating fashion. "But we suddenly thought we'd take Judith's box with us. Then it won't be in your way any longer," she added cunningly.

"What do you want to take the box for?"

"Mummy's longing to see it. And I've got some shells we want to put in the little drawers."

"Oh, very well. It's in the bottom of the Red Cross cupboard. But don't bring it back, because I really don't have space for a lot of bits and pieces. Now, Jennifer, stop pretending you're going to be sick. It's only malt, and very good for you."

They rescued the box from its hiding place, bade Matron goodbye, and escaped, Judith carrying her new treasure, and Loveday an overnight bag in each hand. Down the stairs, down the long corridor, scuttling along as quickly as possible without actually breaking into a run. Through the dining-room, across the hall . . .

Deirdre Ledingham was pinning games lists onto the green baize notice-board. "Where are you two going?" she asked bossily.

"Home," Loveday told her, and without waiting for more, shot out of the open door and down the stone steps, leaving the head-girl to stand with her mouth open.

It was a wonderful day, a real Saturday, cold and windy, with great white clouds scudding across the starch-blue sky. The Carey-Lewis car was already there, parked on the gravel, with Mrs. Carey-Lewis behind the wheel, waiting for them, and Pekoe the Peke sitting on the passenger seat beside her.

The car, in itself, was glorious enough: a new Bentley, navy-blue, and with a long, sleek bonnet and huge silvery headlamps. Despite the cool air, Mrs. Carey-Lewis had let the hood down. She wore her fur coat, and had wrapped a brilliant silk scarf around her head to keep the wind from blowing her hair into her eyes.

She raised an arm as they appeared. "There you are, darlings. I thought you were never coming. You're five minutes late."

"We went to get Judith's box. Mummy, this is Judith."

"Hello, Judith, lovely to see you. Heavens, that looks heavy. Put it all on the back seat, and then, Loveday, you sit in the back, and take Pekoe with you, and Judith can sit by me. What a gorgeous morning. I couldn't resist putting the hood down, everything is smelling so delicious. Pekoe, don't make a fuss. You know you love sitting in the back. Hang on to him tight, Loveday, otherwise he'll see a sheep or a cow or something and want to chase it. Now, everybody settled . . ."

With no more ado, she switched on the ignition, the powerful engine purred, and they were off. Judith settled back in the padded leather seat and heaved a great, secret sigh of pleasure, because for the past few days she had lived in the certain apprehension that something . . . anything . . . was going to happen to put a stop to their plans. But it hadn't, and it was all right. They swept out through the gates and down the road, and Saint Ursula's disappeared, into the past, behind them.

Loveday chattered. "We decided at the last moment to bring the box, and Matron was livid, wasn't she, Judith? I don't know why she's so bad-tempered all the time, I don't know why she can't be like Mary. I don't think she likes Judith and me very much, do you, Judith? Mummy, who's home this weekend? Anybody exciting?"

"Not really. Only Tommy Mortimer, down from London."

"Oh, *ho!*" Loveday's tone was arch. She thumped her mother on the shoulder. "Tommy *Mortimer*. He's Mummy's boy-friend," she explained to Judith. "He brings her gorgeous chocs from Harrods."

"Oh, Loveday, you are ridiculous." But her mother didn't sound annoyed in the least, simply amused. "You mustn't believe a single word this child says, Judith, but you've probably found that out for yourself already."

"It's perfectly true and you know it is. Athena says he's been swooning over you for years and that's why he's never married."

"Athena talks even more rubbish than you do."

"Have you had a letter from Athena?"

"Oh, darling, what a silly question. You know she's hopeless at letters. But we did have a scrawl from Edward to tell us that he's in the Second Pair for Rackets. And Jeremy Wells turned up this morning. Pops asked him over, and he and Pops and Tommy have disappeared into the woods to shoot pigeons."

"Jeremy. Oh good, I haven't seen him for ages." Kindly she explained him to Judith. "He's nice. He used to be Edward's tutor when Edward was trying to get into Harrow. And sort of an old boy-friend of Athena's. He used to take her to parties when she was about sixteen. His father is our doctor. And Pops simply loves Jeremy, because he's frightfully good at rugby and cricket, and he's Captain of the County Team."

"Oh, darling, he doesn't love him just for those reasons."

"Well, he always goes to Twickenham when Cornwall are playing, and to Lords in the summer. And he's forever on about what a wonderful *shot* Jeremy is, and how many pheasants he's bagged."

Diana Carey-Lewis laughed ruefully. "That's true enough," she admitted, "but I still think there's more to their friendship than just blasting away at anything that flies . . ."

Judith stopped listening. She was beginning to be a bit nervous, because so many names were being bandied about. So many people and so much going on, and all so casual, so worldly, so infinitely alien to anything she had ever experienced before. She hoped that, during the next two days, she would be able to cope with all the social activity, and would not commit some gauche and unknowing blunder and so embarrass everybody, especially herself. And as for Loveday, she had never heard any child speak to her mother in such a way, gossiping away as though they were contemporaries, and teasing her about her boy-friend. Tommy Mortimer. He, more than anybody who had been mentioned, was a source of wonder. The mothers Judith had known simply did not have boy-friends, or if they did, kept the fact thoroughly secret. But it seemed that Mrs. Carey-Lewis was quite shameless about—and even rather proud of—her gentleman admirer. She did not care if all her family . . . which, presumably, included her husband . . . knew, and was happy to let them all discuss her little affair, and treat it as a great joke.

It was, Judith decided, all going to be extremely interesting.

By now they had left the town behind them, driven through a small fishing village, and climbed the steep hill onto the empty country which lay beyond. The narrow road wound and twisted, following the reasonless contours of meandering drystone walls, the boundaries of random farms, the buildings of which could be glimpsed, low-roofed and ancient, huddled down against the wind. Gentle hills, crowned with cairns of granite rock, swept down to the coast and the cliffs, and the dazzling, sun-speckled sea. Far out to sea, tiny fishing boats butted out into the swell, and overhead sea-gulls, spying a man ploughing behind a horse, swooped and screamed and hovered, waiting to pounce on the freshly turned earth.

It was a very different country from the other side of Cornwall. Judith said, "It's so beautiful."

Mrs. Carey-Lewis smiled. "Have you never been on this road before?"

"No. Never. Not as far as this."

"It's not very far from Penmarron. Nowhere in Cornwall is very far from anywhere else."

"It is, if you haven't got a car."

"Didn't your mother have a car?"

"Yes. An Austin Seven. But she wasn't very fond of driving it, so we mostly went to Porthkerris by train."

"Oh, that's a shame. Didn't she like driving?"

"No. She was very nervous. She said it was because in Colombo she always had a driver. But that was silly, really, because she could drive perfectly well. She just thought she couldn't."

"What is the point of having a car," Loveday asked, "if you never drive?"

Judith felt that perhaps she had been rather disloyal, and should now stick up for her absent mother.

"Well, it's better than being like my aunt Louise, who drives her Rover at about a hundred miles an hour, and usually on the wrong side of the road. Mummy used to dread going anywhere with her."

"I think I should too," said Mrs. Carey-Lewis. "Who's Aunt Louise?"

"She's my father's sister. I'm going to spend holidays with her while Mummy's away. She lives in Penmarron."

"I hope she isn't going to drive *you* at a hundred miles an hour."

"No, she's going to buy me a bicycle."

"Sensible lady. But it's a shame that your mother wasn't fond of driving, because there are so many divine coves and beaches all around this part of Cornwall, and there's no way of finding them unless you have a car. But never mind, *we'll* be able to show them to you, and it'll be all the more fun for us because you've never seen them before."

She fell silent for a moment, and then, "What do you call your mother?" she asked.

Which was, thought Judith, a fairly odd question.

"Mummy."

"And what are you going to call me?"

"Mrs. Carey-Lewis."

"Very right and proper, too. My husband would approve. But shall I tell you something? I simply hate being called Mrs. Carey-Lewis. I always think people are talking to my mother-in-law, who was old as God and twice as frightening. She's dead now, thank goodness, so at least you don't have to worry about *her*." Judith could think of absolutely nothing to say to this, but it didn't matter, because Mrs. Carey-Lewis just went on talking. "I really only like being called either Diana, or Darling or Mummy. And as I'm not your mother, and Darling sounds a bit affected, I think you'd better call me Diana." She turned her head to smile at Judith, who saw that the brilliant blue of her patterned headscarf exactly matched her eyes, and wondered if Mrs. Carey-Lewis knew this, and knowing, had chosen it from some drawer to knot it around her head.

"But wouldn't you mind?"

"No. I'd like it. And it's easier to start right away. Because once you begin by calling me Mrs. Carey-Lewis, then you'll find it impossible to change to Diana, and I don't think I could bear that."

"I've never called a grown-up by their Christian name before."

"It's so ridiculous. We're all given lovely Christian names, and so we should use them. Mary Millyway, whom you're going to meet, is Loveday's nanny—or at least she *was* Loveday's nanny when Loveday was a baby. But we never called her Nanny, because Mary is such a pretty name. And anyway, I can't bear that word, nanny. It conjures up images of the most tiresome mothers." She put on a false, but deadly accurate, upper-class voice. " 'Nenny's so crawss because I kept Lucinda up after her bedtime.' Sickening. So let's start as we mean to go on. Say my name now, aloud."

"Diana."

"Shout it to the world."

"Diana!"

"Much better. Now, let's make as much noise as we can. One, two, three, all together . . ."

"DIANA!"

Their voices were blown away, up into the sky, by the wind. The road, a grey ribbon, wound ahead of them, and they were all laughing.

After another ten miles or so, the scenery, abruptly, changed again, and they were in a district of running streams and deep wooded valleys. Rosemullion lay at the foot of one of these, a cluster of whitewashed cottages, a farmyard, a pub, and an ancient church with a square tower, surrounded by leaning gravestones, yellow with lichen. A curved bridge led over a sweet-flowing stream, and then the road, steeply, climbed again, and at the crest of the hill it levelled off and the impressive gateway came into view, curved walls enclosing tall wrought-iron gates, which stood open and framed a prospect of a long wooded driveway, winding out of sight and into the distance. Diana changed down, and the Bentley swung in through the entrance.

"Is this it?" Judith asked.

"Yes. This is it. Nancherrow."

As the road wound on, twisting and turning and never seeming to reach anywhere, Judith fell silent. Everything was suddenly a bit scary, remote and overpowering. She had never known such a long approach to any establishment, and began to suspect that Nancherrow was not a house at all, but a castle, perhaps with a moat and a drawbridge and even a headless ghost, all of its own. She found herself filled with the anxious apprehension of the unknown.

"Are you feeling nervous?" Diana asked. "We always used to call it avenue fever. That sinking feeling when you're coming somewhere new."

Judith wondered if she was a thought-reader as well as everything else.

"It's such a long drive."

"What do you imagine it's all going to look like?" She laughed. "Don't worry, it's not a bit frightening. No spooks. They were all incinerated when the old house burnt down in 1910. My father-in-law simply shrugged his shoulders and built another, a great deal larger and much more convenient. Such a relief," she said, smiling, "because we have the best of both worlds and not a ghost or a secret passage in the place. Just the most wonderful home that we all adore."

And when they came at last to Nancherrow, Judith saw exactly what she meant. It was a sudden and abrupt encounter. The surrounding trees thinned and fell behind them, the wintry sun glittered down once more, the road turned a final corner, and the house stood revealed. It was of local granite, and slate-roofed, like any traditional farmhouse, with long windows on the two floors, and a line of dormer windows above these. It stood back, beyond a carriage sweep of pale sea-pebbles, and its eastern wall was smothered with clematis and climbing roses. The front door was set in the round tower, castellated at its top like some Norman keep, and all about stretched green lawns, spreading to vistas of shrub and woodland, ornamental flower-beds, and yellow and purple carpets of daffodils and crocus. To the south, which was the front of the house, these lawns took the form of terraces, bisected by flights of stone steps. In the distance could be glimpsed the blue horizon, and the sea.

And yet, for all its splendour, it wasn't overwhelming or frightening in any sort of way. From that very first moment, Judith fell in love with Nancherrow, and immediately felt that she understood Loveday much better. Because now she knew exactly why Loveday had run away from her school in Hampshire, found her way back to this magical place, and made her mother promise never, ever, to send her far away again.

The Bentley drew to a dignified halt outside the front door, and Diana switched off the engine.

"Well, there we are, my ducks, safe and sound."

They piled out, gathering up possessions, and filed indoors, Pekoe importantly leading the way, and Judith, loaded with her cedarwood box, bringing up the rear. Up a flight of stone steps they went, through a circular flagged porch, and then inner glassed doors, to the central hallway which lay beyond. It all seemed enormously large and spacious, but despite the size of everything and the generous proportions, the ceilings were not overly high, so that the immediate impression was of a country house, a family house, friendly and unpretentious, and Judith at once felt much easier, and at home.

The walls of the hallway were panelled in natural wood, and polished floors were scattered with worn and faded Persian rugs. The wide staircase, thickly carpeted, rose in three straight flights to the upper landing, and sunlight streamed down through the wide stair window, curtained in folds of heavy yellow silk brocade. In the middle of the hall was a round pedestal table, on which stood a lustre tureen crammed with a moon-burst of white narcissi. As well, a worn leather Visitors' Book, a dog lead or two, somebody's gloves, a stack of mail. Opposite the staircase was the fireplace, the mantelpiece much carved and ornamented. In its hearth lay a bed of dead ashes, but Judith guessed a dry log or two and a puff with the bellows would soon bring the fire back to flaming life.

As Judith stared about her, taking it all in, Diana paused at the table, to unknot her silk scarf and stuff it into the pocket of her coat. "Off you go then, Loveday, and take care of Judith. I think Mary's in the nursery. The boys are coming in for lunch at one, so don't be late. Be in the drawing-room by a quarter to." And with that, she picked up her letters and was on her way, walking away from them, down the long wide hallway furnished with lovingly polished pieces of antique furniture, mammoth porcelain vases, and ornate mirrors. Pekoe followed, close on her elegant, high-heeled heels. A languid wave of her hand was their dismissal. "Don't forget to wash your hands . . ."

They watched her going, as Judith had observed her leaving the shop, that day when she had first seen her, obscurely fascinated, rooted to the ground, somehow unwilling to turn away. They stayed until she reached the closed door at the far end of the passage, opened it to a blast of sunshine, and was gone.

Her exit, and its abruptness, presented an interesting insight into the Carey-Lewis mother-and-daughter relationship. Loveday was allowed close intimacy, and to speak to her mother as though she were a sister, but the privilege demanded its own price. If she was treated like a contemporary, then she was expected to behave like an adult, and take social responsibility for her own guest. This, it seemed, was the norm, and Loveday took it in her stride.

"She's gone to read her letters," she explained unnecessarily. "Come on, let's find Mary."

With that, she headed up the stairs, lugging their overnight bags. Judith followed at a slightly slower pace, burdened by the weight of the box, which was beginning to feel extremely heavy. At the top of the stairs was another long passage, replica of the one down which they had watched Diana make her airy exit. Loveday broke into a run, the bags thumping against her skinny legs. "Mary!"

"Here I am, pet!"

Judith had little experience of either English nannies or English nurseries. Nannies she had seen on the beach at Porthkerris, stout fierce ladies in sturdy cotton dresses, hatted and stockinged in the hottest of weather, knitting, and constantly adjuring their charges either to go into the sea, come out of it, put on a sun-hat, eat a ginger biscuit, or to come away from that nasty child who might have something catching. But she had never, thankfully enough, had to have anything very much to do with any of them.

As for nurseries, the word conjured up nothing more exciting than Matron's sick-room at Saint Ursula's, with its brown linoleum floor, uncurtained windows, and a strange smell compounded of Germoline and cinnamon.

Consequently, she entered the Nancherrow nursery with a certain amount of trepidation, which was instantly dispelled as she realized that all her preconceived ideas had been totally off the mark. For this was not a nursery at all, but a large, sun-filled sitting-room, with a great bay window, and a window-seat which took up much of the southern wall and afforded a view out over the garden, and that distant, seductive vista of the sparkling horizon.

It had an open fireplace, and bookcases crammed with books, proper sofas and chairs with flowery slip-covers, a thick Turkey carpet, and a round table covered with a heavy blue cloth patterned with birds and leaves. Other delights stood all about. Cheerful pictures, a radio on the table by the fireside, a portable gramophone and a stack of records, a basket of knitting, and a pile of magazines. The only concessions to nursery life were the tall fire-guard with its polished brass rail, a battered rocking-horse without a tail, and an ironing board.

This was set up, and at it Mary Millyway had been hard at work. A wicker basket of washing stood on the floor, a pile of immaculately ironed linen was stacked on the table, and a blue shirt lay, half-done, upon the board. And there was that good, reassuring smell of fresh warm cotton, reminding Judith of the kitchen at Riverview House, and, so, of Phyllis. And she smiled, because it felt, a bit, like coming home.

"Well, here you are . . ." Mary had set down her iron, abandoned the shirt, and opened her arms to Loveday, who, dropping the bags onto the carpet, had flung herself into them for a huge hug. She was lifted from the floor as though she weighed no more than a feather, and swung to and fro, like the pendulum of a clock. "There's my wicked baby." A kiss was pressed onto the top of Loveday's curly dark head, and then she was set down with a thump, as Judith came through the door.

"So this is your friend! Laden down like a donkey. What's this you've brought with you?"

"It's my cedarwood box."

"It looks as though it weighs a ton; put it on the table, for goodness' sake." Which Judith, gratefully, did. "Why did you bring that with you?"

Loveday explained. "We wanted to show it to Mummy. It's new. Judith got it for her Christmas. This is Judith, Mary."

"I guessed as much. Hello, Judith."

"Hello."

Mary Millyway. Neither stout nor old nor fierce, but a tall and raw-boned Cornishwoman no more than thirty-five. She had coarse fair hair and a freckled face, and strong features that were pleasing, not because they were beautiful in any way, but because they all matched each other, and somehow looked exactly right. Nor was she wearing any sort of uniform, but a grey tweed skirt and a white cotton blouse with a brooch at the collar, and a smoky-blue Shetland cardigan.

They observed each other. Mary spoke.

"You look older than I thought you'd be."

"I'm fourteen."

"She's in a form above me," Loveday explained, "but we're in the same dormitory. And Mary, you've got to help because she hasn't got any home clothes, and all mine are going to be too small for her. Is there something of Athena's she can borrow?"

"You'll get into trouble, borrowing Athena's things."

"I don't mean Athena's proper clothes, something that she doesn't want any more. Oh, you know what I mean . . ."

"I certainly do. Never known such a girl for wearing things once, and then throwing them away . . ."

"Well, find something. Find something *now*, so that we can get out of our horrible uniforms."

"I'll tell you what"—Mary calmly and firmly picked up her iron again—"you take Judith and show her where she's sleeping . . ."

"Which room is that?"

"The pink one at the end of the passage . . ."

"Oh, goody, Judith, that's the prettiest . . ."

". . . and then when I've finished my ironing I'll have a look in my special drawer and see what I can find."

"Have you got heaps of ironing to do?"

"Won't take me more than five minutes. Off you go, and by the time you come back I'll be ready."

"All right." Loveday grinned at Judith. "Come on."

She was already off, out of the room and away, and Judith, pausing only to grab up her bag, had to run to keep up with her. Down the long passage, with doors closed on either side, but glass fanlights above them, so all was light and airy. At the far end the passage took a turn to the right, and another rambling wing was revealed, and for the first time Judith realized the extent of the house. Here, long windows allowed views of the lawns at the back, spreading to tall hedges of escallonia, and beyond these, the pasture fields of farmland, stone-walled, and grazed by herds of Guernsey cows.

"Come on." Loveday had paused for an instant, waiting for her to catch up, so there was no time to stand and gaze and take it all in.

"It's all so big," Judith said in wonder.

"I know, it's huge, isn't it, but it has to be because there are so many of us, and there are always people coming to stay. This is the guest wing." Now, as she went ahead, Loveday opened and closed doors, allowing a sight of the rooms which lay beyond. "This is the yellow room. And a bathroom. And this is the blue room . . . Tommy Mortimer's usually in here. Yes, he is, I recognize his hairbrushes. And his smell."

"What does he smell of?"

"Heavenly. The stuff he puts on his hair. And then this is the big double room. Don't you adore the four-poster bed? It's frightfully old. I expect Queen Elizabeth slept in it. And another bathroom. And then this is the dressing-room, and it's got a bed too, in case they've got a baby or something awful like that. Mary puts a cot up if it's a real baby. And another bathroom. And then it's you."

They had reached the last door, and Loveday, with certain pride, led the way into it. Like every other room in this delectable house, it was panelled in wood, but it had two windows, and these were hung in a chintz of toile de Jouy. The carpet was pink as well, and the high brass-ended bed had a cover of white linen, crisp as new snow, hem-stitched and embroidered with daisies. A luggage rack stood at the end of the bed, and Judith set down her bag, and it sat there looking humble and small and somehow vulnerable.

"Do you like it?"

"It's simply *lovely*."

She saw the kidney-shaped dressing-table, skirted in the same toile as the curtains, and on this stood a triple mirror, and a china tray patterned in roses, and a little porcelain mug filled with velvety polyanthus. There were a huge Victorian wardrobe and a proper armchair with pink cushions, and beside the bed a little table with a lamp and a carafe of water with a tumbler fitted over its neck, and a cretonne-covered tin, which Judith knew would be filled with rich tea biscuits. Just in case she might be hungry in the middle of the night.

"And this is your bathroom."

Quite overwhelming. She went to inspect it and saw the black-and-white-checkered floor, the huge bath, the wide-mouthed gold taps, immense white towels, bottles of bath-oil and glass bowls of scented talcum powder.

"My *own* bathroom?"

"Well, you share it with the room on the other side, but there's nobody staying, so you've got it all to yourself." Loveday returned to the bedroom, to fling wide the window and hang out of it. "And this is your view, but you have to peer a bit to see the sea."

Judith joined her, and they stood side by side, leaning their arms on the stone sill and feeling the chill, sea-scented wind on their faces.

Craning her neck, she dutifully admired the view of the sea, but what was a great deal more interesting was the immediate vista below them. A large cobbled yard boxed in on three sides by single-storey buildings roofed in slate. In the middle of this yard stood a dovecote, and white pigeons flew all about, to settle, to preen themselves, to fill the air with their satisfied cooing. Around the sides of the courtyard were wooden tubs planted with wallflowers, as well as other, more mundane, evidences of domestic activity: a game larder, large as a wardrobe; some dustbins; a washing line strung with snowy tea-towels. Beyond the courtyard could be seen a gravelled road, and then mown grass, rolling away to a line of trees. These, not yet in leaf, leaned from the sea-wind, and tossed their branches in the fresh breeze.

There did not seem to be anybody about, but as they watched a door opened, and a girl in a mauve cotton overall emerged. They stared down at the top of her head. She carried a tin bowl of vegetable peelings, which she tipped into one of the rubbish bins.

"That's for Mrs. Mudge's pigs," Loveday whispered importantly, as though they were spies and must not be observed. The girl in the overall did not look up. She clanged the lid down upon the bin, paused to feel the tea-towels, checking for dryness, and then disappeared indoors again.

"Who's that?"

"That's Hetty, the new kitchen maid. She helps Mrs. Nettlebed. Mrs. Nettlebed's our cook; and she's married to Mr. Nettlebed, and he's our butler. She's sweet, but he can be terribly bad-tempered. Mummy says it's his stomach. He's got an ulcer."

A butler. It was all becoming grander and grander. Judith leaned out a little farther and peered below her.

"Is that the stable where you keep your pony?"

"No, that's the boiler-house and the wood-shed and the coal-house and things like that. And the gardeners' lav. The stables are a bit away, so you can't see them from here. I'll take you after lunch to meet Tinkerbell. You can ride her if you like."

"I've never ridden a horse," Judith admitted, not admitting at the same time that she was frightened of horses.

"Tinkerbell's not a horse, she's a pony. She's adorable and she never bites or bucks." Loveday thought for a moment. "It's Saturday, so maybe Walter will be there."

"Who's Walter?"

"Walter Mudge. His father farms Lidgey . . . that's the Home Farm, and he helps Pops run the estate. Walter's really nice. He's sixteen. He sometimes comes at weekends to muck out the horses and help the gardener. He's saving up for a motor bicycle."

"Does he ride as well?"

"He exercises Pops' hunter when Pops hasn't the time. If he has to sit on the bench, or go to some meeting or other." Abruptly, Loveday withdrew her head. "I'm getting cold. Come on, let's do your unpacking."

They did it together. There wasn't very much to unpack, but everything had to be put in its right, important place. Judith's hat and coat were hung in the wardrobe, the coat on a fat pink velvet hanger. The inside of the wardrobe smelt of lavender. Then her night-dress was laid on the pillow, her dressing-gown hung on the back of the door, her brush and comb arranged on the dressing-table, clean underclothes laid in a drawer, toothbrush and face-flannel placed in appropriate places in the enormous bathroom. Her diary and her fountain pen she put on the bedside table, along with her clock and her new Arthur Ransome book.

When they had finished, she looked about her and decided that her insignificant possessions made little impact on the beautiful, luxurious room, but Loveday had no time to stop and stare. Impatient as ever, she was already bored by housewifely activities. She kicked the empty bag under the bed and said, "That's done. Now let's go find Mary and see if she's dug up something for you to wear. I don't know about you, but if I don't get out of this horrible uniform very soon, I'm going to start screaming."

And she was out of the room and off again, racing away back to the nursery, thundering down the passage as though defying every school rule that had been drummed into her wayward head, because she was home again, and free.

Mary had finished her ironing, folded down her board, and set the iron to cool. They found her kneeling in front of a tall armoire, which was the most impressive piece of furniture in the room, with the deep bottom drawer opened and various garments set, in neat stacks, around her.

Loveday couldn't wait. ". . . What have you found? It doesn't have to be smart. Anything will do . . ."

"What do you mean, anything will do? You don't want your friend looking like something out of a jumble sale . . ."

"Mary, this is a *new* jersey. Athena got it last hols. What's it doing in this drawer. . . ?"

"You may well ask. She caught the elbow on a bit of barbed wire. I mended it, but would she wear it? Not her, the little madam."

"It's gorgeous, cashmere. Here . . ." Loveday tossed it over to Judith, who caught it, and it was like catching thistledown, so weightless and soft was the wool. Cashmere. She had never owned a cashmere jersey. And this one was holly-red, one of her most favourite colours.

". . . now, here's a nice gingham blouse, with a Peter Pan collar. Dear God knows why Athena threw that out. Bored with it, no doubt. And a pair of shorts. She had those at school for playing hockey. I kept them because I thought they might do for Loveday." Mary held them up for general inspection. They were navy flannel, pleated like a little skirt.

Loveday approved. "The very thing. Those'll do, won't they, Judith? Oh, Mary, you are brilliant." She stooped to hug her, winding skinny arms in a stranglehold around Mary's neck. "You're the best Mary in the world. Now, Judith, go right away and put them on, because I want to show you *everything* else."

Judith carried the borrowed clothes back to her bedroom. She went in and closed the door behind her, and laid the shorts and the jersey and the blouse ceremoniously on the bed, the way her mother did when she was going to change for a party. In truth, although it was a perfectly ordinary Saturday, Judith felt a bit as though she *was* about to change for a party, because everything about this delectable house—the very atmosphere—had a party feel to it.

But . . . and this was even more important . . . for a moment she found herself alone. She could scarcely remember the last time when she had been truly on her own, with nobody to talk or ask questions, or jostle or barge, or tell her to do something, or to stop doing something, or ring a bell or claim her attention. She discovered that this was the most wonderful relief. Alone. By herself, in her own private bedroom, surrounded by space and quiet, and pretty eye-pleasing objects, and peace. She went to the window, opened it, and leaned out to watch the white pigeons, and to listen to their gentle cooing.

Alone. There had been so much going on, and for so long. Weeks. Months, even. Christmas at Plymouth, and all the business of packing up Riverview House and shopping for school and finally saying goodbye. And then Saint Ursula's, where it was not possible to be private for a single second.

Alone. She realized how much she had missed the luxury of solitude, and knew that its occasional comfort would always be essential to her. The pleasure of being on one's own was not so much spiritual as sensuous, like wearing silk, or swimming without a bathing suit on, or walking along a totally empty beach with the sun on your back. One was restored by solitude. Refreshed. She watched the doves, and hoped, just for the moment, that Loveday would not come searching for her. It was not that she did not appreciate Loveday, who was being endlessly kind and hospitable. It was just that she needed time to reassemble and reorientate a personal sense of identity.

From far away, from a distant line of woodland, there came a crack of guns. The menfolk, still blasting away at pigeons. The sudden sound, splitting the quiet, caused the white doves to flutter from their perches and fly around in some agitation until they deemed it safe to settle again. She watched them reassemble, pout their snowy breasts, start in once more on their preening.

Loveday did not come. She was probably searching for some suitably ragamuffin garment, as far removed as possible from the rigid discipline of school uniform. So, after a bit, Judith closed the window, took off her own uniform, and, slowly savouring the novelty, dressed herself in Athena Carey-Lewis's cast-offs. Moving to and fro, she washed her hands (Chanel soap) and brushed her hair, tying it back with a fresh navy-blue ribbon. Only then did she go to inspect herself in the long mirror set in the wardrobe door. And it was amazing, because she looked so different. Sleek and expensive. Another girl, almost grown up, and totally new. She saw her own complacent expression and could not help smiling. She thought of her mother, because this seemed exactly the sort of experience that they should be sharing, but at the same time she was pretty sure that her mother, at that moment, would scarcely have recognized her.

The door burst open. "Are you ready?" Loveday demanded. "What *have* you been doing? You've taken ages. Goodness, you look nice. It must be something to do with Athena. She always looks sensational, even if she put on an old sack she'd look wonderful. Perhaps she magics everything she wears, and the magic stays. Now, what do you want to do *now?*"

Judith said feebly that she didn't mind, but this was true, and she couldn't think of anything else to say. In her present state of euphoria any ploy suggested would seem perfect.

"We could go and look at Tinkerbell, but it might take rather long, and it'll be lunch soon. So let's explore the house, and I'll show you every single room, and then you'll know your way around."

Judith had been right about Loveday. Loveday had pulled on a disreputable pair of jodhpurs which were already far too short for her skinny shins, and a sweater the dark purplish shade of ripe damsons. The colour of this accentuated the violet-blue of Loveday's extraordinary eyes, but so lacking was she in any sort of personal conceit that it was unlikely she had chosen the jersey for this reason, but rather because it had darns in the elbows and had been worn and washed into a comfortable shapelessness.

She agreed. "All right. We'll explore. Where do we start?"

"At the top. In the attics."

Which they duly did. These slope-ceilinged apartments went on forever— store-rooms, box-rooms, two small bathrooms, and four bedrooms. "These are the maids' rooms." Loveday wrinkled her nose. "They always smell a bit, of sweaty feet and armpits . . ."

"How many maids are there?"

"Three. Janet's the housemaid and Nesta's the parlourmaid and Hetty helps Mrs. Nettlebed in the kitchen."

"Where does Mrs. Nettlebed sleep?"

"Oh, she and Nettlebed have a little flat over the garage. Now we'll go down the back stairs, and you've seen the guest wing, so we'll start with Mummy's room . . ."

"Are we allowed?"

"Oh, yes, of course, she doesn't mind, provided we don't fiddle and squirt all her scent." She opened the door and pranced ahead of Judith. "Isn't it gorgeous? She's just had it redecorated, a frightfully fancy little man came all the way down from London to do it. Pops was furious because he painted the panelling, but I think it's rather nice, don't you?"

Which Judith decided was the understatement of all time. She had never seen such a bedroom, so huge, so feminine, so filled with charming and beguiling objects. The walls were pale, neither white nor pink nor peach, and glowed with sunlight. There were tremendously thick swagged draperies smothered in roses, and inside these a drift of filmy white curtains which stirred, coolly, in the breeze which blew, from the sea, in through the opened window. The wide, snowy double bed was draped in the same filmy white, and stacked with lacy and embroidered pillows, and there was a canopy over it with a little gold coronet at the centre, so that it looked like a bed in which a princess might choose to sleep.

"But just look at the *bathroom*. This was all new too . . ."

Wordless, Judith followed and gazed; shining black tiles, and rose-tinted mirrors, white porcelain, and a thick white carpet. A carpet in the bathroom! The utter, final luxury.

". . . and see, her mirror's got lights all round, like an actress's dressing-room, and if you open the mirrors, there are cupboards behind, for all her make-up and smells and stuff."

"What's that?"

"That? Oh, that's her bidet. It's French! It's for washing your bottom."

"Or your feet."

"Pops was *horrified*."

They doubled up with mirth, holding their sides, staggering with laughter. A thought occurred to Judith. Controlling her giggles, she went back into the sweet-scented, flowery bedroom, looked about her, but found no single trace of masculine occupation.

"Where does your father put his things?"

"Oh, he doesn't sleep here. He's got his own bedroom at the far end, over the front door. He likes the morning sun, and he has to be out of the way because he snores so much and keeps everybody awake. Come on, I'll show you more . . ."

They left the entrancing bedroom and continued on their way. "This is where Athena sleeps, and Edward's in here. And these are bathrooms. And then Mary's here next to the nursery, because it used to be the night nursery, and she's just stayed there. And this is the nursery bathroom, and it's got a little sort of kitchen in the corner so that she can make tea and things. And this is my room . . ."

"I would have known."

"How?"

"Clothes on the floor and ponies on the wall."

"And the Pony Club rosettes, and all my teddies; ever since I was born I've been collecting them. I've got twenty now, and they've all got names. And my books and my old doll's house, because Mary said she didn't want it cluttering up the nursery. And my bed faces *this* way, so that I can watch the sun coming up in the mornings . . . now come on, because there's still heaps to look at. This is the housemaid's cupboard, where all the brooms and things are kept, and this is the linen room, and another little room which is only used if we're packed out with guests." By now they had come full circle and were back again at the top of the main staircase. At the far side of the landing, one last door stood shut. ". . . and this is where Pops sleeps."

It was not a very large room, and it seemed, after the splendour of the rest of the house, austere and rather dark. The furniture was heavy and Victorian, the single bed narrow and high. All was immaculately tidy. The curtains were dark brocade, and a man's ivory-backed brushes lay neatly in the dead centre of the high chest of drawers. There was, as well, a photograph of Diana in a silver frame, but little else of a personal nature. It was a room which gave nothing away.

"It's dreadfully gloomy, isn't it? But Pops likes it that way, because it's the way it's always been. He hates change. And he likes his bathroom, because it's round . . . it's in the tower, you see, over the porch, and he can sit in his funny old bath and hear people arriving and listen to their voices and decide who they are. And if he doesn't like them, then he just stays in the bath until he hears them go away again. As you can gather, he's not very sociable."

"Does he know I'm staying?" Judith asked in some trepidation.

"Oh, heavens, yes, Mummy will have told him. Don't worry, he'll like you. It's just *her* boring friends he prefers to avoid."

After that, they went downstairs, and started off on the last lap. Judith by now was beginning to feel a bit bemused and confused. And hungry. It seemed hours since breakfast. But Loveday was inexhaustible.

"Now, the hall you've seen. And this is Pop's study, and the gents' cloaks. It's got this most wonderful lav, just like a men's club, and Pops closets himself in here for hours every morning after breakfast and reads *Horse and Hound*. Look, isn't it impressive? Mummy calls it his throne room. And then in *here* is the billiard-room, sometimes the men come here after dinner and play for hours, right into the night. Or it's good for wet afternoons. And this is Pops' study, and here's the dining-room . . . all laid for lunch, as you can see. And this is the little sitting-room, but we don't use it unless it's a freezing-cold winter night. I shan't take you into the drawing-room because you'll see that anyway, before lunch. Come and meet Mrs. Nettlebed."

And so they came at last to the kitchen, the heart of any house. This was the same as most other Cornish kitchens, except that it was much larger, and in place of the ubiquitous Cornish range stood a huge cream-coloured Aga. But there was the same familiar ration of dark-green paint, the same rack for airing clothes hoisted high to the ceiling, the same dresser, loaded with china, the same immense scrubbed table in the middle of the floor.

At this stood Mrs. Nettlebed, arranging bits of glacé fruit onto the top of a trifle. She was a small dumpy lady in a pink overall with a white apron over it, and she wore a concealing, and particularly unbecoming, white cotton cap, low on her brow. Her face was flushed, and her ankles swollen from standing, but when Loveday burst in upon her . . . "Hello, Mrs. Nettlebed, it's us . . . !" there were no frowns, nor requests to keep out of the way; she was dishing up the lunch, for heaven's sake. Instead, Mrs. Nettlebed's round cheeks bunched up into a besotted expression of pure delight. Loveday, it was instantly obvious, was her treasure and her joy.

"My dear life. There's my baby! Come and give Mrs. Nettlebed a nice kiss now . . ." She held her hands wide, her sticky fingers spread like a starfish, and leaned forward, all ready for the kiss which Loveday pressed upon her cheek. "Look at the size of you! You've grown. Soon be bigger than me. This the friend you've brought . . ."

"She's called Judith."

"Pleased to meet you, Judith."

"How do you do."

"Come for the weekend? That'll be some fun. Up to high jinks you'll be with this little tinker."

"What's for lunch, Mrs. Nettlebed?"

"Shooter's stew and mashed potato, and boiled cabbage."

"Is there nutmeg on the cabbage?"

"I wouldn't serve cabbage without nutmeg."

"In that case I'll probably eat it. Are the men in yet?"

"Just heard them in the yard, counting up the bag. Rabbit pie for lunch tomorrow. They'll be in the gunroom, I expect, cleaning guns. Shouldn't be more than ten minutes."

"Ten minutes." Loveday made a face. "I'm starving." She went to the dresser, opened a tin, and took out a couple of rich tea biscuits. She gave one to Judith and crammed the other into her mouth.

"Now Loveday . . ."

"I know. I'll spoil my appetite and I won't eat any of your lovely lunch. Come on, Judith, let's go and find Mummy and see if she'll give us a drink."

They found Diana in the drawing-room, peacefully curled up in the corner of a vast cream sofa, reading a novel. She was smoking, with a jade holder, a fragrant Turkish cigarette, and on the small table at her side stood her ashtray and a cocktail. As they burst in upon her, disturbing her quiet, she raised her head to smile a welcome.

"Darlings, there you are. What fun. Have you been enjoying yourselves?"

"Yes, we've been all over and seen every single room, and we've been to say hello to Mrs. Nettlebed, and now can we have a drink?"

"What do you want to drink?"

A mirrored table stood against one wall, neatly arranged with bottles and shining clean glasses. Loveday went to inspect its offerings. She said, "I really feel like Orange Corona, but there isn't any."

"That dreadful fizzy stuff that turns your mouth orange? Perhaps there's some in the larder. Ring for Nettlebed and find out if he has a bottle tucked away."

The bell was in the wall above the table. Loveday pressed her thumb upon it. Diana smiled at Judith. "What do you think of my darling house?"

"It's beautiful. But I'm not sure that this room isn't the nicest of all." It was too. Panelled and with a parquet floor scattered with rugs, it was filled with sunlight and flowers. No humble daffodils here, but more exotic hot-house blooms, all purple and white and fuchsia, and in one corner stood a blue-and-white china tub and a camellia tree, its dark glossy branches loaded with deep-pink flowers. The thick curtains and the covers were cream bro-cade, and all the sofas and chairs were filled with fat satin cushions, in the palest of greens and pinks and blues, looking just like so many delicious, enormous boiled sweets. Magazines were neatly aligned on a central table, the journals mandatory to any self-respecting country house. *The Tatler*, for social gossip; *The Sketch*, for theatre and ballet; *The Illustrated London News*, for current events; and *The Sporting Dramatic*, for racing. As well, *The Field*, *Horse & Hound*, the latest *Vogue* and *Woman's Journal*, and a stack of daily newspapers which did not look as though they had even been opened.

Judith longed to be alone, to stare forever, to take in every detail, so that if she never came again to this house, she would be able to keep a perfect picture of it in her mind. The tall mantelpiece was white-painted, and upon it stood a row of engaging porcelain figures, a Meissen monkey-band. Over the mantelpiece hung a portrait of Diana, her slender shoulders draped in smoke-blue chiffon, and a shaft of light turning her corn-coloured hair to gold. There was laughter in the painted blue eyes, and the ghost of a smile on her lips, as though she and the artist shared the most intimate and amusing of secrets.

Seeing her staring, "Do you like it?" Diana asked.

"It's *just* like you."

Diana laughed. "Wonderfully flattering. But then de László was always a flatterer."

The view from the tall windows was by now familiar. The formal terraced gardens sloped down to meld with shrubs and rough-grassed meadows bright with daffodils. To one side stood a French window, which gave out onto a small enclosed terrace, private as a little room within the garden. This was backed by a conservatory, and through the glass could be seen a climbing jasmine, a burgeoning vine, and a lot of enviable, old-fashioned wicker furniture. All conjured up thoughts of summer, baking sunshine, lazy afternoons, and long cool drinks. Or perhaps China tea in very thin cups, and cucumber sandwiches.

Lost in charming imaginings, she was joined by Loveday.

"That's Mummy's special spot. Isn't it, Mummy? She lies here and sunbathes without any clothes on."

"Only if there's nobody about."

"Well, I've seen you doing it."

"You don't count."

At this juncture the door behind them quietly opened and a deep voice was heard. "You rang, madam?"

Mr. Nettlebed. Loveday had already told her that he had stomach ulcers and so an unpredictable disposition, but this had not prepared Judith for his distinguished and awesome appearance. He was a tall man, white-haired and quite handsome in a gloomy way. A bit like a reliable undertaker. His clothes confirmed this impression, for he wore a black jacket and a black tie and sponge-bag trousers. His face was pale and lined, his eyes hooded, and so impressive did he look that Judith wondered how anybody plucked up the nerve to ask him to do anything, let alone give him any sort of an order.

"Oh, Nettlebed, thank you," said Diana. "Loveday wants some drink or other . . ."

"I want Orange Corona, Mr. Nettlebed, and it's not on the table."

This demand was followed by a long and pregnant silence. Nettlebed did not move, merely fixed Loveday with his cold gaze, as though he were piercing a dead butterfly with a long steel pin. Nor did Diana speak. The silence continued. Became uncomfortable. Diana turned her head and looked at Loveday.

Loveday, with a resigned expression on her face, started all over again.

"Please, Mr. Nettlebed, would you be very kind and see if there is some Orange Corona in the pantry?"

The small tension was immediately dispelled. "Certainly," said Nettlebed. "I think there's a crate on the larder shelf. I shall go and ascertain."

He began to withdraw, but Diana spoke. "Are the men back yet, Nettlebed?"

"Yes, madam. They're cleaning up in the gunroom."

"Have they had a good morning?"

"A number of rabbits and pigeons, madam. And two hares."

"Heavens. Poor Mrs. Nettlebed. What a lot of gutting and cleaning."

"I will probably assist her, madam."

He went, closing the door behind him. Loveday grimaced. "I will probably assist her, madam," she mimicked. "Pompous old ass."

"Loveday." Diana's voice had turned icy.

"Well, that's what Edward calls him."

"Edward should know better. And you know perfectly well that you never ask Nettlebed, or anybody, to do anything for you without saying please, and then thank you when they've done it."

"I just forgot."

"Well, don't forget."

She turned back to her book. Judith felt awkward, diminished and gawky, as though the reprimand had been for herself, but Loveday was undismayed. She went to lean, in wheedling fashion, over the back of the sofa so that her curly dark head almost touched her mother's sleek golden one.

"What are you reading?"

"A novel."

"What's it called?"

"The Weather in the Streets."

"What's it about?"

"Love. Unhappy love."

"I thought all love was happy."

"Oh, darling. Not always. Not every woman is lucky." She reached for her drink, the little triangular cocktail glass filled with silvery liquid. At the bottom of the glass, like a rare pebble, or some strange sea-creature, lurked an olive. She took a sip and then laid the glass down, and as she did so, the door of the drawing-room opened once more, but it was not Mr. Nettlebed, returned, who stood there. "Pops!" Loveday left her mother's side and fled into his outstretched arms.

"Hello, my baby." They hugged and kissed, he stooping his height to hers. "We've missed you. And here you are, back again . . ." He ruffled her hair, smiling down at his youngest child as though she were the most precious creature on earth.

(So loved was Loveday. By everybody. Feeling a bit out of it, observing the sort of demonstrative behaviour that she herself had never experienced, Judith found it hard not to feel a small pang of envy.)

"Diana." With Loveday hanging on to his sleeve like a puppy, he crossed over to where his wife sat, and bent to kiss her. "I'm sorry, my darling, are we late?"

She tilted her head to smile up into his face. "Not at all. It's only a quarter to one. Did you all have a good morning?"

"Splendid."

"Where are Tommy and Jeremy?"

"Tommy's on his way. Jeremy's cleaning my gun for me . . ."

"The kind boy."

Standing on the sidelines, listening to this exchange, Judith deliberately assumed a bland and smiling expression, hiding her shock at his appearance. For Colonel Carey-Lewis was a complete surprise, being so old, and privately she decided that he looked more like Diana's father than her husband and could easily be Loveday's grandparent. True, he held himself with the upright stance of a soldier and moved with the easy, long-legged lope of a perpetually active man, but his hair, what there was of it, was white, and his eyes, set deep in his lined face, were the faded blue of some ancient countryman. His wind-burned cheeks were cadaverous, and his nose long and beaky over a trim military moustache. He was tall and very sparsely built, dressed in venerable tweeds and moleskin knickerbockers, and his storklike stockinged shins ended in brogues polished to a chestnut shine.

"He said it was the least he could do."

With this, he straightened up, loosed himself from Loveday's clutch, smoothed his hair with his hands, and turned to Judith.

"And you must be Loveday's friend?"

She looked up into his eyes, and saw them both watchful and kindly, but for some reason, dreadfully sad. Which was strange again, because his reunion with wife and daughter had clearly given all of them so much delight. But then he smiled, and some of the sadness was erased. He moved towards her, hand outstretched.

"How very pleasant that you could come and stay."

"Her name's Judith," Loveday told him.

Judith said, "How do you do," and they shook hands formally. His fingers, enclosing hers, felt dry and rough. She smelt the sweet reek of his Harris tweed jacket, and realized instinctively that he was just as shy as she felt. This made her like him very much, and long to be able to put him at his ease.

"Has Loveday been taking care of you?"

"Yes. We've been all over the house."

"Good. Now you know your way around." He hesitated. He was not good at small talk and so it was fortunate that at this moment they were interrupted by the appearance of a second gentleman, with, hard on his heels, Nettlebed, who bore before him, like a votive offering, a bottle of Orange Corona on a silver salver.

"Diana. Are we all in disgrace for taking so long?"

"Oh, darling Tommy, don't be so silly. Good morning?"

"Great fun." Tommy Mortimer stood for an instant rubbing his hands together, as though grateful to be indoors and out of the cold, and looking forward to a comforting drink. He too was dressed for shooting, in elegant tweeds and a canary-coloured waistcoat. His face was boyish, good-humoured and smiling; his skin smooth and tanned and immaculately barbered. However, it was difficult to guess how old he was, because his thick hair was nearly white. But somehow this only served to accentuate the springy youthfulness of his step and the whole rather theatrical manner of his arrival. *Here I am*, it seemed to say. *Now we can all start having a wonderful time.*

He crossed the room to drop a kiss on Diana's cheek, and then turned his attentions to Loveday.

"Hello there, wicked one! Got a kiss for your honorary uncle? How's school? Have they turned you into a little lady yet?"

"Oh, Tommy, don't ask such stupid questions."

"You could at least," said her mother, "introduce Tommy to your friend."

"Oh, I *am* sorry." Loveday, palpably showing off a bit, proceeded to make a great production of this. "This is Judith Dunbar who's at school with me, and this, ta-ra, ta-ra, is Tommy Mortimer."

Tommy laughed, amused by her impudence. "Hello, Judith."

"How do you do."

The Colonel, however, had had enough of trivial formalities. It was time for a drink. Nettlebed, at the table, poured these. Dry martini for Mr. Mortimer, beer for the Colonel, Orange Corona for the girls. Diana, lazily sipping her own martini, refused a refill. Tommy, holding his glass, came to settle himself on the sofa beside her, half-turned to face her, with an arm gracefully disposed along the back of the cushions. Judith wondered if he was an actor. She had little experience of the live theatre, but had been to enough films, squashed into the Porthkerris cinema with Heather beside her, to recognize the contrived arrangement of limbs, the outstretched arm, the gracefully crossed legs. Perhaps Tommy Mortimer was a famous matinée idol, and she was just too stupid and inexperienced to know about him. But if he was, then surely Loveday would have told her.

Nettlebed, having dealt with drinks, departed.

Judith sipped her Orange Corona. It was delicious, fizzy and strong and very sweet. She hoped that the fizz would not make her burp. Standing a little apart from the others, she endeavoured to swallow slowly and carefully, thus avoiding any possible embarrassment. Concentrating on this problem, she did not notice the last member of the shooting party enter the room.

He came quietly, on rubber-soled shoes, so none of the others heard him either. A much younger man, bespectacled, dressed in corduroys and a hefty ribbed sweater, he paused just inside the open door. Judith felt his eyes upon her and looked up, and saw him watching her, as once she had watched him. For an incredulous instant they stared at each other in some bewilderment, and then he smiled, and after that there could be no doubt at all, because everything about him was totally familiar.

He came across the room to her side. He said, "It is you, isn't it? The girl on the train?"

Judith was so delighted that she was unable to speak, so she simply nodded.

"What an extraordinary coincidence. Are you Loveday's schoolfriend?"

Her own face was creeping up into a smile. She could feel it, without any conscious volition on her own part. If she had wanted to, she couldn't have stopped smiling.

She nodded again.

"What's your name?"

"Judith Dunbar."

"I'm Jeremy Wells."

She found her voice at last. "I know. I guessed."

"Jeremy! I didn't realize you'd come." From the sofa, Diana had spied him. "You must have tiptoed in. Are you introducing yourself to Judith?"

He laughed. "I don't need to. We've already met. In the train. Coming down from Plymouth."

Immediately, they were the centre of attention. Everybody was suitably amazed by the coincidence, and wanted to hear all the details of their meeting. How they had shared the compartment, and gazed from the Saltash Bridge at the naval men-of-war, and finally said goodbye in Truro.

"How's your little sister? The one with the gollywog?" Jeremy asked.

"She's gone. Back to Colombo with my mother."

"Oh dear. I didn't know. You'll miss them."

"They'll be there by now. And then they're moving on to Singapore. My father's got a new job."

"Will you be joining them?"

"No, not for years."

It was lovely. It was like being a grown-up, dressed in Athena's expensive clothes, and sipping a drink, and having everybody delighted because she had a friend of her own. She kept taking covert glances at Jeremy Wells's face, just to make sure that he was really here at Nancherrow, part of the Carey-Lewis clan, and yet, himself. She remembered how, in the train, when he opened the window, the end of his long muffler had lain across her knee. She remembered telling Phyllis all about him. *He was really nice*, she had said. *I wouldn't mind meeting someone like him.*

And now it had really happened. He was here. Now she knew him properly. It had really happened . . .

From the hall, the gong for luncheon rang out. Diana finished her drink, handed the empty glass to Tommy Mortimer, rose to her feet, gathered her party around her, and led the way through to the dining-room.

The Colonel said, "Now you must explain to me how you and Jeremy came to meet."

"It was in the train from Plymouth. Just after Christmas. We were in the same compartment."

"And what had you been doing in Plymouth?"

"Staying with my aunt and uncle. He's an Engineer Captain, at Keyham. We spent Christmas with them."

"We, being. . . ?"

"My mother and my little sister and me. And then he got off at Truro, and we went on to Penmarron."

"I see. Did you realize he's now a doctor?"

"Yes. He told us that. And . . . Diana told me this morning that his father is *your* doctor." She hesitated a little over saying Diana's name to her distinguished and elderly husband in such a familiar way, but the Colonel didn't seem to notice. He was probably very used to his wife's casual attitude to the formalities of life.

"He's a good lad." He glanced down the table to where Jeremy sat. "Great cricketer. Captains Cornwall rugby team. Watched them play last year. Went to Twickenham. Great thrill."

"Diana told me about that too."

He smiled. "In that case, I mustn't be a bore. Now, tell me about your family. They're in the East?"

"Yes, Colombo."

"Have you lived there?"

"I was born there. I didn't come home till I was ten. My mother was having Jess. She's four now."

"Is your father with the Civil Service?"

"No, he's in shipping. With a firm called Wilson-McKinnon. He's being moved to Singapore, and they'll all be going there quite soon." She added, "My mother didn't really want to go, but I expect she'll like it once she gets there."

"Yes, I expect she will."

She thought that he was being very courteous and hostly, conversing and making her feel at home just as though she were someone really important. He sat at the head of the long dining table, with Loveday and Judith placed on either side. Diana was at the far end, with Tommy on her left and Jeremy at her right. Mary Millyway, who had appeared as they all settled down at the table, had taken her seat between Jeremy and Loveday. She had combed her hair and powdered her nose, and was composed and perfectly at ease, talking to Jeremy, whom she had obviously known forever, imparting the latest gossip of the legendary Athena, and in return being brought up-to-date on his progress and work at Saint Thomas's Hospital.

The meal, as described in the kitchen by Mrs. Nettlebed, had not sounded exciting, but it was, in fact, delicious. The Shooter's stew was dark and rich, enhanced by fresh mushrooms and a winy sauce; the mashed potatoes were creamy and smooth . . . good for soaking up the thick gravy . . . and the cabbage, lightly dusted with grated nutmeg, was green and sweet and crisp as nuts. To drink there was water, or beer for the men. Nettlebed, having handed around the vegetables, and seen that all the glasses were filled, had withdrawn, soft-footed, from the room. Judith was relieved to see him go. She found it hard to ignore his chilling presence, and his cold regard was enough to make anybody use the wrong knife or fork, knock over a glass of water, or drop one's linen napkin on the floor.

So far, however, she had committed none of these crimes, and without Nettlebed lurking around the back of her neck, she was beginning to enjoy herself.

"And how about yourself?" the Colonel asked. "Are you going to manage on your own? Are you enjoying Saint Ursula's?"

She shrugged. "It's all right."

"What about school holidays?"

"I'm going to live with my Aunt Louise."

"Where is that?"

"In Penmarron. Near the golf course."

It was at this moment that one of those inexplicable silences fell around the table . . . everybody coming to a pause in the general conversation. So when Judith added, "The house is called Windyridge," hers was the only voice.

Across the table, Loveday began to giggle.

"What's the joke?" her father asked.

"I wouldn't call it Windyridge. I'd call it Fartyedge," whereupon she dissolved into shrieks of laughter, and would probably have choked on her stew, or done the nose-trick, had not the Colonel thumped her on the back, and so, by a whisker, saved the day.

Judith was both embarrassed and apprehensive, expecting a storm of reprimands, or, at the worst, a furious order to leave the room at once. Such language, and at the lunch table too.

But nobody seemed in the least shocked, just marvellously amused, and everyone around the table dissolved into mirth as though Loveday had made some brilliantly funny remark. Mary Millyway did murmur, "Oh, *really*, Loveday," but nobody, least of all Loveday, took the slightest bit of notice of her.

When she had stopped laughing, and wiped the tears from her cheeks with a tiny lace-edged handkerchief, Diana observed, sotto voce, "What a frightfully good thing Nettlebed wasn't in the room. Loveday, you really are naughty, but you're so funny I suppose it doesn't matter."

The first course was finished, and the bell rung for Nettlebed to return and

clear the plates. The pudding was then served. Syrup tart and bottled plums
and Cornish cream. The Colonel, having done his duty by his daughter's
guest, now turned his attention to Loveday, who had a great deal to tell
him about the iniquities of school, the unfairness of Deirdre Ledingham, the
impossibility of learning algebra, and the hatefulness of Matron.

He listened to this routine moaning with polite attention, neither arguing
nor interrupting, and Judith guessed that he had probably heard it all before.
Her respect for him grew, because he clearly knew that none of Loveday's
complaints, if analysed, would prove to have the slightest substance. Perhaps
as well he had accepted the fact that Loveday, come hell or high water, was
a survivor, and if she couldn't get her own way by wheedling and charm, she
would resort to the depths of blackmail. Like running away from her first
boarding-school, and refusing, on pain of death, to return.

Judith spooned cream over her syrup tart and turned her attention to other
conversations. Tommy Mortimer and Diana were laying plans for London; for
the coming Season, for the Chelsea Flower Show, and Wimbledon and Henley and Ascot. It made fascinating listening.

"I've got tickets for the Centre Court and the Royal Enclosure."

"Oh, heaven. I shall have to buy some hats."

"How about Henley?"

"Oh, let's go. I always adore Henley. All those dear old codgers in their
pink ties."

"We'll get a party together. When are you next coming up to town?"

"I hadn't really thought. Perhaps in a couple of weeks. I'll drive up in the
Bentley. I have to order a clothe or two, and have fittings and such. And find
a decorator to do something about Cadogan Mews, before Athena gets back
from Switzerland."

"I know a marvellous man. I'll give you his number."

"How kind. I'll let you know when I'm on my way."

"We'll do a theatre, and I'll give you dinner at the Savoy."

"Heavenly." All at once, Diana became aware of Judith. She smiled. "I'm
sorry, we're being boring, laying plans. And this is your day, and nobody's
talking to you. Now, tell me, what do you want to do this afternoon?" She
raised her voice slightly, commanding attention. "What does *everybody* want
to do this afternoon?"

Loveday said, "I want to ride Tinkerbell."

"Darling, that sounds a little selfish. What about Judith?"

"Judith doesn't care for riding. She doesn't like horses."

"In that case, perhaps it would be kind to do something that *she* wants to
do."

"I don't mind," Judith said, fearing some sort of argument, but Loveday
didn't seem to care about arguments or rows or anything. "Oh, Mummy, I
really want to ride Tinkerbell. And you know it's not good for her not being
regularly exercised."

"I don't want you going out on your own. Perhaps Pops can come with
you."

"She won't be on her own," the Colonel told her. "Young Walter's working down at the stables this afternoon. I'll send word to him to have the horses saddled up and ready."

"But, Pops, why can't *you* come with me?"

"Because, my pet, I must go and do some work. I've letters to write, and calls to make, and an appointment with Mudge at four o'clock." Down the table he indulgently regarded his wife. "And how are you going to spend the rest of the day?"

"Oh, Tommy and I are all arranged for. I've asked the Parker-Browns over for some bridge. But that still doesn't solve the problem of our guest . . ." Judith felt dreadfully embarrassed, as though she had become, all at once, a tiresome nuisance, and it was made even worse by Diana turning to Mary Millyway. "Perhaps, Mary . . . ?"

She was, however, interrupted by Jeremy Wells who, up to now, had kept out of the discussion. He said, "Why don't I do something with Judith? We'll all go down to the stables together, and she and I will take the dogs and go on down to the cove." He smiled at Judith and she was filled with gratitude, because he had seen her predicament and come, so easily, to her rescue. "Would you like to do that?"

"Yes, I'd love it. But you don't need to bother; I mean, I'm all right on my own."

Diana, clearly thankful to have everything settled, overrode her feeble objections. "Of course you can't be on your own. It's a lovely idea, provided Jeremy's parents won't mind him spending the entire day here. After all, you are only down for the weekend, and they'll be longing to have a sight of you . . ."

"I'll go back after tea. Father's on call today anyway. But we'll have the evening together."

Diana beamed. "Well, isn't that splendid? Everything settled and everybody happy. Judith, you'll love the cove, our own darling little beach. But put on a jacket or get Mary to lend you an extra jumper, because it's always cold down by the sea. And Loveday, don't forget your hard hat. Now . . ." She pushed back her chair. "Why don't we all go to the drawing-room and have a cup of coffee."

The invitation, it seemed, did not include the two girls. When the grown-ups had gone, they stayed in the dining-room to help Mary and Nettlebed clear the table, and only then went upstairs to prepare for their expeditions. Extra pullovers were produced for both of them, and Loveday's jodhpur boots, her string gloves, and her hard hat all run to earth.

She said, "I hate this hat. The elastic's too tight under my chin."

But Mary was adamant. "It's nothing of the sort, and you're to keep it on."

"I don't see why I should have to wear it. Lots of girls don't."

"You're not lots of girls, and we don't want you bashing your brains out on a rock. Now, here's your crop, and two toffees for your pockets." She took a glass jar from the mantelpiece and doled out a toffee each.

"What about Jeremy and Walter?" Loveday asked, and Mary laughed, and gave her two more, and sent her on her way with a pat on the behind. "Off with you," she said. "And when you get back, I'll have tea ready for you both, here, by the fire."

Like puppies escaping, they galloped downstairs and along the passage which led to the drawing-room door. Outside this, Loveday paused. "We won't go in," she whispered, "otherwise we'll get *caught up*." She opened the door and put her head around it. "Jeremy! We're ready."

"I'll meet you in the gun-room," came his voice. "In one minute. I'll bring Pekoe with me. Tiger's there already, drying off after this morning."

"Right. Have lovely bridge, Mummy. See you later, Pops." She closed the door. "Come on, we'll go to the kitchen first and get some sugar lumps for Tinkerbell and Ranger. And if Mrs. Nettlebed gives us sweets, don't tell her Mary's already given us toffees."

Mrs. Nettlebed did not give them sweets, but tiny fairy cakes fresh out of the oven, which she had just made for drawing-room tea. They were warm, and too good to keep, so they ate them then and there, raided the sugar basin, and went on their way. "Have a good time now . . ." Mrs. Nettlebed's voice floated after them.

The back passage led to the gun-room, which smelt pleasantly of oil, and linseed, and old mackintoshes, and dog. Locked cabinets of guns and rods stood all around the wall, and gaffs and waders and rubber boots had their own special racks. Tiger, snoozing in his bed, had heard them coming and was up and ready for them, and raring to go for another bit of exercise. He was a huge black Labrador, with a square nose and dark eyes and a tail that wagged like a piston.

"Hello, darling Tiger, how are you? Have you had a lovely morning finding dead rabbits and shot pigeons?" Tiger made pleased noises in the back of his throat. He was enormously friendly, which was a good thing, because he was too big and strong to be anything else. "And are you going to come for a lovely walk?"

"Of course he is," said Jeremy, coming through the door behind them with Pekoe under his arm. He put Pekoe down on the floor, and while he pulled on his jacket, which he took from a hook on the wall, the two dogs made much of each other, Tiger nuzzling at the little Peke, and Pekoe lying on his back and waving his paws, as though he were swimming upside down.

Judith laughed. "They look so funny together."

"Don't they just." He grinned. "Come on then, girls, no hanging about. Walter will be waiting."

They trooped out, by way of a second door which led into the cobbled yard where the white pigeons fluttered around the dovecote. It was a bit like walking out into winter, and Judith was taken aback by the cold of the air. Indoors, inside the centrally heated house, so filled with pale sunshine and the scent of flowers, it was easy to be lulled into the belief that warm spring had truly arrived, but a nip in the wintry air instantly dispelled any such illusion. It was still bright, but there was a sharp east wind coming in off the sea, from time to time blowing dark clouds across the face of the sun. Judith reminded herself that it was, after all, still only the middle of February, but, despite her extra sweater, she shivered. Jeremy noticed the shiver and said, in a comforting manner, "Don't worry. Once we get moving you'll be as warm as toast."

The stables lay a little way from the house, screened from sight by a coppice, discreetly landscaped, of young oak trees. A gravelled roadway led towards these, and as they approached, the stables came into view, purpose-built and very trim, forming three sides of a square, and with a yard in the middle. In this yard, the two mounts were ready and waiting, already saddled up and tethered to iron rings set in the wall. Tinkerbell and Ranger. Tinkerbell was a charming little grey pony, but Ranger was a great bay, seeming, to the wary Judith, the size of an elephant. He looked frighteningly strong, with powerful quarters, and muscles fairly rippling beneath his polished, groomed coat. Approaching, she decided to keep her distance. She would pat the pony, and even feed it a lump of sugar, but would give the power-house of the Colonel's hunter a very wide berth.

A young man stood with the animals, engaged in tightening the girth strap of the little grey. He saw them coming, finished his task, slapping down the saddle-flap, and stood waiting, with a hand resting on the pony's neck.

"Hello, Walter," Loveday called.

"Hello, there."

"You're all ready! Did you know we were coming?"

"Mr. Nettlebed sent young Hetty down with word." He ducked his head at Jeremy. "Hello, Jeremy. Didn't know you were down."

"Got a weekend off. How are things with you?"

"Oh, not too bad. Coming out with us, are you?"

"No, not today. We're going down to the cove. Taking the dogs. This is Loveday's friend, Judith Dunbar."

Walter turned his head slightly, and nodded at Judith. He said, "Hello."

He was an extraordinarily good-looking young man, slim and dark and sunburnt as a gypsy, with black hair that covered his head in curls, and eyes dark as coffee beans. He wore corduroy breeches, a thick shirt striped in blue, and a leather waistcoat. Around his brown neck was knotted a yellow cotton handkerchief. What age was he? Sixteen, or seventeen? But he looked older, totally mature, and already sported a man's dark shadow of a beard. He made Judith think of Heathcliff in *Wuthering Heights,* and she could perfectly well see why Loveday was so keen to spend her afternoon riding Tinkerbell. Even Judith could understand the lure of the horse if one was to have the dashing companionship of Walter Mudge.

They stood and watched them mount. Walter eschewed the offer of a leg-up, and swung himself up into the saddle with an effortless grace that suggested that he might, just slightly, be showing off.

"Have fun," Judith told Loveday.

She raised her crop. "You too."

Hooves clattered across the yard, and then changed sound as the horses reached the gravelled road. In the bright, cold light, the little entourage made an attractive sight. They broke into a trot, disappeared around the oak coppice. The hoof-beats faded.

"Where will they go?" Judith asked.

"Probably down the lane to Lidgey, and then on up to the moor."

"It makes me wish I liked horses."

"You either like them, or you don't. Come on, it's too cold to stand."

They went the way that the riders had taken, and then turned off to the right, where the path sloped down through the gardens towards the coast. The dogs shot ahead and were soon lost to view. "They won't get lost, will they?" Judith, feeling responsible for their well-being, was anxious, but Jeremy reassured her. "They know this walk as well as anybody. By the time we've reached the cove, they'll be there, and Tiger will already have had a swim."

He led the way and she followed, along a winding gravelled path which led in the direction of the sea. The formal lawns and flower-beds were left behind them. They passed through a small wrought-iron gate, and the path narrowed and plunged downwards into a jungle of semi-tropical vegetation; camellias, late-flowering hydrangeas, stately rhododendron, lush clumps and thickets of bamboo, and tall-stemmed palms, their trunks matted with what looked like very thick black hair. High overhead, bare branches of elm and beech soughed in the wind, and were filled with hosts of cawing rooks. Then a stream appeared from the undergrowth of creeping ivy and moss and fern, and bubbled and tumbled its way down a rocky bed, alongside where they walked. From time to time the path crossed and then re-crossed the flowing water, by means of ornamental wooden bridges, contrived in designs that were vaguely oriental and made Judith think of willow-pattern plates. The running water and the wind in the trees made the only sound; footsteps were deadened by a thick compost of dead leaves, and only when they crossed the bridges did the wooden planking ring with their tread.

Over the last bridge, Jeremy paused, waiting for Judith to catch up. There was still no sign of the dogs.

"How are you doing?"

"All right."

"Well done. Now we come to the tunnel."

He set off once more. She looked and saw that, ahead, the sloping path plunged into a cavern of gunnera, that monstrous prickly-stemmed plant, with leaves large as umbrellas. Judith had seen gunnera growing before, but never in such daunting profusion. They stood there, sinister as creatures from another planet, and it took a small effort of courage to duck her head and follow her guide, and in the tunnel the light from the sky was shut away. It was like being underwater, so damp was everything, so aqueous and green.

She scrambled to keep up with him, her feet slithering on the steepening path. She raised her voice. "I don't like gunnera," she told him, and he looked back, to smile over his shoulder.

"In Brazil," he told her, "they use the leaves as rain shelters."

"I'd rather be wet."

"We're nearly out of it now."

And indeed, moments later, they emerged from the primeval gloom of the tunnel and stood once more in the glittering light of the bright winter afternoon. And Judith saw that they had come to the rim of a disused stone quarry. The path turned into a zigzag flight of roughly hewn steps which led to the foot of this. The stream, which had never been out of earshot, now appeared once more, to fling itself over the edge of the cliff in a sparkling waterfall, pouring down into a rocky crevasse, emerald green with moss and fern, and misted with damp. The sound of it filled her ears. The walls of the quarry were hung with mesembryanthemum; its floor, littered with rocks and boulders, had become, over the years, a wild garden of bramble and bracken, tangled honeysuckle, ragged robin and butter-yellow aconites. The air was sweet with the almond-scent of gorse, and as well, the cool tang of seaweed, and she knew that they were close, at last, to the beach.

With some care, they scrambled down the precipitous makeshift stairway. At the bottom the path, now reduced to a narrow thread, followed the stream, twisting its way between the gaunt shapes of the boulders, until they came to the far side of the quarry and the original entrance. Here a shallow grassy bank sloped up to a wooden gate. The stream plunged into a culvert and disappeared, and they climbed the bank and then the gate, and jumped down onto the Tarmac of a narrow farm road. On the far side of this was a low drystone wall, and then, finally, there were the cliffs and the sea. Descending through the grounds of Nancherrow, they had been sheltered by vegetation, but were now exposed to the full blast of the wind pouring in from the southeast. The sun was out, the sea intensely blue, flecked with white-caps. They crossed the road and climbed the far wall by means of a stile. The cliffs were not steep. A turfy track led down to the rocks, through prickly gorse and bracken and clumps of wild primroses. The tide was out, and a curving sickle of white sand came into view. Their friend the stream now appeared yet again, spilling down the cliff and so onto the sands, and there flowing out to join the breakers by means of a freshwater channel which sliced the beach in two. The wind buffetted. Gulls hung screaming overhead, and the thunder of the waves was continuous, creaming up onto the shore, and then drawing away again, with a tremendous hissing sound.

As Jeremy had promised, the dogs were already there, Tiger wet from his swim and Pekoe digging a hole, having scented some buried and noxious scrap of offal. Otherwise, there was no living soul to be seen. Only the dogs and the gulls, and they themselves.

"Does anybody ever come here?" she asked.

"No. I think most people don't even realize that the cove exists." He climbed down, negotiating boulders and awkward corners, and Judith scrambled after him. They reached, at last, a wide shelf of rock overhanging the sand, where crannies were studded with sea-pink, and yellowed with lichen.

"You can see, the beach is steep, so that when the flood-tide comes up, the water is twenty feet deep or more, and clear as glass. Good for diving." He smiled at her. "Can you dive?"

"Yes. My father taught me, in the pool at the Galle Face Hotel."

"You'll have to come in the summer and show off your prowess. It's such a perfect place. This rock is where we have picnics, no fear of the Thermos flasks being washed away by the high tide. And it always seems to be sheltered and more or less out of the wind. Why don't we sit down for a moment?"

Which they did, shifting about a bit to find a bearable perch on the hard rock. And Judith was cold no longer, but warmed by exercise, by the dazzling sunshine striking through her thick sweater, by the easy and undemanding presence of her companion.

She said, "I don't know if you know the beach at Penmarron, but it's quite different from this. It's big as a desert, and deserted too, and if you want to get out of the north wind, you have to go up onto the dunes. It's very beautiful, but this is more . . ." She searched for the right word.

Jeremy supplied it. "Domestic?"

"Yes, that's just what I mean. I . . . am glad you brought me to see it. But I hope you don't feel that you had to. I'm very good at doing things on my own."

"I'm sure you are. But don't worry. I wanted to come. I always like it here. Refreshment of the soul, perhaps." He sat with his elbows resting on his knees, squinting out to sea through his spectacles. "Do you see the cormorants on that rock? Sometimes in warm weather, the seals come and bask. The dogs go mad. Don't know what to make of them."

They fell silent. Judith thought of Loveday and Walter, by now probably cantering over the moors, but the tiny twinge of envy she had known as they set off, looking so competent and dashing, was gone. Better to be here, in this place, and with this nice man. Being with him was almost as good as being on one's own.

After a bit, she said, "You know it all so well here, don't you? I mean Nancherrow. And the Carey-Lewises. As though it were your own home and your own family. And yet it isn't."

Jeremy leaned back on his elbows.

"It's a sort of second home. You see, I've been coming here for years. I got to know the Carey-Lewises because of my father being family doctor, and then, as I grew older, and started playing rugby and cricket, the Colonel sort of took me under his wing, and gave me every kind of encouragement and support. He's a great *aficionado*. He was always at all my matches, cheering on the home team. And later, he began to ask me to shoot with him, which was immensely kind, because my own father has never had the time to indulge in that sort of sport, and so could never return the Colonel's hospitality."

"And the children? I mean, Athena and Edward. Are they your friends too?"

"They're a good deal younger than me, but yes, they are my friends. When Athena was first going to dances, I used to be given the responsibility of being her partner, not that she ever danced with me, but I was considered reliable enough to take her to the party and bring her home in one piece."

"Didn't you mind that she didn't dance with you?"

"Not particularly. I always knew plenty of other girls."

"She's very beautiful, isn't she?"

"Ravishing. Just like her mother. Men fall about her like ninepins."

"And Edward?"

"Edward I got to know very well, because when I was a medical student I was perpetually short of cash, so the Colonel offered me a holiday job. I suppose, for want of a better word, you'd call it being a tutor. Edward was never particularly academic, and he needed extra coaching to get him through his exams, and finally into Harrow. And I coached him in tennis and cricket, and we used to go over to Penzance and sail with the club there. It was great. So you see, I spent a good deal of time around and about."

"I see."

"What do you see?"

"Why you seem to be part of the family."

"One becomes absorbed. And you? Had you any idea what to expect when you were invited to Nancherrow for the weekend?"

"Not really."

"The first impression is something of an experience. But I don't think you've been overwhelmed."

"No." She thought about this. "But only because they're all so nice. If they weren't, it would be a bit frightening, because it's all so . . . rich. I mean, butlers and ponies and nannies and shooting parties. I've never known anyone in England with a butler. In Ceylon it's different because everybody has servants, but most people here just have a cook-general. Is . . . is Colonel Carey-Lewis frightfully rich?"

"No more so than any other Cornish landowner . . ."

"But . . ."

"The money is Diana's. She was the only child of an immensely wealthy gentleman called Lord Awliscombe. When he died she was well provided for."

Diana, it seemed, had been blessed with everything. "She must have had a very special fairy godmother. To be so beautiful, and wealthy and charming. Most people would settle for just one of those things. And not just beautiful, but still so young. You can hardly believe she's got grown-up children."

"She was only seventeen when she married Edgar."

"Edgar. Is that the Colonel's name?"

"It is. He's much older than Diana, of course, but adored her all her life and finally won her. And it's been a great marriage."

"If he loves her so much, doesn't he mind about people like Tommy Mortimer?"

Jeremy laughed. "Do you think he should mind?"

She was embarrassed, as though she had sounded like some dreadful prig. "No, of course not. It just seems . . . he seems . . ." She floundered. "I wondered if he was an actor."

"All those expansive gestures and the mellifluous voice? An easy mistake to make. No, he's not an actor. He's a jeweller. His family owns Mortimer's, the silversmiths in Regent Street. You know, where people go to buy immensely expensive wedding presents and engagement rings and such. My mother went there once, but just to get her ears pierced. She said she came out feeling like a millionaire."

"He's not married? Tommy Mortimer, I mean."

"No. His great cry is that he loves only Diana, but I think the truth is that he enjoys being a bachelor and playing the field, and has always been reluctant to give up his freedom. But he is Diana's close friend. He looks after her when she disappears up to London, and he comes down here from time to time when he feels in need of a little relaxation and a spot of fresh air."

But it was still difficult to understand. "Doesn't the Colonel *mind?*"

"I don't think so. They've worked out their own lives, they each have their own interests. Diana has this little mews house in London, and she needs to escape to the big city from time to time. And Edgar hates London, and only goes there to see his stockbroker, or watch the cricket at Lord's. And he never goes to Diana's house, but stays at his club. He's essentially a country-man. Always has been. *His* life is Nancherrow, and the farm and the estate, and his hunting and his pheasants, and his bit of salmon fishing in Devon. Also, he's a magistrate, and sits on the County Council. A perpetually busy man. Besides, as I've already mentioned, he's a great deal older than Diana. Even if he wanted to, he couldn't keep up with the sort of pleasures that she enjoys."

"What are those?"

"Oh, shopping and bridge, and dining out in London, and going to night-clubs and concerts and the theatre. She took him to a concert once, and he slept most of the way through it. His idea of a good tune is 'If You Were the Only Girl in the World,' or 'Land of Hope and Glory.' "

Judith laughed. She said, "I do like him. He's got such a kind face."

"He *is* kind. He's also painfully shy. But you seem to have found plenty to talk about, and broken the ice with him . . ."

At this juncture, their peaceful interlude was brought abruptly to an end. The dogs, having had enough of the sand and the sea, came in search of them, scrabbling their own way up over the rocks. Tiger was soaking from his second swim, and Pekoe's fur was encrusted with damp sand. Their behaviour seemed to indicate that they were bored with hanging about and wished to continue their walk. At the same time, the sun disappeared behind a large sinister cloud, the sea turned grey, the wind was cold, and clearly the time had come to move on.

They did not return by the way they had come, through the gardens, but rejoined the farm lane and walked on along the coast for a mile or more and then struck inland, up a steep valley tunnelled by wind-stunted oaks, which followed the course of a shallow river. By the time they had reached the head of this, they were just about up onto the moor, but a right-of-way led back towards Nancherrow through pasture fields filled with herds of grazing dairy cattle. Between these fields, instead of gates, were ancient stiles, slabs of granite set across deep ditches. "Early British cattle grids," Jeremy remarked, leading the way over these obstacles, "and a great deal more efficient than gates, because hikers and ramblers can't leave them open." Tiger took the stiles as a matter of course, but Pekoe stalled at the first one and had to be carried over them all.

It was nearly five o'clock and the afternoon dying by the time they got back to the house. Clouds, by now, filled the sky, the sun was gone for good, the light fading.

Judith was tired. As they trudged up the last bit of the drive, "Will Loveday be back?" she asked.

"Bound to be. Walter wouldn't risk being caught by darkness."

By now even the dogs were dragging their heels, but they were very nearly home. The trees thinned, the driveway curved, and the house came into sight, with lights shining from windows and the glassed front door. They did not, however, enter through this door, but by the way they had come, around to the back and through the gun-room.

"House rule," Jeremy explained. "No dogs in the main part of the house until they've dried off. Otherwise all the sofas and rugs would be in a perpetual state of filth." He filled the enamel bowls with fresh water and stood and watched the dogs drink. Finally quenched, they shook themselves and settled gratefully in their baskets.

"That's it," said Jeremy. "Let's go and find Mary. She'll be expecting us, with her kettle on the boil. I want to wash my hands. I'll meet you in the nursery."

Judith went tiredly upstairs to her room. But it was different now. Not new, but familiar. She was returning to Nancherrow, not seeing it for the first time. She was one of the occupants, accepted, and this was *her* room. She pulled off the thick sweater and threw it down on the bed, and went into *her* bathroom to use the scented soap and dry her hands on her own bath towel. Then she brushed her hair, tangled by the wind, and tied it neatly back off her face. Her face in the mirror was rosy with exercise and fresh air. She yawned. It had been a long day, and was not yet over. She turned off the light and went in search of tea.

Jeremy was there before her, already sitting at the tea-table with Mary and Loveday, and buttering himself a hot scone.

"We didn't know where you'd *gone*," Loveday said as Judith joined them. "You've been such ages. Mary and I thought we'd have to send out a search party." Judith pulled out a chair and joined them. It was bliss to sit down. The fire was blazing, and Mary had drawn the curtains against the darkening evening. "Did you love the cove?"

"It was beautiful."

"How do you like your tea?" Mary asked. "Milk and no sugar? You'll need a good strong cup after walking all that way. I've just been telling Jeremy, he had no need to take you all that long way."

"I didn't mind. I liked it. Did you have a good ride, Loveday?"

Yes, Loveday had had a perfect afternoon, with plenty of adventure, and Tinkerbell had jumped a four-barred gate, and Ranger had been spooked by an old sack blowing on a thorn hedge, but Walter had been brilliant and managed to control his panic and calm him down again. "I really thought we were going to have the most *frightful* disaster." And on the top of the moor they had galloped for miles, it had been heaven, and the air so clear they could see forever. And it had all been heaven, absolute heaven, and she couldn't wait to go out with Walter again. "It's more fun even than with Pops, because Pops is always so *careful*."

"I hope Walter didn't take any risks," said Mary sternly.

"Oh, Mary, you're such a fusser. I'm perfectly able to take care of myself."

They finally stopped eating and drinking when they were all so filled with hot scones, iced fairy cakes, shortbread, and marmite sandwiches that they couldn't eat another thing. Jeremy leaned back in his chair and stretched enormously. Judith was fearful that the chair would crack up under his weight. But it didn't. He said, "I don't want to, but I'm simply going to have to go, otherwise I shan't be home in time for supper."

"How you can think of eating another meal after all those scones, I can't imagine," Loveday told him.

"Speak for yourself."

He pulled himself to his feet, and as he did so, the door opened and Diana appeared.

"Well, here you all are, gorging, and how cosy you look."

"Have you had your tea, Mrs. Carey-Lewis?"

"Yes, and the Parker-Browns have gone, because they've got some cocktail party they have to attend, and the men have collapsed with newspapers. Jeremy, you look as though you're about to leave us."

"I'm afraid so. On my way."

"It's been divine seeing you. My love to your parents . . ."

"Well, thank you for the lunch and everything. I'll put my head around the door and say goodbye to the Colonel and Tommy."

"Do that. And come again soon."

"I don't know when that'll be, but I'd love to. Goodbye, girls. Goodbye, Judith. It was great meeting you again. Goodbye, Mary . . ." He kissed her. "And Diana." He kissed her as well, went to the door, opened it, raised a hand, and was gone.

"He never was one to waste time," said Diana with a smile. "Such a dear boy." And she came to settle herself in the corner of the nursery sofa, close to the fire. "Do you girls want to come down for dinner, or do you want to have nursery supper with Mary?"

"Do we have to change if we come down for dinner?" Loveday asked.

"Oh, darling, what a silly question, of course you have to."

"In that case, I think we'll just stay up here and eat scrambled eggs or something."

Diana raised her lovely eyebrows. "What about Judith?"

Judith said, "I love scrambled eggs, and I haven't got a dress to change into."

"Well, if that's what you both want, I'll tell Nettlebed. Hetty can carry up a tray for you." She reached into the pocket of her pale-grey cardigan and produced her cigarettes and her gold lighter. She lit one and reached for an ashtray. "Judith, what about that beautiful box you brought with you? You promised you'd show it to me after tea. Bring it over here and we'll look at it now."

And so the next ten minutes or so were spent in displaying once more the charms of the cedarwood box and the intricacy of the little lock. Diana was gratifyingly enchanted, admired every aspect of Judith's treasure, opening and shutting the tiny drawers, promising her collection of cowrie shells to fill one of them.

"You could use it as a jewel box. All your rings and treasures. They'd be safe as safe."

"I haven't got any rings. Or treasures."

"You'll acquire them." She lowered the lid for the last time, and fastened the latch. She smiled at Judith. "Where are you going to keep it?"

"I suppose at Aunt Louise's . . . I'll take it at half-term."

"Yes," said Loveday, "beastly old Matron won't even spare a corner of her Red Cross cupboard."

"Why don't you leave it here?" Diana asked.

"*Here?*"

"Yes. At Nancherrow. In your bedroom. Then, every time you come to stay, it will be waiting for you."

"But . . ." (She was going to be asked again, was all she could think. This visit was not a one-off. She was going to be invited to return.) "But won't it be in your way?"

"Not in the very least. And the next time you come, you must bring some clothes and leave them here as well, just as though this were your other home. And then you won't have to wander around in Athena's cast-offs."

"I've loved wearing them. I've never had a cashmere pullover."

"Then you shall keep it. We'll hang it in your cupboard. The beginning of your Nancherrow wardrobe."

Lavinia Boscawen, who had long ago come to terms with the fact that the very old need little sleep, lay in her downy double bed, with her head turned towards the window, and watched the night sky lighten with the dawn. The curtains were parted, drawn back as far as they could go, because the darkness, the out of doors, with its starlight, and night scents and sounds, she had always believed too precious to be shut away.

The curtains were very old . . . not as old as Mrs. Boscawen herself, but as old as the years she had lived in the Dower House, which was nearly fifty years. Sunshine and wear had faded and shredded them; the thick interlining, like the wool of an old sheep, protruded here and there, and the braid on the pelmets and the elaborate tiebacks had unravelled and hung in little thready loops. No matter. Once they had been pretty and she had chosen and loved them. They would see her out.

This morning it was not raining. For that, she was grateful. Over the winter, there had been too much rain, and although at eighty-five she had stopped striding up and down to the village or going for long healthy hikes, it was still pleasant to be able to step out of doors and into the garden, and to spend an hour or two pottering about in the sweet fresh air, mulching the roses or making tidy plaits of daffodil leaves once the golden flower-heads had died back. For the latter task, she had a patent kneeler, which her nephew Edgar had designed and had made for her in the estate sawmill. It had a rubber pad to protect her old knees from the damp, and sturdy handles which were good for grasping when she wanted to haul herself to her feet again. Such a simple device, but so practical. Rather like Edgar himself, whom, because Lavinia had never been blessed with family of her own, she had always cherished as a son.

The sky paled. A fine, cold day. A Sunday. She remembered that Edgar and Diana were coming for luncheon, bringing with them Loveday, and Tommy Mortimer, and Loveday's schoolfriend. Tommy Mortimer was an old acquaintance, encountered on the many occasions when he abandoned London and escaped for a country weekend to Nancherrow. Because he was Diana's friend, attentive, affectionate, and the source of an endless supply of flowery compliments, Lavinia had initially been deeply suspicious of him, suspecting nefarious intent, and, on Edgar's behalf, resentful of his constant attendance on Edgar's wife. But, as the time passed, Lavinia had made up her own mind about Tommy Mortimer, realizing that he offered no threat to any person's marriage, and so she was able to laugh at his extravagant ways and become quite fond of him. As for Loveday's schoolfriend, she was an unknown quantity. But it would be interesting to discover what sort of a girl that naughty, wayward child would choose to bring home for the weekend.

Altogether, quite an occasion. For luncheon there would be a pair of ducklings, fresh vegetables, a lemon soufflé, and bottled nectarines. On the larder shelf was an excellent Stilton. Lavinia must remind Isobel to cool the hock.

Isobel. Lavinia had, in old age, few worries. In her middle years, she had come to the conclusion that it was useless to worry about matters over which she had no control. These included her own eventual death, the weather, and the unhappy way things seemed to be going in Germany. So, having dutifully read the newspapers, she would resolutely turn her mind to other things. A new rose to be ordered; the trimming of the buddleia; her library books and letters to and from old friends. Then there was the progress of her tapestry carpet, and the daily conference with Isobel concerning the general smooth running of the little household.

But Isobel *was* a bit of a worry. Only ten years younger than Lavinia, she was really getting beyond all the cooking and the caring, which had been her life for forty years. From time to time Lavinia gathered up her courage and brought the conversation around to the subject of Isobel's retirement, but Isobel always became immensely huffy and hurt, as though Lavinia were trying to get rid of her, and, inevitably, there would always be a day or two of sulky umbrage to be dealt with. However, compromises had been made, and now the postman's wife climbed the hill from the village each morning. Employed to do "the rough," she had gradually infiltrated beyond the kitchen doors and taken over the rest of the housework—polishing floors, scrubbing the slates of the porch, and generally keeping everything shining, sweet-smelling, and trim. At first, Isobel had treated this good soul with cool disdain, and it said a lot for the postman's wife that she had stuck out a long period of non-co-operation, had finally broken through Isobel's hostility, and made friends.

But she did not come on Sundays, and the luncheon would mean a lot of work for Isobel. Lavinia wished she could help a bit, not that she could do much, being incapable of so much as boiling an egg. But Isobel's prickly pride was always at stake, and at the end of the day it was easier all round if nobody interfered.

Somewhere, out in the garden, a blackbird sang. Downstairs, a door opened and shut. She stirred on her piled linen pillows, and turned to reach out a hand for spectacles, which lay on the bedside table. It was quite a large bedside table, as big as a small desk, because of the number of small but important objects it was necessary to keep close to hand. Her spectacles, her glass of water, a tin of rich tea biscuits, a small pad of paper and a sharp pencil in case she got a brilliant idea in the middle of the night. A photograph of her late husband, Eustace Boscawen, staring sternly from its mount of blue velvet, her Bible, and her current book, *Barchester Towers*. For, perhaps, the sixth time, but Trollope was such a comforting man; reading him was like having someone take you by the hand and gently lead you back into an easier past. She struggled for her spectacles. One thing, she told herself, at least you haven't got a set of dentures grinning at you out of a tumbler. She was proud of her teeth. How many old women of eighty-five still had their own teeth? Or, at any rate, most of them. And the ones that had gone the way of all flesh had gone from the back and didn't show. She was still able to smile and laugh with no fear of embarrassing anybody with a gap-toothed grimace or a slipped plate.

She looked at the time. Seven-thirty. Isobel was on her way upstairs. She could hear the stairs creak, the old footsteps across the landing. A cursory knock, and the door opened, and she appeared bearing on a tray Lavinia's early-morning glass of hot water in which floated a slice of lemon. She shouldn't continue this old tradition; Lavinia could do perfectly well without it; but Isobel had been serving early-morning hot lemon for fifty years, and she had no intention of stopping now.

She said, "Morning. Some cold it is." She made space on the table, and set down the tray. Her hands were gnarled and reddened, the knuckles swollen with arthritis, and she wore her blue cotton, and a white apron with a bib. In the old days she had covered her head with a voluminous and unbecoming white cotton cap, but Lavinia had finally persuaded her to abandon this badge of servility, and she looked a great deal better without it, revealing frizzy grey hair scraped back into a little bun fastened with huge black hairpins.

"Oh, thank you, Isobel."

Isobel crossed the room to close the window, shutting out the blackbird's voice. Her stockings were black; she had swollen ankles over worn strapped shoes. She should be lying in bed herself, being brought warm comforting drinks. Lavinia wished she did not always feel so guilty.

She said, on impulse, "I do hope you're not going to have to do too much today. Perhaps we should stop having luncheon parties."

"Now, don't start that again." Isobel fussily settled the curtains, giving herself something more to see to. "You carry on as though I was just about dead and buried."

"I don't do anything of the sort. I just want to be sure you don't wear yourself to a frazzle."

Isobel gave a snorting laugh. "Little chance of that. Anyway, it's all on the road. Table laid last night, when you were eating your supper off a tray, and all the vegetables done. Lovely Brussels sprouts, they are, just a touch of frost and they're some crisp. I'm going down now to make the soufflé. That Loveday wouldn't thank me if there wasn't a soufflé."

"You spoil her, Isobel, just as everybody does."

Isobel sniffed. "All spoilt, those Carey-Lewis children, if you ask me, but doesn't seem to have done them any harm." She stooped and picked up Lavinia's fine wool dressing-gown, which had slipped from the chair onto the floor. "And I never approved of them sending Loveday off to that school . . . what's the point of having children, if you send them miles away?"

"I suppose they thought it was all for the best. Anyway, that's all in the past now, and she seems to be settling down at Saint Ursula's."

"Good sign she's brought a friend home. If she's making friends, she can't be too put out."

"No. You're right. And we must remember that it's nothing to do with us."

"Maybe so, but we can have our opinions, can't we?" Having made her point, Isobel went to the door. "Like a fried egg for your breakfast?"

"Thank you, Isobel dear, that would be a treat."

Isobel departed. Her footsteps faded, treading cautiously down the curved staircase. Lavinia imagined her taking the steps one at a time, a hand on the balustrade. The guilt would not go away, but what to do? Nothing to be done.

She drank her hot lemon water, thought about the lunch party, and decided that she would wear her new blue dress.

Loveday's behaviour the following morning made it perfectly clear that Great-Aunt Lavinia was one of the few people—or perhaps the only person—capable of exerting any sort of influence on her wayward personality. To begin with, she got up early in order to wash her hair, and then dressed without the slightest objection in the clothes which Mary had set out for her the night before: a checked woollen dress with shining white collar and cuffs, white knee-socks, and black patent-leather shoes with straps and buttons.

Finding her in the nursery having her hair dried and brushed by Mary, Judith started to worry about her own appearance. Seeing Loveday looking so unusually pretty and smart made her feel really pathetic, like a penniless relation. The holly-red cashmere sweater was just as perfect as ever, but . . .

"I can't go out for luncheon in *shorts*, can I?" she appealed to Mary. "And the uniform's so ugly. I don't want to wear a uniform . . ."

"Of course you don't." Mary was understanding and practical as always. "I'll look in Athena's wardrobe and find you a nice skirt. And you can borrow a pair of Loveday's white socks, just the same as the ones she's got on, and I'll polish up your shoes for you. Then you'll be smart and bright as a new penny . . . Now keep still, Loveday, for goodness' sake, otherwise we're never going to get this mop dry."

The skirt, shamelessly purloined from Athena's cupboard, was a tartan kilt, with leather straps and buckles at the waist. "Kilts are lovely things," Mary pointed out, "because it doesn't matter how fat or thin you are, you can always make them fit."

She knelt and wrapped it around Judith's waist, and fixed the straps.

Loveday, watching, giggled. "It's a bit like fixing Tinkerbell's girth."

"Nothing of the sort. You know how Tinkerbell blows himself out like a little balloon. There. Perfect. And it's the right length, too. Just to the middle of your knee. And there's a bit of red in the tartan that picks up the red of your jersey." She smiled and heaved herself to her feet. "Lovely, you look. As though you wouldn't call the King your cousin. Now take your shoes off and Mary will shine them up so you can see your own face."

Breakfast at Nancherrow wasn't until nine o'clock on Sunday mornings, but even so, by the time the nursery party put in its appearance, the others were already there, tucking into hot porridge and grilled sausages. The big dining-room was full of early wintry sunshine, and there was the delicious smell of fresh coffee.

"I'm sorry we're late . . ." Mary apologized.

"We wondered what you were all doing." Diana, at the far end of the table, wore a pale-grey flannel coat and skirt, so immaculately cut that it rendered her slender as a wand. A blue silk blouse turned her eyes to sapphires, and there were pearl-and-diamond studs in her ears, and a triple string of pearls gleamed at the base of her throat.

"Getting ready took us a bit of time."

"No matter." She smiled at the girls. "Seeing such an elegant pair, I can perfectly understand. You've done brilliantly, Mary . . ."

Loveday went to kiss her father. He and Tommy Mortimer were equally formal, wearing suits with waistcoats, stiff-collared shirts, and silken ties. The Colonel laid down his fork, so that he had an arm free to hug his daughter. "I hardly recognize you," he told her. "A real little lady, wearing a dress. I was beginning to forget what your legs looked like . . ."

"Oh, Pops, don't be silly." Looking as though butter wouldn't melt in her mouth, Loveday clearly had no intention of behaving that way. "And look, you greedy old thing, you've got *three* sausages. I hope you've left some for us . . ."

Later in the morning, they drove the short distance to Rosemullion, all five of them disposed in great comfort in the Colonel's enormous Daimler. For church, Diana had put on a grey felt halo hat with a flirty little veil, and because the day, although bright and sunny, was chill, had wound a silver-fox fur around her shoulders.

The car was parked by the churchyard wall and they filed up the path with all the other village people, between the old gravestones and the ancient yews. The church was tiny and very, very old, even older, Judith guessed, than the one at Penmarron. It was so old that it seemed to have sunk into the very earth, so that from the outdoor sunlight one stepped down into a chill gloom, smelling of damp stone and woodworm and mouldy prayer-books. The pews were hard and hideously uncomfortable, and as they settled themselves in the front pew, a cracked-sounding bell began to toll from the tower high above them.

At a quarter past eleven, the service commenced. It all took rather a long time because the vicar, the verger, and the organ were all, just like the church, extremely ancient, and became, from time to time, rather muddled. The only person who seemed to know what he was doing was Colonel Carey-Lewis, who stepped smartly up to the lectern to read the lesson, read it, and then stepped smartly back into his pew again. A rambling sermon was duly delivered, the subject of which was unclear from start to finish; three hymns were sung; a collection taken (ten shillings from each grown-up and a half a crown from Judith and Loveday), and finally the blessing and it was all over.

After the seeping cold of the church, emerging into the sunshine felt positively warm. There they stood about for a bit, while Diana and the Colonel exchanged a few words with the vicar, his sparse white hair blown on end by the breeze, and his surplice billowing and flapping like a sheet hung on the line. Other worshippers, on their way home, tipped their hats and spoke respectfully. "Morning, Colonel. Morning, Mrs. Carey-Lewis . . ."

Loveday, becoming bored, began to hop on and off a lichened gravestone. "Oh, let's *go*." She tugged at her father's arm. "I'm hungry . . ."

"Morning, Colonel. Lovely day . . ."

At last everybody drifted away, and it was time to move. But the Colonel now looked at his watch. "We have ten minutes in hand," he announced. "So we shall leave the car here and walk. A little exercise will do us no harm, and we shall all work up a good appetite for lunch. Come along, girls . . ."

So they set off, taking the narrow winding road which led up the hill from the village. Tall stone walls stood on either side, smothered in ivy, and bare elm trees soared up into the pristine sky, their highest branches filled with cawing rooks. The hill steepened and everybody became rather breathless.

Diana said, "If I'd known we were going to walk, I shouldn't have put on my highest-heeled shoes."

Tommy put an arm around her waist. "Shall I sweep you into my arms and carry you?"

"I hardly think that would be very seemly."

"Then I shall simply *urge* you forward. And just think how splendid it will be coming back again. We can run all the way. Or slide on our bottoms, like tobogganists."

"That would at least give everybody something to talk about."

The Colonel, ignoring this banter, strode ahead, leading the way. The lane took yet another right-angled turn, but it seemed that here, on the steep corner, they had reached, at last, their destination. For, in the high wall on the right-hand side of the road, appeared an open gateway. Beyond this a narrow drive curved away between grass verges and neatly clipped hedges of escallonia. It was something of a relief to be on level ground, although the path was gravelled with sea-pebbles, which made noisy walking.

Tommy Mortimer trudged gamely. Physical exercise was not one of his passions unless he happened to be wielding a tennis racket or carrying a gun. "Do you think," he asked wistfully, "that I shall be offered a pink gin?"

"You've been for lunch here before," Diana reminded him briskly. "You'll be given sherry, or perhaps Madeira. And you're not to ask for a pink gin."

He sighed, resigned. "Dear girl. For you I would drink hemlock. But, admit, Madeira does have tones of Jane Austen."

"Neither Jane Austen nor Madeira will do you any harm."

The little party rounded the curve of the escallonia hedge, and the Dower House stood before them. It was neither large nor imposing, but possessed a certain dignity of style that at once impressed. A square house, symmetrical and solid, harled and whitewashed, with Gothic windows, a grey slate roof, and a stone porch smothered in clematis. Sitting there, tucked into the shelter of the hill, it had the aspect of a place that had turned its back upon the world, slumbering secretly through the passing years, for a longer time than any person could remember.

There was no need to knock, nor ring a tinkling bell. As the Colonel approached, an inner door was opened, and an elderly woman emerged into the porch. She wore a parlourmaid's uniform, with muslin apron and a muslin cap set square on her grey head and trimmed with velvet ribbons.

"I thought you'd be here directly. We're all ready for you."

"Good morning, Isobel."

"Morning, Mrs. Carey-Lewis . . . lovely, isn't it, but chilly yet." Her voice was shrill and very Cornish.

"You remember Mr. Mortimer, Isobel?"

"Yes, of course. Good morning, sir. Come along in, and we'll get the door closed. Take your coats, shall I? My life, Loveday, you're growing. And this is your friend? Judith? Let me have your furs, Mrs. Carey-Lewis, and I'll put them safely . . ."

Judith, unbuttoning her green school overcoat, looked covertly about her. Other people's houses were always fascinating. As soon as you went through the door for the first time, you got the feel of the atmosphere, and so discovered something about the personalities of the people who lived there. Riverview, although transient and somewhat shabby, had been home simply because Mummy was always there: playing with Jess; or in the kitchen, writing out shopping lists for Phyllis; or ensconced in her chair by the fireside, with all her small and pretty possessions about her. Windyridge, on the other hand, had always felt a bit impersonal, rather like a golf club, and Nancherrow, under Diana's influence, became a luxurious London flat on an enormous country scale.

But the Dower House had an impact that Judith had never experienced before. It was truly like stepping back in time. So old—certainly pre-Victorian—so perfectly proportioned, so quiet that, over the murmur of voices, the slow tocking of the grandfather clock was clearly audible. The floor of the hallway was flagged in slate and laid with rugs, and an airy circular staircase rose from this, curving up beneath a Gothic window, curtained in wheaten linen. There was as well a fascinating smell compounded of age, antique furniture polish, and flowers, with a faint undertone of damp stone and cold cellars. No central heating here, just a bright fire burning in the grate, and a square of sunshine slanting across the floor from an opened door.

". . . Mrs. Boscawen's in the drawing-room . . ."

"Thank you, Isobel."

Leaving Isobel to carry the coats upstairs, Diana led the way, towards and through this opened door. "Aunt Lavinia!" Her voice was warm with genuine pleasure. "Here we all are exhausted after trudging up the hill. Edgar made us. You are a saint to tolerate such an invasion . . ."

"But you've all been to church! How good you are. I didn't come, because I felt I couldn't bear, just yet, another of the vicar's sermons. Loveday, you monkey, come and give me a kiss . . . and dear Edgar. And Tommy. How splendid to see you again."

Judith hung back, not so much because she was shy but because there was so much to look at. A pale room, flooded with golden sunshine which streamed through tall south-facing windows. Soft colours, pinks and creams and greens, faded now but never bright. A long bookcase crammed with leather-bound volumes; a glass-fronted walnut cabinet containing a set of Meissen fruit plates; an ornate Venetian mirror over the white-painted mantelpiece. In the grate a small coal-fire flickered and the sunshine diminished the brightness of the flames but sparked into rainbow brilliance the faceted drops of a crystal chandelier. And there were flowers, and more flowers. Lilies, with their drowning scent. Everything dazzled.

". . . Judith."

She realized, with a start, that Diana had already said her name. How awful if Mrs. Boscawen thought Judith ill-mannered or offhand. "I'm sorry."

Diana smiled. "You're looking mesmerized. Come and say how do you do." She flung out an arm, coaxing Judith to come forward to join them. She laid a hand on her shoulder. "Aunt Lavinia, this is Loveday's friend, Judith Dunbar."

Suddenly she did feel shy. Mrs. Boscawen waited, sitting very upright in a low-lapped chair, half-turned towards the light, with her blue woollen dress flowing to her ankles. She was old . . . well into or perhaps beyond her eighties. Her cheeks, beneath a surface dusting of powder, were netted with wrinkles and at her side, ready to hand, leaned a silver-handled ebony cane. Old. Wonderfully old. But her faded blue eyes sparked with interest, and it was not hard to see that once she had been very beautiful.

"My dear." Her voice was clear and only a little tremulous. She took Judith's hand in her own, and held it. "How delightful that you were able to come with the others. Not very exciting, perhaps, but I do love meeting new friends."

Loveday said bluntly, "The reason I asked Judith to come and stay is because her family are all in Colombo and she hasn't anywhere to go."

Diana frowned. "Oh, Loveday, that sounds rather a chilly invitation. You know you asked Judith because you wanted her. You would give me no peace until I'd phoned Miss Catto."

"Well, anyway, it was *one* of the reasons."

"And a thoughtful one," Aunt Lavinia reassured her. She smiled at Judith. "But Colombo does seem a long way away."

"They're only there for a bit. Just long enough to pack up the house and then move on to Singapore. My father's got a new appointment there."

"Singapore! How romantic that sounds. I was never there, but I had a cousin who was on the Governor General's staff, and he said it was one of the jolliest spots. Parties all the time. Your mother will have the time of her life. Now . . . come and find somewhere for yourself to sit. Such a lovely day, I couldn't bear to huddle around the fire. Edgar, will you deal with the drinks? See that everybody has a sherry. We've ten minutes to spare before Isobel rings her gong. Diana, my dear, what news of Athena? Is she back from Switzerland?"

At the base of the window was a long cushion. With attention elsewhere, Judith went to kneel upon it, to look out over the deep, roofed veranda to the sloping garden which lay beyond. At the foot of the lawn stood a coppice of Monterey pines, and lying across the topmost branches of these was drawn the distant blue line of the horizon. The sight of this, the juxtaposition of dark conifer and a seemingly summer sea, induced the most extraordinary sensation of having come abroad; as though they had all been magically transported from Nancherrow to some Italian villa washed in the sunlight of a southern land, and standing high on a hill above the Mediterranean. The illusion filled her with a dizzying pleasure. "Do you like gardens?" Once again, the old lady was addressing her.

"I like this one especially," Judith told her.

"You are a child after my own heart. After luncheon we shall put on coats and go out and look around."

"May we really?"

"*I'm* not going to," Loveday interrupted. "It's far too cold and I've seen it a thousand times before."

"I don't suppose anyone else will want to," Aunt Lavinia observed gently. "Like you, Loveday, they know the garden well. But that won't stop Judith and me taking a little time for ourselves and enjoying a small walk and some fresh air. And we can have a chat, and get to know each other. Now, how are you getting on, Edgar? Ah, my sherry. Thank you." She raised her glass. "And thank you all, so much, for being here."

"Judith." Behind her, the Colonel said her name. She turned. He smiled. "Lemonade."

"Oh, thank you."

She sat, where she had knelt, with her back to the window, and reached to take the tumbler from his hand. Opposite, Loveday, who had for some reason chosen to share a capacious armchair with Tommy Mortimer, and sat squashed close to his side, had also been given lemonade. Across the small space which divided them, she caught Judith's eye, and her urchin face broke into a grin, and she looked, all at once, so wicked and so pretty, that Judith's heart brimmed with affection for her. Affection, and gratitude too, because Loveday had already shared so much with her, and now, because of Loveday, she was here.

". . . now these are my first little bulbs to come up, aconites and early crocus and snowdrops. It's so sheltered here, you see, that on New Year's Day I always make a practice of coming out into the garden and finding out how they're coming along. And I throw out all the horrid dusty holly, and find just the tiniest bunch of little blooms, just enough to fill an egg cup. And then I feel that the year has really started and the spring is on its way."

"I thought you were meant to wait until Twelfth Night. To throw the holly away, I mean. What's that pink flower. . . ?"

"*Viburnum fragrans.* It smells like summer, slap-bang in the middle of winter. And this is my buddleia, but it looks a little sad just now. In summertime it's a riot of butterflies. It's quite big, isn't it, and I only planted it two or three years ago . . ."

They stepped out, side by side, down the sloping gravel path. Aunt Lavinia, true to her word, had not forgotten her promise, and when lunch was over, had sent the others back into the drawing-room to entertain themselves as best they might, and brought Judith out of doors for a little tour. For this expedition, she had put on a pair of stout gardening boots and an immense tweed cape, and tied a scarf over her head. Her cane kept her steady, and was useful for pointing.

"As you can see, my land slopes all the way down the hill. At the very bottom is the vegetable garden, and the Scots pines are my southern boundary. It was all terraced when we came here, but I wanted a garden in compartments, like outdoor rooms, each with its own character, rather unexpected and secret. So we planted escallonia and privet hedges and trained the gateways into arches. The path draws the eye, don't you think? Makes one long to explore and find out what lies beyond. Come. I shall show you. You see?" They passed beneath the first archway. "My rose garden. All old-fashioned roses. This is Rosamunde, the oldest rose of all. It looks a little droopy now, but when it flowers, the petals are striped in pink and white. Like little girls in party dresses."

"How long have you lived here?"

Once more, Aunt Lavinia paused, and Judith decided that it was particularly pleasant to be in the company of a grown-up who seemed to be in no hurry whatsoever, and happy to chat as though she had all the time in the world. "Nearly fifty years now. But, you see, my home, when I was a child, was Nancherrow. Not Diana's house, but the old house, the one that burnt down. My brother was Edgar's father."

"So you've always lived in Cornwall?"

"Not always. My husband was a King's Counsel and then a Circuit Judge. We lived first in London, and then in Exeter, but always returned to Nancherrow for our holidays."

"Did you bring your children, too?"

"My dear, I never had children. Edgar and Diana are my children, and their children like grandchildren to me."

"Oh, dear, what a shame."

"What? That I never had children? Well, you know, every sadness brings its own recompense. And perhaps I should have been a hopeless mother. Anyway, let's not dwell on past history. What were we talking about?"

"Your garden. And your house."

"Oh, yes. The house. (This is the most beautiful pink lilac. I try not to let it grow too tall and leggy.) The house. It was the Dower House for Nancherrow, you see. My grandmother lived here when she was just as old as I am. And when my husband retired from being a Circuit Judge, we rented it off the estate, and later on we were able to buy it. We were very happy here. My husband died here, lying peacefully in a long chair on the lawn outside the house. It was summer, you see, and quite warm. Now. Next, we come to the children's garden. I think you'll like this the best of all. Has Loveday told you about the Hut?"

Judith, bewildered, shook her head. "No."

"No, I don't suppose she would. She never played here very much. The Hut was never hers the way it was Athena's and Edward's. I suppose because she was so much younger than they, and didn't have a sibling to share it with."

"Is it a Wendy house?"

"Wait and see. My husband had it built because Athena and Edward used to spend so much time with us. They spent whole days down here, and when they were older, were allowed to sleep out, so exciting and so much more fun than a tent, don't you think. And then, in the morning, they cooked their own breakfast . . ."

"Has the Hut got a *stove?*"

"No, because we were dreadfully afraid of fire and the children being burnt to a frizzle. But there's a brick fireplace a safe way off, and Athena and Edward used to fry bacon and boil up their billycans. Come along, let's go and look at it. I popped the key into my pocket, just in case you wanted to see inside . . ."

She led the way, and Judith, filled with eager anticipation, followed; through the gate in the privet hedge, and then down a flight of stone steps into a little orchard of apple and pear trees. Here the grass was rough and long, but drifts of snowdrops and blue scillas lay in swathes around the gnarled trunks of the fruit trees, and the first shoots of daffodils and lilies pushed their way, like green swords, through the rich earth. Clearly, before too long, all would become a springtime riot of yellow and white. Above, on a bare branch, a blackbird perched, singing his heart out, and across the orchard, tucked into a sheltered corner, stood the Hut. It was constructed like a log cabin, with a pitched shingle roof, and two windows on either side of a blue-painted door. At the front was a deep porch, with wooden steps, and a fret-worked rail, and it wasn't a child-size house, but a proper place, where grown-up people could come and go without ducking their heads, nor crouching on baby chairs.

She said, "But who comes here now?"

Aunt Lavinia laughed. "You sound desolate."

"It's just so sweet, and secret. It ought to be played in all the time, and cared for . . ."

". . . but it is cared for. I care for it. I keep it aired and fresh, and each year it gets a good coat of creosote. It's well-built, and consequently, quite dry."

"I can't think why Loveday never told me anything about it."

"Keeping house has never appealed to her. She prefers to muck out stables and be with her pony, and is none the worse for that. And, from time to time, there *are* children. The Rosemullion Sunday School always hold their annual picnic in this orchard, and then the Hut comes into its own again, but there are quite often the most terrible fights, because the boys want it to be a Red Indian fortress, and the girls like playing mummies and daddies. Look, here's the key. Go and open the door for me, and I'll show you the inside."

Judith took the key and went ahead, ducking beneath the trailing branches of the apple trees, and so up the two steps to the porch. The key fitted smoothly and turned sweetly. She turned the handle and the door swung inwards. There was the good smell of creosote, and she stepped inside. It wasn't dark at all, because there was a third window on the back wall. She saw the two bunks, built on either side, beneath the slope of the roof; the wooden table and the two chairs; the bookshelves, the mirror, the framed picture of a bluebell wood, the rag rug upon the floor. An upturned orange crate did duty as a kitchen cupboard, stacked with odds and ends of china, a sooty kettle, and a blackened frying pan. The windows were hung with blue-checked curtains, and there were blue blankets and cushions on the bunks. Above her head, a paraffin lamp hung from a hook on the main beam. And she imagined the Hut in darkness, with the lamp lit and the curtains drawn, and the thought occurred to her, rather sadly, that perhaps at fourteen she should be too old for such innocent joys.

"So what do you think of it?"

Judith turned and Aunt Lavinia stood in the open doorway.

"Perfect."

"I thought you would be charmed." The old lady sniffed the air. "Not damp. Just a bit cold. Poor little house. It needs company. We need babies, don't we? A new generation." She peered about her. "Any signs of mice? Naughty field-mice get in sometimes and eat holes in the blankets and build nests for themselves."

"When I was little—about ten—I think I'd have sold my soul for a play-house like this."

"A nest of your own? Another little field-mouse."

"I suppose so. Sleeping out on a summer night. Smelling damp grass. Looking at the stars."

"Loveday would never dream of sleeping here alone. She said there were funny noises and spooks."

"I'm not usually afraid out of doors. But dark houses, sometimes, can be quite scary."

"And lonely, too. Perhaps that's why I spend so much time in my garden. Now . . ." Aunt Lavinia adjusted her headscarf and drew the folds of her tweed cape about her. "I think it's getting rather chilly. Perhaps it's time to return to the others. They'll be wondering what has happened to us . . ." She smiled. "Can you guess what Loveday will be doing while she waits for us? She will be playing spillikins with Mr. Mortimer."

"Spillikins? How do you know?"

"Because that is what she always does when she comes to visit me. And despite her waywardness, Loveday is a slave to tradition. I am glad you are her friend. I think you are a good influence."

"I can't stop her being naughty at school. She's always getting order marks."

"She is very naughty. But charming. Her charm, I fear, will be her downfall. Now, lock the door, and let us be off."

Saint Ursula's
Sunday, 23rd February.

Dear Mummy and Dad,

> I am sorry I didn't write a letter last Sunday, but I was away for the weekend and I didn't have time. Miss Catto was very kind and allowed me to go to the Carey-Lewises with Loveday.

Here, Judith paused, chewed her pen, and grappled with a dilemma. She loved her parents, but knew them well, and was wise to their harmless shortcomings. Which made it difficult to tell them about Nancherrow, simply because it had all been so unbelievably wonderful, and because she was afraid that they wouldn't understand.

For they themselves had never enjoyed such a glamorous life-style, and did not even have friends with large houses, who took luxury and ease for granted. Living as they did in the Far East, and bound by the strict conventions of the British raj, they had become ingrained by rigid lines of class distinction, social and racial strata, professional seniority, and the unspoken rule seemed to be that you knew your own place, high or low, and stayed in it.

So, if she extolled, at length, the beauty and charm of Diana Carey-Lewis, then Molly Dunbar, never the most confident of women, might suspect that comparisons were being made, and that Judith was inferring that her mother was both plain and dull.

And if she went into elaborate detail about the size and grandeur of Nancherrow, the gardens and the lands, the horses in the stables, the staff of servants, the shooting party, and the fact that Colonel Carey-Lewis was a magistrate and sat on the bench, then her father, in his rather humdrum way, would maybe feel a little hurt.

And if she enlarged on the socializing which had continued the entire weekend, the casual cocktails, the afternoon bridge, the formal mealtimes, perhaps it would seem as though Judith were bragging in some way, or even covertly criticizing her mother and father for their own simple and unambitious way of life. And the last thing she wanted to do was to distress them in any way. One thing was for sure. She was not going to mention Tommy Mortimer, otherwise they would panic, decide that Nancherrow was a sink of iniquity, and write to Miss Catto forbidding Judith ever to return again. Which was unthinkable. What she needed was some point of reference, an event that she could share. Inspiration struck. Jeremy Wells, putting in such an unexpected appearance, and giving up his afternoon to take Judith under his wing and show her the cove. It was a bit like having him come to her rescue for a second time. With him to write about, the remainder of the letter would be easy. She drew the writing paper towards her and started off again, the words flying across the paper.

The house is called Nancherrow, and the most extraordinary thing happened. There was a young man there for the day, shooting pigeons with Colonel Carey-Lewis, and he was called Jeremy Wells, and he was the young doctor we met in the train from Plymouth to Truro after staying at the Somervilles'. Wasn't that a coincidence? He is very nice, and his father is their family doctor. On Saturday afternoon, Loveday rode her pony Tinkerbell so he very kindly came on a walk with me, and we went along the coast. It is very rocky there, with tiny beaches. Not a bit like Penmarron.

On Sunday morning we all went to church at Rosemullion and afterwards went out to lunch with Mrs. Boscawen, who is Colonel Carey-Lewis's aunt. She is very old, and it is a very old house that she lives in. It is called the Dower House. It is full of very old-fashioned things, and she has a maid called Isobel who has been with her for years. The house is on a hill, so that you can see the sea, and it has a sloping garden, all terraces and hedges. One of these is an orchard, and in it is a sweet little wooden house for children to play in. It is, actually, full-sized and properly furnished, but Jess would simply love it. Mrs. Boscawen (I have to call her Aunt Lavinia) took me to look at it after lunch, and we had a talk and she was very friendly. I hope that, one day, I shall go again.

Mrs. Carey-Lewis says I can go again to Nancherrow to stay, which is very kind of her. I have written my bread-and-butter letter. Next weekend is half-term, and I'm going to Windyridge. We have four days off, from Friday to Monday. I got a postcard from Aunt Louise and she is coming to fetch me in her car on Friday morning and we're going to Porthkerris to buy the bicycle.

I took my Chinese box to Nancherrow and have left it there for the time being, because there is nowhere at school to put it. Mrs. Carey-Lewis gave me some cowrie shells for one of the little drawers.

Work is all right, and I got seven out of ten for the History Test. We're doing Horace Walpole and the Treaty of Utrecht. Longing to hear about the new house in Orchard Road, Singapore. You'll hate saying goodbye to Joseph and Amah.

Lots of love and love to Jess,

Judith

She was at Windyridge, standing at the window of her bedroom, staring out at the view of the golf course and the distant bay, but not able to see anything very clearly because everything was drowned in soft and relentless rain. As well, her eyes kept filling with childish and stupid tears, because she suffered, quite suddenly, from the most acute homesickness.

Which was strange, because this was half-term, and she hadn't experienced such depression since Molly had said her last goodbyes and left Judith at Saint Ursula's. Somehow, at school, there wasn't time to be homesick, because there was always so much to do, so much to achieve, so much to learn, to think about, and remember; so many people scurrying around, so many bells clanging, all interspersed with copious bouts of enforced exercise, that by the time she climbed into bed, that classic hour for weeping privately, she was always too tired to do much more than read for a moment or two and then fall fast asleep.

And at Nancherrow, speaking of her parents and Jess in the course of conversation, politely answering polite questions, had aroused no pangs of yearning nor need. In truth, during that magic weekend, she had scarcely thought of Mummy and Dad, as though they were part of a disappeared world which had temporarily ceased to exist. Or perhaps because Judith, wearing Athena Carey-Lewis's clothes, had taken on some new identity which had nothing to do with family; a person absorbed only in the present, and the next exciting thing that was going to happen.

Now, she thought of Nancherrow in a wistful fashion, wishing that she were there with Loveday, in that place filled with sunshine and flowers and light, instead of Aunt Louise's soulless house stuck up on the hill, and with only three middle-aged women for company. But then common sense came to her rescue, for the whole of Cornwall was being drenched with rain, and Nancherrow would be suffering with the rest. There had been much gloom in the dormitory when they awoke to the dismal weather, and mackintoshes and rubber boots had been ordered as the rig of the day. At ten o'clock, the boarders streamed out of the front door and splashed through puddles to the various cars which waited to bear them away for the mid-term holiday. Aunt Louise, always punctual, was there in her old Rover, but no car had yet arrived for Loveday and she had complained bitterly because she was forced to wait, kicking her heels, until somebody turned up.

(In a way, that was a good thing because Judith did not particularly want to have to introduce Aunt Louise to Diana. The two ladies would have little in common, and Aunt Louise would doubtless make snide remarks about Mrs. Carey-Lewis all the way home.)

Despite the weather, however, it had been quite a good morning. They had stopped in Penzance to do some shopping, and gone into the bank to get spending money for Judith for the weekend. (But not money for the bicycle, because Aunt Louise had promised to pay for that.) And they had gone into the bookshop and had a good browse, and Judith had bought a new fountain pen, because some girl had borrowed hers and ruined the nib. Then they had coffee in a tea-shop, and ate Kunzle cakes, and then came back here. The journey, through the rain, sitting beside Aunt Louise as she had clashed her gears and pressed her polished brogue hard down upon the accelerator, was hairy, to say the least of it, and Judith had closed her eyes and expected instant death as Aunt Louise overtook a lumbering bus on a bend, or sped over the narrow brow of a hill with no idea of what might be coming on the other side. But somehow they had reached Penmarron, and the longing for Riverview and Mummy and Jess started as they drove through the village, because it seemed all wrong to be staying on the main road and not taking the turning that led, by way of lanes, down to the estuary and the railway station. And when they got to Windyridge, that was all wrong as well, the house rearing up in front of them through the swirling mist, and the treeless, manicured garden offering no sort of welcome or comfort.

Hilda, the housemaid, had come to the door to help carry suitcases. "I'll take them upstairs now," she announced, and Judith followed her thick black cotton legs, and although she knew the house as well as she knew Riverview, this was the first time she had ever stayed here, and it was strange and alien and didn't smell right, and all at once she longed to be anywhere else in the world. Just not here.

And for no practical reason; simply a sort of emotional turmoil, a panic of misplacement. Because her room, Aunt Louise's erstwhile spare bedroom, was very nice, and her possessions, brought from Riverview, were neatly disposed or hidden away in cupboards and drawers. And her desk was there, and her books on a shelf. And flowers on the dressing-table. But nothing else. And yet, what else was there to want? What else was there to fill this terrible void that felt like a great hole in her heart?

Hilda had made a few banal observations about the dirty weather, the proximity of the bathroom, the fact that lunch was at one, and then departed. Judith, left alone, went to the window and succumbed to these ridiculous tears.

She wanted Riverview, and Mummy and Jess and Phyllis. She wanted all the familiar sights and sounds and smells. The sloping garden and the view of the peaceful estuary, filling and flowing with the tides, and the day broken by the reassuring chunter of the little steam train. The shabby charm of the flower-filled sitting-room, and the sound of Phyllis clashing pots in the scullery as she prepared vegetables for lunch, to the perpetual accompaniment of Jess's piping voice. Smells were even more invidious and nostalgic. The clean mixture of Vim and Yardley's lavender soap which emanated from the bathroom; the sweet scent of privet from the hedge by the front door; and the gusty tang of seaweed at low tide. And cooking smells, mouth-watering when you came indoors hungry. A cake in the oven, or onions frying . . .

It was no good. It did no good. Riverview had gone, let to another family. Mummy and Dad and Jess were away across the oceans on the other side of the world. Crying like a baby would not bring them back. She found a handkerchief and blew her nose, and then unpacked, wandering around the room, opening drawers and doors, locating clothes and finding something to wear that wasn't uniform. No cashmere sweaters here. Just an old skirt, and a Shetland pullover that had been washed so often it was no longer scratchy. She brushed her hair, and was calmed by this, and tried to think of cheerful things. The new bicycle, to be bought in Porthkerris this afternoon. Four days of freedom from school. She would cycle to the beach and walk on the sand. Perhaps go and see Mr. Willis. She would telephone Heather and make some plans with her. The prospect of seeing Heather again was enough to cheer anybody up. Gradually her misery dissipated; she tied her hair back in its ribbon bow and went downstairs in search of Aunt Louise.

Over lunch, which was chops and mint sauce and stewed apples, Aunt Louise showed some curious interest in the visit that Judith had paid to the Carey-Lewises. "I've never been there, but I hear the garden is fairly spectacular."

"Yes, it is, and full of lovely things. There are hydrangeas all the way up the drive. And camellias and things. And they've got their own little beach."

"What's the child like?"

"Loveday? She's wicked, but nobody seems to mind much. She's got a terribly nice nanny called Mary who does all the ironing."

"You'll be getting ideas above your station."

"No, I won't. It was different, but it was nice."

"What did you think of Mrs. Carey-Lewis? Is she really as flighty as her reputation?"

"Has she got a reputation?"

"Very much so. Always off to London, or little trips to the south of France. And rather raffish chums."

Judith thought of Tommy Mortimer, and decided, once again, that it would be prudent not even to mention his name. She said instead, "There was a terribly nice man there called Jeremy Wells. He's a doctor, and Mummy and I met him on the train when we came back from Plymouth. We shared a compartment. He wasn't staying at Nancherrow. He was just there for the day."

"Jeremy Wells?"

"Do you know him?"

"No, but everybody knows about Jeremy because of his sporting prowess. He captains the Cornish rugby team, and played for Cambridge. He scored three tries in his last Varsity match. I remember reading about it in the newspaper. The hero of the day."

"He plays cricket too. Colonel Carey-Lewis told me."

"Well, you have been hobnobbing with celebrities! I hope you won't find it too dull here."

"I'm really looking forward to buying the bicycle."

"We'll do that this afternoon. I've been told that Pitway's is the best shop in Porthkerris, so we'll go there. And Mr. Pitway has a van, so we'll get him to deliver it here just as soon as he can. I don't think you should ride it home on the main road until you've got the hang of it. You can practise around the village, and learn to stick your hand out when you're turning a corner. I don't want to have to write to your mother and tell her that you've ended your days under the wheel of a lorry."

She laughed as though this were a great joke, and Judith laughed too, although she didn't think it was particularly funny.

"As for the rest of the weekend, let's hope it stops raining, so you can be out and about. On Sunday, I'm afraid I have to abandon you, as I'm playing golf all day. As well, Edna and Hilda are going home for some celebration, an old aunt's eightieth birthday, and they have to be there to help with the tea. So you'll be on your own, but I'm sure you'll be able to amuse yourself."

The prospect of a day on her own was not unattractive, but it would be even more fun spending the empty Sunday with the Warren family. She said, "I thought I might telephone Heather, if you didn't mind. Perhaps I could go there on Sunday. Or Heather come to me."

"The little Warren girl? What a good idea. I'll leave it to you. It's good to keep up with old friends. Now, have some more apple? No? Well then, ring for Hilda to come and clear the table and then I'll have my cup of coffee and we'll leave for Porthkerris about two-thirty. You'll be ready?"

"Yes, of course." She could hardly wait.

The rain, relentless, continued. Through it, they drove to Porthkerris, which looked its most gloomy, with gutters running with water, and the harbour filled with sullen grey sea. Pitway's Bicycle Shop stood at the bottom of the hill, and Aunt Louise parked the Rover up a neighbouring alley, and they went inside. The shop smelt of rubber and oil and new leather, and there were bicycles everywhere, ranging from toddlers' trundle toys to racing bikes with dashing drop handlebars, which Judith considered a bit of a swizz, because pedalling along with your head between your knees and with nothing to look at but the road surely destroyed the whole object of the exercise.

Mr. Pitway appeared, in his khaki overall, and the great decision commenced. In the end, they all agreed on a Raleigh, dark green and with a black saddle. It had a chain-guard, and three speeds, and good fat rubber handgrips, and its own pump for blowing up the tyres, and a little bag at the back of the saddle with tools and a small can of oil. It cost exactly five pounds, and Aunt Louise gallantly took out her wallet and peeled out the notes.

"Now, Mr. Pitway, I want this delivered as soon as possible. How about this afternoon?"

"Well, I'm alone in the shop just now . . ."

"Rubbish. You can get your wife to hold the fort for half an hour. Just pop it in your van and bring it over. Windyridge, Penmarron."

"Yes, I know where you are, but—"

"Splendid. That's all fixed. See you about four o'clock. We'll be looking out for you." She was already half-way out of the door. "And thank you for your help."

"Thank you," said the hapless Mr. Pitway, "for your custom."

He kept his word, clearly intimidated by Aunt Louise. The afternoon had improved slightly, and although the skies were still grey, and the world sodden and dripping, the rain, obligingly, had stopped, and when, at five to four, the blue van turned in at the gates of Windyridge, Judith, who had been watching for its arrival, was able to rush out and help Mr. Pitway unload the precious cargo. Aunt Louise, who had also heard the car, followed hard on her heels, just to make sure that all was in order and the bicycle had not been marked or damaged in any way during its short journey. For once she could find no fault. She thanked Mr. Pitway and gave him half a crown for his trouble and to pay for the petrol. He received his pourboire in an embarrassed but grateful fashion, waited until Judith had mounted the bike and done a couple of turns around the path which circled the lawn, and then touched his cap, got into his van, and drove away.

"Well," said Aunt Louise. "And how's that?"

"It's absolutely perfect. Oh, thank you, Aunt Louise." Hanging onto the handlebars, she planted a kiss on Aunt Louise's unreceptive cheek. "It's the most lovely bike and the most lovely present. I'll really look after it, and it's the best thing I've *ever* had."

"Always remember to put it in the garage, and never leave it out in the rain."

"Oh, I won't. I never will. I'm going for a ride now. Round the village."

"You know how the brakes work?"

"I know how everything works."

"Off you go then. Enjoy yourself."

And with that, she went indoors to her knitting, her afternoon tea, her novel.

It was heaven, like flying. Spinning down the hill, and cycling through the village, seeing again all the small remembered shops and the familiar cottages of the main street. She sailed past the post office and the pub, passed the turning which led to the Vicarage, and then free-wheeled, at tremendous speed, down the wooded hill which led to the far boundaries of the estuary, where the causeway curved to the far side of the water. She took the lane that circled the violet farm and cycled on, splashing through puddles, along the bumpy track that ran parallel to the little railway line. It was always sheltered here, and the south-facing banks were starred with wild primroses. It didn't matter about the dismal grey skies. The air was sweet and smelt of damp earth, and the fat tyres of the bicycle skimmed over the bumps and puddles, and she was on her own and totally free, and filled with endless energy, as though, if asked, she could have travelled to the ends of the earth. She felt like singing, and there was nobody about to hear, so she sang.

> "*The winds are blowing*
> *The snows are snowing*
> *But I can weather the storm . . .*"

The end of the lane and the first of the houses. The big important houses of Penmarron, with their shadowed secret gardens enclosed by high stone walls. Pine trees towered overhead, noisy with cawing rooks. The railway station. Riverview House.

She put on the brakes and stopped, steadying herself with a foot on the ground. She had not meant to come, but it was as though the bicycle had found its own way, like a trusty horse, and brought her to her old home, without any conscious volition on her own part. She stared up at the house, and it was all right. Poignant, but not unbearably so. The garden looked cared for and the early narcissi were flowering in the orchard. And somebody had hung a child's swing on one of the apple trees. It was good to know that children lived here.

After a bit, she rode on, under the trees and past the spring where fresh water flowed into a pool that had always been a good place to catch tadpoles and frogs. The track leaned upwards and came out on the main road by the church. For a moment she thought of going on down to the beach and calling on Mr. Willis, but it was getting late, the afternoon was fading, and she had no lights on the bicycle. Next time she went to Porthkerris, she would buy a pair. A big headlight and a red tail-light. But right now was time to head for home.

The road ran uphill with fields on one side and the golf links on the other. Pedalling furiously, she soon discovered that it was much steeper than she had ever imagined, and even with her three-speed gear, finally ran out of puff. Alongside the club house, she gave up and dismounted, resigning herself to walking the rest of the way and pushing the bicycle. It occurred to her that perhaps this was why they were called push-bikes . . .

"Hello, there." Judith stopped and turned to see who had called. A man was coming through the club-house gate, and down the steps which led to the road. He was dressed for golf, in baggy plus-fours and a yellow pullover, and wore a tweed cap at a rakish angle, which gave him a faintly suspect appearance, like an untrustworthy bookmaker. "You must be Judith, or I'm muchly mistaken."

"Yes, I am," said Judith, without any idea who he could be.

"Your aunt told me you'd be here for the weekend. Short leave from school." He had a florid complexion and a moustache and a pair of bright and knowing eyes. "You don't know me, because we've never met. Colonel Fawcett. Billy Fawcett. Old friend of Louise's, from India. *Now*, I'm her next-door neighbour."

Recognition dawned. "Oh, yes, I remember. She told Mummy and me about you. You were a friend of Uncle Jack's."

"That's right. Same regiment, up on the North-West Frontier." He eyed the bicycle. "What's this you've got?"

"It's my new bike. Aunt Louise bought it for me today. It's got a three-speed, but I still can't get it up the hill, so I've got to push it."

"That's the worst of bikes, but I must say, it's a handsome piece of kit. Walking, are you? I'll walk with you if I may . . ."

It was rather annoying to have her solitude disturbed, but she said, "Yes, of course," and they set off once more, he falling into step beside her.

138

"Have you been playing golf?" she asked him.

"Just a practice round, on my own. I have to improve my game before I can give your aunt any sort of competition."

"She's very good, I know."

"Splendid player. Hits the ball like a man. And a deadly putter. How does it feel to be back in Penmarron . . . ?"

They talked on, in a polite and stilted fashion, for the rest of the way. When they reached the turning for Windyridge and the bungalows which lay beyond, the lane was level and Judith could have mounted her bicycle and ridden on, and left Colonel Fawcett behind, but this seemed a bit rude, so she couldn't.

At the gateway of Windyridge she paused again, expecting him to say his goodbyes and carry on, but he did not appear anxious to end their encounter. It was now nearly dark, and from beyond Aunt Louise's drawn sitting-room curtains, light shone out into the dusk, and Colonel Fawcett was clearly tempted by this tacit invitation. Hesitating, he made great play of pushing back the cuff of his pullover and squinting at the face of his wristwatch.

"Quarter past five. Well, I've a few moments to spare, so why don't I come in with you and pay my respects to Louise? Haven't seen her for a day or two . . ."

Judith could think up no objection to this, and anyway did not suppose that Aunt Louise would mind. And so, together, they went through the gate and up the gravelled path.

At the front door, "I have to put my bicycle in the garage," she told him.

"Don't worry. I'll let myself in."

Which he did. Without ringing the bell or even knocking on the glass panel of the inner door. He just opened it, and shouted "Louise?" and she must have made some reply, for he went in and slammed the door shut behind him.

Left alone, Judith made a private grimace at his retreating back view. She was not certain if she liked Colonel Fawcett and certainly did not approve of his high-handed behaviour. But perhaps Aunt Louise was fond of him and did not object to his bursting in on her, unexpected and uninvited. Thoughtfully, she wheeled the bicycle into the garage and stowed it with some care, well out of reach of the Rover. With Aunt Louise's driving, one never knew.

Deliberately taking her time, she closed and bolted the garage doors. She was reluctant to go indoors. It would be all right if she were able to slip upstairs to her own room and there wait until Colonel Fawcett had departed, but the design of Windyridge precluded escape. Through the front door, and she was with them both, in Aunt Louise's lounge hall, and there was no way of sneaking off without being blatantly rude.

She found him already settled by the fire, looking as though he had been there forever, and Aunt Louise, her afternoon tea-tray removed by Hilda, was pouring him a drink.

"And how are you going to spend your weekend?" He had taken his first large strong mouthful, cradling the glass in his hand with loving, stubby fingers. "Made plans? Done your staff work?"

Aunt Louise returned to her knitting. She had not taken a drink for herself, because it was too early and the sun not yet over the yardarm. She was strict with herself about such rules. Living alone, one had to be.

"We haven't talked about it very much. I'm playing golf on Sunday with Polly and John Richards, and a friend they've got staying. He's a member of Rye, and apparently a very good golfer . . ."

"So how are you going to spend your day?" Billy Fawcett cocked an eye at Judith.

"I'll probably visit my friend in Porthkerris. I'm going to telephone her."

"Can't have you kicking your heels on your own. Always available if you need a bit of company." Judith pretended not to hear this.

Aunt Louise changed needles. "It would be splendid if Mrs. Warren can have Judith on Sunday because Hilda and Edna are taking the day off as well. Might be a bit dull in the empty house."

"I can always go out on my bicycle."

"Not if it's pouring with rain. You'd need one of those rain capes people wear that come right down to your ankles. And at this time of the year, goodness knows what the weather's going to do."

Billy Fawcett laid down his tumbler, and contorting himself slightly, reached into his plus-four pocket for cigarette case and lighter. He lit up, and Judith saw that his fingers were stained with tobacco. His moustache looked a bit frizzled, too, as though it had been well-smoked.

"How about a visit to the pictures?" he suddenly suggested. "I was in Porthkerris this morning, and they're showing *Top Hat* at the cinema. Fred Astaire and Ginger Rogers. Should be quite a good show. Why don't you let me take you both? Tomorrow evening. My treat, of course."

Aunt Louise seemed a bit taken aback. Perhaps this was the first time that Billy Fawcett had offered to pay for *anything*.

"That's very good of you, Billy. What about you, Judith? Would you like to go to the cinema and see *Top Hat*? Or perhaps you've already seen it?"

But no, Judith had not seen it, but had been wanting to for ages. And she had seen photographs, in a film magazine which Loveday had smuggled into the dormitory, of the glamorous pair, twirling and gliding over the dance floor, she in a dress adrift with feathers. And one of the girls in the fifth form had already sat through the film twice, in London, had fallen in love with Fred Astaire, and had his debonaire photograph glued inside the cover of her rough notebook.

On the other hand, she would have preferred to go to the cinema with just Heather; together they could have eaten bull-eyes and swooned contentedly in the stuffy darkness. It wouldn't be quite the same with Aunt Louise and Billy Fawcett.

"No. I haven't seen it."

"Would you like to go?" asked Aunt Louise.

"Yes." There wasn't much else to say. "Yes, I'd love it."

"Splendid." Billy Fawcett slapped his tweeded knee with his hand, approving a decision well made. "That's settled then. When shall we go? Six o'clock house? I'm afraid you'll have to be the chauffeur, Louise, as my old banger's coughing a bit. Have to take it to the garage."

"Very well. If you come here at five-thirty and we'll all go together. It's very kind of you."

"A pleasure. Two lovely ladies to escort. Who could ask for more?" He reached for his tumbler, drained the whisky, and sat on, smoking, with the empty glass in his hand.

Aunt Louise raised her eyebrows. "The other half, Billy?"

"Well." He gazed into the empty glass, as though surprised to see it in such a sad state. "Well. If you insist."

"Help yourself."

"How about you, Louise?"

She glanced at the clock. "A small one. Thank you."

So he heaved himself to his feet and went to the drink-tray to do the honours. Watching him, Judith thought he looked quite frighteningly at home. She wondered about his bungalow, and decided it was probably quite awful, cheerless and cold. Perhaps he was dreadfully poor, and couldn't afford cosy fires and bottles of whisky and resident housekeepers and all the comforts of life that lonely bachelors needed. Perhaps that was why he seemed to be insinuating himself into Aunt Louise's well-ordered and affluent life. Perhaps . . . horror of horrors . . . he was, in his own way, *courting* Aunt Louise, with marriage in mind.

It was an idea so dreadful that it scarcely bore thinking about. And yet, why not? He was an old acquaintance of Jack Forrester's, and Aunt Louise clearly found his company amusing, or she would have sent him packing long ago. She was not one to suffer fools gladly. So perhaps she was just sorry for him, and their relationship had simply evolved, over the passage of time. Such things happened.

"Here you are, my dear . . ."

Judith watched her carefully, but she received the drink in her usual practical fashion, and placed it on the table by her side. No covert glances took place, no secret smiles. Judith relaxed slightly. Aunt Louise was far too sensible to make any rash decisions, and what could be more rash than making any sort of commitment with a penniless old boozer like Billy Fawcett?

"Thank you, Billy."

Good old Aunt Louise. Judith decided to forget her instinctive fears; put them out of her mind. But she discovered that the idea, once planted, had taken root, and knew that there was no way of ignoring its possibility. She would simply have to watch and wait.

The next morning she rang Heather. Mrs. Warren answered the telephone, made a few pleased and welcoming noises when she realized who was on the line, and then went to fetch her daughter.

"Judith!"

"Hello."

"What are you doing?"

"It's half-term weekend. I'm with Aunt Louise."

"Got the bike, have you?"

"Yes, we bought it yesterday, in Pitway's. It's super. I went for a long ride yesterday evening. Only thing is, I want to get some lights."

"What kind is it?"

"A Raleigh. It's dark green. Three speeds."

"That's lovely."

"I want to see you. I wondered if I could see you tomorrow. Could I come over?"

"Oh, darn it."

"What's wrong?"

"We're going up Bodmin for the weekend to visit my gran. Dad's got the car and we're leaving in about five minutes. Won't be back till late Sunday night."

"I can't bear it." It was too disappointing. "Why do you have to go away *this* weekend?"

"It's all arranged. And I didn't know you'd be home. You should have let me know."

"I've got Monday off, too."

"No good. I'll be back to school Monday. Could you come for tea Monday?"

"No, because I've got to get back to Saint Ursula's by four o'clock."

"Oh, that's some nuisance," said Heather. "I'm really vexed. I've been wanting to see you. Hear about everything. What's it like? Made any friends, have you?"

"Yes. One or two. It's not bad."

"Missing your mum?"

"Sometimes. But it doesn't do any good."

"Have they got there? Colombo, I mean. Had a letter, have you?"

"Yes, lots. And they're all right, and Jess is all right."

"Elaine was asking after you the other day. Now I can give her some news. Look, I'll see you Easter holidays."

"Right."

"When do your holidays start?"

"First week in April."

"Well, ring me up right away and we'll fix something. Mum says can you come and stay a couple of nights."

"Say yes, I'd love to."

"I've got to go, Judith. Dad's hooting the horn and Mum's putting on her hat and flapping around like a flea in a blanket."

"Have a good weekend with your gran."

"You, too. Don't forget. See you Easter."

"I won't."

" 'Bye."

She went, feeling flat, to tell Aunt Louise the bad news. "The Warrens are going to Bodmin for two days to stay with Heather's gran. So they aren't going to be here tomorrow."

"Oh dear. How disappointing. Never mind, you'll be able to get together next holidays. And with a bit of luck tomorrow will be fine and dry. If it is I'll get Edna to make you a picnic and you can go out on your bicycle. Perhaps down to the beach. Or up to Veglos Hill. All the wild primroses are out up there. You can bring me back the first bunch of the season."

"Yes. I suppose so." But it was still disappointing. She slumped into an armchair with her legs sticking out in front of her and sucked at a strand of hair which had escaped from its ribbon. She thought about the empty Sunday, and hoped that Aunt Louise would not tell Billy Fawcett about the change of plan. She opened her mouth to say this, thought about it, decided not to, and closed her mouth again. Better not to say anything. Better not to betray any inkling of her instinctive antipathy towards the harmless old codger whom Aunt Louise so clearly looked upon as a close friend.

After another drizzly morning, Saturday afternoon blossomed into sunshine, blinking in and out behind huge clouds which drifted inland from the sea. Aunt Louise announced that she would garden, so Judith helped her, grubbing weeds out of the soft damp earth and carting away, in a wheelbarrow, the dead wood that Aunt Louise had pruned from various rose-bushes and shrubs. They did not come indoors until half past four, but there was plenty of time to wash hands and tidy up and have a cup of tea before Billy Fawcett presented himself, marching up the path from the gate, eager and ready for the evening out.

They piled into the Rover, Billy in the front seat, and were on their way.

"What have you two been doing today?" he wanted to know.

Aunt Louise told him. "Gardening," she said.

He turned in his seat to grin at Judith, and she saw his yellowed teeth and his twinkling eyes.

"Not much of a holiday, when the memsahib puts you to work."

She said, "I like gardening."

"How about tomorrow? Get hold of your chum?"

Judith looked out of the window and pretended not to hear him, so he repeated his question. "Managed to fix something up?"

"Not really" was all she could think of to say, praying that Aunt Louise would keep her mouth shut and the subject would be dropped. But Aunt Louise, unprimed and so unsuspecting, let spill the beans. "Unfortunately, Heather's away for the weekend. But no matter, they'll meet up in the holidays."

Judith knew it wasn't her fault but still could have screamed at her.

"So you'll have to fill in your own time, eh? Well, if you need a bit of company, I'm just down the road."

He turned back to face ahead once more, and Judith, rude as Loveday, put out her tongue at the back of his head. He might have seen her in the driving mirror, but even if he did she didn't care.

This evening Porthkerris, as they came coasting down the hill into the town, presented a very different face to the dismal one it had shown yesterday morning. The sky had cleared and the last rays of the setting sun washed all the old grey stone houses with a golden-pink light, so that they took on a pale translucence of seashells. The breeze had dropped and the sea was silvery and still, and on the great crescent of the beach, far below the road, a man and a woman walked together, stitching, behind them, a double line of footprints on the firm, smooth sand.

As the car descended into the maze of narrow streets, the Saturday-evening smell of freshly fried fish and chips drifted from an open door. Billy Fawcett raised his head and sniffed, flaring his nostrils, like a dog on a scent.

"Fairly makes your juices run, eh? Fish and chips. Perhaps after the show, we should all have a fish supper?"

But Aunt Louise didn't think this a good idea. Perhaps because she did not want to deal with any wrangles of the bill and who should pay. "Not this evening, Billy, I think. Edna is expecting Judith and me at home, and she's going to give us a cold supper." Billy Fawcett was clearly not invited to share in this frugal feast. Judith had it in her heart to feel a bit sorry for him, but then Aunt Louise said, "Perhaps another time," which made things a bit less rude. She wondered what he would have for his supper. Probably a whisky and soda and a packet of potato crisps. Poor old thing. But still, she was glad that Aunt Louise was not asking him back to Windyridge. By the time the film was over, she guessed that she would have had enough of his company.

Aunt Louise parked the car near the bank, and they crossed the road to the cinema. There was no queue, but a lot of people seemed to be going in. Billy Fawcett strode ahead and lined up at the ticket office to pay for the seats. Aunt Louise and Judith gazed at the display of shiny black-and-white photographs which advertised the film. It was clearly going to be very romantic and funny and glamorous. A thrill of anticipation shivered down Judith's spine, but Aunt Louise only sniffed. "I do hope it's not going to be *silly*."

"I bet you love it, Aunt Louise."

"Oh, well. I'll enjoy the catchy tunes."

They turned from the photographs, and Billy Fawcett had disappeared from view. "Where on earth has he gone *now?*" Aunt Louise asked, rather as though he were a dog on a picnic, but he appeared almost right away, having been to the newsagent next door to buy a small box of Cadbury's Milk Tray chocolates. "Have to do the thing in style, eh? Sorry to keep you waiting. Now, in we go."

The inside of the cinema—which had once been a fish market—was cramped and stuffy as ever, smelling strongly of the disinfectant which was regularly squirted around in case of possible fleas. A girl with a torch showed the way to their seats, but she didn't shine the torch, because the lights had not yet gone down. Judith was about to edge her way into the row, but Billy Fawcett intervened: "Ladies first, I think, Judith. Let's see your aunt comfortably settled." Which meant that Judith sat between them, with Aunt Louise on her left and Billy Fawcett on her right. Once they were settled, with coats disposed of, he opened the box of chocolates and handed them along. They only tasted a bit stale, but then they had probably been sitting on the newsagent's shelf for years.

The lights dimmed. They watched trailers for the next show . . . A thrilling western set, apparently, in South America. *The Stranger from Rio.* A blonde actress dressed in picturesque tatters, but with her maquillage intact, struggled, panting, through pampas-grass. The hero, in a tremendous sombrero, driving his white horse through a river, meanwhile whirling a lariat over his head. "Showing at This Theatre. Next Week. The Chance of a Lifetime. Not to Be Missed."

"I shall miss it," said Aunt Louise. "It looks rubbish."

Then there was the news. Herr Hitler strutting around in his breeches, reviewing some parade. The King talking to shipbuilders after a launch in the north of England. Then some funny shots of puppies at a dog show. After the news there was a Silly Symphony about a chipmunk, and then, at last, *Top Hat.*

"Thank goodness for that," said Aunt Louise. "I thought it was never going to start."

But Judith hardly heard her. Settled deep in her seat, her eyes glued to the screen, she was caught up in the old familiar magic, the total submergence in the sight and sound of the story that was being told. And before long, there was Fred Astaire on a stage, twirling and tapping his way through the "Top Hat" number, walking, strolling, juggling his cane, but somehow always dancing. And then the plot thickened, and he met Ginger Rogers and pursued her, and they sang, "Isn't This a Lovely Day to Be Caught in the Rain?" and danced again, only together this time. And then he and Edward Everett Horton somehow got mixed up, both dressed the same and swapping over a briefcase, and Ginger Rogers thought that Fred Astaire was Edward Everett Horton and became enraged, because Edward Everett Horton was married to Ginger's best friend Madge . . .

It was at this juncture that Judith became aware that something funny was going on. Billy Fawcett was restless, shifting around and generally distracting her attention. She changed her position slightly, in order to give his legs more space, and as she did so, felt something on her knee. And the something was Billy Fawcett's hand, which had alighted, as though by mistake, but stayed there, heavy and uncomfortably warm.

The shock of this destroyed all concentration and pleasure. *Top Hat,* with its glitter and charm, simply ceased to exist. The dialogue, the jokes, the laughter were unheard. She continued to stare at the screen, but saw nothing.

and all thought of following the plot flew from her mind, as she grappled with an alarming and totally unexpected crisis. What was she meant to do? Did he know that his hand was on her knee? Did he perhaps think it rested on the narrow arm which divided the cramped velvet seats? Should she tell him? And if she did, would he take his hand away?

But then his fingers tightened and gripped and began to knead, and she knew that his intrusion was no accident, but planned. Fondling, his hand moved higher, under her skirt, up her thigh. In a moment he would reach her knickers. In the darkness, in the warmth, she sat in terrified horror, wondering where he would stop, and what was she to do, and why was he doing it, and how could she possibly alert Aunt Louise . . .

Up on the screen, something amusing had taken place. The audience, Aunt Louise included, burst into peals of laughter. Under cover of this sound, Judith pretended she had dropped something, slid out of her seat, and landed on her knees, jammed in the fusty darkness between the two rows of seats.

"What on earth," Aunt Louise demanded, "are you doing?"

"I've lost my hair-slide."

"I didn't think you were wearing one."

"Well, I was, and I've lost it."

"Leave it then, and we'll find it at the end of the film."

"Shh!" came a furious whisper from the row behind. "*Stay quiet, can't you?*"

"Sorry." With some difficulty, she wriggled back into her seat again, this time squeezed so close to Aunt Louise that the arm-rest dug into her rib-cage. Surely now he would take the hint and leave her alone.

But no. Another five minutes, and the hand was there again, like a creepy crawly creature that no amount of bashing with a rolled-up newspaper would kill. Fondling, moving, creeping upward . . .

She sprang to her feet.

Aunt Louise, not unnaturally, became exasperated. "Judith, for heaven's *sake*."

"I have to go to the lavatory," Judith hissed.

"I told you to go before we left home."

"*Shsh! Other people are watching; do you mind being quiet?*"

"Sorry. Aunt Louise, let me by."

"Go the other way. It's much quicker."

"I want to go *this* way."

"*Well, go or sit down; you're spoiling everyone's pleasure.*"

"Sorry."

She went, clambering over Aunt Louise's knees, and the knees of all the other irritated and inconvenienced members of the audience who happened to be sitting in their row. She sped up the dark aisle and through the curtain at the back and found the dirty little ladies' cloakroom, and went in and locked the door, and sat in the smelly place and nearly cried with disgust and despair. What did he want, the horrible man? Why did he have to touch her?

Why couldn't he leave her alone? She didn't mind about missing the picture. The very idea of going back into the cinema gave her the shivers. She just wanted to get out into the fresh air and go home, and never ever have to see him or speak to him again.

"Let's go to the cinema," he had suggested, without blinking an eye, letting Aunt Louise believe that he was offering the treat out of the goodness of his heart. He had fooled Aunt Louise, which alone rendered him both astute and dangerous. Why he had fondled her knee, and slid his hateful fingers right up her thigh, was incomprehensible, but that alone made her feel desecrated, because it was horrible. From the start, she had not much liked Billy Fawcett, but simply thought him rather pathetic and ridiculous. Now she felt ridiculous too, and demeaned as well. So demeaned that she knew she could never bring herself to tell Aunt Louise what had happened. The mere idea of looking her in the eye and saying *Billy Fawcett tried to put his hand up my knickers* was enough to make her burn with shame.

One thing was for sure. She would go back into the cinema, the way she had come, and would not budge until Aunt Louise stood up, took Judith's seat beside Billy Fawcett and let Judith take her own place. This could be achieved by standing and arguing, and with the help of the infuriated couple who sat behind them. Thus Aunt Louise would be forced, out of sheer embarrassment, to do as Judith insisted, and if she was angry afterwards and demanded to know what on earth Judith had been thinking about, what a way to behave, et cetera, et cetera, then Judith would take no notice of her because, indirectly, the whole situation was Aunt Louise's own fault. Billy Fawcett was *her* friend, and she could jolly well sit next to him, and Judith was pretty sure that, come hell or high water, he wouldn't dare to put his hand up Aunt Louise's knickers.

The sky, which had been clear with a brilliant full moon, suddenly darkened, and a wind sprang up from nowhere, pouncing on and howling about the house on the hill with the voice of lost ghosts. She lay in bed and was terrified, and stared at the square space of the window, waiting for what was inevitably going to happen, and not knowing what it was. She knew that if she got out of bed and fled to the door, with escape her only hope, then she would find the door locked. Over the sound of the wind, she heard footsteps on the gravel, and then a thump, as the top of a wooden ladder was set against the windowsill. It was coming. He was coming, climbing silently as a cat. She stared and her heart thudded, and she lay still because there was nothing else to do. He was coming, with his evil intentions, and his manically twinkling eyes, and his hot and fumbling fingers, and she was lost because even if she screamed she knew that no sound would come out of her mouth, and nobody would hear. Nobody would come. And then as, petrified, she watched, his head came over the edge of the windowsill, and although it was dark, she could see every feature on his face, and he was smiling . . .

Billy Fawcett.

She sat up in bed and screamed, and screamed again, and he was still there, but it was daylight now, it was morning and she was awake, and the terrible image stayed only for a second, and then mercifully faded, and there was no ladder, only her own open window and the morning light beyond.

A dream. Her heart thudded like a drum with the terror and reality of her own overwrought imagination. Gradually it stilled. Her mouth was dry. She drank from the glass of water by her bed. Lay back, trembling and exhausted, on the pillows.

She thought about facing Aunt Louise over bacon and eggs, and hoped that she was not still cross about yesterday evening and the disastrous visit to the cinema. Judith's frightening dream had faded, but the practical problem of Billy Fawcett was as real and immediate as ever; it lay on her heart like a weight, and she knew that no amount of chewing over the debacle of their night out was going to solve this problem, or, on consideration, do any good whatsoever.

"*Let's go to the cinema.*" So kindly and well-meaning. And all the time, he had been planning *that*. He had deceived them both, which rendered him cunning, and so an enemy to be reckoned with. His violation was incomprehensible. She only knew that, somehow, it was all mixed up with sex, and so, was horrible.

From the start Judith had not found him likeable . . . not like dear Mr. Willis, or even Colonel Carey-Lewis, with whom she had formed an instant rapport . . . but simply something of a caricature—ridiculous. And now the awful thing was that she felt ridiculous too, because she had behaved like an idiot. As well, there was Aunt Louise to be considered. Billy Fawcett was an old acquaintance, a link with Jack Forrester and their halcyon days in India. To tell would be to destroy her faith and end their friendship. And Judith, distraught as she was, did not have it in her to be so cruel.

Because Aunt Louise had been very good about the disastrous visit to the cinema, saying no word until she and Judith were back at Windyridge and alone. After the film was finished, and the audience stood for the scratchy rendering of "God Save the King," they had filed out, into the cold and blowy darkness, and piled into the Rover, and returned to Penmarron. Billy Fawcett had kept up perky conversation all the way, repeating and recalling amusing scraps of dialogue from the film, and whistling the tunes.

"*I'm putting on my top hat
Tying up my white tie . . .*"

Judith stared at the back of his head and wished him dead. As they approached the gates of Windyridge, he said, "Drop me here, Louise my dear, and I'll make my own way home. Splendid of you to drive us. Enjoyed myself."

"We enjoyed ourselves too, Billy. Didn't we, Judith?" The car halted, and he opened the door and clambered out. "And thank you for our treat."

"A pleasure, my dear. 'Bye, Judith." And he had the effrontery to stick his head through the door and send her a wink. Then the door slammed shut and he was on his way. Aunt Louise turned in through the gate. They were home.

She had not been really angry, simply puzzled, and at a loss to know what on earth had got into Judith. "You behaved like a maniac. I thought you'd caught a flea or something, hopping about like a person with Saint Vitus' dance. Losing things, and dropping things, and then disturbing a whole row of innocent people who were only trying to enjoy themselves. And all that fuss about sitting in *my* seat. I've never seen such behaviour in my life."

Which was all quite reasonable. Judith apologized, told her that the mythical hair-slide had been a favourite, the visit to the lavatory highly essential, and that she had only asked Aunt Louise to shift seats because she thought it easier for Aunt Louise to move, rather than to endure Judith's clambering across her knees and possibly kicking her. She had, actually, only been thinking of Aunt Louise's well-being, when she made the suggestion.

"My well-being! I like that, with the couple behind me calling me every sort of name and threatening to call the police . . ."

"But they wouldn't have."

"That's not the point. It was very embarrassing."

"I am sorry."

"I was quite enjoying the film too. I didn't think I would, but it was amusing."

"I thought it was funny too," Judith fibbed, because, in fact, after the moment when the fumbling started, she couldn't remember anything about it at all. She added, hoping to put Aunt Louise off any possible scent, "It was kind of Colonel Fawcett to take us."

"Yes, it was. Poor old boy, he's pretty hard-up. Not much of a pension . . ." The row, it seemed, was over. Aunt Louise, having divested herself of coat and hat, went to pour herself a sustaining whisky and soda, and carrying this, led the way into the dining-room, where Edna had left them cold mutton and sliced beetroot, her idea of a suitable post-cinema snack.

But Judith was not hungry. Simply dead-tired. She toyed with the mutton and drank some water.

"You all right?" Aunt Louise asked. "You look dreadfully pale. The excitement must have been too much for you. Why don't you pop off to bed?"

"Would you mind?"

"Not a scrap."

"I'm sorry about everything."

"We'll talk no more about it."

Now, the morning after, Judith knew that she wouldn't. For this she was grateful, but still felt miserable. Not only miserable but grubby, and itchy and uncomfortable. Contaminated by the unspeakable Billy Fawcett, and as well physically unclean, as though her body had absorbed the frowstiness of the stuffy little cinema, and the fetid lavatory where she had fled for refuge from his prowling hand. And her hair smelt of cigarette smoke, which was disgusting. Last night she had been too tired to have a bath, so she would have one now. The decision made, she flung back the rumpled sheets and went across the landing to turn on the taps full-blast.

It was wonderful, scalding hot, and deep as she dared. She soaped every bit of herself, and washed her hair as well. Dried, and scented with talcum powder, and with her teeth scrubbed, she felt marginally better. Back in her room, she kicked all yesterday's clothes aside—to be dealt with, at some point, by Hilda—and found clean ones. Fresh underclothes and stockings and a crisply ironed shirt. A different skirt and a dusty-pink pullover. She rubbed her hair on her towel and then combed it back from her face, put on her shoes, tied the laces, and went downstairs.

Aunt Louise was already at breakfast, buttering toast and sipping coffee. She was dressed for golf, in tweeds and a cardigan, buttoned over a manly shirt. Her hair, confined in its net, was immaculate. As Judith came in, she looked up.

"Thought you'd slept in."

"I'm sorry. I decided to have a bath."

"I had mine last night. Something about going to the cinema always leaves one feeling perfectly filthy." Judith's misdemeanours apparently were forgiven and forgotten. She was in cheerful mood, looking forward to her game. "How did you sleep? Did you dream of Fred Astaire?"

"No. No, I didn't."

"My favourite was the actor who pretended to be a clergyman." Judith helped herself to bacon and eggs and took her seat. "Being *English* made him somehow so droll."

"What time are you playing golf?"

"I said I'd meet them at ten. We'll probably tee off about half past, and then have a late lunch in the club. How about you?" Aunt Louise glanced at the window. "It looks quite a promising day. Do you want to go off on your bicycle, or is there something else you'd like to do?"

"No. I think I *will* go up Veglos, and look for primroses for you."

"I'll get Edna to make a sandwich, and pack it in a haversack. And maybe an apple and a bottle of ginger beer. She and Hilda are off at half past ten for Auntie's birthday. Some cousin is going to come and pick them up in his motor car. Funny. I never even knew they *had* a cousin who owned a motor car. And I'd like you to wait until they've set off, and then you can take the back-door key. I'll take the front-door key, and that way we're independent of each other. And I'll make sure all the windows are locked as well. You never know. Such funny people around. In the old days I never thought of locking doors, but then Mrs. Battersby was burgled, and one can't be too sure. And you'd better take a raincoat, in case it rains. And be home before dark."

"I have to be. I haven't any lights."

"How silly. We should have thought of lights when we bought the bicycle." She poured her second cup of coffee. "Well, that's all settled." She stood, and carrying the coffee cup, went from the room, headed for the kitchen and Edna, and gave orders for Judith's picnic.

Later, brogued and wearing a beret, and with her clubs stowed on the back seat of the Rover, she departed for the golf club, locking the front door firmly behind her. Judith saw her off, and then went back indoors by way of the kitchen. Edna and Hilda were dressed in their finery for the momentous birthday party.

Hilda wore a beige coat buttoned low, and a halo hat, and Edna had put on her good coat and skirt and a purple tammy with a brooch pinned to it. Of the two sisters she was Judith's least favourite, endlessly complaining about her varicose veins and her sore feet, and displaying a remarkable ability always to look on the black side of any situation. Getting a laugh out of her was a bit like getting blood from a stone. However, she was good-hearted, and Judith's picnic had been hastily assembled and waited for her on the kitchen table, packed in a small haversack.

"Thank you so much, Edna. I hope it wasn't too much trouble."

"Didn't take no time. Only meat paste. Madam says you're going to take the back-door key with you. And leave the door open for us coming back. About nine o'clock we'll be home."

"Goodness. What a long birthday party."

"There'll be all the clearing up to do."

"I'm sure it will be fun."

"Well, I hope so, I'm sure," said Edna gloomily.

"Oh, come on, Edna," Hilda chipped in. "Everybody's going to be there. It'll be screeches of fun."

But Edna only shook her head. "Eighty's too old, I always say. And Auntie Lily's stuck there in her chair and her ankles so swollen she can scarcely rise to her feet. And heavy! Takes two people to get her on the lavvy. I'd rather be down graveyard than in a state like that."

"It's not for us to choose," Hilda pointed out. "Anyway, she still likes a laugh. Split her sides she did, when her old goat ate all the washing off Mrs. Daniel's clothes-line . . ."

The argument, which might have gone on forever, was brought to a close by the cousin in his car. Like a couple of flustered hens, the sisters were galvanized into action, gathering up their handbags and umbrellas, the tin containing the cake they had baked, and the bunch of daffodils wrapped in a bit of newspaper.

"See you tomorrow."

"Have a good time."

She watched them, shrill with excitement, climb into the ramshackle vehicle and be driven away. She stood waving and they waved back. The exhaust pipe exploded clouds of black smoke, and they were gone.

She was alone.

And Billy Fawcett knew she was alone. The spectre of his presence, lurking in his bungalow just down the road, meant that there was no time to hang about. She fetched her raincoat from its hook in the cloakroom, rolled it up, and stuffed it into the haversack, on top of the picnic. With this slung across her shoulder, she let herself out of the back door, and ceremoniously locked it. In the garage, she stowed the enormous key in with all the spanners of her tool-bag. Then she wheeled the bicycle out onto the gravel, took a quick look around to make sure that he was nowhere to be seen, mounted the bicycle, and sped away.

It was a bit like escaping. Furtive, swift, and secret. But the awful thing was that, as long as Billy Fawcett was around, this was how it was always going to be.

Veglos Hill lay four miles from Penmarron, a distinctive landmark despite its modest elevation. Narrow lanes led up to and around it, and all about was moorland, small farms, and copses of oak and hawthorn, stunted and deformed by the constant winds. On its flattened crest were cairns of rock, bun-shaped granite boulders, piled upon each other, and the way to the summit lay beyond an encircling drystone wall. The lower slopes of the hill were thick with brambles, bracken, and gorse, and turfy paths wound their way up through the thickets. Wild flowers grew abundantly. Bell heather, and celandine and primroses, and in summer the ditches overflowed with the belled spires of foxgloves.

And yet it was an ancient place, and atmospheric. On the upper slopes of the hill, in the lee of the cairn, could be discerned the remnants of habitation, the hut circles of stone-age man. On a day of rain, with the mist swirling in from the ocean, and the Pendeen fog-horn moaning out through the murk, it was not hard to imagine that the ghosts of those small dark men were still in possession of Veglos; just out of sight but watching.

When they lived at Riverview House, the Dunbars had sometimes come to Veglos, in springtime, or September when the dark blackberries were ripe for picking. It was always a day's expedition, and because the hill was too distant for Jess's short legs to walk, their mother had plucked up her courage and driven them in the little Austin. Phyllis always came too, and everyone, even Jess, carried a bit of the picnic.

Judith remembered these occasions as particularly happy days.

But this was the first time she had come by bicycle, and it was a tiring ride, uphill most of the way. But finally she made it, and the hill lay just above her, beyond the drystone wall. Access to the path was by means of a stepped stile, which meant that the bike could go no farther, so she abandoned it, half-hidden by gorse and brambles, settled her haversack, and started out on the long walk.

The day was cool but fair, with clouds sailing across the pale sky and a faint sea haze blurring the horizon. The turf felt springy and sweet beneath her feet, and as she climbed, she paused from time to time, to draw breath and see how the countryside had opened up, spread before her like a map.

The sea was all-embracing; to the north, the blue bay curved to the distant lighthouse, and to the south, glimmering in the haze, lay Mount's Bay and the English Channel.

At last, she achieved the summit, and the cairn reared up above her. The final climb was a scramble up the face of this, finding toe-holds and finger-holds, scrabbling up the thorny gullies, and at last emerging at the top, in the teeth of the wind, and with all the world at her feet. It was now nearly one o'clock, and hunkering down for shelter in the lee of a yellow-lichened rock, she felt the sun warm on her cheeks.

It was all very peaceful and solitary, with only the sough of the wind and bird-song for company. She rested and gazed, filled with a good sense of achievement, and took her bearings. She saw the tidy patchwork of fields, small farms reduced by distance to toy-size; a man ploughing behind a horse, with a cloud of white gulls at his heels. The Lizard was drowned in the diffused light, but she could discern the pale outline of Penzance, the church tower and the dome of the bank. Beyond Penzance, the coast stretched out of sight. She thought of the road which led out along the cliffs to Rosemullion and Nancherrow. She thought of Loveday and wondered how she was spending this day. She thought of Diana.

She wished Diana were here, now. Just Diana. Sitting beside her, with nobody else to listen, so that Judith could confide, could tell her about Billy Fawcett, could ask her advice. She could ask Diana to tell her what on earth she was meant to do. Because even on the top of Veglos Hill, Billy Fawcett sat on her shoulder like a black dog. It seemed that you could cycle and walk until you were physically exhausted and ready to drop, but nothing would still the ever-present and restless anxieties which rat-raced around in the inside of her head.

The worst was having nobody to tell. All morning her subconscious mind had been milling over every possible confidante, and always she came up with a blank.

Mummy. Out of the question. A world away. And even if she were *here*, at Riverview, Judith knew that her mother was basically too innocent, too vulnerable to be landed with such a shocking dilemma. She would become flustered and get into one of her hysterical states, and more harm would be done than good.

Phyllis. Now working for Mrs. Bessington in Porthkerris. But Judith did not know where Mrs. Bessington lived, and could not see herself ringing the bell, facing up to the unknown Mrs. Bessington, and demanding an interview with her cook-general.

Aunt Biddy then. Aunt Biddy would listen, and probably scream with laughter, and then become indignant, get in touch with Aunt Louise and precipitate a row. Relations between the two disparate aunts had never been close, and spilling the beans to Aunt Biddy would fairly put the cat among the pigeons. The resultant carnage and its consequences did not bear thinking about.

Heather. Or Loveday. But they were both younger than Judith, and just as naive. They would only gape or giggle or ask a lot of unanswerable questions, and a fat lot of good *that* would do.

Which brought all responsibility back to herself. By fair means or foul, she simply had to deal with Billy Fawcett on her own. And if her worst fears were realized and for some unimagined reason Aunt Louise lost her head, succumbed to his blandishments and agreed to marry him, then Judith was leaving Windyridge, packing her bags, and going to Plymouth to live with Aunt Biddy. Provided he stayed in his bungalow down the road, she reckoned she could deal with him. But at the first inkling that he was about to become Mr. Louise Forrester and take possession of Windyridge, then Judith was off.

So a sort of decision had been achieved. With weary resolution, she tried to put it all out of her mind, and set about enjoying her solitary expedition. Exploring all the cairns took up a bit of time, and then she ate her picnic, and sat in the thin warmth until clouds covered the face of the sun and it grew chilly. She gathered up her haversack and made her way down the slope to where the turfy dells were filled with primroses. She began to pick, tying the bunches with strands of wool when they became too plump to hold. Crouching, she grew stiff. When the third bunch was completed she stood, painfully easing the cramps from her shoulders and her knees. She looked up and saw the black sky moving in from the west, and knew that, very soon, it was going to start to pour with rain, and that the time had come to head for home. She opened her haversack, hauled out her raincoat, and put it on. The primroses went in, on top of the remains of her picnic. She buckled the straps, slung it across her back, and ran all the way down the path to where she had hidden her bicycle.

She was only half-way back to the village when the sky turned the colour of granite and the rain fell. It came not gradually, but in a deluge, and in moments she was extremely wet. It didn't matter. In fact, it was rather enjoyable, pedalling along with the rain in her face, and her hair dripping drops down the back of her neck, and the bicycle gamely splashing its way through the puddles. Up the hill (too steep to pedal, so she had to push) and then through the village, and on by the main road. She was passed by cars and the local bus, trundling its wet way towards Porthkerris, the faces of passengers blurred beyond the foggy windows. It was cold, and with the rain a keen wind had risen, but she glowed with exertion and exercise, even if her hands were frozen.

Windyridge at last. Down the lane and in through the gate, and up the garden path. In the garage, she parked the dripping bicycle, took the back-door key from the tool-bag, and scurried for the house. She would have a hot bath, hoist her wet clothes on the kitchen pulley to dry, make herself a cup of tea.

It was good to be indoors. The kitchen was warm and, without Edna and Hilda, seemed very quiet. Only the old clock ticked from the wall, and the hot coals of the range hummed in the draught. She took off her sodden raincoat and dropped it on a chair. She found empty jam jars and filled them with water, and set the primroses into them so that they could have a drink and recover from their journey. She left the jam jars and the haversack on the kitchen table and went out of the kitchen and across the hall, and started upstairs.

As she did so, the telephone standing on the hall chest rang. She turned back and went to answer it, but before she could say anything, it spoke to her.

"Judith."

She froze.

"You there, Judith? Billy Fawcett here. Looking out for you, saw you come home. Bit worried about you in this monsoon. Thought I'd check." His voice sounded a bit woozy. Perhaps, already, he had been at his whisky bottle. "Come around and have a cup of tea with you." She scarcely breathed. "Judith? Judith, are you there. . . ?"

Gently, Judith replaced the receiver on its hook. She stood motionless with the calm of desperation, and her mind crystal-clear. Billy Fawcett, on the prowl. But she was all right. Thanks to darling, darling Aunt Louise, the front door and all the downstairs windows were locked. Only the back door had she left open . . .

She sped back the way she had come, through the kitchen and the scullery; retrieved the key, slammed the door shut, and locked it from the inside. The old-fashioned mechanism, well-oiled, slid into place. Downstairs, now, all was safe. But the upper floor . . . ? She raced back into the hall and up the stairs, taking the treads two at a time, because there was not a second to waste. Last night, in her dream, he had armed himself with a ladder and come that way, finding her open window and setting the ladder against its sill. The dream flooded back in all its horror. His head and shoulders appearing, silhouetted against the night, and his yellow-toothed smile, and his knowing eyes . . .

In the bedrooms, on the landing, windows stood open. She raced from room to room, closing and snibbing every one. Aunt Louise's bedroom was the last, and as she scrabbled with the latch, she saw, through the curtain of rain, Billy Fawcett, mackintoshed and dripping, come through the garden gate and set off at a brisk clip up the gravelled path. Before he could catch sight of her, Judith flung herself onto the carpet, and rolled, like a log, into the cramped and stuffy gloom beneath Aunt Louise's enormous mahogany double bed.

Her heart raced, and it was hard to breathe.

Looking out for you, saw you come home. She imagined him at his window, armed with his tumbler of whisky and possibly a pair of binoculars, as though ensconced in his frontier fort, and watching for Afghans to kill. Spying, he had waited. Waiting, he had been rewarded for his patience. And he knew that she was totally alone.

Through the drip of the rain, she heard his feet on the gravel. The thump of his fist on the front door. The pealing of the bell from the kitchen. It shrilled through the empty house. She lay motionless.

"Judith. I know you're there."

She stuffed her fist into her mouth. She remembered the little larder window, always open, and was momentarily terrified. But common sense came to her rescue, because only the tiniest baby could squeeze through that window, and anyway it was screened with a fine wire mesh to keep out the wasps and the bluebottles.

His footsteps moved away, tramping off around the side of the house, out of hearing. He was going to try the back door. She remembered its dungeon lock and took courage.

She lay silent, listening, ears as sensitive as those of a suspicious dog. Only the drum of the rain, the whispering tick of Aunt Louise's little bedside clock. Tick-tick-tick, it went, very quickly. She waited. After what seemed like eternity, he returned to the front door, his footsteps crunching back into earshot.

"Judith!" A bellow from beneath the window, and she nearly jumped out of her skin. Soaked and frustrated, he was clearly losing control of his temper, and was giving up any attempt to be either ingratiating or friendly. "What do you think you're playing at? Bloody rude. Come down and let me in . . ."

She did not move.

"*Judith!*" Now he renewed his onslaught on the front door, hammering at the solid wood with the fury of a man demented. Once again, from the kitchen, came the furious jangling of the bell.

Its clangour finally ceased. A long silence. The wind whined, nudging at the windows, rattling their frames. And she was grateful for the wind, and the relentless rain, because surely he couldn't stand there forever, getting nowhere, getting drenched. Soon, surely, he would chuck in the sponge, admit defeat, and go.

"Judith!" But now it was a wail. A last, sad, token appeal. He was losing hope. She did not respond. And then she heard him say, quite loudly, for a man who had only himself to talk to, "Oh, bloody fucking hell." And he shuffled about a bit on the gravel, and then began to walk away down the path to the gate.

He was going at last. Leaving her alone.

She waited until the footsteps were almost inaudible, then rolled out from under the bed, crawled to the window, and under cover of Aunt Louise's curtains, took the most wary and cautious of peeps. He was already through the gate, and over the top of the escallonia hedge she could see the top of his head as he stumped disconsolately back to his bungalow.

He was gone. Relief rendered her weak as a kitten; she felt like a balloon with all the air let out, a wrinkled, wobbly scrap of coloured rubber. Her knees crumpled and she sank down onto the floor and, for a bit, she simply stayed there. She had won that skirmish, but it had been a bitter victory and she felt too drained, and had been too frightened, for any sort of triumph.

And she was cold. Judith was still soaked from her bicycle ride, and shivering, but lacking the strength in her limbs to get to her feet, get to the bathroom, put in the plug, and turn on the hot tap.

He was gone. Suddenly, it was all too much. She felt her face crumpling like a baby's. She leaned her head against the hard, polished side of Aunt Louise's dressing-table and let the tears, silently, stream down her cheeks.

The following afternoon, Aunt Louise drove Judith back to Saint Ursula's. Judith was dressed once more in school uniform, and the mid-term break was over.

"Hope you've enjoyed yourself."

"Very much, thank you."

"It was just unfortunate I had to leave you on Sunday, but I know you've never been a child who needs company all the time. Just as well. Can't stand demanding children. Pity about Heather Warren, but we'll make some plan during the Easter holidays."

Judith did not want to think about the Easter holidays.

She said, "I really like my bike."

"I'll keep an eye on it for you."

She couldn't think of anything else to say because the bike was really the only good thing that had happened during the weekend, and all she wanted, now, was to get back to normality, to the routine and the familiar surroundings of school.

The only thing that she really regretted was that she had never gone to call on Mr. Willis. There had been time and opportunity that morning, but she had made excuses to herself and let the chance slip. Friendship, she knew, should be constant, but somehow Billy Fawcett had spoiled even that.

Saint Ursula's
March 8th, 1936.

Dear Mummy and Dad,

I've missed a week again, because I was with Aunt Louise for half-term. Thank you for your letter. I am longing to hear about Singapore and your new house in Orchard Road. I am sure it will be lovely, and you'll soon get used to it being a bit hot and steamy. It will feel funny having yellow Chinese faces around you, instead of black Tamil faces. And at least Mummy won't have to drive a car, ever again.

The weather at the weekend wasn't very good. Aunt Louise bought me the bicycle. It is a green Raleigh. On Sunday she played golf with some friends, so I biked to Veglos Hill with a picnic. There were lots of primroses. I telephoned Heather but didn't see her because she was going to Bodmin to stay with her gran.

So much for the weekend. Nothing more that could be safely told. But the letter was not yet long enough, so she ploughed on.

It was quite fun coming back to school and seeing Loveday again. Her sister Athena has come back from Switzerland and was at Nancherrow for the weekend. She brought a boyfriend with her, but Loveday said he was dreadfully dull and not nearly as nice as Jeremy Wells.

Sorry this is such a short letter but I have to go and swot for my History Test.

With love from

Judith

Louise Forrester's golfing friends, Polly and John Richards, were an ex-naval couple, who, on retirement, turned their backs to Alverstoke and Newton Ferrars, and instead bought a solid stone house near Helston, with three acres of garden and commodious outbuildings. Polly Richards' father had been a successful brewer, and some of his wealth had obviously trickled down to her, for they enjoyed a far less penurious life-style than most of their pensioned contemporaries, and were able to employ a couple to care for them, a daily cleaner, and a full-time gardener. The couple were an ex–chief petty officer and his wife who rejoiced in the name of Makepeace, and the gardener was a silent, morose man who worked from dawn to dusk, when he put away his tools and sloped off to his badger's holt of a cottage tucked away beyond the glasshouses.

Untrammelled by domestic chores, the Richardses were able to enjoy a packed, active social life. They kept a yacht at Saint Mawes, and the summer months were totally occupied in sailing this craft around the inland waters of southern Cornwall, and racing her in various regattas. All through the year they had a stream of visitors to stay, and when they were neither sailing nor entertaining, they headed for the fairways and the bridge tables of the Penmarron Golf Club. It was thus that they had met Louise, and it was over many friendly tussles on the links that they had all become well-acquainted.

Polly telephoned Louise. After a few pleasantries, she got down to business.

"Frightfully short notice, but you couldn't come and play bridge tomorrow evening, could you? That's right, Wednesday the twenty-second."

Louise consulted her diary. Apart from a hair appointment, it was blank.

"How very kind. I'd love to."

"You are a brick. We've got an old chum of John's staying, and he's longing for a game. Could you be here at six? It's a bit early, but then we can have a rubber before dinner, and you won't be too late getting home. It's a hell of a drive, I'm afraid." Polly's breezy language went with her sailing, and she was legendary for the oaths that were clearly audible as their craft headed for some marker buoy, scudding, close-hauled, across the choppy grey waters of the Falmouth Passage.

"Don't worry your head about that. I shall look forward to it."

"See you tomorrow then."

And without further ado, Polly rang off.

It *was* a long drive, but worth the effort, as Louise knew it would be. A splendid evening. John Richards's friend was a Royal Marine General, a handsome man with a wicked eye, and plenty to say for himself. The drinks were lavish. The dinner, and the wine, excellent. As well, Louise held good cards all evening, and played them impeccably. With the last rubber played, the score was settled and small amounts of money changed hands. Louise found her purse and stowed away her winnings. The clock on the mantelpiece struck ten o'clock, and she snapped shut the clasp of her handbag and announced that it was time for her to set off for home. They pleaded with her to stay, to play one more rubber, to have one for the road, but, though tempted, she stuck to her guns and refused their kindly offers.

In the hall, John helped her into her fur coat, and after goodbyes had been said, accompanied her out into the dark, wet night, and stowed her safely in behind the wheel of her car.

"You'll be all right, Louise?"

"Right as rain."

"Drive carefully now."

"Thank you so much. A splendid evening."

She drove, with her windscreen wipers pumping to and fro, and the road ahead shining wetly in the beam of the headlights, black as satin. She went by way of Marazion, towards Penzance, and as she approached the turning that led onto the main highway for Porthkerris, decided, impulsively, that the night was so unpleasant and the drive so long, that she would take the shorter route, the narrow lane that led up and over the moor. It was an awkward road, high-hedged and winding, with blind corners and summits, but she knew it well, there would be no traffic and it cut at least five miles off her journey.

The decision made, she turned left instead of right and, moments later, turned again, up the steep, wooded incline that led to the empty downs. The sky was black and there was not a star to be seen.

Four miles ahead of Louise, and travelling in the same direction, Jimmy Jelks, at the wheel of a ramshackle truck, was on his way back to Pendeen. His father, Dick Jelks, farmed a down-trodden smallholding in that neighbourhood, kept pigs and hens, grew potatoes and broccoli, and was renowned for having the muckiest farmyard in the district. Jimmy was twenty-one and lived at home, bullied by both his parents and the butt of every cruel joke, but as he lacked both the wit and the expertise to go courting, it seemed unlikely that he would ever escape.

He had driven to Penzance early that afternoon, with a load of broccoli to sell at the market. He was meant to return as soon as this was safely accomplished, but his father was in a dirty temper, and so, with cash in his pocket, Jimmy was tempted to put off time, drifting around the market, and having a crack with any person who could be bothered to talk to him. Eventually, craving company, he had yielded to the temptation of the open door of the Saracen's Head, and there stayed till closing time.

His progress, now, was not speedy. Beneath him the old truck rattled and shook. Dick Jelks had bought it, fourth-hand, from a coal merchant, and from the start it had suffered from every sort of mechanical complaint. Windows, once opened, refused to close; handles fell from doors; the mudguards had succumbed to rust, and the radiator grille was tied on with binder wire. Starting the engine was a recurring battle of wills, involving a cranking handle, enormous physical exertion, and often painful injuries, such as sprained thumbs or agonizing clouts over the knee. Even when it finally shuddered into life, the truck stayed resolutely uncooperative, refusing to go into any forward gear higher than second, frequently boiling, blowing its ancient tyres, and backfiring with such explosive force that any person unfortunate enough to be standing nearby feared an instant heart attack.

Tonight, having stood in the rain all afternoon, it was behaving in a more pig-headed fashion than usual. The headlights, never very bright, seemed to be losing heart, achieving only a candle glow to show the way ahead. And from time to time the engine coughed, like a consumptive, and faltered, threatening to stop altogether. Painfully grinding up and down the undulating moorland was almost too much for it, and after hauling its way up a steepish hill and achieving the level ground which lay beyond it, it finally gave up the ghost. The lights died, the engine coughed its last, and the wheels, exhausted, rolled to a sudden stop.

Jimmy pulled on the handbrake and cursed. Outside, all was blackness and rain. He heard the thin keening wind; saw the pinprick light of a distant farmhouse, and knew that it was too far away to be of any use to him. He turned up his coat collar and, reaching for the starting handle, clambered down onto the road and went around the front of the truck to do battle. It was only when he had been cranking for five minutes, injured his shin, and bloodied his knuckles, that the truth dawned on his fuddled brain. The battery was flat and the bloody bitch of a truck was not going to move again. Almost in tears of rage and frustration, he flung the starting handle back into the cab, slammed the door shut, and with hands in his pockets and his shoulders hunched against the rain, set off to walk the seven miles back to Pendeen.

Louise Forrester, headed for home, found herself in a good mood; pleased that she had chosen to come this way, enjoying the challenge of the journey, the solitary isolation of the unlit country road, the gratification of being the only person out and about so late and on such a filthy night. As well, she loved to drive, and was always stimulated by the sensation of being in charge, in control, behind the wheel of her powerful car. Accelerating, she got a physical thrill from the response of the engine, and experienced a young man's excitement as she manoeuvred the Rover around narrow, tight corners without ever losing speed. All of it gave her a kick. She thought of the song, but could not remember the words, so made up some of her own—

"*I get a kick out of you*
Driving too fast with my life in the past . . ."

I am, she told herself, behaving as skittishly as that flighty creature, Biddy Somerville. But it had been a good evening. This exhilarating journey home, over the empty moors, was a fitting way to end the day. A flourish. She had never been a woman to do things by halves.

The road sank before her, winding down into a shallow valley. At the foot of this she crossed a small stone humpbacked bridge, and then began to climb again. She changed down to third and, its headlights pointing to the sky, the powerful car charged up the hill and was over the brow like a steeplechaser.

Her foot was still hard down on the accelerator. She saw the truck, unlit and abandoned, but only a split second before she hit it. The shattering crash, the noise of tearing metal and breaking glass, was horrendous, but Louise was not aware of anything. The impact caused her to be flung forwards, out of her seat, against and through the windscreen, and at the consequent post-mortem the police doctor gave it as his opinion that Mrs. Forrester had died instantly.

But it was impossible to be certain. Because, for perhaps half a minute after the collision, nothing much happened. Only splinters of glass trickled to the roadside and a wheel, askew in the air, slowly ceased to rotate. In the dark and the rain and the solitude, there had been no witness to the disaster, and so nobody to send for, nor bring, help. The shambles of the wreckage, lightless and torn and twisted almost beyond recognition, was simply *there*, unsuspected; the two shattered vehicles locked together like a pair of copulating dogs.

And then, with startling suddenness and a thud that boomed through the black night like a clap of thunder, the Rover's petrol tank ignited and blew up, and the flames exploded, consuming, staining the dark heavens with scarlet. The conflagration, like a warning beacon, alighted the world, and a dark cloud of evil-smelling smoke was blown across the sky, contaminating the sweet damp air with the stench of burning rubber.

Deirdre Ledingham opened the library door. She said, "So *there* you are . . ."

Judith looked up. It was a Thursday afternoon, and she had a free period and had come to the library to do some reading for an English literature essay she had to write on Elizabeth Barrett Browning. But she had been diverted by the latest issue of *The Illustrated London News*, which Miss Catto considered educational, and had delivered to Saint Ursula's every week. Its pages were devoted to a variety of subjects as well as news: archaeology; and horticulture; and nature articles, covering the life-styles of strange, tree-creeping creatures, and birds with names like the lesser-bar-tailed godwit. But Judith was not all that keen on zoology and had been deep in a disturbing account of the creation and development of the Hitler Youth in Germany. This movement was not, it seemed, a bit like Boy Scouts, who never appeared to do anything more sinister than put up tents, light campfires, and sing "Underneath the Spreading Chestnut Tree." Instead, the young lads seemed like soldiers, dressed in shorts and military caps and swastika armbands. Even their activities appeared arrogant and warlike, and there was one picture of a group of the handsome blond youngsters that filled Judith with a special foreboding. Because they should all have been playing cricket or football or climbing trees, but instead were marching at some civic ceremony, grim-faced and well-drilled as a squad of professional soldiers. She tried to imagine how she should feel, should such a parade come goose-stepping down Market Jew Street, and found the prospect unimaginably awful. And yet, in the photographed faces of the crowds gathered to watch the boys strut by, was nothing but pleasure and pride. This, it seemed, in Germany, was what ordinary people *wanted* . . .

". . . I've been looking for you everywhere."

Judith closed *The Illustrated London News*. "Why?" she asked. As the weeks of term had passed and the routine of school became as familiar as home, her confidence had grown and she had lost some of her awe of Deirdre Ledingham. Egged on by Loveday, who stood in awe of nobody, she had decided that Deirdre's bossy self-importance at times verged on the ridiculous. She was, as Loveday frequently pointed out, just another girl, for all her air of authority, her badges, and her thrusting bust. "What for?"

"Miss Catto wants to see you in her study."

"What about?"

"No idea. But you'd better not keep her waiting."

After that first interview, Judith was no longer terrified of Miss Catto, but even so, she had enough respect for the headmistress to do as she was told. She stacked her books and screwed the top on her fountain pen, and then went to the cloakroom to wash her hands and tidy her hair. Neat, and only slightly apprehensive, she knocked at Miss Catto's study door.

"Come in."

She was there, behind her desk, just as before. Only today it was grey and cloudy and the sun did not shine, and the flowers on her desk were not primroses but anemones. Judith loved anemones, with their pinks and purples and sea-greens. All the rich bold colours of the spectrum.

"Judith."

"Deirdre said you wanted to see me, Miss Catto."

"Yes, my dear, I do. Come and sit down."

A chair awaited her. She sat facing Miss Catto. This time there was to be no small talk. Miss Catto came straight to the point.

"The reason I sent for you has nothing to do with school, nor your work. It is about something quite different. But I am afraid it is going to come as something of a shock, so I want you to prepare yourself . . . You see . . . it's your Aunt Louise . . ."

Judith stopped listening. She knew instantly what Miss Catto was about to tell her. Aunt Louise was going to marry Billy Fawcett. The palms of her hands went clammy, and she could almost feel the blood drain from her cheeks. The nightmare was going to come true. The thing that she prayed would never happen, was happening . . .

Miss Catto's voice continued. Inattention was a cardinal sin. Judith pulled herself together and tried to concentrate on what her headmistress was saying. Something about last night. ". . . driving home, at about eleven o'clock . . . she was alone . . . nobody about . . ."

The truth dawned. She was talking about Aunt Louise and her car. Nothing to do with Billy Fawcett. Judith felt her lips part in a sigh of relief, and knew that the colour was coming back into her face in an almost shameful blush.

". . . an accident. A really terrible collision." Miss Catto paused, and Judith looked at her and caught on Miss Catto's calm features an expression of puzzlement and concern. "Are you all right, Judith?"

She nodded.

"You understand what I'm trying to tell you?"

She nodded again. Aunt Louise had had a car smash. That was what it was all about. Aunt Louise, driving, as always far too fast, overtaking on bends, scattering sheep or hens with a blast of her horn. But now, it seemed, her luck had run out. "She's all right, though, isn't she, Miss Catto?" Aunt Louise in the local hospital, with a bandage on her head, and her arm in a sling. That was all. Just wounded. "She is all right?"

"Oh, Judith, no. I'm afraid she's not. It was a fatal accident. She was killed instantly."

Judith stared at Miss Catto, her face filled with defiant disbelief, because she knew that something so violent and final simply couldn't be true. And then saw the pain and compassion in Miss Catto's eyes, and knew that it was. "That is what I have to tell you, my dear. Your Aunt Louise is dead."

Dead. Finished. Forever. Dead was a terrible word. Like the last tick of a clock, or the snip of a pair of scissors, severing a thread.

Aunt Louise.

She heard herself take a deep breath that sounded like a shudder. She said, very calmly, wanting to know, "How did it happen?"

"I told you. A collision."

"Where?"

"Up on the old road, the road that goes over the moor. A truck had broken down, been abandoned. No light. She drove into the back of it."

"Was she going very fast?"

"I don't know."

"She was always a terrible driver. She went terribly fast. She overtook things."

"I think, probably, that this accident was not her fault."

"Who found her?"

"There was a fire. It was seen, and the police were alerted."

"Was anyone else killed?"

"No. Your aunt was alone."

"Where had she been?"

"I think out to dinner with friends. Near Helston."

"Commander and Mrs. Richards. She used to play golf with them." She thought of Aunt Louise driving home through the darkness as she had driven herself countless times before. She looked at Miss Catto. "Who told you?"

"Mr. Baines."

Judith's mind was a blank. "Who's Mr. Baines?"

"He's your aunt's solicitor in Penzance. I believe he takes care of your mother's affairs as well."

She remembered Mr. Baines. "Does Mummy know that Aunt Louise has been killed?"

"Mr. Baines has sent your father a telegram. He will, naturally, follow this up with a letter. And I, of course, will write to your mother."

"But what about Edna and Hilda?" For the first time, real distress sounded in Judith's voice.

"Who are they?"

"Aunt Louise's cook and her housemaid. They're sisters. They've been with her for years . . . they'll be terribly upset."

"Yes, I'm afraid they are. They didn't realize that your aunt had not returned home. The first suspicion they had was when one of them took up her early-morning tea-tray, and found the bed unslept in."

"What did they do?"

"Very sensibly, they telephoned the vicar. And then the local constable went to call on them, and break the sad news. They were naturally very distressed, but have decided to stay together, in your aunt's house, for the time being."

The thought of Hilda and Edna, alone and bereaved in the empty house, comforting each other and drinking cups of tea, was somehow sadder than anything else. Without Aunt Louise, their lives would have no direction, no purpose. And it was all very well thinking they'll get other jobs, because they were not young and resilient like Phyllis, but middle-aged and unmarried, and hopeless on their own. And if they didn't get other jobs, where would they live? What would they do? They were inseparable. They could never be parted.

She said, "Will there be a funeral?"

"In due time, yes, of course."

"Will I have to go?"

"Only if you want to. But I think you should. And I shall of course come with you, and stand by you all the time."

"I've never been to a funeral."

Miss Catto fell silent. Then she rose to her feet and came out from behind her desk and crossed the room to the window, where she stood with her black gown bundled about her like a shawl, as though for comfort. For a little while she gazed through the window, at the damp and misty garden, the sight of which, Judith decided, offered no sort of solace.

Miss Catto, it appeared, was of like mind. "What a sad day," she remarked. She turned from the window and smiled. "Funerals are a part of death, Judith, as death is part of life. That is a desolate thing for someone of your age to come to terms with, but it is something that everybody has to do. And you're not alone. Because I am here to help you through it. To accept it. Because death really is part of life, in fact the only thing in life of which we can all be totally certain. But such words of comfort sound very banal when tragedy strikes so close to home, and so suddenly. You are being very brave, and unselfish. Thinking of others. But don't feel constrained. Don't keep your grief to yourself. I know I'm your headmistress, but just now I'm your friend. You can say what you want, what you think. And don't be afraid to cry."

But tears, with their easing, had never seemed further away.

"I'm all right."

"Good girl. Do you know what I think? I think it would be nice to have a cup of tea. Would you like that?"

Judith nodded. Miss Catto went to the side of the fireplace and pressed the bell. She said, "It's the classic remedy for everything, isn't it? A nice hot cup of tea. I can't think why I didn't think of it before." She did not return to her desk, but settled herself in the small armchair by the hearth. The fire was laid, but not lit, and without saying anything she reached for a box of matches and, leaning forward, struck a match, and kindled the crumpled newspaper and the dry sticks. Sitting back, she watched the flames catch and flicker over the coals. She said, "I only met your aunt a couple of times, but I liked her so much. There was no nonsense about her. Concerned and capable. A real person. I felt quite at ease knowing you were in her charge."

Which brought the conversation, quite naturally, to the vital question. Judith gazed out of the window, and tried to make her voice as casual as she could. "Where will I go now?"

"We must talk about that."

"I have Aunt Biddy."

"Of course. Mrs. Somerville, living in Plymouth. Your mother told me all about the Somervilles, and I have their address and their telephone number. You see, Judith, when parents are abroad, we have to be able to be in touch with all the close relations. Otherwise our responsibility would really be too great."

"Aunt Biddy always said I could go to her if I wanted. Does she know about Aunt Louise?"

"Not yet. I wanted to talk to you first. But I will tell her."

A knock sounded on the door. Miss Catto said, "Come in," and one of the housemaids put her head into the room. "Oh, Edith, how good of you. Could you bring us a tea-tray? Two cups, and perhaps some biscuits."

The girl said that she wouldn't be more than half a tick, and withdrew. Miss Catto continued as though there had been no interruption.

"Would you like to spend your holidays with your Aunt Biddy?"

"Yes. I would. I love her and Uncle Bob. They're really nice and fun. But the thing is, they won't be in Plymouth forever. Sooner or later, they'll leave Keyham and Uncle Bob will probably go back to sea. Aunt Biddy talked about buying a little house. They've never owned a place of their own . . ." Her voice trailed away.

"Is there anyone else?"

"There's Mrs. Warren. Heather Warren was my great friend at Porthkerris School. Mr. Warren's the grocer, and my mother liked them all very much. I'm sure, some time, I could go and be with them."

"Well, whatever." Miss Catto smiled. "We'll work something out. Just remember that you are surrounded by friends. Ah, here's our tea-tray. Thank you, Edith; just put it down on that table . . . Now, Judith, why don't you get off that uncomfortable chair and come and sit here, by the fire . . . ?"

So, Muriel Catto told herself, the worst is over, the sad news broken, and the child seemed to have accepted it, and kept her composure. Twice before in her career as a headmistress had she had to perform this unhappy task, telling one of her girls that either a mother or a father had died, and she was always left feeling like a murderer. Because the messenger becomes the murderer. Until the fatal words are spoken, the loved one concerned is still alive, waking, sleeping, going about his business, making telephone calls, writing letters, going for walks, breathing, seeing. It was the telling that killed.

From the start of her career, she had laid down rigid rules for herself; impartiality and not a hint of favouritism. But Judith, unconsciously, had somehow breached these defences, and strictly unmaternal as she was, Miss Catto found it troublingly hard to ignore this special interest and to turn her back to the child's appeal. She had settled well at Saint Ursula's, and seemed popular with her contemporaries, despite her very different upbringing and background. Her work was steady and satisfactory, and she did her best at games. The Carey-Lewis connection was a bonus, and even Matron had found no cause to complain of her behaviour.

And now this. A trauma that could well and truly rock the boat, cause deep withdrawal, and terrible inner disturbance. As she had sat at her desk, outwardly composed, but inwardly sick with apprehension, waiting for the child to knock at the door of the study, Muriel Catto had been mortified to find herself wishing that this shocking tragedy had happened to almost any other girl in her school.

It wasn't just that Judith was so isolated, with family abroad and no siblings for comfort or company. It was something to do with *her*. Her stoic acceptance of the long parting (not once had she indulged in tears or tantrums); a disarming directness, and a certain sweetness of disposition that had to be inbred, because Miss Catto knew that this was a quality which could not be taught.

As well, she found her appearance charming. All the natural disadvantages of the average teenager were there, the long gawky legs, the bony shoulders, the freckles and the over-large ears, but somehow, on Judith, they were not unattractive, simply engendered a certain coltish appeal. And there was more. Eyes that were truly beautiful. Grey-blue and very large, fringed with dark, bristly lashes, their pupils clear as crystal water. And, like a much younger child, every inner thought was mirrored on her expressive face, as though she had never learned the art of deviousness. Miss Catto prayed that she never would.

They drank the hot, comforting tea, and talked, not about Aunt Louise, but about Oxford, where Miss Catto had spent her childhood. ". . . such a wonderful place to be brought up. The city of dreaming spires and bells and bicycles and youth and infinite knowledge. We had an old house in the Banbury Road, so big and rambling, and it had a walled garden and a mulberry tree. My father was a Professor of Philosophy, and my mother was an academic as well, always writing, or working, or deep in research. In term time, the house was invaded by a constant stream of undergraduates, coming and going for tutorials, and I always remember the front door as being perpetually open, so that nobody ever had to ring the bell, and so consequently every room was swept by draughts." She smiled. "There's a smell, isn't there . . . an ambiance, about the house in which one lives as a small child. And you smell it again, unawares—old books and polish and old furniture, and the damp mustiness of ancient stone; and suddenly you're back there, and about eight years old."

Judith tried to imagine Miss Catto at eight years old, but failed. She said, "I know what you mean. In Colombo our house smelt of the sea, because we lived right on the ocean, and there was a temple-flower tree in the garden, and at night it smelt very sweet and strong. But there were other smells too. Disinfectant and drains, and the stuff Amah used to squirt to kill the bugs."

"Bugs! Horrible. I hate insects. Were there lots of bugs?"

"Yes. Mosquitoes and spiders and red ants. And sometimes snakes. Once we had a cobra in the garden and Dad shot it with his rifle. And tik polongas used to hide in the bathroom. They came up the drains. We had to be dreadfully careful because they're so poisonous."

"How frightening. I'm not very brave about snakes . . ."

"There were snake charmers in the Pettah when we went to shop. They sat on the grass cross-legged and blew pipes, and the snakes used to come writhing up out of baskets. Mummy hated them, but I loved to watch." Judith took another biscuit and ate it thoughtfully. She said, "I've never been to Oxford."

"I think you should go. To University, I mean. It would mean staying on here, and taking matriculation, but knowing your scholastic abilities, I think you should have no difficulty in passing the examination and getting an entry into Oxford."

"How long would I have to stay there?"

"Three years. But what an opportunity it would be for you. I can't think of anything more magical than being given three years just to immerse yourself in knowledge . . . and not algebra or zoology, neither of which I think you are particularly interested in . . . but maybe English literature and philosophy."

"Would it cost a lot of money?"

"It isn't cheap. But none of the best things in life come cheaply."

"I don't like asking for something my parents maybe couldn't afford . . ."

Miss Catto smiled. She said, "It was just a suggestion, an idea. We have plenty of time to work out practicalities. Now, would you like another cup of tea?"

"No, thank you. That was lovely."

A silence fell. Not constrained. Now, much more relaxed. Tea had been a good idea. Judith's natural colour had returned; the worst of shock was over. Time, now, to speak. To bring the conversation gradually round to the question that Miss Catto knew she had to ask.

She said, "If you want to, you know, you can always use my telephone in here, and speak to any of your friends. You must give me time to ring up Mrs. Somerville, and let her know the situation, but perhaps you might like to talk to Edna or Hilda, or any of your friends in Penmarron."

Judith, with her face turned to the flames of the fire, hesitated for a moment, and then shook her head. "No. I don't think so. Not just yet. But it's very kind of you."

"I think probably Mr. Baines will want to see and talk to you, but that won't happen for a day or so. And by then we should know any arrangements that have been made for the funeral."

Judith took a deep breath, and then let it all out again. She said, doubtfully, "Yes."

Miss Catto leaned back in her chair. She said, "I just have to ask you one more thing. Please don't think I'm intruding, and you don't have to tell me if you don't want to. But I have the feeling that when I began to tell you what had happened . . . you . . . you imagined it was going to be something quite different. I may of course be wrong." There was a long silence. Judith continued to stare into the fire. Then her hand went up, and she began to twist at a strand of hair that had escaped from its ribbon. "Was there something that was worrying you? What was it that caused you to look so frightened?"

Judith bit her lip, then mumbled something.

"I'm sorry," said Miss Catto. "I didn't hear."

"I thought she was going to get married."

Miss Catto, totally taken aback, could scarcely believe her ears. "*Married?* You thought Mrs. Forrester was going to get *married?* Whom did you think she was going to marry?"

"Colonel Fawcett."

"And who is Colonel Fawcett?"

"He's her neighbour." Touchingly, Judith corrected herself. "He *was* her neighbour. An old friend from India."

"And you, perhaps, didn't want her to marry him."

"No."

"You didn't like him."

"I hated him." She turned her head from the fire, and looked straight into the headmistress's eyes. "He was horrible. If he married Aunt Louise he would have come to live in her house. I know. I didn't want him there."

Miss Catto, instantly understanding the situation, stayed cool. This was no time for emotional sympathy.

"Did he bother you?"

"Yes."

"What did he do?"

"He took us to the cinema and he put his hand on my knee."

"Oh. I see."

"He did it twice. Right the way up my leg."

"Did you tell Mrs. Forrester?"

"No." Judith shook her head. "I couldn't."

"I don't think I could have told her either, had I been you. It's a very difficult situation." She smiled, somehow masking her inner fury at the whole tiresome, distasteful world of dirty old men. She said, "At Cambridge, we used to call them gropers or garter-snappers."

Judith's eyes widened. "You mean . . . you mean, it happened to *you?*"

"All young female undergraduates were considered fair game. We swiftly learned avoiding tactics, and developed our own defences. Of course, there were a lot of us girls, safety in numbers, and the comfort of confidantes. But you didn't have that reassurance, so it must have been very much worse for you."

"I didn't know what to do."

"I don't suppose you did."

"I don't *think* she would have married him, but once the idea got into my head, I couldn't get rid of it. It was always there. I didn't know what to do."

"Well, that is something you don't have to worry about any more. In a very drastic and tragic way, your problem has been solved. They always say that some good comes out of every situation, however devastating. And what a good thing you've told me. Now, you can get the whole sorry affair in perspective."

"If we go to the funeral, I expect he'll be there."

"I have no doubt that he will. And you shall point him out to me. You shall say, 'There is Colonel Fawcett,' and I shall have the pleasure of hitting him over the head with my umbrella."

"Will you *really?*"

"Probably not. Imagine the headlines in the *Western Morning News*. 'Local Headmistress Attacks Retired Colonel.' It wouldn't do much good for Saint Ursula's, would it?" Not much of a joke but, for the first time, she saw Judith, spontaneously, smile and then laugh. "That's better. Now"—she looked at her watch—"you must be off and I must get on with all I have to do. It's just about time for games. I expect you'd like to have a little chat with Loveday. I'll get Deirdre to tell Miss Fanshaw that you're both excused hockey, so that you can be together for a bit. Take a walk round the grounds, or go and climb a tree or sit in the sun-trap. You'll feel better when you've talked it all over with Loveday."

"I shan't tell her about Colonel Fawcett."

"No. I think we shall keep that to ourselves." She rose from her chair, and Judith, instantly, got to her feet. "Now, it's over. I am so sorry about your aunt, but you have taken it well. And you are not to fret about your future, because that is my responsibility. All I can do is assure you that you are in safe hands."

"Yes, Miss Catto. And thank you. And thank you for the tea."

"Off you go then . . ." But as Judith went through the door, she reverted. She was the headmistress again. ". . . remember not to run in the corridor."

Saturday, 28th March.

Engineer Captain's House
Keyham Terrace
Keyham
Plymouth.

My dear, poor Judith,

Just had a long telephone call with nice Miss Catto, who sounds dear and sympathetic. My darling, I am shattered for you, what a perfectly ghastly thing to happen to poor Louise; I always knew she drove like a Jehu but somehow never imagined anything would come of it. She always seemed to me to be indestructible, and although I was never very kind about her, I know that she was a good sort, despite her sometimes cutting tongue. Miss C. tells me that your parents have been informed, and that she's writing to your mother. Also asked if Bob and I could field you for Easter hols. Darling, I can't think of anything we'd like more, but we're devilled with problems. Your grandparents have both been ill, and I've been trying to keep an eye on them. As well, looking for a house in Devon to buy so that we can have some sort of permanency in our lives. Think I've found one, but it's going to need rebuilding before we can take possession. Finally, Uncle Bob leaves Keyham in June, and is joining HMS *Resolve* based at Invergordon on the Cromarty Firth, about a thousand miles in the far north. Nothing but rain and kilts and sporrans. It is not a shore job, so

I shall have to go and look for yet another house, to rent this time, so that I can be with him.

You'll gather from all this gabbling that I think we won't be able to have you for the Easter holidays, but by summer we should be more or less established, and please, please, come to us then. Miss Catto assures me that she'll see you are cared for, and she sounds so sensible that I shan't worry about you, but just look forward enormously to seeing you in the summer.

Dear pet, I am so sorry this has happened. Let me know when the funeral takes place, not that there is much likelihood that I shall be able to be present. My father is ill again, and my mother struggling to take care of him. Cries for help come all the time, so I must try to find some sort of a resident housekeeper to keep an eye on the old pair.

Uncle Bob joins me in sending our love. He says keep your chin up.

Always kisses,

Aunt Biddy

Sunday, 5th April.

Dear Mummy and Dad,

I know that you have got telegrams and that Miss Catto and Mr. Baines are both writing to you. It was dreadfully sad about Aunt Louise and I shall miss her very much, because she was so kind to me. I was homesick for you all when I first went to Windyridge for the half-term, but I very soon stopped because Aunt Louise was very good about everything and didn't fuss at me. I know she was a terrible driver, but Miss Catto said that the accident wasn't her fault, because this truck had been abandoned just over the brow of the hill, and she hit it.

As for me, please don't worry. I could have gone to Aunt Biddy for the Easter holidays, but she is very occupied just now with a new house which she has bought, and Grandfather Evans being ill. But I am sure that I could stay with the Warrens in Porthkerris for a bit, and Miss Catto has even mentioned going to Oxford to stay in the big house where her parents live. I would quite like that, because Miss Catto thinks I might do well enough in exams to get a place at Oxford University, so it would be interesting to see the town. And then I can go to Aunt Biddy in the summer.

I am so sorry for Edna and Hilda, but perhaps they will find another job where they can be together. It was horrible being told about Aunt Louise because a car smash is such a violent thing, and she wasn't very old. Miss Catto says that death is a part of life, but even so you don't want death to happen quite so quickly.

The funeral was last Thursday. Miss Catto said I didn't need to go if I didn't want to, but I thought I'd better. I wore uniform and Matron made me a black armband for mourning. Miss Catto said that she would take me, but Mr. Baines came in his car and took both of us. He was very nice to us both and I sat in the front beside him. The service was in Penmarron Church and there were lots of people there, a lot of whom I didn't know.

But we arrived just at the same time as the Warrens, and Mrs. Warren gave me a huge hug and introduced herself to Miss Catto, and said that any time I wanted, I could go and spend holidays with them. Wasn't that really kind of her?

In church, we sang "The Day Thou Gavest, Lord, Is Ended," and there were a great many flowers everywhere. The vicar said nice things about Aunt Louise. Hilda and Edna sat just behind us and cried, but their cousin was there with his motor car, and he took them away when the service was over. They were both in black and looked dreadfully miserable.

After the service, we all went out after the coffin. It was a very cold day, but a blue sky and a cold north wind blowing in from the sea. In the churchyard, all the grass on the top of the walls was blowing sideways and you could smell the sea and hear the rollers. I am glad it wasn't raining.

It was terrible seeing the coffin go down into the hole and knowing that Aunt Louise was in it. The vicar gave me some earth and I threw it in, and Miss Catto threw in a bunch of primroses and Mr. Baines a rose, which I thought was nice of him. He must have known how much Aunt Louise liked roses. It wasn't until that moment that I realized that she was really dead for ever. Then we all said goodbye to everybody and came back to Penzance and Mr. Baines took Miss Catto and me out to lunch at the Mitre, but I kept thinking of the day we had lunch there, Mummy, and missed you and wished you had been there.

Most of the village people were there, and I spoke to Mrs. Berry and Mrs. Southey. Mrs. Southey gave me a rather whiskery kiss.

Here, Judith became a bit stuck. Memories of the funeral were blurry. Other known faces had swum into her vision from time to time, but it was hard to put names to them. Billy Fawcett had been there, but she didn't even want to write his name. She had spied him, at the end of the service, as she stepped out into the aisle with Miss Catto behind her, and made her way out towards the main door. He was standing at the very back of the church. She saw him, and he was looking at her, and with a new courage, bolstered by the presence of her headmistress, she met his eye and stared him down. He turned away, but before he did this, she saw on his face an expression of pure hatred, directed at herself. The bolted doors of Windyridge were not forgotten, and his own humiliating defeat unforgiven. She did not care. In the churchyard, he was not amongst the mourners at the graveside. Offended and truculent, he had already taken himself off, and for this small mercy Judith felt grateful. But his was a recurring spectre, still haunting her dreams. Perhaps, with no Aunt Louise to keep an eye on him, keep him company, and pour free whisky down his thirsty throat, he would chuck his hand in, leave Cornwall, and go and find somewhere else to spend his twilight years. Scotland perhaps. There were lots of golf courses in Scotland. She wished he would go and live in Scotland, and then she would never, ever have to see him again. But then he probably didn't *know* anybody in Scotland; in truth, he was so horrible, she couldn't imagine him having a single friend anywhere. So, in all likelihood he would stay just where he was, dug in to his rented bungalow, haunting the club house in Penmarron like a lost dog, and from time to time driving himself to the shops of Porthkerris in order to stock up on the necessities of life. He would always be around, and she had the sense to realize that she would never be totally free of him until the day when he turned up his toes and died. Shivering in the graveyard wind, she found time to wish that it was *he* they were about to inter forever in his grave, and not Aunt Louise. It was all so dreadfully unfair. Why should Aunt Louise be snatched away to eternity while still in the prime of her useful and busy existence, while that gruesome old groper lived on, spared to go about his horrid business?

Unseemly reflections for such a sad and overwhelming occasion. But then she spied Mr. Willis, and was so grateful to see him there, she put Billy Fawcett out of her mind. Mr. Willis stood respectfully a little way off, shy of intruding into anybody's private sorrow. Shaved and scrubbed, he wore a shiny blue suit with straining buttons, and a collar that looked as though it were about to choke him. He carried his bowler hat, and Judith, who had remained dry-eyed all through the service, was touched to tears by the obvious trouble to which he had gone. Before going from the churchyard, she left Miss Catto and Mr. Baines, who were having a few words with the vicar, and made her way across the tufty grass between the ancient headstones to greet her old friend.

"Mr. Willis."

"Oh, my dear." He put his bowler on, in order to get it out of the way, and took both her hands in his own. "Some awful thing to happen. You all right, are you?"

"Yes, I'm all right. Thank you so much for being here."

"Awful shock when I heard the news. Went up to the pub Thursday evening, and Ted Barney told me then. Could hardly believe it . . . that softhead, Jimmy Jelks . . ."

"Mr. Willis. I never came to see you at half-term. I felt so badly. I meant to come . . . but somehow . . . I never did. I hope you weren't hurt . . ."

"No, I reckoned you'd have plenty to do without coming that long way down to the ferry."

"Next time I'm in Penmarron, I promise I'll come. I've got so much to tell you."

"How's your mother and Jess?"

"All right, as far as I know."

"Who's going to take care of you now?"

"Oh, Aunt Biddy in Plymouth, I expect. I'll be all right."

"Tragedy's bad enough, but this is cruel luck on you. Still, Great Reaper strikes, and there's not much we can do, is there?"

"No. No, there's not much. Mr. Willis, I have to go. They're waiting. I'm so glad I saw you." They were still holding hands. She looked at Mr. Willis and saw his eyes suddenly fill with tears. She leaned up and kissed his leathery cheek, which smelt of Lifebuoy soap and tobacco, all mixed up together.

"Goodbye, Mr. Willis."

"Goodbye, my handsome."

Recalling all this was a bit sad, because perhaps she wouldn't go to Penmarron ever again, and perhaps their goodbye at the funeral was to be forever. And she remembered further back, to many happy, stolen afternoons spent in his company. Fine days when he leaned against the rotted hulk of a rowboat, smoked his pipe and yarned companionably, while waiting for the tide to rise, and the coal-boats to move in over the sand-bar. And wet, cold winter days, which were even better, because then they fugged up together in his little shack, and brewed tea on the old pot-bellied stove.

But no time for brooding, because she had to finish her letter.

For a moment or two, she debated as to whether she should mention Mr. Willis's presence at the funeral. She had always kept him something of a secret from her mother, partly because she wanted no interference, and partly because of the doubtful status of the so-called Mrs. Willis. And then thought, oh, bother it, because really in the present circumstances Mr. Willis and his private life-style were no more important than a storm in a teacup. He was Judith's friend, and that was how it was going to stay. And if Mummy read between the lines and found some hidden and sinister inference, it would be six weeks before Judith got a letter in reply to this one, by which time the whole world might have changed.

Besides, she wanted to write about Mr. Willis.

> Mr. Willis was there too. Do you remember him? He's the ferryman and works for the Harbour Authority. He looked very smart and he had a bowler hat and he asked after you and Jess. I thought it was good of him to be there, and shave and dress himself up and everything.
>
> Tomorrow afternoon Mr. Baines is coming to school and I have to see him to talk about what he calls family affairs. I suppose to do with school and things, but have no idea what this means. I hope he doesn't use long words that I won't understand, and I just hope he is able to help Edna and Hilda get another position.
>
> And I hope you are all well, and that Dad isn't too unhappy about Aunt Louise. Miss Catto says she died so quickly she never knew what happened, and that she loved driving, but this isn't much comfort when you are so far away, and were so fond of each other. Please don't worry about me. We break up on Friday, 10th April.
>
> Lots of love,
>
> *Judith*

"Well, there you are, Judith . . ."

Mr. Baines, presumably with Miss Catto's permission, had already established himself behind her desk, and littered it with his briefcase and a lot of documents. He was a very tall man, with brindled hair like a rough-coated terrier, and enormous horn-rimmed spectacles, and in his tweed suit and checked shirt looked the very epitome of a successful country solicitor. His firm, of which he was one of the senior partners, had been long-established in Penzance, and occupied offices in an enviable Regency house in Alverton. Judith knew this because every Sunday the Saint Ursula's crocodile walked that way to church, and because she knew that the firm were the Dunbar family lawyers, had always taken time to admire the charming proportions of the little house, and to read the old names—Tregarthen, Opie & Baines—on the highly polished brass plate by the front door. She had, however, never met Mr. Baines until the day of Aunt Louise's funeral, when he had been extremely considerate and kindly, driving them in his car, and standing them lunch at the Mitre, and generally making the dismal day as bearable as he possibly could. Because of this, she felt, now, as though the social ice had already been broken, which was a good thing. She had no idea what he wanted to say to her, but at least they didn't have to edge into acquaintance-ship, and could dispense with the polite and time-consuming formalities which she imagined were the norm on such occasions. "How are you getting along?"

She told him that she was getting along very well, and he came out from behind the desk and brought forward a chair for her to sit on. Then he returned to Miss Catto's throne and settled himself once more at his papers.

"First of all, before anything else, I want to set your mind at rest about Edna and Hilda. I think I have found a position for them with an old client of mine who lives up near Truro. I'll arrange for the sisters to go for an interview, but if they take the job, I think they'll be very happy and comfort-able. A single lady, about the same age as Mrs. Forrester, and pleasant work-ing conditions." He smiled. When he smiled he looked much younger, and even quite attractive. "So you don't have to worry about them any more."

"Oh, thank you." Judith felt most grateful. "You are clever. It sounds abso-lutely right for them. And I know they would want to stay together."

"So that's one thing out of the way. The next is that you know I cabled your father to let him know about Mrs. Forrester? Well, I had a cable back a couple of days ago, and he sends you his love. He says he'll be writing to you. Have you written to your parents?"

"Yes, and I told them all about the funeral."

"Well done. A sad letter to have to compose." He moved a paper or two, getting things into order. For a moment it seemed as if he didn't quite know how to start. "Now. Just remind me. How old are you? Fourteen? Fifteen?"

Which seemed a funny thing to say. "I'll be fifteen in June."

"Ah, yes. My eldest girl is just eight. She's starting at Saint Ursula's next year. It is fortunate that you are already established here. You'll get an excel-lent education. Miss Catto and I were talking, and it is her opinion that you are University material." He smiled. "Would you like to go on to University?"

"I haven't really thought about it. I'm just afraid that it would be dreadfully expensive."

"Yes," said Mr. Baines. "I see." A silence fell, but before it could become uncomfortable, he pulled himself together, drew a folder towards him, picked up his fountain pen and said, "Well. Down to business."

Judith waited politely.

"Before she died, your aunt drew up a comprehensive will. Generous annuities have been arranged for Hilda and Edna. Everything else, her entire estate, she has left to you."

Judith continued to wait.

Mr. Baines took off his spectacles. His eyes, without them, wrinkled up in a peering fashion. Across the desk, she met his gaze. "All her worldly possessions."

Judith found her voice. "It sounds an awful lot."

"It is a lot," said Mr. Baines gently.

"All for me?"

"All for you."

"But . . ." She knew that she was behaving stupidly, yet Mr. Baines was being very patient. He waited, watching her. "But why me? Why not Dad? He's her brother."

"Your father has a sound job, a career, with a regular salary, recent promotion, and future security."

"But, I . . . well, I thought people like Aunt Louise, ladies on their own, left their money to charity, or cats' homes. Or the golf club. The golf club was always having whist drives or bridge afternoons to pay for new central heating, or cloakrooms or something."

Mr. Baines allowed himself a smile. "Perhaps your Aunt Louise had decided for herself that the cloakrooms were entirely adequate."

It was almost as though he didn't understand. "But why *me* . . . ?"

"She had no issue of her own, Judith. No children. No dependants. No family. Over the years, she told me a lot about herself. In her day, when she was a young woman, girls didn't have jobs or careers, and few were encouraged to go to University. If you were beautiful and wealthy, it didn't really matter, but for the ordinary, middle-class daughter, the only prospect of any sort of a life was marriage. Your aunt was neither wealthy nor beautiful. She told me this herself. In England, she had little success with young men, and so eventually her parents shipped her out to India to find a husband for herself. She remembered this without rancour, and yet as a sort of humiliation. She was only one of many . . . unattached, quite pretty girls, all sailing across the world with one thought in mind."

"You mean, getting married?"

"The worst was that they were known, collectively, as the Fishing Fleet, because they were on their way to fish for husbands."

"Aunt Louise would have hated that."

"In her case, the story had a happy ending, because she married Jack Forrester and shared many good years with him. She was lucky. But she knew others who had not fared so well."

"Do you think that she minded about not having children?"

"No, I don't think so."

"Then what are you trying to tell me?"

"Oh dear, I'm not doing this very well, am I? What I am trying to tell you is that your Aunt Louise was very fond of you. She saw, I think, a great potential. She did not want you to go through what she had to go through. She wanted you to have what she never had. The independence to be her own person, to make her own choices, and to do those things when she was young, with all her life before her."

"But she did. She married Jack Forrester and she had a lovely time in India."

"Yes. For her it worked. But she didn't want you, ever, to have to take that risk."

"I see." It all began to sound a bit overwhelming and something of a responsibility. Worrying, even.

"Could you say it all again? About the worldly possessions, I mean."

"Of course. She has left you her house, and everything in it. But, most important, her capital investments."

"But what would I do with her house?"

"I think it should be put on the market and the resultant sum of money invested." He laid down his pen and leaned forward, his arms crossed on the desk top.

"I can see you're having a bit of difficulty taking this all in, and I don't blame you. What you have to understand is that your Aunt Louise was a very wealthy lady. And I mean *very* wealthy."

"*Rich?*"

"Let's just use the word wealthy. 'Substantial' is another good word. She has left you substantially provided for. You probably had no idea of what she was worth because, although she lived comfortably, it was with no sort of ostentation."

"But . . ." It was puzzling. "The Dunbars were never rich. Mummy and Dad were forever talking about economizing, and I know my school uniform was dreadfully expensive . . ."

"Mrs. Forrester's fortune was not Dunbar money. Jack Forrester was a soldier, but as well a man of considerable private means. He had no brothers or sisters, and so everything he had he left to his wife. Your aunt. She, in turn, hands it on to you."

"Do you think she knew he was rich when she married him?"

Mr. Baines laughed. "Do you know, I don't imagine she had the faintest idea."

"It must have been a lovely surprise for her."

"Is it a lovely surprise for you?"

"I don't know. It's hard to imagine, exactly, what it all means." She frowned. "Mr. Baines, does Dad know about all this?"

"Not yet. I wanted to tell you first. I shall, of course, let him know the situation as soon as I return to my office. I shall send him a cable. And as for what it means, I shall tell you." He spoke with some relish. "It means security and independence for the rest of your life. You can see yourself through University, and if you marry, you need never be beholden to your husband. The Married Woman's Property Act, one of the best bits of legislature ever seen through Parliament, ensures that you will always be in control of your own affairs, able to deal with them and handle them by yourself, just as you see fit. Does the prospect alarm you?"

"A bit."

"Don't be alarmed. Money is only as good as the people who possess it. It can be squandered and wasted, or it can be used prudently, to enrich and enhance. However, for the time being, you don't have to worry about responsibility. Until you are twenty-one, the inheritance will be put in trust and administered by trustees. I shall be one of them, and I thought perhaps we should ask Captain Somerville to join the team."

"Uncle Bob?"

"Does that sound a good idea?"

"Yes." Mr. Baines had obviously done his homework. "Of course."

"I'll get something drawn up. And meantime, I'll arrange for some sort of allowance for you. Now you're on your own, you'll need to buy clothes, books, birthday presents for friends . . . all the small expenditures that parents or guardians normally deal with. You're too young for a cheque-book, but in another year you should qualify for that. So, perhaps, a post-office savings account. I'll see to that."

"Thank you very much."

"You'll be able to go shopping. All women want to go shopping. I'm sure there must be something that you've been yearning for."

"I wanted a bicycle for ages, but Aunt Louise bought me one."

"Is there nothing else?"

"Well . . . I *am* saving up for a gramophone, but I haven't got very far."

"You can buy a gramophone," Mr. Baines told her. "And a stack of records."

She was charmed. "Could I really? Would I be allowed? Would you let me?"

"Why not? It's a modest-enough request. And perhaps there is something in Mrs. Forrester's house that you would like to keep? You are far too young to be lumbered with bricks and mortar, or a collection of furniture, but maybe a little piece of china, or a pretty clock . . . ?"

"No." She had her desk, her books, her bicycle (at Windyridge). Her Chinese box (at Nancherrow). Extra possessions would only become a burden. She thought about the elephant's-foot umbrella stand, the tiger-skin rugs, the horns of the deer, Uncle Jack's golf trophies, and knew that she wanted none of them. Windyridge had been a house filled with another person's memories. Nothing in it meant anything to her. "No. There's nothing I want to keep."

"Right." He started to gather together his documents. "That's it then. No more questions?"

"I don't think so."

"If you do think of anything, you can telephone me. But we'll certainly have another meeting, and I'll be able then to fill you in with details . . ."

At this moment the door of the study opened, and they were joined by Miss Catto, her black gown flying, and the usual bundle of exercise books tucked under her arm. Judith, instinctively, sprang to her feet. Miss Catto looked from her to Mr. Baines. "Not interrupting, am I? Given you enough time?"

Mr. Baines, too, stood, towering over the pair of them. "Plenty of time. All has been explained, if not discussed. You may once more take possession of your study. And thank you for letting us have the use of it."

"What about a cup of tea?"

"Thank you, but I must get back to my office."

"Very well. Judith, don't go just yet. I want a word with you."

Mr. Baines had packed his briefcase, and now buckled the strap. He came around from behind the desk.

"Goodbye then, Judith." He beamed benevolently down on her. "For the time being."

"Goodbye, Mr. Baines."

"And thank you again, Miss Catto."

Judith went to open the door for him, and he loped from the room. She closed the door behind him, and turned to face her headmistress. There was a moment's pause, and then Miss Catto said, "Well?"

"Well what, Miss Catto?"

"How does it feel to know that University is no longer a financial problem, because security so simplifies life?"

"I never knew Aunt Louise was wealthy."

"It was one of her greatest assets. A total lack of pretension." Miss Catto dumped the exercise books onto her desk, then turned to lean against it, so that her eyes were on a level with Judith's. "I think your aunt has paid you a great compliment. She knew that you are not, and will never be, a fool."

"Mr. Baines says I can buy a gramophone."

"Is that what you want?"

"I'm saving up for one. And a collection of records like Uncle Bob's."

"You are right. Listening to music comes second only to reading." She smiled. "I have more news for you. I think tonight in your diary you are going to write, 'This Is My Lucky Day.' I spoke to my mother on the telephone and she was charmed at the thought of your coming to spend part of the Easter holidays, or even all of them, at our house in Oxford. But you've had another invitation, and you must feel perfectly free to accept this if you want. I have had a long chat, again on the telephone, with Mrs. Carey-Lewis. She was deeply distressed to hear about Mrs. Forrester's death . . . she read the news and the account of the funeral in *The Cornish Guardian*, and rang me right away. And she says that of course you must go to Nancherrow for the whole of the Easter holidays. She has space and more to spare, she is very fond of you, and they would consider it a great honour if you would accept their invitation." She paused, and then smiled. "You look so astonished! Are you pleased, as well?"

"*Yes*. Yes. But, your mother . . ."

"Oh, my dear, you would be so welcome in Oxford. At any time. But I think Nancherrow would probably be much more fun. I know what pleasure you and Loveday find in each other's company. So, for once, don't think about anybody but yourself. You must do what *you* want to do. Really."

Nancherrow. A month at Nancherrow with the Carey-Lewises. It was like being offered a holiday in Paradise, unthought of and unimagined, but at the same time Judith found herself terrified of behaving in an ungrateful or churlish manner. "I . . . I don't know what to say . . ."

Miss Catto, recognizing an agonizing dilemma, took matters into her own capable hands. Laughing, she said, "What a decision to have to take! So why don't I take it for you? Go to Nancherrow for Easter, and later on, perhaps, you can come and spend a few days with us all in Oxford. There. A compromise. Life is made up of compromises. And I don't blame you a bit for wanting so much to go to Nancherrow. It's a dream of a place, and Colonel and Mrs. Carey-Lewis I am sure are the most kind and generous of hosts."

"Yes." It was said. "Yes, I would like to go."

"Then you shall. I'll speak to Mrs. Carey-Lewis and accept, conditionally, on your behalf."

Judith frowned. "Conditionally?"

"I must square things off with your mother. Get her permission. But I can send a cable and we should have her reply in a day or so."

"I'm sure she'll say yes."

"I'm sure she will." But Judith was frowning. "Is something else worrying you?"

"No, it's just that . . . all my things. Everything I have is at Aunt Louise's house."

"I mentioned that to Mrs. Carey-Lewis, and she says that they will take care of all of that. The Colonel will send one of his farm lorries over to Mrs. Forrester's, and take it all back to Nancherrow. Mrs. Carey-Lewis told me that you already have your own bedroom there, and even one or two of your possessions, and swears that there is plenty of room for everything else."

"Even my desk and my bicycle?"

"Even your desk and your bicycle."

"It's as though I'm going to *live* with them."

"Wherever you go, Judith, you must have a base. That doesn't mean that you aren't free to accept other invitations. It just means that, while you're growing up, you'll always have a home to go back to."

"I don't know how anybody can be so kind."

"People are kind."

"I really want to come to Oxford. One day."

"And so you shall. There's just one more thing. Because of your aunt's generosity, and because one day you will be a woman of some substance, you need never feel that because you are accepting generosity and hospitality, you are at the same time accepting charity. You are totally independent. Being financially secure is truly a life-enhancer; it sweetly oils the wheels of life. But remember: to talk of money, the excess of it or the lack of it, is vulgar to the extreme. One either boasts or whines, and neither makes for good conversation. Do you understand what I am trying to say?"

"Yes, Miss Catto."

"Good girl. The most important thing to remember, to be grateful for, is that your aunt has bequeathed to you not just her worldly goods, but a privilege that comes to few. And that is the right to be yourself. An entity. A person. Living life on your own terms with no other person to answer to. You probably won't appreciate this until you are older, but I promise you that one day you will realize the importance of what I am telling you. Now, I've got history essays to correct, and you must be on your way." She looked at her wristwatch. "A quarter past three. You've missed your last form period, but it isn't time yet for games, so you've a little time in hand. You can go up to the library and do some reading . . ."

The very idea of going to the library was claustrophobic; the stuffy, dusty room, the light filtering down from the closed windows, the smell of old books, the heavy silence. (Talking was forbidden.) If she had to go and sit in the library, she would suffocate. With the courage of desperation, she said, "Miss Catto."

"What is it?"

"Instead of going to the library . . . what I would really like, more than anything, is to go somewhere and just be by myself. I mean really by myself. I would like to go and look at the sea and think and get used to everything that's happened. Just for an hour, until tea-time. If I could go down to the sea . . . ?"

Miss Catto, for all her composure, bucked visibly at this outrageous and unheard-of request.

"Go to the *sea*? By *yourself*? But that means walking through the town."

"I know we're not allowed to, but couldn't I, just this once? Please. I won't talk to anybody or eat sweets or anything. I just want to have a bit of . . ." She had been going to say *peace*, but this seemed a bit rude, so she substituted "time to myself" instead. "Please," she said again, and Miss Catto, against all instinct, recognized a cry from the heart.

But still she hesitated. It meant breaking one of her strictest school rules. The child would be seen, people would talk . . .

"Please."

Miss Catto, with much reluctance, gave in. "Very well. But only once and never again. And only because you've plenty to think about, and I appreciate that you need the time to sort it all out. But don't tell anybody, not even Loveday Carey-Lewis, that I allowed you. And you must be back in good time for tea. And no sneaking into cafés for ice-creams."

"I promise."

Miss Catto sighed deeply. "Off you go then, but I think I must be mad."

"No," Judith told her, "not mad." And escaped before the headmistress could change her mind.

She walked out of the school gates into a pale, still afternoon, not bright, but with the clouds somehow lit up by the hidden sun. There was no wind, but from the south there moved a milky air that was not strong enough even to stir the branches of trees. Most trees were budding, but some were still bare, and it was so quiet that a dog barking or a car starting split the hush like an echo. She walked and the little town was deserted. Later, when the schools emptied, it would be loud with the sparrow-chatter of homebound children, larking on the pavements, and kicking stones into the gutters, but at this hour only a few tardy shoppers stood about, waiting for buses, or staring at the window of the pork-butchers, trying to decide what to buy for the evening meal. On the stone seat outside the bank, a couple of old men sat in wordless communion, leaning on their sticks, and when the bank clock struck the half hour, a gathering of pigeons rose and fluttered about for a bit in an agitated sort of way before settling once more, to strut and preen.

The pigeons made her think of Nancherrow, and the best was knowing that she was going back, to stay for the whole of the Easter holidays; and she was going not because Loveday had pleaded with her parents, but because Diana and Colonel Carey-Lewis had asked her, had liked her, had wanted her to return. She would go back to the pink bedroom that Diana had promised would always be hers, where the window looked down onto the courtyard and the doves, and where her Chinese box awaited her. And she would wear Athena's clothes and become, once more, that other person.

But the strange thing was that she felt like that other person even now, because everything, already, was different. In the stilled streets, with not another child to be seen, her solitude changed the look and the feel of everything. Familiar buildings presented themselves in an entirely new light, as though she had never been in the town before, exploring some foreign city for the first time. It was like having a third eye, for perceiving light and shade and stone and shape; an unexpected alley, the stealth of a darting black cat. In shop windows, she saw herself trudging by, dressed in the bottle-green tweed coat and horrible hat that proclaimed her as a Saint Ursula's child. But within, she was that real person, that sleek and adult being who wore cashmere jerseys and would one day emerge, like a butterfly escaping its chrysalis.

She turned down Chapel Street, by the antique shops and the Mitre Hotel, and the carpet shop. Outside this stood rolls of Axminster and patterned linoleum, and the man who sold second-hand junk was sitting in an armchair by his doorway smoking a pipe and waiting for custom which, today, was clearly not going to arrive. As Judith went by, he took his pipe out of his

mouth, gave her a crack of his head, and said "Hullo," and she would have
stopped to talk had she not given her promise to Miss Catto.

At the end of Chapel Street a cobbled ramp led down to the harbour. The
oily tide was in, and the fishing boats moved gently, as though breathing,
their masts on a level with the road. There was a strong smell of fish and salt
and sea-wrack, and on the docks men were working, baiting lines for the
night's catch.

For a bit she watched them. She thought about Aunt Louise, and tried to
feel genuinely grateful, though sad, but was incapable of feeling anything very
much. She thought about being rich. No, not rich. Mr. Baines had eschewed
that vulgar word. Very wealthy, he had said. I am very wealthy. If I wanted I
could probably buy . . . that fishing boat. But she didn't want a boat any more
than she wanted a horse. So, what did she want, above all else? Roots, perhaps. A home and a family and a place to go to that was forever. Belonging.
Not just staying with the Carey-Lewises, or Aunt Biddy, or Miss Catto, or
even the cheerful Warren family. But all the money in the world couldn't buy
roots, and she knew *that* if she knew nothing else, so she cast about for other
mad extravagances. A car. When she was old enough, she could buy a car.
Or a house. A house was a new and beguiling fantasy. Not Windyridge, which
she had never much liked anyway, but a granite barn, or a stone cottage with
a palm tree in the garden. It would face the sea and have an outside staircase,
and there would be geraniums all the way up the steps. Geraniums in earthenware pots. And cats. And a dog or two. And inside there would be a stove
like Mr. Willis's, and she would cook things.

But that was in the future. What for *now?* She was going to be able to buy
a gramophone, but surely there were other heart's desires to be fulfilled. In
the end, she decided that perhaps she would have her hair cut, in a page-boy
bob like Ginger Rogers's. And buy green knee-socks to wear at school instead
of stuffy brown lisle stockings. Some time, she would go to Medways and buy
the socks for herself. With her own money.

She left the harbour and the boats and walked on, along the edge of the
sea, past the outdoor swimming pool, and onto the Promenade. Here were
shelters where people could sit out of the wind and feed crusts to the ravenous
gulls, and on the far side of the road, hotels, white as wedding cakes, stared,
with blank windows, out to sea. She leaned on the ornate iron railings and
gazed down at the stony beach and the silvery mill-pond ocean. Tiny waves
ran up onto the shingle, and broke, and were sucked away again, dragging a
rattle of pebbles behind them. It was rather a dull beach, not nearly as spectacular as Penmarron, nor as beautiful as the cove at Nancherrow, but the sea
was constant and changeless, like the very best, most reliable sort of friend.
It made her feel strong enough to try to sort out some of the momentous
confusion of the day.

The right to be yourself, an entity, a person. That was Miss Catto, with her
M.A. (Cantab) and her self-sufficiency and her fierce independence. Perhaps
she would become like Miss Catto, do brilliantly at University, achieve a first

or even an honours degree, and become a headmistress. But she didn't really want to be a headmistress. Any more than she wanted to be a wife.

If you marry, you need never be beholden to your husband. That was Mr. Baines who, presumably, knew all about such matters. But marriage, with its complications, wasn't something that, at the moment, Judith felt like contemplating. She was pretty certain that it involved things that went on in a double bed, and the memory of Billy Fawcett's groping hands (although set into brisk perspective by Miss Catto herself) was still vivid enough to put her off the thought of any sort of physical contact with men. Of course, if you married, it would obviously be a very special man, but even so, none of it, veiled in her own total incomprehension, presented the smallest likelihood of pleasure.

Perhaps she would never get married, but that wasn't an immediate problem, and so not much point in bothering over it. For a bit it was simply going to have to be a case of taking one thing at a time. Easter holidays at Nancherrow, and then back to school. School for four years, and after that, with a bit of luck, a voyage to Singapore. The family once more, Mummy and Dad and Jess, and the lovely blazing sunshine of the East, and the smells of the streets and the scents of the night, and the dark velvet skies, like jewel boxes filled with diamond stars. After Singapore, perhaps England again. Oxford or Cambridge. A bicycle in the High, or punting on the Backs. Her imagination ran out of images. She found herself yawning.

She was weary. Tired of being a grown-up, with all a grown-up's decisions and dilemmas. She wanted Loveday. To giggle and whisper with, and to concoct plans for their time together at Nancherrow. As well, she was hungry, so that it was quite a relief to hear, from behind her, from the top of the town, the bank clock strike the hour of four. Time to start back if she was to get any tea. Bread and butter, jam if they were lucky, and heavy cake. Tea with Loveday suddenly seemed very appealing. She turned her back on the sea, crossed the road, and set out at a brisk trot on the long walk back to school.

Diana Carey-Lewis hated, above all things, writing letters. Even scribbling a postcard to thank for a dinner-party or a weekend was a task that she habitually put off for as long as possible, and almost all of her day-to-day business was conducted on that admirable invention, the telephone. But Edgar was insisting that she simply had to write to Judith's mother, Molly Dunbar.

"Why do I have to write to her?"

"Because you have to offer your condolences on the death of Mrs. Forrester, and because it is only thoughtful and polite to reassure her that we shall take care of her daughter."

"I'm sure she needs no reassurances from me. Miss Catto will have made all the right noises, in her usual estimable fashion."

"That is not the point, Diana my darling. You must write *yourself*. I am sure Mrs. Dunbar will be expecting some sort of contact, and it's up to you to start the ball rolling."

"Why can't I ring her up?"

"In Singapore? Because you can't."

"I could send her a cable." She thought about this, and then began to giggle. "How about,

'*Faint not, nor fear;*
Your child is here,
Being fed on sweets
and ginger beer . . . ?' "

But Edgar was not amused. "Don't be facetious, Diana."

"Why can't *you* write? You know I hate writing letters."

"Because *you* have to do it. Do it this morning, and get it over with and be sure to be tactful and gentle and sympathetic."

And so here she was, martyred, sitting at her desk and summoning the energy to get on with the tedious task. Reluctantly she reached for a sheet of her thick, blue-embossed writing-paper, took up her wide-nibbed fountain pen, and started in. Once begun, and with a growing sensation of virtue, she proceeded to cover sheet after sheet of paper with her enormous and almost illegible scrawl. There was, after all, no point in doing things by halves.

Nancherrow,
Rosemullion,
Cornwall. Friday 10th April.

Dear Mrs. Dunbar,

I was so dreadfully sorry to read in the paper about the death of your sister-in-law, Mrs. Forrester. I did not know her personally, but can perfectly comprehend your shock and sadness when the news reached you. It is difficult for me to write of such matters when we have never been formally introduced, but please know that I and my husband both send you and Mr. Dunbar our deepest sympathy in your tragic loss.

We have, however, met. Just the once, when we were buying school uniforms for our offspring in Medways in Penzance. I remember the occasion well, and hope that you do not feel that this letter comes from a total stranger.

I have invited Judith to come and spend the Easter holidays with us. We have already had her to stay for a weekend and she was a charming guest and a perfect companion for my own naughty Loveday. Our house is large, with many guest bedrooms, and Judith already has made herself at home in my pretty pink room, and this will now be hers, for as long as she wants. Edgar, my husband, is arranging for all her possessions to be conveyed from Windyridge to here. One of the men will go over in a farm lorry, and I am sure Mrs. Forrester's maids, who are still living there, will help to pack up all Judith's clothes and other bits and pieces.

I promise you that she will be loved and cared for. But not processed. I know she has relations in Plymouth and grandparents in Devon, whom she will probably wish to visit. As well, an old school friend in Porthkerris, and Miss Catto, I know, would be happy to take her home to Oxford at any time. But it is good for Judith to feel that she has some sort of security, and Edgar and I will do our best to see that she gets this.

Please don't imagine that her being here is going to cause extra trouble or work. We have plenty of staff and Mary Millyway, who was Loveday's nanny, is still with us. She keeps an eye on the girls, and sees to their well-being, and if I am in London, which I frequently am, then my darling Mary Millyway is a great deal more responsible than silly I could ever be.

If I am in London, which I frequently am . . . Diana's concentration wandered. She laid down her pen and leaned back in her chair, and gazed from the window at the misty April garden, the drifts of daffodils, the fresh young green of the trees, the hazy sea. Right now, with the Easter holidays almost upon her, was not the time to escape, but she had not been to London for too long, and all at once, like a drug, she craved simply to take off.

London was glamour, excitement, old friends, shops, theatres, galleries, music. Dining at the Berkeley and the Ritz; motoring down to Ascot for Gold Cup Day; lunching in clandestine fashion at the White Tower with some other woman's husband; or dancing the small hours away at the Mirabelle, the Bagatelle, or the Four Hundred.

Cornwall was, of course, home; but Nancherrow belonged to Edgar. Cornwall was family, children, servants, guests; but London was her own, and hers alone. Diana had been an only child, with immensely wealthy, older parents. When her father died, his estate in Gloucestershire and the tall house in Berkeley Square were both inherited, along with his title, Lord Awliscombe, by a distant male cousin. But, on her marriage at seventeen to Edgar Carey-Lewis, part of Diana's considerable dowry had included the mews cottage off Cadogan Square. "You'll be living in Cornwall," her father had told her, "but bricks and mortar is always a good investment. And it sometimes makes sense to have a bolt-hole of your own." She did not question the reasoning behind this statement, but never ceased to be thankful for his foresight and perception. Without it, sometimes she wondered if she would have survived, because it was only there, within the miniature walls of her own little house, that she could truly feel that she belonged to herself.

A scrap of music slipped into her head. A wistful Noël Coward song, to which she and Tommy Mortimer had danced during their last evening to-gether at Quaglino's.

I believe
The more you love a man
The more you give your heart
The more you have to lose . . .

She sighed. When the Easter holidays are over, she promised herself, I shall go. I shall take Pekoe and my Bentley and I shall drive to London. Something to think about. Something to look forward to. Life was nothing without something to look forward to. Cheered by the prospect, she picked up her pen once more, and settled down to complete her letter to Molly Dunbar.

> So please don't worry about a thing. Judith will be happy, I am sure. During the holidays, the house is always filled with friends and family, and if she falls ill or comes out in spots, I shall let you know instantly.
>
> I hope you are enjoying Singapore and your new house. It must be lovely to be warm all the time.
>
> With best wishes,
> Yours,
>
> *Diana Carey-Lewis*

Finished. She blotted her signature, and skimmed through the pages she had covered, then folded them into a thick wedge and jammed them into an envelope. She licked the flap and thumped it down with her fist, and then wrote the address, which Miss Catto had dictated to her over the telephone.

All done. Duty honoured. Edgar would be delighted with her. She got up from her desk, and Pekoe unwound himself from her feet, and together they went from the room, down the long passage to the hall. Here, on the round table in the centre of the floor, stood a silver salver, its purpose expressly for the collection of mail. She tossed the letter down upon it. Sooner or later, somebody, probably Nettlebed or Edgar, would find it, stamp it, and post it.

> *I believe*
> *The more you love a man*
> *The more you give your heart*
> *The more you have to lose.*

All done. And in a month's time, she would be on her way to London. Suddenly light-hearted, she stooped and gathered Pekoe into her arms and kissed the top of his sweet, smooth head. "And you'll come with me," she promised him, and together they went out through the front door and into the cool, damp freshness of the April morning.

Saint Ursula's,
Saturday, 11th April 1936.

Dear Mummy and Dad,

> Thank you for sending the cable to Miss Catto and saying that I can spend Easter with the Carey-Lewises. Miss Catto was very kind as I told

you and said I could stay with her parents in Oxford, but she has postponed the invitation, and says I can go another time, so is not offended. In fact, she made the decision for me.

This is the first day of the holidays and it's ten-thirty in the morning, but I am still here, and someone from Nancherrow is going to come and collect me at eleven. My luggage is all sitting outside the front door, but it's not raining, so that's all right. It is funny being in school with only a few members of staff, it feels quite different, and I am writing this in the Junior Common Room without another soul about. Being on one's own makes everybody much nicer, as though you were a proper person and not just a girl. The funny thing is that everything smells quite different too, not of other people and chalk dust, but of the odd-job-man's smelly pipe. He comes in to screw on door handles and fix windows and he smokes this noxious old pipe all the time.

The reason I didn't go home yesterday, with Loveday, is because Mr. Baines wanted to take me shopping in Truro to buy a gramophone. He says he has let you know that Aunt Louise very kindly left me a legacy in her Will. I can't believe it yet and it's going to take some getting used to. I feel a bit badly about Jess, but I suppose at the moment she is too little to feel cross about something like that. Anyway, Mr. Baines came yesterday afternoon, and we drove to Truro. I'd never been there before, and it is beautiful and very old, with a cathedral and lots of little narrow streets, and the end of the river snaking up, with boats moored. Lots of trees going down to the water, and a Bishop's palace. When we'd done the shopping (gramophone and three records), we went to the Red Lion for tea, and he explained that I must have an allowance, and he's opened a post-office savings account, and is going to put *five pounds* every month into it.

It seems a dreadful lot, but I don't suppose I shall spend it but save it up and then I will get Interest. He explained it all to me. He is so nice and I don't feel a bit shy with him. Afterwards we came back to Penzance and he took me home and I met his family. A lot of small children making the most dreadful noise, and the baby kept spitting out its bread and butter and spilling its milk. Even worse than Jess at her naughtiest. He thinks that Windyridge should be sold. He's found another job for Hilda and Edna, and—

"Judith!" Matron, in her usual bossy fluster. "For heaven's sake. I've been looking all over for you. What are you doing? The Nancherrow car is there, and they're waiting. Now hurry up."

Judith, so rudely interrupted, sprang to her feet, trying to gather up the pages of her letter and screw the cap onto her fountain pen all at the same time. "Sorry, Matron. I was just writing to my mother . . ."

". . . never known such a girl. There's no time to finish, so put it away, and come now. Have you got your coat and hat? And all your bits and pieces . . . ?"

Her impatience was catching. Judith bundled the unfinished letter into her attaché case, put away her pen, and dealt with the locks, and Matron scooped it up, almost before it was closed. By the time Judith had pulled on her coat and jammed on her hat, Matron was on her way, a bustle of starched apron, out of the door and down the long polished corridor. Judith had to sprint to keep up with her. Down the stairs, through the dining-room, the hall, out of the open front door.

A split second in which to recognize that it was a beautiful morning, with a starch-blue sky and sailing clouds and the sweet smell of the rain which had fallen during the night. Her luggage had already been disposed of and the car waited, in splendid isolation, in the centre of the gravel. Not the Daimler nor the Bentley, but an old shooting-brake of huge proportions, panelled in wood and built high off the ground, like a bus. Beside it, leaning against the bonnet and yarning companionably, stood two male figures. One was Palmer, one of the Nancherrow gardeners, wearing his old working clothes and, in deference to the occasion, a battered chauffeur's cap. The other was a stranger, young and blond, dressed in a white polo-necked pull-over and a pair of shapeless corduroys. A stranger. But when he saw Judith and Matron emerge through the door, he pushed himself away from the shooting-brake and came across the gravel to meet them, and as he came, Judith realized that it wasn't a stranger at all, because she recognized him from the many photographs which stood about at Nancherrow. This was Edward. Loveday's brother. Edward Carey-Lewis.

He said, "Hello there." He held out his hand. "You're Judith. How do you do? I'm Edward."

He had his mother's blue eyes, and strong, chunky features. Full-grown and broad-shouldered, he still wore the youthful face of a boy, for his skin was tanned and very smooth and fresh-complexioned, and his friendly grin was a spontaneous flash of even white teeth. Despite the informality of his clothes, and his scruffy old leather shoes, there was a lovely cleanness about him, like a shirt that has been bleached and hung in the sunshine to dry. His appearance was so unexpected and so glamorously adult that Judith wished that she had not had to jam her hideous hat on her head in such a hurry, and had taken time to comb her hair.

But, politely, she shook his hand. "Hello."

"We thought you'd forgotten to come. We're early, I know, but we've got some things to do in Penzance. Now, everything's in the car. Are you ready?"

"Yes, of course. Goodbye, Matron."

"Goodbye, dear." Matron's eyes, behind their spectacles, gleamed with the vicarious thrill of a brush with upper-class life; the shooting-brake, the chauffeur, the handsome and confident young man. "Have a lovely holiday now."

"Yes, I will, and the same to you . . ."

"Thank you for finding her, Matron . . ." Edward, smoothly, took charge, relieving Matron of the attaché case, which she still held, and urging Judith forward with a touch of his hand on her back. "And," he added over his shoulder, "tell Miss Catto we'll take good care of her."

But Matron did not go instantly indoors. She stood, her apron and her veil flapping in the breeze, and watched them clamber up into the shooting-brake, slam shut the doors, and drive away. Looking back, as they rattled down the drive between the rhododendrons, Judith saw her still there, waiting until the bulky vehicle finally disappeared from her sight.

She settled herself in her seat, and pulled off her hat. "I've never known Matron so amiable."

"Poor old cow. Probably the most exciting thing that's going to happen to her all day." A lock of fair hair fell across his forehead and he put up his hand to push it back. "Sorry it's us come to fetch you, but Pops has got some meeting or other, and Ma's taken Loveday to a pony-club camp. We spent much time boxing that wretched pony, but Walter Mudge has gone with them, so Ma shouldn't have anything too arduous to do once they get there."

"Where have they gone?"

"Oh, I don't know. Some great place over the other side of Falmouth. Do you like horses?"

"Not particularly."

"Thank God for that. One in the family's quite enough. I personally could never be doing with them. One end bites, the other end kicks, and they're bloody uncomfortable in the middle. Anyway, that's why Palmer and I are here. You know Palmer, don't you?"

Judith looked at the back of Palmer's red neck. "I've seen him at Nancherrow, but I don't think we've ever been introduced."

"That's all right," said Palmer over his shoulder, "I know all about you. Coming to stay for a bit?"

"Yes. Easter holidays."

"That'll be nice. Join the throng, that's what I always say."

"In another month," Edward explained, "I'd have been able to come and fetch you myself, because I'll be driving by then. I mean, officially. I drive around Nancherrow, but I'm not able to go out onto the main road until I'm seventeen. It's such a bloody bore, but there's nothing to be done about it, specially as I've got a law-abiding father who sits on the bench. So I had to haul Palmer out of his turnip patch and get him to do the necessary."

"I've never seen this shooting-brake before."

"No, I don't suppose you have. It only comes out on emergencies or special occasions. It's about thirty years old, but Pops won't get rid of it, because he says that it doubles conveniently as a lunch-hut on wet-day shooting parties. And it's good for meeting people at stations and hauling supplies when the house is full. Incidentally, do you mind if we don't go straight home? I've got to go to Medways to get measured for a new tweed, and it seemed a good idea to kill two birds with one stone. Do you mind hanging around for a bit?"

"No." In fact, she felt quite pleased, because hanging around meant more time spent in the company of this engaging young man.

"It won't take long. You can go and shop. And Pops gave me a fiver and said I could give you lunch. He said something about the Mitre, but it's such a stuffy old place, and I get a little bored with roast beef and gravy, so I thought we might find somewhere else." He leaned forward. "Palmer, what's that pub called, in Lower Lane?"

"You can't take the young lady into a pub, Edward. She's under age."

"We can pretend she's older."

"Not in that school uniform you can't."

Edward looked at Judith. She hoped that she wasn't about to blush. But he only said, "No, I suppose not," which was a bit depressing, as though she had been closely examined, and had not come up to scratch.

She said, "*You* can go into a pub if you like. I'll get a sandwich and eat it in the car."

Which made him laugh. "What an accommodating girl you are, to be sure. Of course you won't sit in the car. We'll find somewhere splendid that isn't the Mitre."

Judith said nothing to this. The Mitre had always been her idea of a really expensive and special place to be taken for lunch. But now, it seemed, it was not only dull, but stuffy, and Edward had other and, no doubt, more lively ideas. Wherever they went, she hoped she would be able to deal with it all, and order the right sort of drink, and not drop her napkin or have to go to the lavatory in the middle of the meal. Being given lunch by Edward Carey-Lewis would be quite different to being given lunch by Mr. Baines, but despite all these private anxieties, it was impossible not to feel rather excited.

By now they were in the middle of the town, bowling along Alverton towards the Greenmarket.

"If you drop us by the bank, Palmer, that'll do. And perhaps pick us up at the same spot in a couple of hours."

"That'll suit me. I've got a couple of errands to do for the Colonel."

"And you'll get yourself a bite to eat?"

Palmer was amused. "Don't worry about me."

"I won't. One thing for certain is that you're not too young for the pub."

"I never drink when I'm working."

"Well, I'll believe it, but thousands wouldn't. This is perfect, Palmer. Drop us here." He leaned across Judith and opened the door. For a moment she hesitated, debating as to whether or not to put her hat on again. Wearing a hat with school uniform was an unbreakable rule, and she would never have dared to go bare-headed in term time. But this was holidays now, and she felt irresponsible and daring. Besides, who would see her, and who, when it came down to brass tacks, could possibly care? So, the hateful hat was abandoned, and left where it lay, on the floor. She got out of the brake, followed by Edward, who slammed shut the door. The imposing vehicle moved away, down the street. They watched it go, and then turned and walked together down the sunny, crowded pavement in the direction of Medways.

It was funny coming back. The same gloomy interior, polished counters, high-collared assistants. But different. Because the last time she had come through the doors, she had been with her mother, and both of them were tentatively feeling their way into a new life of separation and Saint Ursula's. And on that day, she had seen Diana and Loveday Carey-Lewis for the first time and had covertly watched them together, dazzled by their companionship and Diana's beauty and charm. And there had been no inkling, no possible idea, of how close she was to become to those two intriguing, butterfly characters.

But it had happened. And here she was, less than a year later, strolling casually into the shop with Loveday's glorious elder brother, and already accepted as one of the Carey-Lewis clan. But the credit was not all Judith's, and she knew this. Circumstances, in an extraordinary way, had taken over her life. Such a short time ago, the future had promised nothing more than taking leave of her family, and settling down to the acceptance of four years of boarding-school and Aunt Louise. But Aunt Louise had died, and her going had opened the doors of Nancherrow to Judith, and allowed her vistas of opportunity and possibility that seemed to stretch forever.

"Good morning, Edward."

Her deep and rather disturbing reflections were interrupted, in timely fashion, by the appearance of the tailor, emerging from some dim back room. Alerted, he was ready to set to work, with his tape measure slung around his neck, and his bald head glistening as though polished.

"Morning, Mr. Tuckett." He and Edward shook hands. The occasion, it appeared, was one of traditional formality.

Mr. Tuckett's eyes travelled to Judith. He frowned. "This isn't young Loveday, is it?"

"Good God, no. This is her friend, Judith Dunbar. She's staying at Nancherrow."

"Well, that explains it. I thought it couldn't be Loveday. Now. The Colonel spoke to me on the telephone this morning, and said you'd be on your way. Tweeds for shooting, he said."

"That's right. I've grown out of everything."

Mr. Tuckett eyed Edward, and allowed himself the ghost of a grin. "Yes, I see what you mean. They must have been feeding you well at that place you're at. Now, do you want to choose the tweed first, or shall we get on with measuring you up?"

"Let's do the measuring first. Get it over."

"Very well. If you'd like to come this way . . ."

"You'll be okay, Judith?"

"Yes. I'll wait."

"Find a chair."

But when they disappeared into Mr. Tuckett's holy of holies, discreet behind a black curtain, she went upstairs, to the school department, and bought herself three pairs of knee-socks so that she would never, unless directed, have to wear brown lisle stockings again. For some reason this small gesture of defiant independence made her feel much more confident, and she ran downstairs quite cheerfully, found a chair, and settled down to wait for Edward.

She had to wait for quite a long time. But eventually Edward and Mr. Tuckett reappeared from beyond the curtain, Edward hauling his sweater back over his head.

"Sorry about that," he apologized.

"It's all right."

Mr. Tuckett explained. "A whole new set of measurements. A man's measurements now. This shooting suit should last Edward for some time to come."

Next came the choice of tweed, which took almost longer. Edward, surprisingly enough, was very picky. Thick books of samples were produced, piled on the counter, and mulled over. Much discussion took place concerning the relative advantages of Harris tweed and Yorkshire tweed. Was it to be dog-tooth, herring-bone, or plain lovat? The samples were turned, examined, and turned again. Finally Edward made his choice, a Scottish thornproof, in a sludgy green, with a faint red-and-fawn overcheck. Considering it, Judith approved. "It's very non-committal," she told him. "You'll blend in, and you won't show in the undergrowth, and yet it's quite suitable for lunch parties, or even going to church."

Mr. Tuckett beamed. "Exactly, miss." He folded back the corner of the chosen tweed and fastened it with a pin. "I shall order it immediately, and start work as soon as it arrives. We should have your shooting suit ready for you before the end of the holidays. Now, there's nothing more you're needing? Shirts? Neckties? Socks?" He lowered his voice discreetly. "Underwear?"

But Edward had had enough. It was time to be off. Mr. Tuckett saw them to the door, with as much flourish and dignity as Nettlebed himself, and bade them good afternoon.

Safely on the pavement, Edward let out a sigh of relief. "Phew. That's over. Let's go and find a drink and something to eat."

"I thought you were enjoying yourself."

"Up to a point. But it all takes time."

"I love the tweed."

"Better than dog-tooth anyway. And least I shan't look like a second-rate bookie. Now, come on . . ." And he put a hand beneath her elbow and steered her across the road, narrowly missing two cars and a bicycle.

"Where are we going?" Judith asked, skipping along to keep up with Edward as he strode down the pavement.

"I don't know. We'll find somewhere."

What he found was a pub, but it had a garden so Judith didn't need to go into the bar. The garden was very small, with a low stone wall, and over this was a good view of the harbour and the sea beyond. There were some tables and chairs dotted about, and it was fairly sheltered from the breeze and so not too cold. He established her at one of these tables, and asked what she wanted to drink. Judith said she would have Orange Corona which was still her favourite, and he laughed and went indoors, ducking his head under the low doorway, and presently came out again, with her orange and a tankard of beer for himself and a luncheon menu, handwritten on a dog-eared card.

"I'm afraid it's not quite as up-market as the Mitre, but at least we're spared that deathly hush, broken only by the sounds of belches, or worse, and the mouselike scrape of cutlery on china." He frowned at the bill of fare and turned down the corners of his mouth in an exaggerated grimace. "Toad in the Hole. Sausages and Mash. Home-made Cornish Pasties. Let's go for the pasties."

"All right."

"Do you like pasties?"

"Love them."

"And for afters you can have trifle, jelly, or an ice-cream. Also home-made."

"I mightn't have any room when I've finished the pasty."

"Probably not." He looked up as a woman in a pinafore came out of the pub to take their order. Edward gave it, in a lordly manner belying his sixteen years. He was really, Judith marvelled, extraordinarily sophisticated.

"We're going to have the pasties."

"Righty-ho." He grinned up at her, and she added, "My love."

It was a good place to be. He was right. Much better than the Mitre. Not cold, because she had a coat on, and fun to sit in the open air, with the high sky and the blowing clouds and the wheeling, gliding gulls making their endless racket around the masts and decks of the fishing boats. The tide was in, and on the far side of the bay, St. Michael's Mount appeared to be floating on the blue sea, the crenellations of the castle sharp as a cut-out in the clear air.

She leaned back in her chair and sipped her drink. She said, "When did you break up?"

"Two or three days ago. Athena's still in Switzerland. God knows if or when she's coming home."

"I didn't realize that you were back already."

"Why should you?"

"I thought Loveday might have told me."

"Some hope. She thinks of nothing but that wretched Tinkerbell." Across the wooden table, he suddenly smiled. "Do you relish the prospect of coming to Nancherrow for a whole *month*, or does it leave you with a sinking heart?"

She had the wit to realize that she was being teased.

"No. No sinking heart."

His smile faded. Suddenly serious, he said, "Ma told me about your aunt being killed like that. Ghastly. I'm sorry. It must have been the hell of a shock."

"Yes, it was. But I'm afraid she never drove very carefully."

He said, "I went to her house."

"You *did?*"

"Yes. Palmer and I were detailed to take the farm truck over and bring back all your stuff. My first day of freedom and I was working like a dog."

"That was kind of you."

"I didn't have much option."

"How . . . how did Windyridge look?"

"A bit bleak."

"Were Edna and Hilda there?"

"The two old maids. Yes, they're still in situ, and helped us sort out all your stuff. Everything ready and packed up. Very neat."

"It was always rather a bleak house . . ." She wondered if he had spied Billy Fawcett prowling about, watching all that was going on, but decided not to ask any questions. She screwed up her nose. ". . . and full of extraordinary relics of Aunt Louise's life in India. Skins and elephant's feet and brass drums."

"I didn't really go into that bit of the house, so I can't remark on her taste."

"And my things?"

"I think Mary Millyway has dealt with them. Arranged your belongings, probably unpacked your clothes. Ma told me very firmly that the pink bedroom is now yours."

"She's been so kind."

"No skin off her nose. And she likes a mass of people around." He looked up. "Oh, hurray, here come our pasties. I was beginning to feel faint with hunger."

"There you are, my love." The plates were slapped down before them. "Get round those and there won't be much wrong with you."

The pasties were, indeed, enormous, steaming and fragrant. Judith took up a knife and cut hers in two, and bubbling morsels of steak and potato slipped out from between the folds of pastry. She smelt the onion, and her mouth watered. A breeze gusted from the sea and blew her hair over her face. She pushed it back and smiled at her companion.

"I'm so glad," she told him, in a burst of content that was almost happiness, "that we didn't go to the Mitre."

Returning to Nancherrow, bowling down the hill into Rosemullion, Edward was visited with yet another brilliant idea. "Let's go and call on Aunt Lavinia. I haven't seen her yet, and perhaps we can prevail on Isobel to give us a cup of tea."

"I'm still full of pasty."

"So am I, but that doesn't matter." He leaned forward and gave Palmer a thump on his solid shoulder. "Palmer, you don't have to get back to work, do you?"

"I've got these things I picked up for the Colonel. He's waiting for them. I said I'd be straight back."

"In that case, you can drive us up the hill and dump us, and we'll walk home."

"Whatever you want."

"Okay. We'll go." He sat back once more, pushing his forelock out of his eyes. "You'd like that, wouldn't you, Judith? Lavinia's always good for a gas."

"If that's what you want, yes, of course. But will Aunt Lavinia mind us dropping in on her with no warning?"

"She won't mind. Always adored nice surprises."

"It's only half past three. Perhaps she'll be resting."

"She never rests," Edward informed her shortly.

And indeed, he was quite right, and Aunt Lavinia was not resting. They walked into the house without so much as a by-your-leave, and found her in her sun-filled drawing-room, sitting at her desk and dealing with her correspondence. In the grate, a little fire flickered, and, as before, the charming room dazzled and sparkled with reflected light. When the door burst open, she turned abruptly in her chair, putting up a hand to remove her spectacles. Her expression, finding herself so rudely disturbed, was a little surprised, but only for a second. Recognizing Edward standing before her caused her features to fill with delight.

"My dear!" She laid down her pen. "What a splendid surprise. Edward. I didn't even know you were home."

She flung out an arm, and he went to embrace and kiss her. Judith saw that today she was dressed far less formally than she had been for the remembered Sunday luncheon, and wore a heavy tweed skirt, thick stockings, and sensible shoes. A long cardigan was buttoned over a cream silk blouse, revealing a glint of gold chain and a loop of pearls.

"We decided to drop in. We're on our way back to Nancherrow from Penzance. We got Palmer to drop us and we're going to walk home."

"Heavens, what energy. And Judith as well. Better and better. In school uniform. Have you just broken up? What a treat for me. Now, both come and sit down and make yourselves comfortable, and Edward, you must tell me everything you've been up to . . . how long have you been back?"

She leaned back in her chair, Edward drew up a low stool, and Judith went to sit in the window and watched them both, and listened, and heard about life at Harrow, and the possibility of becoming Head of House, and the success, or otherwise, of the rugby football team. And he was asked about examination results and the possibility of going to Oxford or Cambridge, and they talked of mutual friends, and the boy whom Edward had brought home for the summer holidays, and Judith marvelled that anyone so old should be so astute and interested; that a person who had never had family of her own could be so perceptive of the younger generation, and so aware of the truly important aspects of that generation's life. She guessed that it was probably because she had always been deeply involved with the Carey-Lewis children, and because of them had never allowed herself to become out of touch.

Finally, she had heard it all, and was content, and only needed to be brought up-to-date. "And what were you up to today, the pair of you?"

Edward told her. About picking Judith up from Saint Ursula's, and getting his new tweed measured, and then eating pasties in the garden of the little pub.

"Oh, how envious I am. Nothing more delicious than a good pasty eaten in the open air. And now I expect you're hungry again." She pushed back her cuff and looked at her small gold wrist-watch. "It's nearly four o'clock. Why don't you pop into the kitchen, Edward dear, and ask Isobel to bring us a tea-tray. With a bit of luck, she'll have some shortbread for us. Or perhaps hot toast and gentleman's relish?"

"Delicious. I was wondering when you'd bring up the subject of tea." Edward got to his feet, stretched enormously, and departed in search of Isobel. As the door closed behind him, Aunt Lavinia turned to Judith. "Now, I can talk to you." She put on her spectacles and inspected Judith over the top of them. Her expression, now, was serious once more. "I didn't want to speak in front of Edward, but I was so distressed for you when I heard that your aunt had died in that dreadful motor-car accident. Are you all right?"

"Yes. I'm all right."

"Such a tragic thing to happen, and most of all, to you, with your family abroad."

"It would have been much worse if everybody hadn't been so kind. Miss Catto, and Mr. Baines, and Diana. Everybody, really."

"Diana has a very generous spirit. And the most important thing is that you have been made so welcome at Nancherrow. That was a great comfort to me, when she told me her plans for you. It stopped me worrying for you. It means that you have a loving home to come to, and nothing is unbearable provided you've got some sort of a family, even if it isn't your own."

Judith felt that it was necessary to explain. "Actually I do have a bit of family in this country, because I've got Aunt Biddy and Uncle Bob. They're great, but she's rather occupied with a new house just now, and both Uncle Bob and my Cousin Ned are in the Navy. But they're always there, and I know I can always go to them. But even so, being at Nancherrow makes everything different."

"And such a cheerful house! Always something going on. Sometimes I think poor Edgar becomes quite bemused. You'll be happy there, I know, but do remember, dear Judith, that if for any reason you do feel a bit blue or depressed or lonely, or you want to talk about things, or just mill problems over, I am always here. At the Dower House. And after years of being married to a barrister, I have become an excellent listener. You won't forget, will you?"

"No. I won't forget."

"And now I can hear Edward coming back. I sent him because Isobel adores him, and usually I don't have my tea until half past four, and I didn't want there to be a sulky face brooding in the kitchen. But for Edward she will make toast and gentleman's relish, and for the remainder of the day will be wreathed in happy smiles."

Nancherrow,
The same day, but later.

Now I can finish the letter. As you can see, I am here, back in my same bedroom, but it is really mine now because I have all my things. They look quite at home, and Mary Millyway moved the bed so that I have space for my desk and my books. It is six o'clock and a beautiful evening and beyond my window I can hear the doves in the courtyard, and if I stick my head out of the window I can actually hear the sea.

Such a surprise. Edward, Loveday's brother, was there to fetch me from school with one of the gardeners driving Colonel Carey-Lewis's shooting-brake. We went to Penzance and to Medways, because he had to have a new suit measured, and then we went out for lunch, and then on the way back called in to have tea with Aunt Lavinia, Mrs. Boscawen, at the Dower House. We had hot toast, and then, after, walked home, much farther than I'd remembered, and it was a relief finally to arrive. Edward is very nice. He is nearly seventeen and at Harrow and going to Oxford, I think, when he leaves school. It was he who went to Windyridge to fetch all my things. He saw Edna and Hilda, who are still there, but they have another post to go to.

I haven't seen Loveday or Diana yet, as they're not back from a pony-club rally, and I haven't seen Colonel Carey-Lewis either. Only Mary Millyway, who came to help me unpack all my clothes and settle in. Later on, when I go down for dinner, I shall see them all.

Please write soon and tell me everything you are doing so that I can imagine it. Or tell Dad to take some snaps so that I can see if Jess is growing. I want to know if she is going to school, or having lessons. And is Golly still alive, or has he been eaten by a snake?

Rather a muddled letter, but there has been so much to tell you. Everything is changing so quickly, that sometimes it is quite difficult to keep up with it all, and from time to time I find myself wondering if I have remembered to tell you everything. I wish I could be with you and talk about it all. I suppose growing up is always a bit lonely.

Lots of love, and please don't worry. I'm all right.

Judith

1938

*I*n Singapore, in the Orchard Road bungalow, Molly Dunbar, sleeping, awoke with a start, in a sweat of panic, consumed by some incomprehensible and nameless fear. Almost in tears, *What is wrong?* she asked herself, *what has happened?* Ridiculous, because it was not even dark, but mid-afternoon, and the huge contraption of the mosquito net hung overhead hoisted to the high ceiling. Siesta. No ghouls, snakes, or night-time intruders. Yet her teeth were clenched, her breathing shallow and uneven, and her heart thumping like a drum. For a moment or two, she simply lay rigid, waiting for the dreaded whatever-it-was to pounce. But nothing pounced. The panic slowly subsided. A nightmare, perhaps, but any dream, if it had existed, had flown from her mind. Deliberately, she paced her breathing, forced tense muscles to relax. After a little, the reasonless terror evaporated, and the void it left slowly filled with a sort of passive, exhausted relief.

So, nothing. Just her own imaginings flying in all directions, as usual, even as she rested, safe in her own bedroom, with her husband beside her. Her eyes moved over the familiar surroundings, searching for reassurance and some sort of comfort. White walls, marble floor; her dressing table, draped in frilled white muslin; the ornate teak wardrobe, marvellously scrolled and carved. Chairs of rattan, and a cedarwood chest. Alongside this, the door stood open into Bruce's dressing-room, and overhead, in the high ceiling, the paddles of the wooden fan revolved, churning leaden air into a semblance of cool. Two lizards crouched on the opposite wall, still and lifeless as bizarre brooches pinned to a lapel.

She looked at her watch. Three o'clock on an April afternoon, and the heat so humid, so intense, as to be almost unbearable. She lay naked beneath a thin lawn wrapper, and her cheeks, and neck, and hair and the small of her back all trickled with sweat. On the far side of the bed, Bruce slumbered, snoring lightly. She turned her head and watched him, and envied him for his ability to sleep away the overpowering heat of this tropical afternoon. And yet, she knew, at four o'clock, he would wake on the dot, to rise, shower, dress in fresh clothes, and return to his office, there to work for another two or three hours.

She stirred, closed her eyes, and almost immediately opened them again. It was impossible to lie, wakeful, for another second. Cautiously, so as not to wake her husband, she sat up and swung her legs over the side of the bed, drawing her thin wrapper about her, and pushing her feet into a pair of thong sandals. Treading softly, she crossed the room, and went through the slatted doors that led onto the veranda. This was wide and shady, enclosing the entire perimeter of the bungalow, and had a sloping roof which allowed no ray of sunlight to permeate the interior, and here too the ubiquitous fans revolved overhead. At the far end, by the opened doors of the drawing-room, chairs and tables were grouped. An outdoor sitting-room where Molly spent much of her time. Blue-and-white planters were filled with hibiscus and orange blossom, and beyond the veranda's shade, the garden simmered under a sky bleached with heat. No breeze stirred the palm tree nor the frangipani nor the flower of the forest, but as she stood there, a tree-rat scampered up the stem of the bougainvillea, disturbing a shower of blossom. The petals floated down and settled on the veranda steps.

It was immensely quiet. Jess, servants, dogs still slept. Molly walked the length of the veranda, the leather soles of her slippers slapping on the wooden floor. There she sank into one of the long rattan chairs, her feet supported by the foot-rest. Alongside this particular chair was a cane table, where were collected all the small necessities of her leisurely, sedentary life: her book, her sewing-box, magazines, correspondence; her engagement diary (very important), and her embroidery. Today, as well, it bore a three-week-old copy of the London *Times*, which Bruce had arranged to be sent out from Home on a regular basis. He said that he liked to read what he called "the proper news," although Molly suspected that all he ever studied in any depth were the rugby results and the cricket scores.

Normally, Molly did not read *The Times*. But now, for want of anything better to do, she picked up the newspaper, unfolded and opened it. The date was March the fifteenth, and the headlines leaped at her like a spectre in the dark, for, on the twelfth of March, Nazi Germany had occupied Austria.

Old now, of course, because they had heard of the occupation on the wireless three weeks ago, almost as soon as the shocking event had taken place. But Bruce, though grim-faced, had not talked about it very much, and for this Molly had been grateful, because it meant that she could simply push it out of her mind. There was no good being pessimistic. Perhaps something would happen to make everything all right. And anyway, there was always so much else to occupy her thoughts, like seeing that Jess did her lessons, and arranging menus with Cookie, and keeping her social commitments up-to-date. The latter, in particular, she found very demanding.

But now . . . alone and unobserved, and with no person to remark on her reactions, she drew upon her courage, and resisted the temptation to toss the horrible news aside. There was a photograph. Hitler, driving in state through the streets of Vienna, his car flanked by German troops, and the pavements crammed with crowds. She studied the faces in these crowds and was filled with bewilderment, for, though some clearly mirrored the horror of what had finally happened, too many were jubilant, cheering the new leader and raising flags emblazoned with the black and broken cross of Nazism. It was incomprehensible. How could any patriot welcome such an invasion? Searching for some answer to this question, she began to read the account of how it had all taken place, and once started could not stop, for the sombre words, the measured prose caught her attention, drawing an extraordinarily vivid picture of outraged subjugation. Finished, if this, she asked herself, had been allowed to happen, then what on earth was going to happen next?

Nothing very good. In London, in Parliament, the mood was grave. In the House of Commons, Winston Churchill had stood to speak. For years he had been treated as a sort of Cassandra, preaching doom and destruction, while others went hopefully about their business. But now it seemed that he had been right all along, and his warnings tolled like a death knell. ". . . Europe is confronted with a programme of aggression . . . only choice open . . . to submit or take effective measures . . ."

Enough. She folded the newspaper and dropped it to the floor by her side. Effective measures meant war. Even a fool like herself could understand the implication. The storm-clouds, which had appeared over the horizon of Molly's uncomplicated life even before she had left England to sail for Colombo, had neither dissipated nor disappeared, but grown and gathered and now threatened to blacken out the whole of Europe. And England? And Judith?

Judith. Molly knew that she should be ashamed. She should think of others, nations already violated and peoples suppressed, but uppermost in her mind was the safety of her child. If there was a war in Europe, if England was involved, then what would happen to Judith? Should they not, perhaps, send for her right away? Forget about school, jettison all the plans they had made for her, and bring her out to Singapore with all convenient speed? War would never touch them here. They would all be together again, and Judith would be safe.

But even as the idea occurred to her, she was fairly sure that Bruce would not agree to it. A strong supporter of the Government, a rabid Conservative and a staunch patriot, he could not imagine any situation where England could be in mortal danger, invaded or suppressed. Should Molly argue, she would be reminded by Bruce of the impregnability of the Maginot line, the overwhelming superiority of the British Navy, and the global power of the British Empire. Judith would be perfectly safe. Ridiculous to panic. Stop being so silly.

She knew all this, because she had heard it all before. When Louise Forrester had killed herself in that dreadful car smash, and the cable had come from

Mr. Baines, informing them of the tragic event, Molly's first instinct had been not grief for Louise, but concern for Judith, and she had been all for getting a passage on the first boat Home, and returning to England to be with her abandoned daughter. But Bruce, although clearly shattered by the news of his sister's death, had become intensely British, keeping his feelings to himself, with a stiff upper lip, and his feet on the ground. Worse, he had insisted to his distraught wife that there was no point in taking impulsive action. Judith was at boarding-school, Miss Catto was in command, and Biddy Somerville close to hand, if needed. The emotional return of her mother would make things no easier for Judith. Far better to leave her in peace, to get on with her studies, and let events naturally take their course.

"But she has no *home*. She has nowhere to go!" Molly had wept, but Bruce remained adamant.

"What good would you do?" he demanded, losing his patience.

"I could be *with* her . . ."

"By the time you reached her side, this crisis will be over, and you will be totally extraneous."

"You don't understand."

"No. I don't. So calm down. Go and write her a letter. And don't fuss. Children hate parents who fuss over them."

And there was nothing she could do, because she had no money of her own, and if Bruce would not go to the shipping office, book her passage and pay for it, then Molly was helpless. She did her best to come to terms with the situation, but the next two or three weeks were like a period of grieving, longing for physical contact with Judith, to see her sweet face, embrace her, listen to her voice, comfort and counsel her.

But at the end of the day she realized Bruce had been maddeningly right. Had Molly sailed, it would have been five or six weeks by the time she reached Judith's side, and in that period, all the problems miraculously had sorted themselves out, and the void left by the death of Louise was filled by this benevolent, if unknown, family called Carey-Lewis.

Judith's virtual adoption was accomplished in an orderly and businesslike way. Miss Catto wrote, in essence giving Colonel and Mrs. Carey-Lewis an excellent reference, and adding that, in her opinion, their proposed hospitality could be nothing but beneficial to Judith. She had made good friends with young Loveday Carey-Lewis, the family were old-established and much respected in the county, and Mrs. Carey-Lewis had expressed, with deep sincerity, her desire to take Judith into their home.

Then, hard on the heels of Miss Catto's letter, had come one from Mrs. Carey-Lewis herself, written in huge, almost illegible handwriting, but on the most expensive, headed, thick blue paper. Despite herself, Molly was both impressed and flattered, and, once she had deciphered the handwriting, found herself touched and disarmed. And Judith, clearly, had made an excellent impression. Molly allowed herself to feel quite proud. All she could do was simply hope that her daughter would not be overwhelmed by the grandeur of what was clearly an establishment of the landed gentry.

Nancherrow. She remembered that day in Medways when she had seen Diana Carey-Lewis for the first and only time. Their lives had touched only for a moment—ships passing in the night—but she still retained a vivid image of the beautiful youthful mother, the bright-faced ragamuffin child, and the peke with its scarlet lead. Asking, "That's Mrs. Carey-Lewis," she had been told. "Mrs. Carey-Lewis of Nancherrow."

It would be all right. No point in hesitating, no reason for reservations. Molly wrote back, grateful and accepting, and did her best to push down the unworthy sensation that she was giving Judith away.

Bruce was smug. "I told you it would all work out."

His attitude she found intensely irritating. "It's easy to say that now. What would we have done if the Carey-Lewises hadn't come up trumps?"

"Why suppose? Everything's settled. I always said Judith could take care of herself."

"How do you know that? You haven't seen her for five years!" Annoyed by him, she became perverse. "And I don't think she should spend all her time at Nancherrow. After all, Biddy's still around. She would love to have Judith, at any time."

"They must make their own arrangements."

Molly sulked for a moment, unwilling to let him have the last word. "It's just that I can't help feeling that I've lost her to strangers."

"Oh, for God's sake, stop agonizing. Just be grateful."

And so she had suppressed her slight twinges of resentment and envy, and told herself firmly how lucky she was, and concentrated on being grateful and writing letters to her daughter. And now it was two years later—Judith would be seventeen in June—and in all that time scarcely a week had passed without the arrival, at Orchard Road, of a fat envelope addressed in Judith's handwriting. Long, loving, dear letters, with all the news that any mother would want to hear; each to be read and reread, savoured and finally filed away in a huge brown cardboard box in the bottom of Molly's wardrobe. Judith's life, no less, was contained in that box; a virtual record of everything that had happened to her since that unforgotten day when she and her mother had said their last goodbye.

The early letters were all of school, lessons, the new bicycle, and life at Windyridge. And then the shock of Louise's death; her funeral, the first mention of Mr. Baines, and the astonishing news of Judith's inheritance. (None of them had ever realized the extent of Louise's wealth. But so satisfactory to know that Judith would never have to ask a husband for money, one of the least agreeable aspects of married life.)

Then the first visits to Nancherrow, and Judith's gradual absorption into the Carey-Lewis clan. Which was a bit like reading a novel with far too many characters . . . children and friends and relations, to say nothing of butlers, cooks, and nannies. Bit by bit, however, Molly sorted out all the various individuals, and after that it wasn't too difficult to follow the plot.

Later again, and more school news. Concerts and plays, hockey matches, examination results, and mild epidemics of measles. A Christmas with Biddy and Bob in their new house on Dartmoor; a half-term with the Warrens in Porthkerris. (Molly was pleased that she had kept up with Heather. It would have been sad had Judith become too grand for old friends.) Then, a summer trip to London with Diana Carey-Lewis and Loveday, to stay in Diana's little Mews house, and to be taken on a positive round of shopping and luncheons, culminating in an evening at Covent Garden, to see Tatiana Riabouchinska dance with the Russian Ballet.

All the trials and treats of an ordinary girl, growing up. And Molly, her mother, was missing it all. It is so unfair, she told herself on a surge of resentment. It is all wrong. And yet she knew that she was not isolated. Her anguish was shared by thousands of other British wives and mothers. Whether in Singapore or England, one was never in the right place, and always yearning for the other. Either braving the cold and rains of Home, and dreaming of the sun; or else sitting as she sat now, staring at the sun-baked gardens of Orchard Road and seeing only the path at Riverview on a misty evening, and Judith walking up towards the house from the railway station. Walking, and then seeing her mother, and pressing her cheek against Molly's cheek, saying her name. Touching. Sometimes, Molly held the sheets of Judith's letters to her cheek, because Judith's hand had touched the paper; the closest she was ever able to get.

She sighed. From behind her, from indoors, the bungalow was stirring. Amah's soft voice from Jess's bedroom, rousing the child from her sleep. Siesta was over. On the far side of the lawn, the garden boy appeared, diligently lugging an overflowing watering can. Soon Bruce would emerge, neatly turned out for the office, and later it would be time for afternoon tea. The silver teapot, the cucumber sandwiches, the finely sliced crescents of lemon. How shaming should Ah Lin, the butler, find his mistress sitting here dressed only in her wrapper. She must pull herself together, make her way back to her bedroom, to shower and dress and do her hair and then present herself once more as a respectable memsahib.

But before she could make this enormous effort, she was joined by Jess, fresh and clean in a sleeveless sun-frock, and with her milk-fair hair smooth as silk from Amah's ministrations with the hairbrush.

"Mummy!"

"Oh, darling." She put out an arm to scoop her small daughter into an embrace, to plant a kiss on the top of her head. Jess, now six, had grown tall and slender in the heat of Singapore, like a flower that relishes the warmth and the damp. Her face had lost some of its baby curves, but her eyes were still round and cornflower-blue, and her cheeks, her bare arms, and legs were all gently tanned to the delicious colour of a freshly laid brown egg.

Her appearance caused Molly a pang of guilt, for she had been so taken up with thoughts of Judith that Jess, for a moment or two, had slipped quite out of her mind. "And how are you?" The guilt rendered her voice especially loving. "How pretty and cool you look."

"Why are you in your nightie?"

"Because I've been lazy and I haven't dressed yet."

"Are we going to the club to swim?"

Molly, gathering her thoughts, remembered plans already laid. "Yes, of course we are. I'd forgotten."

"And afterwards can we play croquet?"

"Not this evening, my pet. There won't be time. I have to come home and change and go out for dinner."

Jess took this information totally in her stride. By now she had become resigned to the fact that her parents went out most nights, and if they did not, then entertained in their own home. There was scarcely an evening when they sat on their own.

"Where are you going?"

"To a Guest Night at the Selaring Barracks. The Colonel has invited us."

"What are you going to wear?"

"I thought perhaps my new lilac voile. The one the dressmaker finished last week. What do you think?"

"Why don't I come and look in your wardrobe and help you choose?" Jess was intensely keen on clothes, and spent much time tottering around in her mother's high-heeled shoes, or draping herself in beads.

"What a good idea. Come, we'll go together before Ah Lin catches me looking such a mess."

She swung her legs over the side of the long chair, holding her wrapper modestly about her. Jess took her other hand and skipped her way down the length of the veranda. The little tree-rat was still scuttling about in the branches of the bougainvillea, and the petals drifted down, to pile, where they had fallen, in a profusion of magenta.

There had been a time when Judith had become disillusioned by Christmas. This was during the Riverview years, when Molly Dunbar's lack of enthusiasm for the annual festival, her reluctance to deck the house with holly, and even her disinterest in traditional food engendered a flat sensation of anticlimax, so that by four o'clock on Christmas afternoon, Judith was ready to retire with her new book and be quite glad that the day was nearly over.

It had not, of course, been entirely Molly's fault. Circumstances were difficult for her. She had never made friends easily, and with no young relations to fill the house, it was not easy to whip up a whirl of social gaiety for her two young daughters. Without the moral support of a husband to dress up as Father Christmas, fill stockings, and carve turkeys, her naturally passive nature won the day, and she ended up taking the line of least resistance.

But, along with so much else, now it was all changed. Three Christmases had come and gone since those singularly unfestive times at Riverview; each different, and, in retrospect, each even better than the one before. First, those two weeks in Keyham with Aunt Biddy and Uncle Bob. That holiday had done much to restore Judith's confidence in the essential magic of the celebration. Then, the first Christmas at Nancherrow, with the house aglitter with decorations and awash with presents. All the Carey-Lewises gathered and a good many others as well, and the fun had never stopped, from Christmas Eve and Midnight Service, to the long walk home after the Boxing Day meet of the local Hunt. And Diana had given Judith her first long dress, pale-blue paper taffeta, and she had worn it for Christmas dinner and afterwards waltzed with the Colonel, round and round the drawing-room floor.

Last year, 1937, she had returned to the Somervilles, not to Keyham, but to their new house on the edge of Dartmoor. And Ned and a friend had been there, a young sub-lieutenant from Ned's ship. A lot of snow had fallen and they had gone sledging, and one evening had driven down to Plymouth for a memorable party in the Wardroom of one of His Majesty's cruisers.

And now it was to be Nancherrow again, and at seventeen Judith was as excited as a very small child by the prospect, and counting the days until the end of term. From Loveday, who still returned home every weekend, she had gleaned, on Monday mornings, scraps of pleasurable information concerning plans laid, parties arranged, and guests to be invited.

"We're going to be the most enormous houseful. Mary Millyway is counting sheets like a maniac, and Mrs. Nettlebed is up to the eyes in mincemeat and puddings and cakes. I can't tell you how delicious the kitchen smells. And spicy and drunk with brandy. And Athena's coming from London, and Edward's going to Arosa to ski, but he's promised he'll be back in time."

Which caused a small tremor of anxiety in Judith's heart, because how awful it would be if he didn't make it. Edward was grown up now, had left Harrow, and had done his first term as an undergraduate at Cambridge, and seeing him again was part of the excitement and anticipation that she was experiencing. In fact, quite a big part. She wasn't in love with him, of course. Being in love was something that you fell into with film stars or matinée idols or other beings safely unattainable. But his presence added such life and glamour to any occasion that it was hard to imagine any sort of celebration being complete without him.

"I do hope he is. What about Jeremy Wells?"

"Mummy didn't say. He's probably working, or being with his own parents. But I bet he'll turn up some time. He always does. And Mummy's asked the Pearsons, from London. They're sort of second cousins of Pops', but they're quite young . . . I suppose about thirty. They're called Jane and Alistair, and when they got married, I was their bridesmaid. Saint Margaret's, Westminster. Frightfully *posh*. They've got two children now, and they're coming too, with their nanny."

"What are the children called?"

"Camilla and Roddy." Loveday screwed up her nose. "Don't you simply hate that name, Camilla? It sounds like underclothes. They're very little. Let's hope they don't howl all the time."

"They'll probably be very sweet."

"Well, they're not going to be allowed into my bedroom, that's for sure."

"I wouldn't worry. Nanny will keep an eye on them."

"Mary says if their nanny starts turning Mary's nursery upside down, she'll give her what for. Oh, and on Saturday, Pops and I went out into the plantation and chose a tree . . ."

A bell clanged, and there was no time for more. Judith headed for her French class, hugging herself with pleasure, because, in truth, it all sounded as though it was going to be the best Christmas ever.

Meanwhile, at Saint Ursula's, Christmas took off on a suitably religious note with the onset of Advent. At morning assembly, they sang Advent hymns:

> "O come, o come Immanuel
> And ransom captive Israel . . ."

and out of doors the days were short and the dark evenings long. In art class, Christmas cards were designed and paper decorations made. During the music period, carols were practised, the choir struggling with the hideously difficult descants to "The First Nowell" and "O Come All Ye Faithful." Then there was the annual party, with a different theme each year. This year was to be Fancy Dress, the costumes made of paper and to cost no more than five shillings. Judith had stitched some crêpe-paper frills into a gypsy outfit on Matron's sewing machine, and looped curtain rings onto her ears with thread, but Loveday simply glued a lot of old newspapers together, put on her riding hat, and went as *The Racing News*. Her costume fell apart during the course of the energetic games they played, and she spent the rest of the evening in her navy-blue knickers and the old Aertex shirt which she had worn under all the layers of *The Daily Telegraph*.

Even the weather contrived to add to the seasonal build-up, turning bitterly cold, unusual for this temperate, sea-girt claw of England. Snow had not fallen, but hard frosts turned lawns to silver, and rendered the playing fields so hard that all games were cancelled. In the gardens, frozen palm trees and semi-tropical shrubs drooped pitifully, and it was hard to imagine that they could ever recover from their cruel experience.

But there were more important things to think about. At last, the final morning of term, the annual Carol Service in the chapel, and then home. Already, on the gravel sweep before the front door, cars and taxis and buses were assembling, to bear away the chattering throng of schoolgirls. Having said goodbye to Miss Catto, and wished her a Merry Christmas, Judith and Loveday, with arms full of books and shoe-bags dangling, escaped, out into the bitter air, and freedom. Palmer was there, with the shooting-brake already loaded, and they climbed on board, and were away.

At Nancherrow, the girls found preparations already hotting up: fires blazing everywhere, and the huge spruce erected in the hall. Even as they came in through the front door, Diana was there, running down the stairs to meet them, with a garland of holly in one hand and a long festoon of tinsel in the other.

"Oh, you darling creatures, there you are, safe and sound. Isn't it utterly freezing? Shut the door and keep the cold out. I didn't think you'd be here so quickly. Judith, sweetheart, heaven to see you. Goodness, I think you've grown."

"Who's here?" Loveday asked.

"Only Athena so far, and not a cheep yet from Edward. But that just means that he's having a good time. And the Pearsons come tonight. They're driving down from London, poor things. I hope the roads aren't too ghastly."

"What about Nenny and Camilla and Roddy?"

"Darling, don't call her Nenny. That's a private joke. They're all coming tomorrow, by train. And then Tommy Mortimer's coming the next day, and he's being sensible and taking the train as well. What a lot of people to go and meet at the station."

"So, where is everybody?"

"Pops and Walter Mudge have taken the tractor and the trailer, and gone to find me masses more holly. And Athena's writing Christmas cards."

"Hasn't she done her Christmas cards yet? They'll never get to anybody in time."

"Oh, well. Perhaps she'll just put Happy New Year." Diana thought about this, and giggled. "Or even, Happy Easter. Now, darlings, I must get on. What was I doing?" She gazed, as though for inspiration, at her tinsel and her holly. "Decking halls, I think. So much to do. Why don't you go and find Mary?" Already, she was drifting off in the direction of the drawing-room. ". . . get unpacked. Settled in. I'll see you at lunch . . ."

Alone in her pink bedroom, once she had orientated herself, checked on her possessions, and spent a few icy moments hanging out of the opened window, the first thing Judith did was to change, get out of her uniform, and put on proper, comfortable grown-up clothes. Once she had accomplished this, she was ready to deal with her unpacking, and was kneeling beside the opened suitcase rummaging for a hairbrush, when she heard Athena's voice, calling her name.

"I'm here."

She paused in her rummagings, her face towards the open door. She heard the swift light footsteps, and the next instant, Athena was there. "Just popped along to say hello, and Seasons Greetings and all the rest of it." She came into the room and flopped languidly down on Judith's bed. She smiled. "I've just seen Loveday, so I knew you'd come. How's everything?"

Judith sat back on her heels. "Fine."

Of all the Carey-Lewis family, Athena was the one whom Judith knew least well, and consequently, at first encounters, was always slightly over-whelmed and a bit shy. It wasn't that she wasn't friendly, or funny, or easygoing as an older sister, because she was all those things. It was just that she was so sensationally glamorous and sophisticated that the impact of her presence was apt to stun. As well, she was not often at Nancherrow. Done with débutante dances and Switzerland, she was now totally adult, and spent most of her time in London, roosting in her mother's little house in Cadogan Mews and leading a sybarite's life of pleasure. She didn't even have a proper job (she said that a job would interfere with lovely, impromptu arrangements), and if questioned about her idleness, merely smiled in dazzling fashion and murmured something about a charity ball she was helping to organize, or an exhibition to publicize some scrofulous painter or sculptor, whose incomprehensible work she professed to admire.

Her social life appeared to be non-stop. Men buzzed about her, the proverbial bees around a honey-pot, and whenever she was at Nancherrow, she spent much time on the telephone, placating lovelorn swains, promising to get in touch when she returned to London, or else concocting some unlikely story as to why she was, at the moment, unavailable. The Colonel was at one time driven to remark that she had had him on a bed of sickness so many times, it was a wonder he was not already dead.

But Judith was sympathetic. In a way, it must be a terrible responsibility to be possessed of such beauty. Long blonde hair, flawless skin, and enormous blue eyes fringed with black lashes. She was as tall as her mother, slender and long-legged, and she wore very red lipstick and very red nails and was always dressed in lovely new clothes, in the height of fashion. Today, because this was country, she wore trousers, cut like a man's, and a silk shirt, and a camel-hair jacket, with padded shoulders and the glitter of a diamond brooch pinned to the lapel. Judith had not seen that brooch before, and guessed that it was the latest gift from some adoring male. That was another thing about Athena. She was perpetually being given presents. Not only for Christmas and birthdays, but all the time. And not just flowers and books, but jewellery and charms for her gold bracelet, and expensive little furs of sable and mink. Sitting there on the bed, she filled the room with the romantic fragrance of her perfume, and Judith imagined the huge cut-glass flagon, pressed upon her by some man mad to possess her, and set down carelessly, to join the dozen or so others on her dressing-table.

But, despite all this, she was very sweet; and very generous about lending clothes and giving advice about hair, and for some reason not in the least swollen-headed. Men, she implied, without actually saying so, were really something of a bore, and she was always perfectly content to escape their attentions and spend a little—but not too much—time with her family.

Now she curled up her legs, and settled herself comfortably down for a chat.

"Adore the colour of that jersey. Where did you get it?"

"In Plymouth, last Christmas."

"Of course. You weren't with us, were you? We missed you. How's school? Aren't you getting utterly sick of it? I nearly went mad with boredom when I was seventeen. And all those ghastly rules. Never mind, it'll soon be over and then you can whiz off to Singapore. Edward said he never realized how stultifying Harrow was until he left. I think Cambridge has opened up a whole new world for him."

"Ha . . . have you seen him lately?"

"Yes, he came and spent a night in London with me before setting off for Arosa. We had a lovely time, steaks and champagne and lots of catching up on news. Do you know what he's doing? You won't believe it. He's joined the University Flying Club, and he's learning to fly an aeroplane. Don't you think that's frightfully brave and heroic?"

"Yes, I do," Judith said with total truthfulness. The very thought of learning to fly an aeroplane she found quite terrifying.

"He adores it. Says it's the most magical thing in the world. Floating about like a sea-gull and looking at all the little fields."

"Do you think he'll be back for Christmas?"

"Bound to be. Some time or other. What are you going to wear for Christmas feasties? Have you got something new?"

"Well, yes, I have. It's not exactly new, but I haven't worn it yet."

"It's new, then. Tell me."

"It's made out of a sari. Mummy sent me one for my birthday, and your mother helped me draw a picture, and we took it to her dressmaker and she made it." It felt very companionable, discussing clothes with Athena in such a grown-up way. Loveday never talked about clothes, because they bored her and she didn't care how she looked. But Athena was instantly interested.

"Sounds sensational. Can I see it? Is it here?"

"Yes, in the wardrobe."

"Oh, do show."

Judith got off her knees and went to open the wardrobe and to reach for the padded hanger on which hung the precious dress, shrouded in black tissue paper.

"The paper's meant to keep the gold thread from tarnishing. I don't quite know why," she explained as she peeled it aside. "It was awfully difficult to design, because we wanted to use the border pattern, but Diana worked it out . . ."

The last sheet of paper drifted to the floor and the dress was revealed. She held it up in front of her, spreading the skirts to reveal their width. So fine was the silk that it all weighed nothing, just felt light as air. Around the deep hem and the cuffs of the little sleeves the gold key pattern of the sari's border glittered with reflected light.

Athena's jaw dropped. "Darling, it's divine. And what a colour. Not turquoise and not blue. Utterly perfect." Judith felt warm with delight. It was reassuring to have Athena, of all people, so genuinely enthusiastic. "What about your shoes?" She narrowed her eyes. "Gold or blue?"

"Gold. Sort of sandals."

"Of course. And you must wear gold jewellery. Huge earrings. I've got just the thing, I'll lend them to you. Goodness, you're going to devastate every man in the room. It's really heavenly, and I'm madly jealous. Now wrap it all up in its parcel, and put it away before it starts tarnishing or whatever it's meant to do."

She sat and watched while Judith, with some difficulty, accomplished this, and replaced the dress in the safety of the wardrobe. Athena then yawned enormously and looked at her wrist-watch.

"Goodie, it's a quarter to one. I don't know about you, but I'm simply starving. Let's go down before Nettlebed starts banging his gong." She rose gracefully from the bed, ran a hand over her shining hair, and was ready and waiting. "You haven't done much unpacking. My fault for interrupting you. Never mind. You can do it later. Isn't it heavenly to know it's holidays and you've got days and days? All the time in the world."

Judith was awakened by the wind, a gale which had risen during the night, and was now howling in from the sea, clouting at the window and rattling the casement. It was still dark. She had opened the window a fraction when she went to bed, but now the draught tore at the curtains, causing them to dance like ghouls, so after a bit she got out of bed and, shivering in the bitter air, shoved the window shut and closed the snib. Still it rattled, but the curtains were stilled. She turned on the bedside light, and saw that it was seven o'clock in the morning. Dawn had not yet started to lighten the stormy morning, so she jumped back into her warm bed again and pulled the eiderdown up over her shoulders. By now thoroughly wide awake, she lay and thought forward to the day ahead, and back to yesterday evening. Nancherrow was slowly filling up. The latest guests, Jane and Alistair Pearson, had arrived in time for dinner, having survived a long and icy car journey from London. The entire family had streamed out into the hall to greet them, hugging and kissing beneath the laden boughs of the glittering, fairy-lit Christmas tree. The new arrivals were an attractive pair, looking younger than their years, and bringing with them a buzz of London sophistication, he in his navy-blue overcoat and foulard scarf, and she in scarlet with a white fox collar. She had tied a silk scarf over her hair, but in the warm indoors, she unknotted and pulled this off, and her hair was dark and loose against the soft fur of her collar.

". . . oh, darling . . ." Diana was clearly thrilled. ". . . wonderful to see you. Was it a ghastly journey?"

"Frightfully skiddy, but Alistair never turned a hair. We thought it was going to snow. Thank goodness we didn't have the kiddywinks and Nanny with us. She'd have been frightened stiff."

"Where's your luggage? In the car?"

"Yes, and about a million parcels for under the tree . . ."

"We'll bring them in. Where's Nettlebed? Nettlebed!"

But Nettlebed was already there, making his way up the passage from the kitchen. "Don't worry, madam, I'll see to everything."

Which, of course, he had, and the Pearsons had been duly installed in the big bedroom with the four-poster bed, where, at this moment, they presumably still slept, unless, like Judith, they had been disturbed by the storm.

This showed no sign of abating. Another sudden squall assaulted the house, and rain spattered and streamed down the windowpane. Judith hoped that it was not going to continue all day, but the weather was the least of her worries. Far more pressing was the fact that although parcels were already piling up under the tree, Judith had not yet got a single present for anybody. But now wide awake, she lay and brooded about this for a bit, and then got out of bed and pulled on her dressing-gown and went to sit at her desk and start on a list. In a long line, she wrote seventeen names. Seventeen presents to buy and only three days in hand before the great day. No time to be lost. Swiftly, she made a plan, cleaned her teeth and washed her face, brushed her hair, got dressed, and went downstairs.

It was now eight o'clock. Breakfast at Nancherrow started at half past eight, but she knew that Colonel Carey-Lewis, relishing a little peace, was always early, able to eat his eggs and bacon in silence, and read the bits out of yesterday's newspaper that he had had neither time nor opportunity to peruse the day before.

She opened the dining-room door, and he was there, sitting in his chair at the head of the table. Startled, he lowered his paper and looked up over his spectacles, his expression clearly dismayed at this disturbance. But when he saw Judith, he politely rearranged his features into a semblance of pleasure. She thought, not for the first time, that he was probably the most courteous man she had ever met.

"Judith."

"I'm sorry." She closed the door. In the grate a fire had been kindled, and the coals gave off a bitter, acrid smell. "I know I'm interrupting you, and you don't want to talk a bit, but I've got a problem, and I thought you might be able to help me."

"But of course. What is it?"

"Well, it's this . . ."

"No, don't tell me until you've got something to eat. We shall discuss your problem then. Never make any sort of a decision on an empty stomach."

She smiled, and was filled with affection for him. Over the years she had been coming to Nancherrow she had become deeply fond of the Colonel, and their relationship had very soon lost its initial shyness, and become, if never intimate, then easy. As for him, he treated Judith, if not as one of his own daughters, then certainly as though she were a favourite niece. And so, obediently, she went to the sideboard, helped herself to a boiled egg and a cup of tea, and then returned to the table to sit beside him.

"Now. What is it?"

She explained. "It's Christmas presents. I haven't bought any. I couldn't at school, and there wasn't time before I came here. I've sent the family ones off, of course, ages ago, because you have to if they're to get to Singapore in time, but that's all. And I've just made a list, and I've got to get seventeen for everybody here."

"Seventeen?" He looked mildly amazed. "Are we really as many as that?"

"Well, we will be, by Christmas."

"So what do you want me to do?"

"Well, nothing really. I just wondered if there was a car going to Penzance, so that I could go too and shop. I didn't want to say anything to Diana, because she's got so much to do here, with all her guests arriving and everything. But I thought maybe *you* might be able to fix something."

"You were quite right to come to me. Diana's spinning like a top. Impossible to get a sensible word out of her." He smiled. "Why don't you and I go together, to Penzance, this morning?"

"Oh, but I didn't mean that you had to drive me . . ."

"I know you didn't, but I have to go in anyway, to the bank, and it may as well be this morning rather than any other time." He raised his head to gaze from the window as another assault of rain and wind was driven in from the sea. "There's little else one can do on such a day."

"Do you *really* have to go to the bank?"

"Yes, I really do. As you know, I'm not much of a shopper, so all my loved ones receive for Christmas an envelope with a bit of cash inside. It's so unimaginative that I try to make it more exciting by seeing that the bank notes are new ones, fresh and crisp. And those I shall collect this morning."

"But that won't take you a moment, and I shall be at least two hours. I don't want you hanging about, waiting for me."

"I shall go to the club, read the papers, see a few friends, and at the appropriate moment, buy myself a drink." He shot his cuff and looked at his watch. "If we waste no time, we can be in Penzance by ten o'clock, which should ensure that, without too much pressure, we should be back here in time for lunch. We must arrange a rendezvous. I suggest the Mitre Hotel at half past twelve. So that will allow you two and a half hours to make your purchases. If Diana is anything to go by, two hours is insufficient. A mere flea-bite. It takes her half a day to choose a hat."

He so seldom made any sort of a joke that Judith wanted to hug him, but didn't. Instead, "Oh, you are kind," she told him. "I'm so grateful. You've taken such a load off my mind."

"You must never keep your worries to yourself. Promise me that. And I shall enjoy your company. Now, be a dear girl, and pour me another cup of coffee . . ."

In Penzance the weather was no better. In fact, if anything, worse. Streets ran with rogue water, and overflowing gutters were awash with scraps of rubbish and broken twigs torn from trees. Beleaguered shoppers struggled with umbrellas, only to have them blown inside out, and hats were torn from heads, to go bowling away into oblivion. From time to time, slates, dislodged from roofs, came sailing down to smash to smithereens on pavements, and so dark was the morning that lights inside shops and offices burnt through the daylight hours. From the beach could be distinctly heard the sullen crash of high-tide rollers, and talk was all of disaster: flooded houses, fallen trees, and the vulnerability of the swimming pool, promenade, and harbour.

It felt a bit like being in a siege, but not unexciting; bundled up in rubber boots, a black oilskin, and with a woollen hat pulled down over her ears, Judith fought her way from shop to shop, gradually becoming laden with parcels, packages, and carrier bags.

At half past eleven, she found herself in W. H. Smith, the stationers, having bought presents for everybody except Edward. She had left his present to the last for two reasons. She couldn't think what to get for him, and she couldn't allow herself to be totally certain that he would actually be at Nancherrow for Christmas. *He'll be back from Arosa*, Diana had promised, but one couldn't be *sure*, and Judith so longed to see him again that she had become deeply superstitious about the whole business. It was a bit like taking an umbrella on a picnic as an insurance against a possible downpour. If she didn't buy him a present, then he would be bound to turn up, and Judith would have nothing to give him. But if she did, perhaps she was tempting Providence, and sure as eggs were eggs, he would decide, at the last moment, to stay on in Arosa with his friends. She imagined the telegram from Switzerland being delivered to Nancherrow; Diana, opening the envelope and reading the message aloud. TERRIBLY SORRY, STAYING ON HERE FOR CHRISTMAS AFTER ALL. SEE YOU ALL AT NEW YEAR. Or something. Perhaps . . .

"Can you get out of my way, please?" An irritated lady, trying to get to the counter with a box of writing-paper, disturbed these morose reflections.

"Sorry . . ." Judith gathered up her bundles and moved aside, but the small incident had brought her to her senses. Of course she must buy a present for Edward. If he didn't come home for Christmas, then she would give it to him later on. Surrounded by piles of lovely new books, she thought about getting him a book, but then decided against it. Instead . . . Feeling strong and determined, she plunged once more out into the wind and the rain and set off up Market Jew Street in the direction of Medways.

Even this old-fashioned shop, usually quiet and rather dull, was touched by the seasonal cheer. Paper bells hung from the lights, and there were more customers than usual—homely ladies buying sensible grey woollen socks for their spouses, or agonizing over the collar size of a new shirt. But Judith didn't want to buy socks for Edward, and she was certain that he had plenty of shirts. Debating the problem, and with water dripping from her oilskin into a small pool in the middle of the polished floor, she might have stood forever had not the most elderly of the salesmen approached her, and, faced by him, she was galvanized into decision.

She said, "A scarf?"

"For a Christmas present, is it?"

"Yes." She thought about it. "Something bright. Not navy blue or grey. Red, perhaps."

"How about tartan? We've got some lovely tartan scarves. They're cashmere, though, and quite pricey."

Cashmere. A tartan cashmere scarf. She imagined Edward with such a luxury knotted casually around his neck.

She said, "I don't mind if it's a bit expensive."

"Well, let's have a look then, shall we?"

She chose the brightest, red and green with a dash of yellow. The salesman retreated to wrap it for her, and she got out her cheque-book and her pen, and waited for him to return. Standing at the counter, she looked about her with some affection, for this fuddy-duddy old shop had been the unlikely venue for momentous memories. It was here that she had first set eyes on Diana Carey-Lewis and Loveday; and it was here that she had come that special day with Edward, and helped him to choose his tweed, and afterwards he had taken her out for lunch.

". . . there you are now, miss."

"Thank you." He had wrapped the scarf in holly paper.

"And this is your bill . . ."

Judith wrote her cheque. As she did this, the door from the street opened behind her. There was a momentary gale of a draught, and then the door closed again. She signed her name, tore off the cheque, and handed it over.

From behind her, a voice said her name. Startled, she turned, and found herself face to face with Edward.

Speechless shock lasted only for an instant, to be almost immediately replaced by a joyous leaping of her heart. She could feel the smile spreading across her face, her jaw drop in wonderment.

"*Edward!*"

"Surprise, surprise!"

"But what are you *doing* . . . ? How did you *get* . . . ? What are you *doing* here?"

"Came looking for you."

"I thought you were still in Arosa."

"Got back this morning, on the night train from London."

"But . . ."

"Look"—he laid a hand on her arm and gave her a little shake—"we can't talk here. Let's get out." He looked down at the plethora of carriers and parcels by which she was surrounded. "Is this all yours?" He sounded disbelieving.

"Christmas shopping."

"Have you finished?"

"I have now."

"Then let's go."

"Where to?"

"The Mitre. Where else? Isn't that where you're meeting Pops?"

She frowned. "Yes, but . . ."

"All will be explained." He was already gathering up her packages, and with two hands filled, making his way towards the door. Swiftly, she collected up the few items he had left on the floor, and hurried after him. He opened the heavy glass door with his shoulder and stood waiting until she had gone through, and then they were out in the rain-driven streets, heads down against the wind, crossing the road with Edward's usual lack of care and attention, and running down Chapel Street headed for the warmth and shelter of the old Mitre Hotel. Inside, he led her into the lounge, which smelt beery and of last night's cigarettes, but where there was a welcome fire, and no other people to disturb them.

They proceeded to make themselves at home. Edward piled all her packages in a neat pile on the floor, and with this accomplished, "Come on, get that soaking coat off and warm yourself up," he told her. "Shall I order some coffee? It'll probably taste disgusting, but with a bit of luck it'll be hot." Looking about him, he found a bell by the fireplace and went to press it. Judith unbuttoned her oilskin and laid it, for lack of anywhere better, over the back of an upright chair, where it slowly dripped, like a faulty tap, onto the faded Turkey carpet. She pulled off her woollen hat and shook her damp hair loose.

A very old waiter appeared at the door. Edward said, "We'd like some coffee, please. Lots of it. Perhaps two pots. And biscuits."

Judith found a comb in her bag, and tried to do something about her hair. There was a mirror over the mantelpiece and if she stood on tiptoe she could get a reflection. She saw her own face, her cheeks rosy from the wind and her eyes bright as stars. Happiness shows, she thought. She put her comb away, and turned to face him.

He looked wonderful; unshaven, but wonderful. Very tanned and hard and fit. Having ordered the coffee, he had divested himself of the sodden ski jacket, and beneath it wore corduroys and a navy-blue roll-neck sweater. The corduroys were dark with wet, and when he came to stand near the roaring fire, they steamed gently in the heat.

She said, "You look great."

"So do you."

"We didn't know you were coming home."

"I never sent a telegram or anything. But I was always coming. I wouldn't miss Christmas for all the skiing in the world. And if I'd said *when* I was coming, then Ma would have been fussing about meeting trains and all that crap. Better to be without deadlines, specially when you're travelling from Europe. You never know if you're going to catch the train, or if the ferry's going to run."

Judith understood his point of view, and decided that it was a very good philosophy. But . . . "So when did you get here?" she asked him.

He reached into his trouser pocket for his cigarettes and lighter, and she had to wait for his answer until he had got the cigarette going. He blew out a cloud of smoke, and smiled at her. "I told you. Night train. Got in at seven o'clock this morning."

"With nobody there to meet you."

He looked around for somewhere to sit, and chose an ancient armchair which he shoved and shunted across the carpet in order to be close to the fire. Into this he then collapsed.

"So what did you do?"

"It seemed a bit early to start ringing home and demanding transport and I'm too mean to take a taxi, so I left all my stuff at the station, and walked up to Pops' club and beat on the door until somebody let me in."

"I didn't think you were a member of your father's club."

"I'm not, but they know me, and I spun a sob story and got let in. And then I told them I'd been travelling for two days, I was tired and dirty, so they let me have the use of a bathroom, and I soaked in hot water for an hour, and then some kind lady cooked me breakfast."

She was filled with admiration. "Edward, what a nerve you've got."

"I thought it was rather a bright wheeze. Super breakfast. Bacon and eggs and sausages and scalding, very hot tea. And bless my soul, just as I was finishing this gargantuan feast—I hadn't eaten for about twelve hours—who should walk in but Pops."

"Was he as astonished as I was?"

"Just about."

"You are naughty. He might have had a heart attack."

"Oh, don't talk rubbish. He was just very pleased to see me. And he sat down and we had more tea together, and he told me he'd brought you into town to do your Christmas shopping, and was meeting you here at twelve-thirty. So I came to look for you and hurry you up."

"What made you think of Medways?"

"Well, you weren't in any other shop, so I finally ended up there." He grinned. "Successfully."

The very thought of him, in this appalling weather, trudging around Penzance in search of her touched Judith deeply, and filled her with a warm glow.

She said, "You could have just sat cosily in the club and read a newspaper."

"I didn't feel like sitting cosily anywhere. I've been sitting in stuffy trains for too long. Tell me how've you been . . ."

But before she could tell him, the antique waiter returned with a tray bearing coffee pots, cups and saucers, and two extremely small biscuits on a plate. Edward reached once more into his trouser pocket, produced a fistful of coins, and paid him. "Keep the change."

"Thank you, sir."

When he had gone, Judith knelt on the worn hearthrug and poured the coffee. It was black and smelt a bit funny, but was at least hot.

". . . what have you been doing with yourself?" he persisted.

"Nothing much. Just school."

"God, I'm sorry for you. Never mind, it'll soon be over, and you'll wonder how on earth you endured it. And Nancherrow?"

"Still standing."

"Stupid girl, I meant what's going on. Who's there?"

"Everybody, I think, now that you've arrived."

"What about friends and relations?"

"The Pearsons, from London. They came last night."

"Jane and Alistair? Good, they're good value."

"And I think their children and Nanny are arriving this evening, by train."

"Oh, well, I suppose we all have a little cross to bear."

"And Tommy Mortimer's coming for Christmas, but I'm not quite sure when."

"Inevitable." He put on Tommy Mortimer's mellifluous voice. "Diana, my darling girl, a tiny martini?"

"Oh, come on, he's not as bad as that."

"I rather like the old codger, as a matter of fact. And has Athena produced no panting swain?"

"Not this time."

"That at least is a cause for celebration. How's Aunt Lavinia?"

"I haven't seen her yet. I only got back from Saint Ursula's yesterday. But she's coming for Christmas dinner, I know."

"Majestic in black velvet, dear old girl." He drank some coffee and screwed up his face. "God, this *is* disgusting."

"Tell me about Arosa."

He put down his cup with a derisory clatter, and it was clear that he was going to drink no more. But, "Terrific," he told her. "All the tows working and not too many people. Fantastic snow, and sun all day long. We skied all day and danced most of the night . . . there's a new bar, Die Drei Husaren, where everybody goes. We were usually swept out at four in the morning." He burst into song. " 'Girls were made to love and kiss, and who am I to disagree with this.' We made the band play that every night."

We. Who was we? Judith suppressed an unworthy pang of envy. "Who was with you?" she asked.

"Oh, just friends from Cambridge."

"It must have been wonderful."

"You've never skied?"

She shook her head. "No."

"One day I'll take you."

"I can't ski."

"I'll teach you."

"Athena told me you're learning to fly."

"I've learned. I've got my pilot's licence."

"Is it frightening?"

"No, it's bliss. You feel quite inviolable. Superhuman."

"Is it difficult?"

"Easy as driving a car, and a million times more fascinating."

"I still think you're dreadfully brave."

"Oh, of course," he teased her, "the original intrepid birdman." Suddenly, he pushed back the woollen cuff of his sweater and squinted at his watch. "It's a quarter past twelve. Pops will be here before long to bear us all home. The sun's over the yardarm, so let's have a glass of bubbly."

"Champagne?"

"Why not?"

"Shouldn't we wait for your father to come?"

"Why? He hates champagne. You don't hate it, do you?"

"I've never drunk it."

"Then now is a good time to start." And before she could object, he sprang to his feet and went once more to press the bell for the waiter.

"But . . . in the middle of the *day*, Edward?"

"Of course. Champagne can be drunk at any hour of the day or night, that's one of its charms. My grandfather used to call it the rich man's Eno's. Besides, what better way is there for you and me to start Christmas?"

Judith sat at her dressing-table, leaned anxiously towards the mirror, and applied mascara to her eyelashes. It was the first time she had ever used mascara, but Athena's Christmas present to her had been a beautiful casket of Elizabeth Arden cosmetics, and the least she could do to say thank you was to try to deal with the complications of make-up. There was a little brush with the mascara box, which she had wet under the tap and then made a sort of paste. Athena's tip had been to spit on the mascara, she said that made it last longer, but spit seemed a bit disgusting and Judith had reverted to tap-water instead.

It was seven o'clock on Christmas evening, and here she was dressing herself up for the climax of Christmas dinner. She had set her hair, with Kirby grips, in a lot of little snail-like curls all over her head, and had cleaned her face with the new cleansing cream, and put on foundation cream, and a dusting of deliciously scented powder. The rouge was beyond her, but the mascara a challenge; luckily, it went on all right, and she managed not to stick the brush in her eye with possibly fatal consequences. Finished at last, she sat back, carefully not blinking, and waited for it to dry. Her reflection stared back, wide-eyed as a doll, but marvellously improved. She could not think why she had not tried mascara before.

Waiting, she listened. Beyond the closed door, the house was filled with small, distant sounds. A clatter of dishes from the kitchen, and Mrs. Nettlebed's voice raised as she called to her husband. Farther away still, the faint strains of a waltz. *The Count of Luxembourg*. Probably Edward trying out the radiogram, in case his mother decided that they should dance after dinner. And then, much closer to hand, splashings and raised childish voices from the guest bathroom, where Nanny Pearson was endeavouring to get her charges ready for bed. But they were both tired out, over-excited after the long day, and from time to time the childish voices broke into yowls and wails as they whined and grizzled and probably hit each other. Judith allowed herself a pang of sympathy for Nanny Pearson, who had been chasing after them all day. By now she must be longing for them to be unconscious in their beds, so that she could go to the nursery, put up her swollen ankles, and gossip with Mary Millyway.

The mascara seemed to be dry. Judith unpinned her hair and brushed it out, and coaxed the ends under into a gleaming page-boy. Now, the dress. She slid out of her dressing-gown and went to her bed, where she had laid out the butterfly-blue concoction in readiness for just this moment. She lifted it, weightless as gossamer, over her head, thrust arms into sleeves, felt the thin silk settle over her body. She fastened the tiny button at the back of the neck, and then did up the zip at the waist. It was a bit long, but once she had put on her new high-heeled sandals, that problem was solved. So, nearly there. The gold earrings, which Athena had so kindly lent her, screwed into lobes. The new lipstick, Coral Rose, the new scent, and she was ready.

She stood, and for the first time surveyed herself in the long mirror set in the centre of the wardrobe. It was all right. In fact, it was marvellous, because she looked really good. Tall, slender, and, most important of all, grown up. Eighteen at least. And the dress was a dream. She turned, and the skirts floated out around her, just like Ginger Rogers's; just the way they would float if Edward asked her to dance with him. She prayed that he would.

Time to go. She turned off the lights and went out of her room and along the passage, and the thick carpet felt soft through the thin soles of her sandals. From beyond the bathroom door came steamy smells of Pears soap, and Nanny Pearson's voice, admonishing. "What's the sense in being so stupid?" She thought about looking in to say goodnight, but decided against it, in case Roddy and Camilla started yowling again. Instead, down the back stairs, and so to the drawing-room. The door stood open, and she took a deep breath and went through, and it felt a bit like walking onto the stage in a school play. The huge pale-coloured room danced with firelight, and lamplight, and glittering Christmas baubles. She saw Aunt Lavinia, majestic in black velvet and diamonds, already ensconced in an armchair by the fireside, with the Colonel and Tommy Mortimer and Edward standing grouped about her. They held glasses and were talking, and so did not notice Judith, but Aunt Lavinia spied her immediately and raised her hand in a little gesture of welcome, and the three men turned to see who had interrupted them.

Conversation ceased. For an instant there was silence. Judith, hesitating at the door, was the one to break it.

"I'm the first down?"

"Dear God, it's Judith!" The Colonel shook his head in wonderment. "My dear, I hardly recognized you."

"What a perfectly gorgeous apparition!" That was Tommy Mortimer.

"I don't know why you all sound so surprised," Aunt Lavinia scolded them. "Of course she looks beautiful . . . and that colour, Judith! Just like a kingfisher."

But Edward didn't say anything. He just laid down his glass and crossed the room to her side, and took Judith's hand in his own. She looked up into his face, and knew that he didn't have to say anything, because his eyes said it all.

At last he spoke. "We're drinking champagne," he told her.

"*Again?*" she teased him, and he laughed.

"Come and join us."

Afterwards, in the years to come, whenever Judith recalled that Christmas dinner at Nancherrow in 1938, it was a bit like looking at an Impressionist painting: all the sharp edges blurred by the softness of candle-light, and the muzziness of a little too much champagne. The fire was lighted; logs flamed and crackled, but looming furniture and panelled walls and dark portraits retreated and merged, to become no more than a shadowed backdrop for the festive table. Silver candelabra marched down the centre of this, with, all about, sprigs of holly, scarlet crackers, dishes of nuts and fruit and Floris chocolates, and the dark mahogany was set with white linen place-mats and napkins, the most elaborate of the family silver, and crystal glasses fine and clear as soap bubbles.

As for the ten people who sat around the table, Judith was never to forget exactly how they were placed, and how they were dressed. The men, of course, in formal evening wear, dinner jackets, starched, snow-white shirts, and black bow-ties. The Colonel had decided upon a wing-collar, which made him look as though he had stepped straight from the gilded frame of some Victorian painting. And as for the women, it was as though they had all gone into conference beforehand, like royalty, to be certain that no colours clashed, and no lady would outshine the others.

The Colonel sat at the head of the table, in his usual huge Carver chair, with Nettlebed hovering behind him, and Aunt Lavinia at his right hand. Judith sat between her and Alistair Pearson; beyond him was Athena, looking like a summer goddess in sleeveless white shark-skin. On the Colonel's other side was Jane Pearson, bright as a parakeet in her favourite red, and with Edward at her left hand. This meant that Edward sat opposite to Judith, and from time to time she looked up and caught his eye, and he would smile as though they shared some splendid secret, and raise his wineglass to her, and sip champagne.

Alongside him was his younger sister. Loveday at sixteen was still on the cusp of being a teenager and becoming an adult, but for some reason this uncomfortable state did not bother her in the very least. She still lived for her riding, and spent much of her days down at the stables, mucking out and cleaning tack in the company of Walter Mudge. Clothes were as unimportant to her as they had ever been; stained and shrunken jodhpurs were her usual garb, paired with any old sweater she'd found in the nursery airing cupboard. And so, tonight, she wore no jewellery, her dark curls were artless as always, and her vivid face, with those amazing, violet eyes, shone, innocent of make-up. But her dress—her first long dress, chosen by Diana in London and given as one of Loveday's Christmas presents—was sheer enchantment. Organdie, the vivid green of young beech leaves, cut low over Loveday's shoulders and deeply ruffled at neck and hem. Even Loveday had been seduced by it, and dressed herself up without a word of complaint. Which was a great relief to everybody, in particular Mary Millyway, who knew the contrary ways of her erstwhile charge better than any of them.

Beside Loveday sat Tommy Mortimer, and then, at the far end of the table, Diana, in a slinky satin dress the colour of steel. As she moved, or as the light caught the folds, this shade subtly altered, so that sometimes it seemed blue, and sometimes grey. With it, she wore pearls and diamonds, the only dash of colour her scarlet nails and lipstick.

Conversation buzzed, voices rising as the wine and the delicious feast went down. First, paper-thin, rosy slices of smoked salmon; then turkey, bacon, sausages, roast potatoes, buttered sprouts and carrots, bread sauce, cranberry jelly, thick dark gravy rich with wine. By the time the plates were cleared from the table, Judith's dress was beginning to feel uncomfortably neat, but of course there was more to follow. Mrs. Nettlebed's Christmas pudding, her brandy butter, mince pies, and dishes of thick Cornish cream. Then nuts to be cracked and sweet little tangerines to be peeled, and crackers to be pulled. The formal dinner degenerated into a children's party, with unbecoming paper hats worn askew, and painful jokes and riddles to be read aloud.

But finally it was all over and time for the ladies to leave. They rose from the table, now littered with torn paper, chocolate wrappings, ashtrays and broken nutshells, and withdrew, headed for the drawing-room and coffee. Diana led the way. As she went, she paused to stoop and kiss her husband. "Ten minutes," she told him. "That's all the time you're allowed to drink your port. Otherwise the evening will fall to pieces."

"And how are we going to spend the rest of it?"

"We shall dance the night away, of course. How else?"

And indeed, by the time the men did join the ladies, Diana had organized everything: the sofas and chairs pushed aside, the rugs rolled back, and the radiogram stacked with her favourite dance records.

The music was another thing Judith was always to remember; the tunes of that evening, that year. "Smoke Gets in Your Eyes" and "You're the Cream in My Coffee," and "Deep Purple" and "D'Lovely."

> The moon is out,
> The skies are clear
> And if you want to go walking, dear,
> It's delightful, it's delicious, it's d'lovely . . .

She danced that one with Tommy Mortimer, who was so expert that she didn't even have to think about what her feet were meant to be doing. And then it was Alistair Pearson's turn, and that was quite different, because all he did was to march her briskly around the room, rather as though she were a vacuum cleaner. After that there was a waltz, for Aunt Lavinia's benefit, and she and the Colonel were quite the best and showed them all up, because they were the only pair who knew how to reverse properly, and Aunt Lavinia lifted the heavy velvet skirts of her dress with one hand, revealing diamond-buckled shoes, her feet twinkling and turning with all the lightness and vitality of the young girl that she had once been.

Waltzing was a thirsty business. Judith went to pour herself an orange juice, and turned from the table to find Edward at her side. "I've left the best till the last," he told her. "Done my duty to all friends and relations. Now come and dance with me."

She laid down the glass and went into his arms.

> I took one look at you,
> That's all I had to do
> And then my heart stood still.

But her heart wasn't standing still. It was thumping so hard she was sure that he must feel its beat. He held her very close and sang the words of the song softly into her ear, and she wished the music would go on forever and never end. But of course it did and they drew apart, and he said, "You can have your orange juice now," and went to fetch it for her.

For a moment there was a bit of a lull, as though everybody was beginning to feel slightly exhausted and grateful for a breather. Except Diana. For her every moment had to be filled, and when the music started up again, it was that old classic "Jealousy," and she instantly went over to the armchair where Tommy Mortimer reclined, took him by the hand, and pulled him to his feet. Dutiful as ever, he drew her towards him, and the pair of them, alone on the floor, danced the tango.

They did this with the expertise of professionals, but, as well, in the most satirical of ways, their bodies pressed close and arms held high and rigid. Every step and pause and swoop was exaggerated, and, unsmiling, they stared intensely into each other's eyes. It was an extraordinary performance, but, as well, extremely funny and, on the final chord of strumming guitars, ended triumphantly, with Diana bent backwards over Tommy's supporting arm, he looming passionately over her, and her blonde head very nearly touching the floor. Only then, as Tommy lifted her upright to a storm of applause, did Diana allow herself to dissolve into laughter. She went to sit by Aunt Lavinia, who was wiping tears of mirth from her eyes. "Diana, my darling, your tango was brilliant, but keeping a straight face even more so. You should have been on the stage. Oh dear, I don't know when I've enjoyed myself so much, but you know, it's nearly midnight. I really should call it a day, and go home."

The Colonel, trying not to look too eager, instantly moved forward. "I shall drive you."

"I hate to break up the party." She let him help her up out of her chair. "But the best time to go is when you're really enjoying yourself! Now, my wrap, I believe, is in the hall . . ." She moved around the room, kissing and saying good night. At the door, she turned. "Darling Diana . . ." She blew a final kiss. "Such a perfect evening. I'll telephone in the morning."

"Sleep in, Aunt Lavinia, and have a good rest."

"Maybe I will. Good night, everybody. Good night."

She was gone, with the Colonel in attendance. The door closed behind them. Diana waited for a moment, and then turned, and stooped to help herself to a cigarette. For an instant the atmosphere felt strange, as though they were all children, left on their own without grown-ups to spoil their fun.

Her cigarette lighted, Diana surveyed her guests. "What shall we do now?" Nobody seemed to have any bright suggestions. "I know." Suddenly her smile was brilliant. "Let's play Sardines."

Athena, still sipping champagne, let out a groan. "Oh, *Mummy*. Grow up!"

"Why not Sardines? We haven't played for ages. Everybody knows how to play, don't they?"

Alistair Pearson said that he'd played, years ago, but had forgotten the rules. Perhaps if somebody could . . . ?

Edward explained. "One person hides. The house is dark. We turn off all the lights. The others wait here. We count a hundred and then all go off in search. If you find the hider, you don't say anything. Just sneak in and hide alongside, until everybody's crammed into a laundry basket or a wardrobe or wherever the hiding-place happens to be. Last one in is the booby."

"Oh, yes," said Alistair, not sounding over-enthusiastic. "I remember now."

"The only rule is," Diana chipped in, "that we must all stay downstairs. There's masses of space, and if we go upstairs somebody's bound to wake the children . . ."

"Or get into bed with Nanny Pearson . . ."

"Oh, *Edward*."

"By mistake, of course."

"But how," asked Alistair, doggedly determined to get everything straight, "do we pick the person who's going to hide first?"

"We draw cards. Spades are high, and the highest card wins." Diana went to her bridge table, opened a drawer, and took out a pack; arranged them face down, in a clumsy fan, and went from one to the other so that each could pick. Judith turned her card over. The ace of spades. She said, "It's me."

Loveday was dispatched by Diana to switch off all the lights. "Every single light in the house?" she asked.

"No, darling, not the upstairs landing. Otherwise there'll be a nanny-panic and people falling downstairs."

"But that'll mean we can *see*."

"Scarcely anything. Quickly, off you run."

"Now." Edward took charge. "We'll give you a count of a hundred, Judith, and then we'll come after you."

"Anywhere out of bounds?"

"The kitchen, I think. I don't suppose the Nettlebeds are finished in there yet. Otherwise you've got a free rein."

Loveday returned to them. "It's really dark and spooky," she announced with some satisfaction. "You can scarcely see a *thing*."

Judith was gripped by a tremor of anxious fear. Ridiculous, but she wished that the high card had been picked by one of the others. She had never admitted to anybody the state of nerves to which she was reduced by these sort of games, and had always found even hide-and-seek in the garden something of an ordeal, because she usually spent most of the time wanting to go to the lavatory.

But there was nothing to be done, except to brave it out.

"Let's start, then. On your marks, Judith. Ready, steady, go."

They had started counting before she was even through the door. *One, two, three* . . . She closed the door behind her, and was overwhelmed by inky blackness. It was like having a dense velvet bag put over her head. She was gripped by panic, searching in her mind for some bolt-hole to crouch in before they all came, like hounds, baying after her. She shivered, but behind the door they were still counting. *Thirteen, fourteen, fifteen.* By now, however, her eyes were becoming used to the dark, were able to see, at the far end of the hall, the faint gleam filtering down the staircase from the light that burnt upstairs, outside the nursery door.

Which made everything a bit better. And there was no time to be lost. She went forward, cautious as a blind person, uncertain, and terrified that some chair or table was about to trip her up. Where to hide? Endeavouring to orientate herself, to measure distances, known so well but now totally confusing, she paced her own timorous footsteps, and calculated her whereabouts. On her right the small sitting-room, and then farther on, the dining-room. On the other side lay the billiard-room and the Colonel's study. As she went down the hall, the pale light from upstairs drew her onwards. She moved to the left, her hand touched the wall, and she let the moulding of the cornice guide her; bumped into a table, felt the cold brush of leaves against her bare arm. Then, the upright of a doorway. Fingers fumbled across the heavy panelling, found the handle, turned it, and slipped inside.

The billiard-room. Black-dark now. Softly she shut the door behind her. She smelt the familiar smell, musty baize and cigar smoke. Cheating, she felt for the electric switch and turned it down. The billiard-table was instantly illuminated, swathed in dust sheets. All was neat and orderly; cues standing in their racks, ready for the next game. No fire, but the heavy brocade curtains drawn close. She got her bearings, and then turned the light off again, and sped across the huge room, her feet making no sound on the thick Turkey rug.

The tall windows in this room had a deep, high sill, where sometimes, on a wet afternoon, she and Loveday perched, watching some game in progress and endeavouring to keep the score. Not a very imaginative hiding-place, but she could think of no other, and the seconds were speeding by. She pushed a curtain aside, gathered up her long skirts, and scrambled up onto the sill. Then, swiftly, dealt with the curtains, drawing them close, settling their folds, so that they would appear undisturbed and no betraying chink of light could give her away.

It was done. She had made it. She was here. She moved sideways, and leaned her shoulders against the mouldings of the shutter. It was dreadfully cold, like being in a very tiny, cold room, because the glass of the windows was icy, and the thick curtains kept out all the warmth of the radiators. Outside, the sky was dark, swept with grey clouds, which parted from time to time to reveal the twinkle of starlight. She looked out into the darkness and saw the silhouettes of winter trees, restless, tossing their heads in the wind. She hadn't noticed the wind before, but now, shivering, she was very aware of it, piping at the edge of the windows, like something that wanted to be let in.

A sound. She raised her head to listen. Far off, a door opened. A raised voice. "We're *coming!* Ready or not!" They were done with counting. Now, they were on her scent; on the hunt. She thought about going to the lavatory, and then, firmly, didn't think about it. She hoped they would all find her before she died of cold.

She waited. The wait seemed to last forever. More voices. Footsteps. A shriek of feminine laughter. Minutes passed. And then, very softly, a door opened and was closed again. The billiard-room door. She was terribly aware of the looming presence of another person, and was all at once terrified. But no sound. The thick carpet would muffle any sound, but she was suddenly quite certain that footsteps were creeping towards her. She held her breath, in case breathing betrayed her. Then a curtain was gently drawn back, and Edward whispered, "Judith?"

"Oh," an involuntary sigh of relief that the waiting and the tension were over. "I'm here," she whispered back.

He vaulted lightly up onto the deep windowsill, and drew the curtain behind him. He stood, and was there, tall and solid and very close. And warm.

"Do you know how I found you?"

"You mustn't talk. They'll hear."

"Do you know?"

"No."

"I smelt you."

She stifled a nervous giggle. "How horrible."

"No. Lovely. Your scent."

"I'm freezing."

"It's bloody cold. Here." He drew her towards him, and began to rub her goose-pimpled arms briskly, rather as though he were drying a dog. "My God, you *are* frozen. How's that? Is that better?"

"Yes. Better."

"It's like being in a little house, isn't it? With a wall and a window and just enough space in between."

"Outside, there's a wind. I didn't know there was a wind tonight."

"There's always a wind at night. It's a present from the sea. Tonight it's a Christmas present." And with that, and no further ado, he put his arms around her, pulled her close, and kissed her. She had always imagined that being kissed for the first time, properly, by a man, would be terrifying and strange, and an experience that she would need to get used to, but Edward's kiss was hard and competent, and not strange in the very least, just wonderfully comforting, and obscurely what she had been dreaming of for months.

He stopped kissing her, but continued to hold her, pressed to his shirt-front, rubbing his cheek against her cheek, nuzzling her ear. "I've been wanting to do this all evening. Ever since you came through the door looking like . . . what was it Aunt Lavinia said . . . a beautiful kingfisher."

He drew away, and looked down at her. "How could such a funny little cygnet grow into such a beautiful swan?" He smiled, and there was enough light to see his smile. She felt his warm hand move from her shoulder, move down her back, caressing her waist and her hips through the thin folds of the blue silk dress. And then he kissed her again, but it was different this time, because his mouth was open, and his tongue was forcing her lips apart, and now his hand was cupping her breast, kneading the soft flesh . . .

And it all came back. Mercifully out of mind for so long, the horror returned, and she was in the cinema again, the dark, grubby little cinema, and Billy Fawcett's hand was on her knee, groping, violating her privacy, working its way . . .

Her panic reaction was totally instinctive. What had been pleasurable and delightful became all at once menacing, and it was no good telling herself that this was *Edward* because it didn't matter who it was; she simply knew that she couldn't deal with this sexual intrusion. She didn't want it, any more than she had wanted it or been able to deal with it when she was fourteen years old. She could not have stopped herself had she wanted to, but sharply brought up her arms and shoved hard against Edward's chest.

"*No!*"

"Judith?" She heard the bewilderment in his voice; stared up into his face, and saw his puzzled frown. She said again, "No, Edward." She shook her head violently. "No."

"What's the panic? It's only me."

"I don't want. You mustn't . . ."

She pushed him away from her, and he let her go. She backed off, so that once more her shoulders were pressed against the bony strappings of the shutter. For a moment, neither of them spoke. The silence lay between them, accompanied only by the pipe of the wind. Gradually, Judith's stupid, reasonless panic died away, and she felt her racing heart settle down to its normal beat. *What have I done?* she asked herself, and was filled with shame because she had wanted to be so grown up, and instead had behaved like a gauche and flustered idiot. Billy Fawcett. She suddenly wanted to scream with rage at herself. Thought about trying to explain it all to Edward, and knew that she never could.

She said, at last, "I'm sorry." It sounded pathetically inadequate.

"Don't you like being kissed?" Clearly, Edward was totally confused. Judith found time to wonder if any girl had ever treated him thus. Edward Carey-Lewis, that privileged, gilded youth, who had probably never, in all his life, had any person say No to him.

"It's all my fault," she told him bleakly.

"I thought that was what you wanted."

"I did . . . I mean . . . Oh, I don't know."

"I can't bear you to sound so wretched . . ." He took a step towards her, but in some desperation, she put up her hands and held him off. "What is it?"

"Oh, it's nothing. It's *nothing* to do with you."

"But . . ."

He stopped. Turned his head to listen. Beyond the curtains the billiard-room door was opened and gently closed. Discovery was close at hand, and too late now to make amends. In some despair Judith gazed up at Edward's profile, and told herself that she had lost him forever. There was time to say no more. The curtain twitched aside.

"I thought you might be here," whispered Loveday, and Edward stooped to give her a hand, and hoist her up onto the windowsill to join them.

That night the old dream returned. The nightmare that she had thought buried and forgotten forever. Her bedroom at Windyridge, and the open window, and the curtains blowing, and Billy Fawcett climbing up his ladder to get at her. And lying paralysed with terror, watching and waiting for his head to appear over the sill, his bright and knowing eyes, and his yellow-toothed smile. And, as he came, jerking awake in a sweat of fear, sitting bolt upright and with her mouth open in a silent scream.

It was as though he had won. He had spoilt everything for her, because in some ghastly, gruesome way she had confused him with Edward, and Edward's hands had become Billy Fawcett's hands, and all her basic inhibitions had leapt into life, and she was too young and too inexperienced to know how to deal with them.

She lay in her darkened bedroom at Nancherrow and wept into the pillow, because she loved Edward so much and she had ruined everything, and nothing was ever going to be the same again.

But she had reckoned without Edward. In the morning, still asleep, she was wakened by him. She heard his soft knock, and her door open. "Judith?" It was dark, but the ceiling light was abruptly switched on, assaulting her eyes with its hard glare. Thus dragged out of sleep, she sat up, blinking and confused.

"Judith."

Edward. She stared at him stupidly. Saw him shaved, dressed, clear-eyed and ready for the new day, looking not at all as though he had climbed into bed at three o'clock in the morning.

"What is it?"

"Don't look so alarmed."

"What time is it?"

"Nine." He went to the window to draw back her curtains, and her room was filled with the grey light of the late-December morning.

"I've slept in."

"Doesn't matter. Everybody's sleeping in this morning."

He returned to the door to turn off the light, and then came to settle himself, without ceremony, on the side of the bed. He said, "We have to talk."

Memories of last night came flooding back. "Oh, Edward." She felt as though she were about to succumb once more to unstoppable tears.

"Don't look so anguished. Here . . ." He stooped and retrieved her dressing-gown from the rug by her bed. "Put this on, otherwise you'll die of cold." She did as she was told, shoving her arms into the sleeves, and bundling it around her. "How did you sleep?"

She remembered the horribly familiar dream. "All right," she fibbed.

"I'm glad. Now look, I've thought everything through, and that's why I'm here. What happened last night—"

"It was my fault."

"It wasn't anybody's fault. Perhaps I misjudged the situation, but I'm not going to apologize because, by my reckoning, I didn't do anything to apologize for. Except, perhaps to forget how young you still are. Dressed up and looking so glamorous, it seemed to me that you'd grown up in a minute. But of course, nobody can do that. They just look as though they have. You don't change inside."

"No." Judith looked down, watched her own fingers pleating the edge of the sheet. She said painfully, "I did want you to kiss me. I wanted to dance with you, and then I wanted you to kiss me. And then I spoilt it all."

"But you don't hate me?"

She looked up into his eyes, his straight blue gaze. "No," she told him. "I'm much too fond of you to hate you."

"In that case, we can wipe the slate clean."

"Is that why you came and woke me up?"

"Not entirely. I just wanted to be certain that we understood each other. Because there mustn't be any tension or disagreement between us. Not because of you and me, but because of everybody else in the house. We're all going to be together for a few days yet, and nothing would be more uncomfortable than any sort of an atmosphere, non-speaks, loaded remarks or gloomy faces. Do you understand what I'm saying?"

"Yes, Edward."

"My mother is as sharp as a needle when it comes to other people's relationships. I don't want her sending you long quizzical looks or asking me loaded questions. So you won't droop around, will you, doing an imitation of the Lady of Shallot?"

"No, Edward."

"Good girl."

Judith did not reply to this, because she couldn't think of anything to say, simply sat there churning with mixed emotions.

Relief was uppermost. Relief that Edward wasn't going to ignore and despise her for the rest of her life; that he still wanted to talk to her, to remain friends. And that he didn't think of her as a two-faced little cock-teaser. (She had gleaned this sophisticated phrase from Heather Warren, who had learned it from her brother Paddy. Paddy had a girl-friend whom he much fancied, but with whom, despite her dyed hair, short skirts, and enticing ways, he had got nowhere. *She's a bloody little cock-teaser*, he had finally told his sister, and gone off in a filthy temper, and at the first possible opportunity, Heather had relayed this fascinating information to Judith, making it perfectly clear that such behaviour counted, with men, for less than nothing.)

So, relief. But, as well, Judith found herself touched by Edward's good sense; prompted mainly by concern for his mother and her Christmas house party, but surely, too, he had been thinking a little bit of her.

She said, "You're completely right, of course."

"So," he smiled. "Family loyalties?"

"They're not my family."

"Close as . . ."

Which filled her with love for him. She put up her arms and pulled him close and kissed his smooth cheek. He smelt fresh and lemony. The nightmare of Billy Fawcett had flown again, chased off by Edward and the clear light of morning, and love was back where it belonged. She lay back on the pillows. "Have you had breakfast yet?"

"Not yet. Sorting things out seemed more important."

"I'm starving," Judith told him, and found, somewhat to her surprise, that this was true.

"You sound like Athena." He got off the bed. "I'll go down. How long will you be?"

"Ten minutes."

"I shall wait for you."

1939

*S*peech Day at Saint Ursula's took place, by tradition, during the last week of July, on the last day of the summer term, and at the end of the school year. It was an occasion of great ceremony, following a time-honoured pattern of procedure. Assembly of parents and girls in the Great Hall, a prayer, a speech or two, prize-giving, the School Hymn, a blessing from the Bishop, and then afternoon tea, served either in the dining-hall or the garden, according to the clemency of the weather. All over, everybody escaped, home for the summer holidays.

The wording of the invitation to this annual function was, as well, unchanging.

> The Governors of Saint Ursula's School for Girls, and Miss Muriel Catto (M.A. Cantab) . . . Speech Day . . . The Great Hall at 2 P.M. . . . Please be in your places by 1:45 P.M. . . . RSVP to the Headmistress's Secretary . . .

A nice, thick, gold-edged card, and copperplate script. A bit, thought some parents, like a Royal Command.

But dutifully, they turned up, obediently on time. By ten to two the impressive oak-panelled hall was jam-packed with humanity, and, despite opened windows on all sides, extremely warm, for prayers had been answered and out of doors bloomed a perfect summer day, without a cloud in the sky. Normally the Great Hall was an austere place, draughty and chill as an unheated church, its only decoration a stained-glass window depicting the martyrdom of Saint Sebastian, some Rolls of Honour, and a shield or two. But today it fairly burgeoned with flowers and greenery, pot plants brought in from the greenhouses, and the scent of these, lying heavy on the warm air, was almost overpowering.

At the north end of the hall stood an elevated stage, flanked by two flights of wooden steps leading up from the auditorium. This was where Miss Catto took Morning Prayers, standing behind her lectern, delivering daily instruction, admonitions, and generally keeping her school more or less on its toes. Today however, it was fronted by a positive flower-bed of potted pelargoniums, and set with a spaced row of throne-like chairs, all ready for the platform party. It was the arrival of this illustrious group—the Bishop, the Chairman of the Governing Board, the Lord Lieutenant of the County, Lady Beazeley (who had been dragooned into giving away the prizes), and Miss Catto—which the assembled company now awaited.

Two-thirds of this consisted of parents and families, all dressed to the nines. Mothers sported garden-party hats and white gloves, flowered silk frocks and high-heeled shoes. Fathers were mostly in dark suits, except that here and there stood a man in service uniform. Smaller siblings wore smocks of liberty lawn and hair ribbons, or were decked out in sailor suits, with white lanyards and pipe-clayed shoes. Their protestations could be clearly heard as they grizzled plaintively, complaining of heat and boredom.

Edgar and Diana Carey-Lewis were part of this throng, as were Mr. Baines, the solicitor, and his wife. The smaller Baines children were not present. Prudently, they had been left at home with their nurserymaid.

The remainder of the auditorium, at the front of the Hall, was filled with girls; the smallest in the front on kindergarten benches, and the seniors at the back. All of them wore their regulation party frocks, long-sleeved cream tussore, and black silk stockings. Only the very littlest were permitted to be cool in white socks. At the end of each row of girls sat a member of staff, formally attired, and wearing her black gown. But even these archaic garments were rendered, today, quite glamorous, because every mistress had donned her academic hood, the carefully arranged folds revealing silken linings of ruby red, emerald green, or sapphire blue.

Judith, sitting in the very back row of the school party, pushed back the cuff of her dress to look at her watch. Two minutes to two. In a moment they would come, the platform party, summoned from Miss Catto's study by the Head Girl, Freda Roberts. Judith was a prefect, but she had not been made Head Girl. Remembering the dreaded Deirdre Ledingham, for this small mercy she was endlessly grateful.

Behind her, a little boy squirmed in discomfort. "I want somefin to drink," he whined, and was instantly shushed.

She was filled with sympathy for him. Speech Day was always an ordeal, and being eighteen and knowing that this was the very end of school, and the very last Speech Day ever, somehow didn't make it any more bearable. The tussore dresses were heavy and airless, and she could feel trickles of sweat starting under her arms and behind her knees. To divert her thoughts from her own discomfort, she began to make a mental list of positive and cheering events that had happened or were about to happen.

The most important was that she reckoned that, with a bit of luck, she would have passed her Matriculation. Results wouldn't be published until later on in the year, but Miss Catto was confident, and already had started to make arrangements for Judith to go to Oxford.

But even if it all worked out, that wouldn't be for another year, because in October a passage had already been booked on a P & O boat bound for Singapore, and she was going to spend ten months, at least, reunited with her family. *One thing at a time*, she had told herself all those years ago, leaning over the rail of Penzance promenade and watching the grey sea splashing onto the pebbled beach. *Finish school, pass exams, and then go back to the Far East and be with Mum and Dad and Jess.* Jess was eight now. Judith could hardly wait to see them all.

More immediately, there were other good things. The end of school-days, freedom, and summer holidays. For these, plans had been laid: two weeks in August to be spent in Porthkerris with Heather Warren and her parents, and later on, perhaps, a visit to Aunt Biddy. The dates for this had not yet been fixed. "Just ring me and let me know when you want to come," Biddy had told her in a letter. "It's an open invitation, so I'll leave the timing to you."

Otherwise, Nancherrow. Which meant Edward.

She sat in the stuffy school hall, and was suffused with blissful anticipation. The events of Christmas, his abortive advances behind the drawn curtains of the billiard-room, her childish rejection of these, and his subsequent handling of the unhappy situation had finally tipped the scales of Judith's relationship with Edward, and she had secretly opened her heart to him, and fallen, totally, in love. She could not imagine how any man, so attractive and desirable, could be, as well, so understanding and patient. Because of him, the harmless incident, which could have precipitated a most destructive embarrassment, slipped away unnoticed, like water streaming beneath a bridge. Gratitude and admiration were both part of loving. Propinquity . . . (She had looked the word up in the dictionary. "Nearness in place," it told her. "Close kinship") . . . was even stronger.

Separation, as well, played its part. Separation, like the wind, blowing out a small candle, but causing a strong flame to burn even brighter. Judith had not seen Edward since January. He had spent his Easter vacation on a ranch in Colorado, invited by a fellow undergraduate, a bright young American student who had won a scholarship to Cambridge. The two young men had sailed in the *Queen Mary* from Southampton to New York, and then travelled by train to Denver. It all sounded enormously adventurous, and although Edward was not much of a correspondent, he had sent Judith a couple of postcards, with highly coloured pictures of the Rocky Mountains, and Red Indians selling baskets. These treasured mementoes she kept within the leaves of her diary, along with a snap that she had stolen from Loveday's photograph album. If Loveday had noticed its disappearance, she had said nothing. As for right now, this very moment, he was in the south of France, having gone straight there from Cambridge, with a party of young friends, to stay in somebody's aunt's villa.

When Diana told the girls of this latest ploy, she was consumed by rueful laughter, shaking her head in wonder, while clearly delighted by evidence of her precious son's popularity. "It's so extraordinary, the way he always falls on his feet! Not only does he make rich friends, but they all seem to have houses in the most exotic spots. And, what is more, ask him to stay. Which is nice for Edward, but a bit sad for the rest of us. Never mind. Hopefully, for a bit of the summer, he'll come home."

Judith didn't mind. Anticipation, looking forward to seeing Edward again, was all part of the joy.

The other tremendously exciting thing that had happened was that Mr. Baines had said that Judith could buy a little car of her own. She had spent the Edward-less Easter holidays learning how to drive, and had, unbelievably, passed her test first go. But it was a bit difficult, at Nancherrow, to find something *to* drive. Diana's Bentley and the Colonel's Daimler were out of the question, because both were so grand, and she was terrified of so much as denting a bumper. And their family runabout was the old-fashioned shooting-brake, so enormous it was a bit like driving a bus.

She had explained her predicament to Mr. Baines. ". . . it's just that if I want to go and buy something in Penzance, I have to wait until somebody else is going in a car, and then get a lift, and it's not always convenient for anybody."

He had been most understanding. "Yes, I see," he had said, and fallen silent, considering the problem, then made up his mind. "You know, Judith, I think you should have a car of your own. You're eighteen and perfectly responsible. And of course you should be able to come and go just as you wish, without being a burden on the Carey-Lewises."

"*Really?*" She could scarcely believe her ears. "A car of my own?"

"You'd like that, wouldn't you?"

"Oh, more than anything, but I never imagined you'd suggest such a thing. And if I did get one, I'd really look after it and wash it and put petrol in and everything. And I'd use it. It used to make me so frustrated when Mummy wouldn't drive the Austin because she was frightened. There were so many lovely places we could have gone, and so many lovely things to see, like gardens and secret beaches. But we never did."

"Will you do those things?"

"Not necessarily. But so wonderful to know I *can* if I want to. And there's something else I could do that's been bothering me for ages. It's Phyllis, who used to work for us at Riverview. She got another job in Porthkerris, but then she married her young man and went to live at Pendeen with him. He's a miner, and the mine company gave them a little house to live in, and now she's had a baby, and I'd really like to go and see her. If I had a car I could do that."

"Phyllis. Yes, I remember Phyllis, answering the door when I came to see your mother. She was always smiling."

"She's a darling. One of my best friends. We've kept in touch, and written postcards and letters, but I haven't seen her since I said goodbye four years ago. Even when I was staying in Porthkerris it wasn't possible, because there was only one bus a week, and it was far too far to bike."

"It's ridiculous, isn't it?" said Mr. Baines with some sympathy. "We live in this small county and yet are remote from each other as creatures in the moon." He smiled. "A car of your own, and independence, seems to me a necessity and not a luxury. But don't count on it. Finish school, and pass your Matriculation and we'll consider the matter. I'll have a word with Captain Somerville."

And there the matter had rested. But Judith was full of hope because, at the end of the day, she couldn't imagine Uncle Bob saying No.

It occurred to Judith that perhaps, with luck, she would get the car *before* she went to stay with the Warrens, and would be able to drive herself to Porthkerris. Loveday had been invited as well, to join the cheerful household over the grocer's shop, but had not yet committed herself, because she had a new pony to school, and various gymkhanas and events which she planned to enter, and hopefully win. If, however, she was presented with the added lure of a car of their own in which to travel, there was every possibility that she would make up her mind and come, if only for a few days. The thought of herself and Loveday bowling across the county in a little sports two-seater, with their suitcases piled on the back seat, was so dizzying that she would have liked, then and there, to share it with Loveday, but Loveday was sitting two rows ahead, and so it would have to wait.

Loveday, at seventeen, was also leaving Saint Ursula's forever. She had never been made a prefect, and academically had got no farther than sitting her School Certificate examination, but had made it perfectly clear to her long-suffering parents that, without Judith, Saint Ursula's would be unbearable.

"But, darling, what are we going to do with you?" Diana had asked in some perplexity.

"I'll stay at home."

"You can't simply *moulder* here. You'll turn into a cabbage."

"I could go to Switzerland, like Athena."

"But you always said we were *never* to send you away again."

"Switzerland's different."

"I suppose you could go. Not that it did Athena much good. All she learned to do was ski, and fall in love with her instructor."

"That's why I want to go."

And Diana had dissolved into laughter and hugged her youngest child, and said that she would see.

Two o'clock. A small disturbance at the back of the hall, and the entire company rose, thankfully, to its feet. At last the occasion was under way. It was a bit, thought Judith, like a wedding, with all the flowers, and everybody in their best, mothers fanning themselves with hymn sheets, and the bride about to swan into view on the arm of her father. So strong was this illusion that, as the Bishop led the small procession down the aisle, she half-expected an organ to start belting out some toccata or other.

But there was, of course, no bride. Instead, the platform party took their places on the stage. The Bishop stepped forward and delivered his short prayer. Everybody sat. The ceremony proceeded.

Speeches. (The Chairman of the Governors droned on forever, but Miss Catto was brisk, brief, and even quite funny, raising a welcome and spontaneous laugh or two.)

Prize-giving. Judith thought she might get the Senior English Prize, which she did, and then went up again for the Senior History Prize; a bonus, because that had not been remotely expected. Finally, the last prize of all. The coveted Carnhayl Cup.

Judith by now was stifling a yawn. She knew perfectly well who was going to get the Carnhayl Cup. Freda Roberts, who spent her days running around being obsequious, and sucking up to all the mistresses.

The Carnhayl Cup, Miss Catto was explaining in her clear voice, was presented annually to the girl who, by the popular vote of her entire staff of teachers, had contributed most to the school. Not simply academic work, but those three essential Cs: Capability, Character, and Charm. And the winner this year was . . . Judith Dunbar.

She felt her mouth drop open in an unbelieving and unbecoming gape. Somebody gave her a dig in the ribs and said, "Go on, you idiot," and she scrambled to her feet for the third time and went, feeling quite weak at the knees, to collect her prestigious trophy. So wobbly were her legs that she tripped going up the steps, and just about fell flat on her face.

"Well done," said Lady Beazeley with a beaming smile, and Judith took the cup and bobbed a curtsey and returned to her place to a storm of applause and with cheeks, she knew, red as beetroots.

Then, finally, the School Hymn. The music mistress, already in her place, crashed out a chord on her piano, everybody rose to their feet, and eight hundred voices just about raised the roof.

> "He who would valiant be
> 'Gainst all disaster
> Let him in constancy
> Follow the Master."

The power of music had always affected Judith deeply, shifting her moods in an instant between the ephemeral emotions of sorrow and joy. Now, she had come to the end of an era, and knew that never again would she hear the familiar words of Bunyan's great poem without remembering every detail of the moment. The hot summer afternoon, the scent of flowers, the great surge of voices. It was hard to decide whether she felt happy or sad.

"Since Lord thou dost defend
  Us with thy Spirit
We know we at the end
  Shall life inherit."

Happy. She was happy. With the resilience of youth, her spirits soared. And, singing, another cheerful thought occurred to her. With the Carnhayl Cup under her belt she was in a strong position to get possession of her new car before she and Loveday set off for their visit to Porthkerris. They would drive together. Two friends, done with school. Grown-ups.

"Then fancies flee away
  I'll fear not what men say
I'll labour night and day
  To be a pilgrim."

Speech Day was over, everybody departed, the school, the dormitory, deserted. Only Judith remained behind, sitting on her bed, sorting out the contents of her handbag, and putting off time until six o'clock when she had an appointment in the headmistress's study to say goodbye to Miss Catto. Her luggage and her battered trunk were already on their way to the Carey-Lewises in the boot of the Colonel's Daimler. Later, when Miss Catto had finished with her, Mr. Baines had volunteered to come and drive her back to Nancherrow. The time spent with him as they made this journey would be a splendid opportunity to press the case for getting her new car.

Finished with her handbag, she crossed the dormitory and went to lean out of the opened window. Saw the empty lawns sloping to the tennis courts and the shrubbery. All traces of the garden party had been cleared away, and shadows were beginning to lengthen across the trodden grass. She thought of the afternoon when she had seen it all for the first time; the day that she had come with her mother for a little private prowl. In retrospect, the four years which lay between had flown more quickly than Judith could ever have imagined, and yet, in some ways, that long-ago afternoon seemed a lifetime away.

Five to six. Time to go. She turned back to the empty dormitory, retrieved her handbag, and went downstairs. The great stairway stood empty, and everything seemed strangely silent. No chatter of voices, no clangour of bells, no distant tinkle of scales from the music room, as some girl laboured through her practice hour. She knocked on the study door, and Miss Catto called "Come in" and Judith found her headmistress, not sitting behind her desk, but at ease in an armchair, turned to the long window and with her feet up on a stool. She had been reading *The Times*, but as Judith appeared, folded it and dropped it onto the floor beside her.

"Judith. Come along. I'm not going to spring to my feet, because I'm exhausted."

She had removed her gown and hood and tossed them across her desk, and her appearance was quite different without these badges of office. Now it was possible to admire the silk afternoon dress, and to observe her legs, shapely in fine silk stockings. Her navy-blue court shoes had little heels and silver buckles, and, comfortably relaxed after her demanding day, she looked both feminine and attractive, and it occurred to Judith that it was really a shame that Mr. Baines already had a wife and family of his own.

"I don't wonder you're exhausted. You've never stopped all day."

Another armchair had been set in position, and between stood the low table, on which had been placed a silver salver with a bottle of sherry and three small glasses. Judith saw this and frowned. Never had there been so much as a whiff of wine in this room. Miss Catto saw her puzzlement and smiled. "The three glasses are for you and me and Mr. Baines when he turns up. But we won't wait for him. Pour us each a glass, dear, and then sit down."

"I've never drunk sherry."

"Well, this is a very suitable day for you to start. And I think it will do us both good."

So she poured the two glasses, and then settled herself in the cushions of the second chair. Miss Catto raised her glass. "To you and your future, Judith."

"Thank you."

"And before I forget, congratulations on winning the Carnhayl Cup. And remember, it was an almost unanimous vote, and absolutely nothing to do with me."

"It was all a bit surprising . . . I thought Freda Roberts would get it. And I nearly fell over going up those wretched steps . . ."

"Well, you didn't, and that's all that matters. Now, what's the programme for the holidays . . . ?"

The sherry was good. It warmed, and made Judith feel comfortable and at ease. She curled up her legs, as she would never before have dared to do, and told Miss Catto her plans.

"I'm going back to Nancherrow to begin with, and then Mrs. Warren has asked me to Porthkerris for a couple of weeks."

"With your friend Heather." Miss Catto never forgot any person's name. "You'll enjoy that."

"Yes, and they've asked Loveday too, but Loveday can't make up her mind whether to come or not."

Miss Catto laughed. "Typical. Perhaps she feels a bit shy?"

"No, it's not that. It's her new pony. She's been to Porthkerris with me before. We went once, just for a day, and then another time a whole weekend."

"And did Loveday enjoy herself?"

"Enormously. I was rather surprised."

"Three friends is sometimes not a very good number."

"I know, but Loveday and Heather got on like a house on fire, and Mr. and

Mrs. Warren think Loveday's a real character. And Heather's brothers teased and ragged her, but she loved it all and gave as good as she got."

"Splendid for her to get away from the rather rarefied atmosphere of home. To see how other people live and fit in with their ways."

"I'm *hoping* she'll come, and that I'll be able to drive her there, in my own car. Did Mr. Baines tell you about that?"

"He did drop a hint."

"It was his idea. He said I needed to be independent, and perhaps, if I passed my Matric . . ." Judith hesitated, not wishing to sound smug or boastful, "But now, I've won the Carnhayl Cup . . . ?"

Miss Catto, understanding, laughed. "I should think so! Make your point with him while he hasn't got a leg to stand on. Independence! What joy. Now, tell me more. What else is on the cards?"

"I'll probably go and be with Aunt Biddy for a bit. Uncle Bob's at sea, and Ned's joined the Ark Royal, so she's always happy to have a bit of company. We thought we'd go to London for a day or two, and she'd help me buy some new clothes for Singapore. I can't arrive looking too dowdy."

"Most certainly not. Just promise me one thing. Don't fall in love while you're in Singapore and get married and throw Oxford out of the window. You've got all your life to fall in love and get married, but you'll never have the opportunity of going to University again."

"Miss Catto, I have no intention of getting married for *ages*. Certainly not before I'm twenty-five."

"Good for you. And watch out for shipboard romances. I've never had one, but I hear they're lethal."

"I won't forget."

Miss Catto smiled. "I shall miss you," she told Judith. "But it's your life, and time for you to move on, make your own decisions, set your own rules instead of having them set for you by some other person. Just remember that the most important thing is to be truthful to yourself. If you hang on to that, you won't go far wrong."

"You've always been so kind . . ."

"My dear child, such rubbish. Simply doing my job."

"No. More than that. And I always felt badly because I never took up your invitation to stay with your mother and father in Oxford. I would really have loved to go, and to meet them, but somehow . . ."

She hesitated. Miss Catto laughed. "You found a surrogate family of your own. An infinitely more suitable and satisfactory arrangement. After all, there is only so much a headmistress can provide in the way of direction. A feeling of home and belonging has to come from someone else. Looking at you now, I would say that Mrs. Carey-Lewis has done an excellent job. But, too, I think it's time you went back to your own family. Now . . ."

But at this juncture their conversation was interrupted by a firm rap at the door, and the appearance of Mr. Baines.

"I'm not disturbing you . . . ?"

"Not at all," Miss Catto told him.

He gave Judith a pat on her shoulder. "Your chauffeur's reporting for duty. Not too early, I hope?"

Miss Catto smiled up at him from her chair. "We're having a restoring glass of sherry. Sit down and join us for a moment."

Which Mr. Baines did, making himself comfortable, accepting his drink and lighting himself a cigarette, which made him look uncharacteristically racy. They talked. He had already congratulated Judith, during the course of the Garden Party, on winning the Carnhayl Cup, and clearly saw no reason to mention it again, but he was warm with praise for Miss Catto, and the success and general smooth running of the day.

"We were certainly blessed with the weather," she pointed out. "I just wish somebody would edit the Chairman's annual speech. Who wants to listen to a blow-by-blow account of the dry rot in the chapel rafters? Or the measles epidemic in the Easter term."

Mr. Baines laughed. "It's a sort of compulsion. When he stands up to speak at the County Council meetings, everybody settles down for a restoring doze . . ."

But finally it was time to end it all. The sherry glasses were emptied and Mr. Baines looked at his watch.

"Time, I think, to go."

They stood.

"I shan't come and see you off," Miss Catto told Judith. "I hate waving goodbye. But please keep in touch, and let me know what you are doing."

"I will."

"And have a splendid summer holiday."

"I'll do that too."

"Goodbye, my dear."

"Goodbye, Miss Catto."

They shook hands. They did not kiss. They had never kissed. Judith turned and went from the room and Mr. Baines, following, closed the door behind them. Miss Catto was left alone. She stood for a moment, thoughtful and still; then went to pick up the newspaper she had discarded when Judith appeared. The news was becoming graver as each day passed. Now, two thousand Nazi guards, believed armed, had already moved into Danzig. Sooner or later, Hitler was going to invade Poland, just as he had annexed Czechoslovakia and Austria. And that would mean another war, and a whole new generation, on the brink of rich and rewarding lives, were going to be sucked into and decimated by this appalling conflict.

She folded the paper neatly and laid it on her desk. It was necessary, she knew, to remain strong and resolute, but it was at moments like this, just as Judith left her for the last time, that the tragedy of such wastage made her heart feel as though it were being torn apart.

Her gown and her hood lay where she had placed them. Now, she gathered them up, bundled them and held them close, as though for comfort. Speech

Day was a hurdle to be taken every year, and always left her exhausted, but still, no reason to feel so bereft, so anguished. Suddenly tears welled in her eyes, and as they streamed down her cheeks, she buried her face in the fusty black material, silently raging against this imminent war; mourning for youth, for Judith, and for opportunities that would be lost forever.

August now, and a wet Monday morning. Summer rain, soft and drenching, streamed down upon Nancherrow. Drifting in from the south-east, low grey clouds obscured the cliffs and the sea, and heavy-leaved trees drooped and dripped. Gutters ran and drain-pipes gurgled, and the weekly wash was postponed for a day. Nobody complained. After a long spell of hot, dry weather, the sweet coolth was welcome. The rain fell with relentless steadiness, and thirsty flowers and fruit and vegetables absorbed the moisture with gratitude, and the air was filled with the incomparable scent of newly damp earth.

Loveday, with Tiger at her heels, emerged into the outdoors by way of the scullery, stepped out into the yard, and stopped for a moment to sniff the air and fill her lungs with this sweet invigorating freshness. She wore gumboots and an old raincoat, pulled over her shorts and a striped cotton sweater, but her head was bare, and as she set off in the direction of Lidgey Farm, the rain descended upon her hair, causing the dark locks to curl more tightly than ever.

She took the road that led towards the stables, but turned off before reaching them, following, instead, the rutted lane that led up onto the moors. Here the ancient lichened stone walls were divided from the lane by a deep ditch, now running with water, and gorse grew in prickly thickets aflame with yellow flowers smelling of almonds. There were foxgloves too, in profusion, and pale-pink mallow, and tangles of wild honeysuckle, all the way up the lane, and the dark granite of rock wore velvety patches of saffron-coloured lichen. Beyond the wall were pasture fields, where Mr. Mudge's Guernsey milk cows grazed, the grass a brilliant green between the random whale-shaped crests of hidden boulders, and overhead gulls, flying inland with the weather, wheeled and screamed.

Loveday enjoyed rain. She was used to it, and it exhilarated her. Tiger ran ahead, and she followed him, quickening her pace to keep up with his enthusiasm. After a bit, she became very warm and unbuttoned the raincoat, and let it flap around and behind her, like a useless pair of wings. She went on and the lane zigzagged, to and fro, up the hill. Lidgey lay just ahead, but she couldn't see it because of the misty cloud. Which didn't matter, because she knew it was there, just as she knew all of Nancherrow, the farms and the estate, like the back of her hand. The acres of land which belonged to her father were her world, and blindfold, she knew that she could have found her way quite safely to any corner of it. Even down the gunnera tunnel, through the quarry, and so to the cliffs and the cove.

At last, the final bend in the lane, and the Lidgey farmhouse loomed out of the murk, above and ahead of her; solid and squat, with farm buildings and stables and piggeries all about it. Mrs. Mudge's kitchen window shone out like a yellow candle, but that was not surprising considering the gloomy conditions, because Mrs. Mudge's kitchen, even on the brightest of days, was inclined to be a lightless place.

She reached the gate which led into the farmyard and paused for a moment to get her breath. Tiger was already through and ahead of her, so she climbed the gate and crossed the mucky yard, rich with the reek of cattle manure. In the middle of the yard a stone midden was heaped with this, steaming gently, festering away until such time as it would be ripe for spreading on fields and ploughed in. Around the place, Mrs. Mudge's brown hens squawked and pecked, foraging for goodies, and on the top of the midden wall, her handsome cock stood tiptoe and stretched his wings and crowed his heart out. Loveday picked her way across the slippery cobbles, and went through a second gate and into the farmhouse garden. A pebble path led to the front door, and here she toed off her rubber boots and, in socked feet, let herself indoors.

The ceiling was low, the little hall dim. A wooden staircase rose to the upper floor. She put her thumb on the iron latch of the kitchen door and pushed it open, to be assailed by the warm smell of Mrs. Mudge's cooking. Vegetable broth and warm bread. "Mrs. Mudge?"

Mrs. Mudge was there, standing at her sink peeling potatoes, surrounded as always by a certain chaos. She had been rolling pastry at one end of her kitchen table, but because the kitchen was living-room as well, the other end of the table was piled with newspapers, seed catalogues, ironmonger's brochures, and bills waiting to be paid. Uncleaned boots stood by the range, tea-towels hung over it, and washing aired on a rack, yanked by a pulley to the ceiling. Mr. Mudge's long johns were much in evidence. There was, as well, a dresser, painted blue, its shelves crammed not only with mismatched items of china, but curling postcards, packets of worm-pills, old letters, dog leads, a syringe, an old-fashioned telephone, and a basket of mud-encrusted eggs waiting to be washed. Mrs. Mudge's hens were careless where they laid, and a favourite place to search for eggs was at the back of the sheep-dog's kennel.

Loveday scarcely noticed the clutter. The Lidgey kitchen always looked this way, and she liked it. It was somehow very cosy. And Mrs. Mudge was comfortably grubby as well, standing there flanked by blackened saucepans, dishes of hen-food, and all the unwashed crocks and bowls of her morning's labour. She wore a wraparound pinafore and her rubber boots. She wore these boots all the time, because she was constantly in and out of the house, flinging crusts to the hens, or fetching kindling, or heaving baskets of dirty clothes out of the wash-house, and it was scarcely worthwhile taking the boots off. The flagged floor and the worn rugs were distinctly dirty, but the dirt didn't show too much, and Mr. Mudge and Walter saw nothing to complain about, so well fed were they, so cared for, and so unbothered about such trivial matters. (And yet, Loveday knew, the dairy, for which Mrs. Mudge was solely responsible, was hygienically spotless, scrubbed and disinfected. Which, considering the number of people who drank her milk and ate her butter and cream, was perhaps just as well.)

Mrs. Mudge turned from her sink, with a potato in one hand and her lethal knife, a much-honed old carver, in the other. "Loveday!" As always, she looked delighted. There was nothing she enjoyed so much as an unexpected interruption. A good excuse to put the kettle on, make a pot of tea, and gossip. "Well, this is some nice surprise."

She was toothless. She had false teeth but only wore them for company or occasions like the Church Feast, when she had dreadful trouble with macaroon crumbs. Being toothless made her look quite old, but she was in fact quite young, in her early forties. Her hair was straight and lank, and on her head was a brown beret which she wore as constantly as her rubber boots and for the same reason. "Walked up, did you, in this dirty weather?"

"I've got Tiger. Do you mind if he comes in?" Which was a pretty silly question because Tiger was already in, soaking wet and sniffing at Mrs. Mudge's pig bucket. She swore cheerfully at him, and aimed a kick, so he retreated to the rag-rug by the range and settled down to clean himself up, with sloppy, slow licks.

Loveday pulled off her raincoat and draped it over a chair, then reached out and took a bit of raw pastry and ate it. Mrs. Mudge cackled with laughter. "Never known such a maid for raw pastry."

"It's delicious."

"Want a cup of tea, do you?"

Loveday said yes, not because she particularly wanted one, but drinking tea with Mrs. Mudge was part of tradition. "Where's Walter?"

"Up the top field with his father." Mrs. Mudge abandoned her potatoes and filled her kettle and put it on to boil. "Want to see him, did you?"

"Well, he wasn't at the stables this morning, and by the time I'd got there he'd turned the horses out."

"Went down to the stables early, he did, because his dad wanted him to help stank up one of the walls. Two cows got out onto the road last night, pesky brutes. What did you want Walter for?"

"Just to tell him something. But you can give him the message. It's just that I'm going away tomorrow to Porthkerris, for a week, so he'll have to see to everything for the horses. But there's plenty of hay, and I cleaned all the tack last night."

"I'll tell him. Chase him off and make sure he don't forget." Reaching up, Mrs. Mudge took her tea-caddy, decorated with portraits of Royalty, from the mantelshelf, and then her brown teapot from the side of the range. "Why are you off to Porthkerris?"

"I'm going to stay with the Warrens, with Judith. They've asked me to go too. Judith's going for two weeks, and I very nearly said no, but then I thought it might be rather fun. But I feel a bit badly about leaving the new pony, but Pops said he thought I *should* go. Besides, and you'll never believe this, Mrs.

Mudge, Judith and I are going to drive ourselves! Judith's gone off today with Mr. Baines, the solicitor, and he's going to help her buy a car for herself. And she's only eighteen. Don't you think she's a lucky mucker? It's going to be new, too. Not second-hand."

Mrs. Mudge, clattering cups and saucers, paused open-mouthed at this news.

"A car of her *own*! You can hardly believe it, can you? And going off, two young ladies, on your own. Just hope you don't have a crash and kill yourselves." Having made the tea, Mrs. Mudge took, from an earthenware crock, a saffron loaf from which she proceeded to cut inch-thick slices. "The Warrens? Is that Jan Warren, the grocer?"

"That's right. He's got a daughter called Heather. She was Judith's friend at Porthkerris school. And she's got two frightfully good-looking brothers called Paddy and Joe."

Mrs. Mudge let out a crow. "*Oh* . . . so that's why you're going!"

"Oh, don't be silly, Mrs. Mudge, of course it isn't."

"Don't know them well, of course, but the Warrens are distant kin of mine. Daisy Warren was a cousin of my Aunt Flo. Aunt Flo married Uncle Bert. Big family they are, the Warrens. And Jan Warren was a *one* when he was a young man, wild as a goat, none of us ever thought he'd settle down."

"He's still the most dreadful tease."

Mrs. Mudge poured the tea, pulled out a chair, and settled down to a good chat.

"What else is going on, down at the house? Full up yet, are you?"

"The very opposite. Pops and Judith and I are the only ones there. Athena's still in London, and Edward's being frightfully grand in the south of France, and as usual we don't know when he's coming home."

"What about your mother?"

Loveday made a face. "*She* went off yesterday, to London. She drove the Bentley and took Pekoe with her."

"She went to *London*?" Mrs. Mudge looked amazed, as well she might. "With you all coming home, and the middle of the holidays?" And indeed, Diana Carey-Lewis had never done such a thing before. But Loveday, despite feeling a bit put out at her mother's defection, thought that she understood.

"Between you and me, Mrs. Mudge, I think she got a bit depressed and miserable. She needed to get away. Athena always cheers her up, and I suppose she wanted a change."

"What does she want a change for, then?"

"Well, admit, everything is a bit depressing, isn't it? I mean the news, and everybody talking about war, and Edward's joined the Royal Air Force Reserve, and I think that frightens her. And Pops is a bit down in the mouth as well, and insists on listening to all the news bulletins, full-blast, and they're digging up Hyde Park for air-raid shelters, and he seems to think we're all going to be gassed. Not much fun to live with reality. So she just packed a suitcase and went."

"How long is she staying away?"

"Oh, I don't know. A week. Two weeks. As long as she needs, I suppose."

"Well, if that's how she's troubled, better out of the way. I mean, it's not as though she's *wanted*, is it? Not with the Nettlebeds and Mary Millyway there to keep an eye on things." Mrs. Mudge took a long noisy suck at her tea, then thoughtfully dunked her slice of saffron cake in what remained in her cup. She liked it that way, all soft and pappy, on account of having no teeth. "I don't know, it's not a good time for any of us really. Except that I don't suppose Walter will have to go. Farming's a reserved occupation, his dad says. He can't run this place single-handed."

"What if he wants to join up?"

"*Walter?*" Mrs. Mudge's voice was filled with proud scorn. "He won't rush to volunteer. Never did like being told what to do. Never out of trouble when he was at school, just because of the rules and regulations. I can't see Walter saying 'Yes, sir' to any sergeant-major. No. He'd be better staying here. More use."

Loveday finished her tea. She looked at her watch. "Oh dear, I suppose I'd better be getting back. That's another thing. I've got to take an extra can of cream with me because Mrs. Nettlebed's run out and she wants to make a raspberry fool for dinner. That's really why I came, that and to tell Walter about going away."

"Well, there's plenty of cream in the dairy, if you want to help yourself, but mind and bring my can back."

"I can't, because I'm going away tomorrow. But I'll tell Mrs. Nettlebed."

The dairy was cold and glistened with cleanliness and smelt of the carbolic soap which Mrs. Mudge used to scrub the slate floor. Loveday found the cream and a sterilized can, and filled the can with a long-handled dipper. Tiger, refused entrance, whined at the open door, and went into ecstasies of pleasure when she emerged into the farmyard again, tearing around in circles as though he had believed himself to be abandoned forever. She told him he was stupid, and he sat and smiled at her.

"Come on, fat-head, we've got to go home."

She went back across the farmyard and climbed the gate, and then sat there for a bit on the top rail. While she had chatted to Mrs. Mudge, a breeze had got up and the rain eased off a little. Somewhere, above the clouds, the sun was shining, and odd rays penetrated, as they always seemed to do in Bible pictures. The mist, like a filmy curtain, was parting, and now it was possible to glimpse the still silver sea.

She thought of Walter, and the coming war, and felt grateful that he would not be leaving Nancherrow to be a soldier, because Walter was part of Nancherrow, part of everything she had known all her life, and she was terrified of change. Besides, she was very fond of Walter. He was rough and foul-mouthed, and rumour had it that he was beginning to spend far too many of his evenings in the Rosemullion pub, but still, he was a constant in her existence, and one of the few young men she knew with whom she felt entirely at ease. Ever since he went to prep school, Edward had been bringing friends home to stay, but they seemed to Loveday to come from a different world, with their drawling upper-class voices, and their sometimes effete behaviour. While Loveday mucked out the stables, or rode with Walter or her father, they lay about in deck-chairs or played not very energetic tennis, and their dinner-table conversations were all of people she did not know, had never met, and had no desire to meet.

Walter, for all his wild ways, she found enormously attractive. Sometimes, when he was grooming one of the horses, or carting hay, she would covertly watch him, and be filled with satisfaction by the strength and ease of his body, his tanned and muscled arms, his dark eyes and his raven-black hair. He was like some beautiful gypsy out of a D. H. Lawrence book, and her first stirrings of physical sexuality, a sort of ache deep in her stomach, were engendered by Walter's presence. It was a bit the same with the Warren boys over at Porthkerris. With their Cornish voices, their horseplay, and their teasing, Loveday was never for a moment either shy with them or bored. It occurred to her that perhaps this preference for . . . she searched for the right word. Lower-class was horrible. Ill-educated was worse. She hit upon real . . . real people, had something to do with the way she had been brought up, treasured and petted all her life within the safe haven of Nancherrow. Whatever. It was her own secret, shared with neither Judith nor Athena.

Walter. She thought about War. Every evening they all listened, willy-nilly, to the nine o'clock news, and every evening world events seemed to be worsening. It was like the build-up to a monumental disaster—an earthquake or a terrible fire—with no person able to do anything to prevent it. The chimes of Big Ben sounding nine o'clock had begun to sound to Loveday like the trumpets of doom. She was far more concerned about the prospect of war than any of her family realized, yet could not begin to imagine how it would be, particularly within the context of her own home, her family, and their immediate world. She had never been much good at imagining things, always hopeless at essays and compositions. Would there be bombs, dropping from black aircraft, and explosions and houses falling down? Or would the German Army land somewhere, London, perhaps, and march across the country? And would they come to Cornwall? And if so, how would they cross the Tamar, which only had a railway bridge? Perhaps they would build special pontoon bridges or paddle themselves across the water in boats, but that did seem a bit primitive.

And if they came, what would happen? Almost every man Loveday knew, and certainly all of her father's friends, had a gun with which to blast off at pheasants and rabbits, or to put some injured dog or horse out of its misery. If everybody went with guns to meet the Germans, then surely the invaders wouldn't stand a chance. She thought of the old Cornish song, belted out by the crowds in the stands at county rugby matches.

And shall Trelawney die, my boys
And shall Trelawney die?
Then forty thousand Cornishmen
Shall know the reason why.

Tiger, impatient, was wheeking at her. She sighed and put dismal thoughts from her mind, and climbed down off the gate and set off at a trot, down the rutted lane, the cream can swinging to and fro as she ran. To cheer herself up, she thought about tomorrow, and going to Porthkerris to stay with the Warrens. Seeing Heather and Paddy and Joe again; and sitting on the crowded beach and eating ice-creams. And Judith's new car. Perhaps it would be a little MG with a folding hood. She could not wait to see the new car.

With all this going through her mind, by the time she reached home, her good spirits were quite restored.

August 9th, 1939.
Porthkerris.

Dear Mummy and Dad,

I am sorry I have not written for such a long time. I shall just have to try to give you all the news very quickly, otherwise this letter will be as fat as a newspaper. As you can see, I am at Porthkerris with the Warrens, and Loveday has come too. She wavered for a bit, because she has got this new pony called Fleet, and is schooling it for some gymkhana, but in the end she decided to come, just for a week, which is fun for all of us. It's a bit of a squash, but Mrs. Warren doesn't seem to mind, and Paddy is now working on his uncle's fishing boat, so is away a good deal of the time. So Loveday's got his bed, and I'm in with Heather. Heather's left school as well, and she's going to do a secretarial course right here in Porthkerris, and then maybe go to London and get herself a job.

The weather is absolutely gorgeous and Porthkerris is full of visitors, in shorts and sand-shoes. Joe has got a job working at the beach, he cleans out the beach-huts and puts away the deck-chairs, and yesterday when we went to swim, he sneaked us all free ice-creams.

There's a new girl working in the shop, she's called Ellie; I think she's about sixteen. She dyed her hair blonde with a peroxide bottle, but despite the fact that she looks so dotty, Mrs. Warren says she's the best assistant they've ever had, and got the hang of the cash register in no time.

It's funny knowing I never have to go back to school. Haven't heard about Matric yet, of course, but I got the History and the English Prizes on Speech Day, which was great, and the Carnhayl Cup as well, which was a dreadful surprise and made me feel wobbly. But it was worth winning because, because of getting it, Mr. Baines and Uncle Bob put their heads together and let me buy a car of my very own as a sort of reward. Mr. Baines and I went to the garage in Truro together, and chose it. It is a little dark-blue Morris with four seats, and too sweet. There was a sports car with a folding roof as well, but Mr. Baines said that if I turned it over (which of course I wouldn't), I would probably break my neck, and he reckoned the Morris was more suitable. Whatever, I absolutely love it, and I drove it back to Nancherrow myself, all the way through Camborne and Redruth and Penzance, with Mr. Baines, in his car, trundling along behind me like a sort of bodyguard! It's the best thing I've ever had since Aunt Louise bought me my bike, and just as soon as I can, I'm off to Pendeen to see Phyllis and her baby. In my next letter, I'll tell you about her.

Anyway, it meant that Loveday and I were able to come here under our own steam, instead of having to be chauffeured in the Nancherrow shooting-brake. I can't tell you what fun it was, driving ourselves, and we made the journey very slowly, *savouring* it. It was the loveliest day, all the hedges smothered in foxgloves, and we took the road over the moor, and in the distance the sea was the deepest blue. We sang quite a lot.

Just before we left, Diana Carey-Lewis went off to London for a bit. Colonel Carey-Lewis looked a bit down in the mouth when she told him she was going away, but he's fairly depressed about everything himself, and never stops reading newspapers and listening to the wireless, and I think the poor man just got on her nerves. In the end, however, he made the best of it, and saw her off in her car and told her to have a good time. He really has to be the dearest and most unselfish of husbands, and who can blame him for being concerned about the way things are going? It must be agonizing for a man who fought in the trenches all through the last war. I am glad that you are all in Singapore and away from it all. At least there, you will be safe from whatever happens in Europe.

I must go. Loveday and Heather want to go to the beach, and Mrs. Warren has packed us a picnic. I can smell hot pasties. Can you think of anything better than eating hot pasties after a swim? I can't.

My love to you all as always. I'll try to write again soon.

Judith

Unlike Nancherrow, mealtimes at the Warrens' house were, by necessity, informal affairs. With two men at work, starting at different hours, breakfast was very much a movable feast, and Mr. Warren was in his shop, and Joe away to the beach, long before any of the girls were even out of bed. At midday, Mrs. Warren fed her husband whenever there came a lull in business and he was able to escape from his sides of bacon, his packets of tea, and pounds of butter. Having been on his feet since early morning, he needed to sit down for a spell, to cast his eye over the local paper, to enjoy a bowl of soup, a slice of bread and cheese, and a cup of tea. Mrs. Warren did not sit down. While her husband ate, she ironed, or made a cake, or washed the kitchen floor, or stood at the sink and peeled pounds of potatoes, listening companionably while he read out snippets of news, like cricket scores, or how much the Women's Institute of Saint Enedoc had made with the Bring & Buy Sale. When he had finished his tea and rolled and smoked a wrinkled cigarette, he returned to work, and then it was Ellie's turn for refreshment. Ellie did not fancy soup. She made herself meat-paste sandwiches, and crunched away on chocolate biscuits, all the while telling Mrs. Warren what Russell Oates had said to her while they were queueing for the cinema, and did Mrs. Warren think she should have a permanent wave? She was a flighty girl, and mad on boys, but Mrs. Warren had known her since she was just a little thing at the Porthkerris school, and enjoyed Ellie's company. She liked her because she had a bit of go in her, and was a real worker, bright as a new penny and always friendly with customers.

"Jeanette MacDonald's on this week," Ellie would tell her. "With Nelson Eddy. I always think they're a bit soppy, but the music's nice. Saw James Cagney last week, it was some frightening, gangsters and that in Chicago."

"How you can watch all that shooting and killing, Ellie, is beyond me."

"It's exciting. And if it gets too bloody, I just go down under the seat."

Loveday stayed her week, and it was a constant source of wonder to Judith the way she fitted in and adapted to life in the crowded house over the grocer's shop, so diametrically different in every way from the establishment in which she had been brought up. The Carey-Lewises were "gentry" . . . there was no getting away from that uncomfortable-sounding word. And Loveday had been raised accordingly, spoilt and indulged, surrounded by devoted nannies and butlers, and worshipped by besotted parents. But ever since her first visit to Porthkerris, when they had both still been at school, Loveday was entranced by the Warrens and everything about them. Loving the novelty of living bang in the middle of a busy little town, of stepping out of the door straight into the narrow cobbled street that led down to the harbour. When Mr. Warren or Joe started in on their teasing, she gave as good as she got, and for Mrs. Warren, she learned to make her own bed, help with the dishes, and peg laundry out in the yard at the back of the wash-house. The grocery shop, always milling with customers, was a constant diversion, and the freedom that the Warren offspring took for granted, Loveday found precious. "I'm going now" was all you had to shout up the stairs, and nobody asked where you were going, or when you would be home again.

But most of all she enjoyed the fun of the crowded beach where she, with Judith and Heather, spent much of their time. The weather never stopped being perfect, with a cool breeze, and days of cloudless skies, and the sands bright with striped tents and sun-umbrellas, and noisy with cheerful parties of holiday-makers. Diana had bought Loveday a new bathing-suit, a two-piece, to which Loveday added a pair of dark glasses, so that she could blatantly stare at people without being observed. As well, Judith suspected, Loveday hoped they made her look like a film star. So slender and tanned and dazzlingly pretty, she inevitably drew admiring glances, and it was never long before some young man bounced a beach ball their way, and so a new acquaintance would be struck up. Scarcely a day passed but the three girls were invited to join in a game of rounders or volleyball or to swim out to the raft and sunbathe on the soggy coconut matting.

Nancherrow Cove had never been so diverting.

But the time flew by, and almost before they realized, it was Loveday's last day. The evening meal at the Warrens was the one time when the whole family, and anyone else who happened to be about and in need of sustenance, foregathered around the long, scrubbed table in Mrs. Warren's kitchen, to talk, laugh, argue, tease, and generally catch up on the day's affairs. There was never any question of changing, or dressing up. A cursory hand-wash was all that was expected, and everybody sat down in the clothes they had worn all day, the men in open-necked shirts and Mrs. Warren still wearing her pinafore.

The meal was served at half past six, and though never less than a feast, was traditionally referred to as "tea." A leg of lamb would be served, or a capon, or grilled fish, accompanied by mashed and roasted potatoes, three dishes of vegetables, sauces and pickles, jugs of dark, rich gravy. For "afters" there were jellies and custards, dishes of cream, and then a home-made cake, or biscuits and cheese, all washed down with large cups of strong tea.

This evening it was just family. The Warren parents, Joe, and the three girls, bare-armed and cool in the sleeveless cotton dresses they had pulled on over their bathing-suits after a day on the beach.

"We're going to miss you," Mr. Warren told Loveday. "Won't be the same without you around the place, driving us all mad."

"Do you really have to go?" Mrs. Warren asked, sounding a bit sad.

"Yes, I've got to go. I promised Fleet I'd be back, and we've lots of work to do together. I just hope Walter's been riding her, otherwise she'll be frisky and nappy as anything."

"Well, you've certainly had the sunshine." Mr. Warren grinned. "What's your mum going to say when you go home black as a little Indian?"

"She's in London, so she won't be there. But if she was there, she'd be jealous. She's always trying to get brown. Sometimes she sunbathes with no clothes on."

Joe raised his eyebrows. "Tell her to come to our beach then. We could do with a side-show or two."

"Oh, you stupid thing. She doesn't do it on crowded beaches. Just privately, sometimes, in the garden or on the rocks."

"Can't be so private if you know she does it. Go peeping, do you?"

Loveday threw a bit of bread at him, and Mrs. Warren heaved herself to her feet and went to put the kettle on.

She left the next morning, fetched by Palmer in the Nancherrow shooting-brake. Not the most suitable of vehicles for the steep hills, narrow streets, and tight corners of Porthkerris, and by the time he turned up, Palmer was in something of a fluster, because he had totally lost his bearings in the unfamiliar warren of cobbled lanes, and made it to the door of Warren's Grocery more by luck than good management.

However, he was there. Loveday's suitcases were humped downstairs and out through the shop, and everybody emerged onto the pavement to see her off, with lots of kisses and hugs and promises that, before long, she would come again.

"When will you be back?" she asked Judith, hanging out of the open window of the brake.

"Probably Sunday morning. I'll ring you up and let you know. Send my love to everybody."

"I will . . ." Shuddering, the shooting-brake started up and moved, with monstrous dignity, away. "Goodbye! Goodbye!"

They all stood waving, but only for a moment, because almost immediately the huge vehicle turned the sharp corner by the Market Place and was gone.

At first it felt a bit strange without Loveday. Like all the Carey-Lewis family, she had that gift of adding a certain unexpected glamour to almost any gathering. But it was nice too, to have just Heather for company, and to be able to talk about the old days and old friends, without feeling that they were leaving Loveday out of the conversation, or having to explain painfully to her who so-and-so was, or when such-and-such had happened.

They sat at the kitchen table and drank tea and discussed how they would spend the day, and decided against going to Porthkerris beach, because, although Loveday had wished to do nothing else, being without her seemed a good opportunity to travel a little farther afield.

"After all, I've got the car. Let's drive somewhere really inaccessible." They were still trying to make up their minds where to go when Mrs. Warren joined them, treading up the stairs for a breather from the shop, and she made the decision for them.

"Why don't you go off to Treen? Won't take you long in the car, and the cliffs'll be some lovely on a day like this, and probably not a soul there. Mind, it's a real scramble to get down to the sands, but you've got all day, haven't you?"

And so they went to Treen, by way of the Land's End Road, Pendeen, and Saint Just. Bowling along, Judith was reminded of Phyllis.

"I must come and see her one day. She lives somewhere near here, but I don't know quite where. I'll have to write her a letter, because she most certainly isn't on the telephone."

"You can do that this week. And we can go to Penmarron too, if you want."

Judith wrinkled her nose. "No, not really."

"Make you homesick, would it?"

"I don't know. I just don't want to risk it." She thought of the little railway station and Riverview and perhaps going to call on Mr. Willis. But those were the happy memories, and there were others which were better left buried. "Perhaps it's better just to remember it the way it was."

At Treen, they parked the car by the pub and walked across the fields, bathing-things and picnics in haversacks on their backs. Another cloudless day with bees humming in the bell-heather, and the sunlight diffused by heat, shimmering on a lazy sea the colour of jade. The cliffs were tremendously high, and the sickle of the cove lay far beneath them, but they made the long, slightly hair-raising descent down the precipitous path, and when they finally reached the sands, it was like being abandoned on a desert island, for there was not another person to be seen.

"We don't even need to wear bathing-suits," Heather pointed out, and so they stripped and ran naked into the gentle breakers, and the water was icy and smooth as silk, and they swam until too cold to stay in the water any longer, and then emerged, and walked up the baking sand to reach for towels and dry themselves and lie, sun-bathing, on the rocks.

They talked. Heather confessed that she now had a proper boy-friend, one Charlie Lanyon, the son of a prosperous timber merchant out at Marazion. She had met him at a Cricket Dinner, but was keeping Charlie something of a secret from her family because she could not stand the inevitable brotherly teasing should Joe discover their friendship.

"Charlie's really nice. Not really *good*-looking, but *nice*-looking. Nice eyes, and a lovely smile."

"What do you do with him?"

"Go to the Palais de Danse, go to the pub, have a glass of beer. He's got a car, and we usually meet up by the bus stop."

"You'll have to take him home sometime."

"I know, but he's a bit shy. We're leaving it for the time being."

"Does he work with his father?"

"No, he's at technical college in Camborne. He's nineteen. But he's meant to be going into the business."

"He sounds really nice."

Heather smiled. "He is," she said.

Judith, lying on her back, shaded her eyes with her hand, and fell silent. For a bit, she deliberated as to whether she should tell Heather about Edward. As Heather had confided, she felt that she should too, but then decided against it. For some reason, what she felt for Edward was too precious, too tenuous to share with any person, even Heather. Heather, she knew, would never betray a trust, but secrets once spoken were gone forever.

The sun was too bright; her shoulders and thighs were beginning to burn. Painfully, she rolled over onto her stomach and made herself as comfortable as she could on the shelf of relentlessly hard rock. She said, "Are you going to get engaged?"

"No. What's the point in getting engaged? If there's a war, he'll be called up, I suppose, and we shan't see each other for years. Besides, I don't want to get married, and be lumbered with kids. Not yet. You can do that any time." Suddenly she began to giggle.

"What's so funny?"

"I just remembered. That Norah Elliot and what she told us behind the bicycle shed. About how babies start . . ."

Judith, remembering only too well, was consumed by mirth. ". . . . and we thought she was disgusting, and that she'd made it all up, and only someone as horrible as Norah Elliot could think up something so awful."

"And of course she was right after all . . ."

When they had finally controlled their laughter, and wiped the tears from their eyes, Heather said, "Who told *you?*"

"What? About sex?"

"Yes. I mean, Mum told me, but your mum wasn't there."

"Miss Catto told me. She told all my class. It was called Physical Education."

"Golly, that must have been embarrassing."

"Funnily enough, it wasn't. And we'd all been doing biology, so it didn't come as too much of a surprise."

"Mum was sweet. She said it didn't *sound* too nice, but loving someone made it really special. You know. Emotions and all that."

"Do you feel like that about Charlie?"

"I don't want to go to bed with him, if that's what you mean . . ."

"No. I mean . . . do you love him?"

"Not that way." Heather thought about this. "It's not like that. I don't want to be tied down."

"So what do you want? Still a job in London?"

"Eventually. Have my own little flat, a proper salary . . ."

"I can see you in a black dress with a white collar, sitting on the boss's knee and taking dictation."

"I'm not sitting on no boss's knee, I can tell you that."

"Won't you miss Porthkerris?"

"Yes, but I'm not going to stay here for the rest of my life. I know too many girls with a string of babies and they've scarcely ever been out of the town. I want to see the world. I'd like to go abroad. Like Australia."

"Forever?"

"No. Not forever. I'd always come back eventually." Heather sat up and yawned. "It's some hot, isn't it? I'm hungry. Let's have something to eat."

They spent all that day in the sunshine, on the rocks and the sand, and in the sea. During the afternoon the tide moved in, over the sizzling beach, and the shallow breakers did not feel so cold, and they were able to float, staring up at the sky and rocked by the gentle swell of the summer waves. By half past four, some of the heat had gone from the sun, and they decided to call it a day and tackle the long climb up to the top of the cliffs.

"Seems a shame to go," said Heather as they pulled on cotton frocks and stuffed their haversacks with wet bathing-things and the detritus of their picnic. She turned to look at the sea which, in the altering light, had miraculously taken on a different hue, for now it was no longer jade but a deep aquamarine blue. She said, "You know, it won't ever be like this again. Not ever. Just you and me, and this place and this time. Things only happen once. Do you ever think that, Judith? It can be a bit the same, of course, but never *quite* the same."

Judith understood. "I know."

Heather stooped and slung her haversack onto her back, shoving her bare arms through the straps. "Come on then, off we go. Mountaineering."

And indeed it was a long and demanding climb, if not quite so hair-raising as the journey down. Reaching the summit without mishap was something of a relief, and they paused for a moment to catch their breath, standing on the thick turfy grass, and looking down into the deserted cove, seeing the unchanging cliffs and the empty, tranquil sea.

Things only happen once.

Heather was right. *It can never be quite the same.* Judith wondered how long it would be before they came to Treen again.

They were back in Porthkerris by six, sunburnt, salty, and exhausted. The shop already had its CLOSED sign up, but the door was open and they went in and found Mr. Warren, shirt-sleeved, in his little office, tidying up the books for the day. As they appeared, he raised his head from his column of figures.

"Well, look who's turned up here. Have a good day, did you?"

"Perfect . . . we've been to Treen."

"I know. Mum told me." His eyes moved to Judith. "You had a phone call, about an hour ago."

"I did?"

"Yes. He wants you to ring him." He laid down his pen and searched about on his desk. ". . . here it is. I wrote it down." He handed the scrap of paper over. On it were written two words. "Ring Edward." "He said you'd know the number."

Edward. Judith felt herself suffused with joy, like a dry Turkish sponge soaking up water. It rose from the soles of her feet to the top of her head, and she could feel the smile tugging at the corners of her mouth. Edward.

"Where did he ring from?"

"Didn't say. Just said he was home."

Heather was agog. "Who is it, Judith?"

"Only Edward Carey-Lewis. I thought he was still in France."

"You'd better ring him now then." Judith hesitated. The telephone which stood on Mr. Warren's desk was the only one in the house. Heather caught her hesitation. "Dad won't mind, will you, Dad?"

"I don't mind. Make yourself free, Judith." And he pulled himself to his feet.

Judith felt deeply embarrassed. "Oh, please don't feel you have to go. It's nothing private. Only Edward."

"I've finished in here for the moment. I can do the rest of it later. I'm going up to have a beer . . ."

Heather, with her black eyes sparkling, said, "I'll come and pour it for you. Give me your haversack, Judith, and I'll get our wet things out on the line . . ."

With consummate tact, they left her on her own. She watched them go, companionably, up the stairs, and then took Mr. Warren's seat behind his desk, lifted the receiver of the old-fashioned telephone, and gave the operator the Nancherrow number.

"Hello." It was Edward.

She said, "It's me."

"Judith."

"I just got back. Mr. Warren gave me your message. I thought you were still in France."

"No, I got home last Thursday, to a practically empty house. No Ma, no Judith, and no Loveday. Pops and I have been leading a bachelor existence."

"But Loveday's back?"

"Sure, but I've hardly seen her. She's been down at the stables all afternoon, schooling the new pony."

"Did you have a good time in France?"

"Amazing. I want to tell you about it. When are you coming back?"

"Not for another week."

"I can't wait. How about this evening? I thought I might drive over to Porthkerris and take you out for a drink or something. Would the Warrens mind?"

"No, of course they wouldn't mind."

"Well, say eight o'clock. How do I find you?"

"You come down the hill and head for the harbour. It's just behind the old Market Place, Warren's Grocery. The shop door will be locked but there's a side door that's always open and you can get in that way. It's a bright-blue door with a brass handle."

"Unmissable." She could hear the smile in his voice. "Eight o'clock. I'll see you." And he rang off.

She sat for a little, dreamy and smiling, going over everything he had said and every nuance of his voice. He was coming. He wanted to tell her about France. *I can't wait.* He wanted to see her. He was coming.

She must change, bath, wash the salt out of her hair. No time to lose. Galvanized into action, she sprang from the chair and ran up the stairs, taking the steep treads effortlessly, two at a time.

She was in her bedroom applying lipstick when she heard the car come around the corner of the street and draw to a halt outside the shuttered windows of the grocery. She laid down the lipstick and went to the open window and hung out, and saw, far below her, the dark-blue Triumph and Edward clambering, long-legged, out of it. He shut the door behind him with a soft clunk.

"Edward!"

At her voice, he paused and then stared upwards, a figure foreshortened by her angle of vision.

"You look like Rapunzel," he told her. "Come down."

"I won't be a moment."

She turned back into her bedroom, collected up her white shoulder-bag, took a last swift glance at her reflection, and then went out of the room, ran down the flights of stairs, out through the blue door, and so onto the street, where long shadows lay on cobbles still warm from the heat of the day, and, leaning against the shining bonnet of his car, Edward waited for her. He held out his arms, and she went to him and they kissed, first one cheek and then the other. He was wearing rust-red linen trousers and espadrilles and an open-necked blue-and-white shirt. The sleeves of this were rolled up to his elbows, and he was very brown and his hair bleached by the Mediterranean sun.

She said, "You look wonderful."

"You, too."

His informal appearance reassured her. She had resisted the temptation to dress up, and after her bath pulled on a clean cotton dress, butcher-blue and striped in white. Her legs were bare and her feet cool in white sandals.

"I'm jealous," he told her. "I think you've achieved a better tan than I have."

"We've had amazing weather."

He pushed himself away from the car and stood, with his hands in his trouser pockets, gazing up at the face of the tall, narrow stone house. "What a splendid place to be staying."

"It goes up in stages," Judith explained. "There are three storeys on this side, but only two at the back. I suppose because, like the rest of the town, it was built on a hill. The kitchen's on the first floor, with a door that goes out into a yard at the back. That's where Mrs. Warren grows her pot plants and hangs her washing. She hasn't got a garden."

"Am I not to be invited in?"

"Yes, of course, if you want. But there's nobody in except me. There's a summer fair up at the rugger field, and Heather and her parents have gone to ride on the roundabouts and shy coconuts and win prizes."

"Pink plush elephants?"

She laughed. "Exactly so. And Joe—that's Heather's brother—has gone off with his mates for the evening."

"So where shall we go? Which is the fashionable night-spot this season?"

"I don't know. I suppose we could try the Sliding Tackle."

"What a good idea. I haven't been there for years. Let's go and see what's happening. Do you want to drive or shall we walk?"

"Let's walk. It's hardly worth taking the car."

"In that case, *en avant*."

They set off, strolling abreast down the narrow street that sloped to the Lifeboat House and the harbour. A thought occurred to Judith. "Have you had anything to eat?"

"Why? Do I look particularly hungry?"

"No. But I know as well as you do that dinner at Nancherrow is at eight, so I presume you've missed out."

"You're right. I haven't eaten and don't need to. I've decided that, at home, we all eat far too much. I suppose it's all to do with Mrs. Nettlebed's cooking. I can't imagine why my parents aren't as fat as butterballs, but they munch away four times a day and never put on an ounce of weight."

"It's all to do with something called metabolism."

"Where did you learn that long word?"

"Oh, we were well educated at Saint Ursula's."

"*Were* well educated," Edward repeated. "Isn't it marvellous to know it's all behind you? I couldn't believe it when I finally left Harrow. I used to have nightmares about going back, and wake up in the night in a sweat of apprehension."

"Oh come on, it can't have been as bad as all that. I bet you get a lump in your throat when you hear boyish voices singing old school songs."

"No, I don't. But I admit, I probably will when I'm fifty."

They turned the corner of the Lifeboat House and set out along the harbour road. It was such a fine and golden evening that the street was still crowded; all the summer visitors out and about, ambling along the edge of the quay, pausing to lean over the rail and stare down at the fishing boats; licking ice-creams or eating fish and chips out of cones of newspaper. You knew they were visitors because they wore such peculiar clothes, were lobster-red from the unaccustomed sun, and spoke in the accents of Manchester, Birmingham, and London. The tide was high and the sky filled with greedy gulls, and some of the old residents who still lived in harbour-side houses had carried kitchen chairs out of doors, there to sit, black-clad and vociferous, to enjoy the last of the day's warmth and watch the world go by. Outside the Sliding Tackle a group of young holiday-makers, sunburnt and noisy, sat at a wooden table and downed their beer.

Edward made a face. "I hope it's not too dreadfully crowded. Last time I was here it was winter, and there was just one or two old boys inside, getting a bit of peace from their wives. Come on, though, we'll give it a try."

And he led the way inside, ducking his head beneath the crooked lintel of the doorway. Judith, at his heels, stepped into semi-darkness and was at once assailed by the reek of beer, spirits, and hot humanity, clouds of cigarette smoke, and the din of raised, convivial voices. She had not admitted so to Edward, but this was her first visit to the Sliding Tackle, because it was a pub that the Warren menfolk kept strictly to themselves. Now, she looked about her with some curiosity, trying to discover what was so special about the place.

"This is worse than I'd imagined," Edward observed. "Shall we make a run for it or stay?"

"Let's stay."

"Right. You stand here and grab a table if one comes free. I'll get the drinks. What do you want?"

"A shandy. Or a cider. It doesn't matter."

"I'll get you a shandy." He left her, expertly shouldering his way towards the bar, and she watched his progress, relentlessly shoving a path for himself, but at the same time being enormously polite. "So sorry . . . Excuse me . . . Do you mind . . . ?"

He was within shouting distance of the distracted barman when, with startling luck, the party who had been sitting at a table under the tiny peep-hole of a window began to gather themselves together and make as if to depart. Judith, with a swiftness that surprised even herself, was onto them in an instant.

"I'm so sorry, but are you leaving?"

"That's right. We've got to get back up the hill to our boarding-house. Want the table, do you?"

"It'd be nice to sit down."

"I know. Like the Black Hole of Calcutta in here."

There were four of them and they took a bit of time, but Judith stood very close, guarding against intruders, and as soon as they were out of the way, eased herself onto the narrow wooden bench and put her handbag down beside her, laying claim to a space for Edward.

When he returned to her, carrying his tankard and her glass, he was gratifyingly delighted by her cleverness. "What a brilliant girl you are." He carefully set down their drinks and then slid onto the bench beside her. "How did you accomplish that? Make mad faces and frighten them off?"

"No. They were going anyway. Back to their boarding-house."

"What a bit of luck. Murder having to stand all evening."

"I never realized the Sliding Tackle was so *small*."

"Tiny." Edward reached for a cigarette and lit it. "But everybody wants to come here. There are plenty of other pubs in the town, but I suppose the visitors all think this place is picturesque. Which of course it is. But, God, it's crowded. There's not even space for a humble game of darts. You'd probably spear someone's eye out. Anyway"—he raised his glass—"cheers. It's so good to see you again. It's been so long."

"Since Christmas."

"As long as that?"

"Well, you were in America all over Easter."

"So I was."

"Tell me about France."

"It was splendid."

"Where did you go?"

"To a villa up in the hills behind Cannes. Near a village called Sillence. Very rural. Surrounded by vineyards and olive groves. And the villa had a terrace wreathed in vines, where we had all our meals, and in the garden was an icy little swimming-pool, contrived by damming the stream which ran down from the mountain-top. And there were cicadas, and pink geraniums, and indoors it smelt of garlic and sun-oil and Gauloise cigarettes. Heaven."

"Whom did the villa belong to?"

"A rather nice older couple called Beath. I think he was something to do with the Foreign Office."

"So you didn't *know* them?"

"Never met them before in my life."

"Then, how . . ."

Edward sighed and, painfully, explained. "I went to London to go to some party with Athena. And there I met this jolly girl, and over the course of dinner, she told me her aunt and uncle had this villa in the south of France, and she had been invited out to stay, and the invitation included a chum or two."

"Edward, you are the . . ."

"Why are you laughing?"

"Because only you could go to a party in London and end up spending two weeks in the south of France."

"I thought it was rather clever of me."

"She must have been frightfully pretty."

"Villas in the south of France tend to make girls pretty. Just the way that a socking bank balance renders the most hideous of women sexually attractive. To a certain type of man."

He was teasing. She smiled. At Christmas, when Edward had told her about his Swiss holiday, she had been unable to suppress a pang of jealousy of the unknown girls who had skied with him, and with whom he had danced the nights away to the tunes of Richard Tauber. *Girls were made to love and kiss.* Now, however, perhaps because she was that much older and that much more sure of herself, she didn't feel jealous at all. After all, Edward, returning to Nancherrow and finding no Judith, had lost no time in getting in touch, and coming to find her. Which seemed to indicate that she was a *bit* important to him, and that he hadn't lost his heart to another, nor left it in the south of France.

"So what happened next, Edward?"

"Sorry?"

"You said the invitation included a chum or two."

"Yes, it did. And she'd fixed things up with a girl-friend, but all the chaps they fancied were already committed to other arrangements. So . . ." He shrugged. "She asked me. And being one who never says No to a good offer, I instantly accepted before she had time to change her mind. And then she said, 'Bring a Friend,' and off the top of my head I suggested this chap called Gus Callender."

It was the first time Judith had heard the name. "Who's he?"

"A dark, dour Scot from the wild Highlands. He's at Pembroke with me, doing Engineering, but I didn't really get to know him until this summer, when we both had rooms on the same stair. He's quite a shy, reserved sort of fellow, but terribly nice, and he immediately sprang to mind because I was pretty certain that he wouldn't have any plans made for the vacation. At least, none that couldn't be changed."

"And did he fit in with the rest of the house party?"

"Of course." Edward sounded surprised that Judith should for a moment question his impeccable social judgement. "I knew he would. One of the girls fell wildly in love with his brooding, Heathcliff looks, and Mrs. Beath kept telling me that she thought he was a *pet*. As well, he's something of an artist, which added an extra dimension. He did an oil painting of the villa, and had it framed and left it with the Beaths as a thank-you present. They were more than delighted."

He sounded, Judith decided, an interesting character.

"An engineer and an artist. Funny mixture."

"Not really. Think of all those technical drawings. Geometry at its most complicated. And, as it happens, there's every chance you'll meet him. After we'd driven home, and finally arrived in Dover, I suggested he came back to Nancherrow with me, but he had to return to darkest Scotland and spend a bit of time with his old mum and dad. He doesn't talk about his family much, but I get the impression that they're not the most exciting parents in the world."

"So why is there every chance I'll meet him?"

"He'll maybe come later on. He seemed quite tempted by the idea. Didn't exactly jump at it but then he never, obviously, jumps at anything." Edward looked at Judith, and found her laughing. He frowned. "What's so funny?"

"I hope he's not chinless and boring, otherwise Loveday will crucify him."

"Loveday's a pain in the arse. And of course Gus isn't chinless. All Scotsmen have chins."

"Has he ever been to Cornwall?"

"No."

"If he's a painter then he'll become bewitched, as all painters do, and never want to leave."

"Knowing Gus, I think his career is safe. He's far too conscientious for diversions. Traditionally the Scots have a tremendous respect for education. That's why they're so clever and invent things like mackintoshes and inflatable tyres and tar-macadamed roads."

But Judith had talked enough about Gus Callender. "Tell me more about France. Tell me about the drive. Was it beautiful?"

"It was great going south, but it wasn't so much fun coming back. After Paris, the roads to Calais became choked with traffic and we had to wait half a day before we got a berth on the ferry."

"Why was that?"

"Panic. War nerves. All the little British families holidaying in Brittany and Belgium suddenly deciding to cut short their stay and scuttle for home."

"What did they think was going to happen?"

"I don't know. I suppose the German Army suddenly bursting through the Maginot Line and invading France. Or something. Bad luck on the hoteliers. You could imagine the long faces of Monsieur and Madame du Pont of the Hôtel du Plage, watching their bread and butter drive away down the road and back to England."

"Are things *really* as bad as that, Edward?"

"Pretty bad, I reckon. Poor old Pops is racked with apprehension."

"I know. I think that's why your mother ran away to London."

"She's never been much use at facing up to cruel facts. Brilliant at keeping them at bay but not much use at facing up to them. She telephoned last night, just to make sure we were all surviving without her, and to give us the London news. Athena's got a new boyfriend. He's called Rupert Rycroft and he's in the Royal Dragoon Guards."

"Goodness, how smart."

"Pops and I have got bets on how long it will last. A fiver each way. I'm going to get another beer. How about you?"

"I'm all right. I've not finished this yet."

"Don't let anyone sneak my seat."

"I won't."

He left her to fight his way once more back to the bar, and Judith was alone. Which didn't matter because there was so much, and so many people, to look at. A mixed bunch, she decided. Two or three old men, clearly locals, sat, firmly established, on the wooden benches which flanked the fireplace. They nursed tankards in work-worn hands, and talked amongst themselves with smouldering cigarette stubs glued to their lower lips. They looked, she decided, as though they had been sitting there since opening time, which they probably had.

And then there was a rather grand group of people, probably staying at one of the big hotels up on the hill, but making this foray Downalong, to visit the Sliding Tackle, and see how the natives lived. They had upper-class, hooting voices, and looked thoroughly out of place, but even as she observed them, appeared to decide that they had had enough, for they were finishing their drinks, laying down the empty glasses, and preparing to depart.

Their going created a gap, not instantly filled, and Judith was left with a clear view across the room to the bench which stood at the far end. A man sat there alone, a half-filled tumbler on the table before him. He was watching her. Staring. She saw the unblinking eyes, the drooping, nicotine-stained moustache, the tweed cap pulled low on his brow. Beneath bristling brows his pale gaze was unblinking. She reached for her shandy and took a mouthful, and then quickly laid the glass down again because her hand had started to shake. She could feel her heart pumping in her breast, and the blood drain, like water through a sieve, from her cheeks.

Billy Fawcett.

She had neither seen him nor heard news of him since the day of Aunt Louise's funeral. As the years had passed—and now being fourteen seemed a lifetime away—the trauma of her girlhood had gradually faded. But never totally disappeared. Lately, older and better informed, she had even tried to find some sympathy for his pathetic sexual aberrations, but it was almost impossible and helped not at all. On the contrary, the memory of him had almost destroyed her relationship with Edward, and he, of course, was the reason that she had never wanted to return to Penmarron.

During her first few visits to the Warrens, while still a schoolgirl, she had lived in terror of meeting Billy Fawcett by chance; in the street perhaps, or walking out of the bank or the barber's shop. But the dreaded scenario never took place and gradually, as the years went by, her fears abated and she took heart. Perhaps he had moved from Penmarron, left his bungalow and the golf club, and gone to live up-country. Perhaps, happy thought, he was dead.

But he wasn't dead. He was here. In the Sliding Tackle. Sitting at the other end of the room and staring at her, his eyes burning like two bright pebbles in his florid face. She looked for Edward, but Edward was jammed in at the bar, buying his beer, and she could scarcely scream for help. *Oh, Edward, come back*, she begged silently. *Come back quickly.*

But Edward loitered, exchanging a few friendly remarks with the man who stood next to him. And now Billy Fawcett was pulling himself to his feet, picking up his tumbler, and making his way across the flagged floor to where Judith sat petrified, mesmerized as a rabbit by a snake. She watched him come, and he looked the same, but a bit more decrepit, down-at-heel, and shabby. His cheeks were flushed and netted with purple veins.

"Judith." He was there, steadying himself with his knotted old hand on the back of a chair.

She said nothing.

"Mind if I join you? Take a seat?" He pulled the chair from the table and cautiously lowered his bottom onto the seat. "Saw you," he told her. "Recognized you the moment you came through the door." His breath stank of old tobacco and whisky. "You've grown up."

"Yes."

Edward was on his way. She looked up, her eyes a mute appeal for help, and Edward, in some confusion, visibly bucked at finding the broken-down old stranger sitting at their table. He said politely, "Hello there," but there was not much friendliness in his voice and his expression was wary.

"My dear boy. I apologize . . ." The word took a bit of saying, so Billy Fawcett tried again. ". . . apologize for interrupting, but Judith and I are old friends. Had to have a word. Fawcett's the name. Billy Fawcett. Ex-Colonel, Indian Army." He eyed Edward. "I don't think we've had the pleasure . . . ?" His voice trailed away.

"Edward Carey-Lewis," said Edward, but did not put out his hand.

"Delighted to meet you." Fumbling around for something to occupy his hands, Billy Fawcett caught sight of his whisky, took a great slug and then slapped the glass back on the table. "And where are you from, Edward?"

"Rosemullion. Nancherrow."

"Not familiar, dear boy. Don't get around much these days. What do you do for a living?"

"I'm at Cambridge."

"Dreaming spires, eh? Blue remembered hills. Much have I travelled in the realms of gold." His eyes narrowed, as though hatching some plan. "I suppose, Edward, you wouldn't have such a thing as a cigarette on you? Seem to have run out."

Silently, Edward reached for his packet of Players and offered it to Billy Fawcett. With some difficulty he extricated one, and then dug in a sagging pocket to produce a lethal-looking metal lighter. It took some concentration to turn the wheel and produce a flame, and then to apply the flame to the end of the cigarette—by now looking a bit bent—but he finally achieved this, took a long drag, coughed appallingly, slurped down another mouthful of whisky, and then settled his elbows on the table, looking as though he intended to stay forever.

He became confidential. "Judith used to live next door to me," he told Edward. "With her Aunt Louise. Penmarron. Great times we had. Wonderful woman, Louise. My best friend. My only friend, come to that. You know, Judith, if you hadn't turned up, I'd have probably married Louise. She had a lot of time for me before you turned up. Good friends. Missed her like hell when she killed herself in that car of hers. Missed her like hell. Never felt so alone. Abandoned."

His voice shook. He raised a mottled hand and wiped away a dribbling tear. He had reached the maudlin stage of drunkenness, inviting sympathy and wallowing in his own self-pity. Judith stared into her shandy. She did not want to look at Billy Fawcett and was too appalled and ashamed to look at Edward.

Billy Fawcett rambled on. "Different for you though, eh, Judith? You didn't do too badly, did you? Scooped the lot. Knew which side your bread was buttered on. Didn't matter about me. Buggering everything up for me. Didn't even speak to me at Louise's funeral. Ignored me. And got the lot. Louise always said she'd look after me, but she didn't leave me a bloody thing. Not even one of Jack's bloody golf trophies." He brooded on this injustice for a bit, and then fired his broadside. "Conniving little bitch." A bit of spit flew through the air and landed on the table, too close to Judith's hand.

A long silence ensued, and then Edward shifted slightly in his chair. He spoke quietly. "You don't want to listen to any more of this shit, do you, Judith?"

She shook her head. "No."

Edward rose unhurriedly to his feet, towering over the old drunk. "I think you'd better go," he told him politely.

Billy Fawcett's apoplectic face, wearing an expression of confused disbelief, stared up. "Go? Young whipper-snapper, I'll go when I'm ready, and I've not done yet."

"Yes, you are. You're finished. Finished with drinking and finished with insulting Judith . . . now, go."

"Fuck off," said Billy Fawcett.

Edward's response to this was to take hold of the collar of Billy Fawcett's sagging jacket and yank him to his feet. By the time he had done his protesting . . . "Don't you dare lay your hands on me . . . don't you dare . . . treating a feller like a common felon . . . I'll have the law on you . . ." Edward had propelled him neatly away from the table, across the threshold, and out of the open door. There he dumped him on the cobbled pavement where Billy Fawcett, shocked and legless, collapsed into the gutter. There were a good many people around, and all of them witnessed his humiliation.

"Don't you come back here," Edward told him. "Don't you ever show your bloody face in this place again."

But, even flat on his back in the gutter, Billy Fawcett still retained a spark of fight. "You damned bastard," he yelled. "I never finished my drink." So Edward strode back into the bar, picked up the remains of the whisky, carried it out into the street, and flung its contents into Billy Fawcett's face.

"It's finished now," he said, "so go home."

Whereupon Billy Fawcett passed out.

Joe Warren, ambling homewards down Fish Street after an evening spent in the company of his mate, Rob Padlow, stepped out on the harbour road by the Sliding Tackle just in time to witness a riveting scene. A lot of people standing about, in various attitudes of shock and horror, an old geezer lying supine in the gutter, and a tall, fair young man in shirt-sleeves dousing his head in whisky, before striding back into the pub again.

Joe had not intended calling in at the Sliding Tackle, but such dramatic doings called for investigation. The old geezer appeared to have passed out, so he stepped over his legs and followed his assailant into the pub, where he was further astonished to find him sitting at the table under the window, and in the company of Judith.

Judith looked white as a sheet. Joe said, "What was all that about?" and she raised her head and saw him standing there, but all she could do was shake her head. Joe's eyes turned to her companion. "You're Loveday's brother?"

"That's right. Edward."

"I'm Joe Warren." He pulled out the chair from which Billy Fawcett had been so forcibly removed and sat down. "What did you do that for?" he asked Edward mildly.

"He's an offensive old drunk, so I helped him out into the fresh air, and then he swore at me and said he wanted to finish his drink, so I helped him finish it. Simple as that."

"Well, he's out for the count now. Did he upset Judith?" He frowned at her. "You're some pale. Are you all right?"

Judith took a deep breath and let it all out again. She was determined not to shake, nor cry, nor behave like an idiot in any sort of way.

"Yes, I'm all right. Thank you, Joe."

"You know the old geezer?"

"Yes. It's Billy Fawcett."

"Do *you?*" Edward asked Joe.

"Only by sight, because he spends his time in here two or three evenings a week. Usually pretty docile, though. Nobody's had call to throw him out before. Bother you, did he, Judith?"

"Oh, Joe, it's all over."

"Well, you look like you're going to faint away." Joe got to his feet. "I'm going to get you a drink. Won't be a moment."

And was gone before Judith could stop him. She turned to Edward. "I haven't finished this drink yet," she pointed out miserably.

"I think Joe has something a little stronger in mind. Tell me, was that old toad really a friend of your aunt's?"

"Yes."

"She must have been mad."

"No, not really. Just kind-hearted. And she and her husband had known him in the old days when they were all in India. I suppose she felt sort of responsible for him. They played golf. He lives in a horrible little bungalow in Penmarron. Oh, Edward, how's he going to get himself home?"

"I left him surrounded by gawping voyeurs. I expect one of them will be sufficiently misguided to take pity on him."

"But shouldn't we *do* something?"

"No."

She said, "I always thought he wanted to marry Aunt Louise. He was after her comfortable house, of course, and her money and her whisky."

"Sounds as though he was always a bit of an old soak."

"I hated him."

"Poor Judith. How horrible."

"And he . . ." She thought about Billy Fawcett's hand creeping up her leg, and wondered how on earth she could possibly explain to Edward and make him understand. But at that moment Joe returned to them, and the opportunity slipped away. He held out the tiny glass of brandy. "Get this down you and you'll feel better."

"Joe, you are kind. And you won't say anything, will you, to your parents? It's over now. I don't want anybody to know."

"I didn't see anything to talk about. An old drunk in a gutter. Nothing to do with you. Perhaps I'll just go and have a look and see what's happening." Which he did, returning in a moment with the news that some charitable passer-by had taken pity and telephoned for a taxi; Billy Fawcett had been bundled into this and was already on his way. Having delivered his message, Joe announced that he was going home.

"Can't I buy you a drink?" Edward asked.

"No, I'm tanked up already. Need my bed and my beauty sleep. Night, Judith."

"Good night, Joe. And thanks again."

"You get that brandy down you, my love . . ." And he was gone.

For a bit nothing was said. Judith sipped her brandy, and it burnt like fire in her throat, but slipped comfortably into her stomach and helped to still the panic of her heart.

Beside her, Edward lit another cigarette, and reached out to draw the ashtray towards him. "I think you need to talk, don't you?" he said at last. "Because if you do, I'm perfectly prepared to listen." She didn't say anything, simply sat staring at her hands. "You hated him. Surely not just because he was a bit of a boozer."

"No. It wasn't that."

"So what was it?"

She began to tell him, and once she had started it wasn't as difficult as she thought it was going to be. She told him about the departure of Molly and Jess, the closing of Riverview, and herself left in the care of Louise Forrester. Then the appearance of Billy Fawcett on the scene, and his apparently close friendship with Louise.

"I never liked him from the moment I first saw him. There was something so"—she wrinkled her nose—"sleazy about him. And he was always so jolly and twinkling and . . . untrustworthy, somehow."

"Did your aunt not see that in him?"

"I don't know. *Then,* I was terrified that she'd marry him, but now, with hindsight, I'm pretty certain she'd never have taken such a stupid step."

"So what happened?"

"He took us to the cinema. It was *Top Hat.* And I had to sit next to him, and he started groping and squeezing my leg." She looked at Edward. "I was fourteen, Edward, I hadn't got the faintest idea what he was up to. I panicked and fled from the cinema, and got a terrible row from Aunt Louise afterwards." She frowned. "You're not going to laugh, are you?"

"No. I promise. Did you tell Aunt Louise?"

"I simply couldn't. I don't know why. I just *couldn't.*"

"Is that all?"

"No."

"Tell me the rest then."

So she told him about the wet Sunday when she had been left on her own, and had gone to Veglos on her bicycle in order to get away from Billy Fawcett. "He used to watch us from his bungalow. I'm sure he had field-glasses. And he knew I was on my own that day because Aunt Louise, in her innocence, spilt the beans. Anyway, when I got home . . ."

"Don't tell me he was waiting for you?"

". . . I was scarcely indoors when he telephoned and said he was coming over. And I locked all the doors and windows and bolted upstairs and hid under Aunt Louise's bed. And for about ten minutes he shouted and swore and banged on doors and rang bells and tried to get at me, and I just lay under the bed in total terror, and I'd never been so frightened and I never have been since. I had nightmares about him. I still have sometimes. The same nightmare, that he's coming into my bedroom. I know it's childish, but when I saw him this evening, I was simply petrified with terror . . ."

"Am I the first person you've ever told about all this?"

"No. After Aunt Louise was killed, I told Miss Catto."

"What did she say?"

"Oh, she was sweet, but very matter-of-fact. Just said that he was simply an old groper and I wasn't to think about it any more. But you can't help what goes on inside your head, can you? If I could do something physical, like murder Billy Fawcett, or squash him like a beetle, perhaps it would be easier. But I can't help it if my psyche jumps up and down like a screaming idiot every time his name comes up or I'm reminded of him."

"Is that what happened at Christmas when I kissed you behind the billiard-room curtains?"

She was so embarrassed by the memory, by Edward even mentioning the incident, that she could feel the blush, like fire, creeping up into her cheeks. "It wasn't a *bit* like Billy Fawcett, Edward. You mustn't think that. It was just that, when you . . . touched me . . . it all went wrong."

"I think you have a trauma."

She turned to him, almost in tears of despair. "But why can't I be shed of it? I don't want to live with it for the rest of my life. And I'm still frightened of him, because he hates me so much . . ."

"Why does he hate you so much?"

"Because I wouldn't let him near me. And because when she died, Aunt Louise left me all her money."

"I see. I never knew that."

"I was told never to tell anybody. Not because it's a secret but because Miss Catto said it was vulgar to talk about money. Your mother knows, of course, and your father. But that's all."

"A *lot* of money?" Ruefully, Judith nodded. "But how perfectly marvellous."

"Yes, it is, rather. It means I can buy people presents, and now I've got my own little car."

"And for this, Billy Fawcett will never forgive you?"

"He was at Aunt Louise's funeral. That day he looked as though he would like to kill me."

Now, Edward did smile. "If looks could kill, we'd all be dead long ago." He stubbed out his cigarette, and put his arms around her, and bent to kiss her cheek. "Darling Judith. What a very unpleasant storm in a very small teacup. Do you know what I think? I think you need a catalyst of some sort. Don't ask me what, but suddenly something will happen, it will all work out and you will be shed of all your hang-ups. You mustn't let one unhappy memory come between you and love. You are far too sweet for that. And not every man will be as constant and patient as I am."

"Oh, Edward, I'm so sorry."

"There's nothing to be sorry about. Just be sure to let me know when it's all behind you. And now, I really think I should take you home. It's been something of an evening."

"The best bit was just having *you* here."

"When are you coming back to us at Nancherrow?"

"Sunday, next week."

"We'll be waiting for you." He got to his feet and stood until she had extricated herself from the narrow bench. Outside, the dusky evening bloomed. The sun had gone, slipped behind the sea, and the sky deepened to sapphire-blue. Small waves lapped at the quay and the harbour was ringed with the riding lights of fishing boats. There were still a few people around, relishing the twilit warmth, and reluctant to call it a day and go indoors; but Billy Fawcett had gone.

Edward took her arm and together they walked slowly back to where he had left his car.

He telephoned the next morning. Judith was in the kitchen helping Mrs. Warren to deal with the breakfast dishes when Ellie came galloping up the stair from the shop.

"Judith, that's a phone call for you. Says it's Edward."

"Edward!" Mrs. Warren made a coy face. "He's not losing any time."

Judith pretended not to hear. Still tied up in a blue-and-white striped apron, she went downstairs and into Mr. Warren's office. "Edward?"

"Good morning."

"It's only nine o'clock. What are you ringing up about?"

"I wanted to ask if you'd slept well."

"Oh, silly thing. Of course I did. I'm sorry about what happened last night, but there wasn't an awful lot I could do to stop it. Did you get back safely? Stupid question, of course you did."

"Yes, I got back. But . . ." he hesitated. "This is the other reason I phoned. The thing is, there's a slight panic on here."

Judith's heart sank. "Something wrong?"

"No, not really. Well, yes, then. Aunt Lavinia took ill last night. Apparently, the day before, she'd been out gardening, and stayed too long, and caught a bit of a chill. She went to bed but her condition deteriorated, and now she's got pneumonia. Poor Isobel rang Mary Millyway, and the doctor's been coming and going, and there's a full-time nurse taking care of the old girl, but everybody's a bit worried. It all happened so quickly."

"Oh, Edward, I can't bear it." Aunt Lavinia, so seemingly indestructible. "She's not going to die, is she?"

"Well, she's pretty old. We all have to die sometime, I suppose, but none of us wants her to die just yet."

"Is your mother home?"

"Pops phoned her late last night. She's driving back today."

"What about Athena? Athena so *loves* Aunt Lavinia."

"Athena took off for Scotland with Rupert Rycroft . . . I think they went at the beginning of the week. We dithered a bit as to whether we should let her know or not, and then Pops decided that if the worst happened and Athena didn't even know Lavinia was ill, then she'd never forgive him. So he

268

got the number from Ma, and put a trunk-call through to some remote glen or other, but Athena had already left for the hills and so all he could do was leave a message."

"Poor Athena. Do you suppose she'll come home?"

"I don't know. It's a hell of a long way. We'll have to see."

"And Loveday? Is she all right?"

"Yes, she's all right. A bit tearful, but Mary Millyway's a motherly comfort, and Loveday'll be fine once Ma's home again."

"Are you able to go and see Aunt Lavinia?"

"Pops has been. She knew him, but she's clearly very ill. If I get the go-ahead, I'll maybe go to the Dower House with him this afternoon."

"It doesn't sound very hopeful, does it?"

"Don't be despondent. She's a tough old bird. At the end of the day, she'll probably outlive us all."

"I'll come back to Nancherrow today if it would help."

"That's what you mustn't do. I only told you because I thought you'd be upset if you weren't told. I know that you feel about Aunt Lavinia very much the way that the rest of us do. But don't cut short your holiday. We'll see you next Sunday, or whenever. And, incidentally, Gus'll be here as well. There was a message for me when I got back last night. He's driving down from Scotland, on his way already."

"Oh, *Edward*. What an inopportune time for more visitors. Can't you put him off?"

"No. I don't know where he is. Probably Birmingham, or somewhere gruesome. Can't get hold of him."

"Poor man. He's going to arrive to a sort of pandemonium."

"Oh, it'll be all right. He's a very easy guest. He'll understand."

Judith decided that men—even Edward—could be at times extremely thick. He had spent his life inviting friends back to Nancherrow, and took entirely for granted the domestic upheaval and organization that these prolonged visits involved. Now, she had a mental picture of poor Mary Millyway, with a family crisis on her hands, and enough to see to at the best of times, having to deal with this extra chore: alerting Mrs. Nettlebed to the fact that there would be an extra mouth to feed; taking clean sheets from the linen cupboard; organizing Janet to get ready one of the spare rooms; seeing to towels and fresh soap; checking on coat-hangers in the wardrobe and rich tea biscuits in the tin by the bed.

"Perhaps I *should* come back."

"You're absolutely not to. I forbid it."

"All right. But I am sorry for you all. Send my love to everybody. Give your father my love."

"I will. Try not to worry."

"And love to you."

"The same, by return." She could hear the smile in his voice. " 'Bye, Judith."

Gus Callender, at the wheel of his dark-green Lagonda, left Okehampton behind him and roared up the steep hill which led out of the little market town and into the high country beyond. It was a bright and breezy August morning, and all about him was pleasingly new and unfamiliar because he had never come this way before. A verdant countryside of pasture and stubble fields, lying gold in the late-summer sunshine. In the distance, friezes of ancient elms marked the boundaries of the hedgerows.

He had been driving for two days, taking his time, relishing the freedom of being on his own, and the satisfying surge of his powerful car. (He had bought the Lagonda a year ago with the money he had been given for his twenty-first birthday, and it was just about the best present he had ever had.) Leaving home, of course, had been a bit of a facer because his parents had thought that, having had those two weeks in France, he would be content to spend the rest of his vacation with them. But he had explained, and cajoled, and promised to return before too long, and his mother had made the best of it, and bravely waved him off, flapping her handkerchief like a little flag. Despite all his resolutions he had, momentarily, been consumed by a ridiculous guilt, but as soon as she was out of sight he was able, without too much difficulty, to put her out of mind.

He drove from Deeside to Carlisle, then Carlisle to Gloucester. Now he was on the last leg of the long journey. After Scotland (wet) and the Midlands (grey), it felt like arriving in a totally new world, sun-washed and pastoral. At the summit of the long hill, Dartmoor came into view, the deserted miles of tor and bog subtly changing colour as billowing cloud shadows rolled across, blown by the western wind. He saw the curving shapes of slopes that seemed to lean up into the sky, the emerald green of bogland, the cairns of granite, carved by the wind into primeval, yet oddly modernistic sculptures. And his painter's eye was caught, and his fingers itched for pencil and brush, and he longed to stop, then and there, and somehow try to capture, on his sketch-pad, this place and this light forever.

But if he stopped, he knew that he would be there for the rest of the day, and he was due, expected, at Nancherrow sometime during the course of the afternoon. Painting must wait. He thought of France and the picture he had done of the Beaths' delectable villa. Thinking of the villa, he began to sing the song that would always be the theme of the holiday, heard on the radio, or played on the gramophone, while they sunbathed by the pool, or sat on the terrace in the blue-scented evenings, drinking wine, watching the sun slip behind the mountains of the Midi, and the lights of Sillence come on one by one, spangling the opposite hillside like Christmas decorations on a dark tree.

La mer
Qu'on voit danser le long des golfes clairs
A des reflets d'argent

La mer
Des reflets changeants
Sous la pluie.

Launceston. He recalled a small bridge, and realized that he had already crossed the county boundary. He was in Cornwall. Ahead lay the wastes of Bodmin Moor. Somewhere there was a pub called Jamaica Inn. It was half past eleven, and for a bit he debated with himself as to whether he should stop there for a drink and something to eat, and then decided against it. Instead he would press on to Truro. Before him the road lay empty. He accelerated and allowed himself to revel in an unaccustomed and uncharacteristic elation.

La mer
Au ciel d'été confond
Ses blancs moutons
Avec les anges si purs
La mer bergère d'azur
Infinie.

Truro drowsed in its valley in the noonday sun. Approaching, he saw the spire of the cathedral, the silver glint of tree-fringed water. He drove into the town, into the wide main street, parked outside the Red Lion, went inside, and found his way to the bar. It was very dark and wood-panelled, smelling beery and cool. One or two old boys sat around reading newspapers and smoking their pipes, but Gus settled himself at the bar, and having ordered his half-pint of bitter, asked the barman if it was possible to have something to eat.

"No. We don't do meals down here. Have to go up to the dining-room for something to eat."

"Do I have to book a table?"

"I'll send word up to the head-waiter. On your own, are you?"

"Yes, just myself."

The barman drew his half-pint and set it down on the counter. "You travelling, are you?"

"Yes. I've got my car outside."

"Come far?"

"Yes, actually. From Aberdeen."

"Aberdeen? That's up in Scotland, isn't it? Some drive. How long's it taken you?"

"Two days."

"You've come a long way. How much farther have you got to go?"

"Right to the end. Beyond Penzance."

"Good as John o'Groat's to Land's End, isn't it?"

"Just about."

"Live in Scotland, do you?"

"Yes, born and bred."

"You haven't got no accent, if you'll excuse me saying so. We had a Scotsman in here a month or two ago, from Glasgow, and I couldn't make out a word he was saying."

"Glasgow's a tricky accent."

"Tricky all right."

A couple of new customers came through the door and the barman excused himself, left Gus, and went to serve them. Alone, Gus felt for his cigarettes, took one, and lit it. At the back of the bar, behind the shelves of bottles, the wall was lined by a mirror. In its murky depths, beyond the bottles, bits of his own reflection stared back at him. A dark young man, looking, he decided, older than his years. Dark-eyed, dark-haired, pale-skinned, clean-shaven. He wore a blue cotton shirt and had knotted a handkerchief around his neck in lieu of a tie, but even this informality did nothing to dispel the image of a dour fellow. Sombre, even.

Cheer up, you gloomy sod, he told his reflection. *You are in Cornwall. You've made it. You're here at last.* As though his reflection didn't already know. *You've come a long way,* the barman had remarked, but he had spoken a subtler truth than he realized.

Gus raised the glass to himself. *You've come a long way.* He drank the cool, woody beer.

It was Edward Carey-Lewis who had first started to call him Gus, and the nickname had stuck. Before that, he had been Angus, the only child of two elderly parents. His father, Duncan Callender, was an astute and successful Aberdeen business man who had pulled himself up, from humble beginnings, by his bootstraps, and by the time Angus arrived on the scene had already amassed a tidy fortune in the ship's chandlery business. As well, over the years, his interests had diverged to include a wholesale ironmongery business and large chunks of city property; tenement blocks and terraces of low-rent housing.

Angus's early childhood had been spent in the heart of Aberdeen, in a solid granite town house set in a small walled garden. The garden had a front lawn and a back green for the washing line, and a small patch of earth where his mother grew runner beans and cabbages. A small world for a small boy, and he was perfectly content.

But Duncan Callender was not. He had got where he was by his own hard work, honesty, and fairness, and so had earned the respect of both his work force and his colleagues. But that was not enough. For his only son he had ambitions, and was determined to raise and educate him a gentleman.

Accordingly, when Angus was seven, the family moved. From the comfortable, unpretentious house that had been home, to an enormous Victorian mansion in a village on the banks of the River Dee. From here, Duncan

Callender commuted each day to his office in Aberdeen, and Angus and his mother were left to make the best of it. After the city streets, the shops, and friendly rattling trams, the majestic hills and straths of Deeside were both strange and overwhelming, and their new abode only slightly less so, with its plethora of fumed oak and stained glass, tartan carpeting and fireplaces large enough to roast an ox if one felt so inclined.

As well, a large number of servants had to be employed in order to run this massive establishment. Where, before, Mrs. Callender had managed very nicely with a cook and housemaid, she now found herself expected to give orders to a resident indoor staff of six and two gardeners, one of whom lived in the lodge by the entrance gate. She was a devoted wife and mother, but a simple soul, and found it a sad trial to be always struggling to keep up appearances.

In Aberdeen, she had felt comfortable; knowing her own place in the world, and safe in the dignity of a modest, well-run home. But on Deeside, she was totally out of her depth. Neither fish, fowl, nor good red herring. She found it almost impossible to communicate with the village folk, and became convinced that their dour faces and monosyllabic responses to her tentative advances proved that they thought little of her, and were not impressed by the wealth and style of such newcomers.

Her other neighbours, the old noble families who had occupied their castles and estates for generations, were even more terrifying, alien as creatures from another planet. Lady This and the Marquis of That, with their beaked noses and their lanky tweeds. Mrs. Huntingdon-Gordon, who bred Labradors, and reigned, like some all-powerful warlord, in an archaic keep on the hill. And Major-General Robertson, who read the lesson in church on Sundays rather as though he were barking out orders for battle, and never bothered to lower his voice even when he was being rude to the minister.

It was a very difficult period, but for Angus did not last long. At eight years old he was despatched to boarding-school, an expensive preparatory in Perthshire, and his childhood was virtually over. At first he was teased and bullied. Because of his Aberdeen accent; because his kilt was too long; because he had the wrong sort of fountain-pen, and because he came top of his class and was dubbed a swot. But he was a well-muscled boy and good at football, and after he had bloodied the nose of the lower-school bully, in full view of everybody who happened to be in the playground, he was left alone and swiftly settled down. By the time he returned to Deeside for the Christmas holidays, he had grown two inches and his accent was a thing of the past. His mother secretly grieved for the child she knew she had lost, but Duncan Callender was delighted.

"Why do you no' ask some of your new pals home?" he asked, but Angus pretended not to hear him and went out of doors to ride his bicycle.

Finished with prep school, he went on to Rugby, where he earned the reputation of a reliable all-rounder. It was at this period that he discovered the joys of the art room, and a latent ability to draw and paint that he had never even suspected he possessed. With the encouragement of a sympathetic art master, he began filling a sketch-book, all the time developing his own style. Pencil drawings, tinted by a pale wash of colour . . . the playing fields; a boy working at a potter's wheel, a master striding across a windy quad on his way to class with an armful of books and his black gown billowing like fat black wings.

One day, leafing through a copy of *The Studio,* he read an article on the Cornish painters, the Newlyn School. Illustrating this was a coloured plate of a work by Laura Knight: a girl standing on a rock and watching the sea. The sea was peacock-blue, but the girl wore a sweater so it couldn't be all that hot, and her hair was copper-red, dressed in a single plait which fell across one shoulder.

His attention caught, he read the article, and for some reason it set his imagination ablaze. Cornwall. Perhaps he would become a professional artist, and go and settle in Cornwall, as so many had done before him. He would wear bizarre paint-stained clothes, grow his hair, smoke Gitanes; and there would always be some besotted, devoted girl around, domestically inclined, of course, but beautiful. She would live with him in his fisherman's cottage, or perhaps a converted barn, with an outside staircase of granite blocks and a blue-painted door, and there would be geraniums growing scarlet in earthenware pots . . .

The illusion was so real that he almost felt the warmth of the sun, smelt the sea-wind scented with wild flowers. But a fantasy. He looked up, across the deserted art room, through a tall window to a wintry midland sky. A schoolboy's fantasy. He could never be a professional painter because he was already committed to maths and physics, streamed for Cambridge University and a degree in engineering.

But dreams and fantasies were too precious to abandon altogether. He took out his penknife and carefully removed the colour plate. He slipped it into a folder containing some of his own drawings, and suppressing his conscience, spirited it away. Later he mounted and framed it, and the unknown girl by the Cornish sea made an impressive decoration for the walls of his study.

In other directions too, Rugby widened his experience. Too self-contained to make close friends he was, nevertheless, popular and from time to time invitations were proffered, to spend part of the holidays in other people's country houses, in Yorkshire, or Wiltshire, or Hampshire. These, politely, he accepted, was kindly received, and managed not to perpetrate any obvious social gaffes.

"And where is it you come from?" some mother would ask him, over the first cup of tea.

"Scotland."

"You lucky boy. Whereabouts?"

"My parents have a place on Deeside." And then, before she started talking about salmon fishing, a beat on the Dee, and grouse moors, he would change the subject, and ask if he might have a slice of gingerbread. After that, with a bit of luck, the subject would not be raised again.

Returning home after these visits was invariably something of an anticlimax. The truth was that he had outgrown his elderly parents, the hideous house felt claustrophobic and the days endless, broken only by lengthy and tedious mealtimes. His mother's loving attentions stifled him, and his father's embarrassing pride and interest only made matters worse.

But all was not gloom. When he turned seventeen, an unexpected bonus came his way, albeit a mixed blessing. Word, it seemed, had gone around the neighbourhood that the Callender boy, despite the distinct disadvantage of his parents, was not only good-looking but perfectly presentable, and if any hostess was in need of a spare man . . . ? Engraved invitations began to arrive, bidding Angus to various functions to which his mother and father were not invited. Reel parties and summer balls, where his partners had names like Lady Henrietta McMillan, or The Honourable Camilla Stokes. By now he was able to drive a car, and at the wheel of his father's ponderous Rover he duly got himself to these formal events, correctly attired in full Highland rig, starched white shirt, and black tie. His training in those country houses in Yorkshire, Wiltshire, and Hampshire now stood him in good stead, and he was able to cope with the formality of massive dinner parties, and afterwards dance until the small hours—smile, be attentive to all the right people—and generally acquit himself to everybody's satisfaction.

But it all seemed a bit like play-acting. He was who he was, with no illusions as to his background or breeding. Driving the long road home after one of these dances, the dark and empty landscape sombre and the sky lightening with the first touch of dawn, the thought occurred to him that, since he was seven years old and the family had left Aberdeen for good, he could remember no place where he'd felt comfortably at home. Not his father's house certainly. Not school. Not the hospitable country establishments in Yorkshire, Wiltshire, and Hampshire, where he had been made so welcome. However much he enjoyed himself, he always felt that he was standing apart and watching others. And he wanted to Belong.

Perhaps one day it would happen. Like falling in love. Or hearing a voice. Or walking into a strange room and finding it instantly recognizable, even though you'd never seen it before in your life. A place where no person would condescend, and he would need no label, no tag. Where he would be made welcome simply because he was himself. "Angus, my dear fellow. How good of you to come, and how splendid to see you."

But matters, unexpectedly, were to improve. After the uneasy years of adolescence, which, for Gus, were more painful and difficult than for most of his contemporaries, Cambridge came as a revelation and a release. From the first moment, he thought it the loveliest city he had ever seen, and Trinity a dream of architecture. During his first few weeks, he spent much of his leisure time simply walking; gradually learning his way about the ancient, time-drenched streets and courtyards. Raised as a Presbyterian, he attended Morning Service in King's Chapel for the sheer joy of listening to the singing, and it was there that he heard for the first time the Gregorian "Miserere," and found himself pierced by reasonless joy as the boys' voices soared to heights that were surely unachievable, unless perhaps by angels.

After a bit, as he became more familiar with his new surroundings, the visual impact of Cambridge stirred his painter's instinct, and before long his sketch-book was filled with swift, pencilled impressions. Punts on the willow-fringed Backs; the Bridge of Sighs. The inner courts of Corpus Christi, the twin towers of Kings College, silhouetted against the enormous skyscape of the flat fenlands. The sheer size and pureness of proportion and perspective he found a challenge; the brilliant hues of sky and lawns, stained-glass windows, autumn foliage cried at him to be set down on paper. He felt surrounded, not only by deep wells of learning but by a beauty that was not of nature, but, astonishingly, contrived by man.

His college was Pembroke and his subject engineering. Edward Carey-Lewis, as well, was at Pembroke, but reading English and philosophy. They had arrived as freshmen at the same time, the Michaelmas term of 1937, but it was not until the last term of their second year that they finally got to know each other and became friends. There were reasons for this. Studying different subjects, they did not share tutorials. Their rooms were in different parts of Pembroke, and so the normal, casual, neighbourly chat was precluded. And while Gus played cricket and rugger, Edward appeared to have no interest in team games, and instead spent much of his time with the University Flying Club, endeavouring to achieve his pilot's licence.

Consequently, their paths seldom crossed. But inevitably, Gus saw Edward about the place. At the far side of the College Dining Hall on the formal occasions when all undergraduates were bidden, in some splendour, to dine in. Or buzzing down Trinity Street in his dark-blue Triumph with always a pretty girl or two squashed in beside him. Sometimes, he was glimpsed across a crowded pub, the hub of a noisy gathering, and usually the one to be picking up the bill for a round of drinks, and, with each encounter, he struck Gus as being yet more blessed, confident, handsome, and pleased with himself. An instinctive antipathy (born of envy?—he would not admit this, even to himself) matured into dislike, but, with inborn discretion, Gus kept his feelings to himself. There was no point in making enemies, and he had, after all, never even spoken to the fellow. It was just that there was something about him that was just too good to be true. Edward Carey-Lewis. No man could have it all. There had to be some worm in the bud, but it was not Gus's business to winkle it out.

So, he left it at that, and concentrated on his studies. But fickle fate had other ideas in mind. This summer term, in 1939, Gus Callender and Edward Carey-Lewis were allocated rooms on the same stair at Pembroke, and shared a miniature kitchen, known as a "gip-room." One late afternoon, boiling up a kettle to make a pot of tea, Gus heard footsteps running up the stone stairway behind him, to pause at the open door. And, then, a voice. "Hello, there."

He turned and saw Edward Carey-Lewis standing in the open doorway, a lock of blond hair flopping over his forehead, and his long college muffler wound about his neck.

"Hello."

"You're Angus Callender."

"That's right."

"Edward Carey-Lewis. It seems we're neighbours. What are your rooms like?"

"Okay."

"Making tea?" An unashamed hint.

"Yes. Do you want some."

"Have you got anything to eat?"

"Yes. Fruitcake."

"Good. I'm starving."

And so Edward came, and they sat at the open window of Gus's room, and drank tea out of mugs, and Gus smoked a cigarette, and Edward ate most of the fruit-cake. They talked. About nothing in particular, but within fifteen minutes Gus realized that as far as Edward Carey-Lewis was concerned, he had been utterly and completely wrong, for Edward was neither snobbish nor stupid. His easy ways and his straight blue gaze were entirely genuine, and his confidence of manner sprang, not from a rarefied upbringing but from the fact that he was clearly his own man, considering himself no better and no worse than any of his contemporaries.

With the teapot emptied and the cake depleted, Edward pulled himself to his feet and started nosing around Gus's rooms, reading the titles of his books, leafing through a magazine.

"I like your tiger-skin hearthrug."

"I bought it in a junk-shop."

Now Edward was looking at Gus's pictures, moving from one to the other like a man about to purchase.

"Nice water-colour. Where's that?"

"The Lake District."

"You've got quite a collection here. Did you buy them all?"

"No. I painted them. Did them myself."

Edward turned his head to gape at Gus. "Did you really? What a frightfully talented fellow you are. And good to know that if you fail your Tripos, you can always keep the wolf from the door by dabbling with your paintbrush." He went back to his inspection. "Do you ever use oils?"

"Yes, sometimes."

"Did you do this one?"

"No," Gus admitted. "I'm ashamed to say I tore that one from the pages of a magazine when I was at school. But I like it so much I take it everywhere; hang it up where I can look at it."

"Was it the pretty girl who caught your boyish fancy, or the rocks and the sea?"

"The whole composition, I suppose."

"Who's the artist?"

"Laura Knight."

"It's Cornwall," said Edward.

"I know it is. But how can you tell?"

"Couldn't be anywhere else."

Gus frowned. "Do you know Cornwall?"

"I should do. I live there. Always have. It's my home."

After a bit, "How extraordinary," said Gus.

"Why extraordinary?"

"I don't know. It's just that I've always been enormously interested in the Cornish painters. It seems to me amazing that so many incredibly talented people should congregate in such a remote place, and yet remain so influential."

"I don't know much about that, but Newlyn's inundated by artists. Colonies of them. Like mice."

"Have you met any of them?"

Edward shook his head. "Can't say I have. I'm afraid I'm a bit of a philistine when it comes to art. At Nancherrow we have a lot of sporting pictures and dark family portraits. You know the sort of thing. Wall-eyed ancestors with dogs." He thought for a moment. "Except that my mother was painted by de László. It's very charming. It hangs over the drawing-room fireplace." Suddenly, Edward seemed to run out of steam. Without ceremony, he yawned enormously. "God, I'm tired. I'm going to go and have a bath. Thanks for the tea. I like your rooms." He ambled towards the door, opened it, and then turned back. "What are you doing tonight?"

"Nothing much."

"A few of us are driving out to Grantchester for a drink in the pub there. Want to join us?"

"I'd like to very much. Thank you."

"I'll bang on your door about a quarter past seven."

"Right."

Edward smiled. "See you then, Gus."

Gus thought he had misheard. Edward was already on the way out. "What did you call me?"

Edward's head came round the edge of the door. "Gus."

"Why?"

"I suppose I think of you as Gus. I don't think of you as Angus. Angus has got red hair, and huge brogues like tank treads, and voluminous knickerbockers contrived from ginger tweed."

Gus found himself laughing. "You'd better watch it. I hail from Aberdeenshire."

But Edward was unfazed. "In that case," he said, "you'll know exactly what I'm talking about." And on this exit-line he withdrew, closing the door behind him.

Gus. He was Gus. And such was Edward's influence that after that first evening, he was never again to be called anything else.

He found himself, all at once, extremely hungry. Upstairs, in the half-empty dining-room—fusty, old-world Turkey carpets and starched white table-cloths, and lowered voices over the timorous scrape of cutlery—he ate his way through soup, and boiled beef with carrots, and Queen of Puddings, and then, feeling a new man, paid his bill and escaped once more into the open air. He walked for a bit down the cobbled pavements until he found a book-shop and there went in, and bought an ordnance-survey map of the west of Cornwall. Back in his car, he lit a cigarette, and opened out the map and planned his route. Nancherrow. Edward, over the telephone, had given him a few vague instructions, but now, working on a scale of an inch to a mile, Gus decided that only an idiot could lose the way. Truro to Penzance, and then the coast road that led to Land's End. His finger traced its way across the stiffened paper and stopped at Rosemullion, clearly marked with church and river and bridge. And then, Nancherrow, the word written in italics, a dotted line for the approach road, a tiny symbol for the house. It was good to find it there, set down by some knowledgeable geographer. It made his desti-nation real, not simply a name, casually spoken, nor a figment of his own imagination. He folded the map and laid it on the seat beside him; dealt with his cigarette, switched on the ignition.

He drove, down the bleak backbone of the county where evidence of de-funct tin-mines reared its head, old engine houses and crumbling stacks. Not beautiful. And when would he come to the sea? He was impatient for the sea. But, at last, the road sloped downhill ahead of him, and the countryside was changing. To his right appeared a range of hillocky sand-dunes, and then a deep estuary, and finally he was rewarded by a first sighting of the Atlantic. A glimpse, no more, of green rollers pouring in over a sand-bar. Beyond the estuary, the road turned inland, and there were pasture fields filled with dairy herds, or others south-sloping and planted with market-produce, all bounded by irregular drystone walls which looked as though they had stood forever. Palm trees grew in cottage gardens, houses wore the chalky patina of lime-wash, and narrow lanes led away from the main road, dipping down into wooded valleys, invitingly signposted with obscure or saintly names. All slumbered in the warm afternoon sunshine. Trees threw dark shadows, sun-speckled on dark Tarmac, and there was an extraordinary air of timelessness, as though here it would always be summer; the leaves would never fall from those ancient trees, and the gentle slopes of farmland would never know the cruel blast of winter gales.

Presently, ahead, shimmering in a glare of diffused light, Gus saw the other sea, the great sweep of Mount's Bay, a shout of blue, the horizon blurred. A flock of small craft was out on the water, a regatta, perhaps. The dinghies, redwings, scudded into the breeze, close-hauled, scarlet sails keeling, headed for some distant buoy.

And it was all piercingly familiar, as though he had seen it all before, and was simply returning, to a place long-known and deeply loved. *Yes. Yes, there it all is. Just the way it always has been. Just the way I knew it would be.* The sheltering arm of the harbour pier, the coppice of tall-masted boats, the air alive with the scream of gulls. A small steam train, chuffing out of the station and along the curve of the shore. A terrace of Regency houses, windows blinking the bright light, gardens rich with magnolia and camellia bushes. And over all, flowing in through the open window of the car, the fresh, cool, salty smell of tide-wrack and the open sea.

> *La mer*
> *Les a bercés*
> *Le long des golfes clairs*
> *Et d'une chanson d'amour*
> *La mer*
> *A bercé mon coeur pour la vie.*

It was all part of it. He felt like a man returning to his roots, as though everything he had ever done, every place that he had ever lived, had simply been a waiting time, an intermission. Which was strange, but, analysed, perhaps not strange at all, because he was simply witnessing, albeit for the first time, an experience that had become totally recognizable through the Cornish artists whose work he had studied and followed so avidly. Laura Knight and Lamorna Birch and Stanhope and Elizabeth Forbes and countless others. And he remembered his boyhood fantasy, born in the art room at Rugby: of coming to live in Cornwall, to embrace the Bohemian life, and to paint; to buy himself a white sun-washed cottage, and plant geraniums at the door. And he smiled, remembering that the fantasy had included a vague and undefined female companion. No person in particular, and she had never been given a face, but she had of course been young, and beautiful and eminently paintable, and an excellent cook. His mistress, of course. And, driving, Gus laughed out loud, at the innocence of his own lost youth and the harmless dreams of the gormless boy he had once been. And then ceased to laugh, because now that he was *here*, now he had actually *come*, the dreams seemed perfectly viable and not in any way beyond the bounds of possibility.

By now these recollections had brought him through the town and out into the country on the other side. He had climbed a hill, steep as the roof of a house, and reaching its summit, saw that the terrain, once more, had changed abruptly, and the fields of isolated farms swept up to moorland, tan-coloured and crowned with cairns of rock. The sea, to his left, was ever-present, but now its tang was overlaid by the sweet, mossy scent of stream and bogland, and he heard, from far off, the long, bubbling call of a curlew.

And there was the other dream, also long-forgotten and put out of mind, but all at once suddenly poignant and very real again: that one day, he would come to a house, a place never visited before, and there, instantly, utterly, would know that he belonged, as he had never belonged either in the gloomy

Victorian mansion on Deeside, or the hospitable homes of his schoolfriends. Cambridge was the closest he had ever got to this particular fantasy, but Cambridge was a university, a seat of learning, an extension of school. Not a bolt-hole, but a corner of the world where one put down roots, returned to, knowing that it would always be there, unchanged, making no demands, comfortable and comforting as an old pair of shoes. One's own. *Gus. Dear Gus. You're back.*

Long forgotten. Just as well. Day-dreams were the prerogative of the very young. With some firmness Gus put it all out of his mind and set his thoughts once more on the immediate task of not losing his way. But just then he saw a cross-roads, and a wooden signpost with the name "Rosemullion" printed upon it, and realized that he had only another ten miles or so to go, and common sense flew out of the window, to be replaced by the reasonless excitement of a boy returning from school for the holidays. Coming home. And that was peculiar in itself, because *coming home,* for Gus, had never been a thought to fill him with much pleasure. On the contrary, going home had become something of a painful duty, which he undertook with deep reluctance, loyally returning to be with his parents, but never lasting more than a couple of days before he began searching, desperately, for any excuse to leave. His mother and father could not help being elderly, set in their ways and pathetically proud of their only child, but for some reason, this only made matters worse. It wasn't that Gus was ashamed of them in any way. In fact, he was rather proud of them, and his father in particular. But he had become distanced from the old man, had little in common with him, and resented having to search for things to say and struggle with the most banal of conversations. And all this was because the doughty Duncan Callender had been determined for his son to become a gentleman; had insisted on an expensive private education, and so elevated Gus away from him, into a world that he and Gus's mother had never known, and would never know.

It was a cruel situation. Ironic. But it was not Gus who had built the barrier which lay between them all. Even before he had left Rugby, he had forced himself to come to terms with the uncomfortable situation and his own uneasy conscience, and had finally, firmly, shed all sense of blame. This was important, because otherwise he was going to have to spend the rest of his life with a millstone of guilt slung about his neck.

Loveday, shut into the fruit-cage, picked raspberries. It was good to have something to do, because everything just now was so horrible. Anxiety and fear for Aunt Lavinia pervaded the house like a heavy cloud, affecting everything and everybody. For her father, it had even taken priority over the news and, instead of listening to the wireless, he now spent his time on the telephone: talking to the doctor; to Diana in London; getting messages through to Athena in Scotland; arranging for day- and night-nurses to be in constant attendance at the Dower House. There had been some discussion as to whether Aunt Lavinia should be moved to hospital, but in the end it was decided that the physical demands of a journey by ambulance, and the distress of finding herself in strange surroundings, would most likely do more harm than good, and Aunt Lavinia should be allowed to remain, peacefully, where she was, in her own house and her own bed.

It was Loveday's first experience of possibly mortal illness. People died, of course. She knew that. But not her own close family. Not Aunt Lavinia. From time to time, she made a real effort to imagine life without the old lady, but she had always been so much part of Nancherrow, and her influence, on all the family, so strong and benevolent that Loveday found it impossible. It didn't, in fact, bear thinking about.

She moved down the line of canes, picking the sweet red fruit with both hands, and dropping them into the sturdy basket which she had slung, by a piece of string, around her waist. It was afternoon, bright and sunny, but a nippy wind blew in from the sea, and because of this, she had pulled on an old cricket sweater of Edward's, yellowed and darned. It was far too long, drooping down over her cotton skirt, but the sun lay on her shoulders, warm through the thick wool of the sweater, and Loveday was grateful for its brotherly comfort.

She was on her own because, after lunch, her father and Edward and Mary Millyway had all gone up to the Dower House. Pops had made an arrangement to speak to the doctor, Edward was going to sit with Aunt Lavinia for a bit, and Mary had accompanied them in order to keep poor old Isobel company. They would sit in Isobel's kitchen and drink tea. Isobel, perhaps, needed comforting more than any of them. She and Aunt Lavinia had been together for over forty years. If Aunt Lavinia died, it was likely that Isobel would not be far behind her.

"How about you, my darling?" her father had said to Loveday. "Do you want to come as well?"

And she had gone to him, and put her arms around his waist and pressed her face into the front of his waistcoat. He understood, and held her close. Muffled, "No," she told him. If the worst happened, she wanted to remember Aunt Lavinia the way she was, alert and gracious and joining in all the family jokes. Not an aged and sickly lady, bedridden, slipping away from them. "Is that awful? Should I come?"

"No. I think you shouldn't come."

She wept, and he kissed her and dried her eyes with his huge, clean white linen handkerchief. They were all very kind to Loveday. Edward gave her a hug and said, "Anyway, there has to be somebody here when Gus arrives. He's coming sometime this afternoon, and it wouldn't be hospitable if there was nobody to meet him. You can be a one-man reception committee."

Loveday, still sniffing a bit, didn't think that this was much of an idea. "Have I got to hang about?"

Mary laughed. "No, of course not. Do what you want. I'm sure Fleet would appreciate a good gallop."

But for once Loveday did not feel like riding Fleet. She wanted to stay within the confines of Nancherrow, where she felt safe and secure. She said, "I rode him yesterday."

"Then perhaps you could pick raspberries for Mrs. Nettlebed. She wants to make jam. You could help her hull and weigh the fruit."

Which wasn't wildly exciting, but at least better than doing nothing. Loveday sighed. "All right."

"That's my girl." Mary gave her a comforting cuddle and a kiss. "And we'll send your love to Aunt Lavinia, and tell her once she's a bit better, you'll be up to see her. And don't forget, your mother's driving back from London today. She'll be tired and distressed, and we don't want her to arrive home and find nothing but a lot of sad faces. For her sake, try not to worry too much."

So, she had picked raspberries. It took a bit of time to fill the two baskets that Mrs. Nettlebed had given her, but finally they were both brimming with ripe, perfect fruit. She had eaten some, but not many. Now, carrying a heavy basket in either hand, she made her way up the leafy passage between the canes, and let herself out of the fruit-cage, carefully latching it behind her, so that no bird could find its way in, gorge itself silly on berries, and then batter itself to death as it tried to fly to freedom.

In the kitchen, she found Mrs. Nettlebed icing a chocolate cake, with lots of swirls and little bits of crystallized fruit.

She dumped the baskets onto the table. "How's that, Mrs. Nettlebed?"

Mrs. Nettlebed was gratifyingly appreciative. "Lovely. You're a real sweetheart."

Loveday leaned across the table, scooped a gob of icing out of the mixing bowl, and sucked it off her finger. She decided that the taste of chocolate and the taste of raspberries did not mix. "And look at you, Loveday! You're a real mess. That jumper's covered in snags and raspberry juice. You should have put on a pinny."

"It doesn't matter. It's only an old one. Do you want me to help you make jam?"

"Haven't time now. Do it later, I will. And you've better things to do, because the visitor's arrived."

"The visitor?" Loveday's heart sank. Picking raspberries, she had forgotten about Edward's wretched friend, come to stay. "Oh, bother, is he here already? I hoped he wouldn't come till Edward was back." She wrinkled her nose. "What's he like?"

"No idea. Nettlebed let him in, took him up to his room. He's probably there now, unpacking. You'd better go up and say how do you do and make him welcome."

"I can't even remember his name."

"It's Mr. Callender. Gus Callender."

"Do I *have* to? I'd much rather make jam."

"Oh, Loveday! Get on with you." And Mrs. Nettlebed gave her a soft slap on the bottom and sent her on her way.

Reluctantly, Loveday went. Up the back stairs and down the guest-room passage. Half-way along, his door stood open. She reached it and paused, hesitating. He was there, standing with his back to her, his hands in his pockets, staring out of the open window. His luggage was stacked on the wooden rack at the foot of the bed, but the cases were closed and he seemed to have made no effort to start in on his unpacking. Her feet, in worn gym shoes, had made no sound on the carpeted passage, and she realized that he was totally unaware of her presence, which made her feel uncomfortable and a bit shy. From the courtyard below the window, she could hear the doves cooing. After a bit, she said, "Hello."

Thus startled, he swung around. For an instant they faced each other across the room, and then he smiled. "Hello."

Loveday found herself disconcerted. This was not what she had expected. What she had expected was a clone of the various youths whom Edward had brought home during the holidays of his school-days. They had all seemed to be cut from the same pattern, and she had found it hard to warm to any of them. But here was a different breed altogether and she instantly recognized the fact. For one thing, he looked older than Edward, more mature and expe-rienced. Dark and thin, rather serious. Interesting. Not someone who would make facetious remarks, nor treat her, Edward's little sister, like an idiot. Up to now, Walter Mudge and Joe Warren had been her yardsticks for the sort of man she was beginning to find disturbingly attractive, with their blatant masculinity and their easy ways. Gus Callender, oddly enough, looked a bit like both of them: the same dark hair and dark eyes, but he was taller, less stockily built than either Walter or Joe, and when he smiled, his whole face changed and he didn't look serious any longer.

Suddenly, she stopped feeling shy.

"You're Gus Callender."

"That's right. And you must be Loveday."

"I'm sorry there's nobody here but me. And I was picking raspberries."

She advanced into the room and perched herself on the high bed.

"That's all right. Your butler . . ."

"Mr. Nettlebed."

". . . made me welcome."

Loveday looked at his luggage. "You don't seem to have done much un-packing."

"No. To be truthful, I was wondering whether I should."

"What do you mean?"

"Mr. Nettlebed led me to believe that there are some problems. An illness in the family. And that Edward had gone to see his aunt . . ."

"Great-aunt. Lavinia. Yes. She's got pneumonia. And she's frightfully old, so it's rather worrying."

"Not a very good time to have people to stay. I feel that perhaps I should, tactfully, take myself off."

"Oh, you *mustn't* do that. Edward would be so upset and disappointed.

Anyway, everything's ready for you and we're all prepared, so there wouldn't be much point, would there?"

"I just wish Edward had called me, and told me the situation. I'd never have come."

"He couldn't because she's only been ill a little time, and he didn't know where you were. How far you'd got. Anyway, don't fuss about it. It makes no difference whether you're here or not." Which didn't sound very friendly. "Everybody would be very cross with me if I let you escape. And I know Mummy will want to meet you. She's been in London, but she's driving home today because of Aunt Lavinia. And Pops is having a word with the doctor, and Mary Millyway is cheering Isobel up. And Judith, she's my friend, she lives here quite a lot, she's still in Porthkerris." By now Gus was beginning to look a bit bemused, as well he might. Loveday made an effort to clarify the situation. "Mary Millyway used to be my nanny, she's heaven, she does everything; and Isobel is Aunt Lavinia's old maid."

"I see."

"They'll all be back in time for tea, I know, so you'll see Edward then. What time is it now?"

He looked at his wrist-watch, heavy gold and leather-strapped to his sinewy wrist. "Just on three o'clock."

"Well." She considered. "What would you like to do?" She was not very good at being hostessly. "Get unpacked? Or go out for a walk, or something?"

"I'd like some fresh air. I can unpack later."

"We could go down to the cove. You could swim, if you want, but there's a chilly wind. I don't mind cold water, but I hate coming out into a cold wind."

"Then let's not swim."

"All right, we'll walk. Tiger's gone with Pops, otherwise we could have taken him with us." She slid off the bed. "It's rather a steep, slippy path to the sea, so have you got rubbery shoes on? And perhaps a pullover? It might be a bit nippy on the cliffs."

He smiled at her bossiness. "Okay on both counts." He had tossed a sweater over the back of a chair, dark-blue Shetland wool and suitably thick. Now, he took this up, slung it over his shoulders, and knotted the arms round his neck like a muffler. "Lead the way," he told Loveday.

Because he was a newly come visitor, she did not take him down the back stairs, but along the passage, down the main stairway, and out through the front door. There was parked his car, and Loveday, diverted, paused to admire it.

"Goodness, what a dashing vehicle. Does it go frightfully fast?"

"It can do."

"It looks brand-new. Shiny headlamps and everything."

"I've had it about a year."

"Sometime, I'd love a ride."

"You shall have one."

They began to walk. Rounding the corner of the house, the wind pounced upon them, chill and salty. Overhead, huge white clouds bowled across the starch-blue sky. They went across the terraced lawns, and so onto the path, hemmed in by thickets of shrub and incongruous palms, that led down towards the sea.

After a while, this path became too narrow to walk abreast, so they fell into single file, Loveday leading the way, going faster and faster, speeding ahead of Gus, so that it took some concentration and a good deal of physical effort to keep up with her flying feet. He wondered if she was doing this on purpose, a tease, as he cantered along in her wake, ducking his head beneath the tunnel of gunnera, and slipping and sliding his way down the precipitous steps that fell to the floor of the quarry. Then, across the quarry and over the gate; a farm lane, and a stone stile (a bit like a steeplechase), and finally, the cliffs.

She was waiting for him, standing on grassy turf stained purple with thyme. The wind, rumbustious, tore at her cotton skirt and sent it ballooning about her long tanned legs, and her vivid face and her violet eyes were brimming with laughter as, gasping slightly, he reached her side.

"You run like a rabbit," he told her, when he had got his breath.

"Never mind. You kept up."

"You're extremely lucky that I didn't do myself some irreparable bodily harm. I thought I was going for a walk, not a marathon run."

"But worth it. You must admit, worth it."

And Gus looked, and saw the dark-turquoise sea, the scrap of beach, and the mammoth breakers hurling themselves against the rocks at the foot of the cliffs. Surf sizzled like soapy foam and spray, in rainbow-shot explosions of water, sprang twenty feet or more into the air. It was all very invigorating and very spectacular. And then Loveday shivered.

"Are you cold?" he asked her.

"A bit. Usually, we go down onto the rocks, but the tide's high today and we'd get drenched in spray."

"Then let's not go."

So, instead, they found shelter from the wind behind a huge boulder, yellow with lichen and stonecrop. Loveday settled herself on a thick cushion of turf, drew up her knees, and wrapped her arms around them, snuggling into her sweater for warmth. Gus lay beside her, legs outstretched, his weight supported by his elbows.

She said, "This is better. We can't see the sea but we can hear it, and at least we won't get soaked." She closed her eyes and turned up her face to the sun. After a bit, "That's *much* better," she said. "Warmer now. I wish we'd brought something to eat."

"I'm not, actually, hungry."

"I am. Always. So's Athena. I think Athena's coming home. Because of Aunt Lavinia. She's been in Scotland. You live in Scotland, don't you?"

"Yes."

"Whereabouts?"

"Aberdeenshire. On Deeside."

"Near Balmoral?"

"Not very."

"Are you near the sea?"

"No. Just the river."

"But rivers aren't the same as the sea, are they?"

"No. Not a bit the same."

Loveday fell silent, thinking about this, digging her chin into her knees. "I don't think I could live away from the sea."

"It's not so bad."

"It's worse than bad. It's torture."

He smiled. "As bad as that?"

"Yes. And I know because when I was about twelve I was sent off to boarding-school in Hampshire, and I nearly expired. It was all wrong. I felt like an alien. Everything was the wrong shape, the houses and the hedges and even the sky. I always felt the sky was sitting on top of my head, pressing me down. It gave me terrible headaches. I think I would have died if I'd had to stay there."

"But you didn't stay?"

"No. I lasted half a term and then I came home. Ran away. I've been here ever since."

"School?"

"In Penzance."

"And now?"

"I've left school."

"Is that it?"

She shrugged. "I don't know. Athena went to Switzerland. I might go to Switzerland. But then, on the other hand, if there is a war, I mightn't."

"I see. How old are you?"

"Seventeen."

"Too young to be called up."

"Called up for what?"

"The war. The services. Making munitions."

Loveday looked horrified. "I'm not going to stand at a conveyor belt and make bullets. If I don't go to Switzerland, I'm not going anywhere. If there's a war, it's going to be quite difficult enough to be brave and courageous right *here*. At Nancherrow. I certainly couldn't be brave and courageous in Birmingham or Liverpool or London. I'd go mad."

"Not necessarily," Gus said, endeavouring to calm her down, and rather wishing that he had not raised the subject in the first place. She brooded for a bit, and then, "Do you think there's going to be a war?" she asked.

"Probably."

"What will happen to you?"

"I'll be called up."

"Right away?"

"Yes. I'm in the Territorial Army. The Gordon Highlanders. My home regiment. I joined the battalion in 1938, after Hitler walked into Czechoslovakia."

"What does being a Territorial mean?"

"A part-time professional soldier."

"Are you trained?"

"Up to a point. Two weeks in a TA camp every summer. I am now quite capable of firing a gun and slaying the enemy."

"Provided he doesn't slay you first."

"Yes. That's a point."

"Edward's going into the Royal Air Force."

"I know. I suppose you can say we both saw the writing on the wall."

"What about Cambridge?"

"If the balloon does go up, then we shan't return. Our final examinations will have to wait."

"For the end of the war?"

"I suppose so."

Loveday sighed. "What a waste." She thought about this. "Does everybody at Cambridge feel the same way as you and Edward?"

"By no means. Political attitudes vary widely amongst the undergraduates. Some are left wing as they can possibly be, without taking the final step and becoming committed Communists. The more courageous of these have already disappeared, gone to fight the war in Spain."

"Terribly brave."

"Yes. Brave. Not particularly sensible but enormously brave. And then there are others who believe that pacifism is the answer, and others again who carry on like a lot of ostriches, sticking their heads in the sand and carrying on as though nothing nasty was ever going to happen." Thinking about his, he suddenly laughed. "There's one impossible fellow, called Peregrine Haslehurst . . ."

"I don't believe it. Nobody could be called that."

"I promise you, it's true. From time to time when at a loose end, he seeks me out and graciously allows me either to pour him or buy him a drink. His conversation is invariably trivial, but should more serious matters come up for discussion, his attitude always strikes me as light-hearted to the point of lunacy. As though a new war held no more threat than a cricket match, or the Wall Game at Eton, which is where Peregrine whiled away his boyhood years."

"Perhaps he's just pretending. Perhaps he's really just as apprehensive as the rest of us."

"The English sang-froid, you mean? The stiff upper lip? The genius for understatement?"

"I don't know. I suppose so."

"Characteristics I find intensely annoying. They make me think of Peter Pan, flying off with his little sword to do battle with Captain Hook."

"I hated Peter Pan," said Loveday. "I simply hated that book."

"How extraordinary, so did I. *'To die will be an awfully good big adventure.'* That must be the stupidest line that any man ever wrote."

"I don't think it would be a bit adventurous to die. And I don't suppose Aunt Lavinia thinks so either." Loveday fell silent, thinking about Aunt Lavinia who, for a moment or two, she had actually forgotten. She said, "What time is it?"

"Half past four. Someone should buy you a watch."

"They do but I always lose them. Perhaps we should go back." She unfolded her long legs and abruptly stood up, all at once impatient to be off. "The others should be home before long. I do hope nothing awful's happened."

He decided that anything he said to this would sound empty and hollow, so he said nothing. It had been pleasant sitting in the sun with his back to the rock, but he pulled himself to his feet and felt the smack of the wind, chill through the thick wool of his sweater. "Then let's make a start; and this time how about keeping to a reasonable pace?"

He spoke light-heartedly, knowing that it wasn't much of a joke. Not that it mattered, because Loveday was not listening. She had paused, turned away from him, as though reluctant to leave the cliffs and the gulls and the tempestuous sea, and return to reality. And in that moment, Gus saw, not Loveday, but the Laura Knight girl, the picture that he had stealthily removed, so long ago, from the pages of *The Studio*. Even her clothes, the worn tennis shoes, the striped cotton skirt, the aged cricket sweater (rather charmingly stained with raspberry juice) were the same. Only the hair was different. No russet plait lying like a heavy rope over one shoulder. Instead Loveday's chrysanthemum mop of dark, shining curls, ruffled by the wind.

Slowly, they retraced their steps, following the path down which Gus had hurtled after her. Now, Loveday seemed in little hurry. They crossed the floor of the quarry, and scrambled up the steps that rose to the top of the shaly cliff. Then, up through the woods, stopping from time to time to pause for breath, to loiter on one of the small wooden bridges and watch the dark waters of the stream flow away beneath their feet. By the time they finally emerged from the trees, and the house had appeared, standing above them, Gus was warm with exertion. The sheltered gardens basked in the sun, streaming down across closely mown lawns, and he stopped for a moment to shed his sweater, stripping it off over his head and slinging it over his shoulder. While he did this, Loveday waited for him. He caught her eye, and she smiled. As they set off again, "It's so annoying," she told him, "because on a really hot day, by the time you've got this far, all you really want is another swim . . ."

She stopped abruptly. A sound had caught her ear. Her smile died, and she stood very still, listening. From far off, Gus heard the engine of an approaching car. Looking, he saw it: a stately Daimler emerging from the trees at the head of the drive, crossing the gravel, and drawing to a halt by the side of the house.

"They're back." Walking up from the cove, chattering inconsequently, Loveday had seemed quite cheerful, but now her voice was filled with apprehension. "Pops and Edward are back. Oh, I wonder what's happened . . ." And, abandoning Gus, she ran ahead, racing across the grass and up the slopes of the terraces. He heard her calling to them. "Why have you all been so long? What's happening? Is everything all right . . . ?"

Gus, praying that it was, followed at a deliberately slow pace. All at once, his confidence ebbed away, and he found himself wishing that he were any place but here, that he had never come. Under the circumstances, Edward had every excuse to forget altogether about his Cambridge friend, so casually invited to stay; and on seeing him would feel compelled to feign pleasure and welcome. For a moment Gus wished heartily that he had followed his original instinct, which had been to put his suitcases back into his car and drive away. It was Loveday who had persuaded him to remain. Probably mistakenly. This, most certainly, was not the time to be an unknown guest.

But it was too late now to rectify the situation. Slowly, he climbed the wide stone stairway which bisected the top terrace, and stepped forward onto level ground. The Daimler stood there, parked alongside his own car, the doors still open. Its occupants formed a little group, but Edward, seeing Gus, detached himself from this and came forward, smiling and with his arms outstretched.

"Gus! Great to see you."

So clearly delighted was he that all reservations melted. Gus was filled with gratitude. He said, "You too."

"Sorry about all this . . ."

"I'm the one who should be sorry . . ."

"What have you got to be sorry for?"

"It's just that I have this gut feeling that I shouldn't be here."

"Oh, don't be a bloody idiot. I asked you . . ."

"Your butler told me about your aunt being so ill. Are you sure it's all right if I stay?"

"You being here isn't going to make any difference one way or another. Except you'll help to cheer us all up. And as for Aunt Lavinia, she seems to be holding her own. And she's such a tough old bird, I refuse to believe that she's going to do anything else. Now, did you have a good drive? How long did it take? I hope you got some sort of a welcome and that Loveday didn't abandon you to your own devices. I left her with strict instructions to take care of you."

"And so she did. We've been down to the cove."

"Wonders will never cease. She's not usually that social. Now, come and meet my father and Mary . . ." Edward turned back to the others and stopped, frowning in some puzzlement. "Except that Mary seems to have disappeared."

He shrugged. "Hopefully to alert Mrs. Nettlebed and tell her to get the kettle on. But, at least, meet my father. Pops!"

The Colonel was deep in conversation with his daughter, and clearly doing his best to comfort and reassure her. But, on hearing Edward call him, he stopped talking and looked up, saw Gus, and set Loveday gently aside. He came forward, his brogues crunching on the gravel, tall and tweedy and scarecrow-thin, and if he harboured any reservations about a stranger's turning up to stay beneath his roof at this particular and inopportune moment, he kept them to himself. Gus saw only the gentle expression in his pale eyes, and the shy smile of genuine pleasure.

"Gus, this is my father, Edgar Carey-Lewis. And, Pops, this is Gus Callender."

"How do you do, sir."

The Colonel thrust out his hand, and Gus took it in his own. "Gus, my dear fellow," said Edward's father. "How good of you to come, and how splendid to see you."

The following morning, at ten o'clock, Edward Carey-Lewis rang Warren's Grocery in Porthkerris and asked to speak to Judith.

"Who shall I say?" inquired the unknown female and very Cornish voice.

"Just Edward."

"Hold on."

He held on. *Judith there? Tell her she's wanted.* The female voice, presumably screeching up a flight of stairs, reached him distantly, over the receiver. He waited. She came.

"Hello?" Her voice was thin with anxiety. "Edward?"

"Good morning."

"What is it?"

"It's okay. Good news."

"Aunt Lavinia?"

"She seems to have pulled through. We got word from the Dower House. Apparently she woke up this morning, asked the night nurse what on earth she was doing sitting by her bed, and demanded a cup of tea."

"I simply don't *believe* it."

"So Pops and Ma shot straight off to see the old girl and check on the general situation, and I thought I'd better ring you."

"Oh, you must all be so *relieved*. Darling old thing."

"Wicked old thing, more like, giving us all such a scare. And everybody flying back from all points of the compass to be here. Ma arrived last night, looking pretty exhausted, and Athena and Rupert are already on their way from Scotland. Like Gus, we don't know where they are, so we can't ring them and tell them to turn round and go back to Auchnafechle or wherever it is they were staying. The whole thing has turned into a complete circus."

"That doesn't matter. All that matters is that she's going to get better."

"When are you coming back?"

"Sunday."

"If she's fit for visitors, I'll take you to see her."

"Sunday morning. I'll be back on Sunday morning."

"It's a date, then. How are you?"

"Beginning to wish I was with you all."

"Don't wish too hard. It's a bit like living in the middle of Piccadilly Circus. But I miss you. There's a hole in the house without you."

"Oh, Edward."

"See you Sunday morning."

"Goodbye. And thank you for ringing up."

Rupert Rycroft, on his first morning, slept in. When he did wake, opened his eyes and stared blearily at the opposite wall, he found himself disoriented. There had been so much travelling, so many strange beds, in such a short space of time, and now, seeing the end of a brass bed, striped wallpaper, and thickly flowered curtains, half-drawn, he couldn't work out where the hell he was.

But only for an instant. Recollection flooded back. Cornwall. Nancherrow. He had finally got Athena home, having flogged the length of the country, and Rupert had driven the entire way. From time to time, Athena, half-heartedly, had offered to take the wheel, but Rupert preferred to be in charge of a situation, and his car was too precious to him to be trusted to the hands of another. Even Athena.

He fumbled a bare arm out from beneath the covers and reached for his watch. Ten o'clock. He lay back with a groan. Ten o'clock in the morning. Horrors. But the Colonel, seeing him to his room, had said, "Breakfast's at eight-thirty, but catch up on your sleep. We'll expect you when we see you," and some automatic trigger in Rupert's brain had done what it was told. Which was the same, in a converse sort of way, as knowing one had to be on parade at seven-thirty in the morning, however stunned with alcohol from the previous night's partying.

They had arrived at half past midnight, and only Athena's parents were there to greet them, the remainder of the house party having already retired to bed. Athena, who for most of the way had been quite alert and chatty, fell silent for the last hour or so of their journey, and Rupert knew that she was both longing for, and dreading, arrival. Longing to be there, safe in the bosom of her family, and dreading the news that she feared they were going to impart. It was such a private anxiety that Rupert knew he could not intrude, and so he said nothing and left her in peace.

But, at the end of the day, it turned out that everything was going to be all right: the old aunt who had been so ill was not, after all, going to expire. Rupert's gallant sacrifice of a week's grouse-shooting, and his marathon effort to get Athena back to her family, had been for nothing. Unnecessary. It took a bit of swallowing, but he kept his expression doggedly pleased.

Athena, however, was, quite naturally, ecstatic. She stood with her mother in the high, lighted hallway of Nancherrow, and hugged enormously, and their endearments and explanations and unfinished sentences and rejoicings sounded like a positive collision of emotions.

"I can't believe it . . ."

"Such a long way to come . . ."

". . . I was so afraid she was going to be dead . . ."

"Oh, my darling . . ."

". . . we've driven all day . . ."

"So tired . . ."

". . . she's really going to get better . . . ?"

". . . hope so. Such a long way. Perhaps we shouldn't have told you . . ."

". . . I had to be here . . ."

". . . spoilt your holiday . . ."

". . . it doesn't matter . . . nothing matters . . ."

Rupert had already met Diana Carey-Lewis. She had been with Athena in the little town house in Cadogan Mews when Rupert arrived to bear Athena off to Scotland. He had thought then, and still thought, that they looked more like sisters than like mother and daughter. Tonight, at this late hour, Diana was, very sensibly, already wrapped in a floor-length dressing-gown of rose-pink wool, but the Colonel remained fully dressed. Over the heads of the two incoherently happy women, Rupert looked up to meet the eye of his host; saw the elderly velvet dinner-jacket and the silk bow-tie, and knew a comfortable familiarity. Like his own father, the Colonel clearly changed for dinner every evening. Now he came forward, with his hand outstretched.

"Edgar Carey-Lewis. How enormously kind of you to bring Athena home to us. And now it must seem to you that all your efforts have been spent on an empty cause." And he was so apologetic and so sympathetic that Rupert put his own private chagrin behind him, and did his best to reassure the older man.

"Don't think that, sir. It's a case of all's well that ends well."

"That's generous of you. Even so, something of a disappointment for you to lose out on your shooting." And then, disarmingly, and with perhaps an inappropriate spark of interest in his fading eyes, "Tell me, how were the grouse?" he asked.

"We had two great days."

"What sort of a bag?"

"Over sixty brace. Some splendid coveys."

"Now, I suppose, you'll be keen to get back?"

Rupert shook his head. "Not worth it, sir. I was only offered a week."

"I'm sorry. We've spoilt everything."

"Don't think that."

"Well, you're more than welcome here. Stay as long as you like." He eyed

Rupert approvingly. "I must say, you're taking it all very well. If I were you, I'd be chewing the rugs. Now, why don't I pour you a nightcap?"

Ten o'clock in the morning. Rupert climbed out of bed and went to draw back the curtains. He found himself looking down into a cobbled courtyard filled with the cooing of white fan-tailed doves; there were tubs of geraniums, and a line of starch-white washing blowing in the breeze. Beyond the court-yard were verges of grass, and in the middle distance a clump of trees, heavy with leaf. By leaning out of the window and craning his neck a bit, he was rewarded by the view of the blue horizon. All was washed in the clear sun-shine of a perfect summer's morning, and he decided, philosophically, that if he could not be at Glenfreuchie slaying grouse, then this place was, quite certainly, the next-best thing. He withdrew from the window, yawned, and stretched enormously. He was ravenously hungry. He headed for the bath-room and began to shave.

Downstairs was a bit disconcerting because there didn't seem to be any-body about. But by means of a bit of reconnoitring, Rupert found the dining-room, occupied by a tall and stately gentleman who was clearly the butler. Nettlebed. Athena had talked of Nettlebed.

He said, "Good morning."

The butler turned from the sideboard, where he had been rearranging dishes on the hotplate.

"Good morning, sir. Captain Rycroft, is it?"

"That's right. And you're Nettlebed."

"I am, sir." Rupert advanced and they shook hands.

"I'm desperately late."

"The Colonel said that he'd told you to sleep in, sir. But I'm sure you'd like something to eat . . . There's bacon and sausages here, and if you'd like a fried tomato, Mrs. Nettlebed will be happy to oblige. And coffee. But if you'd prefer tea . . . ?"

"No, coffee's fine." Rupert looked at the table, the great long mahogany length of it with only a single place laid at one side. "I seem to be the last."

"There's only Athena to come, sir. And Mrs. Carey-Lewis said not to expect her until luncheon."

"No. She'll need her sleep." He helped himself to the bacon and sausages, and Nettlebed poured his coffee.

"You had a long journey, sir?"

"Just about the length of the country. Tell me, where is everybody else?"

Nettlebed told him. "The Colonel and Mrs. Carey-Lewis are up at the Dower House . . . they go every morning, to visit Mrs. Boscawen and be certain that the nurse has everything under control. And Edward has driven Mary Millyway into Penzance to do some household shopping and pick up supplies for Mrs. Nettlebed. And Loveday has taken Mr. Callender off in search of some picturesque spot where he can do some sketching."

"Who's Mr. Callender?"

"Mr. Gus Callender, sir. Edward's friend from Cambridge. Apparently, he is something of an amateur artist."

"And he's staying too? What a houseful you have to deal with. No wonder Edward has gone off in search of rations."

"Nothing out of the ordinary, sir," Nettlebed assured him modestly. "We're used to a full house, Mrs. Nettlebed and I."

"So, when I have finished my breakfast, and until Athena puts in an appearance, what do you suggest I do with myself?"

Nettlebed allowed himself a smile, appreciating the young gentleman's assurance. "The morning papers are in the drawing-room, sir. Or, as it's such a pleasant morning, perhaps you would like to read them out of doors, in the sunshine. You'll find garden chairs outside the French windows. Or you may prefer to take a little exercise? A walk, perhaps . . . ?"

"No. I think the exercise can wait. I shall lie in the sun and scan the news."

"An excellent idea, sir."

He took *The Times* from the drawing-room, carried it out of doors, but in the end did not read it. Instead, he settled himself in a long cane chair and gazed through narrowed eyes at the pleasing prospect of the garden. The sun was warm, and a bird was singing somewhere, and below him a gardener was mowing the tennis-court, drawing swaths of green behind him, ruler-straight. He wondered if, later on, he would be expected to play. And then stopped thinking about tennis, and instead, brooded over the question of Athena.

Thinking back, it was hard to work out just how he had landed himself in this dilemma, which had metamorphosed as he was least expecting it, and at a most inconvenient time. He was twenty-seven, a cavalry officer, a captain in the Royal Dragoon Guards, and a man who had always treasured and guarded his fairly wild bachelor existence. A new war was imminent and he would be in the thick of it, posted off to some God-forsaken spot, to be shelled, shot at, wounded, or possibly killed. Right now the last thing he needed was to get married.

Athena Carey-Lewis. He and a couple of his Regimental cronies had driven from Long Weedon to London for a party. A cold winter evening, a warmly lit first-floor drawing-room in Belgravia. And almost immediately, he had spied her across the room, and thought her sensationally beautiful. She was, of course, deep in conversation with an overweight and vacuous-looking man, and when he made some footling joke she laughed, smiling up into his eyes. And her smile was enchantment, and her nose just the wrong shape, and her eyes blue as very dark hyacinths. Rupert could scarcely wait to get his hands on her. Later, and not before time, their hostess introduced them. "Athena Carey-Lewis, darling. Surely you must have met before? No? Athena, Rupert Rycroft. Isn't he heaven? All leathery and sunburnt. And his glass is empty! Give it to me, and I'll get you a refill . . ."

After the party he dumped his cronies, and got her into his car, and they went to the Mirabelle and then the Bagatelle, and it was only because he had to be back in Northamptonshire and be on parade at seven-thirty in the morning that he finally took her home, dropping her at the door of a little house in Cadogan Mews.

"Is it your house?"

"No, it's my mother's."

"Is she there?"

"No. Nobody's there. But you can't come in."

"Why not?"

"Because I don't want you to come in. And because you've got to get back to Northamptonshire."

"Shall I see you again?"

"I don't know."

"Can I phone you?"

"If you want. We're the only Carey-Lewises in the book." She dropped a kiss on his cheek. " 'Bye." And before he could stop her, or even accompany her, she was out of the car and across the cobbles, opening her front door, slipping inside, and closing it firmly behind her. He sat for a moment gazing at it, wondering, in a slightly tipsy fashion, whether he could have imagined the entire encounter. Then he sighed deeply, put his car into gear, and roared noisily away, down the Mews and beneath the arch at its end. He only just made it back to Long Weedon in time for morning parade.

He telephoned, but there was never any answer. He wrote a letter, a post-card, but got no reply. Finally, on a Saturday morning, he presented himself at the front door of the little house, beat upon it with his fist, and when Athena opened it, wearing a silk dressing-gown and bare feet, he thrust a bunch of flowers at her and said, "Flee with me to Gloucestershire."

She said, "Why Gloucestershire?"

"Because that is where I live."

"Why aren't you in Northamptonshire, schooling horses?"

"Because I'm here, and I don't have to report back until tomorrow evening. Please come."

"All right," said Athena peaceably. "But what shall I be expected to do?"

He misunderstood. "Nothing."

"I don't mean that. I mean what sort of clothes. You know. A clothe for a ball, a clothe for muddy walks, a tea-gown perhaps?"

"Jodhpurs."

"I don't ride."

"Never?"

"No, I hate horses."

Rupert's heart had sunk, because his mother talked and thought of nothing else. But it didn't sink all that far and he persevered. "Something for dinner, and something for church," was all he could come up with.

"Goodness, what a riotous time we're going to have. Does your mother know I'm coming?"

"I gave her a storm warning. I said I might bring you."

"She won't like me. Mothers never do. I've got no conversation."

"My father will love you."

"That's no good at all. It just makes trouble."

"Athena, please. Let me come in, and you go and pack. There's no time to stand here arguing."

"I'm not arguing. I'm just warning you that I might be the most frightful failure."

"I'll cross that bridge when I get to it."

Athena's visit to Gloucestershire was not a success. Rupert's family home was Taddington Hall, a vast Victorian pile set in gardens of austere formality. Beyond these lay the estates, the parklands, the Home Farm, cultivated woodland, a trout stream, and a pheasant shoot famous for the number of dead birds which came tumbling yearly from the sky. His father, Sir Henry Rycroft, was Lord Lieutenant of the County, Colonel of his old Regiment, Master of Foxhounds, and Chairman of the local Conservatives, as well as running the County Council and sitting as a JP on the bench. Lady Rycroft was just as active with her committee work, and when she wasn't organizing the Girl Guides, or the Cottage Hospital, or the Local Education Board, then she fished, gardened, and rode to hounds. The appearance of Athena came as something of a shock to both parents, and when she did not turn up, on the dot, for breakfast, his mother saw fit to question Rupert.

"What is she doing?"

"Sleeping, I suppose."

"She surely heard the bell."

"I wouldn't know. Would you like me to go and wake her?"

"Don't even suggest it."

"All right, I won't."

His father chimed in. "What does the gel *do*?"

"I don't know. Nothing, I suppose."

"But who *is* she?" Lady Rycroft persisted. "Who are her people?"

"You wouldn't know them. They're Cornish."

"I've never seen such an indolent gel. Last night, she just *sat*. She should have brought some *work* with her."

"You mean stitchery? I don't suppose she knows how to thread a needle."

"I never thought, Rupert, you'd take up with a *useless* gel."

"I haven't taken up with her, Mother."

"And she doesn't *ride*. Quite extraordinary . . . I must say . . ."

But at that moment the door opened and Athena appeared, wearing grey flannel trousers and a pale-blue angora sweater and looking pretty as a powder-puff. "Hello," she said, "I didn't know which room I was meant to have breakfast in. It's such a huge house, I sort of got *lost* . . ."

No. Not a success. Rupert, being the elder of two sons, was in line to inherit Taddington, and his mother had strong and immovable ideas about the type of girl he should marry. The first priority was that she should be well-born and well-connected; he was, after all, a captain in the Royals, and in such a regiment, the social standing of the wives was immensely important. Then, a bit of money wouldn't go amiss, though there was, as yet, no need for him to go hunting for an heiress. And it didn't really matter what she looked like, provided she had the right sort of voice and a decent pair of hips for breeding future Rycroft males and so ensuring the continuation of the line. Good on a horse, of course, and capable, when the time came, of coping with the management of Taddington, the unwieldy, rambling house and the acres of garden, all devised on the vast and ostentatious scale so loved by the Victorians.

Athena was the very antithesis of their dreams.

But Rupert did not care. He was not in love with Athena and he was not about to marry her. But he was enchanted by her looks, her slightly dotty conversation, her sheer unpredictability. Sometimes she maddened him; at others, he found himself touched to the heart by her childlike lack of guile. She seemed to have no idea of the effect she had upon him, and was quite likely to drift off on a weekend with some other young man, or disappear without warning to ski at Zermatt or to visit an old friend in Paris.

Finally, with August coming up, he had pinned her down. "I have a long leave coming up," he told her, without preamble, "and I've been asked to shoot grouse. In Perthshire. They say you can come too."

"Who say?"

"The Montague-Crichtons. Jamie Montague-Crichton and I were at Sandhurst together. His parents are sweet, and they've got this wonderful shooting lodge right up at the head of Glenfreuchie. Nothing but hills and heather and peat-fires in the evening. Do say you'll come."

"Will I have to ride a horse?"

"No, just walk a bit."

"Will it rain?"

"With a bit of luck, it won't, and if it does, you can sit indoors and read a book."

"I don't mind doing anything really. I just hate being expected to do things."

"I know. I understand. So come. It'll be fun."

She hesitated, biting a rosy lower lip. "How long will we have to stay there?"

"A week?"

"And at the end of the week, will you still be on leave?"

"Why do you ask?"

"I'll make a deal with you. If I come to Scotland with you, then will you come to Cornwall with me? And stay at Nancherrow, and meet Mummy and Pops and Loveday and Edward? And the darling doggies and all the people I really love?"

Rupert was both taken unawares and enormously gratified by this unsolicited invitation. So little encouragement had Athena shown him, so casually had she dealt with his pursuit of her, that he could never be certain whether she enjoyed his company or simply put up with him. The last thing he had ever expected was that she would ask him to her home.

With some effort he concealed his pleasure. Too much delight might scare her off, cause her to change her mind. He made as if to consider the proposition and then said, "Yes. Yes, I think I could probably do that."

"Oh, goody. In that case, I'll come to wherever it is with you."

"Glenfreuchie."

"Why do Scottish places always have names that sound like sneezes? Do I have to go and buy lots of scratchy tweeds?"

"Only a good raincoat and a pair of proper shoes. And a ball gown or two for Highland dancing."

"Heavens, how grand. When do you want to go?"

"Leave London on the fifteenth. It's a long drive, and we'll need a bit of time."

"Spending the night en route?"

"If you like."

"Separate rooms, Rupert."

"I promise."

"All right, I'll come."

Glenfreuchie was as much a success as Taddington had been a failure. The weather was perfect, the skies blue, and the hills purple with heather, and on their first day Athena cheerfully walked for miles, sat with Rupert in his butt, and kept her mouth shut when he told her to. The rest of the house party were friendly and informal, and Athena, with nothing expected of her, blossomed like a flower. At dinner that night, she wore a deep-blue gown that turned her eyes to sapphires, and all the men fell mildly in love with her. Rupert was filled with pride.

The next morning, much to his surprise, she was up bright and early, all ready for another day on the hill. Anxious that she should not overtire herself, "You don't need to come," he told her, as she sat at the dining-room table and consumed an enormous breakfast.

"Don't you want me?"

"More than anything. But I shan't be in the least hurt if you choose to spend the day here, or even the morning. You can join us all with the lunch baskets."

"Thank you very much, but I don't want to be a lunch basket. And I don't want you to treat me as though I were a wilting violet."

"I didn't realize I was."

For the first drive of the day, Rupert drew the top butt, which involved a climb not far short of mountaineering, trudging up a long, daunting slope through knee-high heather. It was another glorious August morning. The clear air was filled with the sound of bees and heather linties singing their hearts out, and the splash of small peat-stained burns tumbling down the hillside to join the river at the foot of glen. From time to time they paused to cool their wrists and douse their faces in the ice-cold torrent, but, hot and sweaty, they finally made it, and the view from the summit made it all worthwhile. A fresh breeze blew from the north-west, from the plum-blue slopes of the distant Grampians.

Later, standing in the butt with Athena beside him, he waited, silently and patiently, with the rest of the guns. From the north, hidden from the butts by a fold of hills, a line of beaters was marching in across the simmering moor, armed with flags, sticks, and a good deal of foul language, and driving the coveys of grouse before them. The birds had not yet got up, but it was a classic moment of intense excitement, and all at once Rupert was suffused with a sensation of total, piercing happiness, the sort of reasonless ecstasy that he had not experienced since he was a very small boy.

Turning, he bent impulsively and kissed Athena's cheek.

She laughed. "What's that for?"

"No idea."

"You should be concentrating, not kissing."

"The thing is . . ."

From down the line came a bawl of "Over," and a single grouse sailed overhead, but by the time Rupert had pulled himself together, raised his gun and fired, it was too late. The bird sailed on unharmed. From down the line came a voice, clearly audible in the still air. "Bloody fool."

"I told you," said Athena smugly, "to concentrate."

They returned to the Lodge at six o'clock that evening, sunburnt and weary. Trudging down the last stretch of the track that led from the hill, Athena said, "I shall get straight into a very deep, dark-brown, peaty, hot bath. And then I shall lie on my bed and probably fall asleep."

"I shall wake you."

"Do that. I should hate to miss dinner. I'm ravenous."

"Jamie said something about country dancing tonight."

"Not a *ball*?"

"No. Just rugs rolled back and gramophone records."

"Heavens, what energy. The only thing is, I don't know how to do country dances."

"I shall teach you."

"Do you know how to do them?"

"Not really."

"How perfectly awful. We shall spoil it for everybody."

"You couldn't spoil anything. And nothing could spoil today."

Famous last words. As they went indoors, Mrs. Montague-Crichton, who had not joined the party on the hill, being otherwise engaged in domestic duties, came down the stairs.

"Athena. Oh, my dear, I am so sorry, but there's been a telephone call from your home." Athena stood stock-still, and Rupert saw the colour drain from her cheeks. "It was your father. Just to let you know that Mrs. Boscawen is very ill. He explained to me that she is quite elderly. He thought, perhaps, that you might want to go home."

It was Athena's reaction to this message which changed everything for Rupert. Because, like a child, she burst into tears. He had never seen any girl so instantly devastated, and her noisy weeping quite upset Mrs. Montague-Crichton who, being Scottish, did not believe in letting your feelings show. Realizing this, Rupert put an arm around Athena and led her firmly upstairs and into her bedroom, shutting the door behind them in the hope that that would drown the sound of her sobs.

He half expected her to throw herself face-down on her bed and succumb to grief but, still sobbing and gasping, she was already getting her suitcase out of the wardrobe, throwing it open on the bed, and packing it with clothes gathered up in handfuls from drawers, and stuffed into the case any old way. He had never seen anybody do this before, except in films.

"Athena."

"I have to go home. I'll get a taxi. Get a train."

"But . . ."

"You don't understand. It's Aunt Lavinia. Pops would never ring if he thought that she was going to be all right. And if she dies I just can't bear it, because she's been there *forever*. And I can't bear Pops and Mummy having to be miserable without me being there being miserable with them."

"Athena . . ."

"I've got to go right away. Be an angel and find out about trains, I suppose from Perth. See if I can get a sleeper or something. Anything. Oh, why do I have to be such a long way away?"

Which made him feel as though, in some way, he was to blame. Her distress tore him apart, and he couldn't stand the sight of her being so unhappy. He said, "I'll take you . . ."

To this incredibly unselfish suggestion he expected a reaction of tear-sodden gratitude, but instead Athena, unpredictable as always, became quite irritated and impatient with him. "Oh, don't be *silly*." She had the wardrobe doors open and was pulling garments off their hangers. "Of course you can't. You're here." She flung the clothes onto the bed, and went back for more. "Shooting grouse. That's what you've come for. You can't just walk out and leave Mr. Montague-Crichton short of a gun. It would be too rude." She bundled up her blue evening gown and jammed it into a corner of the suitcase, then turned to face him. "And you're having such a perfect time," she told him tragically. Fresh tears filled her eyes. ". . . and I know you've been looking forward to it . . . for . . . so . . . *long* . . ."

Which was all true but didn't make anything any better, so he took her in his arms, and let her cry. He was totally overwhelmed. Always so trivial and light-hearted, he had never imagined Athena to be capable of such intensity of emotion, such love, such involvement with her own immediate family. Somehow, perhaps deliberately, she had kept these deeper feelings from him, but now, Rupert felt, he was seeing the hidden side of her face, the whole person that was Athena.

His handkerchief was filthy, covered in sweat and gun oil, so he reached for a face towel and gave her that in which to blow her nose and wipe her eyes.

He said again, "I shall take you. We were going to Cornwall anyway, it just means we'll arrive a bit sooner than we intended. I'll explain to the Montague-Crichtons, and I know they'll understand. But I must have a bath, and I must change into some clean clothes. I suggest you do the same. After that, we'll leave just as soon as you're ready . . ."

"I don't know why you're being so sweet."

"Don't you?" He smiled. "These things happen." And even to himself it sounded a pretty stupid thing to say. In fact, it was the understatement of the year.

🌿

Everybody was enormously kind and sympathetic. Rupert's car was fetched from the garage and brought to the front door. Somebody else humped their suitcases and stowed them in the boot. Jamie promised to ring Nancherrow and let Athena's father know what was happening. Mrs. Montague-Crichton made sandwiches and filled a Thermos. ". . . just in case." Goodbyes were said, and at last they were off, rolling down the long glen road that led to the highway.

Athena had stopped crying, but she said dolefully, gazing from the window, "I can't bear it all being so beautiful. I've hardly got here, and now we're going away again."

"We'll come back," he told her, but somehow the words had a hollow ring to them, and she made no reply.

By the time they had crossed the Border and were approaching Scotch Corner, darkness had fallen, and Rupert knew that if he did not sleep, he would be likely to nod off over the wheel and deposit the pair of them in a ditch. He said, "I think we should stop at the hotel and book in for the night. Tomorrow morning, we can set off at sparrowfart, and with a bit of luck we'll do the rest of the journey in the day."

"All right." She sounded exhausted, and he put a smile in his voice to try and cheer her up.

"Separate rooms."

Athena was silent. After a bit, she said, "Is that what you want?"

Which threw him slightly. "Isn't that what *you* want?"

"Not necessarily." Her voice was very casual, non-committal. She stared ahead at the dark road, beyond the long beam of his powerful headlights.

He said, "You owe me nothing. You know that."

"I'm not thinking of you. I'm thinking of me."

"You're *sure* that's what you want?"

"I'm not in the right mood for being alone."

"Mr. and Mrs. Smith, then."

"Mr. and Mrs. Smith."

And so they slept together, their weariness and his desire assuaged in the anonymous and undisturbed comfort of an enormous double bed. And the last, unasked question was answered, because he discovered that night that Athena, for all her affairs, her strings of admirers, her little weekends in Paris, was still a virgin. Finding this out was somehow the most touching and marvellous thing that had ever happened to him; as though, gratuitously, she had given him a priceless present which he knew he was going to hold close, and treasure, for the rest of his life.

Hence, the dilemma. It had, as it were, crept up on him from behind and his subconscious had known it was there, approaching, ready to pounce at any moment, while all the time he had been robustly telling himself that Athena was simply another relationship, another girl. Lies. What was the point in lying to himself, when the truth was that the prospect of any sort of an existence without her would be insupportable? She had, in fact, become his future.

There. It was done. Accepted. He took a deep breath, and let it all out on a long sigh of relief.

"You sound very gloomy."

He turned his head, and Athena was there, standing in the open French windows, and smiling down at him. She wore a sleeveless cream linen dress, and had knotted, like a cricket silk, a blue-and-cream-spotted scarf around her slender waist.

"You look like a matinée star," he told her, "making an entrance. Anyone for tennis?"

"And you look like doom personified. But rather comfortable. Don't get up." She stepped out onto the grass, and dragged a second chair closer to where he lay. On this she perched, sitting sideways, so that she faced him. "What was the sigh for?"

He reached out and took her hand. "Perhaps it was a yawn. How did you sleep?"

"Like a log."

"We didn't expect you until lunch-time."

"The sun woke me up."

"Have you had breakfast?"

"Cup of coffee."

"Actually, I wasn't yawning. I was thinking."

"So that's what you were doing? It sounded dreadfully exhausting."

"I was thinking that perhaps we ought to get married."

Athena looked a bit stunned. After a bit, she said, "Oh, dear."

"Is it such an awesome suggestion?"

"No, it's just come at rather a funny time."

"What's funny about it?"

"I don't know. Everything, really. Aunt Lavinia dying and then not dying, and us racing home from Scotland . . . I just feel I don't quite know what's going to happen next. Except that we seem to be teetering on the verge of a horrible war."

It was the first time Rupert had ever heard her make a serious and considered statement about the situation in Europe. And in all the time they had spent together, she had presented a face so trivial and light-hearted and sweet that he had never brought the subject up, simply because he didn't want to spoil anything; he wanted her to stay that way.

Now he said, "Does it frighten you?"

"Of course it does. The very idea turns me to jelly. And I hate *waiting*. And listening to the news. It's like watching sand go through an egg-timer, and each day everything gets more and more ghastly and hopeless."

"If it's any comfort, we're all in it together."

"It's people like darling Pops that I agonize for. He's been through it all before, and Mummy says he's despairing, though he does his best to hide it. Not for himself, but for all of us. Specially Edward."

"Is it because of a war that you don't want to get married?"

"I didn't say that."

"Can you imagine being the wife of a regular Army officer?"

"Not really, but that doesn't mean that I wouldn't quite like it."

"Following the drum?"

"If the balloon goes up, I don't suppose there'll be much of a drum to follow."

"That's true enough. So, for the time being, I haven't very much to offer you, except probably years of separation. If you don't think you can deal with that, I shall perfectly understand."

She said, with total confidence, "Oh, I could easily deal with *that*."

"So what couldn't you deal with?"

"Oh, silly things that you probably don't think are important."

"Try me."

"Well . . . I'm not being rude or critical or anything, but I don't think I'd fit frightfully well into your family. Admit it, Rupert, I didn't make much of an impression."

He was sympathetic. "My mother is a bit of a battleaxe, I know, but she's not a fool. She's capable of making the best of any situation. And my inheriting Taddington, and taking over responsibility, is, with a bit of luck, decades away. As well, I respect my parents, but I have never been intimidated by them."

"Goodness, you're brave. Do you mean you'd fly against their wishes?"

"I mean that I intend marrying someone I love, not the Lady Master of Foxhounds, nor the prospective Conservative candidate."

Which for some reason made her laugh, and all at once she was his own dear Athena again. He put his hand around her neck, drew her close and kissed her. When he had finished kissing her, she said, "I certainly don't fall into either of those categories."

He lay back in his chair. "Which deals with one silly thing. What's the next objection?"

"You won't laugh?"

"I promise."

"Well, the thing is, I've never really wanted to get married."

"To get married, or to be married?"

"To get married. I mean, weddings and such. I hate weddings. I don't even like going to them. They always strike me as being the most ghastly ordeal for everybody. Particularly the poor bride."

"I thought her wedding day was meant to be every girl's dream."

"Not mine. I've attended too many, sometimes as a bridesmaid and sometimes as a guest, and they're all the same, except that each seems just a bit more extravagant and pretentious than the last. As though the whole idea was to outdo the last performance, and put on an even more costly and theatrical show. And weddings take months to organize, and there are fittings and invitation lists and old aunts being coy about the honeymoon, and having to have somebody's perfectly hideous cousin for a bridesmaid. And then hundreds of appalling wedding presents. Toast-racks and Japanese vases and pictures that never, in a million years, would you want to hang on the wall. And you spend all your time writing insincere thank-you letters with your fingers crossed, and everybody gets tense and miserable and there's lots of bursting into tears. The miracle is that anybody ever gets married at all, but I bet most girls have nervous breakdowns on their honeymoons . . ."

He listened patiently to all this until Athena finally ran out of breath. Her outburst was followed by a long silence. Then she said, sounding sulky, "I told you it was a silly reason."

"No," Rupert told her, "not silly at all. But I think you concentrate on inessentials. I am talking about a lifetime, and you are jibbing at a single day. A tradition. I think, the way the world is going, we are perfectly entitled to throw tradition out of the window."

"I hate to say it, Rupert, but my mother would be devastated."

"Of course she wouldn't. She loves you, and she'll understand. Now, we've talked it all through, pros and cons. And as for a wedding, when it comes to the push, nobody really needs to be there except you and me."

"Do you really mean that?"

"Of course."

She lifted his hand and pressed a kiss on it, and when she looked up at him again, he saw that her eyes were bright with unshed tears.

"So silly to want to cry. It's just that I never thought this could happen. That you could have a best friend and a lover all rolled in one. You are my Scotch Corner lover, Rupert. It sounds like something to eat, doesn't it? But the best-friend bit is the most important, because that's what lasts for always."

"That's right," Rupert told her, and he had to make something of an effort to keep his voice steady, so touched was he by her tears, and so filled with protective love. "That's what's really important."

"Have you got a handkerchief?"

He gave her his clean one, and she blew her nose.

"What time is it, Rupert?"

"Just about noon."

"I wish it was lunch-time. I'm starving."

It was not until the Saturday, the final day of her stay in Porthkerris, that Judith set off for Pendeen to see Phyllis. The reasons for the delay were various. It wasn't that she didn't *want* to see Phyllis, nor felt that in any way she was performing a duty, it was just that there was always so much going on, and the days raced by with alarming speed. As well, there was the complication of communication, and the amount of time it took to get in touch by letter. Judith had sent Phyllis a picture postcard, suggesting one or two dates, and finally had received Phyllis's reply, written on lined paper torn from a notebook.

> Saturday would be best come around three and well have tea. Im about a mile beyond Pendeen. Row of cottages on the left. Number two. Cyril's on weekend shift at Geevor but Anna and me will be waiting. Love Phyllis.

Saturday. "It's my last day!" she protested to Heather. "Oh, bother, I wish we could have fixed it before."

"Doesn't matter. Mum wants to go to Penzance and buy a hat for Daisy Parson's wedding, and if I don't go with her she'll come home with something that looks like a po. You and I can do something in the evening. Get Joe to take us to the Palais de Danse."

And so, Saturday afternoon and she was on her way, driving up the hill and out of the town. Past shops, her old school; between terraced rows of stone houses, each one step higher than its neighbour. The bay, the harbour sank down behind her, and she reached the cross-roads and took the turning for Land's End.

The weather was still fine, hot and sunny, but a brisk wind blew in from the sea, and the Atlantic was freckled with white-caps. Clouds sailed across the sky, and as the car ground its way, in third gear, up onto the moor, she saw their shadows bowling across the russet hills. At the summit, the view was spectacular—the shelf of green farmland, distant cliffs, yellow gorse, jutting headlands, the clear horizon and the indigo sea. For a moment she was tempted to draw in to the side of the road, roll down the window, and just sit and look at it all for a bit, but Phyllis was waiting and there was no time to be wasted.

Im about a mile beyond Pendeen. Row of cottages on the left. Phyllis's directions were not hard to follow, because once through Pendeen, and past Geevor Mine, where poor Cyril was, at this moment, labouring deep underground, the countryside abruptly changed, becoming bleak. Primeval; almost forbidding. No more pretty little farms set in green pasture fields, patchworked by stone walls dating back to the Bronze Age; and not a single tree to be seen, however stunted by the wind.

The terrace of mining cottages, when she came upon it, stood isolated, reasonless, in the middle of nowhere. It resembled nothing so much as a row of upended bricks, cemented together and then dropped, haphazard, and abandoned where they had fallen. Each brick had a window upstairs and a window downstairs and a doorway, and all were roofed in grey slate. They were separated from the roadside by a stone wall, and then small, downtrodden front gardens. The garden of number two boasted a patch of rough grass and a few pansies and a lot of weeds.

Judith got out of the car, collected up the sheaf of flowers and small packages she had brought for Phyllis, opened a rickety gate, and started up the path. But she was only half-way before the door opened and Phyllis, bearing the baby Anna in her arms, came running to greet her.

"Judith! Been looking out the window, waiting for you to come. Thought you might have got lost." She stared out at the road, her face incredulous. "That your car, is it? I couldn't believe it when you said you'd come in your own car. It's lovely. Never seen anything so *new* . . ."

She had changed. Not aged, exactly, but lost weight, and with it some of her bloom. Her skirt and knitted jumper hung about her, as though once they had belonged to a much larger person, and her straight hair looked dry as straw. But her eyes shone with excitement, and nothing could stop her smile.

"Oh, Phyllis." They hugged. All those years ago it had been Jess in Phyllis's arms who had impeded their embrace. And now it was Anna who got in the way, but not enough to matter except that her expression was deeply disapproving.

Judith laughed. "She looks as though we're doing something dreadfully wrong. Hello, Anna." Anna stared balefully. "How old is she?"

"Eight months."

"She's wonderfully chubby."

"Got a mind of her own. Come on inside, the wind's teasy, and we don't want to stand here with the neighbours watching . . ."

She turned and went back in through her front door, and Judith followed, walking straight into a small room which was clearly the only living space. Little light penetrated the window, so it was a bit dark, but a Cornish range kept it warm, and one end of the table had been carefully set for tea.

"I've brought you some bits and pieces . . ." She unloaded the packages onto the free end of the table.

"*Judith*. You didn't need to do that . . ." But Phyllis's eyes gleamed with happy expectancy at the thought of surprises in the offing. "Just hang on a mo, till I get the kettle on, and then we can have a cup of tea." Hoisting the baby to her shoulder, she went to do this, and then drew out a chair and sat down, with Anna on her lap. Anna reached for a teaspoon, and stuffed it, dribbling, into her mouth. "She's teething, the little love."

"Perhaps we should put the flowers in water."

"Flowers! Roses! You know, I haven't seen roses in years, not like these. And the smell. What can I put them in? I haven't got any vases."

"A jug would do. Or a jam jar. Tell me where to find one."

Phyllis began, gently, to unwrap the tissue paper from the long-stemmed buds. "There's an old pickle jar in that cupboard. And the tap's out the door at the back, in the wash-house. Oh, just look at those! I'd forgotten how beautiful they are."

Judith went to open the cupboard door, unearthed the pickle jar, and carried it through the door at the back of the room, down two steps, and out into a cavernous wash-house, a double-height lean-to, tacked on to the back of the two-room cottage. This had a flagged floor and flaking whitewashed walls, and smelt of household soap and the soggy wood of the draining-board. Cold and damp struck chill. In one corner, like a great monster, brooded a clothes-boiler, and there was a clay sink with a tin-bath tucked beneath it. The sink had one tap, and a flight of open wooden stairs led to the upstairs room. The baby clearly slept with her mother and father.

At the back of the wash-house was a half-glassed door, ill-fitting and the source of a sneaky draught. Through this could be seen a cement yard, a washing-line strung with blowing nappies and work-shirts, a rickety perambulator, and a sagging privy. This dismal spot was probably where Phyllis spent much of her time, lighting the fire under the boiler to deal with her family wash, or carrying a kettle of hot water through from the range in order to wash a sinkful of dishes. Imagining the hard labour involved simply to deal with the ordinary chores of everyday life caused Judith some distress. No wonder Phyllis looked so thin. What was almost impossible to understand was how any person could have put up such a house in the first place, without thought for the woman who was going to have to work in it. Only a man, she decided bitterly.

"What are you doing?" Phyllis called through the open door. "I'm going mad, waiting."

"Just coming." She turned on the lone tap, filled the pickle jar, and carried it back to the front room, closing the door firmly behind her.

"Gloomy old place, that wash-house, isn't it? And it's icy in winter unless you've got the boiler going." But Phyllis said this quite cheerfully, and clearly did not think that there was anything untoward in such primitive conditions. She placed the roses, one by one, into the pickle jar, and then sat back to admire them.

"They change everything, don't they, flowers? Make a place look quite different."

"Open the other things, Phyllis."

It took some time, with Phyllis unknotting string and folding paper, to be put aside for use at some later date. "Soap! Yardley's Lavender. Just like your mum used to use. I'll save it for best. Put it in a drawer with my knickers. And what's this then?"

"That's for Anna."

"Oh, look. A little coat." Phyllis held it up. "She's hardly ever had a new thing for herself, been living in hand-me-downs since the day she was born. Look at it, Anna. Isn't that lovely? You can wear it next Sunday when you go to see Gran. And so soft, that wool. Like a little princess, you'll be."

"And this is for Cyril. But you eat them if he doesn't like them. I thought about cigarettes, but I didn't know if he smoked."

"No, he doesn't smoke. Has a glass of beer, but he doesn't smoke. Gets to his chest. Coughs something awful. I think it must have something to do with working down the mine."

"But he's all right?"

"Oh, he's all right. Sorry about him not being here today. You never met him, did you, not even after all that time I was with your mother?"

"I'll meet him another day."

"In a way," said Phyllis, "it's easier without him. We can have a proper chat." She took the wrapping-paper from the final parcel. "Oh, my life. Chocolates. Cyril's mad on chocolate. Look, Anna, at the ribbon and the pretty box. See the little kitten and the puppy in their basket? It's lovely, Judith. It's all lovely. Some kind, you are . . ."

She smiled, dizzy with delight, but there was the shine of tears in her eyes, and Judith was filled with guilt. Such small things she had brought with her, and here was Phyllis almost weeping with gratitude.

She said, "I think the kettle's boiling," and Phyllis said, "So it is," gathered Anna, and leaped up to her feet to rescue the spitting kettle, and to make the tea.

Over the years, they had always kept in touch, if sporadically, by means of letters and Christmas cards, but still, there was much to talk about, and details to be filled in. Uppermost, however, in Phyllis's mind was the fact that Judith, at eighteen, was actually the owner of a car. And could drive it! To Phyllis it seemed little short of a miracle; undreamt of. She couldn't get over it.

"When did you get it? How on earth did you *manage?*"

In Phyllis's language, manage meant pay for. "I can't manage a new dress," one said, or "We can't manage a holiday this year."

Judith hesitated. It seemed dreadfully unfair to sit in this mean little cottage, with Phyllis looking so worn, and to talk about money. Here there was clearly so little to spare. But it was one of the things that she was determined to get off her chest. Somehow, when it all happened, it had not been possible to write it down in a letter to Phyllis. Words simply made it all seem so materialistic and greedy. But in the old days at Riverview, Phyllis had become

Judith's dearest friend, and most trusted of confidantes, and she didn't want this to change, which it would if untold secrets were left to lurk between them.

". . . it was Aunt Louise, Phyllis," she said at last. "I never wrote to you about it, because I wanted to be with you when I did tell you. You see, when she died, she left me all her money, and her house . . . and everything. In her Will."

"Oh!" Phyllis's jaw gaped as she took in this astonishing piece of news. "I didn't think things like that happened to real people. I thought they were just like stories in *Peg's Paper*."

"I couldn't believe it either. It took me ages to get used to the very idea. Of course, it's not mine to spend until I'm twenty-one, but Mr. Baines, the solicitor, and Uncle Bob Somerville are my trustees, and if I need something very badly, or they think I should have it, then I'm allowed."

Phyllis had gone quite pink with excitement. "I'm that *pleased* for you . . ."

"You're so dear. And I'm so lucky, I feel a bit ashamed . . ."

"What's there to be ashamed about? Mrs. Forrester wanted you to have it, why shouldn't you? Couldn't have happened to a sweeter person. And she'd have thought it all over, mark my words, she was no fool. Good-hearted lady, I always thought, even though she had a funny way with her. Downright, I suppose you'd call her . . ." Phyllis shook her head, clearly bewildered. "Life's funny, isn't it. There you were, with sixpence a week pocket money, and now you've got your own car. Just imagine! And driving it too. Remember your mum, like a flustered chicken every time she had to get that little Austin started. Mind, she had reason to be nervy, when you think of Mrs. Forrester ending up the way she did. Ghastly, that was. Great fire up on the moor. You could see it for miles. And it was *her*. Couldn't take it in, when I read the paper the next morning. Couldn't believe it. Mind, she was some dangerous driver. Every soul in West Penwith knew that. Didn't make it any easier, though."

"No," Judith agreed. "It didn't make it any easier."

"I worried about what would happen to you. At the time, I mean. And then I thought you'd probably make your home with the Somervilles. Haven't asked about them, have I? How is Mrs. Somerville? I was some fond of her, always made me laugh, she did, with her funny ways. I used to look forward to the times when she came to stay at Riverview. No airs about her."

"As far as I know, they're all in splendid form. My grandparents died, you know, within months of each other, and though it was sad for Mummy and Aunt Biddy, I think it was a bit of a relief as well. Aunt Biddy spent so much time on the road, driving to the Vicarage to make sure they were all right and not starving to death or anything."

"It's a terrible thing, old age. My granny got like that. Living alone and couldn't be bothered to feed herself, or else forgot. I'd go up there sometimes and find not a scrap of food in the house, and her just sitting there with the cat on her knee. I can understand your Aunt Biddy, feeling relief."

"She's got a dear little house near Bovey Tracey. I've been to stay there two or three times. But mostly, of course, I'm with the Carey-Lewises at Nancherrow. I'm going back there tomorrow . . ." Even as she said this, she could hear the pleasure in her own voice, and feel the smile on her face. Edward. Tomorrow she would see Edward again. She didn't think about him all the time; she didn't brood about him, nor long for him to be there. She was neither lovesick nor moonstruck, but nevertheless, when he sprang to mind, or his name was casually mentioned in conversation, it was impossible to ignore this leap of the heart, this sensation of dizzying happiness. And it occurred to her then, sitting in Phyllis's poor little house, that perhaps the distillation of happiness was being without a person, and yet knowing that very soon you were going to be with that person again. ". . . tomorrow morning."

"Lovely. By this time, it must feel like they're your own family. When you wrote and let me know you were going to stay with them, I stopped bothering about you. I reckoned you'd be all right. And then, that young man you met again there . . ."

Judith frowned. For a moment she couldn't think whom Phyllis was talking about. "Young man?"

"You *know*. You wrote and told me. That young man you met on the train, the evening you all came back from Christmas at Plymouth. And there he was, at the Carey-Lewises . . ."

Realization dawned. "Oh! You mean Jeremy Wells."

"That's right. The young doctor. Still around, is he?"

"Yes, he's still around, but stop looking so coy. We scarcely see him now. When he left Saint Thomas's, he came back to Truro and went into practice with his father, so now he's a busy country doctor with little time for socializing. But sometimes he fills in for his father, if somebody's ill. I had the most dreadful 'flu last Easter, and he turned up and was terribly kind."

"Don't you fancy him any more? You were some taken with him on the train."

"That was *years* ago. Anyway, he's over thirty now. Miles too old for me."

"But . . ." Phyllis, obviously, had no intention of being fobbed off with this and was intent on pursuing the subject of Judith's love life. But, even with Phyllis, Judith did not want to share the secret of Edward. Casting about for some way of steering the conversation into a more mundane direction, she was saved by the sight of Anna.

"Phyllis. I think Anna's going to sleep."

Phyllis looked down at her child. Anna, having drunk milk from a tin-mug and eaten her way through a plate of bread and butter, now had her thumb firmly plugged in her mouth. Her eyes drooped drowsily, long lashes drifting down over rosy cheeks.

"So she is." Phyllis's voice dropped to a whisper. "Didn't sleep this morning. I'll put her in her pram. She can have a bit of a nap . . ."

She rose to her feet, gently cradling the child in her arms. ". . . there's my little love now. Mum'll put you in your pram." She opened the door at the back of the room and stepped down into the wash-house. ". . . have a sleep and your dad will soon be home . . ."

Judith, alone, stayed where she was. The wind was getting up, piping across the moor from the cliffs, nudging at the ill-fitting window. Nursing her teacup between her hands, she looked about her and decided, sadly, that really it wasn't much of a place. Shabby, thin on the ground, everything she saw spoke of little money and hard times. All was clean as a bleached bone, of course, but just about as cheerful. The floor was laid with linoleum, cracked in places and so worn that its original pattern was all but gone. A washed-out rag-rug lay by the hearth and the single easy chair bulged horsehair from a hole in its faded velvet upholstery. She saw no wireless, no telephone, no pictures on the wall. Only a tradesman's garish calendar, hung from a drawing-pin. The polished brass knobs of the range and the sparkling brass fender were just about the only cheerful items to be seen. She remembered Phyllis crocheting doilies for her bottom drawer, and wondered what had happened to these treasures. There was certainly no sign of them here. Perhaps in her bedroom . . .

But Phyllis was returning. Judith turned as she closed the door. "Is she all right?"

"Fast asleep, little soul." She picked up the teapot and refilled their cups. "Now"—she settled herself back in her chair—"kept the best to the last. Tell me about your mum and Jess . . ."

Which took a bit of time. But Judith had brought with her the last letter from Singapore and a wallet of snapshots taken by her father. ". . . this is their house . . . and this is Jess with the Chinese gardener."

"Look at the size of her."

"And this is one taken at the Singapore Cricket Club for some party or other. Doesn't Mum look pretty? And here they are swimming. And here's Mum going to play some game of tennis. She's taken it up again, she plays in the evenings when it's cool."

"It must be a wonderful place . . ." Phyllis leafed once more through the photographs.

"Do you remember how she didn't want to go? And now she loves it! And there's so much going on. And parties on naval ships and in the Army barracks. Of course, it's terribly hot, much hotter than Colombo because it's so damp and steamy, but she seems to have got used to that. And everybody sleeps all afternoon."

"And now you've finished school, you'll be joining them! Just imagine that. When are you going?"

"I've got a passage booked in October . . ."

"That's no time. How long are you going to stay out there?"

"A year. And then, with a bit of luck, University." She thought about this, and then sighed. "I don't know. Phyllis, I really don't know."

"What do you mean, you don't know?"

"I don't know what I'll do if there's a war."

"That Hitler, you mean? He's no call to stop you being with your mum and dad and Jess."

"I suppose the shipping lines will go on functioning. Unless all the liners are turned into troop-ships, or hospital ships or something."

"Oh, they'll still sail. You've got to go. You've looked forward to it for so long." Phyllis fell silent, and after a bit, shook her head. "Terrible, isn't it? Everything so uncertain. So wrong. What's that Hitler got to be so greedy about? Why can't he leave people alone? And those poor Jews. What's so bad about being a Jew? No soul can help the way he was born. All God's creatures. I can't see no call to turn the world upside down, tear families apart . . ."

All at once, she sounded desolate and Judith tried to cheer her. "But *you'll* be all right, Phyllis. Mining's so important. It's bound to be a reserved occupation. Cyril won't have to go and be a soldier. He'll just go on working at Geevor."

"Some hope," Phyllis told her. "He'll go, all right. Made up his mind, he has. Reserved occupation or not, if war breaks out he's going to join the Navy."

"He's going to join the *Navy*? But why should he join the Navy if he doesn't have to?"

"The truth is," Phyllis admitted, "he's fed up with tin-mining. His father was a miner, but Cyril never wanted to be one. He's wanted to go to sea ever since he was a little boy. Merchant Navy or something. But his father wouldn't hear of it, and living out here, there wasn't much else Cyril could do. Left school at fourteen, and that was it."

Distressed as she was for Phyllis, Judith felt some grudging sympathy for Cyril. She couldn't think of anything worse than being forced underground if you didn't want to go. But, even so, he was a married man now, with responsibilities. "You mean, if war comes, then he's going to grab his chance?"

"Something like that."

"But what about *you*? And the baby?"

"I dunno. Suppose we'll manage."

So now, a new anxiety. Questions leaped to mind, but one was more important than all the others.

"Who owns this house?"

"The Mine Company. They offered it to Cyril before we were married. If they hadn't, we'd still be courting. We hadn't even a stick of furniture, but our families helped. My mum gave us our bed, and Cyril's gran let us have this table and a few chairs."

"Do you have to pay rent?"

"No. It's like a tied cottage."

"So . . . if Cyril goes to war, will you have to get out?"

"They wouldn't allow me to stay here on my own. They'd need it for someone else."

"So what would happen?"

"I'd go back to Mum's, I suppose."

"The house at Saint Just? Phyllis, there wouldn't be space for you all!"

"There'd have to be."

"Oh, it's too cruel."

"I've tried persuading him, Judith. To see it my way. Cyril, I mean. But he's that stubborn. I told you, all he ever wanted was to go to sea." She sniffed. "Sometimes I think he's praying for the war to start."

"You mustn't even think of such things. I'm sure he's not. He can't have any idea of the dangers he'll face; not just the sea, but guns and torpedoes and submarines and bombs."

"I've told him all that. But you can't stop a man going off to fight for his country. You can't grudge a man the only thing he's ever wanted."

"Well, I think it's terribly unfair. What about what *you* want . . . ?"

"What *I* want? Do you know what I want? I think about it sometimes. Somewhere to live that's pretty, with flowers and a real bathroom. Proper spoilt I was, living with you all at Riverview. It was the first bathroom I'd ever seen, and the water always hot out of the tap, and the smell of your mother's soap. And the garden. Never forget that garden, sitting out on summer afternoons and having tea picnics, and all that. And flowers everywhere. I planted pansies out the front, but there's no sun there. Nothing but wind. And not a scrap of earth out in the yard at the back. I'm not complaining. It's a roof over our heads, I know, and probably the best place I'll ever get. But it doesn't cost nothing to dream, does it?"

Judith shook her head. "No. Nothing."

They fell silent once more, because all at once there didn't seem to be much else to talk about. Everything was just too dreadful and depressing. In the end, it was Phyllis who broke the gloomy spell. She sat back in her chair and suddenly grinned. "I don't know what we're doing," she said, "sitting here like two old men at a funeral." And Judith remembered, with love and gratitude, that however dire a situation, Phyllis had always been able to find the funny side of it. "Long faces like we were both going out to be shot."

"What was it your mother used to say, Phyllis? Don't worry, it might never happen."

"And if it does, it'll all come out in the wash." Phyllis took the lid off the teapot and peered at its contents. "Looks stone-cold and black as ink to me. Why don't I put the kettle on again, and we'll have a fresh pot?"

It was late in the afternoon before Judith finally said her goodbyes and set off on the drive back to Porthkerris. The day had fallen apart. As she and Phyllis talked, clouds had gathered and thickened, rolling in from the sea, bringing with them a drenching mist that spread inland, like fog. Anna had had to be wakened from her sleep and brought indoors again, out of the rain, and Phyllis opened the door of the range, just for the cheer of seeing the flaming coals. Now, the windscreen wipers swung to and fro, and the surface of the twisting moorland road was lead-coloured and wet, a dark-grey satin ribbon winding up onto the soggy moor.

Depressing enough without the weight of concern for Phyllis which now occupied Judith's mind. *We've got a house,* Phyllis had written to her. *We're going to be married.* And then later, *I'm going to have a baby,* and it had all seemed so *right,* so exactly what Phyllis had always wanted and, more, deserved. But reality was a disillusionment, and it had been painful to tear herself away from Phyllis, and leave her, abandoned in that unlovely, primitive cottage, stuck in the middle of nowhere. After they had said goodbye, and she had turned the car in the road and set off on her homeward journey, Phyllis and the baby had stayed in the open doorway of the cottage, waving goodbye, and she had watched their reflections in the wing mirror, growing smaller and smaller as she drove away, and Phyllis was still waving, and then the road took a turn and they were lost from sight.

Unfair. It was all grossly unfair.

She thought of Phyllis in the old Riverview days. All of them had loved her, depended on her, and treated her as one of the family, which was of course the reason she had stayed with them, right to the end. Remembering, it was impossible to recall any occasion when she had been either grumpy or ill-tempered, and her kitchen had always provided a warm haven of laughter and chat. She remembered walks with Phyllis, picking wild flowers and learning their names and then arranging them in a jam jar for the middle of the kitchen table; and the pleasing sight of Phyllis, crisp in her pink-and-white-striped cotton overall, chasing Jess up the stairs, or carrying picnic teas across the lawn to where they sat beneath the mulberry tree. Most poignant, she remembered the sweet talcumy smell of Phyllis after she'd had her bath, and how her hair fluffed out when she'd just shampooed it . . .

But getting sentimental was of no use. After all, Phyllis had chosen to marry Cyril, had indeed waited years to marry him. The life of a miner's wife was bound to be hard, and Phyllis, the daughter of a miner, knew this better than anyone. And the baby was sweet, and they presumably had enough to eat, but . . . the unfairness of it.

Why should Phyllis, of all people, have to live and bring up her child in such conditions, just because her husband was a miner? Why couldn't miners have nice houses like the Warrens? Why should being a grocer be so much more rewarding than being a miner? Surely people who did horrible underground work should get more money than people who had pleasant occupations. And why should some people, like the Carey-Lewises, be so rich, so privileged, so . . . and it had to be said . . . spoilt, when a really wonderful person like Phyllis had to boil water before she could wash her dishes, and make the journey across the yard, whatever the weather, when she wanted to go to the lavatory?

And if there was a war, then Cyril was going, leaving Phyllis and her baby behind. Not, it seemed, for any deeply patriotic reason, but simply because he had always longed to get away from Pendeen and the tin-mining, and go to sea. She wondered how many thousands of young men there were in the country who felt the same. Young men who had scarcely ever left their native villages, except perhaps for a church bus-trip to the nearest town, or a Darts Championship outing.

The bicycle she knew, once invented, had revolutionized rural life in England, because for the first time a boy could travel five miles and court a girl in the next village, and this mobility had considerably minimized inbreeding and congenital deformities in isolated communities. If a simple bicycle could achieve so much, then surely a modern war would blow to pieces and scatter forever social conventions and traditions that had been respected since time immemorial. In her present mood, Judith decided that perhaps, at the end of the day, that wouldn't be a bad thing, but the immediate prospect of national mobilization, bombs and gas attacks, was still pretty scary.

So what would happen to Phyllis and Anna? *They wouldn't allow me to stay here on my own. I'd go back to Mum's, I suppose.* Dispossessed. A married woman without the dignity of her own home, however humble. *Do you know what I want? Somewhere to live that's pretty, with flowers and a real bathroom.*

If only there was something that could be done. If only there were some way of helping. But there wasn't. And even if there was, it would just be interfering. All Judith could do was keep in touch, return to Pendeen to visit as often as she could, and be around, if necessary, to pick up the pieces.

The church-tower clock was striking five as she drew in by the pavement outside Warren's Grocery. The shop was still open, and would stay so for another hour. Saturday evenings were often a busy time, as people popped in to buy last-minute provisions to see them through the empty Sabbath; a bit of extra bacon for breakfast, tinned peas and Bird's Custard powder for the huge midday meal. This evening, however, as Judith went through the door, it seemed to be busier than usual, with half a dozen customers queuing to be served, and only Heather behind the counter, looking a bit flustered, but doing her best to hold the fort.

This in itself was surprising. Heather, though perfectly competent, seldom worked in the shop, and was only called in to lend a hand at times of crisis.

"Did you say half a pound of sugar?"

"No, a pound. And I don't want granulated, I want castor . . ."

"Sorry . . ." Turning to get the other bag down from the shelf, Heather caught sight of Judith and threw her eyes heavenwards, but whether this was a plea for help or a silent scream of exasperation, it was impossible to tell. She was clearly near the end of her patience.

"Perhaps I'd better have a pound and a half."

"Well, make up your mind, Betty, for goodness' sake."

Judith said, "Where's your father, Heather, and Ellie?"

Heather, pouring sugar into the scales, jerked her head. "Upstairs."

"*Upstairs?*"

"In the kitchen. You'd better go."

So Judith left her to her confusion, and wondering what on earth was going on, went through the back shop and up the store steps to the kitchen. Its door, always open, was, this evening, firmly closed. Through it she heard the sound of noisy sobs. She opened it and went in, and found both Warrens and Ellie sitting around the kitchen table. It was Ellie who wept, and from the look of her she had been at it for some time, for her face was bloated and swollen with tears, her dry blonde hair all awry, and in her hand she clutched a uselessly sodden handkerchief. Mrs. Warren sat close to her while her husband faced the pair of them across the table, his arms crossed over his chest and his usually cheerful face dauntingly stony. Judith was filled with apprehension. She closed the door behind her. "What's happened?"

"Ellie's had a bad time," Mrs. Warren told her. "She's been telling us. You don't mind Judith knowing, do you, Ellie?"

Ellie, incoherent with sobs, wailed once more, but shook her head.

"Now, stop crying if you can. It's all over."

Judith, bewildered, pulled out a chair and joined the little group. "Has she had an accident or something?"

"No, nothing like that, though bad enough." Mrs. Warren laid her hand over Ellie's and held it tight. Judith waited, and Mrs. Warren told her the dreadful story. Ellie had been in the cinema, watching Deanna Durbin. She'd meant to go with her friend Iris, but Iris had dropped out at the last moment, and so Ellie had gone alone. And half-way through the film a man had come in and taken the seat next to Ellie, and presently he had laid his hand on her knee, and pushed it right up her leg, and then she had seen . . .

At this point Ellie's mouth opened like a baby's, and she started to howl once more, the tears spurting from her eyes like rain-water from a gutter.

"What did she see?"

But what Ellie had seen was, so far as Mrs. Warren was concerned, unspeakable. She went very pink, averted her eyes, pursed her lips. Mr. Warren, however, did not suffer from such delicate scruples. He was, clearly, beside himself with anger. "His fly buttons were open, the dirty bugger, and his thing sticking out . . ."

"Gave Ellie the fright of her life. There, Ellie, there. Don't cry no more."

". . . so she did the sensible thing. Got out and came here to us. Said she was too upset to go home. Hadn't the nerve to tell her mum."

But this had all happened before. Young girls, even streetwise kids like Ellie, did not tell their mothers, nor their aunts. They were too ashamed; they did not have the words to explain. They simply fled, to hide in the ladies' lavatory, or to bolt, hysterically weeping, out into the street, desperate for some sort of sanctuary.

She said, knowing what the answer would be, "Did you speak to the manager of the cinema?"

Ellie, mopping her eyes with the wad of handkerchief, managed a few words through her sobs. ". . . No . . . couldn't . . . and who'd believe me? . . . say it was just a story . . . as if I could make up something . . ." The prospect was clearly so dreadful that tears flowed anew.

"But did you see the man's face?" Judith persisted.

"I didn't want to look."

"Have you any idea what age he was? Was it a young boy? Or . . . older?"

"He wasn't young." Pathetically, Ellie made a real effort to pull herself together. "His hand was all bony. Feeling me. Right up my leg, under my skirt. And he smelt. His breath. Like whisky . . ."

Mrs. Warren said, "I'm going to make a nice cup of tea," and got to her feet, to fetch the kettle and fill it under the tap.

For a moment, Judith sat silent. She thought of Edward. What was it he had said? *I think you need a catalyst of some sort. Don't ask me what, but something will happen and it will all work out.* A catalyst. A reason to fight back, to finish Billy Fawcett for good and finally to heal the trauma he had inflicted upon her all those years ago. Sitting at the Warrens' kitchen table, she had no doubt at all of the identity of poor Ellie's groper, except that now he was worse than just a harmless old groper, because not only had he groped, but exposed himself. The very thought gave her the shudders. No wonder poor Ellie was in such a state. As for herself, she had stopped feeling the slightest pity for Billy Fawcett, and anger was a great deal more healthy than useless compassion. A catalyst. A reason to fight back. Or could it be termed revenge? Either way, she didn't care. Only knew what had to be done, and that she was going to take the greatest pleasure in doing it.

She took a deep breath and said firmly, "We must tell the manager of the cinema. And then we must all go to the police and press charges."

"We don't know who he is," Mr. Warren pointed out.

"I know."

"How do you know? You weren't there."

"I know because I know him. And because he did the same thing to me when I was fourteen."

"*Judith!*" Mrs. Warren's voice, her expression, mirrored her unbelief and her shock. "He *didn't?*"

"Yes, he did. He didn't actually expose himself, but I'm pretty certain that, sooner or later, that was on his agenda. He's called Colonel Fawcett. Billy Fawcett. He lives in Penmarron. And he's the most horrible person I've ever known in all my life."

"You'd better tell us."

So she told them. The whole story, from the time she had been staying with Aunt Louise at Windyridge. The visit to the cinema, his attempt to break into the house when she was on her own, his malevolent appearance at Aunt Louise's funeral, and finally the debacle of her night out at the Sliding Tackle with Edward Carey-Lewis.

By now Ellie, diverted by the drama of the saga, had stopped crying. When Judith came to the bit where Edward emptied the whisky into the old man's face, she even began to smile.

But Mrs. Warren saw nothing funny in the story. "Why didn't you *tell* us about all this?" she kept demanding indignantly.

"How could I tell you? What was the point? What could we do?"

"Stop the old villain."

"Well, that's what we can do now. Because of what's happened to Ellie."
She turned to Ellie, put an arm around her thin shoulders, and gave her a
little hug. "You did exactly and utterly the right thing, coming here and
telling Mrs. Warren about it all. If I'd had more sense, I'd have told Aunt
Louise, but I wasn't as brave as you. And you're not to let it worry you, Ellie,
you're not to let it spoil things for you. Most men are sweet and kind and fun,
it's just some of them that make everything so ugly and frightening. Now, we
must be sure that it never happens again. Tell the police, and make sure that
Billy Fawcett comes up in front of some judge or magistrate or court and gets
punished, so that he never, never does it again. I'll stand up as a witness for
the prosecution if necessary, and if he gets sent to jail, I'll be delighted. I
don't care. I only know that I want to be finished with him, for Ellie and for
me, and for all the other young girls he's fumbled, for once and for all."

After this long and fervent speech, she sat back in her chair to draw breath.
Her audience, for the moment, seemed to be silenced. Then Mrs. Warren
spoke. "Well, I must say, Judith. I haven't ever heard you on about something
like that before."

Despite herself, Judith laughed. Suddenly, she felt wonderful. Strong,
adult, filled with a relentless determination. "Perhaps that's just as well." She
turned to Mr. Warren. "What do you say?"

"I say, *right*." And he rose to his feet. "Now. Right away. No point in
wasting another moment. And you're coming with Judith and me, Ellie,
whether you want to or not. You'll be all right. We'll be with you all the time,
and back up every word you say. And afterwards, I'll take you home to your
mum, and together, we'll explain to her. Just remember, no real harm's been
done, and if a bit of good comes out of it, then you've done your bit." He
patted Ellie's shoulder and stopped to plant a comforting kiss on the top of
her tousled straw-coloured head. "Wasn't your fault, girl. None of it was your
fault."

And so it was done. It all took rather a long time. At the police station,
the sergeant on duty had never had to deal with such a delicate case before—
nicked bicycles and drunks-in-charge being his usual bill of fare—and was
obliged to feel his way through the necessary procedures, charge-sheets, and
other essential forms. Then the information had to be spelt out and written
down, with agonizing slowness. Ellie's distress, rekindled by the bleak offici-
ality of the police station, did nothing to help, and she had to be prompted
at every turn. When finally, painfully, the work was completed, Ellie then
had to be delivered home, a visit which involved yet more explanations,
reactions of shock and fury, and eventually innumerable cups of restoring tea.
But at last everybody calmed down, and Mr. Warren and Judith, both feeling
wrung-out, were able to return home. They found the shop shuttered and
closed, and upstairs in the kitchen, Heather, Mrs. Warren, and Joe waited for
them with the evening meal ready to be set on the table. But Mr. Warren
was not ready, instantly, to eat.

He said, "I'm going to have a drink." And went to the cupboard where, for times of crisis, he kept a bottle of Black & White whisky. "Who's going to join me? Joe?" But Joe, amused by his father's uncharacteristic behaviour, shook his head. "You, Mother? Heather? Judith, then?" But there were no takers, and so he poured himself a hefty tot and tipped it, neat, down the back of his throat. After which, he slapped down the empty tumbler and announced himself ready and able to carve the roast of pork.

Later, with the talk all over, the dishes done and the kitchen neat once more, Judith went downstairs to Mr. Warren's office and telephoned Mr. Baines. It was, necessarily, a fairly long call, and at first he was a bit put out that she had never before confided in him and told him of her unhappy girlhood experience with the dreaded Billy Fawcett. But his slight crossness did not last for long, and after that he was his usual calm, understanding, and helpful self. He said that Mr. Warren and Judith had done exactly the right thing, and it was about time the old bounder had a halt called to his nefarious activities. As for having to go to court when the case came up at the Bodmin Assizes, Mr. Baines promised to do his level best to make sure that Judith would not have to appear as a witness, but that he would be there in her stead, state her case, and handle everything.

Judith was deeply grateful, and told him so. He said, "Think nothing of it. That's what I'm here for," and then changed the subject and asked how she was enjoying herself at Porthkerris. They talked for a little while about nothing in particular, and finally said goodbye and rang off.

In bed that night, in the quiet darkness, Judith lay and stared at the ceiling, and decided that, in a strange way, today had been the end of a beginning. Not simply the last day of her holiday with the Warrens, nor the fact that she had managed finally to get to see Phyllis, but the knowledge that, at last, the saga of Billy Fawcett was over. *I would like to murder Billy Fawcett,* she had told Edward, *or squash him like a beetle.* But, at the end of the day, she had done better than that. With the help of Mr. Warren, the weeping Ellie, and the lugubrious police sergeant, she had set the wheels of the law in motion; thus putting paid to Billy Fawcett's horrid activities, and laying her own personal ghost forever. So the score was settled and she knew that never again would he haunt her nightmares, scrambling up his ladder to get at her through an open bedroom window. Never again would she awake petrified and silently screaming. And never again would he come between her and that which she desired most. It felt marvellous. Like being relieved of an aching load, a spectral shadow that had been hanging around at the edge of her mind for four years, and had very nearly destroyed her relationship with Edward.

Which led her reflections, quite naturally, back to him. She was returning to Nancherrow tomorrow morning, and she would see Edward again. If Aunt Lavinia was well enough, then he and Judith would go to the Dower House together, to visit her. A chance, perhaps, to be alone with him, away from all the others; to have opportunity and time to talk. To tell him that he had been right about the catalyst. To explain what had taken place. And generously to give him the chance of saying "I Told You So."

It would be like a new beginning, because now she was another person. Now, there was no need for rejection and childish terrors, because there was nothing left to be frightened about. To test herself, she imagined being kissed by Edward, just as he had kissed her last Christmas, as they stood, hidden, behind the billiard-room curtains of Nancherrow. She remembered his arms about her, his hand fondling her breast, the pressure of his mouth on her mouth, and then his tongue, forcing her lips open . . .

She was suddenly consumed by the pressure of desire, a pain, deep in her abdomen, a flush of breathless warmth. She closed her eyes and turned, abruptly, onto her side, curled up like a baby, her arms wrapped tight around her knees. Alone and in the darkness, she smiled, because it felt like coming to terms with some wonderful truth.

At Nancherrow, Rupert Rycroft, alone in his bedroom, changed for dinner. He had already bathed and shaved for the second time that day, and now pulled on pants and socks, buttoned himself into a clean white shirt, and tied his bow-tie. This involved standing in front of the mirror, and he had to sag at the knees a bit, on account of he was taller than most men. When he had dealt with the tie, he paused for a moment, inspecting his own reflection, the ordinary, undistinguished face which had been staring back at him from mirrors for the whole of his life. Ears a bit too big, sleepy eyes that drooped at the corners, and a chin that was inclined to run into his collar. On the bonus side, however, a trim military moustache helped to tie all these uncoordinated features into some sort of order, and the cruel suns of Palestine and Egypt had tanned his skin to leather, and etched a network of wrinkles around his eyes and mouth, imparting an impression of maturity, a man older and more experienced than his years.

He hoped.

His dun-coloured hair was thick and soft, and after his bath, quite uncontrollable. But Mr. Trumpers Royal Yacht lotion and a good deal of tamping down with a pair of ivory-backed hair brushes brought it back into line again, rigidly disciplined to the short-back-and-sides of a regular soldier.

He turned from the mirror, pulled on his trousers, and then tried buffing up his shoes a bit with his dirty handkerchief. They didn't look much better, and he thought wistfully of Private Stubbs, his soldier-servant, who, with spit, a bone, and a fair ration of elbow grease, could produce a gleaming shine, even on a pair of square-bashing boots.

But no Stubbs. The shoes would have to do. He pulled on the silk-faced dinner jacket, gathered up small belongings and stowed them in pockets, then turned off the lights, went out of the room, and made his way downstairs.

It was seven o'clock, and dinner not until eight. But, in the drawing-room, Rupert found Colonel Carey-Lewis, on his own, already changed, sitting in an armchair, reading his newspaper and enjoying a restoring whisky and soda before the hordes of the house party descended to shatter his peace. Rupert had hoped for exactly this. It was just what his own father did when Taddington bulged with guests.

Disturbed, the Colonel lowered his paper and managed not to look too put-out.

"Rupert."

"Please don't get up, sir. I'm sorry. I'm a bit early . . ."

"Not at all. Not at all." The newspaper was folded and set aside. "Pour yourself a drink. Come and sit down." Rupert, grateful at the prospect of a bit of Dutch courage, went to do as he was bidden. "Hope you're comfortable. Enough hot water? Good bath?"

"Splendid, thank you, sir." Carrying his drink, he went to sit by the Colonel's side, perched on the fireside stool, with long legs folded like jack-knives. "I was feeling a bit hot and sweaty. Athena made me play tennis . . ."

Despite the fact that Rupert had planned this interlude alone with his host, he had, at the same time, slightly dreaded it, because, for all his charm, it was patently clear that inconsequential chat was not Colonel Carey-Lewis's forte and that, basically, he was a shy man. But fears proved groundless. They slipped easily into conversation, and their common interests gave them plenty to discuss, and shooting, horses, and the Regular Army, quite painlessly, broke the ice. Then the Colonel asked about himself, and Rupert told him about Taddington, and his parents, and his career. Eton, Sandhurst, the Royal Dragoon Guards. Postings to Egypt and Palestine and now the Equitation Centre in Northamptonshire.

"The trouble is, Long Weedon is too close to London. The temptation is to buzz up to town at every opportunity, and then of course one has to buzz back, usually in the early hours of the morning with a crashing hangover, and somehow be on parade on time."

The Colonel smiled. "That is simply one of the problems and disadvantages of youth. Any word of the Royals being mechanized?"

"Not so far, sir. But to be truthful, in a modern war a cavalry regiment does seem to be a bit of an anachronism."

"How would you feel about tanks?"

"I'd be sorry to say goodbye to the horses."

The Colonel shifted in his chair. He raised his head and his pale eyes gazed through the open window, to the gardens that lay beyond, washed in the gold of the evening sun. He said, "I'm afraid we will have to go to war. So many months slipped by, filled with compromise and treaty. For no point, as far as I can see. Hopes are extinguished, one by one. Just as Austria was extinguished, and then Czechoslovakia, and now Poland. And suddenly, it's too late. Poland is just a question of time. Hitler has no reason to mobilize. The German Army is ready to march the instant they are given the word. It must be soon. The first fortnight in September, before the rains of October. Before the muds of November can halt their tanks."

"And Russia?"

"The great question mark. If Stalin and Hitler sign a pact, then Russia gives Germany the go-ahead to proceed. And that will be the start." He looked back at Rupert. "What about you? What will happen to you?"

"Probably back to Palestine."

"This will be a war of air power. Edward will fly with the Royal Air Force." He reached for his glass, and abruptly finished his drink, tossing it down his throat as though it were medicine. "Pour me another, there's a dear fellow. And how is your own glass?"

"I'm all right, thank you, sir." Rupert got to his feet and went to refill the Colonel's tumbler, and then returned to his place. "Actually," he said, "I wondered if I could have a word with you."

A gleam of humour crossed his host's features. "I thought we *were* having a word."

"No, it's . . ." Rupert hesitated. He had never done this before and was anxious not to make a hash of it. "I would like to ask your permission to marry Athena."

There followed a moment's astonished silence, and then Colonel Carey-Lewis said, "Good God. Why?"

Which was an unexpected reaction and a bit of a facer. But Rupert did his best.

"Well, I'm extremely fond of her, and I think she is of me. I know it's not much of a time to get married, with war on its way and no certainty of our futures, but I still think it would be a good idea."

"I don't know what sort of a wife she'd make."

"You sound doubtful, sir."

"She's always been such a fly-by-night. I suppose her mother all over again."

"But you married her mother, sir."

"Yes, I married her. And she has never ceased to entertain and beguile me. But by the time I married Diana I had loved her for years. You and Athena haven't known each other all that long."

"Long enough, sir."

"Have you discussed it all with her?"

"Yes. Yes, we've discussed it."

"Army wife. Years of separation. All that?"

"Yes. All that."

"And the future. The far future, when this terrible disaster that is hanging over us all is a thing of the past. What then?"

"I can't say. I can only tell you that when my father dies, Taddington will come to me."

"Athena and Gloucestershire? Is that a good idea? She hates horses, you know. Won't go within a bloody yard of one."

Rupert laughed. "Yes. I know that."

"And you still want to marry her?"

"Yes. I do."

"When?"

"I think as soon as possible."

"Takes months to plan a wedding."

"We . . . well, we wouldn't have that sort of a wedding, sir. Athena has a horror of big weddings. I'm afraid it will be rather a disappointment to Mrs. Carey-Lewis, but we thought something very small, or even a Registry Office. I could get a special licence."

"Oh, well. It'll save me a bit of money. I suppose we have to be grateful for small mercies."

"I really do love her, sir."

"I love her too. She's a sweet and funny girl and I have always thought her quite enchanting. I am just sorry that you will have to face up to such uncertainty, but if worse comes to worst and you are torn apart, then Athena can always come back to Nancherrow and wait for you here."

"I hoped you'd say that. My parents, of course, would welcome her and make her as happy as they could, but she and my mother are chalk and cheese and I don't think the arrangement would be very comfortable."

The Colonel said drily, and with some perception, "It's clearly unfortunate for you that your intended has no love of horses."

"Yes. Unfortunate. But not the end of the world."

"In that case, we seem to have talked it through. All I can say is, yes, you may marry her, and I wish you both all the good fortune and happiness that this cruel world will allow you."

"There's just one thing, sir . . ."

"And what is that?"

"When the others come down, don't say anything. I mean, don't announce an engagement or anything. If you don't mind."

"Why not?"

"Well, we've talked about it, Athena and I, but I haven't actually asked her yet. And she hasn't, actually, said yes."

The Colonel looked a bit bewildered, as well he might. "Very well. Not a word, but get it all settled as soon as you can, there's a good fellow."

"I will, sir, and thank you."

"No point in letting these sorts of arrangements hang fire. Strike while the iron is hot, I always say. Otherwise, things are inclined to collapse."

"A bit like a soufflé, sir."

"A soufflé?" The Colonel thought about this. "Yes. Yes. I see what you mean."

The Nancherrow kitchen, on the Sunday mornings when there were a lot of people staying in the house, habitually simmered like a cauldron of furious activity. Despite opened windows and doors, the temperature, on this balmy September day, rose by the moment, causing Mrs. Nettlebed to go red in the face and perspire freely, and her pesky ankles to swell like balloons over the straps of straining shoes.

Nine in the dining-room, and five in the kitchen to feed. No, she corrected herself, not nine in the dining-room, but eight, because Mrs. Carey-Lewis had taken to her bed—a bilious attack, the Colonel had said—and would probably have to be taken a little tray. Mrs. Nettlebed had accepted the bilious-attack excuse without comment, but privately she and Nettlebed had made up their minds that Mrs. Carey-Lewis was simply worn out; all that junketing in London, and then having to come rushing home because everybody thought that old Mrs. Boscawen was on her way out. She wasn't on her way out, of course, because, miraculously, she had rallied, but even so, the anxiety was still there, and the house crammed full of guests. Not very restful. If Mrs. Nettlebed had been Mrs. Carey-Lewis, she too would have retired to her bed, and not got out of it until things had calmed down a bit.

She stood at her kitchen table and rubbed flour, sugar, and butter briskly through her fingers into a large earthenware bowl, rather as if she were making scones. Whatever the season, and however high the temperature, the Colonel always enjoyed his hot pudding, and this Sunday it was to be apple crumble, sweetened with mincemeat and laced with a spoonful of brandy. The apples had already been peeled and sliced and lay, like pale-green petals, in the pie dish, waiting for the crumble. Hetty had prepared the apples, just as she had already peeled pounds of potatoes, cleaned two cauliflowers, chopped a cabbage, and hulled four punnets of fresh strawberries. Now, she was clattering about in the scullery, washing up what Mrs. Nettlebed always thought of as "the oddses," pans and bowls and colanders and kitchen knives and graters.

In the oven, a twelve-pound sirloin of beef on the bone was simmering away to itself, and through the firmly closed door, an aroma seeped—of rich meaty juices, mingled with the scent of the onion Mrs. Nettlebed had tucked into the sirloin's flank. With it would be served roast potatoes, roast parsnips, Yorkshire puddings, horseradish sauce, gravy, and freshly made, red-hot English mustard.

The puddings, just about, were done. Two glass dishes, containing fresh strawberries and a chocolate soufflé, stood ready and waiting on the cool slate shelf of the larder. Once she'd popped the apple crumble into the hot oven, Mrs. Nettlebed would start in on the Yorkshire puddings. Hetty could have made these, but she had a heavy hand with batter.

The kitchen door opened. Mrs. Nettlebed, imagining that it was her husband, did not raise her head from her task, but said, "Do you think we should have whipped cream with the soufflé?"

"Sounds delicious," said a man who was not Mr. Nettlebed. Mrs. Nettlebed's hands were stilled. She jerked her head around and saw, standing in the open doorway, none other than Jeremy Wells. Her mouth fell open in a delighted gape, and it occurred to her that at this moment, bang in the middle of getting Sunday lunch on the road, he was just about the only person whose unexpected appearance could fill her with pleasure.

She said, "Well!"

"Hello, Mrs. Nettlebed. What splendid smells of cooking. What's for lunch?"

"Roast sirloin." She stood there, with her cap askew and her hands all floury, and beamed at him. "Dr. Wells! You're some stranger." (In the old days, when he was tutoring Edward, she had always called him Jeremy, but as soon as he passed his finals and qualified, she had addressed him as "Doctor." She reckoned he deserved it, after all those years of studying books and taking examinations. To save confusion, when talking about him, he was referred to as young Dr. Wells, while his father, rather to that good man's chagrin, was relegated to old Dr. Wells.) "What are you doing here? Did the Colonel send for you? He never said nothing to me."

Jeremy closed the door behind him and came over to the table. "Why should he send for me?"

"Mrs. Carey-Lewis. She's poorly. *He* says a bilious attack, but me and Nettlebed thinks different. Tired out, I'd say, with one thing and another. Did you know Mrs. Boscawen had been ill?"

"Yes, I heard. But she seems to be over the worst of it?"

"Some fright she gave us all. Everybody rushing home from London and Scotland and goodness knows where, thinking that she was about to breathe her last. It was as bad as that."

"I'm sorry."

She frowned. "If the Colonel didn't send for you, then why are you here?"

"Just to see you all." He reached out and took a bit of apple from the pie dish, and ate it. If he had been Loveday, she would have slapped her hand. "Where is everybody?"

"All gone to church. Except Mrs. Carey-Lewis. Like I said, she's in her bed."

"Perhaps I should pop up and see her."

"If she's asleep, then leave her sleeping."

"I will. Have you got a houseful?"

"Bulging, we are." Mrs. Nettlebed reached for her pie dish and began to sprinkle the topping over the apples, pressing the mixture down into a firm crust. "Athena brought her young man, Captain Rycroft, and Edward's got a friend staying, too. A Mr. Callender."

"And Loveday?"

"Yes, Loveday, of course. And Judith's coming back this morning."

"Where's Judith been?"

"Staying in Porthkerris, with the Warrens."

"Is there enough lunch for me?"

"What do you think, you silly thing? Enough and over, I would say. Seen Nettlebed, have you?"

326

"No, I didn't see anybody. Just walked in."

"I'll tell him to lay another place . . . now why don't you go up and see Mrs. Carey-Lewis. And if she's talking about getting up, you just tell her to stay where she is. *Hetty!* You nearly finished in there? There's more to be washed, and I need you to whip some cream for me . . ."

Jeremy left her to it, went out of the kitchen and up to Diana's bedroom by way of the back stairs. He knocked gently at her door, and her voice called to him to come in. He had half-expected drawn curtains and an invalid's gloom, but the room was filled with sunshine. Diana, however, was still in bed, propped up on a pile of downy pillows and wearing a lace-trimmed voile bedjacket. Beside her, with a snow-white, lace-trimmed pillow all to himself, Pekoe lay in state, curled into a ball and fast asleep. Diana had been reading. The book lay open, face-down on the white satin quilt, and her thin red-tipped hand lay upon it.

"Jeremy."

"Hello."

"What are you doing here? Oh, Edgar didn't bother you with a summons, did he? I told him not to get in a fuss."

"No, he didn't call." He closed the door and came to sit, unprofessionally, on the edge of the bed. She looked not feverish but washed out, pale as paper, and as though her fine skin had been pulled taut over the classic bone structure of her face. Her usually immaculate hair was disarmingly tousled, and beneath her astonishing eyes were smudges of exhaustion.

He said, "You're looking worn out."

"I am. But Edgar's telling everybody it's a bilious attack."

"So what have you been up to, to get yourself in this state?"

"You make it sound as though it's all been fun. But at the moment, nothing's fun. Lavinia's been so ill, and there's too much to do. And sometime, Mary and I have got to go and buy thousands of yards of horrible black cotton and somehow make curtains for every window in the house. The truth is, I'm tired and miserable and depressed and I've run out of the energy to go on pretending that I'm anything else. So I came to bed and told Edgar I was feeling ill. He'd much rather I felt ill than have me unhappy."

"Are you worrying about Mrs. Boscawen?"

"Yes, a bit, still. She's not out of the wood yet. She gave us all such a scare. And I was frazzled out anyway, after London and strings of late nights, and then I had to come bolting home. I'd never driven the Bentley so far and so fast before, not by myself. All along that dreadful A30, and the Exeter by-pass choked with traffic."

"But you made it."

"Yes, I made it, to a hysterical Isobel, and having to find nurses, and then everybody coming home, and bringing people to stay. And then to cap everything, Edgar told me last night that this young man of Athena's wants to *marry* her!"

"Captain Rycroft?"

"Who told you about him?"

"Mrs. Nettlebed."

"He's called Rupert. He's terribly sweet. Royal Dragoons. Rather conventional and totally unexpected. But we're none of us to say anything, because apparently he hasn't even *asked* her yet. People are funny, aren't they?"

"I think that sounds rather cheering news."

"Well, it is, in a way, but if they do get engaged, then they're going to insist on a hole-in-the-corner wedding, all terribly quick. A Registry Office, or something, and it all seems a bit joyless. But how can anything be joyful when the papers are full of such gloom and doom and everything gets worse every day and Edgar makes me listen to the nine-o'clock news every night with him, and sometimes I think I'm going to be sick with terror."

Her voice shook, and for the first time Jeremy felt a real concern. In all the time he had known her, he had never seen Diana Carey-Lewis in anything even approaching a state. She had always seemed to him nerveless, insouciant, able to see the ridiculous—and so, funny—side of the most impossibly serious situations. But this Diana had lost her spirit and so her greatest strength.

He laid his hand over hers. "You mustn't be afraid, Diana. You're never afraid of anything."

She disregarded this.

"I've been like an ostrich all this year. Burying my head in the sand, and pretending that it's not going to happen, that some miracle will occur, that some black-hatted idiot will go and get another bit of paper signed, and we'll all be able to breathe again, and go on living. But it isn't any good any longer. Deceiving oneself, I mean. There isn't going to be a miracle. Just another terrible war." To his horror, Jeremy saw her eyes well with weak tears, and she made no effort to brush them away. "After the Armistice in 1918, we told ourselves that it would never happen again. A whole generation of young men wiped out in the trenches. All my friends. Gone. And do you know what I did? I stopped thinking about it. I stopped remembering. I simply put it all out of my mind, shut it away like a lot of old rubbish in a trunk. Fastened the locks, did up the straps, pushed the trunk to the very back of some dusty attic. But now, only twenty years later, it's all starting again and I can't help remembering. Dreadful things. Going to Victoria Station to say goodbye, and all the boys in khaki, and everything fogged in steam from the engines. And the trains rolling out, and everybody waving . . . and mothers and sisters and sweethearts left behind on the platform. And then the pages and pages of Casualty Lists, columns of tiny newsprint. Each name a young man, cut down by war before he'd even had time to live. And I remember going to a party and there was a girl, and she sat on a grand piano and swung her legs and sang 'Let the Great Big World Keep Turning,' and everybody joined in, but I couldn't because I couldn't stop crying."

She was weeping now, dabbing at her streaming cheeks with a useless scrap of lace-edged handkerchief.

He said, "Haven't you anything a little more robust than that?"

"Women's handkerchiefs are always so idiotic, aren't they?"

"Here's mine. A bit bright but spit-clean."

"What a lovely colour. It matches your blue shirt." She blew her nose lustily. "I'm talking too much, aren't I?"

"Not at all. It seems to me you need to talk, and I am here to listen."

"Oh, darling Jeremy, you are the dearest man. And actually, in a funny way I'm not nearly as stupid as I sound. I know there has to be a war. I know we can't go on letting dreadful things happen in Europe—people being suppressed, losing their freedom, being imprisoned and murdered just because they're Jewish." She wiped her eyes once more and pushed his handkerchief beneath her pillow. "Just before you appeared, I was reading this book. It's just a novel, nothing very deep . . . but it makes it all so dreadfully real . . ."

"What is the book?"

"It's called Escape, by some woman called Ethel Vance. And it's about Germany. A finishing school, very chic and cosmopolitan, run by an American-born countess, a widow. Young girls come to her to learn to ski and to study French and German, and music. It's all very charming and civilized. But close by, hidden in the forests beyond the ski slopes, is a concentration camp, and incarcerated there a Jewish actress under sentence of death."

"I hope it is she who is going to escape."

"I don't know. I haven't come to the end yet. But it's chilling. Because it is now. It's going on now, to people like us. It's not something out of history. It's now. And it's so vile that somebody has to stop it. So I suppose it has to be us." She smiled at him wryly, and it was like a watery beam of sunshine on a wet day. "So. Now I'm not going to moan any more. It's so lovely to see you. But I still can't think why you're here. I know it's the weekend, and you're all open-shirted and casually attired, but why aren't you mixing potions and taking surgery and telling people to say 'Aah'? Or perhaps your father's given you the day off?"

"No. As a matter of fact, my mother and father have gone off to the Scilly Islands for a few days' holiday. He said he was going to grab the chance while he could, because, at the rate things are going, only God knows when he'll get another."

"But the practice?"

"We got a locum in."

"A locum? But you . . ."

"I am no longer my father's partner."

"Has he given you the push?"

Jeremy laughed. "Not exactly. But I've been selected by the local medical committee as expendable. For the time being, my father's going to carry on alone. I volunteered to join the RNVR, and I've been accepted by the Medical Director-General. Surgeon Lieutenant-Commander Jeremy Wells, RNVR. How does that sound to you?"

"Oh, Jeremy. Terribly impressive, but frightfully frightening and brave. Do you really have to do this?"

"I've done it. I even went to Gieves and bought my uniform. I look a bit like a cinema commissionaire, but I suppose we'll all get used to it."

"You'll look heavenly."

"I have to report to Devonport Barracks next Thursday."

"And until then?"

"I wanted to see you all. Say goodbye."

"You'll stay, of course."

"If there's a bed."

"Oh, darling boy, there's always a bed for you. Even though we are a bit of a houseful. Did you bring a suitcase?"

He had the grace to look a bit sheepish. "Yes. Packed. On the off chance you'd invite me."

"Did Mrs. Nettlebed tell you about Gus Callender? Edward's chum from Cambridge."

"She said he was staying."

"He's rather interesting. A bit of a dark horse. Loveday, I fear, is besotted."

"*Loveday?*"

"Isn't it astonishing? You know how dreadfully rude and offhand she's always been with Edward's friends. Giving them dreadful nicknames and mimicking their fruity voices? Well, this is quite a different cup of tea. One could almost say, she hangs on his every word. It's the first time I've ever seen her even vaguely interested in a personable young man."

Jeremy found himself much amused. "And how does he take her devotion?"

"I should say quite coolly. But he's behaving very well."

"Why is he so interesting?"

"I don't know. Just different from all Edward's other friends. And he's Scottish, but he's a bit clammish about his family. Reserved, I suppose. A bit humourless? And yet he's an artist. Painting is his hobby, and he's amazingly good. He's already done some charming little sketches. You must get him to show you."

"Hidden depths."

"Yes. I suppose so. And why not? We're all such extroverts, we expect everyone else to lay their lives on the line. Anyway, you'll meet him. And remember, we all seem to have entered a tacit agreement not to tease. Even Edward's being incredibly tactful. After all, we sometimes forget that our wicked baby is nearly eighteen. Perhaps it's time she started falling in love with something that doesn't have four legs and a tail. And I must say he's very sweet with her. It's all rather dear." Suddenly she yawned, and settled back on her pillows, slipping her hand from beneath his own. "I wish I didn't feel too tired. All I really want to do is sleep."

"Then sleep."

"It's made me feel so much better, just talking to you."

"That's what a professional consultation should be all about."

"You'll have to send me a socking bill."

"I will if you don't stay there. Have a really good rest. How do you feel about food? Do you want some lunch?"

She wrinkled her nose. "Not really."

"A bit of soup? Consommé, or something. I'll have a word with Mrs. Nettlebed."

"No. Tell Mary. She'll be around somewhere. And tell her you're staying. She'll find a room for you."

"Right." He stood. "I'll come and see you later on."

"It's so comforting," she told him, "knowing that you're here. Just like the old days." She smiled, a smile warm with grateful affection. "It makes everything so much better."

He left her and went out of the room, closing the door behind him. For a moment he hesitated, knowing that he should go and find Mary Millyway, but not certain where he should start looking for her. And then all thoughts of Mary Millyway were driven from his head by the sound of music. It came from the far end of the long passage that was the guest wing. Judith's room. She was there. She had returned from Porthkerris. Was probably unpacking. And while she did this had put a record on her gramophone, for companionship maybe. For solace.

A piano. Bach. "Jesu, Joy of Man's Desiring."

He stood there and listened, filled with a sweet and piercing nostalgia. Carried back in time, with startling vividness, to Evensong in his school chapel, he recalled the golden summer light streaming through stained-glass windows; the acute discomfort of fumed oak pews, and the pure voices of the young trebles singing the alternating phrases of the classic chorale. He could almost smell the fusty hymn-books.

After a bit, he went down the passage, his footsteps muffled by the thick carpet. Judith's door stood ajar. He pushed it gently open. She did not hear him. Suitcases and bags stood about the floor, but she had, apparently, abandoned them and decided instead to write a letter, for she sat at her desk, intent on her task, and her profile was framed by the open window. A lock of honey-coloured hair fell across one cheek, and she wore a cotton dress of azure blue, splashed with white flowers. Her concentration, her unawareness of his presence, rendered her so vulnerable, and at the same time so lovely, that all at once Jeremy found himself wishing that time could be stopped. Like a film halted at a single frame, he wanted the moment to last forever.

It occurred to him then that eighteen was an amazing age for a girl, suspended, as it were, between gawky youth and the full flower of womanhood. It was like watching the tight bud of a rose unfurl, day by day, and knowing that its full perfection was still to come. This magic metamorphosis did not happen to everyone, of course, and in his life he had come across plenty of overgrown schoolgirls, beefy in Aertex shirts trained over well-developed busts, and exuding about as much feminine allure as a rugby coach on a wet day.

But he had witnessed the miracle happen to Athena. One day a leggy, coltish blonde, and the next, the object of every man's desire. And now it was Judith's turn, and he remembered the little girl he had first talked to in the railway carriage four years ago. And it felt a bit sad. But there was reason as well to be grateful. His father, old Dr. Wells, had served as a Front Line Medical Officer in the First World War, and had talked a bit, though not very much, about his mind-numbing experiences. And so Jeremy knew that the only certainty about the months and years that lay ahead of him, as a naval surgeon on board one of His Majesty's ships, was that from time to time he was going to have to come to terms with loneliness, exhaustion, miserable discomfort, and sheer terror, and that memories of better days would probably be the guardians of his own sanity.

Now. This moment, caught in time like a fly in amber, was a memory.

He had stood there long enough. He was about to speak but the music of Bach, at that moment, came to its stately conclusion. The silence which followed the final chords lay empty, to be filled by the voices of the doves in the courtyard below the window.

"Judith." She looked up and saw him, and for a moment said nothing, while he watched her face pale with apprehension. Then she said, "Diana's ill," and it was not a question, but a statement.

So much for being a doctor. "Not a bit," he told her instantly. "Just tired out."

"Oh." She dropped her pen and leaned back in her chair. "What a *relief*. Mary said she was in her bed, but she didn't tell me you'd been sent for."

"Mary didn't know. I haven't seen Mary yet. I haven't seen anyone except Mrs. Nettlebed. Apparently they've all gone to church. And I wasn't sent for, I just came. And Diana really is all right, so don't worry."

"Perhaps I should go and see her for a moment."

"Leave her. I think she's going to sleep. You can go and visit later on." He hesitated. "Am I disturbing you?"

"Of course not. I was just trying to write to my mother, but I'm not making much of a job of it. Come in. Come and sit down. I haven't seen you for months."

So he stepped into the room, over the unopened suitcases, and lowered himself into a ridiculous little armchair which was far too narrow for his masculine backside. "When did you get back?" he asked.

"About half an hour ago. I meant to unpack, but then I decided to write to my parents. I haven't written for so long. There's been so much going on."

"Did you have a good time in Porthkerris?"

"Yes. It's always fun there. A bit like a three-ring circus. Have you got the day off or something?"

"No. Not exactly."

She waited for him to enlarge on this. When he did not, she suddenly smiled. "You know, Jeremy, you are extraordinary. You never change. You look just the same as you did when I first saw you, in the train coming down from Plymouth."

"I don't know quite how to take that. I always thought there was room for improvement."

She laughed. "It was meant as a compliment."

He said, "I'm on leave."

"I'm sure you deserve it."

"Embarkation leave, I suppose you might call it. I've joined the RNVR. I report to Devonport next Thursday, and Diana has asked me to stay here until I have to go."

"Oh, *Jeremy*."

"It's a bit of a thought, isn't it? But I've been chewing it over all summer, and now it seems to me that the sooner the balloon goes up, the sooner we'll get it all over and done with. And I might as well be in at the start of things."

"What does your father say?"

"I talked it all over with him, and he, fortunately, is of like mind. Which is good of him, because he's going to be the one to carry the burden of a considerable practice, single-handed."

"Will you go to sea?"

"With a bit of luck."

"We'll miss you."

"You can write me letters. You can be my pen-pal."

"All right."

"It's a deal. Now"—he heaved himself with some difficulty out of the little chair—"I must go and find Mary and be given a billet. The others should be back from church at any moment, and I wouldn't mind cleaning myself up a bit before lunch."

But Judith had news of her own to impart. "Did you know I've got a car now?"

"A *car*?" He was much impressed. "Of your own?"

"Yes." She beamed, gratified by his reaction. "Brand-new. A dear little Morris. I'll have to show it to you."

"You can take me for a spin. What a spoilt girl you are. I didn't get a car until I was twenty-one, and then it cost five pounds and looked like a very old sewing-machine on wheels."

"Did it go?"

"Like a breeze. At least thirty miles an hour with all the doors open and a stern wind." Standing in the open doorway, he paused, listening. From downstairs could be clearly heard the sound of voices, footsteps, slamming doors, and Tiger's joyous barking. "The church party would appear to have returned. I must go. See you later . . ."

Home from church. They had all come back, flooding into the house: the family, and the two strangers whom Judith had yet to meet. And Edward was there, with the rest of them. Downstairs. Her heart began to beat with a scarcely suppressed excitement, and she knew that the letter to Singapore would have to wait. She pushed the pages aside, and swiftly did a bit of cursory unpacking. Changed her shoes and washed her hands, and put on some lipstick, and then, after a quick consideration, a splash of scent. That was all. This was no time to start overdoing things. She was at her mirror, brushing her hair, when she heard Loveday's voice calling.

"*Judith!*"

"I'm here."

"What are you doing? We're all home. You've got to come down and see everybody . . . gosh, you're looking super. How was it all? Did you go on having fun? When did you get home? Have you seen Mummy? Poor thing, she's not very well . . ."

"No, I haven't seen her, I think she's sleeping. Jeremy says she's just a bit exhausted."

"*Jeremy? Is he* here?"

"He turned up just before I got home. He's staying for a few days. I think he and Mary are trying to find somewhere for him to sleep. And talk about looking super, just look at you! Where did you get that heavenly jacket?"

"It's Athena's. She lent it to me. It's Schiaparelli. Isn't it divine? Oh, Judith, I have to quickly tell you about Gus before you meet him. He's simply the most wonderful person I've ever met in my life, and we've done lots and lots together, and he never seems to be in the least bit bored with me or anything like that."

Her face, as she imparted this riveting information, opening up her heart and making no effort to conceal her obvious infatuation, shone with a sort of inner happiness that Judith had never seen before. She had always been pretty, but right now, she looked sensational. It was as though, at last, she had abandoned the deliberately cultivated loucheness of adolescence, and had decided, almost overnight, to grow up. As well, there was a sort of brilliance about her, an inner glow that had nothing to do with artifice. Falling in love, Judith decided, suited Loveday almost as well as the little scarlet linen jacket she had borrowed from Athena.

"Oh, Loveday, why should he be bored with you? Nobody's ever been bored with you in all your life."

"No, but you know what I mean."

"Yes, I do, and it's lovely for you." Judith went back to brushing her hair. "What sort of things have you been doing together?"

"Oh, *everything*. Swimming, and showing him the farm, and taking care of the horses, and taking him lovely places so that he can do his painting. He's a frightfully clever artist, I'm quite sure he could make a tremendous success of it; only, of course, he's going to be an engineer. Or a soldier."

"A soldier?"

"A Gordon Highlander. *If* there's a war." But even this prospect cast no shadow on Loveday's radiant bloom.

Judith said, "Jeremy's joined the Navy."

"Already? Has he?"

"That's why he's here. Sort of embarkation leave."

"Goodness." But with the self-absorption of any young lover, Loveday was disinterested in any person but herself and the object of her desire. "I simply can't *wait* for you to meet Gus. But you're not to be too nice to him, otherwise he might like you better than he likes me. Isn't life absolutely extraordinary? I thought he was going to be like all those other drones Edward's brought home, but he's not a bit."

"Lucky for him he's not, otherwise you'd have given him a really bad time."

Loveday giggled. "Do you remember Niggle, and how he nearly fainted away when Edward brought home a dead rabbit he'd shot?"

"Oh, Loveday, poor man, you were gruesome to him. And he wasn't called Niggle, he was called Nigel."

"I know, but admit, Niggle suited him much better. Niggle-Niggle. Oh, do hurry and come down, everybody's there and waiting, and we're having drinks in the garden. And we're going down to the cove this afternoon; it's high tide and we're going to swim . . ."

"I might be going to see Aunt Lavinia."

"Isn't it utterly wonderful that she didn't die? I couldn't have borne it. Now, come on. I can't wait any longer. Stop prinking. You look terrific . . ."

Following Loveday, stepping out of doors through the French windows of the drawing-room, Judith was dazzled by light. The garden was drowned in it; by a glare that the noonday sun drew and reflected from the sea, so that everything shimmered, flickered, shifted in the summer breeze. The restless leaves of the eucalyptus shivered and turned, silver and green; deep-pink petals, dropping from an overblown rose, were chased across the lawn, and the thick white fringe of Diana's garden sunshade, speared through the centre hole of an ornate cast-iron table, danced and jigged in the wind.

This table bore a tray of glasses, ashtrays, pottery bowls of potato crisps and nuts. Beyond the dark shadow of the sunshade, canvas chairs had been set up and arranged in a rough semi-circle, tartan car-rugs spread upon the grass. Nettlebed, gauging the clemency of the day, and knowing that the younger members of the Carey-Lewis clan never stayed indoors if they could possibly be out, had clearly used his forethought and been busy.

Judith looked for Edward, but he was not there. Only three figures waited for them, gracefully arranged, as though they had been posed, set there by some artist, wishful of a little human interest to enliven his landscape. This impression of a canvas—a moment caught in time—was so strong that Judith found herself regarding the scene as though appraising a painting, a brilliant oil, importantly framed in gold, hanging, perhaps, on the walls of a prestigious gallery, its title, *Before Lunch, Nancherrow, 1939.* A work that one would long to own, be impelled to buy, however costly, and keep forever.

Three figures. Athena lay on one of the rugs, propped up on her elbows, with her blonde hair blowing and her face obliterated by an enormous pair of dark glasses. The men had drawn up two of the chairs and sat facing her. One was very dark, the other fair. They had shucked off the jackets of their church-going suits, pulled off their ties and rolled up the sleeves of their shirts, and managed, despite chalk-striped trousers and polished shoes, to look comfortably informal.

Three figures. Athena, and the two young men whom Judith was yet to meet. She repeated their names to herself: Gus Callender and Rupert Rycroft. So, which of them was Gus? Which was the man who had captured the wayward Loveday's heart, and brought about, in mere days, the final transformation from deliberately gawky teenager to radiant young woman, garbed in Schiaparelli, wearing lipstick, and with the light of love shining from her violet eyes?

Loveday, unable to contain her impatience, ran to join them. "Where is everybody?" They had been deep in conversation, but thus interrupted, ceased talking. Athena stayed where she was, but the two young men heaved themselves, with some difficulty, out of their deck-chairs. "Oh, don't get up, you look so comfortable . . ." Judith followed her, out into the sunshine and across the grass, momentarily suffused with the shyness that she still experienced on meeting new people, and hoping it didn't show. Both young men, she saw, were tall, but the fair one was exceptionally lanky and thin, and the taller of the two. ". . . isn't there anything to drink? I'm parched after all that hymn-singing and praying."

"It's coming, it's coming, have a little patience," Athena told her younger sister, and Loveday collapsed onto the rug beside her. Athena turned her dark glasses onto Judith. "Hello, darling, heaven to see you. You seem to have been away for centuries. You haven't met Gus and Rupert, have you? Chaps, this is darling Judith, our surrogate sister. The house always seems half empty when she isn't here."

Athena, like her mother, had the power to make one feel special. Judith stopped being shy. She smiled and said, "Hello," and they all shook hands. Rupert was the very tall one, Athena's friend, who had sacrificed his week's sport to drive her back to Cornwall. Unmistakably Army, and the archetypal Guards officer, with his neat moustache, his relentless haircut, and an undeniably receding chin. And yet he did not look effete at all, because his face had been burnt to leather by some foreign sun, his hand-clasp was firm, and his heavy-lidded eyes looked down at her with an expression that was both amused and friendly.

But Gus was not unmistakably anything. Judith, trying to discover the single element that had finally broken down Loveday's stubborn defences, found herself at a total loss. Gus's eyes were dark as black coffee, his skin was olive, and the deep cleft in his chin looked as though some sculptor had set it there with a chisel. His mouth was wide and sweetly shaped, but unsmiling, and his whole demeanour was one of a man strangely contained, shy perhaps, but certainly giving nothing away. Relating this enigmatic young man to Loveday's ebullient, love-struck confidences was not only confusing but well-nigh impossible. How on earth had it all happened? She did not know exactly what she had expected, but certainly not this.

He had said, "How very nice to meet you," and for a moment a ghost of a smile had touched his lips, and his voice was careful, accentless, and yet without a trace of the inherited upper-class drawl of most of Edward's friends. New ground altogether, Judith decided. And indeed, why not?

"Where are you going to sit? Here, I'll get you a chair." And he went to pull one forward.

"Where *is* everybody?" Loveday asked again.

Athena told her, as the others all settled down once more in the warm sunshine. "Pops has gone up to see Mummy, and Edward's hunting up something to drink. Nettlebed didn't want to put out the booze in case it got too warm in the sun."

"Did you know Jeremy's turned up?"

"Nettlebed told us. Lovely surprise. Mummy'll be thrilled."

Judith said, "He's on embarkation leave. He's going to be a surgeon in the RNVR, and he's got to report to Devonport next week."

"Goodness," said Athena. "How dreadfully plucky. Darling man, just the sort of selfless thing he would do."

"Explain Jeremy," Rupert told her.

"Well, I was trying to, when Judith and Loveday turned up. He's another sort of surrogate member of the family. He's been around forever. His father's our doctor, and he used to be Edward's tutor. I think he arrived when we were all at church."

"He's going to stay," Judith told her. "Until it's time for him to go."

"We must all spoil him and make it very special."

Gus had laid his jacket on the grass beside him. Now he reached out a hand to pick it up, feeling in his pocket for his cigarettes and lighter. As he did this, an object slipped from an inner pocket and fell upon the grass alongside Judith's chair. She saw a small, thick sketch-book, secured with a rubber band. Loveday, sitting at his feet, saw this too and pounced upon it. "Your sketch-pad. You mustn't lose that."

He looked a bit embarrassed. "Oh . . . sorry." He put out a hand to take it, but Loveday hung on to it. "Oh, do let me show Judith. You wouldn't mind. You're so brilliant, I want her to see. Please."

"I'm sure she's not interested . . ."

"Oh, don't be so modest, Gus, of course she is. We all are. Say yes."

Judith felt a pang of pity for Gus, who clearly did not want his essentially private work to be put on display. She said, "Loveday, perhaps he doesn't want us all gawping."

"It's not gawping. It's being interested and filled with admiration."

Judith looked at Gus. "Do you carry a sketch-book with you always?"

"Yes." Suddenly he smiled at her, perhaps grateful for her championship, and the smile transformed his rather solemn features. "You never know when something will present itself, aching to be set down, and then it's agony if you haven't the means to capture it. Some people take photographs, but I'm better at drawing."

"Even in church does it happen?"

He laughed. "It might have. Although I wouldn't have had the nerve to start drawing in church. It's just that it's something I automatically carry around with me."

"Like small change."

"Precisely so." He took the book from Loveday and tossed it into Judith's lap. "Feel free."

"Are you sure?"

"Of course. Just little sketches—nothing very good."

But Loveday excitedly intervened, coming to kneel at Judith's side, slipping the rubber band off the book, laying it on Judith's knee, turning the pages, and keeping up a proud and proprietary running commentary.

". . . and this is the cove. Isn't it lovely? And Gus did it in a *moment*. And here's the rocking rock on the top of the moor, and Mrs. Mudge's barn with the hens on the steps . . ."

As the pages were slowly turned for her, Judith found herself filled with a growing wonder, because she knew that she was looking at the work of a true professional. Each small pencil sketch had been set down with the accuracy and detail of an architect's drawing, and then titled and dated in precise situation. *Nancherrow Cove. Lidgey Farm.* Drawn, he had tinted them with pale washes of water-colour, and the colours were totally original, observed by a true artist's eye, so that an old tin-mine stack stood lilac in the evening light, granite was touched by coral pink, and a slated roof was blue as hyacinths. A palette that Judith—and probably most other people—had never before perceived.

Now, a beach. Breakers rolling in onto creamy sands from a blue and blurred horizon. Another page: Rosemullion church. She saw the ancient doorway with its carved stonework, and the eleventh-century portal supported by Romanesque capitals. And she felt almost ashamed, because Gus had seen the beauty and the symmetry that Judith, coming and going through that doorway on countless occasions, had never taken time to appreciate.

They were only half-way through the book, but "This is the last," Loveday announced. "The rest is just blank." She turned the final page with a flourish. "Ta-ra ta-ra, it's me. Gus did a painting of *me*."

But there was no need to be told. Loveday, sitting on some cliff-top and silhouetted against the sea, wearing a faded pink cotton dress, her feet bare, the wind ruffling her dark curls. And Judith saw that Gus had taken a portraitist's licence, exaggerating the length of her limbs and her slender neck, the jut of her bony shoulders, the louche, uncontrived grace of her pose. Thus, somehow, he had captured the very essence of Loveday, at her most vulnerable; her sweetest. Suddenly, everything was changed, and Judith knew that the relationship between Gus and Loveday was not as one-sided as she had initially imagined, for this was a miniature portrait painted with love, and all at once she felt a bit like a voyeur, disturbing a moment of the most private intimacy.

A silence had fallen. At the edge of this she was aware of the soft voices of Rupert and Athena, chatting away together. Athena was making a daisy chain. Then Loveday spoke again, "Do you like it, Judith?" Abruptly, Judith closed the book, and secured it once more with its rubber band. "Isn't he clever?"

"Very clever." She looked up and saw that Gus was watching her. For a split second she experienced an intense rapport with him. *You understand. I know that you know. Don't say anything.* He had said nothing, but the words came through to her like a telepathic message. She smiled at him, and tossed the sketch-book over, and he caught it as though fielding a cricket ball. "More than clever. Really brilliant. Loveday's right. Thank you for letting me look."

"Not at all." He turned away from her to reach for his jacket, and the spell was broken, the moment over. "It's just a hobby." He stowed the book away in its hiding-place. "I wouldn't like to think my bread and butter depended on it."

Loveday said, "I'd bet you'd much rather be an artist than an engineer."

"I can be both."

"Even so, I somehow don't think you'd end up starving in a garret."

He laughed at Loveday, and shook his head. "I wouldn't be too sure . . ."

Somewhere inside the house, a door slammed. Her attention caught, Athena, with the daisy chain slung between her hands, looked up. "That *has* to be Edward. What has he been doing? I'm simply parched."

Edward. Astonishingly, for a little while, Judith had forgotten Edward. But now Gus and Loveday, and all speculations about them, flew from her head. Edward was nearly here. She looked and saw, from the open French windows, the two young men emerge. Edward and Jeremy, both bearing before them laden trays of bottles and glasses. And she watched them come, treading across the sunlit summer lawn, laughing together over some unheard joke, and just seeing Edward again compounded everything. She felt the lift of her heart, and her body yearned to run and meet him, and knew that this was the instant of total certainty. She loved him beyond all else, had always loved him and always would. As well, she had something wonderfully exciting to tell him . . . a secret to be shared only with Edward. And she told herself that it would be like giving him a marvellous present, a gift that had cost her much, and which she could watch him open. But that was for later. When they were alone together. Just for this moment, it was enough to watch him coming, walking across the grass.

Gus had pulled himself to his feet and now proceeded to shift things about on the table, making space for the two trays. Rupert, however, sensibly decided to stay just where he was, with his elongated frame gracefully draped in the sling of the deck-chair, and his drooping eyes half-closed against the sun.

The trays were finally set down with a thankful thump. "God, that's heavy," said Edward. "The things we do for all you lazy louts."

"We're all dry as dust," Athena complained ungratefully. "What have you been *doing?*"

"Gassing with Nettlebed."

"And Jeremy too. Such a divine surprise. Come and give me a kiss." Which, dutifully, Jeremy did. "And such a lot of new faces for you to meet. Gus. And Rupert. And everybody. Jeremy, you're going to go to sea. You are brave. I can't wait to see you in your uniform. Now, who's going to be barman? I'm dying for a gin and tonic. Have you brought some ice?"

Edward stood between Judith and the sun. She looked up into his face, saw his blue eyes and his lock of fair hair. He stooped, supporting himself on the struts of her deck-chair, to give her a kiss. He said, "You got home safely."

"About an hour ago."

He smiled and straightened up. "What do you want to drink?" And it was enough, and for the moment, she didn't need any more.

With drinks dispensed and everybody settled, they all sat around and discussed plans for the afternoon.

"We're *definitely* going to the cove," Loveday announced. "Anyway, Gus and I are going, whatever anybody else wants. The tide's high at five o'clock, and it'll be quite perfect."

"When do you want to start?" Athena asked.

"Right after lunch. As soon as possible. And take a picnic . . . oh, *do* everybody come." She looked with pleading eyes at Rupert. "*You'd* like to come, wouldn't you?"

"Of course. How about Athena?"

"I wouldn't miss it for anything. We'll all go. Except Pops. Because he's not much of a one for picnics."

"Nor your mother," said Jeremy, who had settled himself, cross-legged, on the grass, and cradled a tankard of beer. "She's having a day in bed."

"Doctor's orders?" asked Athena.

"Doctor's orders."

"She's not ill, is she?"

"No. Just a bit worn out. She'll sleep."

"In that case, let's ask Mary to join us. Perhaps she'll help with the picnic. We can't expect Mrs. Nettlebed to do another *thing* after cooking Sunday lunch for all of us. Anyway, she always puts her toes up on a Sunday afternoon, and rightly so, too."

"I'll help," Loveday offered instantly. "There's a whole new tin of chocolate biscuits and Mrs. Nettlebed's made a lemon cake. I saw it this morning before we went to church."

"And we must have gallons of tea and lemonade. And we'll take the darling doggies."

"It's beginning to sound," said Rupert, "a bit like a military expedition. I expect at any moment to be told to go and dig a latrine."

Athena gave him a slap across his knee. "Oh, don't be so stupid."

"Or pitch a tent. I'm useless at pitching tents. They always fall down."

Athena, despite herself, began to laugh. "What about camp-fires? Are you any good at those? No, on second thought, you don't need to bother because Edward will come, and he's a whiz at lighting fires."

Edward frowned. "What do you want a fire for on a day like this?"

"To cook things."

"Like what?"

"Sausages. We'll take sausages. Or baked potatoes. Or perhaps somebody will catch a fish."

"What with?"

"A trident. A bent pin on a bit of string."

"Personally, I think we should forget about lighting camp-fires. It's too hot and too much trouble. Anyway, Judith and I aren't coming."

Sounds of dismay, distress, and disappointment greeted this announcement. "But of course you must come. Why not? Why don't you want to come?"

"We have a previous engagement. We're going up to the Dower House to see Aunt Lavinia."

"Does she know?"

"Of course. Insists we come. Just for a little while, of course. But she hasn't seen Judith since she was ill. So we're going."

"Oh, well." Athena shrugged. "If it's only for a little while, you can join us later. We'll leave one of the tea-baskets for you to lug down, though, so don't *not* come, or we'll be short of food. Talking of which . . ." She pushed up her dark glasses to look at her watch.

"I know," said Rupert, "you're starving."

"How did you guess?"

"Instinct. Pure animal instinct. But hark . . ." He cocked his head. "You need faint no longer. Help is at hand . . ."

At which point Colonel Carey-Lewis made his appearance, stepping out from the drawing-room, and stalking across the lawn towards the little group that consisted of his three children and their friends. He still wore his church-going suit, and the wind caught his thinning hair and blew it into a coxcomb. As he approached, he smiled his shy smile and tried to smooth his hair down with his hand.

"How very comfortable you all look," he told them. "But I'm afraid I must disturb you." The four young men were already on their feet. "Nettlebed asks me to tell you that luncheon is just about to be served."

"Oh, darling Pops, haven't you had time for a drink?"

"I've had one. A glass of sherry with your mother."

"How is she?" Athena was getting to her feet, brushing bits of grass and daisy heads from her lap.

"All right. Mary's just taken her a bowl of soup. She says she's not feeling up to roast beef. I think she's going to stay where she is for the rest of the day."

Athena went to embrace her father. "Poor darling," she said softly. "Never mind. Come along." And she tucked her arm into his, and they started back towards the house. The rest of them hung behind, collecting glasses and beer bottles and once more stacking the trays.

Without being prompted, Gus picked up one of them. "Where do I take it?"

"If you'll follow me," Edward told him, "we'll head for Nettlebed's pantry . . ."

The small procession straggled indoors, Judith bringing up the rear and carrying an ashtray and a couple of glasses that had been forgotten. Behind her, the garden, deserted, simmered in the sunlight, and the shadow of the umbrella, with its jigging fringe, lay dark on the empty canvas chairs, the tartan rugs.

With luncheon over and the pudding plates cleared, coffee was served, at Athena's request, at the dining-room table. "If we all troop into the drawing-room," she pointed out quite rightly, "we shall collapse into armchairs, go to sleep or start reading the newspapers, and the afternoon will be over before it's even begun."

Loveday was in total agreement. "I don't want any coffee. I'm going to go and start getting the picnic ready."

"Don't get under Mrs. Nettlebed's feet," warned Mary.

"I won't. Will you come with me, Mary, and help? If there are two of us it'll be much quicker. And we want you to come with us," she added, wheedling. "You haven't come to the cove for ages. And we're going to take the dogs."

"You won't take Pekoe. He's curled up on your mother's bed like a little prince. There'll be no budging him."

"Well, we'll take Tiger. *Please* come and help me, Mary."

Mary sighed. It was clear to everybody that she would have quite liked to sit down for five minutes and digest her huge Sunday lunch, but Loveday, as always, got her own way.

"I've never known such a child as you," Mary told her, but she rose to her feet, excused herself to the Colonel, and carrying her coffee cup and saucer, followed Loveday out of the room. "We'll butter splits," Judith heard Loveday telling Mary importantly, "and put the kettle on to make gallons of tea . . ."

Edward was equally impatient, but for another reason. "I think we should skip coffee," he said to Judith, "and go to the Dower House right away. Aunt Lavinia's usually quite perky after lunch, but she gets sleepy later on and dozes off. This is the best moment to catch her at her best."

"Don't stay too long," his father warned. "Half an hour is about as much as she can stand."

"Okay, Pops, I promise."

"When will you be back?" Athena asked.

"I suppose about half past three."

"And you'll join us at the cove?"

"Of course. Expect us when you see us."

"We'll leave one of the tea-baskets on the hall table for you to carry down."

"You make it sound like a penance."

"No. Just a device to make sure you come. It's the perfect afternoon, just right for swimming off the rocks."

"We'll be there. Ready, Judith?"

She stood. The others stayed at the table, their faces turned towards her, smiling. The Colonel and Athena and Jeremy, and Rupert Rycroft and the enigmatic Gus. She said, "Goodbye."

"See you soon . . ."

"Send our love to Aunt Lavinia . . ."

"Send her my special love . . ."

"Tell her I'll be up to see her this evening . . ."

They went. Outside the front door stood a selection of cars, including Edward's own, because he had driven Athena and Rupert to church in it. They got in, and because it had been sitting in the sun, it was boiling, the leather seats hot as griddles.

"God, what a furnace." Edward rolled down windows, creating a small draught. For luncheon, in deference to his father, he had put on a tie again, but now he tore it off, and undid the top button of his blue shirt. "I should have parked in the shade. Never mind, it makes the prospect of leaping into the sea even more inviting. And when the moment comes, it will be extra splendid, knowing that you and I have done our duty."

"It's not really a *duty*," Judith pointed out, even though she did not want to disagree with him, and entirely saw his point.

"No." Edward started up the engine and they moved away, across the blistering gravel into the cool tunnel of the avenue. "But you mustn't expect her to be the same jolly, active Aunt Lavinia we've all known and loved. She's had a hell of a battering, and it shows."

"But she isn't *dead*. That's all that really matters. And she'll get strong again." She thought about this. Aunt Lavinia was, after all, very old. "Or, anyway, stronger." Another thought occurred to her. "Oh dear, I haven't got anything to take her. I should have bought flowers or something. Chocolates perhaps."

"She's overloaded with both. And grapes, and eau de cologne, and boxes of Chanel soap. It's not just the family who care about her. She has friends all over the county, who've come trundling along to pay their respects and celebrate the fact that she didn't actually kick the bucket."

"It must be lovely to be really old and still have lots of friends. It would be awful to be old and lonely."

"Or old and lonely and poverty-stricken. That's even worse."

It was such an un-Edward-like remark that Judith frowned. "How do you know?"

"Old people on the estate . . . Pops used to take me to visit them. Not in a patronizing sort of way, just to have a crack and make sure they were all right. Usually they weren't."

"So what did you do?"

"Couldn't do much. Usually they refused to be budged. Wouldn't go and live with a son or a daughter; were terrified of the stigma of any sort of social assistance. Just wanted to die in their own beds."

"It's understandable."

"Yes, but not very easy to deal with. Particularly when the cottage they inhabit is needed to house a new young ploughman or forester."

"But you couldn't possibly turn them out?"

"You sound like a Victorian novel. No, of course we didn't turn them out. We cherished them and looked after them until they finally passed on."

"And where did the young ploughman live?"

Edward shrugged. "With his own parents, or in lodgings, or something. It was just a matter of making allowances for everybody."

Judith thought of Phyllis, and told Edward about her unhappy circumstances. ". . . it was lovely seeing her, but it was horrid too, because she has to live in such a gloomy place and in such a bleak little house. And if Cyril joins up and goes to sea, then she's got to get out of it because it belongs to the mining company."

"The tied-cottage syndrome."

"It's just so dreadfully unfair."

"But if you want a man to work for you, then you have to give him a house."

"Shouldn't everyone have a house of their own?"

"That's talking about Utopia, which doesn't exist."

Judith fell silent. They were out onto the main road now, running down the hill into Rosemullion. Trees threw dark, speckly shadows onto the Tarmac, and the village drowsed in the heat, set about the small clear river, its banks yellow with kingcups. And Judith thought about Phyllis and then thought that this was a pretty funny conversation to be having with Edward, whom she loved more than anyone she had ever known, and whom she had not seen since the evening of Billy Fawcett's humiliation in the Porthkerris gutter. But it was rather nice too, because it meant they didn't just have love to talk about, but other, deeper topics. And it was easy and natural to talk to him about such things, because she had known him for so long, and he had been part of her life long before he became the whole of it.

Going back to Phyllis. "Do you think it ever will? Utopia, I mean. Do you think things ever will be right for everybody?"

"No."

"And equality?"

"There's no such thing as equality. And why are we onto such serious topics? Let's talk about something tremendously cheerful, and then we will arrive at the Dower House with beaming smiles on our faces, and everybody, including Isobel and Nurse, will be delighted to see us."

Which, of course, they were. Isobel opened the door to them just as Nurse came down the stairs, bearing Aunt Lavinia's luncheon tray. Despite the warmth of the day, Nurse was in full fig: starched apron, white veil, and thick black stockings. She was a formidable figure, and Judith felt quite relieved

344

that she wasn't the one upstairs in bed, being cared for by such a paragon—
the very idea was too intimidating, but then, Aunt Lavinia had never been
one to be intimidated by any person, not even this battleaxe.

She was called Sister Vellanowath. Edward, coming out with this mouthful, introduced Judith, and Judith, shaking hands, had to suppress shameful
laughter. Going upstairs, out of earshot, she thumped his arm with her fist.
"Why didn't you *tell* me she was called that?" she whispered furiously.

"I wanted to give you a lovely surprise."

"She *can't* be called Vellanowath."

"Yes, she can. She is." But he was laughing too.

Aunt Lavinia's bedroom was filled with sunshine, flowers, twinkling silver
and crystal, photographs, books. She lay in bed, propped up by a pile of lace-
frilled, snowy pillows, and with her shoulders wrapped in a Shetland shawl of
the very finest wool. Her white hair was neatly dressed, and as they appeared
through the open door, she took off her spectacles and held wide her arms in
welcome.

"Oh, my darlings, I've been so looking forward to this. So excited, I could
hardly eat my lunch . . . steamed fish and egg custard, and I long for lamb.
Come and give me a kiss. Dear Judith, I haven't seen you for far too long . . ."

She was thinner. Much thinner. She had lost a lot of weight, so that her
face had fallen in on its bones, and her eyes become sunken. But those eyes
were as bright as ever, and her cheeks bunched up as though she didn't know
how to stop smiling.

Judith stooped to kiss her. She said, "I feel guilty, because I haven't brought
you a present."

"I don't want presents, I just want you. And Edward. Dear boy, how perfectly sweet of you to come. I know perfectly well that on a day like this,
you're just dying to go down to the cove and jump into the sea."

Edward laughed. "You've got second sight, Aunt Lavinia, you always did
have. But don't worry, that can wait. The others are all heading off as soon
as Loveday and Mary Millyway have got the picnic ready, and later on Judith
and I will join them."

"In that case, I shan't feel selfish. Come and sit down—there's a comfy
chair—and tell me everything you've been doing. You know, I always thought
being ill would be so boring, but it's not a bit, I've seen more people and old
friends lately than I have in years. Some rather gloomy, I must admit, whispering as though I were about to pass on, but most of them just as sociable as
ever. I'd forgotten I had so many friends. Now . . ." Judith had drawn a chair
up to the bedside, and Aunt Lavinia reached out for her hand and held it
tight. It was an old lady's hand, all bones and knuckles and rings. It felt very
precious. "How was your holiday in Porthkerris? And who have you got staying at Nancherrow? And tell me all about Athena's young man . . ."

They stayed for half an hour, the length of time they had been allotted,
and for all of it they talked and laughed, and brought Aunt Lavinia up-to-
date on every single thing that had happened and was about to happen. They
told her about Rupert and about Jeremy and about Gus . . .

"Gus. That's your friend, Edward? Your father told me that Loveday has at *last* got stars in her eyes. Isn't life amazing, the way little girls suddenly grow up? I hope she doesn't get bruised. And Diana. My darling Diana. How is she holding up?"

So they told her about Diana, and Aunt Lavinia was much distressed, and had to be reassured. "Just tired. She's had so much to do."

"It's all my fault. Giving everybody such a fright. She's been a saint, the dear creature, up here every day, making sure everything is running on oiled wheels. Which, of course, it is. And if Jeremy's at Nancherrow, then he'll keep an eye on her." She did not ask why Jeremy was at Nancherrow, and, as if by tacit agreement, neither Edward nor Judith told her that he was on embarkation leave. She would only worry about him, start to fret about the sad state of the world. Right now, she could, at least, be spared that.

"And are you here for the summer?" she asked Judith.

"Well, for the time being. Later I'm going to go to Aunt Biddy in Devon. We're going to go to London for a few days to buy me some clothes for Singapore."

"Singapore! I'd forgotten you'll be leaving us. When do you sail?"

"In October."

"How long will you stay?"

"About a year, maybe."

"Oh, your mother will be ecstatic! What a reunion you will all have. I am so happy for you, my darling . . ."

But finally, time was up. Discreetly, Edward glanced at his watch. "I think perhaps we should be on our way, Aunt Lavinia . . . we don't want to tire you out."

"You haven't tired me out one little bit. Just made me feel so happy."

"Is there anything you want? Is there anything you need fetched, or anything you need done?"

"No, I have everything." And then she remembered, "Yes. There is something you can do for me."

"What's that?"

Aunt Lavinia let go of Judith's hand (she had been holding it all through their conversation), and turned in her bed to reach for the drawer of her bedside table. The drawer open, she groped inside and withdrew, attached to a crumpled label, a key. She said, "The Hut," and held it out to Edward. He took it.

"What about the Hut?"

"I am the one who takes care of it. I open it regularly and get rid of the cobwebs and the spiders and make sure it is warm and dry. It has been sadly neglected ever since I fell ill. Before you go back to Nancherrow, will you and Judith go and check and be certain that everything is all right? I am so afraid that some of the older boys in the village might come nosing around or do some sort of damage. Not maliciously, of course, just high spirits. Such a weight off my mind if you'd make certain that all is well. It's such a precious place, I would hate to lie here and think of it being unloved."

346

Edward, standing, laughed. "Aunt Lavinia, you're a constant surprise to me. The last thing you need to worry about is the Hut."

"But I do. It's important to me."

"In that case, I promise Judith and I will go and open all the doors and windows and if there is so much as a mouse or a beetle, we will send it on its way."

"I knew," said Aunt Lavinia, "that you of all people would understand."

Outside, the old-fashioned garden slumbered, scented, in the warm Sunday afternoon. Edward led the way along the path, through the rose garden, and down the flight of stone steps that led into the orchard. Here the grass had been scythed and raked into little haystacks, and on the trees the fruit had formed, and was beginning to drop, to lie, rotting and juicy, circled by wasps. The air smelt faintly of cider.

"Does the fruit get picked?" Judith asked.

"Yes. But the trouble is, the gardener's getting a bit beyond it . . . growing old, along with Aunt Lavinia and Isobel. He'll need someone to give him a hand if the apples are to be picked and stored for the winter. I'll have a word with Pops. Maybe Walter Mudge or one of the younger boys could come up one day and do the ladder-climbing."

He went ahead of her, ducking beneath the trailing branches that drooped, heavy with russet fruit. Overhead, in some tree, a blackbird was singing. The Hut, tucked into its sheltered, bosky corner, basked in sunshine. Edward went up the steps, fitted the key in the lock, and opened the door. He stepped inside. Judith followed him.

They stood, very close, in the small space between the two bunks. It still smelt pleasantly of creosote, but was hot and airless, musty with imprisoned heat. A huge bluebottle buzzed around the hurricane lamp that hung from the centre beam, and in a corner was draped an enormous cobweb studded with dead flies.

Edward said, "Yuk," and went to open the windows, all of which had warped a bit, and needed some muscular persuasion. The bluebottle buzzed away into the open air.

Judith said, "What do we do about the cobweb?"

"Remove it."

"With what?"

He delved into the bottom of the orange-box cupboard and came up with a small brush and a battered old dustpan. "Every now and again," he told her, "we had to sweep the floor." And she watched, her nose wrinkled in disgust, while he neatly dealt with the cobweb and its gruesome victims, disposed of all in the dustpan, and then went out of the door and shook the contents out onto the grass. Returning, "What else?" he asked her.

"I think that's all. No sign of mice. No bird's nests. No holes in the blankets. Perhaps the windows need cleaning."

"That'll be a nice job for you, one day when you've nothing better to do." He stowed the dustpan and brush back in their makeshift cupboard and then settled himself on the edge of one of the bunks. "You can play houses."

"Is that what you used to do?" She sat too, on the other bunk facing him across the narrow space. It was a bit like having a conversation in the cabin of a boat, or a third-class railway compartment. "Here, I mean."

"Nothing so feeble. It was the real stuff, camp-fires and all. Peeling potatoes and cooking the most disgusting meals which, for some reason, always tasted sublime. Sausages and lamb chops and fresh mackerel if we'd been fishing. But we were useless cooks. We never got it right, everything was always either raw or burnt black."

"What else did you do?"

"Nothing much. Innocent fun. The best was sleeping in the darkness with the doors and windows open and listening to the sounds of the night. Sometimes it got bloody cold. One night, there was a thunderstorm . . ."

He was so close, she could have reached out and laid her hand on his cheek. His skin was smooth and coppery, his arms downed with fine golden hair, his eyes the same blue as his cotton shirt, the lock of fair hair flopped across his forehead. She sat hugging herself, saying nothing, relishing his beauty, listening to his voice.

". . . lightning split the sky. There was a ship wrecked that night, off Land's End, and we saw the flares bursting in the sky and thought we were seeing comets . . ."

"How strange . . ."

Their eyes met. He said, "Dear Judith. You've become so lovely. Did you know that? And I did miss you."

"Oh, Edward . . ."

"I wouldn't say so if I didn't mean it. And I find it particularly nice, just sitting here, together, un-surrounded by hordes of other people."

She said, "I have something to tell you."

His expression, subtly, altered. "Important?"

"I think it is, to me."

"What is it?"

"Well . . . it's about Billy Fawcett."

"The old goat. Don't say he's raised his head again."

"No. He's gone. Gone for good."

"Elucidate."

"You were right. You said I needed a catalyst, and it happened. It changed everything."

"Tell me."

So she told him. About Ellie and her horrid experience in the cinema. About Ellie's tearful confession to the Warrens and Judith. About Mr. Warren's rage, and their subsequent visit to the police station to make the formal charge against Billy Fawcett of indecent behaviour and harassment of a junior. "It all took ages. The wheels of officialdom grind very slowly. But it was done."

"Good for you. And about time too, the rotten old bugger. What'll happen?"

"I suppose the case will come up the next Quarterly Assizes in Bodmin . . ."

"Meantime, he's stewing with apprehension. That alone should keep his hands off little girls."

"It made me feel very strong, Edward. Very positive. Not afraid any more."

He smiled. "In that case . . ." He put out his hands and laid them on her shoulders and leaned forward across the little space that lay between them, and kissed her mouth. A gentle kiss that swiftly became passionate, but this time she neither drew away nor rejected him, because to let him have his way was all she wanted, and as she opened her mouth to him, it felt as though an electric current streamed into every nerve end she possessed, and her entire body seemed to leap into life.

He stood, and put his arms around her, and lifted her, and laid her down on the bunk where she had been sitting. He sat at her side and arranged cushions behind her head, and stroked her hair away from her face, and then, gently, began to undo the small pearl buttons which fastened the front of her cotton dress.

"Edward . . ." Her voice was no more than a whisper.

"Loving doesn't stop here. This is just the beginning of loving . . ."

"I've never . . ."

"No, I know you haven't. But I have. I have been before, and I shall show you the way." He gently pushed her dress down from her shoulders, and then the white satin straps of her bra, and she could feel the cool air on her naked breasts and he put his head down and buried his face in the smooth skin that lay between them. And she wasn't frightened in the very least, just peaceful and excited all at the same time, and she took his head between her hands and gazed up into his face. "I love you, Edward. I want you to know that *now* . . ." And after that there was neither time, nor opportunity, nor need to say anything more.

A buzzing sound. Not the bluebottle this time, but an enormous droning bumble-bee, dizzy with nectar. Judith opened her eyes and watched it lumbering about in the small pitched ceiling, finally settling to cling to one of the dusty window-panes.

She stirred. Beside her, on the narrow bunk, Edward lay, his arm beneath her, Judith's head pillowed on his shoulder. She turned her head and his brilliant eyes were open, and startlingly close, so that she could see, in each iris, so many variations of blue that it was a bit like looking into the sea.

He said very gently, very quietly, "All right?"

She nodded.

"Not battered, bruised, or wounded?"

She shook her head.

"You were exceptional."

She smiled.

"How do you feel now?"

"Sleepy."

She laid a hand across his naked chest, felt the bones of his rib-cage beneath the firm sun-tanned flesh. She said, "What time is it?"

He raised his arm to look at his wrist-watch. "Half past three."

"So late."

"Late for what?"

"I thought we'd only been here for a moment or two."

"As Mary Millyway is prone to say, time flies when you're enjoying yourself." He sighed deeply. "Perhaps we should stir ourselves. We have to show up at the picnic, otherwise a thousand probing and awkward questions will be asked."

"Yes. I suppose. I know."

He kissed her. "Lie there for a bit. We're not in that much of a hurry. Raise your head and let me loose. I'm getting cramp."

Which she did, and he extricated himself and sat up, with his back to her, and pulled on his shirt and his shorts, and then his trousers, standing to shove in the shirt-tails, deal with his zip, buckle the plaited leather belt. In the orchard, beyond the opened door, the breeze stirred the branches of the apple trees, and shadows flickered on the log walls of the cabin. She heard the blackbird's song, and distant gulls, and from far off, the sound of a car, chugging up the hill out of Rosemullion. Edward left her then, and went through the door, reaching in his trouser pocket for cigarettes and lighter. Judith turned on her side and watched him; his cigarette going, he moved to lean a shoulder against the wooden post of the small veranda, and she thought that his back looked a bit like an illustration out of a Somerset Maugham story— one of the Malayan ones. A bit disheveled and deliciously decadent, with his bare feet and his tousled hair, and the worldliness of his cigarette. At any moment a dusky maiden, wearing a sarong, would come prowling up out of the jungle (the orchard) to entwine herself seductively in his arms and murmur words of love.

Edward. She could feel the smile creep into her face. Now, there could be no going back. They had taken the final step, and he had been wonderfully sweet, claiming Judith for his own in the most complete of ways; choosing her; loving her. They were a pair. A couple. Sometime, somewhere, they would be married, and together forever. About this there was no shadow of doubt, and the prospect filled her with a warm sense of continuance. For some reason, the social rites of this state—proposal, engagement, wedding—never entered her head. They were simply trimmings of convention, unimportant and almost unnecessary, because she felt as though, like pagans, she and Edward had already made their vows.

She yawned and sat up and reached for her own clothes: pants and bra, the cotton dress retrieved from the floor. She slipped it over her head and fastened the buttons and thought that she should comb her hair but she had no comb. Edward, finished with his cigarette, flicked it away and then turned and came back to her, and sat down once more, and they faced each other, just as they had done before, an hour ago, an age ago, a world ago.

She did not speak. After a bit, he said, "We really should go now."

But she didn't want to go just yet. There was so much to say. "I do love you, Edward." That was the most important. "I suppose I always have done." It was wonderful to be able to say the words, not to have to be shy or secretive any longer. "It's like suddenly having everything come true. I can't imagine, ever, loving anybody else."

He said, "But you will."

"Oh, no. You don't understand. I never could."

He repeated himself. "Yes. Yes, you will." He spoke very kindly. "You're grown up now. Not a child, not even an adolescent any longer. Eighteen. With the whole of your life ahead of you. This is just the beginning."

"I know. Of being with you. Belonging with you."

He shook his head. "No. Not with me . . ."

Confusion. "But . . ."

"Just listen. What I'm saying doesn't mean I'm not enormously, intensely fond of you. Protective. Tender. All these things. All the right words. All the right emotions. But they belong to now. This moment, this afternoon. Not exactly ephemeral, but certainly not for always."

She listened, and heard, and was stunned with disbelief. He didn't know what he was saying. He couldn't know what he was doing. She felt the warm certainty of being loved, beyond all else, forever, drain slowly from her heart, like water streaming from a sieve. How could he not feel as she felt? How could he not realize what she knew beyond all doubt? That they belonged together. They belonged to each other.

But now . . .

It was more than she could bear. She searched frantically for loopholes in his argument, reasons for his excuses, for his perfidy. "I know what it is. It's the war. There's going to be a war and you're going to have to go and fight with the RAF, and you might be killed and you don't want to leave me all alone . . ."

He interrupted her. "The war has nothing to do with it. Whether or not there is a war, I have a whole life to live before I commit myself to a single person; settle down. Have children. Take over Nancherrow from my father. I'm not twenty-two yet. I couldn't begin to make a long-term decision if somebody put a gun to my head. Maybe I will marry someday, but not until I'm at least thirty-five, and by then you will have gone your own way, and made your own decisions, and be living happily ever after." He smiled at her encouragingly. "Singapore. You're going to Singapore. You'll probably marry some enormously wealthy taipan or tea-planter and be living a life of tremendous luxury, with all the riches of the East, waited upon by soft-footed servants."

He sounded like a grown-up trying to coax a sulky child into a good humour. "And just think of the voyage out. I don't imagine you'll get as far as the Suez Canal without at least two dozen proposals . . ."

He was talking rubbish. She lost her patience, and rounded on him.

"Don't joke about it, Edward, because it's not in the least funny."

Wryly, "No. I suppose it isn't. I'm whistling in the dark, because I hate to hurt you in any way."

"What you're saying is that you don't love me."

"I do."

"Not the way I love you."

"Perhaps not. Like I said, I feel ridiculously protective about you, as though I were in some way responsible for your happiness. Like Loveday, and yet not like Loveday, because you're not my sister. But I've watched you growing up, and you've been part of Nancherrow and the family all these years. That incident with the wretched Billy Fawcett brought it all home to me. How alone you are, and how vulnerable. It made my flesh creep to think of you being traumatized by that bloody old man. I couldn't stand thinking of it happening again . . ."

She began, at last, to understand. "So you slept with me. You made love to me. *You* did it."

"I wanted to lay his ghost forever. It had to be me, not some incompetent, lusty lout relieving you of your sweet virginity, giving you a miserable time, and destroying all the joys of sex."

"You were doing me a kindness. You were sorry for me. A good deed." She realized that her head was starting to ache. She could feel the pain, like tight strings pulling behind her eyeballs, a throbbing in her temples. "A good turn," she finished bitterly.

"Darling Judith, never think that. Give me the benefit, at least, of loving you with the best of intentions."

But that wasn't enough. Would never be enough. She looked down, away from his eyes. Her feet were still bare. She stooped and picked up one of her sandals, and began to put it on, buckling the leather strap. She said, "I seem to have made a terrible fool of myself. But perhaps that's not surprising."

"Never. Not that. It's not foolish to love. It's just pointless giving all your love to the wrong person. I'm not right for you. You need somebody quite different from me; an older man who'll give you all the wonderful things you rightly deserve, and that I could never find it in my heart to promise you."

"I wish you'd said all this before."

"Before, it wasn't relevant."

"You sound like a lawyer."

"You're angry."

She turned on him. "Well, what do you *expect* me to be?" Her aching eyes were hot with unshed tears. He saw these and said, in some alarm, "Don't cry."

"I'm not crying."

"I can't bear it if you cry. You'll make me feel such a shit."

"So what happens now?"

He shrugged. "We're friends. Nothing changes that."

"We just carry on? Being tactful and not allowing Diana to be upset? Like we did before. I don't know if I can do that, Edward."

He stayed silent. She began to fasten the other sandal, and after a bit, he shoved his bare feet into his shoes and did up the laces. Then he stood, and went to close and latch the windows shut. The bumble-bee had flown. She got to her feet. He went to the door and stood, waiting for her to go out before him. As she did so, he stopped her with his arm, and turned her to face him. She looked up into his eyes, and he said, "Try to understand."

"I do understand. Perfectly. But that doesn't make it any easier."

"Nothing's changed."

Which Judith thought was perhaps the most stupid, untrue thing she had ever heard any man say. She pulled away from him and plunged out into the orchard, running through the grass, ducking beneath the branches, and willing herself not to burst into tears.

Behind her, he closed and carefully locked the door. It was done. It was all over.

They returned to Nancherrow in a silence that was neither painful nor companionable. Sort of half-way in between. Certainly this was not the moment for small talk, and Judith's headache had reached proportions which rendered her incapable of any conversational effort, however trivial. She was beginning to feel a bit nauseous and there were strange tadpole shapes swimming about in her line of vision. She had never had a migraine, but girls at school sometimes had them and had tried to describe the symptoms. She wondered if she was starting a migraine now, but probably not, because she knew they took ages, sometimes days, to develop, and hers had struck out of the blue, like a hammer-blow.

She thought, with sinking heart, of the next stage of this endless day. Arriving home, and then starting out once more, to join the picnic party down at the cove. Walking down the garden, through the gunnera, across the quarry; emerging onto the cliffs, and seeing below them the others, camped upon the traditional rock. Brown bodies, oiled against the sun, brilliant towels spread about the place, straw-hats and abandoned clothes left lying where they had fallen. Voices raised, and the splash as someone dived from the high rock above the pool. And above everything, the glitter of light, the unrelenting brightness of sea and sky.

All too much. As they approached the house, she took a deep breath and said, "I don't think I want to come to the cove."

"You must come." Edward's voice was edged with impatience. "You know they're expecting us."

"I've got a headache . . ."

"Oh, *Judith* . . ." He clearly thought this was some excuse she had invented.

"I really have. It's true. My eyes are hurting and I can see tadpoles and my head's torture and I feel a bit sick."

"Really?" Now he was concerned. He turned his head to look at her. "I say, you do look a bit pale. Why didn't you say?"

"I'm saying now."

"When did it start?"

"A bit ago," was the best she could come up with.

"I am sorry." He was truly contrite. "Poor Judith. In that case, when we get in, why don't you go and take an aspirin or something and lie down for a bit. You'll feel better before long. We can go down to the cove later. They won't be packing up until at least seven o'clock, so there's hours yet."

"Yes." She thought, with longing, of her own quiet room, the curtains drawn against the unforgiving light, the coolth of soft linen beneath her throbbing head. Peace. Solitude. A little space of time in which to gather up her dignity and lick her wounds. "Perhaps I will. You mustn't wait for me."

"I don't want to leave you on your own."

"I won't be on my own."

"Yes, you will. Mary's gone to the cove with the others, and Pops will be doing his Sunday circuit of the farms with Mr. Mudge."

"Your mother will be there."

"She's ill."

"I'll be all right."

"But you will come, when your headache's gone?"

It seemed important to him. To save an argument, she said, "Yes. When it's cooler, maybe."

"An evening swim will do you all the good in the world. Chase the miseries away; clear your head."

And she thought how wonderful that would be, and if only it were possible. But whatever you did, the inside of your head went on churning away, and you couldn't get away from the treadmill of remembering things that you longed to forget.

They were back. Edward drew up outside the open front door, and they got out of the car and went into the house. There, on the table in the centre of the hall, stood the picnic basket, packed with tin boxes and Thermos flasks. But as well, neatly folded on the top of these, were two red-and-white-striped towels, Edward's trunks and Judith's bathing costume. Beside the basket, weighted down with the brass letter-tray, was a note from Athena.

> Don't say we don't think of everything. Bathers at the ready to save you time. Come right away. No hanging about. X. Athena.

Edward read this aloud. Judith said, "You'd better go."

But he clearly felt guilty about leaving her on her own. He put his hands on her shoulders and gazed down into her face. "Are you *sure* you'll be all right?"

"Of course."

"Have you got an aspirin?"

"I'll find one. Just go, Edward."

But still he lingered. "Am I forgiven?"

He was like a small boy, resenting another person's displeasure, needing reassurance that all was right with his world.

"Oh, Edward. It was just as much my fault as yours." Which was true, but so shame-making, it was unpleasant to think about.

It was, however, enough for Edward. "Good." He smiled. "I don't like you being angry with me. I couldn't bear the thought of us not being friends." He gave her a little hug, then let her go and turned to lift the heavy basket off the table and make for the door.

On the way out, he turned for the last time. "I shall be waiting for you," he told her.

Judith could feel the stupid tears again come swimming up into her eyes, and it was not possible to speak. So she nodded, willing him to go, and he walked away from her, through the open door, was silhouetted for an instant against the sunlight, and then gone. The sound of his footsteps on the gravel faded and died into the hot, slumbrous Sunday afternoon.

She stood, and the house was empty and silent. No sound. Just the slow tick of the tall grandfather clock that stood at the foot of the stairs. She saw that it was a quarter past four. Everybody was gone, dispersed. Only she herself, and, upstairs, the invalid, probably asleep in her lavish bed, with Pekoe curled up beside her.

She went towards the staircase, intending to make her way upstairs, but for some reason she felt so exhausted that, instead, she sank down on the bottom stair and leaned her forehead against the cool wood of the banister. The tears now were flowing, and the next thing she knew was that she was weeping, sobbing like a child. It didn't matter, of course, because there was no person to hear, and it was something of a relief just to give way to her misery and let it all pour out. Her eyes streamed and her nose was running, and of course she had no handkerchief, so she tried wiping her eyes on the skirt of her dress, but she could scarcely blow her nose on it . . .

At that moment, she heard footsteps, briskly making their way along the upper landing. At the top of the staircase, they paused. "Judith?"

Mary Millyway. Judith froze, half-way through a deep, gulping sob.

"What are you doing there?"

But Judith, frantically mopping at tears, was not capable of making any sort of a reply.

Mary was coming downstairs.

"I thought you were both back ages ago, and gone to the cove hours before this. And then from the nursery window I saw Edward going down the garden on his own. Mrs. Boscawen's all right, isn't she?" Her voice became sharp with anxiety. "Nothing's wrong, is it?"

Reaching Judith's side, Mary laid a hand on her shoulder. Judith wiped her nose, like an urchin, on the back of her hand. She shook her head. "No. She's all right."

"You didn't stay with her too long? Tire her out?"

"No, we didn't."

"Then what took you so *long?*"

"We went to the Hut to clean out the cobwebs."

"So what are all the tears about?" Mary sat on the stair beside Judith, and laid an arm around her shoulders. "Tell Mary. What is it? What's happened?"

"Nothing. I've . . . I've just got a headache. I didn't want to go to the cove." Only then did she turn her face to Mary. She saw the familiar freckled face, the concerned and kindly expression in Mary's eyes. "You . . . you haven't got a handkerchief, have you, Mary?"

"Of course." And one was produced from the pocket of Mary's striped overall, and handed over, and Judith, gratefully, blew her nose. Being able to stop snivelling made her feel, very slightly, better. She said, "I thought *you* were meant to be going to the cove too, with all the others."

"No, I didn't go. Didn't like to leave Mrs. Carey-Lewis on her own in case she needed something. Now, what are we going to do about this headache? Sitting here like a load of old coal isn't going to get rid of it. How about coming up to the nursery with me, and I'll find something in my medicine cupboard. And then a nice quiet sit-down and a cup of tea. I was just thinking of putting a kettle on . . ."

The comfort of her presence, her aura of normality and good sense, were like a sort of balm. She stood, and helped Judith to her feet, and led her upstairs and into the nursery; settled her down in a corner of the saggy old sofa, and went to draw the curtain a little so that the sun would not shine into Judith's eyes. Then she disappeared into the adjoining bathroom and returned with a glass of water and a couple of tablets.

"Take those now, and you'll be better in no time. Just sit quiet, and I'll get the tea made."

Judith dutifully took the tablets and washed them down with the cold, clear water. She lay back and closed her eyes, and felt the breeze moving through the open window, and smelt the comforting nursery smell of newly ironed linen and sweet biscuits and the roses that Mary had picked and arranged in a blue-and-white jug in the middle of the table. Her hand was still clenched around Mary's handkerchief, and she clung to it, as though it were some sort of a talisman.

Presently Mary returned, bearing teapot and cups and saucers on a little tray. Judith stirred, but, "Don't you move now," Mary told her. "I'll put the tray down on this little stool." She pulled up her old nursing chair and settled herself comfortably with her back to the window. "There's nothing like a cup of tea when you're feeling a bit down in the mouth. Got your period, have you?"

Judith could have lied and said yes, and it would have been a splendid excuse, but she had never lied to Mary, and even now could not bring herself to do so.

"No. No, it's not that."

"When did it start?"

"Sometime . . . this afternoon." She took the steaming teacup from Mary's hand, and her own hand shook a bit and the teacup rattled. "Thank you, Mary. You are a saint. I'm so glad you didn't go to the cove. I don't know what I'd have done if you hadn't been here."

"I don't think," said Mary, "that I've ever seen you cry like that before."

"No, I don't suppose you have . . ."

She drank her tea. In sips; scalding hot and wonderfully refreshing.

"Something happened, didn't it?" Judith glanced up, but Mary was concentrating on pouring a cup of tea for herself.

"Why do you say that?"

"Because I'm not a fool. I know all you children like I know the back of my hand. Something's happened. You wouldn't be in tears for nothing, sobbing your heart out as though you'd lost the world."

"I . . . I don't know if I want to talk about it."

"If you talk about it to anybody, you can talk about it to me. I've got eyes, Judith, I've watched you growing up. I've always been a bit afraid that this might happen."

"What might happen?"

"It's Edward, isn't it?"

Judith looked up and saw in Mary's face neither curiosity nor disapproval. She was simply stating a fact. She would neither judge nor blame. She had seen too much of life, and she knew the Carey-Lewis children, with all their charm and all their faults, better than anyone.

She said, "Yes. It's Edward." The relief of admitting it, saying it out loud, was immense.

"Fallen in love with him, have you?"

"It was almost impossible not to."

"Had a row?"

"No. Not a row. Just a sort of misunderstanding."

"Talked it through, have you?"

"I suppose that's what we've been doing. But all we've discovered is that we don't feel the same way. You see, I thought it was all right to tell him how I felt. I thought we'd passed the stage of pretending. But I was completely wrong, and at the end of it all, I knew all I'd done was to make a complete fool of myself . . ."

"Now don't start to cry again. You can tell me. I'll understand . . ."

With some effort Judith pulled herself together, dabbed at her face with the wadded handkerchief. She drank a bit more tea. She said, "Of course he's not in love with me. He's fond of me, like Loveday, but he doesn't want me for always. The thing is, that it . . . happened once before. Last Christmas. But I was too young then to deal with it . . . I sort of panicked. And we had a row then, and it could all have been most dreadfully difficult and embarrassing for everybody. But it wasn't, because Edward was so sensible and ready to forget what had happened and start all over again. And it was all right. But this afternoon . . ." But of course she couldn't tell Mary. It was too intimate. Private. Even shocking. She sat gazing down at her teacup, and she could feel the traitorous, rosy blush creep up into her cheeks.

Mary said, "Gone a bit too far this time, has it?"

"You could say that."

"Well, it's happened before and it'll happen again. But I feel some vexed with Edward. He's a lovely man and he'd charm the birds out of the trees, but he's no thought for others, nor for the future. Skims over life like a dragonfly. Never knew such a boy, making friends and bringing them home, and then on to the next one, before you could say Jack Robinson."

"I know. I suppose I've always known."

"Like another cup of tea?"

"In a moment."

"How's that headache?"

"A bit better." Which it was. But its easement had left a void, as though the pain had drained her mind of all substance. "I told Edward I'd go down to the cove. Later on. When it's cooler."

"But you don't want to go?"

"No. But it's nothing to do with the way I feel. It's because I don't want to see them all . . . Loveday and Athena and the others. I don't want them looking at me, and asking questions, and wondering what's happening. I don't want to face anybody. I wish I could just disappear."

She waited for Mary to say, "Don't be so silly; no point in running away; nobody disappears; you can't just disappear." But Mary didn't make any of these damping observations. Instead, "I don't think that's such a bad idea," she said.

Judith looked at her in amazement, but Mary's face was quite calm.

"What *do* you mean, Mary?"

"Where's Mrs. Somerville now? Your Aunt Biddy?"

"Aunt *Biddy?*"

"That's right. Where's she living?"

"In Devon. Bovey Tracey. In her house there."

"You're going to stay with her?"

"Yes. Sometime."

"I'm interfering, I know. But I think you should go now."

"Now?"

"Yes. Now. This very afternoon."

"But I couldn't just *go* . . ."

"Now listen, my dear. Just bear with me. Someone has to say this, and there's nobody but me to do it. Your own mother is on the other side of the world, and Mrs. Carey-Lewis, for all her kindness, has never been much use at this sort of thing. I said before, I've watched you growing up, known you since the day Loveday brought you here from school. I've seen you being absorbed by this family, and become part of them, and a wonderful thing it's been. But it's dangerous too. Because they're *not* your family, and if you're not very careful, you're in danger of losing your own identity. You're eighteen now. I think it's time to break loose and go your own way. Now, don't for an instant think that I want to be rid of you. I shall miss you very, very much, and I don't want to lose you. It's just that you're a person in your own right, and I'm afraid that if you live here, at Nancherrow, much longer, you're going to lose sight of that."

"How long have you thought this, Mary?"

"Since last Christmas. I guessed then that you were getting involved with Edward. I prayed you wouldn't, because I knew how it would end."

"And, of course, you were right."

"I don't like being right. I only know that they're a lot of strong characters, these Carey-Lewises. A family of born leaders, you might say. You've landed yourself in a bit of an emotional mess, but the best thing to do at such times is to grasp the nettle. Take the initiative. If for no other reason, it helps to shore up your own dignity."

And Judith knew that she was right. Because much the same thing had happened the evening Billy Fawcett gave such a fright to poor Ellie in the cinema, and Judith had taken control and swept everybody off to the police station to lodge complaints. And afterwards, she had never felt so strong or so positive, and Billy Fawcett had been exorcised for ever.

Aunt Biddy. The very idea of getting away from Edward, and Nancherrow and all of them, just for a little while, was enormously tempting. Just for long enough to get everything in proportion, to deal with heartbreak, and get her life back on the rails again. Aunt Biddy did not know Edward. Aunt Biddy would ask no questions, simply be delighted to have a bit of company, and the excuse for a cocktail party or two.

But the complications of departure were too numerous to be dealt with. "How can I just go? How can I leave? Without any sort of excuse? It would be *too* ill-mannered."

"Well, the first thing to do is to go downstairs to the Colonel's study, and telephone Mrs. Somerville. Have you got her number? Good. So you ring her up and ask her if she'd mind if you turned up this evening. You can make some excuse or other if she asks to know why. You can drive in your little car. It shouldn't take you more than four hours, and with a bit of luck there won't be too much traffic."

"Supposing she isn't there? Or she doesn't want me?"

"She'll want you. You were going to visit her anyway, it's just a question of arriving a bit early. And then we'll make *her* the reason for your going. We'll tell a lie. Say she's unwell, all alone, got 'flu, needs nursing, broken her leg. We'll say she rang you; a call for help, and it sounded so urgent you just got straight into your car, and went."

"I'm useless at telling lies. Everybody will know I'm telling a lie."

"You don't need to tell the lie. I will. The Colonel won't be back until dinner time this evening. He and Mr. Mudge have gone to see some cattle out Saint Just way. And Edward and Athena and Loveday and the others won't come up from the cliffs for two hours or so yet."

"So, you mean . . . I won't have to say goodbye . . ."

"You don't need to see any of them again, not until you're strong enough, and ready."

"I will come back, though. I'll come back before I go to Singapore. I'll have to say goodbye to the Colonel and Diana."

"Of course. And that'll be something for us all to look forward to. But right now, it's expecting too much of you, just to carry on after what's happened. And, as well, I think it's asking too much of Edward."

"It's a sort of catalyst, isn't it?"

"I've no idea what a catalyst is. I only know you can't be anybody but yourself. At the end of the day, you're stuck with that."

"You sound like Miss Catto."

"I could do worse."

Judith smiled. She said, "And what about you, Mary? You're part of the family too, but I don't think of you as being absorbed by them, or ever losing your own identity."

"I'm different. I work for them. This is my job."

"But you could never leave them."

Mary laughed. "Is that what you think? You think I'm going to stay forever, growing older and less useful. Doing a bit of ironing, waiting for Athena to start a string of babies, dealing with another generation of sleepless nights, and strings of nappies, and potty-training? And then having a stroke or something; becoming senile. A burden. Having to be cared for. Is that how you see my future?"

Judith felt a bit embarrassed because, in a shameful way, it was. The devoted servant, the old retainer, sitting shawled in a chair, knitting garments that nobody would ever want to wear, being brought cups of tea, and privately moaned about because she was such a nuisance. She said, "I just can't imagine you being anywhere else except Nancherrow."

"Well, you're wrong. When I'm sixty, I shall retire and go and live in a cottage on my brother's farm up Falmouth way. It belongs to me. I saved up my money, and I bought it from him, for two hundred and fifty pounds. So I shall be independent. And that's how I shall end my days."

"Oh, Mary, good for you. But what they'll all do without you I can't imagine."

"They'll manage. Nobody's indispensable."

"Do they know about your plans?"

"The Colonel does. When I bought the cottage, I told him then. Took him into my confidence. He came and looked at the cottage, and paid for me to have a survey done."

"And Mrs. Carey-Lewis?"

Mary laughed and shook her head. "I don't suppose, for a single moment, that the Colonel has told her. He protects her, you see. From everything. Like a child. Now . . ." Once more Mary became practical. "We're wasting time. Sitting here gabbing isn't going to get the baby bathed. If you're going to go, then we must get moving . . ."

"Will you help me pack?"

"Ring your auntie first," said Mary. "No point in putting the cart before the horse."

Diana awoke. She had slept the afternoon away. She knew this, even as she opened her eyes, because the sun had dropped in the sky, and its beams now slanted down through her western window. Beside her, Pekoe still slumbered. She yawned and stretched, and settled back again on her pillows and thought how perfect it would be if sleep could not only restore one but iron out all anxieties in the same process, so that one could wake with a totally clear and untroubled mind, as smooth and empty as a beach, washed and ironed by the outgoing tide.

But that was not to be. She awoke, and all her pressing anxieties at once crowded about her and raised their heads again. They had simply been waiting for her. Aunt Lavinia, recovered but still so frail. And a war waiting to pounce. When, nobody knew. Two weeks' time, perhaps. A week. Even days. The endless wireless bulletins, and the newspapers, and the headlines that grew graver by the hour. Edgar's expression of anguish tore at her heart. He tried to hide it from her, but did not always succeed.

And the young ones. Jeremy, her stalwart, the strong pillar of so many years. But now on embarkation leave, committed to the Royal Navy, already on his way. He was the first to go, but as soon as war was declared, all the others would be in the front line of the call-up. Her precious Edward to fly those dreadfully dangerous aeroplanes—quite dangerous enough without having some German firing bullets at you at the same time. And his friend Gus, who was already an officer in the Gordon Highlanders. They would never return to the dreaming spires of that lovely city, with nothing to do but absorb knowledge and enjoy themselves. As for Rupert, he of course was a regular soldier, but the added complication there was that he and Athena wanted to get married, and he would be sent off to some inhospitable desert with his horse, and get shot at, and Athena would be left on her own for years and years, wasting her youth. All of them, the *jeunesse d'or*, wasting the precious years that would never come again.

And little Loveday. Seventeen and in love for the first time, without any hope of starting any sort of relationship with the object of her girlish dreams. Diana could not imagine what would happen to Loveday. Dumped down in the middle of another terrible war, it was impossible to imagine how Loveday would react. But then, she had always been totally unpredictable.

She stirred and turned her head to look at her little gold bedside clock. It was half past four. She longed for tea, but hadn't the heart to ring her bell and summon Mrs. Nettlebed to come trudging up the back stairs on her swollen feet. As well, Diana was bored. Perhaps she would get up . . . If she could summon the energy, she would get up, have a bath, get dressed, go downstairs. Jeremy had told her to stay where she was, but he couldn't imagine the boredom . . .

Someone knocked on the panel of her door.

"Who is it?"

The handle turned and the door opened a crack. "It's me. Judith. Are you awake?"

"Yes, I am."

"I'm not disturbing you?"

"Not a bit. I was just thinking how bored I was. I need somebody to talk to."

Judith came in, shut the door behind her, and crossed the room to sit on the edge of Diana's bed. She looked very neat and tidy in a white blouse with a frilled collar, and a blue-and-white-striped cotton skirt. Her hair was smooth and newly brushed and she had cinched her slender waist with a scarlet leather belt.

"How are you feeling now?" Judith asked.

"Oh, better. Just lazy."

"Did you sleep?"

"All afternoon." Diana frowned. "Why aren't you down at the cove with all the others?"

"I had a bit of a headache. Edward went down by himself."

"It's the heat. How's Aunt Lavinia?"

"She was wonderful. Full of chat. Amazing, really, considering what she's been through."

"Do you think she'll ever be able to do all the lovely things she did before?"

"Of course." Judith hesitated for a moment, and then said, "Diana, I've got something to tell you. To explain. I've got to go away. Now."

Astonishment. "Go away? But, darling, why?"

"It's a bit complicated. It's just that I was having tea with Mary, and there was a telephone call . . ."

"I didn't hear it . . ."

"You were asleep, I expect. It's my Aunt Biddy. Biddy Somerville. She's had the most horrible dose of 'flu, and of course Uncle Bob and Ned are both away at sea, and she's on her own, and she hasn't got anybody living in now, just a daily lady who comes up on her bicycle from Bovey Tracey. Anyway, it's a sort of cry for help, and she said would I be able to go and keep an eye on her. Her doctor says she shouldn't be alone."

"But, my darling, how perfectly frightful. Poor woman. Would you like to ask her to come here and be with us?"

"Oh, you are sweet, but I don't think she could make the journey. I think I must go to her. I was going anyway, later on. So it doesn't make that much difference if I go now."

"What a good girl you are." Judith smiled. And it occurred to Diana then that she was looking most dreadfully tired. Her lovely eyes were sunken and the bright lipstick only accentuated the pallor of her cheeks. Poor child, she had been suffering from a headache, but just for an instant Diana wondered what had caused her indisposition. She should ask, she knew, show motherly concern, but in her present state she didn't feel strong enough to deal with any more confidences, any more problems. As well, there was always the possibility that it had something to do with Edward, and for that reason alone, it was much better that she knew nothing. Besides, at the end of the day, much as she loved Judith, Judith was not her child, and for the time being Diana had quite enough on her plate, endeavouring to cope with all the uncertainty of what was going to happen to her own children. So, "Of course you must go if you're needed so badly. How will you get there?"

"I'll take my car."

"You will drive carefully, won't you?"

"Of course."

"When are you setting off?"

"Right now. Mary helped me pack a suitcase. Just one or two things. I don't suppose I shall be there for very long. But I will come back, if I may, because I want to see you all again before I sail for Singapore."

"But of course you'll come back."

"And you'll explain to the Colonel for me?"

"I forgot. You won't have *seen* him. And the others. How horrid to go without saying goodbye to all the others. Can't you just nip down to the cove for a moment before driving away?"

"There's no time. You must say goodbye to them for me."

"I'll do that, but I know they'll all be *terribly* upset."

"I . . . I'm sorry about this. It's sweet of you to understand."

"Oh, darling, not your fault." Judith stood, and moved to stoop and kiss Diana's cheek.

Judith said, "It's only for a little while."

"In that case we won't say goodbye. Just *au revoir*."

"*Au revoir.*"

"Good journey." Judith smiled, and turned and went to the door. But as she was leaving, Diana called her back. "Judith."

"What is it?"

"Is Mary around?"

"Yes."

"Tell her Pekoe needs to go out into the garden for a wee-wee. And ask her to be a saint and bring me a cup of tea."

Judith closed the door behind her, and went down the passage to the nursery. Mary was waiting for her, sitting on the window-seat and looking down into the garden. When Judith said her name, she turned her head, and pulled herself to her feet.

"Did you see Mrs. Carey-Lewis?"

"Yes. She was awake. I've told my lie. It's all right. She didn't ask any questions . . . she just asked me to tell you that Pekoe needs to be taken out to do wees, and she wondered if you'd be a saint and take her a cup of tea."

Mary smiled wryly. "Never ends, does it?"

"I would have felt really guilty leaving without saying goodbye to her."

"No. It wouldn't have done. So. That's it. Now. Time to be off. I'll come and see you away . . ."

But Judith stopped her. "No. Please don't. I couldn't bear it. I'll just start crying again."

"You're sure?"

"Certain."

"Well. Goodbye then." They embraced, hugging enormously. "It's just for a little while, mind. We'll see you soon. Keep in touch. Drive safely now."

"Of course."

"Got enough petrol, have you? There's a garage in Penzance, near the station, open all Sundays."

"I'll fill up there."

"And money? Got plenty of cash?"

"Ten pounds. That's more than enough."

"Don't grieve for Edward," Mary told her. "Don't look back, nor let your heart be broken. You're too young and too lovely for that."

"I'll be all right."

She left Mary, standing alone and at something of a loss, in the middle of the nursery. She went along the passage and ran downstairs. She had already fetched her car from the garage, and Mary had stowed her suitcase on the back seat. She got in behind the wheel and started the engine and put the car into gear. The wheels rolled forward across the gravel. It was agony not crying, but she managed not to.

She told herself, "It's not forever," but it felt like that. And out of nowhere, the words of a poem sprang into her head, and she remembered her mother, reading aloud, long ago, when she was just a little child in Colombo.

> To house and garden, field and lawn
> The meadow-gates we swang upon

She looked in her wing mirror and saw there, framed, the miniature reflection of Nancherrow, washed in sunlight, receding away, all the time becoming smaller.

> To pump and stable, tree and swing,
> Goodbye, goodbye, to everything.

And she remembered coming for the first time, in Diana's Bentley, and seeing the house and the gardens and the distant sea, and being instantly captivated, falling in love. And she knew that she would come back, but knew too that Nancherrow as she had known it would never, ever, be quite the same again.

And then she was into the trees, and it was gone, and Edward was gone, and once again she was on her own.

Part Two

Coming Home

Biddy Somerville's house, perched on the hill above the little town of Bovey Tracey, was called Upper Bickley. Its date was carved into the lintel over the front door, 1820, so it was quite old, solidly built of stone which had been plastered and whitewashed, and with a slated roof and tall chimneys. Indoors the ceilings were low, and floors sometimes crooked. Doors, closed, did not always stay closed. On the ground floor were kitchen, dining-room, sitting-room, and hall. A large cupboard had been converted to a downstairs lavatory, where coats were hung and rubber boots jostled for space with a selection of guns and fishing-rods, game-bags and gaffs. Upstairs were three bedrooms and a bath, and up again, a musty loft packed with sea-chests, old photographs, various items of moth-eaten naval uniform, and Ned's toy trains and jigsaw puzzles, long since forgotten and abandoned but which Biddy could never bring herself to throw away.

The house was reached by a steep, narrow, winding Devon lane—a hazard in itself, and impassable in snow—and the entrance was a farm gate which always stood open.

Beyond the gate, a pebbled approach led to the main door, which was at the back of the house. The garden was not large. Some grass at the front, and unambitious flower-beds, and beyond a few useful outbuildings, a small vegetable plot, and a green for hanging out the washing. Then, sloping up the hill, a paddock where some former owner had kept his ponies. At the top of this stood a copse of stringy pine trees, and a stone boundary wall, and over the wall was the beginning of Dartmoor—a sweep of turf and bracken and heather and bog leaning up to the distant skyline, crowned by brooding tors. In wintertime, the wild ponies, searching for fodder, sometimes made their way down as far as the wall, and

Biddy would take pity on the dear shaggy creatures and feed them hay. In wintertime, the wind blew a good deal of the time and the coast was shrouded in rain, but in summer and on clear days, there was a spectacular southwestern view, over the clustered grey roofs of the little town, to green fields and the hedgerows of farmland, to Torbay and the twinkling sea of the English Channel.

The Somervilles, with a certain amount of courage, had bought Upper Bickley in a state of some dilapidation. It had stood empty for four years, following the demise of the old lady who had lived there for half a century, because her four grown-up children, squabbling and feuding, could not decide what to do with the property. Eventually, an exasperated (and honest) lawyer intervened, told the sullen family to stop wasting his time, take their fingers out and pull themselves together, and at last got them to agree to putting the house on the market. The Somervilles drove from Plymouth to look it over, realized that the asking price was ridiculously low, and snapped it up. There followed the inevitable hiatus of refurbishment. Builders, electricians, plumbers, plasterers, and carpenters trod their booted way through the old rooms, forgot vital pieces of equipment, hammered enormous masonry nails through hidden pipes, hung wallpaper upside down, and put the end of a ladder through the glass panes of the arched staircase window. Biddy spent her time bullying and coaxing them along, alternatively giving them cups of tea and pieces of her mind. Finally, however, Bob pronounced Upper Bickley more or less shipshape, the rattling lorries and vans drove out of the gate for the last time, and Biddy moved in.

It was the first house she had ever owned, and it was so very different from living in naval quarters that the novelty took some time to wear off. She had never been much of a housekeeper or a homemaker, and both Mrs. Cleese and Hobbs—those stalwarts of Keyham Terrace days—were gone. Mrs. Cleese had left because she didn't like the country, greatly distrusted cows, and wanted to stay in Plymouth. And Hobbs was gone because, reaching a certain age, he had been forcibly retired by Their Lordships, and almost immediately died. Biddy, dutifully attending his funeral, swore she heard his creaking boots as he passed on to the great Corporal's Mess in the sky.

Other help had to be found. There was no space in Upper Bickley for a living-in domestic, and anyway, Biddy didn't want a liver-in. Instead, she engaged the services of two local ladies who came each day, one to cook and one to clean. They arrived in tandem, at eight in the morning, and left at twelve. Mrs. Lapford was the cook, and Mrs. Dagg the housemaid. Mrs. Dagg's husband, Bill, was a ploughman and worked with heavy horses on a nearby farm, but turned up, on Saturdays and summer evenings, to do a bit of labouring in Biddy's garden. It was hard to say which of them knew less about growing flowers and vegetables, but Bill was quite good at digging, and of course always able to lay his hands on copious quantities of horse manure. In his care the roses, if nothing much else, flourished.

With domestic problems out of the way, Biddy cast about for social stimulation. She had no intention of spending her days arranging flowers, making jam, knitting socks, or going on bus trips with the local Women's Institute, but finding other diversions proved no problem at all. She already had a wide circle of naval friends living well within reach, and before long made the acquaintance of, and was taken up by, a number of county families residing in impressively old inherited establishments surrounded by acres of land. Newcomers did not always slip easily through the doors of these great houses, but the Royal Navy made one automatically persona grata, and hospitality was generous. Biddy was invited to ladies' luncheons, with an afternoon of bridge or mah-jong to follow. Bob was asked to shoot pheasants, or offered excellent fishing. Together, they attended immensely formal dinner parties, slightly less formal race-meetings, and cheerful, family-orientated tennis afternoons. Gregarious and amusing, they were also meticulous and open-handed about returning hospitality, and so, with one thing and another, in no time at all they found themselves home and dry; accepted.

August 1939, and Biddy was content. The only cloud on her horizon, and it was a great one, was the darkening threat of war.

Sunday evening; half past nine now, and Biddy sat by the open window of her sitting-room watching the dusky shadows gather across the garden and the light fade from the sky. She was waiting for Judith. Bob had been home for the weekend, but after tea had set off in his car, back to Devonport. He did not have to go but, in these tense times, he became edgy if away from his office for more than a day, needing to be on duty in case some vital signal should come through demanding his immediate attention and consequent action.

And so she was alone. But not alone, because she had a dog lying at her feet. The dog was a Border collie, irregularly patched and with an engaging face that was half black and half white. Her coat was deep and thick, her tail a plume, and her name was Morag. She was Ned's dog, a stray which he had found wandering around the dockside at Scapa Flow, filthy dirty and painfully thin, scavenging the dustbins for scraps of food. Much shocked, Ned had tied a bit of rope around her neck and led her off to the local police station, but nobody had reported a lost dog, and he hadn't the heart to leave her there, so walked out again, the collie still at his side, attached to its makeshift lead. With time running out—he had only an hour before he had to be back on board and reporting for duty—Ned found a taxi, loaded himself and the dog into it, and asked to be taken to the nearest veterinary surgeon. The vet was a kindly man, and agreed to take the dog for a night, with a bath and a good meal thrown in, and Ned left her there, got back into his taxi, and returned in the nick of time to his ship, galloping up the gangway like a steeplechaser and just about knocking the Officer of the Watch off his feet.

The next day, after some thought, Ned applied for a long weekend, and rather to his astonishment, was allowed it. He then telephoned the vet, who agreed to keep the dog for another two days. On the Friday, as soon as he was free, Ned reclaimed the collie, and together they caught the ferry across the Pentland Firth and, at Thurso, boarded the night train south.

The following morning at about eleven o'clock, he turned up at his parents' house, unexpected, unannounced, and unshaven, with the Border collie still in tow.

"She's called Morag," he told Biddy over a fry-up of bacon, sausages, tomatoes, mushrooms, and eggs. "She's a Scottish dog, so she's got a Scottish name. I thought she could live with you."

"But, darling, I've never had a dog."

"Time you started. She'll keep you company when Dad's away. Where is Dad, by the way?"

"Shooting pheasants."

"When'll he be back?"

"About five."

"Good, I'll see him. I don't have to leave until tomorrow morning."

Biddy looked at the dog. Her dog. She said her name, and Morag sat up, smiled at her, and thumped her feathery tail. The eye in the white side of her face wasn't quite the same colour as the eye in the black side, and this gave her an engaging expression, as though she were winking.

Biddy said to the dog, "You are rather sweet."

"She adores you. I can tell."

Bob, returning from his shoot, was so delighted to find his son waiting for him at home that he scarcely noticed the collie. And by the time he realized Morag was to be a permanent fixture, Ned had cleaned his gun for him, taking the wind from his father's sails and putting Bob in no position to raise objections.

Which did not mean that all doubt was allayed.

"Won't make messes, will she?"

"Of course not, Dad. She'll do it all in the garden."

"Where's she going to sleep?"

"The kitchen, I suppose. I'll buy her a basket in Bovey Tracey. And a rug. And a collar and a lead. And a feeding bowl. And some food . . ."

But, Bob realized, Ned had already spent much time and money on Morag, to say nothing of vet's bills, as well as squandering a precious long weekend leave in order to bring the dog home to his mother. The thought of further expense, all to come out of Ned's hard-earned sub-lieutenant's pay, was more than his father could stand.

He said, "No. I shall buy them." He looked at his watch. "Now. Saturday evening. We've just time to nip down to the ironmonger's before the shop closes. You may choose the dog's accoutrements. *I* shall foot the bill."

That had all happened two months ago, and now Biddy could scarcely imagine life without Morag. She was a sweet and undemanding creature, loving to go for long walks, but perfectly happy just playing about the garden, if one did not happen to feel like going for a walk, or wanted to play bridge with one's friends instead. This afternoon Morag had missed out on a walk because, despite the fine weather, Bob had spent most of his time indoors, clearing papers from his desk, turning out cupboards, throwing out worn or unwanted items of clothing. With all this accomplished, he had turned his attention to the garage, sorely in need of a good spring clean. To deal with the resultant rubbish, he had built a bonfire, and anything that couldn't be burnt, like broken scythes, old petrol cans, a two-wheeled tricycle, and a rusty lawn-mower, he had piled outside the back door, awaiting the next call of the dustbin lorry.

The inference of all this was only too clear to Biddy. She understood her husband very well, and knew that private, gnawing concern and anxiety could only be dispelled by furious physical activity. As Biddy watched him through the kitchen window, her heart became heavy. It was as though he knew already that war was inevitable and was now bent upon clearing the decks of his ship before battle commenced.

But finally, there was nothing more to be done. He came indoors for a restoring cup of tea at the kitchen table, and they were there together when Judith's telephone call came through. The telephone was in the hall, and Biddy went to answer it. When she returned, "Who was that?" Bob asked.

Biddy sat down again, and took a mouthful of tea, but it had grown cold. "It was Judith."

"What did she say?"

"She wants to come. Here. Now. Today. She's driving up from Cornwall in her car. She says she'll arrive about ten o'clock."

Bob raised his thick eyebrows. "What's up?"

"No idea."

"How did she sound?"

"All right." She thought about it. "A bit bright-voiced. You know. Brittle."

"Did she say why she wanted to come?"

"No. No details. She said she'd explain when she arrived."

"Was she phoning from the Carey-Lewises?"

"Yes."

"Something must have happened."

"Perhaps she's had a row with her friend, Loveday. Or blotted her copybook in some way."

"That doesn't sound like Judith."

"No, it doesn't, does it? Never mind, whatever the reason, she's coming. She can help me make black-out curtains. I bought a bale of the horrible black cotton, but I haven't got around to cutting them out yet. Judith's a whiz on the sewing machine." She stood to empty the mug of tepid tea down the sink, and then to pour a fresh brew from the teapot. Morag, hoping that she was about to be given something to eat, sat on the rag-rug and gazed at Biddy. "It's not suppertime yet, you greedy thing," Biddy told her. "Dear doggie,

Judith hasn't met you yet. She doesn't even *know* about you. If you're nice to her, she'll maybe take you walks." She straightened, and leaned against the sink. "I don't even have to make up her bed, because Mrs. Dagg did the spare room on Friday morning. She was coming to stay later on anyway, and we'd planned to go to London to buy gear for Singapore. So it's just a question of putting the dates forward." Across the table, she met her husband's eye. "Oh, Bob, it's no good jumping the gun, getting too concerned. Whatever. We'll just have to see."

"If something really is wrong, she mightn't want to tell you."

"She will. I'll just ask her. We have a good relationship. Anyway, I can't deal with hidden undertows or unspoken feelings."

"Be tactful, my love."

"Darling, of course I shall be. And you know I adore the child."

Just after eleven o'clock, by which time Biddy was beginning to be anxious, imagining accidents and empty petrol tanks, Judith arrived. From the window, Biddy saw the beams of the car's headlights coming up the hill, and heard the approaching engine. She stood, and swiftly left the room, crossing the hall and switching on the light that hung over the front door. Standing in the blowy darkness, with Morag at her heels, she saw the little Morris come through the open gate.

The headlights were switched off, the door opened, and Judith emerged.

"Oh, darling, what a relief. I almost had you dead." They hugged. "Did you have a dreadful journey?"

"Not too bad. Just long. And I said I'd be here about now."

"I know you did. Just me fussing."

"The last bit is so windey. At one moment I thought I'd lost the way." Judith looked down. "Who's this?"

"Morag. Our dog."

"You've never had a dog before!"

"We've got one now. She's Ned's."

"What a sweet person. Hello, Morag. How long has she lived with you?"

"Two months. Come on, don't let's stand here and talk. Where's your luggage?" Biddy opened the back door of the Morris and pulled Judith's case off the seat. "Is this all?"

"It's all I need."

"I hoped you were going to stay for *ages*."

"You never know," said Judith, but there was no laughter in her voice. "Perhaps I will."

They went indoors. Biddy locked the front door behind her and dumped the case on the bottom stair. In the glare of the rather cold hallway light, they stood and looked at each other. Judith seemed all right, Biddy decided. A bit pale, and much thinner than when Biddy had last seen her, but not ill or anything. Not ill, nor apparently trembling on the verge of tears. But perhaps she was just being brave . . .

"Where's Uncle Bob?"

"Went back to Devonport after tea. You'll probably see him next weekend. Now, what would you like? Food? Drink? I can give you some soup."

Judith shook her head. She said, "Bed. Just bed. I'm exhausted."

"Do you need a hot-water bottle?"

"I don't need anything. Just a bed and a pillow."

"Up you go then. Usual room. And don't get up in the morning. I'll bring you a cup of tea about nine o'clock."

Judith said, "I'm sorry."

"For heaven's sake, what for?"

"For springing myself on you."

"Oh, don't be ridiculous. We always love it when you come." But senti-ment, at this late and vulnerable hour, must at all costs be kept at bay. Con-fidences and confessions could wait until the morning. "Now, off with you. Go and get your head down. And sleep well!"

"I will . . ." Judith gathered up her suitcase and trod up the stairs. Biddy watched her go. Suddenly, Biddy longed for Bob, and wished that he had not had to go. In lieu of his comforting presence, she poured herself a whisky and soda and, carrying her drink with her, went to the kitchen, put Morag to bed, locked doors and windows, and finally took herself upstairs. On the landing, she saw that Judith's bedroom door was shut. From beyond the open window an owl hooted, but all the house was silent.

It was not Biddy who awoke Judith, but the dog. In her sleep, she was aware of the rattle of the door as Morag scratched upon it, and then a thin, insistent wheeking. Scarcely conscious, Judith climbed out of bed, staggered to open the door, let the dog in, shut the door, and fell back into bed again. Almost instantly, she was fast asleep once more. When, at nine o'clock, Biddy offi-cially woke her, bearing the promised cup of tea, Morag was curled up at the end of Judith's bed, a warm and heavy weight on her feet.

"I couldn't think where she'd got to," Biddy said, putting the cup of steam-ing tea down on the bedside table. "I let her out to do wees and then she disappeared. I thought she'd gone rabbitting, but she must have sneaked back into the house." She neither scolded Morag nor hauled her off the bed, simply telling her she was a very clever doggie, and then went to draw back the cretonne curtains, letting in the light of the new day. (My first day without Edward, Judith thought, and wished that it hadn't had to start so soon.) "It's a bit misty, but I think it's going to be fine. How did you sleep?"

One step at a time. That was the only way to get through such an unbear-ably miserable vacuum. Judith made a huge effort and sat up and punched the pillows into position, so that the slats of the bedhead would not dig into her shoulders. "Like a log." She yawned and pushed her hair out of her face. "I was exhausted."

"You must have been. Such a drive on your own. You looked drained." Biddy came to sit on the side of the bed, adding yet more weight to the creaking springs. She wore linen trousers and a checked shirt, as though she were about to step out of doors and get on with a bit of haymaking. Her curly hair, once so dark, was beginning to show threads of grey, and she had put on a bit of weight, but her face was just the same, with lipstick and laughter lines and bright eyes. She said, "I've been having a look at your little car. It's too sweet. You must love it."

"Yes, I do." Judith reached for her tea, which was hot and very strong. Biddy waited for a moment, and then said, "Do you want to talk?"

Judith's heart sank. She tried stalling. "What about?"

"Talk it through, I mean. Something's happened. A row with Loveday perhaps? Or is it more far-reaching than that?"

Her perception, like a needle, was both sharp and painful. "What makes you say that?"

Biddy became a bit impatient. "Oh, darling, I'm not a dimwit. And I'm also a mother as well as an aunt. I don't enjoy undercurrents of feeling, nor nervous silences, nor sulks . . ."

"I'm not sulking . . ."

Biddy ignored this, ". . . and it's not in character for you to make impulsive decisions. So tell. Whatever it is, whatever caused you to leave the Carey-Lewises in such a hurry, I shall understand. My own life was never unblemished. In fact, it's scattered with spots and boils. And it *is* better to talk."

Judith made no reply to this. She drank her tea and tried to marshal her thoughts. Biddy waited patiently. Beyond the window the sky was misty, but the air warm. The small bedroom—light-years away from the beautiful room at Nancherrow that was hers alone—was a bit cramped and shabby, but comfortably familiar, because this was where Judith had always slept when she stayed at Upper Bickley, and nothing had been changed, nor improved, nor refurbished in any way. The cretonne curtains did not match the patterned carpet; the candlewick covers on the twin beds were primrose yellow, and the wallpaper striped in blue and white. Interior decoration had never been Biddy's forte. But there were marguerite daisies in a jug on the dressing-table, and over the old-fashioned fireplace hung a picture of a harbour, with blue sea and fishing boats, which was good for looking at just before you fell asleep.

She sighed and met Biddy's eyes. Biddy was really family, not just pretend. Being here, and being with her, felt a bit like slipping into an old pair of shoes after a day spent in painfully uncomfortable high-heeled sling-backs. She put down the teacup and said, "It's just that I've made the most awful fool of myself."

"How?"

Judith told her just about everything, starting at the beginning, when Edward came to pick her up from school for those first summer holidays, and ending yesterday, when it had all ended, because she thought Edward loved her as much as she loved him, and had told him so, only to suffer the terrible shock and humiliation of his rejection.

She told Biddy just about everything. She did not, however, mention Billy

Fawcett. This, obscurely, had something to do with a certain loyalty for dear, dead Aunt Louise. Nor did she admit to Biddy that she had actually slept with Edward; allowed him to seduce her; and happily surrendered her virginity. Biddy was not easily shocked, but with grown-ups one could never be sure; being made love to by Edward had been an experience of such dizzying delight that Judith did not want, in any way, to be made to feel ashamed or remorseful.

". . . the worst was that there were so many people at Nancherrow . . . all the family, and friends. A real house party. I couldn't bear the thought of them all watching me . . . watching us . . . and not letting them guess what had happened. It was Mary Millyway who suggested that I come to you. She said since I was anyway, I might as well come a few days earlier. And it seemed just about the only thing to do."

"What about Mrs. Carey-Lewis?"

"Diana? She's taken to her bed. Some upset or other. But even if she hadn't been ill, I couldn't have confided in her. She's terribly sweet, but somehow not that sort of person. And it being Edward made it all the more impossible. He's her only son, and she dotes on him."

"Did you tell her you were coming to me?"

"Yes."

"What excuse did you give? What reason?"

"I told a dreadful fib and said that you had 'flu and were all alone and had to be nursed."

"Heavens," Biddy murmured faintly.

"Luckily, she seemed to believe it. I went to say goodbye to her. I didn't say goodbye to any of the others because they'd all gone down to the cliffs to swim. Edward too. I didn't even say goodbye to him."

"Perhaps just as well."

"Yes. Perhaps."

"And how long are you going to stay with us?"

Judith bit her lip. "Just for a bit. Till I've had time to pull myself together. Is that all right?"

"I hope it takes ages, because I love to have you here. Now, do you know what I think? Shall I tell you what I think?" And she told Judith what she thought, and she said things that Judith had heard a thousand times before. Clichés, maybe, but then they had become clichés because all had been proved true, over and over again. A first love is always the love that hurts the most. There's better fish in the sea than ever came out of it. You won't forget Edward, ever, but life doesn't end at eighteen, because it's only just beginning. And finally, time is the great healer. All this will pass. However painful the heart-break, you will recover.

By the time she came to the end of all this, Judith was nearly smiling. "What's so funny?" asked Biddy, looking a bit hurt.

"Nothing. It's just that you sound like one of those tracts people used to embroider in cross-stitch and hang in some other person's bedroom."

"You mean, 'East Or West, Hame Is Best'?"

"Not *exactly*."

"How about,

"The Kiss of the Sun for Pardon
The Song of the Birds for Mirth
You Are Nearer God's Heart in a Garden
Than Anywhere Else on Earth.

"My mother used to have that one hanging in the Vicarage loo. That was all there was to read except the small print on the Bronco packet."

"That's a poem, not a proverb. Or a motto. You know, like 'There's Many a Slip 'Twixt Cup and Lip.' "

"I've just thought of a wonderful one. 'It's at the Corners of Life That the Wind Blows the Sharpest.' It sounds awfully uplifting but it doesn't actually mean a thing."

Suddenly they were both laughing. "Oh, Biddy . . ." Judith leaned forward and put her arms around Biddy and was hugged and patted, and rocked gently to and fro, like a baby with wind. ". . . you are a star. I'm really sorry about everything."

"You can't help loving. And don't feel you have to be cheerful all the time. A little mope won't get me down provided I know what it's all about. The great thing is to keep busy. I've got all the black-out curtains to cut out and sew, and a great list of stuff that Bob says we've got to lay in, like paraffin, in case the war starts and there's an instant shortage. So, lots of shopping. Why don't you have a bath and get dressed? Mrs. Lapford's in the kitchen, frying bacon for you. She'll be frightfully hurt if you don't come and eat it."

Biddy was right. Occupation, preferably fairly mindless, was all-important. The worst was over, it had all been said, and did not need to be mentioned again. Biddy understood.

After a bath, and a few clean clothes out of her bag, she went downstairs, and was warmly greeted by Mrs. Lapford and Mrs. Dagg, who both said how lovely she was looking and how nice it was to have a bit of company again. Then she ate breakfast, and after that she and Biddy sat at the kitchen table and made shopping lists. Paraffin and candles and electric light bulbs. Petrol for the motor mower. Tins of soup. Sewing-machine needles and spools of black thread for making black-out curtains, and screws for fixing the wires to the windows. Then, everyday items. Food for Morag, and butter and macaroni, and a fresh chicken and potatoes, and biscuits and bread. Two bottles of gin, and two bottles of whisky, a soda syphon, tonic water, and three lemons.

"Sounds as though you're planning a party."

"No. Just regular supplies. We'll maybe ask a few people in at the weekend, when Bob's home again. Now, put down crisps and chocolate biscuits . . ."

The list, when completed, was very long. Biddy gathered up her purse and basket and they went out, got into her car, and drove down the hill into the little town.

That afternoon, after they had eaten the lunch that Mrs. Lapford had left for them (lamb cutlets and rice pudding), they took Morag for a walk, and then, returning, started in on the black-out curtains. While Judith set up the old sewing-machine on the dining-room table, filled spools, and fitted a new needle, Aunt Biddy measured the windows and, kneeling on the sitting-room floor, cut the varied lengths. The cotton was black and dense and smelt faintly of Indian ink. "I've never cut out anything so boring in my life," Biddy observed. "I'm just glad I haven't got a huge house with dozens of windows." She handed over the first two lengths, which were for the dining-room. They had to be sewn together (with a French seam for strength) and then a heading stitched, with a casing, and a deep hem, to give them a bit of weight. As soon as the first one was finished, they hung it, threading the wire through the casing, and screwing the little hooks to the window frame, so that the curtain would hang close to the glass.

Completed, it looked horrible, too bulky to be drawn out of sight. They stood back, and surveyed, with little pleasure, the result of all their labour. Biddy sighed. "I've never made anything so unattractive, or so disagreeable. I just hope they work."

"We'll experiment tonight, after dark," Judith told her. "We'll pull it across, and then the proper curtains, and I'll go out into the garden and see if any light shows."

"If there's so much as a chink, we'll be put into prison, or fined. And it's nearly tea-time, and we've only made *one*. The whole house is going to take us forever."

"Well, just be grateful you don't live at Nancherrow. There must be about a hundred and forty-three windows there."

"Who's going to make their curtains?"

"I don't know. Mary Millyway, I suppose."

"Bad luck on her, that's all I can say." Biddy lit a cigarette. "Let's stop now. I'll go and put the kettle on."

So they dumped all the yards of black cotton onto the dining-room table with the sewing-machine, closed the door, and abandoned their task until the next day.

After tea, Judith and Morag went out into the garden and did some weeding, and then Judith picked a bowl of raspberries for supper, and later Uncle Bob rang up, and when Biddy had finished talking, Judith had a bit of a chat with him.

"See you on Saturday," he finished. "Tell Bids I'll be home sometime."

"He says he'll be home on Saturday."

Biddy was sitting at the open window engaged upon stitching, half-heartedly, at a rather knobbly-looking tapestry. "I've been at it for months," she told Judith. "I don't know why I bother. It's going to look awful on a chairseat. Perhaps I should take up knitting again. Darling, you're not waiting for the telephone to ring and for it to be Edward, are you?"

Judith said, "No."

"Oh, good. I just thought. That's the worst agony in the world, waiting for a telephone call. But if you want to call him, you know you can."

"You're sweet, but I don't want to. You see, there wouldn't be anything to say."

Presently Biddy, bored with her stitchery, pierced the needle into the canvas and tossed it aside. She looked at the clock, announced with satisfaction that the sun was over the yardarm, and went to pour herself her first whisky and soda of the evening. Then, taking it with her, she went upstairs to have her bath. Judith read the newspaper, and when Biddy reappeared, in her jewel-blue velvet housecoat, they tried out the new black-out curtains. "It's no good making any more until we're certain that this one works," Judith pointed out, and she went out into the garden while Biddy dealt with the black-out, then drew the thick padded curtains and turned on the light.

"Can you see anything?" she called, raising her voice in order to be heard through all this muffling.

"Nothing at all. Not a glimmer. Really successful." Judith went back indoors, and they congratulated themselves on their brilliance, and then Biddy had another drink, and Judith went into the kitchen to heat up Mrs. Lapford's macaroni cheese and make a salad, and because the dining-room table was still piled with the detritus of their sewing, laid supper in the kitchen.

Over supper and a glass of white wine, they talked about Molly and Jess and going to Singapore.

"It's October, isn't it, that you sail? We haven't got all that much time. We mustn't keep putting off going to London to shop. We must try to make a firm date. We can stay at my club, and maybe go to a theatre or something. Next week, or the week after. Liberty's always have lovely thin cottons and summery cruise clothes, even in the middle of winter. I must say I can't help envying you, getting away from all this dreariness. I'd settle for the boat trip alone, drifting down the Suez Canal and out into the Indian Ocean. You must promise to send me a fez from Aden."

After supper they washed up the dishes, and then went back into the sitting-room, and soon it was time for the nine-o'clock news. Air-raid shelters and sandbags in London; Nazi troops on the march; Anthony Eden flying somewhere or other with a fresh missive from the British Government; mobilization of reservists imminent. Biddy, clearly unable to bear all this gloom for another moment, reached out and turned the knob of the wireless to Radio Luxembourg, and all at once the room, softly lighted by lamps and with the windows open onto the scented, dusky garden, was filled with the voice of Richard Tauber.

> Girls were made to love and kiss
> And who am I to disagree with this

And Judith was back with Edward, and it was last Christmas, the day he had returned from Switzerland and come to find her, and they had run together, laden with packages, through the grey rain-washed streets, and drunk champagne in the lounge of the Mitre Hotel. So piercingly vivid was the memory that she heard the screaming gulls overhead, being tossed by the storm, and saw lights from shop windows streaming out over the drenched pavements, and smelt tangerines and spruce branches, the very essence of Christmas. And she knew that it was always going to be like this. However hard she tried, Edward was always going to be there. I've survived one day, she told herself. One day without him. It felt like the first step of a thousand-mile journey.

By the time Bob Somerville returned to Upper Bickley on the following Saturday morning, a number of disparate events—some quite alarming—had taken place.

Morag had disappeared, to hunt on the moor, and returned with fourteen ticks embedded in her thick coat, all of which had to be painstakingly removed. It was a disgusting task which Judith undertook, because Biddy was too squeamish and Judith had once watched Colonel Carey-Lewis perform the horrid operation on Tiger. De-ticked, Morag then had to be given an antiseptic bath, which she hated so much that, by the end, not only was the dog sodden, but Biddy and Judith as well.

In Austria, at Obersalzberg, Herr Hitler, orating at his generals, announced that the destruction of Poland would commence within days.

Biddy, committed to an afternoon's bridge, took herself off to one of her rather grander friends, and returned for supper in cheerful form, having had good cards and won five and sixpence.

The sinister news broke upon the world that the Nazis and the Russians had signed a non-aggression pact. It seemed that nothing, now, could avert war.

Biddy and Judith, along with the Daggs and the Lapfords, and a large number of local people, presented themselves at the School Hall, and were duly issued with gas masks. They carried them home, carefully and distastefully, as though they were ticking bombs, stowed them under the hall table, and devoutly prayed that they would never have cause to wear them.

Bill Dagg, turning up one warm, humid evening to do a couple of hours' work in the garden, cornered Biddy in the vegetable patch, pulling a couple of lettuces for supper. Leaning on his spade, he engaged her in conversation, and at last came round to his point, which was that the lower quarter of the paddock should be dug, manured, and planted with potatoes. Biddy told him it would take days to dig, she wasn't all that fond of potatoes, and thought that she preferred the green grass of the paddock, but Bill was dogged and determined to get his own way. After all, he pointed out, taking off his cap to scratch his bald head, if that there 'Itler got 'is way, then everyone in England was going to starve. No point good land lying fallow if you could grow something. And if you 'ad potatoes you weren't never going to go 'ungry.

Whereupon Biddy, being bitten to death by midges, allowed herself to be persuaded, and Bill, triumphant, went to find a ball of twine with which to mark out the boundaries of his new potato patch.

Finally, Judith completed the mammoth task of stitching the curtains. The last pair were for Ned's room, and she made her way there in order to hang them up. Ned's was the smallest room in the house, and he slept in a bunk, built over a mahogany set of drawers. The linen curtains were navy-blue, and the walls white, hung with group photographs from his preparatory school, through to his years at Dartmouth Naval College. As well, there was a large coloured poster of a nubile and half-naked girl. He had a desk, with a lamp on it, and a chair, and that was all, because there wasn't space for more furniture. To fix the hooks on the window frame, Judith had to pull the chair over and stand on it and when the black curtains were hung and she turned to clamber down, she suddenly caught sight of Ned's moth-eaten old teddy bear, one-eyed and mostly hairless, sitting on the pillow of the bunk. And the significance of Ted, in juxtaposition to the breasty blonde, was somehow terribly touching. She stood there leaning against the bottom of the bunk, and thought of Ned Somerville, and it made a change from not thinking of Edward Carey-Lewis. And she remembered the good times they had had together, and hoped it would not be too long before she saw him again, because he was the nearest thing she had ever had to a real brother.

From downstairs, Biddy called, "Judith."

"I'm here."

"Have you seen my secateurs?"

"No, but I'll come and find them."

She got down off the chair, replaced it by the desk, and went out of Ned's room, closing the door behind her.

Now, Saturday, the twenty-sixth of August. Bob Somerville drove from Devonport to Upper Bickley, arriving just before midday. Biddy, hearing the sound of his car roar up the hill, dropped what she was doing (cleaning a cauliflower, because Mrs. Lapford didn't come at weekends) and went out through the front door and into the sunshine to meet him just as he emerged from his car, looking both tired and dishevelled. He was in uniform. His cap, with its golden oak leaves, was jammed down over his brow, and his jacket was an old one, so that it sagged a bit around his bulky frame, and the four stripes of gold braid, set with the purple of an engineer officer, had become worn and tarnished. He lugged, from the passenger seat, his battered leather grip and his briefcase, and thus laden, came to kiss his wife.

"I feared you mightn't make it," she told him.

"I'm here."

"Everything's so awful. I thought there might be some panic on."

"There is. It's non-stop. But I wanted to see you both."

She tucked her arm into his, and together they went indoors. At the foot of the stairs, "Do you want a drink?" she asked him.

He shook his head. "Later, Biddy. I'll go up and get out of this filthy gear and into dog-robbers. That should help make me feel myself again. Good smells. What's for lunch?"

"Irish stew."

"Delicious."

Because the black-out curtains were finished with, and the sewing-machine stowed away, they were back in the dining-room again, after a week of eating in the kitchen. Judith had laid the table, and when Bob came downstairs, in old corduroys and a comfortably clean and faded shirt, she went to greet him and be given a crushing and loving hug. Biddy whipped off her cooking apron, and they all went out into the front garden, sat out in the sun, and had drinks. Bob had a beer, Judith a cider, and Biddy a gin and tonic. He asked what had been going on, and they told him about Bill Dagg's potatoes and Morag's ticks. (They did not mention gas masks or the Russian-German Treaty.) And Bob drew the dog to his side and fondled her head and told her she was a stupid, dirty bitch, and she sat very close to him and smiled.

He leaned back in his chair and turned his face to the sun. An aeroplane, making a noise like a bee, slowly crossed the sky. He watched it go, a silvery toy suspended in time and space. He said, "I hope we're not entertaining, or being entertained, this weekend."

"A drink party this evening," Biddy told him. "Here. That's all. Just old friends."

"Who?"

"The Barkings and the Thorntons. No need to make a huge social effort." She hesitated. "But if you want, I'll put them off. They'll understand. I just thought perhaps we all needed a bit of cheering up."

"No. Don't put them off. I'd like to see them." The plane was disappearing, drifting into the far distance behind a vaporous cloud. He said, "Is that all?"

"That's all."

"When are they coming?"

"Half past six."

He thought about this for a bit, and then said, "Why don't we ask Miss Lang?"

Judith frowned. She knew, from previous visits, both the Barkings and the Thorntons. The Barkings were a retired naval couple who had settled in Newton Ferrars, and there bought themselves a small house, with access to the water, and a slipway for their sailing boat. Once hostilities commenced, James Barking would be recalled to active service. Biddy knew this, which was one of the reasons she had invited them. The Thorntons, Robert and Emily, lived in Exeter. He was a solicitor, and as well a captain in the TA battalion of the Devonshire Regiment. Emily Thornton was one of Biddy's bridge and tennis friends.

But Miss Lang . . .

She said, "Who is Miss Lang?"

Biddy told her. "She's an elderly spinster, a retired civil servant, who's come to live here. She has a little stone house at the end of the town, with a yellow front door flush on the pavement and a delectable garden at the back. Bob's in love with her."

"I am not in love with her," Bob protested, quite peaceably. "I just find her enormously intelligent and interesting."

"How old is she?" Judith asked.

Biddy shrugged. "Oh, I suppose about sixty-five. Very trim and slim and alert. We met her at a lunch party at the Morrisons' about three months ago." She paused for a moment, thinking about Miss Lang. And then said, "You're quite right, Bob, I should ask her. I will. You don't think it's rude . . . such short notice?"

"I don't imagine she is a lady who easily takes offence."

"And she won't feel a bit shy or *de trop*, with us all being such old friends?"

"Darling Biddy, you are far too good a hostess to let such a thing happen. Besides, I can't imagine Miss Lang ever being in the least out of her depth. She seems to have spent her life organizing international conferences, attending the League of Nations, and working in embassies in Paris and Washington. I don't see her becoming tongue-tied on account of a few bucolic Devonians."

"I saw her the other day, and I should have asked her then. But it was in the School Hall when we were all getting our gas masks, and she was in a different queue, and anyway, it hardly was the appropriate time for making social arrangements."

"Go and ring her now."

So Biddy went indoors and made the telephone call, and returned with the information that Miss Lang had been delighted with the invitation, did not mind at all about the short notice, and would present herself at Upper Bickley at half past six.

Bob reached for Biddy's hand, and pressed a kiss upon it. "Well done." And then he said he was feeling peckish, so Biddy went back to the kitchen to put on her apron and dish up the Irish stew.

Miss Lang was a little late. The Thorntons and the Barkings had already arrived, been given their drinks, lit their cigarettes, and settled down to the easy conversation of close friends who had all known each other for a long time. After a bit, Judith was able to sneak away to the kitchen, where a tray of chicken vol-au-vents were warming in the oven, and about which Biddy had clearly forgotten. They were only very slightly over-brown. She was standing at the table arranging them on a blue-and-white plate, when she saw, through the kitchen window, the small green car come through the gate and park itself at the front door.

She abandoned the vol-au-vents, and went to greet the last guest. On the doorstep she found a slender lady, white-haired, neatly dressed in a grey flannel skirt and a claret-coloured cashmere cardigan. Low-key, but very elegant.

"Miss Lang."

"I'm late."

"It doesn't matter a bit."

"Somebody telephoned just as I was leaving. Doesn't that always happen?" She had clear grey eyes, alert and intelligent, and looked, thought Judith, a bit like Miss Catto would look in twenty years' time. "Now, who are you?"

"I'm Judith Dunbar, Biddy's niece."

"Of course, she's told me about you. What a pleasure to meet you. You're staying?"

"Yes, for a bit. Please come in." In the hall, she paused. The party, going full-tilt, was clearly audible through the open sitting-room door. "I'm actually, at the moment, dealing with some slightly overcooked vol-au-vents . . ."

Miss Lang smiled understandingly. "Don't say another word. I'm sure they will be delicious. And I can take care of myself." And with that, she crossed the hallway and made her way through the open door. Judith heard Biddy. "And here's Miss Lang, how lovely to see you . . ."

She returned to the kitchen, was relieved to find the vol-au-vents intact because there was every possibility that Morag had smelt them, come to investigate, and devoured the lot. She disposed them in decorative fashion on the plate, and then carried this back into the sitting-room.

There was not much space, and eight people seemed quite a crowd. On Miss Lang's appearance, they had all stood to be introduced, and then rearranged themselves, settled back in chairs, and resumed conversation. Judith handed round the vol-au-vents. The party progressed.

Later, as she sat on the window-seat with Emily Thornton and Biddy, and listened with some amusement to the latest scandal from the tennis club, they were joined by Miss Lang, who gazed from the window at the garden, and the green lawn, across which the evening shadows were lengthening, and said that she had no idea that Biddy grew such splendid roses.

Biddy was quite down-to-earth about her one horticultural success. "It's heavy horse manure," she explained. "I have access to an unlimited supply."

"Would it be very rude if I went out and had a look? They are quite exceptional."

"Of course not. Judith will give you a guided tour . . . you don't mind, do you, darling?"

"I don't mind a bit, except that I don't know all the names . . ."

Miss Lang laughed. "That makes it sound rather as though I expected to be introduced . . ."

She laid down her sherry glass, and Judith led her from the room, leaving Biddy and Emily Thornton happily digging up an even more salacious scrap of tennis-club gossip. They went through the glassed door that led out into the front garden, and the deck-chairs that they had sat in at lunch-time were still there, and a wagtail was hopping about on the grass.

"What a perfectly lovely evening," Miss Lang remarked. "And what a view Mrs. Somerville has. I had no idea of the extent of the view from here. My house is right on the main street, so I have no view, but when I retired I thought better to be close to neighbours and shops, so that when I'm really decrepit and can't drive any longer, I can continue to be independent." In leisurely fashion, they made their way across the grass. "Now, tell me about yourself. Are you the niece who's on her way to Singapore? Now, that rose *is* a darling, and I know her name. Ena Harkness. What a size!" She stooped to smell the velvety bloom. "And a scent that is pure heaven. When do you sail?"

"I'm meant to be going in October."

"How long is it since you've seen your parents?"

"Four years."

"Too long. Too cruel, such separation. How old are you?"

"Eighteen."

"Left school, of course."

"Yes, this summer."

"Matric?"

"I haven't got the results yet."

"Oh, the waiting! Terrible. I remember it. How long are you going to be in Singapore?"

"About a year. If I've passed matriculation, I think I'll get a place at Oxford. I'll have to come back for that."

"But that is wonderful . . . I think some of my happiest years were those at University." She didn't just look like Miss Catto, but sounded like her as well. "And languages. You must try to achieve some languages. You have French, of course. How about German?"

"I've never done German."

"Latin?"

"Not much good at Latin."

"A pity. With Latin, you're half-way to Italian and Spanish. Now, here is a rose whose name I do not know."

"Neither do I."

"So, we must ask Mrs. Somerville."

"I doubt if she'll know either . . . she's not much of a gardener."

"In that case, I shall have to look it up. These four years, while your parents have been abroad, what have you been doing with yourself? Who fielded you for holidays . . . ?"

And she was so interested, and yet so clearly uncurious that Judith found herself quite at ease, and able to speak about the Carey-Lewises and Nancherrow in an objective sort of way, impersonally, as though it were a period in her life which had slipped away and left no trace. Which was strange, because she couldn't talk about it to Biddy or Bob without the misery of Edward flooding back, and the dreaded lump swelling in her throat. She explained about Aunt Louise, and Loveday, and the consequent open-heartedness of Diana and Edgar Carey-Lewis.

Miss Lang listened with the deepest attention. "How kind people are," she remarked. "We forget sometimes, the boundless kindness of people. I won't say you were lucky, because I hate that word. It sounds as though you'd won the jackpot in some no-skill-required sort of competition. But I am so pleased for you, because it must have rendered your life quite, quite different."

"Biddy was always there, of course. I always knew I could come to Biddy."

"But with your new friends you were clearly one of the family."

They had come to the end of the roses. Spek's Yellow was the last. Miss Lang, having admired this, paused, turning to face Judith.

She said, "I have so enjoyed talking to you. I hope I shall see you again."

"I hope so too, Miss Lang."

Miss Lang hesitated. She said, "I haven't spoken to Mrs. Somerville yet, but I wish you all would call me Hester. Which is my name. I'm living here now. This is my home. And I've been Miss Lang for far too long. I think it's time to change my image."

Hester. And Judith remembered that far-off day when Diana Carey-Lewis had said very much the same thing, and Judith and Loveday and Diana had bowled along in the open Bentley and all shouted "Diana" to the wind. She said, "I'd really like to call you Hester."

"That's settled then. Now, the midges are starting to bite. I think it's time we returned to the others."

From Haytor, the view was immense: a sweep of Dartmoor, and villages, tiny as toys spread upon a carpet, valleys and rivers and fields; and in the distance, from Teignmouth to Start Point, the glimmering silver sea. Judith and Bob Somerville, with Morag bounding at their heels, had climbed the five miles by way of a moorland track, and having finally reached their goal, paused to get their breath, sitting in a grassy hollow in the shelter of a handy boulder. Biddy had not come with them. Uncharacteristically, she had taken herself off to church. Lunch, she assured them, was a movable feast. There was no need to hurry back to Upper Bickley. They could take their time.

They sat in a companionable silence. It was a still morning, and the quiet was filled with small country sounds. The lowing of sheep, a dog barking, a car starting up somewhere and climbing a hill. Walking, they had heard bells ringing from small, squat church towers, but the ringing had stopped now. A breeze moved, and stirred the bracken.

Judith plucked a blade of grass and began to shred it with her thumb-nail. She said, "Uncle Bob. Do you think we could talk?"

He had taken out his pipe and his pouch and was occupied in filling the bowl, tamping down the tobacco.

"Of course. You can always talk to me."

"It's about something rather difficult."

"Could that be young Carey-Lewis?"

She turned her head to look at him. He was lighting his pipe from a box of Swan Vestas. The flame died and the tobacco smelt sweet, and smoke rose in a fine grey plume. "Biddy told you."

"Of course she told me." He put the matches back into the pocket of his old tweed jacket, so worn that in places it looked a bit like loosely woven string. "She tells me everything. You knew she would. I'm sorry. Unrequited love is not a happy state."

"It's not Edward. It's about Singapore."

"What about Singapore?"

"I don't think I can go. I've been thinking about it for ages, but I haven't talked about it to anybody. It's horrible, because I feel as though I'm being torn in two directions. In one direction, I want to go most dreadfully. I want to see Mummy and Dad again, and Jess, more than anything. I've waited four years, and looked forward to it every minute, every day. Counted the months and the days. And I know that Mummy's the same. In her letters she's been saying, just another year. And then, just another six months. And then, just another three months. And she's got my room ready for me, and planned all sorts of lovely treats, like having a big party to welcome me, and going down to Penang for a holiday. And I've got my passage booked and everything, and there's nothing to stop me sailing . . ."

She stopped. Bob waited. Then he said, "And the other direction?"

Judith took a deep breath. "The war. Everybody's going to be in the thick of it. Everybody I really love. You and Ned, and all my friends. Jeremy Wells and Joe Warren, and probably Heather as well. And Athena Carey-Lewis and Rupert Rycroft . . . I think she's probably going to marry him, and he's in the Royal Dragoon Guards. And Edward's friend, Gus Callender. And Loveday. And Edward. I know if I go to Singapore, I'll feel like a rat deserting a sinking ship. I mean, I know we're *not* going to sink, but that doesn't stop me feeling that way. And last week Biddy and I got gas masks and stocked up with paraffin and candles, and made all the black-out curtains, and in Singapore all my mother does is to have masses of servants, and go to the club, and dress up and play tennis and go out to dinner parties. I'd have to do that too and it would be tremendously exciting and grown up, but I know I'd feel conscience-stricken every moment of the day. It's not as though there's the smallest likelihood that the war will affect them in any sort of way, just like in the Great War. But to me it would feel like running away, hiding out, and letting everybody else do all the dirty work. Fight the war, I mean."

She fell silent, having more or less run out of words. Bob did not at once make any comment. And then he said, "I see your point, but I'm sorry for your parents, particularly your mother."

"That's the worst bit. If it wasn't for her, I wouldn't even be *thinking* of going to Singapore."

"How old are you?"

"Eighteen. I'll be nineteen next summer."

"You could go for a year, and then return."

"I don't want to risk it. Anything could happen. There mightn't be a boat. I mightn't get back again. I might be stuck out there for years."

"What about University? Oxford. I thought that was the next step."

"Not for a year. And I haven't had my matric results yet. But I feel that Oxford can wait. It's not so imperative as actually *staying* in England. Maybe I *will* be able to go to University, but what is really important, right now, is that I really don't want to run away. Escape. Not be here to do something useful, and be able to share the horrible things that are bound to happen."

Uncle Bob, with his pipe going well, leaned back, settling his tweedy shoulders against the lichened granite. "So, what do you want me to tell you?"

"I hoped you'd help me make up my mind."

"I can't do that. You have to make the decision for yourself."

"It's so difficult."

"I'll just say two things. If you join your parents I am convinced that nobody would think the worse of you, or point the finger of shame. You've all been apart for too long, and after all these years on your own, I think you deserve a little fun. And if you don't go . . . you must realize that it's going to be rough. However, it's your life. You have responsibility only for yourself."

"If I stay in England, will you feel I'm being cruel and selfish?"

"No. I shall feel you are displaying boundless patriotism and selflessness. And I shall also be very proud of you."

Patriotism. It was a funny word, not often spoken aloud, encompassing an emotion even deeper than loyalty to, and affection for, friends. She thought of the song, belted out by the girls of Saint Ursula's on Empire Day or the King's birthday or other appropriate occasions. The words, a paraphrase of Shakespeare:

> *This royal throne of kings, this scepter'd island*
> *This earth of Majesty, this seat of Mars*
> *This fortress, built by nature for her purpose*
> *Against infection and the hand of wars.*

I shall feel very proud of you. Perhaps that was all she needed. She said, "I think I'll stay. I'll ring up the shipping company and cancel my passage, and then write to Mummy. She'll be devastated, I know, but she'll just have to understand."

"I think better to send her a cable first. With LETTER FOLLOWING at the end. And once you've done that, and burnt your boats, you can compose a really good letter, and tell her everything you've just told me. In the Royal Navy we call it 'giving the reasons in writing.' "

"Yes. Yes, you're quite right. That's what I'll do. Right away. As soon as we get back. Oh, the relief of not having to agonize over it any longer. You are a saint, Uncle Bob."

"I just hope you won't regret the decision."

"I know I won't. I feel much better already. And if there is a ghastly fuss, you'll back me up, won't you?"

"I shall be your alternative defence. Now, with that settled, what are you going to do with yourself? Have you thought that far forward?"

"Yes. What I'd like to do is join one of the services, but there's not much point joining up unless I've got some sort of a qualification, otherwise I'll end up cleaning guns, or hanging on to the string of a barrage balloon, or cooking enormous institutional meals. Heather Warren, my friend in Porthkerris, she's going to learn shorthand and typing. I thought perhaps I could do it with her. Shorthand and typing isn't much, but at least it's some sort of a skill. And I thought I'd go back and live in Porthkerris, and perhaps ask Mrs. Warren if she'd have me as a paying guest. I know she would, she's the most hospitable person. I've stayed there so many times, and if Joe joins up, then I could have his room."

"Porthkerris?"

"Yes."

"Not Nancherrow?"

"No. Not just because of Edward. But because I think I've lived with the Carey-Lewises for long enough. I've got to start standing on my own feet. And anyway, Nancherrow is miles from anywhere; if I was trying to learn something, it would be dreadfully inconvenient."

"Do you really *want* to return to Cornwall?"

"Not really. In fact, I think I probably need a bit longer away from it all; I haven't exactly pulled myself together yet."

"Then why not stay here? With Biddy."

"I can't do that. Indefinitely."

"Not indefinitely. Just for the time being. I would like you to stay. I am asking you to stay."

Judith looked at him in some puzzlement. She saw his solid, rugged profile, with its thick eyebrows, and his jutting pipe. And she saw, too, his greying hair, and the deep lines that ran from nose to chin, and all at once it wasn't difficult to imagine him as he would become when he was very old. She said gently, "Why do you want me to stay?"

"I want you to keep Biddy company."

"But she has dozens of friends."

"She misses Ned, and God knows what's going to happen to me. She likes having you around. You'll be able to keep each other in order."

"But I must do *something*. I really want to learn how to do shorthand and type."

"You could do that from here. Go to either Exeter or Plymouth."

"But how would I get to and fro? You've said yourself that the first thing to be rationed is petrol. I wouldn't be able to use my car, and there's only one bus a day out of Bovey Tracey."

Uncle Bob began to laugh. "What a girl you are for details. You'll make an excellent petty officer writer." He sat up and leaned forward to tap out his pipe on the heel of his shoe. "Why don't we take one thing at a time? I'll work something out, I promise. I won't abandon you at a loose end with nothing to do. Just be with Biddy for a bit."

She was suddenly filled with love for him. She said, "All right," and leaned forward and kissed his weather-beaten cheek, and he gave her a hug. Morag, who had been lying in the bracken a little way off, stirred herself and came to find out what they were up to. Uncle Bob dealt her a soft slap on her thickly furred flank. "Come on, you lazy girl," he told her, "we're going home."

It was nearly half past two before they returned, hungry, thirsty, and thoroughly exercised. It had been a splendid walk. They approached Upper Bickley by way of the moor, and reaching it, climbed the stone wall at the head of the paddock and made their way down the tufty grass towards the house. Morag, lively as ever, led the way, leaping the wall like a steeplechaser, and racing ahead to where her water bowl stood by the back door.

Judith and Uncle Bob took it more slowly. At the foot of the paddock, they paused to inspect Bill Dagg's projected potato patch. The area had been neatly squared off and marked with twine, and about a quarter was already dug, grass and weeds removed, and the resultant earth lay dark and loamy. Judith stooped and took a handful, and it smelt sweet and damp, and she let it slip away through her fingers. She said, "I bet that will grow the best potatoes in the world."

"Once dug. A labour that I wouldn't relish. Rather Bill Dagg than . . ." Uncle Bob turned his head to listen. Judith heard it too. A car, slowing, turning to climb the hill. Bob frowned. "Now, who could that be, coming our way?"

They stood, side by side, waiting, their eyes turned towards the open gate. The sound of the engine drew closer and then the car appeared in the road, to turn in at the entrance of Upper Bickley. Tyres ground across the pebbles. A dark Royal Naval staff car, with an officer at the wheel.

Beneath his breath, Bob said, "Bloody hell."

"Who is it?"

"My signal officer."

The car drew to a halt, and out of it stepped a young man in lieutenant's uniform. Bob went to meet him, striding out ahead of Judith, and ducking his tall head beneath the washing-line. Judith hesitated, wiping the earthy palm of her hand on the seat of her trousers, and then, more slowly, followed him.

The lieutenant came forward and saluted. "Captain Somerville, sir."

"Whitaker. What are you doing here?"

"A signal, sir. It came through about an hour ago. I came at once, sir. Thought it best to deliver it by hand."

"In a staff car?"

"I have an idea you'll be needing transport, sir."

The signal was handed over. Standing there, in his dusty shoes and his old tweed jacket, with his hair awry, Bob Somerville read the message. Judith anxiously watched his face, but his expression gave nothing away. After a bit, he looked up. "Yes," he said to Lieutenant Whitaker. "Best delivered by hand. Well done. Thank you." He looked at his watch.

"I'll need fifteen minutes. I must have a word with my wife, eat a sandwich or something; pack."

"Right, sir."

Bob turned to go into the house, but remembered, at the last moment, Judith, who stood there feeling a bit spare and at a loss. "Oh, Whitaker, this is my niece, Judith Dunbar. You'd better fill her in with the details. And if you're nice to her, she'll maybe make you a cup of tea."

"I think I'll be able to survive, thank you very much, sir."

"Fifteen minutes."

"I'll wait, sir."

Uncle Bob went indoors. The front door closed, explicitly, behind him, and Judith knew that right at this moment he did not want anybody around; he just wanted to be alone with Biddy. She felt fearfully apprehensive, her imagination leaping ahead to imminent invasion, some disaster at sea, or dire news of Ned.

"What *is* happening?"

"It's a special appointment," Lieutenant Whitaker told her. "The Commander-in-Chief, Home Fleet, has requested Captain Somerville to join his staff." (A certain relief; none of the terrible things she had feared.) "Forthwith. With all convenient speed. That's why I brought a staff car."

"Where is the Home Fleet?"

"Scapa Flow."

"You're not going to *drive* him to Scapa Flow?"

Lieutenant Whitaker laughed, and at once looked a lot more human. "No. I think Captain Somerville will probably get a ride with the Fleet Air Arm."

"Ned's based at Scapa Flow."

"I know."

"It's all so sudden." She met his eyes, and saw his sympathy, and tried to smile. "I suppose everything's going to start being like this . . ."

Whereupon Lieutenant Whitaker shed officialdom and became a perfectly pleasant and friendly young man. "Look," he said, "why don't we go and sit down somewhere, and have a cigarette."

"I don't smoke."

"Well, I could do with one."

So they went and sat on the stone steps that led up to the drying green, and Morag came and joined them, and it was warm in the sunshine, and he smoked his cigarette, and asked what Judith and Captain Somerville had been doing, and she told him about the walk to Haytor and the view from the top of the hill; and she told him that for the time being she was going to stay at Upper Bickley with Biddy, and even as she said this, she realized that now Uncle Bob was going to have neither time nor opportunity to lay plans for Judith's future. She was simply going to have to deal with those by herself.

Exactly fifteen minutes later Bob reappeared, with Biddy at his side. Lieutenant Whitaker, disposing of his cigarette, sprang smartly to his feet and went to shake Biddy by the hand. Biddy looked a bit bemused, but she had been married to the Royal Navy for a long time, and had learned to be both brave and philosophical about precipitous partings. As for Uncle Bob, he had become, once more, his other self. Back in uniform, back in charge, he looked both distinguished and sanguine, not unfamiliar but somehow distanced, as though he had already moved ahead of them to be absorbed into his real, professional life.

Lieutenant Whitaker relieved him of his luggage and went to stow it in the back of the car. Uncle Bob turned to embrace his wife.

"Goodbye, my darling."

They kissed. "Try to see Ned. Send him my love."

"Of course."

It was Judith's turn. "Goodbye."

"Goodbye, Uncle Bob." They hugged. "Take care," he told her, and she smiled and said that she would.

Lieutenant Whitaker was waiting, holding the door open for Bob. He got into the passenger seat, and the door was slammed shut, and then Lieutenant Whitaker came around the front of the car and got in behind the driving-wheel.

"Goodbye!"

The car went through the gate and was gone. Bob Somerville was gone. Biddy and Judith, waving, stopped waving. They listened until they could hear the car no longer, then turned to each other.

"Are you all right?" Judith asked.

"No. Absolutely shattered." But Biddy managed a wry laugh. "Sometimes the Navy makes me want to spit. Poor man. In and out like a dose of salts, with nothing but a beef sandwich to sustain him. But the darling pet is thrilled to bits. Such an honour. Such a prestigious appointment. And I really am pleased for him. I just wish it hadn't happened so quickly, and that Scapa Flow wasn't right at the other end of the country. I asked about joining him, but he says it's out of the question. So I'll just have to roost here." She looked at Judith. "He told me that you're going to stay for a bit."

"Is that all right?"

"I know I sound silly, but at the moment I simply couldn't bear to lose both of you. Heaven to think you'll be around to keep me company. Oh dear . . ." She shook her head, refuting emotion, ". . . so idiotic, but suddenly I feel a bit weepy . . ."

"Come on," said Judith and took her arm. "Let's go and put the kettle on and make a really strong cup of tea."

Afterwards Judith was always to think of that August Sunday afternoon, and Uncle Bob's going, as the moment when the war really started. The events of the following week—the mobilization of the Royal Navy, the call-up of reservists, the German invasion of Poland, and Mr. Chamberlain's speech declaring war—became in retrospect simply the final formalities preceding the first bout of a mortal struggle that was to continue for nearly six years.

Upper Bickley,
South Devon.
September 13th, 1939.

Dear Diana,

I am so sorry I haven't written to you before, but there has been so much going on, and somehow there hasn't been time. It was horrid leaving you all at such short notice and not being able to say goodbye to anybody, but I know that you understood.

Here Judith crossed her fingers, and delivered the last of her continuing fib.

Aunt Biddy was really very unwell, and I was pleased that I had come. She is much better now, and quite over the bad attack of 'flu.

Uncross fingers again.

Apart from the fact that the war has finally started (in a way quite a relief after those last two dreadful weeks) I've got lots to tell you. The first is that I have decided not to go to Singapore. The reasons for this decision are too many and too complicated to explain, but what it really boils down to is that I felt I simply couldn't go swanning off to the Far East to enjoy myself while everybody at home was getting prepared to fight the war. My being in England isn't going to make a mite of difference, I know, but I would have felt too awful. The worst bit was telling my parents. I cancelled my passage first of all, and then sent them a cable. I got one back almost at once (how can they be so quick?), pages of pleading to change my mind, but I know Uncle Bob is backing me up and I've stood my ground. I wrote them a very long letter with all my reasons and I hope so much that they will realize how things are, and how people feel, in England. Like rolling up sleeves and preparing for the very worst. I hope you don't think that I have been dreadfully selfish. I think my mother does, but then disappointment is so lowering, and the worst is knowing how much she was looking forward to our reunion and how, now, I have shattered her hopes.

Anyway, here I stay.

The other bit of news is that Uncle Bob has gone to Scapa Flow to take up the post of Engineer Captain on the staff of the Commander-in-Chief, Home Fleet. He was specially picked and asked to go, so it was a tremendously exciting appointment, but that doesn't mean that we don't miss him dreadfully. And, of course, Biddy can't go and be with him, so she has to stay here. And, for the time being, I am staying with her.

I expect, before long, she will become involved in Red Cross work, or something, or join the Women's Voluntary Service, but at the moment there is enough to do, just keeping everything going here. Mrs. Lapford, her daily cook, is leaving; she is going to go and cook in some factory canteen near Exeter, because she says she has to do her bit. Mrs. Dagg, who cleans and dusts, is staying, so far. She is married to a farm worker, and has decided that her number-one-priority war work is to keep him well fed!

As for me, I decided, before Uncle Bob left us, that I must learn to do shorthand and typing. I couldn't think where I could find somewhere that would teach me (we're pretty remote here), but everything has worked out. Biddy has a friend called Hester Lang, a retired civil servant who has come to live in Bovey Tracey. She came for bridge the other afternoon, and after bridge, while she was having a drink, we got talking and I told her about the shorthand and typing and she said she would teach me. She's so clearly efficient, I am sure I shall learn in no time. Like having a one-to-one tutor. Once I've got that under my belt, and decent speeds, I think I might join the services. The Women's Royal Naval Service, probably. If for no other reason than the uniform is nice!

I do hope everybody is well. I miss you all so much. I wonder if Mary made all the black-out curtains. I made Biddy's and they took me an entire week and the house is tiny compared with Nancherrow. I hated having to leave you so suddenly, but please give my love to Colonel Carey-Lewis and Mary and the Nettlebeds and Loveday and Aunt Lavinia and everybody.

Just one thing. My matric results were going to be sent to Nancherrow, or maybe Miss Catto might ring you up and tell you about them. Whatever, when you do get news, could you be a saint and either send them to me or perhaps Loveday could give me a telephone call. I long to know. Not that it makes much difference. Now, I don't suppose I shall ever go to University.

My love as always,

Judith

The reply to this missive did not arrive at Upper Bickley until two weeks later. It thumped through the letter box and onto the doormat along with the rest of the mail, a large, fat envelope, addressed in Loveday's childish scrawl, which, along with her hopeless spelling, had been for years the despair of Miss Catto. Judith was surprised, because she had never in her life received a letter from Loveday, let alone known her to write anything more than the most cursory of bread-and-butter notes. She carried the letter into the sitting-room, curled up in a corner of the sofa, and slit the heavy envelope.

Inside were her Matriculation results and sheets of expensive Nancherrow writing paper, folded into a satisfactory wodge. She looked at the Matriculation results first, unfolding the official form with dread-filled caution, as though it might explode. To begin with, scarcely believing, and then flooded with relief and the excitement and satisfaction of a real accomplishment. If she had been with somebody of her own age, she would have leaped to her feet and danced with exultation, but it seemed pretty silly to put on such an exhibition just for herself, and Biddy had gone to Bovey Tracey to get her hair done, so she contented herself with reading the results just once again, then set them aside and started in on the screed from Loveday.

Nancherrow,
September 22nd.

Darling Judith,

We loved getting your letter and it's been sitting in Mummy's desk, but you know how awful she is about writing letters, so anyway, she's asked me to write. A labour of love I can tell you, but it's pouring with rain outside so there's nothing much else I can do.

Before I say another thing, here are your matric results. The envelope came and I simply had to open it, even though it was addressed to you and I read it aloud at breakfast and Mummy and Pops and Mary all cheered. You are brilliant. All those credits and two *distinctions*. Miss Catto will be dancing a fandango. Even if you don't go to University, it doesn't matter, because you'll be able to frame your certificate when it comes, and hang it in the lavatory or somewhere suitable.

You are good not going to Singapore. I'm not sure if I could have been so strong-minded, missing out on all the fun. I hope your mother has forgiven you, it's so hateful being in the doghouse. And tremendous news about your uncle. He must be frightfully efficient and clever to do such a job. I had to look Scapa Flow up in the Atlas. It's practically in the Arctic Circle. I hope he took lots of woolly underfugs.

Here, things are happening. Pearson has left us, gone off to join up with the Duke of Cornwall's Light Infantry. Janet and Nesta are trying to make up their minds what they are going to do, although they haven't been called up or anything. Janet thought she might be a nurse, but Nesta says she's going somewhere to make munitions, she says she's never fancied bedpans. Anyway, I suppose before long they'll both be on their way. The Nettlebeds remain a permanent fixture, thank goodness, they're too old to go and fight, and Hetty's still here too. She's longing to go into the army to be an At and march around in khaki uniform, but she's only seventeen (too young), and Mrs. Nettlebed keeps telling her that she's too gormless to be let loose on a lot of randy soldiery. I think Mrs. Nettlebed is being unkind; she just doesn't want to have to scrub her own saucepans.

Mary's been making black-out curtains. She sewed and sewed, and to help her Mummy got someone called Miss Penberthy to come. She lives in Saint Buryan and she bicycles here every day and sews and she's got the most frightful BO and we have to have all the windows open. As well, there are some rooms still without black-outs, so after dark we can't even open the door. I hope Miss Penberthy finishes the lot soon, and goes away.

Mummy had a Red Cross meeting in the drawing-room, and Pops is putting buckets of water everywhere in case we catch fire. Haven't quite worked this one out yet, but I'm sure there's an answer somewhere. It's getting colder. When winter comes we are going to dust-sheet the drawing-room and live in the little sitting-room. Pops says we must conserve fuel and grow lots of vegetables.

Now, news of Others. Left this to the end because I don't want to leave anybody out.

Aunt Lavinia is all right, she is getting up now for a bit and sitting by the fire. It's horrid for her having yet another war. She's had the Boer War, and the Great War, and now this. Too much in one lifetime.

After you went we all missed you dreadfully, but the others followed pretty sharpish. Jeremy was the first to go, and then Rupert, who shot off to Edinburgh of all places, somewhere called Redford Barracks. The cavalry horses were all moved there from Northampton, I suppose put on trains because it would be far too far for the poor darlings to walk. More about Rupert later.

Then Edward and Gus went. Edward is at some training base, but we don't know where because his address is Somewhere in England. Mummy's got a sort of poste restante number for him, and she hates not knowing exactly where he is. I expect he's having the time of his life, flying around and drinking beer in the mess.

And Gus went to Aberdeen, because that is the HQ of the Gordon Highlanders. It was simply ghastly saying goodbye to him. I didn't cry for any of the others, but I did cry for him. It's so mean, meeting the only man one could ever possibly fall in love with, and then having him whisked away by beastly old Hitler. I cried buckets in bed, but I've stopped crying now, because I've had a letter from him, and written one back. And I've got a photograph of him that I took with my camera, and I've had it en-larged (looks a bit furry, but okay) and framed and it's sitting by my bed, and I say good night to it every night, and good morning in the morning. I bet he looks heavenly in his kilt. I'll try to persuade him to send me a picture of him wearing it.

Now, continuation of Rupert story.

Three days after he left, Athena suddenly announced that she was going to Edinburgh too, and she got into a train and went. Isn't she the *end?* She's living in the Caledonian Hotel. She says it's enormous and frightfully Victorian and that Edinburgh is bitterly cold, but it doesn't seem to matter because every now and then she can see Rupert. If she doesn't mind being cold, then she must be in love with him.

As for me, I am staying put, right here. Mummy is going to get masses of hens and they will be my war-work, and Walter Mudge says he'll teach me how to drive a tractor, and then I can help on the farm. I don't really care what I do, stoking a boiler or cleaning the lavatories, provided nobody says I've got to register or be called up or something gruesome.

Mr. Nettlebed has just appeared to break the glad tidings that petrol's going to be rationed, and we're all on our honour not to fill cans and *hoard*. Goodness knows what we'll do about food, as it's far too far to bicycle to Penzance! Start slaughtering Walter's sheep, I suppose!

Longing to see you again. Come back as soon as you can. Mary says do you want her to send you some winter clothes?

Lots of love, love, love,

Loveday

PS—STOP PRESS! Too exciting. A moment ago, a telephone call from Edinburgh. Pops took it in his study. And Athena and Rupert are *married*. They got married in a registry office there, and Rupert's soldier-servant and a taxi driver were the witnesses. Just exactly what Athena always wanted. Mummy and Pops are torn between delight and fury that they missed the ceremony. I think they really like him. I don't know when she'll come back to us. It can't be much fun being married and living all by yourself in the Caledonian Hotel.

Judith folded the letter and put it back in its envelope, and then put the Matriculation results back as well. It was comfortable, curled up in the corner of the sofa, so she stayed there, and gazed from the window, and thought about Nancherrow. It almost felt like being back there again. And she thought about Athena and Rupert getting married in their registry office, and Miss Penberthy stitching black-out curtains, and Gus in his kilt, and the Colonel and his buckets of water, and Loveday keeping hens. And Edward. Somewhere in England. Training. Training for what? He already had his pilot's licence. But a stupid question to ask oneself. Training for war, of course, to dive from the skies and fire guns and knock out enemy bombers. *He's having the time of his life, flying around and drinking beer.*

Since that last Sunday at Nancherrow there had been no communication between them, so Loveday's was the first news that Judith had received of him. She had neither written to Edward, nor telephoned because she couldn't think of anything to say to him that hadn't already been said, and because she still cringed at the memory of her own naïvety, and the deadening shock of Edward's rejection. And Edward had not written to her, nor telephoned, but then she had hardly expected that he would. He had been constant and understanding for a long time, and no man's patience can last forever. Her final defection, driving away from Nancherrow without even waiting to say goodbye, had probably been the ultimate exasperation. And there was no reason, no need for Edward to pursue Judith. His charmed life would always be filled with lovely women, just waiting, queuing up, to drop into his lap.

But it was still impossible to remember him dispassionately. The way he looked and the sound of his voice, and his laughter and the lock of his hair that fell across his forehead and had constantly to be pushed away. Everything about him that had filled her with delight.

Since coming to Devon, she had tried her hardest to resist the indulgence of day-dreams: that she would hear a car come up the hill and it would be Edward, come to find her, come because he could not live without her. Such fantasies were for children, fairy stories with happy endings, and now—in every sort of way—she was a child no longer. But she could not stop his invading her night-time dreams, and in those dreams there was a place that she came to, and was consumed by a blissful pleasure, because she knew that, somewhere, Edward was there too; was on his way, was coming. And she would awake filled with happiness, only to have that happiness drain away in the cold light of morning.

All over. But now, remembering him did not even make her want to cry any longer, so perhaps things were getting a little better. They could certainly be worse, because she had passed her matriculation, and for the time being such practical comforts were going to have to keep her going. *Self-reliance is all*, Miss Catto had preached, and when all was said and done, two distinctions would hardly fail to be something of a spirit-booster. She heard a door slam, and Biddy's voice. Biddy, home again, with her marcel wave. She pulled herself out of the sofa, and went to find her aunt to share the news.

It was nearly the end of September by the time the shorthand and typing lessons with Hester Lang got off the ground, as Hester had a certain amount of preparation to do. She owned an impressive typewriter—a real one, not a portable like Uncle Bob's—but this had to be cleaned in a shop in Exeter, fitted up with a new ribbon and a shield, so that Judith would be unable to take sly glances at the keyboard. She also purchased a couple of manuals, because it was some time since she had learned the theory of both accomplishments and she needed to do a bit of mugging up. Finally, she telephoned and said that she was ready to start.

The following day, Judith walked down the hill and presented herself at Hester's front door. With one thing and another, it felt a bit like going back to school for the Christmas term; autumn was in the air, and the leaves were turning gold. The days were shortening, and each evening the ritual of doing the black-out came a little earlier . . . soon they would be having tea, at half past four, with the curtains tightly drawn. Judith missed the long twilights, watched from indoors. It felt claustrophobic being shut in with electric light.

But now, at nine o'clock in the morning the day was crisp and clear, and she smelt bonfire smoke from some gardener's pyre of burning rubbish. Over the weekend, she and Biddy had picked pounds of blackberries from the hedgerows around the local farmer's fields, and the same farmer had promised a load of logs, the gleanings of an old elm felled by last winter's gales. Bill Dagg would bring them to Upper Bickley with a tractor and a bogie, and they would be stacked, like peat, against the garage wall. Burning wood would help to conserve their stock of coal, because the way things were going, there could be no certainty of fresh supplies.

Hester's house was grey stone, double-storeyed and one of a small terrace, so that she had a neighbour on either side. Their houses looked a bit dim, with peeling black or brown front doors, and lace curtains framing aspidistras in pea-green pots. But Hester's front door was butter-yellow, and her shining windows were veiled in snow-white net. As well, alongside the old boot-scraper, she had planted a clematis, and this was already well on its way up the face of the house. All of this contrived to give the impression that the little terrace was on its way up in the world.

Judith pressed the bell, and Hester came to open the door, looking, as always, immaculate.

"Here you are. I feel you should be lugging a school satchel. What a heavenly morning. I'm just making coffee."

Judith could smell it, fresh and inviting. She said, "I've only just had breakfast."

"Then have another cup. Keep me company. We don't have to start work right away. Now you've never been in my house, have you? The sitting-room's through there; make yourself at home and I'll join you in a moment."

The door was open. Beyond, Judith found herself in a long room that stretched from the front of the house to the back, because a dividing wall between the original two small rooms had been removed. This rendered everything spacious, and very light. As well, it was furnished and decorated in a style both simple and modern, and not at all what she had either imagined or expected. A bit, she decided, like a studio. The walls were white, the carpet beige, and the curtains coarse linen, the colour of string. The obligatory black-out blind was clearly evident, but furled away, and the bright morning light was diffused through the loosely woven material, almost as though the curtains had been made of lace. A Kelim rug lay over the back of the sofa, and there was a low table composed of a sheet of plate glass supported by two antique porcelain lions, which looked as though they might have come, a long time ago, from China. This table was piled with delectable books, and in the centre stood a piece of modern sculpture.

All very surprising. Looking further, Judith saw, over the fireplace, an abstract canvas, hung unframed; grainy and brilliant, the paint appeared to have been scraped on with a palette knife. On either side of the fireplace, alcoves were shelved in glass, bearing a collection of green and Bristol-blue goblets. And there were other shelves, packed with books; some leather-bound and others with deliciously new shiny jackets—novels and biographies that one longed to read. Beyond the window lay the garden, a long thin lawn, flanked by borders a riot of Michaelmas daisies and dahlias in all the clashing hues of the Russian Ballet.

When Hester returned, Judith was standing by the window turning the pages of a book of colour plates of Van Gogh.

She looked up, then closed the book and laid it back on the table with its companions. She said, "I can never be sure if I appreciate Van Gogh or not."

"He's a bit of a puzzle, isn't he?" Hester set the coffee tray down on a lacquer-red stool. "But I do love his thundrous skies and his yellow corn and his chalky blues."

"This is a lovely room. Not what I expected."

Hester, settling herself in a wide-lapped chair, laughed. "What did you expect? Antimacassars and Prince Albert china?"

"Not that exactly, but not this. Did you buy the house this way?"

"No. It was just like all the others. I knocked the wall down. Put in a bathroom."

"You must have been terribly quick. You haven't been here long."

"But I've *owned* the property for five years. I used to pop down at weekends when I was still working in London. Then I didn't have time to meet people, because I was always occupied in chasing builders and painters and the like. It was only when I actually retired that I was able to settle here and make friends. Do you take milk and sugar?"

"Just milk, thank you." She took the cup and saucer from Hester and went to sit on the edge of the sofa. "You've got such fascinating things. And books. Everything."

"I've always been a collector. The Chinese lions were left to me by an uncle; the painting I bought in Paris; the glass I collected over the years. And my sculpture is a Barbara Hepworth. Isn't it amazing? Just like some marvellous stringed instrument."

"And your books . . ."

"So many books. Too many books. Please, anytime, if you want, borrow. Provided, of course, you bring it back."

"I might just do that. And I will bring it back."

"You're clearly an inveterate reader. A girl after my own heart. What else do you like besides painting and books?"

"Music. Uncle Bob introduced me to music. After that I got a gramophone, and now I've got quite a big collection of records. I love it. You can choose your mood."

"Do you go to concerts?"

"There aren't a lot of concerts in West Penwith, and I hardly ever go to London."

"Living here, that's what I miss. And the theatre. But nothing else, really. I'm very content."

"It was so kind of you to say that I could come and learn shorthand and typing . . ."

"Not kind at all. It will keep my brain working, and make a change from crosswords. I've got everything set up in the dining-room. For typing you must have a good, firm table. And I think three hours a day is enough, don't you? Say, nine to twelve? And we'll give weekends a miss."

"Whatever you say."

Hester finished her coffee and laid down her cup. She got to her feet. "Come along then," she said. "Let's make a start."

By the middle of October, six weeks into the war, nothing very much had happened; no sort of an invasion, nor bombing, nor battles in France. But the horrors of the destruction of Poland kept everybody glued to their wireless sets, or else following the terrible accounts that appeared in the newspapers, and alongside the appalling suffering and carnage that was taking place in eastern Europe, the small inconveniences and deprivations of everyday life were almost welcome, stiffening spines and giving a sense of purpose to the most trivial of sacrifices.

At Upper Bickley, one of these was that Mrs. Lapford had departed, to labour in her factory canteen.

Biddy, in all her life, had never even boiled an egg. But Judith had spent a good deal of time in kitchens, watching Phyllis make semolina puddings and fairy cakes, mashing potatoes for Mrs. Warren, and helping to dish up the enormous teas that were so much part of day-to-day life at Porthkerris. At Nancherrow, Mrs. Nettlebed had always welcomed a bit of help with the jam- and marmalade-making and was grateful if one offered to stand and beat the sugar and eggs for an airy sponge cake until they were the colour of cream. But that was the limit of Judith's experience. However, needs must when the devil drives. She found an old *Good Housekeeping* recipe book, tied on an apron, and took over the cooking. To begin with, there were a good many scorched chops and underdone chickens, but after a bit she began to get the hang of it, and even accomplished a cake, which tasted not bad, despite the fact that all the raisins and cherries had sunk, like lead, to the bottom.

Another inconvenience was that the Bovey Tracey tradesmen—the butcher, the grocer, the greengrocer, the fishmonger—all ceased to deliver. It was the petrol rationing, they explained, and everybody understood and bought enormous baskets and string bags and humped their shopping home. It wasn't too much trouble, but it all took an enormous amount of time, and the climb up the hill to Upper Bickley, laden like a pack-horse, was exhausting to say the least of it.

And it was beginning to get cold. Judith, having spent so much time at Nancherrow, where the central heating was never turned off until the warm spring was well on its way, had forgotten about being cold. Being cold out of doors was all right, but being cold indoors was misery. Upper Bickley had no central heating. Two years ago, when she had come for Christmas, there had been fires lighted in the bedrooms, and the boiler kept going, full-tilt, all twenty-four hours of the day. But now they needed to be parsimonious with fuel, and only the sitting-room fire was lighted, and then never until after lunch. Biddy did not seem to feel the cold. After all, she had happily survived Keyham Terrace, which Judith remembered as the coldest place in the world that she had ever been. Colder, perhaps, than the Arctic. As winter closed in, Upper Bickley would probably become just as icy. Standing on the hill, it faced the teeth of the east wind, and the old windows and doors were ill-fitting and let in every sort of draught. Judith looked forward to the long, dark months without much enthusiasm, and was grateful that Mary had sent her, from Nancherrow, a huge dress box (labelled "Hartnell's") filled with her warmest winter clothes.

Saturday, the fourteenth of October. Judith awoke and felt the frosty air on her face flowing in through the open window, and opening her eyes saw a sky that was grey, and that the topmost branches of the beech tree at the foot of the garden were already gilded with russet leaves. Soon they would start dropping. There would be much sweeping up and burning, and eventually the tree would stand bare.

She lay in bed and thought that if things had gone as they should, and there had been no war, and she had not had to make that enormous decision, then right now, at this moment, she would be in a P & O liner in the Bay of Biscay, being tossed from one side of her bunk to the other and probably experiencing the first nausea of seasickness. But still, en route to Singapore. For a moment or two, she allowed herself to feel dreadfully homesick for her own family. It seemed that she was fated always to live in other people's homes, however hospitable, and sometimes it was really lowering to brood over all that she was missing. She thought of steaming through the straits of Gibraltar into the blue Mediterranean and a forgotten world of perpetual sunshine. Then the Suez Canal and the Indian Ocean, and each evening the Southern Cross rising a little higher in the jewel-blue sky. And she remembered how, when you approached Colombo, there came a smell in the air, long before the smudge that was Ceylon appeared on the horizon, and the smell was of spice and fruits, and cedarwood, blown seaward on the warm wind.

But it was unwise to imagine, unthinkable to regret. Her bedroom was cold. She got up and went to close the window on the dank morning, pausing for a moment to hope that it would not rain. Then dressed, and went downstairs.

There she found Biddy already in the kitchen, which was unusual because normally Judith was always down first. Biddy was bundled in her dressing-gown, and boiling a kettle for coffee.

"What are you doing up so bright and early?"

"Morag woke me, whining and wheeking. I'm surprised you didn't hear her. I came down to let her out, but she just did her wees and then came straight in again." Judith looked at Morag, slumped in her basket with a soulful expression in her mismatched eyes. "You don't think she's ill, do you?"

"She certainly doesn't look her usual cheerful self. Perhaps she's got worms."

"Don't even suggest it."

"We might have to take her to the vet. What do you want for breakfast?"

"There doesn't seem to be any bacon."

"In that case, boiled eggs."

Over breakfast they discussed, in a desultory fashion, how they were going to spend their Saturday. Judith said that she had to go down to Bovey Tracey to return a book borrowed from Hester Lang, and that she would do the shopping. Biddy said good, because she intended to write letters, and she lit a cigarette and reached for her pad and pencil and began to compose the inevitable shopping list. Bacon, and dog meal for Morag, and a roast of lamb for Sunday lunch, and lavatory paper, and Lux . . .

". . . and would you be a dear and go to the wool-shop and buy me a pound of oiled wool?"

Judith was astonished.

"What do you want a pound of oiled wool for?"

"I'm sick of my silly tapestry. I said I was going to start knitting again. I shall make seaboot stockings for Ned."

"I didn't know you could knit stockings."

"I can't, but I found a wonderful pattern in the newspaper. They're called spiral stockings and you go round and round and you never have to turn a heel. And then when Ned wears a great hole in them, he just has to twist them round and the hole ends up on the top of his foot."

"I'm sure he'll love that."

"There's another pattern for a Balaclava helmet. Perhaps you could make him a Balaclava helmet. Keep his ears warm."

"Thanks, but at the moment I've enough to do practising pot-hooks. Write 'wool' down on the list and I'll see if I can get some. And you'd better have a set of needles as well . . ."

Saturday morning in Bovey Tracey was a bit like Market Day in Penzance: filled with country people from all around, come in from remote villages and moorland farms to collect the week's supplies. They crowded the narrow pavements with baskets and push-chairs, stood chatting at street corners, took their turn in butcher's and grocer's to be served, all the while exchanging gobbets of gossip and family news, and only lowering their voices to speak of illness or the possible demise of somebody's Auntie Gert.

Which meant everything took a great deal longer than it normally did, and it was eleven o'clock before Judith, burdened with bulging basket and string bag, made her way to Hester Lang's house and rang the front-door bell.

"Judith."

"I know, it's Saturday, and I'm not here to do shorthand. I just came to return the book you lent me. I finished it last night."

"Lovely to see you. Come in and have a cup of coffee."

Hester's coffee was always particularly delicious. Judith, smelling its fragrance, fresh and wheaten, drifting from the kitchen, needed little persuasion. In the narrow hallway, she dumped her baskets and took the book from the capacious pocket of her jacket. "I wanted to bring it back right away, in case it got dirty, or Morag chewed it."

"Poor dog, I'm sure she'd never do anything so wicked. Go and put it back in its place, and choose another, if you want. I'll be in with the coffee in a moment . . ."

The book she had borrowed was *Great Expectations*, one of a complete set of leather-bound volumes of Charles Dickens. She went into the sitting-room (even on a grey morning it felt light and cheerful), and slipped it back into its place, and was contently reading titles and trying to decide what she should tackle next when, from the hall, she heard the telephone begin to ring. Then, Hester's footsteps as she went to answer it. From beyond the door, which stood ajar, Judith heard her voice. "Eight-two-six. Hester Lang speaking."

Perhaps not Dickens this time. Something contemporary. She took out *The Mortal Storm*, by Phyllis Bottome, and began to read the blurb on the inside of the book-jacket, and then to browse, haphazardly, through the pages.

The call continued. Between long silences, Hester spoke, and her voice was dropped to a low murmur. "Yes," Judith heard her say, "yes, of course." And then another silence. Standing, alone, in Hester's sitting-room, Judith waited.

Finally, when she was beginning to think that Hester would never return to her, the call was abruptly finished. She heard the single ring of the receiver being replaced, closed the book, and looked towards the door. But Hester did not come at once, and when she did appear there was a stillness about her, a deliberate composure, as though she had paused to arrange herself in some way.

She didn't say anything. Across the long room, their eyes met. Judith laid down the book. She said, "Is something wrong?"

"That was . . ." Hester's voice shook. She pulled herself together and started again, this time in her usual quiet and level tones. "That was Captain Somerville on the telephone."

Which was bewildering. "Uncle *Bob*? Why is he ringing you up? Can't he get through to Upper Bickley? The phone was working yesterday."

"It has nothing to do with the telephone. He wanted to speak to me." She closed the door behind her and came to sit on a small upright gilded chair. "Something perfectly terrible has happened . . ."

The room was warm, but Judith felt, at once, chilled. A sense of doom dropped, like a weight, into her stomach. "*What* has happened?"

"Last night . . . a German submarine breached the defences of Scapa Flow. Most of the Home Fleet were at sea, but the *Royal Oak* was there, in the harbour, at anchor . . . She's been torpedoed, lost. Sank so quickly. Over-turned . . . three torpedoes . . . impossible for anybody below decks to escape . . ."

Ned's ship. But not Ned. Ned was all right. Ned would have survived.

". . . about four hundred of the ship's company are believed to be safe . . . the news hasn't broken yet. Bob says I must tell Biddy before she hears it on the wireless. He wants me to go and tell her. He couldn't bear her to be told, by him, over the telephone. I have to go and tell her . . ."

For the second time, Hester's voice faltered. Her beautifully manicured hand came up to brush away tears that had not even fallen. "I am touched that he thought of me, but yet I would rather he had asked any other person in the world . . ."

She had not wept. She was not going to weep.

Judith swallowed, and made herself say it. "And Ned?"

Hester shook her head. "Oh, my dear child, I am so dreadfully sorry."

And it was not until then that the truth—lying in wait, always there—finally pounced, and Judith knew that what Hester Lang was telling her was that Ned Somerville was dead.

Upper Bickley,
October 25th, 1939.

Dear Colonel Carey-Lewis,

Thank you so much for your very kind letter about Ned. It has been the most shattering time, but Biddy is grateful for letters and reads them all. But really isn't able to answer them herself.

After the *Royal Oak* was sunk, Uncle Bob was not able to come at once to be with her, on account of being in Scapa Flow, and the crisis of the attack and its aftermath. But he got home last week for a couple of days; it was really terrible, because he was trying to comfort Biddy, and feeling all the time just as lost and bereft as she does. Now he's gone back to Scapa Flow, and we're on our own again.

I am staying here over the winter. When the spring comes, I'll think again, but I can't leave Biddy on her own until she has got over her grieving. She has a dog called Morag which Ned gave to her, but I am not sure whether she is a comfort to Biddy or a sad reminder. My own sadness is that none of you ever met Ned, nor got to know him. He was such a special person and so dear.

Please send my love to everybody, and thank you again for your letter. Always,

Judith

Nancherrow,
1st November, 1939.

Darling Judith,

We were all so terribly sad about your Cousin Ned being killed. I thought of you for days and wished I could be with you. Mummy says that if you want to bring your Aunt Biddy down for a few days, just for a break, she would love to have you both to stay. But on the other hand, at the moment, she may just prefer to stay in her own house and her own surroundings.

Pops says that the German submarine getting into Scapa Flow was an epic piece of seamanship, but I can't think of one single nice thing to say about Germans and think he is being very magnanimous.

If I give you some news you mustn't think that I think what is happening here is more important than Ned being killed.

First is that Athena is home, and is going to have a baby. Rupert has gone overseas with his regiment and their horses, and the Caledonian Hotel, without him, lost its charms, so she came home. I think he has gone back to Palestine.

The baby comes in July.

Gus is in France with the Highland Division and the British Expeditionary Force. I write to him a lot and get a letter at least once a week. He sent me the photo of him in his kilt and he looks absolutely gorgeous.

I saw Heather Warren the other day in Penzance. She's doing shorthand and typing in Porthkerris and she's going to try to get into the Foreign Office or some sort of Civil Service job. She said to tell you she'd write to you when she had a moment, and to say that Charlie Lanyon is in the DCLI, and he's gone to France too. I don't know who Charlie Lanyon is, but she said that you would know. And Joe Warren's joined the DCLI as well, but Paddy is still fishing.

Edward doesn't write but he rings up every now and then, and we have to talk very quickly because he's only allowed three minutes and then the 'phone goes *ping* and it's all over. He seems to be enjoying himself, and he's got one of the new planes which are called Spitfires. It would be lovely if he got home for Christmas, but I don't suppose he will.

The hens have come and are all fenced in on the back lawn and creating havoc. They have little wooden houses with nesting boxes and doors that shut at night to keep naughty Mr. Fox out. They haven't started laying yet, but once they do I expect we shall live on eggs.

It's getting dreadfully chilly. Pops is being strict about the central heating and the dust-sheets have all gone over the drawing-room furniture and the chandelier is all tied up in a bag to stop it getting dusty. It looks a bit bleak, but the small sitting-room is much cosier.

Mr. Nettlebed has become an air-raid warden. This means that if he forgets to do the black-out, or a chink of light shows, then he has to charge himself with negligence and take himself to court to be fined. Ha ha.

The other unexpected air-raid warden is Tommy Mortimer, but of course he's in London. He couldn't join up because of his age and his flat feet (didn't know he had them), so he's gone into Civil Defence. He came down for a weekend and told us all about it. He says if there are bombing raids he has to stand on the roof of Mortimer's in Regent Street with a bucket of water and a stirrup-pump. If Mortimer's gets bombed, do you suppose there will be diamond rings all over the pavement?

Mummy's okay. Loves having Athena here. They giggle away over *Vogue*, just like they always did, and are trying to knit baby clothes.

Lots of love. Come and stay if you want. Kisses,

Loveday

Upper Bickley,
Saturday 30th December.

Dear Mummy and Dad,

It's nearly the end of the year, and I'm glad it's over. Thank you so much for my Christmas present, which came at the beginning of the month, but which I saved up till Christmas Day to open. It is the most lovely handbag, and just what I needed. I loved the length of silk as well, and shall have it made up into an evening skirt when I can find someone who can do it really professionally. It is the most gorgeous colour. And please thank Jess for her home-made calendar; tell her the monkeys and the elephants were really well-drawn.

It has suddenly got bitterly cold, and there is snow all over Dartmoor and down the road, and blue shadows everywhere, and the roofs of all the houses have got thick hats of snow and Bovey Tracey looks a bit like the pictures of *The Tailor of Gloucester*. Each morning we give hay to the Dartmoor ponies that come down off the hill to shelter from the wind behind the wall, and taking Morag for a walk is a bit like trudging off to the South Pole. The house isn't much warmer—not quite as cold as Keyham but just about. I'm sitting in the kitchen writing this because it's the warmest place in the house. Wearing two jerseys.

Uncle Bob got home for four days over Christmas but has gone again now. I really dreaded Christmas without Ned, but Hester Lang came to our rescue and asked us out for lunch, and we didn't have a tree or tinsel or anything, tried to treat it just like an ordinary day. Hester had a nice couple staying from London, quite elderly but very cultured and interesting, and the talk over lunch was not about the war, but things like art galleries and travelling in the Middle East. I think he was an archaeologist.

Here Judith paused and laid down her pen and blew on her cramped and chilled fingers, and wondered if she could be bothered to make a pot of tea. It was nearly four o'clock, and Biddy and Morag were not yet home from their walk. Beyond the kitchen window, the darkening garden sloped up onto the moor, and all was frozen and white with snow. The only green to be seen were the dark branches of the pines, restless in the east wind, blowing up from the sea. The single sign of life was a robin, pecking nuts from the bag which Judith had hung from the bird table.

She looked at the robin and thought about this sad, grey Christmas, which, somehow or other, and with Hester's help, they had managed to survive. And then, allowing herself the luxury of a wallow in nostalgia, remembered last Christmas, and Nancherrow, with all the lovely house filled with guests, and light and laughter everywhere. Sparkling decorations, and the sprucey smell of the Christmas tree, with presents piled beneath its spreading branches.

And sounds. Christmas carols sung at morning service in Rosemullion Church; pots clattering from Mrs. Nettlebed's kitchen as she prepared enormous quantities of delicious food; Strauss waltzes.

She remembered dressing for dinner, in her own pretty pink bedroom, dizzy with excitement; the scent of make-up and the silken sensation as her first delectable grown-up evening dress slipped over her head. And then, going through the open drawing-room door, and Edward coming to take her hand, to tell her, "We're drinking champagne."

A year ago, only a year. But already another time, another world. She sighed and reached for her pen, and went on with her letter.

Biddy is all right, but still not able to cope with anything very much. It is really difficult because I am still spending the mornings with Hester Lang, doing shorthand and typing, but often Biddy isn't out of bed by the time I've left the house. Mrs. Dagg comes, of course, so she isn't alone, but it's a bit as though Biddy has lost all interest in everything. She doesn't want to do anything, or see anybody. Friends ring her up, but she won't even go and play bridge, and she doesn't really like it if kindly friends drop in.

The only person who refuses to be put off is Hester Lang, and I think she will be the one to ease Biddy back into her circle of friends—I don't know how we would have managed without her. She is so wise and kind. She comes up to Upper Bickley most days, on some excuse or other, and I think next week is planning a bridge party, and insisting that Biddy goes. It really is time she began to see people again. At the moment she's out with Morag, and when she comes back I shall make a cup of tea.

She doesn't talk about Ned, and I don't either because I don't think she is able to yet. It will be better when she gets interested in Red Cross work or something. She is too energetic a person to be doing nothing for the war effort.

I hope all this doesn't depress you, it's no good telling you that Biddy is fine, because she isn't. But I am sure very soon she will be better. Whatever, I am staying with her for the time being, and we get on terribly well, so you mustn't be worried about either of us.

The day after tomorrow, it will be New Year's Day, 1940. I miss you all dreadfully, and sometimes wish I were with you all, but with all that has happened, I know I made the right decision. How worried we would all have been to think of Biddy on her own.

Must stop, because I'm frozen. I shall go and hurl logs on the sitting-room fire and draw the black-out and work up a fug. Biddy and Morag are back, I can see them coming up the path from the gate. We had to dig snow away and cover the path with cinders from the boiler, so that the poor postman (who walks everywhere) could deliver the letters without breaking his leg.

Lots of love to you all. I'll write NEXT YEAR.

Judith

1940

By the end of March, after the coldest winter that most people could remember, the worst of the snow and the ice had finally disappeared, and on Dartmoor only random traces remained, caught in sunless ditches or piled against the more exposed of the drystone walls. As the days lengthened, the warm west wind brought a softness to the air, trees budded and birds returned to their summer habitats; wild primroses studded the high Devon hedges, and in the garden of Upper Bickley the first of the daffodils tossed their yellow heads in the breeze.

In Cornwall, at Nancherrow, the house filled up with sophisticated refugees from London, abandoning the city and arriving to stay for Easter. Tommy Mortimer stole a week's leave from his Civil Defence and stirrup-pump, and Jane Pearson brought her two children for the entire month. Jane's husband, the solid and well-meaning Alistair, was now in the Army and in France, and her nanny, younger than anybody had ever realized, had returned to nursing, gone to run a surgical ward in a military hospital in the south of Wales. Bereft of Nanny, Jane had pluckily undertaken the train journey to Penzance with only herself to amuse and discipline her offspring, and as soon as she arrived, had off-loaded them onto Mary Millyway, while she curled up on a sofa, sipped a gin and orange, chatted to Athena, and generally let her hair down. She was still living in her little house in Lincoln Street, and having such a good time that she made no plans to leave London. Never in her life had she had such fun, out on the town, and lunching at the Ritz or the Berkeley with dashing wing commanders or young Guards officers.

"What about Roddy and Camilla?" Athena asked, rather as though they were puppies, and half-expecting to be told that Jane simply put them into kennels.

"Oh, my daily lady stays with them," Jane replied airily, "or I leave them with my mother's maid." And then, "My dear, I must tell you. Too exciting . . ." And she was off, regaling them with another blissful encounter.

All these casual guests brought with them their emergency ration cards, for buying butter, sugar, bacon, lard, and meat, but as well, Tommy provided a store of unlikely pre-war delicacies from Fortnum & Mason. Pheasant in aspic, chocolate-coated cashew nuts, scented tea, and tiny jars of Beluga caviar.

Mrs. Nettlebed, eyeing these assorted gifts as they were placed upon her kitchen table, was heard to remark that it was a pity that Mr. Mortimer couldn't lay his hands on a decent leg of pork.

The Nancherrow staff was by now much diminished. Both Nesta and Janet had departed, in some excitement, to put on uniform, make munitions, and do their bit for the war effort. Palmer and the under-gardener had both been called up, and the only replacement to be found was Matty Pomeroy, an old-age pensioner from Rosemullion, who came each morning on a creaking bicycle and worked at the pace of a snail.

Hetty, of course, being too young to be of much use to anybody, was still in the scullery, breaking dishes and driving Mrs. Nettlebed demented, but now all the house guests had to buckle to, seeing to their own black-out curtains, making their own beds, and volunteering to wash dishes and hump logs. Meals were still served, in certain formality, in the dining-room, but the drawing-room was closed, swathed in dust-sheets, and the best of the silver had been cleaned, wrapped in chamois bags, and stowed, for the duration of the war, carefully away. Nettlebed, relieved of the tedious chore of polishing silver, which in the old days had filled much of his day, drifted imperceptibly out of doors. This was a gradual progression, started by Nettlebed emerging from the kitchen to make sure that old Matty wasn't idling behind the potting-shed, sneaking ten minutes or so with his smelly pipe. Then he volunteered to dig up a shore or two of potatoes for Mrs. Nettlebed, or to cut a cabbage. Before long, he had put himself in charge of the vegetable garden, planning crops and overseeing Matty Pomeroy, all with his customary thoroughness and competence. In Penzance, he bought himself a pair of rubber boots, and wearing these, dug a trench for runner beans. Gradually, his grave and pallid features became quite sunburnt, and his trousers started to look a bit loose. Athena swore that, at heart, Nettlebed was a son of the soil, and for the first time in his life had found his true vocation, and Diana, much amused, decided that it was rather chic to have a suntanned butler, provided he managed to scrub the earth out of his fingernails before serving the soup.

It was in the middle of these Easter holidays, on the night of the eighth of April, that Lavinia Boscawen died.

She died in her own bed, in her own bedroom at the Dower House. Aunt Lavinia had never fully recovered from the illness which had so frightened and disturbed the family, but had peacefully survived the winter, getting up each day, sitting by her fireside, busily knitting khaki socks. She had not been unwell, nor in any sort of pain. One night, she had simply gone to bed as usual, fallen asleep, and never woken.

It was Isobel who found her. Old Isobel, treading upstairs with Mrs. Boscawen's early-morning tea tray (Earl Grey, a slice of lemon), tapping at the door, and then going in to wake her mistress. She laid the little tray down on the bedside table and went to draw back the curtains and raise the black-out blind.

"Lovely morning," she observed, but there was no response.

She turned. "Lovely morning . . ." she repeated, but knew, even as she said the words, that there was never going to be any sort of reply. Lavinia Boscawen lay quietly, her head on the downy pillow, just as she had gone to sleep. Her eyes were closed and she looked years younger and very peaceful. Isobel, old, and versed in the ways of death, took a silver hand mirror from the dressing-table and held it to Mrs. Boscawen's lips. There was no breath, no movement. Stillness. Isobel put down the mirror, and gently covered Mrs. Boscawen's face with the embroidered linen sheet. Then she pulled down the blind and went downstairs. In the hall, with some reluctance, because she had always hated the horrid instrument, she picked up the telephone, put the receiver to her ear, and asked the girl on the switchboard to put her through to Nancherrow.

Nettlebed, laying breakfast in the dining-room, heard the telephone ringing from the Colonel's study. He glanced at the clock, saw that it was twenty to eight, set a fork precisely in its place, and went to answer the call.

"Nancherrow."

"Mr. Nettlebed?"

"Speaking."

"It's Isobel. From the Dower House. Mr. Nettlebed . . . Mrs. Boscawen's dead. In her sleep. I found her this morning. Is the Colonel there?"

"He's not down yet, Isobel." Nettlebed frowned. "You're quite certain?"

"Oh, I'm certain all right. Not a breath from her lips. Peaceful as a child. The dear lady . . ."

"Are you alone, Isobel?"

"Of course I'm alone. Who else would be here?"

"Are you all right?"

"I have to talk to the Colonel."

"I'll fetch him."

"I'll wait."

"No. Don't wait. He'll ring you. Just stay near the phone, so that you hear it."

"Nothing wrong with my hearing."

"You're sure you're all right?"

Isobel did not answer this. She said gruffly, "Just tell the Colonel to ring me dreckly," and rang off.

Nettlebed replaced the receiver and stood looking at it for a moment or two. Mrs. Boscawen dead. After a bit, he said aloud, "What a bugger," and then went out of the room and made his sedate way upstairs.

He found the Colonel in his bathroom shaving. He wore a paisley dressing-gown over his striped pyjamas and leather slippers on his feet, and had slung a towel around his neck. He had shaved one side of his face, but the other was still white with scented foam, and he stood there, on the bath-mat, with his cut-throat razor in his hand and listened to the news relayed from his portable wireless, which he had placed on the mahogany lid of the lavatory. Nettlebed, approaching, heard the grave, measured tones of the BBC news reader, but when he discreetly cleared his throat and rapped on the panel of the open door, the Colonel, turning to see him, put up a hand for silence, and the two men listened together to the morning bulletin. Grave tidings. German troops had moved into Denmark and Norway in the early hours of the morning. Three troop-ships had sailed into Copenhagen Harbour, ports and islands had been occupied, and the vital sea passages of the Skagerrak and the Kattegat were now under enemy control. In Norway, the German Navy had landed troops in every Norwegian port as far north as Narvic. A British destroyer had been sunk . . .

The Colonel stooped and switched off the wireless. Then straightened, turned to his mirror, and continued shaving. Through the looking-glass, his eyes met Nettlebed's.

"Now," he said, "this is the beginning."

"Yes, sir. It seems so."

"Always, the element of surprise. But why should we be surprised?"

"I've no idea, sir." Nettlebed hesitated, reluctant at such a moment to speak. But it had to be done. "I'm sorry, sir, to disturb you, but I'm afraid I have to impart even more sad tidings." *Scrape*, went the cut-throat razor, leaving a swath of clean skin down the soapy cheek. "Isobel has just tele-phoned, sir, from the Dower House. Mrs. Boscawen has passed on. Last night, in her sleep. Isobel found her this morning and telephoned at once. I told her you would ring, sir, and she is waiting by the telephone."

He paused. After a bit, the Colonel turned, and there was on his face an expression of such anguish, sadness, *loss*, that Nettlebed was made to feel like a murderer. For a moment, a silence lay between them, and Nettlebed could think of no suitable words to fill it. Then the Colonel shook his head. "Oh God, so difficult to take in, Nettlebed."

"I am so very sorry, sir."

"When did Isobel ring?"

"Twenty to eight, sir."

"I'll be down in five minutes."

"Very good, sir."

"And Nettlebed . . . look out a black tie for me, would you?"

At Upper Bickley, the telephone rang, and Judith went to answer it.

"Hello."

"Judith, it's Athena."

"Goodness, what a surprise."

"Mummy wanted me to call you. I'm afraid it's very sad news, but really, in a way, not all that sad. Just sad for all of us. Aunt Lavinia died."

Judith, stunned, could think of nothing to say. She reached for an uncomfortable hall chair and crashed down.

"When?" she managed to say at last.

"Monday night. She just went to sleep and didn't wake up. Not ill or anything. We're all trying our hardest to be grateful for her and not to be selfish, but it feels a bit like the end of an era."

She sounded very cool and grown up and accepting. Judith was surprised. Before, when Aunt Lavinia had been so ill and given the whole family such a scare, Athena, she knew, had gone into hysterics of tears on being told, and had worked herself into such a state that Rupert had had to put her into his car and drive her all the way from the wilds of Scotland to the west of Cornwall. But now . . . Perhaps being married and pregnant had caused this metamorphosis, and enabled Athena to behave in such a rational and objective way. Whatever, Judith was grateful. It would have been unbearable to be given the news by a person in floods of weeping.

She said, "I am so dreadfully sorry. She was such a special person, so much a part of all of you. You must all feel devastated."

"We do, yes, we do."

"Is your mother all right?"

"Yes. And even Loveday. Pops gave us all a little talking to, and said that we must think not of ourselves but of Aunt Lavinia, all peaceful and quiet and not having to fret over this bloody war. Isn't everything too ghastly? At least she's being spared having to read the newspapers and look at all those horrible arrows and maps."

"It was sweet of you to tell me."

"Oh, darling Judith, of course we had to tell you. Aunt Lavinia always thought of you as one of the clan. And Mummy says would you come to the funeral? Not a frightfully jolly prospect, but it would mean a lot to us all if you did."

Judith hesitated. "When is it?"

"Next Tuesday, the sixteenth."

"Will . . . will you all be there?"

"Of course. The whole shooting-match. Not Edward, though, he's incarcerated on his airfield, I suppose waiting to shoot down German bombers. He tried to get compassionate leave, but things being the way they are, the answer was No. But all the rest of us will be. Including Jane Pearson, who's here with her kiddie-winks, and I think Tommy Mortimer wants to come. Too silly, he was here for a few days and then went back to London, and now he's got to come all the way down again. And this, with all of us being asked, 'Is your journey really necessary?' But he was terribly fond of Aunt Lavinia, even though he was always given sherry and never offered a pink gin. But do come. And stay. Everything's ready for you. We never allow anybody into *your* bedroom."

"I'll . . . I'll have to have a word with Biddy."

"Surely she'll be all right. Besides, it's about time we all saw you again. Come on Sunday. How will you get here? Will you drive?"

"Perhaps I should save my petrol."

"Then jump on a train. I'll meet you at Penzance. Petrol's not too much of a problem, because Pops and Nettlebed both get a few more coupons on account of being Civil Defence. Catch the *Riviera* . . ."

"Well . . ."

"Oh, *please* come. Say yes. We're all longing to see you and I want you to admire my bulge. And everybody sends love, and Loveday says she's got a favourite hen and she's called it after you. Must fly, darling. See you Sunday."

Judith sought out Biddy and explained the situation. "They want me to go to Nancherrow. To be there for the funeral."

"Then of course you must go. Poor old lady. What a sadness." Biddy eyed Judith, standing there chewing her lip. "You do *want* to go?"

"Yes, I think so."

"You sound uncertain. Will Edward be there?"

"Oh, Biddy . . ."

"Well, will he?"

Judith shook her head. "No. He can't get leave."

"If he was going to be there, would you want to go?"

"I don't know. I'd probably make some excuse."

"Darling, all that happened half a year ago, and since then you've been living with me like a saintly little nun. You can't languish over Edward Carey-Lewis for the rest of your life. Anyway, all this is hypothetical, because you say he won't be there. So off you go. See all your young friends again."

"I just feel bad leaving you on your own. What about cooking meals? You mustn't stop eating."

"I shan't. I shall buy tiddy-oggies from the baker and eat lots of fruit. And now that you've shown me how, I can boil an egg. And Mrs. Dagg will make me soup, and I simply adore bread and marge."

But Judith remained doubtful. To all outward appearances, Biddy was recovered. Prompted by Hester, she had joined the Red Cross and went to Hester's house two mornings a week, to pack comforts for the troops in France. As well, she had started playing bridge again, and seeing old friends. But Judith, living with her day in and day out, knew that with Ned's death something of Biddy had died as well, so that she could never truly come to

413

terms with the terrible loss of her only child. Some days, when the sun shone and there was a sparkle in the air, a flicker of her old liveliness returned, and she would come out with one of her marvellously funny, off-the-cuff observations and they would both start laughing, and for a moment it would be as though nothing had ever happened. But other days, a depression fell upon her, and she lay in bed and refused to get up, and smoked too many cigarettes, and kept glancing at the clock to see if it was time for her first drink of the evening. Often, Judith knew, she could not resist the temptation to jump the gun, and she would come in from a walk to find Biddy in her armchair cradling the precious glass in both hands, as though her very life depended on it.

She said, "I just don't like to leave you alone."

"I shall have Mrs. Dagg. I told you. And Hester down the road, and all my nice Red Cross ladies. And Morag for company. I'll be all right. Besides, you can't moulder here forever. Now that you and Hester have finished with the shorthand and typing, there's really no reason for you to stay. I don't want you to go, of course, but you must never *not* go just because of *me*. Let's face it, I must be independent. A few days without you will give me good practice."

So Judith was persuaded. She said, "All right," and smiled, because indecision was over and, with Biddy's encouragement, she had made up her see-saw of a mind. All at once she felt quite excited, as though she were planning a holiday, which, of course, she wasn't, and although she looked forward enormously to returning to Nancherrow, the fact remained that the two most special people were not going to be there. Aunt Lavinia because she had died, and Edward because of the exigencies of war. No. Wrong. Not the exigencies of war. Edward was lost to her forever because of Judith's own naïvety and inexperience. He had gone from her life and she had only herself to blame.

But. And it was a big but. Nancherrow was constant, and she was going back, to that place of comfort and warmth and luxury, where responsibilities could be dumped overboard and one could revel in the sensation of being a child again. Just for a few days. It was probably all going to be dreadfully sad, but she would be *there*, returned to her own pink bedroom, her loved possessions, her desk and her gramophone and her Chinese box. She thought of throwing open the window and leaning out, to the view of the courtyard and the glimpse of the sea and the sound of the white fantails cooing around the dovecote. And giggling with Loveday, and just being with Athena and Mary Millyway and Diana and the Colonel. Her heart filled with gratitude, and she knew that it was going to be the next best thing to coming home, and wondered if Aunt Lavinia, wherever she was, realized the wealth of her legacy.

The journey to Cornwall was steeped in nostalgia and memories. Plymouth Station, by now quite familiar, was choked with young sailors and kitbags, a raw draft, headed up-country. They assembled on the opposite platform, being bullied into some sort of line by an exasperated chief petty officer. When the *Cornish Riviera* drew in, they momentarily disappeared from view behind the huge, pulsing steam engine, but were still there as the train moved out of the station, and Judith's last sight of them was a blur of new, stiff navy-blue uniforms and youthful, pink-cheeked faces.

Almost at once the *Riviera* clattered over Saltash Bridge, and the harbour was filled with HM ships, grey no longer but painted all over with camouflage. Then, Cornwall: pink-washed houses, deep valleys, and viaducts. The train stopped at Par. "Par. Par. Par, change for Newquay," the station-master intoned as he had always done. Truro. Judith saw the little city clustered around the tall tower of the cathedral, and remembered coming to buy her gramophone with Mr. Baines, and being given lunch at the Red Lion. And she thought of Jeremy, as she had first seen him, and how he had gathered up his belongings and said goodbye, and left the train at Truro, and she had thought then that she would never see him again, and would certainly never get to know his name.

And at last, Hayle and the estuary, blue in a flood-tide, and on the far side, Penmarron, the gables of Riverview clearly visible through the young green of the April trees.

At the junction, she got her suitcase off the rack and stood in the corridor, not wishing to miss the first sighting of Mount's Bay and the sea. The beaches, as the train clattered along the edge of the coast, were tangled in barbed-wire defences, and there were concrete pillboxes, manned by soldiers, and tank-traps, prepared for an invasion by sea. And yet the bay sparkled in sunshine, just the way it had always done, and the air was filled with the scream of gulls and the strong tang of sea-wrack.

Athena was there, waiting for her. Standing on the platform, and instantly visible with her blonde hair blowing in the breeze. Her pregnancy was patently obvious, for she had made no prissy effort to conceal her shape, and wore baggy corduroy trousers and a man's shirt with the sleeves rolled up and the tails flying loose.

"Judith."

They met half-way down the platform, and Judith put down her case and they hugged. Despite her uncharacteristic ragamuffin appearance, Athena was scented, as always, by some deliciously expensive fragrance. "Goodness, heaven to see you. You've lost weight. I've gained it." She patted her stomach. "Isn't it too exciting? It gets bigger every day."

"When does it arrive?"

"July. I can't wait. Is this all your luggage?"

"What did you expect, cabin trunks and hat boxes?"

"The car's outside. Come on, let's get home."

The car was a bit of a surprise. Not one of the large, dignified vehicles that were so much part of Nancherrow, but a small van in shabby condition, with H. WILLIAMS, FISHMONGER, written in capitals on the side.

"Who's gone into the fish trade?" Judith asked in some amusement.

"Isn't it a scream? Pops bought it second-hand to save petrol. You've no idea how many people you can squash into the back. We only got it a week ago. We haven't had time to paint the name out yet. I don't think we should. I think it's frightfully chic. So does Mummy."

Judith loaded the case into the fishy-smelling interior and they set off. The van backfired a couple of times, and then leaped forward, narrowly missing the edge of the harbour wall.

"So sweet of you to come. We were all terrified you'd back out at the last moment. How's your aunt? Is she holding up? Poor Ned. Such a terrifically ghastly thing to happen. We were all so dreadfully sorry."

"She's all right. Recovering, I think. But it's been a long winter."

"I'll bet. What have you been doing?"

"Learning to do shorthand and type. I've got my speeds and everything now, so there's nothing to stop me joining up or getting some sort of a job."

"When are you going to do that?"

"I don't know. Someday." She changed the subject. "Have you heard anything from Jeremy Wells?"

"Why do you ask?"

"I was thinking about him in the train. When we got to Truro."

"His father called the other day because Camilla Pearson fell off the swing and cut her head open and Mary thought she might need a stitch but she didn't. He said Jeremy's bucketing to and fro across the Atlantic in a destroyer. Merchant-ship convoys. He didn't enlarge, but it all sounds pretty rough. And Gus is in France with the Highland Division, but nothing much seems to be happening *there*."

"And Rupert?" Judith asked, before Athena should start talking about Edward.

"Oh, he's fine. Writes lots of funny letters."

"Where is he?"

"Palestine. A place called Gedera. Only I'm not meant to tell anybody in case a spy is listening. And they're still a cavalry regiment, because they haven't been mechanized yet. I should have thought, after what happened to the Polish cavalry, they'd have turned to tanks pretty sharpish, wouldn't you? But I suppose the War Office knows what it's doing. He writes lots. He's thrilled about the baby. Keeps suggesting terrible names like Cecil and Ernest and Herbert. Rycroft family names. Too awful."

"What if it's a girl?"

"I shall call her Clementina."

"That's an orange."

"Perhaps she'll be an orange baby. Whatever, she'll be divine. I'm rather *into* children now, with Roddy and Camilla about the place. I always thought they were a bit spoilt—remember the whining that Christmas—but Mary Millyway's licked them into shape in no time and they're really sweet. Come out with the most killing remarks."

"And Tommy Mortimer?"

"He's arriving tomorrow. He wanted to bring his frock-coat, but Pops said that would be overdoing it a bit."

"Does it feel funny without Aunt Lavinia?"

"Yes. Strange. Like knowing there's an empty room in the house, with no flowers and the window closed. It's so final, isn't it? Death, I mean."

"Yes. It's final all right."

Afterwards, when it was all safely over, everybody decided that Lavinia Boscawen's funeral was so exactly *right*, that she might have arranged it herself. A sweet spring afternoon; Rosemullion Church filled with flowers, and Aunt Lavinia, peaceful in her coffin, waiting there to greet her closest friends for the last time. The narrow, uncomfortable pews were crammed with assorted individuals, none of whom, for all the world, would have missed out on the occasion. They came from all parts of the county and all walks of life, from the Lord Lieutenant downwards, and space was found for the most humble— the retired sailor from Penberth who had for years kept Mrs. Boscawen supplied with fresh fish, and the gormless youth who stoked the school boiler and cleaned out the primitive lavatories.

Isobel was there, of course, and the Dower House gardener, wearing his best green tweed suit, with a Gloire de Dijon rose in his buttonhole. From Penzance came a threesome of professional men: Mr. Baines, Mr. Eustick (the bank manager), and the proprietor of the Mitre Hotel. From Truro, Dr. and Mrs. Wells. Dowager Lady Tregurra had taken a taxi all the way from Launceston, and looked none the worse for the experience, but other mourners were not so spry and needed some assistance to get themselves from the lych-gate to the church, stumping down the yew-shaded path with sticks and canes, and having difficulty, once settled, with tiresome hearing aids and ear-trumpets. One old gentleman arrived in his wheelchair, propelled by his slightly less elderly manservant, and all the while, as the church filled up, the organ wheezed away, the music scarcely recognizable as Elgar's *Nimrod*.

The Nancherrow party occupied the first two pews. Edgar Carey-Lewis and Diana, Athena, Loveday, and Mary Millyway sat in the front. Behind them were their guests, Judith, Tommy Mortimer, and Jane Pearson, with Mr. and Mrs. Nettlebed. Hetty had been left behind to take care of Camilla and Roddy Pearson. Both Mary and Mrs. Nettlebed were a bit anxious about this arrangement, for Hetty was neither the brightest nor the most reliable of girls, but Mrs. Nettlebed, on departing for the church, had put the fear of God into Hetty, and told her that if she got home and found those children with beads up their noses, then there was going to be trouble.

All of them, by means of lending and borrowing, had managed to deck themselves out in inky black. All except Athena, who wore a flowing maternity dress of cream crêpe, and looked like a beautiful, quite serene, angel.

Finally, everybody was settled. The bell ceased its tolling and the organ wheezed, mid-passage, into silence. From the back of the church, through the door which had been left open, came the sound of birds tweeting.

The aged vicar heaved himself to his feet and at once decided that he needed to blow his nose. This took a moment or two, and everybody sat patiently and stared at him, while he fumbled for his handkerchief, shook it out of its folds, trumpeted into it, and stowed it away again. He then cleared his throat, and at last announced, in quavering tones, that Mrs. Carey-Lewis had asked him to intimate that all would be welcome, after the service, at Nancherrow for refreshment. With this important bit of business dealt with, he opened his prayer book, those of the congregation who could, stood, and the service began.

> I am the resurrection and the life, saith the Lord,
> he that believeth in me, though he were dead, yet
> shall he live . . .

They sang a hymn or two, and Colonel Carey-Lewis read a suitable passage from the Bible, and then there was a prayer, and it was all over. Six men moved forward to hoist Aunt Lavinia's coffin shoulder-high: the undertaker and his burly assistant, the Colonel, Tommy Mortimer, the verger, and the green-suited gardener, looking, as Athena remarked afterwards, a bit like a dear little gnome who had found himself at the wrong party. The coffin (strangely small) was borne away, out into the sunlit graveyard, and the congregation, at varying speeds, followed behind.

Judith, tactfully distanced from the family, watched the ritual of burial, and listened to the words. *Dust to Dust and Ashes to Ashes*, but it was hard to realize that anything so final had much to do with Aunt Lavinia. She looked about her and saw, standing a little way off, the tall figure of Mr. Baines, and she remembered Aunt Louise's funeral, in the bitter wind of the Penmarron churchyard, and how kind Mr. Baines had been to her that awful day. And then she found herself thinking about Edward, and wishing, for his sake, that he could have been here, so that he might have helped to carry Aunt Lavinia to her last resting place; to send her on her way.

Because the Nancherrow drawing-room was out of use, Aunt Lavinia's wake took place in the dining-room. All had been previously prepared and made festive. In the middle of the mantelpiece stood a huge arrangement of young beech leaves and pheasant's-eye lilies, which Diana had spent much of the morning contriving. In the fireplace, logs flamed cheerfully, although the April afternoon stayed so warm that it was possible to leave open the windows and let the cool, salty air into the house.

The great table, extended to its full length, had been laid with a white cloth and Mrs. Nettlebed's baking (two solid days of it), set out for all to admire and then consume. Sponge cakes, lemon-curd tarts, gingerbread, scones; tiny sandwiches of cucumber and gentleman's relish, iced fairy cakes and shortbread biscuits.

On the sideboard (Nettlebed's responsibility) were the two silver teapots, one with Indian tea, the other with China; the silver water jug, milk jug, and sugar bowl; and all the best eggshell cups and saucers. As well (discreetly placed), the whisky decanter, the soda syphon, and a number of cut-glass tumblers. The dining-room chairs had been ranged around the edge of the room. Gradually, these were occupied by the most infirm and tottery, while others stood, or moved about, exchanging small talk. Conversation rose and voices buzzed, and before long it all began to sound a bit like the best sort of cocktail party.

Judith, primed by Diana, helped carry trays and hand around the various goodies, pausing now and then to chat, or take an empty teacup to be refilled. So occupied was she that a little time had passed before there was an opportunity to have a word with Mr. Baines. She was headed for the sideboard, with a cup and saucer in each hand, and found herself, mid-passage, face-to-face with him.

"Judith."

"Mr. Baines. How lovely to see you, and how good of you to come . . ."

"Of course I came. You appear to be very busy."

"They all want more tea. I don't think anybody's used to such tiny cups."

"I want to talk to you."

"That sounds dreadfully serious."

"Be reassured. Not serious. Do you think we could remove ourselves for five minutes or so? There seem to be a number of waitresses, and I am sure you could be spared."

"Well . . . all right. But first I have to deal with these two, because the dear souls are waiting and parched."

"I had a quick word with Colonel Carey-Lewis. He says we may use his study."

"In that case, I'll be with you in a moment."

"Splendid. It should take no more than ten minutes." Loveday passed, with a plateful of scones, and he neatly removed one as she went by. "This will sustain me until you come."

At the sideboard, Judith refilled the cups and carried them back to Mrs. Jennings, who ran the Rosemullion Post Office, and her friend Mrs. Carter, who cleaned the brasses in the church.

"You're some lovely girl," she was told. "We're that dry after all the singing. Any more of that gingerbread, is there? Knew we'd get a handsome tea if Mrs. Nettlebed had anything to do with it . . ."

". . . how she manages with this rationing, I don't know . . ."

". . . she'll have had some put by, you can depend on that . . ."

Judith supplied the gingerbread and left them, munching genteelly and brushing stray crumbs from their lips with dainty little fingers. Then, casually, she eased her way from the room. It was something of a relief to get away from all the high-pitched chatter, and she went down the passage and through the open door of the Colonel's study. Mr. Baines was waiting, leaning against the heavy desk, and peacefully consuming the last of his stolen scone. He took out his silk handkerchief and wiped the crumbs from his fingers. He said, "What a spread."

"I haven't eaten anything. I've been too busy feeding others." She sank into a sagging leather armchair, and it was good to get the weight off her feet and to toe off her uncomfortable, high-heeled black patent leather pumps. She looked at him, and frowned. He had said that it was nothing serious, but his expression wasn't particularly cheerful. She hoped that he had been telling the truth. "What did you want to talk to me about?"

"A number of things. Most important, yourself. How are you?"

She shrugged. "All right."

"Colonel Carey-Lewis told me the sad news of your cousin's death. That was tragic."

"Yes. Yes, it was. He was only twenty. It's terribly young to die, isn't it? And it happened so soon into the war . . . almost before we'd got used to the idea that we actually *were* at war. It just came out of the blue."

"He told me, too, that you'd decided not to join your family, but to stay in this country."

Judith smiled wryly. "You seem to have caught up on everything that's happened."

"I see the Colonel from time to time in the Penzance Club. I like to keep tabs on my clients. I hope you have good news from Singapore . . ."

So she told him the latest tidings from her mother, and then went on and explained about Hester Lang and the shorthand and typing lessons, that had helped, somehow, to fill the long, cold, bereaved winter at Upper Bickley. "I've got my speeds now, so I suppose I can leave Biddy and go and get a job or something, but I feel a bit reluctant just to walk out and leave her alone . . ."

"There is a time for everything. Perhaps it will come sooner than you think. Whatever, you seem to be surviving. Now, there's something else I have to tell you. It's about Colonel Fawcett."

Judith froze. What ghastly item of information was Mr. Baines about to impart? The fact that it mightn't be ghastly never occurred to her because even now mention of Billy Fawcett's name was quite enough to chill her heart with apprehension.

"What about him?"

"Don't look so petrified. He's dead."

"*Dead?*"

"It happened only last week. He was in the bank, in Porthkerris, I think cashing a cheque. And the bank manager emerged from his office and said, very politely, that he would like to have a word about Colonel Fawcett's overdraft, and would Colonel Fawcett like to step this way? Whereupon the old man flew into a fearful rage, all at once turned blue in the face, gave a small choking cry, and fell flat on his back. Immovable. You can imagine the consternation. It turned out that he had suffered a massive stroke. An ambulance was called, and he was wheeled off to the Penzance General, but was found to be dead on arrival."

Judith could think of nothing to say. As Mr. Baines spoke, her initial shock and horror were gradually replaced by an hysterical desire to laugh, because she could picture the scene of Billy Fawcett's demise so clearly, and it all seemed ludicrous rather than tragic . . . not all that different from the evening when Edward Carey-Lewis had deposited him in the gutter outside the Sliding Tackle.

On the verge of nervous giggles, she put a hand over her mouth, but her eyes betrayed her laughter, and Mr. Baines smiled in some sympathy and shook his head, as though at a loss for words.

"I suppose we should put on solemn faces, but I had exactly the same reaction when I was told what had happened. Once he lost his menace, he was a ridiculous figure of a man."

"I know I shouldn't be laughing."

"What else can one do?"

"So many people dying."

"I know. I'm sorry."

"Did he ever go to court?"

"Of course. Up before the judge at the Michaelmas Quarterly Assizes. He pleaded guilty, and his lawyer came out with a lot of irrelevant, extenuating circumstances: old, loyal soldier of the King, traumatic experiences in Afghanistan, et cetera, et cetera. So he got let off with a heavy fine and a telling-off. He was lucky not to be sent to jail, but I think the rest of his life was pretty miserable. Nobody in Penmarron wanted to have much to do with him, and he was asked to resign from the golf club."

"So what did he do with himself?"

"No idea. Boozed, I suppose. All we can be sure of is that he stopped visiting the cinema."

"What a miserable end to his life."

"I wouldn't be too sorry for him. Anyway, it's too late now for sorrow."

"I'm surprised Mr. Warren, or Heather, didn't let me know about him dying."

"I told you, it's only just happened. There was a small item in the *Western Morning News* a couple of days ago. Billy Fawcett was a man neither well known nor particularly well loved."

"That ought to make it sad."

"Don't be sad. Just put the whole unhappy business out of your mind for good."

All this time, Mr. Baines had stayed as she found him, with his tall, angular frame propped against the edge of Colonel Carey-Lewis's desk. Now, however, he stood and went to retrieve his briefcase, which he had placed in the seat of a chair. He put the briefcase on the carpet and sat, crossing one long leg over the other. Judith, watching him, guessed that he was going to take off his spectacles and give them a polish with his silk handkerchief. Which he did, and she knew of old that he was neatly collecting his thoughts.

He said, "Now, down to the real business," and put his spectacles on again, disposed of the handkerchief, and folded his arms. "It is perhaps a little precipitant, but I wanted to have a word before you departed once more for Devon. It's about Mrs. Boscawen's house . . ."

"The Dower House?"

"Exactly so. I wonder what your response would be if I suggested that you should buy it. As I said, it is not the most seemly of moments to mention such a course of events, but I've thought things over, and under the circumstances, decided there was no point in losing time."

He fell silent. Across the room, their eyes met. Judith stared at him, and wondered if he had suddenly taken leave of his senses. But he was clearly waiting for her reaction to this astonishing scheme. She said, "But I don't *want* a house. I'm eighteen. The last thing in the world that I need just now is a *house*. There's a war on, and I'll probably join the services and be away for years. What would I do with a *house* to worry about . . . ?"

"Let me explain . . ."

". . . besides, the Dower House, surely, can't be put on the market. Isn't it part of the Nancherrow estate?"

"Once it was. No longer. As soon as he was able, Mrs. Boscawen's husband bought the freehold."

"Won't Colonel Carey-Lewis want to buy it back?"

"I have discussed it with him, and apparently not."

"You've already talked to the Colonel about this?"

"Of course. I couldn't have approached you without having first heard his views on the subject. It's too important. I needed not simply his approval, but his opinion as well."

"Why is it so important? Why is buying the Dower House so important?"

"Because, as one of your trustees, I consider that property is probably the best investment you can possibly make. Bricks and mortar never lose their value, and, properly maintained, can only appreciate. And this is a good time to buy because house prices have dropped, as they always do in wartime, to an all-time low. I know you are very young, and the future is filled with uncertainties, but still, we must look ahead. Whatever happens, you would have a base. Roots of your own. Another consideration is your family. You, thanks to Mrs. Forrester, are the one with the money. Owning the Dower House would mean a home for your mother and father and Jess to return to when their time in Singapore is over. Or, at least, a base. Somewhere to stay until they are able to find a house for themselves."

"But that isn't going to happen for years."

"No. But it will happen."

Judith fell silent. All at once, it seemed there was a great deal to think about. The Dower House. Belonging to her. Her own home. Roots. The one thing that she had never known and always longed for. Lying back in the capacious armchair, she gazed at the empty fireplace and let her imagination lead her through the old house, with its quiet, old-fashioned rooms, the ticking clock, and the creaking stairs. The drawing-room, sparkling with sunlight and firelight; faded carpets and curtains, and always the scent of flowers. She thought of the dank stone passage that led to the ancient kitchen quarters, and the time-stopped atmosphere that never failed to enchant. She saw the view from the windows, with the line of the horizon lying across the topmost branches of the Monterey pines; and then the garden, leading in terraces down to the orchard, where stood Athena and Edward's hut. . . . Would it be possible to deal with so many diversified memories? At this moment there seemed no way of knowing.

She said, "I can't make up my mind so quickly."

"Think about it."

"I am. You have to understand, I've always dreamt of having a little house of my own, that belonged to nobody but myself. But that was just a dream. And if I can't live in it, then what is the point? If I bought the Dower House, then what would I do with it? It can't be left abandoned, standing empty."

"It needn't stand empty," Mr. Baines pointed out in tones of great reasonableness. "Isobel will go, of course. She's already made plans to live with her brother and his wife, and before she died Mrs. Boscawen arranged for an annuity for Isobel, so that she will be able to end her days with independence and necessary dignity. As for the house, it could be rented. Perhaps to some London family anxious to evacuate themselves to the country. There will be no shortage of takers, I am convinced. Or perhaps we could find a retired couple to caretake, or some person grateful for a roof over their head, and a small regular income . . ." He talked on persuasively, but Judith had stopped listening.

A person grateful for a roof over their head; a person who would care for the garden, and polish and clean the house as though it were her own. Who would think the old-fashioned kitchens the height of luxury and convenience, and would probably burst into tears of joy when she set eyes on the one small bathroom, with its white-painted tongue-and-groove walls, and the lavatory with the dangling chain and the handle with PULL written on it.

". . . the property, of course, is not in the best of order. I suspect a touch of dry rot in the kitchen floor, and there are a few damp patches in the attic ceilings, but . . ."

Judith said, "Phyllis."

Halted mid-stream, Mr. Baines frowned. "Sorry?"

"Phyllis. Phyllis could caretake." The idea expanded, flowered. Alight with excitement, she sat up, leaning forward, with her hands clasped on her knees. "Oh, *you* remember Phyllis. She used to work for us at Riverview. She's Phyllis Eddy now. She married Cyril, her young man, and she's got a baby. I went and saw her when I stayed at Porthkerris during the summer. I took my car. I hadn't seen her for four years . . ."

"But if she's married . . . ?"

"Don't you see? Cyril was a miner, but he's joined the Navy. He's left her. He always wanted to go to sea. He never wanted to be a miner. She wrote to me and told me all this when Ned was killed. She wrote me such a sweet letter . . ."

And she went on to explain to Mr. Baines about Phyllis and her humble circumstances, living in that cheerless cottage miles from anywhere out beyond Pendeen. And because it had been a tied cottage, belonging to the mining company, she had had to leave and return to her mother. ". . . and there are already far too many people living in that house. All Phyllis has ever wanted is a place of her own, with a garden and an indoor lav. She could bring her baby, and *she* could look after the Dower House for us. Wouldn't that be the most perfect arrangement?"

She waited expectantly for Mr. Baines to tell her how clever she was being. But Mr. Baines was too cautious for that.

"Judith, you're not buying a home for Phyllis. You're making an investment for yourself."

"But it's *you* who wants me to buy it, and *you* suggested a caretaker. And I've come up with the perfect answer."

He accepted this. "Fair enough. But would Phyllis want to leave her mother and move to Rosemullion? Wouldn't she miss her family and the company?"

"I don't think so. Pendeen was so bleak she couldn't even grow pansies in her garden. And she was always miles away from them there. Rosemullion's only a walk down the hill. When Anna's old enough, she can go to Rosemullion School. They'll make friends. Phyllis is so sweet, everybody will want to be her friend."

"You don't think she'll find it lonely?"

"She's lonely anyway, with Cyril gone. She might as well be lonely somewhere nice."

Mr. Baines, clearly overwhelmed by this volte-face, took off his spectacles, leaned back in his chair, and rubbed his eyes. Then he put his spectacles on again. He said, "We seem to have gone from one extreme to the other. I think we must slow down a bit and try to steer a middle course. Plan sensibly and sort out priorities. This is a big step we're considering, and an expensive one. So you have to be really certain."

"How much will we have to pay?"

"I would guess in the region of two thousand pounds. There will be bound to be necessary repairs and renovations, but the bulk of these will have to wait until the war is over. We'll get a surveyor in . . ."

"Two thousand pounds. It seems a terrible lot of money."

Mr. Baines allowed himself a small smile. "But a sum that the trust can easily afford."

It was incredible. "Is there really so much? In that case, let's go ahead. Oh, don't argue any more."

"Five minutes ago, you were telling me that you didn't want it."

"Well, admit, it was a bit of a bombshell."

"I have always felt that it was a house filled with happiness."

"Yes." She looked away from him, and remembered once more the Hut, on that summer afternoon, and the smell of creosote and the sound of the bumble-bee buzzing about in the roof. But those memories, however painful, could not be allowed to interfere, to stop her from taking this enormously exciting step forward. Phyllis, uppermost in her mind, was of more immediate importance even than Edward. "The Chinese sell happiness. They put good men into a house, to live in it, and fill it with a tranquil spirit." She turned to smile at Mr. Baines. "Please get it for me."

"You're sure?"

"Quite sure."

So, for a little, they talked, discussing pros and cons, laying plans. In view of the fact that Bob Somerville was unavailable, miles away in Scapa Flow and fully occupied with fighting the war, a trustees' meeting would clearly not be possible. But Mr. Baines would be in touch with him, and as well would contact a surveyor. Meantime, nothing must be said. Especially, Mr. Baines warned with some severity, to Phyllis.

"How about my parents?"

"I think you should write to them, and let them know our intentions."

"They won't get the letter for three weeks, anyway."

"By which time we should have some idea of the way things are going to work out. When do you return to Devon?"

"In a day or so."

"I have your telephone number. I'll call you there when I have any news."

"What will happen then?"

"I think you should come back to Cornwall, and we'll finalize all the arrangements. And once everything is signed and sealed, then you can approach your friend Phyllis."

"I can't wait."

"Just be patient."

"You've been so kind."

He looked at his watch. "I have kept you far too long. By now the tea-party will be over."

"It's not a party. It's a wake."

"It sounded like a party."

"Is it wrong to feel so excited on Aunt Lavinia's funeral day?"

"I think," said Mr. Baines, "that the reason for your excitement would afford her nothing but pleasure."

But a month had passed at Upper Bickley before the telephone call came through from Mr. Baines. A Thursday morning. Biddy had taken herself off to Hester's house and her Red Cross ladies, and Judith was in the front garden gathering the first of the lily of the valley to sweeten the sitting-room. The bunch of slender, wiry stems grew in her hands, and the scent of the tiny bell blossoms was delicious, set in their coronet of pointed leaves . . .

She heard the telephone ring from the house. Paused, in case Mrs. Dagg also heard it and answered the call; but it went on ringing, so she hurried up the lawn and through the garden door into the hall.

"Upper Bickley."

"Judith. Roger Baines here."

"Mr. Baines." She laid the bunch of lily of the valley carefully down on the hall table. "I've been waiting for you to ring up."

"I'm sorry. It's all taken longer than I anticipated. But I think we're home and dry now. The surveyor . . ."

But Judith didn't want to know what the surveyor had had to say. "Are we going to be able to buy the Dower House?"

"Yes. It's all been arranged. All we need now is your presence and a few signatures."

"*Oh.* The relief of it. I thought something awful had come up, some obstruction, or some unknown relation claiming possession."

"No. Nothing so disastrous. The only thing is, it's costing three thousand, and the surveyor's report is not that good . . . "

"Never mind."

"But you *should* mind." She heard the amusement in his voice. "As a householder you should be aware of all the defects . . . no point in buying a pig in a poke."

"Someday, we'll mend the defects. The most important thing is that we've got it." She could tell Phyllis. That was going to be the best bit. Driving over to Saint Just and telling Phyllis. Thinking about it, she simply couldn't wait to see Phyllis's face. She said, "What do you want me to do?"

"Come back to Cornwall as soon as you can, and we'll get all the legalities signed and sealed."

"What day is it today?"

"Thursday."

"I'll come on Monday. Is that soon enough? I need a bit of time to organize things here, meals and such for the weekend. But I'll come on Monday. Biddy and I have been frightfully sparing with our petrol coupons, so I'll drive in the car."

"Where will you stay?"

"Nancherrow, I suppose."

"If you wanted you could stay with myself and my wife."

"Oh, you are kind. Thank you. But I'm sure it'll be all right at Nancherrow. Anyway, I'll ring you up when I know when I'm arriving. Probably lunchtime on Monday."

"Come straight to my office."

"I'll do that."

"Goodbye, Judith."

"Goodbye. And thank you."

426

She put the receiver back on the hook and stood there, smiling in an idiotic fashion for a moment or two. And then gathered up the bunch of lilies of the valley and went down the hall and into the kitchen.

There she found Mrs. Dagg, sitting at the table and having her mid-morning break. This entailed making a cup of strong tea and eating any small scrap of food that she found, set aside, on the slate shelf of the larder. Sometimes it was a mouthful or two of cauliflower cheese, sometimes a cold lamb sandwich. Today her snack was half a tinned peach, left over from last night's pudding, enlivened by a blob of Bird's Custard. While she enjoyed this small repast, Mrs. Dagg usually read the juicy bits out of the morning's paper, but this morning she had forgotten about the juicy bits and was onto more serious stuff.

She looked up as Judith came through the door. Mrs. Dagg was a wiry lady, with tightly permed grey hair, and wore a wraparound overall hectically patterned with peonies. It had been made by one of the Women's Institute ladies out of a length of cretonne left over from somebody's curtains, and the bright colours had caught Mrs. Dagg's eye at the Church Sale last Christmas. The bright colours had been catching Judith and Biddy's eyes ever since.

Usually a cheerful lady, she looked, at the moment, distinctly down-in-the-mouth. She said, "I don't know, I'm sure . . ."

"What don't you know, Mrs. Dagg?"

"These Germans. Look at this picture of what they've done to Rotterdam. Blown it to bits. And now the Dutch Army's surrendering, and they're getting forward into France. I thought they weren't going to get through the Maginot Line. That's what everybody *said*. Hope it isn't going to be like the last time. Trenches and everything. Dagg was in the trenches, and said he'd never seen such mud."

Judith pulled out a chair and sat opposite Mrs. Dagg, and Mrs. Dagg pushed the paper across and continued, without much joy, to consume her tinned peach.

Judith glanced at the black-head-lined page, and saw what Mrs. Dagg meant. The maps, with their thrusting black arrows. The Germans had crossed the Meuse. And where were the British Expeditionary Force? She thought of them all out there: Gus and Charlie Lanyon, and Alistair Pearson, and Joe Warren and the thousands of other young British soldiers.

She said, "They can't *possibly* overrun France!" The photograph of shattered Rotterdam scarcely bore looking at. "It's just an initial attack. I'm sure, in no time, all the arrows will be pointing in the other direction."

"Well, I don't know, I think you're being a bit hopeful, if you ask me. Mr. Churchill says it's going to be blood, sweat, toil, and tears. Mind you, he's quite right, giving it to us straight. No point in thinking it's going to be a doddle, this war. And they wouldn't be starting that there Local Defence Volunteers if they didn't think the Germans were going to come. Dagg's going to join. Says we're better to be safe than sorry. But what good he's going to be I can't imagine. He's got no eye for a gun. Can scarcely pot a rabbit, let alone a German."

As Mrs. Dagg was refusing to be optimistic, Judith folded the paper and set it aside. She said, "Mrs. Dagg, I want to talk to you about something. I have to see my solicitor. Would you be able to keep an eye on Mrs. Somerville for me? Like you did before?"

She had expected instant agreement, reassurance that they had managed splendidly before, and would do so again. But Mrs. Dagg's reaction to her innocent proposal was quite startlingly unenthusiastic. To begin with, she didn't say anything. Just sat, with lowered eyes, and fiddled about with the remains of the peach. Watching her, Judith saw a red mottling stain Mrs. Dagg's neck and cheeks, and her mouth worked as she bit her lips.

"Mrs. Dagg?"

Mrs. Dagg laid down her spoon.

"Mrs. Dagg, what's wrong?"

After a bit, Mrs. Dagg looked up, and across the table their eyes met.

"I don't think," said Mrs. Dagg, "that that's a very good idea."

"But why not?"

"Well. To tell you the truth, Judith, I don't think I can be responsible. For Mrs. Somerville, I mean. Not on my own. Not with you away."

"Why not?"

"When you're not here . . ." Mrs. Dagg's eyes were agonized. "When you're not here, she *drinks*."

"But . . ." Suddenly, Judith's heart was filled with fear, all elation extinguished. "But, Mrs. Dagg, she's always enjoyed a drink. A gin at lunch-time and a couple of whiskies in the evening. Everybody knows that. Uncle Bob knows that."

"It's not that sort of drinking, Judith. It's heavy stuff. Too much. Dangerous."

And she spoke so quietly and definitely that Judith knew that Mrs. Dagg was neither exaggerating nor lying. She said, "How do you know? How can you be sure?"

"By the empty bottles. You know where the empties go, in that crate out in the garage. And then it's set out for the dustbin man each week. When you were away, I came in one morning and Mrs. Somerville wasn't even up, and I went up to see that she was all right, and her bedroom reeked of spirits and she was dead asleep. I've seen drunks sleep like that, but no one else. I couldn't understand it. The empties crate wasn't overflowing, nor nothing like that, so I had a look in the dustbin, and under all the old papers and tins I found two empty whisky bottles and an empty gin bottle. She'd *hidden* them from me. That's how drunks carry on. Hide the evidence. I had an uncle, couldn't stop drinking, and there were empty bottles all over the house, in his sock drawer and down the back of the lav."

She paused, seeing the growing horror on Judith's face. She said, "I'm sorry, Judith. Really. I didn't want to tell you, but I must. I think it's just when she's lonely. She's all right with you around, but I'm only here in the mornings, and with just the dog to talk to I suppose she just couldn't stand the loneliness, and the Captain so far away, and Ned dead." Suddenly, Mrs. Dagg began to cry, and Judith couldn't bear it. She leaned forward and laid her hand over Mrs. Dagg's work-worn one.

"Please, Mrs. Dagg, don't be so upset. You were quite right to tell me. And of course I won't leave her. I won't leave her with you."

"But . . ." Mrs. Dagg found a handkerchief and dabbed at her eyes and blew her nose. Her mottled complexion was beginning to fade. Clearly having spilled the beans and shed responsibility for the awful truth, she was about to feel better. "But you *said*. You said you had to go and see your solicitor. That's important. You can't put it off."

"I won't."

"Perhaps," Mrs. Dagg suggested timidly, "Miss Lang would have her to stay. That's all Mrs. Somerville needs. Just a bit of company."

"No, I can't ask Hester Lang. It's too much to ask, and besides, Biddy would just become suspicious." She thought hard. "I . . . I'll take her with me. Pretend it's a little holiday. The weather's getting nicer and Cornwall will be lovely. We'll drive down together."

"Where are you going to stay?"

"I . . . I *was* going to Nancherrow. To my friends." She could still go, and take Biddy with her, certain of Diana Carey-Lewis's boundless hospitality. *Oh darling, of course you must bring her,* Diana would say. *I've never met her and I've always longed to. What fun. When will you arrive?*

But in Biddy's uncertain state, perhaps Nancherrow was not such a good idea after all. Visions of Biddy becoming tipsy at dinner, under the frosty gaze of Nettlebed, did not bear imagining. "But I won't go there. We'll go to an hotel. The Mitre in Penzance. I'll ring up and book rooms. And I'll be with her all the time, and I can drive her round and take her to where we used to live. It'll do her good. She's been here, with her sadness, all winter. It's time she had a change."

"What about the dog?" Mrs. Dagg asked. "You can't take a dog to a hotel."

"Why not?"

"She might do her business on the carpet."

"I'm sure she won't . . ."

"You could leave her with me, I suppose," Mrs. Dagg suggested, but without much enthusiasm.

"You're very kind, but I'm sure we will manage splendidly. And we can take Morag on walks on the beach."

"Just as well, really. Dagg's not all that fond of dogs. Thinks they should live out of doors, not in the sitting-room."

A thought occurred to Judith. "Mrs. Dagg, have you told your husband . . . about Mrs. Somerville and the empty bottles?"

"Haven't said a word to anyone. Only you. Dagg likes his beer, but he can't stand a drunk. I didn't want him telling me I had to stop working for Mrs. Somerville. You know how some men can be."

"Yes," said Judith, who didn't. "I suppose I do."

"Least said, soonest mended, I always say."

"You are a good friend, Mrs. Dagg."

"Oh, that's rubbish talk." Mrs. Dagg was just about herself again. She picked up her cup, took a mouthful of tea, and instantly screwed up her face. "Disgusting. Stone cold." She sprang to her feet and flung the contents of the cup into the sink.

"Make another pot, Mrs. Dagg, and I'll join you."

"Won't get my housework done at this speed."

Judith said, "Oh, damn the housework."

In Cornwall, the first welcome warmth of the summer had already come. The heat of the sun was tempered by a refreshing breeze that smelt of the sea, and all the countryside was dressed in the sweet, soft colours of May: the fresh green of young leaves and new grass, the creamy candles of chestnut flowers, the pink of rhododendron, the white of hawthorn, and the dusty mauve of lilac spears nodding their heads over garden walls. The sea, tranquil beneath a cloudless sky, appeared luminous, streaked with aquamarine and hyacinth-blue, and in the early mornings a haze lay upon the horizon, to be later burnt away by the warmth of the sun.

In Penzance, the busy streets were washed with light and shadow. Judith came out of the Mitre Hotel and walked up Chapel Street and into the Greenmarket just as the bank clock chimed half past twelve. It was very warm, and she wore a cotton dress and sandals, and her legs were bare. Shop doors stood open, and awnings were out, and crates of fruit and earthy vegetables were stacked outdoors, on pavements. The fishmonger's marble slab was a sea of crushed ice, where lay, displayed, with dead eyes staring, whole cod and pilchards and shoals of glittering mackerel. The newsagent's placards were black with the morning's news—GERMANS REACH THE BELGIAN COAST—and yet, by his door, was the usual innocent, seasonal display of wooden spades and tin buckets, cotton sun-hats, shrimping nets and beach balls, smelling rubbery in the sun. There were even a few visitors about, come from London or Reading or Swindon; young mothers with little children, and old grannies with their ankles already swelling over newly acquired sand-shoes.

She passed through the Greenmarket and so into Alverton, where stood the small, desirable Georgian house that housed the offices of Tregarthen, Opie & Baines. Inside the fan-lighted door, the hallway was flooded with light from the stair window, and in an office, screened from visitors by a small aperture like a ticket-booth, sat the receptionist. There was a bell to ring, so Judith did, *ping,* and the receptionist got up from her typewriter and came to deal with the newcomer.

"Morning." She had a neat grey perm and rimless spectacles.

"I've come to see Mr. Baines. Judith Dunbar."

"He's expecting you. Can you go up? Know the way? First door on the right at the top of the stairs."

Judith went. The stairs had a Turkey carpet, and on the landing were portraits of former partners of the firm, whiskery and watch-chained. The door on the right had a brass plaque upon it, with his name: "Mr. Roger Baines." She knocked and he called "Come in," and she opened the door.

From behind the desk, he stood. "Judith."

"Here I am."

"Right on time, too. What a prompt girl. Come and sit down. How summery you're looking."

"Well, it's a summer's day."

"When did you get here?"

"About an hour ago. We left Upper Bickley straight after an early breakfast. There wasn't much traffic on the road."

"Is Mrs. Somerville with you?"

"Yes, and the dog. We're all settled in at the Mitre. She's taken Morag for a little run on the beach, but I said I'd be back for a late lunch."

"What a good idea to bring her."

"I thought she mightn't want to come, but she jumped at the idea. To tell the truth, I think a bit of a change was exactly what she needed. Besides, she's as excited about the Dower House as I am, and she's looking forward to being shown around."

"How long can you stay?"

"As long as we want, really. We've shut *her* house up, and the Daggs are going to keep an eye on everything."

"Well, that's all very satisfactory. And the weather is delightful. So let's not waste any time, and get down to business . . ."

It didn't take very long. Some papers to be signed (Miss Curtis, the receptionist, was summoned to witness these), and the cheque to be written. Judith had never, in all her life, imagined that she would ever write a cheque for such an enormous amount. "Three thousand pounds." But she wrote it, and signed it, and pushed it across the desk, and Mr. Baines, with a paper clip, attached it neatly to the rest of the documents.

"Is that all?"

"That's all. Except for one or two small but necessary points that have to be discussed." He leaned back in his chair. "The Dower House is, actually, ready for habitation. Isobel leaves this afternoon. At five o'clock, her brother is coming in his motor car to pick her up and bear her away to live with him."

"Is she terribly distressed?"

"No. In truth, I think she's quite excited starting out on her new life at the age of seventy-eight. And she has spent the last two weeks scouring every nook and cranny, determined that you will find neither a speck of dust nor an unpolished tap." He smiled. "Where she gets the energy from I don't know, but the daily help's been in to give her a hand, so with a bit of luck she won't, immediately, die of a heart attack."

"I'd like to see her before she goes."

"We'll go to Rosemullion after lunch. Then she can hand over all the keys and give you your final instructions."

"What about the furniture?"

"That was the other thing I wanted to talk to you about. The furniture was all left, by Mrs. Boscawen, to Colonel Carey-Lewis, for himself and his family. But, as you know, Nancherrow is already fully furnished, and none of the children, at this particular point in time, have their own homes. So what has happened is this. A few special items have been removed, in order that each member of the family shall have his or her own small memento of Mrs. Boscawen. The rest, the bulk of it, stays where it is, at the Dower House, and the Carey-Lewises want you to have it."

"Oh, but—"

Mr. Baines overrode Judith's protestations. ". . . none of it is particularly valuable, nor even in very good order. But, for the time being, it is perfectly usable and will do splendidly until you have the time and the opportunity to acquire some bits and pieces for yourself."

"How *can* they be so kind?"

"I think they're quite relieved not to have to deal with the problem, and as Mrs. Carey-Lewis pointed out to me, if it was all put into a sale-room, it would probably fetch next to nothing. There are also one or two other impediments. Mrs. Carey-Lewis and Isobel have disposed of Mrs. Boscawen's clothes and her more personal effects, and the Colonel has retrieved from her desk any paper he considered of importance, but otherwise nothing else has been cleared out. So there are drawers filled with old letters and photograph albums, and all the accumulated memories of a lifetime which will have to be sifted through. I'm afraid this task will fall to you, but there is no immediate pressure, and anything you find that might be of interest to the Carey-Lewis family you can set aside and give to them. But I am pretty sure that most of it can be consigned to a bonfire."

The word "bonfire" brought up the subject of the green-suited gardener. "What's happening to him? Is he retiring as well?"

"I did have a word with him. He says the entire garden is getting a bit much for him, but he lives in Rosemullion and I'm sure he'd come up the hill a couple of days a week and keep the grass cut and the weeds down. That is, if you want him."

"I'd hate the garden to go to rack and ruin."

"Yes. It would be a shame. But I think before long, we should try and find someone a little younger and more permanent. It might even be worthwhile buying a cottage . . . a gardener's house nearby could do nothing but improve the value of the property . . ."

He talked on, suggesting other various small improvements which could, in the fullness of time, be made, and Judith sat and listened, and decided that it was enormously reassuring just to hear him, in his level voice, coming out with ideas for a future which, right now, seemed so distant, unlikely, and infinitely precarious. The Germans had reached the Belgian coast, the English Channel was threatened, and so was the British Expeditionary Force somewhere in France; old men and boys were volunteering for local defence, and it seemed that the invasion could take place at any day. And yet the sun streamed down, and children splashed in the swimming-pool, and the newsagent was selling shrimping nets and rubber beach balls. And here she sat, in the old-fashioned solicitor's office, unchanged probably for a hundred years, with Mr. Baines, in his traditional tweed, discussing, dispassionately, the possibility of an extra bathroom at the Dower House, new guttering, and the eventual refurbishment of the antique kitchens. It felt like being caught between two worlds, a secure yesterday and a potentially terrifying tomorrow, and for a moment she found herself in a state of confusion, uncertain which was the most real.

She realized that he had stopped talking, just as she had stopped paying attention to what he said. For a moment, a pause lay between them. And then he said, ". . . but that is all for a future date."

Judith sighed. "You seem so certain that there's going to be a future." Which made him frown. "I mean, everything seems to be going so badly for us. The news, I mean. Suppose we don't win the war."

"*Judith.*" He sounded genuinely astonished, even a little shocked.

"Well, admit, nothing looks very hopeful."

"Losing a battle doesn't mean you've lost the war. There are bound to be setbacks. We're fighting a ferociously efficient and well-prepared army. But we won't be beaten. At the end of the day, we'll come through. It may take a little time, but the alternative is not possible. Unthinkable. So never, for a moment, consider the possibility of any other outcome."

"You sound so sure," Judith told him wistfully.

"I am."

"*How* can you be so sure?"

"A gut sensation. Like old people who say, 'I can feel it in my bones.' A certain, unshakeable conviction. As well, I suppose I think of this war as something of a crusade."

"You mean, Good versus Evil?"

"Or George and the Dragon. You mustn't waver. Nor ever lose your nerve."

He was neither flag-waving, nor rattling a spear. And he had a wife and three young children of his own, yet remained so clearly calm and resolute that Judith stopped feeling uncertain and tremulous. Life had to go on, and there would be a future. It would probably be quite a long time before it arrived, and there would undoubtedly be stomach-churning moments of fear and horror to contend with, but defeatism was a useless exercise, and if Mr. Baines, with all his experience of life, could remain so cool and certain, then surely Judith could as well.

She smiled. "No, I won't. At least, I'll try not to." She felt, all at once, quite different, relieved of a load, reckless and almost carefree. "Thank you. I'm sorry. I just needed somebody to talk to."

"What a good thing you chose me."

"Are *you* going to join the LDV?"

"I already have done so. I haven't been issued with a gun yet, nor a uniform, but I have an armband. This evening I am going to the Drill Hall to learn, I imagine, how to present arms with a broom handle."

This image, and his dry voice, made Judith laugh, as they were meant to. Satisfied that all was back to normal, he rose to his feet. "It's a quarter past one. Let us make our way back to the Mitre, for a celebratory lunch with Mrs. Somerville, and then we shall all drive to Rosemullion and you shall take possession of your house."

She had been apprehensive that she would feel like an intruder. That Aunt Lavinia's presence would still haunt the Dower House, rendering Judith reluctant to enter, to open doors without knocking, and make her way through rooms that were the private domain of another person. But, thankfully, it did not feel like that at all, perhaps because it was all so neat, and scoured and clean, as though every vestige of its past owner had been scrubbed, by Isobel, away. There were no flowers; cushions sat fat, uncreased by any occupant. Books and magazines had been tidied away, and no work-bags or spectacles or half-finished tapestries lay on the table beside Aunt Lavinia's chair. As well, certain items were gone, rightly claimed by the Carey-Lewises, but leaving empty gaps, instantly obvious as missing teeth. A corner cupboard filled with Rockingham china, the Venetian mirror over the drawing-room fireplace. The Chinese porcelain bowl, always brimming with pot-pourri, the portrait of Aunt Lavinia as a child that had hung on the landing wall outside her bedroom. In her bedroom, the Queen Anne work-table that served as a bedside table, repository for pills and prayer book, had also gone, and many of her photographs, sepia-brown and framed in silver. Where these had stood, or hung, all that remained were bare table-tops and dark patches of unfaded wallpaper.

None of this mattered. None of it made any difference. The house was no longer Aunt Lavinia's but her own.

After a cheerful and sociable luncheon at the Mitre (roast mutton and caper sauce, and Biddy clearly enjoying the company of a new and solicitous male presence), they had all got into Mr. Baines's car and set off for Rosemullion. Morag, because there was no person with whom to leave her, came too. Biddy sat in the front with Mr. Baines and Judith and Morag sat in the back, and Judith opened the window so that Morag could stick out her piebald face and let the wind blow flat her ears.

"What shall we do with her when we get to the Dower House?" Judith asked. "Isobel won't want her making paw-marks all over the polish, or shedding hairs."

"We'll leave her in the car. Park it in the shade and leave the windows open. Once Isobel's departed, we can turn her loose."

Isobel was waiting for them when they arrived, dressed in her best black coat and skirt, and wearing a straw-hat decorated with cherries that had seen the light of countless summer Sundays. Her two small suitcases stood at the bottom of the staircase, with her large, capable handbag alongside. She was all ready for departure, but there was plenty of time for her to take them around, from kitchens to attics, and to bask modestly in their loud admiration for the amount of hard labour she had put in, washing curtains, polishing floors, starching bedcovers, shining brass, cleaning windows.

As they proceeded, she dropped instructions like favours. *The keys are all on these hooks, at the side of the dresser. Front door, back door, garage, tool-shed, garden door, garden house. The range has to be riddled, night and morning. Best silver's gone back to Nancherrow, but I set out the second best in these drawers. Linen cupboard here, and the laundry van comes on Tuesday. Mind the hot-water tap, because it rushes out, scalding.*

Room by room, they passed through the house, from kitchen to dining-room and drawing-room. Upstairs they were shown the little bathroom, Aunt Lavinia's bedroom, the spare room. Up again to the attics; the bedroom where Isobel had slept, in a white iron bedstead, and opposite this, the other loft where still were stacked the old boxes and cabin trunks, dressmaker's dummies, bundles of magazines tied with string, defunct sewing-machines, rolled scraps of carpet and linoleum, and four empty picture frames.

Isobel said, "I'd have cleared this out but I didn't know what to do with all the rubbish, it not being mine. And Mrs. Carey-Lewis said to leave it. The cabin trunk's full of old letters and photographs . . ."

"Don't worry," Judith told her. "You've done so much, and this can all be gone through and tidied up at any time . . ."

"I gave the floor a sweep, and got rid of a few cobwebs. It's a nice room, with a window and everything. I always thought it would make a lovely bedroom, but then where would we have put all this . . . ?"

Biddy, all this time, hadn't spoken much. But now she crossed the floor and stood under the pitched roof of the dormer window, and gazed out at the view. She said, "You're right, Isobel. It would make a perfect bedroom. You can see the sea. And today, it's so blue." She turned back to smile at Isobel. "Won't you miss the view?"

Isobel tossed her head, and the cherries on her hat rattled against each other. "There's a time for everything, Mrs. Somerville. For me, it's not the same without Mrs. Boscawen. And my brother's house has got a lovely view. Not the same as this, mind, but lovely. Right across the fields to the cream factory."

She had, clearly, got over her grieving, perhaps worked it out of her system in that orgy of spring-cleaning. Now, she was ready, in every sense of the word, to leave. They went out of the attic and downstairs again, and as Isobel descended into the hall, they heard the sound of a car's engine, and in a moment a Baby Austin rattled up the gravel and drew to a halt beyond the open front door. Isobel's brother, come to bear her away.

It all took a bit of time. Isobel all at once became a bit flustered, remembering things she had forgotten to tell. And what had she done with her insurance book? It was found in her handbag. And there were six clean dusters out on the washing-line that had to be brought in. And if they wanted a cup of tea, there was tea in the caddy and a jug of milk on the slab in the larder . . .

But finally Mr. Baines calmed her down, assured her that everything was in apple-pie order and perhaps she shouldn't keep her brother waiting? The little car was loaded, Isobel shook hands with all three of them, was inserted into the passenger seat, and finally driven away without, as Mr. Baines observed, so much as a backward glance.

"I'm glad," said Judith, as they stood dutifully waving until the Baby Austin was out of sight. "Wouldn't it have been awful if she'd got all emotional? I'd have felt as though I was throwing her out."

"And she's going to have a lovely view of the cream factory. What do you want to do now?"

"Have you got to get back to the office?"

"No. My whole day is yours."

"Oh, good. Let's stay for a bit. I'll free Morag and give her some water, and then I'll put the kettle on and we can all have a cup of tea."

Mr. Baines smiled. "You sound like my daughter, playing houses."

"Only, this is for real."

✿

Because it was such a warm afternoon, the tea-party took place on the sheltered veranda, and Mr. Baines dragged forward various items of aged rattan furniture in which they disposed themselves. A few high, vaporous clouds had appeared in the sky, gathering and then dispersing like blown smoke. A breeze rustled the branches of a deep-pink prunus, and petals fell softly as pink snow to form a carpet on the green lawn. Somewhere a thrush sang. While they drank tea out of Aunt Lavinia's rose-entwined bone-china cups, Morag disappeared on a tour of exploration, quartering this new territory and making herself familiar with every interesting smell.

Biddy became a little anxious. "She won't get lost, will she?"

"No."

"How far does the garden go?"

"To the foot of the hill. In terraces. There's an orchard at the bottom. Later, I'll show you." The thrush was singing again. Biddy put aside her cup and saucer, lay back in her chair, and closed her eyes.

Presently, Mr. Baines and Judith left her and did another tour of the house, this time with a beady eye for defects that needed instant attention. The damp patch in Isobel's attic; another in the bathroom. A dripping kitchen tap, the suspicion of dry rot in the scullery. "I'll need to get hold of a plumber," said Mr. Baines, and then took himself out of doors to eye guttering and down-pipes, and note missing slates or rusted hinges. Judith, assured that her presence was not necessary, returned to Biddy. On her way through the kitchen, she took, from its hook, the key of the garden house. Because there was no time like the present. The only unhappy ghost of the Dower House had to be laid as soon as possible, so that there should be not one corner of her new demesne unswept and scoured of memories.

Biddy had stayed as they left her, but Morag had returned and was resting by her side. It was a long time since Judith had seen Biddy do nothing so peacefully. It seemed a shame to disturb her, but she was not asleep. Judith pulled up a wickerwork stool and sat facing her.

"Do you want to see the garden?"

Biddy turned her head. "What have you done with your friendly solicitor?"

"He's inspecting the guttering."

"What a sweet man he is."

"Yes. Special."

"Mrs. Boscawen must have been a very tranquil lady."

"Why do you say that?"

"Because I don't remember ever having been in such a tranquil place. Not a sound. Just birds and gulls and a sunlit garden. And that little sight of the sea."

"When I first came here years ago, I thought it felt like being abroad. The Mediterranean, somewhere. Italy, perhaps."

"Exactly. Pure E. M. Forster. I'd forgotten about Cornwall. I haven't been for so long . . . that last summer at Riverview. It's like the past. Another country. Already Devon seems so far away."

"Is that a good thing?"

"Yes. It's a good thing. Healing. Being somewhere . . . a house like this . . . that has no memories of Ned."

It was the first time, since Ned's death, that Judith had actually heard Biddy say his name. "Is that good too?" she asked.

"Yes. It shouldn't be. I should savour memories, but Upper Bickley is too full of them. I wake in the night and think I hear his voice. I go into his bedroom and bury my face in his blanket, and weep with desolation. It's been such a terrible winter. Without you, I think I couldn't have endured it."

Judith said, "It's over now."

"I still have to go back. Deal with my weaknesses, face up to reality. I know that."

"You don't have to go back. We can stay here. It's my house. We can move in tomorrow, if you want. You can stay for days, or weeks, or months. The whole summer. Why not?"

"Oh, Judith! What a scheme. When did you think this up?"

"Just now. While you were talking. There's nothing to stop us."

"But my poor little house in Devon! I can't just *abandon* it."

"You can let it, furnished, for the summer. Some naval family stationed at Devonport would *jump* at it, so handy and so close to Plymouth. Surely you can send the buzz round the dockyard; you'd let it in no time."

"But the Daggs . . ."

"If you let it to nice people, the Daggs will happily go on working there, keep an eye on the house and the garden for you. Staying here will be like a lovely holiday for you, and you can help me clear out all those boxes in the attic."

Suddenly Biddy laughed. "That won't be much of a holiday." But Judith could see the growing excitement in her expression.

"There's nothing to stop us. Don't you see? There's nothing to stop you just staying here. Come on, Biddy, say yes. Give yourself a chance. You deserve it."

"But you . . . we've agreed that you can't stay with me for always, and I'm so useless on my own . . ."

"I've *told* you. I'm going to ask Phyllis and her baby to come and live here, so you won't be alone. You always loved Phyllis, and Anna's sweet, and even if I do go off to be a Wren or something, the three of you can be here together. Company for each other. And I'll take you to Nancherrow, and once you've met Diana and all of them you won't feel a bit lonely. And you can go and be a Red Cross lady with her instead of with Hester Lang. Don't you see? It all works out so perfectly, it might have been *meant*."

But Biddy, despite herself, was still uncertain. "How about Bob?"

"We'll ring him up and tell him our plan."

"But leaves, and things. I must be there if he has leave."

"It's only a little further than Devon. Or if you wanted, you could nip up to London in the train and meet him there. Please don't think of any more objections. Just agree. Anyway, till the end of the summer."

"I'll think about it," Biddy said feebly, but Judith disregarded this.

"What we'll do is, we'll go back to the Mitre tonight, and spend one more night there, and then we'll buy a bit of food and come back here tomorrow. And we'll make up the beds and pick heaps of flowers. We'll stoke up the range tonight so that it doesn't go out, and then there'll be lots of hot water for baths and things, and that's absolutely *all* we've got to think about."

"And Morag?"

"Oh, Biddy, Morag will love to live here. Won't you, darling creature? She's already perfectly at home. Please, don't think of one more damping thing to say. What's the use of my having a house if we can't all enjoy it?"

Finally, Biddy succumbed. "All right. We'll give it a try. We'll give it a couple of weeks." And then she laughed. "For the life of me, I can't imagine where you got your persuasive powers from. Certainly neither your dear mother, nor your father."

"I'd like to think I get them from you. Now, quickly, before Mr. Baines appears and says it's time to go back to Penzance, come with me and let me show you the garden."

So Biddy got to her feet, and together they stepped out into the sweet warmth of the late afternoon, and went across the grass and along the path that led through the rose garden and down into the orchard. Here, the gnarled old apple trees were misted in young green; they had shed their blossom and the tiny buds of new fruit had already formed. The grass was long, studded with wild poppies and marguerite daisies. Soon, all would have to be scythed down, and raked into little haystacks.

Biddy breathed the scented air. "It's like a painting by Monet." Morag bounded ahead. "What's that little house?"

"Oh. That's the Hut. I've got the key. Aunt Lavinia had it built for Athena and Edward Carey-Lewis. They used to camp out here in the summer-time."

"Do you want to show me?"

"Yes, I think I do."

She went ahead of Biddy, ducking her head beneath the apple branches. She climbed the wooden steps and smelt the warm smell of creosote, and put the key in the door and pushed it open. Saw the bunk, with its scarlet blanket, where she had found and lost her love.

This is just the beginning of loving.

But it had been the end.

It's pointless to give your love to the wrong person.

She remembered the bee, droning around the roof. She looked up, and there were cobwebs there again, and her eyes filled with tears.

"Judith."

Biddy, behind her.

She brushed the tears away, and turned. She said, "So stupid."

"You and Edward?"

"I had to come. I haven't been here since; I had to come today."

"Grasping the nettle?"

"I suppose so."

"Does it still sting?"

"Yes."

Biddy said, "This is yours now. You can fill it with your own experiences, make your own memories. You were brave to come."

"Right now, I don't feel very brave."

"And failing all, you can always use it as an extra spare room. For, possibly, guests who snore?"

And all at once the stupid tears receded, and they were both laughing. And Biddy gave Judith a hug and shooed her out through the door, and they locked it up again, and started back through the orchard. And as they went, they heard Mr. Baines calling them from the house, and hurried back up through the garden to tell him immediately, losing no time, of the plans that they had laid.

"Nancherrow."

"Diana, it's Judith."

"Darling! Where are you?"

"At the Dower House. I moved in yesterday. I'm living here."

"Oh, what bliss. I didn't even know you'd come down."

"I brought Biddy with me. And her dog. We got the keys on Monday, and then yesterday we moved in."

"For good?"

"Not sure about that. Anyway, for the time being. It's heaven. And I have to thank you so much for letting me have all the furniture. I feel I should pay you for it or something . . ."

"Heavens, don't suggest such a thing or Edgar will be mortally offended. I'm afraid we left a few gaps, removing all those goodies, but I really wanted the children to have just one little remembrance of darling Aunt Lavinia."

"The gaps hardly show. One day I'll fill them up with bits of my own. How is everybody?"

"In rude health. We've just had Edward down for a couple of days. Totally unexpected. But his commanding officer gave him a weekend leave, and it was utter bliss to see him again. I can't bear it that you just missed him."

". . . how is he?"

"Looking a bit tired and thin, and he slept a good deal of the time, but by the time he went back to darkest Kent or wherever he is, he was quite himself again. I told him about you buying the Dower House and he was delighted—as, of course, we all are. He said it felt like keeping it in the family, and to tell you that next time he comes down, he's going to descend on you and make sure you're not making any radical changes or improvements."

"What would he imagine I might do?"

"Oh, I don't know. Fling out a ballroom wing or something. When are we going to see you? Come for lunch. Bring your aunt and the dog for lunch. What day? Tomorrow?"

"We can't come tomorrow because we have to go out to Saint Just and talk to Phyllis Eddy. I want her to come and live here too, with her baby girl. I'm hoping that she's going to jump at the idea, but you never know, do you?"

"Darling, *anything's* better than Saint Just. So, what about Friday? Lunch on Friday."

"That would be wonderful. And I want you to rope Biddy into the Red Cross."

"We could certainly do with a little fresh blood. Barbara Parker-Brown's getting dreadfully bossy, and everybody but me's terrified of her. We keep being told that being at war brings out the best in people, but it's certainly brought out the worst in her. Darling, what about all your bits and pieces that are here? Do you want to remove them, or do you want me to keep them for you?"

"I'll take them away, and then you can have your pink bedroom back."

"Too sad. The end of an era. I'll get Mary to pack them up, and we'll send them over with a tractor, or something."

"There's no immediate hurry. How's Athena?"

"Getting more enormous every moment. I'm trimming the cot. White broderie anglaise, too pretty. I'll show you when you come. Friday lunchtime. I'll go and tell Mrs. Nettlebed now, so that she can kill the fatted calf or wring the neck of one of Loveday's old hens. See you then, darling. Thank you for phoning. Heaven to know you're back with us again. Bye-eee!"

The Dower House,
Rosemullion,
Cornwall.
Saturday, 25th May.

Dear Mummy and Dad,

Once more, ages since I have written. I am so sorry, but so much is happening. Most important, don't you adore this writing paper? I found it in a drawer and couldn't resist using it. It was in a box from Harrods, all embossed and waiting for me.

As you can see, we've moved in. Biddy and her dog and me. Biddy loves it, she's unravelled like a length of string, and looks better than she's looked forever. I think she finds this house very peaceful, and it has no memories of Ned. Besides, she's always loved Cornwall, and this afternoon we're going to go down to the sea and swim. I hope she will let Upper Bickley, and stay, at least for the summer, but it's an open-ended arrangement, and she must make up her own mind.

Yesterday, we got into the car and drove to Saint Just to see Phyllis. She's living in her parents' house and there's scarcely room to turn around, but after we'd said hello and everything and had the inevitable cups of tea and slabs of saffron cake, Biddy and I managed to smuggle her out onto the washing-green, and we sat on the grass and invited her to bring Anna and come and live here. (Anna is adorable, toddling around and beginning to say a few words. Luckily, she looks like Phyllis and not like Cyril, whose only good feature seems to have been his lovely eyebrows.) Anyway, the proposal all took a moment or two to sink in, but when it did, Phyllis burst into tears, she was so overcome with delight and gratitude. The arrangement is (with Mr. Baines's approval) that I pay her a sort of retainer for caretaking, so that she won't be strapped for cash, and she's got a bit of Navy pay as well, and won't have to pay rent, so she should be all right. I thought she might be a bit reluctant about leaving her mother and going so far away (it's not far really, in miles, but it certainly isn't next door), but she seemed quite philosophic about this, and when we broke the news to her mother, I think she was quite relieved as well, because, honestly, the Saint Just house is quite unhygienically overcrowded.

On Friday I took Biddy for lunch at Nancherrow. I was a bit anxious about whether she and Diana would get on, as they're rather alike in some ways, and sometimes if people are too alike, they don't make friends. But I needn't have worried because they were gassing away in no time, and shrieking with laughter at the same silly jokes, and Biddy is going to join Diana's Red Cross group, which will give her a bit of war-work to do. Meantime, she has settled down here like a cat with butter on its paws, and like I said, is becoming more relaxed, and her old funny self, with every day that passes.

441

I hadn't realized the strain, for her, of getting through the days in a house so filled with memories of Ned.

I can't wait to show you my lovely new home. Aren't I lucky, being a householder, with roots of my own, and I'm still not even nineteen?

I shan't stay forever. I really want to go and join up with the Wrens, but I have to get everything and everybody settled first. Perhaps at the end of the summer.

Now I must go and help Biddy. One of the attics was left piled with old trunks and bits of carpet, et cetera, and she's started clearing it out. At the moment we have only three bedrooms, and Phyllis and Anna are going to have to sleep in the attic, where Isobel used to sleep. But I think, at the rate we're going, we'll need another bedroom, so as soon as we've disposed of all the clobber, we'll give it a coat of paint and buy some furniture.

The war news is ghastly. The Allies have fallen back to Dunkirk. Colonel Carey-Lewis is convinced that the entire British Expeditionary Force is going to be either annihilated, or captured. It has all happened with such terrible speed, and by the time you get this letter, heaven knows what the state of play will be. But Mr. Baines is utterly certain that, at the end of the day, we're going to win the war, so I have decided to be certain, too.

So you mustn't worry about us. I know it's difficult, when we are all so far away from each other; but I know too that whatever happens, we will be all right.

Lots of Love,

Judith

The Nine Days Wonder, the evacuation of the British troops trapped at Dunkirk, was over. The first men were brought home on the night of May 26, but Dunkirk was ablaze, after days and nights of consistent attack, and the jetties and harbours destroyed. And so what was left of the British Expeditionary Force gathered on the beaches and the dunes, to wait for rescue; patient and orderly, lined up in long, winding queues on the flat French sands.

The troop ships and naval destroyers, under constant gun-fire and air attack, lay offshore, but without means of transport, there was no way that the beleaguered troops could reach them. Consequently, security was lifted, word went out, and the following night, from Dover, a fleet of small boats began to flow across the English Channel. Yachts and barges, pleasure boats, tugs, and tublike dinghies; they came from anchorages and boat-yards at Poole and the Hamble, from Hayling Island and Hastings, Canvey Island and Burnham on Crouch. And the men who skippered these small crafts were old men and young boys, and retired bank managers and fishermen and estate agents, and any person, sufficiently resolute, who had spent his peace-time summers innocently messing about in boats.

Their brief was to get as close to the beaches as they possibly could, load up with troops, and carry them to safety, shuttling to and fro, delivering their exhausted human cargo to the offshore ships which lay waiting. Unarmed, raked by enemy fire, they kept this up until fuel ran out and it was time to return to England for fresh supplies and a couple of hours' sleep. And then, off once more.

Nine days. On June 3, a Monday, the operation ceased. By means of inspired organization and improvisation, to say nothing of individual acts of enormous personal courage, over three hundred thousand troops had been rescued from the beaches of Dunkirk, and ferried home to England and safety. The entire country gave thanks, but forty thousand men had been left behind, to spend the next five years as prisoners of war.

But the Fifty-first Highland Division were not at Dunkirk. This division, including battalions of the Black Watch, the Argylls, the Seaforths, the Camerons, and the Gordons, still remained in France, to fight on alongside all that remained of a disheartened French Army. But it was a losing battle. Each morning, the English newspapers showed the sinister, thrusting arrows of the unstoppable German advance, and it was frighteningly clear that it would be only a matter of days before this last courageous remnant of the British Army was driven to the coast.

Finally, Saint Valéry en Caux, and they could go no farther. Fog precluded rescue by sea, and the battle-weary battalions were surrounded—trapped by the overwhelming might of the German Panzer divisions. On the tenth of June the French Corps capitulated, and hours later all that remained of the Highland Division followed suit. Later, disarmed, they were permitted to march past their general, and, in the rain, gave him *eyes right*. They marched on, into captivity. The Black Watch, the Argylls, the Seaforths, the Camerons, the Gordons. Gus.

Afterwards, in retrospect, Judith was always to remember the war as being a bit like a long journey in an aeroplane . . . hours of boredom interspersed with flashes of pure terror. The boredom was perfectly natural. It was not humanly possible for any person to live through six years of war in the top gear of passionate involvement. But the fear, and the immediacy of that fear, were natural too, and during the dark days of Dunkirk and the fall of France, Judith, and just about everybody else in the country, existed on the tenterhooks of anxiety and suspense.

At the Dower House, the wireless on the kitchen dresser was kept on all through the day, burbling away to itself from early morning to late at night, in order that no single bulletin nor news flash should be missed. In the evenings, Judith, Biddy, and Phyllis all gathered around the wireless in the sitting-room and listened, together, to the nine o'clock news.

As the cloudless early-summer days crawled by, despair was replaced by cautious hope, and then—as the extraordinary operation proceeded according to plan—by thankfulness and pride, and finally, intense relief. A relief that flowered into a sort of triumph. The men were home. They had returned with nothing but rifles and bayonets and some machine guns. Behind them lay, abandoned, massive amounts of equipment. Guns, tanks, and motor vehicles, many of which had been destroyed, along with petrol tanks and oil stores, in the smoking knackers yard which was all that remained of Le Havre.

But the men were home.

Gradually, in dribs and drabs, came news of those who had been rescued, and who had been left behind in France. Palmer, the erstwhile Nancherrow gardener-cum-chauffeur, had made it. As had Joe Warren and his friend Rob Padlow.

Jane Pearson telephoned Athena from London with the glad tidings that Alistair Pearson was safe, hauled out of the sea by a burly yachtsman, warmed by a tot of the best French brandy, and delivered ashore at Cowes. For Alistair, it seemed a suitably civilized conclusion to his adventures. But the Lord Lieutenant's son had been wounded, and was in hospital in Bristol, and Mrs. Mudge's nephew and Charlie Lanyon, Heather Warren's friend, were both posted missing, presumed killed.

But, most personal and important of all—for Diana and Edgar Carey-Lewis, for Athena and Loveday and Mary Millyway and the Nettlebeds and Judith—Edward Carey-Lewis had survived, his fighter squadron having flown successive patrols over the mayhem of Dunkirk, scattering the formations of German bombers, and driving them away from the beleaguered beaches.

From time to time, all through those tense and anxious days, if he could grab the chance and get a clear line, Edward telephoned home, simply to tell his family that he was still alive, and very often his voice was high with the excitement of a sortie only just completed.

As for Gus, after Saint Valéry, all hope was lost for Gus. Gus was gone, with his regiment, into eclipse. They all prayed that he was alive and had been taken prisoner, but so many of the Highland Division had been killed during the ferocious fighting that preceded Saint Valéry, that this alternative seemed only too likely. For Loveday's sake, brave faces were worn, but she was only seventeen, and refused to be comforted.

"The great thing to do," said Mrs. Mudge, "is to keep busy. Least, that's what people say, but it's easier said than done, isn't it? I mean, how can I say that to my poor sister, when she's sitting there worrying herself sick over whether her boy's dead or alive? Missing believed killed, indeed! What a bit of news for the poor soul to get in a telegram. And there wasn't no one in the house with her, her husband was up Saint Austell market, and only the telegraph boy there to make her a cup of tea."

Loveday had never seen Mrs. Mudge so down. Disaster, death, sickness, operations, and fatal accidents were usually the breath of life to her, incidents to be imparted to others, and chewed over with much relish. But this, Loveday supposed, was different. This wasn't young Bob Rogers from over Saint

Austell way, who'd cut his fingers off in the turnip-chopper, nor old Mrs. Tyson, who'd been found dead in a ditch on her way home from the Mothers' Union, but Mrs. Mudge's own flesh and blood, and her sister's only son.

"I feel I should go and be with her for a few days. Just for company. She's got daughters, living up-country, but there isn't nothing like a sister, is there? Talk about old days, you can, with a sister. Her daughters are that flighty, all they talk about is film stars and clothes."

"Then why don't you go, Mrs. Mudge?"

"How can I? Got the cows to milk and the dairy to see to. And the hay-making will be starting in a week or two, and that'll mean trips out to the fields with the tea-bottle and Lord knows how many extra mouths to feed. Hopeless, it is."

"Where does your sister live?"

"Her husband's got a farm up the back of Saint Veryan. Back's the word. Back of beyond, I'd say. A bus once a week if you're lucky. Don't know how she stands it. Never did."

It was half past ten in the morning, and they were sitting at the kitchen table at Lidgey and drinking tea. Helping Walter and his father on the farm, learning to cope with the balky tractor, feeding the poultry and now the pigs (a new acquisition, bought at Penzance market with an eye to bacon rashers), Loveday necessarily spent many of her days at Lidgey. But, just lately, since the black tidings of Saint Valéry had broken, she had taken to escaping here on the smallest excuse, and sometimes with no excuse at all. For some reason, she found the down-to-earth company of Mrs. Mudge more comforting even than the loving sympathy of her mother, Mary, and Athena. Everybody at Nancherrow was being almost unbearably understanding and sweet, but the thing was, that while trying to come to terms with the fact that Gus was dead, and that she would never see him again, all she wanted to do was to be able to talk about him as though he *wasn't* dead. As though he were still alive. Mrs. Mudge was good at this. Over and over again she had said, "Mind you, he might have been taken prisoner," and Loveday was able to say the same thing to Mrs. Mudge, about Mrs. Mudge's nephew. "We don't *know* that he's dead. There must have been such dreadful battles. How can anybody be sure?"

Thus they consoled each other.

Mrs. Mudge had finished her tea. She pulled herself wearily to her feet, went to the range, and poured herself another cup from her huge brown teapot. Loveday looked at her back view, and thought that Mrs. Mudge had lost her bounce. Family instincts were running strong, and she clearly yearned to be with her sister. Something must be done. Loveday's inbred Carey-Lewis sense of responsibility, along with her natural bossiness, rose to the fore. By the time Mrs. Mudge had sat down again, Loveday had made up her mind.

She said firmly, "You must go to Saint Veryan now. Today. For a week, if necessary. Before the haymaking starts."

Mrs. Mudge looked as though she thought Loveday had gone mad. "You're talking some silly."

"I'm not talking silly. I can do the milking. Walter can help me, and *I'll* do the milking."

"You?"

"Yes. Me. Farming's meant to be my war-work. And I can milk. You showed me how when I was little. I may be a bit slow, but I'll soon get the hang of it."

"You could never do it, Loveday. We start at six in the morning."

"I can get up. I can get up at half past five. If Walter can get the cows into the milking parlour for me, then I'll be here at six to start work."

"It's not just mornings, it's evenings too."

"It's no problem."

"Then there's the churns to be cleaned and taken up the lane for the milk-marketing lorry. Eight o'clock in the morning he comes, and doesn't like to be kept waiting."

"I won't keep him waiting." Mrs. Mudge gazed dubiously at Loveday. She was clearly torn between the desire to be at her bereaved sister's side, and a certain discomfiture at the notion that she was not indispensable. "You'll have to clean up after you," she warned. "Walter won't do that for you. That's not men's work. And I'm not coming home to a mucky parlour and dirty churns."

"I promise. You won't. Oh, do let me, Mrs. Mudge. Please. You've just said that the great thing to do is keep busy, and I'm just as miserable and worried as your sister is. I lie awake at night and think about Gus, so I might just as well get up at half past five and *do* something. So if you go to her, you'll be helping both of us."

"You mustn't think I think less of Gus than I do of my nephew. Lovely young man, Gus was. Remember that day when he came up to paint a picture of my barn? Chicken mess and manure all over the place, and he never turned a hair."

"Telephone your sister and tell her you're coming. Mr. Mudge can drive you over to Saint Veryan this evening, and you can stay just as long as you think you're needed."

Mrs. Mudge shook her head in wonder. "I don't know, Loveday, you'll be the death of me. Full of surprises. I never thought of you as being so thoughtful . . ."

"I'm not thoughtful, Mrs. Mudge, I'm selfish. I probably wouldn't do anything if I didn't think I was going to get something out of it."

"You're belittling yourself."

"No, I'm not. I'm being honest."

"That's what you say," Mrs. Mudge retorted. "Others are allowed to say different."

Each morning, at half past eight in the morning, after she had taken the full churns up to the end of the lane, delivered them to the milk-marketing lorry, and brought the empty churns back to the dairy, Loveday walked home to Nancherrow, ravenously hungry, for her breakfast.

It was now the eighteenth of June. Mrs. Mudge had been away for five days, and was returning to Lidgey tomorrow. In a way, Loveday felt rather sorry. Coping with the milking, a marathon task that she had taken on so impetuously, had proved to be something of a challenge and tremendously hard work. At first, she had been both slow and clumsy (nerves), but Walter, alternately swearing at her or handing out a bit of foul-mouthed encouragement ("If you wait, I'll show you how to shift that bloody churn") had been uncharacteristically co-operative, and had seen her through.

Without a lot of chat. Walter was a taciturn fellow. Loveday was not sure if he had been told about Gus. Knowing Mrs. Mudge, she was pretty certain that he had. Whatever, Walter said nothing, and offered no sort of sympathy. When Gus was staying at Nancherrow, the two young men had met one morning down at the stables, and Loveday had introduced them, but Walter had been at his most offhand, the very epitome of a mannerless groom, and Gus, after one or two friendly overtures, lost heart. It had occurred to Loveday at the time that perhaps Walter was jealous, but the idea was so preposterous that she almost immediately put it out of her mind. Walter was a law unto himself, but she had known him all her life and never felt anything but at ease in his company.

Each evening, when the last cow had been milked and the little herd turned out into the fields again, Loveday had set to work, hosing and scrubbing the parlour, taking pride in shining cobbles and pristine milk-pails, determined that Mrs. Mudge, returning, would be able to find no fault. The Lidgey kitchen, on the other hand, was a pigsty of dirty dishes, blackened saucepans, and unwashed clothes. Perhaps, tomorrow, she would find time to muck that out as well. It seemed the least she could do for poor Mrs. Mudge.

She crossed the farmyard and climbed the gate that led into the lane, and sat there for a bit, on the top of the rail, because this was one of her favourite views, and this morning looked particularly bright and sparkling. Earlier, as she had walked to work, all had lain dew-spangled and tranquil beneath the first low rays of the rising sun. Even the sea, shifting gently, unruffled by wind, had turned from grey to the translucence of mother-of-pearl. Now, however, three hours later, it was a silky blue beneath a cloudless sky. A breeze had got up, and she could hear the distant sound of breakers, rolling in at the foot of the cliffs. Gulls were flying high. In the sunlight, the moors were tawny, and pasture fields a brilliant emerald green. She saw the peaceful, grazing cows, and, from far off, heard the furious barking of Walter's dog.

Her mind, curiously, emptied. She hadn't thought about *nothing* for ages, and it felt rather pleasant, like being in limbo, floating in space between two worlds. And then, gradually, the vacuum of mindlessness was filled with the image of Gus, striding up the lane towards her with his painting gear slung in a knapsack over his shoulder. And she thought of him now, in France, and he was walking, or marching, or wounded, but he wasn't dead. His vital presence came across so strongly that, all at once, she was consumed with excitement, the irrefutable conviction that he was still alive. At that very moment, he was thinking about her; she could almost hear his voice, humming towards her as though transported by unseen telephone wires. She closed her eyes in a sort of ecstasy, and sat, clinging with her hands to the top rail of the old farm gate. And when she opened her eyes again, everything was different, and she wasn't even tired any longer, and all the lovely world was brimful with the old possibilities of happiness.

She jumped off the gate and ran down the lane, her legs going faster as the slope steepened, her gumboots thumping like pistons over the loose stones and ruts of dried mud. At the bottom, she vaulted over the second gate, and then, breathless and suffering from an agonizing stitch in her side, had to stop and kiss her knee, which was the classic remedy for stitches. Then, along the path, and across the drive, and into the yard, and through the back door.

"Take your boots off, Loveday, they're caked with dirt."

"Sorry, Mrs. Nettlebed."

"You're late today. Busy, were you?"

"Not particularly. Just hanging around." In socked feet, she came into the kitchen. She wanted to ask if there had been any news, if there was a letter, if anybody had heard anything, but if she did this, then Mrs. Nettlebed and everybody would start asking questions. And until there came some sort of confirmation of Gus's safety, Loveday was not going to whisper a word of her new hope, not to anybody, not even Judith.

She said, "What's for breakfast? I'm ravenous."

"Fried eggs and tomatoes. On the hotplate in the dining-room. Everyone else has finished already. You'd better hurry along and let Nettlebed get cleared up."

So Loveday washed her hands in the scullery and dried them on the roller towel that hung behind the door, and then went out of the kitchen and down the passage. From upstairs came the sound of the vacuum cleaner, and her mother's voice calling Mary. The dining-room door stood open, and she was just about to go through when the telephone began to ring. She stopped dead, and waited, and then, when nobody answered, went on and into her father's study. The room was empty. The telephone, shrilling, stood on his desk. She picked it up and the ringing was stopped.

"Nancherrow." For some reason, her mouth had gone dry. She cleared her throat and said it again. "Nancherrow."

Click, click, went the telephone, and then started buzzing.

"Hello?" She was beginning to sound a bit desperate.

Click, click.

"Who's that?" A man's voice, blurred and distant.

"Loveday."

"Loveday. It's me. It's Gus."

Her legs, literally, turned to water. She couldn't stand, so she collapsed onto the floor, taking the telephone with her.

448

"Gus."

"Can you hear me? This is a ghastly line. I can only talk for a moment or two."

"Where are you?"

"In hospital."

"Where?"

"Southampton. I'm okay. Being shipped home tomorrow. I tried to ring before but everybody's in the same boat and there aren't enough telephones."

"But . . . what . . . what happened? Are you badly hurt?"

"Just my leg. I'm okay. On crutches, but all right."

"I knew you were safe. I suddenly knew . . ."

"There's no time for more. I just wanted to speak to you. I'll write."

"Do that, and I'll write too. What's your address . . . ?"

"It's . . ."

But before he could tell her, the line went dead. "Gus? Gus?" She jiggled the hook on the receiver and tried again. "Gus?" But it was no good. He was gone.

Reaching up, she put the telephone back on the table. Still sitting on the thick Turkey carpet, she laid her head against the cool, dark, polished wood of her father's desk and closed her eyes against the tears, but they streamed out, quite quietly, pouring down her cheeks. She said aloud, "Thank you," and was not quite sure whom she was thanking. She said, "I knew you were alive. I knew you were going to be in touch." And this time she was talking to Gus.

And after a bit, she sat up, pulled her shirt out of her trousers, and wiped her face and blew her nose on its hem. And then she got to her feet and went out of the room, calling for her mother, and calling again, and she fled up the stairs on feet that could have been winged, to be met by Mary, to fling herself into Mary's arms, and to share in hysterical joy the incredible news.

At the Dower House, Biddy, making full use of her new-found energy, had cleared the second attic of its rubbish. All that had been salvaged were the two cabin trunks, and space was found for these on the upstairs landing, their contents being too personal and precious for Judith to feel that she could take responsibility for their disposal.

One was filled with old letters, tied together in bundles with faded silk ribbons; dance programmes, dangling tiny pencils; sheets of music; photographs; albums; birthday books; and a battered leather Visitors' Book, dated 1898. The other held a selection of Victorian finery. Long white gloves with tiny pearl buttons, ostrich plumes, wilted bunches of artificial gardenias, beaded bags, and paste hair-ornaments. All too sentimental and too pretty to throw away. Sometime, Diana Carey-Lewis had promised, she would come to the Dower House and sift through all these old memories. Meantime, Judith had draped the cabin trunks with old curtains of William Morris damask, and thus disguised they would probably stay where they were, undisturbed, for years.

Everything else had been deemed either useless or broken (even the picture frames proved to be riddled with worm); and humped painstakingly downstairs, to be piled alongside the dustbins. The next time the dustbin lorry made its call, the driver was going to be given half a crown in the hopes that he would cart it all away.

And so the attic was now empty. And Judith and Phyllis stood side by side, surveying it and discussing how it should be used. They were on their own, because Anna was out in the garden digging holes in the border with an old tin spoon, and Morag was with her, doing her best to assist in this exercise. From time to time, Phyllis went to the window to glance down, and make certain that neither dog nor child were either tormenting each other, or doing untold harm. But all seemed to be peaceful.

Biddy was in the kitchen. The most unenthusiastic of cooks, she had found, in Isobel's battered and butter-smeared old cookery book, a recipe for making elder-flower cordial. The elder-flowers happened at this moment to be out, the hedgerows were heavy with their subtly scented creamy blossom, and Biddy was fired with enthusiasm. She didn't count making elder-berry cordial as cooking. Cooking was stews and roast mutton and jam tarts and mixing cakes, none of which she had any intention of attempting. But concocting lovely drinks was right up her street, specially if one could gather the ingredients for free, from roadside bushes.

"I think we should turn it into another spare bedroom," Phyllis was saying. "Mrs. Somerville's in the only one there is, and supposing someone else wants to come and stay?"

But Judith did not agree. "Another spare bedroom is just waste of space. I think we should give it to Anna as a nursery. We can put a bed up for her to sleep in, and a few shelves for her books, and perhaps an old sofa. Sofas always look so cosy. And then she can use it as a playroom and have somewhere to make a mess if we have a wet day."

"Judith." It was turning into an argument. "We've already got that great bedroom. This is your house, not mine. You can't give us all this space . . ."

"Well, what about when Cyril gets leave? He's going to want to be with you and Anna. So he'll come here too. Unless, of course, he'd rather go and be with his mum and dad."

"Oh, he won't want that."

"Well, you can't all sleep together. In the same room. It wouldn't be proper. Anna's not a tiny baby any longer."

Phyllis looked at bit embarrassed. "We managed before."

"Well, I don't want you managing in my house. There's no need. So it's settled. This room's for Anna. It's time she learned to sleep on her own. And we'll get a proper-sized bed, so that if I do have another house guest, we can turn Anna out and the visitor can sleep in her bed. How's that for a compromise? And we'll get carpeting for the floor . . ."

"Bit of lino would do."

"Lino's horrible and cold. It must be a carpet. Blue, I think." Imagining the blue carpet, she looked about her. The attic was spacious and airy, but there was only one small dormer window, and the combed ceilings made it a bit dark. "We'll paint the walls white, that'll lighten it up, and perhaps put a Peter Rabbit frieze round the walls. The only thing is, there's no fireplace. We'll have to think up some plan for heating it in the wintertime . . ."

"Paraffin stove would do . . ."

"I don't like paraffin stoves. I always think they're a bit dangerous . . ."

"I love the smell of paraffin stoves . . ."

"But Anna might knock it over, and then we'd all go up in smoke and cinders. Perhaps . . ."

But she got no further, because from downstairs came the sound of the front door slamming shut and a voice, high with excitement, calling her name. "Judith!"

Loveday. She and Phyllis went out onto the landing and hung over the banister, and were rewarded by the foreshortened view of Loveday pelting up the staircase.

On the first landing she paused. "Where *are* you?"

"Up in the attics!"

She came on, up the attic stairs, her face red with exertion and warmth, her curls bouncing, her violet eyes wide with the ecstasy of delight. Half-way up, she was already telling them. ". . . you won't believe it. Gus has just phoned . . ." She was gasping for breath as though she had run the whole way from Nancherrow, not just simply up the Dower House stairs. ". . . he phoned about half an hour ago. From Southampton. Hospital. Wounded. He's on crutches. But he's all right . . ."

Carpets, lino, heaters were all forgotten. Judith let out a yell of triumph, and was waiting with her arms open. They hugged and kissed and danced about like children, and Loveday was still in her filthy old corduroys with her shirt-tails loose, and she still smelt of cows, and it didn't matter, nothing mattered except that Gus was safe.

Finally, they stopped dancing about, and Loveday collapsed onto the top stair. "I've got no breath left at all. I bicycled to Rosemullion, and left my bike by the church yard, and, I promise you, ran all the way up the hill. I simply couldn't wait to tell you."

"You could have phoned."

"I wanted to be *here*. I wanted to see your faces."

Phyllis's face, however, was concerned. "Wounded? Is it serious? How was he wounded?"

"I don't know. Shot in the leg, I think. He's on crutches, but it didn't sound *too* dire. We didn't have time to talk. Just a moment or two and then we got cut off. But he's going home to Scotland tomorrow, and he's going to write . . ."

"How on earth did he get out of France?" Judith wanted to know. "How did he get away?"

"I've just told you, I don't know anything. There wasn't time to tell. Just that he's safe and alive . . ."

"It's like a miracle."

"That's what I thought. I went all weak at the knees. And Mummy says you've all got to come down to Nancherrow this evening, and Pops is going to open some champagne. All of you, Phyllis and Anna and Biddy, so that we can have a real party . . ."

Biddy. For an instant, reading thoughts, they all fell silent. Gus was safe, but Ned would never return. Even Loveday's joy was, for a moment, quenched.

She said, lowering her voice, "Where is Biddy?"

"In the kitchen."

"Gosh, I hope she didn't hear me, bursting in and screaming out my tidings like that. I should have *thought*. But I just didn't think."

"Of course you didn't think. Why should you? We can't stop being happy. Even Ned being dead can't stop us being happy for you. I think we should all go down now and tell her. She's so generous, even if she does feel a bit miserable and bitter, she'll never show it. She's so much better now; even saying Ned's name in quite an ordinary sort of voice. And if she does start looking a bit blue, we'll tell her about the champagne party, and take enormous interest in her elder-flower cordial."

Ardvray House,
Bancharry,
Aberdeenshire.

Friday, 21st June.

My dear Loveday,

At last there is a moment in which to write. When I got back to Aberdeen, I was shoved into hospital again, but everything seems to be going well and I'm home, still on crutches but convalescing. My mother has got a nurse in to do dressings, et cetera . . . she's built like a wrestler and talks all the time, so I hope she doesn't have to be here for too long.

It was wonderful to talk to you, and I'm sorry we were cut off so abruptly, but the hospital switchboards were pretty strict about rationing our calls. It took me a couple of days of trying before I could get through at all, because it wasn't a home-call. If it hadn't been for the fact that, at the moment, I'm not particularly fleet of foot, I'd have jumped the fence, caught a train and come to Cornwall to see you all. Cornwall is much nearer to Southampton than Scotland is, and the long train journey back to Aberdeen took forever.

I got away a day before the capitulation. Responding to the General's directive of *sauve qui peut*, a number of small groups made their way to the little port of Veulles-les-Roses, about four miles east of Saint Valéry. Amongst these groups were some French troops, and men from the Lothians and Border Horse. We went by night, and four miles has never seemed so long, nor so fraught with peril, but when dawn came, we could see the dim shapes of Royal Naval vessels lying offshore (the fog wasn't so bad at Veulles). The cliffs here are tremendously high, but gullies lead down to the beach, and we had to form a queue and wait our turn, because the Royal Navy were landing beach parties, despite the fact that they were already being shelled from Saint Valéry.

One or two chaps were too impatient to wait their turn and went over the cliffs with improvised ropes. By the time it was daylight, the Germans were shelling from both sides, machine guns and snipers as well.

The beach was littered with dead men, and I got hit in the thigh before I'd gone more than a hundred yards. Two jocks in front of me saw what had happened and came back to help, and between them, I managed to lurch and hobble along the two miles of beach to the boats. Just as the three of us got into a boat, the bombers came and one boat was sunk with about thirty men in it. The ships put up a terrific barrage, and two of the bombers were shot down. Finally, soaked to the skin and covered in mud (me covered in blood as well), we were hauled aboard the destroyer, and no sooner did we think we were safe than the enemy started shelling from the clifftops. But we stayed until it was decided that no more men could possibly be on the beach or the cliffs, then pulled anchor and sailed. That was about ten o'clock in the morning of the twelfth of June.

We docked in Southampton, and I was wheeled ashore on a stretcher and taken to hospital, where the bullet was removed from my leg, and all strapped up, et cetera. It didn't penetrate too deeply, and doesn't seem to have done any lasting damage. Now, it's just a question of it healing.

I don't know what will happen now. There is talk of the Highland Division re-forming. If so, I should like to stay with them. But the powers-that-be may have other plans for me.

I send my love to you and all your family,

Gus

This was one letter. But there was another in the envelope, a single sheet, unheaded and undated.

Dearest Loveday,

I thought your father might like to read the enclosed account, but this little note is just for you. It was so wonderful to hear your voice answering the telephone. I thought about you all the time I was waiting to get on that hell-hole of a beach, determined that I was going to make it. It is such a beautiful day here, and the hills are all bloomy in the morning light, and the sunshine sparkling on the river. When I am able to walk a bit better, I shall go down to the bank and try to catch a fish. Write to me and tell me everything you are doing. With all my love, GUS.

The Dower House
Rosemullion.

24th July 1940.

Dear Mummy and Dad,

At two o'clock this morning, Athena had her baby. She had her at
Nancherrow, in her own bedroom, with old Dr. Wells and Lily Crouch, the
Rosemullion district nurse, in attendance. Poor things, having to turn out
at that hour, but old Dr. Wells said he wouldn't have missed it for the world.
It is now seven o'clock in the evening, and I have just come back from
Nancherrow (on my bike both ways), and seeing the new arrival. She is
enormous and looks a bit like a Red Indian papoose, with a very red face
and lots of straight dark hair. She is called Clementina Lavinia Rycroft,
and the Colonel sent a cable to Palestine letting Rupert know that she had
come. Athena is simply delighted, cock-a-hoop, as though she had done it
all by herself (which, in a way, I suppose she had), and sitting up in bed
with the baby beside her in its frilly cot. And, of course, her bedroom is
filled with flowers, and Athena drenched in perfume, and wearing the most
divine white voile negligée, dripping in lace.

Loveday and I are both going to be godmothers, but Clementina is not
going to be christened until her father gets some leave or something, and is
able to be there. It really is exciting, having this little new life, I can't think
why it should be so exciting, because we've all known for months that she
was on the way.

While I was at Nancherrow, old Dr. Wells dropped in again. He said, to
see how everybody was doing, and to check up on mother and child. The
Colonel opened a bottle of champagne, and we wet the baby's head. (He is
a great one for opening bottles of champagne. I am afraid, one day, he is
going to run out because he can't get any more. I hope he keeps one case
at least, for the day when we celebrate Victory.) Anyway, while we were all
sipping away and getting jolly, old Dr. Wells came out with the real reason
for his second visit, which was to tell us that Jeremy is in a naval hospital
somewhere near Liverpool. We were all appalled and shocked, because it
was the first we had heard of this, but old Dr. Wells said that he had not
thought that two in the morning (and with Athena's *accouchement* in full
swing) was an appropriate moment for the breaking of such news. Wasn't
it sweet? And he must have been bursting to tell everybody.

Back to the point. Jeremy. What happened was his destroyer was torpedoed and sunk by a U-boat in the Atlantic, and he and three other men
were in the sea, covered in oil and hanging on to a Carley float for a day
and a night before they were spotted and picked up by a merchantman. It
doesn't bear thinking about, does it? Even in the summer, the Atlantic
ocean must be icy cold. Anyway, he was suffering from exposure and exhaustion and burns on his arm from the explosion, so once the merchantman got to Liverpool, he was bustled off to this naval hospital and is still
there. Mrs. Wells has gone up to Liverpool by train to sit at his bedside.

When he's discharged, he's going to be given sick leave, so hopefully we'll all see him before long. Isn't it wonderful—even miraculous—that he was spotted and rescued? I don't know how people survive under such circumstances, I suppose they do because the alternative is unthinkable.

Invasion fever has swept the country, and we're all donating our aluminium pots and pans to the Women's Voluntary Service, to be melted down and made into Spitfires and Hurricanes. I had to go to Penzance and buy a whole lot of horrible enamel ones which chip and burn, but it can't be helped. The Local Defence Volunteers are now called the Home Guard, which sounds much grander, and everybody is joining. Colonel Carey-Lewis is back in uniform, and because of his experience in the Great War has been made Commanding Officer of the Rosemullion Detachment. They have already been issued with uniforms and guns, and the Rosemullion Village Hall has been turned into the Home Guard HQ, and they've got a telephone, and notice-boards and everything, and learn drill.

As well, all the church bells were silenced, quite soon after Dunkirk, and must only ring out to tell us that the Germans have landed. One poor old chap, rector of a remote parish, never heard about this, or if he had, forgot, and the local bobby found him pulling the rope, the bell clanging away in the belfry, and promptly arrested him. Another man was fined twenty-five pounds for spreading rumours. He was in his local pub telling everybody that twenty German parachutists, disguised as nuns, had landed on Bodmin Moor. The magistrate said that he was lucky not to be put in prison for defeatist talk.

Another thing is, that all the local signposts have been removed, so you come to a remote Cornish cross-road and you don't know which way to go. Biddy doesn't think this is much of an idea. She supposes the powers-that-be imagine that a squad of German Panzers, marching on Penzance, would turn right by mistake and end up at Lamorna Cove. Where, no doubt, someone would try to sell them cream teas.

But, despite our laughs, it is all terribly immediate and close. Falmouth was bombed a couple of weeks ago, and every evening we listen to accounts of the air battles over Kent and the Channel, and can scarcely believe that the fighter pilots are doing so brilliantly, knocking the German bombers out of the sky. Edward Carey-Lewis is one of them, and there are newspaper photographs of the young airmen sitting around in the sun, in deck-chairs and basket chairs; but all kitted up, and just waiting for the warning to *Scramble*, which means another formation of Stukas is on its way. It's a bit like David and Goliath. And of course, the Channel Islands have already been occupied, the Union Jack pulled down and the swastikas flying. At least, there wasn't a lot of fighting and people being killed. No shots were fired, it was quite orderly, and the only resistance was a drunk Irishman who punched a German soldier on the nose.

We're all well here. Biddy's been on duty with the WVS collecting pots and pans for fighters, and Phyllis has finished painting the attic for Anna, and tomorrow a man is going to come and lay the carpet for us. It is blue, with a bit of a pattern, and is going to be fitted right to the walls. I think it will look pretty.

Phyllis is so happy here, and Anna thriving. She's a dear little girl, sleeps a lot and is no trouble. Phyllis is loving, but quite strict with her. Cyril is in the Mediterranean, Malta, I think, but we're not allowed to say. He was sent on a course and is now a qualified ERA, which stands for Engine Room Artificer, whatever that means. I suppose, one up from a stoker. Anyway, he's been made a leading seaman and so has got his hook. He sent Phyllis a photograph of himself, in cotton flannel (hook much to the fore) and pipe-clayed cap. He looks very brown and well. The funny thing is that although I have known about Cyril forever, I've never actually met him. He's not very good-looking, but Phyllis is delighted with the photograph and says he's "improved awful."

I hope you are all well. I'm afraid this is a rather long letter, but this is such an extraordinary time to be living through, I find I want to write it all down.

My love to you both and Jess,

Judith

The Dower House, like all self-respecting gentlemen's residences built in the nineteenth century, had, gathered about its back entrance, a number of out-buildings. An old coach-house, a tool-shed, and a potting-shed; a store for coal and wood, an outside lavatory (known as the Maid's Lav), and a wash-house. This contained the traditional boiler and a momentous mangle, and entailed much laborious carting of water and lighting of fires. The ironing was done on the kitchen table, padded up with blankets and old sheets, using flat-irons which had to be heated up on the top of the range.

When the Boscawens took possession, however, Lavinia Boscawen, with Isobel's well-being in mind, made a number of daring modernizations. The coach-house became a garage. A new lavatory was constructed indoors, down a small passage that led from the scullery, and the Maid's Lav relegated to the gardener, should he be caught short whilst hoeing his turnips. The wash-house was converted into a shed for storing apples, potatoes, and buckets of preserved eggs, and the great scullery sink, the size of a horse-trough and set back-breakingly low, was removed and carted away. Its place was taken by two deep clay sinks with a wringer riveted in position between them. Finally, all the old flat-irons were flung onto the dump, and Isobel was presented with one of the new electric devices.

She had thought she was in heaven.

Phyllis Eddy, years later, thought much the same. After the dismal little house in Pendeen, and then her mother's overcrowded miner's cottage, the domestic arrangements of the Dower House seemed to Phyllis the very height of luxury. To watch boiling-hot water streaming from a tap into a sink or bath never failed to give her a thrill; and dealing with dirty dishes and clothes—something which she had come to think of as an endless drudge—turned into chores that were almost pleasurable, so swiftly and easily were they accomplished. As for the bathroom here, nearly as good as the one at Riverview it was, with the thick white towels on the hot rail, and the cheerful cotton curtains flying in the breeze, and the lovely, remembered smell of Yardley's Lavender soap.

And as for dreaded Monday wash-day, now Phyllis almost looked forward to it. Anna's nappies she dealt with every day, and strung them out on the line like a bunting of white flags. Sheets and bath towels still went to the laundry, but there were four of them living in the house, and all the other bits of household linen, to say nothing of blouses, underwear, cotton dresses, overalls, skirts and slacks, stockings and socks, added up to two big basketfuls every Monday morning.

Usually, Phyllis and Judith tackled this together, while Anna sat on the scullery floor and played with clothes-pegs. Phyllis had a scrubbing board for the whites, and a great bar of Sunlight soap, and when she reckoned some pillowcase or garment had been scrubbed enough, she wound it through the wringer into the other sink, where Judith did the rinsing in clean water. Working in tandem, they usually finished the whole lot and had it out on the line by the end of the hour. And if it was raining, all was draped over the slats of the kitchen pulley and hoisted up into the warm ceiling over the range.

It wasn't raining today. The sky had hazed over and it was very warm, but it wasn't raining. A blustery west wind kept the clouds moving, and every now and then they drifted apart, and there was blue sky with blasts of hot sunshine.

Even with the back door propped open, the scullery was humid and steamy, smelling of soap and clean, wet linen. But at last the final garment, a little pinafore of Anna's, was rinsed, wrung, and tossed onto the heap of damp clothes in the wicker wash-basket.

"That's it for another week," said Phyllis with some satisfaction, and she pulled out the plug to let the soapy water gurgle away, and, watching it go, put up a wrist to push her hair away from her damp forehead. "It's some warm, isn't it? I'm fair sweating."

"Me too. Come on, let's get out into the fresh air." Judith stooped and swung one of the heavy baskets up onto her hip. "You bring the pegs, Anna." And she went out through the door, and the west wind blew on her cheeks and through the thin cotton of her clammy skirt.

The washing green took up the space between the garage and the back door. The grass was speckled with daisies, and a low escallonia hedge, heavy with sticky pink flowers, divided the green from the gravel approach which led to the house from the gate. Together, stooping and stretching, Judith and Phyllis pegged out the lines of laundry. The wind blew pillowcases into square balloons, and filled the sleeves of shirts.

"There'll be nappies at Nancherrow now," Phyllis observed, pegging out a tea-towel. "Who'll be dealing with those, do you imagine?"

"Mary Millyway, who else?"

"I wouldn't want her job. Love children, but never wanted to be a nanny."

"Nor me. If I'd had to go into service, though, I'd have *chosen* to be a laundry maid."

"You need to have your head examined."

"Not at all. Hanging washing is much nicer than emptying some horrible old man's chamber-pot."

"Who's talking about chamber-pots?"

"Me."

"I'd be lady's-maid. Dressing hair and hearing all the Upstairs scandal."

"And dealing with tantrums, and having to sit up until three in the morning? Waiting for Madam to come home from the ball? I think that's—"

"There's a car coming up the hill."

Judith listened. There was. They paused, in mild interest, fully expecting the driver, whoever it was, to travel on up the hill. But the car slowed down, changed down, then appeared through the gates. Tyres crunched over gravel, and stopped at the front door. "Know something?" said Phyllis unnecessarily. "You've got a visitor."

"Yes," said Judith.

"Know who it is?"

"Yes."

"Who?"

Judith dropped the clothes-pegs she had been holding into their basket and tossed Biddy's petticoat in the general direction of Phyllis. She could feel the stupid smile spread and stretch itself across her face. "It's Jeremy Wells."

And she went to meet him.

Jeremy Wells. Over the washing-line, Phyllis watched, covertly, pegging the petticoat in haphazard fashion, and trying not to stare. But it was difficult, because she'd waited a long time to set eyes on Jeremy Wells. The young doctor Judith had met all those years ago on the train from Plymouth, and only fourteen she'd been then, but she'd fancied him. No doubt about that. And then, so strangely, she'd met him again, with the Carey-Lewises of Nancherrow, and Phyllis, on hearing of this extraordinary coincidence, decided, then and there, that it was all *meant*; written in the stars; one of those love affairs that was going to have a happy ending.

Judith, of course, pretended that there was nothing in it. "Oh, don't be so silly," she would say to Phyllis, if Phyllis made coy references to the young doctor. But she'd been proud enough when he joined up with the Royal Navy, and distressed enough when she heard that he'd been blown up in his ship and bobbing about in the Atlantic for goodness knows how long. Phyllis could not decide which was the worse of the nightmares—a flaming ship with red-hot decks, or having to plunge into the dark, deep, cold, inhospitable sea. Neither Phyllis nor Cyril had ever learned to swim. But anyway, he'd been rescued, and now here he was, at last, and looking right as rain as far as Phyllis could see. Pity he wasn't wearing his uniform. She'd like to have seen him in his uniform. Just old grey flannels and a blue cotton shirt, but Judith didn't seem to think the worse of that, because she let him give her a great hug and a kiss on the cheek, and there they were, both talking away nineteen to the dozen, the pair of them grinning like Cheshire cats.

She might have stood there, gawping, forever, but Judith suddenly remembered her and turned her smiling face towards Phyllis, and called her to come and be introduced. Phyllis suddenly felt very shy, but she obediently abandoned the washing, and stooped and lifted Anna in her arms, and went across the grass and through the gap in the escallonia hedge, and across the crunchy gravel, wishing that she looked a bit tidier, not all bundled up in a wet apron.

"This is Phyllis Eddy, Jeremy. She used to help Mummy at Riverview. She's living here with us now. Her husband's in the Navy too."

"Is he? What's his job?"

"He's an ERA," Phyllis was able to tell him proudly. "Leading seaman. Got his hook."

"That's terrific. He must be doing well. Whereabouts is he?"

"Mediterranean, someplace."

"Lucky chap. Lots of sun. Who's this little girl?"

"This is my Anna. But she won't smile for you. She's too shy."

Judith said, "Jeremy's on his way to Nancherrow, Phyllis. He's going to stay with them for a couple of days . . ."

"Lovely," said Phyllis. He wasn't actually good-looking, and he had spectacles, but he had the nicest smile of any man she'd ever seen, and handsome white teeth. And for someone who'd just been blown up, burnt and then nearly drowned, he looked amazingly fit.

He said, "I'm not expected until lunch-time, and I couldn't drive through Rosemullion without coming to see you all, and see the old house, and what you've done to it."

Phyllis smiled to herself in some satisfaction. He had come calling. It was only half past ten. Two hours before he would have to be on his way. Time for a bit of privacy and a proper old chin-wag. She shifted Anna onto her other hip. "Why don't you take Dr. Wells inside, Judith, or out onto the veranda? I'll get the last of the washing out on the line, and then bring you a cup of coffee."

And it felt good, saying that. Like the old days when she'd worked for Judith's mother, and Mrs. Dunbar had had company. Jeremy Wells was company. Almost their first. A cup of coffee wasn't much, but Phyllis would have been prepared to go to any effort, if it would help smooth the path of true love.

There was a great deal to talk about, news to catch up on, tidings of mutual friends to exchange. It was eleven months since they had been together; that hot August Sunday that had started, for Judith, so happily, and ended so disastrously, with her sudden and precipitous flight from Nancherrow. She remembered saying goodbye to them all, as they sat over the remains of Sunday lunch. "See you all later," she had promised, but she had never seen Jeremy again.

Until now. Jeremy, she thought, covertly watching him, had changed. Ten months of war and life at sea had hardened and honed him down, and there were lines on his face that had never been there before, and his charming smile was not quite so ready, but she had never known him as anything but adult and responsible, and so could not mourn the passing of his youth.

They talked about Athena and Rupert and the baby Clementina. "She was enormous," Judith told him, "nearly nine pounds, and she looks like a little Minnehaha."

"I can't wait to meet her."

"We all thought Athena would hand her straight over to Mary Millyway, but in fact she's frightfully maternal, and spends hours lying on the bed with Clementina and talking to her. Too sweet. A bit as though Clementina were a dear little puppy. And Loveday's become a total land-girl . . . she isn't officially one, of course, and she doesn't have to wear that horrid uniform . . . but she works like a beaver, and has all these dozens of hens. She keeps us supplied with eggs as well, because sometimes the post office runs out. And Mr. Nettlebed, besides being an ARP warden, has put himself in charge of the Nancherrow vegetable garden, but he still assumes his old lofty act when he's serving dinner. You'll love it all. It's different, but in a funny way it's just the same."

Then Jeremy asked after the Warrens in Porthkerris and Judith's friend Heather, and she was much touched by his interest, because he only knew the family by hearsay.

"They're all fine. Joe Warren got home from Dunkirk, thank heavens. He got some leave and then went off again, but I don't quite know where he is. Biddy and I went over to Porthkerris and had tea with them one day, and got all their news. Heather's doing frightfully well, she's working with the Foreign Office, somewhere terribly secret and we're not allowed to know exactly *where*. But, so far, nobody's heard anything about her boyfriend, Charlie Lanyon. He was at Dunkirk too, and the Warrens are all simply praying that he was taken prisoner." Which made her think of Gus. "And Gus Callender? Did you hear about him, escaping and getting away from Saint Valéry?"

"My father told me that one. What a miracle."

"You should have seen Loveday's face when she came to tell us. She'd been really miserable, worrying about him, and then she suddenly had a sort of second-sight conviction that he was alive—she told me about it—almost as though she could hear his voice speaking to her. She was on her way back from Lidgey, and she bolted all the way home to Nancherrow, and about five minutes after she got into the house, the telephone rang and it was *him*. From hospital in Southampton. So perhaps it really was 'telepathy.' "

"If people are that fond of each other, I believe that telepathy is perfectly possible . . . besides, Loveday's Cornish born and bred, a real little Celt. If anyone was blessed with second sight, it should be Loveday."

460

And then they stopped talking about the Carey-Lewises, for, after all, Jeremy was going to be with them in an hour or so. Instead, Judith told him the tragic details of Ned Somerville's death, and about Bob Somerville and Biddy.

"She's left Devon and come to live here, with us. Did you know that?"

"Yes, I did. I hoped I'd be able to meet her."

"She got a lift into Penzance this morning. She wanted to get her hair done. I don't know when she'll be back. But everything has worked out so well. I said to Mr. Baines, it was as though it had been meant."

"And Phyllis too?"

"That's the best. She's a darling. And she simply loves it here, she's blossomed like a flower. And we've made a room for Anna, so that when Cyril (that's Phyllis's husband) comes on leave, he can come here and be with Phyllis. I'll show you all over before you go. I still can't believe it's my own house. I used to have fantasies about having a place of my own, very humble fantasies, of course, nothing more than a granite cottage and a palm tree. Just somewhere that belonged to me and where I could put down roots and come back to. And now, this is mine. All mine. I wake in the night sometimes and wonder if it's really true."

"Are you going to stay here?"

"Always. But, immediately, probably not. I shall have to go and do my *bit*. Join the Wrens or something."

Jeremy smiled, but did not pursue the subject. Instead, he asked about her family in Singapore, and she was telling him their latest news when Phyllis appeared with a tray and coffee. She stooped to set it down on the stool between them, and Judith saw that she had laid the tray with Aunt Lavinia's best china, and the coffee smelt fragrant and freshly ground, and there was a plate of shortbread biscuits.

Shades of Riverview.

"You've only put two cups, Phyllis. Aren't you going to come and join us?"

"No, I'm busy in the kitchen and you've got plenty to say to each other. I put sugar, Dr. Wells; I don't know if you take it."

"Yes, I do. How kind. Thank you very much."

Phyllis, with a knowing and faintly coy smile upon her face, went on her way. Judith, hoping that Jeremy had not noticed this, poured coffee and handed him a cup. She said, "We've talked about everybody but you. Your ship being torpedoed and everything." She saw the expression on his face, and added quickly, "But perhaps you don't want to talk about it."

"I don't particularly."

"I don't want to hear if you don't want to tell me."

"It doesn't matter."

"Did your ship go down?"

"Yes. Quite slowly. I clung to that bloody Carley float and watched her go. Stern first and bows last. Then a huge, sucking wave. And then nothing but sea and oil and debris."

"Were many of the ship's company lost?"

"About half. The gunnery officer and the first lieutenant were both killed. My captain was picked up, he's still in hospital."

"Your father said you had burns."

"Yes. My shoulder and back and the top of my left arm. Not too gruesome. No skin grafts. Recovering."

"What happens next?"

"That's for their Lordships to decide."

"Another ship?"

"I devoutly hope so."

"The Atlantic again?"

"More than likely. Convoys. An ongoing battle."

"Are we winning it?"

"We have to. In order to keep the trade routes to America open, and keep the country supplied with food and arms. The U-boats are everywhere, like hunting wolves; but the speed of the convoy is the speed of the slowest ship, and we're still losing far too many merchantmen."

"But aren't you frightened, Jeremy? At the thought of going back?"

"Of course. But you learn to pretend you're not afraid. Everybody's the same. Routine and discipline do much to concentrate the mind. And at least, next time, I'll know what to expect."

It was all very depressing. Judith sighed. "So many battles. The Battle of France. And now the Battle of Britain . . ."

She did not go on. She knew what Jeremy was going to say next.

"And Edward's in the thick of it."

"Yes, I know."

"Have you heard from him?"

"Only family news."

"Doesn't he write to you?"

Judith shook her head. "No."

"And you don't write to him?"

"No."

"What happened?"

"Nothing."

"That's not true."

"Really." She looked at him. "Nothing." But she was useless at lying.

"You loved Edward."

"Everybody does. I think he is a man born to be loved. Fairy godmothers must have been thick on the ground when he was born."

"I didn't mean that."

Judith dropped her eyes. In the garden, the trees rustled in the wind, and a couple of gulls wheeled, screaming, high overhead. When she stayed silent, he spoke again.

"I know how it was. I knew, that last Sunday, when you were all sitting out in the garden at Nancherrow, before lunch. And Edward and I brought the drinks out, and you looked up and saw him, and there was an aura of such joy about you that it seemed like a light bulb being switched on. And he went over to speak to you, and it was as if some magic, glittering ring enclosed the pair of you . . . held you apart from the rest of us."

She found it almost unbearable to be so reminded. She said, "Perhaps that's what I wanted you all to think."

"After lunch, you both left us, and came to see Mrs. Boscawen. And then Edward turned up at the cove, but we never saw you again because you'd gone. You'd left Nancherrow. Something happened, didn't it?"

He knew. There was little point in denial.

"Yes. It happened. It happened, and I thought he felt as deeply about me as I felt about him. I think I always loved Edward, Jeremy, right from the first moment I ever met him. But then, there is something irresistible about a person who can make the most humdrum of occasions into a celebration. And he always had that incredible gift, even when he was a schoolboy." She turned to smile at Jeremy. A wry smile, but he responded instantly with his old, encouraging grin. "But you, of all people, know about that."

"Yes."

"I imagined that he felt the same about me. But of course he didn't."

"He was immensely fond of you."

"But not taken with the idea of a permanent commitment."

"He's too young for commitment."

"That's what he told me."

"And you let that end it all?"

"I'd gone too far, and said too much. I had to back away."

"And leave Nancherrow?"

"I couldn't stay. Not in the house, not with him, and the family. Not seeing him every day. Surely you understand?"

"I can understand the end of love. But not the end of friendship."

"I wouldn't know. Athena might know, perhaps, but I'm not as experienced as she is."

"Are you still in love with Edward?"

"I try not to be. But I suppose you never fall out of love with the man who was the first love of your life."

"How old are you?"

"Nineteen. Just."

"So young."

She said, "I'll be all right."

"Do you worry about him?"

"All the time. At the back of my mind. I look at newspaper photographs of air battles and Spitfires, and although I *think* about Edward, I find it impossible to *identify* him with it all. Perhaps, as well as being charming, he's charmed. One thing we can be certain of: whatever he's doing, he's enjoying it."

Jeremy smiled, understanding. "I know what you mean, and I'm sorry to have pried. I didn't intend to invade your privacy. It's just that I know Edward so well . . . his good points and his faults . . . and I was concerned. Afraid that he'd hurt you."

"It's over now. And I can talk about it. And I don't mind *you* knowing."

"Good." He had finished his coffee. He laid down the cup and looked at his wrist-watch. "Now, if you're going to show me around your property, perhaps we'd better get moving, because before very long I shall have to be on my way."

So they got up off their chairs and went indoors, and the peaceful tranquillity of the old rooms dissolved the last of the constraint that had lain between them, to be replaced by Judith's pride of possession and Jeremy's boundless enthusiasm. He had been to the house, of course, many times, in the days of Aunt Lavinia, but had never ventured farther than sitting-room and dining-room. Now, they embarked on a regular tour of inspection, starting at the top with the new attic nursery, and ending in the kitchen.

". . . Diana and the Colonel let me have all the furniture and stuff that the family didn't want, so I haven't had to buy anything. I know the wallpaper's faded, and the curtains worn, but I always rather like things that way. Even the bare bits in the carpets. It makes it friendly and familiar, like wrinkles on a nice person's face. Of course, there are gaps, where things have gone to Nancherrow, but I can live quite happily with that. And the kitchen works really well . . ."

"How do you heat your water?" He was being comfortingly practical.

"With the range. It's incredibly efficient, provided you remember to feed it twice a day . . . The only thing I really *would* like is a proper refrigerator, but I haven't had time to do anything about that yet, and the shop in Penzance hasn't got one for sale, so I suppose I'll have to go to Plymouth. And Mr. Baines talks about putting in another bathroom, but honestly, we don't really need one. I'd much rather put in central heating, like Nancherrow, but I suppose that will have to wait until after the war . . ."

"You'd have to have an extra boiler for central heating."

"There's room for one beyond the scullery . . ."

She showed him the space that she had in mind, and they spent another satisfactory five minutes discussing the subject, and considering the difficulties of inserting pipes through and around the old, thick stone walls of the house. And then they were joined by Phyllis and Anna, who had been picking peas for lunch, and after a bit more chat Jeremy looked at his watch once more, and said it really was time he took himself off.

Judith went with him to his car. "How long are you staying at Nancherrow?"

"Just a couple of days."

"Will I see you?" she asked a little wistfully.

"Of course. Tell you what, why don't you come down this afternoon, and we'll walk down to the cove together. With whoever wants to come. We could swim."

It was an inviting idea. She hadn't been to the cove for too long. "All right. I'll bike over."

"Bring your bathers."

"I will."

"About three, then?"

"I'll be there. But if they've all made other plans and want you to do something else, just give me a ring."

"I'll do that."

He got into his car, and she stood and watched him drive away. And then went back into the kitchen to sit at the table with Phyllis and Anna and help pod the peas.

The long driveway of Nancherrow was lined with hydrangeas in full flower. In the diffused sunlight filtering through the branches of tall trees, it felt a bit like bicycling along the bed of an azure-blue river. Judith had changed into shorts and an old Aertex shirt. In her bicycle basket were her striped beach towel, her bathing costume and thick sweater, and a packet of ginger snaps to eat after the swim. She looked forward to swimming, and hoped that Loveday, and maybe Athena, were going to join Jeremy and herself.

Out of the trees, and the bicycle tyres rattled over gravel. The haze of the morning had cleared, but the soft west wind still blew. The windows of Nancherrow blinked in the afternoon sunshine, and Loveday's hens, penned into their wire enclosure at the side of the house, clucked and tocked away to themselves, making all the traditional sounds of cheerful, healthy poultry who have just laid—or are about to lay—an egg.

There didn't seem to be anybody about, but the front door stood open. She parked her bike, leaning it against the wall of the house, gathered up her bathing-things and her sweater, turned to go indoors and find everybody, and instantly jumped nearly out of her skin, because Jeremy had appeared from nowhere and was standing right behind her.

"Oh! You brute. What a fright! I never saw you, never heard you!"

He put his hands on her arms, holding her still, as though she were about to escape in some way. He said, "Don't go in."

His face was taut, and under his tan, very pale. A nerve throbbed just above the angle of his jaw-bone. Judith stood bewildered.

"Why?"

"A telephone call. Half an hour ago. Edward's dead."

She was grateful that he held her so steadily, for her knees were trembling, and for an instant she experienced a terrible panic, as though she wasn't going to be able to breathe. *Edward's dead.* She shook her head, in passionate denial. "No."

"He was killed this morning."

"No. Not *Edward.* Oh, Jeremy, not Edward."

"His commanding officer rang up to break the news. He spoke to the Colonel."

Edward. The gnawing fear that had lived with them all for so long, lurking, and waiting, had finally struck. She looked up into Jeremy's face, and saw, behind the spectacles that were so much part of him, that his eyes shone with unshed tears. And she thought, *It's all of us. We all loved Edward, in different ways. Each single one of us, every person who ever knew him, is going to be left with a great hole in his life.*

"How did it happen?" she wanted to know. "Where did it happen?"

"Over Dover. Hell-fire Corner. There was a tremendous enemy raid on the shipping in the harbour. Stuka dive-bombers and Messerschmitt fighters. An immense, intense bombardment. The RAF fighters tore into the German formations. They got twelve enemy planes, but lost three of their own machines. Edward's Spitfire was one of them."

But there had to be a shred of hope. Shock had drained her. Now she found herself suffused with useless rage. "But how do they *know*? How do they *know* he's dead? How can they be *sure*?"

"One of the other Spitfire pilots put in his report at the debriefing. He saw it all happen. A direct hit from one of the Stukas. A plume of black smoke. The plane plummetted down, in a spin, hit the sea. Then exploded. No ejection. No parachute. There's no way any man could have survived."

She listened to his painful words in silence, and the shred of hope died forever. Then Jeremy stepped forward and took her in his arms. She dropped the bundle of towel and sweater onto the gravel, and put her arms around his waist, and thus they did their best to comfort each other, Judith with her cheek pressed against his shoulder, the clean cotton smell of his shirt, the warmth of his body. Standing there, in his embrace, she thought of the family, somewhere indoors. The charmed Carey-Lewises, and the desolation of grief, the enemy, that had invaded the lovely, happy, sun-filled house. Diana and the Colonel. Athena and Loveday. How were they going to come to terms with the agonizing finality of their loss? It scarcely bore thinking about. All that was certain was that she, Judith, had no part in this private desolation. Once, she had felt part of the Carey-Lewises. Sometime, she would probably feel that way again. Now, at this moment, she was no more than an intruding stranger at Nancherrow, a trespasser.

She drew away from Jeremy, gently detaching herself from his arms. She said, "We shouldn't be here, you and I. We shouldn't stay. We must both go away. Now. Leave them."

Garbled words, spoken with urgency, but Jeremy understood.

"You go if you want to. I think you should. Go home. Back to Phyllis. But I must stay. Just for a couple of days. I think the Colonel's anxious for Diana. You know how protective he is of her . . . So I'll hang around. There might be something I can do to help. Even if it's only giving him a bit of moral support."

"Another man in the house. If I were the Colonel, I would want you to stay. Oh, Jeremy, I wish I could be like you. Strong. You have so much to give them all, but at the moment, I don't feel I've got anything. I just want to escape. Go home. Go home to my *own* home. Is that awful?"

He smiled. "No. Not awful at all. If you like, I'll drive you."

"I've got my bicycle."

"Ride carefully. You've had a shock."

He stopped, then, and picked up her rolled towel and her sweater, and brushed the gravel dust and grit from them, and went to stow them back in the basket. Then he took the handles of her bicycle and wheeled it over to where she stood.

"Away you go."

She took it from him, but still hesitated. "Tell Diana I'll be back. Give her my love. Explain."

"Of course."

"Don't go away again without coming to say goodbye to me."

"I won't. And, another time, we'll swim."

For some reason, this caused her eyes to fill with tears. "Oh, Jeremy, why did it have to be Edward?"

"I don't know. Don't ask me."

So she didn't say any more. Just got on her bicycle and pedalled slowly away, and he watched until she was out of sight; gone down the curve of the drive, disappeared into the tunnel of trees.

Why did it have to be Edward?

After a bit, he turned and went up the steps and through the door, back into the house.

Afterwards, Judith had little recollection of that journey from Nancherrow to the Dower House. Her legs, as though they had developed volition of their own, pumped the bicycle pedals, working automatically as pistons, set on driving the machine along. She didn't think about anything very much. Her brain felt as numb as a limb that has suffered some terrible blow. Later, it would start to hurt, and then become agony. For the moment, her only idea was to get home, as though she were a wounded animal headed for its lair, burrow, den, cave, holt, whatever one wanted to call it.

She reached, at last, the gates of Nancherrow, and was out once more, in the sunshine, then was spinning down the hill into the deep valley of Rose-mullion. At the bottom, she turned into the village, and cycled along the road beside the little river. A woman, hanging out her washing, called her name. *Hello! Lovely day!* But Judith scarcely heard and never turned her head.

She cycled on, up the hill until the steepness of the slope defeated her and she had to get off the bicycle and push it the rest of the way. At the gates of the Dower House she was forced to pause for a moment, to get her breath, and then went on, wheeling the bicycle over the pebbles. By the door, she dropped it and let it lie, abandoned, the front wheel still turning slowly, the handlebars askew.

The house waited for her, drowsy in the afternoon light. She went to lay her hands on the wall of the porch, and the old stone was still warm from the sun which had lain upon it all morning. Like a person, she thought. A human being. Living, and with a heartbeat.

After a bit, she went indoors, through the porch, and so into the flagged hall, where the only sound was the slow tick tock of the grandfather clock. She paused, and listened.

"Biddy." And then, again, "Biddy!"

Silence. Biddy, clearly, had not yet returned.

"Phyllis!"

But nor did Phyllis answer.

She went to the end of the hall and opened the glass door that led out onto the veranda. Beyond this lay the garden, and there she saw Phyllis, sitting on a rug on the grass with Anna and Morag, and a few toys for Anna to play with. The rubber ball that Judith had bought the child, and a doll's tea-set, made of tin, unearthed when Biddy had cleared the attic.

She went across the veranda and out onto the lawn. Morag, hearing her footstep, sat up and woofed in a fairly useless manner, and looked around to find out who, or what, had caused her to bark.

"Judith! We weren't expecting you back so soon. Didn't you go swimming?"

"No." Reaching Phyllis's side, Judith sank down on the rug beside her. The thick tartan wool felt comfortingly warm in the sun, like a heavy sweater pulled on after an icy swim.

"Why ever not? It's such a . . ."

"Phyllis, I have to ask you something."

Phyllis frowned at the intensity of Judith's voice. "Are you all right?"

"If I go away . . . if I have to go away, will you stay here and take care of Aunt Biddy for me?"

"What are you talking about?"

"The thing is, I haven't spoken to her, but I think she'll probably want to stay on, at the Dower House, with you. Not go back to Devon, I mean. But you see, you mustn't leave her. She mustn't be left alone. She gets terribly lonely, thinks about Ned, and she starts drinking whisky to cheer herself up. I mean, really drinking so that she gets drunk. It happened before, when I left her in Devon, and Mrs. Dagg told me about it all. It's one of the reasons I brought her to Cornwall with me. I have to say this now, because Biddy isn't here, so this is just between you and me, but you wouldn't ever leave her, would you, Phyllis?"

Phyllis, quite naturally, was mystified. "But Judith, what's all this *about?*"

"You knew I was going. Sometime. To join up. I can't stay here forever."

"Yes, but . . ."

"I'm going tomorrow, to Plymouth. To Devonport. I'll catch a train. I'll sign on there, in the Women's Royal Naval Service. But of course, I'll come home again. I shouldn't get my orders for at least two weeks. And then I'll go for good. But you won't *ever* leave Biddy, will you, Phyllis? Promise me. If you and Anna have to go away, perhaps you could arrange for someone to come and live here, and be with her . . ."

She was, Phyllis realized, working herself up into a high old state, and why? So tense and so urgent, gabbling away, scarcely making sense at all. Phyllis was both bewildered and concerned. She laid a hand on Judith's shoulder, and was reminded of the time she had tried to calm and reassure a nervous young horse.

"Now . . ." Deliberately, she spoke slowly and quietly. "Stop getting so upset. Of course I shan't leave her. Why should I leave her? We all know Mrs. Somerville. Know she likes her little drink of an evening."

"But it's not just a little drink," Judith almost shouted at her. "You don't *understand* . . ."

"I do. And I've given my word. Now, ease down."

It worked. The sudden spurt of annoyance was quenched. Judith bit her lip, said no more. "That's better," said Phyllis encouragingly. "Now, let's talk quietly. About you. I know you've been thinking for months about joining up. But why all at once? So sudden. Going off to Devonport tomorrow. When did you decide all this? What made up your mind?"

"I don't know. It made itself up."

"Has something happened?"

"Yes."

"Just now?"

"Yes."

"Tell Phyllis, then."

And she sounded just the way she used to sound, in the old days at Riverview, when Judith hung about the kitchen, miserably worrying about exam results, or the fact that she hadn't been asked to some birthday party or other.

Tell Phyllis. She took a deep breath, and said it. "Edward Carey-Lewis has been killed. His fighter was shot down over Dover."

"Oh, God."

"Jeremy just told me. That's why we didn't swim. I came home. I just wanted to be home. I wanted you so badly." Suddenly, her face crumpled, like a child's, and Phyllis reached out and pulled her roughly into her arms, and kissed her head, and rocked her as though she had been a baby. "I don't think I can bear it, Phyllis. I don't want him to be dead. He was always *somewhere*, and I can't bear the thought of him not being somewhere. He's not anywhere now. He's just not anything . . ."

"Shh . . ."

Still rocking Judith in her arms, all at once, Phyllis understood. It was all as clear as glass. Edward Carey-Lewis had been the one for Judith. Not Jeremy Wells. Phyllis, for all her certainty and high hopes, had been barking up the wrong tree. It was young Carey-Lewis to whom Judith had given her heart, and now he was dead.

"Shh . . . there now . . ."

"Oh, Phyllis . . ."

"Just cry."

Life was so cruel, thought Phyllis, and war was worse. But what was the point in being brave, and holding feelings tight close? Better to give way, to go with the tide; let nature take its healing course, sweeping all before it, in a dam-burst of weeping.

Three days had passed before Judith returned to Nancherrow. The first day of August, and it was raining; a soft, drenching Cornish rain that fell on grateful gardens and fields and refreshed the air. The swollen river gurgled under the bridge, drowning the kingcups which grew on its green banks; there were puddles in the roads, and great drops of water descended in showers from overhead branches.

In the rain, wearing a black oilskin, but with her head bare, Judith cycled. From the village, she pushed the bicycle up the hill, and then mounted it again at the Nancherrow gates, and went on, down the winding, aqueous tunnel of the drive. Everything glistened and dripped, and the heads of the hydrangeas hung, heavy with moisture.

Reaching the house, she propped the bicycle by the front door, and went in, through the door. And there stopped, diverted by the sight of the old Nancherrow perambulator, strap-slung and classic as a Rolls-Royce. It had been parked in the outer hall, until such time as the rain ceased and Clementina could be wheeled out into the garden for her necessary fresh air. Judith unbuttoned her oilskin and laid it over a carved wooden chair, where it dripped onto the flagstones. Then she went to peer into the pram, to feast her eyes on the lovely sight that was Clementina. Fast asleep, with fat peach-pink cheeks and her dark silky hair on the frilled lawn pillowcase. She had been bundled into a gossamer Shetland shawl, but somehow had fought one arm free, and her starfish hand, with its chubby, braceleted fist, lay, like an offering, upturned, on the little pink blanket. There was something timeless about her peaceful slumber, untouched by any terrible thing that had happened, or perhaps was about to happen. It occurred to Judith that this was what innocence was all about. She touched Clementina's hand, and saw the tiny, perfect fingernails, and smelt the sweet fragrance of the baby, compounded of cleanliness and wool and Johnson's talc. Just looking at her was the most comforting, reassuring thing she had done for days.

After a bit, she left the baby sleeping and went on, into the inner hall. The house was quiet, but there were flowers on the round table which stood at the foot of the staircase, and the usual pile of stamped letters, waiting for some person to post them. She paused for a moment, and then, when nobody appeared, started down the passage to the door of the small sitting-room. This stood open, and across the room, in the bay window, she saw Diana, sitting at her desk. The desk that used to live in the drawing-room, but had been moved in here when the drawing-room was closed up for the war.

The desk was littered with all the usual accoutrements for correspondence, but Diana had dropped her pen and was simply doing nothing but gazing out of the window at the dripping rain.

Judith said her name. Diana turned, and for an instant her lovely eyes stayed blank and unfocused; then cleared in recognition.

"Judith." She held out an arm. "Darling. You've come."

Judith went through the door and closed it behind her, and swiftly crossed the room and stooped to embrace Diana and to kiss her.

"So lovely to see you." She looked thin and pale and unbearably worn, but was elegant and beautifully turned out as ever, wearing a pleated linen skirt and a sky-blue silk shirt with a matching cashmere cardigan slung across her shoulders. As well, her pearls, her earrings, lipstick, eye-shadow, scent. And Judith was filled with enormous admiration, and gratitude too, because to have found Diana dishevelled, untidy, ill-dressed would have made everything seem frightening and hopeless as the end of the world. But she understood, too, that the way Diana looked was her own personal armour, and that the time and the trouble that she had clearly spent upon herself was her own private contribution of courage. She had always been a joy to behold. For her family's sake; for the Nettlebeds and Mary, she was staying that way. Maintaining standards. Keeping up appearances.

". . . I thought you were never coming."

"Oh, Diana. I'm so sorry."

"Darling, you mustn't say things like that, otherwise I go to pieces. You've just got to talk ordinarily to me. What a ghastly day. Did you bike over? You must have got drenched. Sit down for a moment and chat."

"I'm not disturbing you?"

"Yes, you are, but I want to be disturbed. Writing letters was never my strong point, and so many people have written and I simply have to try to answer them. It's so funny, I've always written letters to people, when people die, because it's what was *done*. Good manners. I never realized how much they meant. I read them over and over, even the most banal of condolences, and they fill me with pride and comfort. And you know, the extraordinary thing is that all of them say something different about Edward, as though dozens of people were writing about dozens of different Edwards. Some say how kind he was, or remember a certain amusing incident, or a time when he was particularly thoughtful, or funny, or just devastatingly attractive. And Edgar received the most touching letter from his commanding officer. Poor man, imagine having to write to all those bereaved parents, trying to think of something to say."

"What did he say about Edward?"

"Just how well he'd done, in France and then over Kent. And how he never lost his good spirits, nor his sense of humour, and how his ground-crew loved and respected him. He said at the end he was very tired, he'd had to fly so many sorties, but he never showed his weariness and he never lost his courage."

"The Colonel would have appreciated that."

"Yes. He keeps the letter in his wallet. I think it will stay there until the day he dies."

"How is he?"

"Shattered, lost. But like all of us, trying not to show it too much. That's another strange thing. All of them, Athena and Edgar, and even little Loveday, seem to have found some great resource that the rest of us never even suspected. Athena has her baby, of course. Such a duck, and so good. And Loveday just goes off to work at Lidgey a bit earlier each day. For some funny reason, I think she finds Mrs. Mudge a great solace. And I suppose being brave for other people helps you to be brave for yourself. I keep thinking of Biddy, when her Ned was killed. How perfectly terrible for her to have no other children to keep her going. How lonely she must have been. Even with *you* there. *You* must have saved her life."

"Biddy sent a message. When you want, she'll come and see you, but she doesn't want to intrude."

"Tell her, any day. I'd love to talk. Do you suppose Ned and Edward are somewhere frightfully jolly, making friends?"

"I don't know, Diana."

"Such a silly thought. It just occurred to me." She turned her head and looked out once more at the rain. "When you came, I was trying to remember something that they always read on Armistice Day. But I'm useless at remembering poetry." She fell silent, and then turned back to smile at Judith. "Something about always staying young. Never growing old."

Judith knew instantly what she was talking about, but the words, and their associations, were so emotive that she was not sure if she could say them aloud without breaking down altogether.

Stalling, "Binyon," she said. Diana frowned. "Laurence Binyon. He was Poet Laureate at the end of the Great War. He wrote it."

"What did he write?"

> *"They shall not grow old, as we that are left grow old:*
> *Age shall not weary them, nor the years condemn."*

She stopped, because there had swelled a great lump in her throat, and she knew that she was incapable of speaking the last two lines.

But if Diana noticed this, she gave no indication. "It says it all, doesn't it? How wonderfully brilliant of Mr. Binyon, to pick out the one tiny grain of comfort from a mountain of despair, and then to write a poem about it." Across the space that lay between them, their eyes met. Diana said, quite gently, "You were in love with Edward, weren't you? No, don't be upset that I know. I always knew, I watched it happen. The trouble was, that he was so young. Young in years and young in heart. Irresponsible. I was a little afraid for you, but there was nothing that I could do. You mustn't mourn him, Judith."

"You mean, I haven't the right?"

472

"No, I don't mean that at all. I mean that you're only nineteen, and you mustn't waste your youth, weeping for the might-have-been. Heavens." Suddenly she was laughing. "I sound like Barrie, and that ghastly play, *Dear Brutus*. Tommy Mortimer took me to see it in London, and all the audience were snivelling, except Tommy and me, who were bored to bits."

"No," Judith was able to assure her. "I'm not going to waste my youth. I don't *think*. But I *am* going away. Leaving you all. I went up to Devonport on Tuesday, and signed on with the WRNS. Sooner or later, I'll get my orders and then I'll be off."

"Oh, darling."

"I knew I had to go sometime. I suppose I've just been putting it off. Right now seems as good a time as any. Besides, I've done everything I can. Biddy and Phyllis and Anna are settled at the Dower House, and there, I imagine, they'll stay for the duration. Perhaps from time to time, you can keep an eye on them, make sure they're all right."

"Of course I will . . . Anyway, I'll go on seeing Biddy at the Red Cross. What are you going to do in the Wrens? Something frightfully glamorous, like Boat's Crew? I saw a photograph in the paper the other day. Pretty girls in bell-bottoms. They looked like something straight out of Cowes Week."

"No, not Boat's Crew."

"Too disappointing."

"Shorthand and typing, probably. In the Navy they call it being a writer."

"It doesn't sound very exciting."

"It's a job."

Diana thought about this for a bit, and then sighed deeply. "I can't bear the thought of you going away, but I suppose you must. I couldn't bear saying goodbye to Jeremy, either, when he had to leave us. I can't tell you what a rock he was, just being here with us all, even if it was only for two days. And then he had to go. Back to another ship, I suppose."

"He called in at the Dower House, on his way, to say goodbye. It was he who told me to come and see you."

"I do believe he's one of the dearest men I've ever known. And that reminds me." She turned to her desk, opened tiny drawers, searched through their contents. "I've got a key here somewhere. If you're going to leave us all, you must have a key."

"A *key*?"

"Yes. A key to my house in Cadogan Mews. When war broke out, I had half a dozen spares cut. Rupert's got one, and Athena, of course. And Gus. And Jeremy. And Edward. Edward had one . . . oh, here it is. You'll need to tie a label on it to stop it getting lost." She tossed it across and Judith caught it. A small brass latchkey. She held it in her palm.

"But why are you giving me this?"

"Oh, darling, you never know. In wartime, everybody goes to and fro through London, and hotels will be packed—anyway, they're hideously expensive—and it could just be a little bolt-hole for you, or a place to lay your head for a night. If it doesn't get bombed, or something disastrous. There's no reason, now, for me to go to London, and if I do, and one of you happens to be roosting there, well and good. There's enough space."

"I think that's a lovely idea. How sweet of you, and generous."

"I am neither of those things. And sharing my little house with you all is, perhaps, the least I can do. Are you going to stay for lunch? Do. It's rabbit pie, and there's masses."

"I'd love to, but I must get back."

"Loveday's at Lidgey, but Athena's around . . ."

"No. I think another day. I only wanted to see you."

Diana understood. "All right." She smiled. "I'll tell them. Another day."

Each morning Edgar Carey-Lewis made it his business to collect the morning post from the hall table—placed there by the postman—take it into the privacy of his study, and go through all the letters before handing any of them over to Diana. Ten days after Edward's death, and they were still coming in, from old and young and all walks of life, and he read each one with attention and care, filtering out well-meant, but possibly tactless and clumsy efforts which he feared might upset his wife. These, he answered himself, and then destroyed. The others, he placed upon her desk for her to peruse and deal with, in her own time.

This morning, there was the usual pile; as well, a large, stiffened buff envelope, addressed in black italic script. The pleasing writing caught his eye, and he peered more closely, and saw the Aberdeen postmark.

He carried the bundle of mail into his study, closed the door, sat at his desk, and slit the heavy envelope with his silver paper-knife. From it, he withdrew a letter, and a sheet of card folded in two, and secured with paper-clips. He opened the letter and looked at the signature, and saw that it was signed "Gus," and felt much touched that yet another of Edward's Cambridge friends had taken the trouble to write.

> Regimental Headquarters,
> The Gordon Highlanders,
> Aberdeen.
>
> August 5th, 1940.
>
> *Dear Colonel Carey-Lewis,*
>
> I heard only yesterday about Edward, which is why I have not written before. Please forgive me and understand.
>
> I spent ten years of my life at boarding-school, first in Scotland, and then at Rugby, and never in all that time did I make a close friend, a person with whom I felt entirely at ease, and whose company never failed to stimulate and entertain. By the time I reached Cambridge I had decided that there was something in my make-up—that dreaded Scottish reserve per-

474

haps—that precluded such relationships. But then I met Edward, and all of life changed colour. His charm was deceptive . . . I have to admit that at first I was wary of it . . . but once I got to know him all reservations melted, for beneath that charm lay the strength of character of a man who knows exactly who he is, what he wants, and where he is going.

From those few months when we knew each other, I have a host of good memories. His companionship, kindliness, and boundless capacity for friendship; his laughter and good humour; and his generosity of spirit. The days I spent with you all at Nancherrow, just before war broke out, and the kindness you showed a total stranger, are all part of those memories. Nothing can destroy such happy recollections, and I can only be grateful that I was fortunate enough to know Edward, and to be counted as one of his friends.

Looking through my Cambridge sketch-book I came upon this drawing I did of him. Summer, and a college cricket match, and he had been prevailed upon to make up numbers and play. Without, I may add, much enthusiasm! I drew him as he stood by the pavilion, padded up and waiting to go in. If you wish, I won't be in the least hurt if you toss it into the waste-basket, but I thought that you might like to have it.

The Highland Division is being re-formed, but I am being seconded to the Second Battalion, the Gordon Highlanders, who are already overseas. If I may, I would like to write to you and keep in touch.

With my best wishes to yourself and Mrs. Carey-Lewis, and Athena and Loveday,

Yours sincerely,

Gus

Edgar read the letter through twice, and then laid it aside and took up the makeshift folder. With some difficulty (his fingers, for some reason, were a bit shaky) he prised the paper-clips loose and unfolded the card. Inside was a sheet of cartridge paper, the top edge rough where it had been torn from Gus's sketch-book.

His son. Swiftly sketched in pencil, later washed in colour (Gus's artistic trade mark). Caught in an instant, caught forever. Edward, dressed for cricket, in white shirt and flannels, and with a brilliantly striped silk knotted at his waist. Shirt-sleeves rolled up, muscled forearms, a leather cricket ball cradled in his hand. Face half-turned, suntanned and smiling, and with that stubborn lock of corn-coloured hair falling across his forehead. In a moment, he was going to put up a hand and push it aside.

Edward.

All at once, he found that he couldn't see it properly, because his vision was blurred by tears. Caught unawares, disarmed, he was weeping. He reached into his pocket and drew out a huge blue-spotted cotton handkerchief, and with it wiped the tears away, and lustily blew his nose. It was all right. It didn't matter. He was alone. No person had witnessed that moment of agonizing grief.

He sat there, with the drawing of his son, for a long time. Then, carefully, replaced it in the folder, secured it once more with the paper-clips, and stowed it away in a drawer. Sometime, he would let Diana see it. Later still, he would have it framed, and set it on his desk. Later. When he found himself strong enough to sit and look at it. And live with it.

1942

WRNS Quarters
North End
Portsmouth

Friday 23rd January.

Dear Mummy and Dad,

I haven't received a letter from you since one you wrote just after New Year, and I am so afraid you are not able to write, or perhaps it's just that something has gone wrong with the mails, or there aren't enough ships (for mail) or planes or something. Anyway, I'm going to send this to Orchard Road in the hopes that you are still there, or that somebody will forward it to you. I read the papers and listen to the news every day, and am so anxious for you all, because every day there seem to be more and more Japanese advances, the Philippines and Manila and Rangoon and Hong Kong, and then both the *Prince of Wales* and the *Repulse* being sunk, and now Kuala Lumpur has fallen. Too close to you all. What is happening? Why does nobody seem to be able to stop them? I tried to ring Uncle Bob in Scapa Flow to see if he could get any information about you all, but of course I couldn't get through. Even if I had I don't suppose I would have been able to talk to him.

So then I telephoned Loveday to find out if she had had news from Gus. (Gus Callender, who is with the Second Gordons in Singapore. Some time ago, you wrote and said you had met him at a party at the Selaring Barracks, and he'd come up and introduced himself to you. Remember?) Well, Gus and Loveday write to each other a lot, and I thought she might have had some news, but she hadn't had a letter recently either. She thought he was on some course or doing manoeuvres or something.

So no joy there either.

This morning, I went into Lieutenant-Commander Crombie's office to get some letters signed (he's my boss, the Training Development Officer) and he was reading the newspaper, which I am sure he shouldn't have been doing, and he said, "Your family are in Singapore, aren't they?" Rather unexpected, because he's not usually a very friendly man. I don't know how he knew, I suppose the Wren First Officer must have told him. Anyway, I told him about you all, and told him I was pretty anxious, and he said that things did look black just about everywhere at the moment (we're not doing very well anywhere, even in North Africa), but he assured me that Singapore was invincible, not simply because of its fortress position, but because it will be so heavily defended. I hope he is right, but I don't like to imagine some sort of siege. Please, Mummy, if you get the chance to be evacuated somewhere safer, do go. You can always return when the danger is over.

Now, having got that all off my chest, I shall tell you about me. It's absolutely bitterly cold, and these quarters are like a refrigerator, and there was ice on my drinking water this morning. I woke up and Portsdown Hill wasn't green, but white with snow . . . not very thick, and it's gone now. I'm always quite glad to get to work because at least the hut which is our office is warm. Tomorrow I've got a short weekend, and I'm going up to London for a night. (Don't worry, the worst of the raids seem to be over for the moment.) Staying at Cadogan Mews, which is still standing and hasn't been bombed. Heather Warren is coming to London, too, from her top-secret whatever-it-is. I haven't seen her since the beginning of the war, because by the time I'd moved to the Dower House, she'd started work and had left Porthkerris. We've tried to arrange a meeting two or three times, but she seems to get such odd times off, never at weekends, which is the only time I can manage. But, at last we've fixed it, and I'm really looking forward to seeing her again. I told you, didn't I, that Charlie Lanyon is a prisoner-of-war in Germany. Not much fun for him, but preferable to the alternative.

Anyway, I'm meeting her at the door of Swan & Edgar's, and then we're going out to lunch, and then maybe to a concert. I'd love to buy what Athena calls "a clothe," but now I'm in uniform I don't get clothing coupons, and have to cadge them off Phyllis or Biddy.

Every now and then I get a letter from Nancherrow. Athena wrote, because she wanted to send me a snap of Clementina, who is now eighteen months old and beginning to walk. I must say, she looks rather sweet. Athena's husband, Rupert, is now in North Africa with the Armoured Division. Not cavalry any more, but tanks. She'd had a letter from him, and he sent this joke. A British officer went off into the desert on a secret patrol, all by himself and riding a camel. After a few days, HQ got a signal saying, "Returning at once, Rommel captured," and they all celebrated and jumped up and down. But what he had really said was, "Returning at once, camel ruptured."

Not very funny but I thought it would make Dad laugh.

Please be in touch just as soon as you possibly can, and set my mind at rest about you all.

With lots of love,

Judith

The Wrens' Quarters, where Judith had lived for the past eighteen months, was a requisitioned block of flats in the North End of Portsmouth, flung up by some jerry-builder in the nineteen thirties. It stood at the junction of the main road and a dull suburban street, and for hideousness, discomfort, and inconvenience would have been hard to beat. Built of red brick, and in modern style, it had a flat roof, curved corners, and horrible steel windows. No gardens or balconies softened its soulless façade, and at the back was a cement yard where once the unfortunate tenants had hung their laundry, but which the Navy had converted, with racks and shelters, into a park for the Wrens' bicycles.

Three storeys high, it contained twelve flats, all identical. Access to these was by stone stairways, and there were no lifts. The flats were very small. Sitting-room, two bedrooms, kitchen, and bathroom. There was no central heating, and there were no fireplaces and no chimneys. Only the sitting-room and the narrow hallway had electric heaters built into the wall, and even these, for reasons of fuel economy, had been put out of action. The cold, in winter, was so extreme as to be actually painful.

Ten girls occupied each flat, sleeping in double-decker naval-issue bunks. Four in the sitting-room, four in the main bedroom, and two in the second bedroom, which had clearly been designed for a very small child, or perhaps an equally small and unimportant elderly relation. Judith and a girl called Sue Ford shared this cramped apartment, which was, Judith reckoned, about the same size as the larder at the Dower House, and three times as frigid. Sue was a tall and languorous creature who came from Bath, and she was a Leading Wren in the Signal Office, which meant that she worked in watches, which was just as well because there wasn't space for two people to get dressed, or undressed, at the same time.

The Wrens' mess was in the basement, permanently blacked-out and sandbagged, as it served the double purpose of dining-hall and air-raid shelter. Breakfast was at seven, and the evening meal at seven as well, and sometimes Judith thought that if she was faced with another slice of Spam, another reconstituted scrambled egg, or another hunk of yellow cauliflower out of a piccalilli jar, she would scream.

And so, with one thing and another, it was something of a relief to be getting out, getting away, going to London, even if it was only for a single night. Bundled up in her greatcoat and carrying her overnight bag, Judith checked out at the Regulating Office, and then stepped forth into the bitter morning, intending to catch a bus that would take her to the railway station.

(She could have bicycled, of course, but that would have meant leaving her bicycle at the station, and, perhaps not finding it there when she returned. And her bicycle was such an essential part of existence that she didn't dare risk having it nicked.)

However, she didn't have to wait for a bus, because as she stood at the bus-stop, a Royal Navy truck heaved into view, the young seaman at the wheel spied her, drew up, and leaned over to open the door.

"Want a ride?"

"Yes, I do." And she clambered aboard and slammed the door shut behind her.

"Where to?"

"The station. Thanks," she added.

"On leave, are you?" He drew out into the road again, with a tooth-clench-ing clash of gears.

"Short weekend."

"Where are you off to?"

"London."

"Lucky girl, going up the Smoke. Come from 'ackney, myself. Least, I used to. My mum was bombed out in the blitz. Living with 'er cousin now, in Balham. Bloody cold, i'n't it? Want a fag?"

"Don't smoke, thanks."

"When's your train?"

"Meant to be ten-fifteen."

"*If* it goes on time."

It didn't. It was late, but that wasn't surprising. Late drawing into the plat-form, and late in leaving. She stood about for a bit, stamping her feet to try to keep her circulation going, and then, when at last the passengers were allowed to board, got defiantly into a first-class compartment. Her travel war-rant was for third class, but a draft of young seamen, fully kitted out, were also travelling to London, and she didn't feel strong enough to fight her way along the crowded corridors in search of a seat only to end up sitting on a kitbag wedged in a corner by one of the smelly lavatories. If the ticket collec-tor came around between Portsmouth and Waterloo—which, quite often he didn't—she would simply pay the few shillings extra and stay where she was.

The train was blissfully fuggy and overheated. She took off her coat and hat and flung them, with her bag, into the luggage rack, then settled into a corner by the grimy window. Her only other companion was a Commander, RNVR, already deep in his newspaper and clearly disinclined to chat. Judith, too, had bought a newspaper, a *Daily Telegraph,* but she let it lie on her lap and gazed through the dirty glass at the station, scarcely registering the dam-age of bomb-blast, because it had all become so familiar; a part of life. In her head, she made plans. Get to Waterloo. Get the tube to Sloane Square. Walk to Cadogan Mews. Unpack, and if there was time, change out of uniform and into plain clothes. Then, another tube to Piccadilly Circus . . .

It was then that she became aware of an uncomfortable, dry tickle at the back of her throat, which was always the classic start to one of her miserable colds. As a child, she had not suffered from colds, but since joining the Wrens and living in such close proximity to so many other people, she had endured at least three, one of which had turned into influenza, necessitating a five-day sojourn in the Sick-Bay.

I shall ignore you, she told the tickle, pushing out of her mind the memory of Sue Ford, coming off watch last night with a snivelling nose. *I shall take no notice of you, and you will go away. I've got two days leave, and you're not going to ruin it for me.* She had aspirins in her wash-bag. She would dose herself with aspirin when she got to Cadogan Mews. That should see her through today, and tomorrow could look after itself.

She heard the guard coming down the platform, slamming shut the heavy doors, which meant that hopefully, soon, they would be on their way. And at that moment, she and the Commander RNVR were joined by a third person, a Royal Marine lieutenant in the full fig of his best uniform, and a long, very dashing, khaki greatcoat. He entered from the corridor.

"Sorry. Is that seat taken?"

Which it clearly wasn't. The Commander RNVR scarcely acknowledged his presence, so Judith said, "No."

"Good show." He slid the door shut behind him, divested himself of cap and greatcoat, stowed them overhead, sagged at the knees in order to check on his appearance in the mirror, smoothed his hair with his hand, and finally dumped himself down opposite Judith.

"Phew! Just made it."

Her heart sank. She knew him. She didn't want to know him, but she knew him. Anthony Borden-Smythe. She had met him at the Junior Officer's Club in Southsea, where she had gone with Sue Ford and a couple of young sub-lieutenants. Anthony Borden-Smythe, on his own, had done his best to join their party, hanging about on the edge of the group in a most tiresome fashion, muscling in on conversation, and standing rounds of drinks with embarrassing generosity. But he had proved thick-skinned as a rhinoceros, survived badinage and even insult, and in the end Judith and Sue and their escorts were forced to call it a day and move on to the Silver Prawn.

Anthony Borden-Smythe. Sue called him Anthony Boring-Smith, and said he stemmed from the illustrious Boring family, and that his father had bored for England, and his grandfather had been the famous Olympic borer.

Unfortunately, he instantly recognized her.

"Hello there! Gosh, what a stroke of luck."

"Hello."

"Judith Dunbar, isn't it? Thought so. Remember, we met at the JOC. Terrific party. Shame you had to leave."

"Yes."

The train, at last, had started. But that made everything worse, because now she was trapped.

"Going to town?"

"To London, yes."

"Good show. Me too. Going to meet my mater for lunch. She's up from our place in the country for a few days." Judith looked at him with loathing, and tried to imagine his mater, and decided that she probably resembled a horse. Anthony looked a bit like a horse. A terribly thin horse, with enormous ears and a lot of teeth, and long, long, spindly legs. A small moustache bristled on his upper lip. The only attractive thing about him was his beautiful uniform.

"Where are you stationed?"

She said, "HMS *Excellent*."

"Oh. Whaley. How do you get on with all those gaitered gunnery officers? Not many laughs there, I'll bet."

Judith thought with love and loyalty of the taciturn Lieutenant-Commander Crombie. "Very well, thank you."

"Did my gunnery course there, of course. Never run so far in all my life. Where are you staying in London?"

Judith lied. "I have a house."

His eyebrows raised. "Do you, by Jove?" She did not elaborate on this, letting him imagine six storeys in Eaton Square. "I usually go to my club, but as my mater's in town, I'll probably shack up with her. Pembroke Gardens."

"How nice."

"You fixed for tonight? You wouldn't like to come to Quags with me? I'll give you a spot of dinner. We could dance. Go on to the Coconut Grove. They know me there. I can always get a table."

She thought, I have never known, never met, any man as insufferable as you.

"I'm sorry, but I'm afraid I can't."

"Previous engagement, eh?"

"I'm meeting a friend."

He smiled, suggestively. "M or F?"

"I'm sorry?"

"Male or Female?"

"A girl-friend."

"Terrific. I'll haul in another chap. Make it a foursome. Is she as pretty as you?"

Judith hesitated, trying to make up her mind how she would answer this. Various alternatives sprang to mind.

She's simply hideous.

She's perfectly beautiful, but unfortunately she's got a wooden leg.

She's a physical-training instructor, and she's married to a boxer.

But the truth was best. "She's a very highly powered and influential civil servant."

It worked. Anthony Borden-Smythe actually looked slightly dashed. "God," he said. "Brains. Bit out of my league, I'm afraid."

Having finally punctured his ego, Judith moved in for the kill. "Anyway, we couldn't have come to Quaglino's this evening. We're going to a lecture at the British Museum. Artifacts from the Ming Dynasty of China. Fascinating."

From the other corner, from behind his newspaper, the Commander RNVR made a small snorting sound, which could have signified disapproval, or possibly amusement.

"Gosh. Oh, well. Another time."

But she had had enough. She unfolded her *Daily Telegraph*, and took refuge behind its pages. At once, her small moment of triumph at having finally silenced Boring-Smith was doused by the latest frightening developments in the Far East.

JAPANESE ADVANCE THREATENS SINGAPORE was the headline, and it took certain courage to look at the sketch-maps and to read on.

> Time is running out for the hard-pressed defenders of Malaya. With Kuala Lumpur in Japanese hands and its inhabitants in flight, the Japanese Fifth and Guards Divisions are pressing southwards to Johore State, where the coming battle will decide the fate of Singapore . . . Indian Brigade defeated on the Muar River . . . Lieutenant General Percival's army forced to retreat towards Singapore . . .

She was filled with apprehension. She thought of her parents and Jess, and prayed that by now they were somewhere else, had abandoned the lovely house in Orchard Road and gone. Left Singapore. Gone to Sumatra or Java. Anywhere. Somewhere safe. Jess was ten now, but Judith still thought of her as she had been when they said goodbye: four years old, and weeping and clinging to Golly. Oh God, she prayed, don't let anything happen to them. They are my family, they are mine, and they are so precious. Keep them safe. Let them be safe.

The train stopped at Petersfield. The Commander RNVR alighted, and was met on the platform by his wife. Nobody else got into the compartment. Anthony Borden-Smythe, snoring gently, had fallen asleep. Judith's throat was beginning to feel dreadfully sore. She folded the newspaper and laid it aside and sat looking out at the grey mid-winter day and the frozen fields of Hampshire, and hated the war for spoiling everything.

Diana's property in London, to which she always referred as her little house, had been converted, just before the Great War, from two coachman's dwellings with stabling for horses beneath. The front door stood in the middle, with garage on one side, and kitchen on the other. A narrow steep staircase led straight to the upper floor, which was unexpectedly spacious. A long sitting-room (the venue for many memorable pre-war parties), a large bedroom, a bathroom, another lavatory, and a small bedroom, mostly used as a repository for suitcases, ironing board, and the few clothes that Diana had never bothered to move to Cornwall. It still, however, boasted a bed, and was useful for overflows.

There was no dining-room. This had bothered Diana not a jot, because when she was in London she dined out most of the time, except for rare evenings of solitude which she shared with Tommy Mortimer, eating supper off a tray and listening to beautiful music played on the radiogram.

Mrs. Hickson, who in the old days had worked for Diana, housekeeping when she was in residence, and keeping an eye on the place when she wasn't, was now engaged in full-time war-work, as a tea-lady in the Forces Canteen at Paddington Station. But she lived in a block of council flats nearby, and two or three evenings a week popped in to the Mews to do a quick check-up. Mrs. Carey-Lewis did not come to London now, and Mrs. Hickson missed her company most dreadfully. But she had given keys of the Mews to a number of young service people outwith her own family, and Mrs. Hickson could never be sure if she'd find Athena in residence, or some unknown young flying officer. Sometimes the only evidence of occupation was a few scraps of food in the fridge, or a bundle of sheets on the bathroom floor. In which case, she would tidy up, and remake the beds with clean linen, and take the used sheets home in a paper carrier-bag, to launder herself. She rather enjoyed these brief encounters, and there was nearly always five bob on the dressing-table, to be scooped into her pinafore pocket.

During the early months of 1940, when it had still been a phoney war, Edward Carey-Lewis was the most frequent visitor, usually bringing a friend with him, and using the Mews to entertain a number of dizzyingly pretty girls. Mrs. Carey-Lewis had written herself to Mrs. Hickson to tell her that Edward had been killed, and Mrs. Hickson hadn't been able to stop crying for a whole day. In the end, her supervisor at the Forces Canteen, rightly deciding that Mrs. Hickson's tears were doing nothing for the fighting man's morale, had sent her home.

Miraculously, the little house had survived the blitz. At the height of the raids, a great bomb had dropped nearby, and Mrs. Hickson had been filled with fear. But the only damage done had been a few cracks in the walls, and all the windows blasted in. Broken glass all over the floor and everything—furniture, china, glass, pictures, carpets and rugs—shrouded in a thick layer of brownish, grimy dust. It had taken her a week of evenings to get it cleaned up.

Judith took out her key, turned the latch, and went inside, closing the front door behind her. On her right was the kitchen, and she glanced in, saw the fridge, empty and open, so went to close its door and turn on the switch. The fridge started to hum. Sometime, before the little corner shop closed, she would buy some rations to put in the fridge. But, for the moment, shopping would have to wait.

Humping her grip, she went up the steep stairs, which led directly into the sitting-room. There was no central heating and it felt a bit cold, but later, when she came back again, she would light the gas-fire and it would all warm up in moments. Beyond the sitting-room were the bedroom and the bathroom. The second bedroom and the lavatory were over the kitchen.

She felt blissfully relieved to have finally arrived. Every time she came to the Mews (and, taking advantage of Diana's generous offer, she had been now, from Portsmouth, three or four times), she was assailed by the comforting sensation of coming home. This was because Diana's touch, her style and taste, were so unique and personal, that it felt a bit like walking into a miniature Nancherrow. Comfortably, even luxuriously, appointed: raw-silk curtains the colour of cream, and thick beige carpeting all through the rooms and the passages, the monotone relieved here and there by Persian rugs. Sofas and chairs were covered in a Liberty print, furniture was small-size and elegant. There were pictures and mirrors, fat cushions, family photographs. All that was missing were the arrangements of fresh flowers.

She went through to the bedroom. Cream curtains again, and the downy double bed veiled in a canopy of lace. Chintz bedcover, smothered in roses, and the same roses frilling the dressing-table and the little Victorian chaise longue. Diana had not stayed here since the start of the war, but her perfume bottle still stood on the dressing-table, and the musty air was heavy with her remembered scent.

Judith took off her hat and coat and slung them across the bed, and then sat down and looked at her watch. Half past twelve. No time to change into plain clothes. Heather would just have to take her as she was, in uniform. Her throat felt rough as emery boards, and she had the beginnings of a headache. She unzipped her grip and took out her wash-bag, and went into the bathroom (pink marble and a sheepskin rug) to fill a mug with water and take a couple of aspirin. Then she opened the mirrored cupboard and searched around for a bit, and found a bottle of Glycerine of Thymol, so she gargled with that, and simply hoped that these medications would get her through the day. She washed her hands and face and then went back to the bedroom and sat at the mirror to fix her hair, put on some make-up and scent, inspect her white collar for train smuts, and straighten the knot of her black satin tie (her best, from Gieves). Behind her, the reflection of the bed was not only inviting, but alluring. She thought of climbing between the sheets, with cool pillows and warm hot-water bottles, going to sleep, and being ill in peace.

However, already she was running late for her rendezvous with Heather, and so bed, along with everything else, must wait until later.

She had intended taking the tube to Piccadilly, but as she stepped out into Sloane Street, a bus rolled up, so she got onto that and bought a ticket to

Piccadilly Circus. It was still very cold and grey, with the smell of snow in the air, and the streets of London were battered and dirty, bombed houses gaping like missing teeth and store windows boarded up, with only a peep-hole for window-shopping. Over the park, the barrage balloons flew high, lost in cloud, and the grassy swards were humped with sandbags and air-raid shelters. All the ornate wrought-iron railings had gone, to be melted down for armaments, and the lovely old church of Saint James, which had received a direct hit, was a ruin. In Piccadilly Circus, the statue of Eros had been removed, evacuated to some place of safety, but crowds still sat on the steps of the plinth which had supported the statue, fed pigeons, and sold newspapers.

It was a city at war, and every other person seemed to be in uniform.

The bus stopped, and she got off and walked down the pavement by Swan & Edgar's, and around the corner to the main door. Heather was already there. Instantly visible, with her dark, shining hair, and wearing an enviable scarlet overcoat, and long suede fur-lined boots.

"Heather!"

"I thought you were never *coming*."

"I'm sorry. Ten minutes late. Are you frozen? No, don't hug me, nor kiss me, because I think I'm getting a cold and I don't want to pass on any germs."

"Oh, I don't give a damn for germs." So they hugged anyway, and then started laughing, because it was so wonderful, after so long, to be together again.

"What shall we do?" Heather asked.

"How long have you got?"

"Just today. This afternoon. I've got to be back this evening. I'm on duty tomorrow."

"Tomorrow's Sunday."

"We don't have Sundays where I work."

"It's too bad. I thought you might have come back to Diana's house with me and spent the night."

"I'd have loved to, but I can't. It doesn't matter. My train doesn't go till half past seven. We've all the rest of the day. I'm starving. Let's go somewhere and eat lunch, and over lunch we can decide what we're going to do. Now, where to?"

They discussed this for a bit, rejecting the Kardomah Café and Lyons Corner House. In the end, Judith said, "Let's go to the Berkeley."

"But that's frightfully grand."

"Doesn't matter. It's not allowed to cost more than five bob, anyway. With a bit of luck, we'll get a table."

So they set off in the direction of the Berkeley, walking the short distance back up Piccadilly. Going inside, through the perpetually revolving doors, they were injected into a world of comfort, and warm, expensive smells. There were a great many people about and the bar was packed, but Heather spied a free table and two empty chairs, which she swiftly claimed, while Judith went in search of the restaurant and the head-waiter, to ask if it would be possible to have a table for two. He was rather a nice man, and did not look at her down his nose (a Wren on her own, and not even an officer) but went to his desk to inspect his bookings, and returned to say that if she didn't mind waiting fifteen minutes, there would be a table then.

She said, "I hope it isn't by the kitchen door," and he looked a bit surprised by her self-assertion, but respectful as well.

"No, madam, it will be near the window."

"That's perfect." She treated him to her nicest smile.

"I'll come and fetch you when the table is free."

"We'll be in the bar."

She returned to Heather, making a sly thumbs-up sign, and all at once it began to be fun. They shed their overcoats, and a porter appeared and bore them away to the cloakroom, and then a waiter swam forward and asked what they would like to drink, and before Judith could open her mouth, Heather had ordered champagne.

"By the glass, madam?"

"No, I think a half bottle."

He left them, and Judith muttered, "Shades of Porthkerris Council School," and they began to giggle, and Judith ate crisps out of a little china dish, and Heather lit a cigarette.

Eyeing her, Judith decided that she looked amazing. Not tall, but wonderfully slim, and her dark colouring made her very distinctive. She wore a narrow grey flannel skirt and a fine navy-blue polo-necked sweater, and there was a long gold chain around her neck and gold rings in her ears.

"You're looking terrific, Heather. I meant to change, but I didn't have time."

"I think you look terrific, too. And I like the uniform. Thank God you didn't choose to be an At or a Waaf. Nothing but pockets and buttons and busts. And the hats are a disaster. You've cut your hair."

"I had to. It's not meant to touch your collar. It was either cut it, or have a bun."

"I like it. It suits you."

The waiter returned with their glasses and the bottle which, ceremoniously and efficiently, he opened. The wine creamed into Heather's glass, with not a drop spilt, and then Judith's was filled.

"Thank you."

"A pleasure, madam."

They raised their glasses and drank, and almost at once Judith felt infinitely better. She said, "I must remember. Champagne is the remedy for colds."

They sat sipping champagne and looking about them, at elegant women, and staff colonels, and Free French officers, and young guardees, all talking their heads off, and drinking, and laughing as though they hadn't a care in the world. A lot of them were entertaining ladies who were clearly not their wives, but this only engendered a buzz of piquancy; the wartime affair, the undertones of illicit love. One girl in particular was immensely glamorous, with a mass of red hair and a sinuous figure made even more suggestive by her clinging black jersey dress. She had tiger-claw nails, painted blood-red, and a mink coat was draped from the arm of her chair.

Her escort was a balding group captain, his middle-aged libido fairly panting with youthful lust.

Much amused, "He can scarcely keep his eyes off her," Judith remarked.

"Let alone his hands."

Just as they finished the champagne, the head-waiter appeared to tell them that their table was ready, and to lead them across the crowded restaurant and settle them in their places, flicking open vast linen napkins to lay across their laps, giving each girl an enormous menu to study, and asking if they wished an aperitif.

Which they didn't, because already, they were both feeling extremely happy.

It was a lovely lunch, the restaurant so airy and pretty, so different from the dark, battered, dirty streets beyond the net-veiled windows. They ate oysters and chicken and ice-cream, and shared, between them, a bottle of white wine. They talked, catching up, covering the long months that had passed since they had last been together. Some of it was necessarily very sad. Ned's death. Edward Carey-Lewis. And Mrs. Mudge's nephew, posted missing believed killed, had died on the beaches of Dunkirk. But Charlie Lanyon had been more fortunate, survived the shelling, and was now a prisoner-of-war in Germany.

"Do you write to him, Heather?"

"Yes, I do. Every week. Don't know if he gets them or not, but that's no reason to stop writing."

"Have you heard from him?"

"He's rationed, so he writes to his mum and dad and they give me the news. But he seems to be all right . . . and he's getting some of our food parcels."

"Will you wait for him?"

Heather frowned, astonished. "*Wait* for him?"

"Yes. Wait for him. Stay constant."

"No. I'm not waiting for him. It was never like that with Charlie and me. I just liked him. Anyway, I told you once, I'm not mad on getting married. I mean, I will if I want to. One day. But it's not the be-all and end-all for me. There's too much to life. Too much to do. Too much to see."

"Are there any nice chaps where you're working?"

Heather laughed. "A lot of weirdies. Most of them are so bright they're just about barmy. As for fancying one . . . you wouldn't touch them with a barge-pole. But that doesn't mean they're not interesting . . . scholarly. Very cultured. Just weird."

"What do you do? What's your job?"

Heather shrugged her shoulders, and dropped her eyes. She reached for another cigarette, and when she looked up again, Judith knew that she had clammed up, and not another word was she going to say. Perhaps, already, she feared she had said too much.

"You don't want to talk about it, do you?"

"No."

"But you enjoy it?"

Heather blew out a cloud of smoke. "It's fascinating. Now, talk about you. What's your job?"

"Not very exciting. I'm at Whale Island, the Gunnery School. I work for the Training Development officer."

"What does he do?"

"He researches and develops devices that will help train men to fire guns. Simulation domes. Mock Oerlikons. That sort of thing. Artificial visual trainers. Devices to teach the principles of centrifugal force. It's endless. New ideas crop up all the time."

"Got a boy-friend?"

Judith smiled. "Lots."

"Not one particular one."

"No. Not again."

"What do you mean?"

"Edward Carey-Lewis. I'm not going through that again. I'm going to wait until the war's over, and then I shall probably fall madly in love with some unlikely man, and get married and have strings of babies and become a total bore. You won't want to know me."

"Were you in love with Edward?"

"Yes. For years."

"I never knew."

"I never told you."

"I'm sorry."

"It's over, now."

So they didn't talk about Edward any longer, but got onto more cheerful, positive topics, like Mr. Warren being a sergeant in the Porthkerris Home Guard, and Joe Warren getting recommended for a commission.

"How's your mother?" Judith asked.

"Same as ever. Nothing fazes her. She doesn't write much. Too busy, I suppose. But she did write to tell me when old Flasher Fawcett dropped dead in the bank. Couldn't wait to get that gobbet of gossip down on paper. Remember the carry-on we had that evening, when Ellie came back from the pictures in hysterics because the old toad had shown his all? I'll never forget it, as long as I live."

"Oh, Heather, you weren't even *there*."

"Heard all about it, though. Lived with it for days. My mum couldn't stop talking about it. 'You should have seen Judith,' she kept saying to me. 'Like a real little fury.'"

"He died of apoplexy, I think. Because the bank manager told him he had an overdraft. It was Mr. Baines who told me about it, and all we could do was giggle. Dreadfully unseemly."

"Good riddance to bad rubbish, I'd say. Now, what about the Carey-Lewises? Are they all right?"

So they talked about Nancherrow, and how Diana's grief after Edward's death had been eased, in a small way, by the arrival and constant diversion of her grand-daughter Clementina. Just as, in some obscure way, the undemanding company of Phyllis and Anna had helped to get Biddy Somerville back on her feet again.

"So they're all living together at the Dower House?"

"Yes, and it's working. You've never seen my house. Sometime, when you get some leave, you must come over, and I'll show it to you. You'll love it. I do. I love it to bits."

"I still can't believe you've got a house of your own," Heather marvelled. "Really grown up. I mean, understand, I'm not envious in the very least, because the last thing I'd want would be a house to tie me down. But for you, it must be like a dream come true. Specially with your family so far away." She stopped, and then said, "Sorry."

"Why are you sorry?"

"Tactless. Singapore. I read the paper in the train this morning."

"So did I."

"Have you heard from your family?"

"Not for too long."

"Worried?"

"Yes. Worried stiff. I just hope they've been evacuated. Anyway, Mummy and Jess. Everybody says Singapore won't fall, that it's too well defended, too important, everything will be flung into the battle. But even if Singapore holds, there'll be air raids and every sort of horror. And there doesn't seem to be anything, or any army, capable of stopping the Japanese. I just wish I could find out what's happening." She looked at Heather across the table. "You . . . you couldn't find anything out, could you? I mean, sort of, under the counter?"

The waiter came with coffee. Heather stubbed out her cigarette, and lit another. They sat silent while the black, strong coffee was poured into the little cups. When he had gone, out of earshot, Heather shook her head and said, "No. We only deal with Europe."

"I shouldn't have asked." Judith sighed. "Gus is out there, too. Gus Callender. He's with the Second Gordons."

"You've lost me."

"He was a friend of Edward's at Cambridge. He came to stay at Nancherrow. He and Loveday . . . how do you say? Hit it off."

"Loveday?" Heather sounded incredulous. "Loveday fancied him? She never said anything to me."

"I don't suppose she would. It was extraordinary. She was only seventeen, and it just happened. An instant rapport. As though they'd known each other forever. As though they'd always been a couple."

"If he's a soldier, and in Singapore, he'll be in the thick of it. I wouldn't put my money on his chances."

"I know. I've been thinking that too."

"It's a bloody war, isn't it? Poor Loveday. And poor you. I suppose we just have to sit and wait. See what happens."

"Waiting's the worst. Waiting for news. Trying to pretend that the worst isn't going to happen. Mustn't happen. I want my parents and Jess to stay alive, and be safe, and one day come home and come to the Dower House. And I want Gus to stay alive for Loveday. After Saint Valéry, we thought he was dead, but he managed to escape and get home, and when she heard the news, Loveday was like a person transformed. I can't bear for her to have to go through all that agony for a second time."

"Judith, whatever happens to Loveday, she'll survive."

"Why do you say that?"

"I know her. She's a tough little thing."

"But . . ." Judith was all ready to spring to Loveday's defence, but Heather interrupted her.

"Look, we could go on talking all afternoon, and the day will have gone, and we won't have done anything. In my wallet I've got two tickets for the Albert Hall. The man I work for gave them to me. A concert that's due to start in half an hour. Do you want to go to a concert, or do you want to go shopping?"

"What are they playing?"

"William Walton's Violin Concerto, and Rachmaninoff's Second Piano Concerto."

"I don't want to go shopping."

So they finished their coffee, and paid the bill (with hefty tips all round), collected their coats from the cloakroom (more tips) and plunged out into the bitter cold and Piccadilly. As they emerged, a taxi rolled up to the pavement's edge, from which stepped a naval captain and his homely wife. They waited until he had settled his fare, and then swiftly hopped in, before anyone else could bag the cab.

"Where to, love?"

"The Albert Hall, and we're in a terrific hurry."

The concert was wonderful, everything that Judith had hoped for, and more. The Walton was new to her, but the Rachmaninoff dearly familiar, and she sat lost in the music, transported into a sort of timelessness, the affirmation of another, constant world, set apart from anxiety and death, and battles and bombs. The rest of the huge audience was equally intent, and when the performance was finished, and the last notes had died away, displayed their appreciation with applause for conductor and orchestra, applause that lasted for at least five minutes.

But finally it was all over, and time to leave. Judith felt a bit as though she had spent two hours floating effortlessly in the upper air, and was now having to come down to earth again. So absorbed had she been that her cold was forgotten, but now, as they edged their way up the crowded, carpeted aisle towards the foyer and the main doors, the headache and the sore throat returned with a vengeance, and she realized that she was beginning to feel distinctly unwell.

They had planned to walk back to the Mews, or catch a bus, but when they emerged, with streams of others, into the black, lightless evening, they discovered that it had started to rain, a thin raw sleet, and neither of them had an umbrella.

They stood, bumped and barged, on the wet pavement and discussed their chances of getting a taxi, which were so slim as to be impossible.

"We can't walk, we'll get soaked. Why *didn't* I bring an umbrella?" Heather, always so efficient, was furious with herself.

"*I* couldn't bring one, because I'm not allowed to carry one in uniform . . ."

And then, as they hesitated, trying to decide how on earth they would get home, good fortune beamed upon them. A private car drew up, with a driver, to be claimed by an RAF Wing Commander and his female companion. Clearly, he had had the forethought to arrange his own transport. He opened the door, the woman bundled herself inside, getting into shelter as swiftly as she could, and the Wing Commander was just about to follow when he caught sight of the two girls, illuminated in the tiny light that beamed from the interior of the car, standing forlornly and getting wetter by the moment.

He said, "Which direction do you want to go?"

"Sort of, Sloane Square," Judith told him.

"We're going to Clapham. Why don't we give you a ride?"

It was almost too good to be true. Gratefully, they accepted, and Heather got into the back seat, while Judith sat by the driver. Doors were slammed shut, and the car moved forward into the dark, wet street, with windscreen wipers going full-tilt, and the driver feeling his way by the faint beam of the darkened and hooded headlights.

Behind her, Heather made lively conversation with their saviours. "It's *really* kind of you," she told them. "I don't know what we'd have done otherwise."

"It's always hell getting home after a theatre or a concert. Particularly on a filthy night like this . . ."

Judith stopped listening. She had stood in a puddle and her feet were wet, and she was beginning to feel a bit shivery. When they got back, she would light the gas-fire and work up a fug, but before that happened, there was the small problem of food, because she'd had no time to buy anything.

They were now proceeding down Sloane Street. In the back of the car, chat was still going non-stop. They had finished discussing the concert, and were on to the horror of the Queens Hall being destroyed in the bombings, and the lovely lunch-time recitals that Myra Hess was giving at the church of Saint Martin's-in-the-Fields.

"They're always packed. People just pop in to listen for a bit, on their way to or from their offices . . ."

The Wing Commander leaned forward. "Exactly whereabouts do you want to go?" he asked Judith. "We can take you to the door, if it's not too far out of our way."

"Cadogan Mews." She turned in her seat to speak to him. "But . . ." She hesitated. "The only thing is, I have to go to a shop. There's no food in the house. I came up from Portsmouth this morning and there wasn't time . . . but if you could drop us at our local grocery . . . ?"

He said, "Don't you worry," and because of his kindness, all went smoothly. Judith directed the driver to the ramshackle corner store, which had always been the nearest and the most convenient for the Mews. It sold groceries and newspapers and cigarettes, and while the others waited, she went inside, armed with her Emergency Ration Card, and bought bread and eggs, and tiny amounts of bacon and sugar and margarine and a pint of milk and a jar of dubious-looking raspberry jam. The old woman behind the counter dug out a crumpled paper carrier into which she packed all this, Judith paid the bill, and returned to the others.

"Thank you so much. That's perfect. At least we've got something to eat for tea."

"We couldn't allow you to go hungry. Where to now?"

They were delivered, in style, to the door. In the Mews, in the dim beam of the blacked-out headlights, the cobbles glistened, and a wet cat streaked across, in search of shelter. Judith and Heather got out of the car, effusive with thanks, even offering to pay their share of the fare, but they were dismissed forthwith, told that it was the least any person could do, and get inside, pronto, before they got even wetter.

It sounded like an order, so they did as they were told. As they closed the door behind them, the car was already turning, and on its way.

They stood, very close, in the inky darkness of the tiny hall. "Don't turn on any lights," Judith told Heather, "until I've done the black-out. Stay where you are, or you'll fall over the stairs."

She felt her way into the kitchen and fixed the black-out, and dumped the paper carrier on the table. Then, still in darkness, she emerged once more, trod carefully up the staircase, and dealt with the black-out and the thick curtains of the sitting-room. Only then could she safely press the switch.

"You can come up now," she told Heather, and together they went around all the rooms, even the ones that Judith had no intention of using, so that every gleam of light was sealed away. With this accomplished, Heather made herself at home, divesting herself of damp overcoat and boots, lighting the gas-fire, turning on a few lamps. Almost at once, everything looked quite different, snug and cosy.

Heather said, "I'd die for a cup of tea."

"Me too, but I must take some more aspirin first."

"You feeling awful?"

"Yes, fairly."

"Poor thing. You do look a bit poorly. Do you think you've got 'flu?"

"Don't even suggest it."

"Well, you go and dose yourself, and I'll make the tea." Already she was on her way downstairs again. "Don't worry. I'll find my way around."

"There's some bread. We can make toast by the gas-fire."

"Lovely."

Judith took off her coat and laid it on the bed, and then removed her shoes and damp stockings and put on a pair of fleecy slippers. She took off her jacket as well, and instead pulled on a Shetland sweater that she'd brought up from Portsmouth. Then she took more aspirin and gargled again. Her reflection in the mirror did nothing to cheer. Her face looked peaky and pinched, and there were dark rings, like bruises, under her eyes. If Biddy were here, she would prescribe a hot toddy, but as Judith had neither whisky nor honey nor lemon, the knowledge didn't do her much good.

By the time she went back to the sitting-room, Heather had made the tea and carried the tray up the stairs. They sat by the gas-fire, and made toast on a long fork, and then meagrely scraped it with margarine and spread on the raspberry jam.

"Tastes of picnics," Heather decided with satisfaction. She licked her sticky fingers. "Mum always used to put raspberry jam on splits." She looked about her. "I like this house. Like the way it's all been done. With the pale curtains and everything. Do you come here a lot?"

"Always when I come to London."

"Better than a Wrens hostel, anyway."

"I wish you could stay."

"I can't."

"Couldn't you ring somebody and say you've got a little headache?"

"No. I must be on duty tomorrow."

"When's your train?"

"Seven-thirty."

"Where do you go from?"

"Euston."

"How will you get there?"

"I'll get a tube from Sloane Square."

"Do you want me to come with you? See you off?"

Abruptly, "No," said Heather. And then she added, "Not with that cold. You mustn't go out again tonight. You ought to be in bed." But Judith got the feeling that even if she'd been in the rudest of health, Heather wouldn't have wanted her to go to Euston, because she didn't want Judith to know even the direction in which she was going to travel. It was all so secret as to be quite alarming. Judith simply hoped that her friend was not training to be a spy, because she could not bear the thought of her being darkly dropped from an aeroplane into dangerous enemy territory.

There were still masses they hadn't talked about, but, too soon, it was time for Heather to leave.

"So early?"

"I daren't risk missing that train, because that's the only one that has a car to meet it." Judith imagined some remote country station, the official car patiently waiting, the subsequent drive through miles of winding lanes. And then, arrival. Locked and electrically operated gates, high barbed-wire fences, prowling guard-dogs. Beyond, long avenues leading to the looming bulk of some great country house or Victorian castle. She could almost hear owls hooting.

For some reason, the image made her shiver, a frisson of distaste, and she was grateful for her open, humdrum job, running messages for Lieutenant-Commander Crombie, taking telephone calls, and doing his typing. At least she wasn't locked up in secrecy. And at least she didn't have to work on Sundays.

Heather was getting ready to go. Zipping on her boots again (they'd dried, more or less, in front of the fire), buttoning herself into her lovely scarlet coat, and then tying a Jacqumar silk scarf over her raven-black hair.

She said, "It's been great. A wonderful day."

"Thank you for the concert. I adored every moment."

"We must try to meet again. Not wait for so long this time. Don't come down the stairs. I'll see myself out."

"I still feel I should come with you."

"Don't be silly. Have a hot bath. Get to bed." She kissed Judith. And then suddenly said, "I don't want to leave you. I don't like to leave you."

"I'm all right."

"Keep in touch. About your mum and dad and Jess, I mean. I'll be thinking of you. Let me know if you have news."

"I will. I promise."

"You've got my address? Box number and everything. It's a bit obscure but letters eventually reach me."

"I'll write. Let you know."

"Goodbye, love."

"Goodbye."

A quick hug and a kiss, and she was gone. Down the stairs and out of the door. The door slammed shut. Her footsteps faded as she hurried away down the length of the Mews. She was gone.

Now, no sound but the dripping rain, and the distant hum of sparse traffic making its way down Sloane Street. Judith hoped that there would not be an air raid, but decided that there probably wouldn't, because the weather was so foul. Bombers liked a clear night and a moon. It seemed a bit flat without Heather's company, so she put some Elgar on the radiogram. The first deep chords of a cello concerto stole into the room, and warmed by this, she stopped feeling abandoned. Judith took the tea-tray, carried it downstairs, washed up the few bits of china, and set them to dry on the draining-board. Putting the kettle on to boil, she found a rubber hot-water bottle, filled it, went upstairs again, turned down the bed, and put the hot-water bottle between the sheets. Then she took another couple of aspirin (by now she was feeling really lousy), drew a deep, scalding bath, and soaked in scented steam for nearly an hour. Dried, she put on her night-gown, and then the Shetland sweater. By now, the Elgar was finished, so she switched off the radiogram, but left the fire burning, and the bedroom door open, so that its warmth would permeate. Then she found an old back number of *Vogue* and climbed into bed. She lay back on the soft pillows, flipped through the glossy pages for a moment or two, and then succumbed to exhaustion and closed her eyes. Almost at once, or so it seemed, she opened them again.

A sound. Her heart thudded in alarm. Downstairs. The click of a latchkey. The front door opening, and softly, being closed.

An intruder. Some person had come into the house. Petrified with terror, for an instant she lay rigid, unable to move; and then flung herself out of the bed and ran through the open door, across the sitting-room to the head of the stairs, determined that if the newcomer was foe rather than friend, she would bash him over the head as he mounted, with any heavy object that came to hand.

He was half-way up already, muffled in a heavy overcoat, gold lace gleaming on epaulettes, his cap sprinkled with raindrops. He carried, in one hand, an overnight grip, and in the other a sturdy canvas sailing-bag with rope handles.

Jeremy. She saw him and felt her legs go weak with relief, and had to cling, for support, to the banisters. Not an intruder, breaking in, intent on theft, rape, or murder. Instead, the one person—had she been given the choice—she would have really wanted it to be.

"Jeremy."

He paused, and looked up, his face shadowed by the peak of his cap, and gaunt in the unflattering overhead light of the stairwell.

"Good God, it's Judith."

"Whom did you think it might be?"

"No idea. But I knew the place was occupied as soon as I opened the door, because of the lights being on."

"I thought you were at sea. What are you doing here?"

"I could ask the same question." He came on up the stair, dumped his luggage, removed his sodden cap, and stooped to kiss her cheek. "And why are you receiving gentlemen in your night-gown?"

"I was in bed, of course."

"Alone, I trust."

"I've got a cold, if you must know. I'm feeling rotten."

"Then get back into bed, right away."

"No. I want to talk to you. Are you going to stay the night?"

"I'd planned to."

"And now I've bagged the bedroom."

"No matter. I'll go in with the ironing board and Diana's clothes. I've slept there before."

"How long are you staying?"

496

"Just till morning." He placed his cap on the top of the newel-post, and began to unbutton his greatcoat. "I've got to catch a train at seven A.M."

"So where have you *come* from? Right now, I mean."

"Truro." He shrugged himself out of the heavy greatcoat and draped it over the banister rail. "I had a couple of days' leave, and went to Cornwall to spend them with my parents."

"I haven't seen you for ages. Years." She could not remember how long.

But Jeremy did. "Since I came to say goodbye to you at the Dower House."

"It seems like another life." She suddenly thought of something really serious. "There's nothing to eat here. Just a loaf of bread and a rasher of bacon. Are you starving? The corner shop will be closed, but . . ."

He was laughing at her. "But what?"

"You could always take yourself out for a meal. The Royal Court Hotel perhaps?"

"That would be no fun at all."

"If I'd known you were coming . . ."

"I know, you'd have baked a cake. Don't worry. I have used my foresight. My mother helped me pack a little nosebag." He gave the canvas sailing-bag a kick. "This is it."

Judith peered down into it, and saw the gleam of a bottle. "At least you've got your priorities right."

"There was no need for me to lug it up the stairs. It weighs a ton. I'd have dumped it in the kitchen, only when I saw the lights, my first thought was to find out who was here."

"Who could it have been, but me? Or Athena. Or Loveday. Rupert's in the desert, and Gus is in the Far East."

"Ah, but there are others. Nancherrow's become a home-from-home, a sort of non-stop canteen for young service officers. They come from Culdrose and the Royal Marine Training Camp at Bran Tor. Anyone special, whom Diana takes a shine to, she presents them with a key."

"I never knew that."

"So the club is no longer so exclusive. Do you come here often?"

"Not very. Weekends, sometimes."

"And this is one of them?"

"Yes. But I have to get back to Portsmouth tomorrow."

"I wish I could stay. I could take you out for lunch."

"But you can't."

"No. I can't. Do you want a drink?"

"There's nothing in the cupboard."

"But ample in my ditty-bag." He stooped and heaved it up, and it clanked a bit and looked enormously heavy. "Come on, and I'll show you."

He led the way downstairs again, and they went into the little kitchen, and he dumped the bag on the table and commenced to unload it. The brown linoleum felt chilly under bare feet, so Judith sat on the other end of the table, and it was a bit like watching somebody open a Christmas stocking.

One had absolutely no idea what goody was coming out next. A bottle of Black & White whisky. A bottle of Gordon's gin. Two lemons. An orange. Three packets of potato crisps and a pound of farm butter. A slab of Terry's dark chocolate, and, last of all, a sinister blood-stained parcel, the outer wrapping of which was newspaper.

"What's in there?" Judith asked. "A severed head?"

"Steaks." He spelled it out. "S-T-E-A-K-S."

"Where did you get steaks from? And farm butter? Your mother isn't dabbling in the Black Market, is she?"

"Grateful patients. Is the fridge on?"

"Of course."

"Good. Any ice?"

"I expect so."

He opened the fridge and laid the butter and the bloody parcel alongside the tiny meagre rations which Judith had already placed there, then removed a tray of ice-cubes. "What do you want to drink? A whisky would do that cold good. Whisky and soda?"

"There's no soda."

"Want a bet?"

He found it, of course, a siphon stowed away in an obscure cupboard. From another cupboard, he took glasses, then manhandled ice-cubes out of their tray, poured the whisky, squirted in the soda. The drinks fizzed deliciously, and he handed Judith one of the tall tumblers.

"I looks towards you."

She smiled. "And I raises my glass."

They drank. Visibly, Jeremy relaxed, letting out a satisfied sigh. "I needed that."

"It's good. I don't usually drink whisky."

"There's a time for everything. It's cold down here. Let's go upstairs."

So they went, Judith leading the way, and made themselves comfortable by the fire, Jeremy settling himself in one of the armchairs and Judith curled up on the hearthrug, close to the warmth. She said, "Heather Warren was here today. We made toast for tea. That's why I came up from Portsmouth. To see her. We had lunch together and then went to a concert, but she had to catch a train and go back to her secret Department."

"Where was your concert?"

"The Albert Hall. William Walton and Rachmaninoff. Heather was given the tickets. But, please, tell me about you. What's been happening?"

"Routine stuff."

"You've had leave."

"No, not really. I had to come to London to see their Lordships at the Admiralty. I'm getting promotion. Surgeon-Commander."

"Oh, Jeremy . . ." She was delighted and impressed. "Well done. You'll get your brass hat."

"It's not official yet, so don't go ringing people up and telling them."

"But you told your mother?"

"Yes, of course."

"What else?"

"I'm joining a new ship. A cruiser, HMS *Sutherland*."

"Still in the Atlantic?" He shrugged. He was being cagey. "Perhaps they'll send you to the Mediterranean. It's about time you got a bit of sun."

He said, "Have you heard from your family?"

"Not since the beginning of the month. I don't know why. Except that the news is so ghastly."

"Are they still in Singapore?"

"I suppose so."

"A lot of women and children have left already."

"I haven't heard."

He looked at his watch. "It's a quarter past eight. We'll listen to the nine o'clock news."

"I don't know if I want to."

"It's better to know the truth than to imagine the worst."

"At the moment, one seems as bad as the other. And it's all happened so quickly. Before, when things were really bad, like Dunkirk time, and in Portsmouth during the bombing, I used to comfort myself by knowing that at least *they* were safe. Mummy and Dad and Jess, I mean. And when we were all queuing for rations and eating horrible scrag ends of meat, that *they* were all right, with lovely food and being looked after by masses of servants, and meeting their friends at the club. And then the Japanese bombed Pearl Harbor, and all at once none of it's true any longer, and they are in much greater danger than I have ever been. I wish now that I'd gone to Singapore, when I was meant to. Then, at least, we'd all be together. But being so far away, and no news . . ."

To her horror, her voice had started to shake. No point in trying to say any more, perhaps breaking down in useless tears. She took another sip of her whisky, and stared into the hot bluish flames of the gas-fire.

He said, gently, "I suppose not knowing is the worst torment of all."

"I'm all right. Usually I'm all right. It's just that this evening I'm not actually feeling very well."

"Go to bed."

"I'm sorry."

"Why should you be sorry?"

"We never see each other, and then when we do, I've got a wretched cold, and I'm too jittery to listen to the news, and I'm not very good company."

"I like you just the way you are. However you are. My only regret is that I have to leave you so early in the morning. We're together, only to be almost instantly torn apart again. But I suppose that's what bloody war is all about."

"Never mind. We're together. I was so glad it was you, and not some man I'd never met . . . one of Diana's favoured few."

"I'm glad it was me, too. Now . . ." He got to his feet. "Your spirits are low, and I'm starving. What we both need is a good hot meal, and perhaps a little incidental music. You get back into bed and I'll take charge of the galley." He went to the radiogram and switched on the wireless. Dance music. The distinctive strains of Carroll Gibbons relayed live from the Savoy Hotel. "Begin the Beguine." She imagined the diners leaving their tables, crowding onto the floor.

"What's on the menu? Steaks?"

"What else? Cooked in butter. I'm only sorry that there is no champagne. Do you want another drink?"

"I haven't finished this one yet."

He held out his hand, and she took it, and he pulled her to her feet. "Bed," he said, and turned her and propelled her gently in the direction of the bedroom. She went through the door, and heard him go downstairs, running expertly as though he were descending a ship's ladder, but she did not instantly get back into bed. Instead, sat at the dressing-table and gazed at her pallid reflection in the mirror, and wondered why he had not remarked on her service haircut, a crisp little bob so different from the long, honey-coloured locks of her youth. Perhaps he hadn't even noticed. Some men didn't notice things like that. She was feeling a bit woozy. Probably the whisky on top of the boiling-hot bath and the aspirins. It wasn't an unpleasant feeling. Rather detached. She combed her hair, and put on a bit of lipstick, and some scent, and wished that she had a beautiful frilly bedjacket—the kind that Athena and Diana always wore—that dripped with lace and made one look vulnerable and frail and feminine. The old Shetland sweater was scarcely romantic. But this was Jeremy, so did she want to look romantic? The question caught her unawares, and there didn't seem to be any sensible answer, so she got up from the dressing-table, and plumped and stacked the pillows and got back into bed again, and sat there, sipping whisky and savouring the delicious smells of hot butter and rich steaks that were beginning to emanate from downstairs.

"Begin the Beguine" was finished. Now, Carroll Gibbons, at his piano, played the melody of an old Irving Berlin number. "All the Things You Are . . ."

You are the promised touch of Springtime . . .

Presently, she heard footsteps ascending the stairs once more. The next moment Jeremy appeared at the open door. He had taken off his jacket and tied a workmanlike butcher's apron over his dark-blue sweater.

"How do you like your steak done?"

"I can't remember. I haven't had one for such ages."

"Medium rare?"

"Sounds good."

"How's that drink?"

"I've finished it."

"I'll get you another."

"I shall get falling-over drunk."

"You can't fall over if you're lying in bed." He took her empty glass. "I shall bring it up with your dinner, in lieu of champagne."

"Jeremy, I don't want to eat my dinner alone."

"You won't."

He produced the meal in a surprisingly short time, carrying the heavy tray upstairs, and setting it down on the bed beside her. Usually, when people brought one meals in bed, like breakfast, they forgot something. The marmalade, or the butter knife, or a teaspoon. But Jeremy didn't appear to have forgotten anything. The steaks, on red-hot plates, were still sizzling, served with potato crisps and tinned peas that he had found in the store cupboard. He had even made gravy. There were knives and forks and salt and pepper, and a pot of fresh mustard, and napkins, except that they weren't proper linen napkins, but two clean tea-towels, which was all he had been able to find. As well, two replenished drinks.

She said, "Why should it be re-plenished? You never say to someone, 'Will you plenish me a drink.' "

"True."

"What's for pudding?"

"Half an orange, or a jam sandwich."

"My favourite. The best dinner. Thank you, Jeremy."

"Eat the steak before it gets cold."

It was all quite delicious and immediately restoring. Jeremy had been right. Judith had not realized that she was hungry, and feeling so low in health and spirits, sorely in need of solid sustenance. He had cooked her steak to perfection, blackened and seared on the outside and rosy-pink in the middle. It was so tender that she scarcely had to bite it, and it slipped easily down past her painful throat. It was also extremely filling. Perhaps, after months of coping with dull, unappetizing food, her stomach had shrunk.

Finally, "I can't eat any more," she told him. "I'm completely stuffed." She laid down her knife and fork, and he took away her plate, and she lay back on the pillows in total satisfaction. She said, in cockney, "Mikes a luvverly chinge from Spam," and he laughed. "I haven't got space for pudding, so you can have the orange all to yourself. You never cease to surprise me. I didn't know you could cook."

"Any man who's ever sailed a small boat can cook, even if it's only to fry a mackerel. If I can find some coffee, would you like a cup? No, perhaps better not. It'll keep you awake. When did you start this cold?" All at once, he had become professional.

"This morning, in the train. My throat began to be sore. I think I caught a germ from the girl I share a cabin with. And my head aches."

"Have you taken anything?"

"Aspirin. And I gargled."

"How does it feel now?"

"It's better. Not so bad."

"In my suitcase I have a magic pill. I got them in America, brought some back. They look like small bombs, but they usually do the trick. I'll give you one."

"I don't want to be knocked out."

"It won't knock you out . . ."

From beyond the open door, the programme of dance music was coming to an end, and Carroll Gibbons and his orchestra were playing their sign-off tune. A second or two of silence, and then the chimes of Big Ben tolled out, slow and sonorous and, by association, laden with doom. "This is London. The nine o'clock news." He looked at Judith inquiringly, and she nodded assent. However dire or grave, she must listen, and would be able to cope, simply because Jeremy was there, sitting an arm's length away from her; a man both compassionate and understanding. As well, strong and companionable, his presence creating an extraordinary feeling of security. It was trying to be brave and sensible on one's own that was so wearing. Two people could console each other. Two people could share. Could comfort.

Even so, it was all fairly grim, just about as bad as she'd feared. In the Far East, the Japanese were closing in on the Johore Highway. Singapore City had suffered its second day of bombing . . . trenches and fortifications being dug . . . fierce fighting on the Muar River . . . British aircraft continued to bomb and machine-gun Japanese invasion barges . . . Australian territory under attack . . . five thousand Japanese troops on the islands of New Britain and New Ireland . . . small defending garrison forced to withdraw . . .

In North Africa, in the Western Desert, the First Armoured Division driven back in the face of General Rommel's advance . . . a two-pronged attack on Agedabia . . . an entire Indian division faced encirclement . . .

Jeremy said, "Enough," and got up and went through to the sitting-room and switched the wireless off. The cultured, dispassionate voice of the news reader was stilled. Presently, he returned. "Doesn't sound too good, does it?"

"Do you think Singapore's going to fall?"

"It'll be a disaster if it does. If Singapore goes, then all the Dutch East Indies will go as well."

"But surely, if the island is so important, has always been so important, it should be defendable?"

"The big guns all point south, over the sea. I suppose no one ever expected an attack from the north."

"Gus Callender's there. With the Second Gordons."

"I know."

"Poor Loveday. Poor Gus."

"Poor you."

He leaned down and kissed her cheek, then laid a hand on her forehead. "How do you feel?"

She shook her head. "I don't know how I feel."

He smiled. "I'll take the tray away, and tidy up the kitchen. Then I'll bring you your pill. You'll be all right in the morning."

He went, and Judith was left alone, supine in the warm, downy bed, surrounded by Diana Carey-Lewis's own, carefully chosen luxury: filmy draperies, rose-patterned chintz, the soft light of lamps. It was strangely quiet. The only sound, the falling rain beyond the drawn curtains, and then the rattle of a pane in the first gust of the rising wind. She thought of the wind as though it was an entity, blowing in from the west, covering square miles of empty country before it hit the darkened city. And she lay still, staring at the ceiling, thinking about London and about being in the middle of it, at this moment, on this night, a single human being in a metropolis of hundreds of thousands. Bombed, burnt, and battered, and yet still pulsing with a vitality that sprang from the people who inhabited its streets and buildings. The East End and the dockyards had been nigh destroyed by the German bombers, but she knew that still there stood small terraces of houses, and in them families gathered in snug front-rooms, to drink tea and knit, and read newspapers, and talk and laugh and listen to the wireless. Just as others congregated each evening on the platforms of the Underground, there to sleep as the trains roared to and fro, because it was a bit of company, a bit of a party, and certainly more fun than being on one's own.

And there were the people out of doors on this bitter January night. Anti-aircraft gunners, and fire-watchers on roof-tops, and ARP wardens sitting by telephones in draughty, makeshift huts, smoking fags and reading *Picture Post* to pass the long hours of duty. There were servicemen on leave walking the dark pavements in twos and threes, looking for diversion, finally plunging through the curtained doorway of some likely pub. She thought of the prostitutes in Soho standing in doorways, out of the rain, and shining torches down on their fish-net legs and stilt-heeled shoes. And, at the other end of the scale, young officers, up in town from remote airfields and Army bases, dining their girl-friends at the Savoy, and going on to dance the night away at the Mirabelle or the Bagatelle or the Coconut Grove.

And then, quite suddenly, without volition, without meaning to, she started to think about her mother. Not as she was now. Not at this very instant, half a world away, in hazard from every sort of mortal danger, panicking, probably terrified and certainly confused. But as she *had* been. As Judith remembered her last, at Riverview.

Six years. But so much had changed. So much had happened. Joining up had happened, and the Dower House, and before that, the dark winter that Judith had spent with Biddy at Upper Bickley. The war had happened, and the golden years of Nancherrow, which she had always imagined would continue forever, had ended.

Riverview. Part and parcel of the end of childhood, and so, deeply nostalgic. Riverview. Temporary, maybe; rented, and never their own, but for those four years, it had been home. She remembered the slumbering garden on summer evenings, when the blue waters of a flood-tide slipped in from the open sea to drown the mud-flats of the estuary. And how the little train, all through the day, clattered along the shore, shuttling to and from Porthkerris.

She remembered getting off that train after school, and climbing the steep, tree-shaded path up to the house, bursting in through the front door, calling *Mummy!* And she was always there. In her sitting-room, with tea ready on the table, surrounded by her pretty bits and pieces, and everything smelling of sweet peas. And she saw her mother sitting at her dressing-table, changing for dinner, combing her hair and dusting scented powder across her insignificant nose. And heard her voice, reading a book to Jess before bedtime.

Uneventful years, with scarcely ever a man in the house. Only sometimes Uncle Bob, come with Biddy and maybe Ned, to spend a few days during the summer. The Somervilles' visits had been high spots of their tranquil life, along with the Christmas pantomime performed by the Porthkerris Arts Club, and Easter picnics on Veglos Hill at primrose-picking time. Otherwise, day had slipped into day, and season into season, without anything of much excitement ever taking place. But nothing bad had ever happened either.

But there was, of course, the other side of the coin; the other truth. Molly Dunbar, sweet and pliant, had been an ineffectual mother. Nervous about driving her little car, disinclined to sit on damp beaches in the cold north wind, shy of making new friends, and incapable of coming to any sort of a decision. Prospect of change had always alarmed her. (Judith recalled her hysterical behaviour on learning that she was returning, not to Colombo, which was familiar, but to Singapore, which was not.) As well, she had little stamina, tiring easily, and retiring to her bed on the smallest excuse.

Always, she had needed direction and support. In lieu of a husband to tell her what to do, and how she was to do it, she had turned to women stronger than herself. Aunt Louise, Biddy Somerville, and Phyllis. At Riverview, it had been Phyllis who had run the house, organized everything, dealt with tradesmen, whisked Jess out of earshot whenever the child indulged in one of her tantrums.

Her weakness and her gentle nature were not Molly's fault, simply the way she had been born. But that knowledge, now, made nothing better. In fact, worse. War, disaster, upheaval, discomfort, hunger, privation brought out the best in some women—steadfast courage, enterprise, and a sheer determination to survive. But Molly Dunbar was barren of such resources. She would be defeated. Go under. Destroyed.

"No." Judith heard herself speak the word aloud, an anguished refutation of her own fears. As though it were possible to shut out images of despair, she turned and buried her face in the pillow, her body curled in the foetal position of an unborn child, still safe in its mother's womb. Presently, she heard Jeremy coming back from the kitchen, his footsteps on the narrow staircase, and then across the floor of the sitting-room.

His voice. "Did you call me?"

Still muffled in pillows, she shook her head.

"I've brought you the magic pill. And a glass of water to chase it down."

She did not move.

"Judith." He sat on the edge of the bed beside her, and his weight pulled tight the blankets around her shoulders.

504

"Judith!"

Furious with weeping, she flung herself onto her back and stared up at him with tear-sodden eyes. "I don't want pills," she told him. "I don't want anything. I just want to be with my mother."

"Oh, my darling."

"And you're just being a *doctor*. You're just being horribly professional."

"I don't mean to be."

"I hate myself for not being with her."

"You mustn't do that. Too many people love you. You'll be overwhelmed."

And he was so unfazed by her behaviour and so matter-of-fact that her small spurt of anger died, and she was filled with contrition.

"I'm sorry."

"Do you really feel rotten?"

"I don't know how I feel."

He said nothing to this. Just reached for the pill, which did indeed look like a very tiny bomb, and the tumbler of water. "Swallow this, and then we'll talk."

She took it doubtfully. "Are you sure it won't knock me out?"

"Quite sure. Just make you feel a great deal better and, later, sleep. It doesn't look very palatable, but if you wash it down in one enormous gulp, it shouldn't choke you. It takes a bit of time to start working, so get it down now."

She sighed. "All right."

"Good girl."

With an effort, Judith raised herself onto one elbow, put the pill in her mouth, and chased it down with tinny-tasting London tap-water. Jeremy smiled approval. "Well done. You didn't even gag." He took the glass from her, and she sank gratefully back onto the pillows. "Do you want to try to go to sleep?"

"No."

"Do you want to talk?"

"It's so *stupid*, not to be able to stop *thinking*. I would like to be given a pill that would anaesthetize my brain."

"I'm sorry." And he really sounded sorry. "I haven't got one."

"So *stupid*. I'm twenty years old and I want my mother. I want to hold her and touch her and know she's safe."

The tears, which, all evening, had never been far away, now filled her eyes again, and she felt too weak, and too lacking in any sort of pride, to try to control them. "I've been thinking about Riverview and living there with her and Jess . . . and how nothing much ever happened . . . but it was all so quiet and tranquil . . . and we were happy, I suppose. Undemanding. Nothing to make you feel you were being torn apart . . . The last time we were together . . . and already it's six years . . . a great chunk out of life . . . and now . . . I don't know . . ." It was not possible to continue.

Jeremy said, sadly, "I know. Six years is far too long. I'm sorry."

"I don't know . . . I don't know anything. I just want a letter. Something. So that I know where they *are* . . ."

"I understand."

". . . so stupid . . ."

"No. Not stupid. But you mustn't give up all hope. Sometimes no news is good news. Who knows, even now they may be away from Singapore . . . perhaps en route to India or someplace safer. Communications at a time like this are bound to fall apart. Try not to be too despondent."

"You're just saying that. Jollying me along . . ."

"This is no time for jollying. Or cheering up. Just trying to be sensible. Keep a sense of proportion."

"Suppose it was *your* mother and father . . ."

"I'd be distracted, at my wit's end with anxiety. But I think I'd do my best to try not to give up hope."

Judith thought about this for a bit. Then she said, "Your mother isn't like my mother."

"Now, what do you mean by that?"

"I mean, she's different."

"How do you know?"

"Because I met her, at Aunt Lavinia's funeral. We talked for a bit, at the tea-party afterwards. And she's strong and sensible, and practical. I could just see her, calming frantic patients over the telephone, and never getting important messages wrong."

"You're very perceptive."

"My mother isn't like that. You only met her that once, in the train, and we didn't even know each other then. She isn't strong. She has no confidence, she's never been sure of herself. She's nervous of what others think, and useless at taking care of herself. Aunt Louise was forever telling her she was a fool, and she never stood up for herself, nor did anything to prove that she wasn't."

"What are you trying to tell me?"

"That I fear for her."

"She's not alone. She has your father. She has Jess."

"Jess is only a little girl. She won't be able to make decisions for my mother."

"Jess is ten years old. Not a baby any longer. Some small girls of ten can be quite formidable characters. Full of ideas, and beadily determined to get their own way. Whatever happens, and wherever they end up, I am certain that Jess will prove a source of infallible support."

"How can we *know* . . ." The tears returned, streaming down her cheeks, and Judith fumbled for the edge of the sheet and tried to wipe them away, in a manner so pathetically incompetent that Jeremy could scarcely bear it. He got up off the bed and went into the bathroom, and wrung out a face flannel in cold water, and found a towel and went back to her side. "Here." He put his hand under her chin and lifted her face and wiped it gently clean, and then gave her the towel, into which she lustily blew her nose.

"I don't usually cry like this," she told him. "The last time I cried was when Edward was killed, but that was different. That was the end of something. Definite, and horribly finished. I feel this time as though it's all the beginning of something infinitely worse." She took a long sobbing breath. "I wasn't frightened then."

And she sounded so despairing that Jeremy did what he had been longing to do all evening. He lay beside her, took her into his arms, drew her near to him, enfolding her in the comfort of closeness. She lay passive, grateful, but one hand came up to touch the thick wool of his sweater, and her fingers closed upon it and held it tight, and he was reminded of a nursing baby clinging to its mother's shawl.

He said, "You know, when I was a small boy and despairing about something or other, my mother used to comfort me by saying 'This will pass. One day you will look back and it will all be over.' "

"Did that make things any better?"

"Not much. But it helped."

"I can't imagine you as a small boy. I've only known you grown-up. How old are you, Jeremy?"

"Thirty-four."

"If it wasn't for the war, I suppose you'd be married and have a family . . . that's funny to think about, isn't it?"

"Hysterical. But I think not very likely."

"Why not?"

"Too occupied with medicine. Too busy to go chasing girls. Usually chronically short of cash."

"You should specialize. Become a surgeon, a gynaecologist or something. Harley Street, and a brass plate on the door. Mr. Jeremy Wells, FRCS. And there would be a queue, all down the street, of rich and pregnant ladies mad for your attentions."

"What a pretty thought."

"Doesn't it appeal to you?"

"Not really my style."

"What is your style?"

"My father's, I think. A country GP with a dog in the car."

"Really reassuring."

She was beginning to sound more herself again, but her fingers, white-knuckled, were still fastened to the wool of his sweater.

"Jeremy."

"What is it?"

"When you were clinging to that Carley float in the middle of the Atlantic, what did you think about?"

"Staying afloat. Staying alive."

"Didn't you remember things? Lovely things? Lovely places? Good times?"

"I tried to."

"What in particular?"

"I don't know."

"You *must* know."

It was clearly important to her, and so, Jeremy, endeavouring to ignore the physical arousal of his own body, engendered by her closeness and her clear need of him, made an enormous effort of will, and dredged out of his subconscious the first ill-assorted recollections that came to mind.

"Autumn Sundays in Truro, and the bells of the cathedral ringing out for Evensong. And walking on the cliffs of the Nare, with the sea blue as glass, and all the wild flowers filling the ditches." And now there were others, memories crowding in, images and sounds that still, in retrospect, had the power to fill him with delight. "Being at Nancherrow, I suppose. Early-morning swims with Edward, and walking back up the garden knowing that we were going to eat the most tremendous breakfast. Playing fly-half for Cornwall for the first time, at Twickenham, and scoring two tries. Shooting pheasants in the Roseland thickets on frosty December mornings, waiting for the birds, and the dogs wheeking, and the bare trees like lace against a very pale winter sky. Music. 'Jesu, Joy of Man's Desiring,' and knowing that you had come back to Nancherrow."

"Music's good, isn't it? Constant. It lifts you up into the air. Away from the world."

"That's me. It's your turn now."

"I can't think. I'm too tired."

"Just one," he coaxed.

She sighed. "All right. My house. My own house. My home. It's still Aunt Lavinia's, because she's left so much of herself behind, but it's mine now. And the way it feels, and the clock ticking in the hall, and the view of the sea, and the pines. And knowing that Phyllis is there. And that I can go back whenever I want. Go home. And one day never leave it again."

He smiled. "You hang on to that," he told her. She closed her eyes. He looked down at her face and saw the long lashes, dark against the pale cheeks; the shape of her mouth, the pure curve of jaw-bone and chin. He leaned over and kissed her forehead. "You're tired, and I've got an early start. I think we should call it a day." At once, her eyes flew open in alarm, and her grip on his sweater tightened. Jeremy, telling himself to be resolute, began to ease away. "I'll leave you to sleep."

But she became instantly agitated. "You mustn't go. Please. Don't leave me. I want you to be with me."

"Judith . . ."

"No, don't go . . ." And she added, as though he needed any encouragement, "It's a double bed. There's masses of space. I'll be all right if you stay. Please."

Torn between desire and his own inbred good sense, Jeremy hesitated. Eventually, "Is that a good idea?" he asked her.

"Why shouldn't it be?"

"Because if I spend the night with you, I shall, in all probability, make love to you."

She was neither shocked, nor seemed particularly surprised. "That doesn't matter."

"What do you mean, it doesn't *matter*?"

"I mean, if you want to, I would like you to make love to me."

"Do you know what you're saying?"

"I think I would like it very much." Suddenly she smiled. He had scarcely seen her smile all evening, and he felt his heart turn over and, at the same time, his inbred good sense drain away, like bath-water down a plug-hole. "It's all right, Jeremy. It won't be the first time."

He said, "Edward."

"Of course Edward."

"If I make love to you, will you think of Edward?"

"No." Her voice was very firm. "No. I won't think of Edward. I will think of you. Here. In London. Here, when I really needed you. I still need you. I don't want you to leave me. I want you to hold me, and make me feel safe."

"I can't make love to you with all my clothes on."

"Then go and take them off."

"I can't. You've got hold of my sweater."

She smiled again. Her hold on him loosened, but still he did not move. She said, "I've freed you."

"I am terrified to leave you in case you disappear."

"Don't be terrified."

"I shall be two minutes."

"Try to make it one."

"Judith."

A voice from far off, from out of the darkness.

"Judith."

She stirred. Put out a hand to touch him, but the bed was empty. With an effort, she dragged open her eyes. Nothing had changed. The bedroom was lamp-lit, the curtains drawn, just as it had been as she sank into sleep. Jeremy was sitting beside her, on the edge of the bed. He was dressed, wearing uniform; had shaved. She could smell the clean smell of soap.

"I've brought you a cup of tea."

A cup of tea. "What time is it?"

"Six o'clock in the morning. I'm just on my way."

Six o'clock. She stretched and yawned, and pulled herself up into a sitting position, and he handed her the steaming cup of tea, almost too hot to drink.

She blinked the sleep out of her eyes, still scarcely awake.

"What time did you get up?"

"Half past five."

"I didn't hear you."

"I know."

"Have you had any breakfast?"

"Yes. An egg, and one of the rashers of bacon."

"You must take all your goodies with you. No point in leaving them here."

"Don't worry. I'm all packed up. I just wanted to say goodbye. I wanted to say thank you."

"Oh, Jeremy, I'm the one who should be grateful."

"It was lovely. Perfect. A memory."

For no reason, Judith felt a bit shy. She lowered her eyes, sipped her scalding tea.

"How are you feeling this morning?" he asked.

"All right. A bit dopey."

"Sore throat?"

"All gone."

"You'll take care, won't you?"

"Of course."

"When do you have to get back to Portsmouth?"

"This evening."

"You may find a letter waiting for you, from your family."

"Yes." She thought about this possibility and, suddenly, felt quite hopeful. "Yes. Maybe I will."

"Try not to worry too much. And take care of yourself. I only wish I could stay. Last night we talked, but there are still a thousand things we never got around to talking about. And now there isn't time."

"You mustn't miss your train."

"I'll write. As soon as I get a bit of time to myself. I'll write, and try to say all the things that I wish I'd said last night. On paper, I'll probably make a much better job of it."

"You didn't do too badly. But, some time, I'd love a letter."

"I must go. Goodbye, darling Judith."

"If you take this tea away from me, I'll say goodbye properly."

And he laughed, and relieved her of the cup and saucer, and they embraced, and hugged, and kissed like the friends they had always been, but now, like lovers too.

"Don't get blown up again, Jeremy."

"I'll do my best not to."

"And write. Like you promised."

"I will. Sooner or later."

"Before you go, will you do something for me?"

"What's that?"

"Draw back all the curtains, so that I can watch the dawn."

"It won't be light for hours."

"I'll wait."

So he drew away from her and got to his feet. He stooped to switch off the lamp, and then went to the window and she heard him draw back the silken curtains, and deal with the black-out. Beyond the glass of the window-pane, the winter morning was lightless, but the rain had stopped and the wind dropped.

"That's perfect."

"I must go."

"Goodbye, Jeremy."

"Goodbye."

It was too dark to see, but she heard him move, open the door, and gently close it behind him. He was gone. She lay back on the pillows, and was almost instantly asleep.

It was ten o'clock before she woke again, so, after all, she never witnessed the dawn lighten the sky. Instead, the day was upon her; cloudy but with rags of pale-blue sky. She thought of Jeremy, in some train, thundering north, to Liverpool or Invergordon or Rosyth. She thought of last night, and lay smiling to herself, remembering his love-making, which had been both infinitely tender and at the same time competent, so that her own pleasure had matched his ardour, and together they had mounted to a climax of physical passion. An interlude of magic unexpectedness, and even joy.

Jeremy Wells. Everything was changed now. Before, they had never corresponded. But he had promised that, sooner or later, he would write. Which meant something special to look forward to.

Meantime, she was alone again. Lying in bed, considering her state, she realized that she was recovered. The cold, 'flu, infection, whatever it had been, was gone, taking with it all symptoms of headache, lassitude, and depression. Though how much of this was due to Jeremy Wells, rather than his professional medications and a good night's sleep, it was impossible to say. Whatever, it made no difference. She was herself again, and filled with her usual energy.

But how to spend it? She didn't have to report back to Quarters until evening, but the prospect of an empty, solitary day in London on a wartime Sunday, with neither church bells nor company to enliven her leisure, was not particularly enticing. As well, at the back of her mind, there lurked the possibility of a letter from Singapore. The more she thought about this, the more certain she became that one would be there, in the Regulating Office, in the mailbox labelled with the letter "D." In her mind's eye, she saw it waiting for her, and all at once it became important to return to Portsmouth without delay. She flung back the covers and sprang out of bed, then into the bathroom, to turn the taps full on, and draw another scalding bath.

Bathed, dressed, and packed, she accomplished a little instant housework. Stripped the bed, folded sheets, went downstairs, emptied the fridge and switched it off. Jeremy, seamanlike, had left the kitchen shining and shipshape. Judith scribbled a note for Mrs. Hickson, weighted it down with a couple of half-crowns, picked up her bag, and left, slamming the front door shut behind her. She took the tube to Waterloo, caught the first train to Portsmouth, and there picked up a taxi alongside the ruins of the bombed Guildhall. By two o'clock, she was back at the Wrens' Quarters. She paid off the taxi and went through the main door, and so into the Regulating Office, where the Leading Wren on duty, a sour-faced girl with a disastrous complexion, was sitting behind the desk chewing her nails with boredom.

She said, "You're a bit early, aren't you?"

"Yes, I know."

"Thought you had a short weekend."

"Yes, I did."

"Well, I don't know." The Leading Wren gave her a fishy stare, as though Judith was up to no good. "It's all right for some, I suppose."

Which didn't seem to call for any sort of response, so Judith made none. Just signed herself in, and then went to the wooden grid of the mailboxes. Under "D" there was a thin pile of letters. She took them out and leafed them through. Wren Durbridge. Petty Officer Joan Daly. Then, at the bottom, the thin blue airmail envelope and her mother's writing. The envelope was dog-eared and grubby, as though it had suffered untold vicissitudes and had already been around the world twice. Judith put the other letters back and stood and looked at it. Her instinct was to rip it open and read it there and then, but the unfriendly eye of the Regulating Wren was still upon her, and she didn't want any person watching, so she picked up her bag and went up the cement staircase to the top flat and the tiny, frigid cabin that she shared with Sue. Because it was Sunday, there was nobody around. Sue, probably, was on watch. She pulled off her hat and sat on the bottom bunk, still bundled in her greatcoat, and slit the envelope and took out the tissue sheets of airmail paper, folded into a wad and covered with her mother's handwriting. She unfolded them and began to read.

> Orchard Road
> Singapore
> 16th January.
>
> *Dearest Judith,*
>
> I haven't much time, so this will be rather short. Tomorrow Jess and I sail on *The Rajah of Sarawak* for Australia. Kuala Lumpur fell to the Japanese four days ago, and they are advancing like a tide towards Singapore Island. As long ago as New Year, word went around that the Governor was recommending the evacuation of all *bouches inutiles.* This means women and children, and I suppose saying it in French doesn't sound so insulting as "useless mouths." But since Kuala Lumpur your father, along with just about everybody else, has spent most of his days at the shipping offices, trying to get a passage for Jess and myself. As well, all the refugees are pouring in, and everything is in turmoil. However, at this moment (11 A.M.) he has appeared to say that he has got two berths for us (bribery?) and we sail tomorrow morning. We are only allowed one small suitcase each, as the boat is grossly overcrowded. No space for baggage. Dad has to stay here. He cannot come with us, as he is responsible for the Company office and the staff. I am terrified for his safety and dread the separation. If it wasn't for Jess, I would stay and take my chance, but as always, my loyalties are torn in two. Abandoning the servants and the house and garden is almost as bad, like being pulled up by the roots. What can I do?

Jess is very upset at the thought of leaving Orchard Road and Ah Lin and Amah and the gardener. All of them, her friends. But I have said we are going on a boat, and it will be an adventure, and she and Amah are packing her suitcase now. I am filled with apprehension, but keep telling myself that we are lucky to be going away. When we get to Australia, I shall send you a cable to let you know that we have arrived, and where we are so that you can write to me. Please tell Biddy, as I haven't time to write to her.

The letter had been started in Molly Dunbar's normal, neat, schoolgirlish script. But as the pages progressed, it had deteriorated, and by now was no more than a frantic, ink-blotted scribble.

It is very strange, but all my life, from time to time, I have found myself asking unanswerable questions. Who am I? And what am I doing here? And where am I going? Now, it all seems to be coming terribly true, and it feels a bit like a haunting dream that I have lived through many times before. I wish I could say goodbye to you properly, but just now a letter is the only way. If anything should happen to Dad and me, you will look after Jess, won't you? I love you so much. I think about you all the time. I will write to you from Australia.

Darling Judith.

Mummy

It was the last letter from her mother. Three weeks later, on Sunday, February 15, Singapore was surrendered to the Japanese.

After that, nothing.

HMS *Sutherland*
c/o GPO
London.

21st February, 1942.

Darling Judith,

I said I would write sooner or later, and it seems to be later, because it's just about a month since I said goodbye to you. I could have written a quick note, but that wouldn't have been very satisfactory, and I knew that, if there was a delay, you would understand.

My address is deliberately deceiving. My ship is not crouched in a GPO pigeon-hole, but having a refit in the Brooklyn Navy Yard. (Every British sailor's dream.) For the Royal Navy, New York is Open House . . . I have never experienced such hospitality, and the parties started the moment we were safely in dry dock, and work had commenced. The First Lieutenant (Jock Curtin, an Australian) and myself were wheeled off to a cocktail party in a swanky apartment on the East Side of Central Park, treated like the heroes that we aren't, and made much of. At this particular do (and there have been too many for any person's liver), we met this delightful couple called Eliza and Dave Barmann, who instantly invited us to "weekend" with them in their house on Long Island. They duly scooped us up at the dockside in their Cadillac, and drove us here to their weekend "home." This is a large old clapboard house in a village called Leesport, on the South Shore of Long Island. It took about two hours to get here, not a beautiful drive, all billboards and diners and used-car lots, but the village is off the beaten track and very charming. Green grass, picket fences, shade trees, wide streets, a drugstore, a fire station, and a wooden church with a tall steeple. Just the way I had always imagined America, like those old films we used to see, when the girl wore a gingham dress and ended up marrying the boy next door.

The house is on the water's edge, with green lawns going down to the shore. It's not the ocean, because the Great South Bay is a sort of lagoon, enclosed by the dunes of Fire Island. On the far side of Fire Island is the Atlantic. There is a little marina, with the Stars and Stripes snapping in the breeze, and a lot of enviable yachts and sailing boats at anchor.

So, I've set the scene. Outside, it's cold, but crisp and dry. A beautiful morning. Indoors, where I now sit at a desk looking out over the summer deck and the swimming-pool, it is wonderfully warm, with central heating oozing from decorative grids. Because of this, the house is furnished for summer, the floors uncarpeted and polished, white cotton curtains, and everything very light and fresh. It all smells of cedar, with overtones of beeswax and sun-tan oil. Upstairs, Jock and I each have a bedroom to ourselves, with a bathroom en suite. So, you will gather, we are living in the lap of luxury.

As I said, the kindness and hospitality we have been offered is unbelievable, and even embarrassing, as there is little we can do to return it. It seems to be an integral part of the American character, and my theory is that it stems from the old days of the first pioneers. A settler, spying the distant cloud of dust, and knowing that a passing stranger was on his way, would call to his wife to put another couple of potatoes in the stew. At the same time, he would reach for his gun, which is the flip side of the American coin.

Now, I shan't talk any more about myself, but about you. I think about you every day, and wonder if you have had any news of your family. The fall of Singapore was a disaster, probably the worst defeat ever suffered in the history of the British Empire, and the defence of the city seems to have been thoroughly mishandled and ill thought out. Which is no comfort to you if you have still have had no news. But, remember that the war will end, and though it may take a bit of time, I am sure the day will come when you will all be reunited. The worst is that the Red Cross are not able to communicate . . . prisoners in Germany at least have the benefit of the organization in Switzerland. Whatever, I never cease to hope for you all. And Gus Callender, too. Poor chap. I think of my present circumstances and what he must be enduring, and feel dreadfully guilty. But personal guilt has always been a pretty useless exercise.

Here, Jeremy laid down his pen, his eye deflected by the sight of a small ferry boat chugging out across the still, silvery waters of the Sound, headed for Fire Island. He had already covered pages of writing-paper, and still had not come to the point of his letter to Judith. It occurred to him that, subconsciously, he was putting it off, because it was so personal, and so important, that he feared that he would not be able to find the words with which to frame the sentences. He had started the letter with such confidence, but now, come to the crunch, he was not so sure of himself. He watched the progress of the ferry boat until it disappeared from view, lost behind a thicket of bushes. Then he picked up his pen again, and went on writing.

> Meeting you in London, finding you at Diana's house, was one of the best and most unexpected of bonuses. And I am so grateful that I was there when you were feeling unwell and so miserably worried. Being with you that night, and letting me share, and I hope comfort, in the most basic of ways, has become, in retrospect, a bit like a small miracle, and I shall never forget your sweetness.
>
> The truth is that I love you very much. I suppose always have done. But I didn't realize it until that day you came back to Nancherrow, and I heard "Jesu, Joy" coming from your bedroom, and knew that you were home again. I think you were writing a letter to your mother. I know that in that moment, I finally understood how important you were to me.
>
> Like that personal guilt, falling in love in wartime, making commitments, is a pretty useless exercise, and I am fairly sure that you feel the same way. You loved Edward, and he was killed, and this is not an experience any person would want to go through for a second time. But one day the war will end, and with a bit of luck we'll all come through it, and we'll all go back to Cornwall and pick up the threads of our lives again. When that happens, I would like, more than anything else in the world, for us to be together again, because at the moment I cannot contemplate a future without you.

Here, he stopped once more, laid down his pen, took up the pages and read them through. He wondered if the last paragraph seemed dreadfully stilted. He knew he was not a man able to lay out his deepest feelings on paper. Some, like Robert Burns or Robert Browning, were able to convey passion in just a few well-turned lines, but writing poetry was a gift with which Jeremy Wells had not been blessed. What he had set down would have to suffice, and yet he found himself assailed by self-doubt, and the cold feet of second thoughts.

At the end of the day, he wanted, more than anything, to marry Judith, but was it fair on her even to suggest such a thing? So much older than she, he wasn't, it had to be admitted, much of a catch, with a future no more exciting than the life of a country GP, and one, to boot, short on worldly goods. While Judith, thanks to her late aunt, was a girl of both wealth and property. Would she imagine, would people say, that he was after her for her money? The life that he offered her was that of a rural doctor's wife, and he knew from experience that this was necessarily ruled by endless telephone calls, broken nights, cancelled holidays, and meals that were no more than movable feasts. Perhaps she deserved more than that. A man who would give her what she had never known—a strong and secure family life—as well as an income that matched her own. She had grown so lovely, so desirable . . . just to think of her made his heart turn over . . . that it was only too obvious that men were going to fall in love with her, like apples falling from a tree. Was it being desperately selfish, at this particular moment in time, to ask her to marry him?

He simply didn't know, but he had got so far that he might as well finish. Torn by uncertainty, he reached for his pen once more and ploughed on.

> I am saying all this without having any idea how you feel about me. We have always been friends, or so I like to think, and I would like it to stay that way, so I don't want to write or say anything that might spoil our good relationship for ever. So, for the meantime, this declaration of my love for you will have to do. But, please write to me as soon as you can, and let me know your feelings, and whether in the fullness of time, you might consider our spending the rest of our lives together.
>
> I love you so deeply. I hope this hasn't upset or distressed you. Just re-member, I am prepared to wait until you're ready for commitment. But *please* write as soon as you possibly can, and set my mind at rest.
>
> Always, my darling Judith,
>
> *Jeremy*

Finished. He threw down his pen for the last time, ran his fingers through his hair, and then sat gazing despondently at the pages which had taken him all morning to compose. Perhaps he shouldn't have wasted his time. Perhaps he should tear them up, forget it all, write another letter, this time asking nothing of her. On the other hand, if he did this . . .

"Jeremy."

His hostess, come in search of him, and he was grateful for the interruption.

"Jeremy."

"I'm here." Swiftly he gathered up the pages of his letter, blocked them off, and slipped them under the top cover of the writing-pad. "In the living-room."

He turned in his chair. She appeared through the open door, tall and tanned and with her silver-gold hair bouffant and shining, as though it had just emerged from the hands of an expert hairdresser. She wore a light wool suit and a striped shirt, crisply collared, the cuffs fastened with heavy gold links, and high-heeled pumps emphasized the elegance of her long American legs. Eliza Barmann, and a pleasure to behold.

She said, "We're taking you to the club for lunch. Leaving in about fifteen minutes. Will you be ready?"

"Of course." He gathered up his belongings and got to his feet. "I'm sorry. I didn't realize it was so late."

"Did you get your letter finished?"

"Just about."

"Do you want to mail it?"

"No . . . no, I might want to add something. Later. I'll mail it when I get back to the ship."

"Well, if you're sure . . ."

"I'll just go and tidy myself up . . ."

"Nothing formal. Just a necktie. Dave wondered if, after lunch, you'd like a round of golf?"

"I've no clubs."

She smiled. "That's no problem. We can borrow from the pro. And don't hurry yourself. There's no rush. Except it would be nice to have a martini before we go in to eat."

At the end of April, at the end of a long day, Judith finished typing the last letter for Lieutenant-Commander Crombie (with copies for the Captain, HMS *Excellent*, and the Director of Naval Ordnance) and ripped the pages out of her typewriter.

It was nearly six. The other two Wrens who shared the office had already packed up and set off on their bicycles, back to Quarters. But Lieutenant-Commander Crombie, late in the afternoon, had come up with this lengthy missive, not only Top Secret but Urgent as well, and Judith, with slight resentment, had been left to deal with it.

She was tired. Out of doors, the weather had been lovely, a sweet spring day, with warmth on the breeze, and all the daffodils in the Captain's garden nodding their heads in a most unsettling way. At midday, heading for O Block, mutton stew, and plum duff, she had seen the green slopes of Portsdown Hill leaning up to the sky, and she had stood for a moment and stared with longing at the rolling crest of the hill, smelt the scent of new-cut grass, and felt her whole body respond to this young season of rising sap and renewal. She had thought, *I am twenty, and will never be twenty again.* She yearned for escape and freedom, to be out and about, climbing the hill, breathing the clear air, lying back on spongy turf, and listening to the wind in the grass, and bird-song. Instead, half an hour for the mutton stew, and then back to the stuffy hut that was the temporary headquarters of the Training Development Office.

Now, she sorted out the pages of the document, separating top copy from the three carbons. She set the last aside for its relevant file, and then squared off the others, slipped them into a card folder, and took them to be signed.

This entailed going out of the typists' office, through the main office, where Lieutenant Armstrong and Captain Burton of the Royal Marines were still at their desks. As she crossed the floor, they neither turned nor raised their heads. Familiarity had bred, if not contempt, then a professional lack of interest. At the far end stood a door, with a name plate. *T.D.O.*

The passion for initials was one of the most confusing hazards of war. Lieutenant-Commander Crombie spent much of his working hours trying to drum up the interest of his superiors in the development of a device known as the AVT 1, which stood for Artificial Visual Trainer, Mark 1. Judith, having been typing letters about this wretched contrivance for the past six months, had privately dubbed it the NBG 1, N.B.G. being service parlance for No Bloody Good. Just after New Year, Lieutenant-Commander Crombie had celebrated a birthday, and deciding that he could do with a little humour in his life, she had drawn and coloured a card for him, and written a poem.

> *The NBG 1 is your latest device*
> *At special request and at terrible price*
> *With modifications*
> *And slight alterations*
> *The Galley can use it for cooking the rice.*

The joke fell flat. Lieutenant-Commander Crombie was in no mood for laughs, being worried about advancing years, his possibilities of promotion, and his son's school fees. Because of this, the birthday card was something of a failure, and two days later, Judith had found it in his waste-paper basket.

"Come in."

He was sitting behind his desk, gaitered and unsmiling. At times he wore the expression of a man suffering from a painful stomach ulcer.

"Here's your letter, sir. I've typed the envelopes. If you want to read it through and then give me a buzz, I'll get them off this evening."

He looked at his watch. "Good God, is it as late as that? Isn't it time you were off?"

"Well, if I don't get back to Quarters by seven, I won't get anything to eat."

"We can't have that. If you fetch me the envelopes, I'll see to their dispatch. Then you won't have to starve."

He was a man whose bark was worse than his bite. Early on, Judith had discovered this, and since then had never been in the least in awe of him. Since the fall of Singapore and the eclipse of news of her family, he had become enormously concerned as to her well-being, in an offhand, avuncular sort of fashion; always asking for news, then, as the weeks passed and none came, tactfully not asking.

He had a house in Fareham, where he lived with his wife and son, and shortly after the tidings of the capitulation of Singapore broke upon a horrified world, he invited Judith for Sunday lunch with his family. Not wanting in the very least to go, but much touched, Judith instantly accepted, beaming with grateful smiles, as though the prospect filled her with nothing but pleasure.

On Sundays there were no buses to Fareham, and so she had to bicycle for five miles in order to get herself to his undistinguished house. The visit had been even less successful than the birthday card, because Mrs. Crombie was clearly deeply suspicious of sexual entanglements, and Lieutenant-Commander Crombie not a man adroit with the light touch of casual conversation. To allay doubts, Judith called him "Sir" every other word, and spent most of the afternoon on the sitting-room floor, helping the small Crombie son construct a windmill with his Meccano set. It was quite a relief when the time came to mount her bicycle and pedal the long miles back to Quarters.

But it had been kindly meant.

Leaving him to read through his letter, she returned to her office, put the cover on her typewriter, gathered up the envelopes and her coat and hat. Lieutenant Armstrong and Captain Burton had also decided to clear their desks and call it a day. Lieutenant Armstrong had lit a cigarette, and as she passed them by, "We're going for a drink at the Crown and Anchor," he told her. "Do you want to come?"

She smiled. They had evidently decided that the time had come to switch off, relax, and start enjoying themselves.

"Thank you, but I don't think I've time."

"Pity. Take a rain-check." This was a new phrase that Lieutenant Armstrong had picked up from the lately arrived American forces.

"Thanks," said Judith, who had not yet discovered what it meant. "I will."

Back with her boss, she folded the letters with immaculate precision, put them into their envelopes, stuck them down, and dropped them into his "Out" tray.

"If that's everything, I'll be going."

"Thank you, Judith." He looked up and gave her one of his rare smiles. She wished he would smile more often. Calling her by her Christian name was a one-off as well. She wondered how many of his hang-ups were caused by his cold and clearly jealous wife, and felt sad for him.

"No trouble." She put on her coat and fastened the buttons, and he leaned back in his chair and watched her. "How long," he asked abruptly, "since you had leave?"

She could hardly remember. "Christmas?"

"You're overdue."

"Do you want to get rid of me?"

"The very opposite. But you're looking a bit washed out."

"It's been a long winter."

"Think about it. You could go home, to Cornwall. Back to that house of yours. A spring-time break."

"I'll see."

"If you want, I'll have word with your First Officer."

In some alarm, Judith shook her head. "No. You don't need to do that. I'm due a long weekend, I know. I'll maybe put in for one."

"I think you should." He sat up, and once more became as brusque as ever. "Off with you then."

She smiled at him, with much affection. "Good night, sir."

"Good night, Dunbar."

In the golden spring evening, she cycled back to Quarters; across the footbridge, up Stanley Road, and so out onto the main road that ran north out of the city. Pedalling along, she thought about going on leave, going back to Cornwall . . . just for a few days. Being with Phyllis and Biddy and Anna, and pottering around the house, and kneeling, with the sun on her shoulders, to pull weeds out of the rose borders. It was time the garden hut was creosoted for the new season, and perhaps as well time to start looking for a new gardener. Just a few days, that was all she needed, and a long weekend would do the trick.

It was ridiculous, but almost the worst void that had been left by her loss of contact with her family had been the knowledge that there would be no more letters. For so long—nearly six and a half years—she had lived with the small and pleasurable anticipation of a regular envelope filled with trivial, precious news from Singapore, that she had become conditioned, and each time she returned to Quarters, had to remind herself that there would be nothing to look for in the pigeon-hole labelled "D."

Not even the promised letter from Jeremy Wells. Over two months had passed since they had said goodbye in London, and he had left her sleeping in Diana's bed. *I'll write*, he had promised. *So much to say. Sooner or later.* And she had believed him, and then nothing had come. Nothing had happened. Which was dreadfully dispiriting, and as the weeks slipped by and still no letter came, she became consumed with doubts, not only for him, but also for herself. Inevitably, there dawned the uncomfortable suspicion that Jeremy had made love to her for very much the same reason that Edward had. After all, it had been she, unwell and deeply upset, who had begged him to stay with her, sleep with her, not leave her. *Darling Judith*, he had called her, but how much of his loving had sprung from compassion? *I will write*, he had promised, but he had not written, and by now she had stopped looking for his letter.

From time to time, she had thought of writing to him. Saying, in a jokey sort of way, *You brute; here I am languishing for news, and you said you'd send me a letter. I shall never trust you again.* Or something. But she was nervous of being too precipitant, of saying too much. Frightening him off with her enthusiasm, just as she had frightened Edward away with her untimely declaration of eternal devotion.

There was, after all, a war on, raging, now, all over the world. No time for commitment. (Edward's words.) No time for keeping promises.

But, on the other hand, this wasn't Edward. This was Jeremy Wells, the epitome of trustworthiness and honesty. All that she could imagine was that he had had second thoughts. Distanced from Judith, good sense had prevailed. Their love in London had simply been an interlude, charming but too lightweight and ephemeral to pursue, at the possible expense of an easygoing friendship.

Deliberately clear-headed, she told herself that she understood. But this wasn't true. Because she didn't understand. The truth was that she felt not only disappointed in him, but dreadfully hurt.

These not-very-cheerful reflections lasted her all the way back to Quarters. She cycled around to the back of the ugly building, slung her bicycle in its rack, and went in through the Regulating Office. The Quarters Officer was on duty, a well-upholstered lady in her mid-thirties, who had, in peacetime, been the matron of a small boys' preparatory school.

"Hello there, Dunbar. Working late?"

"Last-minute letters, ma'am."

"Poor girl. It's not fair. There was a telephone call for you. I put a note in your pigeon-hole."

"Oh, thank you . . ."

"Better get a move on, or you'll miss grub."

"I know."

She signed in, and then went to the rack of mailboxes, and found a letter for herself (from Biddy), and the scrap of signal pad on which the Quarters Officer had written, "Wren Dunbar. 1630 hours. Call from Loveday Carey-Lewis. Please ring back."

Loveday. What was Loveday wanting?

But there wasn't time to ring before supper, so Judith went straight into the mess, and ate a slice of corned beef, a fried potato, and a helping of overcooked cabbage. Pudding was a square of sponge cake with a dollop of plum jam on top. It looked so unpalatable that she didn't take it, but went upstairs to her cabin where she kept a cache of apples, to be consumed whenever hungry. Chewing the apple, she went downstairs again, in search of a free telephone. There were three, in strategic spots, dotted about the flats, and in the evenings usually a queue of girls, sitting on the stairs, listening to every word the telephoner was saying, and awaiting their turn. But this evening, Judith was lucky. Perhaps because of the warm weather, most of the Wrens had gone out, and there was a phone free.

She dialled the number for Nancherrow, dropped the coins in, and waited.

"Nancherrow."

She pressed the button and the coins clanked down into the box.

"Who's that?"

"Athena."

"Athena, it's Judith. I got a message to ring Loveday."

"Hang on, I'll get her." Which Athena did by yelling out Loveday's name, and nearly deafening Judith. "She's just coming."

"How's Clementina?"

"Heaven. Are you calling from a pay phone?"

"Yes."

"Won't talk then, darling, or you'll run out of shillings. See you sometime. Here's Loveday."

"*Judith*. Sweet of you to ring back. Sorry about that. I tried to get you, but they said you were working. Look, I'll be terribly quick. Mummy and I are coming to London this weekend, staying at the Mews. Please come up and be with us. Can you? Do try."

"London? What are you coming to London for? You hate London."

"I'll explain. We're coming together. And I really want to see you." She sounded a bit frantic. "I've got so much to tell you. Can you come? Can you get time off?"

"Well, I could try for a short weekend . . ."

"Oh, do. Do. Say it's dreadfully important. Life and Death. Mummy and I are going up tomorrow in the train. No petrol for the poor old Bentley. Tomorrow's Thursday. How soon can you be with us?"

"I don't know. I'll have to see. Saturday, at the earliest."

"Perfect. I'll be there, even if Mummy isn't. I'll expect you unless I hear from you . . ."

"I may not be able to—"

"Oh, of course you can. Make any old excuse. Compassionate grounds. Anything. It's terribly important."

"I'll try . . ."

"Goodie. Longing to see you." *Pip-pip-pip* went the telephone. " 'Byeee." Click. The call was finished.

Judith, in some puzzlement, replaced the receiver. What on earth was Loveday up to now? And why was she coming to London, which she had always sworn she loathed? There was, however, no answer to these questions. The only thing that was perfectly clear was that, tomorrow morning, first thing, she must present herself at the First Officer's lair, and somehow persuade that frightening female into signing a weekend pass for the very next day. If refused, Judith would blatantly cut corners and appeal for the cooperation of Lieutenant-Commander Crombie. The image of him, entering battle on her side, was very reassuring.

The First Officer WRNS was just as uncooperative as Judith had feared, and it took a certain amount of distasteful pleading before she finally, reluctantly, and with little grace, signed the weekend pass. Abasement had worked. Judith thanked her profusely, and then escaped as quickly as she could before the embittered old hag of a spinster could change her mind.

In the outer office, the Wren on duty looked up from her typewriter and raised her eyes in silent question. Judith made a face, and gave her a thumbs-up.

"Good for you," the other girl muttered, "she's in a foul mood this morning. I thought you were doomed from the start." And Judith, leaving her to her typing, walked back to the Training Development Office in high heart, and, unasked, made a cup of coffee for dear Lieutenant-Commander Crombie, just because she was so grateful to be working for him, and not some prune-faced woman with a power complex.

Saturday was a beautiful April morning, without a cloud in the sky. Emerging from the cavernous gloom of Waterloo Station, she decided to indulge in the extravagance of a taxi, and rode in state to Cadogan Mews. In the warm spring sunshine, London looked surprisingly lovely. Trees were in fresh green leaf; bomb sites countrified by new growths of willow-herb; a mallard duck swam on the still surface of an emergency water tank. In the park, purple crocus spread carpets on the grass, and daffodils nodded yellow heads in the sweet breeze. High above, barrage balloons gleamed silver in the sunlight, flags snapped over important buildings, and the faces of passers-by, jostling the busy pavements, were rendered hopeful and smiling by the clement weather.

The taxi stopped in the road, by the stone arch which led into the Mews.

"This do you, luv?"

"Perfect."

Carrying her overnight bag, she walked the cobbled length of the Mews, where the small houses faced each other, with tubs and window-boxes burgeoning flowers. A cat sat in the sunshine and washed himself, and someone had fixed up a rope and pegged out a line of washing, which made it all feel a bit like Porthkerris. She looked up. The windows of Diana's house had been flung wide open, a curtain blew, and the wooden tub at the yellow front door brimmed with velvety polyanthus.

"Loveday!" she called.

"Hello!" Loveday's head appeared at the open window. "You're here. You are marvellous. I'll come down and let you in."

"Don't bother. I've got my key."

She opened the door, and Loveday was standing at the head of the stairs. "I was terrified you wouldn't make it. Did you have to tell frightful lies to get permission?"

"No. Just bow and scrape a bit." She climbed the staircase. "And listen to a lot of codswallop about giving First Officer so little notice, making extra work for her staff, being so inconsiderate, travel vouchers et cetera, blah, blah, blah. All too boring." She dumped her bag, pulled off her hat, and they hugged. "Where's Diana?"

"Shopping, needless to say. We're meeting her at a quarter to one, at the Ritz. Tommy Mortimer's giving us all lunch."

"Heavens, how smart. I've nothing to wear."

"You look stunning just as you are, in uniform."

"I don't know that I do. Never mind, with a bit of luck they won't drum me out of the restaurant for not being an officer." She looked about her. Last time she had come, it had been midwinter and dark and cold. Now, everything was quite different, the pretty room bright with sunshine, cool with fresh air, and filled with flowers. Nancherrow flowers, brought from Cornwall, and Diana's trademark.

She flopped down on one of the huge, ample sofas and sighed with pleasure. "Heaven. It's like being home again."

Facing her, Loveday curled up in one of the big armchairs. "I have to admit, even though I'm not mad on London, it is rather a dear little house."

"Where are we all going to sleep?"

"You and I are sharing the double bed, and Mummy's going in with the ironing board."

"That's not very fair."

"She doesn't mind. She says she prefers privacy to luxury. Anyway, that bed's quite comfortable."

"When did you get here?"

"Thursday. Came up on the train. It wasn't too bad. And at Paddington, Tommy met us with a car, which is always rather comforting." Loveday giggled. "Did you know, he got a medal for being frightfully brave in the blitz? Too modest, he's only just told us."

"A *medal*? What did he get a medal for?"

"He rescued some old girl from her burning house. Plunged in through smoke and fire and hauled her out, by the legs, from under her dining-room table."

Judith gaped in admiration and astonishment. It was not easy to visualize the urbane Tommy Mortimer, silk-shirted and smoothly suited, indulging in such heroics. "Good for him! I hope she was grateful."

"Not a bit. She was livid because he hadn't rescued her canary as well. Ungrateful old bag."

She was laughing. She looked, thought Judith, prettier than ever, and charmingly sophisticated in a fine woollen dress of hyacinth blue, with short sleeves and a white piqué collar. Silk stockings on her slender legs, black patent leather high-heeled pumps, bright lipstick, dark lashes, her violet eyes sparkling. But something was different . . .

"Loveday, you've had your hair cut."

"I know. Mummy said I looked like a gollywog. She wheeled me off to Antoine's yesterday. It took hours."

"I love it."

Loveday tossed her head. "It's a bit short, but it'll grow. I never have time to have it done at home. Incidentally, everybody sends their love. Pops and Athena and Mary and everybody. Including the Nettlebeds. Clementina's a hoot. She's got a ghastly doll's pram and pushes it everywhere."

"What news of Rupert?"

"Battling it out in the Western Desert. But he writes long letters to Athena and he seems to be quite cheerful." She stopped then, and fell silent. Across the room they faced each other, and some of the laughter died from Loveday's face. After a bit, "At least she hears from him. Gets letters." She sighed. "Nothing, I suppose, from your family?"

Judith shook her head. "Not a word."

"I'm so sorry."

"It's like a shutter's come down. But the boat Mummy and Jess were on never got to Australia. That's all we know."

"If they were rescued, I suppose they'll have been taken prisoner."

"I suppose."

"And your father?"

She shook her head again. "Nothing." And then, because it had to be said, "And Gus? I imagine, nothing from Gus, otherwise you'd have let me know."

For a moment, Loveday sat, eyes downcast, her fingers picking at the braid of the armchair. And then, abruptly, she sprang to her feet, and went to stand at the window, looking down into the Mews, her back to Judith, and the sunlight making an aureole of her curly dark hair. Judith waited. After a bit, she said, "Gus is dead."

Judith felt cold with shock, and for a moment unable to think of anything to say. "Then you *have* heard. You've had news."

"No. But I know."

"*How* can you know he's dead?"

Watching, appalled, she saw Loveday shrug her bony shoulders. "I just know." And then she turned to face Judith, leaning her weight against the white-painted sill of the window. "I would know if he was alive. Like I did after Saint Valéry. Then, it was like a telephone message, but without any words. I told you about it, and I was right. He was safe then. But he's dead now. After Singapore fell, every day, I sat on the gate by the Lidgey farmyard, and shut my eyes and thought and thought about him, and tried to get a message to Gus, and to get him to send one back to me. But there's nothing there but darkness and silence. He's gone."

Judith was horrified. "But Loveday, that's the same as killing him *yourself*. You mustn't give up hope. He needs you to keep hoping and thinking about him, all the time."

"Is that what *you* do?"

"Don't speak in that horrible, condescending way. Of course it's what I do. I have to."

"Do you believe your mother and father and Jess are still alive?"

"I said, I have to. For their sakes. Don't you see how important it is?"

"It's not important if I already know Gus is dead."

"Stop saying it, over and over. You've no right to be so certain. Just because it happened once, that telepathy thing, it doesn't mean it's bound to happen again. That time, Gus was in France, quite close. This time he's on the other side of the world."

"Distance makes no difference." Loveday was immovable, stubborn as she had always been once she had set her mind on something, and was determined never to be sidetracked. "Thought transference covers thousands of miles in a millionth of a second. I would know if he was alive. And I *know* that he's been killed."

"Oh, Loveday. Please don't be so final."

"I can't help it. I am."

There didn't seem to be anything else to say. Judith sighed. "Is this what you had to tell me?" she asked at last. "Is this why you wanted me to come to London?"

"That. And other things." Judith waited in some apprehension. Then Loveday dropped her bombshell. "I'm going to get married."

She said it casually, as though imparting some inconsequent piece of information, and for a moment Judith thought that she had totally misheard.

"*What?*"

"I'm going to get married."

"Married." Now, totally nonplussed. "Who?"

"Walter."

"*Walter*. Walter Mudge?"

"Do you know any other Walter?"

The whole idea was so inconceivable that Judith felt quite winded, as though some person had delivered a blow in her solar plexus, and left her without breath to speak. Finally, "But . . . but what has got into you, that you want to marry Walter?"

Loveday shrugged. "I like him. I always have."

"I like him too, but that's no reason to spend the rest of your life with him."

"Don't tell me that he's lower-class, or that it's not fitting, or I shall scream at you . . ."

"I wouldn't dream of saying those sort of things and you know I never would . . ."

"Anyway, I'm going to marry him. I want to."

Before she could stop herself, Judith said, "But you love Gus . . ." and Loveday rounded on her.

"Gus is dead," she shouted. "I've told you. So I'll never marry Gus. And don't tell me to wait for him, because what is the use of waiting for a man who's never coming back to me?"

Judith, prudently, made no answer to this. She thought, I have to be very practical and very cool, otherwise we're going to have the most resounding row, and say terrible things that can never be unsaid, and that's not going to be any help at all.

So she changed her tack. "Look. You're only nineteen. Even if you're right and Gus is dead, there are thousands of other men in the world, just right for you, just waiting to come into your life. I understand about you and Walter. You've always been friends. You work together, and you see him all the time. But that doesn't mean you have to marry him."

Loveday said, "I know I work with him. But I mightn't be able to go on doing that. They're calling up girls of my age, and I'm not an official land-girl or anything. I'm not in uniform, like you."

"But you're doing essential war-work . . ."

"I don't want to risk being called up. Sent somewhere ghastly to make munitions. I'm never going to leave Nancherrow."

"You mean, you'll marry Walter because you're afraid of being called up?" Judith could not keep the incredulity out of her voice.

"I *told* you. You know how I am about being sent away. I get ill. I'd die. You, of all people, should understand."

It was like arguing with a brick wall.

"But, *Walter* . . . Loveday, what have you got in common with Walter Mudge?"

Loveday threw her violet eyes to heaven. "Oh, God, we're back onto that again. You mightn't say it, but you think it. Lower-class, ill-educated farm worker. Marrying beneath me. Lowering my standards . . ."

"I don't think that . . ."

"I've heard it all, particularly from Mary Millyway, who's scarcely talking to me. But I never felt any of those things about Walter, nor about his mother. Any more than you felt that way about Joe Warren or even Phyllis Eddy. Walter's my friend, Judith. I feel at ease with him, I like working with him, we both love the horses, we love to ride, and work in the fields. Don't you see, we're the same sort of people? Besides, he's good-looking. Masculine, and attractive. I always thought Edward's chinless well-bred friends were perfectly ghastly and not attractive in the very least. Why should I sit and wait for some public schoolboy without a brain in his head to come and sweep me off my feet?"

Judith shook her head. "How any girl could have accumulated so many hare-brained prejudices in such a short time is beyond me."

"I thought *you'd* understand. Sympathize. Back me up."

"You know I'd back you up to the ends of the earth. It's just that I'm not able to sit back and watch you making such a mess of your life. After all, you don't *have* to marry him."

"Yes, I do. I'm going to have a baby," Loveday yelled, as though Judith had, all at once, become stone-deaf, and after that, of course, there could be no doubt.

"Oh, *Loveday*."

"Don't sound so dismal. It happens every day. People get pregnant. Have babies. It's no big deal."

"When?"

"November."

"It's Walter's?"

"Of course."

"But . . . but . . . when . . . I mean . . ."

"Don't try to put it delicately. If you're asking when was the baby conceived, I'm happy to tell you. At the end of February, and in the hayloft over the stables. It's a bit banal, I know. Lady Chatterley or Mary Webb, or even *Cold Comfort Farm*. Something nasty in the wood-shed. But that's how it happened, and I'm not in the least ashamed."

"You thought Gus was dead?"

"I knew he was. I was so lonely, and so unhappy, and nobody could do anything to help me. And Walter and I were seeing to the horses, and suddenly I started to cry, and I told him about Gus, and he took me in his arms and kissed away my tears, and I never knew him to be so gentle and so strong and sweet . . . and the hayloft smelt all grassy and fresh, and the horses were below and I could hear them moving about, and it was the most comforting thing that had ever happened to me. It didn't seem wrong at all." She was silent for a little, and then said, "It still doesn't. And I'm not going to be made to feel guilty."

"Does your mother know?"

"Of course. I told her just as soon as I was sure. And Pops too."

"What did they say?"

"A bit astonished, but sweet. Said I didn't have to marry him if I didn't want to. Another little baby in the Nancherrow nursery wouldn't make any difference one way or another, and lovely company for Clementina. And then when I said I *did* want to marry Walter, and not just because of the baby, they bucked slightly, but said that it was my decision, and my life. Besides, they've always had a lot of time for the Mudge family, and with Edward gone, at least they know I won't be leaving them, but I'll always be around. I think that matters to them more than silly things like Walter's background and breeding."

All of which, knowing the Carey-Lewises, was perfectly understandable. In their charmed, upper-class fashion, they had always been a law unto themselves. Their children's happiness came before everything else, and their loyalty to those children would always be of paramount importance, overriding social mores, or the problems of what people would say. Diana and the Colonel, shoulder to shoulder, were clearly making the best of the situation: they would carry on exactly as before, and in the fullness of time, become besotted by their new grandchild. And Judith knew that in the face of such solidarity, the opinions and attitudes of the rest of the world—including herself—simply did not matter.

Which meant that there was no point in any more argument. Diana and the Colonel had already given their blessing, and the most sensible thing that Judith could do was join their ranks and gracefully accept the inevitable, whatever the consequences. This, at the end of the day, was an enormous relief, because now she could stop being indignant and cross, and start being pleased and excited instead.

She said, "They have to be the best. Parents, I mean. I always knew they were." Suddenly she was smiling, despite the prick of ridiculous tears behind her eyes. She pulled herself off the sofa. "Oh, Loveday, I'm sorry, I had no right to be so difficult." And Loveday came to her and they met in the middle of the room, and they were both laughing, and exchanging kisses. "I was just a bit taken aback. Surprised. Forget everything I said. You and Walter will be fine."

"I wanted to tell you myself. To explain. I didn't want you to hear from anybody else."

"When's the wedding?"

"Next month. Sometime."

"Rosemullion?"

"Of course. And a lunch party after at Nancherrow."

"What are you going to wear? White satin flounces and inherited lace?"

"Heaven forbid. Probably Athena's confirmation dress, or something. I shouldn't really get married in virginal white, but we have to keep up appearances."

"How about a reception?" All at once, it began to be rather exciting.

"We thought a morning ceremony and then lunch after . . . I hate afternoon weddings. Real day-breakers. You'll come, won't you?"

"I wouldn't miss it for anything. I'll fix a week's leave right away. Do you want me to be a bridesmaid?"

"Do you want to?"

"Apricot taffeta with net underskirt?"

"Pleated peplum and a Juliet cap?"

"Bouquet of carnations and maidenhair fern?"

It was all right. They were together again. They hadn't lost each other.

"And huge apricot satin court shoes with heels like lavatories."

"I don't want to be a bridesmaid."

"Why ever not?"

"I might outshine the bride."

"Oh, ha-bloody-ha."

"Where are you going to live, you and Walter?"

"There's an old cottage on Lidgey, a bit broken down, but Pops is going to do it up for us, add on a proper bathroom. It's only two rooms, but it'll do for now, and Walter's going to clear all the nettles and old bedsteads out of the garden."

"A real little love-nest. What about a honeymoon?"

"Haven't really thought about it."

"You must have a honeymoon."

"Athena didn't."

"How about a long weekend at Gwithian Road?"

"Or a couple of nights in Camborne? That'd be jolly. Look . . ." Loveday peered at her watch. "It's midday. We'll have to set off for the Ritz in a moment. Let's have a drink. We brought some gin and a bottle of orange squash up from Nancherrow. They're in the fridge."

"Do you think we should? Knowing Tommy Mortimer, it's bound to be a fairly boozy lunch."

"This is just you and me. Anyway, I need one. I've been dreading telling you about it all in case you put on a face like a hen's bottom and told me you'd never speak to me again."

"Is that how Mary Millyway is?"

"Oh." Loveday dismissed Mary. "She'll come round. She's got to. She's the only one who can make Athena's confirmation dress look remotely bridal. Now, you go and tart yourself up for the Ritz, and I'll fix our cocktails." She headed for the stairs, and then, at the top, paused and turned, grinning like the wicked little girl Judith remembered from school-days.

She said, "What price, Saint Ursula's now?"

"Deirdre Ledingham would be shocked silly. Probably give us both an order mark."

"Thank God we're grown up. I never thought it would be much fun, but it is fun, isn't it?"

Fun. Loveday's high spirits were infectious and Judith felt the sudden lift of her own heart. The dark tides of war, with all its anxieties and anguish, receded, and all at once she was filled with the reasonless happiness of childhood, something she had not experienced for a long time. After all, they were both young and pretty, the sun was shining, and the air filled with the scent of spring flowers. Loveday was going to be married and Tommy Mortimer was standing them a slap-up luncheon at the Ritz. Most important of all, they were still friends.

She smiled. She said, "Yes. Yes, it's fun."

Tommy Mortimer's treat was all that anyone could have hoped for. A table in the window of the beautiful restaurant, looking out over the park, and their host at his most charming. He and Diana had already arrived, seated in the foyer, and waiting until the two girls should be catapulted into the magnificent hotel through its revolving door. There followed a good deal of noisy greeting, everybody extremely pleased to see everybody else. Tommy Mortimer, for all his fame and gallantry, looked much as he had, and Diana dressed for London was a sight for sore eyes in a slick little black suit, and with a mad, flirtatious black hat perched over one eye. They did not pause for an aperitif, but went straight into the restaurant, where a bottle of champagne stood chilling in a silver bucket of ice in the centre of their prestigious table.

It was a splendid meal. The sun poured in, the food was delicious, and the wine flowed. Diana was in sparkling form. This was her first visit to London since the start of the war, and yet she might never have been away. Other diners, old friends not seen for years, spied her, and paused to chat on the way to their tables. Others, again, catching sight of her across the room, waved and blew kisses from where they sat.

And she talked excitedly about Loveday's forthcoming wedding as though it were the most wonderful thing that had ever happened, and exactly what she would have planned for her younger daughter.

"That's why we came up to town, of course, to order invitations, and try to buy some sort of a trousseau. We spent all of yesterday scouring the shops, looking for goodies, didn't we, precious?"

"What about clothing coupons?" Judith, ever practical, wanted to know.

"Oh, no problem, darling, I did a tiny deal with Hetty. Gave her a great pile of Athena's cast-offs, and in return she gave me six months' worth of coupons. And she reckoned she'd got the best of the deal. Which of course she had."

"Poor Hetty," Judith had to say.

"Not a bit. She was delighted. She's never had such a wardrobe. *And* she'll get asked to the wedding. And of course, we're going to ask Phyllis and Biddy and Bob."

Bob. Judith frowned. Living away from Nancherrow and the Dower House, she had slightly lost track of events, and mention of Bob's name (Bob had never been part of Cornwall) took her by surprise.

"You mean Uncle Bob? Bob Somerville?"

"But of course. He came down on leave in the spring, just a few days, and Biddy brought him for dinner at Nancherrow. He and Edgar got on like a house on fire. Such a delightful man."

"I suppose Biddy wrote and told me, but I'd forgotten. I wonder if he'll be able to come."

"I do hope so. We're going to be a bit short of attractive men. Just pews full of old buffers with walking-sticks."

"Tell me about the wedding. Tell me all your plans."

"Well . . ." Diana was in her element. "We thought a sort of *fête champêtre* in the courtyard . . . so much more original than a stuffy lunch indoors. You know, hay-bales and barrels of beer and trestle-tables . . ."

"What if it rains?"

"Oh, it won't rain. At least, I don't think it will rain. Not for me. It wouldn't dare."

Tommy laughed at her complacence. "How many guests will come to this beanfeast?" he asked.

"We worked it out on the train, didn't we, Loveday darling? Rosemullion Church holds eighty with a pinch, so no more than that. And in church, we thought pitchers of wild flowers, and swags of cow-parsley. And corn-stooks with white ribbon bows on the end of each pew. Really countrified. Tommy, why that face?"

"I am reminded of *Far From the Madding Crowd*."

"That's far too gloomy. Much more cheerful than that."

"What hymns are we going to sing? 'We Plough the Fields and Scatter'? Or 'Fair Waves the Golden Corn'?"

"Not funny, Tommy. Going too far."

"Can I wear my frock-coat, or am I expected to come in tweeds with a fish-hook in my hat?"

"You can wear anything you like. Corduroys and baler twine, if it'll make you happy."

"Anything that makes you happy makes me happy," Tommy told her, and she mouthed him a kiss and said that perhaps it was time to order coffee.

Her ebullient, light-hearted mood lasted the rest of the day, and swept the two girls along on the coat-tails of her energy and high spirits. With lunch over, the little party dispersed, Tommy to return to Regent Street, Diana and Loveday to head back to Harrods, and Judith to set off, alone, in search of a suitable wedding present for Loveday and Walter. She caught a bus to Sloane Square and Peter Jones, and there wandered about, deliberating over things like saucepans and wooden spoons, doormats and lamps with shades. But none of these items struck her as being particularly interesting or appealing, so she walked out of Peter Jones and into the network of small streets that lay to the north of the King's Road. After a bit, in the midst of small pubs, she came upon a little junk-shop, spilling dubious-looking antique furniture onto the pavement. Beyond its dusty window were velvet-lined boxes of table silver, odd cups and saucers, lead soldiers, ivory chessmen, old chamber-pots, bronze statuettes, and bundles of faded plush curtains. Feeling hopeful, she ventured inside, and as she pushed open the door, a bell jingled. She smelt must and mould; it was dark and dusty, cluttered with looming furniture and coal-scuttles and brass gongs, but, from some back room, an old lady emerged, wearing a pinafore and a considerable hat, to switch on a dim light or two and to ask if Judith was wanting something. Judith explained that she was looking for a wedding present, and the old lady said, "Take your time," settled herself majestically in a sagging armchair, and lit up the stub of a cigarette. And so Judith spent a happy fifteen minutes or so edging her way around the tiny shop, and inspecting various unlikely objects, but finally found exactly what she had been searching for. Twelve Mason's ironstone dinner plates, unchipped and in perfect condition, with the deep blues rich as the sea, and the warm reds unfaded. They were both decorative and useful, and if Loveday didn't want to eat off them, she could always arrange them on some shelf.

"I'll take these, please."

"Righty-ho." The old lady dropped her cigarette stub on the floor, ground it out with the heel of her bedroom slipper, and heaved herself up out of the armchair. It took some time to pack the plates, wrapping each in newspaper and then packing them into an old grocery box, which consequently weighed a ton. Judith paid for her purchase, heaved the bulky burden up into her arms, and headed back to the King's Road where, after a bit of a wait, she succeeded in finding a taxi to drive her back to the Mews.

By now it was nearly half past four, but Diana and Loveday did not return for another hour, laden with packages and parcels, both complaining vociferously of shopper's feet, but still, miraculously, on speaking terms. They had

had a lovely time, the expedition had been all success, but they both were dying for a cup of tea. So Judith put the kettle on and laid a tray, and made hot buttered toast, and a happy half-hour was spent showing and inspecting all the lovely new clothes that had been purchased. And when at last Loveday came to the end, and the room was a drift of garments and tissue paper, Judith fetched the grocery box from behind the sofa where she had hidden it, and dumped it at Loveday's feet and said, "It's your wedding present," and the first plate was unwrapped to gasps of gratifying delight and appreciation from both mother and daughter.

"Oh, they're *heaven!*"

"Don't unwrap any more. They're all the same and there are twelve of them."

"Gorgeous. You couldn't have given me anything more beautiful. We looked at plates, but they're all horrible utility white. These are lovely. *Lovely*. Where did you get them?"

Judith explained. She said, "You'll have to take them back with you in the train, I'm afraid. They're dreadfully heavy. Do you think you'll be able to manage?"

"No trouble. We'll find a porter or a trolley, or something, and Pops is going to come and meet us at Penzance."

Diana said, "They're almost too pretty to use."

"I shall display them," Loveday decided. "I shall get someone to give me a dresser, and I shall display them. They'll cheer my little house up no end. Thank you, darling Judith. Thank you so much."

So it was all very satisfactory. They sat on, drinking tea and eating toast until Diana looked at her little watch and announced that it was time for them all to start getting ready for the evening's entertainment, for Tommy had got tickets for the revue *Strike It Again*, and was taking them all to the theatre.

Because of all these delightful activities, it was not until the next morning that Judith found herself alone with Diana. Loveday was not yet up, and so the two of them breakfasted together at the kitchen table . . . a proper breakfast—boiled Nancherrow eggs and copious cups of freshly brewed coffee. And it was only then that they were able to discuss topics more grave and serious than Loveday's wedding, namely the fate of the Dunbar family, trapped in the Far East by the Japanese war.

Diana wished to know every detail of every single thing that had happened, and when it had happened. And she was so sympathetic and concerned that it wasn't too difficult to talk about the sad progress of events, culminating in the last piece of news which had filtered through, which was that *The Rajah of Sarawak* had never reached Australia.

"Do you think that their boat was torpedoed?"

"It must have been, though there was no official confirmation."

"Too awful. Your poor mother. Thank you for telling me. Sometimes it's good to talk. I deliberately didn't say anything when we were all together yesterday because it seemed rather inappropriate. And I wanted yesterday to be Loveday's. I do hope you didn't think I was being dreadfully casual and uncaring. And whatever happens, you know *we* are always there. Edgar and I. We think of you as another daughter. If ever you need a shoulder to cry on, you only have to pick up the telephone."

"I know that. You're sweet."

Diana sighed, set down her coffee cup, and reached for a cigarette. "I suppose one just has to go on hoping for the best." Sitting there, in her peach satin dressing-gown, and with her lovely face naked of make-up, she looked, all at once, immeasurably sad. Judith waited for her to say something about Gus, because his name, unspoken, hung in the air between them. But Diana stayed silent, and Judith realized that if they were going to talk properly, then she must be the first to say his name. It took a bit of courage, because there was always the chance that Diana might open her heart, confide her own misgivings about Loveday's intentions, and, close as they were, Judith dreaded such confidences, which would leave her caught in the horrid trap of divided loyalties.

She said, "I've always thought that hope was something of a two-edged sword. Loveday's stopped hoping, hasn't she? She's certain that Gus is already dead."

Diana nodded. "I know. Totally convinced. Too tragic. What can one say? I suppose if she feels that strongly, then he must have been killed. They were so close, you see. They had such an instant rapport. It was lovely to watch, extraordinary. He turned up at Nancherrow, out of the blue, and it was as though he'd always been around. Such a quiet, engaging man, and so talented and artistic. And so in love. They never tried to hide their love."

She fell silent. Judith waited for her to continue but, it seemed, she had nothing more to say. Gus was gone, like water flowing away beneath a bridge, and now Loveday was carrying Walter's baby, and was going to marry Walter. Too late for second thoughts, no time for misgivings. Diana and Edgar had, as it were, nailed their colours to the mast, and no person, not even Judith, was ever to know how they truly felt.

After a bit, she said, "Perhaps Loveday's right. Hope isn't much to build your life on. But the alternative is so unthinkable, and if it's all you've got" . . . And then, without thinking, ". . . Jeremy said it was important to keep on hoping . . ." and instantly could have bitten out her tongue, for Diana, at once, was alert.

"Jeremy? When did you see Jeremy?"

"Oh, sometime." Disconcerted, furious with herself, Judith floundered. "January, I think. I can't remember. Just before Singapore fell. He was passing through London."

"We haven't seen him for ages. Was he well?"

"I think so. He's got promotion. Surgeon-Commander."

"Now you mention it, I think his father told Edgar. Clever boy. I must send him an invitation to the wedding. Where is he?"

"No idea."

"But an address?"

"HMS *Sutherland,* care of GPO."

"Too vague. Doesn't tell us a thing. Oh, this damned war. Everybody all over the place. Shattered. Like bits of shrapnel."

"I know." Judith was sympathetic. "But there's not an awful lot we can do about it."

Suddenly Diana smiled. "Darling Judith, what a sensible girl you are. You're perfectly right. Now, pour me another cup of coffee and let's decide how we're going to spend this beautiful morning. Tommy wants to give us all lunch, but if we can get Loveday out of bed, there'll be time for a walk in the park . . . let's not waste a moment . . ."

So, back on course again. But that evening, returning to Portsmouth in the train, Judith sat gazing out of the window, and thought back over the astonishing events of the past two days. Loveday and Walter. Married. A couple. Alone, and without the stimulation of luncheon parties and sparkling company, she felt the euphoria of the weekend fade, and in its place her own private reservations came flooding back. Loveday was, and always had been, a most special friend, but Judith knew her waywardness and her stubborn determination only too well. Loveday's greatest fear had always been that the war should, in some way or another, drag her away from Nancherrow. Threat of official call-up was quite enough to send her into a panic. With Gus, as she believed, dead and lost forever, she had no reason not to turn to Walter. Married to Walter, she would be safe at Nancherrow for always. The workings of Loveday's mind were not difficult to comprehend. But Judith just hoped that what she had been told was true. That Walter, in the hayloft, had seduced Loveday. And that it was not Loveday who, calculating the odds, had seduced Walter.

Two weeks later, to a day, Judith received the official invitation to Loveday's wedding. She discovered it on her return to Quarters from Whale Island, ostentatiously enormous, and squashed in with all the other mail in the appropriate pigeon-hole. Diana, it appeared, had wasted no time. A heavy, tissue-lined envelope and a double sheet of the sort of luxurious, water-marked paper that Judith had forgotten even existed. She imagined Diana wheedling the stationer into unearthing some of his precious pre-war stock, and then persuading the printer to rush her urgent commission through. The result was a marvel of lavish embossed copperplate, almost royal in its splendour. Clearly, it stated, there was to be nothing hole-in-the-corner about *this* occasion.

Inside the invitation was tucked a lengthy missive from Loveday. Judith took the envelope up to her cabin, jammed the invitation into the frame of the mirror over the chest of drawers, and sat down on her bunk to read the letter.

May 14th. Nancherrow.

Darling Judith,

It was so sweet of you to get to London, and to be so sweet, and we loved seeing you. Here's the invite. Isn't it smart? Mummy's such a love, she has to do everything the big way.

Here it's like a three-ring circus, because we have to cram everything into such a short time. I'm still working with Walter, because Mummy and Mary and Mrs. Nettlebed are much more efficient than me, and apart from standing still while Mary pricks pins into me (the confirmation dress actually doesn't look too bad), there doesn't seem to be much I can do except get in the way. When we're not on the farm, Walter and I are trying to get the garden of the cottage cleaned up. He tractored away quantities of old bedsteads, defunct perambulators, buckets with no bottoms, and other undesirable objects, and then turned it all over with the plough, and planted a crop of potatoes. He calls it clearing the land. Hopefully, when the potatoes are lifted, he'll plant some grass or something, and then we shall have a LAWN. The builders are tearing the cottage to bits. (I think Pops has pulled a string with the County Council or something, so unlike him, but the building restrictions are very strict and if he didn't pull a string, we'd never have got anywhere.) Anyway, it's all been gutted and then put together again, and as well as the two rooms, there's a bathroom out at one side and a sort of muck-room at the back with a stone floor, where Walter can shed his boots and take off his overalls and hang them on a peg. A new range and new floors. I think it will be frightfully cosy.

Mummy and Pops spent agonized evenings trying to compose a guest list, as we are so limited with numbers. Pops is being frightfully fair, forty of our friends and forty of the Mudges'. Anyway, all the right people are being asked, including the Lord Lieutenant, and Biddy and Phyllis and dear Mr. Baines and Dr. and Mrs. Wells, and various other close friends. On the Mudge side, it's a bit more tricky because they have so many relations, all, as far as I can see, having married each other's cousins, et cetera. But you'll be pleased to hear that the Warrens (distant relations by marriage) have been invited. I wrote to Heather and asked her too, but she says she can't get away; I'm so glad I don't work at her horrid Secret Department, she doesn't seem to have any sort of life at all.

You will also be glad to know that Mrs. Mudge has bought herself a new set of teeth for the occasion. As well as a blue crêpe dress and a hat "to tone." The hat and the dress tone with each other, not with the new teeth. And she's made an appointment to have a perm.

Mummy's totally optimistic about the weather and is planning her outdoor lunch in the courtyard. Pops isn't so optimistic, and keeps making what he calls "contingency plans," which means moving everything into the dining-room should the heavens open. Mrs. Nettlebed wanted to do it all but, with rationing, it just isn't on, so a caterer has been booked, from Truro. Mummy has told him he is not to produce those sort of trifles that have Bird's Custard and hundreds and thousands. And the Lord Lieutenant has promised a couple of salmon, so with a bit of luck, the lunch won't be too bad.

We're not having champagne, because we can't get any, and Pops says he's keeping his last case for when Rupert gets home and the war is over. But some sort of jolly sparkling wine (South Africa?) and a barrel of beer.

Mr. Mudge confided to Pops that he'd got a cask of neat spirit buried in his garden, and offered it as another form of alcoholic refreshment. Apparently he heaved it up off the rocks after a shipwreck a couple of years ago, and hid it from the Customs and Excise men. Too exciting. Pure Daphne du Maurier. Who would have thought it of him? However, Pops thought it might be a bit dangerous to feed our guests on neat spirit and said to Mr. Mudge that the cask had better stay where it was.

But *frightfully* generous.

Mr. Nettlebed is so funny. You'd have thought he would be really in his element with all these social arrangements being made, but in fact his greatest concern, from the moment we announced our engagement, was *what was Walter going to wear*. Could you believe it? Walter, actually, was just going to wear his one suit that he sometimes puts on for funerals, though I must say it does look a bit odd, because it belonged to an uncle who had longer legs than Walter, and Mrs. Mudge has never got around to taking the trousers up. In the end, Nettlebed cornered Walter in the Rosemullion pub, stood a couple of beers, and talked him into letting Nettlebed take over. And last Saturday, they went to Penzance and Nettlebed wheeled him into Medways and got him to choose a new grey flannel suit and got the tailor to fix it so that it looks really smart. And a new cream shirt and a silk tie. Walter had the coupons, but Nettlebed paid for all the new clothes, he said it was a wedding present. So kind. And with that all accomplished, Nettlebed is looking a great deal more light-hearted, and able to concentrate on counting out the spoons and forks and polishing up the wineglasses.

All this and I still haven't thanked you properly for the plates. We got them home safely, and I think Mrs. Mudge is going to give us a dresser that belonged to her mother, so I can arrange them on that and they will look so handsome. It was really terribly kind of you, and Walter thinks they're lovely too. We've had some other wedding presents as well. A pair of sheets (still with the blue ribbon round them and so, unused, but dreadfully grubby from sitting in somebody's linen cupboard for years), a cushion covered with knitted squares, a boot-scraper, and a dear little Georgian silver teapot.

I do hope by now you have got leave like you said you would, because we really need you because we want you and Biddy to help to do the flowers in the church. They'll have to be done on the Friday evening because they're all wild flowers which fade so quickly. Biddy has said of course. When are you arriving?

Clementina is going to be a bridesmaid. She's far too little, but Athena insists. Really because she's found an old frock of mine, white muslin with pink smocking, and can't wait to deck her daughter out in it. I wish you were here now, to be a part of the fun.

Lots of love,

Loveday

PS We had a cable from Jeremy Wells, saying congratulations, but he can't make the wedding.

The next morning, after Lieutenant-Commander Crombie had scanned the day's Signals, and signed a letter or two, Judith made her request.

"Do you think it would be all right if I took some leave?"

He raised his head abruptly, his sharp eyes pale as sixpences. "Leave? You're actually asking for leave?"

She felt uncertain as to whether he was being sarcastic or affronted.

"I want to go to a wedding. I *have* to go to a wedding," she amended bravely. "It's on May the thirtieth."

He leaned back in his chair and linked his hands behind his head. Judith half expected him to put his gaitered boots on the desk, like a reporter in an American film.

"Whose wedding?"

"A friend. She's called Loveday Carey-Lewis." As though that would make any difference.

"Cornwall?"

"Yes."

"How long do you want?"

"Two weeks?"

He grinned then, and stopped his dry teasing, and she was on firmer footing. "As far as I'm concerned, it's in order with me. You'll just have to clear things with First Officer Wrens."

"You're sure?"

"Of course. One of the other girls can look after me. I'll miss your kindly ministrations but I shall survive. If you recall, I've been trying to persuade you to take some leave for months."

"There didn't seem much reason before."

"But this is important?"

"Yes. It is."

"Off you go then and beard First Officer in her den. Tell her I've given my approval."

"Thank you." She smiled. "That's really kind."

First Officer, however, was not nearly so co-operative.

"Wren Dunbar! You here again? It seems that you live in my office. What is it this time?"

Not an encouraging start. Judith, trying neither to stutter nor stumble, explained her request.

"But you've only just had leave . . . went off to London."

"That was a short weekend, ma'am."

"And now you want two weeks?"

"Yes, ma'am."

She was made to feel that, unfairly, she was asking for the moon. After all, the First Officer pointed out in her best quarterdeck voice, as Dunbar knew very well, right now every single member of the ship's company of HMS *Excellent* was working flat out. Including the two other Wren writers in the Training Development Office. One could scarcely expect them to take on an extra load of work, on top of the long hours they were already having to cope with. Was Dunbar certain that two weeks' leave, at this moment, was absolutely essential?

Judith, being made to feel like a traitor or a rat deserting a ship, murmured something about a wedding.

"A *wedding?* Scarcely compassionate reasons."

"I'm not asking for compassionate leave"—First Officer shot her a beady look—"ma'am."

"Family?"

"No, not family. My best friend." Bullies, she remembered from school-days at Porthkerris, needed to be stood up to. "Her parents looked after me when my own parents went abroad." First Officer's expression of disbelief indicated that she thought that Wren Dunbar was trying to pull a fast one. "Now, I only have an aunt, and I want to go and stay with her. Besides," she finished, "I'm due for leave. I haven't had any since before Christmas. Ma'am."

First Officer lowered her eyes in order to scan Judith's leave chit. "Have you spoken to Lieutenant-Commander Crombie?"

"Yes. He says it's all right, if you say so."

First Officer bit her lip, ostentatiously pondering. Judith, standing on the other side of the desk in subservient fashion, thought how satisfactory it would be to pick up the sturdy naval issue in-tray, and smash it down on top of the other woman's Eton-cropped head. Finally, First Officer sighed. "Oh, very well. But seven days. That should give you plenty of time."

Mean old bag. "Thank you very much, ma'am." She made for the door, but before she could open it, First Officer spoke again.

"Dunbar."

"Yes, ma'am."

"I think you should get your hair cut. It looks rather untidy. Touching your collar."

"Yes, ma'am."

"All right. You can go now."

"A *week?*" Lieutenant-Commander Crombie repeated, when she told him about the unsatisfactory interview. "What on earth's the old—?" He caught himself up just in time. "What is First Officer thinking about! There's no reason why you shouldn't take a fortnight. I'll speak to her."

"Oh, don't," Judith implored, imagining an embarrassing show-down in the middle of the Wardroom. "If you speak to her, she'll never forgive me. She'll think I put you up to it."

"A week . . . scarcely give you time to get there and back again."

"Yes, it does. It's heaps of time. I'll go on the Thursday, and come back on the following Thursday. Please don't say anything, otherwise she'll drum up some crisis and stop all leave."

"Even she couldn't do that."

"I wouldn't be too certain. She even told me to get my hair cut."

Lieutenant-Commander Crombie said, "I think your hair's perfect just as it is," an observation which took them both by surprise. Judith stared at him in some astonishment, and he was clearly taken aback by his own impulsive words, because at once he began to busy himself, unnecessarily rearranging papers on his desktop. "So"—he cleared his throat—"in that case . . . we'd better leave things the way they are. You'll just have to make the most of every day."

"Don't worry." Judith gave him a warm and affectionate smile. "I will."

540

She went, closing the door behind her, and he was left on his own, needing a moment to compose himself, and deeply regretting his thoughtless remark. But it had just slipped out, and she was such a charming and attractive girl. Cornwall. She had her own little house there. He knew, because she had talked about it, described it to him. For a moment he indulged in the rare luxury of his own imagination, allowing himself a young man's fantasy in which she would invite him to accompany her, and there would be nothing to stop his going. Responsibilities of the Royal Navy, his job, his wife, and his son, all abandoned. *A land of summer beyond the seas.* They would walk together on windy cliffs, swim in the blue Atlantic ocean, dine in delectable inns by candle-light, sleep at night with the sound of breaking waves whispering through the open windows . . .

His telephone shrilled, jerking him back to cruel reality. He reached out a hand to lift the receiver. "T.D.O.," he barked, and it was his captain on the other end of the line.

The dream faded and was gone, which, at the end of the day, was probably just as well.

> The Dower House,
> Rosemullion,
> Cornwall.
> Sunday 31st May.

My darling Bob,

Well, the wedding is over, and the happy pair on a three-day honeymoon at the Castle Hotel in Porthkerris.

Goodness, I missed you and wished you had been there, not just because of the occasion, but because of *me*. I've never before been to a wedding without you and it felt very odd. I may add that you were missed by everybody, but I said a little prayer for you, stuck up there in Scapa Flow. Now I'm on my own. Judith, Phyllis, and Anna have all taken a picnic down to Nancherrow Cove, so I am able to sit down and write and tell you all about the wedding while it is still fresh in my mind.

Start on Thursday, when Judith arrived. It was a rather dismal, wet day, but I took the car into Penzance and met her off the *Riviera*. She'd had a tedious journey, having had to change at Bristol and wait two hours for the London train. Standing on the platform, I felt a bit apprehensive. I hadn't seen her for months, and so much that is truly shattering has happened since we were last together. I was afraid that she would have changed in some way, become withdrawn, and that there would be a sort of barrier between us. We have always been so close, and I never want that to change. But it was all right, although I was shocked to see her so colourless and thin. I suppose that's not surprising, because she has been through (and is still enduring) such a harrowing time.

Anyway, we got home to the Dower House, and she behaved exactly like a small girl back for the school holidays, i.e., tore off her uniform and put on comfortable old clothes, and then went from room to room, looking out the windows, touching the furniture, checking every detail of her own little domain. And I must say, it all looked at its best. Phyllis has been working like a slave, polishing floors, washing curtains, and weeding the borders, and Judith's bedroom was shining for her, full of fresh flowers and smelling of clean linen.

That night, after she was in bed, I went to say good night, and we sat and talked for hours. Mostly about Molly and Bruce and Jess. On their account, she is determined to remain resolutely hopeful, but I don't imagine we shall get word of any of them until the end of hostilities. Then we talked about Ned and Edward Carey-Lewis, and I asked about her love-life, but she doesn't seem to have one, and, for the time being, doesn't even seem to want one. Wary, I think. Once bitten, twice shy. Which is understandable. So we talked about Loveday and Walter instead. Neither of us are terribly happy about this wedding, but won't admit it to a soul, not even Phyllis. And certainly neither Diana nor Edgar Carey-Lewis, who are carrying on as though Loveday were marrying the only man they would have chosen for her. And all credit to them for that. Whatever, it's nothing to do with either of us, though I think we would both be happier about it if Loveday *weren't* having a baby. I left Judith, finally, at half past midnight, with a glass of hot milk and a sleeping pill, and the next morning she looked a different person, with some of the strain gone from her face and a bit of colour in her cheeks. What a healing place this is!

So, Friday, she went off on her bike to Nancherrow to see them all, and to inspect Loveday's new house, which is not yet finished. While she was away, Phyllis's mum appeared, having hitched a lift from Saint Just in the vegetable van, and she bore Anna away for the weekend, as Anna was not invited to the wedding, and Phyllis will have much more fun without a foal at foot, as it were. Friday afternoon was spent gathering wild flowers with which to decorate the church, and Friday evening spent decorating. Athena and Diana and Mary Millyway were there as well, and we all worked until it was dark and we could no longer see what we were doing. So we swept up all the mess, and came home.

Saturday. Wedding day, and would you believe it, all the clouds had been blown away and it was the most perfect day. I could imagine Diana crowing with glee. Only *she* could have got away with it. A late breakfast, and then we all got into our rather outworn finery, which I won't describe to you, because I am sure you are not in the least interested. Except to tell you that Judith had no hat, so she put on Lavinia Boscawen's old leghorn straw that she used to garden in. Phyllis trimmed it with a rose-pink ribbon, and Judith looked perfectly sweet.

So, the wedding. We walked down the hill, and all that was missing was the peal of bells. I have to admit, the church looked really lovely, lacy with cow-parsley and garlands of honeysuckle, and great jugs of white marguerite daisies. Gradually the pews filled up until the place was packed. One side rather smart, and morning coats; the other side not quite so formal but twice as dressy, with lots of carnations and maidenhair fern pinned to ample bosoms. Diana looked a dream in pale-turquoise silk, and the Colonel immensely distinguished in a grey frock-coat. Athena Rycroft wore a cream suit, and little Clementina Rycroft was a fairly inefficient bridesmaid, removing her shoes and socks in the porch, scratching her bottom as she walked down the aisle, and ending up on Mary Millyway's knee sucking jujubes.

As for the bride and groom, they made an extraordinarily attractive couple. Walter is really good-looking, in his dark gypsy way, and he'd had a haircut and a shave. The best man was a bit rough at the edges, but managed not to lose the ring, and Loveday looked enchanting in white voile, white stockings, and white ballet slippers. No veil, no jewellery. Just a wreath of marguerite daisies on her shining dark head.

Then, safely over, and photographs outside the church, and a bit of confetti thrown about, and the happy couple driven away (Nettlebed at the wheel) in Diana's open Bentley. The rest of us piled into the two chara-bancs that Edgar Carey-Lewis had arranged, and any leftovers hitched rides in cars. (Hetty, the Nancherrow kitchen maid, who's a bit simple, managed to hop in with the Lord Lieutenant. Perhaps not as simple as she looks.)

Nancherrow was looking suitably festive, with a Union Jack fluttering at the top of the flagstaff, and flowers everywhere, inside and out. The court-yard, sunlit and sheltered from the wind, had been transformed. Hay-bales all around the walls, doves fluttering about, and the dovecote turned into a maypole with fluttering yards of coloured ribbon. Long tables, white damask table-cloths, and all set for luncheon with the best silver and glass. Most important, the bar, laden with bottles and tumblers, and as well a couple of barrels of beer. Caterers' waiters busy as bees, and soon everybody had a glass in their hands, and the fun began.

We sat down to lunch at about half past two, and with rationing, and all things considered, it really was a feast. Everybody had contributed whatever way they could, so there was cold salmon and roast pork, and wonderful puddings coated with cream. I sat between Mr. Baines, Judith's solicitor, and Mr. Warren, from Porthkerris, and we found plenty to talk about. The meal took quite a long time, but finally the Lord Lieutenant got to his feet to propose the toast. By now a good many menfolk (to say nothing of the womenfolk) were well away, and he got a great reception, much applause and a few cat-calls, which were swiftly hushed. Walter made a speech (adequate), and then the best man (incoherent), and after that, we all went on enjoying ourselves. By now it was nearly five o'clock, and we suddenly realized that the bride and groom were on their way, so we all rushed off to the front door and stood about, waiting for them to appear. Which they did, and Loveday flung her bouquet at Judith, who neatly fielded it, and then they got back into the Bentley and Nettlebed drove them, in some state, to the end of the drive, where they changed into Mr. Mudge's old car and rattled off to Porthkerris.

(I'm glad Nettlebed didn't have to drive them all the way to Porthkerris, because, for the first time in his life, he'd been a little indiscreet, and had drunk far too much. Nettlebed, tipsy, is truly a sight to be seen, dignified as ever, despite a certain unsteadiness of the legs. At one moment he was observed waltzing with Hetty. One can only hope that, in the fullness of time, Mrs. Nettlebed will forgive him his lapse.)

So that was it. We all said goodbye and came back to Rosemullion, and Judith and I took Morag for a long brisk walk because the poor doggie had been shut up all day, and then she and I went back to Nancherrow for a family supper with the Carey-Lewises. Afterwards, we washed up the supper dishes, because the Nettlebeds had retired to bed.

Sorry all this has taken so long to tell you, but it's been such a special time. A bit like the Winter Solstice, cheering celebrations (the wedding) in the middle of a long, cold, dark winter (the flaming war). I think it's done us all good to put depressing news, and boredom, and loneliness and anxiety out of our minds, just for a little, and simply enjoy ourselves.

As well, it has given me cause to think ahead, and to consider our own family circumstances. If the worst happens, and Molly and Bruce and Jess never return to us, then I think that you and I and Judith must make every effort to stay together. (In church, I thought about the day when she will be married, and I imagined you giving her away, and me arranging every-thing, and it seemed, all at once, terribly important.) She has got this enchanting house, and it is the one certain thing in her life, so I don't imagine she will ever want to leave it or sell it. In which case, after the war, and when you finally retire, perhaps it would be a good idea for us to try to find somewhere not too far from Rosemullion. Maybe the Helford Passage, or Roseland? Where you could keep a little boat, and we could have a garden with a palm tree. In truth, I don't think I ever want to go back to Devon and Upper Bickley. The house is too full of memories of Ned, and here I have made friends, and a new life, and been able to come to terms—more or less—with the fact that Ned will never return to us. This is a place where I would like to stay, and after two and a half years, I think that I never want to leave. Would you mind, my darling Bob? Would you think about it?

My love. Take care of yourself.

Biddy

1945

Trincomalee, Ceylon. HMS *Adelaide* was the depot ship for the Fourth Submarine Flotilla, a converted merchant cruiser, broad-beamed and with wheel-house aft. Her permanent berth was Smeaton's Cove, a deep inlet enclosed by two jungly promontories, and sitting low in the deep water, her steel decks simmering in the heat, and with a trot of submarines tied up alongside, she resembled nothing so much as a huge, exhausted sow, newly farrowed of a brood of piglets.

The Officer Commanding was Captain Spiros of the Royal South African Naval Reserve, and because his ship served in a purely administrative capacity, two shore-based Wren writers were ferried on board each day to work in the Captain's Office, type out the Submarine Patrol Orders and Patrol Reports, deal with Admiralty Fleet Orders, and amend the Confidential books. One of these was a languid girl called Penny Wailes who, before coming out to the Far East, had spent two years in Liverpool, in the Headquarters of the Admiral, Western Approaches. When she wasn't working on board HMS *Adelaide*, she spent much of her spare time in the company of a young Royal Marine captain, based at Camp 39, a few miles north of Trincomalee. One of his attractions was that he was possessed not only of transport (a Royal Marine Jeep) but as well a small sailing boat, and he and Penny spent most weekends in this little craft, scudding, close-hauled, across the wide blue waters of the harbour and discovering inaccessible coves in which to picnic and swim.

The other Wren was Judith Dunbar.

Because of the apparent glamour of their job, they were much envied by their fellow Wrens, who were left to make their way, each morning, to humdrum establishments ashore. Naval Headquarters, the Offices of the Captain, HMS *Highflyer*, the Pay Office, and the Base Supply Office. But, in fact, Judith and Penny found theirs a fairly demanding existence, both physically and psychologically.

Physically, because their day was very long. The seamen worked in watches, on a tropical routine, which meant that the off-duty watch was finished by two o'clock in the afternoon, to doze the sweltering afternoon away in bunk or hammock or some shady spot on deck, and then at four, when it had cooled down a bit, to go swimming. But the two girls came on board at half past seven in the morning, having already breakfasted and made the journey across the harbour by boat. And they did not return to Quarters until the evening, with the five-thirty Officers' Liberty boat.

The long hours would not have been so bad had they had access to a shower and been able to freshen themselves up during the course of the day, but for reasons of space, close quarters, and the fact that the ship teemed with men, this was not possible. By the time they were done with their typing and duplicating and tedious amendments to Secret Orders, they ended up sweat-stained and work-worn, with white uniforms—pristine each morning— now crumpled and grubby.

The psychological problem stemmed from the fact that they were the only two women on board, and as well, ratings. This rendered them neither fish, fowl, nor good red herring. They were not expected—and indeed had no wish to be—on intimate or even informal terms with the Upper Deck, and the Lower Deck, starved of female company, resented their intrusion, dubbed them Officers' Bits, and watched warily for any signs of favouritism.

Neither Judith nor Penny blamed them. The small detachment of Wrens in Trincomalee had always been hopelessly outnumbered by the sheer weight of men, and now, with the war in Europe over, the ships of the Royal Navy were sailing out from the United Kingdom to join the East Indies Fleet. So scarcely a day passed that yet another cruiser or destroyer slipped through the boom at the mouth of the harbour, to drop anchor and send ashore the first Liberty boat packed with lusty sailors.

Ashore, there wasn't much for them to do except play football, have a drink in the Fleet Canteen, or watch some old film in the Service Cinema, a huge hangar of a place with a corrugated iron roof. They found no familiar streets, no pubs, no cosy picture houses, no girls. There were few European civilians, and the single local native village was no more than a cluster of palm-thatch huts, with mud lanes rutted by the wheels of bullock carts. And that, moreover, and for obvious reasons, was out of bounds. Inland, away from the white palm-fringed beaches, the terrain was unfriendly, infested with snakes, mosquitoes, and ants, all of which were likely to bite.

During the monsoon, matters deteriorated even further, for the football field flooded, the roads became red rivers of mud, and a visit to the cinema, with the rain battering on its tin roof, held about as much delight as sitting inside a drum. Consequently, the ordinary seaman, once the novelty of his new posting had worn off, thought little of Trincomalee. It was known as Scapa Flow in Technicolor, and that was not meant as a compliment.

No pubs, no picture houses, no girls.

The worst, of course, was no girls. If some good-looking and determined young rating did manage to catch the eye of one of the Wrens, and persuade her to go out with him, there was really nowhere to take her, unless she fancied a cup of tea in a dim establishment on the Harbour Road, called Elephant House. This was run by a Sinhalese family, whose idea of really sophisticated entertainment was to play over and over a terrible gramophone record called "Old English Memories."

So, they could not be blamed. But it did not make for easy living, and so touchy was the situation that when the Supreme Allied Commander, Lord Mountbatten, descended on Trincomalee from his mountain eyrie in Kandy, and made an official visit to HMS *Adelaide*, Penny and Judith elected to stay below, in the Captain's office, and not line up on deck with the rest of the ship's company. They knew perfectly well that the great man, seeing them, would pause to speak, and they also knew perfectly well that such an occurrence could only stir up unnecessary ill-feeling.

Captain Spiros, reluctant to let his two Wrens have their way, finally saw their point of view and agreed. After the important visit was over, and the Supremo was gone, he came below to thank them both for their tact. Which was appreciated but not surprising, because he was a popular captain, and an officer of both good sense and charm.

The beginning of August now, and the welcome end of another broiling day. Judith and Penny stood on the Quarterdeck, waiting for the Officers' Liberty boat to take them ashore. As well, headed for a bit of night-life, were two of the submarine commanders, the first lieutenant, and three young sub-lieutenants, all of them looking unnaturally clean and formal in immaculate Number Tens.

In the shelter of Smeatons Cove, HMS *Adelaide* still simmered in the heat. Amidships, the swimming booms were out, trailing rope ladders, and the deep sea churned with activity, as two teams of seamen engaged in a contest of water polo, splashing and cleaving through the water like so many dolphins.

Judith watched them, and thought about getting back to Quarters, tearing off her sweat-dried uniform and running down the path to the Wrens' own private cove, there to plunge from the swimming jetty into the cool, cleansing sea.

Beside her, Penny yawned. "What are you doing tonight?" she asked.

"Nothing, thank goodness. Not going out. Writing letters, probably. How about you?"

"Not much. The Officers' Club with Martin, probably." Martin was the Royal Marine captain with the Jeep. "Or perhaps Full Big Fish at the Chinese restaurant. Depends if he's feeling flush or not."

The ship's boat drew alongside, held steady with boat hooks. In the Royal Navy, a ship was known by her boats, and HMS *Adelaide*'s were shining examples of white paint, scrubbed decks, and immaculately furled ropes. Even her crew, a coxswain and three deck-hands, had surely been picked for their good looks, for they were all bronzed, muscled, and handsome, barefoot, with pipe-clayed hats square on their brows. The Officer of the Watch gave the signal, and Judith and Penny, being the lowest rank, ran down the gangway and boarded first. The others followed: Lieutenant-Commander Fleming, the captain of the submarine HMS *Foxfire*, bringing up the rear. The deck-hands pushed off, the coxswain opened his throttle, and the boat swept away, in a great curve, bows rising, and a shining white wake, like an arrowhead, streaming aft.

At once, thankfully, it became cooler and Judith sat in a corner of the cockpit, on the clean white canvas squab, and turned her face into the breeze. From the harbour mouth blew in the fresh ocean air, and the boat's bows sent up curtains of spray, rainbowed in the late-afternoon sunshine, and she could taste the salt on her lips.

After a bit, they rounded the long, wooded promontory which guarded Smeaton's Cove, and now trees gave way to rocks and feathery palms and strands of white sand. The coastline receded and the harbour—that marvellous natural phenomenon, and one of the great anchorages of the world—opened up before them. In its sheltered haven lay the greater part of the East Indies Fleet. Battleships, cruisers, destroyers, and frigates; sufficient might to strike terror into the most aggressive and fearless of enemies. A cruiser, HMS *Antigua*, was the newest arrival from the United Kingdom, her Quarterdeck shaded by spanking-white awnings and the White Ensign snapping at her stern.

Five minutes or so later, they were approaching their destination, the Naval Headquarters jetty. Speed slowed, the bows of the boat came down, as the coxswain prepared to go alongside. The jetty was a long one, reaching out into deep water, built of concrete and T-shaped, and always busy with the coming and going of boats, and the loading of personnel and stores. On shore, caught in the curve of the beach, lay the complex of N.H.Q., the Signal Office, the Administration block, the office of the Chief Wren. All of these were square and white as sugar cubes, towered over by graceful palm trees and a tall flagstaff, where snapped the White Ensign in the evening breeze. Behind, like a backdrop, rose the jungly slopes of Elephant Hill, a ridge of land about a mile long, pointing like a finger out towards the open sea.

On the summit of this ridge, their tiled rooftops just visible through the trees, stood three important establishments. At the far end, with a view of the harbour that any right-minded human being would die for, was the residence of Captain Curtice, officer commanding HMS *Highflyer*. A little lower down the slope, his commander lived. The third airy and spacious bungalow was the Wrens' Sick-Bay. All of these were surrounded by deep verandas, verdant grounds, and tall palm trees, and from each garden, stepped footpaths wound down through the jungle to the shore and the water. Penny Wailes, suffering from a nasty bout of dengue fever, had once spent a week in the Sick-Bay, and had returned with some reluctance to the primitive simplicity of living in Quarters, missing the cool sea breezes, the forgotten joys of tiled bathrooms, and pleasant hours of total indolence, being cared for and waited on by nurses and houseboys.

The boat was berthed expertly, scarcely grazing the padded fenders. Two of the deck-hands had already leaped up onto the jetty and secured stern and forward ropes to bollards. The officers stepped ashore, formally, in order of seniority. Judith and Penny were the last, and Judith turned to smile down at the coxswain, because she knew him to be one of the friendlier crew members. "Thanks," she said.

"Okay, love." He raised a hand. "See you tomorrer morning." Throttle open, full speed ahead, and *Adelaide*'s boat sped away. The two girls watched it go, trailing a majestic curve of foaming wake, and then, side by side, set off to walk wearily the last leg of their journey back to Quarters.

The jetty was a long one. They had only reached half-way when they heard footsteps pounding down the concrete behind them, and a voice. "I say . . ."

They stopped and turned. The waiting boat had docked and unloaded its cargo of shore-going officers. The man was recognizable in no sort of way, and Judith frowned in puzzlement and, indeed, some annoyance.

"I'm sorry . . ." He caught up with them. A Lieutenant-Commander RN, his starchy Number Tens stiff and new-looking, and the peak of his cap jammed low over his forehead. "I . . . I didn't mean to yell like that, but I saw you, and . . . aren't you Judith Dunbar?"

Still at a total loss, she nodded. "Yes."

"I thought so. I thought I recognized you. I'm Toby Whitaker."

Which didn't help at all. Judith had never known anybody called Toby. She shook her head in some confusion.

By now beginning to look a bit embarrassed, he ploughed resolutely on. "I was your uncle's signal officer in Devonport. Captain Somerville. I came to your aunt's house in Devon, just before war broke out. Captain Somerville had to go to Scapa Flow . . ."

The fog cleared. But of *course*. Memory flooded in. Lieutenant Whitaker. And they had sat in the garden together, at Upper Bickley, and he had smoked a cigarette. The day that, in retrospect, she always thought of as the very beginning of the war.

"Of course I remember. I am sorry," she apologized. "But it was all so long ago."

"I had to have a word."

"Of course." All at once she remembered Penny. "This is Penny Wailes. We work together. We're just on our way back to Quarters."

"Hello, Penny."

"Hi." But Penny had more on her mind than casual introductions. "Look, don't think me frightfully rude, but I'm going on ahead. I have to get changed because I'm going out. I'll leave you two to catch up on each other." She was already moving off. "Nice to have met you. See you tomorrow, Jude."

She gave a casual wave and was on her way, long brown legs and white shoes going at a brisk clip.

Toby Whitaker said, "You work together?"

"Yes. On board HMS *Adelaide*. She's the submarine depot ship. Moored out in Smeaton's Cove. We work in the Captain's Office."

"Who's your captain?"

"Captain Spiros."

"Sounds Greek."

"He's actually South African."

"So that's why you were coming ashore in an Officers' Liberty boat. I couldn't quite work it out."

"It's also why I'm so grubby. We're on board all day and we can't even get to a shower."

"You look all right to me."

"I'm sorry I didn't recognize you. The thing is, I was at Whale Island for two years before I came out here, and because all the sub-lieutenants came through on courses, I know the face of just about every officer in the Navy, but I can never remember any of their names. I keep seeing people, and I know I ought to know them, but of course I don't know them at all. How long have you been here?"

"Only a couple of days."

"HMS *Antigua?*"

"Signal officer."

"I see."

"And you?"

Side by side they walked on, slowly.

"I've been here about a year. I came in September 1944. After D-Day, I volunteered to go overseas, to France, I thought. The next thing I knew I was on a troop-ship sailing through the Indian Ocean."

"What was that like?"

"All right. A few submarine alerts once we'd got through Suez, but thank goodness nothing more. The ship was the *Queen of the Pacific*; in peacetime she was a frightfully luxurious cruise liner. And after Quarters in Portsmouth, she still seemed luxurious. Four Wrens to a first-class cabin, and white bread. I ate so much white bread, I must have put on pounds."

"You don't look like it."

"It's too hot to eat out here. I live on fresh lime juice and salt. Salt's meant to prevent heat exhaustion. In the old days, they called it sunstroke, and nobody would dream of going out of doors without his sola topi. But now, none of us ever wear hats, even on the beach or sailing. Did you know that Bob Somerville's a Rear Admiral now? And that he's in Colombo on the C-in-C's staff?"

"Yes, I did know. In fact, I'd planned to go and call on him when *Antigua* docked in Colombo to take on fresh water. But we didn't get shore leave, so my plans came to nothing."

"That's a shame."

"Have you seen him yet?"

"No. He's only been there just over a month. But I got a letter from him. The phone system here is impossible. There are about four different exchanges and one invariably gets through to the wrong one. He sounded very chipper, and said he'd got a handsome residence to live in, and that if I wanted I could go and stay with him. So next time I get some leave, I might just do that. My last leave, I went up-country to stay with some friends called Campbell who have a tea-plantation near Nuwara Eliya. My parents used to live in Colombo, you see. I lived there too, until my mother took me back to England. The Campbells were friends of theirs."

"Where are your parents now?"

"I don't know." They walked steadily on. "They were caught in Singapore when the Japanese invaded."

"Oh God. How bloody. I am sorry."

"Yes. It's been a long time now. Nearly three and a half years."

"No news?"

Judith shook her head. "Nothing."

"You're related to the Somervilles, aren't you?"

"Yes, Biddy's my mother's sister. That's why I was living with them in Devon." A thought occurred to her. "You must know that Ned Somerville was killed. When the *Royal Oak* was sunk in Scapa Flow?"

"Yes. That I did know."

"Right at the start of the war. So long ago."

"Five years is a long time. What's Mrs. Somerville doing? Does she still live in Devon?"

"No, she's in Cornwall. I have a house there. She came to stay with me soon after Ned was killed, and when I joined up, she simply stayed. I'm not sure if she'll ever go back to Devon."

He said, "We have a house near Chudleigh."

"We?"

"My wife and I. I'm married. I have two small boys."

"How nice for you. How long since you've seen them all?"

"Just weeks. I got a few days' embarkation leave."

Their conversation brought them to the end of the jetty, and once more they stopped to face each other.

"Where are you going?" Judith asked.

"I'm actually headed for Captain Curtice's house. He's an old shipmate of my father's. They were at Dartmouth together. He sent me a signal, bidding me to go and visit, and pay my respects."

"What time are you due?"

"Eighteen-thirty."

"In that case, you have two choices. You can either go that way"—she indicated the narrow path that led along the shoreline—"and climb about a hundred steps up into his garden, or else you can take the less arduous route and walk up the road."

"Which way are you going?"

"By the road."

"Then I'll come with you."

So, companionably, they strolled on, up the dusty white road—scored with the wheel-tracks of countless trucks—that led through Naval Headquarters. They came to the high fence, strung with barbed wire, and the gate. Open, because it was still daylight, but guarded by two young seaman sentries who sprang to attention and saluted as Toby Whitaker passed through. Beyond the gates the main road curved away beneath the palms, but there wasn't much farther to walk and presently they came to another pair of guarded gates, and entry to the Wrens' Quarters.

Judith turned to face him. "This is me, so here we take our leave."

He gazed with some interest at the prospect beyond the gates, and the sloping track leading to the long palm-thatched building that was the Wrens' mess and their recreation room. Its verandas were smothered in bougainvillea, and there was a Flame of the Forest tree and borders burgeoning with flowers. He said, "From here it looks extremely attractive."

"I suppose so. It's not bad. A bit like a little village, or a holiday camp. The bandas, where we sleep, are on the far side, facing out over the cove, and we've got our own private swimming jetty."

"I suppose no man is allowed to set foot?"

"If he's invited, he can. Come to the mess for tea or a drink. But the bandas and the cove are strictly out of bounds."

"Fair enough." He hesitated for a moment and then said, "If I asked you, would you come out with me one evening? Dinner or something? The only thing is, I'm a bit green here. I wouldn't know where to take you."

"There's the Officers' Club. Or the Chinese Restaurant. Nowhere else really."

"Would you come?"

It was Judith's turn to hesitate. She had a number of male friends with whom she regularly went dining and dancing, sailing, swimming, and picnicking. But they were all old acquaintances from the Portsmouth days, tried and true and strictly platonic. Since Edward's death and Jeremy's perfidy, she had resolutely set her face against any sort of emotional involvement, but in Trincomalee, this was proving a complicated business, simply because of the overwhelming number of perfectly presentable young men mad for female company.

On the other hand, Toby Whitaker was someone from the past, he knew the Somervilles, and had a home in Devon, and it would be pleasant to be able to talk about the old days, and Uncle Bob, and Biddy and Ned. As well, he was married. Of course, the fact that one's date was a married man did not, in this unnatural environment, account for much, as Judith had learned from bitter experience. Sexual passions, egged on by tropical moons, whispering palms, and months of enforced celibacy, proved impossible to suppress, and the distant wife and the brood of children were easily banished from mind in the heat of the moment. She had fought her way, more than once, out of just such an embarrassing situation, and had no intention of such a situation happening again.

The silence lengthened, as he waited for her reply. Wary, she considered his suggestion. She did not find him particularly attractive, but on the other hand, he did not look like a pouncer. More likely to spend his time telling her about his children and—dreaded prospect—producing photographs.

Harmless enough. And perhaps ill-mannered and hurtful to refuse outright. She said, "Yes, of course."

"Super."

"I'd like to. But not dinner. More fun to go somewhere and swim. On Saturday, perhaps. I get Saturdays off."

"Perfect. But I'm a new boy here. Where would we go?"

"The best is the YWCA."

He bucked visibly. "The YWCA?"

"It's all right. It's called a hostel, but it's a bit like a little hotel. Not all Holy Tracts and Ping-Pong tables. In fact, the very opposite. You can even get a drink."

"Where is this place?"

"Over on the other side of Fort Frederick. On a beach, with perfect swimming. Men are only allowed there if they're the guest of some female or other, so it's never crowded. And it's run by a splendid lady called Mrs. Todd-Harper. We call her Toddy. She's a great character."

"Tell me more."

"No time now. Too long a story. I'll explain on Saturday." (If conversation should lag, which it well might, Toddy would provide a talking point.)

"How do we get there?"

"We can climb on some naval lorry or truck. They shuttle to and fro all the time, like buses."

"Where shall I meet you?"

"Right here. At the gate, around eleven-thirty."

She watched him go, setting off at a smart pace up the hill, his white shoes already brown with dust. Shed of him, she sighed, wondering what she had let herself in for, and then turned and went through the gate and the Regulating Office (no letters in her small box) and so on, up the driveway. In the dining-hall of the mess, the Sinhalese stewards were already serving an early supper for the watch-keepers. Judith paused to help herself to a glass of lime juice and drink it down, and then went out onto the terrace, where a couple of girls were entertaining their boy-friends who lay, in unaccustomed comfort, on long cane chairs. From the terrace a concrete pathway led to the far side of the camp, where the sleeping bandas and ablution blocks were grouped, in a pleasant haphazard fashion, beneath trees which had been left for shade when this particular section of jungle was bulldozed by the sappers, and the camp erected.

At this time of day, there were always a good many girls about, and a lot of coming and going. The Wrens who worked ashore finished their day at four o'clock, and so had plenty of time for a game of tennis or a swim. From ablution blocks half-naked figures strolled casually, wearing thong sandals and small bath towels and nothing else. Others wandered about in bathing-suits, pegged underwear to washing-lines, or had already changed into the khaki slacks and long-sleeved shirts which were regulation evening wear in this area of malarial mosquitoes.

Malaria was not the only hazard. Not long ago there had been a typhoid scare, which had entailed everybody queuing up for painful injections and suffering the subsequent discomfort. As well, there lurked a host of minor ailments, likely, at a moment's notice, to strike any person down. Sunburn and Trinco tummy inevitably laid low any girl newly out from England and not yet accustomed to the sun and the heat. Dengue fever was like the worst sort of 'flu. Being constantly in a state of sweat brought out rashes of prickly heat and tropical impetigo, and the most trivial of mosquito or ant bite was apt to turn septic if not instantly doused in a solution of Dettol. Part of every girl's kit was a bottle of Dettol, and the ablution blocks always smelt of it, and carbolic fluid that the night sweepers used when they emptied and scrubbed out the thunder-boxes.

Twelve beds stood on either side of the long banda, not unlike a school dormitory, but a great deal more primitive. Each bed had beside it a chest of drawers and a chair. Wooden pegs did duty as wardrobes. The floor was con-crete, and wooden fans, high in the palm-thatch ceiling, stirred the air into some semblance of coolness. Over each bed, like some monstrous bell, hung a white knotted mosquito net.

As always at this hour of the day, a number of separate activities were going on. At the far end of the banda, one girl, wrapped in her bath towel, sat on her bed with a portable typewriter on her bare knees, and tapped out a letter home. Others lay reading books, perusing mail, blancoing shoes, filing their nails. Two sat and gossiped together and giggled over a sheaf of photo-graphs. Another had put a Bing Crosby record on her portable gramophone, and listened to his voice while she wound her wet hair into pin-curls. The record was very old and well-played, grinding and scratching beneath the steel needle.

> *When the Deep Purple falls*
> *Over sleepy garden walls.*

Her own bed; the closest thing to home Judith had known for over a year. She dropped her bag, stripped off her filthy clothes, knotted a bath towel around her waist, and flopped down on the bed, her hands linked beneath her head, to lie and stare up at the revolving paddles of the fan.

It was strange how things happened, a procession of events. Days passed when she didn't even think of Cornwall and Devon, the Dower House and

Nancherrow. This was partly because there was little opportunity for brooding, and partly because she had learned that nostalgia was a pretty useless exercise. Old times, old friends, the old life, were all an age away, a lost world. Her demanding job occupied much of her mind, and quiet interludes of introspection were rendered impossible by the fact that she was never alone, but constantly surrounded by other people, not always likeable or sympathetic.

But then, a moment, a chance encounter. Toby Whitaker, bouncing up out of the blue, catching her unawares. Talking about Upper Bickley and Biddy and Bob, precipitating a flood of recollections that had lain dormant for months. She remembered, exactly, the day when he had turned up to take Bob Somerville away. She and Bob had been for a walk on the moors with Morag, and Bob had still been wearing his old country tweeds and his walking boots . . .

And now, "Deep Purple" and Bing Crosby. "Deep Purple" was inextricably entwined with those last days of the summer of 1939, because Athena had brought the record down from London, and played it constantly on the radiogram in the drawing room at Nancherrow.

> *In the still of the night,*
> *Once again I hold you tight.*

She thought of the group. The picture that had never been painted, but remained in her imagination like a work accomplished, framed, hung upon some wall. *Before Lunch, Nancherrow, 1939.* The green lawns, the blue sky, the sea, the breeze skittering the fringe of Diana's sun-umbrella, its dark shadow cast upon the grass. And the figures who sat about in deck-chairs, or cross-legged on tartan rugs. Then they had all been together, apparently idle and privileged, but each with his or her own private reservations and fears; painfully aware of the coming war. But had any of them had any idea of how it was going to shatter their lives, blow them apart and disperse them all to the far ends of the earth? Her mind's eye travelled around the little group, counting them off one by one.

Edward first, of course. The golden charmer, loved by all. Dead. Shot out of the sky during the Battle of Britain. Edward would never return to Nancherrow, would never again laze on the lawn in the Sunday sunshine.

Athena, diligently constructing a daisy chain. Shining blonde head, bare arms the colour of dark honey. Then not even engaged to Rupert Rycroft. Now she was twenty-eight, and Clementina was five years old, and Clementina had scarcely ever seen her father.

Rupert, prone in a deck-chair, bony knees jutting. The archetypal Guards officer, tall, leathery, drawling-voiced; marvellously confident and entirely without guile. Because he had survived the North African Campaign, and fought his way through Sicily, one somehow imagined that he had been blessed with a charmed life, only to hear the shattering tidings that he had been nigh mortally wounded in Germany, soon after the Allied Forces crossed the Rhine, and had finished up in a military hospital, somewhere in England, where the doctors had amputated his right leg. This news had been conveyed to Judith in a letter from Diana who, though clearly much dismayed, could scarcely conceal her relief that her son-in-law had not actually lost his life.

Gus Callender. The dark, reserved young Scot, and Edward's friend. The engineering student, the artist, the soldier, who had slipped so briefly into all their lives, only to disappear, snuffed out in the mayhem of the fighting during the defence of Singapore. *He is dead,* Loveday had insisted, and because she was carrying Walter Mudge's child, her family had gone along with her conviction, because if any person knew that Gus had survived, then it would be Loveday. As well, *her* happiness and well-being were paramount, and Diana and Edgar wanted to keep her with them forever. So Gus was dead. Only Judith, it seemed, remained unconvinced. She stayed unconvinced until Loveday's wedding, and after that there didn't seem much point in keeping the flame of hope burning. The die had been cast. Loveday was married. And now a Cornish farmer's wife, and the mother of Nathaniel, who had to be the largest, toughest, and most vociferous baby boy Judith had ever encountered. Gus's name was no longer mentioned. He was gone.

And finally, the last. Jeremy Wells.

News of him, too, had filtered out to Judith via letters from home. He had come through the Battle of the Atlantic, and had been posted to the Mediterranean, but that was all she knew. Since the night she had spent with him in Diana's house in London, she had received no word: no message, no letter. She told herself that he had taken himself out of her life, but sometimes, like right now, she yearned to see his homely face again, to be in his reassuring presence, to talk. Perhaps one day he would turn up out of the blue, in Trincomalee, Surgeon-Commander of some cruiser or battleship. And yet, if this happened, and he sought her out, what would they have to say to each other, after all the years of non-communication? There could only be restraint and awkwardness. Time had healed the hurt that he had inflicted, but the wound had left her wary. Once bitten, twice shy. And what was the point of recrimination, and the opening up of old scars?

"Is Judith Dunbar in here?"

The voice, raised, dispelled her thoughts. She stirred, and realized that it was now dark, the abrupt sunset had fallen, and beyond the open palm-thatch shutters, the night was deepening into a dark, jewel-like blue. One of the other Wrens was making her way down the banda towards Judith's bed. She had short dark hair and horn-rimmed spectacles, and was dressed in slacks and a long-sleeved shirt. Judith recognized her. A Leading Wren called Anne Dawkins, who worked in the Pay Office, and boasted a cheerful cockney accent you could cut with a knife.

"Yes, I'm here . . ." She sat up, not bothering to draw the bath towel up over her naked breasts.

"Ever so sorry to burst in, but I've just looked through my mail and I've got one of your letters by mistake. Must have picked it up with mine. Thought I'd better bring it straight over . . ."

She handed it over, an envelope fat and bulky. Judith looked at the address and saw Loveday's writing, and experienced a spooky nudge of coincidence. Toby Whitaker, then "Deep Purple," and now a letter from Loveday. Really strange. Loveday scarcely ever wrote letters, and Judith hadn't had one from her in months. She hoped that nothing was wrong.

Anne Dawkins hovered, still apologetic. ". . . foolish of me . . . don't know what I was thinking of."

"It doesn't matter. Honestly. Thanks for bringing it."

She took herself off. Judith watched her go, and then plumped up her pillows and leaned back against them, slitting the envelope with her thumbnail. From it she withdrew the wodge of folded sheets of airmail paper. Eyeflies were hovering around her face. She set the knot of her mosquito net swinging to chase them away, opened the letter, and began to read.

Lidgey,
Rosemullion.

22nd July 1945.

Darling Judith, don't have a fit, getting a letter from me. I'm sure you think something must be terribly wrong, but have no fear, no bad news. Just that Nat and I have just been for tea with them all at the Dower House, and it seemed so funny without you there, and I missed you so much that I thought I would write a letter. Nat, thank God, is asleep and Walter's gone to the pub to have a jar with his mates. Nat isn't in his bed but on the sofa, right here in the kitchen. If you put him to bed, he yowls and gets out of it again, so I usually let him do this, and then hump him through to his cot. He weighs a ton. He's two and a half now, and the biggest thing you've ever seen, with black hair and nearly black eyes and endless energy and a terrible temper. He never wants to be indoors, even when it's raining stair-rods, and all he wants is to be out on the farm and preferably driving the tractor with his father. He sits between Walter's knees and quite often goes to sleep, and Walter takes no notice of him and just goes on with what he's meant to be doing. The only time he behaves himself is when he's at Nancherrow, because he's a bit scared of Pops and certainly of Mary Milly-way, who doesn't let him get away with a single thing.

Having tea with Biddy, she told me that your Uncle Bob has been posted to Colombo and is already there. Isn't it funny that you have both ended up out there together? Or perhaps not so funny, as now the war in Europe is over I suppose just about the entire Royal Navy will be headed east. I wonder if you've seen him yet, Uncle Bob, I mean; I looked on the map and it's right the other side of the island from Trincomalee, so probably not.

And I wonder if Jeremy Wells will come your way as well? The last we heard of him, he was in Gibraltar with the Seventh Fleet. He spent so long battling to and fro across the Atlantic, it must be heaven to be in the Med. Lots of sunshine anyway.

News of Nancherrow. It's very empty and sad because about two months ago Athena and Clementina packed up and left, to go and live in Gloucestershire with Rupert. Either Mummy or Biddy or someone will have told you that he was dreadfully badly wounded in Germany just after the crossing of the Rhine, and had to have his right leg amputated. (Dreadfully cruel, when you think that he went the whole way in the Western Desert from Alamein to Tripoli, and then into Sicily and all that fighting without a single scratch, only to get clobbered so near the end of the war.) Anyway, he was brought home, and was in hospital for yonks, and then in a sort of rehabilitation place learning to walk with a tin leg. Athena left Clementina with Mary and Mummy, and was away for quite a bit, staying near the hospitals and being with him. But of course he couldn't stay in the regiment with a tin leg, so has been invalided out, and he and Athena are living in a little farmhouse on his father's estate, and he's going to learn all about running the place when his old pa finally turns himself out to grass. It was horrid saying goodbye to Athena and Clementina, but she wasn't too reluctant to go, and I think is simply thankful that he wasn't killed. She's phoned once or twice and says that Gloucestershire is very pretty, and the house will be pretty too, once she's had time to get her hands on it. A bit difficult with everything still rationed, you can't even get curtains or blankets or sheets without clothing coupons!

Nat misses Clementina very much, but on the other hand, likes having all the nursery toys at Nancherrow to himself, without her objecting all the time and hitting him over the head with a doll or a toy truck.

The war being over is a great relief, but everyday life hasn't changed that much, still only a trickle of petrol, nothing in the shops and food as tight as ever. We are fortunate being on a farm, as we can always slay a hen and there are still pheasants and pigeon in the woods, and of course the present of the odd fish. As well as the eggs. We live on eggs and have bought another two dozen white Leghorns to sweeten up the kitty. Digging the vegetable garden at Nancherrow got a bit much for poor Nettlebed, so we've turned one of the bottom fields of Lidgey into a communal vegetable garden, and Walter's father ploughed it up, and he and Nettlebed work it together. Potatoes, cabbages, carrots, et cetera. Lots of beans and peas. Walter's father hasn't been too well, chest pains and a bad cough. The doctor told him to take it easy, but he laughed hollowly (is there such a word?) and goes on as before. Mrs. Mudge is still slaving away in the dairy, et* cetera.

She adores Nat and spoils him rotten, which is one of the reasons he's so badly behaved. He can go to school when he's five. I can't wait.

Now I suppose I must wash up supper-things, which are all over the place, go and close up the hens, and get Nat to bed. There's a pile of ironing which I probably won't do. It's a fairly useless exercise anyway.

Heaven to talk to you. Do write back. Sometimes I don't think about you for days, and other times I think about you all the time, so much so that it seems funny walking down to Nancherrow and having to tell myself that you aren't there.

Love, love,

Loveday

In the exotic environment of the tropics, where the only change of season was the onslaught of the monsoon, and perpetual sunshine was apt to become monotonous, the days and the weeks and the months slipped by with alarming swiftness, and it was easy to lose all track of time. This sense of living in a sort of limbo was compounded by the lack of daily newspapers, or even the time to listen in to service news bulletins, and only the most serious-minded of girls made the effort to follow closely events that were going on in the world. The last truly significant thing that seemed to have happened was the star-burst of VE Day, and that was already three months ago.

Because of all this, the rhythm of the regular working week, broken into neat segments by the high spots of weekends, was even more important than it had been at home, and helped to instil a sense of normality into an essentially abnormal existence. Saturdays and Sundays took on a special significance, empty days of freedom much looked forward to, with time for oneself, and the choice as to whether one should do nothing, or do everything.

For Judith, the best was not having to get up at five-thirty in the morning in order to be at the end of the jetty in time to board HMS *Adelaide*'s first boat of the day. She still woke at five-thirty, her human time-clock being annoyingly reliable, but usually turned over and went back to sleep again, until it became too hot to remain incarcerated under her mosquito net, and high time for a shower and breakfast.

Breakfast this particular Saturday morning was scrambled eggs, and instead of the weekday snatched slice of bread spread with peach jam, she was able to eat these in leisurely fashion, and linger over cups of tea. Presently, she was joined by an eccentric Irish girl called Helen O'Connor, who hailed from County Kerry and had about her a most refreshing air of total amorality, being tall and rake-thin, with long dark hair and the reputation for collecting men as others collected stamps. She wore a gold chain bracelet heavy with charms, which she called her scalps, and if one went to the Officers' Club, she was always there, smooching under the stars, and always with a new, and passionately besotted, escort.

"And what are you about to do today?" she asked Judith, lighting her first cigarette of the day, and exhaling a long, graceful plume of smoke.

Judith told her about Toby Whitaker.

"Is he handsome?"

"He's all right. Married with two kids."

"You'd better watch out. They're the worst. I was hoping you'd come sailing with me today. I've let myself in for a day on the water, and I have the strange feeling I could be doing with a chaperone."

Judith laughed. "Thanks a bunch, but I'm afraid you'll have to find another gooseberry."

"They're thin on the ground. Oh, well . . ." She yawned and stretched. "Perhaps I'll just take my chance. Fight for my virginal honour . . ." Her blue eyes glittered with amusement, and Judith was reminded of Loveday, and suddenly liked her very much.

After breakfast, she went down to the cove and swam, and by then it was time to get ready for Toby Whitaker. She put on shorts and a sleeveless shirt, and a pair of old tennis shoes, and packed a basket to see her through the day. A ragged straw sun-hat, a bathing-suit, and a towel. A book, in case there should fall a pause in the conversation, or Toby should decide to take an afternoon siesta. As an afterthought, she added khaki slacks and shirt and a pair of thong sandals, on the off chance that their day should continue on, through to dinner and the hours beyond.

With the basket slung on a shoulder, she made her way down through Quarters and to the Regulating Office and the gate. She was a bit early, but Toby Whitaker was already there, waiting for her, and the brilliant surprise was that he had, some way or another, laid his hands on a Jeep, which he had parked in a patch of shade on the far side of the road. In this he sat, behind the wheel, peacefully smoking a cigarette, but when he saw her come, he climbed down out of the Jeep, disposed of the cigarette, and crossed the road to meet her. He, too, was dressed in casual gear, blue shorts and a faded shirt, but he was one of those men who, out of uniform, look a bit diminished, undistinguished. Suitably attired for his day out with Judith, she decided that he resembled nothing so much as a conscientious family man setting out for the seaside. (At least he wasn't wearing socks with his sandals, and hopefully wouldn't knot the corners of his handkerchief and wear it as a sun-hat.)

"Hello there."

"I'm early. I didn't think you'd be here yet. Where did you get the Jeep?"

"Captain Curtice lent it to me for the day." He looked very pleased with himself, as well he might.

"Brilliant. They're like gold dust."

"He said it wasn't being used today. I told him about you, and he said that climbing into a lorry was no way to take a girl out for a date. I've got to return it this evening."

Looking inordinately pleased with himself, he took her basket from her. "Let's go."

They piled into the Jeep and set off in the customary cloud of dust, out and along the harbour road that circled the wide curve of the shoreline. Their progress was not fast, because there was a good deal of ill-assorted traffic about: naval trucks and lorries, bicycles and rickshaws and bullock-carts. Gangs of men were working on the sea-wall, and barefoot women, wound in cotton saris, made their way to the market, carrying tiny babies, leading strings of bare-bottomed children, bearing baskets of fruit on their heads. Beyond the sea-wall, the harbour lay filled with the sleek grey warships of the Fleet. Flags snapped at mast-heads, white awnings drummed in the hot wind, and the bugle calls of piped orders floated clearly across the sparkling waters.

But it was all new territory to Toby. "You'll have to be navigator," he told her. "Give directions."

Which she did, guiding him away from the harbour, down the rutted tracks which led through the village, past the Fruit Market, and through the Pettah. They left behind them the bulk of Fort Frederick and Swami Rock, and then were out on the coast road that led the way north to Nilaveli.

No more traffic now, and they had it all to themselves, but it was impossible to put on much speed, because of all the ruts and ditches and stones. So, onwards they trundled.

Toby said, raising his voice so that he could be heard above the sound of the Jeep's engine and the general confusion of wind and dust, "You promised to tell me about the lady who runs the YWCA."

"So I did." It would have been easier not to talk, but perhaps a bit rude to tell him so. "Like I said, she's a great character."

"What's her name again?"

"Toddy. Mrs. Todd-Harper. She's the widow of a tea-planter. They had an estate up in Banderewela. In 1939 they were due to go home, but then the war broke out and the seas were full of submarines and there were no ships, so they stayed in Ceylon. And then, a couple of years ago, Mr. Todd-Harper had a heart attack and died, so she was left on her own. She handed the tea-estate over to some overseer or other, and joined the equivalent of the Women's Voluntary Service out here. She wanted to join the Wrens, but she was too old. Anyway, she ended up being posted to Trincomalee, and told to run the new YWCA. End of story."

"How do you know so much about her?"

"I lived in Colombo until I was ten. The Todd-Harpers used to come down from the hills from time to time, to stay at the Galle Face Hotel, and socialize with all their friends."

"They knew your parents?"

"Yes, but my mother and Toddy didn't have much in common. I don't think my mother approved of her. She used to say she was very *racy*. Total condemnation."

Toby laughed. "So, after all the years, you and she met up again."

"That's right. She was already here when I arrived about a year ago. We had a great reunion. It makes all the difference having her around. Sometimes, if there's a late party and I've got a sleeping-out pass, I stay the night at the hostel, and if she's run out of bedrooms, she gets one of the boys to put a bed and a mosquito net out on the veranda for me. It's heaven, waking in the cool mornings and watching the catamarans sailing in with the night's catch."

Empty country now. Ahead the coastline, fringed with palms, was hazed in the noonday heat. To the right lay the sea, jade-coloured, clear and still as glass. After a bit, the YWCA hostel came into view, a long, low building pleasantly situated between the road and the ocean: palm-thatch roof and wide veranda, deep in the shade of an oasis of palm trees. The only other habitation in sight was a group of native huts about half a mile farther up the beach. Here, smoke rose from cooking fires, and the fishermen's catamarans were pulled up onto the sand.

"Is that where we're going?" Toby asked.

"That's it."

"What an idyllic spot."

"It was built only a couple of years ago."

"I didn't realize Young Christian Women could be so imaginative."

Another five minutes or so and they were there. It was breathlessly hot, but they could hear the sea. They made their way across the white-hot, rather dirty sand, up wooden steps onto the veranda, and so indoors. A long room, open on all sides to get every breath of breeze, was furnished with the simplest of tables and chairs, for dining. A Sinhalese houseboy, wearing a white shirt and a red-checked sarong, was, very slowly, laying these up for lunch. Overhead the wooden fans revolved, and on the seaward side were framed vistas of sky, horizon, sea, and the white-hot beach.

As they stood there, a door at the far end of the dining-room swung open and a woman emerged bearing a pile of freshly ironed white napkins. She saw Judith and Toby standing there, paused for an instant, recognized Judith, beamed with delight, dumped the napkins on a handy table, and came down the length of the room to greet them. "Sweetie!" Arms flung wide. "Heavenly surprise. No idea you were coming today. Why didn't you let me know?" Toddy reached Judith's side, her arms enclosed Judith in a breath-taking embrace, and kisses were pressed upon her cheek, leaving large smudges of lipstick. "You haven't been ill, have you? Years since you've been to see me . . ."

"About a month, and I haven't been ill." Released, Judith attempted furtively to wipe the lipstick from her face. "Toddy, this is Toby Whitaker."

"Toby Whitaker," Toddy repeated. Her voice was tremendously husky, which surprised nobody because she smoked continuously. "I haven't met you before, have I?" She peered at him closely.

Toby, slightly taken aback, said, "No. I don't think so. I've only just arrived in Trincomalee."

"Thought I didn't recognize you. I know most of Judith's boy-friends."

She was a tall woman, scrawny, slim-hipped and flat-breasted as a man, dressed in slacks and a casual shirt. Her skin was brown and leathery as well-tanned hide and wrinkled as a dried prune, but her make-up made up for this, heavily pencilled eyebrows and glistening blue eye-shadow, and a great deal of very dark red lipstick. Her hair, which could only be described as a shock, would, under natural circumstances, have been snow-white (*snow-white hair makes one look so ancient, sweetie*), but had been dyed a cheerful and brassy yellow.

562

"Have you come for lunch? Heaven! We'll have it together. I'll give you all the latest low-down. Luckily, we're not all that busy today. And it's fish. Bought it off one of the boats this morning. Do you want a drink? You must be dying of thirst. Gin and tonic? Gin and lime?" Even as she spoke, she was feeling in the breast pocket of her shirt for cigarettes and lighter, shaking the cigarette expertly from the pack. "Judith, I can't wait to tell you, there was the most ghastly woman in here the other evening. I think she was a third officer. Far too vulgar to be a rating. But frightfully upper-class. Talked at the top of her voice all the way through dinner. Hoot-hoot. As though she were on a hunting field. Too embarrassing. You don't know her, do you?"

Judith laughed, and shook her head. "Not intimately."

"But you know who I'm talking about? Never mind, it doesn't matter." She flicked her lighter and lit the cigarette. With that safely clamped between her painted lips, she was off once more. "Just hope she doesn't turn up again. Now. Drinks. Gin and tonics do for you both? Judith, take . . . ?" She had already forgotten his name.

Toby said, "Toby."

"Take Toby out onto the veranda and make yourselves comfortable, and I'll go and find drinks for us all."

The door swung shut behind her, but her voice could still be distinctly heard, haranguing, giving orders.

Judith looked at Toby. "Your expression is shell-shocked," she told him.

He quickly rearranged it. "I do see exactly what you mean."

"Racy?"

"Racy, all right. Raffish, perhaps." And then, as though he had said too much, "But I am sure, splendid company."

They dumped their baskets and went out onto the veranda. This was furnished with long cane chairs and tables, and was clearly the living area of the hostel. Small groups of girls and a few men were already there, scantily dressed for swimming, relishing the cool, enjoying a drink before lunch. On the beach, others sunbathed, brown bodies laid out on the sand like so many kippers. A few swam, or lazily floated on the gentle waves. Judith and Toby went to lean their elbows on the wooden rail, and observe the scene.

The sand was blinding white. At the edge of the sea, bordered in pale pink, the detritus of fragments of shells, washed up by the breakers. Exotic shells, a world away from the homely mussels and banded wedges of Penmarron. Here lay shards of conch and nautilus, scorpion shells and cowries. Ear-shells with their mother-of-pearl linings, and the lethal husks of sea-urchins.

Toby said, "I'm not sure how long I can wait before I get into that sea. Can we swim out to those rocks?"

"You can if you want to, but I never do because they're covered in sea-urchins, and the last thing you want is a spine in your foot. Besides, I don't like going out that far. There's no shark boom because of the fishing boats coming in and out."

"Have you seen sharks?"

"Not here. But once I was sailing out in the outer harbour, and we were shadowed the whole way home by a shark, lurking under our keel. If he'd wanted, he could have capsized us in a second and munched us up for lunch. It was scary."

A girl was walking up out of the sea. She wore a white bathing-suit, and was slender and long-legged, and as they watched, she put up her hands to wring the water out of her seal-wet hair. Then, stooping to pick up her towel, she strolled on up the beach to join the man who waited for her.

Toby watched her. After a bit, he said, "Tell me, is it true that all the girls out here look so much more attractive than they did at home? Or am I already succumbing to the glamour of rarity?"

"No, I think it is true."

"Why?"

"Circumstances, I suppose. Living out of doors and lots of sunshine and tennis and swimming. It's quite interesting. A new draft of Wrens arrives out from England and they look really awful. Overweight and pudgy and white. Permed hair and faces coated in pancake make-up. And then they start swimming and the perms go all frizzy, so they have their hair cut off. And soon realize that it's too hot and sweaty to wear make-up, and the make-up ends up in the bin. And being so hot all the time takes the edge off everybody's appetite, so they all lose weight. Finally, they sit in the sun and get lovely and brown. A natural progression."

"I can't believe you were ever pudgy and white."

"I wasn't pudgy, but I was certainly pasty . . ."

He laughed. He said, "I'm glad you brought me here. It's a good place. I'd never have found it on my own."

Toddy returned with their drinks, which were icy cold and extremely alcoholic. When these were finished, they had a quick swim, and after that, lunch in the dining-room with their hostess. Grilled fish, so fresh that the plump white flesh fell from the bone, and for dessert a fruit salad of mangoes and oranges and pineapple. And all the way through the meal, Toddy talked, regaling them with juicy gobbets of gossip, some of which had a fair chance of being true, for she had spent half her life in Ceylon and was on Christian-name terms with everyone, from the Vice-Admiral in Colombo down to the ex-tea-planter who now ran the Labour Camp in Trincomalee.

Toby Whitaker, listening politely, smiled bravely on, but it was clear to Judith that he was somewhat dismayed by such blatant scandal, and so, probably disapproving. Which prompted a certain irritation. He had no reason to be stuffy, and she found herself wanting to provoke him, and so egged Toddy on to even more outrageous indiscretions.

Because of all this chat, fuelled by a second gin and tonic (*sweetie, we must have the other half*), lunch took quite a long time, and was finally concluded by Toddy's stubbing out her cigarette, getting to her feet, and announcing that she was going to her room, to get her head down and have a siesta.

"But you'd like coffee? I'll tell Peter to bring it out onto the veranda for you. I'll probably surface about half past four. We'll have tea together. Meanwhile, enjoy yourselves."

So they spent the next hour prone in long chairs in sybaritic fashion sipping iced coffee, and waiting until the lowering sun drew shadows on the sand, and it was time to swim again. Judith went off to change back into her bathing-suit, and when she emerged, saw that Toby was already in the water. She ran down the beach to join him, plunging into the clear green waves, and the coolness of the sea was like silk against sunburnt skin, and the water turned eyelashes to spikes and broke the light into rainbows.

The conditions were so perfect that an hour had slipped by before they finally turned inshore to make their way back to the beach. Until then, their swim had been both lazy and leisurely, but all at once Toby was visited by a violent spurt of energy, or perhaps some basic masculine impulse to show off. Whatever, "I'll race you," he announced, and without preamble, or even giving Judith a chance to collect herself, he sped ahead, sleeking through the water away from her in an enviable Australian crawl. Judith, left wallowing, was slightly put out, and decided to make no effort to compete, for what was the point of embarking on such a hopeless contest? And who would have thought a grown man could be so childish? She saw him reach the shore, stride up out of the surf, and stand triumphantly on the beach, arms akimbo, to watch her studiedly unhurried progress. There was a maddening grin upon his face.

"Slowcoach," he taunted.

Judith refused to rise. The gentle waves propelled her forward. "You took a very unfair advantage," she told him severely.

Another wave, and the sand nudged her knees. She would walk the last few yards. She put down her feet, and stood up.

The stab of pain plunged deep into her left foot, so exquisite, so agonizing, that she opened her mouth to scream, but no sound came out. The unexpectedness, the spasm of shock caught her off-balance and she stumbled and fell forward and her open mouth was filled with sea-water. Choking, on the edge of panic, she felt the sand beneath her fingers, somehow got her face out of the water, and then, careless of dignity, started to crawl on hands and knees.

It had all happened in less than half a moment, but already Toby was there, beside her.

"What the hell's happened?"

"My foot. I trod on something. I can't stand. Don't try and make me stand."

So he put his hands beneath her shoulders and heaved her, like some awful old beached whale, up onto the sand, where she lay, propped up on her elbows. Hair dripped all over her face, and sea-water was streaming down her nose. She put up a hand and knuckled it away.

"All right?"

A ridiculous question. "No, I'm not all right," she snapped and instantly felt remorseful for snapping, for he was kneeling at her side, and the grin was wiped from his face, to be replaced by an expression of acute anxiety and concern.

"Which foot?"

"The left." Ridiculous tears threatened to flood her eyes, and she found herself clenching her jaw against the pain and the fright and the sheer apprehension of what she had done to herself.

Toby said, "Sit quietly." He took her left ankle in his hand, holding it in a firm grasp, and lifted her foot to inspect the damage. Judith closed her eyes because she didn't want to watch. She heard him say, "Oh, God, it's glass. Broken glass. Still there. I'm going to get it out. Grit your teeth . . ."

"Toby, don't . . . !" But it was done, and another spasm of excruciating torture leaped like fire into every nerve end of her body. She thought she would faint, but didn't. Then, gradually, reluctantly, the agony ebbed, and she was aware of the slow, sticky flow of blood, emptying out onto the sole of her foot.

"It's okay. All finished." She opened her eyes. "Brave girl. Look."

He held up a wicked-looking triangle of glass. The shard of some bottle, thrown overboard, shattered on rocks, washed ashore.

"Is that all? Is it all out?"

"I think so. Just the one piece."

"My foot's bleeding."

"That," said Toby, "is the understatement of the year." He stowed the piece of glass carefully in the pocket of his shorts. "Now, put your arms around my neck and hang on." He lifted her, and she felt strangely weightless as he carried her up the length of the beach, and up onto the cool sanctuary of the veranda, where he laid her down on one of the long, cushioned chairs.

Judith said, "I can't . . . I mean, I'll bleed all over Toddy's cushions . . ." but Toby had already gone indoors, to reappear almost at once with a white table-cloth, whisked from a table. This he bundled and folded into a pad and set gently beneath her foot. In seconds it was, rather frighteningly, stained with red.

She heard him say, rather desperately, "We've got to do something."

"What's happening?" It was one of the girls who had been sunbathing on the beach, come to investigate. Brown-faced and with sunbleached hair, she wore the top of her two-piece bathing-suit, and had knotted a cotton scarf into a sarong.

"A mishap," Toby told her shortly.

"Look, I'm a nurse."

His demeanour, at once, changed. "Thank God for that."

"From the naval hospital." She crouched to inspect the damage. "Hey, that's a really bad cut. What was it? Looks too deep for a shell."

"Broken glass." Toby produced the lethal shard from his pocket and displayed its jagged menace.

"God, what a horrible thing to find in the sand! And the size of it! That must have gone in deep." She became practical. "Look, she's still bleeding like a pig. We need lint and wadding and bandages. There must be a first-aid box somewhere. Where's Mrs. Todd-Harper?"

"Having a siesta."

"I'll get her. You stay here, and try to stanch that bleeding."

She went. With someone to take competent charge, and to give him direct instructions, Toby recovered his cool. He sat down on the end of the long chair and did his best to do as he had been told.

"I'm so sorry," he kept saying.

She wished he would stop saying it. All in all, it was a great relief when the nurse returned, bearing the Red Cross box and with Toddy following up hard at her heels.

"Sweetie." Toddy, torn from her siesta, had dressed so swiftly that her shirt hung out of her trousers and the buttons were all in the wrong buttonholes. "My God, what a ghastly thing to happen. Are you all right? Pale as death, and no wonder." She turned an anxious face to the young nurse. "Is it very bad?"

"Bad enough," she was told. "It's a very deep wound. It'll have to be stitched, I should think."

She was, mercifully, not only competent, but gentle. In no time, Judith's injury had been cleaned, dressed with lint, bundled into a mound of cotton wool, and bandaged.

The young nurse fastened the end of the bandage neatly with a safety-pin. She looked at Toby. "I think you should take her to the Wrens' Sick-Bay or the hospital. They'll stitch her up there. Have you got transport?"

"Yes. A Jeep."

"Good enough."

Toddy by now had collapsed into a handy chair. "I feel quite shattered," she announced to the company in general. "And horrified as well. We've had every sort of minor crisis here: jelly-fish stings, sea-urchin spines, even shark scares, but never bits of broken glass. How can people be so careless? But how fortunate we were that *you* were here . . ." She smiled gratefully at the nurse, now engaged in neatly packing all the equipment back into the first-aid box. "Clever girl. I can't thank you enough."

"No problem. If I can use your telephone, I'll see if I can get through to the Wrens' Sick-Bay. Tell Sister to expect a casualty . . ."

When she had gone, "If you'll excuse me," Toby said, "I think I'd better get some clothes on. I can scarcely drive back to Trincomalee in a pair of wet bathing-trunks."

So he took himself off as well, and Judith and Toddy were left alone. They gazed at each other in disconsolate fashion. "What a bloody thing to happen." Toddy fumbled in her shirt pocket for a necessary cigarette, shook one from the packet, and lit up. "I am so sorry. I feel all responsible. Is it agonizingly sore?"

"Not very nice."

"And you were having such a good time. Never mind, there'll be other days. Other good days. And maybe I'll come and visit you in the Sick-Bay. Bring grapes and eat them all myself. Cheer up. We must think in positive fashion. A week maybe, no more, and you'll be up and about again. And just imagine, you'll be able to have a lovely rest. Lie in bed with nothing to do."

But Judith could not be comforted. "I hate having nothing to do."

But it transpired, rather surprisingly, that she did not find it irksome in the very least. She was put into a ward of four, and her bed was by the open doorway that led out onto a wide terrace, shaded by a roof of palm thatch. The posts which supported this were twined with bougainvillea, and the floor of the terrace was scattered with fallen blossom, entailing much sweeping up by the junior houseboy. Beyond, simmering in the heat, lay the garden, sloping steeply down to the shore; and beyond again, the marvellously elevated view of the entire harbour.

Despite its purpose and the inevitable bustle of hospital life, the Sick-Bay was essentially a tranquil place, airy, white-painted, and spotlessly clean; even luxurious, with proper plumbing, pictures on the walls (coloured prints of the Sussex Downs and the Lake District), and fine cotton curtains which billowed and ballooned in the constant breeze.

Judith's three companions were in varying stages of recovery. One had had dengue fever, another had broken her ankle, mistakenly jumping onto a rock during the course of a lively picnic. Only the third girl was really ill, suffering from a recurrent bout of amoebic dysentery, the persistent ailment that everybody dreaded. She lay depressed, pale and debilitated, and rumour amongst the nurses was that, when well enough, she would probably be sent home.

The real bonus was that none of these patients were avid conversationalists. They were perfectly pleasant and friendly, but once they had seen Judith installed, heard the details of her mishap, exchanged names, and generally made her welcome, that was it. The girl with dengue fever had already recovered sufficiently to stitch diligently at her tapestry. The broken ankle was deep in a fat novel called *Forever Amber*. From time to time the girl with dysentery roused herself sufficiently to turn the pages of a magazine, but she clearly had the energy for little else.

At first this tacit non-communication, a total contrast to the perpetual bustle and chat of her banda in Quarters, took some getting used to. But gradually Judith allowed herself to become as self-absorbed as her companions, and, drifting along on her own thoughts, distancing herself, was a bit like setting off on a solitary walk. Something that she had not experienced for longer than she could remember.

At intervals, chatty nurses came and went, taking temperatures, administering pills, or serving lunch, but most of the time the only sound was the radio which burbled away gently to itself all through the day, tuned to a Forces Network that played continuous music, interspersed with short news bulletins. The music was all recorded and apparently chosen at random, a sort of lucky dip, so that the Andrews Sisters ("Rum and Coca-Cola") were sandwiched between a Verdi aria and the waltz from *Coppelia*. Judith found it mildly diverting to try to guess what was coming next.

Which was about the limit of her capabilities. Sister (big-bosomed, starchy, and good-hearted as an old-fashioned nanny) had offered books from the Sick-Bay library, and when these were rejected, come up with a couple of back copies of *Life* magazine. But, for some reason, Judith found herself with neither the desire nor the concentration to read. It was easier and far more pleasant to turn her head on the pillow and gaze out across the terrace and the garden to the astonishing panorama of water and ships, the busy to-ing and fro-ing of boats, the subtly changing blues of the sky. It all looked very crisp and cheerful and business-like, but quite peaceful too, which was odd considering that the reasons for the Fleet being there in the first place were strictly warlike. She remembered the occasion, a few months back, when an Unidentified Object had slipped through the boom and entered the harbour, and there had been a terrific panic, because it was thought that it might be a Japanese miniature submarine, with intent to torpedo and blow the entire East Indies Fleet to Kingdom Come. The intruder, however, turned out to be a whale, seeking a quiet haven in which to produce a baby whale. When her monstrous accouchement was over, and mother and child deemed fit to travel, a frigate escorted them back to the open sea. It was a pleasant domestic event which had kept everybody amused and interested for days.

There was something else about the prospect that was vaguely familiar, but it took a good deal of thought before she finally pinned it down. It wasn't just the way it *looked*, but the way everything *felt*. She puzzled about this for a bit, trying to pin down exactly where and when she had seen it all before. And then realized that the sense of *déjà vu* was all part and parcel of memories of her very first visit to the Dower House, when, with the Carey-Lewises, she had gone for Sunday lunch with Aunt Lavinia Boscawen. That was it. She had looked from the drawing-room window, and seen the garden, sloping down the hill, and the blue Cornish horizon, drawn, straight as a ruler, above the topmost branches of the Monterey pines. It wasn't really the same, of course, but it was sort of the same. Being high on a hill, and the sunshine, and the sky and the sea visible over the tops of jungly trees.

The Dower House. She remembered that special day, and all the days that had followed on, culminating in the one when she and Biddy had moved in and taken possession. And it was not difficult to imagine that she was actually *there*. And alone. No Biddy, no Phyllis, no Anna. Just Judith. Moving from room to preciously familiar room, touching furniture, settling curtains, straightening the shade of a lamp. She could hear her own footsteps on the flagged floor of the kitchen passage, smell musty damp, freshly ironed laundry, the scent of daffodils. Now, she was climbing stairs, her hand trailing on the polished banister rail, crossing the landing to open the door that led into her own bedroom. She saw the brass-railed double bed, where once Aunt Lavinia had slept; photographs in silver frames; her own books; her Chinese box. She crossed the floor to throw wide the windows, and she felt the cool damp air touch her cheeks.

Like a benevolent spell, the images filled her with contentment and satisfaction. For five years it had been her own house, her home. And eighteen months had passed since she had last seen it, on embarkation leave and a few days in which to say goodbye to Biddy and Phyllis. Then it had looked dear as ever, but dreadfully shabby, run-down, and in need of much attention, but nothing could be done because of the war's shortages and restrictions. By now, she decided wryly, it must just about be falling to pieces.

When . . . in a year's time? Two years? Longer, perhaps . . . the war was over and she was able to go home, she would celebrate by indulging herself in a veritable orgy of repair and refurbishment. The first priority would be central heating, to chase away the looming damp of countless wet Cornish winters. So, a new boiler, new pipes, radiators everywhere. With that safely accomplished and everything dry and toasty-warm, her thoughts moved on to other delightful projects. Fresh white paint. New wallpapers, perhaps. Loose covers. Curtains. In the drawing-room, the curtains were faded and shredded by the sun; they had hung for too many years, and by the time Judith and Biddy moved in, were already on their last legs. But choosing a chintz to replace them would not be an easy business, because Judith wanted the new curtains to look exactly the same as the old ones. Who would help her? And then, inspiration struck. Diana. Diana Carey-Lewis. Choosing chintzes was an occupation right up her street. So, Diana.

You know, darling, I'm sure Liberty's would have just the thing. Why don't we pop up to London, and have a heavenly morning in Liberty's.

She dozed. Waking thoughts slid into dreams. Still the Dower House. The drawing-room, filled with sunlight. But now others were there. Lavinia Boscawen, sitting in her chair by the window, and Jeremy Wells. He had come because Lavinia had lost a letter and he was emptying her desk, looking for it.

You've thrown it away, he kept telling her, but she said that she hadn't thrown it away, she'd sent it to the cleaners.

And Judith went out into the garden, and it was raining now, rain pouring down out of a granite-coloured sky, and when she tried to get back indoors, all the doors were locked and wouldn't open. So she rapped on the glass of the window, but Aunt Lavinia had gone, and Jeremy, looking demoniac and with a lot of teeth, was laughing at her.

Visiting hours in the Wrens' Sick-Bay were something of a movable feast, commencing in the early afternoon, and frequently it was ten o'clock at night before the last of the visitors were chased away. Sister's relaxed approach to hospital rules and regulations was a deliberate policy on her part, because she knew the larger part of the girls who came under her care were there because they were vulnerable, run-down, and overtired. And small wonder. All of them, in one way or another, were doing vital and demanding work, and labouring long hours under conditions of debilitating tropical heat. And because there were so few of them, and they were, socially, so in demand, their precious hours of leisure were anything but restful. No sooner had they returned to Quarters from work than they were off again, to play tennis or swim, or attend some party on board one of HM ships, or dance the night away at the Officers' Club.

So, when a new patient was wheeled—for whatever reason—into the Sick-Bay, Sister's prescription for recovery included not simply medicines and pills, but sleep, an unstructured timetable, a few home comforts, and a bit of spoiling. In the old days, it would have been called a rest-cure. In Sister's robust opinion, this regime was plain common sense.

So, there was the minimum of regimentation. Friends dropped in on patients, on their way to or from work, bringing mail from home, clean laundry, a book, a bag of fresh fruit. Young men, off-duty from ships or establishments ashore, drifted in and out, bearing flowers, magazines, and American chocolate, and cluttering up the wards with their masculine presence. If a girl was pretty and attractive, she was quite likely to have three young men perched on her bed at the same time, and if the laughter and the din of voices reached an unacceptable level, Sister would appear, to chase the patient and her entourage out onto the terrace, where they disposed themselves in long chairs, watched the light fade from the evening sky, and indulged in lengthy and flirtatious conversation.

Because that Sunday was her first day in the Sick-Bay, and word had not yet got around that she was both incapacitated and incarcerated, Penny Wailes was Judith's only visitor, dropping in at five o'clock after a day spent sailing with her young Royal Marine. She appeared wearing a shirt and shorts over her bathing suit, and her hair was salty and tousled by the wind.

"Oh, you poor thing, I am sorry. What horrible luck. Quarters Officer told me all about it. I've brought you a pineapple, we got it in the Fruit Market. Anything else you want? I can't stay, because there's a party tonight on board that new cruiser, and I have to go back and have a shower and tart myself up. I'll tell Captain Spiros tomorrow that we'll be short-handed in the office for a bit. How long do you think you'll be here? A good week, I should imagine. And don't worry about all that boring typing. Chiefey and I can manage between us, and if we can't, we'll leave it in a great pile for you to deal with when you come back . . ."

She stayed chattering on for about a quarter of an hour, and then caught sight of the time, sprang to her feet, promised to return, and went. Judith reckoned that that was her lot. No more visitors. But, just after sunset, with the sky dark and the lights switched on, she heard someone say her name, and looking up, saw Mrs. Todd-Harper striding down the length of the ward towards her.

A delightful surprise. "Sweetie!" She was dressed in her habitual uniform of freshly pressed slacks and shirt, but was clearly headed for a festive evening out, with yellow head gleaming like brass, full make-up, a blast of perfume, and a great deal of heavy gold jewellery, chains and earrings and a couple of knuckle-dusting rings. Over one shoulder was slung a bulging basket, and her ringing voice and bizarre appearance created a certain stir, causing conversation to cease momentarily, and heads to turn her way.

Toddy either ignored this attention, or else was blissfully unaware of it. "There you are! Just had to come and make sure you were all right."

Judith was most touched. "Toddy, you didn't come all this long way to see me, did you? And in the dark? And driving yourself?" She thought Toddy was very brave. The first bit of the road from the hostel was quite lonely, and it was not difficult to imagine a gang of robbers or dacoits appearing from the undergrowth with intent to steal or even kill. But, of course, Toddy was experienced, an old hand, and frightened of nothing and nobody. Any dacoit foolish enough to force a confrontation would undoubtedly come off the worst, reeling from a tongue-lashing of invective, or a clout over the head from the heavy club which Toddy, when driving, always kept close to hand. "No problems." She pulled up a chair. "I had to come anyway, to pick up some stores from the NAAFI. I filtered off one or two goodies for you." She disgorged the contents of the basket, laying offerings on the bed. "Canned peaches. Wine gums. And a bottle of dubious bath-oil. God knows what it smells like. Probably Mémoires de Dead Spaniels. What's this great thing at the end of the bed?"

"It's a cage, to keep the sheet off my foot."

"Is it dreadfully sore?"

"A bit."

From beyond the open door, from the darkness of the terrace, came a burst of masculine laughter. Toddy raised her pencilled eyebrows. "That sounds like a good party. I bet one of those boys has smuggled in a hip-flask of gin. I thought of sneaking in a toot for you, but I was afraid Sister would find out and we'd both be in trouble. Now tell me all about your poor footie. What did they do?"

"Gave me a local anaesthetic and stitched it up."

"Ugh." Toddy screwed up her face into the expression of a person who has just bitten into a lemon. "I hope you couldn't feel the needle going in and out. How long have you got to stay here?"

"Maybe ten days."

"And your job?"

"I think they can probably manage without me."

"And Toby Whitaker? Did he do his stuff? Has he been to see you?"

"He's Duty Officer today."

"Quite a nice man, sweetie, but a bit stodgy. Not nearly as much fun as the other chaps you've brought to see me."

"He's married, Toddy."

"But that doesn't mean that he's got to be *stodgy*. I can't think why you went out with him."

"Old times' sake. Ages ago, he was Uncle Bob's signal officer."

"Uncle Bob," Toddy repeated thoughtfully. She knew about the Somervilles, of course, and about the Dower House, and Nancherrow and the Carey-Lewises, because over the months, from time to time, there had been opportunity to sit and talk, and Toddy was a woman always avidly interested in hearing the details of another person's life. But as well, she liked to get names straight, and people compartmented. "You mean, Rear Admiral Somerville. On the C-in-C's staff, Colombo?"

Judith found herself laughing. "Toddy, he's only been in Colombo for a *month*. Even *I* haven't seen him yet. You can't tell me you've already met him."

"No, but Johnny Harrington telephoned the other night, and said that they'd met at some dinner party. And do you remember the Finch-Paytons? They're older than God now, but they used to play bridge with your parents. Well, apparently poor old Mavis Finch-Payton got most dreadfully drunk. She never did know when to stop, of course, but now it's beginning to show."

"You know, I think you should run a gossip column in the *Fleet Newspaper*."

"Don't even suggest it. I'd be sued off the face of the earth . . . Now what's the time?" She looked at the massive watch strapped to her wrist. "Oh, it's all right, I don't have to go just yet."

"Where are you off to?"

"Nothing much. Just having a drink at the club with the new group captain."

"New group captain. New to Trincomalee, or new to you?"

Toddy made a face. "Both, actually. Now, tell me what to bring you when I come again. Perhaps a spicy novel to help pass the time?"

"That would be great. I don't feel much like reading right now, but I am sure that soon, I will."

"So what have you been doing today?"

"Nothing."

"Nothing? I don't approve."

"You said I would love doing nothing."

"I meant having a rest. Not lying here brooding."

"Who said I was brooding? In fact, I was being quite constructive, mentally redecorating my house in Cornwall."

"You promise me that's true?"

"Why are you so concerned?"

"Well . . . it's natural, isn't it . . . ?" For once Toddy seemed a bit lost for words. "You know, when the buzz of life slows down for a moment, everybody's inclined to get a bit broody . . . I know I did when my husband died. One of the reasons I'm doing this job." She floundered a bit. "Sweetie, you know what I mean . . ."

Judith did, but it was clearly going to be up to her to put it into words. "You think I might be lying here worrying myself sick about Mummy and Dad and Jess."

"It's just that horrible worries, that are always there, are apt to recur, to surface, when there comes time to think about them. Like a pause in the conversation."

"I don't let them surface. It's the only way I can deal with them."

Toddy leaned forward and took Judith's hand in her own large brown, red-nailed one. She said, "I'd be a dangerous gossip-columnist but a splendid Agony Aunt. It's not always a good idea to keep things bottled up. I never talk about your family to you, because I don't want to intrude. But you must know that you could always talk to me."

"What's the point in talking? What good is it going to do *them*? Besides, I've got out of the way of talking. The only person I could ever talk to was Biddy, because she knew them well. Apart from Aunt Louise, there was never anybody else, and she was killed in that horrible accident when I was fourteen. Even the Carey-Lewises never knew Mummy and Jess, because it wasn't until after they'd sailed for Colombo, and Aunt Louise died, that I started spending holidays with them at Nancherrow. I told you all about that, didn't I? I told you about the Carey-Lewises? They're blissful and endlessly kind, and the nearest thing to a family of my own, but they never knew Mummy and Jess."

"You don't have to *know* a person before you can be sympathetic."

"Yes. But not knowing means that you can't remember properly. You can't remember *together*. You can't say, 'That was the day when we went on that picnic and it poured with rain, and then the car had a puncture.' Or 'That was the day when we went to Plymouth in the train, and it was so cold that Bodmin Moor was white with snow.' And there's another thing. It's like if you're ill or bereaved or dreadfully unhappy. Friends are wonderful and sympathetic, but they can only be wonderful for just so long. After that, if you go on complaining and moaning and being sorry for yourself, they get bored and stop coming to see you. You have to come to some sort of deal with yourself. A compromise. If you can't say anything cheerful, then don't say anything at all. Anyway, I've learned to live with it now. The uncertainty, I mean. The not-knowing. It's a bit like the war, and none of us knowing when it's going to end. Only we're all in *that* boat together. The worst is birthdays and Christmas. Not writing cards to them all and choosing presents and tying them up and posting them. And thinking about them all day long, and wondering what they're doing."

Toddy said, rather feebly, "Oh, dear."

"There's another reason I sometimes really long for Biddy. People keep memories alive, of grandparents and old aunts, long after they die, just by talking about them. The opposite is just as true. If you don't keep remembering living people, they're just as likely to fade off into obscurity, become shadows. Stop existing. At times it's difficult to remember how Mummy and Dad and Jess even *look*! Jess is fourteen now. I don't suppose I'd even recognize her. And it's fourteen years since I saw my father, and ten years since Mummy left me at boarding-school and said goodbye. However hard you try, it's a bit like those old sepia photographs you find in other people's albums. *Who is that?* you ask, and then, perhaps you laugh. *Is that really Molly Dunbar . . . ? It can't be . . . ?*"

Toddy was silent. Judith looked at her, and saw the sadness in her tough and leathered face, and the shine of unshed tears in her eyes. She felt, at once, remorseful.

"What a long and garbled speech. I'm sorry. I didn't intend to say all that . . ." She tried to think of something more cheerful to say. "At least, whatever happens, I'm not going to be left destitute, because when my Aunt Louise died she left me everything in her will." Which, once said, didn't sound cheerful in the very least, but rather materialistic and greedy. "Not perhaps the right moment to start talking about such things."

Toddy vehemently disagreed. "Not at all. One must be practical. Money, we all know, doesn't buy happiness, but at least one can be miserable in comfort."

"An independence of spirit. That's what my old headmistress used to drum into us. But ordinary, day-to-day independence is terribly important as well. I found that out for myself. And I was able to buy the Dower House, so I've got a home. I don't have to go and live with anybody else. Roots of my own. Even when I was very small, I always thought that had to be the most important thing in the world."

"And so it is."

"Right now, it feels a bit like marking time. Because it's not possible to move forward and make plans until I know for sure what's become of Mummy and Dad and Jess. The only thing that's certain is that someday, somebody is going to tell me. If it's the worst, and they don't any of them come back, at least I've put in ten years of learning to live without them. But that's selfish too, because it doesn't make it any better for them."

"What I think you have to hang on to," said Toddy, "is your own future, beyond the end of the war. But I know that's difficult when you're young. It's easy for me to talk. I've lived a good many years, I'm old enough to be your mother. I can look back and measure the shape and the purpose of everything that's happened in my life. And although some of it was pretty miserable, it all makes sense. And, as far as I see it, there's little chance of your being on your own for very long. You'll marry some dear man and have children of your own, and watch them growing up in that house of yours."

"Too remote, Toddy. Light-years away. An impossible dream. Right now, choosing hypothetical curtains at Liberty's is about the limit of my imagination."

"At least that's a hopeful ploy. Hope is terribly important. Like being constant. Keeping faith. And this hateful war can't go on forever. I don't quite know how or when, but it will end. Someday. Perhaps sooner than any of us imagine."

"I suppose so." Judith looked about her. The ward was emptying, visitors saying goodbye and taking their leave. "I've lost all track of time." She remembered Toddy's date at the Officers' Club and was consumed with guilt. "You're going to be dreadfully late for your group captain. He's going to think you've stood him up."

"Oh, he can wait. But perhaps I should be off. You're all right now?"

"Yes, I'm fine. You were a saint to listen."

"In that case . . ." Toddy gathered up her basket and stood, then stopped to give Judith a peck on the cheek. "Take care. If you want, we'll talk again. Meantime, I'll be back, with some steamy novel or other to help pass the time."

"Thank you for coming."

She went. Down through the ward, and out of the door at the far end. Gone. Judith turned her head on the pillow and looked out at the skyful of stars, and saw the Southern Cross high in the sapphire-blue heavens. She felt enormously tired, curiously. Detached. It occurred to her that perhaps this was how Roman Catholics felt after they had been to confession.

It will end. Toddy's voice. *Someday. Perhaps sooner than any of us imagine.*

Sick-Bay
Trincomalee.

August 16th, 1945.

Darling Biddy,

I don't know why I haven't written for such ages, because for nearly two weeks I've had nothing to do. I've been in Sick-Bay, because I went swimming with Toby Whitaker (Uncle Bob's signal officer in Plymouth before the war) and cut my foot on a horrible bit of glass and so ended up here. Stitches, and the Senior Medical Officer anxious about septicaemia, and then stitches out, and walking with crutches, but now all right, and going back to Quarters this afternoon. Back to work tomorrow.

But this letter isn't about me, and the reason you haven't had one before of course is because I have spent most moments, ever since that first Monday, hanging over the wireless in our ward, and listening to news bulletins. We heard about the bomb being dropped on Hiroshima on the early-afternoon news that day. We were all listening to Glenn Miller, and busy with our various ploys, and we don't usually bother to turn the radio up for the news, but all of a sudden Sister bounced in and turned the wireless up full volume so that we could hear. At first we just thought it was a regular bombing raid by the American forces, but it gradually dawned that it was far more important and horrific than that. They say that a hundred thousand people died instantly, and it wasn't all that huge a city, and the city itself disappeared; obliterated. You will have seen the dreadful pictures in the newspapers and the mushroom-shaped cloud, and the poor survivors, all burnt. In a way it simply doesn't bear thinking about, does it? And the awful thing is that *we* did it, even worse than the bombing of Dresden. And it feels a bit frightening, because all I can think is that now this terrible power is with us, and we're all going to have to live with it for the rest of our lives.

But even so, I'm ashamed to say we all got terribly excited, and felt frightfully frustrated being stuck in Sick-Bay and not out and about, picking up all the news and being part of it all. However, lots of people came and visited, and brought newspapers and things, and bit by bit, the importance of what has happened, and the scale of the destruction of Hiroshima, began to sink in. Then on Thursday, we heard the news that Nagasaki had been bombed as well, and after that it seemed obvious that the Japanese couldn't continue much longer. But we had to wait a few more tense days before the news broke that they had, finally, surrendered.

On that morning, all the ships of the Fleet held Thanksgiving services, and across the water you could hear the hymn "Eternal Father Strong to Save" being sung by all the ships' companies, and the Royal Marine Buglers playing the "Last Post" in memory of all the men who had been killed.

It was a tremendously exciting and rather drunken day, as all rules were waived, and there was a party in the VAD's mess, and people were coming and going all day long, and nobody at all seemed to be doing any work. That night, after dark, there were great celebrations, the whole East Indies Fleet lit up with flares and searchlights, fire-hoses making fountains, rockets exploding, and hooters hooting. On the Quarterdeck of the flagship, the Royal Marine band played—not ceremonial marches but tunes like "Little Brown Jug," and "In the Mood," and "I'm Going to Get Lit Up When the Lights Go On in London."

We all crowded out onto the terrace and watched the fun, the Senior Medical Officer and two other doctors, and Sister and all the patients (some in wheelchairs), and various other hangers-on, and everybody who turned up seemed to have brought a bottle of gin, so it was fairly riotous, and every time a rocket went up, we all yelled and shouted and cheered.

I did too and it was wonderful, but, at the same time, I felt a bit scared as well. Because I know that, sooner or later, somebody will tell me what has become of Mummy and Dad and Jess, and if they have survived these terrible three and a half years. *I've* only survived because I've deliberately not thought about them too much, but now I'm going to have to get my head out of the sand and face up to the truth, whatever it is. As soon as I hear *anything*, I'll send you a cable, and I'll telephone Uncle Bob, provided I can get a line through to the C-in-C's office in Colombo. Things are bound to be a bit disorganized with so much going on. Toby Whitaker dropped in a couple of days ago, and there is talk of the Fleet beginning to move on to Singapore. Already. Perhaps HMS *Adelaide* will go as well. I don't know. We'll just have to wait and see.

Another person who has been to see me two or three times is Toddy. I've told you about her, I know, in other letters, but in case you've forgotten, she has lived in Ceylon since she was married (widow now) and used to know Mummy and Dad in Colombo in the 1930s. About the only person here who *did* know them, and we talked about them for a long time, the first evening I was in Sick-Bay. It was actually the day before the bomb dropped on Hiroshima, but of course we didn't know this was going to happen, and my foot was hurting and I was feeling a bit depressed. And, to cheer me up, she said, "The war will end, someday. Perhaps sooner than any of us will imagine." And the very next day, the bomb happened, and that day was the beginning of the end. Don't you think that was extraordinary?

My love to you and to Phyllis and Anna, and the Carey-Lewises when you see them, and Loveday and Nat, from

Judith

Sooner or later somebody will tell me what has become of Mummy and Dad and Jess.

She waited. Life continued. Day followed day; the customary routine. Travelling by boat each morning to Smeaton's Cove and HMS *Adelaide*. Long, sweltering hours spent typing, filing, correcting Confidential books. Then back to Quarters each evening.

Perhaps now, she would tell herself. *Perhaps today.*

Nothing.

Her anxieties were compounded by the driblets of information that were trickling through from the first of the Japanese prison-camps. A saga of atrocities, slave labour, starvation, and disease. Others spoke of them, but Judith could not.

In the Captain's Office, all who worked there were particularly thoughtful and kind, almost protective, even the Chief Petty Officer Writer, who was renowned for his surly disposition and rough tongue. Judith guessed that Captain Spiros had put the word around, but how he had come to know her family's circumstances was anybody's guess. She supposed that he must have been told by First Officer, and felt touched that on a senior level, there should be so much concern.

Penny Wailes was a particular comfort. They had always been good friends and worked well together, but all at once there developed a real closeness between them, a tacit understanding without anything very much being said. It was a bit like being at school, and having a sympathetic older sister to keep an eye on you. Together, each evening, they made the return journey, and Penny never left Judith's side until they had passed through the Regulating Office and confirmed that there was still no message. No summons. No news.

And then it happened. At six o'clock on a Tuesday evening. Judith was in her banda. She had been swimming in the cove, had had a shower. Wrapped in a towel, she was combing her wet hair, when one of the Leading Wrens who worked in the Regulating Office came in search of her.

"Dunbar?"

She turned from the mirror, her comb in her hand. "Yes?"

"Message for you. You've got to go and see First Officer tomorrow morning."

She heard herself say, quite calmly, "I have to go to work."

"Message says she's fixed it with Captain Spiros. You can go on board on one of the later boats."

"What time does she want to see me?"

"Ten-thirty." The Leading Wren waited for some response, "Okay?" she prompted.

"Yes. Fine. Thanks." Judith turned back to her mirror and went on combing her hair.

The next morning, she blancoed her shoes and her cap, put them out into the sun to dry. She put on clean uniform, white cotton shirt and skirt, still crisp with the creases of the dhobi's iron. A bit like a sailor, going into battle. If a ship went into battle, the entire ship's company put on clean clothes, so that if you got wounded, there was less chance of infection. Her shoes were dry. She laced them up, and put on her hat, and walked out of the banda and into the dazzling sun, down through Quarters, through the gate, down the familiar road that led to NHQ.

The Senior Wren in Trincomalee was First Officer Beresford. She and her staff, a petty officer and two Leading Wrens, occupied three rooms on the upper floor of one of the NHQ blocks, with windows facing out over the long jetty and the harbour beyond. The prospect, ever changing and always busy, was a bit like having a marvellous painting hanging upon the wall, and visitors to her office invariably remarked on this, and paused to gaze, and to ask her how she could possibly concentrate upon her work with such a constant diversion.

But, after nearly a year of coping with the many aspects of her responsible post, the view beyond the window had lost some of its magic, and become quite humdrum, part of her day-to-day life. Her desk was placed at right angles to the view, and should she look up from her papers, or pause to take a telephone call, she was faced by a blank wall, two filing cabinets, and the odd lizard, pinned to the white plaster like a decorative ornament.

As well, there were three small photographs, framed and placed discreetly on her desk, so that they should not obtrude on professional concentration. Her husband, a lieutenant-colonel in the Gunners, and her two children. She had not seen these children since the early summer of 1940, when, persuaded by her husband, she had sent them to Canada to sit out the duration of the war with relations in Toronto. The memory of putting them on the train at

Euston and saying goodbye, perhaps forever, was so horrible and so traumatic that most of the time she blocked it out.

But now the war, so terribly, so precipitantly, was over. Finished. They had all survived. The Beresford family, one day, would be reunited. Together again. Her children had been eight and six when they left for Canada. They were now thirteen and eleven. Every day of the separation had been painful. No day had passed without her thinking about them . . .

Enough. With a little jerk she pulled herself together. This was not the moment to start brooding over her children; in fact, right now, the most inappropriate time to choose. Now was August the twenty-second, a Wednesday, and at a quarter past ten in the morning almost unbearably hot, the temperature creeping upwards as the sun moved into the September equinox. Even the breeze, flowing in from the sea, and the ubiquitous fans churning overhead, did little to cool the air, and First Officer's cotton shirt was already damp and sticking to her neck.

The relevant papers lay on her desk. She drew them towards her and began to read, although, already, she knew them by heart.

A knock at the door. Outwardly composed, she raised her head.

"Yes?"

Petty Officer Wren put her head around the door. "Wren Dunbar, ma'am."

"Thank you, Richardson. Send her in."

Judith went through the open door. Saw the spacious, workmanlike office, the fans churning, the open window on the far wall, framing the familiar prospect of the harbour. From behind her desk, First Officer rose to her feet, as though politely greeting an invited visitor. She was a tall and pleasant-faced woman in her late thirties, with smooth brown hair wound up into a neat bun at the back of her head. For some reason, she had never looked quite right in uniform. It wasn't that it didn't *suit* her, just that it was much easier to imagine her in a twin set and pearls, being the backbone of the Women's Institute, and organizing the flower rota for the church.

"Dunbar. Thank you for coming. Now, pull up a chair and make yourself comfortable. Would you like a cup of tea?"

"No, thank you, ma'am."

The chair was a plain wooden one, and not particularly comfortable. She sat facing First Officer across the desk, her hands in her lap. Their eyes met. Then First Officer looked away, busying herself by unnecessarily neatening a few papers, reaching for her pen.

"You got my message? Yes, of course you did, or you wouldn't be here. I spoke to Captain Spiros on the telephone yesterday evening, and he said it would be in order for you to take the morning off."

"Thank you, ma'am."

Another pause. And then, "How's your foot?"

"Sorry?"

"Your foot. You had an accident with a piece of glass. It's recovered?"

"Yes. Yes, of course. It wasn't very serious."

"Nasty enough, though."

Preliminaries over. Judith waited for First Officer to come to the point. Which, after another painful hesitation, she did. "I'm afraid it's not very good news, Dunbar. I am sorry."

"It's about my family, isn't it?"

"Yes."

"What's happened?"

"We heard, through the Red Cross and Naval Welfare. The two organizations work closely together. I . . . I have to tell you that your father is dead. He died in Changi Prison, of dysentery, a year after the fall of Singapore. He wasn't alone. Others with him did all they could to care for him and nurse him, but of course, conditions were appalling. There were no medicines and little food. There wasn't much they could do. But he would have had friends around him. Try not to think of him dying alone."

"I see." Her mouth was suddenly so dry that she could scarcely speak the words, and they came out in a sort of whisper. She tried again. A bit better this time. "And my mother? And Jess?"

"So far we have no definite information. We only know that their ship, *The Rajah of Sarawak*, was torpedoed in the Java Sea, six days out of Singapore. She was grossly overcrowded in the first place, and she went down almost instantly. There would have been only moments to get away, and the official verdict seems to be that if there were survivors, there could have been no more than a handful."

"Have they found anyone who did survive?"

First Officer shook her head. "No. Not yet. There are so many camps, in Java and Sumatra and Malaya—even some civilian camps in Japan itself. It's going to take some time to clear them all."

"Perhaps . . ."

"I think, my dear, that you shouldn't hold out any hope."

"Is that what you've been told to tell me?"

"Yes. I'm afraid it is."

The fans circled overhead. From beyond the open window came the sound of a boat's engine, approaching the jetty. Somewhere, a man was hammering. They were gone. They were all dead. Three and a half years of waiting and hoping, and now this. Never, ever to see any of them again.

Out of the long silence which lay between them, she heard First Officer say, "Dunbar? Are you all right?"

"Yes." Perhaps she was not behaving properly. Perhaps she should be weeping and sobbing. But tears had never felt so unlikely, so impossible. She nodded. "Yes, I'm all right."

"Perhaps . . . now . . . a cup of tea or something?"

"No."

"I . . . I really am so dreadfully sorry." And there was a break in her voice, and Judith felt sorry for *her* because she looked so distressed and motherly, and because it must have been a terrible ordeal, having to break such devastating tidings.

She said, and was astonished to hear her own voice so expressionless and calm, "I knew about *The Rajah of Sarawak* being sunk. I mean, I knew she must have been, that something must have happened, because she never reached Australia. My mother said she'd write, once she and Jess got to Australia, but I never got any letters after that last one from Singapore."

She remembered the letter, read so often that she knew that last painful paragraph by heart.

> It is very strange, but all my life from time to time I have found myself
> asking unanswerable questions. Who am I? And what am I doing here?
> And where am I going? Now it all seems to be coming terribly true, and it
> feels like a haunting dream that I have lived through many times before.

A premonition, perhaps? But now, nobody would ever know.

"I realized something must have happened to the ship. But still, I told myself they would have survived; got themselves into a lifeboat, or onto a raft. Been picked up . . . or . . ." The Java Sea. Sharks. Judith's own personal nightmare. Blot it out. ". . . but I don't suppose they had a chance. Jess was only little. And my mother had never been much of a swimmer."

"Do you have other brothers and sisters?"

"No."

Once more, First Officer glanced down at the papers on her desk, which Judith now realized were her own, the complete record of her service career ever since that day, the day after Edward was killed, when she had travelled from Penzance to Devonport and signed on for the WRNS.

"It states here that Captain and Mrs. Somerville are your next of kin."

"Yes. I couldn't put my parents, because they were abroad. And he's Rear Admiral Somerville now, over in Colombo, in charge of the Dockyard. Biddy Somerville is my mother's sister." Which reminded her. "I promised I'd send her a cable as soon as I got any news. I must do that. She'll be waiting."

"We can help there. You can write what you want to say, and we'll get one of the Leading Wrens to put it through . . ."

"Thank you."

"But you have other friends in Ceylon, I believe? The Campbells. You spent your last leave with them, up-country?"

"Yes, that's right. They used to know my mother and father."

"I only mentioned them because I think you should take some leave. Get away from Trincomalee. Perhaps you would like to go and stay with them again?"

Taken unawares, Judith painfully considered this suggestion. Nuwara Eliya. The mountains and the cool air, and the rain. The hillsides, quilted in tea-bushes, and the fragrance of lemon-scented eucalyptus. The casually comfortable bungalow, log-fires in the evenings . . . But she hesitated, and finally shook her head.

"Does it not appeal?"

"Not really." That leave, the Campbells had given her a wonderful time, but it couldn't be the same again. Not now. Now, she didn't think she could face a succession of parties at the Hill Club, and hosts of new faces. Rather, she longed for somewhere quiet. A place to lick her wounds. "It's not that the Campbells aren't endlessly kind . . ." She tried to explain ". . . it's just that . . ."

She needed to say no more. First Officer smiled. "I entirely understand. The closest of friends can be exhausting. So, here's another suggestion. Why not go to Colombo, and spend some time with Rear Admiral Somerville? His official residence is in the Galle Road, he'll have plenty of space, and there will be servants to take care of you. Most important of all, you'll be with family. I feel, just now, that's what you really need. Time to come to terms with what I have just had to tell you. Opportunity to talk things over . . . perhaps even make a few plans for your future . . ."

Uncle Bob. At this bleak watershed of her life, Judith knew that there was no man in the world she would rather be with. But . . .

She said, "He'll be working, away all day. I don't want to be a nuisance to him."

"I don't think that's likely at all."

"He *did* say I could go and stay. He wrote to me as soon as he arrived in Colombo. He said then that it would be all right . . ."

"So, what are we waiting for? Why don't we telephone him, and have a word?"

"What about my job? Captain Spiros and *Adelaide?*"

"We'll arrange for a temporary writer to help Wren Wailes."

"When could I go?"

"I think, right away. So we should waste no time."

"How long could I stay in Colombo?"

"That's another thing. You're due two weeks' leave, but I think we should add compassionate leave on to that. Which would give you a month."

"A *month?*"

"Now, don't come up with any more objections, because it is no more than you deserve."

A month. A whole month with Uncle Bob. Colombo again. She remembered the house where she had lived for the first ten years of her life. She remembered her mother, sitting on the veranda sewing, and the cool of the sea-winds blowing in from the Indian Ocean.

First Officer was waiting patiently. Judith looked up and into her eyes. She smiled encouragingly. "Well?"

But all Judith could say was, "You've been so kind to me."

"That's my job. It's settled then?" After a bit, Judith nodded. "Good. In that case, let us make the necessary arrangements."

From:　The Offices of the First Officer WRNS, Trincomalee

To:　Mrs. Somerville, The Dower House, Rosemullion, Cornwall, England

August 22nd 1945.

DARLING BIDDY I AM AFRAID SAD NEWS STOP BRUCE DUNBAR DIED DYSENTERY IN CHANGI JAIL 1943 STOP MOLLY AND JESS PERISHED WHEN RAJAH OF SARAWAK TORPEDOED IN JAVA SEA STOP TELEPHONED BOB IN COLOMBO STOP TOMORROW GOING ON MONTHS LEAVE AND STAYING WITH HIM STOP WILL WRITE FROM THERE STOP PLEASE DON'T BE TOO UNHAPPY FOR ME STOP LOVE TO YOU AND PHYLLIS STOP JUDITH

From:　Somerville, Rosemullion, Cornwall, England

To:　Judith Dunbar c/o Rear Admiral Somerville, 326 Galle Road, Colombo, Ceylon

August 23rd 1945.

TELEGRAM RECEIVED STOP DEVASTATED BY NEWS STOP GRATEFUL YOU ARE WITH BOB STOP ALL OUR LOVING THOUGHTS STOP PHYLLIS AND I ARE HERE FOR YOU TO COME HOME TO STOP BIDDY

Rear Admiral's Residence
326 Galle Road
Colombo.

Tuesday August 28th 1945.

Darling Biddy,

It has taken me a bit of time to get around to sitting down and writing a letter to you. I am sorry. Thank you for the cable. It made me feel much better, just hearing from you and knowing that, although we are worlds apart, we are thinking the same sad thoughts, and perhaps comforting each other. But I wish we could be together. The worst is knowing that they died so long ago and we never knew, and no sort of word ever came through. The conditions in Changi were unspeakable and how any man survived is a miracle. So much disease and little food and no proper care. Poor Dad. But I am assured that he had friends around him, so he wasn't totally alone at the end. As for Mummy and Jess, I simply pray they were killed instantly, when *The Rajah of Sarawak* was torpedoed. To begin with, almost the worst was knowing I had nothing of them, no personal possessions, not a single memento. As though everything had been swallowed up into a great black abyss. And then I remembered the packing-cases, all the bits and pieces we stowed away, when we were still at Riverside and before Mummy and Jess sailed for Colombo. They're in store somewhere. When I finally come home, perhaps we can go through them together.

I think about Phyllis too, because she was so fond of Mummy, and am glad that you and she are together.

As for me, I am safely here with Bob. (Not Uncle any more, he says I am too old.) Living a life of untold luxury.

But I must start from the beginning.

First Officer broke the news to me, and she was just as sweet and sympathetic as anybody could be. I think she expected me to burst into hysterics of tears but I didn't do that until a bit later. She'd heard about Mummy and Dad and Jess through the Red Cross, who are gradually discovering what happened to everybody, tracing missing persons and clearing the prison camps, so it is quite official. She then said I had to go on leave, so we telephoned Bob from her office and he said, "She must come at once."

First Officer arranged everything. Instead of travelling by train from Trincomalee to Colombo (terribly hot and dirty and sooty), I drove to Kandy in a staff car, leaving Trincomalee at six in the morning. Captain Curtice (HMS *Highflyer*) and his secretary were going up there for a staff meeting at Allied HQ. They sat in the back of the car and I sat in the front with the driver, which was nice because I didn't have to talk. The drive is so beautiful, though even in a car it takes a long time, because the road is very windey, passing through roadside villages, tiny children waving to us, monkeys everywhere. Women sitting by their houses, weaving palm leaves into thatch, and men working with elephants. We stopped for lunch at a resthouse near Sigiriya (Captain Curtice stood me lunch very kindly). At Kandy I stayed the night in another rest-house, and then got another lift in another staff car down to Colombo. Got here about five in the evening, delivered to the door.

Bob wasn't at his office, but here waiting for me. As the car drew up he came out of the front door and down the steps, and as I clambered out of the car, in my rather dirty uniform, he simply took me in his arms and hugged me, and didn't say a word.

You know, Biddy, better than anybody, how huge and comforting his hugs are, all smelling of clean shirts and Royal Yacht hair lotion. And it was at that moment that I fell to pieces and bawled like a baby, not so much for poor Mummy and Dad and Jess, but because I was so tired, and it was such a relief just to be with him, and knowing that I was completely safe, and didn't have to think or plan or be brave on my own any longer.

He is looking wonderful. A few more white hairs perhaps, and a few more lines on his face, but otherwise unchanged. No fatter, and no thinner.

His house is lovely, a bungalow but enormous. Gates with a sentry, and lots of servants. It is not on the seaside of the Galle Road, but the other side, and has an enormous shady garden, filled with beautiful flowering trees and shrubs. About six houses down the road is the WRNS Quarters, and almost directly opposite, the house where we used to live before Dad went to Singapore. Isn't that the most amazing coincidence? I don't know who lives there now, I think some Indian Army family.

Bob's house. You go up the steps and into a large hall, and then double doors into a great big drawing-room. This has doors leading out onto the veranda, and beyond again a very large and beautiful garden. Bedrooms and bathrooms on either side. (I have a lovely cool room with marble floor and a shower and lavatory of my own.) As you probably know, he shares the house with a man called David Beatty, a civilian working with the Government. He looks a bit like a professor and is frightfully clever and erudite and speaks at least six languages, including Hindi and Chinese. He has his own study and spends a lot of time working in there, but always joins us for dinner in the evenings, and is very nice and quite amusing in a rather dry and scholastic fashion.

As I said, servants everywhere. The butler is a lovely man, a Tamil called Thomas. He is tall and dark-skinned as a raisin, and always wears a flower behind one ear. He has a lot of gold teeth. He brings drinks and serves at meals, but there are so many lesser servants, he doesn't appear to do very much else. And yet, should he not be here, I am perfectly certain that the entire establishment would fall to bits.

As well, he is renowned for concocting a secret magic potion which is guaranteed to cure hangovers. A useful accomplishment.

To begin with, I didn't do anything for about three days, just slept a lot and lay on the veranda and read books and listened to lovely music on Bob's gramophone (memories of Keyham Terrace, so long ago). He and David Beatty go to work every morning, of course, so I have been on my own, but that was very peaceful, with Thomas hovering, and bringing cool drinks.

I didn't *have* to stay here doing nothing, because Bob has got two cars and two drivers. A naval staff car, with a seaman driver, appears every morning to take him to work and brings him home in the evening. But as well he has his own car with a driver called Azid, and he has said that any time I needed to use it, to go shopping or something, I could. But I didn't feel much like doing anything that required planning or energy.

In the evenings, after dinner, with David Beatty returned to his study, we have talked a lot. Going all the way back and remembering everything and everybody. We talked about Ned and we even talked about Edward Carey-Lewis. And he told me that he's laying plans to leave the Navy. He says he's fought through two World Wars and that's enough for any man, and he wants to have a bit of time to spend with you. As well, the atom bomb has changed the face of the future, sea power will never again be so vitally important, and the Royal Navy, as he has known it all his life, is bound to be cut back, modernized and totally changed. He said that you've been thinking for some time of selling up in Devon and moving to Cornwall. I don't want you to do this on my account, but can think of nothing that would be more wonderful for me. But please don't leave the Dower House until I come home!

This letter seems to be going on forever!

On my third evening, Bob came home and said I'd had enough of sitting about on my own and he was going to take me to a cocktail party on board a visiting cruiser. So I had a shower and put on a suitable dress and off we set, and it was great fun. On the Quarterdeck, and we crossed the harbour in a spanking pinnace. Lots of new faces, people I'd never met before, civilians and Army—a real mixture.

In the midst of all this socializing, Bob introduced me to a man called Hugo Halley, a Lieutenant-Commander RN who also works in the C-in-C's office, and when the party was over, about eight of us (including Hugo) went ashore and had dinner at the Galle Face Hotel. Everything exactly as I had remembered it, only a good deal more crowded. Last Sunday Hugo came for lunch, and then he and I drove down to Mount Lavinia; we meant to swim but the waves were enormous, and a terrific undertow, so we sat on the beach for a bit and then came back to Colombo and swam in the pool at the Officers' Club. There are tennis courts there as well, so maybe one day we'll play tennis. I know that if we were together your ears would be pricking up and you'd be mad for details, so here they are. Hugo is very nice, extremely presentable, is blessed with a dotty sense of ridiculous and isn't married. Not, at the moment, that this matters at all or would make any difference. It's just that he's a very companionable person to do things with. So please don't start weaving fantasies, and dreaming up a white dress designed to look well from the back! Anyway, he has asked me to another party on yet another ship, so I am going to *have* to do something about my wardrobe. Colombo ladies are very chic, and my washed-out Trincomalee garments make me look like a poor relation.

I've come to the end now. It's funny but I'm just beginning to realize how heavy was that great load of uncertainty, never knowing for sure what had happened to Dad and Mummy and Jess. Now, at least, I don't have to lug it around any more. The void their going has left is unfillable, but gradually some sort of a future is starting to be possible again. So I'm all right. You're not to worry about me.

The only thing is, I'm twenty-four now and it's a bit depressing to realize that in all those years I don't seem to have *achieved* anything. I haven't even been properly educated, because of never getting to University. Getting back to England, and picking up the threads, will be a bit like starting all over again, at the beginning. But the beginning of what, I haven't worked out. However, I suppose I will.

Lots of love, darling Biddy, to you and everybody,

Judith

Seven in the morning; pearly and still, the coolest hour of the day. Bare-foot, wrapped in a thin robe, Judith emerged from her bedroom and made her way down the marble passage, through the house, and so out onto the veranda. The mali was watering the grass with a hose, and there could be heard much twittering of birds, over a distant hum that was the traffic in the Galle Road.

She found Bob already there, breakfasting in peaceful solitude, having eaten a slice of papaya and now onto his third cup of black coffee. He was glancing through the early edition of *The Ceylon Times* and did not hear her come.

"Bob."

"Good God." Taken unawares, he hastily laid aside his paper. "What are you doing, up at this hour?"

She stooped to kiss him, and then sat facing him across the table.

"I wanted to ask something."

"Have some breakfast while you're asking." Thomas, hearing voices, was already on his way, bearing a tray with another dish of papaya, freshly made toast, and Judith's pot of China tea. This morning it was a frangipani blossom that he had tucked behind his ear.

"Thank you, Thomas."

Gold teeth flashed a smile. "And a boil' egg?"

"No. Just papaya."

Thomas arranged the table to his satisfaction, and retreated.

"What do you want to ask?"

Grey-haired, deeply tanned, showered, shaved, and dressed in clean whites, with his Rear Admiral's epaulettes heavy with gold braid, Bob both looked and smelt incredibly toothsome.

"I must do some shopping. Would it be all right if I borrowed the car, and for Azid to drive me?"

"Of course. You didn't need to get up so early to ask."

"I thought I'd better. Anyway, I was awake." She yawned. "Where's David Beatty?"

"Already left. Got an early meeting this morning. What are you going to buy?"

"Some clothes. I haven't a thing to wear."

"I've heard that one before."

"It's true. Hugo's asked me out again and I've run out of dresses. Something of a problem."

"What's the problem? Haven't you got any money?"

"Yes, I'm all right for cash. It's just that I've never been much of a shopper, and I don't know if I'm very good at it."

"I thought all women were good at shopping."

"That's a generalization. Everything needs practice, even shopping. Mummy was always a bit timid when we had to go and buy things, and she never had much to spend at the best of times. And by the time Biddy and I were living together, the war was on and it was all clothes coupons and horrible utility frocks. Much easier to make do and mend." She reached for the pot and poured a cup of scalding tea. "The only person I ever knew who was really experienced and expert was Diana Carey-Lewis. She used to whiz through Harvey Nichol's and Debenham and Freebody's like a hot knife through butter, and the shop assistants never got cross or bored with her."

He was laughing at her. "Do you think they're going to get cross and bored with you?"

"No. But it would be nice to have a really resolute girl-friend to come with me."

"I'm afraid I can't oblige, but I am sure that despite your lack of experience you will do very well. What time do you want to start?"

"Before it gets too hot. About nine?"

"I'll tell Thomas to tell Azid. Now, my car will be waiting, so I must go. Have a good day."

Her memories of the streets and shops of Colombo were vague and of their precise location even vaguer. But she told Azid to take her to Whiteaway & Laidlaw, the store that Molly had used to patronize, gravitating in its direction much as ladies, in London, gravitated towards Harrods. Once there, he unloaded her onto the hot and crowded pavement, and asked when he should return to pick her up.

Standing in the blazing sunshine, bumped and barged by passers-by, Judith considered. "About eleven? Eleven o'clock."

"I will be waiting." He pointed down at his feet. "Here."

She went up the steps, under the shade of the deep awning, and in through the doorway. At first, confusion. But then she got her bearings and climbed the stairs, and found her way to the dress department, an Aladdin's cave of mirrors and models, racks and rails and an overwhelming profusion of clothes. She couldn't think where she should start, and was standing dithering, in the middle of the floor, when she was rescued by the approach of a salesgirl, neat in a black skirt and a little white blouse. A bird-boned Eurasian, with huge dark eyes and black hair tied in a ribbon.

"Would you like me to help you?" she asked diffidently, and after that things got a bit easier. *What did you want to buy?* she was asked, and she tried to think. Dresses, to go to cocktail parties. Perhaps a long dress for dancing. Cotton dresses for daytime wear . . . ?

"We have everything. You are very slim. Come, and we will look."

Garments were scooped at random from racks and cupboards, piled on the salesgirl's arm. "You must try them all on." In a curtained changing-room Judith stripped off her shirt and cotton skirt, and suffered dress after dress to be slipped over her head, admired, considered, and then removed as yet another was produced. Silks and cottons and fine voiles; brilliant peacock shades, and pastels and the stark simplicity of white and of black. A ball gown of Indian pink sari silk, with gold stars embroidered around its hem. A cocktail dress of azure blue crêpe de Chine, splashed with huge white flowers. A sheath of wheat-coloured shantung, very simple and sophisticated; and then a black dress, made of mousseline-de-soie, its gauzy skirts lined with petticoats and a huge white organza collar framing the deep neckline . . .

It was agonizing to have to choose, but in the end she bought the ball gown and three of the cocktail dresses (including the irresistible black with the white collar). As well, three dresses for daytime and a sun-frock with a halter neck.

By now all reservations had melted, and Judith had the bit between her teeth. New dresses necessitated new accessories. Purposefully, she set off in search of the shoe department, where she bought sandals and brightly coloured pumps, and a pair of wicked black sling-backs with four-inch heels, to wear with the black dress. Moving on, she found handbags, one gold and one black for evening, and a beautiful soft red hide shoulder-bag. Then scarves and bracelets, a kashmir shawl, dark glasses, and a brown leather belt with a chased silver buckle.

Back on the ground floor now, the cosmetic department, scented and glittering with seduction, counters stacked with pastel-coloured boxes and jars, cut-glass bottles of perfume, golden lipsticks and jewelled compacts, and swansdown powder-puffs set in drifts of chiffon. Mouth-watering. She had long ago used up the last of her supplies of Elizabeth Arden, and Trincomalee did not boast so much as a proper chemist's shop. So she bought lipsticks and scent, and talcum powder and soap, and eyebrow pencils and eye-shadow and mascara, and bath-oil and shampoo and nail varnish and hand cream . . .

She was late for Azid, but he waited there, as she staggered forth into the street, laden with boxes and bags and parcels. Seeing her, he sprang forward to relieve her of her baggage, stow it all in the back of the car, and hold the door open so that she could climb in, to collapse wilting onto the sizzling leather seat.

He jumped behind the wheel and slammed shut his door. In the driving mirror he caught her eye and smiled.

"You have had a good time?"

"Yes, Azid. Thank you. I'm sorry I kept you waiting."

"It is not important."

Driving back to the Galle Road, with white-wrapped packages piled about her, the windows of the car open and the breeze cooling her sweaty face, Judith realized two things. One was that, for at least two hours, she had not thought about Molly, nor Dad, nor Jess. The other was that, although hot and exhausted, she also felt both stimulated and . . . sleek. There was no other word. She mulled over this for a bit, and then came to the conclusion that for the first time in her life, she understood the compulsion that drove women to shop; to buy and spend money, and accumulate about them a plethora of material possessions, luxurious and even unnecessary.

It seemed that shopping could provide consolation if one was unhappy; a buzz of excitement if one was bored; self-indulgence if one had been rejected. Extravagant and frivolous maybe, but better surely than self-pity, turning for comfort to casual lovers, or taking to the bottle.

She found herself smiling. The black dress was delicious. She must go shopping again.

And then remembered all the money she had spent, and added a prudent rider. *But not too often.*

Darkness had fallen. Beyond the open windows a palm tree was silhouetted against a blue velvet sky, pricked with the first stars. Judith sat at her dressing-table and fixed an earring. From the veranda, where Bob Somerville sat, with a whisky and soda and his pipe, came the sound of a piano, dimmed by distance and the closed door, the faint notes seeping through the house like drops of water. He had put a record on his gramophone, music still his constant pleasure and solace. She paused to listen. Rachmaninoff's "Theme on Paganini." She reached for the other earring. With that secured, chose one of the new lipsticks, unscrewed the golden case, and concentrating, carefully painted her mouth. Her reflection, in the soft light, gazed back at her; grey eyes fringed with darkened lashes, smudged shadows beneath her cheekbones, the curve of reddened lips. She had washed her hair, and it lay sleek and short on her head, bleached blonde by the sun.

Perfume. The new bottle. L'Heure Bleu. She touched the stopper to the base of her neck, the insides of her wrists. The scent filled her nostrils and induced a sensation of almost sybaritic luxury, and all at once she thought of Diana Carey-Lewis, and how she would appreciate and approve of this new and sophisticated Judith.

She stood, dropped her robe from her shoulders and let it fall to the floor, slid her feet into the high-heeled sling-backs, and then went to pick up the dress which she had laid out on her bed. She put it on, letting it slip over her head, settled the skirts which billowed filmy as black clouds, and then, in all innocence, reached for the zip.

A real predicament. The zip ran all the way up the back of the bodice and proved impossible to negotiate by the person who happened to be wearing the dress. The salesgirl that morning had zipped her into it and out of it, and Judith had not foreseen a problem. But this was clearly a dress that required the assistance of another person. A lady's-maid, perhaps, or a husband, or even a resident lover. But Judith was the possessor of none of these useful appendages, so it would have to be Bob. She picked up the black evening bag and went out of the room and down the passage in search of him, her high heels tap-tapping on the marble floor, and the weightless dress slipping off her shoulders.

He lay in a long chair, with a single lamp for illumination, his whisky to hand, his pipe for company, and Rachmaninoff. He looked so peaceful that it seemed a shame to disturb him.

"Bob?"

"Hello."

"You have to do up my zip."

He laughed and pulled himself up into a sitting position, and she knelt with her back to him, and he zipped her up with all the expertise of an old married man. Then she stood, and turned to face him. She felt, suddenly, a bit self-conscious.

"Do you like it?"

"Sensational. Did you buy it this morning?"

"Yes. It was frightfully expensive but I couldn't resist it. And new shoes too. And a new handbag."

"You look a million dollars. And you said you didn't know how to shop!"

"It wasn't too difficult. I learned." She sat facing him, at the end of his long chair. "Heavenly Rachmaninoff. I wish you were coming too."

"Where are you off to?"

"Some ship. I think an Australian destroyer."

"Oh, *that* party. Between you, me, and the gatepost, I received an invitation, but declined. Said I'd got a previous engagement. So don't blow the gaff on me."

"I won't. I promise."

"I'm getting a bit long in the tooth for all these late nights. Need an evening to myself every now and again. Early night."

"If you have an early night how shall I get *out* of my dress?"

"You can ask Thomas to unzip you. He's sure to wait up until you come home."

"Won't he be embarrassed?"

"Nothing embarrasses Thomas."

A doorbell pealed. They sat and waited. Heard Thomas padding across the hall to open the front door.

"Good evening, sahib."

"Good evening, Thomas."

"The Admiral is on the veranda."

"Thank you. I'll find my way."

An instant later and he was there, stepping out into the dusk from the bright lights of indoors, wearing Number Tens and looking immensely distinguished. He carried his hat under his arm.

Judith smiled up at him. "Hello, Hugo."

He was offered a drink, but politely declined. They were running a bit late anyway, and would be bombarded with cocktails once they got on board.

"On your way then." Bob heaved himself to his feet. "I'll see you off." He clearly could not wait to be rid of the pair of them and be left in peace with his pipe and his gramophone. He walked them to the front door. Judith kissed him good night, and assured him that she would enjoy herself. They got into Hugo's car and set off for their evening out. As they drove out through the gate, Bob closed the door behind them.

There was a full moon that evening, round and silver as a plate, rising in the east over the roof-tops of the city, and they drove the length of the Galle Road, across the Fort to the harbour on the far side.

An Australian destroyer was berthed at the dockside, her Quarterdeck sparkling with strings of lights, and the cocktail party already in full swing, so that Judith followed Hugo up a gangplank to the buzz of voices and the chink of glasses. It was much the same as the other party, the one that she had come to with Bob, and some of the same faces too, recognizable, but without remembered names to attach them to. Hugo, hand at her elbow, steered her in the direction of the Captain, and they introduced themselves and made the correct noises of appreciation. They were given drinks and offered canapés by attentive hovering stewards. After that, it was down to the old routine of social conversation, fairly meaningless but not unenjoyable.

Presently, Judith, separated from Hugo but quite happily talking to two young Australian lieutenants, felt a hand like a vice close around her wrist, and turning found herself faced by a weather-beaten lady in a tight peacock-coloured dress. "My dear . . . we've met. Bob Somerville introduced us the other evening. Moira Burridge. And you're Judith Dunbar. Divine dress, I love it. Where is the heavenly man?"

Her grip had loosened slightly, and Judith was able to slide her wrist free. One of the young Australian lieutenants, making polite excuses, moved away. The other stayed, stoic, at Judith's side, his smile fixed, as though pleased. "Must find him." Moira Burridge stood tiptoe (she was not tall) and peered around, over other people's heads. She had enormous eyes, pale as grapes, and her mascara was beginning to melt and smudge. "Can't see him anywhere, the brute."

"He . . . he didn't come. A previous engagement."

"Oh, bloody hell. Half the fun of these dos is having a crack with Bob." Disappointed, she returned her attention to Judith. "Who brought *you* then?"

"Hugo Halley."

"*Hugo?*" She was the sort of person who, talking, pushed her face very close to one's own. Judith's instinct was to back away, as discreetly as she could, but Moira Burridge simply pressed nearer. "When did you meet Hugo? You've only been here for about two minutes. You're staying with Bob, aren't you? How long are you going to be in Colombo? You must come and see us. We'll have a party. Now, what day would suit, I wonder . . . ?"

Judith murmured something about not being quite sure what Bob was doing . . .

"I'll give Bob a ring. We've got a flat in the Fort. Rodney's on the staff . . ." A thought occurred to her. "You know Rodney, don't you?" Judith felt a bit of Moira Burridge's spit land on her cheek, but was too well mannered to wipe it away. "You don't? I'll point him out to you . . ."

A steward passed by with a tray of drinks, and as he did so, Moira Burridge, quick as a flash, set down her empty glass and helped herself to a full one.

". . . he's over there." She hadn't even paused to draw breath. "Talking to that two-and-a-half-striper in the Indian Navy." Judith, with some difficulty, located Captain Burridge. He was an enormously tall man with a bald head and a face the shape of a pear, but before she could come up with any suitable comment, Moira Burridge was off again.

"Now, tell me. I haven't got you worked out yet. Some sort of relation, I know. Out from England, or have I got totally the wrong end of the stick?"

Judith said something about Trincomalee.

"Oh, don't say you're stationed *there*. Poor wretch. Ghastly spot. Mosquitoes. Can't imagine why I thought you'd come out from Home. We've got sprogs at home, both at boarding-school. Spend hols with my mother. Haven't seen the poor little brutes for two years . . ."

The only good thing about talking to Moira Burridge was that one was clearly not expected to make any sort of response. From time to time Judith nodded, or shook her head, or smiled faintly, but otherwise Mrs. Burridge, well-oiled by alcohol, simply rattled ceaselessly, pointlessly on. It felt a bit like being run over by a train. Judith, trapped, began to be desperate.

Hugo, where are you? Come quickly and rescue me.

". . . but to be honest, I'm not *actually* looking forward all that much to getting back to England. We've got a house in Petersfield, but it'll be rations and no petrol and *rain*. Worst of all, no servants. We're all so bloody spoilt out here. Where are you dining after this do? Why don't we all join up and have a bite at the Grand Oriental . . . ?"

Horrors.

"Judith." He had come, and not before time. She felt faint with relief. His charming smile was beamed upon Moira Burridge.

"Good evening, Mrs. Burridge, and how are you? Just been having a word with your husband . . ."

"Hugo, you devil. Trust you to be squiring the prettiest girl on board. Just suggesting, how about joining up for dinner? We're going to the GOH . . ."

"How terribly kind." Hugo's expression became one of deep regret. "But I'm afraid we can't. We've been asked out for dinner, and we're late already. I think, Judith, perhaps we should take our leave . . ."

"Oh, what a bloody shame. Have you really got to go? We were having such a good time, weren't we, dear? A real old gas and still masses to talk about." By now she was teetering slightly on her wobbly high heels. "Never mind, there'll be another time. We'll get together then . . ."

Finally, Judith and Hugo managed to ease away. At the head of the gangplank, Judith glanced back and saw that Mrs. Burridge had once more replenished her glass, cornered yet another reluctant guest, and was off again, in full flow.

Safe on the dockside and out of earshot of the Officer of the Watch, "I've never in all my life met such a dreadful woman," she told Hugo.

"I'm sorry. I should have looked after you better." He took her arm and they began to pick their way across the dock, stepping around cranes and crates, and over mammoth cables and chains. "She's a famous menace. I'd be sorry for poor Rodney, except that he's such a boring old fart that he deserves her."

"I thought I was going to spend the rest of the evening with her."

"I wouldn't have allowed you to do that."

"I was planning a really bad headache. A migraine. Hugo, I didn't know that we'd been asked out for dinner."

"We haven't. But I've booked a table at the Salamander, and I didn't want Moira Burridge to know, because otherwise she'd have tried to come too."

"I've never heard of the Salamander."

"It's a private club. I'm a member. We can have dinner and dance. Unless, of course, you'd prefer the GOH with the Burridges? I can always nip back and tell them we've changed our minds."

"You do that and I'll shoot you."

"In that case, the Salamander it is."

They had left his car by the dockyard gates. They got back into it, and set off, leaving the Fort and driving south into a district of wide streets and old Dutch houses that was unfamiliar to Judith. Ten minutes, and they had arrived. An impressive gabled building, set back off the street, with a high gate and a circular driveway leading to the main door. Very discreet; no signs, no flashing lights. There was a doorman, in a green uniform and a magnificent turban, and another minion to park the car. They went up the wide stairway, and through the carved doorway into a marble foyer with pillars and a wonderfully ornate ceiling. Then through another pair of doors, and so to a large enclosed courtyard, open to the sky and surrounded by wide terraces, for dining. In the centre was the dance floor. Most of the tables were already occupied, each lit by a red-shaded lamp, but the dance floor's only illumination was the huge rising moon. A band was playing. South American music. A samba, or a rumba or something. A number of couples circled the floor, some expert, others less so but doing their best to keep time and beat with the insidious rhythm.

"Commander Halley." The head-waiter, in starched jacket and white sarong, came to greet them. They were led to their table, settled in chairs, and huge napkins were unfolded and laid on their laps. The menus were produced. The head-waiter, soft-footed, moved away.

Across the table, their eyes met.

"Is this all right for you?" he asked.

"Amazing. I'd no idea such a place existed."

"It's only been going six months. With a very limited membership. I was lucky enough to get in on the ground floor. Now there's a waiting list."

"Who runs it?"

"Oh, some guy. Half-Portuguese, I think."

"It's a bit like something out of an enormously romantic film."

He laughed. "That isn't why I brought you."

"Why did you bring me?"

"For the food, you ninny."

Presently the head-waiter returned with the wine-waiter in tow, bearing a silver ice bucket containing a large frosted green bottle.

Judith was amazed. "When did you order that?"

"When I reserved the table."

"It's not *champagne*, is it? It couldn't be *champagne*?"

"No, but it's the best I could do. Sahtheffrican."

"Sorry?"

"South African. From the Cape. A humble little sparkling white wine with no background and no pretensions. A true wine buff would sneer. But I think it's delicious."

The cork was drawn, the wine poured, the bucket left by their table. Judith lifted her long-stemmed glass. "Your health," said Hugo, and she took a single mouthful, and if it wasn't champagne, then it was just about the next best thing. Chilled, sparkling with bubbles, deliciously fresh.

He set down his glass and said, "Now. I have two things to say to you before another moment passes."

"What have you got to say?"

"First . . . is something I should perhaps have said before. It's just that you really are incredibly lovely."

She was much touched by this. As well, a bit embarrassed and confused. "Oh, Hugo."

"Now, don't get all flustered. English women are notoriously bad at dealing with compliments. American women, on the other hand, are particularly good at it. They accept kind words and appreciation as no more than their due."

"Well, that's very kind of you. The dress is new."

"It's enchanting."

"What's the second thing? You said you had two things to say."

"That's a bit different."

"So?"

He set down his glass and leaned forward across the table. He said, "I know about your family. I know that you have just been told that none of them survived . . . after Singapore. I know that you have been waiting for three and a half years for news; only to be told that there is no longer any hope. I am so very sorry. And if you want, we won't talk about it again. But I didn't want to start the evening without you knowing that I know. I didn't want words, unsaid, to lie between us, like something we would have to circle . . . a sort of forbidden area."

After a bit, Judith said, "No. No, you're quite right. Perhaps I should have been the first to say something. It's just that I don't find it very easy . . ."

He waited and then, when she didn't finish, said, "I don't mind you talking about it, if you want to."

"I don't, particularly."

"Right."

A thought occurred to her. "Who told you?" she asked.

"Admiral Somerville."

"Did he tell you *before* we met? I mean, did you always know?"

"No, not until last Sunday, when I took you back to the Galle Road after we'd been swimming. You disappeared for ten minutes or so to get changed, and he and I had a bit of time together on our own. He told me then."

"You didn't say anything to me."

"Not an appropriate moment."

"I'm glad you didn't know before. Otherwise I would suspect that you were just being kind."

"I don't understand."

"Oh, you know. *I'm bringing my rather sad niece to a party. I want you to look after her.*"

Hugo laughed. "I promise you. I'm not much use with sad nieces. Run a mile if I see one."

There was a little pause.

And then he said, "So that's it. Subject closed. Over and out?"

"Better that way."

"Talk about something else. When do you go back to Trincomalee?"

"Not for three weeks. I have to report for duty on the Monday morning. Bob's going to see if he can get me a lift up to Kandy, and then I'll go on from there."

"Why don't you fly?"

"It would have to be an RAF plane, and it's not easy getting rides."

"Do you want to go back?"

"Not particularly. The urgency's gone out of it all now. Since the war's finished I suppose it'll just be a case of winding everything down, people gradually being sent home. I think *Adelaide*—that's the submarine depot ship I've been working in—and the Fourth Flotilla will probably get sent to Australia. So I'll have to go to some shore-based job." She reached for her glass, took another mouthful of the delicious wine, and then laid the glass down again. "I've actually had enough of it all," she admitted. "What I would really like to do is to hop on a troop-ship and go home *now*. But that's unlikely to happen."

"And when it does happen? What will you do then?"

"Go home." She had told him about Cornwall, and the Dower House, and Biddy Somerville and Phyllis, that day when they had sat on the beach at Mount Lavinia, and watched the un-swimmable-in breakers pounding up onto the sand. "And I shan't look for a job and I shan't do anything that I don't want to do. I shall grow my hair until it reaches my waist, and go to bed when I want, and get up when I want, and stay out carousing until the small hours. I've lived with rules and regulations for the whole of my life. School; the war; the Wrens. And I'm twenty-four, Hugo. Don't you agree it's about time I sowed a wild oat or two?"

"I certainly do. But everybody of your age has been hit by the war. A whole generation. What you have to realize is that for some others it had the very opposite effect. A sort of release. From conventional backgrounds, dead-end jobs, limited horizons." Judith thought of Cyril Eddy, seizing the opportunity to leave the tin-mine and realize, at last, his life's ambition of going to sea. "I know at least two women, well-bred, and married in their early twenties simply because they couldn't think of anything else to do. Then the war, and relieved of deadly husbands and with access to Free French, Free Poles, and Free Norwegians—to say nothing of the United States Army—they proceeded to have the time of their lives."

"Will they go back to their husbands?"

"I expect so. Older and wiser women."

Judith laughed. "Oh, well. Nobody's the same."

"And it would be a dull world if we were."

She thought he was being very wise. "How old are you?" she asked.

"Thirty-four."

"Did you never want to get married?"

"Dozens of times. But not in wartime. I never relished the prospect of being killed, but I would hate to die knowing that I was leaving behind a widow and a string of fatherless children."

"But now the war's over."

"True. But my future is still with the Navy. Unless I get passed over or made redundant, or put into moth-balls and a deadly shore job . . ."

The head-waiter returned then to take their order, which involved a bit of time because they hadn't even got around to scanning the menu. In the end, they both chose the same things, shellfish and chicken, and the waiter refilled their glasses and padded away once more.

For a moment they fell silent. Then Judith sighed.

"What's that for?" Hugo asked.

"I don't know. The thought of having to return to Trincomalee, I suppose. A bit like going back to boarding-school."

"Don't think about it."

She made up her mind. "No, I won't. And I don't know how we got onto this rather serious conversation."

"Probably my fault. So let's put an end to it now, and start being frivolous."

"I don't quite know how to begin."

"You could tell me a joke, or ask me a riddle."

"Pity we haven't got any paper hats."

"But that would make us conspicuous. If we make an exhibition of ourselves, I might get all my buttons cut off and be asked to leave. Think of the scandal. Drummed out of the Salamander. Moira Burridge would love it, give her something to talk about for months."

"She'd say, serves us right for telling lies and being unfriendly."

"I think we should make plans for the next three weeks, and not waste a moment. So that you return to Trincomalee with a light in your eye and a host of happy memories. I shall take you to Negombo, and show you the Old Portuguese Fort. It's particularly beautiful. And we shall swim at Panadura, which is a beach straight out of *The Blue Lagoon*. And perhaps drive up to Ratanapura. In the rest-house there, old soup plates sit around on tables, filled with sapphires. I shall buy you one, to pin in your nostril. What else do you like doing? Sporting activities? We could play tennis."

"I haven't got my racquet."

"I shall borrow one for you."

"It depends. Are you frightfully good?"

"Brilliant. The picture of manly grace as I leap the net to congratulate the winner."

The band was playing again. Not South American music now, but an old smoochy tune, the melody carried by the tenor saxophone.

> *I can't give you anything but love, baby*
> *That's the only thing I've plenty of, baby . . .*

Abruptly, Hugo stood. "Come and dance."

They stepped down onto the floor, and she turned into his arms. He danced, as she had suspected he would, with easy expertise, neither shifting from foot to foot, nor steering her around the floor like a vacuum cleaner, two hazards that Judith had learned, over the years, to deal with. He held her very close, his head bent so that their cheeks touched. And he didn't talk. And there was no need to say anything.

> *Gee, I'd like to see you looking swell, baby.*
> *Diamond bracelets Woolworth's couldn't sell, baby.*
> *Till that lucky day, you know darn well, baby,*
> *I can't give you anything but love.*

Over his shoulder she looked up into the face of the moon, and felt as though, for a moment, she was being touched by the very edge of happiness.

Half past two in the morning, and he drove her back to the Galle Road. The sentry opened the gates for them, and the car rolled through and around the curve of the driveway, to draw up in front of the portico of the main door. They got out. The air was scented with Temple flowers, and the moon so bright that garden shadows lay black as Indian ink. At the foot of the steps, Judith paused and turned to him. She said, "Thank you, Hugo. It was a lovely evening. All of it."

"Even Mrs. Burridge?"

"At least she gave us a laugh." She hesitated for an instant and then said, "Good night."

He put his hands on her arms, and stooped to kiss her. It was a long time since she had been kissed so thoroughly. And even longer since she had so thoroughly enjoyed it. She put her arms around him, and responded with a sort of grateful passion.

The front door opened, and they were caught in a wedge of yellow electric light. They drew apart, amused and not in the least abashed, and saw Thomas standing at the head of the steps, his dark features betraying neither disapproval nor satisfaction. Then Hugo apologized for keeping him up so late, and Thomas smiled, the moonlight glinting on his gold teeth.

Judith said again, "Good night," and went up the steps and through the open door. Thomas followed, closing and bolting the heavy locks behind him.

After that, the days slipped past, flowing faster as each succeeded another, so that, in the manner of all pleasurable vacations, before one even had time to notice, the days had turned into a week, and then another week, and another. Now, it was the eighteenth of September. Three more days, and it would be time to start out on the long journey back to Trincomalee; to typing endless reports and having to return to Quarters on time; to no shops and no sophisticated city bustle. No lovely, orderly house to come back to. No Thomas. No Bob. And no Hugo.

He had kept his word. *We mustn't waste a moment,* he had said. Even better, he had betrayed no regret at having promised in the first place. Never bored, he was never boring, and although patently delighted by her company and gratifyingly appreciative of the time Judith spent with him, Hugo had remained endearingly undemanding, so that she was able to feel safe and protected, and never for a moment besieged.

By now, they had become so close and so at ease, that they were even able to talk this through, lying on the deserted, blistering sands of Panadura, and letting the sun dry them off after a swim. ". . . it's not that I don't find you enchantingly attractive, and it's not that I don't want to make love to you. And I think that if I did, it could be deeply pleasurable for both of us. But this isn't the right time. You're too vulnerable. Like a convalescent, you need a bit of peace. Time to lick your wounds, get back on course again. The last thing you need is the trauma of a physical involvement. A thoughtless affair."

"It wouldn't be thoughtless, Hugo."

"But, perhaps, foolish. It's up to you."

He was right. The thought of having to make *any* sort of a decision was a bit frightening. She just wanted to sail along on an even keel, drift with the tide. She said, "It's not that I'm a virgin, Hugo."

"Darling girl, I didn't for a moment imagine that you were."

"I've slept with two men. And both of them I loved very much. And both of them I lost. Since then, I've steered clear of loving. It hurt too much. It took too long to heal."

"I would try very hard not to hurt you. But I don't want to mess about with your emotions. Not right now. I've become too fond of you."

"If I could stay in Colombo . . . if I didn't have to go back to Trincomalee . . . if we had more time . . ."

"What a lot of ifs. Would it make things so different?"

"Oh, Hugo, I don't know."

He lifted her hand and pressed a kiss into her palm. "I don't know either. So let's go and swim again."

Azid turned the car in through the open gate, past the sentry and around the curve of the drive, to draw up at the front door. He switched off the engine, and before Judith could do it for herself, had leaped out and snatched her door open.

His attentions always made her feel a bit like Royalty.

"Thank you, Azid."

It was half past five in the evening. She made her way up the steps and through the front door, and across the cool hall and the empty drawing-room, and so out onto the flower-decked veranda. There she found—as she had known she would—both Bob Somerville and David Beatty, relaxed in long chairs after a day's work and enjoying their moment of companionable quiet. Between their chairs stood a low table, set with all the traditional paraphernalia of afternoon tea.

David Beatty was deep in one of his enormous scholarly tomes, and Bob read the London *Times,* sent out each week by airmail. He was still in uniform. White shorts, shirt, long white stockings and white shoes. When he had read the paper, he would go and have a shower and shave and change. But first, he liked to pause for his afternoon tea, a daily ritual that he relished, it being a comforting reminder of the simple domestic pleasures of home, England, and a far-away wife.

He looked up, and dropped the paper. "There you are! I was wondering what had happened to you. Pull up a chair. Have a cup of tea. Thomas has conjured up some cucumber sandwiches."

"How very civilized. Good afternoon, David."

David Beatty stirred and blinked, saw Judith, lowered his book, snatched off his spectacles, and made as if to gather his lanky frame out of his chair and rise. It was a courteous pantomime that took place every time she caught him unawares, and she had become adept at saying, "Don't get up," just before his shoes hit the floor.

"Sorry. Reading . . . didn't hear . . ." He smiled, just to show there was no ill feeling, replaced his spectacles, dissolved back onto the cushions, and returned to his book. Lost to the world. Idle conversation had never been his strong point.

Bob poured tea into the fine white cup, dropped in a slice of lemon, and handed it over.

"You've been playing tennis," he observed.

"How could you tell?"

"My powers of observation and deduction plus the sporty white gear and the racquet."

"Brilliant."

"Where did you play?"

"At the club. With Hugo and another couple. Serious stuff."

"Who won?"

"We did, of course."

"Are you going out tonight?"

"No. Hugo's got to go to some Guest Night at the Barracks. Men only."

"That means too much to drink and dangerous after-dinner horseplay. When you see him next he'll probably have a broken leg. Before I forget, I've fixed that lift to Kandy for you. A car, next Saturday morning. They'll pick you up here, at eight o'clock."

Judith received this information with mixed emotions. She screwed up her face like a child. "I don't want to go."

"Don't want you to go. I'll miss you like hell. But there it is. Stiff upper lip. Duty calls. And talking of duty, I have another message. From Chief Officer Wrens, no less. She rang me this afternoon. Asked if you'd be available tomorrow morning, and if so, if she could ask you to help."

"Help do what?" Judith asked cautiously. She had been in the service long enough to know that one never volunteered for anything, until in possession of all the details. She took a cucumber sandwich and bit into its sweet crunchiness.

"Go and be welcoming to a lot of chaps who deserve it."

"I don't understand."

"There's a ship stopping off, en route for England. The *Orion*. A hospital ship. The first batch of prisoners of war from the Bangkok-Burma Railway. They've been in hospital in Rangoon. They're being allowed ashore here for a few hours, their first step back to civilization. There's going to be some sort of a reception for them at the Fort. Tea and buns, I suppose. Chief Officer's rounding up a few Wrens to act as hostesses, chat the men up and make them feel at home."

"What did you say?"

"Told her I'd have to discuss it with you. I explained that you'd only just been told that your father died in Changi, and perhaps meeting up with a lot of emaciated prisoners would be a bit close to home."

Judith nodded. She had finished her sandwich, and now, absently, took another. Prisoners of war from the Burma Railway. At the end of the war, when the Army moved in with the medical services, the Red Cross (and Lady Mountbatten) hard on their heels, the railway camps had been opened and their horrors exposed. Reports and photographs in the newspapers had stirred waves of disbelief and revulsion only matched by the reaction of the Western world, a universal lowering of the human spirit, when the Allied Armies, moving east, had uncovered the camps at Auschwitz, Dachau, and Ravensbrück.

On the railway, thousands of men had died, those who survived labouring in the steaming jungle for as long as eighteen hours a day. Brutal guards had kept the sick working, despite weakness from hunger, exhaustion, malaria, and the dysentery brought about by the filthy conditions in which the prisoners had been housed.

But now, they were coming home.

She sighed. "I'll *have* to go. If I don't, I shan't be able to look myself in the eye for the rest of my life. It would be dreadfully feeble."

"You never know. It might make you feel better about things."

"After what they've endured, you'd wonder that *any* of them would be fit enough to even come ashore . . ."

"They've had a little time in hospital being cared for, properly fed. And families alerted that they're alive and on their way back . . ."

"What do I have to do?"

"Climb into uniform, and muster at nine o'clock."

"Where?"

"The Galle Road Wrennery. You'll get your orders there."

"Right."

"You're a good girl. Have another cup of tea. And you'll be dining this evening with David and me? I'll tell Thomas that there will be three of us."

That morning, having showered and wrapped herself in her thin robe, Judith had breakfasted on her own, because Bob and David Beatty had already left for work. Breakfast was a grapefruit and China tea. No more. For some reason she wasn't feeling particularly hungry. After breakfast, she went back to her room, and found that Thomas had laid out her clean uniform on the freshly made bed, with cap and shoes blancoed to blinding whiteness.

She dressed, and it felt a bit like that last day in Trincomalee when, loaded with apprehension, she had put on clean uniform and walked down the dusty road to keep her appointment with First Officer. Now, into battle again. She did up buttons, laced her shoes, combed her hair, put on her hat, lipstick, and scent. She thought about taking a bag, and then decided against it. No need. She would be home by midday. But, just in case of emergencies, took from her purse a bundle of rupee notes and stuffed them into the pocket of her skirt.

In the hall, she found Thomas, waiting for her by the open door.

"You would like Azid to drive you?"

"No, Thomas, thank you, I can walk. It's only a few hundred yards down the road."

"It is very good, what you are going to do. Brave men. Those Japanese, by God! I should like you to tell them they have been very brave."

His dark face was suffused with anguish, and Judith felt much touched by his little outburst.

"Yes. You're quite right. And I'll tell them."

She walked out into the glare and the heat, through the gate and down the busy road. Presently the Wrens' Quarters loomed into view, a large Edwardian edifice, white and ornate as a wedding cake, double-storeyed and with a flat roof, crowned by an ornamental balustrade. Once it had been the home of a wealthy merchant, but now had lost a little of its lustre, and the gardens which surrounded it—extensive grounds with walks and lawns—had been built over with palm-thatch bandas and ablution blocks.

She went in through the gate, and the young sentry gave her an appreciative grin and crack of his head. She saw the lorry parked on the gravel, the able seaman behind the wheel deep in an old copy of *Tidbits*. She went up shallow steps, under the shade of an impressive porch and into the lofty hall, which now did duty as a Regulating Office. There were desks, and pigeonholes for mail, and a number of Wrens already there, standing about, and waiting to be told what to do. A young Third Officer seemed to be in charge, with a Leading Wren at her elbow for moral support. She was having some difficulty with names and numbers.

"There are meant to be fourteen Wrens. How many have we got . . . ?" With a pencil in her hand, she endeavoured to count heads. "One. Two . . ."

"Twelve, ma'am." The Leading Wren was clearly the more efficient of the two.

"Two more to come, then." She caught sight of Judith, hovering on the edge of the little group. "Who are you?"

"Dunbar, ma'am."

"Where from?"

"HMS *Adelaide*, Trincomalee. I'm on leave."

"Dunbar." The Third Officer scanned her list. "Oh yes, here you are. Tick you off. But we're still missing one." She looked anxiously at her watch. All this responsibility was clearly getting her down. "She's late . . ."

"No, I'm not." The final volunteer, bursting through the open door, reporting for duty. "It's only five to nine." A small, sturdy girl, brown as a berry, with bright, amused blue eyes and short dark hair which curled around the tally-band of her hat.

"Oh. Good. Well done." Her confident manner had knocked the young Third Officer a bit off course. "Er . . . are you Sudlow?"

"That's right. HMS *Lanka*. I got the morning off."

Finally, it was decided that they were all mustered and ready to go. Orders were given. The lorry would take them to the Fort, where the ex-prisoners would disembark from tenders.

"Why not the dockside?" asked one girl.

"We'd have to arrange buses to transport the men to the Fort. This way, they can walk to Gordon's Green, it's only a short distance. There's a slipway there and jetty. Then, when they're ashore, you meet them and talk to them, and escort them to where the tents have been put up, and refreshments will be served."

"Beer?" Wren Sudlow inquired hopefully.

"No," she was told dismissively. "Tea and buns, and sandwiches and such. Any more questions?"

"How long do we have to stay?"

"As long as you feel you're being of use. Make sure they're enjoying themselves, being led. Put them at ease."

"Is it just *us*, ma'am?" another girl asked, sounding a bit dismayed.

"No, of course not. There'll be nurses from the hospital, and a contingent from the Garrison. And I believe a band to play music. And then, at the reception in the tent, senior officers from all three services and one or two local ministers and dignitaries. So you won't be alone." She looked about her. "Everybody understand? Right. Off you go."

"And the best of British luck," Wren Sudlow finished for her, which made everybody laugh except the Third Officer, who pretended that she hadn't heard.

The fourteen girls duly trooped out into the hot sunshine, and the able seaman, hearing their chatter, jumped down out of the cab and came around to the back of the lorry to let down the tail-gate, and give a helpful heave to any person who happened to need one. Boarded, they settled themselves on the wooden benches that ran fore and aft on either side. When all were loaded, like so many cattle, the tail-gate was slammed shut and secured. A moment later, the engine started up and they were off, bouncing and lurching through the gate and up the Galle Road.

It was fairly breezy, because the flaps of the canvas cover had been rolled up and the truck was open on all sides. Judith and Wren Sudlow, being the last to board, sat side by side at the back.

"What a carry-on," said Sudlow. "I didn't think I was going to make it. Tried to get a lift, but I couldn't, so I had to take a rickshaw. That's why I was nearly late." She looked at Judith. "I don't know you, do I? Are you Colombo?"

"No. Trincomalee. I'm on leave."

"Thought I didn't know your face. What's your name?"

"Judith Dunbar."

"I'm Sarah Sudlow."

"Hi."

"Wasn't that Third Officer pathetic? Wet as a scrubber. I'm not much looking forward to this, are you? Tea and buns in an Army tent doesn't sound like much of a reception after what those poor chaps have been through."

"I don't suppose they're up to dealing with too much excitement."

Behind them the Galle Road, wide and busy with traffic, streamed dustily away between the avenues of tall palm trees. Judith watched it go, and thought of her father, living in Colombo, driving this way day after day, to and from the offices of Wilson-McKinnon. She thought of him dying in the filth and hopeless misery that had been Changi, and tried to remember exactly how he had looked, and the sound of his voice, but it wasn't possible. It was all too long ago. Which was a shame, because right now, this morning, she could have done with a bit of fatherly support, a stiffening of the spine. *Dad, if you're there, I'm sort of doing this for you. Don't let me be too useless.*

Beside her, Sarah Sudlow shifted on the hard bench. "God, what I wouldn't give for a fag." Clearly, she felt just as apprehensive as Judith did. "It's a bit of a facer, isn't it? I mean, drumming up things to *say*. Cocktail party chat is scarcely appropriate, and I dread pregnant pauses." She considered the problem and then came up with a bright idea. "Tell you what, much easier if we do it in pairs. And then if one of us runs out of chat, the other can chip in. What do you say? Shall we stick together?"

"Yes, please," said Judith instantly, and at once felt much better. Sarah Sudlow. She could not imagine a stauncher partner in time of stress.

Familiar landmarks wheeled by. The Galle Face Hotel, the Galle Face Green. The lorry rumbled across a bridge, and so along the road that ran by the eastern shore of the Fort. The sea was a shout of blue, stretching to the horizon; and the wind from the south-west, driving in a steady procession of breakers to crash on the rocks. They reached the point, with the lighthouse at its end forming a natural harbour, sheltered from the weather, and where the water lay still. Here were a jetty and a slipway, and, in position nearby, immaculately ranked and standing to attention, the impressive spectacle of a Sikh pipe band in full ceremonial fig: khaki shorts and tunics, and magnificent turbans. Their drum major was a man of majestic height and stature, carrying a huge silver mace, and with a sash of scarlet silk, lavishly fringed, worn over one shoulder and across his chest.

"I didn't know Sikhs played the bagpipes," said Sarah. "I thought they played sitars and strange flutes for charming snakes."

"They look fairly good, though, don't they?"

"I'll reserve my opinion until I hear the sort of noise they make."

The lorry drew to a halt, the tail-gate was opened, and they all climbed down. Others were there before them. The official reception committee: officers from the Garrison and Naval Headquarters, two ambulances and some naval nursing sisters, their white veils and aprons snapping in the breeze.

Inland stood the Clock Tower, the Government buildings, the Queen's House, and various banks and ministries. On the grassy expanse of Gordon's Green (venue for ceremonial occasions such as Beating Retreat or garden parties for visiting Crowned Heads) could be seen the khaki tents erected by the Army. These had been strung with bunting, and overall, at the head of a tall flagpole, flew the Union Jack.

Orion lay at anchor, about a mile offshore.

"Looks a bit like a pre-war liner on a pleasure cruise, doesn't she?" Sarah observed. "Ironic to know that she's really a hospital ship, and most of her passengers are probably too sick or debilitated even to make the trip ashore. Oh goodness, they're actually coming . . ."

Judith looked, and saw, approaching around the lighthouse point, three tenders in line astern, headed for the jetty. Each was packed with men, rendered, by distance and the dazzling sunlight, into a blur of khaki and pale faces.

"There seem to be quite a lot of them, don't there?" Her chatter, Judith knew, was probably nervous, the flow of words unstoppable. "I must say, I find it all a bit bizarre. I mean, trying to relate the ghastly facts to all this *en fête* business. I mean, flags and bands and everything. I just hope they won't be ... *Heavens!*"

She was silenced, appropriately enough, by the voice of the drum major screaming out his first order, and causing Sarah nearly to jump out of her skin. He had clearly been well primed as to timing. The sunlight flashed on his mace, the side-drums rolled, and, as one man, the pipers hoisted their instruments shoulder-high. After that came an eerie, spine-tingling dirge as they filled their bags, pumping air into the reeds. Then they began to play. Not martial marches, but an old Scottish air.

> *Speed bonny boat like a bird on the wing,*
> *Onward the sailors cry . . .*

"Oh God," said Sarah, "I hope I'm not going to blub."

The tenders drew closer, their passengers crammed shoulder to shoulder. Now it was possible to make out the features of the men aboard.

> *Carry the lad who was born to be King*
> *Over the sea to Skye.*

Not particularly bonny boats, and certainly there were no Kings to step ashore, just ordinary men who had survived hell and were returning to the real and familiar world again. But what a way to make their landfall, greeted by the sound of the pipes. Some person, Judith decided, had been inspired. She had heard pipe bands before, of course, over the wireless or newsreels at the cinema, but had never actually been part of it all, watching and hearing the wild music stream out into the wind and the open sky. It, combined with the circumstances of the occasion, sent shivers down her back and she, like Sarah, felt tears behind her eyes.

She willed them away, and said in as normal and steady a voice as possible, "Why are they playing Scottish tunes?"

"Probably the only ones they know. Actually most of the prisoners are Durham Light Infantry, but I think there are some Gordon Highlanders as well."

All Judith's senses pricked. "Gordons?"

"That's what my Second Officer told me."

"I once knew a Gordon Highlander. He was killed at Singapore."

"Maybe you'll meet up with some of his chums."

"I didn't know any of his friends."

The first tender had come alongside and was tying up. Her passengers, in orderly fashion, began to climb up onto the jetty.

Sarah squared her shoulders. "Come on. Don't hang about. This is where we move in. Nice smiles and a cheerful manner."

After all their apprehension, it wasn't difficult at all. Not aliens from another planet, but ordinary young men, and as soon as she heard them speak, in the reassuringly regional accents of Northumberland, Cumberland, and Tyneside, Judith lost all her reservations. Bone-thin, bare-headed, and with features still wearing the pallor of sickness and malnutrition, yet they were all neat and clean, decently kitted out (by the Red Cross in Rangoon?) in jungle-green cotton battledress and canvas lace-up shoes. No badges of rank or seniority, no regimental emblems. Coming down the jetty in twos and threes, they approached slowly, as though not quite certain as to what to expect, but as the white-clad Wrens and nursing sisters mingled amongst them, talking and shaking hands, their shyness melted away.

Hello. I'm Judith. It's good to see you. I'm Sarah. Welcome to Colombo.

We've even organized a band to play for you.

We're so pleased to see you.

Soon each girl had, quite naturally, gathered about her a number of men, all of them clearly relieved to be told what they had to do.

"We're going to take you up to Gordon's Green, where the tents are."

"Grand."

One of the senior nursing sisters clapped her hands, like a schoolteacher trying to attract attention.

"Nobody needs to walk if they don't feel up to it. We've plenty of transport if anyone wants a ride."

But Judith's group, now swelled to about twenty men, said that they would walk.

"Right. Then let's go."

They set off at an unhurried pace, up the gentle slope that rose from the shore. The pipe band was now playing another tune.

> *Come o'er the sea, Charlie, proud Charlie, brave Charlie.*
> *Come o'er the sea, Charlie and welcome McLean.*
> *For though you be weary, we'll make your heart cheery . . .*

The man next to Judith said, "That Sister. Clapping her hands. We had a teacher just like that at home, when I was a lad."

"Where's home?"

"Alnwick."

"Have you been to Colombo before?"

"No. We stopped by on our way to Singapore, but we didn't come ashore. Officers did, but not other ranks. Suppose they thought we might scarper."

Another of the men chipped in. "Wouldn't have been a bad thing if we had." He had scars on his neck from what looked like boils, and he walked with a painful limp.

"Are you all right, walking? Wouldn't you rather bum a lift?"

"Bit of a leg stretch won't hurt."

"Where's *your* home?"

"Near Walsingham. The fells. My dad's a sheep farmer."

"Are you all Durham Light Infantry?"

"That's right."

"Are there some Gordon Highlanders on board?"

"Yes, but they're in the last tender. Following on."

"A bit unfriendly, playing Scottish music for coming ashore. They should have played Northumberland folk songs, specially for you."

"Like what?"

"I don't know. I don't know any."

Another man moved forward. "Do you not know 'When the Boat Comes In'?"

"No. I'm sorry. Very ignorant."

"What did you say your name was?"

"Judith."

"Do you work in Colombo?"

"No, I'm on leave."

"Why aren't you off enjoying yourself then?"

"I am."

Long afterwards, when it was all over, Judith remembered the official reception for the returned prisoners of war much as she recalled School Speech Days, or garden fêtes in England. All the elements of some churchly fundraising were there. The smell of trodden grass, canvas, and over-heated humanity. The Royal Marine band, out on the Green, playing light selections from Gilbert and Sullivan. The stifling tents seething with khaki-clad men and visiting dignitaries come to pay their respects. (The vicar, the Lord Lieutenant, and Colonel Carey-Lewis would not have looked in the least out of place.) Then, the refreshments. Around the sides of the tent, trestle-tables were loaded with goodies. Buns, sandwiches, and little cakes, all of which melted away in record time, to be instantly replaced from some bottomless source or other. To drink, there was iced coffee, lemonade, and hot tea. (Again, one half expected to spy Mrs. Nettlebed or Mary Millyway in charge of the tea-urn, with Mrs. Mudge alongside dealing with the milk jugs and the sugar.)

So full became the tent that access to the trestle-tables was limited, so having safely delivered their charges, Judith and Sarah were pressed into duty as waitresses, loading trays with full plates and glasses and cups, and making sure that every man got his share of the feast.

By now, there was a lot of talking, and it was all very hot and noisy. But at last the assembled company, finally sated, stopped eating and drifted in twos and threes out onto the Green, to lie on the grass, smoke cigarettes, and listen to the band.

Judith looked at her watch, and saw that it was already half past eleven. Sarah Sudlow was nowhere to be seen, and the stewards were now clearing away the detritus of the party. Her shirt was sticking to her back and there didn't seem to be much else to do, so she left the tent, ducking under the canvas overhang and stepping over a couple of guy-ropes. She faced the sea, and the breeze was blissfully cooling.

She stood for a moment breathing gusts of fresh air and observing the peaceful scene. The lawns of Gordon's Green; the Royal Marine Band (suitably ceremonial in white helmets) now playing tunes from *H.M.S. Pinafore*; the random groups of relaxing men. And then her eye was caught by a single man, who did not lie prone, propped on an elbow, but stood, with his back to her, apparently intent upon the music. She noticed him because he was different. Lanky and fleshless as the others, but not wearing the anonymous uniform of jungle green and canvas gym shoes. Instead, a pair of battered desert boots, the sort that were always referred to by officers of the Royal Navy as brothel-creepers. On his dark head was a Gordon glengarry, the ribbons fluttering in the breeze. A worn khaki shirt, the sleeves rolled up to his elbows. And a kilt. A Gordon kilt. Ragged and faded, the pleats stitched down, in amateurish fashion, with twine. But still, a kilt.

Gus.

For an instant she thought it might be Gus, and then saw at once that he wasn't because Gus was dead. Lost, killed in Singapore. But perhaps he had *known* Gus.

> . . . *I cleaned the windows and I swept the floor,*
> *And I polished up the handle of the big front door,*
> *I polished up that handle so carefullee*
> *That now I am the ruler of the Queen's Navee.*

She walked across the grass towards him. He did not hear her coming, and he never turned.

She said, "Hello."

Startled, he swung around, and she was looking up into his face. Dark eyes, thick brows, cheeks cadaverous, skin netted with fine lines that had not been there before. She experienced an extraordinary physical sensation, as though her heart had ceased to beat and for an instant she had been frozen in time.

It was he who broke the silence. "Good God. Judith."

Oh, Loveday. You were wrong. You were wrong all the time.

"Gus."

"Where did you spring from?"

"Here. Colombo."

He wasn't killed at Singapore. He isn't dead. He's here. With me. Alive.

She said, "You're alive."

"Did you think I wasn't?"

"Yes. I've thought for years you were dead. Ever since Singapore. We all did. When I saw you standing, I knew it wasn't you, because it couldn't be."

"Do I look like a corpse?"

"No. You look wonderful." And she meant it, and it was true. "The boots, and the kilt and the glengarry. How on earth did you manage to hang on to them?"

"Only the kilt and the bonnet. I stole the boots."

"Oh, Gus."

"Don't cry."

But she took a step towards him, put her arms around his waist, and pressed her face into the worn cotton of the old khaki shirt. She could feel his ribs and his bones and could hear the beating of his heart. His arms came around her and they simply stood there, very close, for anybody to see or to remark upon. And she thought of Loveday again, and then stopped thinking of Loveday. For the moment all that was important was that she had found Gus again.

After a bit, they drew apart. If any person had witnessed their display of intimate affection, then no regard was being paid. She had not wept, and he had not kissed her. It was over. Back to basics.

"I never saw you in the tent," she told him.

"I was only there for a little while."

"Do you have to stay here?"

"Not necessarily. Do you?"

"Not necessarily. When do you have to be back on board?"

"Tenders at three o'clock."

"We could go back to the Galle Road. Where I'm staying. Have a drink or some lunch. There's time."

"What I would really like," said Gus, "is to go to the Galle Face Hotel. I've got a sort of date there. But I couldn't just go on my own, because I haven't any proper money. No rupees. Just Japanese paper notes."

"I've got money. I'll take you. I'll come with you."

"How?"

"We'll take a taxi. There's a rank up on the road by the Clock Tower. We can walk as far as that."

"Are you sure?"

"Of course."

"You won't get into trouble?"

"I'm on leave. A free agent."

So they slipped away. Again nobody noticed, and if they did, said nothing. They went through the now nearly empty tent, and across the grass, and out into Queen Street and so up the road to the cross-roads and the Clock Tower. There some ancient taxis waited. The drivers, spying them, instantly leaped to their feet to haggle amongst themselves for the fare, but Judith and Gus got into the first in the queue, which saved a lot of argument.

She said, "You know, I never realized until just now how terribly difficult it must be to be a witness. In court. At a murder trial or something. You could swear blind on the Bible that you had or hadn't seen a person at some vital moment. But I know now that what you actually *see* is governed by what you believe, or think to be true."

"Me, you mean?"

"It wasn't *you*, until I saw your face."

"The best thing that's happened to me forever was seeing yours. Tell me about you. You're on leave. Don't you work here?"

"No. In Trincomalee. You won't remember Bob Somerville, my uncle? I don't think you'd ever have met him. He's a Rear Admiral on the C-in-C's staff. I'm staying with him."

"I see."

"His wife, Biddy, was my mother's sister."

"Was. Past tense."

"Yes. My parents were in Singapore, about the same time as you . . ."

"I know. I met them once at a regimental party at the Selaring Barracks. It was just before Pearl Harbor, when we were still having parties. What happened to them? Did they get away?"

Judith shook her head. "No. My father died in Changi."

"I'm sorry."

"And my mother and my little sister tried to get to Australia, but their ship was torpedoed in the Java Sea. They didn't survive."

"Oh, God. I *am* sorry."

"That's why I'm on leave. A month. To be with Bob. I have to go back to Trincomalee at the end of this week."

"So a few days later and I'd have missed you."

"That's right."

The taxi was driving along the edge of the Galle Face Green. A group of small boys played football, dribbling and kicking regardless of bare toes. Gus turned his head to watch them. He said, "It's not exactly in the same league, but my parents have died as well. Neither starved nor drowned, but quietly, in their own beds, or hospital, or perhaps a nursing home." He turned back to face her. He said, "They were elderly; they were elderly before I was born. I was the only child. Perhaps they, too, thought I was dead."

"Who told you this?"

"A kindly lady, a sort of social worker, in the hospital in Rangoon."

"At Singapore, couldn't you send word to *anyone*? Not even your mother and father?"

"I tried to smuggle a letter out of Changi, but I don't suppose it ever got to them. I never got another chance."

The taxi was turning into the forecourt of the hotel, drawing up in the shade of the deep awning. They went indoors, into the long foyer lined with flowering shrubs in pots and glass-fronted display cabinets containing very beautiful and costly jewellery: gold necklaces and bracelets, sapphire and diamond brooches and earrings, and ruby and emerald rings.

"Gus, you said you had a date."

"I have."

"Who with?"

"Wait and see." Behind the reception desk stood a Sinhalese clerk. "Does Kuttan still work here?"

"But of course, sir. He is in charge of the restaurant."

"I wonder if I could have a word. I shan't keep him a moment."

"Can I say who wishes to see him?"

"Captain Callender. A friend of Colonel Cameron's. Gordon Highlanders."

"Very good. If you would like to wait out on the terrace, perhaps?" He indicated the direction with a fragile brown hand. "Would you like refreshment? Iced coffee or a drink from the bar?"

Gus turned to Judith. "What would you like?"

"Lemonade, perhaps."

"Lemonade for the lady and a beer for me."

"Very good, sir."

They walked on down the polished marble floor of the foyer and out onto the terrace, Gus leading the way, choosing a table, arranging the cane chairs. Following, she wondered at his coolness, his detachment, his air of authority that was inbred and so could never be destroyed. He had not only survived the Burma Railway, but survived, it seemed, with some style. His rags of uniform looked, on him, neither comical nor odd, simply because he wore them with such pride. But there was something more. An inner strength that was palpable, but formidable as well. She found this a little daunting. Sooner or later, she was going to have to tell him about Loveday. In olden days, bearers of bad news quite often had their heads cut off. She decided that she would not volunteer any information until he actually asked the question.

Sitting out on the terrace, their drinks were brought to them. Some children, with watchful amahs in attendance, were swimming in the pool. The breeze rattled the leaves of the palms, and at the end of the garden, beyond the ornamental balustrade, lay the sea.

Gus said, "It's just the same. It hasn't changed."

"You were here?"

"Yes, on our way out to Singapore. I came in a troop-ship, via Cape Town, with a few other chaps from the regiment. We stopped off here for four days, and then caught another boat on. It was a particularly riotous time. Parties and pretty girls." He said again, "A good time."

"Captain Callender."

They had not heard him come, but now he was there. Gus rose to his feet. "Kuttan." He stood, beaming, his white tunic embellished with the red silk epaulettes that were his badge of office; his hair neat and oiled, his superb raj-style moustache immaculately barbered. He held in his left hand a silver tray, on which stood a bottle of Black & White whisky.

"I could not believe my ears, my God, when I was told that you were here. That you are safe and alive."

"It's good to see you, Kuttan."

"And you. God is very good. You have come on the ship from Rangoon?"

"Yes. We sail this afternoon."

"I shall watch your ship sail out into the sea. At dark, all the lights will be on. Very pretty. I shall watch you go home."

"I shall be thinking of you, Kuttan."

"And this is Colonel Cameron's bottle of Black and White that he asked me to keep for him. I have had it, under lock and key, all this time." He looked about him. "Colonel Cameron is not with you?"

"He died, Kuttan."

The old man stared, with sad dark eyes. "Oh, Captain Callender, that is very bad news."

"I didn't want to leave Colombo without letting you know."

"I have never forgotten the days when you stayed here. And Colonel Cameron. A fine gentleman." He looked at the whisky bottle. "I was so sure he would come back to get this, as he promised. He paid for it, that last night. He said, 'Kuttan, you keep this for me. On ice. We will celebrate again on our way home.' And now, he is not coming." He took the bottle off the tray, and set it down on the table. "So you must take it."

"I didn't come for the whisky, Kuttan. I came to see you."

"I am very grateful. Are you going to come to the restaurant for lunch?"

"I think not. I don't have the time to appreciate your delicious food, nor, I'm afraid, at the moment, the stomach for it."

"You have been ill?"

"I'm all right now. Kuttan, you're a busy man. I mustn't keep you from your duties." He held out his hand. "Goodbye, old friend." They shook hands. And then Kuttan stepped back, placed his palms together, and salaamed with much affection and respect.

"God take care of you, Captain Callender."

When he had gone, Gus sat down again, and looked at the bottle of whisky. He said, "I shall have to find some sort of bag or basket to put it in. I can scarcely be observed by all the jocks, carrying it on board *Orion*. It wouldn't do at all."

"We'll find something," Judith promised him. "You can take it back to Scotland with you."

"Coals to Newcastle."

"What will happen when you get home?"

"Not quite sure. Report to HQ in Aberdeen, I suppose. Medical checkups. Leave."

"Were you very ill?"

"No more than anyone else. Beriberi. Dysentery. Sores and boils. Pleurisy, malaria, cholera. They reckon about sixteen thousand Brits died. The men who came ashore today are outnumbered, by three to one, by the others we had to leave on board."

"Do you hate to talk?"

"What about?"

"Singapore, and how it all began. I had a last letter from my mother . . . but it didn't really tell me anything, except confusion and chaos."

"That's pretty much how it was. The day after Pearl Harbor, the Japanese invaded Malaya. The Gordons were manning the coastal defences, but at the beginning of January, we were moved up-country, into Malaya, and joined an Australian brigade. But we didn't stand a hope in hell, and by the end of January, we'd retreated back over the Causeway onto Singapore Island. But it was a doomed campaign, indefensible without air power, and we only had about a hundred and fifty aircraft, because a large part of the RAF were fighting in North Africa. And then there were the refugees. The place was clogged with them. We were sent to do rear-guard action at the Causeway. We held our positions for three or four days, but it was with rifle and bayonet, since we ran out of artillery shells in no time. There was some sporadic talk of trying to escape, get out, to Java or somewhere, but it was only rumour. Then, a week after entering Singapore, the Japanese reached the reservoirs that supplied all the fresh water. There were at least a million people in the city, and the Japs turned off the taps. That was it. Capitulation."

"What happened to you then?"

"We got put into Changi. It wasn't too bad, and the guards were fairly reasonable. I got on a working party, sent out into the streets to repair bomb damage. I got quite good at scrounging supplies and extra rations. I even sold my watch for Singapore dollars, and used them to bribe one of the guards into posting a letter to my mother and father, but I don't know if he ever did, or whether they ever got it. I suppose I'll never know now. As well, he brought me paper and pencils, a drawing-block, and I managed to keep them filled and hidden for the next three and a half years. A sort of record. But not one for human consumption."

"Have you still got them?"

Gus nodded. "On board. With my new toothbrush and my new bar of soap, and a last letter from Fergie Cameron that I have to deliver to his widow."

"What happened next, Gus?"

"Well, we stayed in Changi for about six months, and then the word went round that the Japanese had built wonderful camps for us up in Siam. The next thing we knew, we were all put in steel cattle trucks, travelling north to Bangkok for five days and nights. Thirty of us to each truck, so there was no space to lie down. It was ghastly. We had one cupful of rice each and one cup of water a day. By the time we got to Burma, many of us were really ill, and some had died. At Bangkok we all fell out of the cattle trucks, weak with relief that the ordeal was over. What we didn't know was that it was only just beginning."

The children had stopped swimming, and been ushered, by their amahs, indoors for tiffin. The pool lay still. Gus picked up his glass and downed the last of his beer. "That's all," he said. "No more. Full stop." Across the table, he sent her the ghost of a smile. "Thank you for listening."

"Thank you for telling."

"No more about me. I want to hear about you."

"Oh, Gus, it's pale by comparison."

"Please. When did you join the Wrens?"

"The day after Edward was killed."

"That was grim. I wrote to the Carey-Lewises. I was in Aberdeen then, after Saint Valéry. I wanted so much to go and see them, but there was never the time nor the opportunity before I sailed for Cape Town." He frowned, remembering. "You bought Mrs. Boscawen's house, didn't you?"

"Yes. After she died. It was lovely. I'd always adored the house. It meant I had a home. Biddy, Bob Somerville's wife, came and shared it with me. And Phyllis, who used to work for my mother. And her little girl, Anna. They're still there."

"Is that where you'll return to?"

"Yes."

She waited. He said it, "And Nancherrow?"

"Just the same. Except that Nettlebed has stopped being the butler and become the gardener. He still buttles, of course, and brushes the Colonel's tweeds, but he's much more interested in his runner beans."

"And Diana? And the Colonel?"

"Unchanged."

"Athena?"

"Rupert was wounded in Germany. Invalided out of the Royal Hussars. They're all living in Gloucestershire now."

She waited. "And Loveday?"

He was watching her. She said, "Loveday's married, Gus."

"Married?" His expression became one of total incredulity. "Loveday? Married. Whom did she marry?"

"Walter Mudge."

"The boy with the horses?"

"That's right."

"When?"

"In the summer of 1942."

"But . . . why?"

"She thought you were dead. She was utterly convinced that you'd been killed. There was no word from you, and no news. Just silence. She just gave up."

He said, "I don't understand."

"I don't know if I can explain. But after Saint Valéry, she had this sort of premonition, this revelation that you were alive. And you were. You came back. You weren't killed then, and you weren't taken prisoner. It . . . it made her believe that there was some sort of tremendously strong telepathy between the two of you. After Singapore, she tried it again, thinking about you incredibly hard, and waiting for some sort of sign, or message from you. That you weren't dead, but alive. And none came."

"I could scarcely ring up on the telephone."

"Oh, Gus, you have to try to understand. You know what Loveday's like. Once she's got an idea, a conviction in her head, she's immovable. In some strange way, she convinced us all." She qualified this. "At least, she convinced Diana and the Colonel."

"But not you?"

"I was in the same boat. I had family in Singapore, and no news. But I went on hoping, because I knew that hope was all I had left. I went on hoping for *you*, until the day she got married, and after that there didn't seem to be much point."

"Is she happy?"

"Sorry?"

"I asked, is she happy?"

"I think so, though I haven't seen her for quite a long time. She's got a baby, Nathaniel. He'll be three in November. She lives in a cottage on Lidgey farm. Oh, Gus, I'm sorry. I've been dreading telling you. But it's happened, a fact of life. There's no point in lying to you."

He said, "I thought she would wait for me."

"You mustn't be angry with her."

"I'm not angry." But, all at once, he looked desperately worn and tired. He put a hand to his face, rubbed it over his eyes. She thought of him going home, going back to Scotland, to nothing. No parents, no family. No Loveday.

She said, "We must keep in touch, Gus. Whatever happens, we *must* keep in touch. I'll give you my address, and you must give me yours so that I can write to you." She thought about this, and realized that they were both singularly ill-equipped. She got to her feet. "I'll go and get some paper and a pen from somewhere. And scrounge something for you to hide your whisky bottle in. Wait here, I shan't be a moment."

She left him sitting alone. Went back indoors, paid the bar-bill, and was given a hefty brown paper bag in which to conceal the bottle of Black & White. After that, she made her way to the bridge-room, where she stole a couple of sheets of hotel writing-paper from a desk, and as well, a pencil. When she returned to Gus, she saw that he had not moved. He sat as she had left him, his eyes fixed on the indistinguishable line, between two different shades of blue, that was the horizon.

"Here." She handed over one of the bits of writing-paper and the pencil. "Your address. Where I can get hold of you." He wrote, then pushed them back to her.

Ardvray
Bancharry
Aberdeenshire.

She folded the sheet of paper and stuffed it in her pocket. Then it was her turn.

The Dower House
Rosemullion.

"If I write, will you promise to answer, Gus?"

"Of course."

"We haven't, either of us, got much left, have we? So we must sustain each other. It's important."

Now it was he who folded the paper and buttoned it into the breast pocket of his shirt.

"Yes. Important. Judith . . . I think I must go back now. I mustn't be late for the tender. Miss the boat."

"I'll come with you."

"No. I'd rather go alone."

"We'll find a taxi. Here . . ."

"What's that?"

"Money for the fare."

"I feel like a kept man."

"No, not kept. Just pretty special."

He gathered up his parcel (which still looked like a bottle, despite its wrappings) and they left the terrace, going back through the foyer and out of the door. The doorman called a taxi, and he held the door open for Gus to get in.

"Goodbye, Judith." His voice seemed a little hoarse.

"Promise to write. I'll let you know the moment I get back to England."

He nodded. And then said, "Just one thing. Will you tell them all, at Nancherrow, about today?"

"Of course I will."

"Tell them I'm okay. Say I'm fine."

"Oh, Gus." She reached up and kissed him on both cheeks. He got into the taxi and the door slammed shut. Then he was driven away, out into the road and down the length of the Galle Face Green. Judith, smiling and waving, watched him go, but as soon as the car was out of sight, she could feel the brave smile slipping from her face.

Silently, *Keep in touch*, she called after him. *You mustn't disappear again.*

"Can I get a taxi for you?"

She turned and looked at the doorman, attentive and resplendent in his bottle-green uniform. For a moment she couldn't think what she was meant to be doing, nor where she was meant to be. But no point in returning to the Fort. She would go home, take a shower, flake out on her bed.

"Yes. Another taxi. Thank you."

The Galle Road once more, but now driving in the opposite direction, in a degree of comfort, and not lurching about at the back of a three-ton lorry.

Will you tell them all, at Nancherrow, about today?

She thought about Walter Mudge, and Nathaniel and Loveday. The marriage that should never have taken place. The child who should never have been conceived, nor born. Loveday was her closest friend. No person in the world could be better company, and nobody could be more infuriating. Staring out of the window at dusty pavements, passers-by, and the wheeling avenue of palms, she could scarcely bear to contemplate the bleak home-coming that awaited Gus. It was so dreadfully unfair, and not what he deserved. Heavy-hearted, and angry on his behalf, she took her resentment out on Loveday, silently raging.

Why do you always have to be so pig-headed, so impetuous? Why didn't you listen to me, that day in London?

I was already having a baby. Loveday, shouting at her, as though Judith were a fool. Loveday giving as good as she got.

You made such a mess of everything. Gus is alive and he's coming home, and he's got no family because his old parents have died. He should be coming to Nancherrow, to find *you* waiting for him. It could all have been so perfect. He should be coming home to *you.* Instead he's going back to Scotland, and an empty house, and no family and no love.

What's to stop him coming to Nancherrow? He was Edward's friend. Mummy and Pops thought he was great. Nothing to stop him.

How can he come to Nancherrow, if you're married to Walter? He loved you. He was in love with you. He's spent all this time building foul railways in Burma, and telling himself that you were waiting for him. How can he come to Nancherrow. You must be without heart or imagination to suggest such a thing.

He should have let me know he was alive. Now, she sounded sulky.

How could he? Like he said, he could scarcely ring you up on the telephone. He only managed one letter, and that was to his parents, and he can't be certain that they ever even *got* it. Why didn't you go on hoping? Why didn't you wait for him?

I can't think why you're so involved all of a sudden.

I'm not *involved.* But I do feel responsible. He must *know* he has friends. We mustn't let him disappear again. But I don't think he'll return to Nancherrow, and I doubt if he'd come and visit me at the Dower House either, because he knows that we all live on top of each other, and sooner or later he'd have to see you again. Can't you see, you've put me in an intolerable position?

We surely weren't his only friends.

But you know how he *loved* Cornwall. It was a sort of heaven for him, with you there and his painting. How can you be so hard? Why do you always make such a mess of everything?

You don't know that I've made a mess of everything. You and I have hardly seen each other for five years. How do you know I'm not happy with Walter?

Because he was the wrong man. You should have waited for Gus.

Oh, shut up.

Now the taxi was slowing down, drawing into the side of the road. She saw the familiar gates, the sentry. She was home. She got out of the taxi, paid the driver off, and went through the gates.

And then, on this extraordinary day of extraordinary events, the last extraordinary thing occurred, that was to drive all preoccupation, all thoughts of Gus and Loveday from Judith's mind. The doors of Bob's bungalow stood open, and even as she trod up the drive, he was there, running down the wide steps, and striding across the neatly raked gravel to meet her.

"Where have you *been?*" He had never in his life been angry with her, but now he sounded quite distraught. "I've been waiting since midday. Why weren't you back? What have you been doing?"

"I . . . I . . ." Completely knocked off course by his outburst, she could scarcely find the words to explain. ". . . I met someone. I've been at the Galle Face Hotel. I'm sorry . . ."

"Don't be sorry." He hadn't been angry, just anxious. He put his hands on her shoulders and held her, as though at any moment she might start falling apart. "Just listen. This morning I got a telephone call from your Second Officer in Trincomalee . . . A signal's come through from Portsmouth, HMS *Excellent* . . . Jess survived Java. Jakarta . . . *The Rajah of Sarawak* . . . a lifeboat . . . a young Australian nurse . . . internment camp . . ."

She watched his craggy face, his eyes keen with excitement, his mouth opening and shutting, making words that she scarcely understood.

". . . tomorrow, or the next day . . . RAF . . . Jakarta to Ratmalana . . . she'll be here."

It finally sank in. He was telling her that Jess was alive. Little Jess. Not drowned. Not killed in the explosion. Safe.

". . . the Red Cross will let us know when she's due to arrive . . . we'll go together and meet her off the plane . . ."

"Jess?" It took an enormous effort even to say her name.

Abruptly, Bob pulled her into his arms and held her so closely she thought her ribs would snap. "Yes, Jess," and there was a break in his voice that he didn't even try to conceal. "She's coming back to you!"

"Pretty exciting day for you."

"Yes."

"Your sister, the group captain said?"

"Yes."

"How old is she?"

"Fourteen."

It was five o'clock in the afternoon. Judith and Bob—driven in certain state in his staff car—had presented themselves at the RAF station, Ratmalana, at a quarter past four. There, the station commander had met them, and escorted them to the mess, where they had been given cups of tea, waiting until word came through from the Control Tower to say that the plane from Jakarta would be landing in a matter of moments.

"Think you'll recognize her?"

"Yes, I think so."

They walked from the mess across the dusty parade ground, towards the Control Tower. Bob Somerville and the group captain had gone on ahead, both in uniform, and deep in service talk. The junior officer—a flight lieutenant in some sort of attendant duty (Secretary? First lieutenant? Aide-de-camp? Equerry?)—had fallen into step beside Judith, and now engaged her in conversation. He had a huge fighter-pilot moustache, and wore his battered cap at a slight angle. She guessed that he enjoyed a reputation as something of a ladies' man. Whatever, he was clearly relishing the bonus of a youthful and not hideous female, and one, moreover, tricked out in an attractive dress; a nice change from the ubiquitous khaki drill of the Women's Auxiliary Air Force.

"Will you be in Colombo for long?"

"I really don't know."

Outwardly cool, inside she was trembling with nerves. Suppose the plane never came? Suppose, when it did land, there was no Jess on board? Suppose something awful had happened, some hitch or other? Or an explosion, causing the aircraft to drop out of the sky, and killing all the passengers?

"Do you work for the Admiral?"

"No, I'm just staying with him."

"Wizard show." He was doing his best, but she didn't want to talk.

In front of the Control Tower, they joined the others, and, as well, some ground crew, wearing grubby overalls and in charge of maintenance trucks and fuel tankers. On the far side of the runway stood hangars and neatly parked groups of aircraft, Tornadoes and Hurricanes. The runway was clear. The wind filled the airsocks.

For a bit nobody said anything. It was a moment of acute anticipation. Then the flight lieutenant broke the silence. "She's coming now." Judith felt her heart leap. The random groups of ground crew began to peel off, re-assorting themselves, clambering into their trucks. A batsman, in a scarlet vest, appeared on the far end of the runway. Shading her eyes, staring up into the sky, Judith could see nothing for the dazzle of the lowering sun. Straining her ears, heard only silence. She wondered if the flight lieutenant had been blessed with extra-sensory powers. Perhaps his moustache was sensitive as the whiskers of a cat, and he was able to . . .

And then she saw the plane, a silver toy, suspended in light. She heard the hum of the engines as it floated down out of the south-west, losing height, beamed in on the runway, wheels down, coming in to land. It touched down in a blast of thundering noise, wheels smacking the runway, and Judith instinctively put up a hand to shield her face against the resultant turmoil, the blown clouds of choking dust.

After that, once the dust had subsided, another five minutes of hanging about, waiting for the Dakota to come slowly taxiing back from the end of the runway, to halt finally in line with the Control Tower. The propellers were still. The heavy bulkhead doors opened from the inside, and makeshift steps trundled up. The passengers alighted in dribs and drabs and began to walk across the concrete apron. An RAF Squadron Leader, a group of American pilots; three neatly dressed Tamils, bearing briefcases. Two soldiers, one of them on crutches . . .

Finally, just as Judith was about to give up hope, she was there, clambering down the steps. Skinny and brown as a boy, wearing shorts and a faded green shirt, and with sun-bleached hair clipped in a crop. Clumsy leather sandals that looked as though they were two sizes too big; a small canvas rucksack slung over one bony shoulder.

She paused for a moment, orientating herself, clearly a bit lost, anxious and apprehensive. Then, bravely, the girl set out after the others, ducking beneath the wing of the plane; coming.

Jess. At that moment they might have been the only two people in the world. Judith went to meet her, searching, in that bony, stony little face, for some trace of the chubby child, the sweetly weeping four-year-old to whom she had said goodbye all those years ago. And Jess saw her, and stopped dead, but Judith went on, and it was wonderful, because Jess's eyes were upon her, and they were just as blue and as clear as they had ever been.

"Jess."

"Judith?" She had to ask, because she couldn't be sure.

"Yes. Judith."

"I thought I wouldn't know you."

"I knew I'd know you."

She held out her arms. Jess hesitated for an instant longer, and then flung herself forward and into Judith's waiting embrace. She was so tall now that the top of her head reached Judith's chin, and holding her felt like grasping something very brittle, like a starved bird, or a twig. She buried her face into Jess's rough hair, and it smelt of disinfectant, and she felt Jess's skinny arms latch tight around her waist, and they were kissing each other, only this time there were no tears.

They were allowed their little time together, and, when they joined the three patient men who waited, were met with great kindness and tact. Jess was greeted in the most casual of tones, as though she made the momentous journey from Jakarta every day of her life. Bob did not even attempt to kiss her, simply rumpled her hair with a gentle hand. She didn't say much, and she didn't smile. But she was all right.

The group captain walked back with them to where the car waited in the shade of a palm-thatch awning. There, Bob turned to him.

"I can't thank you enough."

"A pleasure, sir. A day I won't forget."

And he didn't immediately go, but waited, seeing them off, saluting smartly as the car moved away, and standing waving until they passed through the guarded gates, and out onto the road, and could see him no longer.

"Now"—Bob settled himself comfortably and smiled down at his small niece—"Jess. You're *really* on your way."

She sat between them, in the back of the huge car. Judith couldn't stop looking at her, wanting to touch her, smooth her hair. She seemed all right. There were three hideous purple scars on her right leg, each about the size of a half-crown, and you could see the bumps of her ribs beneath the thin cotton of the threadbare shirt. But she was all right. And her teeth were too big for her face, and her hair looked as though it had been chopped off with a carving knife. But she was all right. She was beautiful.

"When you saw Uncle Bob, did you recognize him?" Judith asked.

Jess shook her head. "No."

Bob laughed. "How could she? How could you, Jess? You were only four. And we were together for such a little while. In Plymouth. And it was Christmas."

"I remember Christmas, but I don't remember *you*. I remember the silver tree, and someone called Hobbs. He used to make me dripping toast."

"You know something, Jess? You talk like a little Australian. I like it. It reminds me of some good cobbers of mine who were shipmates in the old days."

"Ruth was Australian." She pronounced it "Austrylian."

"Was she the girl who looked after you?" Judith asked.

"Yeah. She was great. In my bag I've got a letter for you from her. She wrote it yesterday. Do you want it now?"

"No. Wait till we get back. I'll read it then."

By now, they had left Ratmalana behind them, and were bowling back, north, along the wide road that led to the city. Jess gazed, with some interest, from the windows.

"It's a bit like Singapore used to be."

"I wouldn't know. I was never there."

"Where exactly are we going?"

"To my house," Bob told her. "Judith's been staying with me."

"Is it a big house?"

"Big enough."

"Will I stay there?"

"Of course."

"Will I have a room by myself?"

"If that's what you'd like."

Jess didn't reply to this. Judith said, "I've got two beds in my room. You could sleep with me if you'd rather."

But Jess did not want to commit herself. "I'll think about it." And then, "Could I change places with you, so I can see out of the window?"

After that, she didn't say anything more, simply sat with her back to Bob and Judith, intent on all that passed them by. Countryside at first, little farms and bullock-carts and wells, and then the first of the houses, wayside shops and ramshackle filling stations. Finally, they entered the wide length of the Galle Road, and it was only when the car slowed and swung in through the gate that she spoke again.

"There's a guard on the gate." She sounded a bit alarmed.

"Yes. A sentry," Bob told her. "He's not there to stop us getting out, just to make certain no unwelcome guests come in."

"Is he your own sentry?"

"Yes, my very own. And I have a gardener too, and a cook, and a butler. They're all my very own. The gardener has filled the house with flowers for you, and the cook has made a special lemon pudding for your dinner, and the butler, who is called Thomas, cannot wait to meet you . . ." The car drew up, and stopped. "In fact, he is there, already, come to greet you."

It was a great welcome. Thomas was already down the steps and opening the door of the car, hair freshly oiled, hibiscus blossom tucked behind his ear; beaming with joy and delight, gold teeth flashing, he helped Jess out, stroking her head with his huge dark hand. He gathered up her rucksack and led her indoors, with an arm about her thin shoulders, and generally carried on as though she were his own lost child, and he her loving father.

". . . you have had a good journey? On the aeroplane? You are hungry, yes? Thirsty? You would like refreshment . . ?"

But Jess, looking a bit overwhelmed, said that what she really wanted was to go to the lavatory, so Judith stepped in, retrieved the rucksack, and led her down the passage to the quiet sanctuary of her own cool bedroom.

"You mustn't mind Thomas."

"I didn't."

"He's been so excited, ever since we knew you were coming. The bath-room's in here . . ."

Jess stood in the open door, and simply looked at the shining marble, the polished taps, the gleaming white porcelain.

"Is this all for you?" she asked.

"You and me."

"There were only two lavs in the whole of the camp at Asulu. They stank. Ruth used to clean them."

"That can't have been very nice." Which was painfully inadequate but the only comment she could think of.

"No, it wasn't."

"Why don't you go and spend that penny, and then you'll feel better."

Which Jess did, without bothering to close the door.

Presently, Judith heard the tap running and the splashing sounds of hands and face being washed.

"I don't know which towel to use."

"Any towel. It doesn't matter."

She sat at her dressing-table, and for want of anything else to do, began to comb her hair. Then Jess returned, and perched herself on the end of one of the beds. Through the mirror, their eyes met.

"Better now?"

"Yeah. I was really wanting to go."

"It's agony, isn't it? Have you made up your mind? Do you want to sleep in here with me?"

"Okay."

"I'll tell Thomas."

"I thought you'd look like Mummy, but you don't."

"I'm sorry."

"No. Just different. You're prettier. She never wore lipstick. When I got out of the aeroplane, I thought you mightn't be there to meet me. Ruth told me, if you weren't there, I was just to stay at the RAF station until you came."

Judith laid down her comb, and turned to face Jess.

"You know something? I was just the same. I kept telling myself that you weren't going to be on the plane. And then seeing you . . . it was such a relief."

"Yeah." Jess yawned. "Do you live here with Uncle Bob?"

"No. Just staying. My job's in Trincomalee. That's the big Royal Naval harbour over on the east side of Ceylon."

"The rehabilitation officers at Asulu couldn't find anybody for me. We had to stay in the camp until they'd found out where you were."

"I can't imagine how they even begin to deal with such problems. Like looking for a needle in a haystack. What happened was that I was finally told that both Mummy and Dad had died. You too, for that matter. And I was given a bit of a holiday, it's called compassionate leave, and Bob asked me to come here."

"I've always known that Mummy was dead. Ever since the ship went down. But I only just got told about Dad. They'd had a message from the Red Cross in Singapore. He died in prison. He died in Changi."

"Yes, I know. I haven't really come to terms with it yet. I try not to think about it too much."

"Women died in Asulu, but they always had friends."

"I think Dad would have had friends too."

"Yeah." She looked at Judith. "Will we stay together? You and me?"

"Yes. Together. No more being apart."

"Where shall we go? Where shall we live?"

"Cornwall. To my house."

"When?"

"I don't know, Jess. I don't know yet. But we'll fix something. Uncle Bob will help. Now"—she looked at her watch. "It's half past six. This is when we usually shower and change, and then we sit out on the veranda for a bit. Have a drink. And then dinner. It's early tonight because of you. We thought you might be a bit tired, need your sleep."

"Is dinner just you and me and Uncle Bob?"

"No. David Beatty will be there as well. He shares the house with Bob. He's a very nice man."

"In Singapore, Mummy always put on a special dress for dinner."

"We usually change, too. Not to be smart but to be cool and comfortable."

"I only have these clothes."

"I'll lend you something of mine. It should fit, you're almost as tall as I am now. Another pair of shorts, and perhaps a pretty shirt. And I've got a pair of red-and-gold thong sandals you can have."

Jess stuck out her legs and looked with distaste at her feet. "These are horrible. I haven't worn shoes since forever. It was all they could find."

"Tomorrow we'll borrow Bob's car and go shopping. We'll buy a whole new wardrobe for you, and warm clothes too, for getting back to England. A thick pullover. And a raincoat. And proper shoes and warm socks."

"Can you buy those sort of clothes in Colombo? In Singapore nobody ever wore anything warm."

"Up in the mountains, it gets quite damp and chilly. That's where they grow the tea. Now, what do you want to do? Take a shower?"

"I'd like to go and look at the garden."

"Why not take a shower first, and get changed, and then you'll feel a new girl? There's everything you need in the bathroom, and when you've finished, you can choose something to put on, and then go and find Bob, or explore the garden before it gets dark."

"I've got a toothbrush." Jess reached for her rucksack. She undid the straps, and from its depths produced the toothbrush, and a small bar of soap and a comb. Then something bundled in a washed-out rag, which, on being carefully unwrapped, was seen to be a little pipe, like a recorder, fashioned from a bamboo stalk.

"What's that?"

"One of the boys in the camp gave it to me. He made it himself. It plays proper tunes. Once, we had a concert. Ruth and one of the Dutch ladies organized it." She laid the pipe on the bed beside her and began to grope in her rucksack once more.

"What happened to Golly?"

"He was blown up on the ship," Jess told her in dispassionate tones. From the rucksack she withdrew a folded wad of paper, lined sheets torn from a yellow scratch-pad. She held it out. "This is for you. From Ruth."

Judith took it. "It looks a very long letter. I'll keep it for later." And she put it on her dressing-table, weighted down with the heavy cut-glass bottle of L'Heure Bleu.

She showed Jess how to work the shower and then left her to it. When, after some time, she emerged again, she was naked, except for the smallest face towel, which she had wrapped around her waist. Her wet hair stood up in spikes, and she was so thin that it was possible to count every rib. But her childish breasts had already started to swell, like little buds, and she no longer smelt of disinfectant, but Rose Geranium soap.

They spent some time choosing clothes, and finally decided on a pair of white tennis shorts and a blue Chinese silk shirt. When this had been buttoned, and the sleeves rolled up over Jess's spiky elbows, she took up her comb and flattened her damp hair.

"You look perfect. Feel comfortable?"

"Yeah. I'd forgotten about silk. Mummy used to wear silk dresses. Where will Uncle Bob be?"

"On the veranda, I expect."

"I'm going to go and find him."

"You do that."

It was good, for a moment, just to be alone, exhausted by emotion and suffused with gratitude, but still cool-headed. It was important to maintain this coolness, because that way she could rebuild her relationship with Jess, from the ground floor as it were. On Jess's side, the reunion at Ratmalana, the spontaneous display of physical affection had been triggered not by remembered love but sheer relief that she had not been forgotten nor abandoned. Ten years was too long for love to survive and, in that time, too much had happened to Jess. But it would be all right if Judith was patient, took her time, did not intrude, and carried on treating Jess as though she were already grown up. A contemporary. She was back. A beginning. Apparently normal, composed, and untraumatized. Go on from here.

After a bit, she stood up and shed her clothes, and showered and dressed again in thin trousers and a sleeveless shirt. She put on some lipstick, and took up the bottle of L'Heure Bleu, and touched the stopper at the base of her neck and behind her ears. Then laid the bottle down, and picked up the yellow pages of the Australian girl's letter.

Jakarta,

September 19th, 1945.

Dear Judith,

My name is Ruth Mulaney. I am twenty-five years old. I am an Australian.

In 1941 I finished my nurses' training in Sydney and went to Singapore to stay with friends of my mother and father.

When the Japs invaded Malaya, my father cabled that I must get home, and I managed to get a passage on *The Rajah of Sarawak*. She was an old tub of a boat and overcrowded with refugees.

We were torpedoed six days out in the Java Sea at about five o'clock in the evening. Jess's mother had gone below for a moment and asked me to keep an eye on Jess.

The ship sank very quickly. There was a lot of screaming and confusion. I grabbed Jess and a single life-jacket, and we jumped overboard. I was able to hang on to her, and then a lifeboat came and we managed to get into it. But we were the last, because it was already too full, and if others tried to board, we had to push them away, or hit them with oars.

There weren't enough boats or lifebelts or floats. We had no water nor emergency rations in the boat, but I had a water bottle and so did another woman. There were Chinese with us and Malays and a Lascar crewman. Four children and an elderly lady who were on board died on the first night.

We were adrift that night and the next day and another night. The next morning we were sighted by an Indonesian fishing boat and taken in tow.

They took us to Java, to their village by the beach. I wanted to go to Jakarta to try to get another boat to take us to Australia, but Jess was ill.

She had cut her leg somehow, and it was septic and she ran a fever and was badly dehydrated.

The other survivors went on, but we stayed with the fishermen in their village. I thought Jess was going to die, but she's a strong little tyke and managed to pull through.

By the time she was fit to be moved, Japanese planes were appearing in the sky. Finally we got a ride in a bullock-cart on the road to Jakarta and walked the last fifteen miles. But the Japanese were already there, and they picked us up and put us in a camp at Bandung, with a lot of Dutch women and children.

Bandung was the first of four camps. The last, at Asulu, was the worst of all. It was a labour camp, and all of us women were made to work in the rice fields, or clean drains and latrines. Jess was young enough, so not made to work. We were always hungry and sometimes starving. One punishment was that everybody had no food for two days.

We ate rice and sago gruel and soup made of vegetable scraps. Sometimes the Indonesians threw a bit of fruit over the wire, or I was able to barter for an egg or a little salt. There were two other Australian women, nurses. One of them died, and the other was shot.

Jess was never really ill again, but suffered sores and boils which have left some scars.

We tried to have a little school for the children but then the guards took all our books away.

We knew that the war was ending because some brave women had smuggled in bits of a wireless and put it together and hidden it.

Then, around the end of August we were told that the Americans had bombed Japan and that the Allied Forces would be landing in Java. After that, the Commandant and the guards all disappeared, but we stayed in the camp because there wasn't anywhere else to go.

An American plane flew over and dropped crates with parachutes, with canned stuff and cigarettes. That was a good day.

Then the British came, and the Dutch husbands who had survived their camps came as well. I think they were pretty shocked when they saw the state we were in.

There are two reasons why it has taken so long for the word to get through to you that Jess is alive.

One is that trouble is brewing in Indonesia, because the Indonesians don't want the Dutch back as colonists. This has slowed everything up.

The other reason is that Jess was listed under my name, as Jess Mulaney, and we told everybody we were sisters. I did not want her to be separated from me. We did not even tell the Dutch women that we weren't sisters.

I was afraid of being repatriated before her and having to leave her behind, and so I didn't say anything until it was time for us to leave. Only then did the Army know that she was really Jess Dunbar.

Over these three and a half years Jess has witnessed some terrible events, atrocities and deaths. All of these she seems to have learned to accept, and to keep her head down. Kids seem to be able to detach themselves. She's a great little person and very courageous.

During this time together, we have become very close and important to each other. She flies tomorrow and is very miserable about saying goodbye. At the same time, she accepts that there is no way we can stay together any longer.

To make things easier, I've said it's not goodbye forever, and one day she must come to Australia and stay with me and my family. We're pretty straight-down-the-middle-type folk. My father is a building contractor, and we live in a small house in Turramurra, a suburb of Sydney.

But I'd be grateful if, when she is a bit older, you'd let her make the trip.

I go home soon after Jess just as soon as there is a passage on a boat, or a flight on a plane.

Take care of our little sister.

Regards,

Ruth Mulaney

She read the letter through twice, and then read it again, and folded it, and put it into the top drawer of her dressing-table. *Take care of our little sister.* For three and a half years, Ruth had been Jess's security, however tenuous. This was where her love and her loyalty lay. And she had had to say goodbye, and leave it all behind.

Now, it was dark. Judith got up and went out of her bedroom, and in search of Jess. She found her alone, on the lamp-lit veranda, turning the pages of one of Bob's massive old photograph albums. As Judith appeared, she glanced up. "Come and see these with me. They're so funny. Mummy and Dad. Ages ago. Looking so young."

Judith settled herself beside Jess on the cushioned cane settee, and laid an arm around her shoulders.

"Where's Uncle Bob?"

"He's gone to change. He gave me this to look at. This is when they lived right here, in Colombo. And here's one of you in a terrible *hat*." She turned another page. "Who are these people?"

"Those are our grandparents. Mummy's mother and father."

"They look like they're old."

"They were. And dreadfully dull. I used to hate going to stay with them. I don't think you liked it much either, even though you were just a baby. And this is Biddy, Uncle Bob's wife. Mummy's sister. You'll love her. She's funny, makes you laugh all the time."

"And this?"

"That's Ned when he was about twelve. Their son. Our cousin. He was killed at the start of the war, when his ship was sunk." Jess said nothing. Simply turned another page.

Judith said, "I read the letter. Ruth sounds a special person."

"She is. And she was brave. Never frightened, not of anything."

"She says you were pretty brave too." Jess, elaborately, shrugged. "She said, in the camps, you were sisters."

"We pretended to be. At first. And then it was sort of real."

"It must have been rough, saying goodbye to her."

"Yeah."

"She says, when you're a bit older, she wants you to go to Australia and stay with her."

"We talked about that."

"I think it's a great idea."

Jess's head shot up and, for the first time, she looked into Judith's face. "*Could* I? Could I go?"

"Of course. Absolutely, of course. Say, when you're about seventeen? That's only three years away."

"Three *years!*"

"You'll have to go to school, Jess. When we get back. You'll have a lot of catching up to do. But you wouldn't have to go away. You could go to Saint Ursula's, where I was. You could be a day-girl."

But Jess was not interested in talking about school. "I thought you'd say I wouldn't be *able* to go." She was clearly determined to stick to the point. "I thought it would be too expensive. Australia's such a long way from England . . ."

"It won't be too expensive, I promise. And maybe, when you come back from Australia, you could bring Ruth with you, and then she could stay with us."

"You mean it?"

"I mean it."

"Oh. I'd like that better than *anything* in the world. If I could have just a single wish, that's what it would be. That was the worst about saying goodbye this morning. Thinking I'd never, ever see her again. Can I write to her and tell her? I know her address in Australia. I learned it by heart in case I lost the bit of paper."

"I think you should write a letter tomorrow. Not waste a moment. And then you can both start looking forward to it. It's important, always, to have something to look forward to. But . . ." She hesitated, "Meantime, perhaps you and I should begin to make more immediate plans."

Jess frowned, "Like what?"

"I think it's time we went home."

Judith was packing. It was an occupation which she had always found something of a chore, but was now made more complicated by the fact that there were two people to pack for, and four separate items of baggage in which to pack. Two for Wanted on Voyage, and two for Not Wanted on Voyage.

For the Not Wanted on Voyage bit, she had invested in large, sturdy leather suitcases, girthed with buckled straps. Strong enough, one hoped, to survive being manhandled by the dockyard maties of both Colombo and Liverpool, and not fall apart should they be dropped from a great height. For Wanted on Voyage, she was using her own suitcase, that she had brought from Trincomalee, but for Jess had purchased a capacious brown hide hold-all.

Whiteaway & Laidlaw, that Harrods of the East, had not let them down.

As for clothes, the great shopping expedition had taken most of a day, and Judith had let rip, casting prudence aside. She knew that in England clothes rationing was tighter than ever, and once they got home, there wouldn't be a hope of buying anything very much. To say nothing of the fact that it would probably take some time for all the formalities of officialdom to filter through varying pipelines, and until they did, neither she nor Jess would have access to clothes coupons, let alone food-ration books, petrol coupons, identity cards, and all the restrictions of wartime that still dogged a beleaguered and long-suffering nation.

So, for Jess, a complete wardrobe, from underclothes upwards. Shirts, sweaters, skirts, woollen knee-stockings, pyjamas, four pairs of shoes, a thick dressing-gown, and a warm and sensible raincoat. All this lay on Jess's bed, in neat folded bundles, destined for the hold of the troop-ship. For the voyage home, she set aside only the most essential of basics. The ship, they had been told, was packed to the gunwales with returning troops, and personal space was at a premium. So, cotton shorts and jumpers, a cardigan, a thin night-dress, canvas gym-shoes. And, for the day that they disembarked, a pair of trousers and a soft, tan suede jacket . . .

Now, four o'clock in the afternoon, it was so breathlessly hot that it was almost impossible to realize that, in three weeks' time, she and Jess would actually be *glad* of all these heavy, scratchy, thick garments. The very effort of folding a Shetland sweater was a bit like knitting in a heat wave, and she could feel the sweat trickling down the back of her neck, and the dampness of hair sticking to her forehead.

"Missy Judith." Thomas's soft voice. She straightened and turned, pushing her hair out of her face. She had left the door open, to create a through-draught, and now saw Thomas standing there, diffident at interrupting.

"What is it, Thomas?"

"A visitor. He is waiting for you. On the veranda."

"Who?"

"Commander Halley."

"*Oh.*" Instinctively, Judith put her hand over her mouth. Hugo. She felt really badly about Hugo, because, since Jess's return a week ago, she hadn't seen him, hadn't been in touch, and—if truth be told—scarcely thought of him. And, during the last few days, so much had there been to do, so many arrangements to be made, that an appropriate moment had never presented itself in which to pick up the receiver and dial his number. As the days slipped by, guilt niggled, and this very morning she had written a stern note to herself, RING HUGO, and stuck the bit of paper in the frame of her mirror. And now he was *here*. *He* had taken the initiative, and she felt both ashamed and abashed at her fall from social grace. "I . . . I'll be with him in a moment, Thomas. Will you say?"

"I shall bring you afternoon tea."

"That would be lovely."

Thomas bowed, and glided away. Judith, feeling at a distinct disadvantage, abandoned the packing, washed her sweaty hands and her face, and tried to do something about her lank hair. Her sleeveless cotton dress was neither clean nor fresh, but would have to suffice. She pushed her bare feet into a pair of thongs and went to abase herself.

She found him standing, a shoulder propped against the post of the veranda, his back to her, gazing out over the garden. He was in uniform, but had tossed his hat down on the seat of a chair.

"Hugo."

He turned. "Judith." His expression was neither reproachful nor cross, which was a great relief. Instead, he looked, as always, delighted to see her.

"Oh, Hugo, I'm filled with shame."

"Why ever?"

"Because I should have telephoned you long before now and given you some idea of what was going on. But there's been so much to do, and I just never got around to it. Too rude. I am sorry."

"Stop grovelling. I never even thought about it."

"And I'm looking disgustingly grubby, but everything clean's already been packed."

"You look fine. And certainly cleaner than I do. I've been to Katakarunda all day; just thought I'd drop in on my way to the Fort."

"I'm so glad you did. Because we're going tomorrow."

"So soon?"

"I put a note on my dressing-table to ring you this evening."

"Perhaps it's I who should have been in touch with you. But knowing the situation, I didn't want to intrude."

"I would never have left without saying goodbye."

He put up his hands in a gesture of surrender. "Let's forget it. You're looking frazzled and I'm feeling frazzled. Why don't we both sit down for a moment, and simply relax?"

Which was just about the best idea anybody had had all day. Judith collapsed into Bob's long chair, with her feet up on the leg-rest, and lay back on the cushions with a sigh of relief, while Hugo pulled up a stool and sat facing her, leaning forward, his elbows supported by his bare brown knees.

"Now, let's start at the beginning. You're leaving tomorrow?"

"I've been trying to pack all afternoon."

"What about the Wrens? Your job?"

"I'm on indefinite compassionate leave, and when I get home, I'll get a compassionate discharge. All fixed. Chief Officer Colombo's arranged the whole deal."

"How are you getting back?"

"Troop-ship. Bob fixed us a couple of berths at the very last moment."

"The Queen of the Pacific?"

"That's right. Oddly enough, the same old liner I came out in. But this voyage, it's going to be really close quarters. Families from Ceylon going home, and a draft of Royal Air Force from India. But it doesn't matter. All that matters is that we'll be on board." She smiled, feeling guilty again. "It's an awful thing to say, but it does help having a Rear Admiral as a relation. Bob hasn't just pulled strings, he's been winching hawsers. Blasting away on the telephone, pulling rank. He's done it all."

"And Trincomalee?"

"I never went back. I'm never going back."

"What about your gear? The stuff you left behind."

"Anything special, I brought with me to Colombo; all that got left behind were a few books and some washed-out clothes and my winter uniform. I don't care what happens to any of that. Not important. As well, last week Jess and I went to Whiteaway and Laidlaw, and spent an entire day buying the shop out. So we're both kitted up for all eventualities."

He smiled. "I like the way you said that."

"Said what?"

"Jess and I. It sounds as though you'd never been apart."

"Wasn't it a miracle, Hugo? Wasn't it like something out of a dream? I maybe *sound* as though we've never been apart, but I still wake in the night and wonder if I've imagined it all, and I have to turn on the light so that I can look at her, lying in the next bed, and know that it's really true."

"How is she?"

"Amazing. So resilient. Later, we may have problems. Physical, or psychological. But so far, she seems to have emerged with colours flying."

"Where is she now?"

"Bob took her to the zoo. She wanted to look at the alligators."

"I'm sorry I've missed her."

"They'll be back sometime. Stay till they come."

"I can't. I've been bidden for drinks with the C-in-C, and if I'm late I'll be court-martialled."

At this point they were interrupted by Thomas, approaching down the length of the veranda, and bearing the tea-tray. Hugo reached forward and pulled up a table, and Thomas, with his customary formality, set down the tray, bowed, and withdrew.

When he had gone, she said, "I know Bob told you all about Jess, and the camp in Java and everything, but did he tell you about Gus Callender?"

"Who's Gus Callender? Do you want me to be mother and pour the tea?"

"Please. He obviously *didn't* tell you. It was just the most extraordinary thing. It all happened on the same day. The morning of the day that we knew that Jess was alive. You know about the hospital ship? *Orion?* With the men from the Burma Railway?"

"Yes. She was here for a day, sailed that evening."

"Well, I went to welcome the men who came ashore . . ." He handed her a cup and saucer, and she smelt the fresh scent of China tea and the tang of lemon, but it was too hot to drink, so she let it rest on her lap. ". . . and there was this man there, a captain in the Gordon Highlanders . . ."

She told him about the bizarre encounter. Believing that Gus was dead, and suddenly finding him alive. Going with him to the Galle Face Hotel; the touching reunion with the old waiter; the bottle of Black & White whisky. She told him how Gus had looked, and how he had been dressed, and how, at the end, she had put him in another taxi, headed for the Fort and the hospital ship, and said goodbye.

". . . and then I came back here and even before I'd got into the house, Bob had appeared and was telling me that Jess was alive. Two people I thought had gone forever. All in the same day. Wasn't that the strangest thing, Hugo?"

He said, "Quite amazing," and clearly meant it.

"The only thing is, I don't feel as happy about Gus as I do about Jess. His old parents died while he was in prison and working on the railway; he was told in Rangoon that they had died. He hasn't got any other family. No brothers or sisters. I feel it's going to be rather a dismal homecoming for him when he does get back to Scotland."

"Where's his home?"

"Aberdeenshire, somewhere. I don't know. I never knew him all that well. He was a friend of friends, in Cornwall. He stayed with them during the summer before the war. That's when I met him, and I've never set eyes on him since. Until I saw him again, standing there on Gordon's Green."

"Has he got a home to return to?"

"Yes. I think it's some sort of a great big estate. There certainly seemed to be plenty of money. He was at Cambridge, and before that he'd been at Rugby. And he drove around in a very elegant, supercharged Lagonda."

"Sounds as though he should be all right."

"But *people* matter, don't they? Family. Friends."

"If he's served in a Scottish regiment, he'll be surrounded by friends."

"I hope so, Hugo. I really hope so."

Her tea had cooled. She lifted the cup and drank some, and felt heated, and yet refreshed, all at the same time. Still thinking of Gus, she said, "But I *must* keep in touch."

"And who," asked Hugo, "are *you* going back to?"

She laughed. "A jolly houseful of women."

"And Jess?"

"Sooner or later, she'll have to go to school. Perhaps later. She deserves a bit of time to settle in, get her bearings, have some fun."

"Friends and family?"

"Of course."

"No loving swain, waiting to claim you? Waiting to jam a wedding ring on your finger?"

It was sometimes hard to tell whether or not Hugo was joking. She looked up into his face, and saw that he was not.

"Why do you ask?"

"Because if there were, I should say he was a lucky man."

She took her cup and saucer and leaned over to put it back on the table. "Hugo, I would hate you ever to think I had simply used you."

"I would never think that. I just happened to be around when you were having a bad day. I only wished we'd had more time together."

"We said all this before. I don't think it would have made any difference."

"No. Probably not."

"But that doesn't mean that it wasn't the *best*. Meeting you, and all the things we did together. And the war over, and knowing that it hadn't killed off all the trivial, frivolous, fun things people *used to do* before it all began. Like 'I Can't Give You Anything But Love, Baby,' and dancing in the moonlight, and wearing a new dress, and shrieking with laughter about that dreadful Moira Burridge. Nothing mattering too much, and yet terribly important all at the same time. I'm really grateful. I can't think of anyone else who could have brought it all back, made it real again, so sweetly."

He reached out and took her hand in his. "When I get back to England—whenever—shall we see each other?"

"Of course. You must come and visit me in Cornwall. I have a dream of a house, so close to the sea. You can come for summer holidays. By yourself, or with some luscious lady friend. In the fullness of time, you can bring your wife and children, and we'll all go bucket-and-spading together."

"I like that."

"What do you like?"

"Clear intentions."

"I don't want to cling to you, Hugo. It was never like that. But I don't want to lose you either."

"How shall I find you?"

"Phone book. Dunbar, the Dower House, Rosemullion."

"And if I ring you up, you promise you won't say, 'Who the hell are you?'"

"No. I don't think I'd ever say that."

He stayed for a little longer, and they went on talking, about nothing in particular, and then he looked at his watch and said it was time that he was off. "I have to make some telephone calls and write a letter and present myself to the C-in-C in good working order, and five minutes before the appointed hour."

"When's that?"

"Six-thirty. Cocktails. State occasion. Lord and Lady Mountbatten, no less."

"Will Moira Burridge be there?"

"Heaven forbid."

"Send her my regards."

"If you don't watch out, I'll give her your address in Cornwall and say you can't *wait* to have her to stay."

"You do, and I'll shoot you."

She went with him to the door, and down the steps to where his car stood parked on the baking gravel. He turned to her. "Goodbye."

"Goodbye, Hugo."

They kissed. Both cheeks.

"It's been great."

"Yes. Great. And thank you."

"I am so pleased, so pleased, that it all worked out for you."

She said, "It hasn't worked out yet. But it's begun."

The Queen of the Pacific
Med.

Friday 12th October, 1945.

Dear Gus,

I'm sitting on a rather draughty promenade deck, surrounded by squalling children and distraught mothers, and a large number of very bored aircraftmen. Nothing to sit on, so we all squat around the deck, like a lot of refugees, getting grubbier by the day, because there are few washing facilities!

But I must explain. Easier to begin from the moment I said goodbye to you outside the Galle Face. I got home that day to be told by Bob (Uncle, Rear Admiral Somerville) that my little sister Jess had been found in an internment camp in Java. First you and then her! A day of miracles. Bob, with pheasant-shooting in mind, called it a Right and Left.

She is fourteen now. She flew back to Colombo from Jakarta in a USAF Dakota, and Bob and I met her at Ratmalana Air Station. She is skinny and sun-browned, and will soon be as tall as me. She is well.

So we had a week of tremendous organization, the upshot of which is that we're both on our way home. I'm getting a compassionate discharge, and we'll go back to the Dower House together.

I have thought of you so much . . . perhaps by now you are already back in Scotland. I shall send this to the address you gave me, and post the letter when we get to Gib.

It was the most wonderful thing, finding you again and being able to spend a bit of time together. I was just terribly sorry that I had to tell you about Loveday being married. I quite understand that, perhaps for a bit, you won't want to come to Cornwall, because of her. But when you've settled back at Ardvray and picked up the threads of your life, perhaps you'll feel differently. When this happens, you know the most enormous welcomes wait for you. Not just me, but Nancherrow as well. Anytime. Just come. And bring your sketch-book!

Please write to me and let me know how things are going and what your plans are.

With my love,

Judith

The Dower House,
Rosemullion,

Sunday 21st October.
TRAFALGAR DAY

My darling Bob,

They're home. Safe and sound. I hired a huge taxi, and went on Friday to scoop them off the *Riviera* at Penzance. The train came in, and there they were on the platform, surrounded by mounds of luggage. I don't think I've ever been more excited.

Both are looking well, if tired and a bit emaciated. Jess bears no relation at all to that fat, spoilt little baby girl who stayed with us that Christmas at Keyham. Except, those blue eyes are just as bright, and she has talked a lot about you and the little time she spent with you in Colombo.

The most touching was when she saw Phyllis again. As the taxi arrived at the Dower House, Phyllis and Anna, with Morag in tow, came out of the door to meet us. Nobody said anything to Jess, but she took one look at Phyllis, and was out of the taxi before it had even stopped, to cast herself into Phyllis's arms. I think Anna is a bit jealous, but Jess is particularly nice to her; she said that she spent a lot of time in the camps helping to look after the smaller ones.

Judith showed me the letter from that sweet Australian girl who looked after Jess when they were interned. What hell they went through together. I am sure that, sooner or later, Jess will begin to speak of her ghastly experiences. I am equally sure that, when she does, it will be to Phyllis.

This morning I went to church and said THANK YOU.

Now, it's Sunday afternoon, a chilly October day, all leaves blown from trees, showers and a nippy wind. Judith has taken Jess to Nancherrow to have nursery tea with them all, and Loveday and Nat. They set off, walking, about an hour ago, bundled up in raincoats and rubber boots. At the first opportunity, we must get a bicycle for Jess. It's really an essential, because only a teaspoonful of petrol every week, and Judith's car is still on chocks in the garage and totally out of commission until she gets a petrol ration for herself.

In the house, we are a bit of a squash, but managing comfortably. Anna's moved in with her mother, and Jess has got Anna's room. But I think the time has come for me to fly this nest and start building another one for you and me. I saw a lovely house in Portscatho last week, three bedrooms and two bathrooms, not in the village but up on the hill, looking out over the sea. It's only half a mile from the village shop, and a couple of miles from Saint Mawes. (Mooring for your boat?) It's in good nick, and we could move in tomorrow if we wanted, so I think I shall put in an offer and get it. I spoke to Hester Lang on the telephone the other day, and she has promised to come and stay, and help me over the move. I want to be all settled in and ready for when you come home and we can be together again.

As for Phyllis, the great news is that Cyril has decided to stay in the Navy on a regular basis. He has done really well, is now a petty officer, with an excellent war record, and a DSM for gallantry. I think it is very important that we get Phyllis settled. With Molly gone, I feel a bit responsible for her, after these years that we have lived, quite happily, together. It will depend on how much of his pay Cyril has been able to save, but they must have a home of their own, somewhere for him to come for his leaves. Perhaps a little terrace house in Penzance. If more than they could afford, would we be able to chip in a little? I am sure Judith would help, but she's got Jess to think about now, and her schooling, et cetera. I'll have a word with her when some of the excitement has died down.

So that's about it. If I don't stop now I shan't catch the post. Think of me, splashing down the hill to push this letter into the letter-box. I shall take Morag with me for a little exercise. She is getting older now, but still keen as mustard if you breathe the word "Walkies."

Darling Bob. How lucky we are. Now, I can't wait for you to come home. Don't linger too long.

My love as forever

Biddy

"I'd forgotten how long this road is."

"We seem to be going on forever."

"It's because we're walking. On bikes it doesn't seem anything."

The Nancherrow drive looked a bit unkempt, filled with pot-holes and puddles, and the verges on either side were beginning to encroach. The hydrangeas were long over, their flower-heads browned and papery, sagging with moisture from the showers which had been blown in from the sea, and continued, all through the afternoon. High above, the branches were bare, tossing in the wind, and beyond them the pale sky, scudded with grey, watery clouds.

"The first time I ever came to Nancherrow, the drive was so long and twisty, I was sure the house was going to be quite spooky, when we finally reached it. But of course, it wasn't. It's quite new. You'll see. And then, when I read *Rebecca*, I was reminded of Nancherrow, and seeing it all for the very first time."

"I've never read *Rebecca*."

"You haven't had much chance. But what a treat you've got in store. Heaps of treats. I shall feed you books, like we feed Morag dog-meal."

"I had one book when I was little that I always remember. I got it for Christmas. It was huge and coloured and filled with pictures and stories. I wonder what happened to that?"

"It was put in store, I expect. With all our other stuff. Crates of it. We'll have to get it from the depository. Things that belonged to Mummy. Ornaments and bits of china. It'll be like opening Pandora's box . . ."

The trees were thinning. They were nearly there. Around the last curve of the drive, and the house stood before them, but a squall was driving in, hiding, like a grey curtain, the view of the sea. They stopped, and stared for a moment, raincoats dripping, mufflers blowing in the wind.

Then Jess said, "It's really *big*."

"They needed a big house. They had three children, and lots of servants, and lots of friends always coming to stay. I had a room of my own. The pink room. After tea, I'll show you. Come on, or we're going to get soaked again."

They ran across the gravel, reaching the sanctuary of the front door just as the rain lashed down once more. There, they shed raincoats, toed off their rubber boots. Then Judith opened the inner door and, in socked feet, she and Jess went into the hall.

Unchanged. Just the same. The same smell. It was a bit chilly, perhaps, despite the logs which smouldered in the huge hearth, but an arrangement of chrysanthemums and autumn foliage stood, bright as flames, in the middle of the round table, where still lay the dog leads, the Visitors' Book, the small stack of mail waiting to be collected by the postman.

No sound. Only the tick of the old clock.

"Where is everybody?" Jess whispered, sounding a bit overawed.

"I don't know. We'll go and look. Upstairs first."

On the half-landing, they heard the faint strains of the nursery wireless floating along the passage. The nursery door stood ajar. Judith pushed it gently open, and saw Mary, intent on a pile of ironing. She said her name.

"Oh, *Judith*." The iron was put down with a thump, and Mary's sturdy arms opened for her. "I can't believe you've come back to us. And that you're really *here* again. It's been so long! And this is Jess? Hello, Jess, it's lovely to meet you. Look at your heads, you're soaking. Walk down, did you?"

"Yes. All the way. We've only got one bike. Where's Loveday?"

"She'll be here directly. Walking down from Lidgey with Nat. She had to help Walter pen a couple of calves."

"How is Nat?"

"He's a holy terror." Mary had a bit more grey in her hair, and a few more lines on her face, and she was thinner too, but in a funny way it rather suited her. There were darns in her blue cardigan, and the collar of her blouse was a bit frayed, but she still smelt of Johnson's Baby Soap and fresh ironing.

"Seen Mrs. Carey-Lewis, have you?"

"No. We came straight upstairs to find you."

"Then let's go down now, and tell her you're here."

Pausing only to switch off her iron, turn off her wireless, and put another log on her little fire ("Good thing we've got plenty of trees on this place, otherwise we'd all be dying of cold"), she led them out of the nursery, back down the stairs, and along the hall to the door of the small sitting-room. She tapped on the panel, opened it a crack, and put her head around the edge of the door.

"Someone to *see* you!" And, dramatically, she flung the door wide open.

And there they were, sitting on either side of the fireplace, Diana with her tapestry, and the Colonel with the *Sunday Times*. At his feet, old Tiger lay asleep, but Pekoe, who had been dozing on the sofa and now suspected robbers, sat to attention and let loose a cacophony of barks. Diana looked up, snatched off her spectacles, cast aside her sewing, and sprang to her feet.

"Pekoe, be quiet. It's only Judith. It's *Judith*." Pekoe, deprived of pleasure, sank sulkily back onto the cushions. "Judith. Oh, darling. It's been a thousand years. Come and let me hug you to bits." She was slender, tall, and as lovely as ever, despite the fact that her corn-coloured hair had faded to silver. "You've come back, my precious third daughter. And you're looking utterly wonderful! And you've brought *Jess*. Jess. I'm Diana Carey-Lewis. We've heard so much about you, and this is the very first time we've ever met . . ."

Released from Diana's embrace, Judith turned to the Colonel, who was now standing, patiently awaiting his turn. He had always looked younger than his years, and now it seemed as though time had caught up with him. And, as well, his clothes, which hung in shabby fashion on his lanky frame—a very elderly tweed jacket, and a pair of washed-out corduroy trousers in which, in the old days, he would not have been seen dead.

"My dear." Formal; as always, a little shy. She took his hands in hers and they kissed. "How pleased we are to have you home again."

"Not nearly as grateful as I am to be here." Now Tiger, ever courteous, had heaved himself into a sitting position, and Judith stooped to fondle his head. She said sadly, "He's looking old." He was too. Not fat, but heavy and arthritic, and his dear muzzle was quite grey.

"We're none of us getting any younger. I should start looking for another Labrador puppy, but somehow I haven't got the heart . . ."

"Edgar. Darling, you must say hello to Jess."

He put out his hand. "How do you do, Jess? I must introduce you to my dog, Tiger. This is Jess, Tiger." He smiled, his gentle, charming smile which no child could ever resist. "You've come a long way. What do you think of Cornwall, eh? Doesn't rain like this *all* the time."

Jess said, "I actually remember Cornwall."

"Do you, by Jove? That's going a long way back. Why don't we sit down, and you can tell me about it . . . here, on this stool by the fire . . ." He pushed aside some magazines and papers. "How old were you when you left?"

"I was four."

"I didn't realize you were as old as that. Well, of course you have memories. *I* can remember when I was two. Sitting in my pram, and some other child pushing a bit of butterscotch into my mouth . . ."

At this moment, Mary, raising her voice slightly, announced that she was going to go and put the kettle on for tea, and everybody agreed that this would be a splendid idea. When she had taken herself off, Diana sank back into her chair, and Judith sat on the end of the sofa that Pekoe was not occupying.

"Darling, what a time you've had. You look thin. Terribly elegant. Are you all right?"

"Of course I'm all right."

"Loveday's dying to see you and show you her wicked Nat. They'll be here in a moment. And little Jess! What a brave child. Such experiences. Biddy telephoned the moment she got the cable from Bob. She'd already told us that . . ." Realizing what she had been about to say, and with Jess in earshot, Diana stopped. She glanced at Jess, sitting there with her back to them, deep in conversation with the Colonel. She mouthed *Jess was dead.* Judith nodded. ". . . then, to *hear*. To be told it wasn't true. You must have nearly died of joy."

"It was pretty exciting."

"And, darling, so dreadfully sad about your parents. Unthinkable. I was going to write, but you didn't give me time. Biddy told me all the awful things, but before I could put pen to paper, we learned you were on your way home. What sort of a voyage did you have?"

"Scarcely a voyage. More an endurance test. The boat was packed. Three sittings for meals. You can imagine."

"Ghastly. Talking of meals, the Nettlebeds send their love and say they'll see you soon. They have the whole of Sunday off now, and they've gone to Camborne to visit some ancient relation in a nursing home. Was it heaven to get back to the Dower House? Isn't the garden looking pretty? I gave Phyllis some cuttings . . ."

Brittle with excitement, she chattered on, and Judith sat and tried to look as though she was listening, but wasn't. She was thinking about Gus Callender. Was now the moment to tell Diana and the Colonel that Gus was alive? No, she decided, it wasn't the moment. The first person to be told, and in private, was Loveday. Later today, somehow, somewhere, Judith would do this.

". . . where is little Jess sleeping?"

"In Anna's room. There's plenty of space. Anna's gone in with Phyllis. Just for the time being."

"And what plans have you made for Jess?"

"I suppose I'll have to go and see Miss Catto, and see if she'll take her at Saint Ursula's."

"But, my darling, of course she will. Oh, isn't it too extraordinary how life goes full-circle. Oh, what am I thinking of? I haven't told you about Athena. She's going to have another baby. In the spring, I think. Too exciting. I can't tell you how we missed them when they went. The house was totally empty without a child in it . . ."

No sooner were the words out of her mouth than, *bang* on cue, could be heard the piercing tones of Nathaniel Mudge, on his way from the kitchen, and in full spate of argument with his mother.

"I don't want to take my boots off."

"You've got to. They're covered in mud."

"They *not* covered in mud."

"They are. You've trodden mud all across the kitchen floor. Now come here . . ."

"No . . ."

"Nat . . ."

A howl. Loveday had clearly caught him and was forcibly removing his boots.

Diana said faintly, "Oh dear."

A moment later, the door burst open and her grandson catapulted into the room, bereft of footwear, his cheeks scarlet with indignation, and his bottom lip sticking out like a shelf.

"What's this all about?" Diana asked, and Nat told her in no uncertain fashion. "Mum's taken my boots off. They're new boots. They're red. I was wantin' to *show* them to you."

Trying to placate, "We'll see them another time," Diana told him soothingly.

"But I want you to see them *now*."

Judith got up from the sofa. As she did so, Loveday appeared in the open doorway. Looking exactly the way she always had, a ragamuffin teenager, and not in the least like the mother of that formidable three-year-old. She wore trousers and an old pullover and a pair of red socks, and her hair still bounced up from her head in dark, lustrous curls.

There was a pause, while they simply stood there, grinning at each other. Then, "Well, look who's here," said Loveday. "God, it's good to see you." They met, and hugged and kissed perfunctorily, just the way they always used to. "Sorry we're a bit late, but . . . Nat, don't put your fingers near Pekoe's eye. You know you're not allowed to."

Nat glared at his mother with defiant brown eyes, and Judith, for all her good intentions, dissolved into laughter.

"You seem to have met your match."

"Oh, he's a horror. Aren't you, Nat? You're very sweet, but you're a horror."

"My dad says I'm a little bugger," Nat informed the company in general, and then catching sight of Jess, another stranger, he fixed his gaze upon her and stared without blinking.

Jess, clearly amused, said, "Hello."

"Who are you?"

"I'm Jess."

"What are you doin' here?"

"I've come for tea."

"We brought chocolate biscuits in a bag, my mum and me."

"Are you going to give me one?"

Nat considered this, and then said, "No. I'm going to eat them all myself."

He then set about clambering onto the sofa and commencing to bounce, and for a moment it looked as though the entire afternoon was about to break up into mayhem, but Mary bustled back to save the day, to tell them that tea was on the table, to scoop Nathaniel out of the air, mid-bounce, and to bear him, shrieking, with what one hoped was glee, in the direction of the dining-room.

"She's the only person," said Loveday, with a sort of hopeless pride, "who can do a thing with him."

"What about Walter?"

"Oh, Walter's worse than he is. Come on, Mummy, let's go and eat."

So they all trooped through to the dining-room, the Colonel pausing to put the guard in front of the fire, and bringing up the rear. There, the tea-table had been laid, and set with all the remembered nursery treats, of jam sandwiches and marmite sandwiches, a fruit-cake baked in a ring, and the chocolate biscuits provided by Loveday.

It was a much diminished table from the one that Judith recalled from the old days. All the leaves had been removed, and what remained looked strangely small and inadequate in the middle of the huge, formal room. Gone was the heavy white damask table-cloth, and in its place, humble but practical, blue-and-white-checked seersucker. As it was nursery tea, Mary sat at one end of the table, in charge of the big brown teapot (Judith remembered that all the traditional silver had been put away at the beginning of the war), and with Nat alongside her on a high chair. Nat didn't want to sit on the high chair. Each time he was put onto it, he slid off, until finally Mary set him down with such a thump on his bottom that he heeded the warning and stayed where he was.

The Colonel, facing Mary, had Jess on his left hand. "Would you like a jam sandwich or marmite?" he asked her politely, and Jess said that she would like a jam, while Nat banged on the table with a spoon and announced to the assembled company that what he wanted, and wanted now, was a chocolate biscuit.

But finally he was shushed, fed with a marmite sandwich, the pandemonium subdued, and normal conversation was able to continue. Mary poured tea. Cups were handed round. Diana, warm and charming, and ever the perfect hostess, turned to Jess.

"Now, Jess, you must tell us all the lovely things that you and Judith plan to do, now you're home again. What's the first excitement?"

Jess, with all eyes upon her, became a bit embarrassed. She hastily swallowed a mouthful of jam sandwich and said, "I don't know, really," and across the table caught Judith's eye, a clear signal for help.

"How about the bicycle?" Judith prompted.

"Oh yes. We're going to buy a bicycle for me."

"It might have to be second-hand," Diana warned. "They're terribly difficult to get. Like cars. You can't buy a new car nowadays, and second-hand ones cost more than the new ones do. What else? Are you going to go and look at your old house in Penmarron? Where you used to live?"

"We thought we'd go take the train one day. And go to Porthkerris too."

"What a good idea."

"We can't go into the house. Riverside, I mean, because other people live there now." Uninterrupted, and with all of them listening with kindly interest, Jess's sudden attack of shyness died a natural death. "But we thought we could look at it. And go and see . . ." But she had forgotten the name. Once more, she turned to Judith.

"Mrs. Berry," Judith reminded her. "In the village shop. She used to give you fruit gums. And maybe Mr. Willis, down at the ferry. Only he was *my* friend. I don't think he ever knew Jess."

The Colonel said, "You'll like Porthkerris, Jess. Full of boats and artists and funny little streets."

"And the Warrens," Loveday chimed in. "You must take Jess to see the Warrens, Judith. Mrs. Warren would be frightfully hurt if you went to Porthkerris and didn't go and eat an enormous tea with her."

"What's happened to Heather? I haven't heard from her in years. Is she still in that horrible spy place?"

"No, she's gone to America, on some mission with her boss at the Foreign Office. Last we heard of her, she was in Washington."

"Heavens above. She might have let me know."

Loveday was cutting the cake. "Who wants a bit of fruit-cake?"

Jess, having finished her sandwich, took an enormous slice. She said, "I don't know who Heather is."

"She was a friend of ours, in the old days," Loveday told her. "Judith and I used to go and stay with her and her family. The summer before the war, and the sun never stopped shining, and we spent all the time on the beach. Judith had just got her car, and we felt *frightfully* grown up."

"Was she at school with you?" Jess asked.

"No. She was at another school. We were at Saint Ursula's."

Jess said, "Judith thinks I should go there."

"Another little novice for the nunnery."

"Oh, *Loveday*." Sitting at the end of the table, behind her huge teapot, Mary sounded quite cross. "You really vex me when you say silly things like that. And to Jess, too. Saint Ursula's is a lovely school. You were very happy there. Made enough fuss to be allowed to go there, you did."

"Oh, but Mary, the uniforms! And all those potty rules."

Jess was beginning to look a bit worried. Observing this, the Colonel laid his hand upon her own. He said, "Don't take any notice of that silly daughter of mine. It's an excellent school, and Miss Catto is a splendid lady. She needed to be to cope with Loveday."

"Thank you, Pops, *very* much."

"Anyway"—Diana held out her cup for Mary to refill—"they don't wear uniforms any more. The war put an end to that. And there was another girls' school, from Kent, evacuated onto them, so the uniforms were different anyway. And they had to build Nissen huts all over the garden, because there weren't enough classrooms for all the girls."

"Don't they wear any sort of uniform now?" Judith asked.

"Just school-ties."

"What a relief. I shall never forget that endless clothes list poor Mummy had to go and shop with."

"In Medways, darling. That was the first time we ever saw you. All of us, buying horrible school uniforms. Doesn't it seem an age ago?"

"It is an age ago," said Loveday abruptly. And then, "All right, Nat. All right. You can have your chocolate biscuit now."

By the time tea was finished, the dank October afternoon had faded into darkness. It was overcast now, and the rain falling steadily, yet nobody stood to go and draw the heavy curtains.

"Such bliss," said Diana. "No black-out. I still haven't got used to the freedom of it. Being able to sit indoors and watch the twilight, and not to have to shut it all away. It took us so long to make all the black-out curtains and hang them up, and it only took us about three days to tear them all down again. Mary, don't start clattering about with the teacups, we'll wash them up. Take Nat up to the nursery and give Loveday a few moments to herself." She turned to Jess. "Perhaps Jess would like to go too. Not because we want to get rid of you, darling, but because there are lots of goodies up there you might like to look at. Books and such, and jigsaw puzzles and rather precious doll's-house furniture. But don't let Nat get his hands on that." Jess hesitated. Diana smiled. "Only if you want," she finished.

"Yes, I'd like to go."

Mary wiped Nat's face with a napkin. "Nat doesn't like doll's-house furniture. He likes the bricks, and the little tractors, don't you, my duck?"

She got to her feet and heaved him up into her arms. "Come on, Jess, we'll see what we can find for you."

When they had gone, it was all rather peaceful. Diana emptied the last trickle of the teapot into her cup, and then lit a cigarette. "What a sweet girl, Judith. You should be proud of her."

"I am."

"So confident."

"It's deceptive. She's still feeling her way."

The Colonel had stood, to fetch from the sideboard an ashtray for his wife. He set it down on the table beside her, and she looked up at him and smiled her thanks. "No tears? No nightmares? No ill effects?"

"I don't think so."

"Perhaps a tiny check-over by a doctor might be a good idea. Though I must say, she looks healthy enough to me. Talking of which, old Dr. Wells popped in the other day to have a look at Nat, who was coughing and snivelling, and Mary and Loveday were a bit worried about him. (Nothing wrong, just a chesty cold.) But he did say that Jeremy's hoping to get some leave soon, and come home for a bit. He hasn't had any leave for about two years. He's been stuck in the Med. all that time. Now, where . . . ?"

"Malta," said the Colonel.

"I couldn't remember if it was Malta or Gibraltar. I knew it was *somewhere*."

Judith said, "I should think he'd be demobbed pretty soon," and was delighted with the casualness of her voice. "Considering the fact that he was one of the very first to join up."

Loveday absently helped herself to another slice of cake. "I can't see him settling down in Truro after all that jolly bobbing about on the high seas."

"I can," said Diana. "The perfect country GP with a dog in the back of his car. You never ran into him, Judith?"

"No. I always thought he might come out East with the Fleet. Everybody one knew turned up in Trincomalee sooner or later. But he never did."

"*I* always thought he'd get married. Perhaps Malta doesn't have much local talent." She yawned, and sat back in her chair, and surveyed the crumbly shambles of the tea-table. "I suppose we'd better get rid of this, and go and wash it up."

"Don't worry, Mummy," Loveday told her, through cake crumbs. "Judith and I will do it together. We'll be two little schoolfriends, earning Brownie points."

"What happened to Hetty?" Judith asked.

"Oh, she finally escaped Mrs. Nettlebed's clutches and went off to do her war-work. Ward maid in a hospital in Plymouth. Poor Hetty. Talk about out of the frying pan and into the fire. Will you really deal with all this, my pets? It's actually past six, and we always ring Athena on Sunday evenings . . ."

"Send her my love."

"We'll do that."

The kitchen, large and old-fashioned as ever, and a bit warmer than the rest of the house, felt strangely empty without the Nettlebeds, and Hetty clashing about in the scullery.

"Who scours the saucepans now?" Judith asked, tying an apron around her waist, and filling the old clay sink with scalding water from the brass tap.

"Mrs. Nettlebed, I suppose. Or Mary. Certainly not my mother."

"Does Nettlebed still grow the vegetables?"

"He and Mr. Mudge together. We all eat masses of vegetables, because there's not much else. And although the house is empty this weekend, there seem to be just as many guests as ever; Mummy adopted endless service people who happened to be stationed around and about, and they still trickle in and out. I'm afraid when they all shut up shop and leave, she's really going to miss all the buzz and company."

"How about Tommy Mortimer?"

646

"Oh, he still pops down from London from time to time. With various other old chums. Keeps Mummy amused. When Athena and Clementina left, it was awful for her."

Judith squirted some washing-up liquid into the water, and stirred it up into bubbles, and then put in the first pile of plates.

She said, "How's Walter?"

"He's all right."

"How's the farm going?"

"Fine."

"And Mr. Mudge?"

"He's still working, but he's getting a bit beyond it now."

"What happens when he retires?"

"I dunno. I suppose Walter and I move into the farmhouse. We'll swap houses or something. I don't know."

Her answers were all so laconic, so disinterested that Judith's heart chilled. She said, "What do you do when he's *not* working? I mean, do you go to the cinema ever, or picnics, or down to the pub?"

"I used to go to the pub sometimes, but I can't now I've got Nat. I can always leave him with Mrs. Mudge but, to be truthful, I'm not all that keen on going to pubs. So Walter goes alone."

"Oh, *Loveday*."

"What's that gloomy voice for?"

"It doesn't sound much fun."

"It's okay. Sometimes we have friends in for supper, or something. Except that I'm not much of a cook."

"What about the horses? Do you still ride together?"

"Not much. I sold Fleet, and I never got around to getting another horse. And there isn't a Hunt now, because all the hounds were put down at the beginning of the war."

"Now it's over, perhaps they'll start it up again."

"Yes. Perhaps."

She had found a tea-towel and was drying the plates and cups, very slowly, one at a time, and then setting them down in piles on the scullery table.

"Are you happy, Loveday?"

Loveday took another plate out of the rack. "Who was it who said that marriage was a summer birdcage, set out in a garden? And all the birds of the air wanted to get in, and all the caged birds wanted to get out?"

"I don't know."

"You're a bird of the air. Free. You can fly anywhere."

"No, I can't. I've got Jess."

"Not wanting to get into the summer birdcage?"

"No."

"No lovelorn sailor? I can't believe it. Don't tell me you're still in love with Edward?"

"Edward's been dead for years."

"I'm sorry. I shouldn't have said that."

"I don't mind you saying it. He was your brother."

Loveday wiped another couple of plates. "I always thought that Jeremy was in love with you."

Judith scraped at a stubborn crumb of sticky fruit-cake. "I think you were probably wrong."

"Did you keep in touch? Did you write letters to each other?"

"No. The last time I saw him was in London at the beginning of 1942. Just before Singapore. I haven't seen him, nor heard from him since."

"Did you have a row?"

"No. We didn't have a row. I suppose we just tacitly decided to go our separate ways."

"I wonder why he never got married. He's frightfully old now. He must be thirty-seven. I suppose when he gets back, his father will retire, and then Jeremy will be responsible for all the neighbourhood boils and bunions."

"That's what he always wanted."

The last plate, and then the teapot. Judith pulled out the plug and watched the suds seep away.

"That's the lot." She unknotted the ties of the apron and hung it back on its hook, and then turned, and stood leaning against the edge of the sink.

"I'm sorry." Loveday took the plate from the rack and dried it.

Judith frowned. "What about?"

"Saying that about Edward. I say such horrid things to people these days, and I don't mean to." She put the plate on the top of the stack. "You *will* come and see me, won't you? At Lidgey. You never saw my funny little house when it was finished. And I love the farm and the animals. And I love Nat too, even though he's such a holy terror." She pushed back the ragged cuff of her sweater and looked at her watch. "God Almighty, I must go. My kitchen's a mess, and I've got to get Walter's tea, and get Nat to bed . . ."

Judith said, "Don't go."

Loveday looked a bit taken aback. "I have to."

"Five minutes. I have something to tell you."

"What?"

"You promise you'll listen, and not interrupt, and hear me out?"

"All right." Loveday hitched herself up onto the table, and sat there, shoulders hunched and trousered legs dangling. "Fire away."

"It's about Gus."

Loveday froze. In the draughty, slate-floored scullery, the only sound was the humming of the refrigerator and the slow dripping of one of the brass taps. Drip. Drip. The beads of water fell into the clay sink.

"What about Gus?"

Judith told her.

". . . so then he said it was time he went back to the hospital ship, and we got a taxi for him and said goodbye. And he went. End of story."

Loveday had kept her word. Had made no comment and asked no questions. She simply sat there, motionless as a statue, and listened. Now, she still said nothing.

"I . . . I wrote to him on the troop-ship and posted it in Gib. But he's not replied."

Loveday said, "Is he all right?"

"I don't know. He looked amazing, considering all he'd gone through. Thin, but then he was never very fat. And a bit worn."

"Why didn't he let us *know* . . . ?"

"I've explained. He couldn't. There was only one letter and that was to his parents. They knew nothing about you, and Diana, and the Colonel. Even if they'd got the letter, they wouldn't have known to pass on the news."

"I was so certain he was dead."

"I know, Loveday."

"It was like being certain with every bone of my body. A sort of emptiness. A void."

"You mustn't blame yourself."

"What will happen to him?"

"He'll be all right. Scottish regiments are notoriously clanny. Like family. All his friends will rally around."

Loveday said, "I don't want him to come here."

"I can understand that. To be truthful, I don't think Gus would be very keen on the idea either."

"Did he believe that I would wait for him?"

"Yes." There wasn't any other answer.

"Oh, God." Sitting under the cold overhead light of the scullery, Loveday's face was shadowed and pinched, her violet eyes empty of expression.

"I'm sorry, Loveday."

"Not your fault. All my fault. Everything."

"I hated telling you."

"He's alive. I should be rejoicing. Not sitting here looking like a wet weekend."

"I didn't much like telling Gus, either. That you were married."

"That's different. That was the end of something. For Gus it's the beginning of the rest of his life. At least he's not broke, and possessionless. There's *something* for him to go back to."

"And you?"

"Oh, I've got it all. Husband, son, the farm. Nancherrow. Mummy and Pops. Mary. Everything unchanged. Everything I always wanted." She fell silent for a moment, and then said, "Do Mummy and Pops know about Gus?"

"No. I wanted to tell you first. If you like, I'll go and tell them now."

"No. I will. When you and Jess have gone. Before I go back to Lidgey. It's better that way." Once more she looked at her watch. "And then I simply must go home." She slipped off the table. "Walter will be champing for his tea."

"You're all right?"

"Yes." Loveday thought about this, and then grinned, and the wicked, fearless, stubborn little girl she had once been was suddenly there again. "Yes. I'm fine."

The next morning, Diana came to the Dower House.

A Monday. After breakfast, the little household had dispersed. Anna first, trudging down the hill to the Rosemullion Primary School, her satchel on her back, and a biscuit, for elevenses, in her pocket. Then Biddy had departed, because it was her day in Penzance, for the Red Cross. Jess, who had discovered the Hut in the course of some private explorations and fallen in love with its charm, its privacy, and its smallness, had been supplied with brooms and dusters, and, in high excitement, had gone running down the garden to do a bit of cleaning.

Now, eleven o'clock and she still had not returned. Phyllis was pegging out the weekly lines of washing, and Judith, in the kitchen, made soup. The carcass of yesterday's chicken had been boiled up for stock, and she was at the sink engaged in scraping vegetables, and peeling leeks and onions; she had always found making soup immensely therapeutic (a bit like building a compost heap), and the fragrance, as it cooked, spiced with herbs from the garden, was as comforting as the smell of newly baked bread, or the hot scent of warm gingerbread.

Chopping carrots, she heard the car come up the hill, through the open gate, and draw up outside the front of the house. Expecting nobody in particular, she looked out of the window and saw Diana getting out of the battered little fishmonger's van, which had been bought, to conserve petrol, at the beginning of the war, and done yeoman service ever since.

Judith went through the scullery and out of the open back door. Diana was talking to Phyllis over the escallonia hedge that bordered the washing-green. She wore a narrow tweed skirt and a loose jacket, and carried a large, old-fashioned marketing basket on her arm.

"Diana."

Diana turned. "Oh, darling, not interrupting, am I? I've brought you some Nancherrow vegetables and fresh eggs." She came, in her elegant, polished shoes, across the gravel. "Thought you could use them, and I wanted to have a word."

"I'm in the kitchen. Come on in, and I'll make you a cup of coffee."

She led the way through the back door. In the kitchen, Diana put the basket on the table, pulled out a chair, and sat down. Judith took the kettle and went to fill it, and then set it down on the range.

"Heavenly smell, darling."

"Soup. Do you mind if I go on chopping?"

"Not a bit." She put up her hands to loosen the knot of the silk scarf,

650

draped, so elegantly, about her slender throat. She said, "Loveday told us about Gus."

"Yes. She said she was going to."

"Was she upset when you told her?"

"I think she was fairly shattered. But no tears."

"Darling, tears are for the dead, not the living."

"She said as much herself."

"It's a bit of a mess, isn't it?"

"No. I don't think it's a mess. It's sad that she was so adamant that Gus had died, and it's sad that she didn't have the faith to wait for him to come home. But it's not a mess. It's just that they're not together. They can never be together. Loveday's made *her* life, and Gus will have to make a life of his own. From what Loveday told me, it sounds as though he's going to need a little help."

"He's going to be difficult to help, if he won't answer letters, and won't keep in touch."

"But he was such a friend of Edward's. For that reason alone, I feel we should all rally round. And he wrote such a dear letter when Edward was killed. And sent that sketch he'd done of Edward. It's Edgar's most precious possession. So much more telling than any photograph. It stands on Edgar's desk, so he looks at it every day of his life."

"I know. But it's not easy to rally round when Gus's home is at the other end of the country."

"He could come and stay. Do you think I could write and ask him to come and stay at Nancherrow?"

"No. I don't think that would be a good idea at all. Later, perhaps. But not now."

"Because of Loveday?"

"She doesn't want him here. And even if you asked him, I don't think he'd come. For the same reason."

"So what are we to *do?*"

"I'll write again, in a little while, if only to get some sort of a response out of him. If I could get a reaction, we'd at least know where we stood. How he was faring. How he was settling down again."

"We were so fond of him, Edgar and I. I know he was with us for just a little time, but we became so fond of him . . ." Her voice trailed away. She sighed.

"Diana, don't brood over might-have-beens. It doesn't do any good, looking back, and saying *if only.*"

"Do you blame me?"

"Blame *you?*"

"For letting her marry Walter?"

"You could scarcely stop her. She was having Nathaniel."

"Nathaniel didn't matter. Nathaniel could have been born and lived at Nancherrow with us all quite happily. And if people talked, so what? I've never cared what people said."

The kettle boiled. Judith spooned coffee into the jug and filled it, and set it, for a moment, on the back of the range.

"But she wanted to marry Walter."

"Yes. And we didn't just *let* her; in a way, we encouraged her. Our baby. Edward was gone, and I couldn't face losing Loveday as well. Marrying Walter meant she stayed near us. And we'd always liked him, despite his lack of polish and rough ways. Edgar liked him because he was so good with the horses, and because he'd always been so caring of Loveday, keeping an eye on her on hunting days, and helping her when she started working on the farm. He was her friend. I've always thought that the most important thing, when you get married, is to marry a friend. Passionate love cools down after a time, but friendship lasts forever. I really believed they were right for each other."

"Is there any reason to suppose that they're not?"

Diana sighed. "No. Not really, I suppose. But she was only nineteen. Perhaps we should have been a little more firm, told her to wait . . ."

"Diana, if you'd argued, she'd have just become more and more determined to get her own way . . . that's the way she's made. I tried to argue, that day in London, when she told me she was engaged, and I got my head bitten off for my pains."

The coffee was ready. Judith poured two mugs and set one down in front of Diana. From upstairs there commenced a droning roar, a bit like an aeroplane coming in to land. Phyllis, having dealt with her laundry, was now engaged in Hoovering the landing.

Diana said, "I really thought it would work. It worked for me."

"I don't understand."

"Edgar was never my love, but he was always my friend. I knew him always, right through from when I was a little girl. He was a friend of my parents. I thought he was middle-aged. Ancient. He used to take me to the park, and we'd feed the ducks. And then the war started . . . the First War. And I was sixteen, and wildly in love with a young man I'd met at the Fourth of June, at Eton. He was in the Coldstream Guards, and he went off to France. And then he came home on leave. But of course he had to go back to France, and he was killed in the trenches. By now, I was seventeen. And I was pregnant."

Diana's voice never changed. She said all these things, evoking God knew what memories, and continued to sound as inconsequential as though she were describing a new ravishing hat.

"*Pregnant?*"

"Yes. Too careless, darling, but we weren't very streetwise in those days."

"What happened?"

"Edgar happened. I couldn't tell my parents, so I told Edgar. And Edgar said that he was going to marry me, and that he would be the father of my little baby, and that I would never, ever, have to be worried or troubled for the rest of my life." Diana laughed. "And *that's* what happened."

"And the baby?"

"Athena."

"But . . ." But there was nothing to say.

"Oh, darling, you're not shocked, are you? It was just another sort of love. I never felt I was *using* Edgar. And after all the turmoil and the passion and the tragedy and the despair, being with him was like slipping into a peaceful harbour, knowing that nothing could ever harm one again. And that's how it's stayed. That's how it's always been."

"Athena. I never suspected, not for a single instant."

"Why should you? Why should anybody? Edward was Edgar's first child, but no daughter was more loved than Athena. She looks like me, I know. But there is something of her father there that only Edgar and I would ever see. He was such a beautiful young man. Tall and blue-eyed, and fair. My mother used to call him an Adonis. 'That boy,' she used to say, 'is a veritable Adonis.'"

"Does Athena know?"

"No, of course she doesn't. Why should she ever be told? Edgar's her father. He always has been. It's odd. I haven't even thought about it all for years. In fact, I'm not quite sure why I'm telling you now."

"Loveday."

"Of course. Justifying my actions. History repeating itself. Another hateful war, and a baby on the way, and the constant man one turns to. One's friend." She drank some of her coffee. "I've never told anyone else."

"I would never breathe a word."

"Darling, I know you wouldn't. What I'm trying to say is, Edgar is my life."

"I know."

They fell silent. Judith thought about Tommy Mortimer, and the enigma of his close relationship with Diana that she had never totally understood. But now, knowing the truth, completely understood. *Edgar is my life.* But he was older, set in his ways, a countryman through and through. Diana had lost her love, but never her youth. She had always needed that extra dimension, London, and concerts and parties and shopping and clothes. And lunch at the Ritz. Tommy Mortimer had been the key to that other world.

"Darling, what are you looking so broody about?"

"I was thinking about Tommy Mortimer."

"He was never my lover."

"I wasn't thinking that."

"He's not that sort of man. I don't mean that he's *queer*. Just comfortably sexless."

"When I first came to Nancherrow, and he was there . . . I couldn't work it out."

"Oh, darling, did you think Edgar should fling him from the front door?"

"Not exactly."

"He was never a threat. Edgar knew that. Just a person I needed. And Edgar let me have him. Because he is the dearest, most generous man in the world. And has made me so happy. You see, it really *worked* for me. That's why I thought it was right for Loveday."

"Diana, it was Loveday's decision. Not yours."

At this moment, perhaps fortuitously, they were interrupted. From the front of the house, a door slammed, and then, "Judith!"

Judith raised her voice. "I'm in the kitchen."

"Jess," said Diana. "How awful, I'd totally forgotten she was here." And they were laughing about this when the door burst open and Jess appeared, looking fairly tousled and cobwebby, but loud with satisfaction.

"I've done it all, but I need some stuff to clean the windows." She caught sight of Diana, and hesitated. "I . . . I'm sorry. I didn't know you were here."

"Oh, darling Jess, don't be sorry. Just dropped in to bring some eggs and veggies. What *have* you been doing?"

"Cleaning the Hut. It was filled with cobwebs and dead bluebottles and things, but I swept them all away. And there were two dead mice on the floor. We really ought to have a cat. Have we got any stuff for cleaning windows?"

"I don't know. I'll look in a moment."

Diana smiled. "Isn't it the dearest little house? It was built for my children, Athena and Edward, and they used to spend hours, days, weeks there. Camping out and cooking terrible smelly sausages."

"When the summer comes, I'm going to sleep out there. All the time."

"Won't you be lonely?"

"I shall take Morag with me for company."

"Do you want some coffee?" Judith asked.

Jess wrinkled her nose. "Not much."

"Have a mug of milk, then. And a biscuit or something."

"I want to get the *windows* cleaned."

"Five minutes for a fattening snack, and then you can go and get on with your dusting."

"Oh, all right."

"The milk's in the fridge, and the biscuits are in the tin. Help yourself."

Jess went over to the refrigerator and took out the milk bottle. She said, "Did you ring Saint Ursula's?"

"Yes, and we've got an appointment with Miss Catto tomorrow afternoon."

"Did you speak to her?"

"Of course."

"I don't have to start right away, do I?"

"No. But maybe at half-term."

"When's half-term?"

"About the fifth of November."

Diana said, "Guy Fawkes Day."

Jess frowned. "What's Guy Fawkes Day?"

"It's the most bestial celebration of a ghastly event, and we burn an effigy of poor Guy Fawkes on the bonfire. And let off fireworks and generally behave like a lot of heathens."

"It sounds rather fun."

"Are you going to be a day-girl or a boarder?"

Jess gave one of her elaborate shrugs. "No idea." She took a mug off the dresser and poured her milk.

Judith said, "Day-girl would be nicest, perhaps, but there's the question of transport and petrol. The buses are hopeless. Perhaps a weekly boarder. Whatever. We'll just have to see."

Jess had wrestled open the biscuit tin and found two rich teas. Eating the first, she came to lean against Judith's shoulder. She said, "Judith, I wish you'd look and see if you can find something for me to clean the windows with."

". . . it all rather depends," said Miss Catto, "on how well Jess was grounded at her school in Singapore. How old was she, when she left?"

"Eleven."

"And no sort of schooling since?"

"Not formal teaching. But the Dutch women in the camp were mostly the wives of tea-planters, and so educated and cultured. They did start classes for the children, but the Japanese took all their books away. So they were reduced to story-telling, and general knowledge and learning songs. They even managed a concert or two. One of the boys made Jess a recorder out of a bit of bamboo."

Miss Catto shook her head. She said sadly, "It's almost impossible to imagine."

They sat in Miss Catto's study, venue for so many important and vital occasions. Here Miss Catto had broken the news to Judith about Aunt Louise's fatal car accident. And it was in this room that Mr. Baines had told her about Aunt Louise's legacy, and Judith's life had been changed and enriched ever since.

It was now four o'clock in the afternoon. Saint Ursula's was strangely silent. At three, lessons had finished and all the girls trooped out of doors and up to the games field, there to gallop about on the muddy hockey pitches, or play netball. Only one or two senior girls remained behind, to study in the library, or practise the piano or the violin. From far off could be heard the faint sounds of scales being repeated over and over again.

As far as outward appearances were concerned, Saint Ursula's had changed, and not for the better. The war years had left their mark; they had been years during which Miss Catto had battled on, in charge of not one school, but two, somehow dealing with the pressing and endless problems of insufficient space, meagrely rationed food, black-outs, air-raid warnings, a semi-qualified or elderly staff, and the very minimum of domestic and outdoor help.

As a result, everything bore visible scars. The grounds, if not exactly overgrown, bore no resemblance to the immaculately ordered gardens of yesteryear, and from the window of Miss Catto's study could be seen the six hideous Nissen huts that had been built on what used to be the tennis and croquet lawns.

Even Miss Catto's neat little study looked a bit battered, with papers piled upon her desk, and an old electric kettle sitting in the empty grate. The curtains (which Judith recognized) were quite obviously on their last legs, the pretty, loose covers faded and holey, and the carpet threadbare and worn.

Miss Catto hadn't come out of it all that well either. Still in her forties, she looked a good deal older. Her hair was now quite grey, and there were lines on her forehead and around her mouth. But she still wore that aura of quiet competence, and her eyes were just the same, wise and kindly, and bright with intelligence and humour. Judith, after an hour in her company, had not a single reservation about handing Jess over into her care.

"I think perhaps we'd better start her off in the lower fourth. She'll be with a group of girls a year younger than she is, but they're a particularly nice lot, and I don't want her to be struggling with lessons and perhaps losing confidence."

"I think she's bright. If she's encouraged, I don't expect it will take her too long to catch up."

Jess, clearly, had taken to Miss Catto. At first, a bit overawed and nervous, she had answered Miss Catto's questions with no more than monosyllables, but it hadn't taken long for her to relax and lose her shyness, and after that the formal interview had turned into a chatty conversation, with lots of laughs. After a bit, there had come a knock on the door, and one of the senior girls presented herself and said that she had come to show Jess around the school. This girl wore a grey flannel skirt and a bright-blue pullover, thick white socks, and a pair of scuffed leather saddle shoes. Judith thought that she looked a great deal more attractive than she and Loveday at the same age, bundled as they had been into shapeless green tweed and brown lisle stockings.

"Thank you, Elizabeth, that's very kind. I think half an hour? That should give you plenty of time. And remember to show Jess the dormitories and the gymnasium, and the music rooms."

"Yes, I will, Miss Catto." She had smiled. "Come on, Jess."

They had not yet returned.

". . . has she any languages?"

"I think a little basic French. But she's probably forgotten it all by now."

"Maybe some extra coaching. But we don't want to overload the child. So, down to basics. When do you want her to start?"

"What do you think?"

"I would suggest as soon as possible. After half-term, maybe. That's the sixth of November."

It seemed terribly soon. "Could we discuss it with Jess? I want her to be part of it all. Feel she's making her own decisions."

"You are perfectly right. We'll have a committee meeting, the three of us, when she comes back. And is she going to be a day-girl or a boarder? She could be a weekly boarder if she wanted, but it's not an arrangement that I often recommend. It can be very disrupting, particularly if the child's circumstances are a little unusual. But, again, it's entirely up to you and Jess."

"I don't think she *can* be a day-girl. It's not possible, with so little petrol and so few buses."

"A boarder then? We'll talk about it. I am sure, when she has finished her little tour, she'll be reassured and realize that she's not going to be incarcerated in another terrible prison camp."

"I suppose we'll have to have a clothes list?"

Miss Catto smiled. "You'll be delighted to know that it has been considerably reduced. Scarcely covers a single page nowadays. Rules and regulations have had to go by the board. I sometimes think we were terribly old-fashioned, positively Victorian, before the war. As it is, I love to see the girls all going about in their own cheerful clothes. Children should never be homogenized. Now, each one is very much her own person, and instantly recognizable." Across the desk, they looked at each other. "I promise you, my dear, that I will do my best to make sure that Jess is happy."

"I know you will."

"And you, Judith? How are you?"

"I'm all right."

"And your life?"

"I never got to University."

"I know. I know all about you, because I see Mr. Baines from time to time, and he fills me in on your news. I was truly devastated about your mother and father, but at least you still have Jess. And, what is more, are able to make a home for her." She smiled. "But don't get bogged down in domesticity, Judith. You have too good a brain for that, too bright a future."

"I couldn't go to University now."

Miss Catto sighed. "No. I don't suppose you could. It would be a sort of regression. Never mind. We had a good try . . . Have you seen Loveday Carey-Lewis?"

"Yes."

"Is she happy?"

"She seems to be."

"I could never quite make up my mind what was going to become of Loveday. Usually I can gauge the pattern, the direction of a child's life; have some idea of how she will fare once she's left her school-days behind. But not Loveday. It was either euphoria or disaster, and I could never make up my mind which."

Judith considered this. "Perhaps half-way in between?"

Miss Catto laughed. "Fair enough. Now, how about a cup of tea? Jess will be back in a moment, and I've got a few chocolate biscuits for her." She rose to her feet, hitching her tattered black gown up onto her shoulders. "The days of parlourmaids and tea-trays are long gone. So I boil my own kettle, and do very nicely for myself."

"I never thought of you being domesticated."

"I'm not."

The Dower House,
Rosemullion.
Saturday 3rd November.

Dear Uncle Bob,

I am sorry I have not written before, but I have been busy seeing people with Judith and cleaning the hut in the garden where I am going to sleep when it is warm enough.

Thank you very much for having me to stay in Colombo. I enjoyed it, specially the alligators.

I am starting school on Tuesday. I didn't think I would want to be a boarder, but I am going to be because Miss Catto says they do lots of special things at weekends, like acting and having reading aloud and going on expeditions. And I am going to be allowed to telephone Judith whenever I want. But in the evenings, not during the day.

Miss Catto is very nice and quite funny.

Morag is very well.

I hope you are well too.

Please give my love to Mr. Beatty and Thomas.

With love from

Jess

PS Biddy sends her love.

"I don't want you to come in, Judith. I want to say goodbye to you on the front-door step. If you come in, it will just make it all go on for longer."

"Is that what you really want?"

"Yes. That nice girl, Elizabeth, said she'd be there to meet us and show me my dormitory and everything. She said she'd be waiting at the door."

"That was kind of her."

"And she said that for the rest of the term she would be my special prefect, and if I got lost or anything, I was to go and find her and she'd help."

"That sounds a good arrangement."

They were very nearly there. Judith turned the car off the main road and up the hill, through the estate of small houses, to where stood the school gates. It was half past two in the afternoon, and raining, a steady mizzle of a sea-mist, gently drenching the wintry gardens and the bare trees. The windscreen wipers had been going ever since they left Rosemullion.

"So funny," said Judith.

"What's funny?"

"History repeating itself. When Mummy brought me to Saint Ursula's for the very first time, I said exactly the same thing to her. 'Don't come in. Say goodbye on the doorstep.' And that's what she did."

"But this is different, isn't it?"

"Yes. Thank goodness, this is different. I said goodbye, and I thought it was for four years. It seemed forever. It *was* forever, but luckily I didn't know that at the time. You and I don't really have to say goodbye. Just *au revoir*. Because Phyllis and Biddy and I will never be far away. Even when Biddy moves, and gets a new house, we're all going to be quite near each other. And the next thing we know, it'll be Christmas."

"Will it be a proper one?"

"The best."

"Will we have a Christmas tree, like Biddy did at Keyham?"

"White and silver. Reaching half-way up the stairs."

Jess said, "It'll be funny without you."

"I'll miss you too."

"But I won't be homesick."

"No, Jess. Knowing you, I don't think you will."

Their parting did not take very long. As she had promised, the senior girl, Elizabeth, was there, at the big main door, waiting for them. Seeing the car, she shrugged herself into a mackintosh and came out to greet them.

"Hello. Here you are. What a horrible day. Did you have a very foggy drive . . . ?"

Her self-possession and friendly manner entirely diffused any possible awkwardness or tension. "I'll take your suitcase and your hockey stick. Can you manage the rest? And then we'll go straight upstairs and I'll show you where you're sleeping . . ."

Everything was duly carted indoors. Elizabeth, tactfully, busied herself out of earshot. On the front-door step, in the drizzling rain, Judith and Jess faced each other.

Judith smiled. "This is it, then. This is where I leave you."

"Yes." Jess was composed, but quite adamant. "Right here. I'll be all right now." And so cool, and so in charge of the situation was she, that Judith felt ashamed of her own misgivings, and the knowledge that, given the smallest encouragement, she might behave like the most sentimental of mothers and start brimming at the eyes. "Thank you for driving me."

"Bye, Jess."

"Goodbye."

"Love you."

They kissed. Jess gave her a funny little grin, turned away, and was gone.

Judith wept a bit in the car going home, but only because Jess had been so great, and because the Dower House was going to feel empty without her, and because they had been allowed so little time together. And then she found a handkerchief and blew her nose and stopped crying, and told herself briskly not to be such a fool. Jess, at Saint Ursula's, was going to flourish, like a little plant: mentally stimulated, perpetually occupied, and enjoying the company of girls of her own age. She had lived too long with grown-ups. Had lived too long with hunger and deprivation and bereavement, and all of the horrors of a cruel and adult world. Now, at last, she would have time and space in which to rediscover the joys and the challenges of a normal childhood. It was what she needed. It had been, at the end of the day, the only sensible thing to do.

So, all for the best. But it was hard not to feel a bit empty and bereft. Trundling back across the mist-driven moor, Judith decided that what she needed was a bit of contemporary company, and so would go and see Loveday. She hadn't been to Lidgey yet, simply because all her time lately had been taken up with Jess. Making the promised expedition to Penmarron; taking the train to Porthkerris, exploring the fascinating little town, calling on the Warrens and being given one of Mrs. Warren's classic teas. As well, Jess had to be kitted out for Saint Ursula's. The clothes list was nothing like as long and complicated as it had been in Judith's day, and thanks to Whiteaway and Laidlaw in Colombo, Jess was well supplied with all the necessary clothes. But there were a great many other, ill-assorted items that she didn't have, and these all had to be tracked down in Penzance's denuded shops. A hockey stick, hockey boots, writing-paper, a paint-box. A science overall, a fountain-pen, sewing scissors, and a geometry set. And, last but not least, a Bible and a "Prayer-Book with Hymns Ancient and Modern," both mandatory for any self-respecting High Anglican establishment.

And then, it all had to be packed.

So Loveday had been somewhat neglected. But now, this afternoon, the opportunity presented itself; she would keep her promise, go and visit, and spend an hour or two with Loveday and Nat. She wished she had thought of it before, so that she could have bought flowers in Penzance for Loveday and perhaps a toy or some sweets for Nat. But too late now. Presents would have to wait until later.

She drove past Rosemullion and up the hill, past the gates of Nancherrow, and so on for about a mile, until she reached the turning that led down to the farm. The lane dipped, narrow and rutted as a stream-bed, sunken between granite hedges and thickets of gorse. At its head stood a wooden signpost, LIDGEY, and the stone platform where Walter left the churns each day to be picked up by the milk-marketing lorry.

It was a bumpy, jolting, winding mile to the main farmhouse, but half-way down, on the left-hand side, stood the low stone cottage that the Colonel had had renovated when Loveday and Walter were married. It hugged the curve of the hill, its slate roof gleaming in the rain, and was instantly recognizable by the line of washing which slapped and billowed in the wet wind. She came to the gate, which stood open, propped by a boulder, beyond which led a grassy track, melding into what should have been a garden, but wasn't. Just the washing-line, and a few more gorse bushes, and some toys lying around. A rusted tricycle and a tin spade and bucket. She stopped the car and turned off the ignition, and heard the wind. Somewhere, a dog barked. She got out of the car, walked up the granite flagged path, and opened a paint-scarred door.

"Loveday!"

She was in a tiny lobby hung with old coats and waterproofs, and with mud-caked boots awry upon the floor.

"Loveday!"

She opened a second door. "It's me."

Kitchen, living-room, all in one. Almost a replica of Mrs. Mudge's. A simmering Cornish range, clothes strung on a pulley high overhead, flagged floors, a few rugs; the table, the clay sink, the dogs' bowls, the pig-bucket, the piles of old newspapers, the dresser laden with odds and ends, the sagging sofa.

Nat lay on the sofa, his thumb plugged into his mouth. He was fast asleep. He wore grubby overalls, soaking wet where he had peed into them. The wireless, perched on one of the shelves of the dresser, burbled away to itself. *We'll meet again, don't know where, don't know when.* Loveday was ironing.

As the door opened she looked up. Judith said, unnecessarily, "It's me."

"Well." Loveday set down the iron with a thump. "Where have you turned up from?"

"Saint Ursula's. Just left Jess there."

"Oh God, is she all right?"

"She was amazing. Matter-of-fact. No tears. I was the one who nearly blubbed."

"Do you think she'll like it?"

"Yes, I think so. She's got permission to ring me up if she's feeling blue. The one who's feeling really blue is me, so I've come for a bit of cheering."

"I'm not sure if you've come to the right place."

"Looks fine to me. I'd die for a cup of tea."

"I'll put the kettle on. Take your coat off. Sling it down somewhere."

Which Judith did, but found nowhere to sling it, because there was a pile of washing on one chair, a huge sleeping tabby-cat on another, and Nat, out for the count, on the sofa. So she went back to the little lobby and draped her waterproof on a peg, over a pair of mud-stained black oilskin trousers.

"I'm really sorry I haven't been before, Loveday, but I haven't had a moment, there's been so much to do for Jess . . ." Judith went over to the sofa and gazed down at the sleeping Nat. His cheeks were brightly red, one more so than the other, and he clutched in his fat fist an old rag of a blanket, with the remains of a ribboned hem. "Does he always sleep in the afternoon?"

"Not usually. But he didn't get to sleep till two this morning. I had a terrible time with him. I'd think he might be teething." Loveday filled the kettle at the sink, and went to put it on the range. "To be truthful, I never know when he's going to sleep and when he's awake. He's always been a terror about sleeping. And when he does, I leave him because it's the only bit of peace I get. That's why I was trying to get the ironing done."

"Perhaps if we wake him now, he'll be more likely to go to sleep tonight."

"Yes. Perhaps." But Loveday did not sound too keen on the idea. "Once he's up, he's up, and that's it. And it's too wet to put him outside to play."

But I know we'll meet again some sunny day, mooned the wireless. She went over to the dresser and switched it off. "Soppy tune. Just listening for a bit of company. I'll clear all this away and make a bit of space for you . . ."

She began bundling up the unironed washing, but Judith stopped her. "I'll do it. Let me finish it while you make the tea. I like ironing. And you wake Nat, and then we can all have tea together . . ."

"Are you sure? Seems a bit hard . . ."

"What are friends for, dear?" Judith asked in Mary Millyway's voice, and she picked a crumpled shirt off the top of the pile and spread it out on the board. "Is this meant to look immaculate when it's finished? Because if so, I'll have to damp it down a bit."

"No. Doesn't matter. Just folded, so that I can get it into Walter's shirt drawer." Loveday dumped herself down on the sofa beside her sleeping son. "He's wet himself, the little villain." But her voice was indulgent. "Hey, Nat. Wake up. We're going to have tea." She laid a hand on his round stomach, and bent to kiss him. Occupied with Loveday's ironing, Judith thought she looked terrible. She seemed tired out, with dark rings under her eyes. Judith found herself wondering if there ever came a day when the little house was neat, or even moderately clean and tidy, and decided that probably it never did.

Nat's eyes opened. Loveday lifted him and set him on her knee and cuddled him for a bit, talking to him until he was properly awake. Staring about, he spied Judith. "Who that lady?"

"That's Judith. You met her the other day. At Granny's."

Nat's dark eyes were like two juicy raisins. "I don't amember her."

"Well, she remembers you, and she's come to see you." She stood, lifting Nat up into her arms. "Come along, I'll get your trousers changed."

"Can I come too and see the rest of the house?" Judith asked.

"No, you can't," she was told firmly. "It's much too untidy. If you'd told me you were coming I'd have kicked all the clutter under the bed. I need notice before I give guided tours. A bit like a Stately Home. Next time, I'll show you."

There was a door at the far end of the kitchen, and she disappeared through this, leaving it ajar behind her, so that Judith had a glimpse of the huge brass bedstead. Doing her best to smooth out the wrinkles of the bone-dry, crumpled shirt, she listened to Loveday's voice chatting to Nat. Heard her opening and shutting drawers, running taps, flushing the lavatory. Presently, they returned. Nat, in clean overalls and with his hair brushed, looked as though butter would not melt in his mouth. Loveday set him down on the floor, found a little truck for him to play with, and left him to his own devices.

The kettle was boiling. She reached for the teapot.

"I've done *one* shirt."

"Oh, don't do any more. Switch off the iron. If you want to help, you can lay the table . . . The cups are in that cupboard. And plates, too. There's a bit of saffron cake in the bread bin, and butter in that dish on the top of the fridge . . ."

Between them, they assembled a makeshift tea-table, pushing a few papers and copies of *The Farmer's Weekly* to one side in order to make space. Nat was invited to join them but declined, preferring the floor with his truck, which he pushed around the floor making meh-meh-meh noises to make it real. Loveday let him be.

She said, "I'm sorry about the mess and not letting you look."

"Don't be silly."

"I'll give it a spring clean and then send you a formal invitation. It's actually very sweet and the new bathroom's lovely. Tiled and hot pipes for the towels and everything. Darling Pops was really generous. Only thing is, we've only got the one bedroom. I know Nat would sleep better if he was on his own, but there's not much we can do about it." She poured Judith's tea. "Your house always looks so tidy, not a thing out of place."

"That's Phyllis, and we haven't got a lively three-year-old knocking about."

"It's never so bad on a good day. He plays out of doors most of the time. But when it's wet, it's impossible, nothing but mud being tracked in and out."

"Where's Walter?"

"Oh, somewhere. Up the top field, I think. He'll be back soon, for the milking."

"Do you still help with that?"

"Sometimes. If Mrs. Mudge isn't around."

"How about today?"

"No, not today, thank God."

"You're looking tired, Loveday."

"So would you if you hadn't got to sleep until three in the morning."

She fell silent, sitting there with her bony elbows propped on the table-top, her hands wrapped around the mug of hot tea, her eyes downcast. The long, dark lashes lay on her pale cheeks, and Judith looked, and saw to her dismay that they shone with seeping tears.

"Oh, Loveday."

Loveday, in a sort of angry denial, shook her head. "I'm just tired."

"If there's something wrong, you know you can tell me."

Loveday shook her head again. A tear escaped, dribbled down her cheek. She put up a hand and roughly brushed it away.

"It's no good keeping things to yourself. It doesn't do any good."

Loveday said nothing.

"Is it you and Walter?" It took some courage to say, because Judith knew she was quite liable to have her head bitten off, but she said it. And it was said. And Loveday hadn't flown at her. "Is there something wrong between you?"

Loveday muttered something.

"I'm sorry?"

"I said, there's another woman. He's got another woman."

Judith felt herself go quite weak.

Carefully, she laid her mug on the table. "Are you sure?"

Loveday nodded.

"How do you know?"

"I know. He's been seeing her. Evenings, at the pub. Sometimes he doesn't get home till all hours."

"But how do you *know?*"

"Mrs. Mudge told me."

"*Mrs. Mudge?*"

"Yes. The word got through to her from the village. She told me because she said I ought to know. Have it out with Walter. Tell him to lay off."

"Is she on your side, or his?"

"My side. Up to a point. I think she reckons that if a man goes off chasing a fancy piece, then there's something wrong with his wife."

"Why doesn't she give him hell? He's her son."

"She says it's not her business to interfere. And I must say, she never has. I'll give her that."

"Who *is* this woman?"

"She's a mess. She came down to Porthkerris during the summer sometime. Turned up with some phony painter or other. From London. She lived with him for a bit, and then they either had a row, or he found someone else, so she moved out on him."

"Where's she living now?"

"In a caravan, up the back of Veglos Hill."

"Where did Walter meet up with her?"

"Some pub or other."

"What's her name?"

"You're not going to believe this."

"Try me."

"Arabella Lumb."

"It can't be true."

And suddenly, incredibly, they were both laughing, just for a moment, and Loveday still with tears on her cheeks.

"Arabella Lumb." The name, on repetition, sounded even more unlikely. "Have you ever seen her?"

"Yes, once. She was at Rosemullion one evening, when I went for a beer with Walter. She sat in the corner by the bar all evening, eyeing him, but they didn't talk because *I* was there. Old gooseberry. Getting in the way. She looks like a great bosomy tinker . . . you know, Mother Earth stuff. Bangles and beads and sandals and green varnish on her rather dirty toe-nails."

"She sounds ghastly."

"She's sexy, though. It exudes from her. Lush. Like a huge, over-ripe fruit. A sort of excitement. I think the word is 'palpable.' Perhaps we should look it up in the dictionary."

"No. I think you've got it right."

"I have a horrid feeling that Walter is besotted." Loveday sat back in her chair and felt in the pocket of her trousers, to produce a battered packet of cigarettes and a cheap lighter. She took one of the cigarettes and lit it. After a moment she said, "And I don't know what to do."

664

"Take Mrs. Mudge's advice. Have it out with him."

Loveday sniffed enormously. Then she looked up and, across the table, her lovely eyes met Judith's. "I tried last night." Her voice was despondent. "I was angry and I was fed up. Walter got home at eleven o'clock, and he'd been drinking whisky. I could smell it. When he gets drunk, he gets aggressive, and we had the most terrible row, and we woke Nat up because we were shouting and yelling at each other. And he said he'd do what he bloody pleased, and see who he bloody wanted. And he said it was my fault anyway, because I was such a bloody useless wife and mother, and the cottage is always such a mess, and I can't even cook properly . . ."

"That's unkind and unfair."

"I know I'm not much good at cooking, but it's horrid being told. And there's another thing. He doesn't like me taking Nat down to Nancherrow. He resents it, I think. As though *he* was being diminished in some way . . ."

"Of all men, Walter has no right to have a chip on his shoulder."

"He says I'm trying to turn Nat into a little sissy. He wants him to be a Mudge, not a Carey-Lewis."

It was all understandable, but bewildering too. "Does he love Nat?"

"Yes, when Nat's being good or amusing or funny. Not when he's tired and demanding or needing attention. Sometimes, days go by and Walter doesn't even speak to him. He can be a moody devil. And lately, he's been really impossible."

"You mean, since Arabella Lumb came on the scene?"

Loveday nodded.

"It's surely not serious, Loveday? All men have those dotty times, when they go off the rails and lose all sense. And if *she's* got her big guns trained on him, it doesn't seem to me that he stands much of a chance."

"She isn't going to go away, Judith."

"She might." But even as Judith said this, it didn't sound very hopeful. "You've been happy with Walter. I think you've just got to grin and bear it, and wait for him to come to his senses. It's no good having it out, having rows. It'll just make everything worse."

"Bit too late to say that."

"I'm not being much help, am I?"

"Yes, you are. Just being able to talk about it helps. The worst is, no one to talk to. Mummy and Pops would"—she searched for the right word—"*explode*, if they knew."

"I'm surprised they don't already."

"The only person who *might* have got the buzz is Nettlebed. And you and I both know that Nettlebed would never breathe a word to either of them."

"No. No, he never would."

All this time Nat had been lying on his stomach, intent on his game. Now he decided that he was hungry. He scrambled to his feet and came over, to stand on tiptoe and peer at the contents of the table.

"I want somefin to eat."

Loveday stubbed out her cigarette in a handy saucer, stooped and hoisted him up onto her knee. She pressed a kiss on the top of his thick dark hair, and with her arms encircling him, buttered a slice of saffron bread and gave it to him.

He munched noisily, staring, unblinking, at Judith. She smiled at him. "I meant to bring you a present, Nat, but there wasn't a shop. Next time I come I'll bring you something. What would you like?"

"I like a car."

"What, a little car?"

"No. A big car what I can get inside."

Loveday laughed. "You're a boy for the main chance, aren't you? Judith can't buy you a *car*."

Judith ruffled his head. She said, "Don't listen to your mother. I can do anything I want."

By the time tea was over it was well past five o'clock. Judith said, "I really must go. Biddy and Phyllis will be wondering what's happened to me, imagining terrible dramas with Jess."

"It was lovely seeing you. Thanks for coming."

"I'm glad I did. Next time, I'll do *all* the ironing." She went to retrieve her raincoat. "And you must bring Nat up to the Dower House one day. For lunch or something."

"We'd like that. Wouldn't we, Nat? Judith, you won't say a word, will you? About what I've told you."

"Not a word. But you must keep on talking to me."

"I'll do that."

Loveday scooped Nat up in her arms, and they came to the open door to see Judith away. Outside, the mist had thickened and all was grey, and drenched and dripping. Judith turned up the collar of her coat and prepared to make a wet dash for the car, but Loveday said her name, and she turned.

"Have you heard from Gus yet?"

Judith shook her head. "Not a word."

"Just wondered."

Judith drove home through the dark, dismal evening, into Rosemullion, up the hill, and so through the gates of the Dower House. The kitchen window glowed warm and yellow through the gloom, and someone had left the light on over the front door. She put Biddy's car in the garage, where her own small Morris still crouched, wheel-less, set up on wooden blocks and draped with a grubby dust-sheet. The necessary petrol coupons had not yet come through from the appropriate authority, and until they did, there was no point in getting someone to put the wheels back on, charge up the battery, and discover whether the neglected little car had weathered its years of disuse.

She crossed the gravel and went into the house through the back door. In the kitchen, she found Phyllis rolling pastry, and Anna sitting at the other end of the table, trying to do her homework.

"I've got to write a sentence with the word 'spoken' in it."

"Well, that shouldn't be too difficult . . . Judith. Where have you been? We thought you'd be back hours ago."

"I went to see Loveday and Nat."

"We wondered if something had gone wrong with Jess, and you'd been kept."

"I know. I should have rung. No worries. Quite self-sufficient. She wouldn't even let me go in with her. I had to say goodbye on the doorstep."

"That's a relief. Feels funny without her, doesn't it? As though she'd lived here always. Anna's going to miss her, aren't you, Anna? Now, come on, get that homework done."

Anna sighed elaborately. "I can't think what to say."

Judith came to the rescue. "How about 'I have telephoned Jess and spoken to her'?"

Anna considered this. "Can't spell 'telephoned.'"

"Then put 'seen.' 'I've seen Jess and spoken to her.'"

"That'll do." With fingers clamped around her pencil, Anna wrote, the tip of her tongue clamped, in serious concentration, between her teeth.

"Want a cup of tea, do you?"

"No, thanks, I've had one. Where's Mrs. Somerville?"

"In the drawing-room. She's been waiting for you to come back. She's all agog. Got something to tell you."

"What?"

"Not for me to tell."

"I hope it's something cheerful."

"Go and find out then."

So Judith went, shedding her wet raincoat on the way. She opened the drawing-room door onto a snug scene. Lamps had been lit, and the fire blazed. In front of this, on the hearthrug, lay Morag. Biddy sat in her armchair, close to the flames, and was engaged in knitting a square. Knitting squares was about the limit of her capabilities. She made them out of odds and ends of wool, and when she had a dozen or so in hand, wheeled them into the Red Cross, where some other lady, slightly less handless, crocheted them together into gaudy patchwork blankets. These were then parcelled off to the Red Cross in Germany, and distributed to camps still filled with sad, homeless displaced persons. Biddy called it her peace-work.

"Judith." She laid down her knitting and took off her spectacles. "Everything all right? No problems with Jess?"

"Not a one."

"Good for her. She's such a funny little mixture. A small girl one moment, and so mature the next. She'll do splendidly, I'm sure, but it does feel a bit empty without her. Where've you been?"

"Seeing Loveday." Judith went to draw the curtains against the dank dusk of the dark November evening. "Phyllis said you had something to tell me."

"Yes. Exciting. What time is it?"

"Quarter to six."

"Let's have a drink. Whisky and soda. What do you say?"

"I say yes. I'm bushed."

"Emotionally drained, darling. You sit down and be cosy and I'll bring you one."

She got up and went from the room, because, traditionally, the bottles and glasses were always kept in the dining-room. Judith, alone, put another log on the fire, and sank into the other armchair. Emotionally drained, Biddy had said, and it was true. But what Biddy didn't realize was that it was not leaving Jess that had drained Judith as much as her conversation with Loveday. And, what was sure, could not be enlightened.

After a moment, Biddy returned with the two drinks. She gave one to Judith and then sat down again, placing her glass, with some care, on the table at her side. She lit a cigarette. Finally, with everything nicely to hand, "Now," she said.

"Tell."

"I've got the house. The house at Portscatho. Heard from the estate agent this afternoon."

"Biddy, that's wonderful."

"I can move in any time after the middle of January."

"So soon?"

"But there's lots to be done. I've been thinking, making lists. I shall have to go to Devon, and finally sell Upper Bickley."

"Whom are you going to sell it to?"

"The naval family who've been living in it, renting it, all through the war. They've been wanting to buy it for two years, but if I'd sold it, then I'd have had to put all my furniture into store. As it is they've been looking after it for me."

"Do they still want to buy it?"

"Can't wait. So what I have to do is go to Bovey Tracey and sort it all out, and make inventories of what I've got, and then arrange for packers and removal men, and all that sort of thing. I'm going to ring Hester Lang this evening, and ask if I can stay with her. Easier to deal with everything if I'm on the spot. So . . ." She reached for her drink, and raised the glass. "Cheers, my darling."

"Here's to Portscatho."

They toasted the new house. Judith said, "When are you planning to go?"

"I thought sometime next week. And I'll stay there, with Hester, for a bit."

Judith became alarmed. "But you'll be back for Christmas?"

"Only if you want me."

"Oh, Biddy, you *must* be here for Christmas. I've promised Jess a proper Christmas, and I've never done one, so I'll need lots of guidance and help. And we've got to have a tree, and a proper Christmas dinner with all the trimmings. You must come back."

"All right then, I will come back. Just until the middle of January. And then I'll make my great move. I want to be all settled in before Bob comes home."

"It's terribly exciting, but goodness, we'll miss you."

"I'll miss you all too. And without Phyllis I'm going to have to start learning how to housekeep all over again. But one must keep moving forward, even old crocks like me. Now, there's another thing I thought of. When I go to Hester's, I'll take the train, and leave you my car. You must have wheels, and I can manage without them, because if I'm desperate I know Hester will lend me hers."

"Biddy, that's too unselfish."

"No, it's not. And I've got some out-of-date petrol coupons salted away. Strictly speaking they're illegal, but the filling station up the road are very accommodating about turning a blind eye. So you should be all right." She picked up her knitting once more. "It really is rather thrilling, isn't it? I can't believe I've actually got the house. Exactly what I've always had in mind. And the lovely thing is that we're not very far away from you. Just an hour's drive. And it's got this view of the sea, and you can walk down the lane to the rocks, and swim. And the garden's *just* big enough."

"I can't wait to see it."

"Can't wait to show it to you. But not until I've got it all in order, and am thoroughly dug in."

"You're as bad as Loveday. She wouldn't let me look around her cottage because she said it was too untidy."

"Oh, poor Loveday. You must have caught her unawares. How was she? And was Nat creating?"

"No. He was rather sweet. He wants me to give him a car he can ride around in."

"Heavens, what a greedy boy."

"Not a bit. Why shouldn't he have one?" Judith stretched. The warmth of the fire, and the whisky, had made her feel sleepy. She yawned. "If I can find the energy, I shall go and have a bath."

"Do that. You look a bit washed out."

"It's been one of those days. Everything happening. Changing. People moving on. First Jess and now you. I don't feel unhappy about Jess, but I didn't have her for very long. What we had was all good, but it was over too soon."

"You've done the right thing by her."

"Yes. I know that. It's just . . ." She shrugged. "Everything."

Everything. Judith thought about horoscopes. She didn't often read horoscopes, but when she did, they always referred to clashings of planets—Mercury being in the wrong aspect to the Sun, or Mars being fiery somewhere, and so creating havoc in one's own particular birth sign, which happened in her case to be Cancer. Perhaps this was a particularly tempestuous and active phase, and the limitless heavens had it in for her. She only knew that since the day she had been told that Bruce and Molly had both died, she had been bombarded by unimagined events. Hugo Halley had been one of them, and finding Gus alive, and Jess, miraculously, returning safe and sound from Java. But already, Jess was gone; streamed into her new life. And now, Biddy too was on her way. Sooner or later, Phyllis and Anna would be off as well, to make a new home for themselves and Petty Officer Cyril Eddy.

But, perhaps most lowering of all, were the private preoccupations. Her growing concern for Gus, alarming and frustrating all at the same time. And being party to confidences which she had never wished to hear: Athena not being Edgar's daughter; and that wretched Walter Mudge carrying on with Arabella Lumb, and making Loveday so miserably unhappy.

She said, rather feebly, "Everything happens so quickly."

"Now the war's over, we're all changing gear, changing speed, doing our best to return to some sort of normality. People's lives can never stand still, otherwise we'd all come to a grinding halt and atrophy."

"I know that."

"You're tired. Go and have a bath. You can take the last drop of my Floris Stephanotis, as a tremendous treat. And Phyllis is cooking Mr. Woolton's Special Economy Vegetable Pie for supper. I think we should make it an occasion. I shall open a bottle of wine."

And she looked so sparky and delighted with her bright idea that Judith, despite herself, had to laugh. "You know something, Biddy? Sometimes you have the most brilliant notions. What am I going to do without you?"

Biddy changed needles and set off on another row. "Lots of things."

The Dower House
Rosemullion.
14th November.

Dear Gus,

I wonder if you ever got my letter that I wrote on the troop-ship and posted in Gib? I sent it to Ardvray, but perhaps you haven't gone home yet. Anyway, I'll send this one to Gordon HQ in Aberdeen, and then you'll be sure to get it.

We got back here about the nineteenth of October and it was wonderful to be home. I have been busy with Jess. She has gone to my old school as a full boarder. Miss Catto, the headmistress, used to be my headmistress, and is particularly kind and understanding. I haven't seen Jess since I left her, but she has written us some cheerful letters and seems to be settling down.

I have seen them all at Nancherrow. Loveday too. Her son Nat is large and lively, and she adores him. I managed to buy him a second-hand pedal-car, and he loves it so much that he wants to take it to bed with him.

I wonder what you are going to do for Christmas? I am sure you will have lots of good friends in Scotland who will be queuing for your company.

Please write and let me know what is happening and that you are all right.

With my love,

Judith

The Dower House,
Rosemullion.
5th December 1945.

Dear Gus,

Still no word from you. I wish you didn't live so far away, so I could come in search. Please send me something, if only a postcard of the municipal flower-beds of Aberdeen. You promised you would keep in touch and reassure me, and if you want to be left alone, and don't want any more letters, just say and I shall completely understand.

Here, we are a diminished household. Biddy Somerville has gone off to sell her house in Devon. She has bought another at a place called Portscatho, near Saint Mawes. Think she plans to move there about middle of January. She took her dog, Morag, with her. Jess loved the creature, so I think I shall give her a dog of her own to take the place of Morag when they leave us for good.

Here Judith paused, while she swithered about what to say next, and how to say it. *I don't want Gus to come here,* Loveday had insisted. But perhaps, for once in her life, Loveday should take second place in the priority stakes. Her problems, though dire, were not in the same league as Gus Callender's. Whatever happened to her, she was surrounded by loving and supportive family, while Gus seemed to have nobody close to see him through his rehabilitation after the horrors of the Burma Railway. As well, obscurely, as the days went by with no letter or message from him, Judith's anxiety for Gus was growing. "No news is good news" was the old saw, but instincts told her, loud and clear, that all was not well with him.

She took a deep breath, made up her mind, picked up her pen once more.

Biddy will be back for Christmas. We are a houseful of five females, but if you would like, please come and spend Christmas with us. Perhaps you aren't on your own, but I don't know, because you've never written to me. If you do come, I shan't force you on Nancherrow, or Loveday, or anything. I promise. And you can spend your days exactly as you want.

If I am interfering, and being a nuisance to you, please say. I won't write again until I hear from you.

With my love,

Judith

As Christmas loomed, the weather deteriorated, and Cornwall showed its nastiest face: granite skies, rain, and a bitter east wind. The old ill-fitting windows of the Dower House did nothing to keep this out, bedrooms were icy, and because a fire was lighted in the drawing-room at nine o'clock every morning, the log pile diminished visibly, and an emergency telephone call had to be put through to the supplier, namely Nancherrow Estates. The Colonel did not let them down and delivered the new load himself, tractoring it up the hill with the laden bogie trundling along behind. Yesterday had been a Sunday, and Phyllis, Judith, and Anna had spent most of the day stacking the logs in a neat pile against the garage wall, where the overhang of the roof would keep them protected from the worst of the wet.

So now, Monday again and it was still raining. Phyllis, that staunch traditionalist, had done her washing, but there was no way that she was going to hang it out of doors, which meant that it had all been hoisted onto the kitchen pulley, where it steamed wetly over the warmth of the range.

Judith, battling with a recipe for a wartime Christmas pudding (grated carrots and a spoonful of marmalade), broke an egg into the mixture, and began to stir. From the hall, the telephone rang. She waited hopefully for Phyllis to take the call, but she was cleaning the attic bedrooms and clearly did not hear the ringing, so Judith found a paper bag, put her floury hand into it, like a glove, and went to take the call herself.

"Dower House."

"Judith, it's Diana."

"Good morning. What a revolting day."

"Ghastly. But you got your logs."

"Yes. Your saintly husband delivered them, and we're all cosy again."

"Darling, I've got such exciting news. Jeremy Wells is home. On leave. And the best is, that it isn't just leave, it's demob leave. He's going to be demobbed and come home for good. Isn't it unbelievable? Apparently he put in for it, on account of having been in the RNVR for so long, and also because old Dr. Wells is really too old and worn to struggle on his own for much longer. And they're letting him go . . . Judith? Are you still there?"

"Yes. Yes, I'm here."

"Not a comment, so I thought the line had gone dead."

"No. I'm listening."

"Isn't it exciting?"

"Yes. It's wonderful. I'm really glad. When . . . when did you hear?"

"He got home on Saturday. Rang me this morning. He's coming to Nancherrow on Wednesday, to spend a few days. So we thought we'd have a real coming-home party. Wednesday evening. Loveday and Walter and Jeremy and you. Please come. Edgar's going to open the last of the champagne. He's been keeping it all this time, and I simply pray it hasn't gone all *funny*. If it has, he'll just have to find something else. You will come, won't you?"

"Yes, of course. I'd love to."

"About a quarter to eight? Such heaven to have you all with me again. Good news of Jess?"

"Yes, good news. She's a star at hockey, and she's got into the second eleven."

"Clever little thing. And Biddy?"

"She phoned on Saturday. Sold the house, so now she can pay for the new one."

"Send her my love when she rings again."

"I will . . ."

"See you Wednesday, darling."

"Lovely. I look forward to it."

She put down the telephone, but did not immediately return to the kitchen. Jeremy. Back. Demobbed. No longer safely far away in the Mediterranean, but home for good. She told herself that she was neither sorry nor glad. She only knew that before they could resume any sort of an easy relationship, all must be brought out into the open, and she must be prepared to face him with the hurt and disappointment and even resentment that he caused her. The fact that it had all happened three and a half years ago was neither here nor there. Jeremy had given a promise and broken it, and consequently made no attempt either to explain his perfidy nor excuse himself. So. A confrontation . . .

"What are you doing, standing there by the telephone and staring into space?"

Phyllis, descending the stairs with her dustpan and dusters. Spying Judith, she had paused, half-way, in some puzzlement, a hand on her pinafored hip.

"Sorry?"

"Got a face on like a bulldog, you have. Wouldn't want to come up against you on a dark night." She came on down the staircase. "Was that someone on the telephone?"

"Yes. Mrs. Carey-Lewis."

"What's she said, then?"

"Oh, nothing." To add a little weight to her words, Judith put on a cheerful smile. "Just asking me to dinner on Wednesday." Phyllis waited for further information. "Jeremy Wells is back."

"Jeremy." Phyllis's jaw dropped in clear delight. "Jeremy Wells? Well. That's lovely. On leave, is he?"

"No. Yes. Demob leave. Back for good."

"I never! Think of that. Can't imagine a piece of news I'd rather hear. So what's the face for? I'd have thought you'd be over the moon."

"Oh, Phyllis."

"Well, why not? He's a lovely man. Been a good friend to you ever since that day you met him on the Plymouth train; and like a rock, he was, when Edward Carey-Lewis was killed."

"I know, Phyllis."

"He always fancied you, Jeremy did. Any fool could tell. And it's about time you had a man about the place. A bit of fun. Stuck here with a lot of women. That's not what's meant for you."

Somehow this was the last straw. Judith lost her patience.

"You don't know anything about it."

"What do you mean, I don't know anything about it?"

"Just that. And I've got a Christmas pudding to make." On that telling exit line she marched back, down the stone passage, to the kitchen. But Phyllis was not to be so easily put off and simply followed hard on her heels.

"We're not leaving it there . . ."

"Phyllis, it's really none of your business."

"It had better be. Who else is there now, but me? Someone's got to give you a slice of their mind, if you're going to start flouncing around at the very mention of Jeremy's name." She stowed her dustpan and duster away in the cupboard, and then returned to the attack. "Have you had a row with him or something?"

"Everybody asks me that. No. No, we didn't have a row."

"Well then . . . ?"

It was impossible to argue. "Non-communication. Misunderstanding. I don't know. I only know that I've neither seen nor heard from him for three and a half years."

"That was the war. War's over now." Judith said nothing. "Look, you're making a real dog's dinner of that pudding. Move over and let me have a go at it . . ." Not unwillingly, Judith relinquished the wooden spoon. "Feels a bit dry, doesn't it? I'll maybe put another egg in." She stirred, in experimental fashion, and Judith sat on the edge of the table and watched her. "What are you going to wear?"

"Hadn't even thought."

"Well, think now. Something glamorous. You're so lovely now, like a real film star when you've got all your make-up on. What you want to do is knock him off his feet."

"No, Phyllis. I don't think that is what I want."

"All right then. Be pig-headed if you want to. Keep it all to yourself. But I'll tell you one thing. Best to let bygones be bygones. No point in harbouring grudges." She broke the second egg into the bowl and began to beat the mixture as though the entire situation were its fault. "Shouldn't go cutting off your nose to spite your face."

There didn't seem to be any comment to make to this observation. But Judith was left with the uncomfortable feeling that perhaps Phyllis was right.

Rupert Rycroft, ex-Major, the Royal Dragoon Guards, stepped, dot-and-carry, from the portals of Harrods, crossed to the edge of the pavement, and there paused, debating as to his next move. It was twelve-thirty, the lunch hour, and the December day was bitterly cold, with a sharp, raw wind, but mercifully it was not raining. His Westminster meeting had taken up most of the morning, and his foray into Harrods what remained of it. The rest of the day he could call his own. He thought about flagging down a taxi, driving to

Paddington, and then returning by train to Cheltenham, where he had left his car in the station park. Or he could go to his club for lunch, and *then* make his way to Paddington. Feeling peckish, he opted for the latter.

But although—or perhaps because—there seemed to be so many people out and about, office-workers and Christmas shoppers, and young men in uniform, and older men with brief-cases, all spilling up out of the Underground or hopping off loaded buses, there was a distinct dearth of taxis. If one heaved into view it was invariably already occupied. Had he been spry and able, Rupert would have been happy to take a Number 22 bus to convey him down to Piccadilly. He had never been troubled by false illusions of his own grandeur. But his leg precluded the physical effort of getting himself onto a bus, and worse, getting himself off the bloody thing at the other end. So, a taxi it had to be.

He waited, a tall and personable figure, suitably outfitted in a heavy navy-blue overcoat, regimental tie, and bowler hat. He carried, not the mandatory furled umbrella, but a walking-stick which had become like a third leg to him, and without which he still had some difficulty in getting around. Stairs and steps were a particular problem. As well, in his other leather-gloved hand, was a dark-green Harrods carrier-bag. This contained a bottle of Harvey's Tio Pepe sherry, a box of cigars, and a Jacqumar silk scarf, a present for his wife. Shopping in Harrods did not, in Rupert's book, count as shopping. In other stores, he was inclined to feel a bit lost, demeaned, or embarrassed, but buying things in Harrods was like spending money in a splendidly exclusive and reassuringly familiar gentleman's club, and so, enjoyable.

He was about to give up all hope when a taxi appeared at last, trundling down the other side of the street. Rupert hailed it, raising his carrier-bag like a flag, because if he raised his stick he would probably fall over. The driver spied him, did a neat U-turn, and drew alongside.

"Where to, sir?"

"Cavalry Club, please."

"Righty-ho."

Rupert stooped to open the door. Doing so, he faced the stream of oncoming pedestrians, and in that instant he forgot about getting into the cab, because his eye, and his total attention, were caught by the sight of the young man who was walking towards him. Tall—almost as tall as Rupert himself—vaguely familiar, shabbily dressed, unshaven and gaunt. Painfully thin. A lot of black hair brushing the upturned collar of his battered leather jacket, old grey flannels, and scuffed and unpolished shoes. He carried a grocery box, from which protruded a head of celery and the neck of a bottle, and his dark, deep-set eyes glanced neither to left nor right, but stared ahead, as though all that was of consequence was the direction in which he was headed.

Five seconds, no more, and he was striding past Rupert and on his way. Others closed in behind him. Hesitate and he would be gone. Just before it was too late, Rupert raised his voice and shouted after him. "Gus!"

He stopped dead, frozen, like a man shot. Paused, and turned. He saw Rupert standing by the taxi, and their eyes met. For a long moment nothing much happened. And then, slowly, he retraced his steps.

"Gus. Rupert Rycroft."

"I know. I remember." Close to, his appearance was even less encouraging, and the darkly stubbled jaw made him look like a down-and-out. All Rupert knew about Gus was that he had been a prisoner of war with the Japs. Believed killed, he had, instead, survived. But he knew nothing more. "Did you think I was dead?"

"No, I knew you'd made it. I married Athena Carey-Lewis, so word got through to us from Nancherrow. It's splendid to see you again. What are you doing in London?"

"Just down for a bit."

At this moment, the taxi-driver, getting fed up with all the argy-bargy, chipped in. "Do you want to take this cab, sir, or don't you?"

"Yes," Rupert told him coldly, "I do. Hang on a moment." He turned back to Gus. "Where are you going now?"

"Fulham Road."

"Are you living there?"

"For the moment. I've been lent a flat."

"How about lunch?"

"With you?"

"Who else?"

"Thanks, but no. I'd disgrace you. Haven't even shaved . . ."

A refusal, but Rupert quite suddenly knew that if he let Gus out of his sight, he would never find him again. So he persisted. "I've all day. No appointments. Why don't we go back to your place, and you can clean up and then we'll go to a pub, or something. We can talk. Catch up on things. It's been a long time."

But Gus still hesitated. "It's a pretty crummy place . . ."

"No matter. No excuse." The time had come for action. Rupert opened the taxi door, and stood aside. "Come on, old boy, get in."

So Gus did, sliding across to the far side of the seat, and setting his grocery box on the floor between his feet. Rupert followed at his slightly less agile pace, easing his leg into position, and then slamming the door shut.

"Still the Cavalry Club, sir?"

"No." He turned to Gus. "You'd better tell him."

Gus gave the man his Fulham address, and the cab moved out into the thin stream of traffic. Then he said, "You got shot up."

It was not a question. "Yes. In Germany, just months from the end of hostilities. Lost my leg. How did you know?"

"Judith told me. In Colombo. On my way home."

"Judith. Of course."

"You're out of the Army?"

"Yes. We're living in Gloucestershire in a house on my father's estate."

"How is Athena?"

"Same as ever."

"Still ravishingly beautiful?"

"I think so."

"And you have a little girl, I believe?"

"Clementina. She's five now. Athena's having another baby in the spring."

"Loveday used to write to me, and give me all the family news. That's how I knew. What do you do in Gloucestershire?"

"Mug up all the things I should have known years ago . . . about running the estate and the farms and the forestry and the shooting. The Army, I have decided, doesn't really prepare a man for civilian life. For a little, I mulled over the idea of going to the Agricultural College in Cirencester, but I think perhaps, instead, I shall stream my meagre talents in another direction."

"What's that?"

"Politics."

"Good God, what a thought." Gus was feeling in the pocket of his jacket, to produce a packet of cigarettes and a lighter. He lit a cigarette, and Rupert saw the unsteady tremor of his hand, and the long, spatulate fingers stained brown with nicotine. "What put that into your head?"

"I don't know. Yes, I do know. After I got out of hospital, I went off to see the families of some of the men in the regiment who'd been killed when I was wounded. Tank crews and such. Men I'd fought with all the way through the Western Desert and Sicily. Decent men. And their families lived in such mean and squalid surroundings. Industrial cities, back-to-back housing, smoking chimneys, everything filthy and ugly. It was the first time in my life I'd ever seen for myself how the other half live. Frankly, I found it sickening. And I wanted to do something to make it better. To make this a country that people could live in with pride. It sounds a bit naïve and idealistic, but I feel strongly it's what I should be about."

"Good for you. If you think it will make any difference."

"I had a meeting this morning at the House of Commons, with the Chairman of the Conservative Party. I'd have to be accepted as the prospective candidate for some constituency or other . . . probably a Labour stronghold that one could never win in a million years, but all good experience. And then, in the fullness of time, and with a bit of luck, a Member of Parliament at Westminster."

"What does Athena think of the idea?"

"She's behind me."

"I can see her, sitting on a Conservative platform and wearing a flowery hat."

"That won't happen for a long time yet . . ."

Gus stubbed out his cigarette and leaned forward to speak to the driver . . . "It's on the right-hand side of the road, just beyond the hospital . . ."

"Okay, sir."

They had, it seemed, just about arrived. Rupert looked from the window of the cab with some interest, being unfamiliar with this part of London. His own stamping ground, which included the Ritz, the Berkeley, his club, and the large town establishments of his mother's friends, was enclosed by clearly laid-down borders on the four points of the compass: the river, Shaftesbury Avenue, Regents Park, and Harrods. Beyond was unknown country. Now, he saw evidence of much bomb damage, craters temporarily enclosed by hoardings, and empty walls where once had stood a small terrace house. Everything looked a bit ramshackle and down-at-heel. Small shops spilt their wares out onto the pavements: a greengrocery, a newsagent, a second-hand furniture store, and the Eel-and-Pie Café, its windows damp with steam.

Then the taxi stopped, and Gus got out, stooping to retrieve his grocery box. Rupert followed. On the kerb, he began to reach into his trouser pocket for his loose change, but Gus was there before him.

"Keep the change."

"Thanks very much."

"Come on," said Gus. He crossed the pavement, with Rupert behind him. Between the café and a little grocery stood a narrow door, peeling dark-brown paint. Gus produced a latchkey and opened this, and led the way into a dank and airless hallway, with stairs rising up into the gloom. There was linoleum on the floor and the stairs, and a fusty smell compounded of stale cabbage, tom-cats, and uncleaned lavatories. When the door shut behind them, it was almost totally dark.

"I told you it was crummy," Gus said, and started up the stairs. Rupert transferred his stick to his carrier-bag hand and gamely followed, hauling himself upwards by the banister rail.

On the turn of the stairs, a door stood open, revealing a dank bathroom, curling linoleum, and the source of the lavatory smell. Up again to the first-floor landing. The stairs continued, rising into the half-lit gloom, but they were faced by another door, and Gus opened this with his key and led the way into a large, high-ceilinged front room with two long windows facing out over the street.

The first thing that struck Rupert was the intense cold. There was a fireplace, but no fire, and the grate was a graveyard for dead matches and cigarette stubs. A small electric heater stood by the fender, but this was not switched on, and even if it were, it was hard to imagine that its two little bars could do much to alleviate the chill. The walls were covered with a hectically flowered wallpaper, the sort that Athena always referred to as a bee's nightmare, but this was now faded and dirty and beginning to peel at the corners. The curtains, narrow and far too short, had clearly been intended for some other room, and on the black marble mantelpiece stood a green vase filled with dusty pampas-grass. Looming sofas and chairs upholstered in worn brown moquette bore a few limp cushions, and a table, perhaps intended for dining, was piled with old newspapers, magazines, a dirty cup and saucer, and a worn attaché case, spilling what looked like old letters and bills.

Not, Rupert decided, a cheerful spot.

On the table, Gus set down his grocery box. Then he turned and faced Rupert. "Sorry. But I did warn you."

It was no good prevaricating. "I've never seen anything so depressing in all my life."

"You said it yourself. How the other half live. It's not even a flat. Just rooms. I use the bathroom on the stairs, and the kitchen and the bedroom are on the other side of the landing."

"What the hell are you doing here?"

"I was lent it. I didn't want to go to an hotel. I wanted to be on my own. Some other person had been staying here, and left it filthy. I haven't got around to cleaning it up. Actually, I've had 'flu and been in bed for three days. That's why I haven't shaved. And I had to go out this morning, because I'd run out of food and stuff. Had to get something to eat. It's a bit tricky because I haven't got a ration card."

"If you don't mind my saying so, you could be better organized."

"It's possible. Do you want a drink? I've got a bottle of dubious whisky, but it'll have to be tap-water. Or you could have a cup of tea. Nothing much else, I'm afraid."

"No. Thank you. I don't want anything."

"Well, sit down and make yourself comfortable. I'll get changed. Give me five minutes. Here . . ." He delved into his grocery box and produced a *Daily Mail*. "You can read this while I'm gone."

Rupert took the newspaper, but did not read it. Once Gus had left him, he dropped it on the table, and then set down his Harrods bag alongside Gus's shopping. He crossed the room and stood at the window, looking down at the traffic of the Fulham Road through the fog of uncleaned glass.

His mind was in something of a turmoil, and he found himself thinking back, and trying to sort out all the facts that he could remember about Gus Callender and that golden summer of 1939 when they had all been together at Nancherrow. He had arrived, out of the blue, driving a dashing Lagonda, come from Scotland, a Cambridge friend of Edward's. A reserved, self-contained young man, with dark good looks and an unmistakable aura of affluence. What had he told them about himself? That he had been at school at Rugby; that his father's home was on Deeside, a country known to be rich with the immense estates of landed gentry, old nobility, and even royalty. Somewhere, there had been a lot of money. So what had happened?

He remembered other aspects of Gus, less materialistic. The manner in which he had slipped into the life-style of a family whom he had never met before, and become, obscurely, one of them. His talent for drawing, painting, and portraiture. The sketch of Edward, which held pride of place on Edgar Carey-Lewis's desk, was the most telling and perceptive likeness that Rupert had ever seen. And then, little Loveday. She had only been seventeen, but her love for Gus, and his care for her, had touched all their hearts.

After Singapore fell, it was Loveday who was so certain, so convinced that Gus was dead that she had somehow persuaded her family that he was never going to return. At that time, Rupert was in North Africa with the Armoured Division, but letters came from Athena telling him every detail of all that had taken place, or was about to happen.

At the end of which, Loveday had married Walter Mudge.

He sighed deeply. He realized that he was growing cold, and that his stump had started to throb, sure sign that he had been on his feet for too long. He turned from the window, and as he did, Gus came back, looking slightly improved, having shaved, combed his long thick hair, and changed into a navy-blue polo-necked sweater and a venerable tweed jacket.

"Sorry to keep you waiting. You should have sat down. Are you sure you don't want that drink?"

"No." Rupert shook his head. He couldn't wait to get away out of this place. "Let's find a pub."

"There's one just down the road. Can you walk that far?"

"Provided you don't expect me to sprint."

"We shall amble," said Gus.

The pub was one of those old ones which, somehow, had escaped the bombing, although buildings on either side had been blown to smithereens, leaving the Crown and Anchor isolated, sticking up out of the pavement like an old tooth. Inside it was dark and comforting, with a lot of mahogany and brass, and aspidistras in pots, and a fireplace where burnt a coke-fire, which made it all smell a bit like old railway-station waiting-rooms.

At the bar they ordered two beers, and the barmaid said she would make them sandwiches, but she could only manage Spam and pickles. So they settled for Spam and pickles, and carried their beers over to the fireside, where they found an empty table, and, once Rupert had shed his overcoat and his bowler, made themselves comfortable.

"How long have you been in London, Gus?"

"I've rather lost track of time." Gus was lighting another cigarette. "What day is it today?"

"Tuesday."

"I arrived on Friday? Yes, that's right. And was immediately struck down with 'flu. At least, I think that's what it was. Didn't see a doctor or anything. Just stayed in bed and slept."

"You all right now?"

"I feel a bit feeble. You know how it is."

"How long are you staying?"

Gus shrugged. "No plans."

Rupert felt that he was getting nowhere, and it was about time he stopped tiptoeing around the point. He said, "Look, Gus, do you mind me asking questions? Because if you do, I'll shut up. But you must realize I'm naturally anxious to know how the hell you've got yourself into this situation."

"It's not as bad as it looks."

"That's not the point."

"Where do you want to start?"

"Colombo, perhaps? That's where you met up with Judith?"

"Yes, Judith. That was one of the best things, finding her again. She's such a sweet person, and so kind to me. We didn't have much time, just a couple of hours, and then I had to get back on board again. I had a bottle of whisky with me. Black and White. The old waiter at the Galle Face Hotel had kept it for Fergie Cameron to come back to, but Fergie had died, so he gave it to me."

"When did you get back to England?"

"Oh, I don't know. About the middle of October, I suppose. London, and then we were all wheeled back to Aberdeen. Did you know that my parents died?"

"No, I didn't know. I'm sorry."

"I was told they had died when I got to the hospital in Rangoon. They were quite an elderly pair. Already middle-aged when I was a small child. But I would have liked to have seen them again. I wrote to them from Singapore, from Changi, but they never got the letter. They thought I was dead, and my mother had a massive stroke; she lay in a private nursing home for three years, and then she died. During this time my father went on living at Ardvray, with housekeepers and servants to look after him. He wouldn't move back to Aberdeen. I suppose he thought he might lose face. He was a very stubborn old man, and very proud."

Rupert frowned. "What do you mean? Move *back* to Aberdeen. I thought you'd always lived at Ardvray."

"Everybody always thought that. They assumed it; imagined vast estates, grouse moors, established landed gentry. And I never put them right, because it was easier for me to go along with the assumption. But the truth is that my family was neither landed nor gentry. My father was a humble Aberdonian, who made his own money, and pulled himself up by his bootstraps. When I was small, we lived in a house in Aberdeen, with the trams going by at the foot of the garden. But my father wanted better things for me. I was his only child. He wanted me to be a gentleman. So we moved away from Aberdeen, to Deeside and a hideous Victorian house where my mother was never happy. And I was sent to a private prep school, and so on to Rugby, and then to Cambridge. A gentleman, with background and breeding. For some reason, background and breeding were important in those days, before the war. I wasn't ashamed of my parents. In fact, I had a lot of time for both of them. I admired them. But at the same time, I knew that they were socially unacceptable. Even saying that screws me up."

"What happened to your father?"

"He died—a heart attack—soon after my mother. When I got back to Aberdeen, I thought, at least, that I would be fairly well off, have enough money to start over again. But, it all came out. The cash had dribbled away. The bottom falling out of the property market, costs of hospital fees for my mother, keeping Ardvray going for one old man, paying the servants, the cook, the gardeners. He never thought to lower his standards in any way. Then, his capital. Stocks and shares. I'd never realized he'd so much invested in Malaya, rubber and tin. And, of course, that was all gone."

Rupert decided that this was no time to mince words. "Are you broke?" he asked bluntly.

"No. No, I'm not broke. But I'm going to have to get a job of some sort. I've put Ardvray on the market . . ."

"How about your car? The enviable Lagonda?"

"Fancy you remembering that! It's in a garage in Aberdeen somewhere. I haven't got around to reclaiming it yet."

"I'm sorry, Gus. It doesn't sound much of a home-coming."

"I never thought it would be." Then quietly, "But at least I'm home."

They were interrupted here by the barmaid bringing their sandwiches.

" 'Fraid they're not up to much, but it's all I can manage. Put a bit of mustard inside, I did, then you can pretend they're ham."

They thanked her, and Rupert ordered another couple of beers, and she took away the empty glasses. Gus lit another cigarette. Rupert said, "How about Cambridge?"

"What about Cambridge?"

"I can't remember what you were reading . . ."

"Engineering."

"Could you go back to University, and finish your course?"

"No. I couldn't do that. I couldn't go back."

"How about your painting?"

"I haven't done anything since we were liberated by the Army and taken to the hospital in Rangoon. The desire to draw seems to have left me."

"You're so bloody good, I'm sure you could make a living that way."

"Thank you."

"That sketch you did of Edward. Brilliant."

"That was a long time ago."

"A talent like yours doesn't die."

"I'm not sure. I'm not sure of anything. In hospital, they kept urging me to start drawing again. They brought me papers, pencils, paints . . ."

"You mean in the hospital in Rangoon?"

"No, not in Rangoon. I've been in another hospital for the last seven weeks. A psychiatric hospital in Dumfries. The doctors put me there because I fell to bits. I couldn't sleep. Nightmares. The shakes. Floods of tears. A sort of breakdown, I suppose . . ."

Rupert was appalled. "My dear man, why didn't you tell me before?"

"So boring. Shameful. Not very proud . . ."

"Did they help you?"

"Yes. They were amazing. Wise and patient. But they kept trying to make me go back to my drawing and I had a total mental block about it. So I refused, and they gave me a basket to make instead. There were lovely grounds, and a nice little VAD used to take me for walks. And there was sky and woods and grass, but it never seemed real. It was like looking at somebody else's world through a thick pane of glass, and at the same time knowing that none of it had anything to do with me."

"Do you still feel that way?"

"Yes. That's why I came to London. I thought that if I came to the most anonymous, crowded, stressful place I could think of, and survive it, then I could go back to Scotland and start again. One of the chaps who was in the hospital with me said I could use his flat. It seemed a good idea at the time. But then I got here, and I got 'flu, and it stopped being such a good idea." He added hastily, "But I'm okay now."

"Do you want to go back to Scotland?"

"I haven't decided."

"You could go to Cornwall."

"No, I couldn't."

"Because of Loveday?"

Gus did not reply. The barmaid came back with their drinks, and Rupert paid her for them, and left a hefty tip on her tray.

"Oh, thanks, sir. You haven't eaten your sandwiches yet. They'll get all dry."

"We'll eat them in a moment. Thank you so much."

The fire was dying. She noticed this, and paused to shovel another load of coal onto the embers. For a moment all was smoky and black, and then the flames started to flicker once more.

Gus said, "Loveday was the worst."

"Sorry?"

"Being told by Judith that Loveday was married. It was the thought of Loveday and Nancherrow that kept me alive on that fucking railway. Once I had dysentery so badly that I was just about dead, and it would have been the easiest thing in the world just to slip away, but I didn't. Somehow I clung on. I wouldn't allow myself to die, because I knew I had to get back to her, because she would be waiting. I thought she would wait. But she thought I was dead, and she didn't wait."

"I know. I'm sorry."

"I kept her image, like a private photograph. Water was the other thing. Thinking about water. Peat-brown Scottish burns, tumbling like beer over boulders. Water to watch, flowing by, or rolling in on some empty beach. Water to listen to, drink, swim in. Cold running water. Cleansing, healing, purifying. The cove at Nancherrow, and the sea at high tide, deep and clear and blue as Bristol glass. The cove; and Nancherrow. And Loveday."

After a bit, Rupert said, "I think you should go back to Cornwall."

"Judith has asked me. She has written to me. Three letters. And I've never answered any of them. I tried once or twice, but it wasn't any good. I couldn't think of anything to say. But I feel bad. I promised I'd keep in touch, and I haven't. By now, she's probably abandoned all thought of me." A ghost of a smile crossed his sombre features. "Tossed me aside like a worn glove or a sucked orange. And I don't blame her."

"I don't think you should stay here, in London, Gus."

Gus picked up his sandwich and took an experimental bite out of it. "It's not bad, actually." But Rupert didn't know if he was talking about the sandwich or London.

"Look"—he leaned forward—"if you don't want to go to Cornwall, and I totally understand your feelings, then come to Gloucestershire with me. Now. Today. We'll get a cab to Paddington, and a train to Cheltenham. My car's there. We'll drive home. You can stay with us. Not Cornwall, but lovely country. Athena will welcome you with open arms, I know. You can stay as long as you want. Just, please, for my sake, don't go back to that ghastly flat."

Gus said, "This is meant to be the end of the line. I can't go on running away."

"Please come."

"You're really kind. But I can't. Try to understand. It's *myself* I have to come to terms with. Once I've done that I can start edging out again."

"I can't leave you."

"You can. I'm fine. I'm over the worst."

"You won't do anything stupid?"

"Like topping myself? No. I won't do that. But don't think I'm not grateful." Rupert reached into his breast pocket and took out his wallet. For an instant, Gus looked mildly amused. "And I'm all right for cash. I don't need a hand-out."

"You insult me. I'm giving you my card. Address and telephone number." He handed it over, and Gus took it. "Promise you'll give me a ring if things get rough, or you need anything."

"That's very kind."

"And the invitation to stay still stands."

"I'm all right, Rupert."

After that, there didn't seem to be much else to say. They finished their sandwiches and the beer, and Rupert retrieved his overcoat and his bowler. He gathered up his stick and his Harrods bag. They left the pub, and went out into the bitter, grey afternoon, and walked for a bit until a taxi came trundling down the road. Gus hailed it, and as it drew into the pavement's edge, they turned to each other.

"Goodbye."

"Goodbye, Rupert."

"Good luck."

"My love to Athena."

"Of course."

He got into the taxi, and Gus slammed the door shut behind him.

"Where to, sir?"

"Paddington Station, please."

As they moved off, he turned in the seat to look back through the window.

But Gus had already turned and was walking away from him, and a moment later was lost from view.

That evening, just before nine o'clock, having talked it all through with Athena, Rupert Rycroft put through a trunk-call to the Dower House. There, Judith and Phyllis were enjoying an undemanding evening together, by the fire, with their knitting, and listening to a light operetta, *Vienna Blood,* on the wireless. Now, this was over, and they waited for the news. Then, beyond the closed door, the telephone began to ring.

Judith said, "Damn." Not because she particularly wanted to listen to the news, but because the telephone still lived in the hall, and on this cold December night, it was chilly out there. She laid down her knitting, pulled a cardigan over her shoulders, and braved the icy draughts.

"Dower House."

"Judith, it's Rupert. Rupert Rycroft. All the way from Gloucestershire."

"Goodness. How lovely to hear you." It was likely, she decided, to be a longish conversation, so she reached for a chair and sat down. "How are you all? How's Athena?"

"We're all well. But that's not why I'm calling. Have you got a moment?"

"Of course."

"Bit complicated, so don't interrupt . . ."

She didn't. He talked, and she listened. He had been in London for the day. Seen Gus Callender. Gus, living in some down-at-heels rooms in the Fulham Road. They had gone to a pub for lunch together, and there Gus had told Rupert all that had been happening to him since he got home. The death of his parents, the evaporation of his father's fortune, the long spell in the psychiatric hospital.

"Hospital?" It was alarming news. "Why didn't he let us *know?* He *should* have let us know. I wrote to him, but he never replied."

"He said. Three letters. But I don't think he was capable of writing back."

"Is he well now?"

"I wouldn't know. He looked ghastly. Smoking like a chimney."

"But why is he in London?"

"I think he just wanted to be somewhere totally on his own."

"Couldn't he afford to go to an hotel?"

"I don't think it's quite as bad as that. But no, he didn't want to go to an hotel. Like I said, he wanted to be on his own. Come to terms. Prove to himself he could cope. Some friend lent him the key of this terrible place, but as soon as he got to London, he went down with 'flu. So perhaps that's why he was looking so ropy, and the flat was so filthy."

"Did he talk about Loveday?"

"Yes."

"And?"

Rupert hesitated. "He didn't say much. But I think her defection had much to do with his breakdown."

"Oh, Rupert, I can't *bear* it for him. What can we do?"

"That's why I'm calling. I asked him to come back to Gloucestershire with me. Stay here, with Athena and me for a bit. But he wouldn't come. He was perfectly charming about it all, but utterly adamant."

"So why are you ringing me?"

"He's closer to you than he is to me. It was you who found him again, in Colombo. And you're not part of the family. Athena and I are a bit close to home. We thought perhaps you might help."

"How?"

"Go to London, perhaps. I've got his address. Go and see him, try to get him away. I think he might come to Cornwall, if he came with you."

"Rupert, I asked him to come. In my letters. In the last letter I even invited him for Christmas. I don't think he wants me interfering . . ."

"I think that's something you have to risk. Could you go?"

"Yes. I could."

Rupert hesitated. "The thing is, I don't want to push you, but I don't think we should put off any time."

"You're worried, aren't you?"

"Yes, I really am."

"In that case, I can go right away. Tomorrow if you like. Biddy's not here, but Phyllis and Anna are. I can leave the house." She thought ahead, making swift plans. "I could even drive to London. It might be better than going in the train, because it would give me a bit more leverage, having a car there."

"What about petrol?"

"Biddy left me a stack of illegal coupons. I'll get the local garage to swap them for me."

"It's a long drive at this time of the year."

"It's all right. I've done it before. And there's not much traffic on the roads. If I go tomorrow I can spend the night at the Mews, and then go to Fulham first thing the next morning."

"When you see him, you may think I'm making a mountain out of a mole-hill, but I don't think I am. I think, more than anything else, Gus needs old friends. Nancherrow is out of the question, and that only leaves you."

"You'd better give me his address." She found a pencil, and as he spoke, scribbled it down on the cover of the telephone book. ". . . it's about half-way down the Fulham Road, past the Brompton Hospital, on the right-hand side of the road."

"Don't worry. I'll find it."

"Judith, you're a saint. You've taken a load off my mind."

"I may not be able to do any good at all."

"But you can try."

"Yes. I'll try. And thank you for ringing. I've been so worried about him. I hated saying goodbye to him in Colombo—he seemed so vulnerable, and so terribly *alone*."

"I think that's just what he is. Let us know how you get on."

"Promise."

They talked a little more, and then said goodbye, and Judith put down the receiver. She realized that she was shivering, chilled to the bone, not only by the temperature of the hall, but by the knowledge that all her fears for Gus had been confirmed. After a bit, she got up and went back to the drawing-room to put another log on the fire and crouch by its comforting blaze.

The news was just about over. Phyllis reached over and switched off the wireless.

"That was a long call," she remarked.

"Yes. It was Rupert Rycroft. About Gus Callender."

Phyllis knew all about Gus, because over the course of the weeks that had gone by since Judith returned home, Judith had told her about their meeting in Colombo, and how she had had to be the one to tell him that Loveday had married Walter Mudge.

"What about him?" Phyllis asked.

Judith explained. Phyllis laid down her knitting and listened, and her expression became much distressed.

"Oh, poor man. Hardly seems fair, does it? Could Rupert do nothing for him?"

"He asked him back to Gloucestershire, but Gus wouldn't go."

Phyllis looked a bit alarmed. "So what does he want you to do?"

"Go to London, and try to persuade Gus to come here, I suppose."

"He's not violent, is he?"

"Oh, Phyllis, poor man, of course he's not."

"You never know with these mental cases. Read awful things in the papers . . ."

"It's not like that." She thought of Gus. "It would never be like that."

"So you're going?"

"Yes, I think I must."

"When?"

"Tomorrow. Waste no time. I'll drive. Come home on Thursday."

There was a long pause. And then Phyllis said, "You can't go tomorrow. Tomorrow's Wednesday. The Nancherrow dinner party. Jeremy Wells. You can't miss that."

"I'd forgotten."

"*Forgotten!*" Phyllis began to be indignant. "How could you forget? Why should you go rushing off to some other person's friend, when you've got your own life to think about? Your own future. Put it off for a day, going to London, I mean. Go on Thursday. It's not going to kill anybody, you putting it off for a day."

"Phyllis, I can't."

"Well, I think that's very rude. What's Mrs. Carey-Lewis going to think? What's Jeremy going to think, believing he's going to see you again after all these years, and finding you flying off to London to see some other man?"

"Gus is not just some other man."

"Seems to me he is. Even if he was a friend of Edward's, that's no cause to mess everything up for yourself."

"Phyllis, if I didn't go, I wouldn't be able to look myself in the eye for the rest of my life. Don't you understand what he's been through? Three and a half years of sheer hell, building that railway through the steaming jungle; sick and ill, nearly dying of dysentery; beaten and brutalized by the cruellest and most sadistic of guards. Seeing his friends dying or being killed. Or worse. Can you wonder he's had a breakdown? How can I think of myself or Jeremy under these circumstances?"

This outburst silenced Phyllis. She sat gazing into the fire, still looking mulish but at least not arguing any more. And then she said, "It's like the Germans and the Jews. I don't know how human beings can be so inhuman to each other. Jess said things to me. She told me things. Sometimes, when we were alone together, doing a bit of cooking, or when I said good night to her after she'd gone to bed. Perhaps it wasn't so bad for her and that Australian girl. At least they weren't having to build railways. In that last camp they were in, Asulu, the conditions were so bad, and so little food, that ten of the women, led by the doctor, had gone to the commandant to complain. And he had them all beaten, and their heads shaved, and locked them in a bamboo cage for five days. It haunted me, that, Judith. If they could do that to women and children . . ."

Judith said, "I know." Jess had never told her, but she had spoken to Phyllis, and for this Judith was grateful, because it meant that all the horrors were not being bottled up. She said again, "I know."

Phyllis sighed. "Well, that's it then. When are you off?"

"First thing tomorrow morning. I'll take Mrs. Somerville's car."

"Do you think he'll come back with you?"

"I don't know."

"If he does, where's he going to sleep?"

"He'll have to have Mrs. Somerville's room."

"I'll clean it up. Change the sheets. You'd better ring Mrs. Carey-Lewis."

"I will. In a moment."

"You're looking washed out, with all this. Like a nice hot cup of cocoa, would you?"

"Adore one."

"I'll go and make it, then." Phyllis rolled up her knitting and stuck the needles through the ball of wool. "It'll cheer us up a bit before we go to bed."

Back in the hall again, Judith dialled Nancherrow.

"Hello."

"Diana, it's Judith."

"Darling."

"Sorry to ring so late."

"What's it about?"

Once more, explanations. From time to time, Diana made little painful cries of horror, but apart from that, she was very good and neither asked questions nor interrupted.

". . . so I'm going to London tomorrow. If it's all right with you, I'll stay at the Mews, and hopefully bring Gus back with me on Thursday."

"My dinner party! My coming-home party!"

"I know. I'm sorry. I can't make it."

"Darling, I can't bear it! We're planning such a festive meal."

"I'm really sorry."

"Oh, bother. Why do these things always happen at the wrong time?"

This was unanswerable, so Judith said, "What about Loveday?"

A long silence, and then Diana sighed audibly. "Yes. I see."

"Loveday doesn't want Gus to come to Cornwall. She doesn't want to see him. She told me so."

"Oh dear, it's all so difficult."

"I don't think you should tell her about Gus. If he comes to the Dower House, I don't think she should know. There's no reason for her to be told."

"But she's bound to find out sooner or later."

"Yes, but not immediately. From what Rupert said, it doesn't sound as though Gus is in any state to cope with emotional confrontations."

"I hate secrets."

"I do too. But just for a day or two, until we see how things work out. You go ahead with your dinner party, and tell Loveday that I've had to go away. And tell the Colonel and Jeremy Wells not to say anything either. If Gus comes back with me, and stays here for a bit, of course Loveday will have to know. But, immediately, I think we should all keep our mouths shut."

For a long moment, Diana was silent. Judith held her breath. But when Diana spoke again, all she said was, "Yes. Of course. You're right, of course."

"I'm sorry about spoiling your party."

"I think darling Jeremy will be sorry too."

He had been given his old, familiar bedroom, and found his own way upstairs, lugging the battered green naval-issue suitcase. It was so long since he had been at Nancherrow that he didn't immediately unpack, but dumped the suitcase on the luggage rack at the foot of the bed and went to open the window and gaze out, with some satisfaction, at the long-remembered prospect. It was nearly midday. From time to time the fitful sun gleamed out from behind the clouds. There was a string of washing waving on the line, and the doves strutted on the cobbles or clustered on the platform of their dovecote, cooing away to themselves, and presumably complaining about the cold. It was a moment to be relished. From time to time, he had to remind himself that the war was over, and he was really back in Cornwall for good. This was one of them; and he knew that, with a bit of luck, he was never again going to be long separated from this magical place that always felt like his second home. And he felt enormously grateful that he had been allowed to live, had not been killed, and so was able to return.

Presently he closed the window and turned to deal with his suitcase, but as he did so, heard swift footsteps in the passage outside, and the voice of his hostess.

"Jeremy!" She flung open the door and was there, wearing sensible grey flannel trousers and a huge pale-blue mohair sweater, yet still managing to look fragile and intensely feminine. "Darling! Sorry I wasn't there to greet you; on the telephone as usual. How are you?" She kissed him lovingly, and then settled herself on his bed, clearly having long chats in mind. "Did you have a good drive?" as though he had come for a hundred miles instead of just from Truro. "Goodness, how lovely to see you again. And you look wonderful. Mediterranean tan. Darling, do I spy a grey hair at your temple?"

A bit embarrassed, Jeremy put up a hand to touch this lowering evidence of advancing age. "Yes, I think you do."

"Don't worry. I think it's rather distinguished. And look at me. Silver as a sixpence. Now, listen, I've got so much to tell you I don't know where to start. Most important, you know Judith's home?"

"Yes, I know. My father told me. And he told me about her parents dying, and Jess coming back."

"Poor little thing, she's had such a ghastly time, but really so brave. I hate to call her sensible, because it's such a *deadening* word, but I've never known anybody with so much good sense. Besides being so frightfully pretty. And the most heavenly figure. But Judith isn't the absolutely vital thing I have to talk about . . . Jeremy, you remember Gus Callender? He stayed here, that last summer."

"But of course. Loveday's love. The guy who was killed in Singapore."

"Darling, he wasn't killed. He survived. Prisoner of war. Burma Railways. Too horrific. Judith met him in Colombo on his way home. She told him that Loveday was married, and of course he was dreadfully upset. And then, as soon as she got back here, she told Loveday about Gus being alive, and Loveday told Edgar and me."

All that Jeremy could think of to say was, "Good heavens."

"I know. It's all a bit tricky, isn't it? Anyway, he went back to Scotland, and sort of *disappeared*. Judith wrote to him—I think she was a bit worried about him and felt responsible, but he never replied. And *then*, yesterday, Athena's Rupert was in London, and he found Gus there. Mouldering around the streets and looking like a down-and-out. Too depressing. But he persuaded Gus to come out to lunch with him, and Gus told him that he'd had a perfectly horrid nervous breakdown and had been in a sort of loony-bin, and his old mum and dad had died while he was in prison, and all the family wealth had disappeared . . . a total tale of woe. Rupert was dreadfully upset. He tried to get Gus to go home to Gloucestershire with him, but Gus wouldn't budge."

"Where's he living?"

"Some sordid flat, in a horrid bit that nobody ever goes to."

"So what's happened?"

"Oh, dear, this is taking such a long time, isn't it, but it is rather important. What's happened is that Judith has gone to London today to see if she can do anything to help. Maybe bring him back to the Dower House."

"What about Loveday?"

"Loveday has told us all that she doesn't want to see Gus. I think she feels a bit ashamed. Not that she has a thing to be ashamed about. But one does see . . ." Her voice trailed away. She looked hopefully at Jeremy. "You see, don't you, Jeremy darling?"

He sighed. "Yes, I suppose I do."

"It's all a bit depressing, because this evening I'd planned a lovely coming-home party for *you*, and Nettlebed had plucked pheasants, and Mrs. Nettlebed was going to make a plum fool, and Edgar was blissful, down in the cellar choosing a wine. But then Judith rang last night to tell me she was off to London, and Loveday telephoned to say that Walter couldn't make it either, so we've decided to forget about it for the time being. It's too disappointing."

"Don't worry," Jeremy assured her bravely. "It was sweet of you even to think of it."

"Well. I suppose. Another time." She was silent for a moment, and then looked at her tiny gold watch. "I must go. I promised Edgar I'd telephone the grain merchant about the hen food. It hasn't come, and the poor loves are starving." She got to her feet. "Lunch at one all right?"

"Perfect."

She went to the door, and then, with her hand on the knob, turned back to him.

"Jeremy, if Gus *does* come back with Judith, we're not saying anything to Loveday. Just to begin with. Till we see how he is."

Jeremy understood. "Right."

She shook her head, her expression much distressed. "I hate conspiracies, don't you?" But before he could reply to this, she was gone.

She left him with his unpacking still not done, and his mind in something of a turmoil, because this new peace-time life seemed to be beset by problems, decisions to be made, and matters—which had hung fire for far too long—to be finally clarified.

Only a few formalities remained before he left the RNVR for good, with an excellent chit from the Surgeon Captain, and a small gratuity from a grateful country. But he had returned home to find his old father deep in gloom. A Labour Government was now in office, and talk was all of a projected National Health Service which was going to change the whole face of medical care, and render out-of-date the old tradition of family doctoring. This, Jeremy felt, could be nothing but a good thing, but realized that his father was too elderly to deal with the upheaval that it would entail.

So, instead of returning to practice in Truro, perhaps this was the moment to change? A new location, and a new partnership; young men, and modern methods. A colleague in the Navy had already approached him about this, with an idea that Jeremy found intensely attractive. He could not commit himself, however, until he had spoken to Judith.

She was his last and most pressing quandary. He longed, above all, to see her again, and at the same time, dreaded a confrontation that might end forever his long-cherished dreams. Over the years since that night they had spent together in London, he had constantly thought of her. From the mid-Atlantic, from Liverpool, Gibraltar, and Malta, started letters that were never finished. He had, time after time, run out of words, lost his nerve, crumpled up the halting pages and thrown them in the trash-bin. Telling himself, what's the use? Telling himself that by now he would be forgotten, she would have found someone else.

She wasn't married. He knew that much. But Diana's revelations about Gus Callender filled him with disquiet. The implications, for Loveday, of Gus's return were perfectly understandable, but now Judith, it seemed, was deeply involved as well. The fact that she had opted out of Diana's coming-home party, and gone flying off to London to be with Gus, did not bode well for Jeremy Wells. But then, Gus had been Edward's friend, and Edward had been the great love of Judith's life. Perhaps that had something to do with it. Or perhaps her compassion had turned to a deeper emotion. Love. He didn't know. He had not known anything for far too long.

Suddenly he wanted, more than anything else in the world, a drink. A pink gin. Unpacking could wait until later. He went through to the bathroom and washed his hands and put a comb through his hair, and then went out of the room and downstairs in search of liquid cheer.

Judith took a last look around, to be sure that she had forgotten nothing. Bed stripped, breakfast cup and saucer washed and rinsed and left on the draining-board to dry. Refrigerator switched off, windows closed and locked. She picked up her small overnight bag, went down the narrow stairs, out through the front door, and slammed it firmly shut behind her.

It was nine o'clock in the morning and still only half light. The sky was dark and overcast, and during the night there had been quite a sharp frost. In the Mews, lights still burnt inside the little houses, spilling squares of yellow onto the icy cobbles. No flowers in tubs and window-boxes, but someone had bought a Christmas tree and propped it up against the wall by their front door. Perhaps, today, it would be brought indoors, to be decorated and strung with fairy lights.

She heaved her bag into the boot of Biddy's car and got in behind the wheel. The car didn't like being left out overnight in the cold, and it took two or three coughing attempts before the engine started, but it finally chunt-ered into life, exuding clouds of exhaust. She switched on the side lights and drove down the length of the Mews, and out through the archway at the far end.

It felt strange to be back in London without barrage balloons floating about overhead, and with street lamps shining. But evidence of bomb damage and the deprivations of war were still all about, and driving up Sloane Street, she saw that, although shop windows had been un-boarded and replaced with plate glass, the Christmas displays within the lovely stores bore no resemblance to the lavish luxury of pre-war days.

At this hour, there were still a good many people about. Mothers hurrying children to school, office-workers being sucked in droves down the warrens of the Underground, or queuing patiently for buses. Everybody looked a bit worn and harassed, as did their clothes, and some of the women appeared shabby as peasants, bundled up as they were in overcoats, boots, and head-scarves.

At the top of Sloane Street she turned left at the lights, went down the Brompton Road, and so into Fulham. Driving, she told herself, *one thing at a time.* She had been telling herself this ever since she left Rosemullion early yesterday morning. *Fill up the car tank and the spare petrol cans.* (Wayside garages might not be very accommodating about taking illegal petrol coupons.) *Get to London. Get to the Mews. Spend the night.* Now, it was *Find Gus's flat. Ring the bell. Wait for him to come to the door.* If he didn't come, then what should she do? Break the door down? Ring for the police or the fire brigade? And if he did, then what was she going to say? She thought of Diana. Diana was never at a loss for words. *Darling Gus. Hello. It's me. Lovely morning!*

She drove past the Brompton Hospital and, slowly, began to search for street numbers, over shop-fronts or doorways. Nearly there. Between two side streets, a line of little shops, their owners emerging to stack crates of Brussels sprouts on the pavement, or set up their newspaper stands. She saw the Eel-and-Pie Café, one of Rupert's landmarks, and drew in at the kerbside. Got out of the car, and locked it. The narrow door was wedged between the café and a small grocery. On the doorjamb were two bells, labelled with names written on scraps of card. One read NOLAN, the other PELOVSKY. Not much help. She swithered for a moment, and then pressed PELOVSKY. She waited.

Nothing happened, so she pressed it again. If nothing continued to happen, she would try NOLAN. Her feet, in fur-lined boots, began to feel cold, the iciness of the pavement seeping up through rubber soles. Perhaps Gus was still in bed, asleep. Perhaps the bell didn't work. Perhaps she should seek sanctuary in the Eel-and-Pie Café and get a cup of tea . . .

Then, footsteps, some person approaching down a flight of stairs. She watched the door. A latch clicked and it swung inward and there, at last, unbelievably, was Gus.

For a moment, without words, they simply stared at each other, Judith momentarily silenced, simply because she was so relieved to have actually run him to earth, and Gus clearly totally bewildered at finding her on his doorstep.

She had to say *something*. "I didn't know you were called Pelovsky."

"I'm not. It's some other chap."

He didn't look too bad. Not as awful as she had feared. Dreadfully thin and pale, of course, but shaved and dressed casually in a thick polo-necked sweater and corduroys.

"You should change the card."

"Judith, what the *hell* are you doing here?"

"Come to see you. And I'm frozen. Can I come in?"

"Of course. Sorry . . ." He stepped back, making way for her. "Come along . . ."

She went through the door and he closed it behind them. It was almost dark, and there was a stale, unpleasant smell hanging in the airless atmosphere.

"Not much of an entrance," he apologized. "Come on up."

He led the way, and she followed him up the gloomy stairs. Reaching the landing, she saw the door on the opposite wall standing ajar, and they went through into the room that lay beyond, with its eye-assaulting wallpaper and meagre curtains. In the hearth a small electric fire burnt resolutely, its two bars emanating a faint warmth, but the dirty windows were still frosted with rime, and it was dreadfully cold.

He said, "You'd better keep your coat on. Sorry it's all a bit sordid. I spent yesterday morning trying to clean it up a bit, but there's not much improvement."

There was a table. She saw that he had pushed papers and files and the remains of yesterday's newspaper to one end, and at the other was evidence of breakfast, a teacup and a crust of toast on a plate.

She said, "I've disturbed you."

"Not a bit. I'm finished. Make yourself comfortable . . ."

He went over to the fireplace and took a cigarette packet and a lighter from the mantelpiece. When he had lit the cigarette, he turned and leaned his shoulders against the mantelpiece, and across the worn hearthrug they faced each other. Judith sat on the arm of one of the bulky sofas, but Gus stayed where he was, on his feet.

There was no point in beating about the bush. She said, "Rupert phoned me."

"Ah." As though all were immediately clear. "I see. I thought it must be something like that."

"You mustn't be cross with him. He was really concerned."

"He's such a nice chap. But I'm afraid he caught me on a bad day. 'Flu and such. I'm better now."

"He told me you'd been ill. Been in hospital."

"Yes."

"Did you get my letters?" Gus nodded. "Why didn't you reply to any of them?"

He shook his head. "I wasn't in much of a state to communicate with

694

anybody, let alone getting words down on paper. I'm sorry. Ungrateful. And you were so kind."

"When I didn't hear, I got really worried."

"You mustn't worry. You have enough problems of your own. How's Jess?"

"She's fine. Settled in at school."

"What a miracle for you, finding her again."

"Yes. But, Gus, I've not come here to talk about Jess . . ."

"When did you come to London?"

"Yesterday. I drove up. I've got the car outside, parked in the street. I spent the night at Diana's house. And then I came here. Rupert had given me your address. It wasn't too difficult to find."

"Are you Christmas shopping?"

"No, I haven't come to shop. I came to find you. No other reason."

"How gratifying. That was very good of you."

"I want you to come back to Cornwall with me."

He said instantly, and without any hesitation, "I can't. Thank you, but no."

"Why do you have to be in London?"

"It's as good a place as any."

"For what?"

"To be on my own. Get myself sorted out. Get used to living on my own, standing on my own feet. A psychiatric hospital is an emasculating experience. And sometime I've got to start looking for a job. I have contacts here. Old schoolfriends, chaps who were in the Army. A sort of network."

"Have you seen any of them yet?"

"Not yet . . ."

She did not completely believe all this talk, but guessed that he was trying to reassure her, and so get her off his back.

"Is it so important? To have a job?"

"Yes. Not pressing, but necessary. Rupert probably filled you in with the details of my father's demise. By the time he died, his capital, one way or another, had melted away to a mere trickle. I can no longer enjoy the life of a gentleman of leisure."

"Knowing you, I wouldn't imagine that would be a problem."

"No. But it does raise a certain need for positive action."

"But not *immediately*. You must give yourself a chance. You've been ill. You've had a rotten time. It's mid-winter and it's cheerless, and Christmas is only just around the corner. You can't be alone at Christmas. Come back with me. Now." She heard herself pleading. "Pack a bag and lock the door and we'll go home together."

"Sorry. Really sorry. I can't do that."

"Is it Loveday?" she asked, scarcely daring to ask.

She thought he would deny it, but he didn't. He nodded. "Yes."

"You wouldn't *have* to see Loveday . . ."

"Oh, come on, Judith, don't be too stupid. How could we not? It's unreal to imagine that we wouldn't have to meet."

"We wouldn't have to *say* anything . . . tell anybody . . ."

"And what would you expect me to do? Go around in a false beard and a pair of dark glasses, speaking in the guttural tones of a displaced Mittel-European?"

"We could call you Mr. Pelovsky."

It wasn't much of a joke, and he didn't find it funny. "I don't want to bugger everything up for her."

You don't need to. Walter Mudge and Arabella Lumb are already, very competently, seeing to that. She bit the words back, even as they sat on the tip of her tongue, which was a good thing. Said, they could never be unsaid.

Instead, "Loveday's not as important as you, Gus. The person we must think about is you."

He did not answer this. "Look, if you don't want to come to Rosemullion, then let me take you to Gloucestershire, and I'll leave you there with Rupert and Athena. They'd love to have you, I know."

His face expressionless, his dark eyes sunken and sombre. She was getting nothing out of him at all, and having hung on to her patience all this time, Judith began to be angry. There is nothing in this world more infuriating than a stubborn, immovable man.

"Oh, Gus, why do you have to be so shuttered and pig-headed? Why won't you let any of us help?"

"I don't need help."

"That's ridiculous! Selfish and horrible. You're considering nobody but yourself. How do you imagine *we* all feel, with you being on your own, and no family, and no home and . . . nothing. We can't do anything for you if you won't help yourself. I know you've been through hell, and I know you've been ill, but you've got to give yourself a chance. Not sit in this horrible flat, brooding over your woes, brooding over Loveday . . ."

"Oh, shut *up*."

For a terrible moment, Judith thought she was going to burst into tears. She got up from the sofa and went over to the window and stared down at the traffic in the street, until the hot pricking behind her eyes had subsided and she knew she wasn't going to cry after all.

Behind her, he said, "I'm sorry."

She didn't reply.

"I'd love to come with you. Part of me yearns to come with you. But I'm scared of myself. Of what might happen. Of falling to bits again."

"Nothing could be worse than this place," she muttered.

"Sorry?"

"I said, nothing could be worse than this."

A silence fell. After a bit, she heard him say, "Look, I've run out of cigarettes. I'll just go down and get some from the newsagent. Stay here. Don't go. I'll be a moment. Then I'll make you a cup of tea or something."

Judith did not move. She heard him leave the room, his footsteps running down the dark stairway. The street door opened and slammed shut.

Cold, tired, and disheartened, she let out a long, tremulous sigh. What to do next? What to say? She turned and looked about her at the depressing room. Wandered over to the table and picked up the day-old newspaper, which seemed to present the only diversion. Its ill-folded pages had concealed other possessions now revealed: a worn attaché case, lying open, piled with old papers and letters and bills; a cardboard folder; a scratch-pad and a canvas-bound book, or album, secured with a thick rubber band. Intrigued, she dropped the newspaper and drew it towards her. Saw the filthy cover, stained and greasy, and the dog-eared corners. She remembered Gus's voice, as they had sat together on the terrace of the Galle Face Hotel, and he told her about the last days of Singapore. How he had sold his watch for Singapore dollars, and bribed a prison guard to bring him paper and pencils and a drawing-block.

His sketch-book. *A sort of record. But not for human consumption.*

She knew she shouldn't pry, and didn't want to. But her hands seemed to possess some independent compulsion of their own. She eased off the rubber band and opened, at random, the sketch-book. Pencil drawings. Very detailed. Page after page. A long line of emaciated men, half-naked, backs weighed down with the burden of wooden railway sleepers, making their way in single file through the jungle. A drooping figure, lashed to a stake, left to dehydrate and die in the pitiless sun. A Japanese guard, rifle butt raised over a skeletal prisoner lying prone in the mud. Then, another page. An execution, blood spurting like two red sticks from a severed neck . . .

A rising nausea tasted sour in her mouth.

She heard the street door slam shut, and Gus's footsteps on the stair. She slammed the sketch-book shut, and stood pressing the covers down with the palms of her hands, as though shutting the lid on a box of living, lethal, squirming horrors.

Enough. She said it aloud. "This is *enough.*"

He was at the door. "Did you say something?"

Judith turned on him. "Yes, I did. And I'm not leaving you here, Gus. I'm not asking you to come away with me, I'm *telling* you. And if you don't come, then I shall stay here and nag at you until you do."

Bewildered by her outburst, his eyes moved from her face to the table-top, and he saw the book lying there, and the rubber band that had kept it shut beside it. He said, very quietly, "You shouldn't have opened it."

"Well, I did. And I've looked. You oughtn't to carry it around with you, as though those were the only memories you've ever had. They'll always be there. They'll never disappear. But, one day, they'll fade, if you let them. And you can't do it on your own. You've got to *share.* It's no good if you don't come back with me. It's all wasted. I've driven all this way, and Biddy's car doesn't do much more than forty-five miles an hour, and I had to miss Diana's coming-home party for Jeremy Wells, and now I've got to drive all the way back again, and all you do is stand there like a mummified zombie . . ."

"Judith . . ."

"I don't want to talk about it any more. But for the last time, *please*. If I don't set off now, I'll never get home. Such a long way, and it'll be dark by four . . ."

Suddenly, it was all too much: her disappointment, his refusal to listen to her, the terrible contents of the sketch-book. Her voice broke, and she could feel her face crumple. Finally, she burst into emotional and exhausted tears. "Oh, *Gus* . . ."

He said, "Don't cry," and he came and put his arms around her and held her until the worst of the weeping was over. "Did you really give up a party, with Diana and Jeremy and all of them . . . for me?"

Searching for a handkerchief, she nodded. "That doesn't matter. It can happen another time." She blew her nose.

He said, "I don't like to imagine you driving alone, all the way back to Cornwall. At forty-five miles an hour."

With her fingers, Judith wiped the tears from her cheeks. "There's not much you can do about it."

"Yes, I can." For the first time, he smiled. "Just give me five minutes."

They went west by way of Hammersmith and Staines, and so out onto the A30. Judith drove, because she thought that perhaps Gus might want to sleep, and anyway she was accustomed to the idiosyncrasies of Biddy's old car. Gus sat beside her and followed their route on a tattered road-map, and sucked boiled sweets because he said he was too well-mannered to smoke cigarettes in somebody else's car. At Hartley Wintney, the last of suburbia slipped away behind them. After that the towns they drove through were country towns, with markets, and pubs called the Red Lion and the King's Head, and crooked red brick houses lining the main streets. Salisbury, Crewkerne, Chard, and Honiton. At Honiton they stopped the car, and while Gus filled the tank from the last of the spare petrol cans, Judith went in search of sustenance and returned with two dubious pasties and a couple of bottles of ginger beer. They ate this meagre picnic in the car.

"Pasties," Gus said with satisfaction, and bit into his. He chewed for a moment, and then looked at Judith in some dismay. "This doesn't taste like a pasty."

"What does it taste like?"

He took another mouthful and chewed some more. "Mouse and mud wrapped in a face flannel?"

"You can't expect a Mrs. Nettlebed pasty. Not after six years of war. You need the best steak for a proper one, and most people have forgotten what steak even looks like. Anyway, this is Devon. In Devon, they're not called pasties. They're called tiddy-oggies."

"Where did you glean that bit of useless information?"

"Anyone who's been in the Navy knows they're called tiddy-oggies."

Gus said, "Well, shiver me timbers."

They drove on. The London clouds had disappeared, and the evening was clear and cold. The winter sun, round and red as an orange, lay low over the hills of Dartmoor. Exeter. Okehampton. Launceston. Dark now, headlights full on, only the emptiness of the moor on either side of the narrow road.

Cornwall.

Gus fell silent. For quite a long time he didn't say anything, and then, "Did you ever have fantasies, Judith?" he asked.

"What sort of fantasies?"

"Oh, you know. When you were a child, growing up. Galloping away through the desert on the saddle of a handsome sheikh. Or saving the life of a drowning yachtsman, only to discover he was your favourite film star."

"Not those, no. Not specifically. But I used to pretend that the *Cornish Riviera* was the *Orient Express,* and I was on my way to Istanbul with secret papers to deliver, and various sinister spies on my tracks. Agatha Christie stuff, frightfully exciting. How about you?"

"Mine weren't nearly so adventurous. I don't think I was a particularly adventurous youth. But they were very real to me. There were three of them. Quite separate. One was that I would come to Cornwall, where I had never been, and embrace the life of a Bohemian painter. I would live in a white-washed fisherman's cottage with cobbles at the door, and grow my hair and wear a hat like Augustus John, and espadrilles, and a French workman's *bleus.* And I would smoke Gitane cigarettes, and have a studio, and amble down to some delectable pub where I would be so famous and revered that people would crowd around and buy me drinks."

"That's harmless enough. But why Cornwall, if you'd never been here?"

"I knew it from pictures, paintings, works of art. Articles in *The Studio.* The Newlyn School. The Porthkerris School. The colour of the sea and the cliffs; the extraordinary quality of the light."

"As a painter you would have been a success. I'm sure of that."

"Maybe. But it was my little hobby. That's what my father called it. So it was Cambridge and engineering. A totally different direction." He paused, seeming to ponder something. "Perhaps ours is the last generation that will ever do what it is told."

"What were the other two fantasies?"

"Pictures again. A Laura Knight, a print I tore from a magazine and framed, and took with me to school, home, University. A girl on a cliff. Wearing an old sweater and a pair of tennis shoes. Brown as a gypsy, and with a plait of russet hair falling over one shoulder. Beautiful."

"Have you still got it?"

"No. Another Singapore casualty."

"And the third day-dream?"

"That was less specific. Harder to explain. It was finding a place, a house; somewhere where I would belong. Be at ease with myself. Made welcome for no reason of background or affluence or reputation. Able to drop my guard and present my own face."

"I would never have thought that was a problem."

"It was, until I met Edward Carey-Lewis. After I met Edward, everything changed. Even my name. Before Edward, I was Angus. After Edward, I became Gus. We went on holiday to France together. And then he asked me to Nancherrow. And I'd never been to Cornwall, but I drove, alone, all the way from Aberdeenshire. And as I crossed the county border I was obsessed by this extraordinary feeling that I was coming Home. That I'd seen it all before. It was all entirely recognizable, and very dear. And when I got to Nancherrow, everything came together, as though it had been orchestrated. Contrived. Intended. At Nancherrow I found Loveday; and when Edward introduced me to his father, the Colonel said, *Gus, my dear fellow. How pleased we are to see you. How splendid to have you here*, or something like that. And they all stopped being fantasies and were real. All the dreams, just for a little while, were true."

Judith sighed. "Oh, Gus. I don't know whether it's the house or the people who live in it. But you're not the only person who has felt that way about Nancherrow. And it's not *all* in the past. Edward has gone, I know. And I suppose, for you, Loveday has as well. But there's still the future. What is there to stop you becoming a painter? Living down here, getting a studio, working at a talent that you love, and perhaps should exploit. There's nothing now to stop you."

"No. Nothing. Except my own non-existent confidence. My lack of will. Fear of failing."

"That's just *now*. You've been ill. *Now* isn't going to last forever. You'll get better. Stronger. Things will change."

"Maybe. We'll see." He stirred in his seat, easing his cramped limbs. "You must be tired, poor girl."

"Not far now."

He rolled down his window, and they were momentarily assaulted by a blast of cold, fresh air. He turned his face and took a huge breath of this. He said, "You know something? I can smell the sea."

"Me too."

He closed the window. "Judith."

"What is it?"

"Thank you."

Holding a Wedgwood mug filled with strong, steaming tea, Judith knocked on the door of Biddy's bedroom.

"Gus?"

She opened the door to a blast of icy-cold air. The windows were wide open, the curtains flapping in the draught, and the weight of the door was almost torn from her hand. She closed it hastily behind her, and the curtains subsided a bit.

She said, "You have to be *freezing*."

"I'm not." He was lying in bed propped up with pillows, with his hands linked behind his head. His pyjama jacket was blue, and the night's stubble showed dark on his chin.

"I've brought you a mug of tea." She put it down on the table beside his bed.

"You're a saint. What time is it?"

"Half past ten. Do you mind if I close the window? The draught goes all the way through the house, and we're trying to keep it warm."

"I'm sorry. I should have thought. It was just so good to feel the fresh air on my face. The hospital was grossly overheated, and London air always feels a bit heavy and stale, to say nothing of the noise of the traffic."

"I know what you mean." She closed the old sash window and stood for a moment looking out at the day. The sky was watery and washed with clouds. There had been a shower, and soon there would be another. Puddles glittered on pathways, and the bare branches of the trees dripped onto the shaggy winter grass of the lawn. The wind whined, thumped against the house, rattled the window frame. She turned and came back to lean on the brass rail at the foot of Biddy's double bed.

"How did you sleep?"

"Not too badly." He had pulled himself up into a sitting position, his knees drawn up beneath the covers, his long fingers wrapped around the warmth of the mug, a lock of black hair falling across his forehead. "It was still dark when I woke. I've been lying here watching the sky fill with light. Should I have been up at sparrow-fart, for breakfast?"

"I told you last night, no. I only disturbed you now because I have to go to Penzance to buy some food, and I wondered if you wanted me to get anything for you."

"Cigarettes?"

"Sure."

"And some shaving soap . . ."

"Tube or bowl?"

"Can you still get bowls?"

"I can try."

"I'll need a brush."

"Is that all?"

"I think so. I'll give you some money."

"Don't worry. I'll bill you when I get back. I shan't be long. Home for lunch. Phyllis has made a rabbit-and-pigeon pie. Can you eat rabbit and pigeon?"

"If I can eat a tiddy-oggy, I can eat anything."

She laughed. "Get up when you feel like it. Have a bath if you want. The morning paper's in the drawing-room, and I've lit the fire." She went to the door and opened it. "See you later."

" 'Bye."

When she returned, at a quarter to one, the kitchen was filled with the good smell of the rabbit pie, and Phyllis was putting a pan of Brussels sprouts on to boil. Judith set her laden baskets on the end of the scrubbed table and unloaded her loot. "I managed to get some fresh mackerel, we can have them for supper. And a marrowbone for soup. And our sugar and butter rations. They seem to get smaller every week."

"Has Mr. Callender got a ration card?"

"I'll have to ask him. I don't suppose he has."

"He's going to need one," Phyllis warned. "Man that size, he'll eat twice as much as we do."

"We'll have to fill him with potatoes. Is he up?"

"Yes, up and about. Came in here to say hello, and then went out into the garden for a bit. He's in the drawing-room now, reading the paper. Told him to keep the fire up. Put a log on every now and again."

"How do you think he's looking?"

"Some thin, isn't he? Poor soul. Doesn't bear thinking of, what he's been through."

Judith said, "No." The last of the groceries were unloaded, and all that remained were the things that she had bought for Gus. She gathered them up and went in search of him, and found him looking entirely at home in the depths of Biddy's armchair, reading the paper. When she appeared, he set this aside.

"My conscience is already pricking, because I'm being so lazy."

"That's what you're meant to be. Do you want a drink or something? I think there's a bottle of beer."

"No, thanks."

"Here are your things." She sat on the fireside stool and handed them to him one by one, out of a well-used paper bag. "Yardley's Lavender shaving soap in a cedarwood bowl, no less. They'd got them in for Christmas, and the chemist produced it from under the counter. And a badger brush. And cigarettes. And this is a present from me."

"Judith! What is it?"

"Look and see."

It was a large and quite heavy parcel, wrapped in white paper and tied with twine. He took it onto his knee and unknotted the string and tore away the paper, revealing a thick pad of foolscap cartridge paper, the box of H. B. pencils, the black enamel Winsor and Newton paint-box, the three beautiful sable brushes.

She said quickly, "I know you don't feel like painting just now, but I'm sure you will soon. I hope it's all right. I got it all in the art shop. The paper probably isn't the quality you'd like, but it was the best they had . . ."

"It's perfect, a wonderful present." He leaned forward and put his hand on her shoulder and drew her towards him, and kissed her cheek. "You are the sweetest person. Thank you."

"I won't boss and interfere any more. I promise."

"I don't think I'd mind too much even if you did."

They had lunch, the three of them, in the warm kitchen, and after the pie and bottled plums with top-of-the-milk cream, Judith and Gus put on water-proof jackets and went out into the windy, showery afternoon. And they walked, not down to the sea, but on up the hill from Rosemullion on the road that led to the moors. Then they left the road and struck off across the waste of winter grass, brown bracken, and heather clumps, taking the winding sheep tracks that led to the cairn on the summit of the slope. And cloud shadows chased them up from the sea. There were gulls and curlews flying about overhead, and when they finally scrambled up the rock and stood, braced against the wind, all of the country was spread about them, and they were encircled by the horizon.

They returned home by a different route, which made it a very long walk indeed, and it was half past four and darkness had fallen before they finally turned in through the Dower House gate. Anna was home from school, dili-gently sitting at the kitchen table and struggling with her homework. As they appeared, wind-blown and exhausted, through the door, she laid her pencil aside and looked up, intrigued to meet at last the strange man who had come to stay, and about whom her mother had told her so much.

Phyllis had the kettle on, for tea.

"You've been some time. You must be dead on your feet."

"It feels funny going for a walk without Morag. We'll have to get a dog of our own. Hello, Anna. This is Gus Callender. You haven't met him yet, have you?"

Gus, unravelling himself from his muffler, smiled at her. "Hello, Anna."

Anna became suffused with shyness. "Hello."

"What are you doing?"

"Homework. Sums."

He pulled up a chair and sat beside her. "Money sums. Those were always the most difficult . . ."

Phyllis was spreading slices of saffron bread with margarine. She said, not looking up, "Jeremy Wells rang, from Nancherrow."

Judith felt her heart give an involuntary leap and was instantly much an-noyed with it, for being so foolish. "What did he want?"

"Oh, nothing much." Another slice and more margarine. "Just asking if you'd got back. Said you had. Said you and Mr. Callender had gone for a walk."

"How did the coming-home party go?"

"Mrs. Carey-Lewis put it off. You couldn't be there and Walter had some business or other."

Judith waited for Phyllis to elaborate on this, but she didn't. She was clearly still a bit peeved about the whole business of Jeremy. To placate her, "Does he want me to call?" Judith asked.

"No, he said not to bother. Didn't matter. Nothing important."

Eleven o'clock, an hour from midnight, and still he had not returned.

Loveday, curled up in a corner of the sofa, sat and watched the face of the clock, and the slow minutes ticking by. The wind had got up, pouring in from the sea, to howl at the windows of the little house and set the doors rattling. From time to time, from the kennels, she could hear Walter's dogs barking, but did not venture out to investigate what had disturbed them. A fox, maybe. Or a badger, rooting around in the dustbins.

He had gone at seven. Finished the milking, washed up and changed, and was away in the car, not stopping even to eat the shepherd's pie she had made for his tea. It was still there, in the bottom oven, probably by now congealed and dried out. It didn't matter. She had let him go, holding a sulky silence, because if she said anything, made objections, protestations, demanded explanations, she knew that there would be a blow-up—yet another row between them, concluded by the ear-stopping slamming of the door as he took himself off. They seemed to have nothing left to say that was remotely constructive, and all that was left were cruel and hurtful words to be exchanged.

Her mother's blithe invitation to Jeremy Wells's coming-home dinner party at Nancherrow had filled Loveday with something like panic, because, in his present state of mind, she could not trust Walter to put on his best face, and if he didn't, then her parents could not help but sense ill feeling, and would start to ask questions. Even telling Walter about the invitation needed a bit of courage, and it was almost a relief when he said he had better things to do than go to fancy dinner parties, and anyway, he had already made his plans for that evening.

"You used to like Jeremy."

"He's all right."

"Don't you want to see him again?"

"Will soon enough. And if he wants to see me, he can come up to the farm and find me here."

So Loveday had telephoned her mother, with excuses for Walter, only to be told that the little party had been cancelled for the time being, because Judith couldn't come either.

"What's she doing?" Loveday had asked.

"She's gone to London."

"London? What for?"

"Oh, I don't know. Christmas shopping? Anyway, darling, it's all off for the moment. We'll have it another night. How's Nat?"

"He's fine."

"Kiss him for me."

So that was one thing not to worry about, but there was still plenty else.

Since the afternoon when Judith had come for tea, and Loveday had confided in her, relations between her and Walter had deteriorated at an alarming rate, and she was beginning to believe that he didn't just not love her any more, but actually hated her. He hadn't spoken kindly to Nat for four or five days, and if they did all sit down to a meal together, Walter endured it in silence, reading a newspaper or thumbing over the pages of the latest *Farmer's Weekly*. At first, she had tried asking questions about the farm and the animals—about all they had in common now—but he responded with monosyllables, and she was left defeated. Lately, she hadn't even tried to break through his sullen and quite frightening antipathy. She had the terrible feeling that, if she pushed too far, he might actually stand up and hit her.

A quarter past eleven. Restless, Loveday decided to make a mug of cocoa. She got off the sofa and put a pan of milk on the range to heat, and then, for company, switched on the wireless. Radio Luxembourg was always good for a bit of music. She heard Bing Crosby singing "Deep Purple," Athena's favourite tune of that last summer before the war. When Gus had come to Nancherrow.

She thought about Gus. Most of the time she didn't think about him, because memories of what she had done filled her with such anguish and regret and self-disgust that she was sure that that must be exactly how *he* was thinking of her. At nineteen, she now realized, she had been pathetically feeble, and at the same time, childishly set on getting, as always, her own way. Refusing to countenance the fact that perhaps she was mistaken in her unshakeable conviction that Gus had died in Singapore; totally determined to stay forever at Nancherrow, and never be torn from the loving arms of her family; grabbing at the first straw which came her drowning way, which happened to be Walter. With hindsight, she knew now that Arabella Lumb was simply a sort of catalyst, bringing everything to a head. If it hadn't been Arabella, it would have been something, or someone, else. The only really good thing that had come out of the entire disaster was Nat.

She was pretty sure that she would never see Gus again. *I don't want him to come here*, she had told Judith, but it wasn't because she didn't *want* to see him, simply that she was so ashamed of what she had done to him. And if *she* thought all these lowering things about herself, then what could *he* be thinking? Love, without the strength of faith, and trust, was not much good to anybody. If, by now, he had put her out of his mind, and set his face in a totally different direction, then she could not blame him. She only blamed herself.

But it had been a lovely time.

Waiting for the milk to boil, she felt the tears welling into her eyes, but whether they were for Loveday or for Gus, she didn't know.

From the bedroom, she heard Nat. Crying, calling for her. She set the milk aside and paused, in the faint hope that he might settle and go to sleep again, but of course he didn't, simply yowled louder, so she went through and picked him up out of his cot, bundled in a big blanket, and brought him back to the kitchen and settled him down on the sofa.

"What are you crying about, then?"

"I want Mummeeee."

"I'm here. Don't cry any more."

He plugged his mouth with his thumb and lay watching her from beneath drooping lids. She found a mug and made the cocoa, then went back to him and talked for a bit, giving him sips of the warm, sweet drink which he loved. Presently, he went back to sleep again. When she had finished the cocoa, she put the mug on the draining-board, switched off the wireless, and lay down beside him, her arm beneath his sturdy, warm little body, his blanket tucked around the two of them. His hair was soft against her lips. He smelt sweet and soapy. After a bit, she closed her eyes. They slept.

She woke at seven. The electric light had burnt all night, and she could see the face of the clock and knew at once that Walter was not in the house, had never come back. Nat slumbered peacefully on. She eased her arm from beneath his weight, and, cautiously, sat up and slid off the sofa, replacing the folds of the blanket around his chubby body.

She stretched. Spending the night in such a cramped and awkward fashion had left her limbs aching and a crick in her neck. Outside, the wind had dropped a bit, but it was still fairly stormy, and up here on the face of the hill there was little shelter. She listened for the dogs, but there was no sound of their barking. She guessed that Walter, done with his night on the tiles, had returned to the farm for the morning milking, and had let them out of the kennels on his way down to the byre. She wondered, in a detached sort of way, if he was suffering from an appalling hangover, or even the prickings of a guilty conscience. Probably no on both counts. Whatever. It didn't matter. Once it would have mattered, but after last night her husband's welfare was no longer of any concern.

She went to the range and opened the bottom oven door and took out the solidified remains of the shepherd's pie and scraped them into the pig-bucket. Then she riddled out the ashes and made up the fire. The range, simmering gently, was set for another day. That was all she was going to do.

In the lobby, she took her thick raincoat down from its peg and pulled it on. Tied a woollen scarf around her head, and trod her socked feet into rubber boots. She went back into the kitchen and gathered Nat up into her arms, swaddling him like a baby into his thick blanket. He didn't wake. She turned off the light and walked out of the darkened kitchen, out of the door, and into the cold black wind of the December morning. She needed no torch, knowing every step of the way, every stone and stile by heart. She went by the footpath that led by the fields, and, at the bottom of the hill, joined the lane that led to Nancherrow. Carrying Nat, Loveday set out on the long walk home.

At seven o'clock in the morning, Nettlebed was always the first down. In the old days, even at this early hour, it had been his practice to dress up to the formality and importance of his position. But the years of war, during which he had worn the hat of vegetable gardener as well as that of butler, had put an end to such grandeur and, instead, he had invented for himself a sort of compromise. Striped flannel shirt, detachable white collar, a black tie, and a navy-blue V-necked pullover. Over these, if engaged in mucky work like cooking or plucking pheasants, or shining up the brass, he tied on a blue-and-white-striped butcher's apron, which Mrs. Nettlebed had decided was acceptably practical and did not demean his standing in any sort of way.

Morning rounds followed a changeless routine. Unlocking and opening the outside front door. Drawing back curtains in dining- and sitting-rooms, opening windows a chink to let the fresh air in and the smell of cigar smoke out. Then, through to the kitchen. A kettle on the Aga for the Colonel's early-morning tea. Unlock the scullery door that led out onto the courtyard. After that, down the back passage to the gun-room, where Tiger still slept. (Over the years, Pekoe had insinuated himself into Mrs. Carey-Lewis's bed-room, and slept there, with her. He had a token basket in the corner of the room, but everybody knew that he preferred the foot of her bed.)

Tiger was stiff in the mornings, and Nettlebed was sympathetic towards the old dog, because he too suffered from rheumatics, being sixty-five now and on his feet most of the day. When the east wind blew, his swollen knees gave him gyp.

"Come on then, boy," he coaxed, and Tiger heaved himself to his four feet and lumbered out through the door into the black dark and the pesky wind. Nettlebed went with him, because if he didn't he couldn't be sure that Tiger had done his business.

This morning it took ages, and Nettlebed was chilled to the bone by the time they finally returned indoors. It was sad to see a good dog ageing. Nettle-bed had never had that much time for dogs, not having been born and bred an outdoor gentleman, but he was fond of Tiger. Tiger had seen the Colonel through all the years of war and much sadness. A day did not pass when Nettlebed did not think of Edward.

With Tiger waddling and wheezing at his heels, he went back to the kitchen. There the old dog settled down on his blanket by the Aga. The kettle was boiling. Nettlebed warmed the small white teapot. The clock said half past seven. He reached up for the tea-caddy, and as he did this, heard the scullery back door fly open, letting in a gust of wind that swept across the flagged floor. Startled, "Who's that there?" he called, and went to look.

"Only me, Nettlebed." Loveday kicked the door shut behind her, because her arms were filled with a shapeless blanketed bundle that could only be young Nat. She looked, thought Nettlebed, like nothing on earth, muddy boots and all bundled up in scarves, for all the world like a refugee.

"Loveday! What are you doing here at this unholy hour?"

"I just walked down from Lidgey."

He was horrified. "Carrying Nat?"

"Yes. All the way. I'm exhausted. I hadn't realized he weighed so much." She came through the scullery and into the kitchen, and laid Nat carefully down on the huge scrubbed table, making a pillow with a corner of the blanket and settling her son as comfortably as she could.

Nat never stirred. Loveday straightened cautiously, her hands pressed to the small of her back. "Ah." She let out a small sigh of sheer relief.

Nettlebed's astonishment turned to indignation.

"You shouldn't be carrying Nat all that way. You'll do yourself an injury, and that's a fact."

"I'm all right. But it's cold out." She went over to the Aga and laid her hands on its warm surface for a moment, and then crouched to talk to Tiger.

"Hello, my lovely."

Tiger's tail went *thump-thump*. They had always adored each other.

Nettlebed, heavy-hearted, watched the little scene. He feared, and guessed, the very worst. He had known for some time that there was trouble afoot at Lidgey. It was Nettlebed's custom a couple of evenings a week—no more—to take himself down to the Rosemullion pub, there to have a crack with one or two old cronies, play a game of darts, enjoy a beer. He had noticed Walter with that woman, Arabella Lumb she was called, and Nettlebed recognized bad news when he saw it. He had seen them together more than once, tucked away together at a corner table, and it was obvious to any man with two eyes in his head that they had not met by chance.

Walter Mudge was playing fast and loose. Once, Nettlebed had quite liked young Walter, but that was in the days before he'd married Loveday, when he'd kept his place (the stables) and delivered milk and cream at the back door. When it was announced that he and Loveday were to be man and wife, Nettlebed and Mrs. Nettlebed had strongly disapproved, but, respecting the wishes of their employers, kept their counsel. All that Nettlebed had been able to do was to get Walter into a decent suit for the wedding, so that he did not shame the family in front of the Lord Lieutenant and their smarter friends.

But just lately, he had begun to think that perhaps he would have done better to strangle Walter Mudge with a necktie, drop him in the sea, and take the consequences.

Tiger was dozing again. Loveday stood up, leaning her back against the Aga. "Where's Mrs. Nettlebed?"

"Up in the flat. She's taking the morning off. Her varicose veins are playing her up something awful. Crucified with them, she is."

"Oh, poor thing. Perhaps she should have an operation. I am sorry."

"I'm doing the breakfast this morning. Like a cup of tea, would you?"

"Maybe. In a moment. Don't bother. I can make one myself." She unwound the woollen muffler from her head and stuffed it into the pocket of her coat. Nettlebed saw the dark bruises of tiredness beneath her eyes, and despite the long walk from Lidgey, there was no colour at all in her cheeks.

He said, "Everything all right, Loveday?"

"No, Nettlebed. Not all right. All wrong."

"Is it Walter?"

"He never came home last night." Biting her lip, she met his sad and concerned gaze. "You know about her, don't you? Arabella Lumb. I was pretty sure you did."

"Yes." He sighed. "I guessed."

"I think it's all over. Me and Walter, I mean. I *know* it's over. Right from the beginning, I suppose, it was one huge, horrible mistake."

"Have you come home?"

"Yes. And I'm not going back."

"What about young Nat? He's Walter's boy."

"I don't know about Nat. I don't really know about anything. I haven't had time to think it all through." She frowned. "I have to get it all clear in my head before I face them all. Pops and Mummy and Mary. I think what I would really like is to be on my own for a bit. Go for a walk. Clear my head."

"Haven't you walked far enough already?"

"I won't take Nat." She looked at the comatose child, still sleeping soundly on his makeshift bed. "If they see Nat, they'll know I've come. I don't want them to know just yet . . . not until I've worked out all the answers to all the questions."

Listening to her steady voice, watching her, it occurred to Nettlebed that this was a Loveday he had never known before. No tears, no tantrums, no histrionics. Simply a stoic acceptance of a miserable situation, and no word of resentment or blame. Perhaps, he told himself, she has finally grown up, and he was filled with a new respect and admiration for her.

He said, "I could take young Nat up to our flat. Mrs. Nettlebed will keep an eye on him for the time being. Then nobody will know he's around until you want them to. Until you come back."

"But what about her varicose veins?"

"She's only going to keep an eye on him. Not carry him around."

"Oh, Nettlebed, you are being kind. And you won't say anything, will you? I want to do all the talking myself."

"Breakfast's at half past eight. I'll keep mum till you're back."

"Thank you." She came over to him and put her arms around his waist and gave him a little hug, pressing her cheek against the wool of his pullover. He could not remember her ever having done such a thing before, and for a moment felt quite taken aback, and not quite sure what to do with his hands. But, before he could return her embrace, she had moved away from him, to stoop over the table and gather the slumbering Nat into her arms, and hand him over. The boy seemed to weigh a ton, and Nettlebed's rheumaticky knees sagged slightly beneath the load. But he carried the child across the kitchen and up the narrow back stairs that led to his private quarters over the garage. When he returned, having left Nat in the care of his astounded wife, Loveday had gone, and taken Tiger with her.

Waking was a bit like floating upwards out of a deep, dark pool of water. Black to begin with, and then lightening to indigo, and then azure, and then breaking surface into dazzling light. He opened his eyes and was astonished to find that it was still dark; the sky beyond the window a night sky, pricked with stars. From downstairs, from the well of the hall, he heard the gentle chimes of the grandfather clock, softly striking seven o'clock. He could not remember when he had last slept so long, so soundly, so totally undisturbed. No dreams, no nightmares, no waking in the small hours with a scream on his lips. The sheets were smooth and unrumpled, sure sign that he had scarcely moved, and the whole length of his body felt at peace, relaxed and cool.

He thought back to yesterday, trying to fathom the reason for this unfamiliar blissful state, and recalled a day of ordered tranquillity, a great deal of exercise, and an enormous amount of fresh air. In the evening, after darkness had fallen, he and Judith had played Picquet together, and there had been a Brahms concert to listen to on the wireless. When it was time for bed, Phyllis had made him a mug of hot milk and honey, laced with a teaspoonful of whisky. Perhaps this magic potion had knocked him out, but he knew that, far more likely, it was the extraordinary, timeless, healing quality of Lavinia Boscawen's old house. A sanctuary. He could think of no other word.

So rested, he realized that his limbs were filled with an unfamiliar and long-forgotten energy. He could lie no longer. He got up, went over to the open window and leaned out, with his elbows on the sill, and smelt the cold air and the tang of the sea, and heard the soughing of the wind in the Monterey pines at the foot of the garden. By eight o'clock, the sun would be rising. He was assailed by his old dreams of water, deep and cold and clean, waves breaking on a shore; the sound they made, creaming over rocks.

He thought of the new day that lay ahead. The sun, slipping up over the rim of the horizon, and the first rays of dawn streaking the twilit skies with pink, and that light reflected in the lead-grey, shifting sea. And he was once again obsessed by the old desire to set it all down, translate it into his own language. To capture, with pencil and brush-strokes and washes of colour, the layers of fading darkness and prisms of light. And he was so grateful for this resurgence of his own creative instinct that he found himself trembling in a sort of ecstasy.

Or perhaps it was the cold. He stepped back from the window and closed it. On the dressing-table were neatly stacked the drawing-book and the pencils and paints and sable brushes that Judith had bought for him. He looked at them, and told them, *later. Not just now. When there is light in the sky, and shadows, and the glitter of rain on grass, then we shall get to work.* He stripped off his pyjamas and swiftly dressed. His cords, thick shirt, the heavy polo-necked sweater, his leather jacket. Carrying his shoes (like any corridor-creeper with romantic aspirations), he opened his bedroom door, closed it gently behind him, and made his way down the stairs. Quietly, the old clock tocked the seconds away. He went through the kitchen, put on his shoes, and tied the laces. Then, slip the bolts of the back door, and out into the cold.

It was too far to walk. He remembered, from the old days, the length of the Nancherrow drive, and he was impatient to be there. So he opened up the heavy door of the garage, where roosted, parked fore and aft, the two elderly cars. And Judith's bicycle. He took hold of the handlebars of this and wheeled it out onto the gravel. It had a front lamp, which he switched on, but was short of a rear. No matter. At this hour, there would be little about on the country road.

The bicycle, having been originally purchased for a fourteen-year-old girl, was far too small for him, but that didn't matter either. He swung his leg over the saddle and set off, spinning down the hill and through Rosemullion with his bony knees sticking out sideways. Over the bridge, and he was forced to dismount again, in order to push it up the steep hill. At the Nancherrow gates, he mounted once more and pedalled down the dark, tree-lined road, lurching and rattling along a rutted driveway that once had been immaculately tar-macadamed. High above him, the empty branches of the elms and beeches tossed their heads in the wind, making weird creaking noises, and from time to time a rabbit scuttled across the wavering beam of light from the little headlamp.

Out of the trees, and the house loomed, a pale bulk. Over the front door, light shone from behind a curtained window. The Colonel's bathroom. Gus imagined him standing at his mirror, shaving himself with his old-fashioned cut-throat. The wheels of the bicycle rattled over the gravel, and he feared that the bathroom curtain would be twitched aside, and the Colonel would peer down to spy the sinister, lurking figure. But this did not happen. By the front door, he left the bicycle, propped against the wall. He switched off the headlamp, cautiously made his way around to the front of the house, and finally stepped onto the grass.

The sky was lightening. Beyond the leafless trees, beneath a long smudge of charcoal cloud, the sun was edging up out of the sea, blood-red and smoothly rounded, and the lower half of the cloud already tinged with pink. The stars were fading. There was the smell of moss and damp earth in the air, and all was clean and newly washed, pristine and pure. He went down the slope of the lawns and so joined the path that plunged down through the woods. He heard the stream, the tumble and splash of water. Following it, he crossed the small wooden bridge and ducked his head beneath the tunnel of the gunnera. By the time he got to the quarry it was light enough to see the steps cut in its side, and to cross the rocky floor between the thickets of bramble and gorse. Over the gate and onto the road, and then the stone wall and the stile, and he was on the top of the cliff.

There he paused, because this was why he had come. The tide was out, and the beach of the cove, a grey sickle of sand, was rimmed by a dark circle of seaweed and tide-wrack. The sun was up now, and the first long shadows lay across the turfy cliff-top. And he remembered the day, that August afternoon, the summer before the war, when he had met Edward's sister for the first time, and she had brought him down to the cove. They had sat, sheltered from the wind, and it had felt like being with a person whom he had known for the whole of his life. And when it was time to go, and she had stood and turned to watch the sea, he had recognized her as his girl on the cliff, the Laura Knight picture that was one of his most precious possessions.

He looked for that particular rock, where once he and Loveday had been together. And it was then that he saw them, and screwed up his eyes in disbelief against the dazzle of the new sun. She sat with her back to him, crouched against the rock, the dog pressed close against her side, her outflung arm around his neck. For a second he thought that he had gone mad again, was not yet recovered, was suffering from some self-induced hallucination. But then, instinctively, sensing his presence, Tiger raised his head, sniffed the air, heaved himself to his feet, and came lumbering up over the grassy, boulder-strewn cliff-top to deal with the intruder. He barked, his warning bark. *Who are you? Keep off!* And then his old eyes saw Gus, and he didn't bark any more, but came on, tail thumping, ears flat, as fast as his arthriticky legs would carry him, all the while making pleased noises in the back of his throat.

He reached Gus's side, and Gus stooped to fondle his head, saw the grey muzzle and the weight of Tiger's years. "Hello, Tiger. Hello, old boy."

And then he straightened, and looked, and she was standing there with her hands in her pockets, her back to the sea. The woollen muffler had slipped back off her head, and he saw her dark curls, lit from behind by the sun, like an aureole.

Loveday. Nothing had changed. Nothing. He felt the lump swell in his throat, simply because he had found her again, and she was still there. And it felt almost as though she had known he would come, and had been waiting for him.

He heard her call his name. "Gus," and the wind caught the word, and sent it flying inland, over the winter fields. "Oh, *Gus.*" And she was running up the slope towards him and he went to meet her.

Saturday morning, and Jeremy Wells overslept. This was probably because he hadn't got to sleep until the early hours of the morning, having drunk three cups of coffee after dinner, and enjoyed an excellent glass of brandy with the Colonel. So, had lain wide-eyed, his brain racing, listening to the rising wind and the rattling of the window-pane, and turning on the light every now and then to check the time. In the end, he'd left the light on and read for an hour or two, but it had all been a bit unsatisfactory.

And he overslept. Not by much, but breakfast at eight-thirty was a Nancherrow rule, and he didn't get downstairs until a quarter to nine. In the dining-room he found Diana, the Colonel, and Mary Millyway, by now onto toast and marmalade and second cups of coffee or tea.

He apologized. "I am sorry. I never woke up."

"Oh, darling, it doesn't matter a bit. Nettlebed's done breakfast this morning, so it's boiled eggs. I think we've eaten all our bacon ration." She was opening her mail, her place surrounded by half-read letters and torn envelopes.

"What's happened to Mrs. Nettlebed?"

"She's having the morning off. She's got the most terrible varicose veins, poor pet. Perhaps you could have a look at them. We're trying to persuade her to have them seen to, but she's terrified of an operation. Says she doesn't want The Knife. I must say I can see her point. Heavens, here's an invitation to a drinks party. In Falmouth. Why do people think one is going to use up one's entire petrol-ration for a measly glass of sherry?"

This was not a question that demanded an answer. The Colonel was deep in *The Times*. Passing him on the way to the sideboard, Jeremy laid a hand on his shoulder. "Good morning, sir."

"Oh, Jeremy. Hello there. Good morning. Sleep well?"

"Not particularly. A combination of black coffee and a howling gale."

Mary joined him at the sideboard. "It's dropped a bit, but it's still blowing." She took the cover from the coffee-pot and felt it with her hands. "This seems a bit cold to me. I'll go and make you a fresh pot."

"You don't have to, Mary. I can drink tea."

"But you always were a coffee person. I know that. Shan't be a mo." And she went from the room.

Jeremy took his boiled egg from the padded basket shaped like a hen, poured a cup of strong tea because he could always move on to coffee later, and went to sit at the table. The Colonel silently handed him a neatly folded *Western Morning News*. Diana was deep in her mail. At Nancherrow, conversation at breakfast had never been encouraged. Jeremy took up his spoon and neatly sliced the top off his egg.

By twenty to nine, Nettlebed was starting to get edgy, because Loveday still had not returned. It wasn't that he was imagining an accident, nothing disastrous like falling off the edge of the cliff and breaking her ankle. Loveday knew the cliffs like the back of her hand and was sure-footed as a little goat. But his responsibility for her irked. He already regretted his collusion, and simply wished that she would come back, now, before he was forced to come clean and break the news to the Colonel that not only had Loveday left her husband, but had, at the same time, disappeared.

Preoccupied, he wandered, in a most uncharacteristic way, around the kitchen, going to the window, taking a mouthful of tea, carrying a single saucepan through to the scullery, mopping up a bit of spilt milk, going back to the window.

Not a sign of the wretched girl. His concern, by now, was touched with irritation. When she did turn up, he was going to give her a slice of his mind, in the same way that a mother will smack a child who has just almost been run over by a bus.

At ten to nine, fed up with hanging around and watching the clock, he let himself out of the scullery door and walked across the courtyard, and out onto the back drive, where he stood in the wind and looked for her, down the length of the garden and towards the sea. But there was nobody on the path from the woods. From his vantage point, however, he could see the big garage where all the family cars were housed, and one of the doors to this stood open. He went to investigate and saw that the little fishmonger's van was gone. The implications of this were seriously ominous. Unless, of course, a robber had come by in the night and driven it away. But if a robber had come, he surely would not have taken the van, with Mrs. Carey-Lewis's Bentley sitting there just asking to be nicked.

By now in something of a state, he returned to the house, but this time went in through the gun-room door. And there found Tiger, tired out and fast asleep in his basket.

"Where's she gone?" he asked, but Tiger only blinked and went back to sleep again.

And then the third thing happened, which clinched everything. As Nettlebed went back to the kitchen, he heard, from upstairs, from his own flat, the unmistakable roars of rage from Nathaniel Mudge.

Time's come, he told himself.

At that moment, Mary Millyway appeared through the door from the passage, bearing, in her hands, the dining-room coffee-pot. "Just going to . . ." she started, and then stopped. "What's that racket?"

Nettlebed felt like a schoolboy caught pinching apples. "It's Nat Mudge. He's up in the flat with Mrs. Nettlebed."

"What's he doing here?"

"Loveday left him. Seven-thirty this morning."

"Left him? Where's she gone, then?"

"I don't know," Nettlebed admitted miserably. "She went off for a walk. Said she needed to clear her head, think things through. Said she'd be back by breakfast-time. And she's not."

"Think things through? What does that mean?"

"You know. Her and Walter."

"Oh God," said Mary, which was an indication of her despair, because in all the years they had worked together, Nettlebed had scarcely ever heard her blaspheme.

"She took Tiger, but Tiger's back in the gun-room." Nettlebed went on, in the tones of one determined to make a clean breast. "And the little van's not in the garage."

"Think she's run off?"

"I don't know."

Nat's screams by now had reached a crescendo. Mary set down the coffee-pot. "I'd better go and see to that child. Poor Mrs. Nettlebed, she'll be demented." She set off, across the kitchen and up the narrow stairs. "Who's making all that din then, Mary wants to know?"

So one problem at least was being dealt with. Nettlebed, left alone, untied the strings of his butcher's apron and laid it over the back of a chair. He smoothed his sparse hair with his hands and went, upright and dignified, to find the Colonel and lay bare his soul.

He went into the dining-room and closed the door behind him. Nobody took much notice. He cleared his throat.

The Colonel looked up from his paper. "What is it, Nettlebed?"

"Could I have a word, sir?"

"Of course."

Now both Mrs. Carey-Lewis and the young doctor were paying attention.

"It's . . . rather delicate, sir."

Mrs. Carey-Lewis chipped in. "Delicate, Nettlebed? How delicate?"

"Family, madam."

"Well, we're all family here, Nettlebed. Unless it's something you particularly don't want Jeremy and me to hear."

"No, madam."

"Well, please tell us all."

"It's Loveday, madam."

"What about Loveday?" The Colonel's voice was sharp. He knew a crisis when he saw one.

"She turned up in my kitchen this morning, sir, at half past seven. With young Nat. Walked down from Lidgey. There seems . . ." He cleared his throat and started again. "There seems to have been some trouble between the young couple. Between Walter and her."

A long pause. And then Mrs. Carey-Lewis said, "Has she left him?" and her voice no longer teased.

"It would appear so, madam."

"But what's *happened?*"

"I think, madam, that Walter's eye has been caught by another person. A young woman. He has been meeting her in the pub at Rosemullion. He never came home last night."

The three of them were staring at him, wordless, and in apparent total astonishment. *They never had any idea,* Nettlebed told himself, which made nothing any easier for him.

The Colonel spoke. "Where is she now?"

"That's it, sir. The trouble. She went off for a walk, to be on her own. Said she'd be back at half past eight, for breakfast."

"And it's now nearly nine."

"Yes, sir. And she's not back, sir. But she took Tiger with her, and Tiger's home, in the gun-room. And the small van has gone from the garage."

"Oh." Mrs. Carey-Lewis sounded despairing, and small wonder. "Don't say she's run away."

"I blame myself, madam. I let her go, and then I never heard her return. I was seeing to the breakfast. And with this wind banging about, madam, I suppose I never heard the little motor car."

"Oh, Nettlebed, nothing could be your fault. She's very naughty and wicked to go off like that." She thought about this. "But where on earth would she go? And where is Nat?"

"Mrs. Nettlebed had him with her up in our flat. He was asleep, but he's woken now. Mary's with him."

"Oh, the poor, darling precious." Mrs. Carey-Lewis abandoned her letters, pushed back her chair and rose to her feet. "I must go and see the little boy . . ." As she passed the Colonel, she paused to hug him and drop a kiss on the top of his head. "Don't get in a state about it all. She'll be all right. We'll find her . . ." And she was gone from the room.

The Colonel looked up at Nettlebed, who met his eyes. He said, "Is this so-called affair news to you, Nettlebed?"

"Not entirely, sir. I have seen Walter and the young woman together more than once, in the pub at Rosemullion."

"Who is she?"

"She's called Arabella Lumb, sir. Not a nice type at all. No better than she should be."

"You never said anything to us."

"No, sir. Not my place. And I'd hoped that it would blow over."

"Yes." The Colonel sighed. "I see."

Another pause, and then for the first time, Jeremy Wells spoke. "You're quite certain she's not still down on the cliff?"

"As certain as I can be, sir."

"Do you think I should go and look?"

The Colonel considered this suggestion. "It might be as well. Just to set our minds at rest. But I think that Nettlebed's prognosis is probably right. And Tiger would never have come back to the house without her."

Jeremy stood up. "I'll go anyway. Have a scout around."

"That would be good of you. Thank you." The Colonel, too, rose to his feet, folded his newspaper, and laid it neatly on the table by his plate. "And I think, before we do or say another thing, I must make my way to Lidgey, and find out what the hell is going on."

Within the space of half an hour, Jeremy had jogged, at a brisk pace, down to the cliff, done a thorough reconnoitre, and then jogged back up the hill again. It was a good thing he was fit.

He found them all in the kitchen, Diana and Mary and the Nettlebeds and young Nat, still in his pyjamas, and finally placated by food, a serious breakfast which he was on the point of finishing, sitting at the end of the kitchen table. Mary was beside him, and the others were disposed about the place in various attitudes, gathered together for company, as people will in times of uncertainty or anxiety. Before opening the door, he had heard the buzz and murmur of their voices, and Nat's high-pitched pipe demanding attention, but as he went into the room, they all stopped talking and looked at him. He shook his head. "Not a sign. I went right across the beach to the other headland. Loveday's not there."

"Didn't think she would be," said Nettlebed, but Diana thanked him for going to check. Mrs. Nettlebed, her stout legs encased in heavy elastic stockings, had a teapot handy, keeping warm on the Aga. "Like a cup, would you, Dr. Wells?"

"Thank you, but I won't."

"Do you think . . . ?" Diana started, and then stopped and glanced at Nat, stuffing a toast-crust into his face. "Jeremy, we're trying not to say too much in front of you-know-who."

Mary said, "Little jugs have big handles."

"Perhaps, when he's finished his breakfast, you should take him up to the nursery, Mary. Find something for him to put on that isn't pyjamas." She gazed forlornly at Jeremy. "I wonder what's happening. I do wish Edgar would come back and tell us . . ."

Which he did, almost as soon as the words were out of her mouth. He had walked to Lidgey, because it wasn't worth getting the car out and driving the long way round by the road. And he'd walked back. Came across the court-yard, and in through the gun-room. They heard the resounding slam of the door. The next moment he was with them, pulling off his tweed cap, and with an expression on his face as sombre and angry as Jeremy had ever seen it.

He said, "Mary, take the boy away," and when she had whisked Nat out of the kitchen, and the door had closed behind them, the Colonel came to the table and pulled out a chair and settled himself into it.

They all waited in some trepidation, and he told them the sorry saga. Arriving at the big farmhouse, he had gone inside, and there found the Mudges in a state of what could only be called shock.

Mr. Mudge, silenced by disbelief and shame, had scarcely spoken a word, but Mrs. Mudge, who had always enjoyed relating disaster, even if it happened to be her own, had vociferously and indignantly (in between countless cups of tea) given the Colonel a lively account of all that had taken place.

Walter had not returned in time to see to the milking, and his two old parents had finally done it themselves. Not until they were finished, the cows turned out again, and the milking parlour cleaned and scoured, did their errant son appear, still in his good clothes and looking much the worse for wear.

He had shown no remorse. When taxed, he had told the Mudges that he had had it, up to here; was chucking his hand in, moving on. He was fed up with Nancherrow, with Lidgey, with the Carey-Lewises, with serfdom. Fed up with the responsibilities of wife and child, with a marriage that he had been forced into, and in-laws who looked down their noses at him. He was getting out. He'd been offered a job in a garage out Nancledra way, and he was going to live up Veglos Hill, in her caravan, with Arabella Lumb.

When the Colonel was done, there was a long silence, during which the only sounds to impinge were the heavy tick of the kitchen clock and the faint hum of the electric refrigerator. They were all behaving, thought Jeremy, like a lot of mustered ratings waiting for Captain's Orders. Only Diana opened her mouth as though to make some remark, caught her husband's uncharacteristically steely eye, and prudently closed it again.

"So that's the situation. I've done my best to reassure the Mudges. They can be held responsible in no way for the behaviour of their son. I've also asked them, for the time being, to keep their mouths shut. Mudge will have no trouble in doing this, but Mrs. Mudge is a naturally garrulous lady. However, they realize that no good can come from a lot of gossip, though I'm afraid that it won't take more than a day for the tidings to spread through the entire district of West Penwith. Discretion goes for all of us as well. For Loveday's sake. The first person to be enlightened and prepared must be our solicitor, Roger Baines." He reached into his breast pocket and took out his gold hunter watch. "Ten o'clock. He should be in his office by now." The Colonel rose to his feet. "I shall go and speak to him, on the telephone from my study." He looked about him, from one grave face to another. All nodded agreement to his proposals. And then his gaze alighted on the face of his wife, and his expression softened and he smiled. "I'm sorry, my darling Diana, you were about to say something."

"It's just that . . . I thought Loveday might have gone to Judith. Judith would be just the person she would turn to."

"Wouldn't Judith have telephoned us by now?"

"Maybe not. Maybe they're still talking."

"It's an idea. Do you want to ring up the Dower House?"

"No," said Diana. "I don't think we should telephone. Telephone calls can be rather remote and perhaps distressing. If Loveday isn't there, Judith might become very upset. I think somebody should go to the Dower House and explain the situation to Judith." She turned her head and, across the table, her lovely eyes met Jeremy's. She smiled persuasively. "Jeremy would go for us, I'm sure."

"Of course." He wondered if she knew what she was doing to him. Or, perhaps, for him.

"And you can telephone us when you get there. Just to let us know, one way or the other."

Jeremy stood up. He said, "I'll go now."

Judith, for once, was on her own. It being a Saturday, there was no school for Anna, and Phyllis had accepted the offer of a lift from Mr. Jennings, whose wife ran the Rosemullion post office; and right after breakfast, at eight o'clock, Mr. Jennings's old Austin had rolled up at the back door, and Phyllis and Anna had climbed into it and been conveyed away, in some style, to Saint Just and a day with Phyllis's mother.

Now it was past ten o'clock in the morning, and the other occupant of the Dower House, Gus, had not yet appeared. The door of his bedroom remained firmly closed, and Judith was pleased, because that meant that he was sleeping in and having a really good rest. When he finally made an appearance, she would cook him a breakfast, but until he did, there were other ploys to occupy her mind.

Because she had decided that this was a good opportunity to do what she had been meaning to for ages, namely, measure the drawing-room windows for new curtains, the old ones being by now so tattered that every time one drew them, another rip appeared. It would have been perfectly possible to do this with Phyllis around, but the thing was that Phyllis was so efficient and diligent that the moment one started to do a job, she was there edging one out of the way, giving the odd instruction or two, and ending up by doing the job herself. A small irritation, but viable.

And so she had found the step-ladder, and the yardstick and tape-measure, and had set to work. Her clothing coupons had finally come, from some Ministry or other, and she'd worked out that there were enough for new curtain material, provided she used old curtains, or excess cotton sheets, as the linings. As soon as she had calculated the measurements, and decided how many yards would be needed, then a letter could be written to Liberty's of London, and patterns requested. She would cut a bit off the old curtains and send that as well, because the colours must be neither too gaudy nor too strong.

Balanced on top of the step-ladder, and with her tongue, in concentration, clenched between her teeth, Judith measured the pelmet, and was just deciding that it might look better if it was two inches longer, when she heard the front door open and shut. A twinge of annoyance because, at the moment, she really didn't want to be disturbed. She stopped measuring and waited, hoping that the visitor, whoever it was, would hear nothing, think the house empty, and go away again.

But he, or she, didn't. Footsteps across the hall, and then the drawing-room door opened and Jeremy walked into the room.

He was wearing a thick, tweedy sweater, and had knotted a scarlet muffler around his neck, and her first thought was that he looked so exactly the same, so unchanged, that the years that had flown by since their last encounter might never have happened. And the second thought was identical to her reaction that night in London, when she had felt so ill and so unhappy, and he had turned up at the Mews, unexpected and unannounced, and she had watched him climb the stairs and known that, had she been given the choice, he was the only person she would have really wanted to see.

Which was unexpected and rather annoying, because it left her defence-less, and she had intended being quite firm and cool with him.

He said, "What are you doing?"

"Measuring the window."

"Why?"

"I'm going to have new curtains."

And then he smiled. "Hello."

"Hello, Jeremy."

"Can you come down? I want to talk to you, and if you stay up there, I'll get a crick in my neck."

So, cautiously, she descended, and he came to give her a hand down the last wobbly steps. When she reached the floor, he went on holding her hand, and then he gave her a kiss on the cheek, and said, "It's been so long. Wonderful to see you again. Are you on your own?"

"Phyllis and Anna have gone to Saint Just . . ."

"I've just driven up from Nancherrow . . ."

"They've gone to see Phyllis's mother."

"Loveday's not here?"

"Loveday?" Judith looked into his face, and realized then that he had not come to the Dower House simply to see her. Something was amiss. "Why should Loveday be here?"

"She's disappeared."

"Disappeared?"

"She's left Walter. Or rather, Walter's walked out on her. Look, it's rather complicated. Why don't we sit down and I'll explain."

She hadn't lit the fire, and the room was cold, but they sat on the wide window-seat, a spot not exactly *warm* but at least touched by the early sun. And quite simply, but lucidly, Jeremy told her all that had been happening at Nancherrow during the course of the morning, starting with Loveday's and Nat's arrival from Lidgey, and ending with the Colonel's findings and conclusive pronouncement.

". . . so it's all over. The marriage seems to have fallen to bits. And we don't know where to look for Loveday."

In growing dismay, Judith had listened to the sorry tale. Now, she couldn't think of anything to say, because it was all even more awful than she could ever have imagined.

"Oh dear." Which was fairly inadequate, given the circumstances. "I can't bear it for her. Poor little Loveday. I know she's been having a miserable time. Walter being so unkind. I knew about Arabella Lumb too, but I couldn't say anything because Loveday particularly asked me not to."

"So she didn't come to you?"

Judith shook her head. "No."

"Is Gus about?"

"Yes, of course he is. He's staying with me."

"Where is he?"

"Upstairs. He hasn't woken yet. He's still asleep."

"Are you sure?"

Judith frowned. Jeremy sounded suspicious, as though she were telling terrible fibs. "Of course I'm sure. Why shouldn't I be sure?"

"Just a thought. Perhaps you'd better go and look. Or I will, if you'd rather."

"No." Her voice was cool. "I'll go. I don't mind."

She was still holding the tape-measure. Now, she neatly wound it over her hand and laid it down on the cushion of the window-seat, and then she got up and went out of the room, and up the staircase.

"Gus?"

No response.

She opened the door of Biddy's bedroom, to be met with the sight of the empty bed, the sheets thrown back, the indentation on the pillow where his head had lain. The window was closed. On the dressing-table stood his few possessions: wooden-backed hairbrushes, a bottle of pills, and the sketch-book and paint-box that she had given him. His blue pyjamas had been flung across a chair, but his clothes were gone, his shoes, his leather jacket. And Gus was gone too.

Bewildered, she closed the door and went downstairs again. "You're right," she told Jeremy. "He's not there. He must have got up early, before any of us were awake. I never heard anything. I thought he was just sleeping."

Jeremy said, "I have a feeling he's with Loveday."

"Loveday and Gus?"

"We must call Nancherrow . . ."

But, as he said this, the telephone started to ring. Judith said, "Perhaps that's Diana now . . ." and she went out into the hall to answer it, and Jeremy followed, so that he was with her when she picked up the receiver; by her side.

"Dower House."

"Judith."

It wasn't Diana. It was Gus.

"Gus. Where are you? What are you doing?"

"I'm in Porthkerris. Telephoning from your friends, the Warrens."

"What are you doing *there?*"

"Loveday wants to explain. She wants to talk to you."

"She's with you?"

"Of course."

"Has she spoken to her mother and father?"

"Yes. Just this moment. They were first, you're second. Look, before I put her on, there are three things I have to say to you. One is that I'm very sorry, but I stole your bicycle and it's still at Nancherrow, where I parked it, sitting by the front door. The second thing is that I'm taking your advice, and I'm going to be a painter. Or try to be. We'll see how it goes."

It was almost too much to take in, or even to begin to understand.

"But when did you . . . ?"

"There's a last thing I have to say. I've said it once, but I have to say it again."

"What's that?"

"Thank you."

"Oh, Gus."

"Here's Loveday . . ."

"But . . . Gus . . ."

But he was gone and, instead, Loveday on the line. Loveday's voice, high with excitement, gabbling away as she used to, when they were both children, young and irresponsible, and without a care in the world.

"Judith. It's me."

And Judith was so grateful, so relieved to be speaking to her, that she forgot all about being anxious, or even a bit cross.

"Loveday, you are the *end*. What have you been up to?"

"Oh, Judith, don't fuss. First is that I've spoken to Mummy and Pops, so you don't need to worry about them any more. And I'm with Gus. I went down to the cliffs, all on my own, just to try to work out what I was going to say to everybody, and I took darling Tiger with me, and we were sitting brooding in the dark and watching the sun come up, and the next thing I knew Tiger was going *woof-woof*, and I looked round, and there was Gus. He didn't know I was going to be there. He just came, because *he* wanted to be back on the cliffs too. And by then I'd decided that I was never going to go back to Walter, so it was all specially wonderful, magical, and we were together again. And I didn't even know he'd come *back* to Cornwall. I didn't even know he was with *you*. And suddenly he was just *there*, exactly at the moment when I was wanting him most."

"Oh, Loveday, I'm so happy for you."

"Not one scrap, not one fraction, of how happy I am for myself."

"So what did you do?"

"We talked and talked. And then I thought I couldn't bear to stop talking, and we must go on having a bit more time together. So we went back to the house, and tiptoe, tiptoe, I put Tiger back into the gun-room, and Gus started up the fishmonger's van, and we drove over the moor to Porthkerris."

"Why Porthkerris?"

"About as far as we could get without running out of petrol. No, not that silly reason. We chose Porthkerris because we knew, here, we could find a studio for darling Gus. To work in and hopefully to live in, and never go back to horrid Scotland. He's always wanted to paint. Always and always. But of course we didn't know how to begin to look for a studio. And then I thought of the Warrens, and I knew that if anybody knew Porthkerris, it would be Mr. Warren, and he would be able to tell us whom to go and see, and maybe know of some studio that would be for rent or to buy. And we couldn't go anywhere else because neither of us had any money or cheque-books or anything. Darling Gus counted the change in his trouser pocket and it added up to fifteen and fourpence halfpenny. Too stupid and no use to either of us. So we came here. And they were utterly adorable, as always, and Mrs. Warren cooked us the biggest breakfast you've ever seen, and Mr. Warren's been blasting away on the telephone, and just as soon as I've rung off, we're all going to look at a flat on the North Beach. Just a studio, but it's got a sort of bathroom and what's known as a kitchenette. I don't even know what a kitchenette is, but I'm sure it will be perfectly adequate . . ."

She might have wittered on forever, but Judith decided that the time had come to interrupt.

She said, "When are you coming home?"

"Oh, this evening. We'll be back this evening. We haven't *eloped* or anything like that. We're just being together. Planning things. Planning our lives."

"What about Walter?"

"Walter's gone. Pops told me. Arabella Lumb has won the day, and good luck to her."

"And Nat?"

"Pops spoke to Mr. Baines. They reckon I can keep Nat. We'll have to see. And Gus says he's always wanted a little boy, and he thinks it's quite a good idea to start married life with the bonus of a ready-made family." She fell silent for a moment, and then said, in an entirely different voice. "I always loved him, Judith. Even when I knew he was dead, but it was difficult for me to explain it to you all. Gus was the only man I ever truly loved. When you said he'd come back from Burma it was the worst and the best thing I'd ever been told. But it wasn't very easy to talk about it. I know I've been impossible . . ."

"Oh, Loveday, if you weren't impossible, you wouldn't be you. That's why we all love you so much."

"Come tonight," said Loveday. "Come to Nancherrow this evening. Let's all be together. Just like it used to be. Only Edward gone. But I think he'll be there too, don't you? I think he'll be around somewhere, drinking our health . . ."

Judith said, through her tears, "He wouldn't miss it for all the world. Good luck, Loveday."

"Love you."

She put down the receiver, and was in floods.

"I'm not crying because I'm miserable, I'm crying because it's all so happy. Have you got a handkerchief?"

Of course Jeremy had got a handkerchief. He fished it, pristine-clean and neatly folded, from his pocket, and gave it to her, and she blew her nose and wiped away the foolish, reasonless tears.

"I gather," said Jeremy, "that all is well."

"Blissful. They're together. They're in love. They always have been. He's going to go for his painting, and live in a studio at Porthkerris. With a kitchenette."

". . . and Loveday."

"Probably. I wouldn't know. She didn't say. It doesn't matter." Weeping was over. "I'll keep your handkerchief. I'll wash it for you."

She tucked it up the cuff of her sweater and smiled at him, and all at once, there were just the two of them. No other diversions. No other people. Just themselves. And, for the first time, perhaps a little constraint, a certain shyness. Hedging, "Would you like a cup of coffee, or something?" Judith asked.

"No. No, I don't want coffee, or Gus or Loveday or anyone else. I want you and me. It's time to talk."

Which, of course, it was. They went back into the drawing-room, and returned to the deep window-seat, and now the low sun was shining, every now and then, onto all the old-fashioned furniture, and the faded rugs, and sparking rainbow lights from the drops of Lavinia Boscawen's crystal chandelier.

Judith said, "Where do we start? To talk?"

"At the beginning. Why did you never answer my letter?"

She frowned. "But you never wrote."

"I did. From Long Island."

"I never got a letter."

He frowned. "Are you sure?"

"Of course I'm sure. I waited and waited. You said you were going to write, that morning in London. You promised you would write, and you never did. I never got a letter. And I decided you'd simply changed your mind, got cold feet; decided that, after all, you didn't want to keep in touch."

"Oh, Judith." He let out a sigh that sounded more like a groan than a sigh. "All these years." He reached out, and took her hand in his. "I did write. I was staying in a house in Long Island, and I just about tore myself to pieces trying to get the right words down. And then I took the letter back with me to New York, and sent it off by service mail, the post-box on board HMS *Sutherland*."

"So what happened?"

"I imagine a ship was sunk. The Battle of the Atlantic was at its peak. And the mail, and my letter, would all have ended up at the bottom of the ocean."

She shook her head. "I never thought of that." And then, "What did the letter say?"

"It said a lot of things. It said that I would never forget that night we spent together in London, when you were so unhappy, and I had to leave in the early morning in order to join my ship. And it told you how much I loved you. How much I'd always loved you, from the moment I first saw you sitting in the railway carriage at Plymouth, and looking out of the window to see the Fleet, as we rattled across the Saltash Bridge. And then it was all compounded by finding you again at Nancherrow, and hearing the sound of 'Jesu, Joy of Man's Desiring' come from your bedroom, and knowing that you were there, and how utterly important and essential you were in my life. And at the end of the letter, I asked you to marry me. Because I had got to the pitch where I couldn't imagine a future without you. And I asked you to write. To answer. To say yes, or no, and to set my mind at rest."

"But you got no answer."

"No."

"Didn't that strike you as rather odd?"

"Not really. I never considered myself much of a catch. And I'm thirteen years older than you, and I've always been short on worldly goods. You had everything. Youth and beauty and your financial independence. The world was your oyster. And perhaps you deserved better than the life of the wife of a country GP. So, no. When I received no reply from you, I didn't think it was odd at all. Just the end of everything."

Judith said, "I should have written to you, perhaps, but I wasn't that sure of myself. We'd slept together, and made love, I know. And it had all seemed so perfect. But Edward loved me because he was sorry for me. He wanted to give me the sort of joy he thought I was missing out on. And I was so afraid that your motives were the same. That I was having a bad time, and you provided the comfort."

"Never that, my darling."

"I see now. But I was younger then. Not all that sure of myself. Inexperienced." She looked at him. "There's something we haven't talked about. Jess. I have Jess now. She's part of me. We're family to each other. Whatever happens to me happens to Jess as well."

"Would she mind if I happened to you? Because I would like very much for all three of us to be together. I always remember her in the train, being terribly naughty and throwing her Golly at you. I can't wait to see her again."

"She's fourteen now, and very grown up. And poor Golly is no more. He died at sea."

"I'm filled with shame. I've never said a word to you about your parents, nor about Jess. Just talked about myself. But I was so terribly sad for you. And then so thankful when my father told me Jess had come back. She's gone to Saint Ursula's?"

"Yes, and she's happy. But until she's grown up and able to stand on her own feet, she's my responsibility."

"Darling Judith, that's nothing new. You've been shouldering responsibilities since the day I first met you. Responsibility for yourself, and Biddy Somerville, and Phyllis, and a home of your own. And then the war, and being in the Wrens." Again, he sighed. "That's my only reservation."

"I don't understand."

"Perhaps, before you settle down to married life, you might want a bit of time just to enjoy yourself. Like Athena used to, before the war. You know, be frivolous, buy hats and go to night-clubs. Be taken, by dashing men, to lunch at the Ritz. Go cruising in private yachts, and sip martinis on sun-splashed terraces."

Judith laughed. "What flights of imagination. You make it sound like a nightmare."

"But seriously?"

He was being very sweet. She thought about it, and then said, "Did you ever meet, in the Navy, a man called Hugo Halley?"

"No, I don't think I did."

"He was really nice. I met him in Colombo when I was staying with Bob Somerville. And the war was over, so we didn't have to think about that any more. And we did all those sorts of things that you've just been talking about. And we weren't in love, and there were no strings attached, and it was just the most fun, glamorous time. So I know about it. And I've experienced it. Just for a little while. So when we get married, I promise you I won't spend the rest of my life feeling frustrated or cheated in the smallest way."

"Did you really say that?"

"Say what?"

"When we get married?"

"I believe I did."

"I've got grey hairs now."

"I know. I've seen them, but I'm much too polite to remark."

"I'm thirty-seven. Dreadfully old. But I love you so much, I can only hope that being old isn't going to matter."

He waited for her to say, *Of course, it doesn't,* but she didn't. Instead, she simply sat there, her face a study of intense concentration. "Why are you so deep in thought?"

"I'm doing calculations. And I was never very quick at mental arithmetic."

"Calculations?"

"Yes. Did you know that the exactly right age for people to get married is for the wife to be half the man's age plus seven?"

A conundrum. Nonplussed, Jeremy shook his head. "No."

"So you're thirty-seven. And half thirty-seven is eighteen and a half. And eighteen and a half plus seven is . . . ?"

"Twenty-five and a half."

"Well, I'm twenty-four and a half, so it's near enough. Spot on. If we hadn't waited three and a half years, we'd have been all wrong for each other. It might have been a disaster. As it is . . ."

Suddenly, she was laughing, and he kissed her open laughing mouth, and it all took quite a long time, and he felt the physical arousal of his body, and the thought flashed through his mind that it would be a brilliant idea to gather her up in his arms, head for the nearest suitable spot, and make long and passionate love to her. But common sense lurked at the edge of his mind, and told him that now was not the right moment. The dramas of Nancherrow were at the head of the agenda, and when he did make love to her again, he wanted it to be unhurried, timeless, and, if necessary, to last an entire night.

Gently, he let her go. Drawing apart, he put up a hand to smooth a lock of honey-coloured hair away from her face.

He said, "Who was it who made that statement about the hurly-burly of the chaise lounge, and the deep deep peace of the double bed?"

"Mrs. Patrick Campbell."

"I knew you would know. Shall we, for the moment, pull ourselves together, and try to make some plan for our future?"

"I'm not sure if, just now, I'm capable of making plans."

"Then I shall make them. Except that I haven't even decided anything for myself yet, let alone you and Jess."

"Are you going to go back to Truro and take over from your father?"

"Is that what you would like?"

Judith was honest. She said, "No. I'm sorry, but the awful thing is I never want to leave this house. I know one shouldn't let bricks and mortar rule one's life, but this place is so special. Not just because of Aunt Lavinia, but because it's been a sort of haven for so many people. A home. Biddy came here when she was so broken up about Ned. And then Phyllis and Anna. And Jess, coming home to here, after all she'd been through. And even Gus, who fell to bits and thought he was never going to be happy again. Do you understand?"

"Completely. So, cross Truro off the list."

"Won't your father be very upset?"

"I don't think so."

"So what will you do?"

"I have an old naval colleague. A good friend. A Surgeon-Commander RNVR called Bill Whatley. He put an idea to me, a couple of months ago, when we were both in Malta. Supposing the two of us started up a new practice, right here? In Penzance?"

Judith, scarcely daring to hope, stared at Jeremy. "Could you do that?"

"Why not? The war is over. We can do anything. Bill's a Londoner, but he wants to settle his family in the country, preferably by the sea. He's a great sailing man. We talked it over at length, but I didn't want to commit myself until I knew how the land lay with you. I didn't want to come blundering back into your life if you didn't want me around. A bit embarrassing, having a lovesick old flame on your doorstep."

"Penzance is scarcely my doorstep. And if you're a GP in Penzance, it's too far away to live here. Night calls and things like that."

"There'll be two of us in the practice together. I can commute. We shall build a beautiful modern surgery, with desirable residence incorporated. A useful flat, for night shifts."

"With kitchenette?"

But Jeremy was laughing. "You know something, my darling? We are splitting hairs. Crossing bridges we haven't even come to. We must allow the future to take care of itself."

"Such clichés. You sound like a politician."

"Oh well. I suppose I could do worse." He looked at his watch. "Good God, it's a quarter to twelve. And I'm forgetting entirely the reason why I came here to see you in the first place. I suppose I ought to get back to Nancherrow, or Diana will think that I've joined the club, and eloped as well. Will you come with me, my darling Judith?"

"If you want."

"I do."

"Shall we tell them all? About you and me?"

"Why not?"

For some reason the prospect was a bit daunting and shy-making. "What *are* they going to say?"

"Why don't we go and find out?"